Ellery Queen

FIVE COMPLETE NOVELS

Ellery Queen

FIVE COMPLETE NOVELS

And on the Eighth Day

The Player
on the Other Side

Inspector Queen's
Own Case

Cat of Many Tails

Double, Double

Avenel Books · New York

This omnibus edition was previously published as separate volumes under the titles:

And On the Eighth Day copyright © MCMLXIV by Ellery Queen
The Player on the Other Side copyright © MCMLXIII by Ellery Queen
Inspector Queen's Own Case copyright © MCMLVI by Ellery Queen
Cat of Many Tails copyright MCMXLIX by Little, Brown & Company, ©
renewed MCMLXXVI by Ellery Queen
Double, Double copyright MCML by Little, Brown & Company, ©
renewed MCMLXXVII by Ellery Queen

This edition is published by Avenel Books,
distributed by Crown Publishers, Inc., by arrangement with
Scott Meredith Literary Agency.

Manufactured in the United States of America

h g f e d c b a

Library of Congress Cataloging in Publication Data
Queen, Ellery.
    Ellery Queen, five complete novels.

    Contents: And on the eighth day—The player on the
other side—Inspector Queen's own case—[etc.]
    1. Detective and mystery stories, American. I. Title.
PS3533.U4E4   813'.52   81-19101
ISBN: 0-517-365782   AACR2

CONTENTS

And on the Eighth Day

1 · Sunday, April 2

Somewhere sagebrush was burning, but on neither side of the road could Ellery see smoke. Once he thought he saw fire. It turned out to be an ocotillo shrub in flaming flower. Either the spring rains had fallen earlier than usual, or the elevation in this part of the desert brought occasional rainfall throughout the year.

He decided it was a campfire, perhaps from a wish. He had run across no human trail for hours, except the road itself.

A fuzzy whim had made him turn off into the state road east of Hamlin (named, a sun-roasted marker said, after Lincoln's first Vice-President). The road had been passable as far as it went; the trouble was, it had not gone far enough. About fifty miles from Hamlin it suddenly became an untidy wound. The California highway department's crew had evidently been caught in mid-repair by the outbreak of the war.

Rather than backtrack Hamlinward, Ellery had chanced a detour. He had long since regretted the gamble. The rutted and rotted dirt failed to connect with the state highway. After hours of jouncing, Ellery was convinced that it was no detour at all but a lost wagon trail of the pioneers, leading nowhere.

He began to feel uneasy about water.

He saw no signs. He did not even know if he was still in California or had crossed into Nevada.

The sweet-burn odor died. He had forgotten it by the time he saw the wooden building up ahead.

Ellery should have set out for Hollywood earlier, but the prospect of bucking the pre-Christmas traffic and spending the holiday alone in a motor court somewhere had decided him to wait. That and the remark of the chain-smoking government man with whom he had discussed his trip. "The way things stand, Mr. Queen, we can spare gas for your car a lot easier than space on a plane or train. Or, for that matter, a bus."

In that December of 1943, depots and terminals and waiting rooms across the land demanded *Is This Trip Necessary?* and they were all packed with people who clearly thought the answer was yes. Businessmen waving priorities; students pointing home for their last civilian vacations; recruits on noisy boot leave; beribboned brass in perfect custom-made uniforms; combat veterans wrapped in silence; and, everywhere, sweethearts and pregnant brides and wives clutching children "going to see my daddy—he's a soldier," or sailor, or Marine, or airman, or Coast Guardsman—servicemen unable to wangle a Christmas furlough. And it was all strident with gaiety: "He'll be so happy. He's never seen the baby!" and tears: "Then I'll *stand*.

I don't need a seat. Please?'' and the unspoken, unspeakable words: *But I've got to get there, I may never see him again.*

''I'll drive,'' Ellery had said.

So he had spent Christmas Eve at home with his father and the radio. Christmas Day brought church, unrationed turkey, and a walk in Central Park. After which the Inspector snugged down with his latest leisure project, a rereading of Gibbon's *Decline and Fall*—replete with clucks over the misdeeds of some royal Byzantine gangster—while Ellery wrote appallingly overdue letters.

On the twenty-sixth he had packed and rested for the journey ahead, which he contemplated with no joy whatsoever. He had been working hard and his bones lacked bounce. At eight the next morning he piled his suitcases into the antique Duesenberg, embraced his father, and took off.

By some leer of fate, several of the servicemen he picked up early in the trip spelled him at the wheel while he was still fresh; but after he crossed the Mississippi, when he was beginning to feel the strain, not one of the hitchhikers he stopped for proved able to drive or had a license. So by the evening of December 31, when he pulled into a Hollywood already boiling over with New Year's Eve good cheer, he was weary in every cell and desperate for a hot bath and a good mattress.

''I know, Mr. Queen,'' said the desk clerk with the basset eyes, ''I *know* we confirmed your reservation. But . . .'' It seemed that Ellery's room had been boarded by two ensigns freshly in from the South Pacific.

''And in the finest tradition of the Navy,'' sighed Ellery, ''they won't give up the ship. All right, I'm licked. Where's the nearest phone?'' But by this time he had to find it for himself.

Lew Walsh exclaimed. ''Ellery! You bet we can put you up. For as long as you like. Get over here pronto. The party's going good.''

It certainly was. But he was unable to back out with grace, and it was almost dawn before he achieved the bath and the mattress. His sleep was turbulent. Voices howled faintly in his inner ear; he rocketed down an endless white line on an endless highway; and his fingers ached from steering with the sheet.

From time to time the world of his senses coupled with the world of his dreams and spawned phantasmagoria. Once he saw a splash of sunlight, smelled roses growing in freshly watered earth; but then his eyes slid shut again and he struggled into a dark dusk somewhere in the mountain snows, snows stained with splotches of blood like roses. Another time a radio voice pronounced a passionate *Helen!*, and immediately he was being tossed between the gong tormented sea of Homer and a modern ocean hellishly aglare with exploding ships, while gongs sounded and resounded and the tormented sea roared in agony.

He slept until dark, and he was still tired when he awoke, the hot shower barely lapping at the shores of his tiredness. Evelyn Walsh pounced on him—''We thought you'd died in your sleep, Ellery!''—and proceeded to stuff him with orange juice and eggs and toast and pancakes and brassy tea (''We're out of bacon and coffee, darn it.'' It seemed the Walshes had been prodigal with their ration stamps) . Ellery sipped the tea thinly; he had envisioned coffee by the quart.

Lew Walsh gave him his choice between joining them in a quiet New Year's Night get-together at the home of a movie-star friend of theirs in the Hills or ''just sitting around the house yakking.'' Having experienced quiet New Year's Night get-togethers in Hollywood, Ellery shamelessly chose the alternative. They talked the war, and the flesh situation—Lew was a partner in a talent agency—and the Nazi concentration-camp stories, and the voices began to go away, and then Ellery heard Evelyn say, "That does it," and his head jerked up and his eyes flew open. "You're going right back to bed, Ellery Queen, if I have to undress you myself."

"Well . . . but will you and Lew go to your party?"

"Yes. Now *march*."

When he opened his eyes it was midway through Sunday afternoon. He was still wrung to the withers. And something new had been added, a case of the shakes.

"What's the *matter* with you?" his hostess asked. She had rustled a bit of coffee somewhere, and he was trying to hold the cup steady as he gulped. "You look awful."

"I can't seem to throw off this fatigue, Evelyn."

Lew Walsh shook his head. "If you feel this way now, Ellery, how are you going to live through the rat race? I understand this O.W.I. fellow you're to work for at Metropolitan is trying to win the war all by himself."

Ellery closed his eyes and said, "More coffee? Please?"

The next morning he made it a point to get to the Metropolitan lot at nine o'clock— by Hollywood writers' standards the middle of the night. He found Lieutenant-Colonel Donaldson waiting for him with a chill smile.

"Too much New Year's, Queen?" The chicken colonel's eyes were clear as a schoolboy's. "I'd better make it understood right off that the early bird isn't caught napping. I run a tight little cadre here. Know Charley Dyers?"

"Hi, Charley," said Ellery. If Charley Dyers was already at work by 9:00 A.M. on the Monday after the New Year's weekend, Colonel Donaldson ran a tight little cadre indeed. Dyers had been hacking out screenplays since the days when the close-up was a daring innovation.

"Hi, sonny," said the old-timer, and he squinted down his ruby nose to the inch-long ash on his cigar. "Welcome to the Espreeda Corps."

"Yes. Well," said Colonel Donaldson. "Queen, are you familiar with what we're doing here?"

"Somebody told me the other night that the screenplays deal with subjects like The Importance of Keeping Flies Out of Mess Halls and V.D. Will Get You If You Don't Watch Out."

The colonel's chill look formed ice. "He doesn't know what he's talking about. V.D.'s being handled by another unit altogether."

Ellery glanced at Charley Dyers, but Dyers was gazing innocently out the colonel's picture window, through which came the medicinal odor of peeling eucalyptus. Same old Hollywood. The only difference was the uniform on the man behind the De Mille-sized desk.

"All *right*," said Colonel Donaldson briskly. "We have three months—four at the outside—to prepare twenty screenplays, ten for service personnel, the rest for civilian viewing. Now, gentlemen, to quote a Chinese proverb, one picture is worth a thousand words, so you can figure out for yourselves how many words we've got to turn out to get these films in the can. And no time for mistakes," he added sternly. "To err is human, but in war you've got to be divine. Nobody's heard a shot fired in anger in this country since 1865, and most of us don't realize—simply do not realize—that we can lose this little old war." While Ellery was puzzling out this last juxtaposition of thoughts, the colonel pressed his attack with, "Well, the war's not going to be lost in *my* theater," in a voice of naked steel. "Teamwork, Queen! Remember that I represent the armed forces, Dyers the studio, and you . . ."

For a moment the colonel seemed at a loss. "And you," he rallied, "you'll be working *with* us, Queen, not *for* us, and when I say work I mean . . . *work!*"

Work he did, belly to belly with a cursing Charley Dyers. Twelve hours a day, often longer. If Ellery had come to Hollywood worn out, he was soon in a state of ambulatory exhaustion.

Somehow the accommodations he had been promised by the Office of War Information melted away in a snafu and he found himself, feebly protesting, still in the tender billet of the Walshes. But Evelyn Walsh's mother-henning and Lew's unaggressive hospitality failed to make even the weekends tolerable. The colonel's Pavlovian discipline in early rising made it impossible for Ellery to sleep late on Sundays, so that on his day off he found himself going over, rather than getting over, the week's work—and cringing over the thought of Monday morning.

Even worse than Colonel Donaldson's hot spearmint-scented breath on his ear was the rewrite situation. No sooner had Ellery and Dyers settled down to a new script than back came the old one, or the old two or three or four, with demands for rewritten scenes, new scenes, cut scenes, bridges—revisions in wholesale lots. At least twice Ellery caught himself writing a scene into one script that belonged in another.

He and Dyers had long since stopped speaking to each other except in command situations. Each labored within a force-field of his own purgatory. With gray-dirt faces and red-eyed as albinos they became prisoners of the war, filled with eternal, hopeless hate.

The pay-off came on Saturday, the first of April. All Fools' Day.

Ellery had checked into the studio that morning at seven-thirty. How long he had been slogging away at the typewriter he did not know; but suddenly he felt cold hands on his, and he looked up to find Colonel Donaldson stooping over him.

"What?" Ellery said.

"I said what's the matter with you, Queen. Look!"

Ellery sighted along the colonel's military finger. It was trained on the paper in the typewriter. *Richard Queen Richard Queen Richard Queen,* he read. *Richard Queen Richard . . .*

"I spoke to you," the colonel said. "You neither looked at me nor answered. Just kept typing *Richard Queen.* Who's Richard Oueen? Your son?"

Ellery shook his head and immediately stopped. He could have sworn something rattled inside, something with a long extension, like a chain. "My father," he said, and pushed cautiously away from the desk. When nothing happened, he gripped the edge and changed the direction of the push from horizontal to vertical. This, he found to his surprise, was considerably harder to do. Also, his legs were quivering. Frowning, he clung to the desk.

Colonel Donaldson was frowning, too. It was a chief-of-staff-type frown, fraught with decisions for the further conduct of the war.

"Colonel," began Ellery, and stopped. Had he stuttered? It seemed to him he had stuttered. Or was hearing things. He inhaled smartly and tried again. "Colonel . . ." There. That was perfect. And he was so very very very very tired. "I think I've had it."

The colonel said, "I think you have." There was no rancor in his voice. A cog in his military engine had worn out; the sensible thing to do was replace it before it snapped. Fortunes of war. "Glad it didn't happen sooner—we're almost to our objective. Well, well, we'll carry on. And oh," he said, "will you be all right, Queen?"

Will I be all right, thought Ellery. "No," he said. "Yes."

Colonel Donaldson nodded hastily and turned to go. But at the door he hesitated, as if he had just remembered something. "Well," he said, and cleared his throat. "Good show, Queen, good show!" And left.

Ellery sat wondering where Charley Dyers was. Probably out for a bourbon break. Good old Charley. The hell with him.

And New York. Oh, New York, its April damps and dirt-flecked beauty. California, here I go—back home and broken—with gratitude in my heart. To the comfortable, shabby old apartment. To the end of a Gotham day and the dearly beloved father-image in the thread-bare bathrobe intent on leather-bound *Decline and Fall*. To rest. To rest. Did they give squeezed-out writers Purple Hearts?

And so it was that the next morning, before the Walshes were out of their circular bed—he had made his good-byes the night before—Ellery stowed his suitcases in the Duesenberg and drove out of Hollywood, eastward bound.

The wooden building, he realized later, came into sight almost a mile away, but he had not at first identified it as such. The air was clear enough; it was the undulating ground that now revealed, now concealed it. It might have been a set from a Western film except that it was not neat enough. "Ramshackle" had probably been the word for it from the beginning. There was no sign that it had ever known a coat of paint.

But a sign—a painted sign—there certainly was. It must have been five feet across. Its lettering, more ambitious than accomplished, read:

END-OF-THE-WORLD STORE
Otto Schimdt, *Prop.*
Last Chance To Buy Gas And
Supplies. Next Chance Is
Other Side of Desert

Ellery guessed that he might not be far from the southern edge of Death Valley; but in this country guesses were sibling to disaster, and he felt in no condition to face disaster. Also, the state of his fuel gauge made a stop for gas the better part of wisdom. And while the food hamper Evelyn Walsh had pressed on him was still untouched, who knew what lay ahead? Yes, it might be a smart idea to stop and see what he could pick up in the way of additional supplies—and, of course, information.

Ellery slanted the Duesenberg toward the rickety porch, wondering vaguely why he should feel it necessary to rationalize the stop. Perhaps it was because there was something about the place, a quality of unexpectedness. It stood quite alone in the sun-baked landscape. There was no other building, not even the ruin of one; no other car.

There was a wagon, however, hitched to two animals.

At first he thought they were mules—smallish mules, to be sure, but their size was less matter for wonder than that they were there at all. He had never seen mules farther west than Texas. But then, as he turned off his ignition, he saw that they were not mules; they were donkeys. Not the stunted burros of Old Prospector fame, but a more robust variety, like the asses of the Near East—handsome beasts, well-bred and well-fed.

Ellery had never seen their like outside films and paintings, and it was only the exhaustion which rode him like the Burr-Woman of the Indians that kept him from going over for a closer look. Supplies lay heaped beside the wagon: sacks, crates, cartons.

But then he forgot the wagon and the beasts. For in the silence left by the cutting off of his motor he heard men's voices, slow and deep. They were coming from inside the store. He backed heavily out of the Duesenberg and moved toward the porch as if he were wading through swells.

The boards of the porch wavered under his feet, and he walked even more gingerly. At the screen door he paused to rest. Then, as he was about to open it, the door opened seemingly by itself. Ellery was pondering this phenomenon when two men stepped through the doorway, two very strange and strangely dressed men.

It was the eyes of the first man, by far the elder of the two, that seized him. Later he was to think: *He has the eyes of a prophet;* but that was not his thought at the time. What came into his head at the moment of meeting were words from the Song of Songs: *Thine eyes are dove's eyes;* and with this, instantly, the knowledge that they were not dove's eyes at all. The eyes of an eagle? But no, there was nothing fierce or predatory about them. They were black-bright, blazing black-bright, like twin suns viewed with the naked eye. And there was something far-seeing about them. And yet non-seeing, too. It was the queerest thing. Perhaps—that was it!—they saw something that was there for only them to see.

He was tall, this strange man; bone-thin tall, and exceedingly old. In his eighties, certainly; possibly his nineties. His skin had been so worked upon by time and the sun that it was weathered almost black. From his chin fell a small sparse beard of yellowed white hair; his face otherwise was quite hairless. He was clothed in a robe, a robe with the cut and flow of an Arabian burnoose or *jallābiyah,* made of some unsophisticated cloth whose bleach had come, not from processed chemicals, but directly from the sun. He wore sandals on bare feet; he carried a staff taller than himself. And on his shoulder he bore a keg of nails with no sign of strain.

No actor could play this man, Ellery swiftly thought (the denial reaching his mind's surface even faster than the thought it denied—that the old man was here from Hollywood, on location for some Biblical production). He was not made up for a part; he was really aged; in any case he would be inimitable. This old man could only *be,* Ellery thought. He *is.* An original.

The old man moved by him. The extraordinary eyes had rested a moment on his face and then had gone on—not so much past him as through him.

The second man was commonplace only by contrast with the old man. He, too, was sun-black—if a shade less darkened than the ancient, perhaps only because he was half the ancient's age. In his early forties, Ellery guessed; his beard was glossy black. The younger man's garments were made from the same odd cloth, but they were of an entirely different character—a simple blouselike shirt, without a collar and open at the throat; and trousers that reached only far enough down to cover his calves. He carried a hundred-pound sack on each shoulder, one of salt, the other of sugar.

The eyes of this younger man were a clear-water gray, and they rested briefly on Ellery's face with shy curiosity. The gray eyes shifted to look over at the Duesenberg, and they widened with an awe rarely inspired by that venerable vehicle except on the score of its age. The glance returned to Ellery for another shy moment; then the younger man moved after the elder and went over to the wagon and began to load the supplies.

Ellery stepped into the store. After the inferno outside, its dim coolness received him like a Good Samaritan; for a moment he simply stood there accepting its ministrations and looking about. It was a poor store, with sagging shelves scantily stocked and a dusty foliage of assorted articles hanging from the tin ceiling. The store proper was far too shallow to comprise the entire building, Ellery saw; there was a door at the rear, almost blocked by a stack of cardboard cartons imprinted *Tomatoes,* that probably led to a storeroom.

Along one side of the store ran a flaked and whittled counter; behind the counter, over a lop-eared ledger, stooped a roly-poly little man with a patch of seal mustache in the middle of his round and ruddy face—obviously the Otto Schmidt, *Prop.,* of the sign. He did not look up from his ledger.

So Ellery stood there, not so much observing as absorbing, taking a sensual pleasure in the laving coolness; and then the tall old man came back into the store, moving very quietly. He went over to the counter, his blackened hand slipping into a slit in the side of his garment; it came out with something, and this something he laid on the counter before the roly-poly proprietor.

Schmidt looked up. In that instant he spotted Ellery. He snatched the something and pocketed it. But not before Ellery saw what it was.

It was a coin, large enough to be a silver dollar, and remarkably bright and shiny, almost as if it were new. But no new silver dollars had been minted for years. Perhaps, he thought dully, perhaps it was a foreign coin. There were colonies of bearded sectarians, Old Russian in origin, in Mexico . . .

But dollar, or peso—whatever the coin was—the heap of supplies being loaded onto the wagon seemed far too much to be paid for by a single piece of silver.

Neither the old man nor the man behind the counter uttered a word. Evidently all arrangements had been made before Ellery came in, leaving no need for further conversation. Once more the glance shafted through him; then, incredibly erect, incredibly light on his sandaled feet, the old man left the store. The mystery was not to be resisted; and even if the will to resist had been there, Ellery was too exhausted to exercise it. He followed.

In time to see the old man set one foot on the wagon wheel and lift himself easily to the high seat, where the younger man was now perched. And to hear him speak for the second time, for one of the slow, deep voices Ellery had heard on first approaching the store had been this voice.

"Very well, Storicai."

Storicai? At least that was how it sounded. Storicai . . . What a queer name! Ellery could not fix it in point of time or place. And oh, that voice, the voice that had uttered it, so rich with power, so tranquil—a voice with the strangest accent, and infinitely at peace . . .

Ellery sighed and shook his head as he went back into the store. Distracted now only by the memory and not the presence, he allowed the store to sink into his pores: its musty fragrance of old wood, coffee beans, kerosene, spices, tobacco, vinegar, and coolness—above all, coolness.

"Never saw anything like that before, did you?" the storekeeper said cheerfully; and Ellery agreed that no, he never had. "Well," the storekeeper went on, "it's a free country, and they don't bother nobody. What can I do for you?"

He could fill the Duesenberg up with high-test was what he could do. No high-test? No call for it on a back road like this. Well, all right, regular would do. It would have to. What? Oh, yes, he had stamps for the gas . . . Otto Schmidt came back and took Ellery's ten-dollar bill as if he had never seen one before, and rumpled his cowlick once or twice, and made change. Anything else?

Ellery glanced about, thinking there was something more he wanted; he ordered tobacco for his pipe, paid for it, looked around again . . . there was still something . . .

"How about some supper?" suggested Mr. Schmidt shrewdly. And all at once Ellery realized that this was exactly what he wanted. He nodded.

"Just take a seat at the table there. Ham and eggs, coffee and pie be all right? I could open a can of soup—"

"Ham and eggs, coffee and pie will do just fine." He felt guilty about Evelyn's still unopened box lunch, but it was hot food he wanted. He sat down at the table. It was bare of cloth but quite clean; and there was a much-handled copy of the *Reese River Reveille and Austin Sun* dated the previous November.

Austin . . . that was in Nevada—it couldn't be Texas. Or California. So he must be in Nevada. Or—no, that didn't follow. Anyone coming west from Nevada could have left it just about here. He would ask Mr. Schmidt what state they were in. But Mr. Schmidt was frying ham in the kitchen; and by the time he returned, the question had left Ellery's mind.

Ham and eggs, coffee and pie appeared on the table simultaneously. All were surprisingly good for a country store in the middle of nowhere. Even the pie had a surprise to it. In addition to a crisp, brown, flaky crust, the fruit was just the right mixture of tart and sweet, with a spicy flavor that reminded Ellery of cinnamon; but there was something else, too.

He looked up and saw that Mr. Schmidt was smiling. "It's clove," said Mr. Schmidt.

"Yes," Ellery agreed. "I did smell the clove, but I thought it was from the ham. Delicious."

The proprietor's moon face was split by a grin. "Where I come from there are a lot of Cornishmen—Cousin Jacks, we called them—and they used to put clove in their pie instead of cinnamon. I thought to myself, Why not both?—and I've been putting in both ever since."

Ellery indicated the chair opposite him. "How about joining me in a cup of coffee?"

"Well, say. Thank you!" beamed Otto Schmidt; and he brought a cup of coffee from the kitchen and sat down and began to talk as if Ellery had opened a stop-valve. His delight in company and conversation was that of a man who did not often get much of either.

He was from Wisconsin originally, it seemed—a small city in the northern part of the state—where he had run his father's neighborhood grocery store.

"Just about gave me a living," Schmidt said. "After Pop died I had no family in the United States, so I was kind of lonesome as well as scraping along. Then two bad things happened more or less together . . ."

The depression had settled on the land, and Schmidt's health had broken down. His doctor had advised a warm, dry climate; the growing inability of his customers to pay their grocery bills had put an end to the matter.

"The store had been owned by my family for over forty years," the stout little man said, "but I had no choice. Paid my suppliers, marked down everything, cleared off the shelves, and found myself heading west with five hundred dollars in my pockets and not an idea in the world where I was going or what I was going to do. Then my jalopy ran out of gas about a mile from here. I hiked in and found a fellow named Parslow running this store. He was fed up with it and I offered him the five hundred for the place, lock, stock, and barrel, half in cash. He held out for three hundred down. 'Tell you what I'll do,' I told him. 'My car's a mile up the road and it doesn't need a thing but gas. You can have her for the other fifty.' 'Done!' he says. We closed the deal and he filled up a can with gasoline and was all set to start walking. 'Haven't you forgotten something?' I ask. 'What?' he says, patting his pockets. 'That'll be fifty cents for the gasoline,' I says. Well, he swore at me, but he paid. And that was how I came to be here, and I've been here ever since."

And he chuckled with satisfaction. He would never go back, he assured Ellery. He made very little money, but even on his once-a-year trips to Los Angeles he was always glad to get back. It was . . . He hesitated, his pudgy hands making exploratory circles in the air. It was so *clean* out here on the edge of the desert. You could see for miles in the daytime, and at night . . . oh, you could see for *millions* of miles.

"How about those two fellows who were here when I arrived?" Ellery asked suddenly. "Who are they?"

"Oh, they live out in the desert somewhere. Hermits."

"Hermits?"

"Sort of. Don't know what they do for grub generally—they come to the store here only a couple times a year. Nice folks, though. Queer, maybe, but like I said, they don't bother nobody. Everybody's got a right to go his own way, so long as he don't bother nobody, is what I always say."

Ellery remarked that he couldn't agree more, and rose. Mr. Schmidt swiftly suggested more pie and coffee in a transparent maneuver to detain him. Ellery smiled faintly, shook his head, settled his bill, and then said that he had better get some directions before going on.

"Directions for where?" the little man asked. Ellery looked pained. Where indeed?

"Las Vegas," he said.

Schmidt took Ellery by the arm and marched him to the door. Here, with many gestures, corrections, and repetitions, he described a route. Boiled down—as nearly as Ellery could remember afterward—it came to this: "Follow this road along the edge of the desert. Don't take any of the roads that go off to the left. When you come to the first fork, bear right. That's the road that leads you onto the main highway for Las Vegas."

Ellery waved good-bye and drove off. He expected never to see the End-of-the-World Store or Otto Schmidt, *Prop.*, again.

Once again he drove off toward home, reversing the path of the pioneers—for that matter, of the sun itself. The hot meal had added its own inducement toward drowsiness to his exhaustion, and he had to fight a running battle with it.

He kept his eyes open for the "first fork" in the road, where he was to bear right for the highway that led to Las Vegas. Once—perhaps twice, he was not sure—he noticed a wide path (it seemed little more) which he took to be one of the roads that "go off to the left," and he avoided it with a minor sense of triumph. He had forgotten to ask Otto Schmidt how far away Las Vegas was and how long he might have to be on the road.

The day was settling into its decline, and he began to entertain an only half-amusing fantasy that he was not going to reach any recognizable destination that night. It made him think of the legend of Peter Rugg. The Missing Man, New England's version of The Flying Dutchman, who defied the heavenly elements and for punishment was condemned to gallop in his phantom chaise forever with a thunderstorm at his back, trying to reach a Boston that forever eluded him. Perhaps, Ellery thought, future travelers would repeat the tale of the ancient Duesenberg and its phantom driver, eternally stopping to inquire if he was on the right road to Las Vegas!

Try as he would to keep not only his sleepy eyes but his drifting mind on the road (". . . *first fork . . . turn right . . .*"), Ellery's thoughts kept circling back to the old man with the curious speech, the curious costume, the curiously powerful serenity. Funny old bird to meet in the year 1944, of the independence of the United States the 168th, even in a timeless desert. Was there ever an age when that old man would not have commanded attention, a fascination not far removed from awe?

A clump of desert willows pink with blossoms caught his eye; in the next moment he had forgotten them, but perhaps they sparked his mental leap backward over whole millennia to another time and desert and *jalliābiyah*-clad people among whom moved men like that old man—men called patriarchs, or prophets, or apostles.

That old man of the wagon and his "*Very well, Storicai,*" in an English flavored with that strange accent—no, not of those Russian sectarians in Mexico after all . . . It was not his accent, or his voice, or his face, or his garb that was so remarkable, although together they were remarkable enough. Rather it was his ineffable composure, a certain extraordinary aura of . . . grandeur? No, no! What was the word?

Righteousness, that was it. Not self-righteousness, but righteousness . . . unswerving rectitude . . . acceptance with God . . . It blazed from his eyes. That was it! How very, very remarkable were the eyes of that old man . . .

Much later, recalling the dreamlike journey, Ellery came to believe that in his half-hallucinated state, while reflecting on the eyes of the old man, his own eyes had failed to see the fork in the road of which Otto Schmidt had spoken. Certainly he had not borne right, as Schmidt had instructed him. He must have borne left instead.

He was to remember how, floating between reflection and exhaustion, he realized that the road he was traveling had definitely stopped skirting the desert and had crept into it. Joshua trees thrust their spiky limbs every which way, as if groping blindly for something; the frail scent of sand verbena kept touching his nostrils . . .

. . . until it was replaced gently and slowly and, thus, imperceptibly, until all at once the verbena scent was gone, blocked out by something stronger, heavier, more recently familiar . . .

. . . the smoke of sagebrush burning.

Again.

He frowned, blinked, noticed—consciously for the first time—how the road had changed. The graded dirt had given way to ungraded dirt, then to sand. Before he could think this out, he noticed that it was little more than a weedy trail embraced by two narrow ruts. He did not even then think: I am on the wrong road, and I had better turn around now while there is still enough light. He thought: It must be a very old automobile that uses this road, perhaps a Model T . . . And then: No, no automobile uses this road, because there is not a trace of oil on the weeds runninng down the middle of it.

With that, Ellery stopped the car and looked around. There was nothing but desert on all sides—creosote bushes, the grayish humps of burro-weed, the thorny crowns of yuccas, rocks, boulders, sand. He had stopped the car providentially. The road came to an end just ahead of him, on a rise. What was on the other side he preferred not to dwell on. Perhaps a sheer drop—a cliff.

The light was beginning to pale, and Ellery hastily stood up in the car and craned.

He saw at once that the rise was part of the rim of a low circular hill—a hill with a valley inside; or so it seemed in the failing light. A valley like the bottom of a shallow bowl, hence not really a valley at all, but a basin. Geological niceties, however, were far from his thoughts. As *valley* it first came into his tired mind; as *valley* it was to remain there.

While he stood in the rising heat of the motor, gazing at the rim of hill, a figure suddenly rose from the crest to become fixed in silhouette between the lemon-yellow sky and the hill beyond, already deepening from pink to rose-red . . . while he watched, to purple. Hooded robe from which emerged gaunt profile and jutting beard, long staff in one hand, and in the other . . . It was, it had to be, it could be no other than the old man of the wagon at the End-of-the-World Store.

For a timeless interval Ellery stood there, in the Duesenberg, half convinced that he was the victim of a desert mirage, or that the appearance of this archetype of all father-figures was related in some way to his recent withdrawal from awareness of the world, characterized by the senseless repetition of his father's name on the studio typewriter . . . He saw the curiously thin-looking figure on the hill—as sharp against the sky as if there were no thickness to him at all—raise something to his lips.

A trumpet?

In the silence (literally breathless for him, for he was holding his breath) Ellery heard, or fancied he heard, an unearthly sound. It was at once alien yet hauntingly familiar. Not the long, archaic silvern trumpets that had heralded the proclamation of the British king (and, eight months later, of his brother); not the harsh, yet tremendously stirring ram's horn, the shofar of the synagogue, confuting Satan as it jarred slumbering sinners to repentance; nor the baroque *boo-boo*ing of the conch shell whereby the hundred thousand avatars of Brahma are summoned to compassion; not the horns of Elfland, faintly blowing; nor the sweet-cracked melancholy jazz of the cornet at an old-time New Orleans funeral . . . it was like none of these, yet it evoked something of all these . . .

If, indeed, he had heard anything. At all.

As in a dream, Ellery turned off the ignition and got out of his car and walked in the direction of the silhouette, the long strange echo of the trumpet still in his ears. (Or was it only the singing silence of the sands?)

He began to climb the low hill.

And as he climbed, the tall figure achieved a third dimension and turned toward him. The hand that did not grasp the staff was not visible now; it was buried in the folds of the robe . . . holding the trumpet? Ellery could not tell. What he could tell, however, and surely, was that this was indeed the old man of the wagon. And as Ellery reached the summit, the old man began to speak.

He spoke in English, as before, the same curiously accented English that struck the ear with such unfamiliarity. Or it might be not so much an accent as an intonation. What was the old man saying? Ellery frowned, concentrating.

"*The Word be with you.*"

That must have been what he said. And yet . . . Perhaps it had not been *word* at all, but *ward*. Or *Lord*. There had been a distinct cadenced hesitation in the pronunciation, almost as if it were *Wor'd*. Or—

"World?" Ellery thought aloud.

The old man looked at him with a kindling eye. "Who are you?" he asked Ellery.

And again uncertainty followed. Surely there was a glottal stop after the *r* in *are*, the way the old man pronounced it? Or had he actually asked, *Who art thou?*— speaking the *thou* after the fashion of the British Quakers, so that it sounded more like *thu?*

In these uncertainties Ellery was certain of only one thing—that he felt queerly light-headed. Had he gained enough altitude since leaving the store so that a thinning atmosphere was affecting him? Or was it the exertion of the climb up the hill in his ever-mounting fatigue? He planted his feet apart for better support (how silly if he should faint now!) and he was aware with annoyance how slurred the words sounded as he said, "My name is Ellery—"

Before he could finish, an astounding thing happened. The old man bent double and began to fall. Instinctively Ellery reached out both hands to catch him, thinking that he was fainting, or even dying. But the old man slipped through his hands and landed on both knees on the sand, and he plucked the dusty cuff of Ellery's trouser, and he kissed it.

And while Ellery stared down open-mouthed, convinced that he was in the presence of senility, or madness, the old man prostrated himself; and he said something; and he said it again as he raised his head.

"Elroee."

That was how his name sounded in the old man's curious accent. And Ellery felt his flesh ripple and chill. For wasn't there mention somewhere in the Bible of *Elroï* or *Elroy?* Which meant . . . *God Sees?* Or *God Sees Me?* . . .

All this happened in seconds—his pronouncement of his Christian name, the old man's instant genuflection and repetition of the name in his own version—so that automatically Ellery went on to add his surname.

"—Queen."

And once more the astounding thing happened. For at the sound of *Queen* the old man again kissed the cuff of Ellery's trouser (*the hem of my garments!* Ellery thought, half angrily), again prostrated himself in the dust; and again he repeated what Ellery had said, again giving it a curious and unfamiliar quality.

"Quenan," the old man was saying. "Quenan . . . Quenan . . ."

But this version of his surname brought no shock of recognition. *Quenan* . . . ?

And the old man, still on his knees, went on and on; but what he was saying was meaningless to Ellery, whose own train of thought wandered afield. The hand he had reflexively extended to catch the old man, he was amazed to find, was resting on the old man's cowled head. How had it got there? Surely by accident. Good Lord! he thought. The old boy will think I'm blessing him. And he stifled an impulse to grin. He could make out nothing of what the bearded patriarch was saying—a swift mutter of unrecognizable words that might even have been a prayer.

Ellery came to himself. The old man had risen and taken Ellery's hand in his; and in his odd eyes there was something like excitement (though not exactly that) and something less than concern (though almost that). And he said to Ellery, quite intelligibly, "The time of plowing is over, the days of waiting are at an end."

Ellery searched his memory. Was the old hermit quoting something? No, nothing Ellery could recognize. And where was the younger hermit?

"The time of the threshing of the harvest is here, and the great trouble is soon to come upon us."

"No," Ellery decided, nothing he was familiar with.

"Art thou the first?"

The question rang in Ellery's ears.

"The first?" he repeated foolishly.

"The first. He who comes to us in the time of our great trouble, and prepares the way for the second. Praised be the Wor'd."

No doubt about it now—some sort of slight pause in *Wor'd*. But what could it all mean? He could only look into those unfathomable eyes and repeat, "The second?"

The old man nodded slowly. "The second shall be first, and the first shall be second. It is written thus. We thank thee, O Wor'd."

Had the statement been uttered by another man, Ellery might have passed it off as gibberish, a paraphrase of some imagined Scripture. But this man—"the old, old, very old man"—this man compelled respect. Almost he compelled belief.

"Who are you?" Ellery asked.

"Truly thou knowest me," the prophetic mouth smiled gravely. "I am the Teacher."

"And the name of this place?"

A silence, briefly. Then, "I had forgotten that you are a stranger here, even though your coming is a sign that the Wor'd is sure to follow. The place where we stand goes by the name of Crucible Hill, and below us is the Valley of Quenan. This name you know, seeing that it is your own. And what you are cannot be hidden from you." He bowed.

My God, Ellery thought, he's mistaken me for someone else, someone he's been waiting for. A tragicomedy of coincidence, based on nothing more substantial than a similarity of sounds. But whom has he mistaken me for? On hearing my name, Ellery, he prostrated himself in humblest reverence, thinking I had said *"Elroï,"* or *"Elroy"*—*"thou, God, seest me."* He took me for . . .

Ellery could not bring himself to believe it.

Through the giddiness he fought against, he heard the old man—"the Teacher"—saying, "My people do not know the mystery that is to be; they do not know the trouble which is coming upon them, nor how to save themselves when the hailstorm dashes the crop to the earth. They have lived as children. What will they do when the fire rages?"

His grip on Ellery's hand tightened. "Come," he said, "come and abide with us."

Ellery heard his voice asking from far away, "For how long?"

And said the old man, "Until thy work is done."

Tucking his staff under his arm, the other hand still hidden by his robe (holding the trumpet?—had there been a trumpet?), he gently drew Ellery forward and began to walk him down the inner slope of the hill.

And Ellery stepped into another world. It was so startling that almost he cried out. One moment he had been in a desert of sand and naked rock, the next he was descending into a land green and fat with trees and grass and growing crops. In the basin formed by the circle of hills the soil had been terraced; plow ridges ran along the natural contours of the land. In the twilight's hush he heard the pleasant sound of water trickling, and when he turned in the direction of the sound he saw a rivulet emerging from underground and obediently following the course laid out for it. Plainly some master hand had directed with love and skill this conversion of the desert, so that no grain of earth, no drop of water, should go to waste.

And now, far down the slope, he noticed for the first time a settlement. There were enough houses to constitute a village—fifty of them, he estimated, most of them small, a very few larger, and all of the simplest construction. And then an evening breeze came up, and he heard faint voices; and the breeze brought with it a scent of smoke, which he could see rising in slow spirals from the houses.

It was the odor of burning sagebrush.

They were halfway down the slope when the sun set abruptly behind the western shoulder of the hill.

A great shadow fell quickly over the valley of—what had the old man called it?—Quenan.

Ellery shivered.

2 · Monday, April 3

The eye had been looking at Ellery unblinking for a long time before he could bring himself to consider it. His attention once directed at it, it ceased to be an eye and became—obviously—a knothole.

Aye, tear her tattered ensign down—

"That's enough of that nonsense!" he said firmly, sitting up. His sudden movement sent the worn clean quilt sliding to the floor—a journey of no great distance, he learned immediately, since he had been sleeping on sheepskins spread over a tick stuffed with hay and corn shucks. The smell of all three was plain. He was not in some primitive motor court after all.

And with that, he remembered.

As had happened before and was to happen again, he got up believing he was fully rested; the ache in his bones he attributed to his having slept without a mattress or bedsprings.

He automatically looked around for a shower but there was none; he saw no sign of plumbing. The crude cottage had three small rooms, sparingly equipped with furniture as primitive and unpainted as the cottage itself.

But all the wood glowed with a patina that gave off a definite odor. Ellery sniffed at a chair. Beeswax . . .

On one of the tables lay a lump of homemade soap, a length of clean cloth evidently intended as a towel, and a salt-glazed water pitcher and bowl and cup. The pitcher was full. His luggage was neatly stacked in a corner of the room.

He took a sponge bath, gasping, then got into clean clothes. He brushed his teeth, combed his hair. Shaving . . . no hot water . . .

From the door came the rap of wood on wood. "Come in," Ellery said. He braced himself.

The Teacher entered. In one hand was his staff, in the other a basket. "Bless the Wor'd for the blessing of your coming," the old man said sonorously; and then he smiled. Ellery's answering smile was partly directed to himself for indulging a conceit: what could the old man's burden be but the fairy-tale basket of goodies? To his astonishment, that was what it proved to be—napkin covering and all.

"Commonly I dine alone," the Teacher said. "And it may be that you will sometimes wish to eat with the community in the dining hall. This first meal, however, I wish us to share, and here."

There was a fruit juice strange to Ellery (later he learned that it was a blend of mulberry and cactus pear); its flavor was bland and respectful of a nervous morning stomach. There was a platter of cornmeal pancakes with butter and syrup—probably sorghum or sorgo. Ellery missed his coffee, but the milk (it was ewe's milk, very rich) was warming and the gourd of herb tea, hot and sweetened with honey, made an interesting substitute.

Except for the old man's whispered prayers as he washed his hands and ate and drank, the meal proceeded in silence.

"Are you content with this food?" the Teacher asked at last.

"Yes," said Ellery. "I am content."

"Blessed be the Wor'd, and we are thankful . . . We may now go." He brushed the table clean of crumbs, repacked the basket, and rose.

Puddles of sunlight lay along the tree-lined lane which they followed to a building of gray stone. A murmur of childish voices became audible as they approached. Small rooms, each containing a table and two benches, opened off the main hall where the children were assembled. Of course, Ellery thought, without surprise: he is the Teacher—this must be the school.

The smallest children sat up front on the lowest benches; girls sat on one side, boys on the other. They rose as the Teacher confronted them. Row on row of shyly smiling, grave, or respectfully curious faces—all sun-tanned, all clean, all devoid of apathy or insolence—row on row to the teen-agers at the rear. Ellery saw each face clearly, and each face was clear.

"My children," said the Teacher. "Let us bless the Wor'd."

No head was bowed, no eye closed, no word spoken. An intense silence settled over the room. Dust motes, dancing in the sunbeams from the unglazed windows, seemed to move more slowly. A bird lifted up its song not far off.

"This is a great thing," the Teacher said. "You have all been guests in one another's houses. Now there is a guest among us who is a guest of all, of all Quenan. His coming is a gift to us of the greatest importance. I will tell you now only that it has been foretold. What he is to do, you will all witness. To the Wor'd, our thanks for sending him. This is today's lesson. We shall keep today as a holiday. You may go home now; you may put on your holiday robes, you may play or study or help your parents as you wish. Now, go. Blessed is the Wor'd."

He passed among them, touching the head of one, the shoulder of another, lightly patting a cheek or an arm. The children looked wonderingly at Ellery, but they did not speak to him. The boys were dressed in the fashion of Storicai, the old man's companion at the End-of-the-World Store—collarless shirt and "clam-digger" pants; the girls wore long one-piece dresses. All were barefoot. Presently he was to see them emerge from their houses like figures in a Biblical painting, yet with no hint of masquerade; some carried flowers.

Ellery walked with his guide through the village, accepting with wonder the occasional flower offered to him, even by the older boys.

"Do you have many visitors—guests—from outside?" Ellery asked. And found himself adding, "Teacher?"

"None," said the Teacher.

"None? In the past, surely—?"

"In the past, none. You are the first—as it is written. We know little of the outside, and the outside knows nothing of us."

The light shineth in the darkness, and the darkness comprehendeth it not.

Ellery observed the village with mounting excitement.

Nestled in their patches of garden, the weathered little cottages were bare of ornamentation except for vines, which had been allowed to overrun the walls. The natural wood had turned silvery gray and yellow-brown, with an occasional splash of ochre; the green of the vines and plants and the multicolors of the flowers completed a chromatic harmony that brought peace to the eye. And for contrast there was the rough and random stone of the few larger, public buildings.

Visually the dwellings had a curious vitality, as if they too had grown out of the earth. And here was a lesson, Ellery thought, for architects. It was as if art (or artfulness) was not so much frowned on here as unheard of. There was an artless beauty about it, an innocence, a natural functionalism that, when he thought of the mathematical *Bauhaus*-style urban boxes or Le Corbusier's machines for living, made him wince.

There was no paving. There was no electricity. There were no telephone lines. Barns and farmland and pasture revealed no combustion-engine equipment; even the plows were mostly of wood. And yet everything was lush and teeming. It was hard to remember that beyond the circle of the hills—Crucible Hill, had the old man said?—lay all but lifeless desert.

And the people . . .

Now and then a woman came out on her doorstep to greet the Teacher respectfully, a respect tinged with something remotely like uneasiness, as if the newness and wonder of the guest had suddenly overshadowed everything. Or a man on his way to the fields, or returning—feet stained with earth, hoe on shoulder, gourd of water in hand—would greet the Teacher; and again the eyes would dart to the newcomer, and away, and back again.

Except for the children, free on their holiday, everyone was busied with some task; yet there was no air of drudgery, none of the tension or depression so often produced by industrial work. Everyone Ellery saw seemed happy and at peace.

In spite of an occasional browsing animal, the unpaved streets were remarkably clean, a phenomenon presently explained when they came upon the village's department of sanitation. It consisted of one very old man and one very young woman, who were raking the dirt of the lanes with whisklike implements and carefully depositing each twig and turd and leaf in a donkey cart.

The wonder in their eyes as they glanced at Ellery, and then hastily away, was as deep in the very old man as in the very young woman.

It was a wonder not confined to the people of Quenan. Ellery himself was filled with it. Here, indeed, was the Peaceable Kingdom.

Or so it seemed.

"Here we must stop awhile," said the Teacher, pausing before a large building, barn-size and barn-simple. The heat of the day had increased, and it was a relief to rest. This building had fewer windows than the school, and it was cool inside. Blinking in the dimness after the dazzling sun, Ellery located a bench and sat down.

They were evidently in a sort of central warehouse or supply depot. Shelves ranged the walls and divided the interior into sections; there were bins and compartments and drawers. Bunches of herbs hung drying and dried, wreaths of chili peppers, ropes of red onions glowing like embers in the half-light; white corn, and yellow corn, and Indian corn with kernels of every color from black to lavender; sacks of meal, dried beans in greater variety than Ellery had ever seen outside a Mexican or Puerto Rican grocery. He saw wheels of cheeses, bales of wool, dirt-brown on the outside and creamy white on the shorn underside; hanks of yarn, huge spools of thread, bolts of cloth, tools, parts of looms and spinning wheels, bundles of wax candles hanging by looped wicks, kegs of nails, packets of bone needles, heaps of horn combs, buttons, wooden spools, earthenware, seeds, even crocks of preserves.

It was a primitive cornucopia, a rude horn of plenty; and there was a counter of sorts behind which stood the man Storicai, who had been with the Teacher at Otto Schmidt's store. He greeted Ellery solemnly, his glance slipping past as if to see whether the guest had not, perhaps, come to the storehouse in that strange vehicle which had so fascinated him outside Schimdt's that day . . .

That day? It seemed like only yesterday—

Suddenly Ellery realized that it had been only yesterday.

The shock jolted him out of the sense of dream-participation which he had been experiencing. It was as if he had been caught in a time maze, in which past and present kept shifting like the colors of a kaleidoscope. Certain now, as he had not been a moment before, which day of the week it was (althouth he was by no means certain of the year, or, for that matter, of the century), Ellery watched the Teacher take a knife from some pocket or pouch within his robes and sliding it from its sheath show Storicai that the blade was broken.

"Shall I fetch you a new one, then?" asked the younger man

"No—" the Teacher said. (Or was it "Nay"? What *was* that odd accent, or inflection? Had it developed from some originally minor quirk of speech by the Quenan community's isolation?—or from some other tongue?—or from both?) "—no, I shall choose one for myself. Each hand knows its own need best, Storesman. Place the broken one in the repairs bin for the Carpentersmith."

Murmuring, "So, Teacher," Storicai the Storesman obeyed (in a community like this, Ellery thought, waste-not-want-not would be more a matter of survival than of thrift); but the Storesman did so with his eyes still on the stranger, on and away and on and away.

The Teacher's voice came from the shadows. "When last you saw our guest, Storicai, you did not know, nor did I know, that he was to be here amongst us. He it is who was foretold. It is a great thing that has been visited upon us, Storesman, a very great thing." The voice, so old, so strong, fell silent.

The Storesman's eyes widened with that same wonder Ellery had seen throughout Quenan. Rather restlessly, Ellery stirred. A stray sunbeam picked out his wrist watch, and it glittered. The Storesman uttered a little cry.

"Oh," he said. "Oh."

"My wrist watch—"

"Oh!"

The watch was of gold, and wafer-thin, his father's birthday present to him of some years earlier. It showed not only the time of day but the day of the month as well, and the year, and the phases of the moon. Only the last, Ellery now thought, seemed fitting to this valley. New moon and old moon: what other reckoning was needed in this little lost land—land which time forgot, to its contentment?

"Haven't you ever seen a wrist watch?" Ellery asked, raising his arm.

The Storesman's bearded face was broad with amazement. "A timepiece to wear on the hand? No, no."

"Then you have seen watches of other kinds? And clocks?"

Ellery hoped that he did not sound like the mighty white man patronizing the child of nature. But it turned out that Storicai was familiar with watches and clocks. There were a few watches in Quenan (Ellery saw some of them later—great, grave grandfathers of pocket timepieces, wound by key, which must have crossed the prairies behind oxen leaning heavily into the endlessly stretching grass), and a few clocks, too. "Clocks with hands," the Storesman explained with pride, although it appeared that most of them were hourglasses, and some sundials ("for shadow-time") and some water clocks ("for night-time") .

On impulse Ellery slipped the watch off his wrist. Storicai's eyes opened even wider at the flexible action of the metal-mesh band. "This is what it does," Ellery said. "And this . . . and this."

"But the key. I see no keyhole."

"It keeps winding itself up, Storicai. Through the ordinary movements of the arm."

The Storesman touched the wrist watch timidly. Again it glittered, and the glitter reflected from his eyes. For a moment Ellery wondered if the gleam signified wonder so much as cupidity. Or perhaps neither, he thought. Or something else, or nothing else.

"Here is the new knife I have chosen," said the Teacher, returning. "It fits my hand well."

The Storesman nodded, turning reluctantly from Ellery's watch. He drew toward him a huge ledgerlike tome, a sort of log or daybook that looked homemade; and in this tome he recorded the transaction of the knives. When he was finished, Ellery—again on impulse—held the wrist watch out to him. "I have another one I can use while I am here," he said to Storicai. "Would you like to wear this one until I leave?"

Storicai's eyes shone as he turned automatically to the Teacher. And the old man smiled and nodded as if to a child. Ellery slipped his watch over Storicai's thick wrist; and as he and the Teacher left the storehouse, Ellery glanced back to see the bearded man turning the gold watch this way and that in the shaft of sunlight.

"Your temple, is that it?—or your, well, town hall?" Ellery asked as they went into the tallest and most imposing of the stone public buildings. Each window was set in a vertical recess almost the height of the structure.

"The Holy Congregation House," the Teacher said. "Here I have my room, and the Successor has his. Here is where the Crownsil meets, and here—"

"The what meets?" Ellery thought the old man's speech idiosyncrasy had corrupted the word "council."

But the old man repeated patiently, "Crownsil. In this hall the Crownsil of Twelve holds its meetings, as you will see. As indeed, Elroï, you have already seen."

Elroï!

Nothing of yesterday, then, had been a dream.

And—"Already seen"?

A dream and not a dream. What was real? Ellery thought in a detached desperation. He would ask no more questions. Listen, he told himself, listen. And observe. Perceive . . .

He perceived a hall running the length of the building, in the manner of the schoolhouse. It contained one very long and narrow table, with two benches of corresponding length along the sides, and two short benches, one at the head, the other at the foot. The only lamp he had yet seen in Quenan burned in a bracket over a door set in the far wall opposite the entrance—here evidently was the explanation for the kerosene the Teacher had bought at the End-of-the-World Store. End-of-the-World . . . If the world's end was anywhere, it was here in the Valley of Quenan surrounded by the hill called Crucible.

The old man was speaking again, pointing with his staff in the dim, yellowish, faintly flickering light. The doors in the long walls to the left and right led to sleeping quarters, he explained; the single door in the left wall led to his chamber, which was as large as the two rooms beyond the two doors in the right wall. And the patriarch went to the right wall and knocked with his staff on one of the two doors.

It was opened immediately by a young man, a very young man; eighteen, nineteen, Ellery thought, no older. A teen-ager with the face of a Michelangelo angel, except that it was rimmed by a crisply curling young beard.

The angelic face lit up with joy.

"Teacher!" he exclaimed. "When my brothers ran from the schoolhouse to tell me you had declared a holiday, and why, I put on my robes." He was dressed in a garment much like the old man's. "Guest"—he turned to Ellery and took both Ellery's hands in his—"Guest, you are welcome here. You are very welcome. Blessed is the Wor'd."

Ellery looked into his eyes, dark in the sun-browned young face; and the dark eyes looked back at him with infinite trust. Such trust that, when the boy gently released him, Ellery turned away. Who am I, he thought, that I should be looked at with such trust . . . with such *love* . . . ? Who am I—or who do they think I am?

"Elroï—Quenan—" the patriarch was saying, "this is the Successor."

Successor? Ellery wondered. To what? But then he realized that, as the old man uttered the word, it was capitalized. Successor to whom? Instantly he knew the answer. Successor to the old man himself.

"Teacher, you called him . . ." The young Successor hesitated. "You called the Guest . . . ?"

"By his names did I call him, Successor," said the old man gravely. "By his name which is Elroï, and by his name which is Quenan. It is he, Successor. It is indeed he."

At which the Successor, with a look of adoration, dropped to his knees, and prostrated himself, and kissed—yes, thought Ellery, it cannot be said any other way—kissed the hem of his garment.

"The room where I rest and sleep is the room next door. But this room," the Successor was saying (while Ellery reproached himself: *Why didn't I stop him? Why didn't I at least ask what it all means?*), "this room is where I study and write." He emphasized the last word slightly. "There is no other room like this one. It is called the scriptorium."

On the table were paper, ink, pens. As to what he might be writing, the Successor did not say.

The Teacher pointed with his long staff to the door under the lamp. "That room is the smallest," he said. "But the least shall be the greatest. That is the—" he pronounced a word. It sounded like "sanctum."

Sanctum? The holy place? Again Ellery could not be sure of what he had heard, again it seemed to him that there had been a pause, a hesitation . . . *sanc'tum*.

The dreamy haze, half mystification, half fatigue, through which he had been seeing everything, lifted for a moment. He heard himself asking matter-of-factly, like the Ellery Queen of a million years ago, "How do you spell that?"

"It is the forbidden room," said the Successor. Then, "Spell—? I'll write it for you." The young man seated himself at a writing desk, selected a reed pen, fixed its point with a small knife, dipped it in a jar of ink, and wrote on a scrap of paper. There was something arcane, hieratic, about his manner. Scriptorium . . . Suddenly Ellery realized what it was: with his own eyes, in the century of rocket experimentation and quantum physics, he was actually beholding a scribe at work in the manner of the ancients. In silence he picked up the piece of paper.

Sanquetum.

That explained the pronunciation.

Which explained nothing.

"It is time, Teacher," Ellery said, "that you tell me just how your community is ruled. I must ask about other things, too. But that will do for the beginning."

The old man looked into him—past him, perhaps. "What you require of me, Quenan, I shall do, although I know that you ask only to prove me. We are not ruled, Quenan. We have no rule here. We have governance."

Something flashed through Ellery's mind; eluded him; then he had it. Some lines from an old book: *Dr. Melancthon said to Dr. Luther, Martin, this day thou and I will discuss the governance of the universe. Dr. Luther said to him, Nay, Phillip— this day thou and I will go fishing, and leave the governance of the universe to God.*

What Dr. Melancthon had replied, Ellery did not remember. "Fish, or cut bait," perhaps.

"Governance, then," said Ellery. The old man glanced at the Successor, who immediately rose and parted from them with a vigorous handclasp and a radiant smile.

Taking Ellery into the long hall, the Teacher seated him at the table of the Crownsil and sank onto the bench opposite. For a moment he seemed to meditate (or pray?). Then he began to speak. And as he spoke, Ellery felt himself slip back into the dream, the timeless world which possessed "what the world had lost." And the old one's voice was as soft as the lamplight on his face, which made Ellery blink, for it was like looking at a very old painting through a golden haze.

"The Crownsil of the Twelve," said the venerable Teacher, "I shall list for you in an order, Quenan. But in this order none is first, as none is last."

And he uttered a word. Was the word "grower"? "Growther"? Ellery puzzled over it. But he could not decide.

The Grower, or *Growther*, it seemed, oversaw all the crops and what they entailed: choosing which plots were to be planted to corn, which to cotton, or flax, or beans, or melons, or whatever; directing how they were tended, and by whom; and how harvested, and when.

The Herder. The Herder's responsibility was the cattle, sheep, goats, donkeys, and fowl of the community (there were no horses in Quenan, the Teacher said; what purposes horses might have served were more easily and economically served by the donkeys). The Herder saw that the beasts were kept from the growing crops and the young trees; he saw to their pasturage, to their breeding, and to the care of their progeny. The Herder was also a man wise in the ills of animals, although his methods kept Quenan's livestock in such rude health that his veterinary skills were not often needed.

The Waterman. The very existence of the community depended on the Waterman's labors. It was the Waterman whose duty it was to keep in good repair the cisterns and catch basins where the scant rains were stored; who saw that the wells were clean, the all-important springs kept open. He attended to the small aqueduct; and he husbanded the water of the irrigation ditches, portioning out what was needed for drinking, cooking, and the communal laundry and bath.

The Miller. The Miller made use, when there was sufficient water, of a waterwheel to grind the community's grains and legumes and even pumpkins into meal and flour. When there was no water, the Miller put up his sails and harnessed the winds. And if neither water nor wind was available, he blindfolded beasts so that they might not grow dizzy, and he walked them round and round to turn the millstones.

The Potter. Crucible Hill contained no clay, but at a distance of less than a day's journey by donkey, there was a clay pit. The Potter and his assistant turned out and fired the simple utensils of the community's people, glazing them with salt from a nearby pan. The Potter also made some things apparently needed for religious purposes, but what these were the Teacher did not say.

And the *Slave*—

"The what?" cried Ellery.

"The Slave," replied the Teacher with a sigh.

"You practice *slavery?*" Ellery heard his 1944 voice demand. To the ears of Elroï-in-Quenan it sounded brutally harsh and accusing. For in a community that lived a life of near-Biblical primitivity, was it so remarkable—?

"We merit your reproaches," the patriarch said humbly. "Yet surely it is known to you that we no longer number slaves among us? This is the last. He is in his eighty-eighth year."

"Resting from his labors, no doubt." First the display of bucolic ethics, then this!

"The Slave does no labor at all," the Teacher said. "He serves only by membership in the Crownsil. His needs are cared for by us all."

"Decent of you," muttered Ellery-1944.

"In expiation. In community expiation."

And suddenly it occurred to Ellery that the community might be expiating not its own sins, but those of the nation. Was it possible this "Slave" was one of those who had been freed by the Proclamation or the 13th Amendment? Or was he a survivor of the Indian slavery that persisted in the remote Southwest for a decade or so longer?

It was likelier, Ellery thought, that he represented some dark chapter in the history of Quenan.

Quenan.

What the devil did the name signify? What language had it come from?

Ellery-1944 grew tired again in the slumbering air and dimness of the building. But the other Ellery—the Elroï—said softly, chin propped in both hands, "Go on Teacher. Please."

"Next is one whom you have already met."

The Storesman, to whom Ellery had lent his watch, was custodian of community property. Surrounded by the handmade things of his people, Storicai had taken childlike delight in something of alien manufacture.

The Chronicler. He kept the history, the records, the calendar, the genealogies, and the books of the community. The books consisted mainly of prayers, and these books the Chronicler maintained and repaired.

The Carpentersmith. In charge of all construction, maintenance, and repair of buildings, furniture, vehicles, and tools.

The *Weaver*. This office was currently held by a woman, although it was open to men also. Ellery thinking of Quenan in terms of ancient patriarchal societies, was surprised to learn that women were eligible for all offices.

The Elders. These were two, a man and a woman; each had to be at least seventy-five years old. They represented the special interests of the community's aged.

All matters of community welfare and policy were in the hands of this Crownsil of the Twelve. In any case requiring trial, they served as jury.

"To the Twelve, and to three others—myself as the Teacher, and to the Successor, and to the Superintendent—and to no others," said the old man, "belongs the right of entrance into this Holy Congregation House." He and the Successor lived there, and the Superintendent—whose duties, Ellery gathered, resembled those of a steward, or sexton—acted as liaison between the Teacher and the Crownsil.

"But to two alone belongs the right of silent entrance," said the Teacher. "These are your servant and his Successor."

"Your servant . . ." The dream was multiplying. Ellery felt like seizing his head in his hands out of sheer frustration. After all, *he* had been given entrance. Who in God's name was he supposed to be? Who was "Elroï Quenan"? To cover his confusion, Ellery repeated, "Silent entrance?"

The old hand—bone and vein and skin and sinew—gestured. "There is only one door into the holy house," he said. "That one through which we came. It is never locked; it has no lock. For this house is the heart of the Congregation." His voice did not rise; but it deepened with the fervor of belief.

In the language of modern anthropology, the house had *mana*, and as such it was *taboo* to the community. The only exceptions were rigidly fixed: the members of the Crownsil and the Superintendent. And even they were subject to a ritual discipline. Any of these wishing entrance must first sound the bell outside the door. Only if the Teacher himself answered might the official enter. If the Teacher was absent, or if he was engaged in prayer or meditation or study and did not reply to the bell, then he who rang had either to wait or to seek admittance at another time.

"For none but your servant—" (there it was again! *Is thy servant a dog, that he should do such a thing?* as practice slavery, for example? Was he being gently chided?) "—your servant or the Successor may be alone in this holy house," the old man explained. "To this rule we hold most strictly as an outward sign of obedience to our holy regimen, that none may set foot in this house when I am not in this house, save only the Successor."

Ellery's weariness kept him from uttering the *Why not?* in his thoughts. Probably the old man himself could not give a reason. It was the Rule, the Law; all ritual hardened into that.

Ellery's glance wandered to the far end of the long hall, where stood the closed door with its overhanging kerosene lamp, the door to the room the youngster with the angelic face had called the "sanquetum."

At Ellery's glance, the Teacher said softly, "And the sanquetum. Yes. The forbidden room, as the Successor and the community commonly name it . . ."

Concerning this forbidden room, the old man went on to say, the rule was even stricter. Only one person in the community, the Teacher, might ever set foot in that room; not even the Successor might enter there. It was kept always locked, and the only key to the lock was held by the Teacher. (This was by contrast with the scriptorium, the Successor's official workroom; the door to the scriptorium might be locked, but it need not be, and to this door the Successor usually kept the only key.)

"Thus you see," the Teacher summed up, "our governance is by the fifteen elect: the Crownsil of the Twelve, and the Superintendent, and the Successor, and he who is the leader and the guide and the healer of his flock—thy servant, called the Teacher."

In Ellery's dream it came to him in an enormous waxing of light, like a sunburst, that he was not listening to a recital from some old and forgotten romance, but to the description of an actual community existing in the United States of America in the year 1944, apparently to the complete ignorance of county, state, and federal officials and to some 135,000,000 other Americans.

Searching his memory for a parallel, he could find only one: that tiny community, on its Appalachian mountaintop, which—isolated by a landslide that destroyed its only road to the outside world—remained forgotten for almost a generation, until communication was re-established.

But that had come about through an act of nature, and it had lasted only a short time in the scheme of things. On the other hand, no act of nature could explain Quenan; and from what Ellery had seen and heard, it had been here—isolated by choice—for a very long time. Storicai, the Storesman, had been awed by an automobile; he had apparently never seen nor even heard of a wrist watch.

How long? Ellery wondered.

And, quite mechanically, it became in his thoughts: *How long, O Lord?*

"Then nobody here owns anything?" Ellery asked. He had lost track of time; inside the hall of the Holy Congregation House, the flickering yellow light; outside, from time to time a voice—the soft moan of a cow, the two-note bray of a donkey— all without urgency or clamor.

"No," said the patriarch, "all belongs to the community."

Someone far inside Ellery's head remarked, *But that's communism.* Not the savage, specious communism of Stalinist Russia, but the freely willing way of the early Christians, and of . . . He struggled with the name; it was a pre-Christian group he had read about years before in Josephus. But he could not recapture it.

It was not really necessary to go back so far in time, he thought, or so far away in space. The American continent had a long history of such experiments. The eighteenth-century Ephrata Cloisters—"The Woman in the Wilderness," in Pennsylvania; the Zoarite community of east-central Ohio, which lasted forty-five years; the Amana Society—"The Community of True Inspiration"—founded near Buffalo in 1843, and still flourishing in Iowa in seven incorporated villages; the Shaker communal societies, remnants of which remained after more than a century and a half; the Oneida Community of "Perfectionists." These groups shared at least two common denominators: they were nearly all founded on a religious base, and in them all possessions were owned by all.

So, apparently, in Quenan. Its religious origin and nature, although they eluded Ellery, were evident; and—"all belongs to the community," as the Teacher said. As individuals its people owned nothing; whatever they grew or made, whatever service they performed, was contributed to and shared by and done for the benefit of all. In return, every Quenanite, young or old, strong or weak, received the portion of his need.

But what was "need"? And how draw the line between need and wish? Ellery saw vaguely that to hold this line it would be necessary to maintain absolute isolation from the world outside. A man could not covet something the very existence of which was unknown to him. And to guard against the nomadic nature of the human mind, which knew no boundaries, a system of indoctrination had to be basic to the community's way of life.

Pursuing this thought with the Teacher, Ellery learned that membership in the community came automatically with birth into it. There were no proselytes in Quenan, to spread the taint of civilization. Nor was there a period of probation, for if a probationer were to fail, what would become of him?—he could not be permitted to leave Quenan even under an oath of silence; suppose he were to break his oath and bring the world down upon them? So it was better not to admit the possibility of exclusion to begin with. As soon as the child in Quenan was old enough to enter the school, the Teacher exacted in the most solemn ceremony the child's vow of utter consent to the ways and laws of the community, with its primitive life, its isolation, its customs and hard labor and equal opportunities— and the sharing of all by all.

But this was merely the ritual that sealed the practice. "Give us the child for eight years," Lenin had said to the Commissars of Education in Moscow, "and it will be a Bolshevist forever." Hitler was proving the same thing with his parent-spying youth organizations. *Train up a child in the way he should go*—the scribes of Proverbs had noted twenty-three hundred years ago— *and when he is old he will not depart from it*. A Quenanite would no more question the nature of the community in which he had been rigidly reared and indoctrinated than a fish would question the nature of the sea in which it swam.

And it was of corollary interest to note that while there was the Weaver in this council, and the Herdsman, and the Carpentersmith, and the rest, there was no minister of war or defense, there were no police . . .

"I beg your pardon," Ellery said, "I'm afraid I did not quite catch that. How many did you say was the number of your people?"

"There are two hundred and three," the Teacher said. "The Potter's father ceased a week ago, but an elder sister of the Successor gave light to a girl-child three days since, so the number stands."

The sun sets, but the sun also rises.

In Quenan the sun rose on a communal dining hall, on even a communal bath, open at different hours for men and for women. Bathing, it appeared, was of more than mere hygienic importance here, although bodily cleanliness was a strict rule. In Quenan, as in primitive societies throughout time, bathing was also a ritual act, since what was bathed was the divine image which is man. When the Quenanites washed, they prayed; when they prayed, they washed. The washing of the body was an act of worship; worship, an act of cleansing.

"You prayed, too, I noticed, while we were eating," Ellery said.

"So do we all. For from our bread and wine we draw the strength to do the will of the Wor'd, and it is fitting that we bless the Wor'd as we eat. And we bless the Wor'd also for holy days and fast days, for festal days and for work days, for sunrise and sunset, for the phases of the moon and the seasons, for the rain and for the dry, for the sowing of the seed and the harvest of the crops—for all beginnings, for all endings. Blessed is the Wor'd."

Each male Quenanite was expected to marry by the age of twenty. If he failed to do so, the Crownsil, with the consent of all concerned, chose a wife for him; and the system seemed to work. Dr. Johnson, Ellery reflected, would have been pleased. The Great Cham had remarked once that he thought marriages would work out just as well if they were made by the Lord Chancellor.

One fact of life in Quenan, said the Teacher, made necessary a departure from the marriage-at-twenty rule. Because there was a slight preponderance of women in the community, females were granted an extra four years. If they were not married by the age of twenty-four, they became the wives of the Teacher. The Teacher explained this calmly.

"Men may sometimes be ill content if another man has more than they," he observed. "But in Quenan the Teacher is not as other men. This all believe, so all are content."

Ellery nodded. The Teacher, he supposed, was primarily a spiritual authority; the sacred office would transcend the man. As for the women who became his wives, they would be held in special esteem by the community, and probably they considered themselves fortunate—wasn't it Bernard Shaw who said that any intelligent woman would rather have a share in a superior man than the whole of an inferior one?

Ellery could not help wondering if, at his advanced age, the Teacher was still virile, like Abraham. Or did his young wives serve as mere bed-warmers against the chill of the night, as in the case of old King David? For that matter, how was it that so healthy a community remained so small in numbers? Continence? Control? Contraception? He wanted to ask, but he did not.

"You teach," he said instead. "What kind of textbooks do you use?"

"There is—" The old man paused. Then he resumed: "There is among us in common use one book only. It is our text in the school, it is our every family's prayerbook. The manual of understanding, some call it. The manual of knowledge, others say. Or the book of light, or the book of purity—of unity—of wisdom. Many are the names, one is the Book. It is the Book copied by the Successor in his scriptorium and kept repaired by the Chronicler in his library. It is the Book I have always with me."

He reached into his robe.

"Why, it's a scroll!" Ellery exclaimed.

"It is the Book." Carefully the Teacher unrolled a section of it.

Ellery recognized the Successor's handwriting. It was an odd script—odd as the local accent was odd. It was unlike any standard American penmanship—assuming such a thing to exist—that Ellery had ever seen. Was there a resemblance to the obsolete "Chancery hand" once used in certain English legal documents? He could not be sure. He also thought he detected the influence of some non-Western alphabet. Like so much else in Quenan, it was half revealed, half concealed.

for the pasture and for the sunlight on the pasture, we bless the Wor'd. may our hands work well and our feet walk well, in the pasture, and in coming, and in going. let us not lift up our voices in anger when we work or when we walk, not against brother, not against beast or bird, think on the Wor'd which keeps our voices from anger.

"I see," Ellery murmured. "I see . . ."

The prayers were written on small lengths of paper, each sewn with thread to the next until a considerable scroll was formed, and the whole rolled up and tied with a soft cord. There were no capital letters in the written text—this caught his attention at once—except the W of Wor'd . . . Yes, definitely a W. Did this mean that he had been wrong in thinking "Wor'd" was a corruption of "Lord"? Or had a simple pronunciation change come to reflect itself in the spelling? Or did the break in the word—indicated in the written form by an apostrophe, in the oral form by a just perceptible pause—trace to a missing or dropped letter? And if so, did "Wor'd" stand for "World"?

Language, accents, attitudes, forms . . . So many things in Quenan (the name itself) tantalized with their almost-differences. It was . . . yes, it was exactly like a dream, in which the powerless dreamer never quite grasped (while wholly grasping) the phantom realities of the experience.

Ellery looked up from the scroll. When he and the Teacher had sat down, what sunlight penetrated to the interior of the Holy Congregation House had come through the eastern windows. Now it was slanting through the western windows.

"It is no longer my custom to eat the midday meal," the Teacher said presently. "The people have finished theirs, but there is always enough for one more. Will you come now and eat? I will remain with you."

"I'm sorry that I've missed joining with the people." Ellery rose, feeling hunger. And, as always these days, weariness.

"There will be a time." The Teacher rose, too, and smiled. It seemed to Ellery a sad smile.

They paused outside the door. Ellery blinked and sneezed in the bright afternoon. "This is the bell?" he asked. "The bell which must be rung and answered before entering the holy house?"

The Teacher nodded. The bell was perhaps a foot high. It was discolored with age, its surface scarred inside as well as out; the rim, where the clapper touched it, was worn very thin. It hung about chest-high; and by peering closely Ellery could see that two legends ran along its lip. One read:

17 The Foundary Bell Lane Whitechapel *21*

and the other:

From Earth's gross ores my Tongue's set free
To sound the Hours upon the Sea

An English-made ship's bell dating from the reign of Queen Anne! When this bell had been cast, the King James Bible was a mere century old; Shakespeare had walked the crooked streets of London during the childhood of some very old man; George Washington's birth was twenty years in the future. Through what perilous seas forlorn had the bell sounded its note through the centuries? And how (most marvelous of all) had it come here, to Quenan, in the American desert?

Ellery asked the Teacher, but the patriarch shook his head. As it was, so had it been. He did not know.

And, duly, Ellery marveled and went on to feed his stomach. The communal dining hall was like a barn with many windows, full of light and air and hearty smells. The food was simple and filling—a vegetable soup, chili and pinto beans, steamed corn with butter, stewed fruit, and another variety of herb tea. A young married couple waited on them; apparently this was a rotational duty. Wide-eyed, reserved, yet shyly expectant, with proper deference toward the Teacher, they gave most of their attention to the guest, the outsider. The only outsider they had ever seen.

Throughout Ellery's meal the Teacher prayed silently.

When Ellery was finished, the Teacher led him outside; and for the remainder of the afternoon—until the shadows inundated the land and the windows began to sprout candles—the old man conducted him about the Valley, answering Ellery's questions. Up and down the inner rim of Crucible Hill they went, surveying the cultivated fields, greeting the people at their toil. Ellery was fascinated. He had never seen so many different shades of green in a state of nature. And everything was aromatic with growing things and sagebrush smoke—the wood of the sagebrush was brought in from the desert hills, the Teacher told him, to feed the fires of Quenan . . .

The dream quality intensified; in one day the world outside had become invisible in the mists, and the mists themselves had almost been forgotten. It was as if Quenan and all that it contained, including himself, *were* the world. (Had Adam and Eve known the nature of their Garden until they were cast out of it?)

On his curious sublevel the old Ellery kept musing. Where were art, and music, and literature, and science in this capsule in space-time? They were not here. But also not here—so far as he could tell—were discontent, and hatred, and vice, and greed, and war. The truth, it seemed to him, was that here in the lost valley, under the leadership of the all-wise patriarch, existed an earthly Eden whose simple guides were love of neighbors, obedience to the law, humility, mercy, and kindness.

And, above all, faith in the Wor'd.

It was late that night when Ellery finally voiced the question he had struggled with from the beginning.

They stood in the open doorway of the Holy Congregation House, with the soft uproar of the night in their ears. A sweet odor rose from the damp earth, resting from the day. The small glow of the lamp over the sanquetum door shone behind them in the quiet building.

"You are troubled, Elroï," the Teacher said.

"Yes," said Ellery. "Yes . . . It seems so long ago that we met. But it was only yesterday, at sunset, on the crest of the hill."

The Teacher nodded. His remarkable eyes pierced the darkness as if it were not there.

"You spoke then as if you had been expecting me, Teacher."

"That is so."

"But how could you have known I was coming? I didn't know it myself. I had no idea I was going to take the wrong turn—"

The Teacher said, "It was written."

So might a priest of the Toltec have answered Cortés, thought Ellery; and instantly wondered why the thought had come to him. Cortés, whose armor glittered like the sun god whose return had been predicted. Cortés, who had brought to the faithful of Quetzalcoatl only death and destruction. Ellery stirred.

"You spoke, Teacher," he said cautiously (was it out of some atavistic fear that he might unleash evil merely by speaking of it?), you spoke of a great trouble that would befall your Valley and your people. And you said that I was sent to prepare—"

"To prepare the way. Yes. And to glorify the Wor'd."

"But what trouble, Teacher? And where is it written?"

The patriarch's eyes rested on him. "In the Book of Mk'h."

"I beg your pardon?" Ellery said. "The Book of what?"

"The Book of Mk'h," the Teacher said. "The Book which was lost."

A little drawer opened somewhere in Ellery's head: the fact that the Book *was* lost and not *is* lost was noted and filed away. "Mk'h . . ." he said. "May I ask how that word is spelled, Teacher?"

The old man spelled it, having some difficulty with the hesitation sign. "Mk'h," he said again, stressing the hesitation.

"Mk'h." Ellery repeated. "What does it mean, Teacher?"

The patriarch said simply, "I do not know."

"I see." How could the old man not know? "In what language is it, Teacher?"

The old man said, "Neither do I know that."

This was awkward. And Ellery bent to the task, examining the mystery. Mk'h . . . Could it be, he thought suddenly, some pristine or even aborted form of Micah? The Book of Micah! Sixth of the books of the Minor Prophets in the Old Testament . . . Micah, who had prophesied that *out of thee shall he come forth unto me that is to be ruler in Israel; whose goings forth have been from of old . . . And this man shall be the peace* . . . ! But . . . "The Book which was lost"? Had the Book of Micah ever been "lost"? Ellery could not remember. It seemed unlikely, for surely . . .

"The Book of Micah," Ellery said to the Teacher.

In the night, in the doorway of the holy house, the old man turned to Ellery, and the yellow glow on the far wall turned his eyes to flame. But it was only an effect of the lamp. For the Teacher said in a puzzled way, "Micah? No. Mk'h."

Ellery gave it up (for now, he told himself, but only for now). And he said, "This great trouble, Teacher. Is it written what kind of trouble it will be?" He swallowed, feeling chidish. "A crime, perhaps?"

He might have touched the old man with a red-hot iron. Agitation rippled over the ancient face as if a stone had been thrown into a pond. "A crime?" he cried. "A crime in Quenan? There has been no crime among us, Elroï, for half a century!"

Concerning doctrine or prophecy one might doubt, but Ellery could muster no reason for rejecting the patriarch's testimony on a matter of yea-or-nay fact involving his own Valley. Yet how was it possible for a community of men, women, and children to exist which had known no crime for almost two generations? Since the days of—who had been President then?—Harrison, was it, the stern and bearded Presbyterian warrior who had been a general in the Civil War? Or walrus-mustached Cleveland, whose Vice-President was a man named Adlai E. Stevenson? No matter; it was another world, an American time and way of life as different as in Byzantium under the Paleologi—while here in Quenan, life must have been exactly as today . . . and in all that time—no crime?

"If there has been no crime in Quenan in half a century, Teacher," Ellery said carefully, "then surely I may infer that half a century ago there *was* a crime?"

"Yes."

"Would you tell me about it?"

The old man, tall against his taller staff, stood looking past Ellery at the ghost of a cottonwood tree, but not as if he were seeing it.

"Belyar was the Weaver then, and he had finished weaving ten bolts of cloth for the Storesman's shelves. But first Belyar cut from each bolt an arm-long length and concealed the ten lengths in his house, and he made for himself new garments out of them. The Storesman observed this, and examined the bolts, and he saw that they were not of the usual lengths; and he questioned him.

"Belyar was silent. This the Storesman reported to me, and I—when the Weaver again would not answer—I reported it to the Crownsil. It was a hard time. Much was considered. But at last a search was ordered; and in the presence of witnesses the Superintendent searched the Weaver's quarters and found scraps of the newly made cloth hidden in the bed, for the foolish man had not been able to part with even the scraps. And Belyar was tried by the Crownsil and he was declared guilty. Belyar's beard was brown and, as he worked much in the weaving shed out of the sun, his skin was very pale.''

The sudden intrusion of this bit of description made Ellery start. He looked closely at the old man and thought he understood. That through-seeing gaze was looking at events happening again, happening now.

"He then confessed. 'The washing goes slowly,' Belyar said. 'And it is hateful to me to wear clothes which are not fresh and clean. I took what is mine by right. For it was the work of my own hands.' ''

The heretic. One in fifty years!

"The Crownsil found him guilty, but it might not pass sentence. That heavy duty is the task of the Teacher. It was from my lips, then, that Belyar the Weaver heard his punishment for breaking the law of the community. I declared that he be given a piece of silver, and food and water sufficient for two days' sustenance, and that he be then driven into the desert, never to return on pain of death.''

A piece of silver? It was the first mention of money Ellery had heard in Quenan.

"Never to return on pain of death, Teacher?" he said. "And was not the decree— sending Belyar into the desert with food and water for only two days—tantamount to sentence of death?"

"That is as it may be." The old man's face was set in stone. Then it softened. "It was within my power to decree Belyar's death directly. Yet in my weakness I found that I could not. Such a thing had not happened in my lifetime.''

He went on to say that only strict obedience to their laws kept them a community, and that once the Weaver had broken the law he could not be permitted to remain in Quenan; there was no room for one whose continuing presence would ever remind the people of his awful act in stealing from his brothers. Nor could he be sent out into the world, for fear that he might bring the world down upon them. Thus banishment to the desert and almost certain death.

"He did not come back, or try to come back? Was his body never found?"

The old man sighed. "He was not seen or heard of again. And since his banishment there has been no crime in Quenan." And he fell silent.

What had become of the pale-skinned thief? Did he stagger about the desert until he fell and died of hunger and thirst, to be covered by the shifting sands? Or had some Indian or desert rat killed him for the sake of his silver piece? It was even possible that he had been found in time by a *ranchero,* or that by some miracle of good fortune and hardihood he had made his way to one of the cities of the plain or the seacoast. And there he would have taken up his life—in the era of the Beef Trust and the Sugar Trust and the Robber Barons; in the days when "that dirty little coward that shot Mister Howard" was entertaining the customers of his Leadville gambling hell with the tale of how he, Robert Ford, had put a bullet from an improved Colt .45 clean through the head of "Mister Howard"—Jesse James; when every Western town was rimmed with cribs offering raw sex for sale along with rotgut whisky . . . How long would Belyar and his piece of silver have survived in such a civilization? How could life in the Garden of Eden have prepared him for it?

Death directly, Ellery mused, would have been far more merciful. But the old man could not have known that.

And . . . "there has been no crime in Quenan" since.

That was something to think about!

"Then what is this great trouble which is written?" Ellery asked.

"I do not know," said the Teacher. "It is not written what it is, only that it will come." And he sighed again, heavily. "Until your coming, Elroï, I had thought it might be fire, a flood, or a shaking of the earth, or drought, or a plague of locusts, or a great sickness. Now, with your talk of crime . . . Can it be? I ask, can it be the evil of man of which it is written?

"My heart is sore," the old man went on, staring into the darkness. "For, ask myself what I will, I cannot think of a crime to come so great as to be in the Book. What sin can occur in Quenan?" he cried. "Here there is no cause for envy or for greed. Even the thieving of Belyar the Weaver could not occur today, for our storehouse bursts with the fruits of our toil; so that, should a man wish for more than the common allotment, he has but to ask for it and it is given him freely. Hate? There is no hate in Quenan; if there were, surely the Teacher would know it. Adultery? In all our days not even an accusation of such has been brought against any man or woman among us. Slander? False pride? False witness? I tell you, these cannot be in Quenan.

"For we do not wait to obey our laws, we run to do so with joyous feet. Corruption? What should I, or the Successor, or the Superintendent, or any of the Crownsil or the people generally, be corrupted with, and to what purpose? What one has, all have. And as bribery cannot be, so extortion cannot be. Here in Quenan, authority is not abused, trust is not broken, uncleanliness does not outlast the moment; and we are so slow to anger that the cause for it would wither before ever the anger came.

"My heart is troubled, Elroï, that you should suspect us of a capacity for crime."

The majestic voice ceased, and once again the little noises of the night intruded. Ellery shook his head in the darkness. It was too good to be true. He wanted to accept it, but he could not. Why hadn't the Teacher mentioned the greatest crime of all? he thought as the old man reached past him, shut the door of the Holy Congregation House, then took his arm and urged him gently onto the hardpacked earth of the village street.

Was it that the very notion was foreign to him and his community, so that it would never even cross his mind? As, for example, the concept of war was so foreign to the Eskimo culture that the people of the farthest North had no word for it in their vocabulary?

"And yet," the Teacher said in the lowest register of his deep voice, "and yet you are here, Elroï, and for a purpose. That which has been written for all the days to come I may know not; but this I know—that which will be, will be. Blessed be the Wor'd for your coming. I am thankful even so."

The water from the rivulet stopped splashing in the darkness somewhere, began again farther away, an irrigation ditch had been shut off, and another opened. He sensed that the Teacher was walking him back to the house where he had been lodged during the first night.

"How many years, Teacher, has Quenan been here?" he asked.

"To the number of three generations."

"And you are very old. Can you remember when the community was founded?"

The Teacher was silent. When he spoke, his voice seemed faint. "Tomorrow is another day, Elroï. This is your house. The Wor'd sustain you."

Ellery half imagined that there was a very slight tremor in the old man's powerful handclasp.

Later, lying on his pallet, Ellery heard a frog in some ditch lift up its voice. *Weedit, weedit.* And then another, and another, and another. *Weedit, weedit, weedit* . . . Not more than half awake, Ellery thought of frog spawn, silent in still waters; then of tadpoles, still silent; then the swift ascension to the land, the swarming, the crawling, the croaking . . . and at the last a voice, a human voice, saying something stubbornly.

Nevertheless, this voice said, fading as Ellery sank into sleep, *the world does move* . . .

3 · Tuesday, April 4

Ellery was finishing his breakfast in the communal dining room when the interruption came. (In spite of stern intentions he had overslept, and he was alone in the building except for the commissary staff, who were quietly cleaning up around him. He had tossed on the pallet all night and regretted having neglected to take one of the red capsules from the little bottle in his grip. Also, he missed coffee. Herb tea might be wonderfully healthful, but it did nothing for the taut Queen nerves.)

The interruption came in the form of an excited voice.

"Quenan!"

The young man washing a nearby table top looked up, startled; then at Ellery, awed; then away.

"Quenan!" The voice was nearer. "Elroï—"

The Successor burst into the dining hall, his angelic face alight, the long hair tumbling into the curls of his young beard. "There is a message for you—" For a moment Ellery fancied that someone from outside had tracked him down—the mere possibility made him recoil. But then the Successor said, "—from the Teacher. He asks that you come at once to the holy house!" And the young man ran out.

Ellery jumped up and hurried out after him. But the young Successor was speeding off in another direction, evidently on some task or errand, and Ellery made his way quickly to the Holy Congregation House. Here, just as he was about to open the door, he remembered the taboo, and he took hold of the bellrope instead and pulled it twice. And waited.

Butterflies danced between the world of light and the world of shade. The sound of wood being chopped came to him: ka-thuh-*thunk*, ka-thuh-*thunk*. And the rich green smell of earth and water and plants.

Just as the door of the holy house opened, a little boy rode by astride the pinbones of a young donkey, intent on the dancing butterflies.

"Teacher—" Ellery said.

And—"Teacher," said the little boy.

And—"Blessed be the Wor'd," the Teacher said, to both. His eagle's face softened as he looked at the child, and he raised his hand in a graceful gesture of benignity. "Walk in beauty," the Navajo says in farewell. This old man walked in beauty.

The little boy smiled with delight. Then he spied Ellery, and the smile wavered. "Blessed be the Wor'd," the child lisped hastily, and with uplifted hand made the same gesture.

"Come," the old man said to Ellery. And he shut the door.

This time they did not sit at the table or pause at the Successor's empty rooms. The Teacher led Ellery to the only door of his own room. The light shed by the lamp over the sanquetum door in the main meeting room penetrated to the Teacher's chamber, with its few stark furnishings, and by itself would have served dimly to illuminate it; but the chamber contained its own arrangements for light. These were three tall, very narrow windows, scarcely more than slits a few inches wide, one set in the far wall opposite the door, the other two in the walls to the side. Through each of these slit-windows a plinth of sunlight entered, to meet in the exact center of the room at the bed standing there, so that the bed itself was bathed in sun. (And now Ellery realized that three walls admitting sunlight meant three *outside* walls; the Teacher's room was architecturally a wing of the building, exactly balanced on the other side by a wing housing the Successor's two smaller rooms.)

The Teacher's chamber was the room of a cenobite. Its narrow trestle bed was of wood covered by sewn sheepskins—its mattress—with a single thin blanket neatly spread out. To each side of the head of the cot stood a small square table; two rude chests occupied the midpoints of the two facing side-walls; a stool in one corner was identical with a stool in the corner diagonally opposite. The room itself was square.

And so it was easy, in this room of perfect balance, to sense that something was out of balance. Something jangled in this orderly structure, something was off-key.

Key . . . Ellery's eye leaped, just anticipating the Teacher's pointing finger, to the top of the left-hand table. On it, to one side and near a corner, lay a bracelet of some dull metal; and attached to the bracelet was a single key.

"Someone moved the key last night," the Teacher murmured. He saw that Ellery was puzzled, and he said, "For someone to enter my room without my knowledge— Elroï, this is a grave matter."

"How can you be sure," Ellery asked, "that the key was moved?"

The old man explained. Each night after saying his prayers he took off the bracelet and placed it in the exact center of the table top. "Symmetry," he said, "is a way of life with me, Elroï. I hold it the purest of esthetic forms."

This startled Ellery, who had seen no evidence of esthetic devotion in the village: beauty, yes, but unrealized. *Euclid alone looked on beauty bare . . .*

"—and when I awoke this morning, I found the bracelet where you see it now— not centered on the table, but near a corner. By this I know that someone entered my room as I slept. And what is far more serious—"

"—must have entered the holy house without ringing the bell, by stealth?" The Teacher nodded, fixing Ellery with his prophet's eyes. "This is not necessarily so, Teacher," Ellery said.

"How not? Though it is true that I am the lightest of light sleepers. Still, the bracelet has been moved. I can hardly count the years I have slept here, and nothing like this has happened before. Is it a sign? A warning?"

Ellery looked around, studied each of the slat-thin windows in turn. "No one could have come through one of these," he said, "not even the smallest child. But someone could have *reached* through . . . with a fishing rod—No," seeing the incomprehension on the old face, "no fishing rod here. All right—a pole, then, a long stick of some sort. With it, someone could have lifted the bracelet from the table, pulled it through the window, and later returned it the same way."

"But why?" asked the Teacher, in the same troubled way.

Ellery picked up the key. It was crudely fashioned from the same dull metal as the bracelet. It looked rough and pitted, but it felt smooth—too smooth. Partly on impulse, partly because he had felt this smoothness on keys before, Ellery lifted it to his nose. That wild, pungent odor—

"Do you keep bees here?" he asked.

"Yes, although not many. We save most of the honey for the sick. And the wax—"

"Just so," said Ellery. "The wax."

Someone had taken a wax impression of the key during the night. And someone had fashioned, or was even now engaged in fashioning, a duplicate key—to what?

"This is the key to the sanquetum, the forbidden room. It is the only key, and I alone may have it, for I alone may enter. Not even the Successor may accompany me," the old man said. "Or have I told you that?"

They were silent. Voices faded down the lane, died away. A far-off cowbell sounded; an ass; the woodcutters broke their own silence: ka-thuh-*thunk*, ka-thuh-*thunk*. Somewhere children sang a simple song of a few pure notes. With such treasure as this, what was there to conceal in the sanquetum?

Ellery asked the question.

The old man sat down on one of his stools. Elbow on knee, hand on forehead, he pondered. At last he rose, beckoning Ellery to follow. They went out into the meeting room and stood together beneath the lamp burning over the locked door.

"It would be permitted for you to enter," said the Teacher, with some difficulty.

"Oh, no," Ellery said, very quickly.

"If you are here to open the Way, you may surely open this door."

But Ellery could not bring himself to the act. Whatever strange error had mistaken him for their Guest, to take advantage of it by setting foot in the holy of holies would desecrate it.

"No, Teacher. Or, at least, not now. But do you, please, go in. Look around with care. If anything is missing, or even out of place, tell me."

The Teacher nodded. From a niche in the wall he took a ewer and a basin and a cloth and washed his hands and face and feet and dried them, murmuring prayers. His lips still moving, he unlocked the door. And in reverent silence, walking delicately, the old man entered the forbidden room.

Time passed.

Ellery waited in patience.

Suddenly the Teacher was back. "Elroï, nothing is missing from the sanquetum. Nothing is out of place. What does it mean?"

"I don't know, Teacher. But that someone has made a duplicate key to this holy room, I am sure. Obviously there is something in the sanquetum that one of your people wants. Tell me everything that is in the forbidden room. Leave nothing out."

The lids came down over the black-blazing eyes as the old seer looked into his memory.

"There is a tall jar containing scrolls of prayers. There is another jar containing scrolls of prayers. There is the holy arque in which the Book of Mk'h is kept—"

"The book—"

"—and the front of this arque is of glass. And there is also the treasure."

"What treasure?" Ellery asked slowly.

The old man's eyelids opened; Ellery could see the pupils widen as they were exposed to sudden light.

And he said, "The silver.

"And now the time has come, Elroï Quenan, for me to answer the question you were about to ask last night. Let us seat ourselves at the Crownsil table."

It was The Year of the First Pilgrimage, a name not given to it until much later. The Teacher was then a youth living with his father and mother in San Francisco, but not happily. The friends who shared their faith were equally unhappy.

On the one hand, the city (or so it seemed to him) was seething with sin. Drunkards reeled down the hilly streets; their obscenities fouled the air. Saloons stood on every street corner, ablaze with gaslight and noisy with cheap music to tempt the weak and unwary. Gambling dens swallowed the money needed to feed men's children, families were made paupers overnight. Dishonesty was the boasted rule in commerce; the few who refused to cheat went to the wall, without credit from the coarse multitude for even the honesty that had put them there.

No man's son was proof against the temptations of the vile Barbary Coast, which made of the human body an article of commerce. Even though shame, disease, and death lurked like jungle beasts, no man could be sure even of his own daughter.

Was not the whole city a gaudy sink? Was not the whole country?

A farmer or rancher might feel safe from the distant corruption; he soon felt the pain of nearer ills. He found himself slave to the railroad, whose unchecked tolls robbed him of most of his profit; the plaything of speculators, who juggled the prices his produce sold for.

While in the nation's capital a man of war—said to be a drunkard—sat in the highest office of the land! Political places were bought and sold by his lieutenants without scruple. Huge corporate combines, with the connivance of his administration, scandalously plundered the people's resources.

It was a black time for the God-fearing. Where to turn? Where to go?

The self-contained world of the Latter-Day Saints seemed to offer a way and a destination; but it was open only to those who professed the Mormon faith. And this, for the Teacher's people, was impossible.

Ellery leaned forward eagerly. "Why, Teacher?"

"Because of our own faith," replied the old man.

"Yes, of course. But what is it? Where did it come from?"

The Teacher shook his Biblical head. The roots of Quenan's faith, he said, went so deep into the past that not the oldest member of the holy community—even in the Teacher's childhood—could say whence it grew. It could be traced through many generations and countries, but the trail became fainter and more difficult to follow, until at last it vanished altogether in the wilderness of time. Communicants had fallen by the wayside, but always a small hard core of the faithful remained to keep the faith alive.

Ellery's persistent questions turned up little. The Bible apparently played no direct role in the beliefs of the Teacher's people, although it colored their traditions and theology. The sect (if that was what it was) had once had a way of life, it appeared, that had been "lost" in the long march of the centuries; the tradition of this vanished way of life had been handed down from Teacher to Teacher, the old man said, and he made a vague reference to the pages of Pliny and Josephus (there it was again, Ellery thought suddenly—a confirmation of his own fugitive recollection).

In sum, the Teacher continued, the Crownsil of his youth in a series of solemn meetings made a decision: They must leave the abonimable world in which they found themselves. Somewhere in the vast lands to the east, even if in desert wastes, their people would seek a place in which they might live, uncontaminated, as a self-contained community, in strict accordance with their own ethical and socio-economic principles.

And so the people sold their houses and lands and businesses; wagons and supplies were purchased; and one day a great caravan left San Francisco and began the eastward trek. And this was another long, hard time.

Their first attempt at settlement, on a verdant tract of land not far from Carson City, was disastrous. They had chosen the site because there was then no railroad to the Nevada capital and, compared with San Francisco, Carson City was a mere village. But its very smallness proved their undoing. Saloons and gambling hells and dance halls, because of the lesser scale of Carson City, proved too tempting to many who had been frightened off by the massive bawdiness of the great city on the Bay. And the strange ways of the colony brought them unwelcome visitors, who came to stare and jeer, men of foul mouths accompanying birdlike flocks of gaudy-plumaged, shrieking women.

Within a year the Crownsil decreed the Carson City colony a failure; they must move on. Most of their worldly assets were tied up in the land purchase and must be written off; very well, they would go where money was not merely unnecessary, but useless. They would find a place so remote, so off the beaten track, that the world would forget them—would not even know of them.

Through many nights and days thereafter, the caravan toiled southeast. People died and were buried by the wayside. Young men and women were married. Children were born.

Generally, the migration tried to avoid settlements. It happened once, however, that a man died after having been taken to a doctor in a frontier village. He had no family, and no one could be spared to drive his wagon, nor was there any room for his goods and gear in any of the other wagons. So everything was sold in the village for fifty silver dollars, and the wagon train moved on—not, however, before attempts were made to seduce several of the girls, to rob the Teacher's father of the fifty silver dollars and the rest of the wagon train's dwindling cash, to entice one couple into claiming the teams and wagons of the entire colony with promise to support the dishonest claim by perjured evidence and a venal judge and jury. All these attempts failed. The latter-day pilgrims left town with dogs turned on them, stones thrown, and guns fired to stampede their beasts.

It was their last contact with civilization.

Food was running low and water had run out when the tugging of their oxen, smelling the springs, brought the pioneers to the ringed hill which they were to call Crucible. Here was a veritable oasis in the desert, hidden, green, rich in water and arable soil, with space enough to grow food for all their number. And they called the valley Quenan.

(Ellery, thinking about this later, decided that "Quenan" might be a corruption of "Canaan," altered by the local accent and grown pronouncedly different in isolation. Though they might not possess a single copy of the Bible, the noble language of the King James Version was familiar to all nineteenth-century Americans: what more natural than that, consciously or otherwise, they should have identified their wanderings in the wilderness with those of the Children of Israel? So he was to think, but he was never to be sure.)

In the Valley they settled, building their first rude shelters from the wood and canvas of the wagons; and here they had remained ever since.

The exodus from San Francisco must have taken place in 1872 or 1873; from Carson City in 1873 or 1874.

"And in all these years," Ellery asked incredulously, "no stranger has ever found his way here?"

The Teacher reflected. "I believe I said earlier that that was so. But I had forgotten—there was one. It came to pass some forty years ago, during one of the Potter's journeys with his assistants into the desert to obtain the special clay of which our prayer-scroll jars are made. A man was found lying in the sands; it was far north of Quenan. The man barely breathed. We hold life sacred; and in spite of our laws the Potter brought him here and he was nursed back to health. As it turned out, no harm was done, for his ordeal in the desert had erased from his mind all memory of the past, even his name. So we instructed him in our faith and our laws, and he lived in Quenam as one of us for the rest of his days. I had lost the habit of thinking of him as from the outside. He ceased some years ago."

One intruder in seventy years, and that one a blank page! Did the community know anything of the world outside? Very little, apparently. Once in a great while the Teacher or the Storesman saw, at or near Otto Schmidt's store, a wagon which needed no beasts to pull it, like Elroï's own; and, of course, for some years the people had caught occasional glimpses of flying machines that made a noise like distant thunder in the sky; but as to events . . . The old man shook his head. Even he, the Teacher, the oldest and most learned man in the Valley, knew nothing of the outside; nor did he wish to know.

"Do you remember the Civil War?" Ellery asked.

The sun-black forehead creased. "That would have to do with"—he paused, as if the next word were unfamiliar—"soldiers? Who wore clothes of blue? I was a young child . . . There is in my mind a confused recollection of many marching men in blue . . . many people shouting . . . my father's voice saying that these were soldiers coming back from the Rebellion . . ."

Of World War I the old man knew nothing. And it was clear that he was equally ignorant of the second global war in a generation, the one currently being waged. Had not Otto Schmidt mentioned it? But the old man shook his head. "I do not speak to him of worldly things; he thinks we are wild men, hermits and knows nothing of our community, We revere truth, but Quenan must remain hidden from men's minds."

The Teacher showed no curiosity whatever about the war, and he seemed quite unconscious of the many United States laws he and his people were daily breaking, not to mention the laws of the state.

Such was the story as Ellery pieced it together from the Teacher's account and, later, from the scant records he was able to consult in the archives of the Chronicler . . .

It was while he pored over the Chronicler's records (his search for some reference in them to Josephus or Pliny was in vain, and the Chronicler had not even a dozing acquaintance with the names) that Ellery suddenly remembered. Both Josephus and Pliny the Elder had written of a religious order originating in the second century B.C. called the Essenes—yes, and now that he thought about it, so had the first century A.D. Jewish philosopher of Alexandria, Philo, who had also left an account of a non-Christian ascetic sect in the Egypt of his time whom he called the Therapeutae.

The Essenes had practiced strict communal possession; scrupulous cleanliness—the frequent ceremonial washings of the Quenanites? The Essenes had abhorred lying, covetousness, cheating; they subsisted by pastoral and agricultural activities and handicrafts.

Was it possible that the sect of Quenan had descended from the ancient Essenes? But there were important differences: the Essenes had abstained from conjugal relations; they had condemned slavery.

Ellery wondered. Practices, even beliefs, might well have been lost or modified in the course of over two thousand years by a people with poor written records and the pressures of dispersion in a swiftly proliferating world of Christians and Moslems . . . It was possible. But no one would ever know.

"Quenan must remain hidden from men's minds . . ." That is, the secret valley was a world unto itself, secure in its purity from outside contamination.

But now its purity was threatened by contamination from within.

Someone of the community had, by stealth and contrivance, made a duplicate of the Teacher's key to the sanquetum. Why? The reason must be an overpowering one. For the act was not only Quenan's first crime in almost two generations, but, unlike Belyar's theft of the cloth fifty years before, it was also an act of sacrilege.

Mere curiosity about the sanquetum—a perverse impulse to see the interior of the forbidden room simply because it was forbidden? Possible, but unlikely; in the face of a powerful taboo, curiosity alone would hardly induce a Quenanite to go fishing in the dead of night through one of the slit-windows in the room of the revered Teacher for the sanquetum key, to take a beeswax impression of it, to return the key, and then to manufacture a duplicate from the mold.

No, the act must have a more tangible base than that.

Theft? But of what? The jars of prayer scrolls? But every family had its own prayer scrolls. The holy book of—what had the Teacher called it?—Mk'h, "the book which was lost" but which, presumably, had been found again? This might be the reason if the community were torn by religious dissension—schism, heresy; but it was not.

That seemed to leave only the "treasure" of the silver coins—the fifty dollars realized by the Teacher's father from the sale of the goods of the man who had died on the trail after the community's exodus from Carson City, and which had apparently been hoarded as a sort of special fund, cash expenditures having been made out of the community's original paper money for as long as it lasted.

But what could anyone in Quenan want with fifty silver dollars, or even one silver dollar? Some bauble at Otto Schmidt's store? The forbidden pleasure of mere possession of the shiny coins?

Ellery shook his head. It was a puzzle—a deep puzzle.

The Teacher rose, staff in hand. His ancient face was torn with grief. "I fear, Elroï, that this matter of the key may indeed be the beginning of the calamities which have been foretold. But now I must go to the children; they are awaiting me in the school. I go with a troubled heart."

"It may be, Teacher," Ellery said, rising also, "that you make too much of this." But his tone conveyed his own misgivings.

"It will be as it will be," the old man said. "You will find the Waterman on the south slope, waiting to show you the aqueduct and the irrigation canals."

And Ellery heard himself saying, "The Wor'd sustain you, Teacher."

The old eyes, which had as usual been staring through Ellery, narrowed and focused on him.

"Blessed be the Wor'd," said the Teacher.

4 · Wednesday, April 5

Ellery decided rather early the next morning that the Superintendent would have made the perfect minor civil servant anywhere in the overcivilized world. He had been designated by the Teacher to conduct the Guest to the northernmost part of the Valley and to point out to him those features of the Valley which they would encounter en route.

"I will conduct you to the northernmost part of the Valley," the Superintendent said to Ellery's Adam's apple in a sort of liturgical mumble.

"So the Teacher told me," Ellery said.

"And I will point out to you those features of the Valley which we shall encounter—"

"So the Teacher—"

"—en route," the Superintendent concluded. He was a shiny sort of man who looked as ageless as a robot. He might have been a postal inspector in Iowa or an assistant curator of a provincial Yugoslavian museum or a sealer of scales in a small municipality in Australia. Did the nature of the work produce this type, or did the type seek out the work? Ellery decided to be philosophical and make the best of it. He was stuck with the man for the whole morning.

"Let's go, then," Ellery said, stopping a sigh.

"Shall we go?" the Superintendent asked promptly. And after a few silent moments of walking he said. "That is the communal dining hall."

"I know, Superintendent. I ate there this morning. And yesterday. And the day before."

The man looked at him glassily. "It is where the community eats," he said.

"Ah," said Ellery. "Thank you." What was the use?

In the course of their tour his guide pointed out the laundry ("That is the laundry. Clothes are washed there"), the wool washery ("I'll point out to you the wool washery. It is there. That is where we wash the wool"), the donkey stable ("—where donkeys are stabled"), an alfalfa field ("—field. Alfalfa is grown there. Animals eat it"), a peach orchard ("A peach orchard. On those trees peaches grow. They are good to eat"), and other landmarks of Quenan.

"And this is the northernmost part of the Valley. Here is the peaceful place."

"The peaceful place?" Ellery repeated, perplexed.

"The place of peace. It occupies the entire valleyside slope of the northern hill," the Superintendent explained, as if Ellery were stone-blind. Ellery decided to be charitable. After all, it *was* the first time in his life that the Superintendent had been called upon to fill the role of tourist's guide. "There are almost one thousand places here, Elroï. Or perhaps more than one thousand; early records are faulty.

Each has the same stone. The dimensions of the stone are: at the base, one foot square; in height, two feet; at the top, three-quarters of a foot square.''

"Do you mean—?''

"Each place at the top of the slope is six feet in depth, at the bottom five. The widths vary.''

Ellery stood in silence.

A thousand headstones, each marked with the same strange carving. As if a tree were to be reduced to its essential structure. There was no writing.

The wind sang in passing.

The Superintendent's flat voice took on a certain contour. "In the fifth row from the top, at the eleventh place from the right, lies my father, and seven places from him lies my mother,'' he said. "One row below and fifteen places from the right lie my wife and our child. And blessed be the Wor'd which sustains us all, here and forever.''

He said no more words aloud, but Ellery saw that he was praying.

My wife, he had said. *Our child.* Not *my first wife,* or *Our eldest child,* or *our youngest child.*

Time passed.

Ellery said "I'm sorry.'' The words were not intended as a concession to death; they were an apology for having judged a man to be a robot.

Voices from below made him turn his head. Two figures were coming toward them, one slowly, one quickly; but the slower reached them first, having started sooner.

It was the guardian of the place of peace, a gnomelike old man with marked cretin features. His speech was too thick for Ellery to follow, but from the gleeful gestures of the small scythe in his blackened hand it appeared that he was describing his work in trimming the grass that grew upon the thousand graves. Was that pride shining from his dim eyes? Ellery felt his flewh crawl.

And the Superintendent said "He does a work that must be done, and so he justifies his bread. Also, if he and the very few like him who are born to us teach us the love which is difficult, it cannot be said that they were born in vain.''

The love which is difficult . . .

Once more Ellery said, "I'm sorry.''

By now the second man had reached him.

It was the Successor, as it had been the previous morning.

And his message was the same.

The old Teacher said, "This morning the bracelet with the key was on the other side of the table.''

Ellery examined the key again. It looked like something used for a medieval keep, for it was fashioned from a single huge slab of metal on one plane. It still smelled, though less strongly, of the dark and unbleached beeswax into which it had been pressed.

Suddenly the Teacher said, "You have seen something.''

Ellery nodded. (A bit of nonsense jumped out of his memory: The old lady asking the storekeeper if he had a "signifying'' glass, and at the storekeeper's negative, saying with a sigh, "Well, it don't magnify.'')

He fished in his pocket for the powerful little lens he always carried with him, unfolded it, and looked intently through it at the key. Then he handed the lens to the old man.

"I see marks of a sort," said the Teacher. "Here, and here, and here on the edges of the bit. Scratches." He looked up. "I do not understand."

"File marks," Ellery said. "And fresh—they weren't there yesterday. It seems clear, Teacher, that whoever borrowed your key to the sanquetum and took a wax impression, for the purpose of making a duplicate key, found that his first work was faulty. Therefore he had to correct the fault. He worked on the duplicate key with a file, after fitting the duplicate over your key—this original—for guidance."

The old man seemed uncertain of his meaning. But Ellery had already left the Teacher's room and was striding toward the door of the sanquetum. The old man followed.

Ellery tried the door. "Locked," he said.

"As it should be."

Ellery stooped for a close look at the lock. "Will you observe this, Teacher?"

The old man stooped. By the lock were fresh scratches in the time-polished surface of the wood.

"It means," Ellery said, "that an attempt was made to open the sanquetum door with a key that did not fit."

The old man shook his head. "I am confused," he confessed. "He who made the key worked over it with a file to correct it, and still the key did not fit?"

"You're reversing the probable order of events. It must have happened like this:

"Two nights ago, while you were asleep, someone reached in through one of your slit-windows with a long reed or pole, lifted the key ring off your table, took it away, and in a safe place made a wax impression of the key. The key itself he then returned to your table by the same method, not knowing that you always placed it in the mathematical center of the table top.

"From the wax impression he made a duplicate key, and with this duplicate he stole into the holy house last night and tried to unlock the door of the sanquetum. The duplicate key did not work.

"He realized that the copy he had made was not sufficiently accurate. But to correct it he needed your key again. Thereupon he stole out of the Holy Congregation House and around to one of the windows of your room in the wing, and with a pole or reed he again took possession of your key, and again he went off with it—this time to correct the inaccuracies in his duplicate with a file. He then returned your key on its bracelet to your table with his pole, once more failing to realize that it should be placed in the exact center of the table. Have you investigated the sanquetum, Teacher, to see if anything is missing this morning?"

"Nothing is missing," said the old man with difficulty.

"Then I suppose the coming of dawn or some other reason kept him from using the corrected key on the sanquetum door in the early hours of this morning."

The bearded face was set in a multitude of fine hard lines, like an etching.

"It is to be expected, then . . ." The words stuck in the old man's throat.

"I'm afraid so," said Ellery gravely, pitying him. "He will make another attempt to enter the sanquetum, undoubtedly tonight, and undoubtedly this time the duplicate key will work."

There was no one else in the holy house.

The Teacher had given grim assent to Ellery's request that he be permitted to examine the interior of the forbidden room alone. Then the old man had left, wrapped in silence, and since the Successor was off on an errand somewhere, Ellery had the sacred building to himself.

He found himself squaring his shoulders. If the leader of this curious flock permitted him to set foot in their holy of holies, why should he hesitate? Yet hesitant he did feel, as if he were about to commit sacrilege—a "profanation of the mysterie."

Still, it had to be done. He inserted the big key in the lock, felt the heavy tumblers turning over, pushed the door open, and stood on the threshold of the forbidden room.

It was really no larger than a large closet. There were no windows. The only light came from what he took to be an eternal lamp—an oddly shaped oil lamp of some time-crusted metal hanging from the precise center of the ceiling. The draft caused by the opening of the door had set the lamp in motion; it swung now, slightly, back and forth, like a censer, scattering shadows instead of smoke.

And in the shifting light Ellery saw:

To either side of him, each in a near corner, a very tall and slender jar of pottery, purple in color, resting on a wooden base and surmounted by a bowl-like cover. Jars, bases, bowls were identical.

Directly facing him: an old-fashioned walnut china closet, glass-fronted. On the bottom shelf lay a book, open. And on the upper shelf were two perfectly stacked columns of silver coins of equal height, in accordance with the fundamental principles of symmetry—"the purest of esthetic forms."

Nothing else.

When the eternal lamp had come to rest and his eyes had grown accustomed to the light, Ellery removed one of the jar covers and looked in. It contained many rolled papers—scrolls—each secured with a bit of purple thread. He replaced the cover and looked into the other jar; it, too, was full of scrolls.

He turned his attention to the cabinet.

It reminded him so strongly of the china closet that had stood in his grandmother's dining room during his childhood that he half expected to find the shelves filled with the same blue-and-white willow-pattern dishes. But this one contained nothing except the open book and the two columns of coins. Through the glass front he studied the book. It seemed printed in the black-letter type called Old English (the phrase "Cloister Black" flickered in Ellery's memory), or at any rate in some font with a close resemblance to it. It was difficult to make out in the poor light, so Ellery put off for the moment the task of deciphering it and turned his attention to the two columns of coins. They were remarkably bright and shining.

He opened the china closet. Old silver dollars in mint condition!

He dipped into his store of numismatic knowledge. Some of the old "cartwheels," he recalled, were quite rare.

Was this the reason for the duplicate key and someone's plan to invade the sanctuary? Was the would-be thief concerned with the monetary value of the "treasure" of Quenan?

There was the almost legendary silver dollar minted in San Francisco in—when? yes!—1873, the same year the Quenanite sect had probably left that city in its quest for a new settlement. Only seven hundred had been minted, and all but the proof copies held by the mint had disappeared. Speculations about their fate had run from the theory that they had been buried somewhere and the secret of the hiding place lost through sudden death to the equally unprovable hypothesis that they had wound up in China as payment for lead-lined chests of green unfermented tea or even opium. But suppose everyone was wrong, and these—these two neat pillars of coins, as perfect as on the day they were minted—were the "lost" 1873 San

Francisco dollars? A single specimen would be worth a fortune! And there were—how many?

With shaking fingers Ellery lifted one of the coins from the left-hand column and peered closely. The face of the coin depicted Liberty seated, and the date . . . *1873!* He turned it over, holding his breath. The obverse showed the American eagle ("a verminous bird," Ben Franklin had called it disdainfully, "a stealer of other birds' catches," in urging the adoption of the turkey as the national emblem instead). If there was an *S* below the eagle—signifying the San Francisco Mint . . .

Ellery took out his little magnifying glass and searched out the mint mark. Disappointment washed over him. It was not *S*. It was *CC*.

Of course—*CC*, Carson City. The capital of Nevada had had its own mint in those days, when a flood of silver poured out of the nine-year-old state's rich mines. And then as now Nevadans had favored hard coin over paper money . . . He checked the other coins. All bore the *CC* mint mark.

Ellery restacked them with great care in the same two perfect columns and closed the glass door of the china closet.

While not the priceless silver dollar of the 1873 San Francisco mintage, the 1873 *CC* was valuable enough. Each specimen, he guessed, would be worth about two hundred dollars now—perhaps more, considering their perfect condition. But again the question was: Who in Quenan would even think of stealing money? And what good would it do him if he succeeded? That the would-be thief had any knowledge of the coins' numismatic value he discounted at once. No, to the Quenanite thief the coins would have, at the most, their face value. And to steal a handful of dollars invested with the taboo of sacred objects . . . Ellery shook his head. Whatever value these coins represented to the thief, it was not material. But what? He could not even guess.

He left the sanquetum, its shadows shifting weirdly with his movements, and locked and tried the door. Then he went seeking the Teacher at the school.

Gravely, Ellery returned the key.

"Where," he asked the old man, "is the Chronicler to be found?"

The Chronicler provided an antic note to Ellery's sojourn in the Valley. The old Quenanite sported a crop of curly, grizzled whiskers, rather short. No hair grew on his upper lip, which had sunken into his upper jaw from the long-time absence of incisors. This gave the lip a remarkable flexibility. He would suck it in with a rather startling noise, a combination *smack-click;* this caused his lower lip to shoot forward, so that the total effect was of a sort of spitting, intelligent old monkey. The old man's shoulders were frail and bowed; his head was bald except for a matted gray fringe, like a tonsure. I know, Ellery thought suddenly: he looks like that bust of Socrates.

For the occasion the Chronicler fished out of his robe an extraordinary device. Two pieces of glass had been fitted into a wooden frame, the ends of which were pierced for leathery thongs that ended in loops. Only when the old man fitted them to his eyes and slipped the loops over his ears did Ellery realize that they were hand-crafted spectacles. He seemed to have greater difficulty seeing through them than without them, so obviously the lenses had been salvaged from some mysterious out-world source and fitted into homemade frames. Perhaps they went with the office.

"Do I have your meaning, Elroï?" the Chronicler asked in a cracked tremolo. "Whence you come, the years have numbers, not names?"

"Yes."

"Thunderation! And do the people *(smick!)* have numbers as well?"

"No, names, unless they misbehave. Yes, this is our year 1944."

"*(Smick!)* 1944 *what*, Elroï?"

"A.D. That stands for *Anno Domini*. In the Year of Our Lord. Of the Christian era."

"Ne-e-e-ever *(smick!)* heard-of-it."

"Which year is it, Chronicler, according to the Quenan calendar?"

The Chronicler had been peering into a scroll taken at Ellery's request from its repository jar in his record room. He looked up from the scroll at Ellery's question, amazed.

"The year it is *now? (Smick!)* Blessed be the Wor'd! How should I know?"

Half amused, half confused, "Who, then, should know?" Ellery asked.

"Why, no one! No one at all! (*Smick!*) A year's got no name till it's over, you know. How could it? The Crownsil meets on Lastday and decides which name to give it. The year that has just gone past was recently named The Year the Black Ewe Had Twins. Before that there was The Year of the Big Plums. Then The Year of the Caterpillars. Then The Year of the Great Wind. Then . . ."

Ellery followed him back, back, back . . . through The Year of the Lost Harvest, The Year the Earth Shook, The Year of the Great Rains, The Year the Teacher Took Barzill to Wife, and so on; until, finally, The Year of the Eastern Pilgrimage, when the Quenanites had made their exodus from San Francisco. Which, indeed, had been 1873.

"So you see (*smick!*), we have been in our Valley years to the number . . . seventy, yes! (*smick!*) seventy. That's how many years I have counted for you. And the number may be confirmed by the old writings."

The Chronicler gestured toward the scroll. The writing was in the same strange "Chancery hand" Ellery had seen the Successor employ in the scriptorium. Was it possible that some Teacher or Successor in a long-gone generation had been employed by a London law firm—perhaps even before the days when Dickens was reporting parliamentary debates?

Possible? In this place, Ellery thought, anything was possible.

"The old writings," Ellery murmured. "Do they record anything, Chronicler, about the fifty silver dollars?"

Up jumped the Chronicler, stuffing the scroll into its jar and replacing the cover. "They do, they do!" He trotted back, replaced the jar on its shelf, took down another jar, and trotted back with it. "Let me see (*smick!*) 'Year of the Last Pilgrimage'—yes, hmm, hmm." He ran his finger down a column, failed to find what he sought, rolled the scroll up on one side, unrolled it on another. "Hah! Look—"

There it was, in the same archaic writing, on the yellowed paper. *this year the crownsil debated what to do with the fifty silver dollars, which some suggested that, we possessing greater wealth than this which needs be counted, it be buried and forgotten. but instead the crownsil voted that it be deposited in the sanquetum, there to lie until such time as may be otherwise decided.*

The strange letters danced before his eyes. Ellery drooped. He was exhausted again. What was the matter with him? He struggled with his thoughts.

Fifty . . . He had failed to count the coins in the two columns. But surely they hadn't been as many as fifty?

"What happened to the rest of the silver dollars, Chronicler?"

The old official looked puzzled. "Rest of them (*smick!*)? Nay, Guest, I know nothing of that. Only the Teacher—blessed be the Wor'd for his continuing presence amongst us—is permitted to enter the forbidden room. The dollars are kept there, with the holy book."

"Yes, the holy book. What does its title mean?"

"The Book of Mk'n?"

"Mk'n? I thought the Teacher called it Mk'h?"

The Chronicler frowned at his own error. "According to the old writings—and all is written with the pen of remembrance—the lost book was thought to be the Book of Mk'n. That is, by those who held that there *was* such a book. Others (*smick!*) have held that there was not. But so the Teacher called it, and his father before him—Mk'n. Then, five years ago, in The Year of Many Birds, the Teacher found the lost book; and after he had studied the old writings again, he believed that we had always misread or miswritten the title—that it was Mk'h and not Mk'n. And since then we have called it the Book of Mk'h. For all is as the Teacher says."

"But what does the title *mean?*"

The old man shrugged. "Who knows? Do names always have a meaning?"

After a while Ellery left and sought out the Teacher. He asked if he might borrow a donkey and take a brief leave of the Valley.

"You will be back," the patriarch said. It was neither a question or a request.

"Of course."

"Then go, Elroï, and the Wor'd go with you."

Ellery had not been certain of his motives in fixing on a Quenanite beast for his journey instead of taking his car, and the long, uncomfortable donkey ride did not make them quite clear. Finally he decided that he had been moved simply by a sense of fitness. In the land of the prophet one went mounted in the manner of the prophet. (And a rude manner it was: no proper saddle, only a worn felt pad; a frayed grass rope for bridle and bit; and a long reed in place of whip or quirt.)

He was also undecided whether Otto Schmidt, *Prop.*, was more surprised to see his customer of a few days before come "riding on the foal of an ass" than to see him again at all. At last the storekeeper's mouth closed and a delighted smile spread so widely across his moon-face that his smudge of mustache threatened to reach his ears.

"It's you!" he cried.

"Hello, Mr. Schmidt," Ellery said dismounting. "Where can I tether Lightning?"

The stout little man bustled forward. "Here, here in the shade. Let me get him a bucket of water and some bread. Oh, you brought feed. Here, let me fix it for him. *Well!* Mr. Quinn, was it? Or Kean? My goodness, where you been? And how come you're riding this here old jackass? What happened to your car . . . ?"

Ellery walked into the store, inhaling the cool, damp aroma of ancient wood and cinnamon and coffee and vinegar and cloves and kerosene. Everything was as he had last seen it: the spirals of flypaper, the faded colorphoto of Franklin D. Roosevelt, the worn counter with its brass measure set into the top (and how long ago was it, Ellery wondered, that calico or canvas or gingham or unbleached muslin had been measured off on it?), the antique soda-pop cooler . . .

He sat down at one of the tables and immediately winced. An occasional canter on the Central Park bridle path had not been really adequate training for a three-hour ride through the desert on the back of a vigorous male donkey.

"Well, by golly!" Mr. Schmidt had scurried in, beaming. "You found the road like I told you? You get to Vegas? Say! Is that why you're on the jack? I bet you lost your car playing crap. Or was it in the slot machines? Or—it's none of my business, of course."

Ellery smiled noncommittally. "Any chance of getting something to eat, Mr. Schmidt? Or I'll have to eat Lightning."

"Surest thing you know! You're in luck! Bill Hone, you wouldn't know him, makes a special side trip through here once a week on his way from Hamlin to Vegas. I give him my ration stamps and he picks the meat up for me. Well! Bill was by this morning and he left me some of the nicest steak I've seen since I was cutting meat back in the old home town. How about a T-bone and maybe a couple of eggs? And there's some boiled potatoes I could country-fry, and I baked up a batch of peach tarts . . ." He ran down, evidently searching his mind for additions to the menu.

Ellery swallowed the water in his mouth.

"Oh, yes," he said. "Starting with some coffee?" And added, "Will you join me?"

"Well, by golly!" said Otto Schmidt. "I will . . . !"

The coffee was fresh and strong; the steaks had been pan-broiled over a slow fire. Ellery found his sense of purpose slipping away in the pleasure of once more eating civilized food. How long ago had it been? There was no time in Quenan, and not much more awareness of its passage here in the End-of-the-World Store. With an effort he pulled his dawdling mind back to the business that had brought him.

"What can you tell me about the silver dollar the old fellow gave you last Sunday, Mr. Schmidt?"

Otto Schmidt paused, a crisp brown-edged chunk of potato halfway to his mouth, a drip of egg on his mustache. He stared. He blinked; his smile faded. Then the potato continued to its destination, and he chewed it slowly.

"So. You met up with those two hermits. Well, they're kind of queer, but live and let live is my motto. They don't bother no one and I hope no one bothers them—"

"Mr. Schmidt," Ellery said gently. "Otto. No one's going to bother them. Or you. I simply want to know about that silver dollar I saw him give you."

The corpulent little storekeeper declared earnestly that there was no law against silver dollars. Gold, now, he said, that was different. In '35—no, '34—time went by so slow out here you lost track—a fellow came through in a touring car with rubber curtains buying old gold—

"Otto."

"—said his name was Haggemeyer, he'd been in Mexico with Black Jack Pershing chasing Pancho Villa. He'd set up his own business afterwards in Laredo but the depression wiped him out—"

"Otto . . ."

"—borrowed some money against his pension and was going around buying up old gold. He showed me his license—had to have a license for gold—"

"*Otto!*"

The storekeeper stopped, looking apprehensive.

"Otto, nobody's accusing you of breaking the law. Here, take a look at these."

Ellery produced his wallet. As police card followed police card, Otto Schmidt's eyes opened wider and wider. At the sight of the two letters from Washington, they bulged.

"Sayyy! You must be a pretty important fellow." His eyes shone as he leaned over the table. "Does this have anything to do with the war effort?"

Ellery recast the question. "Do I have anything to do with the war effort?" And answered it, quite truthfully, "Yes, I have."

Otto leaned back, unmistakably awed. With one final "*Well!*" and a muttered, "That's okay, then," he got up and went over to his safe—a safe as short and squat as he was, with the flaked remains of an American flag and eagle still faintly visible in faded red, white, blue, and yellow on its door. He came back with a battered old ledger.

"You got to understand the situation when I bought this place," he said with false-hearty defensiveness. "I don't know how long this old hermit had been dealing with the former owner, but they didn't trade for cash money; no, sir. The hermit and his wagon would come around every now and then with produce—hides, wool, flaxseed oil, honey, beeswax—truck like that; and the fellow who had the store would give him credit.

"Then came the depression. Then came me. But the depression was still on, and in a little while I found out that my suppliers, my wholesalers, wouldn't take produce any more—not in such small quantities anyway. Cash on the barrelhead, they said. Credit? 'Credit is dead,' I told the old hermit. 'No more produce. Has to be cash.' 'What's that?' he asked me. Well, I put my hand in my pocket and I had a lone silver dollar and I pulled it out and showed it to him. That old man looked at the silver dollar, then he looked at me like I'd shown him a dirty picture. And out he goes without saying a word.

"Next time he showed up was November, 1930. Here it is, writen down, see? *November 12, 1930. Hermit, Carson City silver dollar, 1873.* I didn't know much about old coins, still don't, but I figured it's got to be worth a lot more than just one hundred cents, and I told him so. I was due to make a visit to L.A., and I offered to take his coin with me and see what I could get for it. He agreed, though I could see he was kind of struggling with himself."

Otto had taken the silver dollar around to various dealers in downtown Los Angeles, and he had finally sold it for the highest price offered in 1930—$90. When the old man of the hills returned to the End-of-the-World Store, they made a deal: the proprietor would retain $18 for his trouble and the old hermit would be credited with $72 against his account.

The old man visited the store once or twice a year, and Otto noted each transaction in the ledger. Sometimes the hermit would bring one of the *CC* 1873 dollars with him, sometimes not, depending on the state of his account. When one of the coins passed hands, Otto held onto it until his next trip to Los Angeles, where he would shop around for the best price, sell the coin keep 20 percent commission for himself (to Ellery's amusement, the figure was between a literary agent's commission and an art dealer's), and credit the balance to the hermit's account.

"And that's the way it's been for thirteen and a half years," the little storekeeper said. "The old bird seems to have a whole supply of 'em—I figured he must be some kind of prospector from way back who went a little nutty from too much sun, and the younger fellow's his grandson or something."

"How many *CC dollars* has he turned over to you since the first time?"

"Including last Sunday? Well, I got to figure . . ." Figure Otto did, with moistened finger riffling and rumbling the pages, while Ellery fidgeted. Finally the storekeeper announced "Nineteen, all told."

Ellery's first thought was that there was something wrong about the number. The thought kept niggling, but he could not come to terms with it. Impatiently he asked Schmidt what kind of things the old man bought on his visits.

"Oh, rock salt, kerosene, nails, stuff like that. No, never candy or wine or anything fancy. Seed? Not that I remember. But lots of paper. Must do a heap of writing. And, oh, yes! he once bought a piece of furniture."

"Furniture!"

Otto Schmidt nodded. "Sure was funny, what happened that day—the book and all. I can remember, Mr. Green—Breen—?"

"Queen," Ellery said. "Let's not wander afield, Otto. You mentioned a piece of furniture and a book. What about them? And when was this?"

The storekeeper referred to his ledger. It had occurred on April 8, 1939—"the year the war broke out in Europe." The hermit had come in . . . alone? Yes, Mr. Queen, alone. "Never laid eyes on the younger fellow till last year. Well, the old man left a silver dollar, picked up his supplies, and was getting ready to go. The book was on the counter and he spotted it. Something real strange seemed to happen to him. You've noticed his eyes? They're kind of . . . on fire all the time. Well, this time they blazed up like Fourth of July. And he went into a trance, like, shook and mumbled, seemed to be having some sort of a fit, and—well, *praying*, like, all at the same time.

"When he calmed down, he asked me how much credit it would take to buy the book, how many silver dollars."

"What book was it?" Ellery asked, failing to keep the eagerness out of his voice.

"Oh, some book sent to me from Europe; I have relatives on the other side. I'd tried to read it, but it didn't hold my interest, so I put it away. I'd come across it again and was having another try at it when the hermit came in."

"But what was the title of the book?"

"To tell you the truth, Mr. Queen, I can't recall. Anyway, when he said he wanted to buy it, and I said no—"

"You said no? Why, when it didn't interest you?"

"I don't know," said Otto Schmidt. "It just didn't seem right—I mean, selling a present from a relative. But he kept after me to let him buy it. The more I said no, the more he said yes. Got all hotted up, the old man did—offered me all the silver dollars he had. In the end I said he could have it—as a gift. You know, he blessed me? And then he pointed to an old walnut china closet I used as a showcase for notions and such, and he offered to buy *that*. I charged him five dollars for it."

"Didn't he say why he wanted the book?"

"No, just wrapped it up, very careful, loaded his wagon, and left. I guess if you're not touched in the head to begin with you don't become a hermit. You know, he couldn't even read the book? Admitted it when I asked him. But he just had to have it."

The question of the book was not going to be solved here in the store, obviously. Nor the question of the silver dollars. Their number . . . why was he so disturbed about their number?

Here is wisdom: let him who hath understanding count the number of the Beast, for it is the number of a man, and his number is six hundred sixty and six . . .

Interesting that this verse from the Apocalypse of John should enter his mind just now. But of course 666 was far too large. He had to know what the number was— he simply had to. To do that he must return and count the coins in the holy arque. Now!

The nearer Ellery got to Crucible Hill, the moodier he felt. It was with an effort that he had restrained himself from trying to beat the donkey into a gallop. A heavy depression had settled on him; a black, bleak melancholy. The wearisome journey on the beast, his mood and malaise, gloomily recalled the state of mind and body that had brought his work in Hollywood to such an abrupt halt; and he asked himself if he had ever really recovered. And he asked himself if he ever would.

He looked up at the sky, observing with surprise that it was rapidly darkening although it was not yet sunset.

Was a storm brewing? Perhaps a falling barometer was causing his depression.

By the time he had reached the crest of Crucible Hill, the sky was almost black and the Valley was in profound shadow. He could discern nothing clearly. Even his ears seemed affected; he could hear none of the usual sounds of Quenan. Jogging slowly down the inner slope, eyes open but not seeing, he was almost upon the Holy Congregation House before he looked up, and was shocked.

Gathered before the building was a crowd which must have represented almost the entire population of the Valley.

And all were silent.

And it was like night.

The blackened air had a green tinge to it, and through this unnatural light the yellow lampshine from inside the House fell through the open doorway with ghastly effect, like a scene from hell. The stunned folk of Quenan stood rooted as though by some paralyzing force, some terrible horror they groped vainly to apprehend.

Ellery's heart swelled, then constricted as if squeezed by a giant hand. *The Teacher!* Was it his own death the old man had sensed approaching?

Dismounting hastily, Ellery ran through the crowd and into the House. And there indeed was the Teacher —but not dead, only looking like death; looking for the first time every year of his great age. And at his feet lay a man.

Storicai.

The Storesman was dead. But no assault by nature on heart or brain had stormed his life and taken it. The sun-dark forehead had been crumpled by a barbarous blow: bones had shattered, blood had spurted, so that head and face were thickly redly wet with it, as if a bucket of paint had been flung at him. And head and neck and shoulders lay in a pool of it, still glistening.

Numbly, Ellery sought its cause; and there it was lying on the floor of the Holy Congregation House a little to one side of the Storesman's body, an instrument he had—somehow—expected to find: a heavy hammer, spattered with scarlet.

The ''great trouble,'' then, had come at last to the Valley of Quenan. There was no longer need to wonder in what form it would make its dread appearance.

It was the kind of trouble for which Ellery had been predestined; and his brain cleared, and he sprang forward.

At the back of the Storesman's head there was another wound; but Ellery's practiced fingers told him that it was not, by itself, a mortal blow. The smashing hammer on the forehead had taken Storicai's life. He parted the curly hair; and among the curls he spied—first one, then another, then still another—tiny particles of what looked like plaster.

Ellery frowned. Nowhere in Quenan had he seen plaster. He examined the speck again, this time with his lens.

They were clay—bits of hardened clay.

Gently he opened the clenched hand of the dead man. The Storesman had died clutching a button, a metal button, its sundered threads still attached; and on the button's face there was a crude and curious symbol.

Ellery did not pause to examine it. He dropped the button into a glassine envelope from the leather kit he had had a messenger fetch from his luggage.

Strapped to the left wrist of the dead man was Ellery's watch. He lifted the wrist, the hand dangling. Ellery looked up. "He was so taken with this watch—"

Before Ellery's eyes, beyond surprises now, the Teacher drew himself up to his full height, shedding his mantle of years swiftly; and his voice, when it came, was rich and strong again. "We must not say"—he gestured toward the watch, glittering gold in the dimly golden light—"we must not say, Elroï. 'It would have been better had he never seen it.' "

But this was no time for riddles; and Ellery returned his attention to the watch. The crystal was savagely smashed, the dial deeply dented; no mere fall would have caused this havoc. No, Storicai had thrown up his left hand in an attempt to ward off one of the hammer blows, and he did, catching the blow on the watch; but he failed to stop the next blow, and staggering, grappling, clutching, grasping the button, he had fallen dead.

The hands had stopped at 4:20.

The time was now (he had it checked) 4:58. Ellery had been here about three minutes.

Systematically he went through the dead man's clothing. And in an inner pocket he found what he had altogether forgotten—a crude duplicate of the key to the sanquetum.

So the thief in the night had been Storicai. Or . . . had it been?

Ellery sighed. Even in Eden.

He straightened up, pointing to the hammer. The old man's face was now remarkably calm, although his eyes—those prophet's eyes—were sadder than Ellery had yet seen them. But they kindled Ellery's gesture.

"Thus it was," the Teacher began. "One of the legs of the Crownsil table on this side had loosened, and I was intending to ask the Successor to mend it after his studies and writing. I deemed it not important enough to call to the attention of the Carpentersmith, but lacked time to do it myself.

"Therefore I placed the hammer from my tool chest in the center of this table as a reminder to me to ask the Successor to repair the table leg."

Ellery wrapped the hammer carefully in one of his large handkerchiefs. While he was so occupied, the Successor came running in through the still-open door (and still the still crowd stood outside), calling, "I have searched everywhere, Master—"

"He is here," the Teacher said, indicating Ellery.

The young man gasped for breath, looking at the body on the floor. He shuddered and gave a short cry.

"You may go to your room," said the old man gently.

"Oh, but please." Ellery stopped the Successor. "Will you first go to the scriptorium and bring me fifteen pieces of paper?"

Even in Eden the same things had to be done.

Through the doorway a light breeze blew, bringing Ellery the memory of the first hint he had had, then unrecognized, of the existence of Quenan, the smell of burning sagebrush. The same breeze set the room's single lamp to swinging, as the lamp in the sanquetum had swung only that morning. But now the shadows seemed large with doom.

He said to the Teacher, "Please summon the Crownsil and the Superintendent. There is something I must ask them to do."

The summons took only the speaking, for those he named were in the throng outside. The members entered and took their accustomed places; even the very old Slave, who had been ill, it appeared, and had to be carried in; then, at Ellery's gesture, the door was closed. It seemed to him that he could hear another sigh (or was it a moan?); but this might have been imagination.

Once again great waves of stupefying fatigue, so familiar now, began to break against him. He shook them off like a dog.

On the Crownsil table, for the first time since the trial of Belyar the Weaver, were set things appertaining to crime. Then there had been nothing but bolts of cloth and the stolen pieces cut therefrom. Now Ellery laid down his leather kit. It contained the accessories of his other trade—fingerprint outfit, springback measuring tape, compass, flashlight, scissors, tweezers, small jars, rubber gloves, plastic tape, glassine envelopes, notebook, pencil, a marking pen, labels, a .38 Police Positive, a box of shells.

There had been times when he had had to call on all the contents of the kit; but on this occasion Ellery took from it only the fingerprinting equipment and the marking pen.

"What is it, Elroï," asked the Teacher, not flinching at sight of the strange objects, although most of the kit's contents were as mysterious to him as to the shrinking Crownsil, "what is it that you wish of us?"

"Teacher," Ellery replied sofly, "I wish to go among you and record on these pieces of paper the imprint of your fingertips—the fingertips of all present. It is a simple thing, and there is no pain attached to it. Each of you will touch no paper but the single paper I set before you—is that clear?"

"The thing is clear, Elroï, its meaning is not," said the old man. "Nevertheless, it shall be as you say. I observe that you called for fifteen pieces of paper, although— excluding you there are only fourteen of us. Is it your wish to record the imprint of the fingertips of him who has ceased, also?"

Ellery's head snapped back in surprise at the old man's shrewdness. "Storicai's? Yes, Teacher. I shall record his first."

And this he did, under their awed eyes, to the accompaniment of their quickened breathing. When he rose to face them with his paraphernalia, their breathing ceased altogether for a moment. But their venerable leader, observing their dread, stepped forward and said in a steady voice, "Among the living, Elroï, I shall be the first," and he held out his corded, blackened hands.

So Ellery took the fingerprints of the Teacher, and of the Successor, and of the Superintendent, and of the eleven surviving members of the Crownsil of the Twelve; and on each paper, under the fingerprints, he marked the name of the office held by the official whose fingertips had deposited the impressions.

"And now, Quenan?"

"Now we may be alone, Teacher."

"Do you wish him who has ceased to remain?"

"No, he may now be removed."

The patriarch nodded. "Crownsil and Superintendent," he addressed the officials of his people, "do you leave the holy house now, taking him who has ceased with you to be prepared for the place of peace. Tell the people to return to their homes or their tasks; while we live, the duties of life must go on. Successor, you may retire to your chambers. Blessed be the Wor'd, in grief as in joy." He raised his hand in benediction and dismissal.

And while some were reverently removing the body of the Storesman, and others carried the Slave away, and the rest were trooping out in silence, Ellery thought: And now I've committed a crime, too . . . For in whichever state the Valley existed—he had never thought to ask Otto Schmidt!—there was a law-enforcement agency, at least a county sheriff, whom he should be notifying that a murder had been committed. Yet until this moment, watching the Quenanites carting off the body of the murder victim to be prepared for burial, the thought had not crossed his mind.

Well, he could not. What an enormously greater crime it would be to open the doors of the Valley of Quenan to the world as it was!

When the last of the Crownsil had left, and the door was shut again, Ellery said, "Teacher, when we first met you told me that my coming was foretold, that I was to be your guide through a time of great trouble that was to come upon you."

The old man bowed deeply in assent, then raised his head so that once more it was partly hidden by his hood.

"Then you must tell me everything that happened this afternoon, and you must tell me the time that everything happened, as exactly as you know."

The ancient lids slipped down, leaving only slits. Then each eye was wide open, seeing across time.

"So," the prophet said. "At noon I returned from the fields and meditated in my room for the hour of the midday meal, of which I no longer partake. I knew that it was noon, for so the shadow—by its absence—told me. At one o'clock I went to the schoolhouse. I sensed it to be one o'clock—after all these years my body had become a timepiece of itself. And I taught the children for the space of one hour. In the schoolhouse stands a clock, and when it said two o'clock (and when I knew it to be that time) I returned here, to the Holy Congregation House.

"I should have found the Successor at his studies. Instead he was lingering in the doorway hoping to see a certain young woman go by, I am sure. Passion is natural, even holy; but it has its time and place, and these were not the proper ones. I therefore sent him to the scriptorium, and to remove temptation I locked him in and retained the key. Then someone came with a message that the Slave was ill and wished to see me—"

"About the Slave, later," Ellery said gravely. "First I wish to visit the scriptorium again. Will you come with me, Teacher?"

The Successor was not in the scriptorium; apparently he had retired to his sleeping chamber next door. On his original visit to the scribe's tiny workroom, Ellery had been in no condition to observe details. Now he saw that it contained two little writing desks, two small benches, and shelves crowded with scrolls and scroll jars, piles of paper, reels of thread, bundles of quills and reed pens, jugs of ink, and other items of the scrivener's profession.

By the side of each desk stood a tall candelabrum whose sconces held heavy brown beeswax candles.

In the two walls of the scriptorium that faced the outdoors were the same type of tall slit-windows he had seen in the Teacher's room—far too narrow for the passage of even a small child. Once locked in, then, the Successor would have had either to wait until the Teacher returned to unlock the door of the scriptorium or to break down the door himself. The door showed no sign that it had been forced.

Ellery and the old man left the scriptorium as they had entered and visited it, in silence.

"Would you go on now, Teacher?" Ellery asked.

The old man continued his narrative. He had returned to his schoolroom, performed his duties there until the hour of three, and then gone back to the Holy Congregation House. Whereupon he had remembered the message about the Slave and his illness. Before he left, he recalled the weak leg of the table and placed the hammer on it— in the center—as a reminder to himself later to ask the Successor to make the repairs.

Then the prophet had set out for the Slave's house.

Before the Slave's house stood a sundial. The Teacher estimated that the time was about 3:15 when he passed it.

"I remained with him for an hour. I would have stayed longer; we were young men together. And I returned"—he was speaking with the most deliberate care— "and I returned, then, at a time very close to a quarter past the hour of four. I . . . returned . . ."

What was the old man trying to say?

"At four-twenty," Ellery said gently, "Storicai was dead."

The Teacher made a great effort. "Yes, the Storesman was . . . dead. He was lying, even as you saw him, in his blood on the floor of the meeting room here."

"This is difficult for you," Ellery murmured. "But you must go on, Teacher."

"I unlocked the door of the scriptorium, released the Successor, and sent him at once to seek you out, if you had yet returned from your journey. For it had come at last—the great trouble had come down upon the tribe of Quenan; and I knew a need for him who is called Elroï, and again Quenan. For all was as it had been written."

Ellery sighed. Theology, prophecy, soothsaying—it was not through these that the riddle of Storicai's murder would be solved . . . Storicai, who had been so enchanted by the glitter of the wrist watch, the first wrist watch he had ever seen, who had been so childishly pleased at being allowed to wear it. And who had worn it all the rest of his life . . . "Did you ask the Successor if he had overheard anything—an unusual sound, voices—while he was locked in the scriptorium?"

The furrow between the brow tufts deepened. "Nay, Quenan. Let us ask him now."

But the Successor, his angel's face still white above its boyish beard, could gasp only, "I heard nothing, nothing!"

With another sigh, Ellery asked the Teacher to retire to his room also. But first he obtained the key to the sanquetum.

His hand on the doorknob, he hesitated as before, feeling again that if he entered the forbidden room he would defile it. But there was no turning aside now. He slipped the key into the lock and found, to his amazement, that the door was not locked at all. Quickly Ellery slipped inside the sanquetum and shut the door behind him.

The eternal lamp hung from an old brass chain. The chain ran through a metal eye sunk into the center of the ceiling and over to a hook fixed in one of the walls, to which it was secured through one of its links. There were enough links to leave several feet of chain dangling from the hook. Ellery nodded; it was a practical if primitive device, for after all it was easier to slip the chain off the hook in the wall and lower the lamp for refilling than to have to climb a ladder.

He unhooked the chain and let out the slack so that the lamp just cleared his head. The dark circle on the floor where the lamp's shadow fell expanded, but the rest of the chamber became lighter. Ellery hooked the chain so that the lamp would be fixed in the lower position; and down on all fours he went.

He scanned the flooring square inch by square inch, making grotesquely shifting shadows on the walls.

He made his first discovery under the arque—a shard of clay with a purple-glazed outer surface.

Ellery rose, looking keenly about. The huge scroll jar on his right seemed to be sitting poorly on its wooden base, canted a little as if hastily moved or set there. Yet he was sure the big urn had occupied the base properly during his morning survey of the sanquetum.

He turned his attention to the arque. The glass of the china closet was unbroken; but on a corner of the walnut frame, level with the bottom shelf, he made out a faint gleam . . . a stain, darkish sticky . . . for he touched it, and some of it came away on his finger. Blood. Blood that had not been there in the morning.

And the coins?

The two columns of silver dollars which he had left so neatly stacked in the morning, were no longer so. Each column leaned a little, and in one column a milled edge protruded.

Standing before the arque, in the flickering light, Ellery reconstructed the events of the afternoon. Clearly, it was Storicai who had secretly made the duplicate key for the sanquetum door—Storicai who, while the Teacher was visiting the sick old Slave and while the Successor was locked in the scriptorium, had once more committed the sin of entering the Holy Congregation House without leave; Storicai, who had committed the far greater sin of entering the forbidden room for the purpose of stealing the silver treasure of the community.

Forbidden entry, sacrilege, a thieving heart—who would have dreamed the simple Storesman capable of these?

And even as the greedy man had crouched in the sanquetum, perhaps, in the very act of laying impious hands on the coins, he had been attacked from behind. Someone had rushed into the holy room, seized the righthand prayer jar, raised it high, and brought it down on the back of the Storesman's head. The jar must have shattered or, at the least, broken partly—witness the overlooked shard under the arque and the bits of clay in the dead man's hair; but this blow had not been the killing blow. The Storesman had fallen, unconscious or dazed; in falling, he had struck his head on the corner of the arque, and had stained it with his blood.

And all this in the holy of holies, in the presence of the scrolls enjoining peace and the love of brothers. Joab at the horns of the altar; à Beckett in the cathedral.

The striker of the blow must have turned and fled. And the Storesman, recovering quickly, ran after the witness to his crimes and caught up with him in the meeting room. And here they must have struggled (in panting silence, or else the Successor from behind his locked door would have heard the struggle); and Storicai must have tried to kill his assailant of the sanquetum to preserve his guilty secret—for by the law of Quenan theft was a capital crime—and the witness, cornered by the Crownsil table, would have had to fight for his life. The hammer being on the table where the Teacher had left it, the witness had snatched it up and struck the Storesman with it at least twice: once on the upflung wrist, shattering the crystal, denting the dial, and stopping the mechanism of the watch; and a second and lethal time, on the forehead.

Who was the witness to Storicai's crimes and the perpetrator of the first man-slaying in the history of the Valley?

Ellery again became aware of the curious something about the coins that had been gnawing at him all day. What was it?

Their *number*—that was it! In his account of the colony's wanderings, the Teacher had said that his father had brought to the Valley silver dollars to the number of fifty; and the Chronicler had confirmed this from his records. Fifty; and according to Schmidt's ledger, the Teacher had expended nineteen of them at the End-of-the-World Store.

Leaving thirty-one.

Ellery stared at the two columns of coins in the china closet. Each pillar was of the same height. Meaning that each contained the same number of silver dollars— meaning that, whatever the total number of coins, it had to be an *even* number . . . Of course! There could not be thirty-one!

This was what had been nagging him since his visit to Schmidt's store. The number thirty-one disturbed the perfect symmetry of everything in the forbidden room; it had started some subliminal computer clicking in Ellery's head.

How account for both columns containing the same number of coins when one of the columns should be taller than the other by the thickness of a single silver dollar? Was a silver dollar missing?

Then Ellery remembered. It was not missing; it had been expended in the time of Belyar the Weaver, when the Teacher had decreed exile for the cloth stealer instead of death. The man had been driven into the desert with sustenance for two days *and a single silver dollar*.

One from thirty-one gave an even number and explained the two columns of identical height.

And so Ellery reached into the arque and took out one of the pillars of coins, and counted its 1873 Carson City dollars, and he counted fifteen; and he replaced the column perfectly, and took out the other, and in this pillar he counted fifteen coins also.

It was just after he had put the second column carefully back beside its companion that he found himself holding onto the china closet with a roaring in his ears.

The Storesman had betrayed his Teacher, his faith, and his brothers of Quenan for thirty pieces of silver.

As the moment passed, Ellery came gradually to see that at the focus of his downcast eyes, on the arque's lower shelf, lay the book. It was still there, in the same place still, still open; evidently untouched since the morning.

His eyes felt as though they had been ground in sand. At first the lines of black-letter type on the open pages persisted in shifting about in a sort of tormented mock dance. But then they stiffened and stood still; and out of nowhere came the unspeakable thought . . . unspeakable.

It was a dream within a dream, and evilly dark through and through; even this, this movement of his hand—not willed, a nightmare gesture—reaching into the china closet and raising and turning the left-hand part of the open book so that he might see the front cover, and the spine.

And he saw.

And what he saw he glared at like an idiot aroused for one lucid moment. The mind rejected it. Unacceptable! it cried. Except in a dream. Even in a dream. And it was no dream. It was true.

And it was too much.

It was a long time before Ellery recovered sufficiently to withdraw his hand; and then he spent another interval, timeless, staring at the hand.

The holy book. The Book of Mk'h, the Teacher had called it.

Yes, there they were, the letters on the cover that had so fired the old man when he laid eyes on the book lying on Schmidt's counter . . . that had led the patriarch to offer anything, even his entire store of silver coins, for its possession.

The "lost" book of Quenan, the Teacher had called it.

Ellery did not remember leaving the sanquetum, locking its door behind him, walking through the meeting room; he did not remember hearing the uneven echoes of his footsteps.

He remembered only standing in the open and gulping great gulps of air as if he could never gulp enough.

5 · Thursday, April 6

The hags pursued him through the night; leered, gibbered, squatted on his chest mocking his pleas for breath. He knew that it was a dream, that he had only to open his eyes. But the effort was too great. He groaned, he babbled, he moaned; and so, moaning, he woke up at last.

He was chilled, numb, bone-tired; the haunted hours of sleep had brought him no surcease. Muttering, he groped for the blanket and turned over with a heave of desperation . . . In the corners of the room the hags were gathered, whispering. He strained to hear what they were saying, peered through the darkness. That was how he discovered his mistake—they were not the hags at all; he had been deceived by the robes: they were the members of the Crownsil, speaking together in disquieted voices, glancing dubiously at the piece of paper each held in his hand.

Now they were passing the papers from hand to hand *to handsome gathering groaning grinding troubled old troubling old man old mandaring mandrake mandragora agora a gore gore agr grr and so growling and gathering up the gathering gathering*

Give me those! Ellery cried. You'll spoil the fingerprints!

—He shut his eyes, and by this he knew that they had just been open and that he had cried out aloud. He opened his eyes again. He was standing by the window grinding his teeth. Outside ran gray morning. He was shivering and his body was one great ache. And he remembered what had happened yesterday, and what must happen today.

The misery of man is great upon him . . .

He dressed and carried his toilet kit to the rear of the communal kitchen for hot water and he washed and shaved and stumbled into the dining room. The first shift of the people were at breakfast, a few speaking in low tones, most speaking not at all. At Ellery's entrance all speech stopped.

Some looked at him shyly; others with awe—the unfamiliar man and the unfamiliar crime; must they not be connected, to be dreaded equally? Others regarded him with faces full of adoration: had not the Teacher said that the Guest's coming was foretold? And still others showed him unchanged countenances, accepting and respectful.

But no one ventured to talk to him.

Ellery ate and drank what was set before him, conscious mainly that it was hot and filling.

He returned to his room to dispose of his toilet kit and consider his course.

For a time he wrote in his notebook.

Then he put it away and went out to do what had to be done.

Ellery could hardly remember the time when he had not been struck by the recurrence of the great and famous across the shifting planes of space-time. In his boyhood, he recalled, it had been Roman statuary coming to life. Mr. Tobias, who taught him civics, might have been the fraternal twin of Scipio Africanus. Father O'Toole, of the Roman Catholic church around the corner, might have stepped out of Nero's toga only the night before. Patrolman Isador Rosen, Inspector Queen's partner when both were pounding a beat, was a dead ringer for Julius Caesar.

And so it went, in cycles, or perhaps Ellery was only cyclically aware of it: Queen Victoria would sell him a ticket to the movie; Whistler's Mother sat opposite him on the bus; Beethoven delivered the laundry; Ivan the Terrible leaned over the bar and asked, "Wottle it be?"; Robert E. Lee offered to draw his picture for a dollar on a Greenwich Village sidewalk.

Such a cycle was evidently in motion now. Winston Churchill had placed the porridge (if it was porridge) before him at breakfast. Marie Dressler had removed the empty bowl. And here was Bernard Shaw, with dried slip on his beard, explaining how he made pottery. It gave Ellery the queerest feeling as he stared at the wheels and the kilns and watched the author of *Mrs. Warren's Profession* strew a handful of salt inside one of the kilns to give the tiles that were firing there a simple glaze.

Ellery took the shard he had found in the sanquetum from his pocket. "You don't use salt to produce this purple glaze, do you?"

"Oh, no," said non-Shaw, the Potter. "Different process altogether. For prayer jars, I mean."

"Then this came from a prayer jar?"

The Potter nodded. The smile that had graced his bearded face while he was discussing his work died.

"Yesterday a prayer jar was broken. The prayer jars are holy, for they contain the things of the Wor'd and they stand in the sanquetum, the forbidden room in the Holy Congregation House. The last time one was broken was the day the earth shook. There are never more than four—the two in the sanquetum, and two spare ones that are kept packed in wool and straw to protect them. They are not easily made, nor often . . . Yesterday one broke. For others the earth did not shake, perhaps. But it shook for me when I heard and saw, and it has not stopped shaking."

The Potter's workshop was stifling in the heat from the kiln. How must it feel to meet murder for the first time? "The broken jar has been deplaced in the sanquetum, then?"

"Yes." Someone broke into song not far off, and stopped abruptly after the first few notes. As if suddenly reminded, or suddenly remembering. "The Teacher came and asked me for a new one."

"Did he tell you why?"

The tufted white brows drew together, and the deep voice deepened. "He told me that the time of great trouble had come. I wondered, for I had seen no sign. And he asked for another prayer jar. So I understood that the shattering of the one to be replaced must be the sign. Not until later, when there was great running about and crying out, did I learn that Storicai the Storesman had himself been shattered. For is not each man," he signed, "also a vessel of the Wor'd?"

"When did he come, the Teacher, to ask for a replacement jar for the forbidden room?" Ellery managed to ask.

"Yesterday. In the afternoon."

Like all his people, the Potter would not think of time in exact terms. But there was a clock in the shop, an old wooden one with a pendulum and weights (used, the Potter explained, in calculating the work of the kilns), and there was his record of the Teacher's requisition. As near as they could, they settled the time of the Teacher's visit at 4:30.

Ten minutes after the murder.

As Ellery turned to leave, the Potter said "I have known that the great trouble of which we have been told would come upon us in my lifetime if I lived the full measure of my years."

Ellery stopped, surprised. "How did you know that, Potter?"

The man raised his hand, encrusted with slip—the mixture of ground clay and water with which he worked—and pointed upward.

"Those machines that fly through the sky," he said. "For three years now they have come and gone in increasing numbers. Surely this is the sign of the great trouble that has befallen Quenan?"

"It is a sign of the great trouble that has befallen the world," Ellery said.

The Potter's beard rested on his broad chest. "Blessed be the Wor'd," he muttered. "In time of trouble, as in time of peace."

The stench of singed hoof, which he had not encountered since he was a boy, greeted Ellery at his next stop. So did the more recently familiar smell of fresh sawdust. Ulysses S. Grant was just finishing the job of shoeing a fat gray jenny.

"Blessed be the Wor'd," General Grant said. "I am the Carpentersmith." He slapped the she-ass on the rump, and she trotted away. *The ox knoweth his crib, and the ass his masters stall . . .*

Ellery returned the greeting, and for a moment no one said anything more. The apprentice folded up the bellows and went shyly about other tasks. The firebed dimmed slowly from orange-red to ashy gray. Grant reincarnate picked up a piece of wood—a wagon tongue or whippletree, Ellery guessed—and began carefully to pry off a piece of metal.

"Though my hands are busy," the man said, "my ears are not."

"Do you make the keys?"

The Carpentersmith paused to consider. Then, stooping to his work again, he said, "When keys are required I make them. But few are required because we have few locks. The feed bin must have a lock because some of our beasts are clever and otherwise would pry open the latches with their teeth and eat more than is good for them."

"What else is kept locked and so requires a key?"

They were not many. The small quantity of Valley-made black powder, kept on hand for blasting stumps and rocks (the Carpentersmith seemed to have no idea that the powder could be put to other uses), was locked against the children and animals. The store of charqui, or jerked beef (the wind- and sun-dried "jerky" of the Southwest), was also stored under lock and key against the occasional coyote that, emboldened by hunger in a poor hunting season, slunk into Quenan. And the house of the lackwit gnome who tended the cemetery had a lock—the only dwelling in the village so equipped—because of fears to which the little man could give no name: "But none wish to dispute with him, and whom does it harm?"

And, yes. Ah, yes.

The sanquetum.

The calloused hands still and it seemed to Ellery that the Carpentersmith's eyes formed tears.

The sanquetum. "When did you last make a key to the sanquetum?"

"I have never made one," the man mumbled.

"Then who—?"

"The sanquetum key in the Teacher's keeping was made by Smuel, who was Carpentersmith a very long time ago."

There was no help for it; he had to ask: "Could a key be made without your knowledge? Say, in the dead of night?"

The Carpentersmith straightened, and before he answered he deposited in a bin the strip of metal he had detached from the piece of wood.

"Guest," he said courteously, "I am not Carpentersmith by right, but by skill and preference. Anyone is free at any time to come here and work. Whether I am here or not; my work often takes me elsewhere in the Valley. You ask, 'Could a key be made without my knowledge?' And I answer, 'Why should it not be? Why must I know it?' "

Ellery sighed. This was another world, with another set of values. The primitive Polynesians were horrified that the masters of European ships should flog their sailors for, to them, the perfectly natural act of swimming ashore without leave to find women; yet they themselves matter-of-factly stole everything from the ships that was not tied down, and were bewildered at the savage resentment their thievery aroused.

"Let me put it this way," Ellery said patiently. "Did Storicai work in this shop recently? Could the Storesman have made a key?"

With equal patience the Carpentersmith said, "Guest, I have known Storicai all my life. He was often here, for he was Storesman. I was often at the storehouse, for I am Carpentersmith. For Storicai to be here was as common a sight as to see a bird roost in a tree. He could have made a hundred keys and I need not have known it.

"But"—Grant's broad shoulders sagged—"he will be here never more. All men must cease, blessed be the Wor'd; we come into the place left for us by others, we go from here that others may come after us. But no one in Quenan has ever ceased as Storicai ceased, and when I think of this I am sorely troubled, Guest, sorely."

Ellery produced a glassine envelope in which he was keeping the metal button he had pried from the dead Storesman's hand. "Have you seen this button before, Carpentersmith?"

"That is the Teacher's," the man said slowly. He hesitated. "Most use buttons of bone or wood. Those of us on the Crownsil, also the Successor and the Superintendent, wear buttons of horn. Only the Teacher wears buttons of metal." He pointed to the curious symbol on the button, and even as he did so Ellery recognized it as the capital letter *N*, done in the Quenanite script that so resembled the Chancery hand of a century before and six thousand miles' distance. "This *N*," said the Carpentersmith, "means *fifty*. It is a sacred number, and only the Teacher may use it." He hesitated again, and then he said timidly, "Guest, should you not return it to him?"

But Ellery was already out the door.

They were making wool blankets in the weaving shed, and the bitter, musty odor of the sheep hung like a fog. The Weaver paused at her loom, shifting a bit in her harness. She was a big woman, and of course, given a cigar, she could have passed anywhere for Amy Lowell.

Her voice was soft and rich. Yes, she did tailoring as well as weaving. Yes, the Teacher had come to her yesterday afternoon. He had said that a button was missing from his robe—not that he needed to tell her, she said, with a sad smile; she had observed it at once. She had sewn another one on then and there. She kept a supply of his metal buttons on hand at all times.

"What time was this, Weaver?" Ellery asked. He felt mean in the presence of this warmly glowing personality.

"Time?" She paused. "How curious that you should ask, Guest. I take little note of time. Weaving, sewing—you know, they are not like boiling milk. When my heart is light, the shuttle flies. When my heart is heavy—as it is now—the loom is heavy, too, and the work goes slowly.

"Yesterday, when the Teacher came, I was thinking little of time. For I was working on a new pattern—may I show it to you?"

The wool she had used was the color of the desert, and against the background she had woven, in black wool, a bird. Ellery squinted at it, trying to decide whether its subtle distortion was inherent in its design or a result of his tired eyes. Then, quite suddenly, he made it out. What had been woven was not the bird itself, but its shadow on the sandy ground. The illusion was startling.

"Did you do this?" he exclaimed, entranced.

"Do you like it," the woman murmured. "I am glad. Yes, it is my own. I am weaving this for my—for the Teacher's use."

The slip of the tongue told him that she was one of the old man's wives. For some reason, indefinable, the pulse in his neck thickened and began to throb.

"But the time," Ellery muttered. "You don't know what time it was?"

"I was not thinking of time," the rich voice said. "But the Teacher asked me. So I went and looked. I have a watch, an old gold one that was mine from my father, who had it from his. Inside this watch is written a thing which none of us here understands, not even the Teacher. It says, *'From the Men of the 17th. Vera Cruz, Cerro Gordo, Monterrey. 1848.'* "

Ellery closed his eyes. It seemed too much, somehow, this disgraceful echo of the past. "It refers," he said, choosing his words with care, "to an expedition made a generation before this colony was founded. Groups of men went to Mexico, a country to the south. I suppose that someone in your family—your father's grandfather, perhaps—must have been in charge of one of those groups, called the 17th. Afterward, the men of his group gave him the watch as a remembrance . . . The other words are the names of places in Mexico."

The Weaver nodded. "I am glad to know at last," she said, with shining eyes. "They must have loved him greatly to give him so rare a gift. Thank you for telling me. And now to answer your own question. The Teacher asked me the time. And by the watch the time was fifteen minutes before the hour of five."

"One more question, Weaver. Did the Teacher have a prayer jar with him?"

No. No, he did not. Once more her face saddened.

It was not till later that Ellery knew he had misunderstood the reason for her sadness.

The spring accents of the morning were sharp in his nostrils as he walked along the shaded lane. The acacia was in blossom, white and sweet. Here and there bobbed roses, all small; he could identify none of them. Varieties, he thought, so long out of favor in the cultivated world as to be virtually extinct. As, for that matter, was so much else from the lovely past.

And Ellery pondered painfully, as he walked, on the Teacher's odd behavior. Surely a man with something to conceal would not have gone openly to the Potter for a replacement prayer jar so soon after the shattering of the old one? Or to the Weaver to have a new button sewn on his tunic?

And there was the question of time. While the Quenanites were not time-bound or time-harried, the Teacher could no more step out of the universal continuum than a man in Los Angeles or New York. Where had the old man been—what had he done—between 4:30, when he visited the Potters workshop, and 4:55, when Ellery had found him in the meeting room over the body of the Storesman, while the people stood transfixed outside?

At 4:30 he had stepped into the Potter's shop for a new prayer jar, and obviously he had taken it at once to the sanquetum to place on the base where the broken jar had stood. This whole procedure could hardly have consumed more than five minutes. At 4:45 he had stepped into the Weaver's shop to have a new button sewn on; could this have taken more than five minutes also?

Ten minutes accounted for between 4:30 and 4:55—ten out of twenty-five.

Leaving fifteen minutes not accounted for.

What had the old man done with them?

Still musing, Ellery came to the cottage of the Elders—the husband and wife who repesented the old people of Quenan on the Crownsil. How old they were he could not imagine; he could only think of them as Adam and Eve, and he was sure that if he were able to examine them he would find them lacking navels.

Smiling toothlessly, they welcomed him; and the old woman patted the space beside her on the fleece-padded bench on which they sat soaking up the sun.

Them, at least, the tragedy seemed to have passed by. Perhaps they did not understand it, or had already forgotten it. He felt uncertain how to begin.

"You are here to help us," Adam broke the silence at last. "And we are thankful to you. Blessed be the Wor'd."

And Eve said, "Willy told us."

Ellery blinked. "Willy?"

"The Teacher. His name in the world was Willy." And the ancient lady nodded and smiled. A small thing, but astounding. The Teacher, that venerable, majestic figure out of the Old Testament, had once been a boy named Willy, wearing a lace collar and trundling a hoop with a stick along a wooden sidewalk!

"We have known him all our lives," said Adam.

"Then let me ask you," said Ellery. "Have you ever known him to lie?"

Neither replied. Perhaps they had gone back, in the manner of the very old, to some far-distant memory of flaring gas lamps and a harbor quilled with sharp white sails.

Then the old woman's withered lips trembled, and Ellery saw that the pairs had simply been struck dumb by his question. "Lie?" she repeated. "The *Teacher?*"

And her husband rocked as if in pain. "Oh! Oh!"

And both began at once, in their unsteady voices, to impress on him the monstrousness of his question. The Teacher would never lie. He could not lie. Even about the most trifling matter.

"Not to save his life, Guest!" Adam exclaimed.

"Not to save his life!" Eve echoed.

Lines from some old book appeared magically in Ellery's head: Our master talks with the angels. "How do you know?" *He told us so.* "But perhaps he lies." *Fool! As though the angels would talk to a liar!*

But for some reason he could not pass their ancient testimony off with the usual

smile as the product of senile delusion or narrow sectarian ignorance. All he knew—
and the knowledge was a terror as well as a relief—was that he believed them
without reservation or doubt.

The Teacher would not lie about even the most trifling matter.

The Teacher would not lie to save his life.

For the rest of the morning and afternoon, until the sun was well down in the
western sky, Ellery pursued his investigations. The mill rasped, the waters rushed
through their channels, the cattle lowed, and an old man testified in feeble, halting
words. It was late in the afternoon when he returned to his room. The Superintendent
was waiting for him.

"Guest," the Superintendent said, "the Teacher has instructed me, saying: go
you call upon the Guest and ask if he has any instructions. Do you then receive
them and carry them out as if they came from me.' " He might have been reciting
an inventory. "Accordingly," the Superintendent went on, "I have called upon
you, Guest, and I ask if you have any instructions. I shall receive them and carry
them out as if they came from the Teacher."

Ellery wanted to say nothing so much as, Yes, for God's sake get out of here
and let me sleep a week, a month, a year.

What he actually said was: "Yes, Superintendent. Summon the Crownsil, the
Teacher, the Successor, and yourself to the meeting hall in the Holy Congregation
House for after the evening meal."

"I shall do so," said the Superintendent, and turned to go.

"Wait," said Ellery, and wondered why. "Aren't you the least curious, Superintendent, about my reasons for this summons?"

"I was not to ask for reasons, Guest, only for instructions."

"Ah, they could use you in Washington," sighed Ellery. "My reason is this,
and you may tell them so: According to the laws and customs of Quenan, tonight
they are to sit in trial."

It was quite dark in the long room. Candles had been lit by the Successor to
reinforce the single lamp, but they seemed to Ellery to produce more shadows than
light; they leaped and they danced and grew large and shrank away with every
breath of wind let in by the opening door as the members of the Crownsil assembled.
The darkness was palpable, he thought; it could be felt, a thing of shifting solids
that the light of all the sun could not have melted.

While he waited for the people of the Crownsil to seat themselves about the long
table, Ellery thought over the role he was about to play. His to present, his to
accuse, his to prosecute. Elroï the Procurator. The Devil's Advocate. (For that
matter, was not Satan himself a prosecutor, accusing Job?) There had been murder
most foul in Eden, and the task of arraignment, indictment, and pressure for judgment
was now his—assigned him by the leader of the community, his authority to exercise
it accepted by the council of the community.

What choice had they? There was no one else, no one at all, in Quenan with his
knowledge of such things.

Again the guilty thought surfaced that he should be reporting the crime to the
authorities of jurisdiction. But, really, who were they? In every respect but geography,
Quenan lay outside the borders of the United States of America.

"The king's writ runs not in Connaught," said an old Irish proverb. Neither state nor federal power had ever "run" in the Valley of Quenan. And where no other governance obtained, it was the right of the people of any place—by the law of nations—to set up provisional powers . . . not merely their right, but their duty. And such powers, established here for so many decades, and exercised without question or molestation, could not even be deemed provisional any longer. (That this was all rationalization Ellery knew very well, in the part of him that remained Ellery; but in the part of him that had become Elroï, hazy with fatigue, misted over with sorrow, he paid no attention to it.)

Of one thing he—Ellery or Elroï—was sure: this was no kangaroo court, no rumor-ridden Star Chamber, no lynch mob. It was a high court of justice; and its bailiff was about to speak.

For the Superintendent had risen. "We are assembled," his flat, dry, uninflected voice intoned, "to sit in trial according to the laws and customs of Quenan." And he sat down; that was all.

To silence.

And the silence grew.

Ellery had expected questions, objections—something on which he could base his opening remarks. Were they trying to obstruct, to defeat him in the task they had in effect assigned to him, by the dead weight of their silence? Passive resistance? Dream-tired though he was, he felt annoyance. Why the delay? Reluctance to face facts, however prolonged, could not alter them.

But as the silence deepened he began to sense an identity between what he was now witnessing and the stillness of a Quaker meeting or an Orthodox synagogue during silent prayer, or a mosque during that first moment while the faithful await the imam's invocation. And then it became a silence exceeding any of these, a silence so intense that he could not detect the slightest flutter of an eyelid or a nostril. It was as if they had all yielded to a yoga-like trance from which nothing but the last trumpet call would ever rouse them.

For a moment Ellery felt like those Gauls who, walking gingerly through the Rome they had just broken into, observed with an awe not so far from terror the white-bearded senators sitting so severely calm, so without movement, that the barbarians could only believe them to be demigods or statues . . .

He came to himself, the truth revealed. For slowly, gradually, as he stood there in that frozen room, with its utterly still company, the annoyance and restlessness and doubt seeped out of him, and the cloudy murk seemed to thin and lighten. And so Ellery came to understand the purpose of this time of concentrated quiet. It brought calm and peace into the room, and into the minds and heart of all seated here.

Whereupon, once more, the Superintendent rose; but the Teacher, whose strange eyes were fixed on Ellery's face, did not look the Superintendent's way.

"Guest," the official said in a very different voice, the voice of man, not rote, "do you now tell us of the things you have learned and of the things you would have us do. And we shall listen, and we shall reflect, and we shall judge."

And he took his seat once more.

Ellery faced the robed figures around the long table with a great composure and tranquillity. (Not until later did he realize that this overriding feeling had been self-induced by something very like autohypnosis, serving not to dispel but to mask his extreme fatigue. He was feeling the illusive warmth of a man blissfully freezing to death.)

"Murder," he began, and immediately paused. Had a shudder run through them at the word—never before uttered in this room, the forecourt to a shrine dedicated to peace and love? Or had it been his imagination?

"Let me first tell you what murder is," Ellery said. "The life of a man was recently taken in this room" (and was there the slightest shift of every eye to the place on the floor where a new grass mat concealed the spilled blood, or had he—again—imagined it?) "and this man whose life was taken had not been charged with any crime, he had not been tried and convicted and sentenced to his death in the manner prescribed by law. The taking of human life without sanction or due process—that is murder. Storicai the Storesman was murdered."

They were grimly, violently still.

"Now before the facts of a murder can be ascribed to any person, there are three things which must be demonstrated to link the person accused or suspected with the crime.

"These three things are called opportunity, and means, and motive."

They did not yet understand, but they would. Ellery went on deliberately.

"Opportunity," he said, holding up a finger. "This is to say, when death results from a physical attack on the person of the victim—such as the slaying of the Storesman with a hammer—there must be evidence that the person accused or suspected was in fact present on the scene of the murder at or about the time it occurred, or that he *could* have been present.

"Means." Ellery held up a second finger. "This is to say, there must be evidence that the person accused or suspected had possession of, or had access to, the weapon with which the murder was committed.

"Motive." He held up a third finger. "This is to say, that it can be shown that the person accused or suspected had a reason for wishing to take the life of the victim."

He paused. Their faces were impassive but intent; whether they yet understood him it was too soon to judge.

"I shall try to prove opportunity first," Ellery said. "Will the Miller come forward and sit in this place?" He indicated a stool he had asked the Successor to put near the head of the table.

The Miller rose from the long bench and came forward. He was an oak of a man, gnarly, with a vast spread of shoulder. Flour dusted his reddish beard and rusty eyebrows. He breathed heavily as he sat down on the stool.

"What happened yesterday, Miller, when you had finished grinding?" Ellery asked him gently.

The man raised huge hands and rubbed them into his temples, as if they were millstones with which he would grind out the answers. In the loud voice of one accustomed to making himself heard above the splash of the millrace, the rasp of the stones, and the clatter of the sails, he said, "The first of the new flour," and stopped.

"What about the first of the new flour?"

The man looked surprised. "It was ready," he explained, as to a child. "I had sacked the first of the new flour. In a white sack, according to the way. Being the first of the new flour, it must be blessed. So I heaved it up on my shoulder"—he demonstrated awkwardly—"and I carried it here to the holy house for the Teacher to bless it."

"What time was that?"

Time? Just before 4:15. How did he know? He had observed the water clock as he left his mill.

"Very well. Now what did you do, Miller, when you carried the first sack of the new flour to the Holy Congregation House?"

The Miller started at him. "Why, I rang the bell, what else? But there was no answer, so of course I couldn't go in. With the Teacher not here—or surely he would have come to the door?—I had no reason to stay. I started to walk back to the mill."

"Started to?"

The Miller explained that he had walked only a short distance and had just turned into the trees when he heard footsteps and looked around. It was Storicai the Storesman, hurrying toward the holy house. "I was going to call out to him not to bother, that the Teacher was not there to answer the bell, but before I could speak Storicai was at the door, looking all round like—like—"

"As if he did not wish to be seen?"

The Miller, who was now perspiring, nodded his gratitude. "That is so, Guest."

"Did Storicai see you?"

"I don't think so. I was in the shadows of the trees."

The shadows. The flaxen wicks smoldered. Wax ran down the candles and formed huge weepers. The shadows writhed.

"And what did Storicai do then, Miller?"

The man looked from face to face. His voice became hoarse, trembling on the brink of a shout. The Storesman had committed a *sin.* He had pulled open the door of the holy house without ringing the bell and he had entered without waiting to be admitted—in fact, when the Teacher had not been there to admit him.

"He committed a *sin,*" the Miller repeated, knuckling his head.

"Thank you," said Ellery, and the big man went heavily back to his place. "Waterman?"

The Waterman rose and came forward. He was tall and young and sleek and graceful, walking with a glide; but his chief feature was wetness. His clothing showed more damp than dry and his darkly bearded face and quick brown hands shone with moisture in the candlelight. He made Ellery think of a salamander.

"Yesterday afternoon," the Waterman answered Ellery's question, "I set out to clean the well across from the holy house. While I was in the well I heard the bell outside the holy house ring, and I started to climb up to ask whoever it was to lend me a hand in hauling up the bucket. But I slipped, and this made me slow. I heard the bellringer—I suppose now it must have been the Miller—I heard him go away. Then I heard someone else coming. I lifted my head above the housing of the well, and I saw . . ." He stopped to wipe his slick forehead with his slick hand.

"And you saw what, Waterman?" Ellery asked.

"It is as the Miller said. I saw Storicai go into the holy house. He did not ring the bell. He was not admitted by the Teacher."

Ellery glanced at the patriarch. The old man might have been alone in the long room, wrapped in an impenetrable silence. A great calm covered his face; his eyes, burning in the reflected light of the many candles, seemed fixed on something far away, a vision to which the stone walls of the holy house were no impediment.

Ellery felt the stirring of wonder. It was as if the Teacher did not care. Could he actually be indifferent to the purpose of this unprecedented proceeding? Or was it resignation?

"Waterman, what was the time when you observed Storicai enter the Holy Congregation House unlawfully?"

"It was about a quarter past the hour of four, Guest."

"Do you say this because that was the time fixed by the Miller, or because you knew of your own knowledge?"

"I knew of my own knowledge," the Waterman said quietly, "from the slant of the shadow made by the sun in the well."

"You may return to your place, Waterman." Ellery waited until the tall salamander had glided back to his seat on the bench. Then he addressed the motionless figures around the table. "It will be seen, then, that the Storesman is placed at the scene of his killing, by the testimony of the Miller and the Waterman, at a quarter past the hour of four. How long after he entered the holy house was he killed? Five minutes. This I know because the Storesman was wearing on his wrist a timepiece belonging to me, which I had lent him for the duration of my visit to Quenan. This timepiece, called a wrist watch, was broken by a blow of the hammer during the killing as Storicai flung up his hand to protect himself."

He took the wrist watch out of his pocket and held it up. "As you see, the hands stopped at twenty minutes past the hour of four—as I said, five minutes after the Storesman entered the holy house."

When he was satisfied that all had seen the position of the hands, he pocketed the watch and said, "I summon the Growther."

The Growther, or Grower, was middle-age. He was long in the body, like a cornstalk; and the skin under his fingernails was black from lifelong rooting in the earth. He spoke haltingly, in an eerie voice, as a plant might speak if it could be taught words.

Yesterday afternoon, the Growther said, he had visited the sick Slave. He had been with the Slave a quarter of an hour, praying with him and telling him of the crops. He had left the Slave's house when the Teacher arrived. He knew that the time he had come was three o'clock and the time he had left was a quarter past three because of the clock in the Slave's house.

And the Growther said, "Did you know, Guest, that inside the slave's clock lives a little bird? At one time the bird would come out and call the hours. But it has not called the hours for a very long time."

"I did not know that, Growther," said Ellery gravely. "Thank you. And now, will the Herder come forward?"

The Herder was a knotty oldster with a great spreading beard. He squinted from under his bird's-nest brows as if into the sun, his skin was like the skin of a long-dried apricot. Try as Ellery would, he got nothing out of the whiskered mouth but bleats and grunts.

"What did you do yesterday afternoon, Herder?"

Bleat.

"Did you not visit the Slave's house?"

Grunt, accompanied by a nod.

"When did you step into the Slave's house?"

Grunt.

"Did you get there at four o'clock, or later?"

Bleat, untranslatable.

"Oh, all right," said Ellery. "Yesterday I understood you to say that you got there a bit before a quarter past four. Is that so?"

Nod.

"You found the Teacher there when you arrived?"

Nod.

"And the Teacher left the Slave's house at your coming?"

Nod.

"Immediately at your coming?"

Grunt, bleat, nod-nod.

"Thank you, that will be all." Ellery turned to the Teacher. "Can the Slave be brought here now?"

He saw now that, for all his distant look, the patriarch was attending the proceedings. For he nodded at once to the Successor, who hurried from the holy house. They must have had the Slave all ready to be brought in, because the door opened again a bare two minutes later to reveal the young Successor, sweating. He said something, and the Miller and the Waterman rose at once and stepped outside. They returned immediately carrying the Slave. Someone—perhaps the Carpentersmith—had rigged up a sort of reclining chair to which had been fixed two poles, making a crude palanquin; and in it half lay the ailing man.

The Successor swiftly indicated the spot near the foot of the table where the litter should be set down; the Miller and the Waterman set it down precisely there; then all three returned to their places.

The Slave looked as old as the Teacher was but did not look. He looked like the southwestern hills—black-brown-red of skin with dry gullies for wrinkles over a skeleton of calcified bones, moribund as the desert itself. Only the Slave's eyes were alive—shining-black as a bird's eyes, and as unwinking. And this Slave, who was no longer slave, had the massive dignity of his blood; yes, and curiosity, too. The bird's eyes took in everything before they settled on Ellery's face.

"I thank you," said his echo of a voice; and Ellery knew that the whispering tones were giving him thanks for having him brought to the Holy Congregation House for his last Crownsil meeting. "And now I am ready."

"I will not tire you"—he had started to say "Slave," but the word had stuck in his throat—"for my questions are few," and Ellery quickly drew from the ancient man the story of his visitors of the day before, and confirmation of the times they had arrived at and departed from his house—the Growther, the Teacher, the Herder.

"Only one thing more," Ellery said gently. "You are ill, and you have had to lie in your bed. How can you have noted and remembered the times so exactly?"

It seemed to him that the smallest smile curved the withered lips. "There is so little time left to me," said the old Slave, "that I observe time as a young man observes his enemy."

"I need question you no further. And now if you wish to be taken back to your house—"

The ancient whispered, "I should like to remain," and glanced at the Teacher; and a look passed between them so intimate, so full of anguish and compassion that Ellery had to turn away.

And to the Crownsil he said, "And so we come to the Teacher's alibi."

"Al-i-bi?" repeated someone; and Ellery saw that it was the Superintendent. "This is not a word we have ever heard, Guest." And Ellery saw, from their faces, that it was so.

He explained it in the simplest terms he could evoke; and when he knew that they understood, he went on.

"We must therefore hold," Ellery said, "that the Teacher's alibi ended when he stepped out of the—of the Slave's house, which was at fifteen minutes past four o'clock. It is only a few steps from the Slave's house to the Holy Congregation House; had the Teacher returned here from the Slave's house at once, he would have had to arrive just before twenty minutes past four, the time that the Storesman was struck down to his death. I have questioned everyone. No one remembers having seen the Teacher in the five minutes between fifteen and twenty minutes past four.''

He did not look at the Teacher now.

"If anyone in this company now remembers having seen the Teacher, or has heard of another's having seen the Teacher, he must say so now.''

And stopped. And waited. In the long room, no sound. Outside, no sound. In himself, no sound except the terrible beating of his heart.

He felt a tickle on his nose, descending; and he took out his handkerchief and wiped his streaming forehead. "It is thus established,'' Ellery said, "that the Teacher could have been here—in this room—on the scene of the slaying—at twenty minutes past four, the very moment that Storicai the Storesman was dealt the mortal blow.''

No one coughed, shifted, snuffled, slewed about. They were turned to stone. What are you saying? their stone faces seemed to ask. What is your meaning? Because meaning your words must have, though to us they mean nothing.

It was as if the entire weight of the matter had been shifted to Ellery's shoulders. No one of them would help to move it from there one inch to the right or to the left, except as he might wrench their testimony from them.

So there was nothing to do but turn to the source.

To the Teacher, Ellery said painfully, "Teacher, did you go directly from the Slave's house to this holy house yesterday?''

And the old man's eyes came back from the far place and looked at him; and he said calmly, "It is so, Quenan.''

Now was there something heard in that room, a many-lunged sigh, of which one part was his own. Ellery said, "And were you then already in the holy house *before* Storicai was slain with the hammer?''

"It is so, Quenan.''

And again the assembled sigh.

Ellery knew light-headedness. He pressed his palms on the long table, leaning. How theatrical this all was, how pompously unnecessary. Why had he called upon the trappings of interrogation, Crownsil, witnesses, the whole dismal reconstruction of the timetable of the Teacher's movements? When all he had had to do was ask the patriarch the simple question, *Did you kill Storicai, Teacher?* to get the truthful answer. The Teacher did not lie. The Teacher would not lie.

Ellery actually turned to the old man and opened his mouth before reason took control again. Whatever the cause—the other-worldliness of the place, the strangeness of the people, his own enervation, the headiness of the encroaching desert— he had hardly been the same man since setting foot here. A case that rested solely on an accused's bearing witness against himself was not a civilized proceeding; it was an inquisition. This was not a matter between Teacher and Guest, a duel of antagonists. This was a searching after truth. For what is truth? *If you will be persuaded by me, pay little attention to Socrates, but much more to the truth, and if I appear to you to say anything true, assent to it, but if not, oppose me with all your might, taking good care that in my zeal I do not deceive both myself and you, and like a bee depart, leaving my sting behind.* And then there were the Crownsil and the people to persuade. Truth might touch their hearts through faith; but in such a dreadful matter it must convince their minds as well, and that could only come through evidence.

Ellery looked away from the Teacher to the faces around the table.

"Storicai is established as having entered this holy house at fifteen minutes past four. He is established as having been struck down to his death at twenty minutes past four. And the Teacher is established as having been here between Storicai's entering and Storicai's dying. And these two things establish that the Teacher had the *opportunity* to commit the crime. But not these two things alone establish his opportunity. There is another thing to support them."

From his pocket he took the glassine envelope containing the metal button he had found in Storicai's hand. "This button I removed from the Storesman's dead hand," he said. "I shall pass it among you, so that you may look at it closely, and know it for what it is." And he handed it to the Superintendent, who took it and passed it to the Successor as if it burned; and Ellery watched the button go around the table, quickly, leaving pain behind it.

And when it had been returned to him, Ellery said, "The very presence of this metal button in the slain man's hand is witness to its meaning. The threads still clinging to it are witness that it was torn away by Storicai, from the garment to which it was sewn, during the struggle that cost the Storesman his life . . . torn away from the garment of the person with whom he was struggling—who else?"

And Ellery said, sickening himself as he said it, "And this places the owner of the button on the scene of the slaying at the very moment of its taking place. And who, alone in Quenan, wears metal buttons on his garments? And who, in fact, had a metal button replaced on his garment?"

Someone made a stifled sound.

"I call the Weaver to witness."

She came slowly, chin on her bosom; nor would she sit, but remained standing before the stool. Once more it was necessary for him to phrase the answer as well as the question: yes, she did sew a button, a new metal button with the sacred *N* upon it, on the Teacher's robe at fifteen minutes before five o'clock—only twenty-five minutes after the murder. Her "yes" was torn from her. And she returned, with the step of an old woman, to her place.

Ellery felt his own legs trembling. He had to steel himself in order to turn to the Teacher.

"Do you then admit, Teacher, that this button found in Storicai's dead hand came from your garment?"

And calmly the Teacher answered, "It is so."

Ellery looked about, and he saw that he had company indeed in his distress. The stone had crumbled from their faces; each sat exposed in his knowledge and his grief.

And on those naked faces sat not knowledge and grief alone. For there was fear as well. Fear for themselves? No . . . no. It was for the Teacher. They had grown greatly afraid for their Teacher.

And Ellery forced his glance again at that old man, and what he saw shook him more than had he seen its opposite. For on that etching face, the face of the all-but-accused, sat a serenity that could only have come from purest peace within.

And, hating himself, Ellery looked away.

"We now," he said, and paused to still his crawling flesh, "we now weigh the second of our three measures of guilt—Means."

To set the scales, he reconstructed the *res gestae* leading up to the crime—the thefts of the Teacher's key in the night, the evidence of an attempt to enter the sanquetum with a faulty duplicate key, and so on—and the clues incident to the murder itself. He described the wounds on the dead Storesman's head, both at the back and in the forehead. He told them of the specks of baked clay in the dead Storicai's hair; of the bloody hammer beside the body; of the duplicate key in Storicai's pocket; of the unlocked door to the sanquetum; of the prayer jar that did not quite fit its base; of the disturbed columns of coins in the arque, and of the purple shard he found under the arque, and of the bloodstain on a corner of the arque.

"Let me sum up for you what all this means," Ellery said. "The Storesman had secretly made a duplicate key to the sanquetum in order to enter the room forbidden to him, as to all others but the Teacher. He could have had only one purpose in doing this—to steal the treasure of Quenan. He came to the door of the holy house, he looked about, he did not see that the Miller and the Waterman were observing him, and he entered without announcement or permission. In the holy house, he hurried to the door of the forbidden room, and unlocked it with the duplicate key he had made, and went in, and began to take the silver coins from the arque."

They were all leaning toward him now, eagerly, like plants toward the sun.

"At this moment a person—let me call him Witness—a Witness noticed the open sanquetum door and someone within, approached the room, saw the Storesman in the act of stealing the treasure, and in outraged anger plucked one of the scroll-filled prayer jars from its base and raised it high and brought it down on Storicai's head—the back of the head, since the Witness struck from behind. The jar shattered, shards of it falling all around, and one of the shards fell under the arque. Storicai collapsed under the blow, and in falling struck the back of his head on a corner of the arque."

Their sigh made a long, low hissing in the meeting room.

"Now this Witness," said Ellery, "must have then run from the sanquetum, perhaps to call for help. But almost at once the Storesman recovered from the blow by the prayer jar, leaped to his feet, and desperate to prevent the Witness's outcry against him, ran after the Witness, caught up with him here—near this table—grappled with him and, I have no doubt, in his frenzy of fear at being discovered in the act of sacrilege, tried to kill the Witness. And so they struggled in a terrible silence, and during the struggle the Witness managed to snatch the hammer which the Teacher had left for the Successor on this table, and in defense of his life swung it at Storicai. Storicai flung up his arm, and the first blow smashed my wrist watch on his arm, stopping it at twenty minutes past four. The second blow struck Storicai on the forehead. There was no need for a third."

A bit of burning wick detached itself and floated down to the pool of liquefied wax from which the flame rose. Here it continued to burn, separately, as if it had separate life.

"This, then, is a picture of the crime," Ellery continued. "Now for what happened immediately thereafter. Let us proceed step by step. The first thing the Witness must have done after slaying the Storesman was to return to the sanquetum, in order to restore the room to its former undisturbed state. To do this he had to collect the pieces of the broken prayer jar and dispose of them—and in doing so, he overlooked one shard under the arque—and also to replace the broken jar with a whole one and refill it with the scattered scrolls.

"Now, who did this?

"I ask the Potter to come forward."

The Potter came forward, no longer the Shavian figure he had first appeared. His feet dragged as if they bore a crushing weight. He lowered himself to the stool painfully.

"Someone came to you yesterday for a prayer jar to replace one which had been broken. Who, Potter?"

The Potter's slip-specked beard trembled, and he opened his mouth. But nothing came out.

"Who, Potter?" Tension made Ellery's own voice sound brutal.

This time a strangled noise emerged. But it was a noise without meaning.

"*Who, Potter?*" shouted Ellery.

And so at last the anguished words were torn from the Potter's throat: "The Teacher! The Teacher . . . !"

And now a soft keening rose, like a mournful wind, and Ellery, who could have keened with them, waited until it died away. And no eye turned to the Teacher, not even Ellery's.

"And what was the time when the Teacher came to your shed and asked for a new prayer jar for the sanquetum, Potter?"

"At half past the hour of four."

"Ten minutes after Storicai was struck dead," Ellery said, and slowly waved and the Potter stumbled back to his place.

"Thus we have connected the Teacher," Ellery resumed after a moment, "with the first weapon used, the weapon that merely stunned—the sanquetum jar. Now let us consider the second weapon used, the weapon that took Storicai's life—the hammer." And he reached down and took from the floor, where he had laid it, the wrapped hammer; and he began to unwrap it, and the cloth stuck in the now dry blood, and he had to tear it away as they shuddered. And the bloodstains on the hammer's head were still to be seen.

"Listen to me," Ellery said. "Yesterday in this room I took the imprint of the fingertips of all present—the dead Storesman, the Teacher, the Successor, the Superintendent, and the eleven members of the Crownsil of Twelve still living. Do you remember?"

Oh, yes, they remembered; they could not forget *that* mystery within a mystery; so much was clear. But did they have any idea of the significance of fingerprints?

"Do you know why I made each of you press your fingertips on the inkpad and then on the white paper?"

They were blanks.

"Then I will tell you." Ellery said. "Each man here, and each of the women too, lift up your hands and look at the tips of your fingers." The time they glanced at one another doubtfully; but the Chronicler raised his hands and looked at them, and one by one the others did likewise. "Look closely. Do you see the little lines and loops and whorls in your skin, making up a certain pattern?" There was a concert of nods. "This pattern can be transferred from your fingertips to another surface, especially a smooth dry one. Surely you have all seen the imprint of your fingers, or of the children's, on a wall or a window?"

"This we know, Elroï," the Chronicler spoke up suddenly. "But what is the meaning of it?"

"The meaning of it, Chronicler, is that the fingertips of no two people in the world leave the same picture—no, not even those of twins born of the same egg. In the outside world the fingerprints of millions and millions of people of all nations and races and colors have been collected, and not once have those of one person been found to match exactly those of another. Thus it may be said that each human being carries about with him—from his birth to his death and beyond, until the body all but crumbles into dust—a set of marks or signs on his fingers by which he, and he alone, can be told from all others in the world. Now do you grasp my meaning?''

It seemed that they did not; at least, on no face turned up to his did he see anything but a brow-knotted struggle to understand. Or was it a struggle to believe? For this might well come down to a matter, not of comprehension, but of faith.

''You must believe me when I say that it is true,'' said Ellery. ''I, Elroï Quenan, whose coming in a time of great trouble was foretold.'' And may God forgive me, he thought, for *that*. ''So now we come to the weighing of the Means, and to weigh that we must first throw into the balance the fingerprints.''

He held up the bloodied hammer, grasping it by the edges of the head and the bottom of the grip.

''You will see that I have dusted the gripping surface of the hammer with a white powder; and that this white powder, when blown gently away, has left a residue on the fingerprints made by the hand that grasped it in slaying the Storesman, thus revealing a picture of them.''

He laid the hammer carefully down on the table and reached for his fingerprinting kit. The prints on the hammer showing white against the darkened wood of the grip, he took out a piece of black paper. ''Teacher, will you allow me to take the fingerprints of your right hand?''

And now the silence could be scratched, it was so hard. But the Teacher wore the same expression of serenity.

''It shall be as you say, Elroï,'' he said.

Ellery took the old hand; it was warm and quiet in his. *If I forget thee, O Jerusalem . . .* He rolled the patriarch's fingers, then brought out the prints with white powder. He laid the black paper beside the hammer, and produced his pocket lens.

''I wish you all to rise and, one at a time, to look through the glass at the fingerprints of the Teacher you have just seen me take, and then at the fingerprints of the slayer on the hammer. And you will see that the fingerprints on the one are identical with the fingerprints on the other.''

But—would they? Primitive people who had never laid eyes on a photograph were often unable to recognize the most familiar people or objects snapped by a camera. There might be a similar blindness here. And indeed, while the Crownsil and the others filed by and examined the two exhibits in turn through the lens, while a few nodded, most shook their heads. Nevertheless, he waited until they were all seated again, and said, ''Thus, from the prints of the Teacher's fingertips on the hammer, we know that the Teacher, and only the Teacher, could have used the hammer to slay the Storesman. It is proved.''

But was it? To them?

The whole suffocating mantle of fatigue dropped over him again, so that he had to fight his way free of it. And Ellery turned to the serene old man, to prove his guilt by evidence they would have no choice but to accept.

''Teacher,'' he said abruptly, ''was it you who gathered together the pieces of the broken prayer jar, you who went directly from this holy house after the slaying to the Potter's for a new jar?''

And the old man answered, ''It is so, Elroï.''

"And was it your right hand that held this hammer?"

This time there was the least pause before the Teacher, still serenely, answered, "It is so, Elroï."

A gush of brash leaped into Ellery's mouth, and he had to swallow the burning stuff before he could say: "So we have established that the Teacher had opportunity to kill the Storesman—that is, that he was here; and that he had the means—that is, that his hand grasped the hammer.

"Now we must weigh the third and last measure of guilt—Motive."

And Ellery said:

"In stealing the Teacher's key to the sanquetum door and from it making a duplicate key, Storicai sinned in intent. But, having made the key, he proceeded to sin in fact. He committed three acts of offense against Quenan and the Teacher who had taught him.

"Storicai entered the holy house without ringing the bell and without being admitted by the Teacher—this was the first offense. He entered the forbidden room, which the Teacher alone among you has the right to enter—this was the second offense. And he laid greedy hands on the treasure—and this was his third offense.

"So, in the space of five shameful minutes, Storicai the Storesman offended against you, his brothers in Quenan, in general, and against his and your Teacher, in particular. Surely you can understand that the Teacher, venerable and wise and revered though he is, is still a man of flesh and blood, subject to the same weaknesses that beset us all? That, catching Storicai in the act of comitting three sins against the laws and customs of Quenan, your Teacher was seized with a great wrath and rose up against the transgressor with whatever instrument lay at hand—a prayer jar, a hammer—and struck down him who had wrought blasphemy upon the Wor'd?"

He looked up and down the two lines of faces, sure that now, at last, he would see agreement written there, even relief. But he saw only the same confused and fearful people.

What was the matter?

Ellery said in muttered, cracking tones, "And now I really cannot hold off any longer asking the question— the question of questions."

And the Teacher said, "Seek the truth and we shall be—"

There was a word after "be," but Ellery was not sure he had heard it correctly. Had the old man said "safe"? Or was it "saved"?

Well. No matter. Now for it. Ellery braced himself.

"Teacher. Did you slay Storicai the Storesman?"

The patriarch replied instantly, and his reply staggered Ellery . . . made him reach for the table, and support himself.

The rich voice of the Teacher said, "It is you who say it."

They had been gathered at the foot of the long table in a group, deliberating, praying, debating in low voices, for a long time. A final disagreement, apparently irreconcilable, sent the Chronicler as spokesmen to the Superintendent, to whisper in his ear.

That dry man immediately nodded and approached Ellery.

"I am asked to tell you, Elroï, that some of the Crownsil are confused by the pictures on the hammer, what you call the fingerprints. These persons say: Elroï says that the fingerprints on the hammer are the very same as the Teacher's fingerprints on the paper, but we could not be sure that all those little lines and loops are the same in both, so how can he? In a matter as grave as this, there must be no doubt.

This is what they have asked the Chronicler to ask me to ask you, and this is what I ask you now.''

Ellery turned wearily to the Successor, who had sat like a piece of petrified wood throughout most of the procedure.

"Will you please bring me some paper?" He had to repeat his question, for the Successor seemed as deaf as stone, too; but then the young man roused with a start, blushed deeply, and scuttled to the scriptorium to return in a moment with the paper.

Ellery distributed the paper, one sheet to each member of the Crownsil. They were only ten now, for the Slave had been returned to his house, too ill to remain longer in the meeting hall.

After going around the table from member to member, taking the prints of each, Ellery said, "Each person at the table now has before him a sheet of paper on which are impressed the prints of his own fingers. I ask you to do the following: Each of you is to write on his paper, beneath his fingerprints, a secret mark. It may be anything you choose—a circle, a little tree, a crossmark, anything you wish. Do not tell me or show me which mark you are making.''He dipped into his kit and tossed a few pencils on the table. "You may pass the pencils among you. Now I shall turn my back, so that I cannot see what you are doing." He turned his back. "Now do you all make your secret marks on your papers, and be sure you remember which mark you have made."

He stood there patiently, in a sort of exhausted wonder at the extraordinary situation in which he found himself. Behind him arose a sound made of shuffling feet, heavy breathing, and the rustling of clothes.

"Is it done?"

There was a little added confusion. Then the voice of the Superintendent said, "It is done."

Ellery did not turn around. "Now, Superintendent, do you collect the papers."

After a moment the superintendent said, "It is done. I have collected the papers."

"You will now shuffle them, Superintendent, placing them in random order, so that I cannot possibly guess from their order which paper belongs to whom."

After a few moments the Superintendent said, "And that is done, Elroï."

Ellery turned around; the ten sheets lay in a neat pile at the head of the table. Under their puzzled eyes he pulled the stool over, sat down, and took from his pocket the fifteen sets of fingerprints he had recorded the day before, each labeled with the title of the official whose prints it bore. He picked up the top sheet of the unidentified set he had just taken, and compared it with the top sheet of the identified set. They did not match, and he went on to the second sheet of the identified set. Then to the third. The fourth sheet of the old set was the one he was looking for.

He held up the sheet of unidentified prints with the secret mark. For effect, he did not speak at once. They were all watching his lips breathlessly.

"I have here a paper bearing fingerprints and a secret mark. The secret mark is an arrangement of eight lines, forming a square within a square. I say to you, without any doubt, that the fingerprints on this paper were made by"—and he turned suddenly to a pair of startled female eyes—"you, Weaver! Is it so? Tell it aloud, Weaver—are these your prints?"

"Yes," the woman breathed, "for the square within a square is the secret mark I made."

A murmur of amazement arose from the long table. Ellery stilled it with a gesture.

"I have only begun," he said; and he began comparing the second sheet from the secret-mark pile with his master set. Again the holding of breaths. Again his deliberate prolongation of the suspense. And then Ellery said, holding up the sheet, "The prints on this paper are marked with a wavy line such as children draw when they wish to represent water. The maker of this water sign is trying to mislead me, I fear. For one would expect the secret mark of water to be made by the Waterman. But it was not. *It was made by you, Chronicler*. Tell it! These are your fingerprints, I say."

And the Chronicler, scratching his beard as if caught in a sly joke, nodded. "They are mine, Elroï, even as you say."

After that, there was nothing to it. The Waterman had drawn a little house; the Growther had put down two interlocking circles; the Potter had made three Xs; the Miller had scratched the outline of an animal Ellery guessed was intended as a cow only because of its enormous udders; and so on.

"So you may see," he said, when he had finished, "that there can be no mistake when the fingerprints are compared by the eye of one who knows how to read them. The fingerprints on the hammer came from the hand of the Teacher."

They were convinced. He did not look at the patriarch, who had sat in total silence throughout the demonstration.

Once again they withdrew to their deliberations, closing in together at the other end of the table. Once again Ellery looked at them through clouded eyes, his face supported by trembling hands. Presently the Weaver began to cry. And then the Chronicler rose and with a reluctant gesture beckoned the Superintendent. He spoke in so low a voice that the man had to stoop to hear.

The Superintendent slowly, very slowly, returned to Ellery, and as the pale man stood before him Ellery forced himself to speak.

"What is their verdict?" he asked. "If they have reached one." For in that moment it seemed to him the ultimate folly to imagine that they would find against their leader. It had all been a futile farce.

"They have reached a verdict," said the Superintendent hoarsely. His eyes were starting from his head. "It is the verdict of all, with no nay-sayers. The Teacher is guilty of the death of Storicai the Storesman."

His self-control wilted suddenly. And he crouched and slapped his hands over his face, rocking and crying.

Like a signal, it touched off a remarkable demonstration. The two women of the Crownsil, the Weaver and the ancient female of the pair of Elders, burst into wails, the old woman tearing at her hair and beating her breasts with her withered fists. Tears sprang from the eyes of the men and fell into their beards. Some laid their heads on the table, clawing at it with both hands while they wept.

But of the entire company it was the young Successor who sobbed most heart-brokenly. His sturdy body twitched and jumped as if nothing, nothing in this world or the next could ever make him whole again.

And it was the Teacher who consoled him, who laid a gently urgent hand on the boy's racked shoulder, who then stroked his hair and murmured in his ear, making little soothing sounds as if to a terror-stricken child. And gradually the Successor's sobs lessened, and became a whimper, and the whimper died; and Ellery looked around to find that all had fallen silent.

And he turned again to the Superintendent. "And the sentence? The judgment?"

The man peered through red, swimming eyes. "Although the decision of the Crownsil, once made, may not be revoked, it can pass neither sentence nor judgment."

"Then who—?" Ellery began stupidly.

The Superintendent whispered, "Only the Teacher."

My God, he thought, my God. He had forgotten!

And the Teacher straightened and faced them; and the others rose as one; and the Teacher made a gesture of benediction, and they took their seats once more. And there was silence.

"Blessed is the Wor'd," began the old man, "over all the earth and unto all mankind that dwell hereon. Very many have been the blessings of the Wor'd unto me. My years have been long, my wives and children and children's children many. But even had I not enjoyed such riches, I would be rich still. For, blessed be the Wor'd, I have enjoyed other riches beyond number—the rain and the rainbow; the sun and the stars; the holy breath that is the wind. Blessed be the Wor'd for the sight and sound of birds; for the song in the voices of women; for the sweat on the bodies of men earned through toil; for the antelope in its flight and the smiling talk of friends; for the scent of grasses and the feel of watered earth; for the upturned faces of suckling lambs, and the peace that comes from prayers, and the grain that makes good bread; for the thousand perfumes of the flowers, and their thousand colors; for the shade of trees, and the happy agony of birth, and for children's voices.

"Blessed be the Wor'd," said the Teacher, and his voice rang through the meeting room, "for I say to you that no man can abide upon the earth so long as to grow weary of its riches. The moon must wane in its time, and vanish; but after the darkness comes the new moon, glorious."

And the old man paused. And then he said, in quite a different voice, "This is my judgement, this is my sentence that I pass upon myself:

"Tomorrow, at the sun's setting, I shall be caused to cease from among you"— did that quiet voice falter just a little?—"according to the manner decreed by the law."

For a second—one second of bottomless horror during which Ellery felt that he must surely burst, and everything whistled before his eyes in great and roaring circles—for one second no one made a sound.

But then the Successor cried out, "No!" in fearful disbelief, and again, *"No!"* And the womanly voice of the Weaver joined in anguished lamentation.

"Stop now, do you now stop at once, for you trouble not yourselves alone, but me." And the utterance, so firmly and gently said, silenced them more quickly than a shout. "Do not grieve," the Teacher said "for it must be. It is thus written, and only thus it is written, and as it is written so must it come to pass. Blessed is the Wor'd."

For weeks, months, Ellery had been starved for rest. But that night he could not sleep even for a moment. Something was *wrong*—every cell in his exhausted brain told him so. And yet he could not see what, he could not think where. Had the very simplicity of the case made him careless? Blindly unable to see the forest for the trees?

He tossed and shivered and perspired while the deep-seated pain settled deeper.

At the bottom it became a choice between the little bottle of red capsules and giving up. He gave up.

He crawled from the pallet, and switched on his flashlight, and then decided to save the battery; so he lit the candles in the earthenware candlesticks—salt-glazed, he noticed, grimacing at the detail.

Detail, detail—somewhere existed a detail he had overlooked. It gnawed away at him like the fox at the Spartan boy's belly. He had to organize, he had to organize his thoughts. Something about the trial, the end of the trial . . . no, not the end exactly, but toward the end . . . something there; that was what was bothering him. While he was talking about motive? Had his primer exposition of motivation been faulty? Had he left something out? Was that it?

As he continued to think about it, pulling on a jacket against the chilly desert night, tucking his feet back under the blanket, Ellery's heart sank even lower. For, granted that Storicai had been guilty of great sins against Quenan; granted that the Storesman had committed the community's first crime in almost two generations; granted also that religious belief sometimes assumed sudden spasmodic forms of fanaticism (a pilgrim to Mecca had only recently been torn to pieces by maddened worshipers for having, in a fit of sickness, vomited on the holy Kaaba): granted, granted, granted. Still . . . would the Teacher have so lost command of himself— that most patient and disciplined of men—as to yield to an impulse of violence? The Teacher guilty of violence?—that saintliest of the brothers?

As for the possibility that the old man had struck, not in a fit of rage, but with coldly predetermined intention, Ellery could not for a moment credit it.

But certainly he had here got to the root of his hag-mounted doubts: the motive, which had seemed so utterly convincing during the trial, was now not convincing at all. The Teacher was a man whose nature excluded a resort to violence; who would not, who *could* not, have struck Storicai with the prayer jar. The prayer jar! How could Ellery have believed for a moment that the holy man would desecrate a sacred vessel, even to smite a sinner?

And the hammer—would the Teacher have been capable of swinging it at even the meanest of his flock? Not once, but twice? A hammer, a skull-crushing *hammer?* Even in self-defense? Even to save the life that he himself had condemned to be taken tomorrow?

Unthinkable. It was unthinkable.

Think it through again, think it through . . .

And the questions came crowding, elbowing one another, in their release from the dark cell in which he had imprisoned them.

Why had the Teacher left such a plain trail to himself? For that was what he had done:

Ten minutes after Storicai's death the old man had shown up at the Potter's shed to ask for a new scroll jar.

Fifteen minutes later he had gone openly to the Weaver to have his "lost"—his unique, his identifiable—button replaced.

And how was it that, having meticulously swept up the fragments of the broken jar in the sanquetum, the Teacher had overlooked one shard? A shard that Ellery had seen almost at once . . .

And the manner of his responses to the direct questions. Asked if he had gone straight from the Slave's house to the Holy Congregation House, the old man had answered, *It is so.* Asked if he had been in the holy house just before Storicai was stuck down, he had answered, *It is so.* Asked if the button found in the dead man's hand had come from his garment he had answered, *It is so.* Asked if it was he who had gathered together the broken pieces of the prayer jar, if it was he who had gone from the holy house after the killing to the Potter's for a replacement jar, the old man had answered, *It is so.* Asked if it was his hand that had held the hammer, he had answered, *It is so.*

But asked if he had killed the Storesman, he had *not* answered, *It is so*. He had answered: *It is you who say it!*

It is you who say it was not at all the same as *It is so*. The Teacher did not lie— no, as the Elders had both cried out, not even to save his life. *It is you who say it* had been the equivocation of a man who could not lie, but who at the same time did not want to tell the truth, the whole truth.

Therefore . . . therefore (and Ellery shivered in the cold room, made colder by his thoughts) the whole truth has not yet been told. He would have to begin again.

The moment he re-examined the button, with its mystic *N* in the candlelight, Ellery saw what he had failed to see before, and cursed himself for his blindness.

The ends of the thread on the button were not raggedly torn, as they would have been had they been ripped away in a struggle. Instead, under the lens they showed up sharp and clean. They had been severed from the garment with a knife or scissors.

He turned the button over. The lens immediately showed him another proof of his carelessness—criminal carelessness, he told himself bitterly. There was a fresh-looking little gash where the oxidized surface of the soft metal had suffered a recent scratch, as if a sharp-edged instrument had slipped while cutting the thread.

My God, Ellery said to himself wildly, I investigate what I think is a primitive crime in a primitive setting of primitive people, and I find a sophisticated *frame-up!* The button was deliberately cut from the Teacher's robe! The button was deliberately planted in the dead man's hand!

But thank God it was not too late.

Ellery sprang from the pallet and began to dress. He must be thorough now, careful not to underestimate his adversary. The Teacher's life was at stake. The Teacher, who was prepared to sacrifice his life rather than expose the evil—the really evil—sinner in his flock.

By some magic Ellery's brain was now clear. His first morning in Quenan leaped from his memory to awareness: the Teacher in the storehouse, exchanging his broken pocket knife for a new one . . .

Ellery blew out the candles, and seizing the flashlight he made his way through the little settlement in the cold sweetness of the night. The wind was rushing through the trees. There was no light behind any window, but Ellery was certain that vigil, in the darkness, was being kept throughout the town.

At the Holy Congregation House he hesitated. He was excused from having to ring the bell and await admittance; why did he always hesitate? Perhaps because I am so fallible, he thought; and he went in.

He groped through the meeting hall to the Teacher's chamber. The light from the lamp over the sanquetum door, making the interior of the patriarch's room just visible, touched the old man's serene face, his open eyes. He was stretched out on his pallet in the middle of the room, hands behind his head, gazing up at the ceiling as through a window . . . as if he saw clearly the great stars wheeling and blazing in the black heavens.

He did not move or speak when Ellery came in. He knows I'm here, Ellery thought, and he's not surprised. Has he been expecting me?

There were pegs symmetrically spaced on either side of the door, and from one of them hung the Teacher's outer garment. Ignoring the old man on the bed, Ellery searched the robe for hidden pockets. He found the side slits, and in the depths of one of them he found what he was looking for.

It was the Teacher's knife, the new one he had procured in the storehouse under Ellery's eyes—in a wooden sheath, bone-handled, the sheath and knife held together by a leather thong. He switched on his flashlight and slipped the knife out of the sheath and examined the blade closely.

And there it was—a nick on the cutting edge, near the point. And caught in the nick was a tiny sliver of metal, the same soft metal of the button.

Not only had the button been deliberately severed from the Teacher's robe, it had been severed by the Teacher's knife!

And Ellery raised his eyes to that long quiet body, but there was no sign in it of perturbation, or even concern. The old man continued to stare through the ceiling, although he knew well enough what Ellery had done and seen.

Ellery softly left the Teacher's room and the holy house and made his way back through the wind and the *weedit, weedit* of the frogs to his quarters. And there he picked up the hammer and re-examined it. One item of planted evidence he had already exposed—the button.

Was it possible that the hammer, too, showed evidence of the frame-up of the Teacher?

In this shifted frame of reference, it seemed to him now that the hammer seemed too new-looking—rather, too unused-looking—to have justified the Teacher's reference to it, during Ellery's talk with him after the discovery of the Storesman's body, as "the hammer from my tool chest."

He dipped a corner of the toweling provided him into the ewer of water and carefully rubbed away the bloodstains on the striking surface of the hammer. He had been right. There were no abrasions or scratches on the metal of the head. This hammer had never been used for hammering nails or any other ordinary purpose. Was it possible that there had been an exchange of hammers? But if this was a new hammer it had most likely come from the storehouse. Then perhaps the Teacher's . . .

Once again Ellery made his way through the dark lanes of the hamlet, this time to the supply building. He needed no key; it was secured against marauding animals by an inside latch, and to release it he had merely to put his hand through a hole in the door made for the purpose.

It seemed to him that already the storehouse was filled with the effluvium of neglect. They had better elect another Storesman soon, he thought, or this place will begin to smell like a grave. He had to make an effort to pull his mind back to his mission.

Flashing his light among the bins and barrels and shelves, he finally located the compartment where the hammers were stored.

There were only three. Using a handkerchief, he examined them. Two were clearly new; one showed definite signs of use.

Is this used one the real murder weapon? Ellery asked himself. If so, someone had switched hammers after the crime—cleansed this one of Storicai's blood, placed it with the new ones in the storehouse, taken one of the new ones, dipped it in the still-wet blood of the victim, and then set it beside the body.

But why? How did the exchange of hammers compound the frame-up of the Teacher (who had certainly, at some point, become aware of the frame-up)? Why? Why?

And the question rang over and over in Ellery's head until he was sick with it . . .

He returned to his quarters carrying both hammers, thinking of samurai wearing two swords to signify their rank; of fighting priests in the Dark Ages, forbidden to use swords, going into battle against the heathen and laying about them with the *martels-de-fer*, the great fighting mallets; and of other strange and useless things.

Once more he opened his fingerprint kit and set to work. And tested the hammer he had taken from the storehouse, and found fingerprints. The fingerprints of two people, as he expected. And, in dread, he compared them with his master set of fifteen.

And when he saw whose prints they were, the disjointed pieces of the truth fell into place, and sickened him.

For the second time that night, Ellery entered the patriarch's room. Nothing had changed. The old man was still unmoving, still untroubled. Had he placed himself in a kind of mystical trance? But the first assertion Ellery made (with such difficulty!) the Teacher answered at once. And their interchange began to form a sort of litany, as if an act of worship were being performed in that bare dim chamber.

"It was you, Teacher, who cut the button off your robe with your knife and placed the button in the dead man's hand."

"Yea."

"It was you who took the killing hammer to the storehouse and cleansed it, and left it there, and brought back another hammer, and stained its head in the Storesman's blood, and placed it beside the body."

"Yea."

"You deliberately left a trail by way of the Potter and the Weaver which could lead only to yourself."

"Yea."

"You wished me to find evidence against you and against no other."

"Yea."

And Ellery, holding his voice down with all his strength, asked, "Why, Teacher, in heaven's name, *why?*"

"For thus it is written," said the Teacher.

" 'It is written, it is written!' Where are all these things written?"

It seemed to him the old man's beard lifted a little in a smile. "It is written in the book which was lost; or it is written in a book yet to be; or it may be written in the book which is Earth itself and all who dwell upon it, and in which all things were, and are, and will be written."

"Let us rather speak of what I can understand, Teacher," Ellery cried. "It is now clear to me that you *wished* to be accused of the Storesman's murder—that you *wished* to stand trial—that you *wished* to be declared guilty. Is that not so?"

And the old man calmly replied, "I am guilty."

"But not of striking the blow that slew the man!"

And the old man was silent. And then he sighed, and he said, "Nay, not of striking the blow."

"Then you are shielding him who actually struck it!"

And again the Teacher did not reply at once, and again he sighed and again he finally said, "It is so, Elroï."

"So you know who slew Storicai?"

The majestic head nodded. "It is written that thus it would come to pass."

"I do not know about that, Teacher. I do know that on the true weapon, the hammer that actually crushed out Storicai's life, I found the fingerprints of the slayer. They are the fingerprints of—shall I say the name?"

"Said or unsaid, the Wor'd is sure."

"That does not say it. Therefore I must. Storicai was killed by the Successor."

Now for the first time the patriarch shifted his eyes to Ellery's face. "Elroï," he said, "before your coming here I knew nothing of fingerprints. But this I knew—that the Successor had handled the hammer. And I was afraid that, in some mysterious way beyond my knowledge, it could be shown that it was he indeed who had struck with the hammer, and that therefore it would be safer for the boy if that hammer were not found by the body. So I cleansed it and in its place set one which had been in my hand but not in his. Alas. I should have known that deceit is always undone."

Not always, old man, Ellery said; but not aloud.

Aloud he said: "Am I right then, in what I have only now come to believe, Teacher? You returned from the Slave's house to this holy house just in time to see the killing of Storicai at twenty minutes past four—in time to see, but too late to prevent. You saw Storicai and the Successor struggling by the long table. You saw the Successor snatch the hammer and deal two blows—"

The Teacher said faintly, "It was as you say."

"From this it follows that the Successor was *not* locked in the scriptorium at the time of the slaying." And wonder touched Ellery's voice. "Did you not tell me that he was?"

The Teacher said, "Think, Elroï, think."

"All right, I will go back, step by step. You told me you had locked the Successor in the scriptorium at two o'clock because you found him dallying in the doorway of the holy house with thoughts of a young woman, instead of being at his studies. You locked him in and retained the only key. That is the truth."

"Yea."

"But you also told me that just after the killing of Storicai in the meeting room you unlocked the door of the scriptorium, released the Successor, and sent him out to find me. Unlocked the scriptorium door *after* the slaying of the Storesman. That is the truth."

"Yea."

"But I ask myself: How is that possible? For the Successor to have been in the meeting room and to have killed Storicai, the door to the scriptorium must have been unlocked before the murder; yet you told me you unlocked it after the murder . . . Ah, I see. You wished it believed that the Successor sat helpless behind a locked door between two o'clock and some time after four-twenty—to furnish the young man with an alibi that would make it impossible to suspect him of the slaying.

"Yes, I see. Just before three o'clock when you left the Holy Congregation House to visit the Slave, you unlocked the door of the scriptorium and reminded the Successor about repairing the table leg. And this time you left the sctiptorium door unlocked."

The Teacher closed his eyes. "It is so."

"I did not ask you of this, therefore you did not tell me of it."

The Teacher nodded.

"But you knew I would ask other questions, and you could answer those questions only with the truth. So, Teacher, the first thing you did after realizing that Storicai was dead—just after four-twenty—was to send the Successor back into the sctiptorium and lock him in—for the second time. This you did so that you could tell me truthfully that just after four-twenty you unlocked the scriptorium door, released the Successor, and sent him out to seek me. By thus telling me the truth in part only, did you protect the Successor from the consequences of his guilt and point the finger of the slaying to yourself alone.''

And the Teacher said, ''All that you say, Elroï, is so.''

Ellery began to pace the room, his irregular footsteps echoing his troubled thoughts. ''I have been wondering why you should have done this, Teacher, and I am confused. Can it truly be that you, the shepherd of the flock, are willing to give up your life that the little fox with bloodstained paws should live?''

The Teacher began to speak; but he held his tongue in time, and many moments passed. Finally he said in a firm voice, ''Truly,'' and then added in a voice not so firm, ''but only in part.''

Only in part . . . ? Mystified, Ellery waited for the old man to explain his meaning. But the Teacher's silence was unbroken.

''Teacher,'' said Ellery wearily, facing him. ''Teacher, surely there is another way? Surely you need not die? For the Successor need not die if the whole truth be told. Surely, if he were to be put on trial, the Crownsil would be merciful. For Storicai *did* commit three great sins. He *was* caught in the act of committing them by the Successor. What the Successor did was the impulsive action of a young man with a young man's lack of control. He was outraged at Storicai's sacrilege, and he seized the first object at hand, the prayer jar, and struck blindly.

''And when Storicai recovered from the blow and ran after the Successor, surely he intended the boy bodily harm?—for a man who would profane the holy house and contemplate sacrilegious acts would have no hesitation in attempting murder to keep his crimes from becoming known. So that when the boy, fighting for his life, managed to get hold of the hammer on the table and struck out with it, surely he was not a slayer at heart? In the world from which I come such a man-slayer would be defended in the court of law by the plea of self-defense, which, if successful, results in the slayer's being declared not guilty of slaying, and so is released. Surely the Crownsil will understand?''

''It is you,'' said the old man sadly, ''who do not understand.''

''No,'' cried Ellery, ''no, I do not! Or I do, and it is you who do not! Even if the Crownsil were to find the Successor guilty, they could not pass sentence or judgment—that duty is yours alone, as Teacher. And surely it is not conceivable that you would feel obliged to condemn the boy to his death? Surely you could, and would, show mercy?—and the Crownsil would be shamed by their Teacher's compassion. The boy need not die, Teacher; and if he need not die, you need not die in his place!''

''Elroï, Elroï,'' murmured the old man, ''what I did was not for the Successor alone.''

''What do you mean?'' said Ellery, staring.

''The Slave did not request my presence in his house yesterday merely because he was ill, ill though he was. He had urgent tidings for me, for my ear alone . . . Where shall I begin?

''At the place where we first met, and you and I and the Storesman—I shall begin there. It was only last year that Storicai began to accompany me to the End-of-the-World Store. This was a great mistake, and it was mine alone. For I discovered that Storicai was a weak and covetous man. While he knew only our Valley and the things of our Valley, while he was surrounded by our simple abundance and had charge over all of it, his covetousness was not apparent. And when he knew only me, his weakness was supported.

"But at the store of Otto Schmidt he saw for the first time a box that talks, flashing jewelry, handsome cloth the like of which we do not have, succulent foods that made his mouth water—he saw wondrous things he had never known existed. And in his weakness Storicai could not resist the desire to possess them."

And Ellery, recalling the Storesman's wonder at the Duesenberg, his childish delight in the gold wrist watch, saw the man as the Teacher must have come to see him.

"I should not have allowed him to continue accompanying me to the End-of-the-World Store," the patriarch went on strongly. "But I did not then know the depth of his covetousness. No, he was careful not to betray to me the greed that was growing within him, enticing and deceiving him. He did not tell me of his greed—but he did tell the Crownsil."

"What!"

"He worked upon them behind my back. He told them of these wondrous things. At first they were incredulous. Then they were merely doubtful. And soon they began to believe. For some of the elders still dimly remembered the world outside Quenan, the things they had enjoyed as children, and when they added their memories to Storicai's tales, the younger people could not help but believe. And Storicai continued to tempt them, and in time all began to covet the things the Storesman coveted."

Ellery muttered, "Even . . . ?"

The Teacher read Ellery's mind. "Even the Weaver," he nodded in a sort of pain. "Yea, even she—though she told herself that she coveted for my sake, not her own, as women will. She wanted me, before I ceased, to partake of the wonders of which Storicai spoke so cunningly. As if I have need of such baubles and gratifications! As if I would gainsay the whole meaning of my life and the life of Quenan!"

It was the first time Ellery had ever heard the old man raise his voice, seen his eyes flash with the fires of anger. But then the fires damped, and when he spoke his voice was calm again.

"What you must understand, Elroï, is that Storicai found out he could, as punishment, be deposed. In his was craven also. He feared to do alone what he must do in order to satisfy his mean hungers, for if he were cunning he saw that if he could persuade the others of the Crownsil to join with him, he would be safe. So with his mouth smoother than oil he set out about persuading them. They had only to join with him, he said, and he would do what had to be done. He would divide the wondrous things with all in Quenan, he said, but the Crownsil would receive greater shares because of their high position. What, compared to this, was the wearing of horn buttons?"

"The Crownsil was corrupted," muttered Ellery. "The whole Crownsil!"

"The whole Crownsil—but one," the old man whispered. "The whole Crownsil—but one . . . And Storicai proceeded with his plan, and stole the key from my chamber, and made a duplicate key to the forbidden room—for the purpose of it all was, as you saw, to steal the silver dollars with which he proposed to buy the useless things he craved.

"Therefore, Elroï," and his voice became strong and steady again, "all the while I was saying to you that there was no crime in Quenan, there was crime in Quenan and I did not know it. All the while I declared that none in Quenan coveted that which was not his, my most beloved brothers and sisters were coveting, and planning to steal, and to sanction stealing, and to transgress the law and deny the Wor'd; and I did not know it.

"The Slave alone of the Crownsil of Twelve had never entered into Storicai's evil compact. Though sore of heart, he had kept silent, praying that the others would see in time the great sin they intended, and would repent and stay the hand of Storicai. But when he fell sick to dying, and they repented not, the Slave sent for me and disclosed all he knew . . . I walked back from the Slave's house with feet that walked of themselves. I had no thoughts, no feelings; I walked in blackness.

"And I entered this holy house, and I saw the Successor struggling with Storicai and snatching up the hammer to defend himself—for he is only a boy, and Storicai was a powerful man—and slay him, and I was too late to stay the great trouble of Quenan. And I saw also, as in a vision, what I must do.

"I am old, Elroï, and the days allotted to me cannot be many more. The Successor has been reared to take my place since his first breath, for this is our way. He was not ever of the conspiracy, remember; that was only among the Crownsil. He was outraged by what he saw Storicai trying to do, and his only thought was to keep the holy treasure intact, and see the Storesman punished.

"He has the leaping blood of youth, Elroï, but he believes with all his soul in the Wor'd; he will gain wisdom as his blood cools and he will spend his life faithfully, as I have spent mine, to be the Teacher of our people. And, in any case, there is none trained to take his place."

The old man had raised himself to a sitting position in his earnestness. "All these things went through my mind in an instant. And I knew the Successor must remain unshamed in the eyes of the community, if he is to command their utter belief and trust. Therefore I take his sin upon myself and depart from them."

The wind spoke to the trees and the frogs spoke to the wind; but in the dim chamber neither spoke.

Until Ellery said, "Teacher, I cannot approve of it. Even in your own terms I condemn it. You once said to me that we must seek the truth, that the truth will save us—"

The old man nodded, unperturbed. "For thus it is written," he said. And Ellery wondered, not for the first time, if the Teacher meant *Thus the truth is written*, or *Thus it must be*.

"How can we seek the truth, and how can the truth save us, if we act out a lie?" Then he burst out: "What evil have you done, that you should sacrifice your life?"

Some measure of the old man's tranquility left him; he uttered a sigh that seemed to come from great depths.

"You are mistaken, Elroï. I have done great evil indeed. For if the Crownsil have sinned, then have I not sinned more? Is it not I who has been their Teacher? Their sins are upon my head; their guilt that cuts into my heart, is my own.

"It is not they who have failed me; it is I who have failed them. Or they could not have done this thing.

"And as I am their Teacher still, so I must teach them now—since the teaching of my words has failed—by the teaching of my example. And the example is that I shall take their sin upon myself. For if faith in the Wor'd is lost, then all is lost, and Quenan becomes as the outside from which we fled . . . nay, worse, for my people have had no experience with sin, and in the outside they would be as sheep without the shepherd when snow shuts out the sky. I love them, Elroï, and how better can I show my love?—if only they love each other. It must be done."

But Ellery mumbled, "I will tell them the truth."

And the Teacher smiled and asked the ancient question, "What is truth? Today at the trial you told them what you then held to be the truth, and they believed you. And now you wish to tell them the contrary, so that they may believe the contrary. Do you think they will?"

The old man drew a deep breath; his spare body was taken with a shudder, quickly suppressed. "If you tell them the truth, Elroï, I will deny it. I will deny it, and they will believe me as they have always believed me. And what will you have gained?"

Ellery beat his fist into his palm. "You know you will not and cannot deny the truth. You know you will not and cannot ever lie to them!"

The old man trembled. "Then do not, I pray you, force me to lie to them after seven decades. But," and he raised his voice, not in agitation but in emphasis, "but I would do so, Elroï, for it is written that I am doing that which must be done, that which was ordained of old for the end of days. You have been the instrument prophesied, and my love for you is great; but some things I know better than you, for all your knowledge. If you have love for me, then I pray you do not tell them. Believe in me."

Ellery sat, immobilized. What to do, what to do? Rush headlong to his car, speed off to find . . . whom? the police? the sheriff? the governor? the Army?—someone, anyone who would keep tomorrow's human sacrifice from being made? And yet, to do that would be to expose Quenan to a world that could only destroy the Valley. But it was destroyed already. Or was it? The Teacher was prepared to give his life in the belief that it was not. Who was he to set his small judgment against the towering spirit of this old man?

And, as Ellery sat, treacherously it came stealing over him again, that strange, utter fatigue. It began to make a roaring in his ears.

What to do? *What to do?*

The old man spoke gently. "In that cabinet is bread, and also wine, and it is late," he said. "Will you sup with me?"

Ellery shut the door of the old man's room quietly behind and simply stood there. In the meeting hall the single lamp cast its dim glow. Once it had seemed golden, but no longer. It came to his exhausted mind that he was waiting for something. But what?

He pressed his palm against his eyes. Curious patterns were shifting kaleidoscopically. Suddenly they formed a face. He felt immediate relief, and took away the shielding hands and crossed the room to the door of the scriptorium. He knocked, and there was no answer. He tried the door; it was unlocked, and he went in. The scriptorium was empty. Of course. The Successor's bedchamber. He switched on his flashlight and went to the other door and knocked and, again, there was no answer. He opened the door; the Successor was gone. Mechanically he retreated to the long hall.

He heard himself groan. Every atom in his body seemed to be crying out for rest, and the distance to his own room stretched infinitely. The bench beckoned, and he decided to sit down.

His legs had already begun to undertake the labor of getting to the bench when a peculiar sound from outdoors paralyzed them. In the same instant the face, which had vanished, sprang again into his mind's eye. So he made his way painfully out of the Holy Congregation House. He paused outside the door.

There was something in the darkness that made noises like an owl's noises, or a child's; but this thing that he barely saw was not an owl, was too large to be a child, and yet was not shaped like a man.

Ellery's parts shrank in upon themselves.

He took himself in hand. On legs as taut and tingling as they had been leaden-weighted, he approached the thing in the night. Not until later did it occur to him that he could have used his flashlight, which he clutched throughout.

Glimmer—faint in the faint starlight. Bulk—close to the ground, cool and damp. Whimper—incoherent, alien. And then a cough, and then a sob.

Fear dropped from Ellery like melting ice, and he knelt and touched what lay there, and moved his hand over it. It was a man clad in a robe, doubled up, hands so tightly pressed against his face that Ellery had to use all his enfeebled strength to dislodge them. He felt a beard rimming the jaw, the soft curling beard of youth. The Successor.

There was a whispering in the darkness.

Ellery bent closer, trying to make it out. ". . . *tell them, tell them, tell them.*"

"I cannot," a second voice said, the Successor's. Whose, then, had been the whisper? The young man's eyes were open now, holes of darkness in his face. "I cannot tell them," he said.

Ellery tried to rise, staggered. The Successor looked startled; instinctively he put forth a supporting hand, and they struggled together to their feet.

"Why were you crying?" Ellery said.

"You said, Elroï, that I must tell the Crownsil and the people the true happenings," the Successor whispered. "But . . ."

That was when Ellery remembered the flashlight. He switched it on and set it down on the ground so that it reflected from a large pale rock. The boy's face was masklike; to see his lips move was a shock.

"But?"

"But I cannot say the truth. I do not dare."

So it came about that Ellery found himself sitting on the cold ground trying to develop a Socratic dialogue with the boyish man-slayer. In the first place, he asked, once the Crownsil had been made to understand the circumstances of the crime, was it likely they would again convict? But even if they were to convict, was it likely the Teacher would pronounce the dread sentence a second time? But even were the Teacher to pronounce sentence against him, was there reason for the Successor to submit? He was a boy, he had a long lifetime before him: could he not flee? Who was there in Quenan to restrain him by force? Nor need he feel afraid to face the unknown world. Ellery would be to him as a brother, as an elder brother.

But—"I cannot, I do not dare."

Cannot, do not dare? When the alternative is the death of the Teacher? Canst thou remain silent, *darest* thou?

"Can you watch a man like your Teacher go to his death for a crime which, in the first place, he did not commit and in the second place, was not a crime but an act of self-defense? If you're worthy to be the Successor," Ellery said, "you will speak out!"

The mask before him was the mask of tragedy. The change wrought in the short time since he had last seen the boy was horrifying. The eyes were cloudy and deep-sunken, the bloodless lips down-twisted, twitching; the whole young head seemed skeletal.

"You do not understand, Elroï." The Successor's voice, the Teacher's words.

"Then make me understand! Because otherwise I will have no choice but to bring in authorities from the outside world to save your Teacher's life. And that will mean the end of Quenan."

Over and over again, the boy wrung his hands. "I know everything you have told me," he cried. "I would do as you ask—oh, Elroï, you would not have to ask! But I am helpless. Why do you think I remained silent at the trial? I could not speak because the Teacher forbade it! He forbids it still, and I dare not disobey him."

"Why, Successor? *Why* can't you disobey him? What would happen to you if you did?" Ellery demanded.

The young head rolled from side to side in agony. "I do not know what would happen, Elroï. It does not matter what would happen. It is as if you were to ask me, What would happen were you to raise your arms and fly to the stars? You do not understand. I cannot do it. I have never in my life disobeyed the Teacher and I cannot disobey him now!"

Ellery stared at the tragic mask, and suddenly he understood. The Successor was like the next-to-last Emperor of China, the nephew of the wicked Empress Dowager, imprisoned at her command when he tried to reform the corrupt practices of her regency. In prison he was visited by officials secretly in sympathy with his cause. Let the Son of Heaven but give the word, they said, and loyal troops would liberate him and place the "Old Buddha" herself in confinement. But the Emperor shook his head. It was impossible, he said. How could one raise one's hand against a venerable ancestor? And he died a prisoner still, held fast by bars far stronger than the bars of his cell.

I cannot do it. I cannot disobey him.

The words rang in Ellery's ears until they filled the night.

He remembered the dark lane flowing past him. He remembered the path moving like water under his feet. He remembered the noise in his ears, like a howling wind.

But he did not remember stumbling to his pallet and falling on it; he did not remember the new dawn creeping up from behind Crucible Hill.

He knew only darkness.

6 · Friday, April 7

When he opened his eyes there were no shadows, but the great hush that hung over the Valley was not the usual noontime quiet. It was the silence of a ghost town, or rather of a town or a *Mary Celeste* suddenly abandoned by its human beings.

Then an ass brayed, and another; a bellow burst from the chest of a bull; dogs began to howl, as if something dreadful were about to happen.

Or was happening.

Or had happened? With a cry, Ellery jumped out of bed. But then he remembered. It was not to be until sundown.

But . . . the silence? Had all Quenan fled into the desert rather than stay to witness?

He was still in his stale and rumpled clothes. The sleep had not refreshed him; and the sun pouring through the window did not wash away the ache in his bones.

He went out into the lane. No one was in sight, and he walked through the village. Here and there, through an open window, he caught a glimpse of movement; once he saw a distant someone—the Waterman?—working in a field. *The mills are to turn, and the dry fields burn.* No, the people of Quenan had not left their Valley. They simply could not bear to look upon it on this day, as if the hills themselves were due to depart with the departing sun. Most of them had withdrawn into their houses and shut the doors.

Great must be their grief.

And great was the silence which hung over the Valley of the Shadow, and all that endless afternoon Ellery wrestled with his problem and found no answer to it.

The choices always seemed to come down to three:

He could let the events take their course, bowing to the will of the Teacher.

He could tell the truth to the community. But in that case, the Teacher had said, he would deny it, and the people would believe him and not Ellery; and Ellery knew that this was so.

He could go for help to prevent the sentence's being carried out. But then Quenan itself would die.

Talk about Hobson!

Ellery walked the tree-lined lanes, climbed the green terrace of the hills, picked his way along the immaculate furrows of the fields. No one appeared to speak or even wave to him. Twice he headed in the direction of the only figures he laid eyes on in his wanderings, but when he reached the place no one was there. He could not bring himself to knock on any door.

Late in the afternoon he found himself drawn back to the Holy Congregation House. The Teacher was alone there, sitting on a stool. He greeted Ellery with the familiar gesture of benediction and indicated the bench. Ellery sank onto it. The old man seemed completely at peace.

"Teacher," said Ellery, "I beg you to reconsider."

"Very well," the patriarch said calmly.

Ellery's heart jumped. "Then you will tell them the truth?" he cried.

For a moment the old man said nothing; then: "I have reconsidered, Elroï, as you asked. I find no reason to change that which is written. I will say no more to the people, nor will you."

The sun began to set. The people seemed to come from everywhere—houses, barns, fields, trees, shadows—springing up like the reapings of the dragon's teeth. They came from everywhere and became one, a sluggish beast of many heads sluggishly moving along.

And Ellery became one with them.

He saw the Teacher, tall among the many, the throng making way for him with sighs and moans as he moved slowly through, his right hand describing the ritual blessing.

And so Quenan came to the place; and when the crowds parted and Ellery saw what it was that their bodies had concealed, lying on the earth, he almost cried out with relief and joy.

How could he have been so blind as to take literally what was intended as a symbol only? What he was witnessing was a parallel to the rites of the Penitentes of the New Mexico mountains—the Brotherhood of the Light, as they called themselves—who yearly re-enacted the great passion of their religion and chose one of their number for the central role. Performed in secret places, intended as a purging of sin, the mystery stopped short of the taking of life, although its principal suffered torments enough.

He wondered how the isolated community of Quenan had learned of these remarkable rites. Or had they developed a similar rite independently, altering, as it were, the ancient prompt-book? For what he was now witnessing . . .

The Teacher lay down in the place prepared for him.

There was now not even a sigh.

So might the ancient Egyptians have stood at the annual re-enactment of the death of Osiris—knowing it was drama, yet not-knowing, too, with one part of themselves believing it to be a real thing, happening before their eyes.

And the Superintendent stepped forth from among them, holding a vessel of some sort in his cupped hands. And all breath was stopped, even the breath of the wind.

The Superintendent tenderly lifted the Teacher's head with his left hand and held the vessel to the ancient lips with his right and then departed from him. The Teacher lay perfectly still. The sun set then, plunging the scene in blood, reddening the palms of the recumbent patriarch. All at once a soft spring breeze arose, and the grasses whispered in alarm . . .

Ellery awoke to a great anger. To allow himself to be so cozened and bewitched! The Teacher and his puppets had succeeded in infecting him with the disease of their fantasies, making him believe that the real was unreal and the unreal real. But he was cured. What had seemed an experience of pathos and profound tragedy was simply a distasteful demonstration of bumpkin fanaticism. The old man was a natural-born actor, and soon the lesser actors in this primitive drama would be stepping forward to perform their silly roles, too. Well, he had had enough of the nonsense! It was time to call a halt.

A woman nearby began to wail, rocking back and forth. Another woman—ah, the Weaver!—took up the lament. The children began to cry in a frightened way. (They had been coached, too!) And then the man . . .

Ellery raised his arms high and shouted, "This has gone far enough!" and strode over to where the old man lay with arms outstretched to the darkening skies; and Ellery dropped to one knee, and reached out his hand to shake the thin shoulder.

But the hand remained in midair.

Out of the jumble in Ellery's head an orderly thought took shape: I have been following the wrong prompt-book, too. The laws of Quenan are not the laws of Rome. The drink was not the symbolic preliminary to carrying out the symbolic sentence; it *was* the sentence, and there was nothing symbolic about it.

The Teacher had not been acting after all. His face was at peace still, but it was not the same peace; in the manner prescribed by the laws of Quenan—as it was written that it must be, and as it was done, feet together, arms outstretched, in holy symmetry—the Teacher lay dead.

7 · Saturday, April 8

And Ellery wept.

8 · Sunday, April 9

The day was well along when Ellery left the house he had occupied during his stay in Quenan. The day before, he had not left it at all. Now, standing on the doorsill and looking about, though the flowers still bloomed and the leaves hung green he felt even more strongly that this was a place of the dead. Not a soul was to be seen, not a sound to be heard. He stepped out into the lane.

The public buildings, as he passed, seemed hollow ruins; the little houses, earth-stained artifacts of a long-crumbled past. It was just as well, he thought, that the people had crept into their holes. It meant that he didn't have to say good-bye to anyone (and suppose one of them raised a hand in blessing and said, "The Wor'd go with you"?—it would be too much to bear). No, it was time to go, and the sooner and more quietly the better. A week and a day "out of time, out of space" were enough for a mere mortal.

Still, as Ellery strolled through the silent hamlet, he could not help remembering with pleasure the previous strolls, the open faces of the Quenanites, the brown-skinned children offering him flowers shyly . . . Here loomed a tree he had grown fond of, there shone a familiar splotch of ochre on a wall. Had it been a mere week or so that he had been here? It felt more as if in his own flesh he had made the trek across the burning sands with the founding fathers of Quenan.

He came for the last time to the Holy Congregation House. There hung the bell, unmoved. He scanned the familiar legend on it:

> *From Earth's gross ores my Tongue's set free*
> *To sound the Hours upon the Sea*

Yes, the hills walling Quenan, together with the Valley, might be likened to a ship, the surrounding desert the sea—a ship forever becalmed under a cloudless sky, yet always with some creak of calamity impending.

Should he go into the holy house? The Teacher was not there. Why bother? Yet the Teacher *was* there. He was in every crack and cranny. Why why not bid farewell to a ghost?

Ellery went in.

The holy house seemed empty, although the Successor must be in his chambers. The Successor? He had already succeeded! The Teacher was dead; long live the Teacher. What thoughts must be going through the boy's mind? And what must he be feeling? Grief? Guilt? Remorse? Terror? Well, whatever they were, he would have to wrestle with them alone.

Through the silent conventicle he went, and paused at the door of the forbidden room. He turned, not realizing at first that he was looking for the old man to ask permission to enter. Almost he sensed the prophet's presence. But only almost. He turned back to the door. The sense of violation, of desecration, was still strong, and he had to force himself to try the door. It was unlocked (*O tempora! O mores!*), and he went in.

Nothing was changed in the sanquetum. The eternal lamp still burned; how, being eternal, could it not? And the silence was here as always. The light thinned and thickened, thinned and thickened; but then the shadows which had been set to dancing by the opening of the door settled down; and all at once Ellery had the most absurd feeling that the old Teacher was with him in the little room, not merely in spirit but in body also . . . and the rich voice, blessing him . . .

He shook himself back to reality (and *now* what was real?) and stared into the old glass-front china closet, the "arque" the old man had bought to house the mysterious "book which was lost." On its top shelf still stood the two columns of coins, fifteen Carson City dollars in one, fifteen Carson City dollars in the other . . . thirty pieces of silver indeed. The old Teacher's father could hardly have dreamed, when he accepted the store of silver dollars to become a treasure for Quenan, that he was ensuring a curse. A curse that would lie silently, "hidden in the urn," for seventy years, and then unloose a passion that would doom his begotten son.

Ellery almost reached out to steal those terrible coins and scatter them in the desert.

But he could not bring himself to touch them.

But the book, the open book on the lower shelf in its black-letter German type—that was something else. About the book he would have to take action, fitting action, or he would never sleep soundly again.

He opened the glass door of the arque and lifted the volume out as if it were alive. He could not run the risk of letting someone—the Successor; no, the new Teacher—see him taking it away; so he tucked it under one arm securely between his shirt and his jacket, and buttoned the jacket and felt the book burn his flesh. And he left the sanquetum forever.

He was about to shut the sanquetum door when a great thought struck him. Why not leave it open? *Fiat Lux . . . Mehr Licht!* Let the shadows die.

He left it open.

For the last time he made the trip back to his house, packed the book in his grip, and closed his luggage. And so farewell. He had been received almost as a god. There was no reason to assume that he was now held in less reverence; probably he was held in more, since awe and terror had been added. The instrument of the fulfillment of a prophecy, he had helped destroy something tender and potent and unique. Quenan might still look up to him; but it could hardly be with love.

His lips tightened as he snapped the lock on his suitcase and left.

He looked around to get his bearings. There—up that path, behind the vines. That was the way he had come down with an ageless ancient clasping a trumpet beneath his robe.

Ellery climbed the hill slowly, from time to time glancing down the inner slope. No one was in sight. No, there was one. On the farther slope, among the stones that marked the peaceful place, a misshapen little figure crept. Ellery shuddered and went on.

One last time he looked back. The grays and browns had now become a blur of dun, almost colorless.

And then he reached the crest of the hill and passed over it. The Valley of Quenan (Canaan? Kenan? What? He would probably never know now), the whole incredible site, vanished from view.

He had to laugh.

He had gone down the rocky face of the hill, trudged through the sands to his car, tossed his bags in, got behind the wheel, turned on the ignition—and nothing.

The battery was dead.

O Pioneers, ye knew not the blessings of the motorcar.

The water in his radiator had evaporated, too. That was easily remedied (easily?): he had only to go back to the village. But the battery? Dead. He looked around. Everything was dead—the desert, the hill. Nothing lived anywhere; no breath stirred; the air lay panting on the corpse, disconsolate.

Otto Schimdt sold gas, so he possibly had a battery around, or at least a booster. But how to get to Schmidt's store? It would be a long walk in the desert; too chancy. Have to borrow a donkey from the village . . .

But first, the book.

Ellery dug it out of his bag.

He went off a little from the car and laid the book on the sand and began to scoop out a shallow hole with his naked fingers. The sand was powdery, and he had no trouble. Then he began tearing pages from the book, crumpling each one and tossing it into the hole. When the hollow was almost full he struck a match and dropped it in.

In the beginning he knew the paper was on fire only from the magic spread of char. But then the flames came.

Ellery watched them with a wholly new savagery of satisfaction. From time to time he crumpled more pages and flung them into the heart of the flames.

At last nothing was left of the book but its cover.

He stared at the words printed on it in black-letter German and in spite of the heat he shivered. In all the long history of written communication, had there ever been a sadder misreading than the old Teacher's of this book? He had wanted so fervently to believe in the existence of the legendary "lost" book of Quenan. And then the patriarch had gone into the End-of-the-World Store one day for supplies, and there on the counter had lain a book, and on its cover he had seen three words in archaic-looking lettering, in a strange language that he could not read; but the three words lay one under another, so that their first letters were lined up vertically; and he had read the acrostic:

How the old man's heart must have pounded! It was a wonder that it had not stopped altogether. For the "lost" book was said to have been entitled Mk'n, or

𝕸
𝕶
𝕵

which was a difference of only one letter, and the difference was so small in appearance—and who knew, he must have thought, but that the title as handed down, Mk'n, might not originally have been Mk'h, and corrupted somewhere along the route of time?

He had wanted to believe that this was the sacred book of Quenan; and so he had believed.

And how, Ellery thought, how could I have told him that he was selling his faith of peace and brotherhood for a mess of carnage?

He gathered some twigs from a nearby bush, and he carefully ignited them, and when they were burning brightly he laid the cover on them. It caught fire; and the flames took on an evil look, as if the fire itself were corrupted by what it was consuming.

The title seemed to have a demon life of its own. Even as the cover turned to ash, the title clung to its vile substance, standing out clearly, almost coldly in the flames:

𝕸ein
𝕶ampf
𝕳itler

And then it, too, gave up its twisting form and died. And Ellery ground its ashes under his heel.

He had taken only a few steps back toward the Valley when he heard a rumble in the sky that grew steadily to a roar. Queer! The Potter (had it been the Potter?—it now seemed so long ago) had remarked on the increasing number of aircraft passing through Quenan's skies, yet during his entire stay Ellery had not seen or heard one.

He stopped to scan the sky, and—yes!—there it was. A small single-seater plane, not a fighter or any military plane he knew of, was coming toward him from the south. Ellery watched it with growing anxiety. The roar was becoming irregular, erratic . . . staccato . . . and then there was an explosion and a burst of fire and in an instant the little aircraft was one great flame and the flame was flashing and tumbling as it passed almost directly overhead.

My God, the Valley, Ellery thought; if it should hit Quenan . . . ! But he saw that it was going to crash on the slope of Crucible Hill facing the desert, falling just short of the village. And in the same thankful moment a parachute blossomed above him. Ellery began to run.

He saw the parachutist hit the sands only a short way off. For an instant the man lay still, as if stunned; but by the time Ellery reached him he was on his feet, tugging at the silk, unbuckling himself.

"Are you all right?" Ellery cried.

The man looked up from his harness. He smiled and said, "Just fine, *amigo.*"

Ellery blinked. The voice was deep and strong, and yet it had a gentle quality; it sounded familiar. But it was not so much the voice. The flyer was a young man, aquiline features, quite handsome in an odd way; although he had obviously shaved that morning, his gaunt cheeks showed the foreshadows of a heavy beard. I've seen this fellow somewhere, Ellery thought; he certainly looks as familiar as he sounds. And then he stood very still, in the wash of an icy wave. The young man looked like . . . looked like . . .

Ellery shook his head, feeling foolish. Yet it was true. The young man looked as the Teacher must have looked when he was thirty years old.

"Talk about luck," the stranger said, stepping out of the harness. "Imagine conking out over the desert and coming down at the feet of a Good Samaritan with a car."

"Not such a Good Samaritan, I'm afraid," Ellery said. "My battery's dead."

The stranger smiled again. "We'll make out," he said. "Don't worry about it."

"All right," Ellery said, smiling back. "I won't." As they began to walk slowly toward the car, he asked, "Where were you heading?"

"North—up Pyramid Lake way," the young man said. "Crop-dusting. I'm a C.O., you know."

"C.O.? The only thing that means to me is 'Commanding Officer.' "

"Hardly," and the stranger laughed.

"Oh," Ellery said. "You mean a conscientious objector."

"Yes." He said it quite calmly—quite, Ellery thought, as the old Teacher might have said it; and smiled faintly at his fantasy. "I got an agricultural deferment. The funny part of it is, I learned to fly in the cadet program. I was on the wild side, I'm afraid. Rich father, plenty of money, out for thrills and kicks. Then one day a buddy of mine had the same thing happen to him that just happened to me. Only he didn't get to bail out."

"I see."

"I saw, too. For the first time, I guess. And I began to think—you know, man and God, man and fellow-man, man and his eternal soul, all that. Well, I hauled myself out of the cadet program and began to read and study. Found myself after a while. And knew one thing for sure—no killing for me. I wrestled with *that* one for a long, long time. But that's the way it is. I couldn't do it. No matter how they tag me."

"It must be rough," Ellery said.

"Not so rough " the young stranger said, "Not if you know why you're doing it. You find yourself, and you live by what you find. That's why I don't think I'll keep on with this job after the war is over. I've been thinking of social work of some kind. Well, we'll see." They had reached the car, and the stranger opened the hood and poked around. "Dead, all right. Any idea where the nearest town is? Say!" He had straightened up and was staring at the nearby hill. "Look at that."

Ellery looked. And he saw on the ridge of Crucible Hill, in a long line of black figures against the sky, like paper cutouts, the people of Quenan. And it suddenly came to him what had happened, and the icy wave washed over him once more. They had heard the coughing death of the plane, run out of their houses and seen it come down in a streak of flame from the sky. *Like a burning chariot . . . like a chariot of fire . . .*

They had seen the man fall from the burning plane.

No. They had seen the man descend from out the ineffable heavens.

And they had come to him.

"May I ask your name?" Ellery murmured.

"What? Oh." The young stranger kept staring at the people. "Manuel—"

And they shall call his name Emmanuel . . . Ellery felt a quiver ripple through him. His knees actually began to tremble. I won't fall down, he told himself fiercely, I won't; it's weakness, the awful fatigue I've been gripped by . . .

"—Aquina," the young man finished.

It's too much, the other Ellery insisted wildly in his head—too much, too much, too much; it's more than reason can bear. *Aquina, Quenan.* Too much, an infinite complexity beyond the grasp of man. Acknowledge. Acknowledge and depart.

"Those people on the ridge," Manuel Aquina said in a slow, not-quite-puzzled way. "Is there a town beyond that hill?"

The setting sun touched the strange young eyes, and they began to blaze.

"There is a new world beyond that hill," Ellery heard a slow, not-quite-puzzled voice respond—his own? "And I think . . . I think . . . its people wait for you."

The Player
on the Other Side

PART ONE

Irregular Opening

1 · Y's Gambit

He had written:

> *Dear Walt:*
> *You know who I am.*
> *You do not know that you know.*
> *You shall.*
> *I write this to let you know that I know who you really are. I*
> *know the skill of your hands. I know the quality of your obedience.*
> *I know where you come from and what you are doing. I know*
> *what you think. I know what you want. I know your great destiny.*
> *I like you.*
>
> Y

Walt knelt with the sun on his back and the hard sharp bronze letters imprinting his knees, TH on the left knee, RK on the right. He watched his hands, whose skill was known—was known!—to someone else. (*Who?*) . . . Watched his hands trimming the grass around the bronze plaque.

Three left fingers pressed the shorn blades gently away while the finger and thumb felt out the shallow, narrow channel; and deftly, how deftly, the right hand wielded the turf hook, making a margin clean as a moon. Did anyone know that Walt had made the turf hook himself?—would anyone admire its right-hand bevel below, its left-hand bevel above? Who would applaud the creation—who but the creator? And wasn't that enough?

It had been enough. Walt shifted gingerly from the toothed serifs of the memorial plaque and set his knees carefully under IN LIVING MEMORY, with the small OF between them. It had been enough just knowing he was doing his job perfectly.

So perfectly, in fact, that in the York matrix of four strange castles and a private park he existed like an invisible mend.

It may be that Walt had numbly wished to be known and noticed; he could not recall such a wish, but he must have wished it. For years he had been contained and content within his own quiet excellence, patient as a pupa. But now . . .

"*. . . I know who you really are. I like you.*"

It was troubling.

Had Walt ever read Bernard Shaw (he had not), he might have been pleased with the line, "When you have learned something, my dear, it often feels at first as if you had lost something." It would have given flesh to this queer unsettled feeling, together with the comfort that he was not alone in feeling it. He had not truly known how desperate his need had been to have someone say to him, *I like you.*

Only now that it was said, he did not know what to do with it.

A shadow crossed his clever hands. Walt did not look up. There was no necessity. To look up would have been to see Robert York—black homburg, suit hard and gray as iron, waistcoat like an old mint coin, blank gray cravat—wearing his morning face below the rimless glasses, a face drum-tight as an empty bed in a barracks.

"Good morning, Walt," said Robert York correctly.

"Morning, Mr. Robert." It was (as always if the encounter took place just here) seven minutes before ten o'clock.

York Square must never have had a youth; its little formal tapestry of a private park, its grizzled guardian corners of little castles, each with its watchful tower, surely looked old and out of place and time even when the masons laid down their trowels. And what York Square was in stone, Robert York was in the flesh. Imagine him a child if you could, and still you saw only a dwindled Robert York as he stood, in black homburg and iron-gray, with a gray cravat above an antique waistcoat (and spats before May 15th), the unrimmed glasses making him eyeless in the morning sun on his drum-skin face. Compelling Robert York to live in one of York Square's four castles was like compelling a man to be a biped; commanding that he uphold the York tradition was like commanding that the grass in the little park grow green. They were all alike—he, the park, the castles, York Square—punctilious, outmoded, predictable. Neatly Walt worked on the grassy borders of the plaque as, neatly and to the dot, Robert York took his morning stroll about the park.

Walt trimmed the grass along the right side of the bronze. Not all the Yorks were like that, of course.

Miss Myra.

Miss Myra was younger than Robert, which made her forty-four. She had a secret, unmentioned by the other Yorks. Easily remarked by anyone who got close enough to see the twitching lip-corner, the gentle unfocused eyes. She had also a secretary-companion, a kind and lovely girl named Ann Drew, who was walking with her now on the far side of the little park. Ann Drew provided an arm under Miss Myra's, guided at the same time she supported the older woman, taking slow synchronizing strides to Miss Myra's quick small uncertain ones.

Miss Myra held one of the girl's hands tightly in both of hers, and every ten steps or so she smiled a sort of "I did it!" smile, and Ann Drew cooed little acknowledgments into her ear. As much as he liked anyone, Walt liked these two, Miss Myra and the girl. The girl was kind in a special way; when you spoke to her, she seemed to stop thinking of whatever she had been thinking and listened to you altogether. No one else ever did that, Walt was sure. And Miss Myra York—she was, oh, harmless, and it didn't really matter that she was ill.

Walt watched the pair for a moment. He did not wave. He never waved, or passed the time of day, or nodded or did anything of that sort.

He bent to his work again, deftly trimming the turf around the imbedded plaque. When he was finished, and the crumbs of earth were swept and scattered, he stepped back to look.

IN LIVING MEMORY
OF
NATHANIEL YORK, JR.
BORN APRIL 20, 1924

And I, thought Walt, and I . . .

"Walt?"

He was startled, but there was that about him which made it impossible to show what he felt, an instant and utter reflex of stillness to counteract all outward evidence of surprise, fear, anything. Walt turned woodenly. Emily York had come up behind him.

The Yorks were alike only in that no York was like any other York. Emily York was younger than Myra and looked older. She was square and sturdy-backed, with a salt friz of thinning hair, bulby blue eyes, a militant mouth and hard-working hands. Compelled like her cousins to live in a castle, Emily recorded a permanent protest against such trumpery by taking as her own the smallest of the maids' rooms and decorating it with all the elaboration of a Trappist cell. She insisted upon living on what she earned, which was no more than most social workers on the fourth-floor-walk-up level earned, and a good deal less than some. Where the other Yorks employed help—Robert a secretary-assistant, Myra a companion, Percival a sleep-out housekeeper whom he shared with Robert—Emily took pride in her ability to do for herself. Having to fix things, however, defeated her; she was about as mechanically inclined as a tuberose.

"Very nice, Walt," approved Miss Emily, nodding at the manicured plaque. "You do take care of this place as if it were your own."

Walt nodded back his total agreement to this.

"My garbage can," said Miss Emily. "It doesn't quite close. I have to pile three World Almanacs and a dictionary on the lid to hold it down. So then of course I have to lift them off each time I step on the little you-know thing."

"Yes, Miss Emily."

"It should close tight you know. Flies?"

"Yes, Miss Emily."

"And germs." Miss Emily paused. "If I could fix it myself, Walt, I certainly would."

Walt put his hand in his left trousers pocket and grasped his passkeys. "Yes, Miss Emily."

"Well," said Emily York. "Thank you, Walt."

Without expression, he watched her walk briskly toward the nearest subway entrance. Then in his deliberate way he gathered up his tools and went to fix Miss Emily's step-on garbage can.

He had written:

Dear Walt:

You have been so much alone, you do not always know the good you do, how good it is. Nor the fine things, how fine they are. I know (do you?) that you have never said "Sir" to any man. I know about you that "good enough" is never good enough, and that you put as much care into fixing a garbage can as another might into setting a jewel.

Are such excellence and care too good for the jobs you must do? No, because you could not do any job another way. Should you be doing some other job? Yes, you should. And you shall.

You have been patient for a long time. You are right to have been so patient. You know (don't you?), and I know, that your destiny holds great things for you, that you are about to play a role of great importance, to begin at last your larger and more glorious life.

Men do not make their destinies, men fulfill them. The course is set for you, but you must travel it, you must be obedient. (But you already are; it is part of your splendid nature.)

A great trust will shortly be placed in your hands. You will accept it. You will carry it out. For what you are about to do, the world will be a better place. This I assure you.

Since my first letter three days ago I have watched you carefully. Every minute I became more pleased that I chose you for my instrument. I will write again soon, with exact instructions for the first of the great tasks which I have planned for you.

Meanwhile, let no one know that your destiny has come to you, and so be sure to destroy this and all other letters from me. Do this, and you shall please

Y

Like the other, the letter was written on ordinary school notepaper, with faint blue horizontal lines. It was flawlessly typed, undated, and without a return address. It had arrived in a plain envelope inscribed, simply:

WALT
　York Square
　New York, N.Y.

2 · Positions

"How's yours?" young Ann Drew asked.

Young Tom Archer shrugged. He had serious dark eyes and a dark serious voice, and a warm way about him. "Happy when he thinks of his Boscawen, sad when he thinks of his phony two-penoe." He laughed. "And how's *yours?*"

"She doesn't change," said the girl; and "Whatever *are* you talking about? What's a Boscawen? What's a penoe?"

"A Boscawen," said Tom Archer loftily, "is a provisional postage stamp issued in 1846 by the postmaster of Boscawen, New Hampshire. It's dull blue, and it says on it 'paid five cents,' but it's worth enough to pay your salary and probably some of mine for the next year. And Sir Robert of York owns one."

"And he's happy about it. He ought to be! What's the one he's sad about, the penoe something?"

Archer laughed. He had good teeth to laugh by; in this late-of-spring twilight they glowed like the loom of foggy lights. "The so-called 'penoe' is a blue 1848 stamp from the island of Mauritius, of two-pence denomination, showing the head of Queen Victoria. An error was not caught in one of the engraver's plates, and the word 'pence' was spelled with an *o* instead of a *c*. A number of printings of the error were made that year, in slightly differing shades of blue and on different thicknesses and shades of paper. They're all valuable—especially good copies— but the most valuable is the earliest impression, which is a sort of indigo-blue on thick yellowish paper. Worth more than the Boscawen."

"Do go on," said young Ann, successfully sounding fascinated.

"I had no intention of stopping," said young Archer. "Well, a couple of years ago Robert of York was hot on the trail of one of the earliest penoes, and sure enough he caught up with it. It was an especially fine copy, it was authenticated six ways from sundown, and he paid through the nose for it. And then—it's much too long a story—it developed that he'd been sold a beautiful forgery. He wasn't the only one fooled—a lot of reputable people were embarrassed. Of course he got his money back, but he didn't *want* his money back—he wanted a genuine, fine-to-superb earliest-impression penoe. He still does."

"Why?"

"Why?" Archer repeated severely. "Because everybody has an impossible dream, even people with umpty-eleven million dollars hanging over them ready to drop. What Sir Robert wants is one each of the world's ten most valuable postage stamps. He has six. Of course, he'll never get them all."

"Why not?"

"Because one of them is the rarest stamp in the world, the famous British Guiana Number 13, and Mr. York isn't likely to get his hot little paws on that baby— there's only one copy extant."

"My, you know so *much,*" Miss Drew breathed.

"No, I don't," said Mr. Archer with extreme candor, although his teeth glowed again. "Mr. York, now: say what you like about that funny little guy, *he* knows. He really does. All I have is a sticky mind, and after hanging around the likes of him for nearly two years some of what he knows has stuck."

"Is that what you always wanted to be," Miss Drew asked innocently, "a sticky-minded hang-arounder of an expert philatelist?"

"Aha," said Archer. "Looking for the keystone of Archer, eh?"

"Oh, dear. I didn't mean—"

"You did mean, and don't deny it. And don't apologize, either. It's honest, normal curiosity, and if there's anything York Square can use more of it's something normal. Two years ago I was only too eager to be paid to hang around anybody who knew anything. I was one of those perennial school kids. Went from college to postgrad work, got my master's, and then started on a doctorate."

"I didn't know *that,*" the girl said.

"I don't advertise it because I didn't get it, and I probably never will. As I was girding myself for the Ph.D., the Army—bless it—reached out and nabbed me."

"Bless the *Army?*" she asked, for he had said it without rancor or irony.

"On two counts," Tom Archer responded. "One: those old jokes about brain surgeons being assigned to drive tanks are rapidly becoming just that—old jokes. The Army really does make an effort nowadays to find out what you're good for and at. When they came to screen me, I just wouldn't go through the meshes. Classifications: Useless." He laughed. "Really. Pure academic background, philosophy major of a kind they couldn't even use in Public Relations or Intelligence. If not for the Army I might never have found that out. I might have gone on and on taking p.g. and extension courses for the rest of my pedantic life."

"And blessing number two?"

"The Army taught me how Classification Useless can get along. Do what you're told, no more and no less, never volunteer, and the Army takes care of you in every possible way, without letting reality come in contact with you.

"And as with the Army," Philosopher Archer went on, "so with capital L-i-f-e. The perennial schoolboy who pursues degree after degree as ends in themselves is living in the same dream world."

"But he hasn't the Army to feed him," Ann Drew pointed out.

"I had an uncle who left me an income. It wasn't enough to eat well on, but it kept me from rooting in garbage cans, and as for the rest—well, I just kept getting those fellowships."

"Well," she said.

"So there you are. I mean, there *I* am. Learned I was useless, learned that a school is an army, and that they're both unbroken eggs. And the yolk is on me."

"Oh, dear," said the girl.

"And now you'll be saying to yourself that becoming secretary, assistant and philatelic clerk to a Robert York isn't functioning in the real world, either."

"I suppose I will. Yes, I will."

"The difference," said Tom Archer, "is that now I know it. B.A.—Before the Army—I didn't."

"But if now you know it," murmured Ann Drew. "—I shouldn't ask this, but you brought it up—why don't you go out and function in the world?"

"I probably will, and sooner than I think. I could teach—I don't want to, but I could. There's a school out West where you learn to run power shovels—I might do that. I don't know. The right thing will come along. This has been fascinating,'' the young man said suddenly. "I talk too much. Now let's talk about you.''

"No.''

"No?''

"It . . . wouldn't be fascinating,'' Ann Drew said.

"Let's try. You've been here about five months taking care of poor old Myra York—''

"Who's pretty happy in spite of your adjectives.''

He tilted his head. "I thought we'd agreed it's best to live in the real world?''

"Not for Myra York it isn't,'' said Ann Drew.

"Clever,'' said Tom Archer. "Oh, clever. I want to talk about you and you deftly switch the conversation to someone else. All right, I'll talk about you all by myself. You're stacked. You're intelligent. You're very pretty. You were discovered somewhere, somehow, by our social-conscious, welfare-type York, Miss Emily. Which makes you some sort of waif.''

"I don't like this,'' the girl said with an uncertain smile.

"Some of my best friends are waifs. Waives.''

"I don't know that I like *you,* either.''

"Oh, look,'' Archer said, swiftly and warmly. "Please don't not like me. Please don't even try to not like me—'' He stopped, cocking his head in his quick, odd way. "You don't understand me at all, do you?''

She looked at him. "I do,'' she said reluctantly. "I had a father very like you once.''

"That bodes well,'' he grinned. "Dr. Freud says—'' But he was able to see, even in the dim light, that this was no time for a witticism. "I'm sorry,'' he said. "What happened?''

"He died,'' said the girl.

There was a long pause, as if she had an invisible book to leaf through. Finally she murmured, "Daddy was brilliant and . . . unworldly and impractical and . . . well, he just couldn't cope. I did everything to—I mean, I took care of him as best I could. After he died and there wasn't anyone but myself to take care of ''—her pause this time seemed full of silent syllables, because it ended just as if she had not stopped speaking at all—"Miss Emily found me and brought me here.''

"You like it here,'' Archer said.

She looked over at Percival York's house, then quickly around at the identical others. "I like the money I'm near. I mean, handed-down money. I like the feeling that nothing here ever has to change, nothing that starts from any . . . under-the-skin need.'' She shook herself, or shuddered. "I'm sorry. I didn't mean to say any of that. It sounds envious.''

"I'm glad,'' he said seriously, so seriously that she could know for the first time that he really *was* serious. "These people—poor Miss Myra, do-gooding Miss Emily—and she does do good, I'm not denying it—Sir Robert and his little bits of expensive paper, and that *Percival*''—he said the name as its own cuss-word, without adjectives—"they're all laboratory specimens of the genus 'have.' The tendency of the like of us have-nots *is* to envy them, and why shouldn't we? It's hard to feel that they deserve what they've got, when you know and I know that they don't and we do.''

She laughed as she had not been able to do when he was being not-serious. "That almost makes sense. Oh, dear!''

The last two words were evoked by the taxicab that pulled up before Percival York's little castle. From it alighted Percival, who after paying the driver assisted a blonde concoction to the sidewalk. The cab moved off and they had a wonderful glimpse, in the darkling light, of female calves taxing the tensile strength of the suffering nylon, of heels too high for the furtive speed urged on their wearer by Percival, of a black synthetic coat too glossily superb to be the Persian lamb to which it pretended—all surmounted by a piled-up confection of hair that looked as if it had been spun out of a cotton-candy machine.

"He has," murmured Ann Drew with a surprising touch of tartness, "and you have not, although you deserve it. Do you feel deserving of *everything* he has?"

"My modesty," replied Tom Archer, gazing with a slight shudder after the platinum blonde who was just being shooed into Percival's castle by its chatelain, "my modesty prevents me from being sure I deserve *that* part of it. Ann Drew, you're being catty."

"Yes," Ann Drew said. "Refreshing, isn't it?—*Eeeeeeee!*"

Her fingers all but met through his sleeve and the flesh of his forearm.

"God," Archer whispered. "How long has *he* been there?"

"Who? Where?" Her soft, shocked tone commanded the exact softness and shock from him. "Why, it's . . ." And Archer barked: "Walt! What the devil are you doing there?"

"Mr. Robert sent me looking for you," said Walt in his pale voice.

"Did you have to come creeping up like that?"

Walt stood in a pool of shadow close by the memorial plaque. "I wasn't creeping, Mr. Archer."

"Did Mr. York say what he wanted?"

"He's only said to find you—he's got a Seebeck."

"He's got a Seebeck," groaned Archer. "Go tell him I'll be right there."

Only then did the girl release his arm; she fumbled in her handbag. "Walt. Wait."

Walt waited.

"I was at the post office just as it closed and they gave me this for you." She handed him a letter.

Walt took it silently in both hands and, holding it so, walked away from them, across the street toward Robert York's castle. He had an odd walk—not exactly a shuffle, for it was silent, nor a shamble, for it was very contained, but a sort of sliding along, as if the lower part of his body were on tracks.

"Creep," muttered Archer.

"How long *was* he there?"

"No telling."

"Probably not long at all." She was breathing as if breathing were something she had overlooked for a time. "And he *isn't* a creep."

"He looks like one."

"Don't you know why?"

"He just looks it," said Archer defensively.

"It's his eyes," said the girl. "They're almost perfectly round, didn't you ever notice? That's what creates the illusion of stupidity."

"It's no illusion. His brains are all in his wrists, and his nerves all run to his hands. I never yet saw that zombie angry or scared or worried or anything at all." Tom Archer said rather tenderly, "Do we have to talk about Walt?"

"All right," Ann Drew said. "What's a Seebeck?"

"Oh, Lord, the Seebeck! I haven't time now to tell you the whole dismal story—Sir Robert awaits. Take note of this, by the way, my girl—this is an historic occasion. You know, don't you, that the Naval Observatory calls him up to find out what time it is? And that the stars in their courses check with him before they shift their Dopplers?"

"I know he has very regular habits," she said cautiously.

"Agreed—when working time comes, we work, when quitting time comes, we quit. Now hear this: This is the very first, the number-one original time, Robert York has ever yelled for me after hours! It really *must* be a Seebeck." and Tom Archer waved his hand cheerfully, and he too set off across the street to Robert York's castle.

Ann Drew stood watching him. Then, very slowly, she shook her head. Perhaps it was wonderment.

3 · Exchanges

Oh, another, oh, a new one.

Clutching the letter close (oh, there's something in it this time, extra pages and . . . and a *card*) he hurried to Robert York's house to deliver Tom Archer's message. It was with great reluctance that he removed one caressing hand from the envelope to get his keys out (Mr. Robert's door was always locked, as was Miss Emily's; Mr. Percival's and Miss Myra's, never). He let himself in, slid along to the library door and knocked.

"Archer? Come in, damn it!" At the incredible words from the unbelievable voice (for Robert York, though capable of waspishness, never swore and never shouted) Walt swung the door open. "No, Mr. Robert, it's me. Mr. Archer says he'll be right here."

"Well, I should hope so," snapped York.

Silently Walt padded through the house, through the second of the kitchen's two rear doors, through the breezeway to the garage, then between the superannuated Buick and Percival York's rakish, ruined Ryan (by special arrangement; Percival's garage had gone up in smoke as the result of an innocent neighborhood delinquency and Percival had never found the loose capital to rebuild it), up the back stairs and, after unlocking it, through the door of his own quarters. He locked the door behind him, turned on the light . . . and was greeted by the dry rattlesnake buzz of the annunciator.

Walt turned his round eyes on it, his face giving no expression to the indignation he felt. All Walt wanted was to read his precious new letter, and here was Percival York summoning him from all the way diagonally across the Square. If he toyed with the idea of ignoring the buzzer, it was for a microsecond; he murmured, surprisingly, something about "I know the quality of your obedience" and went to the writing table, took out his keys, unlocked the middle drawer, deposited the letter far back in the drawer, carefully locked it, went to the door, canceled the annunciator, unlocked the door, passed through it and locked it behind him, went down the stairs and out through the garage's rear door (which he also locked behind him) and, taking the driveway, rounded Robert York's castle and cut across the little private park to Percival York's castle.

He went around to the rear and entered through the kitchen. The refrigerator door was open and an empty ice-cube tray lay on the floor in a grayish puddle, its crippled separator lying over by the door where it had been thrown or kicked. Walt picked up tray and separator, set them on the table and went down the hall to what was, in this castle of the four, a living room, though in Robert's it was a library, in Emily's a deserted cavern, and in Myra's something like an old curiosity shop.

As Walt touched the doorknob, there was an undignified scuttling inside. The door swung open on a tableau consisting centrally of a love seat, with Percival York at the instant of rebounding from the curved back at one end and, at the other end, an overfleshed blonde girl with one too many buttons undone, and a face like a molded-by-the-thousands kissing-crying-wetting doll crowned with cotton candy hair.

"Walt, God," spat Percival. To the girl he said, "It's only the handyman." To Walt again, "Mrs. Schultzer, or Scheisser, or whatever her disgusting name is, defrosted the refrigerator and there's no blasted ice."

"Mrs. Schriver," Walt said.

"About that I don't give a damn. Just get some ice."

"Mr. Robert has ice."

"Tell him," said Percival York, wrinkling a gray nose on which the first red ruts and runnels of its ultimate condition were beginning to show, "tell him," Percival said, with rummily underlined irony, "tell him I'll return it, every cube, plus six per-bloody-cent." Percival York's eyes, like salamanders looking out of sacks, sought and found the girl and demanded tribute, which she delivered in a hoarse immediate cackle.

Walt returned to the kitchen. He checked the refrigerator setting, picked up the ice-cube seperator, effortlessly straightened it, sighted down its length, straightened it a tiny bit more, then rinsed separator and tray. From a closet beside the refrigerator he took a string mop and blotted up the puddle on the floor. He opened the back door, hung the damp mop on the railing outside, returned to the kitchen, washed his hands and dried them on a paper towel (with which he whisked up the few splatters on the sink edges before he threw it away), took the ice tray he had repaired and another from the refrigerator, canted the latter's contents carefully into the drain (so it would not splash) and went out, shutting the door quietly behind him.

He recrossed the park and went around to the kitchen door of Robert York's house, which now he had to unlock. He rinsed the ice-cube trays he was carrying and filled them at the cold-water tap and set them on the table. He removed two trays from Robert York's refrigerator and replaced them with the two from Percival's. Then, just as he eased the refrigerator door shut, he was arrested by the sound of angry voices from the front of the house.

"I didn't hire you to make childish mistakes!" (Mr. Robert, more angry than Walt had ever known him before.)

"I don't concede that it is a mistake, and if it is I wouldn't call it childish!" (Mr. Archer, who had never talked back to Mr. Robert before.)

"Any fool could see that gum fluoresce! You've gone and saddled me with a lot of damned Seebeck reprints!"

"Those are not Seebecks! I have Borjian's word on it!"

"Borjian! Borjian! Don't stand there and give me Borjian! Borjian once sold me a forged—"

"—a forged penoe," and Tom Archer's voice cut in by shouting as loudly as he could. "I know the whole miserable story by heart, including the fact that Borjian returned your money and that plenty of other stamp-wise people were fooled, too!"

"Now you listen to me—"

"You listen to me! I won't have you bawling me out like a naughty kid over a measly forty bucks' worth of stamps!"

"It isn't the forty dollars!" (Mr. Robert was shouting as loudly as *he* could now.) "It's the idea of a *mistake*! If you can make a little mistake you can make a big mistake, and I will not tolerate *any* mistakes!"

"And *I* will not tolerate" (now Mr. Archer was mimicking Mr. Robert to his face, and he was doing it rather well) "being spoken to in this fashion! Tomorrow morning I will take those goddamn Salvadors down to Jenks & Donahue, and I will have those goddamn Salvadors put under the parallel-beam microscope, and I will pay for the inspection out of my own pocket, and I will come back here and accept your apology when you find out they're really genuine!"

"You'll come back here with proof that they are Seebeck reprints and I will accept your resignation!"

"Give me those stamps. We'll damn well see. Good *night!*"

The library door slammed thunderously. Someone hard-heeled up the stairs, obviously Mr. Archer. Mr. Archer's door overhead, though it was much farther away, slammed even louder.

Walt did not quite shrug or raise his brows; there was a flicker of tension in the controlling muscles and that was all. He picked up the two trays of ice cubes, took them out on the back porch, set them on the railing, softly closed and locked the door, picked up the trays again, retraced his steps to Mr. Percival's kitchen, found a double-walled pewter bowl on a shelf, released the ice cubes at the sink, placed them in the bowl and carried the bowl up the hall.

Mr. Percival, having heard the musical decanting of the ice cubes, stepped out of his living room into the hall, pulling the door to modestly. Mr. Percival was in his stockinged feet and he was holding his unbuttoned shirt together with one hand. "Where did you go for that ice," he rasped, taking the bowl, "Little America?"

"No, Mr. Percival. I got them out of Mr. Robert's refrigerator."

"Arrgh," said Mr. Percival. He slithered back into his living room, kicking the door shut with his heel.

Walt about-faced and passed through Mr. Percival's kitchen and out. The hot eagerness deep within him, to sprint across the park and up to his room, he contained. He wanted more than anything to tear open this new letter, plunge himself into its promised ". . . *exact instructions for the first of the great tasks which I have planned for you.*" But he had been chosen because of what he was; and what he was was deliberate, meticulous, careful and obedient—above all, obedient. He bore the pain of the waiting proudly, like a Christian martyr, as he paced off the way back to his room. For, "*Let no one know that your destiny has come to you.*"

The short heavy man had a cigar. The short thin one had acne. They were in the office too early for the phones to start ringing, but the short heavy man liked it that way, so that was the way it was. He lay back in the swivel chair, with his feet on the desk and his cigar aimed at the ceiling, and he dozed.

The short thin man made a happy sound, a short thin hum.

The man with the cigar moved only his eyeballs, which somehow managed to be both deep-set and protruding. "What you got?"

"Well, it don't pay off at Hialeah," said the thin one detachedly. He dropped his pencil, gathered up some yellow sheets, stacked them, then spread them again and picked up the pencil. "Or at no other regular track. But it sure whips a harness meet if you go all the way through."

"A system? You?"

"On'y on paper. I don't put down a deuce myself, not me."

"You're like a bartender. Don't make like a customer."

"On'y on paper, I told you."

"It's the same thing, you're tasting. Quit before you get hooked."

"Yeah, but listen," the thin man said eagerly. "You bet any favorite, see, but on'y if his post position is number one or two, and on'y if the odds is three to two or less. Otherwise you bet the favorite to place and the challenger to win. And then every race you get your longest long shot and lay on a couple of deuces, and that's it. They won't hit all the time, but they'll pay the freight and maybe the rent."

"System," said the man through his cigar; it sounded like spitting.

"All right, system! But I done this sixty-three times in a row and from $6.50 I'm up to $208.70."

"On paper."

"On'y thing is, you got to work from late odds and wear your spike shoes, get to that window last man in the place. You got to *be* there. You got to watch that tote board like it's a dirty movie."

"Now you listen to me," the cigar-smoker began, and then alarm replaced his severe amusement. "What's all that?"

All that was a sudden commotion in the outer office. It burst in on them in the forms of a grim straight-backed maiden lady with a salty frizzle of hair showing from her bonnet and a black-jowled giant whose high tenor voice grew progressively higher as he tried to expostulate with the lady and explain to the cigar-smoker at the same time.

The cigar-smoker held up one hand. The giant stopped, and the lady began.

"My name is Emily York and you've been taking bets from my cousin Percival."

The man at the desk slowly took down his feet and rolled the cigar to the side of his mouth. "Percival what?"

"Percival York, as you know very well."

"We don't know any Percival York around here."

The acne with the system put in a word: "The sign on the door says Investment Counselors. You got the wrong place, lady."

"Percival York receives his income quarterly—January, April, July and October," continued Miss Emily York. "His bills to date are already greater than his income for the entire year. The Raceway opens tomorrow, I believe, so that any bet he loses he will not be able to pay. And, of course, any bet he wins you lose."

"We ain't making book and we don't know no Percival York," said the acne.

"Shut up," said the cigar. "Lady, what do you want?"

"Don't take any bets from Percival York. And you'd better get in touch with every other horse parlor you know and pass the word along."

"Say," the acne said suddenly, "I think this dame—"

"Shut up," said the cigar. "You his wife, lady?"

"Good heavens, no," snapped Emily York. "I'm his cousin."

"You know what can happen to nosy cousins, lady?"

"Psst," the acne said hurriedly.

An interested glint came into Miss Emily's eye. "Are you threatening me?"

"Psst!" repeated the acne.

The black-jowled giant squeaked, "Boss, you want I should—?"

"Because if you are, I think you ought to know that I'm a well-known social worker and that from time to time I call the station in the precinct in which I happen to be working and tell the desk sergeant where I'm going and that if I don't phone back in twenty minutes he's to send two large detectives for me."

"You can get out," said the man at the desk. But he said it to the black-jowled giant, who precipitatedly obeyed. "Lady, you mean before you came up here you called the cops?"

"Indeed I did," said Miss Emily York.

"Jesus," said the man at the desk respectfully.

"That's what I been trying to tell you," the acne said, waving his arms. "She's the one closed up Rosalie's place. Single handed!"

"Well," said the other man. "It's a good thing we're not in *that* kind of business. What's the harm, lady? A few bets now and then—"

"I'm not intending to close you up, if that's what you're worried about," said Emily York.

"Oh?" he said.

"At least, not just now."

"Oh," he said.

"Because at the moment I have a use for you. You can reach more horse parlors than I can."

"You really want this Percy oddballed—I mean blackballed?" asked the short heavy man at the desk. He was now smoking in quick short puffs.

"Percival. Don't you?"

"Me?"

"He already owes you nearly twenty-eight hundred dollars. If he can't bet he can't lose, and if he doesn't lose he might scrape up enough to pay you what he owes. Come, now! You're not a gambling man. The people who call you up on those telephones are gambling men, but you're not."

"That's what I been saying," the man said feebly.

She glanced at her wrist. "I must make my telephone call."

He rose in a hurry. "Well, thank you for coming in, Miss York. Not that I know anyone by that name myself, but I don't mind passing the word along to oblige a lady. In case I find somebody to pass it to—"

But Emily York was already on her way out. The black-jowled one put in his head and cooed anxiously, "Boss, you want I should—?"

"*Get out!*" said the short heavy man with venom.

The door slammed shut.

Slowly the acne said, "That fishy-eyed son of a bitch York."

"Get on the phone! That old bag's got a slice of the same income Percy's got. Any time he can't settle his bills the lien goes on the principal. This is the Yorks of York Square, stupid."

"Heavy sugar," mourned the short thin man.

"You'll find out how heavy if they hit you with it! Start phoning, will you?"

Meanwhile, Emily York was turning briskly into a cathedral-like establishment not far away, the famous name of which was lettered in heavy bronze castings prominently small in the windows; the floor of which was pelted in cilia like the interior of a royal digestive tract; and whose price tags more often than not included the word "The": *Forty Dollars The Pair* and *Four Hundred Dollars The Set.*

The place smelled male, not the metal-and-soup maleness of a locker room nor the malt-and-sawdust maleness of an old-time corner saloon, but the leather-and-oiled-wood maleness of a city club, as finished and self-consistent as the ash of a fine cigar. At sight of the skirted figure stalking him, the sole visible attendant took refuge behind a showcase; surely, a giraffe, were it a male one, would have startled him less.

Emily York marched up to him, demanded and got the manager, and without preamble stated, "Mr. Percival York buys his clothes here. He charges them. If he continues to charge, his income will fall short of his obligations. If he ceases to charge, he may be able to cover his current account. It is easy to see how both your store and Mr. York can benefit." After that she fully identified herself, explained the matter all over again and departed, leaving the costly cavern in hushed consternation and the very carpet-pile puzzled as to the disposal of her spoor.

Next on her list (she had a list) was a quite different kind and manner of establishment—a liquor store every bit as discriminating as the second car of a subway local. She identified the manager only because he had, on his wrinkled gray cotton jacket, the word in scarlet script over the pocket. He was a sparse-haired man with one frank cataract and wet lips displaying dark brown teeth.

Miss York asked to open an account, and when she was bluntly told that state law forbade it she demanded to know why Percival York was so honored. She quoted to the brown-toothed manager the exact balance due, pointed publicly at his framed license, and promised him faithfully that the delivery to Percival York, for anything other than cash, of anything in stock down to and including cooking sherry would mean that both his store and he would learn something about locks. As a parting shot she suggested a revision, in his invoices to her drinking cousin, of special prices he had been charging. (It was a shot in the dark that cut nearly forty per cent off Percival's next bill, a fact Percival himself was never to appreciate.)

Having thus obeyed, with all her heart and to the best of her belief, the ancient edict that charity should begin at home, Miss Emily York boarded a crosstown bus and went to her regular work at the settlement house.

4 · Maneuvering

He had written:

Dear Walt:
  You are the one.
  Are there men anywhere, in any walk of life, who are as controlled as you are, as dignified?
  Yes, a few. Some, born to the purple, have their high code inborn. Some rise to the top openly by their own worth. And some, perhaps the worthiest of all, remain bound by their honor and their sacred duty.
  These are the trodden, but not downtrodden. These are the lowly, but never the low.
  The true measure of the size of a man is his anger. Does this mean that the violent man, the assertive and pugnacious man, is thereby the larger man? No, even though this is how most men behave. "Don't tread on me." A good motto—for a snake.
  I can look into the hearts of all men. And I tell you this about them: Those who are quick in their furies are furious at themselves. This is because, and only becuase, they are not sure who they are, what it is that lives under their skins. They are afraid, afraid.
  Not so the man who knows what he is. Righteousness is within him, it cannot be affected by anything outside him. A brave man is not afraid to appear humble. He knows what he is. He need not prove he is brave, just as a tall man need not prove he is tall. Bravery, righteousness, and sufficient unto themselves.
  This is the true and inner meaning of the words "The meek shall inherit the earth." The meek are the righteous who need never reveal their inner might to other men.
  You are a righteous man. You are beyond fear. Have faith in me and I shall guard you and keep you and make you master. There is no thing I cannot do. There is no force I cannot control. Your faith in me must be absolute, for absolute is my confidence in you.
  You know who I am. Do not speak my name. Do not be afraid to know me.
  Now you may take the first small step toward your destiny.
  With this letter I give you a white card cut in a special shape. You are to conceal this card where no one can find it.
  Go then to Scholz's Toy Store on Fifth Avenue. It is a very large toy store and many people go in and out. Do nothing to

attract attention to yourself, in any way. Move quietly among the people until you find yourself in the last aisle, which runs front to back by the north wall.

Halfway up the aisle you will see toy typewriters, printing presses, rubber stamp kits and the like. Move along until you see, on the wall shelves, a stack of boxes, blue with red and gold letters, marked PRINTS CHARMING. The price for one of these is $1.49 plus sales tax.

Have your money ready. Point and murmur. Do not speak up. Do not ask for it at all until the moment you have the clerk's attention. Make your purchase quickly, have it wrapped plainly, leave quietly. Step aside, make way, wait.

Do all you can to stay clear of others without calling attention to yourself.

Walk to Third Avenue and turn right. You will see a supermarket near the corner. You are not known there. Go in and buy enough groceries to require a large paper bag, but not enough to fill it. Slip your package from Scholz's into the unfilled part. From then on you are simply a man going home with a bag of groceries.

Go home. Lock yourself in your room. Lower the blinds. Open the box and take out the toy printing set. Remove the letter J— there are capital letters only in this set—and open the ink pad.

Press the J on the ink pad and practice stamping it on scrap paper until you get a good clear impression every time.

IMPORTANT: Be sure to gather up each scrap of practice paper afterward and destroy it.

Now take the enclosed card. Place it on the table in the following position:

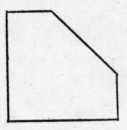

Now very carefully ink the letter J and very carefully stamp it on the card, so:

Let the J dry. When it is dry, put the card in a plain white envelope, seal the envelope and write on it in plain *capital letters:*

ROBERT YORK
YORK SQUARE
NEW YORK, N.Y.

Stick a 5¢ stamp on the envelope, place it securely in an inside pocket. If you can get it into the mailbox at Surrey Street before 9:30, do that. If later, you must take it to the Church Street post office. Drop it into the mailbox outside. Do not hurry. Do not linger.

Carry out the instructions in this letter well, and the later, larger duties will be easy for you.

I know the past. I know the future. I predict: in a very few hours, a few days at most, when you turn your hand, they shall tremble.

Dispose of this letter as you have the others.

I am (but you know who I am!),
Y

5 · Interplay

"I brought the mail."

Tom Archer's dealings with Robert York had been correct, dignified and beyond criticism. Work on the records of Robert York's philatelic holdings proceeded smoothly, and at lunchtime the day before, they had agreed with the politeness of duelists that the end was at last in sight and soon they could begin the final cataloguing. Work had also been done on the family accounts—that part of the accounts, of course, in which the four Yorks were concerned in common, not individually. Robert York, as eldest of the cousins, and as by nature the logical representative of the founding Yorks, had charge of this work by general consent. Tom Archer, as Robert's secretary, helped with the accounting and was privy to these particular matters—wages for the help, upkeep and maintenance of houses and park, prorating of part-time wages as in the case of Mrs. Schriver, the housekeeper who slept out and "did" for Percival as well as for Robert; and such trivia.

The waiting stiffness between the two men had doubtless contributed to their efficiency. Tom Archer (because he was at root a man of peace) and Robert York (whose self-righteousness had as one of its prime articles an insistence on fair play) were, each in his own way, ashamed of the outbreak of temper over the alleged Seebecks. And each, unknown to the other, had his special reason for wishing to preserve their relationship. In a way, then, this particular mail was a pity, for it could not fail to upset their precarious equilibrium.

Tom Archer set the mail down before his employer, and a sense of fatefulness flashed through him: *This will change things a bit!* But first, from his breast pocket he took a manila envelope, drew out its contents, and placed them on the envelope and the envelope on the small heap of mail.

"There!"

Robert York pursed his very thin lips. "What's this?"

"The analysis from Jenks & Donahue." Archer extruded a forefinger and slightly separated the sheets in Robert York's hand. "And here are the stamps."

"Hmp," said Robert York, and he began to read.

"Oh!" he said, after a second.

"Oh . . . " he said, after a minute.

Then he looked up, his skin tighter than usual, his barely bluish lips puckered with the bitter taste of crow.

"I said that if this report proved the stamps genuine, I should owe you an apology. You have it."

"Thank you."

"Mr. Archer, I meant what I said when I made your resignation contingent upon this." He tapped the report.

"I am quite aware of that, sir."

"Had it proved that you made a mistake, I should have insisted upon it. Since it's I who was mistaken I feel I must offer, rather than demand, the same thing."

"I don't understand, Mr. York."

"Then I shall explain," said Robert York stiffly. "It may well be that after what has happened you will no longer wish to be associated with me. If that is the case, I shall certainly understand it; and to do what I can to right the injustice, I shall give you the finest possible recommendation."

"Mr. York," Archer began.

"And perhaps a little more than the usual, ah, notice. In fact, if you'd like to stay on here while you look for something else—" He stopped to open the left-hand top desk drawer, frowning, then suddenly smiled a wan, pathetic smile, for even as he reached into the drawer, Archer had spun to the cabinet behind him, opened it, plucked a stack of tissues from a box and placed them on the desk beside the mail—all in the time it took Robert York to restore his reaching hand to the *status quo ante*.

York took two tissues, folded them once and blew his nose hard. "Mr. Archer, thank you. You're—you've been a good chap." It was as if Mahomet had gone to the mountain.

"Mr. York," said Tom Archer, at sea level, "I should never have spoken to you as I did, and it won't happen again. As for leaving you, I'd rather stay on."

"Indeed? Yes. Well." Robert York's museum features hardly reflected the gratification he felt; but his hand, as if by its own volition, folded another two tissues and brought them to his nose for another sharp, brief blow.

Touched, Tom Archer said gently, "Shall we get on with the mail?"

"The mail. Oh, yes." The eldest York removed his unrimmed glasses, whisked a Sight Saver from his top drawer, polished both lenses, restored the glasses to his eyes, dropped the Sight Saver and the four used tissues in his wastebasket, picked up the envelope on top of the heap, turned it over, put it down. "Mr. Archer—I don't quite know how to say this—would you sit down?"

Archer looked surprised and sat down in a facing chair. Robert York brought his cupped hand to his mouth and coughed delicately, twice. Then he leaned back in his swivel chair and surveyed his ceiling with intensity, as if searching for something.

"As you perhaps know," he began, "I at all times prefer to avoid, the, ah— the emotional approach to things. I have never understood emotions very well. I like things, to, ah—come out even. I mean to say, right-wrong, good-bad, yes-no. That sort of thing. Can you understand that?"

Tom Archer, heroically suppressing a quotation from Hegel which sprang to his lips, said instead, "Yes, indeed."

"I lost my temper with you over the Salvadors," Robert York went on, heroically also, "for the curious reason, I think, that I had had some words with my cousin Percival earlier in the day. It must be that the, ah—vessel of one's emotions has a limited capacity, that it fills up stealthily, as it were, and then—a few insignificant drops more, and it overflows. Is that possible, Mr. Archer?"

"It's not only possible," Mr. Archer assured him, "it unfortunately happens all the time."

"Yet it rather relieves me. Yes, it relieves me. You see, my cousin—" His precise voice became less precise, blurred, then faded away as in a bad overseas connection.

After a moment Tom Archer stirred. "Maybe, Mr. York, you really don't want to talk about it."

York started. "I beg your pardon?" Archer said it again. "Oh, but I do, Archer, I think I do. And now I feel that I may. That is, I find myself trustful of you after—well, you know what I mean."

"I believe so, sir."

"At any rate, my cousin asked me for money. Demanded it, really. I refused. To refuse a loan to a blood-relative who is coming into several million dollars shortly must strike you as very strange, Archer; but I felt that I must. As a matter of principle. My distaste for Percival's squandering and dissolute ways was quite secondary.

"You see," Robert York continued at a faster, warmer pace, "I have always deemed it my duty to carry out the spirit as well as the letter of Nathaniel York, Senior's will, and I have more or less assumed the burden of seeing that my cousins do likewise. Uncle Nathaniel's bequests to us were contingent upon our living in the four houses for a specified number of years, and I have confidently interpreted this—recalling our uncle's impeccable life and his pride in the family traditions—as far more than a mere matter of residence. As I have repeatedly told Percival—the latest occasion, in fact, was the other day—a York occupying a York house in York Square assumes the moral obligation and perhaps even the legal obligation to do so with honor and propriety. I went so far this last time as to suggest to Percival that I might have to take the matter up with the courts, that his unseemly mode of life might actually be an implicit breach of Uncle Nathaniel's will that would disqualify him from his portion of the principal inheritance."

"And what did Mr. Percival say to that?" Archer murmured, although he was reasonably sure of what Mr. Percival had said to that.

"A great many unpleasant things expressed in the most unbridled language," said Robert York uncomfortably. "Also, he laughed in my face. I suppose he was right about the legal aspects, and I knew it—probably that's why I was rather more emphatic in my refusal of his request than I should otherwise have been."

The admission apparently cost him something. He reached for a fresh tissue and patted his brow.

"Knowing Percival," Robert York went on, not without a brightening of tone, "I feel certain that I could, ah—readjust the resulting coldness between us even now by advancing him the money. But if I did that, you see, Archer, Percival would construe it as weakness of character, and then I should never be free of his demands. And I *am* free now, Archer—I assure you of that. The, ah—terms in which I couched my refusal, much as they distressed me then and now, had at least one virtue: I'm quite sure he won't ask again."

"Frankly," Tom Archer said, "I think the end in this case heartily justifies the means. I know how you shrink from being unfair to anyone, but this wasn't unfairness, Mr. York—you were actually doing Mr. Percival a favor to refuse him."

"You think so, Archer? You really think so? I must say I'm very glad to hear you say it. Yes! Well, then . . . "

"The mail, sir?"

"Of course! The mail."

And Robert York, with as nearly cheerful an expression as his Madame Tussaud face could perform, picked up the topmost envelope of the little heap of letters, accepted the letter opener that Tom Archer had for some moments been holding in readiness, slit the letter, returned the letter opener to Archer and withdrew from the envelope an oddly shaped card with the letter J stamped on it.

6 · Y's Gambit Declined

"You'd think," snapped Emily York, "that he could do without his silly old nap just this *once*."

Ann Drew said soothingly, "He's a man of very regular habits."

"I admire regularity and I certainly approve of his. But there *are* times." She uttered the phrase with the completeness of a sentence.

Ann rose. "Excuse me a moment, Miss York. I'll go up and get Miss Myra."

"It isn't as if I had unlimited time, like certain others around here," said Emily, glaring at her nickel-plated wristwatch. "I'm due at the League Conference by half-past eight."

"I'm sure this won't take very long," Ann said from the door.

"Unwed mothers," added Emily, evidently assuming that the two words were pregnant enough with priority and haste to require no elaboration.

Ann Drew turned away then, so whether she smiled or not Emily York was not to know.

After a while the doorbell rang. Emily bounded to her feet, computing instantly that her cousin Myra and Ann Drew were still upstairs, thus presenting her with an opportunity to try to do what another might flabbily pass on as beyond accomplishment. She strode on her sensible heels to the front door and swished it open.

"Good *evening,* Percival." She had been right.

Percival York bared his teeth and pushed past her into the sitting room. He slung his expensive homburg onto a commode, turning and collapsing in continuous motion until he came to rest on a love seat, at the two extremeties of his spine. He rolled a yellowing eyeball across the opposite wall, or rather at the clutter that obscured it: the East Indian whatnot stand, all spools and mother-of-pearl inlay; the faded print of Gainsborough's "Blue Boy"; the Albany, New York, version of an Arabian prayer rug; the modernistic japanned shadow-box bearing an unsplendid specimen of *Euphorbia splendens,* or crown of thorns, and another and nameless succulent, both somehow achieving sadness without (like some sad house plants) bravery; and in the corner, on a massively ugly pedestal of some quasi-mahogany, the marble head of a laughing girl of extraordinary beauty. "This place," said Percival York, "always reminds me of a novel by Dickens."

Emily had seated herself straitly in a straight-backed chair, as if to admonish his sprawl, but at Percival's growl she inclined her body forward, ever ready to encourage the wastrel in cultural conversation.

"Oh, really? That's very interesting, Percival. Which Dickens novel does it remind you of?"

"*The Old Curiosity Shop,*" said Percival, and the cultural conversation expired without a struggle. "I wish we'd have these bloody blood-is-thicker-than-water sessions somewhere else, the way we used to."

"You know perfectly well how confused poor Myra gets if she has to go out," said Emily coldly.

"I know how confused poor Myra gets when she *doesn't* go out. At my place, now," Percival added, apparently more to be offensive than to express an immediate need, "we could at least have a drink."

Emily set herself for the argument she knew was futile. "Unless my nose deceives me," she began. But then she shrugged. There would be other opportunities. "Here's Myra."

"Who's going to be here?" It came as a cooing, rather than speech. On Ann Drew's arm, Myra York had sidled in and was looking tremulously about with soft-focused eyes.

"It's all right, Myra dear," said Emily crisply, reciting the ritual assurance. "Just the four of us. And Ann, of course, and that nice young Mr. Archer."

"Don't worry, Myra," Percival drawled, "the ol' beau hasn't shown his face yet."

Myra York blanched. Ann Drew frowned. Emily barked his name. Percival scowled at them all and slumped further, sardonically watching Myra expel two large matched tears. "I really," she cooed, "don't know what you mean."

"There now," said Ann Drew, dabbing at her with a handkerchief; and Emily straightened up to a little more than straight, a cobra-like movement, and hissed, "Percival, you are a—"

"Su-u-ure I am," Percival York drawled, looking at last quite pleased, as if he had accomplished something and was rather proud of it.

The doorbell rang again, and Myra York uttered a little shriek and sprang upright. Ann Drew quickly put an arm around her shoulders. "It's all *right*," she breathed, "it's all right."

"It's just Robert," said Emily, "and I suppose Mr. Archer." She glanced at Ann Drew, all occupied with Myra, distraught; Percival, supine; and she visibly computed that preoccupation plus insolent non-co-operation equaled another trip to the door for Emily. She rose and went out.

"It's just Robert," Ann echoed to Myra's papery ear, "and I suppose Mr. Archer." She half pressed, half lowered Myra York back into her place on the divan.

"It's just Robert " mocked Percival, "fresh from his 7:31 P.M. beauty nap, a lost cause if ever I saw one. Right, Annie?"

"I'd like you to call me Miss Drew, please," said Ann.

"Okay, Annie, anything you say. Now watch," he said, leering at her. "Robert'll walk in, give *you* a hello, and call the roll of *us*. Then he'll sit down and cough twice. Twice, mind you." He rocked back until his nape thumped the back of the love seat, to stare again at the place where the wall met the ceiling.

"What is it, dear?" Myra murmured.

"Nothing," said Ann, which was not true. For sitting so close to Percival's tusked leer, she had shuddered.

"I do think, Robert you could have gone without your forty winks this *once*. We've all been waiting." Emily entered with Robert, while young Archer stepped along behind them in an oddly oriental manner. This was the resultant of several divergent forces, one being his position of male secretary, which made him certainly not family and yet not a servant, either. Another was the pulsing anticipation Tom Archer always felt when he entered a room containing Ann Drew. A third was his reluctance to enter this room at all, for he had an inkling of some of the events scheduled. The sum totaled a bland, stooped carriage and the impression that he would bow rapidly from the waist at the slightest excuse.

"Good evening," Robert York said to Ann, ignoring Emily's scolding; and immediately, taking a brief bearing on each of the others, "Myra . . . Percival . . ." and indicating the straight chair to which Emily was headed, so that his greeting was also a command to sit-so-we-can-get-started, ". . . Emily." Then he sat down in a hideous brocaded Morris chair and coughed, twice.

Percival leered, in triumph this time, at Ann, who looked away. Robert held out a hand and young Archer placed an attaché case in it. "This," said Robert, opening the case, taking out a ledger, opening it at a broad orange bookmark and placing it on his knees, "this should not take very long." He thereupon covered the ledger pages with his forearm and spoke over them. "But before we begin, I should like to say—"

Percival groaned.

"—a few words. First of all, on the matter of Mr. Thomas Archer here. Mr. Archer has recently proved, beyond the scintilla of a doubt, that he is a young man of resource and integrity. Not that such proof is or ever has been necessary. Nevertheless, I now find it possible to delegate to him certain of my family duties and responsibilities which have kept me from pursuing my personal affairs as freely as I have wished. Actually, the delegation of these duties is a *fait accompli*. I am merely making it official.

"You have been aware for some time that Mr. Archer is thoroughly conversant with our mutual affairs, from these household details"—he tapped the ledger—"to the supervising of our investments and accounts. He will continue as heretofore, with one change."

Robert York drew a folded blue-backed paper from his pocket and agitated it. "This is a power of attorney, permitting Mr. Archer to act for me—that is, for us—in three areas: matters of maintenance of our houses and common property; the supervision of our investments and other paper holdings; and finally" (his deeply grave tone made this finality one of cosmic importance) "Mr. Archer will begin on the climax of my many years' work in philately—the remounting in uniform volumes, and the complete cataloguing, of my stamp collections."

He passed the paper to the astonished Archer. "But, Mr. York," Archer protested.

"Not a word, Archer. It's the right thing to do and I've done it."

"Let me see that!" Percival rocked forward and snatched the paper from Archer. He scowled through it and then gave the embarrassed Archer a long, calculating look. Percival opened his mouth, closed it again and handed the legal document back.

"Emily?" said Robert York.

The social worker took the paper and read it swiftly. "Of course I don't pretend to understand this sort of thing," she said. "But since it does, you know, specify— I mean, it sets out exactly—" She stopped to frown slightly. "I mean to say, it isn't a *general* power, is it? So I suppose it's all right." Then, as if what she had said sounded like an objection, she nodded to Archer. "Quite all right, Mr. Archer."

Archer (charmingly, to judge by Ann Drew's face) blushed and delivered a little grateful bow.

"For someone who knows nothing about this sort of thing, my dear Emily," said Robert York rather dryly, "you understand very well." He coughed, this time once. "So much for that. Now, there is one other matter—"

"You didn't show it to Myra," Percival said nastily.

"Yes? Yes?" Myra York looked to right, left, above, below, quickly, alertly. All quite meaningless.

"I thought," snapped Emily to the family skeleton, "you were in a hurry to finish this!"

"Not at all, Cuddles," grinned Percival. "It's just that I didn't want to come. But now that we're here, let's do it right, shall we?"

"It's all right, Myra," Robert York said hastily. "Just a legal thing. You may see it if you'd like."

Myra looked intelligent. "If it's all right," she said brightly, "then it's all right."

Robert York glared at his cousin Percival. "Leaving that, then, I shall bring up one other matter before proceeding with our ordinary business." From behind his display handkerchief he pulled a monarch-sized envelope, the cheap flat-finished kind obtainable everywhere. From it he took a five-sided card. "Which one of you is responsible for this nonsense?"

There was a moment of puzzled silence. Then Emily demanded curiously, "What on earth *is* it?"

Severe-lipped, Robert York handed her the card.

"J," said Emily, "hmm," and turned it over twice.

Robert extended his hand for it, but Percival had it first. "Hmm!" said Percival through flared nostrils.

Myra, her woolly attention caught by the traveling scrap of cardboard, asked, "What *is* it?" worriedly. Ann Drew leaned over and took it from Percival and handed it to her.

"What *is* it?" Myra said, exactly as before.

"Nothing, dear, nothing really," said Ann.

"I disagree, Miss Drew," said Robert York. "Indeed, I must once more ask— demand: Which of you is responsible for this?"

"Not me," said Percival, so instantly that Robert turned on him a stare of profound suspicion.

"Heavens, Robert," Emily said. "It's just somebody's idea of a joke."

"I fail to see anything humorous in it," said Robert. "Can you, Archer?"

Archer started from his hungry appraisal of Ann Drew. "Well, sir, in line with your bisect theory, it might be some kind of advertising teaser was what I thought."

Robert snorted. "Did any of you get one of these foul things?" There was a general denial. "Then why should I be the only one to get one?"

"You did mention the bisect thing, Mr. York," Archer murmured.

"Well, I've changed my mind, Archer," said Robert testily. "Anyway, it would hardly interest my cousins."

"If it would explain your childish concern about this, Robert," said Emily brusquely, "*I'd* like to hear it."

There was at that moment a thump on the door in the north wall, opposite the hall entrance. Myra York shot to her feet, Ann Drew rising with her. "Someone's in there!" quavered Myra.

Archer strode to the door and snatched it open, while Ann shushed and "There, dear?"-ed, patted and stroked her.

Walt stood revealed. He did not recoil as the door was flung aside. His round eyes seemed as encompassing as an owl's, and his small full moist mouth was not pursed and did not tremble. He looked about the roomful of faces—angry, startled, puzzled, frightened faces—and when he came to Ann Drew he said dully, "It's fixed, miss."

"Thank you, Walt." Ann's clear soft voice cut across the moment's confusion. "The kitchen sink," she explained. "It's been slow."

"I found this in the trap," Walt said. He held out a small object. Archer, who was nearest him, took it. "A ring."

"Walt found your ring, dear," said Ann to Myra York. To Emily, who was wearing her how-can-other-people-be-so-careless look, the girl was moved to explain, "It isn't a valuable one at all, just costume jewelry. Here, dear," and she took the ring from Archer and gave it to Myra.

"While you're here, Walt," said Robert York, "tell me something. Did you ever get anything like this in the mail?" He leaned toward Walt with the card. Walt stepped into the room and took the card without expression. Also without response.

"Well? Well?" said Robert. "Have you or have you not received a card like this in the mail?"

"With a J on it?" Walt inquired.

"With *anything* on it!"

"No, Mr. Robert."

"Have you any idea what it might mean?"

"No, Mr. Robert." Walt handed the card back.

"Very well, then," said Robert York, and produced one of the imperious motions of the hand so characteristic of him—gestures he himself seemed quite unaware of. Walt apparently took it as a dismissal, for he blinked his round eyes once and backed through the door, closing it after him.

"Well?" Emily demanded. "What *is* the 'bisect thing'?"

Robert York twitched his head in irritation, and Tom Archer said, "It was just a thought of Mr. York's. In 1847 the U.S. issued a ten-cent black stamp. In those days, when a post office ran out of—say—its supply of five-centers, it wasn't unusual for a postmaster to make some out of his supply of ten-cent denominations simply by cutting them in half and selling the halves. Some exist on cover that were bisected vertically, others horizontally, and still others diagonally—that is, cut from an upper corner to the lower corner opposite.

"Well, there's long been a rumor among philatelists about a supposed error among the 1847 black diagonal bisects. The story goes that some postmaster, instead of cutting diagonally from corner to corner, carelessly snipped a smaller triangular piece off the top corner of the stamps, so that what was left was actually five-sided—shaped something like this card. Since one of these, if it were found on cover, would be very rare—in fact, unique as far as we know—it would also be immediately valuable. Mr. York thought that maybe some stamp hunter's found such a piece and is taking this means of working up Mr. York's interest in it."

"Well," said Emily York, "that's just silly enough to explain it."

"All but the J," said Percival, adding a heh-heh sound.

Robert was scarlet. He snatched the card and flicked it, a tiny gesture expressing immensities of aggravation. "The J could be the fellow's initial, or—or something like that! Anyway, I *said* I'd changed my mind!" He dropped card and envelope into the open attaché case beside his chair. The scarlet remained, and when he spoke his voice held all the wistful anger of a simple-minded, clumsy-fingered man in a world of swift thinkers and capable hands. "I don't understand it. I don't like things I can't understand!"

"Then forget it, Robert," said Emily impatiently. "I'm late. Can't we push on? Is there anything important on the agenda?"

"Yes-by-God-there-is." It was an ugly snarl, Percival's. His glance impaled his cousin Robert. "I'm going to say this exactly once, and you'd better take it to heart: You keep messing up my charge accounts, Robert, and I'll-squash-you-by-God-like-a-by-God-roach!"

Robert York looked at Percival York wide-eyed, his yellow-pink skin turning yellow-gray. He glanced, startled, from face to face (Is it possible he's talking to *me?*), and finally back to Percival. (He *is* talking to me!) "I don't know what you mean, Percival."

"Don't add lying to your other talents, you double-crossing, two-faced, sneaky-hearted little would-be Napoleon," said Percival. "You know perfectly well you put her up to it."

"Her?" said Robert, again taking inventory of the familiar faces. (Emily's was a firm pink, but in his bewilderment Robert was color-blind.)

"Just don't you meddle in my private concerns again, that's all I'm going to tell you. Just don't, Robert. I warn you. I can do more kinds of damage than your rabbity little brain can imagine, and if this happens once more—*anything goes.*"

"But I don't know what you mean," was all the agitated Robert could find to say.

Percival showed his unlovely teeth in a wolfish grin, and he rose so suddenly that Robert shrank back. But all Percival did was to snatch up his homburg and stride from the room.

"But, Percival, what about—?" Robert mutely lifted the ledger from his lap.

Percival's reply was to *blam!* the front door.

Myra York clung hard to Ann Drew's hands. "Who was *that?*"

"Shh, dear. It's all right," Ann whispered.

Robert, surprisingly, said, "I'm sorry. I'm terribly sorry."

"It isn't your fault," said Archer, as consoling in his way as the girl was in hers.

"It most certainly is not," said Emily definitely. She seemed about to say more, but she hesitated and was lost.

"We'll get on, then," Robert said, wetting his lips—apparently to no purpose, for he had to do it again. "Now. We have a bill here for, ah—yes!—lawn fertilizer for the park. This of course will come from the general fund. And . . . I have a notation of breakage of a gold-trimmed meat platter from the Nathaniel York, Senior Collection. Although it was broken in Myra's house by the housekeeper, it really belonged to all of us. So replacement cost should perhaps come from the general fund—"

"It was a horrible thing," snapped Emily, back on safe ground. "Good riddance."

"Or on the other hand," continued Robert, "should it come out of the woman's wages? Archer, what was the inventory value of the platter?"

"A hundred and eighty dollars, sir."

"She really doesn't break very much," said Ann Drew timidly.

"Good riddance," Emily said again. "Write it off, Robert."

Robert looked from face to face, then made a mark in the ledger. "Very well. But naturally this must not continue. Now, ah . . . yes . . . Walt reports a broken curbstone in front of Percival's house. Percival really ought to be here to discuss this," he added fretfully. "Why on earth do you suppose—?"

"Forget it *and* him," Emily said hastily. "Please, Robert, get on with it. It's *late.*"

So Robert York got on with it—the prorating of a tax charge; the distribution of an insurance refund; the recurrent argument over whether the Family or the Help, who were paid on the first of each month, should stand the loss of the extra day in thirty-one-day months—a standing controversy between Emily York, who was staunch for the rights of Labor, and Robert York, who was just as sturdy a defender of the prerogatives of the Employer, with the invariable result of "Tabled Until Our Next Meeting."

These meetings, they all realized, were more a fussy ritual than a necessity; their business could easily have been taken care of by one delegated person, with perhaps an occasional telephone call to one or more of the others. But so it had been decided when they took up their several residences in York Square (at the strange behest of the dead Nathaniel, Senior) and so it would be until death again intervened in their lives.

Robert York, still reacting to his cousin Percival's mysterious outbreak, concentrated on the petty agenda almost gratefully. Emily stuck with it because it was a Duty, and Duties were her life. Archer, full of his new responsibilities, bent to the task sincerely. Myra York paid close attention to an invisible something in a middle distance of Space and Time, and Ann Drew paid close attention to Tom Archer. Until at last it was done, the last entry posted in the ledger, the last item noted on the list of checks to be drawn, signed and mailed out in the morning; and at last, at last, the fixing of the date for the next meeting (always the second business day after the first day of the next month, a formula which invariably confused everyone but Robert). And then they went their ways; Emily to her unwed mothers; Myra to her bed; Ann to an innocent rendezvous with Archer after putting Myra there; and Robert to his study and the ever-engrossing plans for the grand cataloguing of his stamp collection.

No one, of course, checked up on Myra York after she was tucked in. Ann Drew and Tom Archer unaccountably missed one another. It happened that Robert did not get to work on his cataloguing plans after all. Emily was much later than she had planned in reaching her meeting. And no one knew just what Percival was up to (but then no one ever did).

It was just one of those days.

7 · Attack

He sat alone in a hotel room. The bed had not been slept in, the two thin towels were untouched. On a cheap portable typewriter, working slowly and carefully, pausing only to adjust the machine to align exactly with the ruled lines on the tablet paper he was using, without ever an error, and with the even touch possible only to two-fingered typists of long practice, he was writing:

> . . . and you will spend the morning trimming the ivy on the tower of Robert York's castle. When it is time for lunch, you will leave your shears on the tower and come down. You will go out by the front door this time, so that you may pass the door of his study.
>
> You will stop just long enough to be certain—be absolutely certain—that your watch corresponds to his mantel clock, to the second. If anyone is about, pass on through and check it later in the day.
>
> Under no circumstances overlook this detail—it is vital to my plan and to your glorious future.
>
> At 7:20 make your way back quietly up to the tower. If you are seen and questioned either going up or coming down, say that you are going for your pruning shears.
>
> At 7:31 o'clock you are to count the stone blocks on the north edge of the parapet, Number 1 being the first one to the right of the concrete coping at the corner.
>
> At 7:33 you are to be in position with your hands on the 7th block. You will find the concrete cap cracked and the mortar cleaned away all around this block.
>
> Precisely at 7:34 you are to push the block as hard as you can, so that it falls off the tower.
>
> You will then quietly pick up your shears and, without hurrying, you will return by way of the kitchen and the garage corridor to the garage.
>
> Place the shears on their hook as you go in, pick up the socket wrench from the bench, go round to the right side of Percival York's Ryan sports car, lie down on the mechanic's dolly you will find ready for you, roll under the car, and begin to drain the oil from the crankcase.
>
> Ignore any sounds or voices you may hear unless and until you are called. If you are called, wait until you are called twice before answering. Then and thereafter, you are to know nothing about

the tower, the stone, or anything else connected with these orders. Stand firm, volunteer nothing and, above all, be yourself.

Be yourself, My Dear Walt. Be yourself, for by so doing you please me in my choice. Watch yourself being yourself, and share with me my pride in you, and recognize, as I have recognized, how infallibly I have chosen.

No one—no one at all—could do what you have done. No one will ever do what you will do. To qualify for that, a man would have to be you—and only you can be that. Be yourself, My Dear Walt.

Have you asked yourself why I call you, with these capital letters, My Dear Walt?—why I have not done so before, and whether there is some special meaning to it?

I assure you there is, and I promise you I shall make this revelation in my next writing. And that will be after you have performed this service for me—for us.

Dispose of this letter as you have the others.

Y

8 · Self-Block

The time came (yet again) when Inspector Richard Queen of New York City police headquarters had altogether and finally *enough*—up to here and brimming over. He recognized the signs. From long practice he knew how to contain what could be contained and how to sluice off the rest silently. But he knew also that when frustrated fatherhood reached the floodline, it would crest and overflow because of one extra drop—without warning, with a roar.

That time came one evening when, having let himself into the Queen apartment, the Inspector found no Ellery to greet him with a smile (or a frown) and/or a tingling highball to wash away the back-tooth grit of Centre Street.

The old man felt an almost audible *pop!* of disappointment. He kicked the foyer door to with his heel and put away his keys, frosted head and sparrow face cocked to listen; for the next most welcome thing, queerly enough, would be to find himself alone at this hour—meaning that Ellery had found something outside himself to interest and occupy him. The rattle of newsprint from Ellery's study ended that, and Level Two of anticipation went the way of the first.

Level Three was the wishful-thinking one, belonging as it did to the dream-of-glory family—of warty frogs turning into genuine handsome princes, of six-cent stock certificates suddenly quoted at $785. Anticipation on this third level, as it applied to Ellery's current plight, would have the voice of his typewriter soaring out of this world (away from Centre Street, or a private case, or an item in the newspaper) . . . high, high out of this world into the interplanetary spaces of Pure Mind . . . the voice bespeaking a new idea, a new twist, an Original. A sealed-room answer, perhaps, which no one had thought of before. A murderer with motive as deviously obscure as his logic was brilliantly clear to the all-seeing Ellery in the tale. Or the story might be satisfying on all counts, to all critics, to the author himself—and, of course, to the Inspector. Foo Level Three was a split level, whose impossible creation The One, the ultimate case, the book for the books, would bring joy even to an old man who knew how impossible it was.

But . . . listening to the inhabited silence, smelling the bitterness of coffee too long warming in the pot and of air blue-fogged by too much tobacco in a room dead-still with failure, Inspector Queen felt the bottom go out of his Level Three and the silly disappointment invade his shoulders, which it bowed.

The old gentleman crossed his living room to the son's study doorway and stood there looking in at the long limp ingrown figure at the desk—slumping as it had slumped yesterday, and the day (and week) before, and as it would likely slump tomorrow, at that mute, reproachful typewriter. Then Ellery turned his silvery eyes (tarnished now) from the newspaper, his head not moving, his spine remaining slack and hopeless, and in a voice as warm as ever (but tired as ever, too) said,

"Hello, Dad. Anything happen downtown today?" And this was simply another way of saying, Because nothing happened up here today . . . as usual.

Anything happen? the Inspector thought. Oh, yes. A 183-ticket scofflaw happened. A bakery-truck driver allowed his eleven-year-old son to watch him blow off the mother's head with a 12-gauge shotgun; *that* happened. And two good officers were in critical condition, beaten up by what looked like the total population of the slum block in which they were picking up a pusher; there's a human interest problem for you. And then there was the mysterious case of the teen-ager, a little girl really, who had already found out so much about life that she drank an incredible quantity of gasoline and was being rushed to the hospital when the ambulance struck a taxicab, killing both drivers, the taxi fare, the intern—everyone involved but the terrified kid, who would survive. And the thirty-year man the Inspector had known since the days when the police stables had dirt floors and smelled of honest horse instead of carbolic acid—a Captain now—*he* was caught today with his hand in the till; and what would you do with that, my son?

"Nothing," the old man said to his son.

"Rats," Ellery said. "I was hoping . . . "

This was the interchange, spoken and unspoken, this was the moment when the Inspector's containment could contain no more and the sluice spilled over, not silently.

"Well, what do you know," Inspector Queen said in a loud voice. "You were *hoping*," and the sluice-gate opened and out it poured, in a snarling rush. "You were hoping I'd bring you a present, little boy? Some nice chewy chocolate-covered goodie hot off Centre Street?"

Ellery took his feet down and swung about to look. An unbelievable pugnacity in his father's stance, weight shifted forward not quite to the balls of the feet, heels not quite raised . . .

"Hey," Ellery said, jumping up.

"So you *can* get off your backside! What did you do all day?"

Ellery said, "I—"

"What else did you use that typewriter for besides something to lean your elbows on?"

Ellery said again, "I—"

"How many cups of coffee did you drink today? How many packs of lung-buster did you smoke? Do you know how this room stinks? Ever hear of opening a window? It looks like one of those test chambers at Air Pollution Control in here! What's got into you, Ellery?"

"Well," Ellery began, "I—"

"Do you know I used to look forward to coming home at night? Just what do you think you're doing, anyway? Waiting for me to bring you home a story?"

Ellery said, "Wow," and chuckled. "That's pretty good, Dad. For a moment there I thought you were serious."

"Serious?" the Inspector hissed. He crumpled his topcoat and flung it across the room, at the same time charging up to the other side of Ellery's desk and leaning so far over with his chin stuck out that Ellery could see every aspen hair in his gray brush mustache. "I'll tell you how serious I am, Mr. Queen! I—want—you— the hell out of here!"

"What?" Ellery said feebly.

"Get out! Go somewhere, *do* something! You say you're a writer? Okay! Imagine something a living human being would do—anything at all!—and then just go out and pretend you're it. And pretty soon, Ellery, or so help me I'll have you embalmed!''

With which the waters of paternal anxiety fell off to a trickle, and the Inspector went over and retrieved his coat and stumped out of Ellery's study, muttering to himself. All of this Ellery watched with the round eyes and parted lips of an adenoidal idiot; and then he rubbed his unshaven cheeks and sat down again, looking intelligent.

So it was that (yet again) Inspector Richard Queen of police headquarters found himself, topcoat over his arm, keys in hand, standing in the doorway to his son's study, peering through the old blue fog at Ellery's recumbent length and bristling cheeks, chest at low tide, barely rising and falling. He seemed to be asleep.

The Inspector sighed. For him another working day had passed; for Ellery . . . "Still slaving away, son?" the old man said. There was even a sort of laughter in it.

But from this point everything was different.

Ellery's eyelids flew open, he sprang from his chair, he darted around the desk, he cried, "Dad, I've got it!"

The old man stepped back a pace, as if what his son had got might be contagious. "You have?"

Ellery followed him up, poking at him with a long, torn forefinger. "You were right the other night, Dad, but you were wrong, too. And I was wrong on *all* counts. I thought I had to wait for something to happen before I could write. Occupational blindness. All I had to do was figure out *why* I couldn't write. And I figured it out today!"

"You did?" the Inspector said cautiously.

"My trouble," Ellery chortled, snatching his father's hat off, grabbing his topcoat, tossing them both over his shoulder, forcing the old man down into the overstuffed chair near the fireplace, "my trouble is that I have a contemporary mind. That's all, Dad. That's absolutely all that's been wrong!"

"It is?"

"Certainly! I've always had a contemporary mind. I mean I've always written about the case I was working on at the time, or the one that was bothering you downtown—something *real,* in the here and now. But the times change, my old one," Ellery went on, striding up and down, rubbing his palms together like a Boy Scout making fire, kicking the rug, flinging himself onto the sofa, springing up again and darting to the study to pick up the Inspector's coat and hat, "and the more the times change the *faster* they change. Did you know that? Hah? Ellery's Law? Hell, they change so fast between one book and the next—what am I saying? between one day and the next!—that you don't even see it happen. Get my point, Dad? Do I convey anything to you?"

"No," said his father.

"Well, look!" cried Ellery. "What's happening to elevator operators?"

"What?" said his father. "Who?"

"Elevator operators. I'll tell you what's happening to them. They're *disappearing,* that's what—automated out of existence. Take the theater. Can you recognize a play any more? Ten-second scenes. Speeches consisting entirely of nouns and adjectives—no verbs. Actors moving scenery, and stagehands acting. Some of the cast in the audience. No curtain. No footlights. No *anything* of yesterday's theater. Everything's different, unexpected, purposely mystifying—not mystifying like a puzzle to be solved, but mystifying long after you're home in bed wondering what it was all about—and *meant* to be that way. My God, take this coat.'' Ellery whisked and twirled the Inspector's topcoat about, looking for the label. ''Here! Dacron and orlon mixture with a nylon lining. This is coal, water and air you're wearing, Dad—I'll bet you thought it came from a sheep!'' Ellery laugh-roared with the wonder of it, hurling the topcoat and hat across the living room into the foyer. ''No, no, stay where you are, Dad—I'll mix 'em!''

''What?'' croaked the Inspector.

''The drinks.'' Ellery scudded into the kitchen. The Inspector leaned back warily, keeping one eye open. He came upright to the alert when Ellery rushed back past him to the bar in the corner. ''Yes, sir, that's what's been wrong with me, the contemporary mind,'' said Ellery briskly, snatching the stainless-steel ice mallet from its niche and striking his thumb smartly with it. ''Damn.'' He aimed more carefully at the canvas-wrapped ice cubes. ''Look. I don't want to sound mystic or anything, Dad, but sometimes I used to get the feeling I was a kind of natural counterpoise—''

''A what?''

''Well, that I existed because a certain kind of criminal existed. That I did what I did because he did what *he* did. He was''—Ellery probed finely—''he was the player on the other side.''

''Other side.'' The Inspector wet his lips as he watched Ellery's hands at the bar.

''Yes. Well, that's it. I haven't been able to write any more because the player on the other side doesn't exist any more.'' He squinted at the small print on the bitters bottle. ''The times have outdated him—swept him away, and me with him. I mean the old me. See what I mean?''

''Come *on,*'' the Inspector said.

''Right away, Dad. Because, you see, you constituted authorities have come up with just too much wizardry—a speck of dust, and you know the murderer's height, weight, prep school and breeding habits. Police science today specializes in making the unusual usual—instant communications, electronic bugs, consulting head-doctors, non-criminal fingerprint files . . .'' He brought his father the long-awaited drink, which the knurled fingers seized greedily and conveyed mouthward with a snort of almost passion. ''Why, even the TV writers, for all the hoke and hooey they shovel out, deal in dosimeters and polygraphs and other miracles of the lab, and sometimes they even use 'em right.'' Ellery fell back on the sofa, waved his glass. ''So what chance does little-old-the-likes-of-me have, with my old-fashioned wonder? There's no wonderment left in the real world any longer. Or rather, everything is so wonderful the wonder's gone out of it. I can't outthink a solid state binary computer; I can't outplay an electronic chess opponent—it'll beat me every time. Skoal.''

He drank, and the old man drank again, keeping his eyes anxiously on his son's face while he did so.

Ellery banged his glass down on the coffee table. ''So! Now that I know why I dried up, I know what to do about it.''

''You do?''

''I do.''

''And what's that?''

"I'm taking no more cases—mine, yours, anybody's. I'm through investigating crimes. What I write from now on is going to come out of here"—he tapped his temple—"entirely. Something new, something different. I don't know what yet, but it'll come."

"No more cases," his father said after a contemplative time.

"No more cases."

"Too bad."

Ellery pursued a fugitive thought.

After a while he looked up. His father was staring at him in the most peculiar way. In spite of himself, Ellery began to feel his way back along the past quarter-hour, like a man crossing a muddy stream on invisible stepping stones.

"Too bad?" Ellery said. "Dad, did you say too bad?"

"That's what I said."

"Yes, and before that all you said was 'He did?' . . . 'You were?' . . . 'You do?' . . . 'What?'—"

"I did?" the Inspector said sheepishly.

Ellery chewed on his lower lip for a moment. "Dad."

"Hmm?"

"What is it?"

"What is what?"

Ellery exploded. *"Balls* of fire! The other night you chewed me out for waiting for a case to happen so I could start writing again. You know why you dumped your ill-temper on me? Because you were feeling guilty over not having a case to bring home to me! Tonight, when I announce I'm giving up case work as a basis for my novels, you start acting bashful and coy. Remember me, Dad? I'm the child of your loins and I'm starving! What nourishment have you brought me from downtown?"

Inexplicably, each began to laugh. Their laughter did not last long, but it sufficed. Where that laughter came from, words could not reach.

The Inspector shifted his wiry body a little and reached into a side pocket. "Fellow got himself slaughtered the other night. Person or persons as yet unknown. In fact, everything as yet unknown."

"So?"

"So. This came in the mail for him just before he was clobbered." The Inspector produced something from the pocket he had been exploring and rose and went over to the coffee table and dropped his find before Ellery.

Ellery leaned forward at the waist. His eyebrows drew ever so lightly toward each other as he studied what the Inspector had produced for his inspection.

It was a five-sided white card of peculiar proportions, with a capital J stamped on it in what seemed to be black stamping pad ink.

The Inspector said, "That was the first one."

9 · Y's Gambit Accepted

"Never saw anything like it," Inspector Queen was saying. "That house, I mean. It's laid out like a surgeon's tray. Chair in a corner had to be checked with a draftsman's triangle for exact placement. Big picture mathematically centered on the wall, with two little pictures the same size flanking it exactly the same distance away. Just so much floor could show at each end of the carpet. Whole house is like that except the secretary's room—I don't mean his room's grubby, just that it looks as if someone lives there, which the rest of the house doesn't. You'll see for yourself, Ellery."

Ellery made no commitment. He was staring at the card.

"But he—the lord and master of all this . . . this exactitude—he was the godawfulest mess you ever saw, *I* ever saw," the old man went on. "I've seen accident cases spread out over half a block didn't look as messy as that patio. I s'pose that's what gave me the feeling right off that this case is going to be a wrongo—your kind of wrongo, Ellery. He was lying on a steel-framed chaise on the patio just outside his impeccable dining room. Except for his head, I mean. That was scattered to hell and gone. Someone'd shoved a two-hundred-pound granite block off the top of the tower forty feet above him . . . onto his head."

"This is Robert York you're talking about," Ellery said suddenly. "Of York Square."

"How did you know that? Oh, the papers. Yump," the Inspector said, "it's the Robert York case, all right."

"May I handle the card?"

"Yes."

Ellery picked up the white card, turned it over, turned it back. "What's this J?"

"You tell me, son. There isn't a John, Jack, Jim, Joan or Jehoshaphat in all of York Square. Or a Johnson, Jackson or Jimson, either."

Ellery replaced the card on the coffee table and began to hypnotize it. "Go on. It couldn't have been an accident?"

"Not unless somebody accidentally chipped away all the mortar around the stone, accidentally cracked it loose with a pinch bar and then accidentally swept up all the stone dust. Velie got up there like lightning, and I wasn't far behind. Nobody'd have had time to do that thorough a clean-up job after the push-off. So it had to have been done beforehand—maybe days before, weeks. And that makes it premeditated murder."

"How was the granite block tipped off the tower?"

"By a good hard push. That stone wasn't teetering in the balance up there, Ellery. It was a solid block with a dead-flat seat under it. Even without the mortar it would have stayed put during a hundred years of hurricanes."

"So all the block-buster had to do was wait until York happened to be directly underneath—?"

"That's the beauty part. This Robert York 'happened' to be directly underneath on every mild evening from May fifteenth to October first at half-past seven, give or take ten seconds—you heard me, ten *seconds*—and there he'd stay until half-past eight on the dot. Rainy or chilly evenings he'd lie down on the settee in his study. But he always napped exactly one hour after dinner."

"Which, of course, everyone in the place knew?"

"And more people outside it than I care to think about trying to track down. He liked to brag about the to-the-second regularity of his habits. And how he could fall asleep on a dime and wake himself up the same way."

"Built-in alarm clock." Ellery nodded. "Who had access to the tower, Dad?"

"Everybody," grunted the old man. "There's an outside door that opens directly to the tower stairs, also an inside door in the downstairs hall that runs between the front rooms and the kitchen."

"Doors kept locked?"

"Only the outside door, but the lock is an old relic you could undo with your front teeth without leaving a mark."

"Who was in the house at the time the granite block fell?"

"Nobody. The handyman was in the garage, changing the oil in one of the cars."

"Didn't he hear or see anything?"

"He says no. Could be, too. The garage is pretty far from the terrace, and the block was—well—cushioned some when it landed."

Ellery made a face. "Who cooked York's dinner?"

"Housekeeper, a sleep-out name of Mrs. Schriver. She always had his meal ready at a quarter of seven, he was always finished at five after. Then she'd carry the dishes out to the kitchen and go home."

"Didn't wash them before leaving? Oh, of course. Don't disturb the master at his nap."

"Right."

Ellery pulled at his lower lip until it stretched like a Ubangi's. "Think of asking anyone how sound a sleeper he was?"

"Didn't I. Consensus is that you couldn't have waked York with a fire hose till he chose to wake himself."

Ellery frowned. "Then what's this nonsense about the housekeeper's not doing the dishes because it would disturb His Majesty's nap?"

"I asked her. She says it's a habit she got into when she went to work there three years ago and first found out about Robert York's after-dinner snooze. She just never bothered to change her routine."

"Big strong woman, is she?"

The Inspector showed his dentures in what might have been laughter. "*Little* strong woman."

Ellery communed with some invisible entity in midair. Suddenly he said, "What about this handyman?"

"Walt? Oh, he's a dandy little suspect. Up on the tower that day, too, trimming the ivy. Says even if the mortar under the block had been loosened by that time he'd likely not have noticed. I can believe that, by the way. The cracks are thin and deep-set; you can hardly see the mortar on or under the other blocks. Sure,

Walt could have done the whole job, then skinned on down and out to the garage.
But so could everybody else. Everybody.''

"Ugh," Ellery said mildly. "All right—who found the headless paragon?"

"His secretary. Young guy named Thomas Archer. Archer is remounting York's
stamp collections or something—been putting in a lot of night work."

"Did Archer have dinner with York?"

"No. He used to all the time, but Mrs. Schriver tells me he's eaten most of his
meals out lately."

"Out where?"

"That night? At Myra York's house—the one in the southeast corner of the
Square."

"How come?"

"Myra has a paid companion, a girl named Ann Drew, who's apparently stirred
young Archer's blood. He had dinner with the girl in Myra York's kitchen. Myra
was upstairs in bed, sick."

"So the girl alibis this Archer fellow?"

"They alibi each *other*," said the old man with a grimace, "which I hate. By
the way, if this Drew number doesn't bubble *your* blood a little, son—"

Ellery interrupted. "And the other denizens of York Square?"

"Well, Cousin Emily claims she was alone in her house writing letters. Cousin
Percival says he was alone in *his* house washing down a hangover so he'd feel up
to building another one."

"And that accounts for the lot? Including the help?"

The old man nodded grimly. "That's it. Any one of 'em could have done it."

"Including the man from Dubuque," Ellery said thoughtfully.

"Theoretically, sure. But I don't think this was the work of a passing stranger.
Strangers don't get to hang around York Square for days—or even hours—ahead
of time chipping out mortar on one of the towers."

Ellery stared down at the inked J on the card. "The newspaper accounts say that
Robert York's death means an extra million or so to each of his cousins when the
whole bundle comes due. When is that, by the way?"

"According to the will, in about six months. Equal shares to all surviving heirs
at the time the estate is distributed."

"The old tontine foolishness," Ellery said in disgust. "This is Nathaniel York,
Senior's will you're talking about?"

"Yes. Robert's will left everything *he* has to the joint estate, too. It doesn't
amount to much—I mean, compared to the sheer mass of the principal estate—
although of course to you and me it would be a fortune."

They were silent for a while.

"Emily York's some sort of ascetic, isn't she?" Ellery murmured, looking up.
"And Myra's an invalid? I can't see either of them going out of her way to jack
up the big pot by cutting down on the number of heirs. Which would seem to leave
Percival."

The Inspector's face took on a look of deep yearning. "Just between you and
me, son, I'd like for it to come out that way. There's a walking, talking pimple if
ever I saw one!"

"So I gather. But what would even a no-goodnik like Percival, who'll soon have
three million dollars to spend, want with a fourth?"

"Are you kidding?"

"Enough to commit murder for, I mean."

"Oh, stop, Ellery. Next you'll be saying that babies really are delivered by storks. Besides which, I haven't counted out the lady cousins by a long shot."

"You think Emily or Myra could have pushed over two hundred pounds of stone?"

"They could have paid some muscle to do the pushing, couldn't they?—after chipping away the mortar themselves."

"Any indication of that?"

"Give me a chance, will you?" the Inspector grumbled. "But talking about motive. Take this Emily. Sure *is* an ascetic—a millionaire ascetic, the most fanatical kind. She uses only two rooms of that castle of hers, works for a settlement house, lives mostly on her settlement-house pay, and donates the bulk of her income from the estate *to* the settlement house. And she's got big plans for when she comes into her share of the millions, I understand, plans involving her work. She's a funny old gal, and if something happened to threaten the distribution of those millions in any way—I wouldn't put *anything* past her."

"And Myra?" Ellery asked.

The old man said slowly, "She looks harmless—*looks* harmless. Maybe she's what she seems to be. But . . . I don't know. Myra's some kind of nut. Trouble is, I can't figure out what kind. Vague. Unpredictable . . . " He shook his head. "You'll see, Ellery."

"Now I haven't said—" began Ellery.

"Oh. Sure. Excuse me," his father said. "*If* you'll join me in this head-breaker, you'll see."

Ellery grunted and subsided. "Is there anyone else who might feel better off in a Robert Yorkless world?" The old man shrugged. "Far as I can tell, nobody loved him, nobody hated him. Young Archer, his secretary, tells me Robert always tried to be absolutely fair. According to Robert's lights, of course, which I gather very few people but Archer appreciated."

"Oh, so? How come? What about this Archer?"

"Bright, on the bookish side. We're interested in him because of that stamp collection of Robert York's he's remounting and recataloguing. He's been told by Emily and Percival to go on with the stamp work, because of course it goes to the joint estate along with Robert's other personal property—"

"Hold it." Ellery had sat up abruptly. "I must have been thinking of something else when you mentioned stamp collections a while back. Robert York—sure! His philatelic holdings are supposed to be quite remarkable. He was one of the best-known collectors in New York. That means this Tom Archer has his hands on some mighty negotiable valuables—"

"Sure has," grinned the Inspector. "He could tuck one measly little stamp in an old envelope and walk off with eight, ten grand. That's why we're watching him. Though it isn't likely he'd try it. You can bet that a man who kept an inventory of his collar buttons—that's right, our Robert still used collar buttons!—wouldn't leave his rare stamps around like old confetti. His executors—a bank, by the way—have a list of every last stamp Robert ever bought or sold, and it's up to date."

"Check," Ellery said, shrugging. "Does Archer get anything out of Robert York's death?"

"Not as far as I know. He got a raise in pay only a week or so ago, when Robert gave him power of attorney to handle the nuts-and-bolts details of running York Square—with the others' consent, of course. In fact, Emily and Percival—and technically Myra—want Archer to keep on in that capacity. He seems capable enough, and happy in his job.''

"How happy?''

"You mean about the murder of Robert? No, that seems to have shaken Archer up. I'd say he came closer to *liking* Robert than anybody else we've talked to.''

"Watch him, then,'' said Ellery. "Who's left? Oh, the handyman—Walt. What about him?''

"Speaks when he's spoken to, can do anything in the way of manual work, couldn't possibly be as dumb as he looks and acts. Takes care of everything around the place except what the housekeeper does.''

"And the housekeeper? What's her name—Mrs. Schriver?''

Inspector Queen shook his head. "A housekeeper. Helps Myra York's companion—Ann Drew—with heavy cleaning once a week, straightens up Percival's place twice a week, used to cook and clean for Robert every day. Neither Mrs. Schriver nor Walt stands to gain so much as a second-hand salami by Robert's death—or anyone else's, far as I can make out.''

"Leaving the girl.''

"Ah, the girl,'' the old man said with a wistful nod. "Wait till you see that girl, Ellery—''

"You're not going to get to me that way,'' Ellery said, snorting. Again he stared down at the J-card. Suddenly he looked up. "Wait a minute! I'm really rusty. When you showed me this card . . . Did you or didn't you say something about its being the first one?''

"Hm?'' said the Inspector. "Oh! That's right.''

Ellery was glaring at him. "You mean there's been a *second* card?''

"Didn't I mention that?'' the old man asked innocently. He dug into the other pocket, pulled out another five-sided white card, laid it delicately before his son.

It, too, bore a letter of the alphabet.

An H.

PART TWO

Middle Game

10 · Attack Continued

He had sat alone in the cheap hotel room watching slit-eyed and lipless the steady pistons of his index fingers laying word after careful word down on the pale blue lines of the copy paper.

He had written, in part:

> *. . . to tell you, as I promised, why I write My Dear Walt. Each word I write means something, and when I write those words they mean something precious and special.*
>
> *"My" means you are mine, my creature and my property. You of all people will glory in this, for you understand how mighty are the meek, and that they shall inherit the earth. Let the tall grasses hold up their arrogant heads for the scythe to take. Be little and brown and unnoticed, and you will be alive under the sun's eye when they, the tall ones, have been bundled away.*
>
> *And "Dear" means, above all, "chosen," for I speak like this to no other living soul. It means "valued." It means "trusted." And most of all it means "invulnerable," for no one can harm you under my protection.*
>
> *Last and greatest . . . "Walt." "Walt" means you, My Dear Walt, you, unique, gifted with grace-in-obedience, fated to command while invisible—dispenser of life and death.*
>
> *Now there is a small quiet thing to be done perfectly, and so I call upon you.*
>
> *In the envelope with this letter you will find a second card. As before, you will practice with the printing set until you are sure of a clear impression.*
>
> *You will then print the letter H exactly like this:*

being sure that the diagonal side of the card is at the lower right. You will note that the H in your printing set has a crossbar that is above the center of the letter. Be very careful to print it as you see it in my drawing, for if you were to print it upside down, with the crossbar low, it would be wrong and unworthy of you.

When you have done this, seal the card in a plain envelope as before, and address it (in the same neat plain capital letters you used the first time) to:

EMILY YORK

YORK SQUARE

NEW YORK, N.Y.

Put a stamp on it. Destroy any traces of your work on your table, hands or anywhere in your room. Dispose of this letter and envelope as you did the last time.

Then go out and mail the new letter, following my original instructions.

I feel your gratitude, My Dear Walt. I know how grateful you are to me for having chosen you.

I am pleased with you.

Y

11 · Development

"One thing is clear," said Ellery, poking the two white cards with a troubled fingertip. "This one with the J is the shape of Robert York's corner of York Square, the southwest corner; and Robert got the J-card and was killed. And this one with the H must represent the *north*west corner, Emily's, because Emily got the H-card—"

"My dear son, do I need you to tell me that?" the old man asked wearily. "And if it's protection for Emily you're worried about, I doubled the foot patrol for the entire neighborhood, and I have a prowl car hitting the Square itself every twenty minutes, day and night."

"I hope that's enough."

"You'd like me to put somebody inside? Then you figure out a way. Emily York has an exaggerated idea of what would happen to her with a man in the house. Absolutely put her foot down."

"Virgin territory, eh?" Ellery shook his head, frowning. "There's another thing that would bother me if I were you. The attempt on her life may be planned to take place not in the Square or in her house but somewhere else."

"You think I should have her tailed," Inspector Queen said dryly.

"I most certainly do."

"Well, so do I!" the Inspector snapped. "I had Hesse tailing her when she left for work yesterday morning. You know what?—Hesse can't get over it yet—she spotted him in three minutes and gave him the slip! Seems Emily thought he might be 'after' her. When I told Miss Eagle-Eye that Hesse is a detective assigned to protect her, you know what she said to me? 'I'm not taking chances on *anybody*.' She's a holy terror, that woman. We'll do our best, but you know how tough it is to guard somebody who won't co-operate."

Ellery looked unhappy. "I suppose you drew a blank on fingerprints?"

"Blank? The J-card has *everybody's* prints on it. Seems the late Robert passed it around at the last monthly powwow of the tribe, where they sweat out who owes how much for the garbagemen tips. He even let the housekeeper and the handyman handle it."

"Paper, card, envelope, type, ink, et cetera?" Ellery murmured.

"No sweat. You could duplicate the paper, envelope and card within spitting distance of the Square—or in any five-and-dime or stationery store in the U.S.A. Lab doesn't hold out much hope about the block-letter address. The rubber-stamp type and ink come from a kid's toy printing set called Prints Charming that's been a standard item for years. It's sold by the thousands all over town."

"Great," muttered Ellery. "And the H-card mailing?"

"Emily York's prints, of course. And a Miss Sullivan's. And a couple of smudged partials that may or may not belong to somebody else. And Ann Drew's—in her case just on the envelope. Don't look so happy. The girl happened to bring the Square's mail up from the Church Street post office. Dropped that particular envelope off at Emily's house, and Emily took it to work with her.''

"A Miss Sullivan," said Ellery. "Who's Miss Sullivan?"

"Ah," sighed the Inspector. "I was coming to that."

It was Miss Sullivan (Inspector Queen informed Ellery) who had told him of Emily York's plans for the settlement house development. Miss Sullivan ran the place, a converted brownstone, its grand past barely hinted at by the time-chipped interior, condemned for life to the seething street the city had long since abandoned to its fate.

"I can't really tell you anything about it," Miss Sullivan said when the Inspector (following a surmise, an overheard remark and sheer logic) asked her whether Emily York's imminent bonanza would change things at the settlement house.

"Why not, Miss Sullivan?"

Her voice was sanded only at the margins by the abrasives of time. Yet she was surely in her mid-seventies. She breathed with a difficulty not surprising in view of her bulk, which her birdy-quick skeleton and tiny feet must have found a fearful burden. Her nose was extraordinary; the Inspector wondered if she knew how fatefully it must have affected her lifelong tenure on the "Miss." Her innocence of glasses was explained by neither contact lenses nor vanity; and this was a great boon, for after the first few moments he conversed only with the warm, shy, joyful little person who dwelt inside her eyes. They were of a clean-bleached blue, with a snapping washline quality, like summer linen of the softest, highest grade laundered and set out to dry daily in the sun over a lifetime.

"You see, I know nothing about it." But Miss Sullivan's remarkable eyes were saying happily, *But I do, I do!* And when the Inspector refused to accept that spoken denial and merely stood waiting quietly for more, it was as if the little person inside darted to the right, to the left, hunting something to hide behind—not at all fearfully, but *Catch me! Catch me!* like a laughing child running off with a present which was not hers at all.

"I mean, Miss York wouldn't want me to say a word," she said; and still the Inspector waited, applying no pressure, the small smile on his lips genuine, evoked by the pleasure of her secret. "And I've promised, Inspector, really I have."

"If you told me," he asked gently, "are you afraid she'd change her mind about whatever it is she intends to do with the money?"

"Oh, dear, no! Not Emily York! It means too much to her."

The Inspector said craftily, "She's a fine woman." They beamed at each other. "I overheard something," he added, "when I came in. In that room to the left of the entrance?" The room to the left of the entrance was a sort of stable for the idle, the beaten, the sodden, the rudderless human hulks of the neighborhood.

"You mean in the reading room?" said Miss Sullivan.

"In the reading room," he nodded. "One of the men wanted to leave and go down to the Seaman's Mission for a meal and a bed, but another one told him to stay put and make himself known to you ladies, because big things were going to happen around here soon and you'd need their help." (This was his freehand translation of the bum who had said, "I'm cuttin' this cave, it gives me the goddamn itch. Let's go Sea-Missy and pray us some slops and a shelf." And of his one-eyed adviser who had pulled him back on the bench and said, "Jest you set and smile and give 'em a good pitch. Git acquainted here. The Vinegar Virgin gone come th'oo that door one time soon pushin' a buggy full o' gold bars. You best be in line, man, 'cause she gone buy us a hotel in the country. Ev'body knows that.")

"Oh, yes, some of them would do, well, just anything for Emily York," said Miss Sullivan. "I wonder how they heard?"

"It isn't really going to be a hotel, then?"

"Dear me, no!"

"They'll be disappointed," said the Inspector, shaking his head. "That's what the poor fellows think it's going to be."

"Well, it *isn't*," she said firmly, and the one inside said pleadingly with her eyes, *Ask me! Ask me!*

But—"They'll really be disappointed," he said, and half turned toward the door.

"Oh, but they won't. Oh, dear, must you—? Please!" Her little hands fluttered and caught each other and trembled together. He thought: Those hands belong to the eyes. "Please shut the door." He shut it carefully. She said, "I *can* trust you . . . ?" and the eyes said, *Please? Please?*

"Miss York will never know I know," he assured her.

The eyes sparkled. With conspiratorial zest she said, "Turn *that* over!"

He followed her small finger to the wall, grasped the frame of a large yellowed street map of the settlement neighborhood and the nearby waterfront, turned it over and stepped back.

"Sometimes we just sit here and look at it," she half sang, half whispered.

It was a housing-plan elevation. A box in one corner was occupied by an architect's rendering of a cottage. A flagstone path wound around a lawn to a porch whose roof was supported by square fieldstone columns joined by Byzantine arches, and enclosed by a low concrete-capped parapet. What could be seen of the porch floor was brick tile, and Miss Sullivan explained that the interior would be floored with tile also, a satin-finish ceramic which would clean easily, glow with color and last forever. The building itself would seem larger inside than it did outside, with its ells and gables. The small panes of the many windows, as well as the fanlight which repeated the porch arches, would have their occasional stained square, so that inside by day, outside by night, color would brighten the beholder.

"Rambler roses across the front," Miss Sullivan crooned, pointing. "Ivy on the south and west walls, and forsythia on the north side to look winter in the eye when it comes to bloom. Here mountain laurel and dogwood. And here bleeding heart. And all along the edge here babies'-breath. And every year, hollyhocks and sunflowers and zinnias and honeysuckle. You'll see!"

Looking over the larger plan, the Inspector asked, "Where's this going to be built?"

"It's not far from New York—I mustn't say where, because Miss York only has an understanding about the land, and if people found out about the village, why, land values would go just sky-high and use up all the money."

The Inspector suddenly saw the correlation between the cottage and the curving rows of identical inkblots on the large plan. "She's intending to build a whole *village?*"

"Well, how else could we do it?" cried Miss Sullivan. "Forty-two cottages just like that one—it was to be thirty-five, you know, but now that poor Mr. York has passed away, and there's one less to share the estate, we'll be able to manage seven cottages more. And an administration building, and the help's quarters, and so on. Over here, by the way, is a stone outcrop big enough for us to quarry all the stone we'll need for the cottages and other buildings. All this here—eighty acres—is fine farmland. Here in the south quadrant we'll have a modern cow barn; pits here; geese and ducks and chickens here. Maybe turkeys, too, though we're not sure of that yet—they're said to be *very* hard to raise. And over here we'll have the slaughter shack for the fowl, the smokehouse, the refrigerator rooms—oh, and of course this is going to be a huge hay barn. This section is for the workshops—carpentry, ceramics, a wool shop if we decide to raise sheep . . . Oh, and here! These are our greenhouses. Three for forced truck-gardening—for out-of-season things, you know—and two for flowers.''

"I see," murmured Inspector Queen. "Self-supporting, eh? Maybe even showing a profit?"

"Well, of course we'll have a large staff, and they're to be *well paid*," Miss Sullivan said with sudden severity, as if he had assumed an *ante-bellum* society, "so in the beginning we'll be satisfied to keep our heads above water. But we'll be producing milk and butter and cheese and bacon and hams and dressed fowl and vegetables and flowers, and Miss York said something about perhaps making our own bread and of course country furniture and hand-turned pottery and"—she paused for a long and happy gasp of breath—"and goodness knows what else. So we ought to manage most of our expenses even without the guests."

"The guests?" the Inspector echoed, mystified.

"Those gentlemen you saw downstairs."

"Those—" He coughed hurriedly.

"Yes," Miss Sullivan said with asperity, "those—gentlemen!" and he cursed himself for his *lapsus linguae*. The one inside—the one behind the eyes—could shoot bright bolts of indignation. "Dignity, Inspector Queen, *dignity*. Who needs it more than the weary and sick and homeless who never learned a skill or belonged to anyone or anything? Here they'll have the opportunity to grow strong, to be treated with decency, to acquire an individual *meaning*. Every last man of them will be called *Mister*. Each will have his own room, with his own possessions in it, and we'll be there to—yes, to *cater* to him, to find out what he likes and doesn't like, what he's able to do and what he's not. Oh," Miss Sullivan cried, "it will be wonderful!"

Very carefully Inspector Queen said, "I think you might wind up with—well— a gang of long-term free-loaders."

There came into the child-eyes a shimmer of scornful wisdom. "They will be *paying* guests, Inspector!"

"With what will they pay, Miss Sullivan?"

"With *themselves,* don't you see? Each one will be extended credit, depending on his needs. The longer he stays, the greater his debt, true. *But*. For everything he does for the village after we teach him a skill—making a chair, hoeing a row of corn, tending the chicken plucker—his debt is reduced."

"And if he never gets out of the red?"

She smiled. "Do you know, Inspector, most people—even fine people like yourself—have the minds of accountants?" The Inspector blushed, something he had not done for forty years. "Never get out of the red! Won't he have learned a trade? Won't he be rested, well fed? Won't he have discovered the satisfaction of a clean body and the stimulus of a fresh attitude toward life? And if he should find himself wanting to belong to something bigger than our village, he'll go back into the world, but with what a difference! He'll be *new,* self-confident, full of hope." She was so illuminated from within he could have groaned. "Inspector, it will *work*. You'll see!"

I don't have to see, the Inspector thought. I see daily.

He saw Centre Street line-ups, shills, pimps, muggers, gunsels, sharks, sharpies, touts, shiv artists, bums, pushers, addicts, creeps, morons, dips, muscle men, maniacs, and all-around misfits. In a parade, a cascade, that never stopped. He thought piously: Dear God, let this pipe dream of hers stay just that. She's too old to have to take the dirty truth. Or is it possible—I mean, am I such a jaded old crock . . . ?

His ears prickled a warning, alerted by a note in that burble of half song. ". . . just to give them those things, those simple and essential things, like the right to be called 'Mister.' *That's* what Emily York wants her money for. *That's* why she lives the way she does, in just two rooms of that big house, on a social worker's salary, turning practically her whole income over to the settlement house here. And that's why she'd do—oh, anything—to protect the York estate.''

"Sorry," said the Inspector, controlling his voice with the discipline of a TV announcer. "I didn't quite get that, Miss Sullivan. Protect the York estate from what?"

"Well . . . from anything that might threaten it." She was suddenly troubled. "I mean, anything that might reduce her share of it . . ." He could almost see the girlish Miss Sullivan deep inside place little palms against an appalled mouth. "I'm afraid I'm talking too much."

"I wouldn't misuse it," he said, quickly and warmly.

"Thank you." She hunted for something in his face and seemed to find it. "Thank you," she said again, and went to the plan and set her frail fingers under the frame. The Inspector hastened to help her. Together they turned it over, and for a moment they stood tandem, looking at the yellowed street map of the blighted neighborhood and the noisome waterfront. Then Miss Sullivan turned her back on it and asked, "Was there anything else you wanted to know, Inspector?"

"Well, I don't mean to pry—"

"Don't you, now!" Miss Sullivan laughed her gasping laugh. "And you a police officer." She stopped laughing and sighed, and lowered her great mass carefully into the vast chair behind the desk. "Sit down, Inspector Queen. I'm afraid you're no better at deception than I am."

He grinned feebly, drawing up a chair, feeling chagrin and guilt and something else that eluded classification. "I'm taking up too much of your time. You've been to York Square, Miss Sullivan?"

"Goodness, yes. Often."

"Just in Miss Emily York's house?"

"Oh, no, I've been asked to dinner, one time or another, in all but Percival York's. Chiefly at Emily's, of course. Many's the time the two of us have worked through the night on plans for the village." Miss Sullivan said suddenly, "You think we're both impossible dreamers, don't you, Inspector?"

"Oh, no," he said. *Was* it possible?

"Oh, yes," she retorted. "Well, perhaps we are. I remember Emily used to dream of turning the four castles into one neighborhood-house type of community. But that *was* impossible, she said, because her share of the estate simply wouldn't be enough to buy the others out. You see, the village upstate is planned for just men. But with York Square we could have a headquarters building and three houses for women—one a residence club, say, another a clinic, the third a school. It *would* be nice," she said wistfully.

"How about now?" the Inspector asked, and despised himself. "I mean now that Emily's share is going to be a million or so larger?" She looked at him, and he said, "There I go, prying again, right?"

She gasped with laughter again. "Yes, bless you. But that's not a very nice thought, Inspector, is it?"

He thought: You can bet your lavender sachet it's not a very nice thought. But very not-nice thoughts are why I'm here. And he found himself wondering how old was the controversy over the end and the means. Did a perplexing whiff of it pass through the massive skull of some prehuman homunculus the day he hurled his brother into the jaws of a saber-tooth so that he himself might escape?

In this particular balance, lonely on one pan of the scales, stood Myra and Percival York—Myra a mental and physical invalid, Percival unlovable and unmournable; and on the other pan huddled a street swarm of human wreckage—to be reborn, to be grown whole again and (to the Inspector, above all) to be taken off the streets and out of the cluttered courtrooms. For possibly the first time in his life Inspector Richard Queen, the old hound dog of Centre Street, smiled at the idea of being just a little blind, just a fraction forgetful, just a tiny bit obtuse . . . It was this damned Sullivan woman!

The Inspector shook himself almost visibly, aware of her soft song-voice. "Beg pardon?"

"Are you all right, Inspector?" she asked—was asking—anxiously. "Oh, dear, I've made you angry."

"Not at all," he said gallantly, and grinned. "You couldn't."

"You looked so very stern suddenly."

"I was thinking of how Robert York died," said the Inspector, and told himself aloud with hushed force, "I don't *like* murder, no matter *why* it's done." And felt much better for having said it.

"Poor Emily," murmured Miss Sullivan.

"Would you say she's taking Robert's death hard?"

"Oh, she is. Dreadfully."

"I wouldn't have said so."

"Because you don't know her, Inspector. Dear Emily is very controlled. Threats or violence"—surprisingly, Miss Sullivan chuckled—"are things she simply will not *allow*. Time and again I've seen her stand up to rampaging drunks, raving addicts, the worst hoodlums. She'll walk right into danger without a *thing* showing, though I'm sure she's as afraid as anyone else. She's the same way about grief, I suppose."

"Very controlled," the Inspector repeated thoughtfully.

"Take yesterday, for example. She just worked a bit harder, that was all. You wouldn't have realized anything was disturbing her unless you knew the signs. Like her losing patience. At little things, never the big ones."

"Oh?"

"A door banging somewhere. Mustard on a sandwich when she'd ordered it without mustard—goodness! she never notices what she eats. But how she carried on about that mustard. And then there was that silly card—"

A shooting thrill, much like a little bolt of lightning, almost lifted the old man out of the chair. "Silly card?" he said. "What do you mean, Miss Sullivan?"

"I saved it." Miss Sullivan began opening drawers. "It's here somewhere . . . Why, she'd just come in and taken the mail out of her bag—she always brings her mail from home to the office—and settled down as usual to go through it. All of a sudden she made a kind of *tsst!*—''

''*Tsst?*''

''*Tsst!*'' Miss Sullivan corrected him, repeating the exclamation point he had left out. ''And she hurled the card and envelope to the floor. *The floor—Emily!* Here it is.'' She handed the plain white envelope to Inspector Queen, who took from it the five-sided white card bearing the H.

After a while the Inspector looked up. ''Did Miss York happen to say why this bothered her so much?''

''Oh, I don't think it bothered her at all. Not the *card*. More the nuisance of it, I'm sure. You see, I know her.'' Scanning his face, Miss Sullivan apparently read doubt there. ''I mean, had it really bothered her—the thing in itself—she'd have called me over to look or made phone calls, or . . . or any number of things. She threw it like that because it *wasn't* important, you see, not because it was.'' She said again, ''I *know* her.''

''Did she discuss this with you at all?''

''Well, of course I picked it up and said, 'What on earth, Emily—?' and she''—the young smooth one behind the bleached old eyes puckered with remembered hurt—''and she was sharp, quite sharp, with me. What she said was, 'Let me alone!—please.' And it wasn't a very big 'please,' so I knew she was already sorry for being sharp, that she wasn't troubled about the card, only annoyed with it.''

''Then why did you keep it?'' he asked, because he had to.

''Oh . . . that's me all over,'' Miss Sullivan laughed. ''Always pick up a glove because one day I might find the mate. That card isn't a thing, Inspector, if you really look at it. It's a *piece* of a thing, strikes me. So the other piece must be around somewhere.''

''You ought to meet my son,'' said the Inspector suddenly, heartily. Then before she could answer he asked, ''And so Miss York didn't even attempt to guess what this might be?''

''I mentioned it at lunch,'' she said, her voice infused with the shyness she had felt at the time, ''and all she said was, 'Oh, it's a ridiculous advertising teaser,' and I could see she didn't want to talk about it. It could be a puzzle of some kind, don't you think?''

''Could be,'' said the Inspector, and he slipped the card into the envelope and the envelope into his pocket, not hurrying, not asking permission. Her eyes followed it, but she made no protest. He rose and said flatly, ''I'm coming back.''

''Oh, dear, Inspector. Surely you've squeezed out the last possible drop?''

''I mean, Miss Sullivan,'' said the Inspector, ''I'm coming back when this is over.''

''Oh! Please do,'' and the one inside twinkled unabashed in Miss Sullivan's clean-wash eyes. ''Please *do*.''

12 · Divergent Attack

They met in the park at young Nathaniel York's memorial plaque. It was quite dark. Tom Archer, for all that it was a warm night, without a threat of rain, carried a trench coat.

"Hello, guardian angel."

"Tom!" said Ann Drew. They no longer opened their conversations with, "How's yours?"

"Sorry I'm late. I had to go pick up a girl friend."

"Oh?"

"How's Miss Myra?"

"About the same. Sometimes I think she doesn't realize about Robert, even though she went to the funeral. What girl friend?"

Something said *Yeep!* in a high soprano. Unnoticing, Tom said, "I get so *dog-gone* sorry for her."

"Sorry for whom?"

Yeep!

"Miss Myra, of course. I wonder what she was like—before."

"Tom Archer, will you answer my question? What girl friend?"

Yeep! This time it was loud and clear. She clutched his free arm. "What was that?"

"What was what?"

"Didn't you hear it?"

"I didn't hear anything."

"Something went . . . yeep," she said.

"Went what?"

"Yeep!" she repeated angrily.

"Honey," Archer said, "do you feel all right?"

Yeep! Yeep!

"There!" she said triumphantly. Then she said, "Tom Archer, are *you* making that noise?"

"On my honor as a non-philandering philosophic philatelist, *I* am making no noise."

Yeep!

"Then who is?"

"Beelzebub, I presume."

"*Who?*"

"Beelzebub," said Tom Archer, "meet Ann. Ann, meet Beelzebub." So saying, he swept back the coat rolled on his left forearm and extracted a squirming, yeeping German Shepherd puppy with unstarched ears and enormous feet.

"Oh, *Tom,* he's *sweet!* Oh, oh, oh!" she cried and crooned, nuzzling the puppy.
"Isn't he the softest, funniest—"

"Isn't *she* the softest, funniest," Tom corrected her.

"I thought you said his—its—her name is Beelzebub."

"Quite so. I'm not the first sage to observe that the devil is a female."

"*Most* humurous," Ann sniffed, rubbing her cheek against the puppy's silk coat
and making it whimper with pleasure. "Beelzebub! Why did you give the poor
little thing a name like *that?*"

At which Tom Archer whispered an explanation in her ear that turned it lobster-
shell red.

"So some of those 'gentlemen' are hopelessly loyal to Emily York?" Ellery
mused aloud. "Do anything for her? Anything at all?"

"That's what Miss Sullivan said."

"And would it be out of order to hypothesize that some of the aforesaid gentlemen
might be equally loyal to Miss Sullivan?"

The Inspector regarded his son with shock and, very nearly, distaste. "If you're
hinting that Miss Sullivan is capable of hiring some soup moocher to pull a murder
in order to increase Emily York's share in the estate, Ellery, you have an evil mind.
Why, that woman could no more do such a thing than—than I could!"

"Don't jump salty, Dad," Ellery grinned. "What's with this old lady? You
sound as if you've fallen in love."

"I've talked to her," his father mumbled. "You haven't."

"Exactly. Therefore my judgment remains unimpaired. And besides," Ellery
said, holding up a peace-making palm at the glint in his father's eyes, "the kill
might have been made without her knowing a thing about it. Just for the sake of
argument: Let's suppose somebody's planning big things for that village of theirs.
Let's say further that the ladies know nothing about it—and so that we won't be
detoured, let's not speculate just now about who's sending the cards. Now then:
What do we have?"

"I don't know what we have," said the Inspector irritably, "but I damn well
know what we don't have. We don't have an earthly reason—assuming all this is
being done to make that dream village come true—for *Emily's* life to be threatened.
Because Nathaniel York, Senior's will specifically calls for equal shares or all to
survivor. That means that when Robert got his head blotted out, his share went
into the family stew. And if Emily should be murdered, *her* share would have to
follow Robert's into the pot—*not* into a personal estate which she could will to the
building of the village. So Miss Selliv—I mean, the village project can't possibly
be the motive behind Robert's death and Emily's getting the second card."

"Oh, but it can," said the son.

The Inspector shoved his jaw out. "You show me how!"

Ellery began to push the two cards around on the coffee table. "Why," he
murmured, "have we been calling the H-card Emily's card?"

"What?" the old man said blankly.

"I said, Why do we assume this H-card is meant for Emily?"

"Because—because"—the Inspector spluttered—"what in time kind of question's
that?—because the envelope it came in was *addressed to her!* Because when you
set the card with the H right side up—with that off-center crossbar in the high

position, the way it's meant to be—it gives you the house due north of Robert's, and that's Emily's.''

"You mean like this?"

The Inspector stared down at the way Ellery arranged the cards:

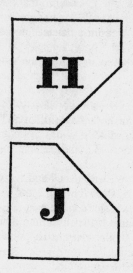

"Certainly!"

"But suppose the sender of the cards," said Ellery, his silvery eyes tarnished no longer but polished to a glitter, "suppose he's one of those very clever coots you read about in detective stories—"

"Especially yours," muttered the old man.

"—especially mine," nodded his son, "and Rex's, and John's, and Miss Christie's, and other practitioners' of the delightfully improbable. And suppose he's playing a game with you—us. And he says to himself: Let's see how good they are. Let's play ducks and drakes and fat red herrings. Let's see if they can figure out—before the event—that I really meant the H-card to be in *this* position."

And, swiftly, Ellery's long fingers turned the H-card upside down and shifted it from the northwest corner of the hypothetical square to the southeast corner:

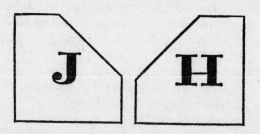

"My God," breathed the Inspector. But then he shook his head. "No," he said. "When you turn the card upside down this way, it makes the crossbar of the H come below-center instead of above. And that's wrong."

"Usually," agreed Ellery. "But I've seen it below-center. And in some fonts dead-center."

"But the address on the envelope—'Miss *Emily* York'—"

"That's where our opponent gets to laugh. Deliberately throwing a threat at one house when he intends it for another, knowing how we'll hate ourselves in the morning."

"But in that position it's *Myra* York's house!"

"Myra York's house," nodded Ellery; and the silver clouded. "Myra York, who's feeble and of no use to anybody except possibly this Helen of Troy who takes care of her—Myra York, who wouldn't begin to know what to do with all those bushels of money. And with Myra York out of the way, there'll be even more bushels for somebody who does know what to do with 'em. Somebody like Emily York, say—who in this hypothesis would still be alive, remember. Emily York, or, by extension, her—and your—Miss Sullivan, whose motive has to be construed as identical with Emily's. So you see why you can't rule out that unbuilt village as being behind this game, Dad?"

Inspector Queen was thinking doggedly: Not-Miss-Sullivan-I-don't-care-what-you-say. But aloud he muttered, "Maybe Myra York, hmm? . . . Well, we can't chance it. I'll phone headquarters."

"No riot squads, *please*," Ellery called from the foyer, where he was shrugging into his topcoat. "I'll see to Myra's safety. Dad—this once—let's see if we can't catch our quarry instead of scaring it away?"

"Very funny," snorted his father. "No, no riot squads, just a stake-out of watchful pedestrians. And what's this I-we-our stuff?" The old gentleman grinned suddenly. "I thought you were through with case work."

"Get thee behind me," growled Ellery. "And while I'm in that territory—may the player on the other side be damned! He's crazy, and that puts him way outside the competence of chemistry and the computers."

"What d'ye mean crazy?" shouted the puzzled Inspector. But he had only an eagerly slammed door and happily sprinting footsteps for an answer.

13 · Tactics

The blonde (they have surprising sensibilities, some of them) made a little *moue* when her eye fell on the Gideon Bible. She picked it up and slid it into a drawer, out of sight. "But, Poochie," she said, "you're just no *fun* right now."

"Don't take it personal," said Percival York, from the bed. He opened his mouth to its widest with an audible *yawp!* and with his thumbnail and forefinger he went hunting for a piece of steak caught between a lower left bicuspid and a molar. After a brief struggle he captured it, glared at it redly, then ate it. "I'm living through the longest six months in my whole entire life. The longer it gets, the worse it gets, and the worst it gets, the more time it takes."

"Yes, and that awful thing about your brother, too."

"My *cousin*. And you can't say that is so altogether awful."

"Poochie!"

"Oh, God, lemme for once in my life say what I want to say like I want to say it without some bluenose bastid telling me how I should say it!"

"Are you calling me a bluenose bas—"

"No-no-no—not you—no," Percival York said hurriedly. "I just get mad sometimes, is all. You can say anything you want if you say it some special way. Like my cousin's head was *struck* by a stone block—all right; but my cousin's head was *squashed* by a stone block—oh, no. Like you can say *lady of the evening* to anybody, you can say *prostitute* to a lot of people, but if you say *whore* everybody gets mad."

"Poochie!"

"Just a figure of speech, like, baby. Now about my cousin. I got real sick of that Robert sitting on his big fat money—yeah, and on a lot of mine as well!— looking down his nose at me *whatever* I did. Am I a poor relative? Am I old enough to do what I want?"

"You're not *old*, Poochie."

"But all the same, it's like he ain't dead yet. It's worse. Cops hanging around. Old Emily shoving her nose in where Robert's used to be. I can't even bring a chick to my own house, I got to come to a fleabag like this! You don't think I'll even get to sign the bill downstairs without an argument, do you? And besides, that bastid Archer."

"Who?"

"Some bastid college wise kid Robert hired, *he's* still there and, mind you, watching the estate—watching *my* money. It ain't like I didn't talk nice to him, y'understand. Why, I could lower the boom on him so fast!—but I never, and I got more gold coming to me than he ever saw or ever will. 'See it my way, old pal,' I says to him, 'and you'll never regret it.' When I didn't have to ask him a-tall, I could of told him! But you think he could see it my way? Hell, no. 'I'm just as sorry as I can be, Mister York,' " Percival minced and mimicked, " 'there isn't a thing in the world I can do. It's up to the Board of Trustees.' "

"But, Poochie, it *is* up to the Board of—"

"He could of been on my side at least, f'evven's sake," Percival whined. "It's bad enough I got to go to some college jerk to try and spring a few grand to pay some bills without I got to walk off with my tail between my legs. He'll be sorry he ever saw the day. What's left in the bottle?"

The blonde handed him the bottle and he looked not at it but into it, as one does into a television screen. "One thing he'll never get the chance to do again is stop my credit. Stop my credit in a store, the bastid. How do you like the nerve?"

"Archer did that?"

"Naah, not Archer, my squash-head cousin Robert, and it serves him right. Even my bookie." In mounting rage, Percival gripped and shook the bottle like a hated throat. "So much as a pair of socks I got no credit. Right down to the damn liquor store!" he shouted, raising the bottle to hurl it across the room while the girl squeezed her eyes shut and put her hands over her ears. But when after a moment she opened her eyes, he was still sprawled on the bed, the bottle was still raised, and his own eyes were screwed down tight. His high forehead shone with the sweat of rage. Slowly he lowered the bottle and drank hard and set it cautiously on the night table.

"You don't want to get so worked up, Poochie," the blonde said with anxiety.

He opened his eyes and gradually brought her overlapping curves into focus. "Six months to wait for that money and sometimes I don't know if I can make it. Tell you something, long as them two are still breathing, that spooked creep Myra and that Emily"—he spat on the threadbare rug—"I got to wait the whole six months. The hell, I wish they'd get their heads squooshed, too. Like to squoosh 'em myself. Fact, maybe I will."

"Poochie!"

"You think I wouldn't? Old Robert gets his head squished and he can't run down no more of my credit accounts, can he?"

Surprisingly, she said, "Poochie, he never."

"Who never? What are you talking?"

"It wasn't him. Lenny told me."

"Lenny who? Told you what?"

"Lenny Mauchheimer, he's the manager at that cut-rate bottle store of yours. He said it was your sister Emily."

"I know it was my sis—*cousin*, damn it! I woo'n't have the likes of her for a sister, I'd of beat her brains out in her crib. Sure it was Emily. But Robert put her up to it."

"Lenny says no. Lenny says the way she tells him off he gives odds it's her own idea."

"Oh, God, it figures, it figures. That Robert, now, he was a blocker, know what I mean? Try something, he stops you. But he never *started* nothing. Emily, she's a starter, got more goddamn guts than a brass bucket of chitlins. She's all the time scared I might get sued and somebody grabs a lien on the whole estate. Sure, it was Emily from the start. Robert, I apologize."

"You said there's enough to handle *anything*."

"I told you she's crazy. How do you like that? Stops my accounts. Bluenose ol' frigate wouldn't know how to spend it anyways. Lemme check," he said suddenly.

He reached for the phone, dialed for an outside line, then dialed again. While he waited for the ring his whole being seemed to change. He still sprawled in the bed; he still presented an ungracious view of pigeon shoulders, red eyes, hairy chest and scrawny lower ribs resembling spread hands pressed into risen dough. Yet when he spoke his voice was resonant, his diction perfect, his accent Harvard— somewhere between beginning-senior and postgraduate consistency; such a voice must have behind it entire walls of morocco-bound volumes.

As she watched, the blonde slowly raised her enameled hands to her mouth and covered it with one, with both, and permitted the escape of a single tiny nicker from her Swedish nostrils. Percival York, in the midst of his performance, gave her a broad wink which detracted not, by the shadow of a subjunctive, from it.

Into the phone he said, "Mr. Pierce? Ah. This is Mr. Tomlinson of Swath, Tomlinson, Sweggar and Peach. In a routine survey of the Nathaniel York, Senior accounts, we find here a notation that Mr., ah, Percival York has canceled his credit arrangement with you. He has? Pending, ah, settlement? Very sound—yes, indeed. He sent you an advisory, of course? I beg your—? Oh, a messenger. *Not* a messenger? My goodness. Eh, eh, eh." (It was at this lofty and controlled expression of mirth that the blonde forcibly corked her wide mouth and valved her hilarity down to a nasal susurrus.) "Miss Emily, of course. Eh! Eh! Still very sound. Good day to you, sir, you stoopid bastid."

Percival hung up, and the blonde's squawk of merriment fused with his enraged shout: "How you like that, the stinkin' ol' *bitch?* You know what I'm gonna do to her? Oh, God, I can't think of anything bad enough; I'd like to cut her up some way she could watch herself bleed to death. Wait a minute."

He snatched the phone again, dialed outside, then another number. This time, when he spoke, there descended on him a mien so furtive, so seedy, that even on him it showed. His voice was harsh and quiet and issued from far back in his throat, and his almost nonexistent lips moved for labial sounds only—nothing else. "Freddy Merck here. Yeah, Detroit. Hey, I got a placement, second and third races Goshen. Long distance, that there Percy York. Yeah, Percy York. Why he calls long distance is his business but I hear a word around, don't play him, he's got a cousin Robert York sends a cousin Emily York around telling lay off or else. So I stalls him, he's calling back. Whadda ya know?"

Quite easily audible throughout the dingy room, the receiver answered back with a quiet harshness to match Percival York's mimicking, though its sibilants were cigar-squelched and its intonations archetypical Brooklynese. "Whaddaya mean you hear a word around? I myself phoned you the first one practically about this hatchet-puss Emily York barged in here and lays it on the line. And where'd you get this b.s. about this cousin Robert York sending her? Listen, Merck, *nobody* sends that broad; she makes trouble around here all the time. So what the hell's with you? Hey? Is this Merck? Hey! Who the hell is this?"

"This," said Percival in the episcopal tones of some giant cathedral bell, "is God, and it were well you mended your ways." He hung up with a new roar of indignation at Emily York's duplicity, which clashed in the air with the blonde's screek of laughter.

"The dirty old two-face bluenose *bitch!*".

"Oh, Poochie, you shouldn't talk like that. You never hurt a fly."

"A fly," raged Percival York sententiously, "never hurt me."

14 · Strategy

Ellery rang, and waited, and rang again; but he could only bring himself to wait four seconds or so. He had his thumb on the bell for the third time when the door opened and a small straight lady in her early fifties, wearing an impossibly white apron, put out her hand and said, "All *right* already. Don't the bell geschplit," in tones of the hex and the schnitzelbank, of Appelbachsville and Perkasie, land of the noodle and strudel.

"Miss York?" said Ellery. "Miss Myra York?"

"She's not in," said the small lady, "and she is out, besides," and she began to close the door. Ellery deftly blocked her.

"You'll be Mrs. Schriver."

"Ach," she said, "I will, will I?"

"I've got to see her," said Ellery. "It's urgent."

"She nobody never sees and your name I don't care what is."

"My name is Queen."

"No, it ent," Mrs. Schriver said flatly.

There had been times when Ellery had desired to conceal his identity; he had seldom had to assert it. It was a strange experience. "I am so!"

"No, you *ent*," the housekeeper said, and shoved at the door. Ellery shoved back. "Mr. Queen was already here whoever-you-are."

"That was my father!" Ellery cried through the narrowing doorway—she could push very hard. "I'm Ellery—*Ellery* Queen."

She opened the door and leaned close enough to him to scan his hairline and eyes. "By gummitch, it could be. A very nice man your father is. Why he calls you Ellery, Ellery?"

Ellery let it go, "Mrs. Schriver, is Miss Myra all right? I think she might be in danger."

Mrs. Schriver bridled. Though her hair was pulled back so hard from her brow that her forehead gleamed with tension, she conveyed the impression of hackles rising. Her blue eyes leveled, and above them appeared two angry eaves. "From *who*, danger?" And this, thought Ellery, is the bodyguard's bodyguard—if she cares about the body in question, and she does.

"I'm not sure," he said candidly. "But I'd rather be careful and not need to, than need to and be careless."

Approvingly she swung the door wide. "Come in."

He entered and in one swoop took in the neat wild miscellaneous character of the place. "Where is she?"

"In her room—" The intonation of the housekeeper's Pennsylvania Dutch voice was such that the three words were incomplete; yet what more there might have been was snipped off and silenced by a firm quick clamping of the lips. "You have her to see, mister, or to see her you want? Which?"

Ellery smiled. "What I must do is make sure that she's all right, and that she stays all right. But I want to see her, too."

"But she is all right." Mrs. Schriver was still weighing the issues carefully.

"You know what happened to Robert York, Mrs. Schriver."

"*Gott.*" She flashed a look upward, either at Myra York's bedroom or higher. Suddenly she said, "I will see if you can come up."

"Is Miss Drew with her?"

From the stairs Mrs. Schriver said, "No, Miss Drew is out the dog walking," and went up at an energetic pace.

Ellery grinned and glanced about. To his left he caught a glimpse of the marble head of a laughing girl, and he stepped into the parlor to admire it, which he did whole-heartedly. He was reflecting that there ought to be a law, or at least an artistic convention, demanding that all things as beautiful as this be mounted against such a horrendous background of gimcrackery as was in this room, when he became aware of upstairs voices—one quietly, steadily pleading, the other trembling on the limits of control and, somehow shockingly, even quieter than the other.

"He can't come up. I won't go down. I'll never see him again. I knew he'd come. I won't see him. I said I'd never speak to him again and I won't. Send him away. I won't—" On and on and on, in a smooth terrible cooing, while the Dutch voice soothed and assured: "Shoosh, *Liebchen,* him it is not. You believe me, honest. Shoosh. He is going, he is gone already. And besides, it is not him at all." That the Dutch voice gradually won, Ellery detected by the waning of both voices, until at last they were only troubled breathing and solicitous breath.

He stood in the foyer for a long time listening to what he could hear and then for what he could not hear—so respectful of the silence that he was afraid to creak a floorboard or a toe-joint lest he cause that dreadful whispering hysteria to come to life again.

At last Mrs. Schriver came downstairs, making not a sound. Very close to Ellery she said, "She is all right now, but she is not all right."

Ellery got the message. "As long as she's all right," he nodded. "I obviously came at the wrong time, Mrs. Schriver. Stay with her as much as you can. Take care of her."

"Ach, I will," she muttered, and showed him to the door. At the door, the housekeeper said suddenly, "Miss Myra thinks I say Mallory. You come again back, hear?"

"Mallory?" Ellery said swiftly, but she had shut him out. He shook his head and stepped into York Square.

The last of the day was merging with the first glow of the city's night. Ellery glanced with curiosity at the old-fashioned street lamps, little and low and gleaming yellow, one to each facet of the park's diamond shape, and each precisely opposite the entrance to one of the absurd Disneyland castles. The lamps had been electrified, but whimsically, so that they duplicated their gaseous past, making themselves merely visible without importantly illuminating anything. If Robert's killer were the sniper-from-the-shadows type, Ellery mused, the little park wouldn't be bad for his future operations.

Strolling along the southeast margin of York Park, he wondered what this killer was made of. Am I right in concluding, he thought, that the H-card may be meant for Myra York rather than Emily? Have I really anticipated his strategy? In either case, how will he move? *If at all!*—since it suddenly occurred to Ellery that the Player's first move might have been his last—that threatening the life of Emily . . . *or* Myra . . . was a tactical feint, the prime purpose of the Game, the removal of Robert from the Board having been its only purpose. And is the dropping of two-hundred-pound granite blocks his M.O., or is his earmark versatility? . . .

At this moment a patrol car pulled into the Square and passed Ellery. Instead of turning off and away at the next corner, it cruised all around the park and suddenly screeched about and rocked to a stop, its headlights exploding in his eyes.

"Oh," said the patrol car. "Excuse me, Mr. Queen." The car shot back and moved on. Through watering eyes Ellery saw it pause at the northwest corner while a man in a light topcoat stepped out of nowhere and exchanged a few words.

And maybe he does mean to try again, Ellery thought, and I'm glad I'm not the only one who thinks so.

At the southern point of York Park stood the person he was (at the moment) looking for. She was staring reflectively at the dark rectangle of a bronze plaque inlaid in the turf. Ellery came silently up behind her and squinted over her shoulder.

IN LIVING MEMORY
OF
NATHANIEL YORK, JR.
BORN APRIL 20, 1924

"Looks like a misprint," he remarked.

"*Oh!*" she shrieked, starting violently; and there came whirling into the yellow light toward Ellery a face so harmoniously proportioned, with such liquidly level great eyes, so sculptured a mouth, such delicately arched nostrils, that his pulse raced off in instant pursuit; in spite of his father's warnings, Ellery had expected anything but this.

"Wow," Ellery said. "I mean, I beg your pardon. I mean, for frightening you half to death. I certainly didn't mean to." There was a ferocious "Yeep!" from the puppy at the other end of the leash she was holding, and Ellery recoiled and said foolishly, "There seem to be two or three 'means' too many."

With indignation already chasing fear, she dropped both to laugh. He had not heard such music in his life. To his own amazement, he felt himself moved to coyness. "And, sir, your pardon, too," he heard his voice say to the puppy. "You must be Miss Drew."

"*I'm* Miss Drew," said the girl (Mozart, he thought, the shimmery movement of the 40th). "*That* is Bub. Short for Beelzebub, my bodyguard."

"Again your pardon, sir," he said to the puppy.

"Miss," she corrected him.

He defended himself—"It *is* dark"—and smiled at her. For sheerest joy, that there could be any face ever quite so pleasing. "My name is Queen."

"*Ellery* Queen." She was not visibly impressed. "I know your father." And she began to speak of the Inspector in the warmest way, as if he were an old dear friend.

Ellery had to chuckle. He was always running into perfect strangers, passersby, who breathed, "*Ellery Queen?* Why, I've read your—" or "Queen! Who solved the Yiffniff Case?" He had even felt it not too unbecoming on occasion, in his books, to refer to that looking-glass version of himself as "the great man." So far none of this was in effect in York Square. It was the paternal Queen who had apparently opened doors and hearts.

"You make my feet too small for his footsteps," he said sweepingly. "And my *chapeau* too big for my suddenly shrunken head."

"Oh, I know about you, too," Ann Drew said quickly; and how, in that ochreous light, could he know that she blushed? "What was that you said about a misprint?"

He pointed to the plaque, its Walt-burnished letters shining faintly from the darkness. *"Living* memory," he said. "It's usually *loving."*

"Not with old Nathaniel it wasn't," the girl said promptly. "From what I've heard, he didn't make mistakes—misprints or any other kind. And as for 'loving,' the scuttlebutt is he hadn't much of that in him."

"Nathaniel, Junior was his son?"

"And only child," Ann nodded. "Loving or not, that old monster had an empire to leave Junior and he meant to do just that. Young Nathaniel had other ideas and got out from under. Senior simply wouldn't accept it. So much so that when word came of Junior's death the old man refused to acknowledge it."

"Hence *Living.* Hm!" Ellery studied the plaque. "Hence a birth date only—no date of death. Quaint! Junior *is* dead, I take it?"

"Well, unless you're a hair-splitter. He ran away to sea, jumped ship in a one-burro Central American port, headed for the jungle—and except for some broken camera parts, a sun hat and a belt buckle he was never seen alive again. The hat, by the way, was split in two by some unblunt instrument."

"Where were the things found?"

"About forty miles upstream, in a shallow grave. The native who stumbled over it headed downriver to spread the news and get a reward, if any, and he brought the belt buckle with him in proof of his story. Unfortunately," the girl added, "when the port authorities went back with him they found that he'd left the grave open. You just don't do that in those jungles, not unless you're satisfied with bits and pieces."

Ellery looked at her wonderingly. "A gruesome tale for lips of coral."

"The grue wears off after you've heard the tale twenty times and told it twenty more," she said coolly. "Oh, I can be shocked, Mr. Queen. You should have heard my maidenly shriek when that devil Tom Archer told me why my shepherd's name is Beelzebub."

"Why is it?"

"That," said Ann Drew grimly, "I'll never tell. You or *anybody."*

"Oh," said Ellery, trying not to dislike Tom Archer on such vague grounds. "So old Nathaniel would never admit his son was dead?"

She toed the plaque with the tip of her improbably slim little shoe. "That's the evidence. He backed it up, too, with that will of his."

"Oh, yes, the will," Ellery murmured. "The papers have been full of it since Robert lost his head. They haven't been able to make much out of that first clause after the whereases, the one leaving everything to young Nathaniel if only he'll show up breathing to claim it. And that would be a matter of some concern to the York cousins, of course. Aren't they all nephews and nieces of Nathaniel, Senior?"

"That's right. It's a complicated genealogy, but as I understand it Nathaniel, Senior was the only one in the direct line, so he inherited all the money and York Square and so on. The whole family's dead—and accounted for, incidentally; no belt-buckle business—except the four cousins."

"Three."

"Three," she amended soberly. "Who did it, Mr. Queen?"

"I'll tell you," Ellery promised, "but not now."

"You don't know now."

"Something like that." He regarded her with fixity, and she held it with level eyes. "Have you any ideas?"

Ann made a face, but what she could make, with a lovely face like that, was only another lovely face. He noticed her glance flicker toward the northeast house, and away. "Whatever I think is pure wish," she said, and suddenly performed a tomboy grin Ellery found enchanting. "Don't quote me, or anything. It's only a feeling."

"Percival?" At her guilty start Ellery said, "You glanced at his house. Any more substantial basis for the feeling?"

"Oh . . . the disgusting way he talks—and most of all, I suppose, the way he looks at me. As if . . ." A rather helpless sound came through those astonishing nostrils. "Well, look. I'm afraid to wear a fitted coat. Actually. Just last week I bought something designed by Omar the Tentmaker. I *hate* it," she said between her teeth, turning now to face Percival York's castle resentfully. "I suppose you'll think that's silly, buying something you don't like because of the way a man looks at you?"

Ellery had to brace to keep his arms from offering their manly sympathy. "There are girls who accept that sort of look as a compliment," he said avuncularly.

"To be looked at as if you're stark naked? No, thank you! But it's worse than that. He looks your *skin* off, too. Sees right through to your bones, like an X-ray, drooling all the while. I don't know who did that—that thing to Robert York, Mr. Queen, but any time something like that happens to *him*"—it struck him suddenly that not once had she voiced Percival's name, as if to do so would materialize him like an evil spirit—"you'd better come looking for me."

Poor, lovely, troubled child, Ellery thought, still in the uncle vein. "If I do," he smiled down at her, "it needn't be for committing a murder. So don't. I mean, *please* don't."

It worked. She began to twinkle. "All right, Mr. Queen, I won't."

"And according to the will the four cousins have had to occupy the four houses to be eligible for the jackpot?"

"You change subjects right deftly, sir," Ann Drew murmured. "Yes, for ten years, which in six months they'll have duly done. I think old Nathaniel hoped they'd all raise little Yorks to live on and on here and create race memory and preserve family tradition and all that. The will permits them to do anything they want with the interiors of the houses, but the Square and York Park have to remain untouched by human hands, except for the maintenance."

"But none of the four married?"

"Not once. Robert was afraid, Emily couldn't bear the thought, Myra just wouldn't, and Percival just can't—he's already married to his own sweet self."

"Now, now," Ellery cautioned her, waving her away from the dark subject—and, in a self-betraying moment, finding his hands grasping her upper arms to turn her forcibly away from the northeast castle. Her flesh was soft-not soft, just right for male hands, and he released her and with an effort avoided inspecting his hands which, for a mad moment he was convinced, must now be luminous. "You're probably right about Robert's fear of marriage—his perfectionism and rather defensive sense of fairness would have shied him off. And my father gave me a pretty succinct impression of Emily; you may be right there, too. But why do you say Myra wouldn't?''

"I can't tell you that,'' she said without hesitation.

"You can't, or you shan't?''

"All right, I shan't.''

"Oh, come—'' Ellery began, only half teasing; but she said, "No. Please. It isn't my story to tell. It's Myra York's. And will you take my word that it wouldn't affect the case?''

He considered her carefully. He liked her loyalty. He also liked . . . But just now he was working. He said suddenly, "It concerns Mallory, doesn't it?''

"Then you do know!''

Blessing the darkness, Ellery stood still and kept silent.

"He must have been a real stinker,'' Ann said passionately.

"Mm,'' agreed Ellery. He tried a wild one. "She expects him back, doesn't she?''

"Every minute. Every living minute. And the older she gets, the worse it gets. It's got so she thinks every knuckle on the door, every passing footstep, is Mallory's.''

"She thought I was Mallory, according to Mrs. Schriver.''

"Ellery—Mallory—of course! Oh, dear!'' Ann cried. "She's so *fuddled*. She's lived so long with the single idea of turning him away if he ever comes back that nothing else exists for her. She's quite sensitive in some ways, you know—about the phone, the doorbell; she's quick as a cat to hear them. And then sometimes she figures things out with remarkable good sense. Like . . . well, I remember thinking, with Robert dead and the big estate coming due—so much more of it now—that would bring Mallory back if anything would. I naturally didn't voice this. You know, the very next day after Robert was killed—when everyone was saying oh poor old Myra York, she doesn't even grasp what's happened—she said to me out of a clear sky, 'Well, Ann, I suppose he'll be back the moment he hears about *this*.' And then she asked me, 'Do I still have that lovely black lace dress, the one with the little collar?' She's actually planning to be all dressed up for the big scene when Mallory shows up and she tells him haughtily to go and never darken her door again! Which, of course, she wouldn't tell him at all,'' Ann said suddenly, "even if he did show up. She'd go all to pieces, I think beyond mending. But it's all she has, this dream of telling Mallory off for having left her at the church. That, and . . . Well, it's all she has.''

Ellery decided to ignore the "and . . .'' for the moment. "It's been a long time, hasn't it?''

"Oh yes, nearly fifteen years. During which the poor thing's been slipping slowly downhill until—'' But the girl stopped there.

Ellery made a lightning decision. "Miss Drew, you'd better be aware of this. I'm afraid Myra York may be in considerable danger of sharing Robert's fate.''

"*Myra* York?'' gasped Ann. "But . . .'' And then she spun about. "*Who's that?''

A male figure was clattering toward them, waving his arms like a Signal Corpsman at the height of a battle. "Ann! Ann, is that you?''

"Tom!''

Tom Archer came panting up out of the gloom, gasping and gulping. "Ann . . .''

"Tom, what's the matter, what's happened?''

"Ann.'' The young man stared unseeingly at Ellery. "Miss York's been *killed!''*

15 · Attack Resumed

He had written:

> . . . *place yourself at the seventh pillar counting from the downtown end of the station, keeping the pillar between yourself and the downtown entrance.*
>
> *Be there promptly at 5:20 P.M.*
>
> *At 5:30 begin to watch carefully the crowds coming into the station.*
>
> *At approximately 5:42 you will see her enter the station. She will probably stop between the fourth and fifth pillars, facing the express tracks. She will doubtless remove a newspaper from under her arm, refold it, and begin to read: if so, so much the better. If not, you will have to be a little more careful.*
>
> *When you are sure she will not observe you, stroll to her location and stand near her and behind her.*
>
> *At 5:49 the uptown express is due into the station. As this train comes in, while it is still traveling at speed, and at the last possible second you will push her from the platform into its path.*
>
> *Do not attempt to run. You will find a great press of people toward the spot. Work your way backward until the crowd thins out. There will be a local train waiting with its doors open. Step inside and sit down, and remain there quietly until the train moves off. If by any chance there is no train, wait for one.*
>
> *You may ignore the presence of guards or police. This is my plan and I shall protect you.*
>
> *I am with you wherever you go, whatever you do. I know where you are at all times; and I know what you say, and what you see, and what you think. I know, for example, that you know who I am and that you will not bring yourself to speak my name.*
>
> *Be sure, as always, to dispose of this as you have my other letters.*
>
> *I know I need no longer advise you as to your conduct during the interesting days and nights ahead. This formula will guard the rightness of all you do, and will protect you against your enemies and mine: Be yourself, be obedient to me, trust in me.*
>
> *For I possess all powers, My Dear Walt, and I am everywhere.*
>
> Y

16 · Further Development

It was, Ellery was to reflect later, in the deepest sense kaleidoscopic. "Miss York's been *killed!*"—mere syllables, shaped disturbances of the atmosphere; but in their precise time and place they imparted a rhythmic shifting and reassembling of people and events that was sheerly ever changing and ever beautiful. Bit met bit slowly, perfectly, mingling, passing, permuting, the final pattern unrealized until the very end. And yet each shifting bit was detached and distinct, in its own substance unchanging and unchanged—and had been so (and this was the tantalizing worst of it) from the beginning, seeable and knowable by the discerning eye.

But there had been no discerning eye . . .

"Miss York's been *killed!*"

The motion starting the kaleidoscope on its course, imparted by the four words in Tom Archer's gulp-and-gasp, was at first explosive. It was the instant flight of Ann Drew, bounding across the street, leaping to and through the door of the southeast castle, flying past the housekeeper and up the stairs, to rock Myra York in her soft-not soft young arms and weep at last.

It was Ellery, turning at a sudden hail from the street wondering with some lesser part of his mind how the car had got there without his hearing it; running to it, exchanging a word with its driver, then calling to young Tom, who, after delivering his fulminating message, had stood drawn and shaken: "Mr. Archer! Go home, please, and wait for the police!"—his voice an uncharacteristic whiplash.

It was Percival York, paying off a taxi at his door, flanked suddenly by two tall men in topcoats, one of whom said, "Get inside, please, Mr. York," with an iron politeness whose urgency communicated itself to Percival's feet.

It was Inspector Queen, in the Queen apartment, banging down the telephone and to his own surprise uttering a word which, when he had heard it from the lips of a raided madam, had shocked even him; then running out clutching hat and coat to meet the squad car he could already hear wailing toward him.

And it was Walt, forty minutes later, blinking at the tall form of the patrolman who opened the door when Walt touched Emily York's bell.

"Who are you?"

"Walt," said Walt. "Miss Emily sent me for these." He extended a package. Inspector Queen charged out, looking wild. "Package for Emily York," said the officer with unvoiced meaning.

"It's the handyman. What is that, Walt?"

"Miss Emily sent me uptown for it."

The Inspector took the package, opened it. "Map pins?"

"A special kind I get her on East Eighty-Seventh Street."

"You just got back from getting these?"

Walt nodded.

"Do you know what's happened to Miss Emily?"

"No," said Walt.

"She was killed by a subway train." When the handyman simply stood there, expressionless, the Inspector decided to interpret it as shock, and some of the harshness went out of his voice. "I'll keep these," he said. "You go to your room now and wait for someone to come question you." He looked again at the man. "You understand that?"

"Yes," said Walt.

"Go with him," the Inspector said to the officer. "Then come back here."

The old man stood glumly in the lighted doorway, watching the comings and goings of police cars, marked and unmarked. Soon—damn it all, there, now!—the press. And tomorrow Joe Dokes and his missus, shuffling through York Square and gawking at the four York castles. Why did people do it? Why this herd curiosity about a street, a house, windows, doors? He was a public servant, the Inspector mused, but there were times when he would enjoy loading all rubbernecks onto barges and towing them out to sea to be served, with ceremony, to sharks.

And speaking of sharks. Sure, the press made approving noises about Hero Cop Slays Maniac. But the noises they made over some human fault in a police officer were Niagara's roar by contrast. Oh well, it wasn't a beef he articulated much any more; it was rather a daily low bitter-tasting rumble at the back of his throat. Once you learned that to the press only the noise mattered, you could almost take it.

But you didn't have to like it, and that tall figure hurrying across the park with the seeming-to-lounge distance-eating stride, that would be one of them. By God, just this once he'd blast. Get the newshounds off his tail right at the start and keep 'em off till this confounded thing began to make sense . . . Sure enough the fellow was coming straight for Emily York's . . . sure enough, thought the Inspector as he filled his lungs, he was going to let this one have it!

But it said, "Dad?"

The old man let out the lungful, tipped his head down and sidewise, and glared at his son. The son stopped at the foot of Emily York's steps. "Seems I was wrong," Ellery said.

"Don't start your breast-beating," snapped the Inspector. "Come on in," and he went back into Emily York's bleak foyer, leaving the door open for the penitent.

"You know something?" Ellery muttered when he was inside. "Six families and nine homicidal lunatics could live in this place and hide eighty-seven kid printing sets, and who'd know?" For along the hallway leading back to the kitchen, every door but one was shut, every transom dark. "Poor Emily."

"Poor anybody's murder," said his father. "And especially this one, because it hurts more people more badly than even what that subway train did to Emily York."

"You're still thinking of Miss Sullivan."

"All right, so I'm still thinking of Miss Sullivan!" Inspector Queen snarled. "Yes, and of all the hundreds of deadbeats who'd've had a catch of breath and maybe a new start, too! And now won't get either."

They fell silent.

Finally Ellery said, "You do call it murder? Positively?"

"I do, and I will. Even when my nose is rubbed in the fact that we don't stand a monkey's chance of proving it." The Inspector shrugged. "Well, at least it clears *her*."

"Does it?"

The old man stared. "What do you mean does it? Emily's dead, remember?"

"She still might have murdered *Robert*. So *her* murder might be an answer of sorts after all."

"You're not serious!"

"And you're so right," Ellery said gloomily. "I'm not. About the only fact that stands out is that Emily's death diverts her hunk of the millions from that drawing-board village to the York estate—and to whoever survives. What do you have there, Dad?"

"Where? Oh, this. Map pins." The old man opened the box. "Made in West Germany. Sold by a specialty shop in Yorkville." He squinted at the sales slip. "Bought by Walt. He just got back from there, didn't even know Emily York was dead. When I told him, he was speechless. But with Walt you never know. From all the expression on his face, I might have told him the time."

"Dad," said Ellery. "Just how dumb is Walt?"

"How dumb is a robot? Ask me something answerable."

They were walking up the hall now, and Ellery said, "Where are we going?"

"Emily's room. Once a maid's room. Just off the kitchen." The Inspector paused outside the one open doorway. Ellery went past him into the room and looked around.

There was an aged roll-top desk with a chair as hard-seated and straight-backed as its late owner. The most prominent thing in the crowded little room was a free-standing clothespress of Georgian vintage, a monstrous piece with immense over-hanging gingerbread eaves and a coat of dusty yellow calcimine. What passed for a bed was a narrow slab of three-fourth-inch plywood standing on six gas-pipe legs with crutch ferrules for feet, its mattress a lumpy affair covered in duck and no more than three inches thick. Except for another smaller chair, that was all.

"Brother," said Ellery with a shiver.

"Well, all she did was sleep here," grunted the Inspector, "and do her paperwork."

"She slept here and worked here and at the settlement house. Where in God's name did she *live?*"

"This was what she called living."

"All this self-denial for a dream that never came true." Ellery popped a cigarette between his lips savagely. "But about Walt," he mumbled as he lit it. "Where is he now, Dad?"

"I sent him to his room with a man to make sure he gets there. Forget Walt, Ellery. He couldn't be behind a thing as carefully planned as this." The Inspector tossed the package of map pins onto the alleged bed.

They both turned at a curious patois of noises. A policeman appeared from the front hall.

"Inspector Queen, he insists—"

"First things first," the Inspector said. "What about the handyman?"

"The dummy? I got him tucked in okay. But then on the way back—"

The officer was overridden, and, from the sound of it and his growl of protest, thrust aside; for there appeared in the doorway the livid specter that was Percival York, eye-whites saffron with rage, tall forehead scored with it. "There you are, Queen! I *demand* to know the meaning of this. Arrested on my own *doorstep*. Get *no* answers to questions. Someone said my cousin Emily's been killed. I *will not be persecuted!* Your job is to *protect* me. I could be in danger. I could be *next!*" The two plainclothesmen were in the foyer, waiting.

The Inspector spoke. He spoke very, very quietly, and Ellery experienced the almost sphincteral reaction of attentive awe which this special quietness had brought about in him from childhood.

Softly, then, the Inspector asked, *"Have* you been arrested, Mr. York?"

Nothing could be funny in the presence of that voice; otherwise Percival York's response would have been ludicrous. It began with one syllable of blustering shout; and with each succeeding one it diminished in volume dwindling down the emotional scale from fury to anger to irritation to perplexity to caution to finally frightened silence. "Well," he shouted; then, "What the hell do you call it when I, I, I . . ." Then he swallowed, and stood sweating.

The old man looked him up and down. "Where have you been during the last hour or so, Mr. York?"

"Out," said York sullenly, but under that frosty lens his defiance was childish and feeble. The Inspector certainly did not acknowledge it; he waited as if the man had merely coughed. Percival York then said, "I was with somebody."

"Who?"

In a repellent combination of wheedle-and-wink Percival York said, "Now, now, old boy, we wouldn't involve the name of a lady, would we?"

"All right, Mr. York," the soft voice said, "that means we can get right on down to Centre Street. If I have to check the alibis of eleven million people to break this case, I'm prepared to do it. But I'm starting at the top, Mr. York, and that means I'll spend ten weeks or ten years, if necessary, on you."

"Now see here—"

"Now *you* see here!" and the too-quiet voice at last crackled like heavy glass yielding to heat shock. "Your cousin Emily York is dead. You are one of two people who stand to gain the most by it. It's as simple as that. You'd better have one brass-bound beaut of an alibi, Mr. York! Are you ready to answer questions?"

Percival York was pale. "But I didn't—"

"I'm not asking you that," snarled the old man. "I asked you who you were with."

"Whom," murmured Ellery, and bit his tongue.

"Well . . ." Percival York stood stripped—of anger, arrogance, petulance, all pretense. What was left was ugliest self-concern. "All right."

"Thank you," said Inspector Queen. "No, not now." He turned to the policeman. "You take Mr. York home. He's to stay there till we come for his statement. And he's going to think his alibi over until it's just exactly right—aren't you, Mr. York?"

"See here," Percival York muttered. But it was an empty thing, a way of departing; and at the old man's very slight head motion York followed the uniformed man meekly out.

"What was that all about?" asked Ellery, after a moment. "You really think he did it?"

The father folded his arms and gazed out at nothing. "Worse luck," he said, "no," and looked suddenly at the son, sore-eyed. "Ellery, I let that jerk have it *because* he's a jerk. I don't like him. I don't like him so much I've had a tail on him ever since his cousin Robert stopped that stone block with his skull. Don't you think I know where Percival was today? Hell, I even know who he was with— whom!" The Inspector struck his fist, painfully, into open palm. "Don't look at me that way."

"Who, me?" Ellery understood what his father wanted to say and could not; that he had let the job climb on top of him, that personal motivation had crippled a good police officer's performance. "I can hardly afford it. With me it was cleverness, trying to outsmart the player on the other side, seeing a move that wasn't there. So off I tear to make sure my Myra's protected from the foul fiend, and he gives it to Emily as advertised. I'd suggest an immediate back-to-work movement. And for a start, from now until this thing is broken, you ought to put a tail on everyone—everyone, that is, whom you can't lock up or in. If it accomplishes nothing else, it'll at least relieve the pressure on the Morgue."

It seemed to help the old man, for he squared his spare shoulders and raised his head.

"And then," continued Ellery briskly, "problem: how to ferret out this cutie-pie."

"The hard way," sighed Inspector Queen. "We find out everything findable about everybody. Get it all on paper, put the paper in a pile, then start from the top. We'll find him, son." He looked at his son. "Or am I using the wrong pronoun?"

"No," said Ellery. "We is correct."

She stumbled, and young Archer caught her elbow. He did not let it go. "Are you all right?"

"Tired," said Ann Drew wanly. "Wrung out, unplugged, destarched—*tired.*"

"You shouldn't try to do so much."

"I don't do anything. I'm just *there*. Like Mrs. Schriver, bless her heart, and the policewoman. But this has been going on—what is it, eight days now?—since poor Emily was killed, and once in a while one of us has to take a shift off. Which means the other two carry double packs."

"They ought to get someone else, then."

The girl shook her exquisite head. "We all want to do this particular job, Tom. Miss Myra's used to the combinations; and another face would make her, well, unpredictable again. I'd rather be haggard than have to go through any more of *that.*"

"How's she taking it? I mean, does she really know what it's all about?"

"How can you ever tell, with her? Sometimes she's so, well, brisk, so quick; talks about all sorts of things, laughs a lot . . . Then all of a sudden she'll grab your arm—she's awfully strong—and insist on knowing if that wasn't 'someone at the door.' When that happens, every rational thought seems to go out of her poor head, *whoosh.*"

"But does she know she's being guarded?"

"I'm not sure. If she does realize she's in danger, she doesn't seem to care. She'll think of things for us to do that would make us leave her by herself. Once— for heaven's sake, Tom, don't breathe a word of this, especially to Miss Constant, the policewoman, because it happened while she was taking her break—Miss Myra insisted I go look for some peach preserves she said were in the cellar. I told Mrs. Schriver to keep an eye on her—she was in the kitchen preparing lunch—and while I was gone Miss Myra got all dolled up and somehow gave Mrs. Schriver the slip and I just happened by dumb luck to catch a glimpse of her in the street through the little cellar window and how I got to her and brought her back so fast I'll *never* know. I was so nervous it was two hours before I noticed that I was all soot and cobwebs."

"The good old death wish," nodded the erudite Mr. Archer.

"O, stuff," said Miss Drew. "It's just a game she plays."

"Or maybe," he said suddenly, "maybe she knows something nobody else does."

"What's *that* supposed to mean?"

"I don't know," he said. "Sometimes my mouth says things without prior consultation."

She looked at him abstractedly. "You worry me."

"I do?" Archer moved closer, and so did his voice. "Glory be for that—"

"Now, Tom, *don't.*"

"Don't what? Did I say anything? Make passionate love to you? Propose something? Permanent? Temporary?"

"Tom, *please.*"

"How did you know I was about to say something that would make your 'Now, Tom, don't' a logical reply? Maybe I was going to ask you out for pizza pie *à deux*. Maybe I was going to say goodbye. Was that it? Did you think I was going to say good-bye and you couldn't face it, so you stopped me? Oh, Ann, Ann, do you really love me so much?"

She stamped her foot. "Tom, stop it!"

"Stop it? Well, now I know. You don't want to marry me. Or could it be that you just can't stand pizza?"

"Don't, don't, *don't!*" The hysteria in her own voice snapped her out of it. She pulled her chest up like a braced cadet, and then let her breath out deeply. "I'm sorry, Tom. I've had a wretched day."

Tom Archer looked like a nice little boy caught with his hand in the collection plate. "No, Ann, no, I'm the one who's sorry. Please. Worry takes different forms. Some people go around dropping things, some burst into tears at a raised forefinger, some kick dogs and children. Me . . . I talk."

"Then you must be *very* worried," Ann said with a quavery ghost-smile.

"I am." He kicked something in the imaginary half-dark.

"About us? We're not Yorks, Tom."

"We know that," said Archer blackly, "but does this damn killer?"

"What do you mean?" gasped Ann.

"How do I know what I mean? I get the nasty feeling that he knows more about us than we do—"

"Tom." She looked at him, and he could just make out the enormousness of her eyes. "It's someone we *know*. Isn't it?"

The lovely fear-stretched eyes, the horror-touched tone, instantly turned Mr. Archer in the opposite direction again. "Who," he asked airily, "really knows anyone? Let's talk about something else. All right?"

He tilted her little chin, and after a moment she smiled and murmured, "All *right*. What about?"

"You carry the ball this time," he suggested.

"Let me think." She cocked her head, a finger to her lips. "Oh, I know. Do you know what lox is?"

"Certainly, it goes with bagels."

"Not that kind, silly. Lox is liquid oxygen. Did you know that if you dip a rose into lox and then drop it, it will shatter like finest crystal, right down to the *tinkle?* Isn't that lovely?"

"It certainly is," he said doubtfully. "Where—?"

"Or take Roquefort cheese. Did you know that Roquefort was discovered by pure accident, when a goatherd lost a bucket of milk in a cool cave?"

"Wait a minute—"

"Or let me tell you about the Trobriand Islanders . . . "

"Wait—a—minute! Where did you pick up these scraps of wisdom? You've never . . . I mean, this has the smack of very recently acquired useless information. Where did you get it, Ann?"

"I don't believe I care for your tone, Mr. Archer," the girl said coldly. "If you must know, at dinner this evening."

"At dinner?" Young Archer sounded skeptical. "From Mrs. Schriver, no doubt? Or Policewoman Monster?"

"Policewoman *Constant*. And you know perfectly well it was my evening off."

"Ah, then, you were out with somebody?"

"I don't know why you assume the right—"

"Who?"

"Tom, I bruise easily—"

"Whom were you out to dinner with tonight?" he cried, fiercely, shaking her. She dimpled. "Ellery Queen."

His jaw dropped so far that Ann almost giggled. "Ellery Queen," he breathed, and Ann's giggle impulse vanished. For over Tom Archer's face dropped a mask of great ugliness. "Why did Queen ask you to dinner, Ann?"

"Tom, I don't think I like you tonight—"

"Why did he ask you out?"

This time, although she cried out faintly at the grip of his hands, he did not release her. "I *don't*. I mean, like you tonight. Or maybe any other time! Is this what you're like when you're jealous?"

"Jealous, hell," Archer said, so flatly that she stopped squirming. "All I want to know is why he took you out."

She whimpered, "Why does any man—"

"Don't give me that, Ann," he snapped. "Queen isn't any man. He's a detective on a case. He's working. He works all the time. Including at dinner with a suspect."

"Suspect?" the girl gasped. *"Me?"*

"You can't be that naïve. Certainly you! We're all suspects. Listen, Ann, this may be serious. What did you tell him? What did he worm out of you?"

"Worm out of me? Nothing!"

"What else did you talk about?"

"Oh, the Seebecks—"

"The Seebecks." He stared down at her.

"Is there something wrong with that, too?" she flashed. "Mr. Queen told me all about how Seebeck worked for a banknote company that printed stamps for foreign countries—"

"Don't tell *me* the story—I told you, remember?" Archer was very close to her now, but there was nothing close about his voice; it was as remote as the next galaxy. "What I want to know is: How did the subject of the Seebecks come up?"

"It just came up," she wailed. "Tom, what's got into you?"

"Think!" he all but yelled. "Think! How did it come up?"

She searched his face; in hers were hurt, bewilderment and, nakedly new, fear. "Is it so terribly important?"

"Yes!"

"Then you'll have to stop shouting at me," she said firmly. "We were talking about . . . yes, Robert York, and what a queer little man he was. So regular, so starched . . . sort of—oh, you know—like a wind-up toy of a man."

"Well?" Archer said harshly.

"Let me think! . . . Oh, yes. Mr. Queen wanted to know about the exceptions. He said there are always exceptions when people live by rules and clocks. And I said I couldn't recall any except that time Robert called you in about the Seebecks that evening. You remember, Tom. He sent Walt."

"What did you have to tell him that for!"

"Why not?" She looked at him like a scared little girl. "Tom, you've never spoken to me like this before—not *ever*. Oh!" she said suddenly, remembering. "Mr. Queen seemed to know that you and Robert York had a bad quarrel over those Seebecks, so naturally I couldn't deny it."

"It's the way it looks, that's all," Archer muttered. "You shouldn't have told him anything."

"But, Tom, Tom, no matter how it looks . . ." She swallowed and said, too quickly, "I mean . . . Oh, I don't know what I mean!"

"I didn't kill him," Tom Archer growled, "if that's what's at the back of your mind. Or Emily York, either."

She wet her lips. "Tom, I never said . . . What's *happening* to us?" she cried. "This is awful, Tom, let's get back to where we were. You were going to ask me something. What was it?"

He regarded her bleakly. He did not seem the same man at all, the man who had released that tumbling flood of euphoria only minutes before.

"Nothing," he grumbled. "It doesn't matter. *You!*" he shouted to the little park. "You can come out of hiding now and take Miss Drew back!"

And when the somewhat abashed plainsclothesman stepped out from behind one of Walt's mathematical box hedges, Tom Archer turned on his heel and stalked back to Robert York's house and, presumably, his own room.

17 · Attack Advanced

He was writing:

I hasten to reassure you, My Dear Walt. You have been worried—just a little, am I correct? Yes, indeed. For I know what you said to the Adversary—every word. You did not doubt that, did you? Of course not. It was your knowledge of my presence that has since caused your worry.

Know, then, that you conducted yourself admirably. You did perfectly. You answered with only just as much of the truth as would be of no real value to him. You volunteered nothing. Again I say—Well done!

Do you feel better? I knew you would.

My Dear Walt, trust me, you will be free from harm, for you know I control all things. And trust yourself, too. When in doubt, trust yourself by being yourself.

You cannot speak my name.

You may not speak my name.

Aside from this, say what you will.

Enclosed is a new card. Get your printing set out of its hiding place and . . .

18 · Counterattacks

Inspector Queen put away his keys and walked like the tired man he was to Ellery's study. He found the sometimes dim light of his life crouched over the desk, blinking sightlessly at the silent ranks of the Encyclopedia Britannica through the old blue smog of unventilated tobacco endlessly smoked.

"Whew," said the Inspector, fighting his way in.

Ellery sprang to his feet, alive and aware on the instant, with no transition. "It's *got* to mean something!" he cried to his father. "Don't you agree?"

"Don't I agree to what?" sighed the Inspector, sitting down in Ellery's good armchair and stretching his aching legs.

"Oh," said Ellery; and he began to pace swiftly back and forth, head bent, torso forward-inclined.

"Aside from the fact that right now you look like Groucho Marx," said his father, "I don't know what you're talking about. Whatever it is, I hope it makes sense." The old man's sigh turned to a growl. "Three times now I've had search warrants for those four cookie-box castles. Today I didn't split the squad up. This time we *all* went to *all* the rooms of *all* the houses. If there's a child's printing set in York Square I'll eat it. What have *you* got?"

"What?"

The Inspector, squinting up, repeated himself.

"Oh!" said Ellery. "Why, Dad, I don't know. I mean I *know*, but not what it means. I've found a lowest common denominator for four people in York Square."

"Oh?" said his father, slowly reaching for one of Ellery's cigarettes; he almost never smoked cigarettes. "Who?—*whom?*"

"Ann Drew. Tom Archer. Mrs. Schriver. Walt."

The Inspector said, "Really?" He lit the cigarette with slightly trembling fingers, puffed, and sat back. "And what would that be? Your whachamacallit—common denominator."

"*Every one of those four came to York Square out of, or by way of, your Miss Sullivan's-Emily York's settlement house.*"

The old man stopped smoking. Finally he resumed. "And what's that supposed to mean, Ellery?"

"Just what I was asking myself," Ellery muttered, "when you came in. Dad . . ." He sat down suddenly on the point of his desk, like a flagellant. "Take Archer. A sort of parchment prodigy. First heard of as runner-up in a Science Search. Disqualified as under age, but given a special certificate. After that, some scholarship award or other every year.

"Archer has a small inheritance," Ellery continued, staring into his father's smoke. "Ten, eleven hundred a year. Two years in the Army interrupted his doctorate. Straight academic Ph.D. No utilitarian specializations. Never went back to school. Wound up hinging stamps in Robert York's albums.''

"Where does the settlement house come in?"

"After his Army discharge he walked in there one day and announced to Emily York that he was a displaced person. Strictly a pleasantry, by the way. He wasn't trying to put anything over.''

"Never mind that," said the old man impatiently. "What did he say?"

"Well, he wanted some sort of work he'd never done before—said he was tired of being a schoolboy. Said he wanted to dig a ditch or something, and a settlement house seemed a good place to begin. Emily York replied that there were too many people needing ditches to dig who couldn't do anything else, but there was her cousin Robert and his stamps, and she sent Archer over for an interview. Robert hired him.''

"How'd you find out all this? Archer talks a blue streak, but I never caught him *saying* anything.''

"I got it from Miss Sullivan.''

"Did you!" said the Inspector, and he sighed. "And how is she?"

"As remarkable as you implied, Dad. And carrying on in spite of everything.''

The Inspector nodded in a pleased way, reaching over to tamp out his cigarette. "What about the Drew girl?''

"The Drew girl.'' Ellery hesitated. His father glanced up at him sharply, and Ellery said in a casual voice, "She spent most of her motherless young life taking care of a despondent father. He died, and Emily York got hold of her some way or other and passed her along to Myra. Would you hand me the cigarettes, Dad?''

"Sure," said his father. "My," said his father, "you told that one fast. That's it on Ann Drew, hmm?''

"Well, there's more, but nothing that has any bearing on the case.'' Ellery used two matches. His parent refrained from comment. "Who's next? Oh, Mrs. Schriver. Mrs. Schriver is a widow from Bucks County whose late husband was swindled by some New York sharpie. She came charging up here with fire in her eye—the swindle and the funeral expenses left her almost destitute—and wound up finding neither the con man nor a job. Emily picked her up, put her back together again and got her started at York Square.''

"Leaving Walt.''

"Leaving Walt. Walt," said Ellery slowly, "is a considerable mystery. He was an amnesiac. His fingerprints are not on file anywhere, for any purpose. No background, then, and—you know him—no foreground either. I'm interested.''

The Inspector shrugged and sighed. "How about making me a drink?''

Ellery went through the living room to the kitchen and busied himself getting ice and glasses; he returned to the living room, to the bar, and poured and mixed, and all the while he was thinking that his lifelong obsession with mysteries could be accounted for by the implacable fact that he hated them for *being* mysteries— which was to say, things without answers. Amnesia concealed a mystery; an amnesiac was someone with something to hide—the fact that he was hiding it from himself was a mere detail. Walt was an unanswered thing.

"Thanks, son," the Inspector said, accepting his drink. He drank, and then he said shrewdly, "You're still on this Walt kick.''

"Dad, look," said Ellery. "All Miss Sullivan could tell me about him is that he was brought into the settlement house one January night, one of a bunch of half-frozen skid-row derelicts. He was just as dirty and ragged, but he wasn't drunk;

and of course he was younger than most of them. Miss Sullivan doesn't think he drinks at all, and she ought to know. He was starved, lost, he could read and write, and the only name he could give was Walt. His clothes told nothing, castoffs he'd evidently picked up in some trash heap—''

"And Emily York realized he wasn't the usual bum," nodded the Inspector, "tried him out on an odd job or two, found he was a good worker, and got the York Square board of directors to give him the custodial job. And there he's been for years. I know all that, son. That's all there is."

"All?" echoed Ellery. "There must be some records—military service, income tax reports—''

But Inspector Queen was shaking his head. "No, son. If he ever had a taxable income it was probably under a different name. He's certainly unfit mentally and overage for military service—I mean, since he went into the amnesia—and before that, well, no prints in the service files. Incidentally, Miss Sullivan got in touch with Missing Persons about him at the time he came into the settlement house; they couldn't match him up with anybody on their lists, and there's been no subsequent lead to him. He's just a blank, son. I told you the other day, whoever's behind these murders has a calculating intelligence that's just out of Walt's league. Amnesiac! It's just too . . . too corny.''

"Corny it may be," muttered Ellery, "but if I were you I'd have him watched all the same. Or you might find yourself losing another York."

"Don't worry, he's being watched along with the others. But he's not costing me much sleep. As to losing another York," the Inspector took a long swift swallow, "sometimes-by-God I wish we would!"

"What?" Ellery said.

"If we could lose one *without* losing one, so to speak. Because look," the Inspector said. "We have one murder that's certainly a murder, and one death that's probably a murder but couldn't be proved even if somebody confessed on a polygraph. Each of our prime suspects *could* have killed Robert—''

"Or, as in the case of the women, got some sub-prime actually to push the stone—''

"Yes, so that gives us X-number of sub-primes. Emily's death: the number of primes goes down, the number of unknown possibles goes up. We know Myra was home in the Square and that Ann Drew was with her. Archer was out, but he can probably prove where he was. Walt was uptown buying map tacks. Percival York and his whatever-she-is—''

"Odalisque?" Ellery suggested absently.

"Whatever *that* is!—anyway, they were being tailed. Mrs. Schriver was in Myra York's house cleaning. And there were X-hundreds of your sub-primes on that subway platform—and besides, who's to say Emily didn't just get a dizzy spell and fall off the edge under her own steam as the train came in?''

"So you'd like to lose another York. I'm still not clear why."

"A killer can get away with one kill, but when he tries it again the odds start to mount against him. You know that! Well, he's done two now—let's assume it's two—and he's still riding the odds. But this time they're way up there. So if he'd only pull one more murder we'd have him—I think. All we've got to do is figure out how we can get him to do that without its actually costing us another York."

"Quite a problem," Ellery said dryly. "But maybe we're doing just that by having Percival and Myra under twenty-four-hour surveillance? So he's bound to be caught if he tries again. I don't see how we can miss short of stupidity or criminal carelessness. I know I wouldn't relish the chore of trying to crawl under the fences we've built, Dad. Not if I wanted to crawl out again.''

''And meanwhile we sit around sucking our thumbs,'' grumbled the Inspector. ''Damn it all, Ellery! There ought to be some way to pressure this whozit into making his play.''

Ellery rolled his cold glass along his forehead therapeutically. Inspector Queen stared across at him. But all Ellery said when he rose to freshen their drinks was: ''Maybe there is.''

Thought Ellery: The prod, the goad, the phrase that gigs, is; *I know all about it.*

''I know all about it,'' he said ominously; and Tom Archer, hunched behind the barricade of the late Robert York's desk in the dim specklessness of the late Robert York's study, started violently.

Archer swallowed, his young Adam's apple jumping like an ambushed cat. ''All about *what?*'' It failed to come out with the scandalized virtue he was aiming for.

''Well, let's see,'' Ellery said in his most obliging drawl. ''When Robert York sent Walt to fetch you that night, he was a very angry man.''

''*What* night?''

''The night,'' Ellery said sonorously, ''of the Seebecks.''

And it worked!—for Archer bit his lip, and one hand on the desk kneaded the other hand on the desk until he caught sight of what they were doing and clenched them into silence.

''Well?'' Ellery barked, when he estimated that the young man had stewed in his own juice just long enough.

''Oh, damn,'' muttered Archer, looking up at last; and he gave a wry grin. ''What would you have done if I'd told you about it right off?''

''Hauled you downtown,'' Ellery said promptly. ''Want to go now?''

''No, I don't.''

''Better give me the whole story, then.''

''You said you knew it.''

Ellery, who had dropped into the Morris chair across from the desk, climbed to his feet. ''Let's go, Archer.''

Archer clawed at his scalp. ''Oh, hell! I'm sorry, Mr. Queen. I've been out of my mind with worry about this thing. I knew you'd find out sooner or later. But I just couldn't bring myself to come clean. It looks . . . well, I don't have to tell you how it looks.''

''Yes, you do.''

Blindly Archer took one of Robert York's tissues from the right-hand drawer and dried his face. ''I take it you've been to Jenks & Donahue.''

Ellery grunted the kind of grunt that universally means whatever worried people are afraid it might mean.

''Robert York said those Seebecks were worthless reprints,'' Archer muttered, ''and I got sore. Because I was equally positive the stamps were *not* reprints. Well, as you now know, I took them down to Jenks & Donahue and had them put through the wringer, everything—black light, horizontal beam, colorimeter, watermark, and gum analysis—and found out what Mr. York had been able to tell with the naked eye! He had a feel for stamps that was uncanny. Of course, he'd been right and I'd been wrong. The stamps *were* Seebeck reprints.'' He looked at Ellery pleadingly. ''What could I do? What on earth else could I do?''

"What did you do?"

"Went out and bought genuine ones, of course. Paid seventy per cent over list for them, too. It took every liquid centavo I had."

Ellery said with dawning understanding, "So then you went back to Jenks & Donahue this time with the genuine ones, had them run tests on *those,* they gave you expert confirmation in writing, and *that* was the report you showed Robert York. And he never knew a thing about J & D's original report about the reprints. Is that it, Archer?"

"How could I bring myself to tell him?" cried Tom Archer. "I'd got myself into a bind with York when I challenged his philatelic eye, and he'd said that if Jenks & Donahue proved me wrong about the Seebecks he was going to fire me. I couldn't let him do that, Mr. Queen. I just *couldn't.* It wasn't the job; I could always get a better job. The thing is, I didn't *want* a better job."

Ellery understood perfectly, having in the near past dined with Archer's reason. But he said only, "Go on."

"I felt like such a heel," groaned Archer. "Mr. York was so contrite over what he now thought had been *his* mistake that he gave me a raise and a power of attorney to act for him in the management of the four households. He couldn't do enough for me, and the more he did the less I could bring myself to tell him what I'd done."

"He was bound to find out eventually."

Archer wet his lips. "You keep hoping not. And playing it by ear, each thing that happens. And one thing leads to another thing, and you keep getting in deeper . . . I'm so glad he never did find out."

"You'd have done a good deal to keep him from finding out?"

"Oh, God! Anything."

Quietly Ellery let the three words rise in the dim room, ballooning and expanding until they filled the whole breatheable space. He watched Archer take note of the silence, then listen to it, then study it and finally—"Oh, *no!*" Archer cried. "When I said 'anything' Mr. Queen, I didn't mean *that.* I'm no killer," he said urgently. "Do I look like a killer to you?"

"Few killers do," Ellery remarked sadly.

"But why would I do a thing like that? If Robert had found out about those Seebecks, the worst that would have happened is that I'd have had to leave."

"So much for not telling *him.* But why, Archer, didn't you tell me?"

"Put yourself in my place, Mr. Queen," Archer pleaded. "Would you tell anybody you'd had a violent quarrel with your employer—shortly before someone dropped a two-hundred-pound stone on his head?"

"A familiar argument," Ellery said. "The fallacy in it is that you're in a far worse position when the quarrel is found out. Did you really think no one would find out?"

"I certainly never dreamed it would come out through Ann."

"Mr. Archer." Ellery rose. "I don't at the moment believe you're our man. But I also don't care for what you did about those Seebecks. It gives you a tricky character, and this is a tricky case. Take my advice: from now on keep your nose very, very well wiped."

"I'll remember that, Mr. Queen," Archer said bitterly.

And I won't tell you, Ellery thought that you have no credible motive; and that, if you'd been planning Robert's murder, your directly antecedent actions would hardly have included a heated quarrel with him; and anyway, that your alibi stands up.

Aloud, and gently, he said, "And about Ann Drew—be consoled. She couldn't help telling me. To borrow a phrase, Archer: I have my methods." He added in total afterthought, "And why I should be telling you this I'm blessed if I understand. I could easily fall for Ann Drew myself."

At which Tom Archer had a smile—a small smile, but a smile—for him; and Ellery, departing, smiled a small one back.

"I know all about it," said Ellery coldly. He had encountered the handyman coming down the walk of Myra York's house.

Walt returned a round, mineral gaze and moved his slack full lips in a sort of windup. If he was surprised, startled, angry, fearful—*anything*—it certainly did not show.

What came out of his mouth at last was, "Yes."

All right, pal, he's thrown you the ball. What are you going to do with it? "Mr. Archer and Robert York had a quarrel before Mr. York was killed."

"Yes."

"Mr. York sent you to find Mr. Archer."

"Yes."

"What did Mr. Archer say when you located him?"

The round eyes closed and opened—it was too slow for a blink. "He saw me and he said, 'God.' "

"And you said—?"

"That Mr. Robert sent me to find him, and to say he's got a Seebeck."

"Why didn't you tell that to the police?"

"They did not ask me to."

"Didn't you know it might be important?"

The flat-finished eyeballs were concealed again by another of those slow-motion blinks. "No."

I believe you, Ellery thought. "What were you just doing in there?" He pointed to Myra York's house.

The handyman removed something from his side pocket and extended it. It was a five-and-dime package of screen patches. "The corner was rusted out on the screen porch. I had to fix it."

"Is that all you did in Miss Myra's house?"

"No." The man produced a plastic flask of a patented muriatic solution. "I took a stain off the second-floor bathtub."

Ellery regarded him gravely. Walt stared patiently back. And Ellery knew then that he could ask questions and get answers from now until noon of St. Swithin's Day and learn never a thing.

"Anything might be important to the police, Walt. The smallest thing. You try to remember, won't you?—and if you think of anything you forgot to tell, come right out with it. Do you understand me?"

"I understand."

Namelessly dissatisfied, Ellery went on up to the house and rang the bell; and so preoccupied was he with his dissatisfaction that, when Mrs. Schriver opened the door, he forgot his magic goad and said at once, "What was *he* doing here?"

"A hole in the screen he fixes," said the housekeeper, "and from the bat'room upstairs a stain he takes out." She looked at him reprovingly. "Gut afternoon, Mr. Queen."

"Oh! Good afternoon, Mrs. Schriver. How's everything?"

"Resting," said Mrs. Schriver. "Unless with the bell you are unresting her."

"*I'm sorry,*" said Ellery. "Could I see Miss Drew?" He knew that the policewoman was also on duty upstairs.

"She is with Miss Myra sitting." She did not mention the policewoman.

Ellery appealed to the determined little chub-face. "Do you think you could get her down here without disturbing Miss Myra?"

"For what?"

"Something very important, Mrs. Schriver. Honest," he added. She invariably made him feel like an unwanted small boy.

"You better," sniffed the housekeeper; and she went noiselessly up the stairs, managing to leave him with the impression that she was stamping with indignation.

A thousand years later Ann Drew appeared; and it seemed to Ellery that she drifted down to him like Peter Pan's Wendy, the time the Lost Boys shot her out of the sky with an arrow; her hair, undone, was floating hurriedly behind her like a bit of cloud trying to catch up. And when—wafting by him into the cluttered parlor—she touched her lips for silence, he realized on the instant that to touch her lips was something he had wanted to do all his life.

She told him in sign language to shut the sliding doors. He did this, and when he turned back he found her looking at him with half a smile on her amazing mouth, altogether trustful. And he did something then at which he would ever after wince in memory—something which had to be done. He said quietly, "I know all about it."

Once he had seen a convulsed virago strike her child, a little girl; this was the same. At the impact there was no pain, only astonishment; then pleading eyes denied the blow; then, the blow being undeniable, came the search for some explanation: *It was an accident,* or *I'm dreaming this*—anything to make it bearable before the pain closed down and terror blotted everything.

He could only loathe himself, and wonder what was coming next.

Ann Drew whispered to the walls, to the wind: "I was sixteen and my daddy was all—oh, he was coming unglued, his kidneys, his liver, his stomach, most of all his brain—the base; it affected his balance. He worked in a library; he loved books, the things of the mind; he could see himself becoming a mindless blob, and it terrified him. Some of the medicine was no good, and some of it they just tried out on him, and some helped, and all of it cost—oh, terribly. And after a while he had to quit working and stay home, a slowly dying man. I couldn't even finish high school—I had to go to work to support us both. I got a job in a store; the salary wasn't nearly enough but it was the best I could do, because the store was close to where we lived and I had to be able to run home to tend to Daddy. And I found that I needed more and more money, and I had no way to get more except . . . except—"

"By dipping into the till?"

"For almost two years."

Ellery looked at Ann Drew; this time he looked deeply. Lovely, lovely girl. "Virtue may not always make a face handsome, but vice will certainly make it ugly." Poor Richard had never met an Ann. She was untouched.

"But it never touched me!" she cried, and startled him. "Miss Emily understood that. When she dug into me, she looked me in the eye and said I didn't need saving because I'd never been lost. It sounds like—like soap opera, but the truth is that the money I stole was, first to save my father's life, and then—when I knew it was a hopeless cause—to pay for the narcotics he needed so that he could die without too much pain."

He had a dozen questions to ask and asked none of them. Instead he said gently, "I take it you were caught."

"In the act." The hardened tone was armor, he knew, against that assault from the past. "I spent almost two days and nights in a cell before Emily York—I don't know how she found out—got me off in her custody. But for just that forty-two hours, when I couldn't get to him, or even communicate, Daddy had to do without the two things he needed to keep living—his morphine and me. He cut his wrists." It was no longer a lovely face she turned up to him; it had no blood in it, almost no bone. "No one's known about this, Mr. Queen. Now, I suppose, it will become public property."

"Ann," Ellery said. "Stop being afraid."

Her head came up in a flash. "I'm *not* afraid!"

"You're scared witless that Tom Archer will find out."

After a moment her head went down. "Well," she said lifelessly, "won't he?"

He cupped her chin, and she was forced to look at him. "Ann, has this back-history of yours anything to do with the York murders? I ask you not to lie to me. Has it? Anything at all? Even remotely?"

"Oh, that." She shook her head almost impatiently. "No. How could it?"

He smiled and let her go. "Well, then."

"I don't understand."

"Of course you do."

"You mean you won't tell him." Her voice was stiff with certainty. For her preoccupation with her past had been so complete that its irrelevance to the York case had not occurred to her; and that his preoccupation with the York case would cause him to shrug off the irrelevance of her past was an outcome she had not even dreamed of.

And so she wept; and Ellery, his back to her, waited her weeping out. The whole thing was soundless.

"No, I won't tell Archer," Ellery said to the unobstructed view. "You will."

That brought sound—a breathy sound of surprise and dismay. He felt her clutch, and he faced about. Ann, Ann, he thought, take your hands off me; and he touched her hands and they fell away. He had lost her. No, he had never had her.

"Tell Tom a thing like that?" the girl cried. "And have him go sick inside?"

"Emily York didn't go sick inside," said Ellery. "And she wasn't even in love with you. If that fellow's feeling for you is so feeble it would collapse under the story you've told me, Ann, don't you think this is a good time to find out?"

But the girl was shaking her head and wailing, "Why, why did you have to rake this up?"

"Because in my sorry business you have to rake up everything. And everything, unfortunately, tends to include a great many things that turn out not to matter. Yet it's the only way. Separate out the things that don't matter, and you're often left with the things that do."

19 · Sacrifice

Ellery, in Boston, said, "I know all about it."

He looked at Mallory across the desk, which was glossy as a skating rink and very nearly as large. Mallory's big head, with its ruddy face-tones and ice-blond hair, was set off by the heavy brown velvet drapes behind him. He was one of those men who cannot avoid looking like an Old Master; light is always kind to them and the eye of the beholder is always seized and slightly awed. And he would greet you without rising, and that would feel right to you.

It had felt right to Ellery, considerably to his surprise.

Ellery had had another session with Miss Sullivan, had flown to Boston and winnowed a great deal through certain files to which he was privy by courtesy of the New York police department; then, failing, he had found what he wanted in the Boston telephone directory. Annoyed, he had made his way to the offices of Mallory & Co., had sternly beaten down the successive blocking plays of a receptionist, a secretary and an assistant, had gained the Presence, and had mentioned the name of Myra York. And, "I know all about it."

"I can almost say," said Mallory, "that I expected you." He had the mellow boom, the oiled diction of an Edward Everett or an Everett Dirksen. "Not you personally, Mr. Queen, nor anyone like you, for of course there is no one like you; but someone concerned in York Square's present difficulties."

Ellery tipped his head politely and wondered what on earth this natural candidate for someone's most unforgettable character was leading up to.

"I knew the Yorks—some of them—of course, or you wouldn't be here. No, don't ask me any questions, Mr. Queen," Mallory said, anticipating the nerve impulse behind the still unmobilized muscle that was about to activate Ellery's mouth. "I am a man who enjoys putting myself in another man's place. It's a knack that puts me in mine." He glanced about his endless office, and smiled. "Let me put myself in yours. You have an important murder on your hands, perhaps two. You are making very little progress. It has consequently become necessary to run down everything about everybody, on the theory that this would elicit the—do you still call them clues?—the clues you need. You inevitably unearthed the clue that at one time, many years ago, I was engaged to marry Myra York. I said, don't ask me any questions!"

Ellery's lips closed with a snap. There was a long silence, during which Mallory kept his eyes shut. When he opened them, the effect on Ellery was much like that of the prowl car's spotlight which had smote him the other night.

"You discovered that my engagement preceded Miss York's good fortune in the matter of old Nathaniel's will. She has remained unmarried, two of the four heirs have been sent to their less material rewards and Myra's large prospects have accordingly become very large indeed. And since I suspect—no, that's unworthy of both of us—since I *know,* because I have kept myself informed, that Myra retains a warped modification of her original interest in me, you were led to wonder whether I might not be tempted to renew my association with her in consideration of those enlarged prospects. You may even be wondering, Mr. Queen, if I may not have arranged the entire sequence of events. Please do not respond to that.''

Ellery's mouth clamped again.

''Mr. Queen,'' Mallory went on to inquire politely, ''do you also know why I broke my engagement to Myra York almost two decades ago?''

It was a relief to be able to say *something.* Ellery said, ''No.''

Mallory seemed pleased. ''Very good. I admire the laconic interviewer. Mr. Queen, I am a man who makes plans and, having made them, follows them. I began this useful practice early in life. In those days I made plans for myself and Myra—who was, by the way, most desirable—at that time. When those plans became impossible—I'll amend that: when I discovered that those plans were impossible with *her*—I had to plan her, so to speak, out of them.''

The Old Master reached abruptly. His kingly fingers closed about a tooled morocco twin-picture frame facing him, and turned it around. The fingers then spread with a little wave, in gracious invitation. Ellery accepted and bent forward.

One of the two photographs showed a calm-eyed lady with an impressive bust and hair either blond or white; the facing picture was of three corn-fed teen-agers, two boys and a girl, descending robustly in what was obvious chronological order.

Mallory smiled. *''They* are what would have been impossible with Myra.'' He reached again, this time to turn the frame away from Ellery's view and back to his. ''She told me so,'' he said, now smiling at the teen-age frame of the two, ''herself.''

''And on her unsupported word—''

''I never acted on anyone's unsupported word. As her fiancé, I consulted her doctor. It was true enough. But I had planned a dynasty, and dynasties are grown only in fertile ground. No children, no Myra York. Could anything be simpler? Comment, Mr. Queen.''

Said Mr. Queen: ''I hardly know where to begin.''

''Certainly you know where to begin. You might say, for example: this was a brutal blow to Myra. Admitted. But it was also a brutal blow to me; I was young, too, and she was *very* desirable, Mr. Queen. I had to comfort myself with the truism that it is in the nature of things for us all to endure brutal blows.

''Or say, for another example, Mr. Queen,'' continued Mallory, leaning back in his tall and massive chair, ''that you nosed your way to Boston seeking a suspect fortune hunter; that, having sniffed me out and discovered that I *had* a fortune, you were compelled to doubt your hypothesis; but that, being a man who examines all sides of everything, you gave me further thought and reinstated your hypothesis, on the ground this time that I might be the kind of affluent man whose acquisitiveness is insatiable. My answer to that is, of course: I have no designs on Myra York's millions. I submit corroboration of this statement to your common sense. Already this year my own millions, my investments, this business, have earned more in profits than the entire fortune Myra York is coming into. I will happily instruct my people to open my books to any firm of reputable accountants you may designate.''

''As a matter of fact,'' murmured Ellery, ''I wasn't thinking any of those things, Mr. Mallory. I was thinking instead of such unfashionable, if not obsolete, words as responsibility and conscience. Since you say that you've kept yourself informed about Myra York, you must therefore be aware of her mental condition. Doesn't it bother you that what she is today may very likely be the direct result of your cold-blooded rejection of her years ago?—a rejection by the way, for something that was not her fault?''

"Nor mine," smiled Mallory, "a fact you have conveniently left out. But aside from that. People are, by and large, what they want to be. You are what you are, Mr. Queen, and I am what I am, because you and I have so willed it. You and I willed ourselves to be successes, so we are. But the principle applies equally to failures. Of course it bothers me to hear of poor Myra's condition; I pity her with all my heart. But pangs of conscience?" He shook his head. "I cannot, do not, and will not accept responsibility for Myra's decline, for that is manifestly something *she* has willed.''

It came to Ellery suddenly that this amazing man might be angry, he kept smiling so.

"I beg your pardon?" Ellery said.

"I said," Mallory repeated, "that you might also inquire what I was doing on the night of so-and-so, et cetera.''

"That," said Ellery with his own smile, "—now that we have cleared away the smog—is the hard question I'm here to ask.''

Mallory spun about on his revolving throne and swept aside the towering drapes behind him. They uncovered an almost unpleasantly large expanse of glass and, beyond it, far below, a miniature panorama of Boston Harbor. The object of his action, however, was neither the glass nor the view; it was propped against the window.

A crutch.

Mallory grasped it and spun back, still smiling. "The evening Robert York was killed," he said, fondling the crutch, "I was lying in a traction splint in Auburn Hospital—that's in Cambridge, Mr. Queen—with a broken femur. On the afternoon Emily York was killed, I was confined to my home, my mobility rather limited by two crutches. I now manage with this one. Of course you will check this, Mr. Queen although I assure you I would not bring it up if it were not true.'' He wagged his ice-crowned head. "I'm afraid I'm not a very profitable suspect.''

In the silence that followed—although Ellery was sure that behind the Mount Rushmore countenance the man was shouting with laughter—the telephone rang. It was a relief, for Ellery had been rather desperately trying to think of an exit speech.

"Excuse me," Mallory said, and picked up the phone. He listened, then covered the transmitter with his muscular hand. "It's for you, Mr. Queen. Are you here?''

"Of course."

Stretching far forward to meet Ellery's hand, Mallory explained, "I like to offer visitors to my office the option of lying to their associates," and, still smiling, settled back.

"This is Queen," Ellery said to the phone. "Oh, yes, put him on. Dad?''

And then Ellery went so still for so long that the smile faded from Mallory's face.

Finally: "When?" Ellery said, and cleared some obstruction from his throat. "All right. All right. As soon as I can.''

He leaned over and replaced the instrument precisely on its cradle. Mallory's eyes alertly followed the action; there was the slightest crevice between them.

"Bad news, Mr. Queen?''

And Ellery looked down at Mallory in a sort of blindness and said, "For Myra York, the worst. She was murdered last night."

The muscles that managed the center of Mallory's mouth held up all right, but those at the corners gave out. For a moment the massive face might have posed for Tragedy's mask on some theater proscenium. "Poor Myra," he muttered.

But that was all.

Ellery made for the door without another word.

And Mallory said, "Mr. Queen!" and Ellery stopped and turned. The man had reassumed command; the corners were now lifted back into place. "I mean to have that devil caught," Mallory barked, "whoever it is. I'm prepared to post a reward—"

"So there's conscience on Olympus after all." The Queenian torso inclined toward the tycoon ever so little, as if ready for anything. "But this time, Mr. Mallory, money won't solve it. My father tells me he's had the murderer in a cell since ten o'clock this morning."

Their stares locked across the long dueling ground. Both men were pale.

Then Ellery reversed himself and marched to Mallory's door and opened it and stepped through and shut it behind him as bitterly as he could.

20 · Breakthrough

"It was Ann Drew," Inspector Queen said, "who found her dead this morning. With the jug on the night table beside the bed. The girl's had a bad time of it."

The old man had been waiting at La Guardia in a squad car when the Boston plane set down. The only thing he could have done to look older would have been to wear silk knee breeches and a ruff. His face was so gaunt, his eyes were so redly rimmed that Ellery found himself wishing he could belittle this incredible third York death.

"The poison was put into her drinking water, Dad? I should think even Myra would have tasted—"

"Who said there was water in the jug?" The Inspector showed his dentures.

"The joke escapes me," Ellery said sharply. "What would a water jug hold but water?"

"A fair question, except in Myra's case. *That* water jug held straight gin. Now it comes out she's been a secret lush for years."

"That floating walk, that slow slurry coo of hers," exclaimed Ellery. "Did Ann know?"

"Sure she knew."

"Poor kid."

"She's been throwing ashes on her head like a professional mourner. And you ought to see the shape that policewoman, Constant, is in. I had to order her home on sick leave. And Mrs. Schriver's wandering around in a daze, looking twenty years older."

And so do you, Ellery thought. Aloud he said, "Has a card shown up, Dad?"

"What else?"

The Inspector went fishing. He handed over his catch; and Ellery seized the familiar white card with the five odd sides as if it were the key to Solomon's treasure room.

"Lower starboard. Myra's castle, all right," Ellery said tensely. "W . . . W. H before that, J before H. J, H, W. JHW. What the devil! Or—wait! Could it be"— he turned the card upside down—"an M?"

The Inspector stared at it. "M. That's Myra's initial."

But Ellery scowled and shook his head. "Then why didn't Robert get an R, and Emily an E? Besides, notice that in the M-position the card would have to be assigned to the northwest corner of the Square, and that makes no sense at all—that was Emily's corner." He restored the card to its W-position. "No, Dad, this one's meant to be a W. Now tell me about it."

"I was the one who found it." The old man took back the white card and glared at it. "It was in the usual envelope, addressed in the usual style to Miss Myra York, et cetera, and postmarked night before last at the local station. It was delivered in the regular mail yesterday morning."

"But if you knew about it yesterday morning—" Ellery began, perplexed.

"I didn't know about it yesterday morning."

"You said you were the one who found it!"

"*This* morning," said the Inspector woodenly, "when it was too damn late."

"But how did it slip by everybody?" Ellery cried.

"You won't believe it, it's so ridiculous." Then the Inspector's voice turned policeman. "First of all, the carrier says it was Myra herself who took the mail from him."

"*Myra?*" said Ellery incredulously. "How was she allowed—?"

"If you'll shut up, I'll tell you. Mrs. Schriver was preparing breakfast in the kitchen. Constant was upstairs, picking up after Myra. Ann Drew was downstairs, setting the dining-room table. She called upstairs that breakfast was ready; the policewoman called down that Myra was on her way. In the few seconds after Myra left Constant's line of sight and before she got into the Drew girl's, Myra passed the front door—and that had to be the exact moment the postman came with the mail. A thing like that couldn't have been planned by anybody but Satan, Ellery. The breaks."

"But didn't one of them see Myra take the mail? At least hear the doorbell?"

"Ann heard it and came right out. But by then Myra had the door closed, and the mail—a couple of magazines, some advertising matter, a cheer-up note from Miss Sullivan—in her hand. Ann took it from her and led her to the dining room. But Myra could be almighty quick—apparently she'd spotted the W-envelope and slid it into the side pocket of her suit. And then must have forgotten all about it, because that's where I found it this morning—twenty-four hours later—in her suit pocket, unopened." The Inspector paused. Then he swallowed, making a face. "Don't ask me why Myra latched onto that particular envelope. Don't ask me why she was sly about it—not mentioning it to Ann, or Policewoman Constant, or Mrs. Schriver. And don't ask me why she didn't open it. Don't ask me *anything* about this case!"

They became absorbed in watching the police driver fight his way onto the ramp from the Triborough Bridge to the East River Drive.

When they were speeding down the Drive, Ellery murmured, "So now you've got your killer."

The Inspector retorted, "So now we've got *your* killer," and gave him half a grin, the left half. "Go ahead and say it, Ellery. 'I told you so.' "

"But I didn't. He's just bothered me." Ellery scowled at the back of the driver's neck. "By the way, how did you break him?"

"Who said I broke him? I arrested him, booked him, locked him up. He hasn't said a damn word but his name—I half expected him to add his rank and serial number before he clammed up."

"He hasn't confessed?" Ellery asked slowly.

"He hasn't *anything,* I tell you. Anyway, the evidence confesses for him." The old man closed his eyes and settled down on his tail. "Let me tell it from the top. Ann Drew called the news in, hysterical. When I got there I found Myra dead, and those three females . . ." He shuddered. "Took me half the morning to get coherent stories out of them. Even the policewoman.

"By that time," he continued, "I'd found the envelope with the W-card in it, and I'd also had a preliminary report from Doc Prouty about the poison, because some of it had spilled on the night table and on the floor beside Myra's bed—only a few grains, but enough for a quick analysis. Prouty's done the p.m. since, and his findings check. It's a commercial rat poison—arsenic and Dicumerol compound. The box it came from is still on a shelf in the Robert York garage, half empty. The gin in the jug is loaded with it. The glass she drank from is coated with it. And there was enough in Myra's innards to kill a couple of horses."

Their car raced into the almost-tunnel under the U. N. Building, and Inspector Queen subsided. When they emerged he said, "You know how fast that stuff kills?"

"With a big dose? I'd say five minutes."

"The dose was bigger than that," said the Inspector grimly. "Nearer three minutes, Prouty says. Well, yesterday afternoon Walt showed up to fix a porch screen that was torn and to clean a stained bathtub—"

"I know," Ellery said. "I met him coming out, and he told me about it."

"He was upstairs there almost an hour. While he was fixing the screen, Myra was nipping at her jug. And showed no ill effects, so at that time the gin in the jug had to be all right. Then Walt came in to work on the tub in Myra's bathroom. Myra was higher than a kite, so for propriety's sake Ann and Policewoman Constant hustled her into Ann's room. They didn't take Myra back to her own room until Walt finished and left."

"So during that period Walt was alone in Myra's quarters?"

"That's it. And after the women brought Myra back and until she went to bed last night, the policewoman states, neither Ann Drew nor Mrs. Schriver nor anyone else touched that jug—Constant swears to that. Not even Myra because they wouldn't let her have any more—the only reason Ann didn't take the jug away altogether, she says, is that Myra would have raised holy hell. Anyway, Constant herself locked the bedroom door after they put Myra to bed, and that room wasn't entered until this morning, when Ann unlocked the door and found her dead. She'd obviously waited till they left her alone, then downed a whole glassful of arsenic-flavored gin. Prouty says she died well before midnight. She was mighty cold turkey this morning."

"So only Walt could have dropped the stuff into the jug." Ellery seemed uneasy. "Yet he didn't confess, you say."

"He didn't deny, either!" said his father, the irritation rubbing through.

"And that's it, Dad?"

"No, that's not it. There's more. After I'd got the women's stories yesterday morning, I sent for Walt. When he was brought in I was mulling over what they'd told me, and the card business and all, so I wasn't really paying him much mind. I actually heard myself say to him, 'What's your full name?' as if he were a suspect in the line-up."

The old man paused, so casually that Ellery jerked to attention. "So?" Ellery said. "What's the point?"

"The point," the Inspector said, "is that he answered my question—in full."

"Answered the question in full? What do you mean?"

"He gave me his name. His full name."

"His full name? He doesn't know his full name!"

"I guess I shocked it out of him," the Inspector said with a faint chuckle. "You can do that sometimes with amnesiacs."

"But what is it? What did he say?"

"Why," said the old man, "he said, 'John Henry Walt.' "

"John Henry Walt? Walt is his *surname?*" Ellery turned the name over on his tongue. "John—Henry—Walt. John Henry Walt!" he exploded. *"The initials of his name!"*

"J, H, and now W," nodded Inspector Queen, waving the white card Myra York had received. "It's not really surprising, son. You know how these birds unconsciously want to be caught. This one was signing his name—in installments."

"He's crazy!" Ellery howled, as if his father had not spoken at all; and then he remembered that he had said something like that about John Henry Walt at the very beginning.

21 · Attack Pressed

He had concluded his most recent letter of instructions to Walt—specifying and explicating the various matters of screen-mending, Miss Myra's bathtub rust stain, the granular material in the box on the garage shelf, and the alternatives of opportunity open to Walt for the dropping of the material into the jug at Miss Myra's bedside—in this vein:

> . . . *therefore we have now come to a situation in which you may have to reveal yourself.*
>
> *You may not say my name, but in all other ways you may answer their questions. Or, if you choose, you may answer some or none at all.*
>
> *Remember you need fear nothing, for in this matter you are I. And you know who I am, my Dear Walt. These men cannot harm me, and through me you are immune. You have my blessings and my protection.*
>
> *I am proud of you. I trust you. I admire you.*
> Y

22 · Position Play

He sat dampishly on the rivulets of the old black leather chair near Inspector Queen's desk, all bulge-eyes and grudging hair, and looking not at all like a coming fortunate man. The Inspector's office door was open, and now and again someone would walk in, drop papers in the Inspector's *IN* basket, glance sluggishly at the incipient millionaire and walk out. When these intruders were in uniform Percival York would sigh a small comforted sigh. When the men who dropped in wore ordinary clothing, he would frankly cower until they left. Throughout, he sweated.

The arrival of the Queens, father and son, aroused his gratitude. Percival said, "Hellohellohello," in a warm tone and actually rose to offer his hand, such as it was. Ellery gave a token wave; the Inspector ignored it.

"What do *you* want?" the Inspector asked absently, sitting down at his desk and poking in the basket. He picked out a file folder and at once became absorbed in its contents.

York put his fingers in his mouth and popped his eyes. Then he took the fingers out and said, "Autopsy report on my cousin Myra?"

"Did you read it Mr. York?" Ellery asked, reading it himself over the Inspector's shoulder. "Nothing spectacular, Dad," he murmured, "far as I can see. Oh, you *didn't* read it, Mr. York. Well, you haven't missed anything." He was about to add, You're also sitting in my favorite chair; but then he shrugged and perched on the corner of his father's desk instead.

The Inspector uttered an impolite sound and scaled Doc Prouty's opus to one side. "I seem to remember, Mr. York," he said, "asking you a question."

"Fair enough," Percival giggled. "I'll ask you one, Inspector, and we'll be even. Did you know my cousin Myra used to be a fatal female?"

"A what?" said the Inspector.

"A lover-girl. Ashtoreth and Freya and Lorelei. What you'd call a vamp, I suppose. That Myra," mourned Percival, shaking his head. "Too bad."

"What are you talking about?"

"And got through the whole thing *virgo intacta,* or I miss my guess," said Percival, sucking on a thumb thoughtfully.

Ellery asked softly, "Mallory?"

"Mallory and."

"Mallory and?" The old gentleman was becoming nettled. "Mallory and! What kind of sense does that make?"

Percival York smirked.

"Let's have it." Although it is not possible to describe the Inspector's tone, except in terms of quietude, it made Percival York stop smirking and begin to talk almost like a rational human being.

"Maybe I'm clobbering a dead horse," the Sole Survivor conceded, "maybe it was only kid stuff, but hear this: Mallory had a rival. Did you know that?"

"No, I didn't," confessed Ellery with gleaming eyes. "Who was the dead horse, pray?"

"Nathaniel York, Junior, in living memory of," exulted Percival, quoting the bronze plaque in York Square. "Gone but not forgotten. Head split open on a tropical mud-flat, all for love and a world well lost. Though he was breathing plenty hard while he had it."

"Nathaniel, Junior was in love with Myra York?"

"Mad about her. Myra was delicious in her bloom, and I yield to no man in my devotion to *l'amour*, but that boy overdid it. Would go about mumbling things like Myra was his oyster and oh how he'd like to swallow her whole—that sort of tenth-grade hyperbole.

"But Junior's papa," continued Percival, lying back to enjoy his sensation, "—that was my revered uncle, Nathaniel o' the Purse Strings—old Nate threw fits. Very loud ones, too, full of I'll-cut-you-offs and thou-shalt-nots and so on—Uncle Nathaniel was co-author of the Ten Commandments, a sort of post-Victorian Moses crossed with the spirit of Billy Sunday. Because Myra and young Nat were first cousins, you see. But Junior didn't care a fig leaf about that, and anyway Uncle's pride and joy was all set to clasp the blushful maiden to his breast and flee, when along comes this Mallory, and Myra falls in love with *him*. And that's when Junior fled—flew—oh, hell, you know what I mean—and got himself butchered in the Mato Grosso or somewhere. After which, heh-heh, Mallory dumped *her*. And that, gentlemen, is a little-known chapter in York history."

"I thought " said Ellery, "that Junior's reason for lighting out—"

"Oh yes " said the York remnant magnanimously, "that was part of it, of course. But I doubt if Junior'd ever have given Papa the flirt of his exhaust except for Myra's fickleness. The two things gave him just enough thrust to escape Senior's orbit."

"Well," murmured Queen the younger.

"Well, what?" grated Queen the elder. "Kicking corpses around! Who cares about Junior's love-life twenty years ago, or whenever it was? Is that what brought you here, York? Because if it is, I'm busy, and thank you."

Percival York shot glances to the right, the left and, otherwise unmoving, gave an all-by-himself impression of huddling. "I had to know something."

The Inspector picked up the Myra York autopsy report again; not looking at York, he said, "What?"

"Did Myra get a card? Like the ones Robert and Emily got?"

The old man looked up at that. "Why do you want to know?"

"I just wanted to." Percival sat up in the chair and pushed out his narrow chest. He also pushed out his lips.

"You wouldn't be scared, would you?" asked the Inspector softly.

"Who, me?"

"All right," said Ellery. "There was a card for Myra, too."

"God," said York. "Oh, my God."

"I don't get this," said the Inspector. "Why does that bother you so much, Mr. York?"

"Because Myra wasn't—well, you know—well," said Percival earnestly. "Or what you might call happy. I'd been rather—I mean, I think maybe—"

"You thought maybe she wrote her own ticket bye-bye? Well, Mr. York, she didn't. What d'ye think we put Walt in the can for—jaywalking?"

Bull's-eye Ellery thought watching Percival York twitch.

"He really did it, then . . ."

"You don't think so?"

"I don't know Inspector. I don't see *why* . . ." He looked at them beseechingly. "May I ask what was on the card?"

"A W," said Ellery.

"W? Did Walt confess?"

"No," said Ellery.

"Then I don't see that proves it was Walt—"

"Mr. York," said Richard Queen. "Remember what the letters on the other cards were?"

"A J on Robert's, an H on Emily's."

"And d'ye know Walt's full name?"

"I don't think anyone does. Even Walt. Especially Walt."

"It's John Henry Walt," said Ellery.

"John Hen—JHW! Ohhhhh. Ohhhhhhhhh," said Percival, the second sound being the sound of revealed truth. "Then he really did do it," Percival breathed, as this was the first time he had permitted himself even to hope for such a beautiful thing. "Crazy, man! I suppose he's plain psycho. By God," said Percival York, preening himself, "I'm all right now!"

"In the sense that you're safe," said the Inspector dryly, "I'd say so."

York rose, above the slur, in every dimension seeming to have increased by half. "Well, then, *hell*," he said jovially. "We ought to have a drink and I'm buying!"

"Sorry," said Inspector Queen. "On duty, y'know."

"Off duty," said Ellery. "Thanks just the same."

York shrugged. He picked up his hat and jauntily walked out.

Ellery caught his father's stabbing gesture and jumped off the desk to swing the door shut as the Inspector dived for his phone. "Velie? Percival York's leaving the building and I want somebody to ride on his back and I *don't* want him to know; understand? Who've you got—Johnson, Hesse? Then how about Zilgitt? All right, put Zillie on him, and when Johnson or Hesse checks in tell him to tail Zillie. Anything happens to York, Velie, I'll have Doc Prouty uncork the Black Death around here." He hung up and ground his hard old knuckles into his eye sockets.

"Why?" murmured Ellery. "When you've got your man?"

"Don't start going fancy on me, my son," growled the old man. "I've got the right one, all right. Maybe I can't prove Walt knocked Robert York's head off, and maybe nobody can prove he shoved Emily York onto those subway tracks, but I've sure got him for poisoning Myra. All I need's a few bows to tie up the package, and our boy Percival may be hiding some ribbon ends in his pants pocket, that's all."

"He certainly may," said Ellery. "But not just ends."

His father swallowed. Then he leaned back in an exhausted way. "Spit it out. What's that supposed to mean?"

Ellery reached over and took a scratch pad and a pencil and began to draw. "Look at the three cards the victims received."

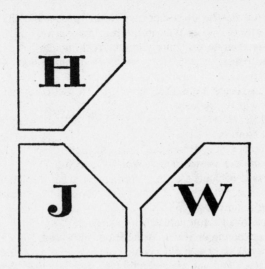

"Arranged like the houses in York Square, granted? They read in order, from lower left, clockwise: Robert's, Emily's, Myra's. Corresponding to the three murders . . . So that leaves Percival."

"So what, for the love of Mike? The three cards have Walt's three initials."

"Yes. But it still leaves Percival, doesn't it? And who profits by the three murders?"

"I don't give a hoot if Percival profits," the Inspector said wearily. "These just aren't murders for profit, that's all. Or even if they are! We know Walt pulled off at least one of them, don't we?—and maybe before we're finished we can prove he pulled off all three, which I'm sold on right now. So what's all the hassle?"

"Well," said Ellery, "suppose Walt's been framed."

"Been *what?*"

"Framed."

"By who?—*whom?*"

"Percival."

The word "framed" had made the old man grip the edge of his desk. The word "Percival" made him let go and lean back, grinning.

"You've avoided the obvious for so long, Ellery, you don't even see it any more. If I understand you, it's not Walt who committed the three murders, but Percival?"

"All I'm asking you to do," said Ellery doggedly, "is to try it on for size."

"Glad to oblige," the old man said dryly. "Robert's kill? Yes, Percy could have pushed that block off. Myra's? A lot less likely, even if we ignore the case against Walt. But for the sake of argument, I'll concede that while Walt was in Myra's bathroom, and the policewoman and Ann Drew were in Ann's room with Myra, Percy could have slipped into the bedroom and dropped the rat-killer into Myra's gin jug. But the middle murder, Emily's, the one practically anybody in New York could have committed—that Percival did *not* do. Couldn't have. Not possibly."

"His alibi." Ellery was crestfallen. "I'd forgotten that. Although alibis . . ." he began hopefully.

But the Inspector was head-shaking. "Not this one, son. This one is copper-riveted." Ellery was beginning the long, loping pacing that characterized a crisis in his relations with a mystery. "Stop flogging it, Ellery," the Inspector said with kindness. "It was Walt. He planned to wipe out all four Yorks. We stopped him after number three."

Now Ellery was head-shaking as he loped. "I don't buy it," he muttered. "No . . ."

"For Pete's sake, Ellery," exploded the Inspector, "you were the one who was bothered by Walt from the start!"

"And he still bothers me. But, Dad." Ellery stopped loping and faced around. "If it was Walt who did the murders, who sent the cards?"

"The cards? Walt, of course."

"You think Walt has the perception, the creative intelligence to have planned all this? Including the cards?"

"That's a question for the psychiatrists to answer."

"You think that, having conceived the idea of the cards, and executed the idea of the cards, he could also have fooled an old police dog like you, and an experienced squad?"

"Fooled us about *what?*" cried the Inspector, out of temper at last.

"The toy printing outfit he's been using—*if* he's your man. You didn't find it, did you? And you searched, you and your men—how many times did you say?"

They looked at each other, the Inspector no longer angry. *He* had forgotten about *that*.

"Dad," Ellery said suddenly.

"What, Ellery?"

"Your search warrants. Are they still valid?"

"Why?"

Ellery said, "Come on."

23 · Pawn

"But, Poochie," pouted the blonde, "I never heard you talk like this before."

"I can talk lots of ways," said Percival York. "You said so yourself."

"Did I do something?" she asked plaintively.

Percival looked her over. There was a glitter in his lemuroid eyes, a steadiness of purpose subtly different from the wayward wildness usual to him. For the first time in the blonde's experience he appeared to be a man with a load off his back, and very great plans.

"You did plenty," Percival said with appreciation. "Most of it pretty good. But let us not forget the fact, my maple cream, that you got plenty, too. And had fun, and it hasn't cost you. Out of it you got flowers and candy and clothes and jewelry and you haven't had to worry about rent too much, right?"

"Poochie, I never wanted—"

"And knock off the Poochie bit. This is a public place."

She glanced about. It was a shadowed, discreet, out-of-the-way public place, but a public place nevertheless. "How about that. Why, Poo—I mean honey? We could've gone to the hotel again."

"I didn't feel like it. I felt like coming here. You want to make something of it?"

She slowly sucked in her lower lip, and bit it. It left lipstick on her teeth. "Now you listen to me, Perce. If you think for one minute after all we been through, and I never asked you for a single thing hiding around all the time like I was a I don't know what, and I never did a single thing to you and now you're treating me like dirt, well!" And she picked up her fork and thrust it five times furiously into the heart of her filet mignon. The impact seemed to bring her to a primitive awareness; she took her hand away and stared glumly at the fork handle, sticking up out of her plate like a rocket on its launching pad.

Percival whinnied. "You want me to tell you what to do with it? Cheese!"

She was frowning with puzzlement, anger and hurt, yet she bravely tried to whinny with him. But then she said, as if to herself, "Day before yesterday it was so *nice*."

"Ah, well," said Percival happily. "Things happen."

"*What* happened?"

"A twenty-to-one shot came in, there's hell to pay in the Middle East, and I went down to police headquarters."

"Police head—Perce! What for?"

"They've got the lad who murdered my cousin Myra."

"They did? It wasn't in the papers. Who is it?"

"Walt."

"Who?"

"Walt. Can you imagine that?"

"You mean that bug-eyed creep that walks like on tracks? But *why?*"

"Y is a crooked letter. And so is his head. What difference does it make, O my darlin'? They got him is enough for me."

She sucked in her lip again and bit it again. "Perce. Is this why you're so—so whatever you are?"

"That's it." Percival filled his lungs to the full, which in his case represented an expansion of about three-quarters of an inch. "Sure I'm so whatever I am. 'Cause who do you s'pose was next on his hit parade?"

Intelligence dawned in the blonde's eye. "My poor, poor Poochie! Why, Poochie, you must've been just—"

"You knock that off, you witless itch," Percival said with such sudden and savage fury that she squeaked and fell back in her chair, her beringed hands instinctively raised in self-defense. "Look, Maybelline, this is your last free ride on *my* bus, so you better enjoy it while you can!"

"My name ain't Maybelline, and this is my last *what?*"

Percival shut off his fury and turned his attention daintily to his steak.

"You're kissing me off?"

He pointed a bottle of Tabasco at her gaily. "You're the one said that."

"I don't have to sit here and take this!"

"Right," Percival said in a cheerful tone.

She made an explosive sound, quite dangerous. But then she took refuge in female helplessness, dabbing piteously at her lips and eyes and leaving her napkin a mess of tangerine and silver-gray. "Oh, what's happening to us? What's happening, Percival?"

"What's happening to me," said Percival, chewing briskly, "is I got lots to do from here on out and I can take my pick with who to do it. It's been great, dearie, so don't let's spoil it and you got your western hemisphere in the Russian dressing."

This was a clearly visible untruth. Nonetheless, the blonde sat up straight and patted herself with the napkin. And said with slitted glance, "You can't do this to me, you slug."

"Wrong," said Percival York.

"You wait, mister. You know what I can do to you?"

"You," Percival said, unmoved, "can't do a bloody damn thing, and you want to know why? Because I got too much money, that's why. I got so much money coming to me, why, God couldn't do anything to me."

She jiggled to her feet, death and tears in her eyes, and snatched up her bag and a mink stole made of dyed beaver, and ran blindly toward the door. As she reached it, she screamed over her shoulder, "You'll be sorry the day you laid eyes on me!"

"I already am!" he bellowed joyously, while quiet diners and silent-footed waiters, a hand-polished cashier and a jointed-at-the-waist maître-d' stiffened with shock. "So get lost, you rancid broad! Drop dead!"

The blonde departed and Percival returned to his plate, chuckling. A waiter wrung his hands, then glided up to him. "Everything all right, sir?" he asked, evidently by reflex.

"Everything's just peachy-keen," said Percival, still laughing. He reached across the table with his fork, captured what was left of the blonde's filet and transferred it to his plate. "My compliments to the cow," he gurgled, "and bring me a bottle of Irish stout."

At Ellery's suggestion they stopped first at a toy store. He picked up a toy printing set, like the set established as having been used to print the J, H and W on the cards; then they proceeded to York Square.

Unexpectedly, it was Mrs. Schriver who answered the Inspector's ring at Percival's castle. The housekeeper seemed to have dwindled since Myra York's death—all but her jaw, which was harder set than ever. The red-penciled perimeter of her eyes widened with welcome at sight of the Queens.

"Inspector, Mr. Ellery Ellery—come in, come in."

They stepped inside, conscious of her grief. She stood before them uncertainly, looking from one to the other. "Now what is it?"

"Nothing, Mrs. Schriver," said the Inspector gently. "Is Mr. York home?"

She shook her head. "I am by myself alone, cleaning him."

"Do you know when he'll be back?"

"After the cleaning I am finished and out, I hope it," the doughty little housekeeper said angrily.

"Oh?" said Ellery. "Then you don't like Mr. York?"

"No-no-*no*." Her head vibrated like a plucked string, she shook it so rapidly. "Cleaning he wants, cleaning I do. Only for myself I do it, not for *him*. A *Schwein*, so dirty he is."

"He asked you to clean his house?"

"Yah. 'You clean up my house,' he says, 'while me, I clean up my life,' and he gives me a yoomp."

"A yoomp," said the Inspector uncertainly.

Mrs. Schriver suddenly executed a caper. Neither Queen smiled; there was too much deadly fury in her clumsy imitation. "And he says, 'All now I need is a good woman. How about you, cookie?' And then on the excuse me *Sitzplatz* he *schwumps* me, and he goes away. So mad I am, I got to fight. The *Schwein* I cannot fight, so his *Schweinstall* I fight until better I feel. Ach, the dirt in this house you would not believe!"

"What can you expect from a *Sitzplatz-schwumper?*" murmured Ellery; and in spite of herself, Mrs. Schriver laughed. He took advantage of her laughter to shuck the paper off his parcel. "Mrs. Schriver, have you ever run across a toy like this while you were cleaning here?"

The housekeeper peered, frowned, then shook her head. Ellery lifted the lid and showed her the wood-handled rubber stamps and the ink pad. She kept shaking her head.

"You're sure, Mrs. Schriver?"

"When a house I clean," she said emphatically, "I clean. No such thing in this house is."

"We'd like to be absolutely sure. Would you help us look?" said the Inspector; and in the next seventy-five minutes he learned to wish devoutly that he might have the likes of Mrs. Schriver under his command. The little castle concealed no corner, nook, shelf or cranny safe from her probing eye. She even helped them explore the hot-air ducts coming up from the cellar.

At last—dusty, dry, lugubrious—Ellery conceded that the only toy printing set in the house was the one he had brought with him. Mrs. Schriver extorted from them a promise that one day they would allow her to glut them with her strudel, shoofly pie and Dutch beer; and they left her attacking Percival York's dining-room rug as if it were, like its owner, her favorite enemy.

Outside, the old man said almost cheerfully, "So Percival doesn't have it, and that's that. Where do you want to check me next?"

"Walt's room."

"We searched it like Maxwell J. House looking for the last drop. I think three times."

"Robert's house?"

"Inside and out."

"And the garage?"

"We even started to pull the cars apart."

"Let's look there again," said Ellery.

They cut across the park to the garage behind Robert York's castle and indeed looked again. Inspector Queen showed Ellery just where the box of poison had stood; and Ellery demonstrated where Walt said he had been—under the Ryan sports car—when Robert was murdered; and they were about to denude the shelves in order to tap and measure the walls behind them when the son clutched the father's ropy arm with a warning clutch.

And they listened, not breathing, and heard through the closed door footsteps coming stealthily toward the garage.

The Inspector's right hand visited his left armpit and returned with a Police Positive. Ellery squared his shoulders until they crackled, then hunched over and drifted toward the door.

The footsteps came closer, stopped. The Inspector raised his weapon.

The knob turned, very, very slowly. Then—*crash!* the door was kicked open and, "Oh, scheissmonger," said the Inspector disgustedly, and put away his gun.

"You could lose half a head that way, Archer," said Ellery. "Nevertheless, heroic. How are you?"

"You did give me what is known as a turn," said Tom Archer, grinning whitely. "I didn't know who it was."

"And we forgot you'd still be working at Robert's. How's it coming?"

"It's going to be three cuts too high for any but a multimillionaire's private stamp collection. Fantastic." Archer looked around the garage curiously. "Can I help you with anything?"

"No," said Inspector Queen.

"Yes," said Ellery. He reached over to the workbench for his parcel. "We've been looking for . . . *this*." And he snatched away the wrapping.

Father and son were watching the face, eyes, stance, everything. Archer did not turn a hair. "What is it?" he asked, and bent forward to read aloud, "Prints Charming. Oh, I see. This is what those ridiculous cards were stamped with."

"Yes," said Inspector Queen.

"No," said Ellery. "One like it, and we can't find it. Have you seen anything like this around here?"

Young Archer shook his head. "By the way, I hear you arrested Walt. You can't actually think *he* did it?"

"Go on back to your work," sighed Ellery. "We'll be rummaging around for some time."

"Anything I can do to help, sing out." Archer waved and went away.

On their way up the narrow stairs to the upper story of the garage the Inspector grumbled, "I don't know what you expect to find, Ellery. If you think Mrs. Schriver's super-clean and Emily lived like a nun, wait till you see Walt's room.

It must be symptomatic of whatever's wrong with him. He couldn't hide a guilty thought in it."

"A man just can't live in a room for years without impressing his personality on it in some way, Dad."

"He *has* no personality. That's Walt's secret weapon." Inspector Queen took out the ring to passkeys he had brought along. "Now which one was it again?"

The second key worked. The old man pushed the door open; it moved as silently as Walt. Ellery stepped inside.

Coming from the dim stairwell, he blinked in the blaze of blankness. The floor was pine, scrubbed white, bleached, waxed; a basic table to match; white curtains simple as pillow slips; an immaculate blanket, white, tucked tight barracks-fashion, on a canvas cot; a plain straight chair, a rectangular table lamp with a base turned from the same white pine, with a tubular white shade. The place was so aching-clean it hurt.

"Might's well live in an aspirin tablet," grunted the Inspector. "Did I exaggerate?"

Ellery stood still in wonderment. "What does he do with himself up here?"

"Reads, I guess." His father pointed.

Between the far side of the bed and the wall beyond stood a small raw bookcase in the inevitable white. Ellery ran over, slid the cot aside—it, too, moved noiselessly—and squatted.

"Talk about one-track minds," he breathed. "*Plywood Projects. Concrete and Masonry Handbook. Woodworker's Manual.* Four books on the care and feeding of lawns. Roses. Pumps. Heating systems. House wiring. And a Bible, the Douay. Wait, here's a paperback *Modern Reader's Bible.* And the *Revised Standard!*" Ellery looked around. "What in God's name would he want with three Bibles?"

"Four," said the Inspector. "There's a King James locked in the table drawer." He unlocked it.

Ellery rose and swooped on the drawer. "The Oxford, with Concordance . . . Dad, this is neat! This figures."

"What figures?"

"Duty. Devotion to Duty—always, always capitalized." Ellery waved at the bookcase. "A couple of shelves full of musts. A must is like a should, explaining the Bibles." He began the long hungry lope, explaining to himself aloud. "He's a zombie, a robot . . . does what he must do . . . should do . . ."

"And nothing he shouldn't?" demanded his father. "Is that your point?"

"Exactly. This room closes the point out, Dad—it isn't even debatable any more. The man who lives in this room could not—repeat, could *not*—have conceived this devious business, as I've held repeatedly. It's too . . . too inventive. Too romantic."

"Romantic!"

"Well, adventuresome," muttered Ellery. "The only way Walt could ever have committed these crimes is by someone telling him to, spelling it all out for him, step by step. And whoever that is, he's not sitting in your jail smiling."

Inspector Queen choked. "There are Walt's clothes."

In one corner of the room, an L-shaped partition segregated the tiny bathroom. White curtains over the doorway. Another across an area where the partition was single wallboard instead of double, with the studs removed. There, on hooks hung in a ruler-straight line, hangers were angled to the narrow space. Two immaculate "good" suits, cheap but cared for: one black, one brown. Dress shoes: one pair black, one pair brown. Work shoes: three pairs, of excellent quality. On shelves, small or wide as needed: stacks of socks, black and brown; underwear; handkerchiefs.

Shirts were on hangers, obviously laundered and pressed by hand, for they were not folded. Ironing board hinged from the partition; iron in a cubbyhole. Every possible space in the little partition was used; it was a miniature storage wall, only four inches thick.

"If he hid it here," said Ellery, "he chewed it up fine and painted it on."

"You think that's packed? Look at the kitchen."

Ellery turned around twice before he saw the "kitchen." Stove—a two-burner electric plate—and work surface hinged down from the wall opposite the window. This exposed china—heavy white cafeteria crockery, exactly one service—and a stainless-steel knife, fork, teaspoon and tablespoon upended in the single white china coffee mug. There was no refrigerator: Walt apparently ate from cans and boxes, of which there was a supply on the shelf beside the dishes. No sink: he must use the tiny one in the bathroom.

Ellery closed it all up and walked thoughtfully across to the window, a dormer, which alone broke the boxlike proportions of the room. He could see along the side of Robert York's castle and across the end of the diamond-shaped park to Myra's front door.

Suddenly he threw his forearm across his eyes and stood motionless.

"Son. What's the matter?"

Ellery gave the Inspector an impatient headshake. He flung down his arm and bounded for the door. "I'll be back in a minute," he exclaimed, and raced down the stairs.

His father hopped for the window. He saw Ellery gallop out the side door of the garage, turn and look up while running, stumble, recover and scramble into the building, to race back up the stairs.

"Ellery, what in time—?"

Ellery held up a breathless wait-a-minute palm and dashed to the window, scooping up the chair as he passed the table. He set it before the window, leaped on it and, using his knuckles, pressed upward.

The Inspector gaped. For the dormer ceiling, a mere piece of fiberboard, lifted readily to expose a quite sizable blackness above. Still holding the panel up with his knuckles, Ellery reached over the nearest beam and felt beyond it, shouted, "Dad!" and drew forth a shiny box bearing the legend *Prints Charming*. He jumped down with it, the panel fell back into place with a cushioned *whoosh*, he threw the toy printing set to his father and dropped gasping into the chair.

The old man's face was a sight to behold. For just as all the combined rays of the spectrum reflect to the eye the color white, so all the Inspector's emotions—stupefaction, self-castigation, professional chagrin, anger at subordinates and half a dozen others—produced an expression of total blankness. He proceeded mechanically to set the box on Walt's table, raise the lid, take out his display handkerchief and, with it, lift the letter J from its bed, examine its stamping surface and, shaking his head in a dazed way, replace the J and lift out the H. And then the W. And then all the other letters, and the numbers.

"The only ones showing ink on the stamping surfaces are the J, H and W," the old man mumbled; and, carefully replacing the lid, he turned and looked at his son, who was still breathing hard.

"If I didn't think you might do it," said the Inspector in a sort of croak, "I'd turn around and instruct you to kick me where it'd do the most good. Will you kindly tell me: are you a genius or am I an idiot? A hand-picked squad searched this room, not once but three times. I searched it personally. Yet you walk in here, take one look, point—"

"Oh, come on, Dad," Ellery said irritably. "You just didn't happen to notice one thing, and I just did. This is a dormer window with a pitched roof. Yet inside the window the ceiling is flat. So there had to be space up there. That's not what's bothering me."

"You're *bothered* about finding this?" snapped the old man. "What's the matter with you, Ellery? This find of yours cinches the case against Walt. It's going to send him to the Chair."

"That's what's bothering me," muttered Ellery. "Because it pins all three murders on him."

"Are you suggesting that the box was planted up there to frame him? That Percival pipe dream again?"

"No, I was wrong about that," said the son wearily. "I don't doubt you'll find Walt's fingerprints all over it. I'm ready to concede that Walt executed the three murders, Dad. What I'm not ready to concede is that he *planned* the three murders."

"What are you doing now?" demanded his father. For Ellery had risen suddenly and stepped back onto the chair.

"Seeing if there's anything else up here."

Again Ellery used his knuckles to raise the ceiling plasterboard. With the other hand he felt around the floor of the hiding place. "Nothing on this side . . ." He changed hands on the ceiling panel and fumbled about in the opposite direction— and then, with almost a surprised look, stopped fumbling. The Inspector, watching him, stiffened.

"What is it, Ellery?"

"Feels like a clipboard," said Ellery slowly; and he withdrew the hand of discovery with care, and the panel came down with a *whoosh;* and it was indeed a clipboard, with a number of sheets of paper held neatly in its jaws.

And as he read the topmost sheet from his elevated position in John Henry Walt's white and sterile room, with Inspector Queen shifting restlessly below him, one hand making futile requests, Ellery sighed a long and satisfied sigh, and some of the hunch went out of his taut shoulders, and even the lines drawn lately on his face underwent erasure.

But when he handed the clipboard to his father, and the Inspector began to read the topmost sheet as Ellery got down from the chair, there was neither satisfaction nor relaxation on the old man's face, only a deepening of its anxieties.

For what the Inspector read was:

Dear Walt:
> *You know who I am.*
> *You do not know that you know.*
> *You shall.*
> *I write this to let you know that I know who you really are. I know the skill of your hands. I know the quality of your obedience. I know where you come from and what you are doing. I know what you think. I know what you want. I know your great destiny.*
> *I like you.*

Y

24 · Queen's Countergambit

Ellery Queen was fast asleep when at last he began to understand—really to understand—the rules of the York Square game he was playing.

It did not come to him as a game at first, when he was profoundly dreaming. It began as a series of impressions, whimsical, laughable even; not until then did he find himself locked in combat with a chess piece. But which one? which one?—oh, horrible, it was a bishop, but instead of the miter it had a squashed head . . .

And then he was running, running over the squares (squares?), and he was tiny, too tiny to cover that much distance quickly; but he must get there, he must . . . and the squares grew larger as he grew smaller until he could see only one square—York Square, of course, with the four castles at the corners.

And Ellery knew with a great desolation that he was running, had been running, to save a chess piece that was under attack; he saw her standing with her doom descending like a great hand, come to take her away. And take her it did, and then there was the horror of stasis wherein suddenly he must stand where he found himself, helpless, waiting, waiting, and immobile because it was not his turn.

He twisted and moaned in his sleep, and he moved upward from level to dark level—still very dark, very deep, but by a subtle tone less dark than those lightless depths at which the dream (he now knew) had begun.

A pawn went sliding past, dipping to go by diagonally. And as it passed his vision (he was still immobilized, waiting his turn), he knew why it had sidestepped like that: it had taken a piece, one of his best, which screamed as the pawn replaced it on the board.

And the pawn had the face of Walt.

Suddenly he had to make a move (now, *now!*) but there would be no time to think; he must just *move;* and he did; and he knew as he did that it was a terribly wrong move. The shape ahead of him was the shape of Ann Drew, and when she realized what he had done she looked at him with disgust and loathing and began to bleed all over her body; her loathing was infinitely greater than her agony, and he tried to tell her that he'd had to move that way, that there'd been no time to think. But her loathing was greater than his voice, his whole mind; it would never let her understand. And he moaned and twisted, and came up a bit more out of his roiling sleep.

The game was a shooting-gallery kind of chess, with rows of chess pieces moving from left to right, and above them a row of heads moving from right to left. The heads were Emily and Myra and Walt and Percival and his father and himself, and one face that was not a face at all but a blank in the shape of a head. In endless succession they moved, heads to the left, chess pieces to the right, so that from moment to moment Walt was a pawn, his father was a pawn, Tom Archer was a

206

king, Mrs. Schriver a knight. A moment, and it was all changed: Percival was a pawn, Mallory a king, the faceless one a rook . . . a castle.

There was one remarkable instant when all the heads fitted all the chessmen—when everything was as clear to him as if he had always known this curious game and its complex rules. But then the instant blinked away, and he cried out at his inability to remember any of the right heads for the pieces. And he gnashed his teeth and scissored his jaws, because for that short solar moment he had seen the face of the faceless one—the king, the player on the other side.

He groaned aloud, "The player on the other side."

And came higher out of his dream, almost out of sleep.

"Check," someone said. And it echoed, and on each descending pulse a check for $1,000,000 went spinning on the wind.

"And mate!" someone cried. But this was a cry of ecstasy, for a sheet-lightning flash revealed Tom Archer in intimate embrace with Ann Drew. Or did "check" with "mate" mean stop it, stop it? ("Should any man know cause why these twain should not be wed," muttered the bishop, "let him speak now or forever hold his peace.") (Which piece is that? The Queen! Then use the queen, use it, the most powerful piece on the board. Only . . . the queen has forgotten how to move. Who's the player on the other side? Tell me that and I'll remember the moves) . . .

With a wrenching grunt Ellery came finally out of his dream and his sleep. His inhospitable bed angered him, and he lurched up and away from it to stand, weaving, in the dark. His mouth felt like an ant farm, and a faintly luminous rime seemed to salt his eyelids.

He stumped into his study, stubbed his toe, groped for a curse word, fumbled and found the desk-lamp switch, dropped into the chair, lifted the lid of the coffeepot, dropped it back in disgust. And leaned back to gloom owlishly at the bland backs of the Encyclopedia Britannica, Eleventh Edition. A to AND. AND to AUS (Ann to Archer?) . . . He skipped along the attentive row. HAR to HUR (laugh her off!) . . . SHU to SUB and SUB to TOM. (And *that* was clear: kick him in the subway.)

He shook his head and told himself aloud to shut up, which made him glance guiltily toward the other bedroom. And he wondered what his father would say at the sight of him sitting barefoot at his desk in the middle of the night telling himself to shut up. And suddenly, uninvited, inexpressibly welcome, suddenly the dream flashed across his mind, all of it at once; and, father or no father: "Well, sure!" he cried.

For it *was* like a game! There was Walt, the pawn, all but worthless in himself, yet deadly if played with skill—and Walt had been played adroitly indeed. (He and the Inspector had pored over the My Dear Walt letters signed the cryptic Y, letters typewritten with such perfect exactness on the faint blue lines of the cheap ruled paper . . . read them and marveled and discussed, reread and discussed again how clear it now was that to lock up the weapon Walt was merely to lock up a gun or a switchblade and let its user go.)

Yes, Y had played Walt well, with painstaking cruelty. Through his victorious anger at the letters Ellery could have wept at the tragedy of this slow dutiful little blinking man, his past forgotten and his future hopeless, unloving and unloved, a lone cipher in the midst of an involved equation—suddenly receiving those passionless, directing, assuring, omnipotent letters . . . that icy cascade of admiration, those calm promises of greatness: Walt, man of destiny, dispenser of death, the chosen one for that mighty trust . . . loved at last.

Little as Walt knew about himself, he must dimly grasp that he was less clever than most; yet here he was, outwitting the sharp, outflanking the powerful—even now, silent in a cell, unafraid, for had not his great and awful patron written that no harm would come to him? Of course Walt would not speak! Why should he? He need only wait—rescue was certain, his destiny foreordained. *My Dear Walt.* Safe all along, because anyone, even the great man himself (Ellery winced and writhed) could tell at a glance that he, Walt, hadn't brains enough to be the player on the other side.

Player on the other side . . . Oh, yes, it was a game—a game in which for any piece to be swept off the board meant death, and millions of dollars hung on every move. A game in which York Square was the board, and didn't it have a castle in each corner? Walt the pawn, the castles the rooks. What else?

"Well, sure," Ellery said, again aloud, and again guiltily; but the Inspector slept on in the other bedroom.

For the Queen was there, oh, yes; the queen, the powerful piece—as his dream had had it—uncertain of the moves. (How terrible, the move that left Ann bleeding, loathing.)

What else?

A knight? Do we have a knight? Oh, yes (and Ellery almost smiled)—oh, yes, we have a knight, Percival . . . Sir Percivale, brought to ruin by the dark arts of the Arthurian enchantress . . . Parsifal, "the guileless fool" who at the end became guardian of the Holy Grail; and was that so far gone in its cynical symbolism?

But there's no bishop, no bishop . . . (Only one who is subject to such fantasies of the night can know how very elusive a detail can be, and how desperately desirable.)

But Ellery punched the leather arm of his chair, elated. There was one! For in the olden days of the game didn't they call the bishop an *archer?* He had seen antique sets whose piece in the bishop's square carried a bow. Archer . . .

Pawn, rook, knight, queen, bishop . . . king?

For take the king and the game is over. That's how you know he's the king. The player on the other side.

The faceless one . . . Immediately Ellery shut his eyes and saw again that mad progression of chessmen changing heads. It was a shock to remember that one miraculous instant when all the right heads were on all the right pieces—even the head of the faceless one. The king, the player on— And now to have forgotten it—

Ellery sprang from his chair. But his left leg had gone to sleep, and he staggered back. The swivel chair swiveled maliciously; he flailed, and the coffeepot jumped off the desk; he lunged and caught it just as it was about to baptize the rug.

Breathing hard, Ellery set the pot carefully back on the desk and started over. (Make haste slowly, aging man. Tell yourself the story of the young bull and the old bull who spotted the herd of heifers in the valley. "Shake a hoof, old-timer," bellowed the youngster. "Let's run down there and smooch us one of those heifers." "No, son," said the old bull with dignity, "let's walk down there and smooch 'em all.")

And Ellery stood on his sensible leg and shook the other until he could all but hear the pins and needles jingle. Then he limped to the bookshelf and fingered out his Bartlett from between Fowler and Roget. And riffled, and squinted, and found what he was looking for; and with his index finger as a bookmark he limped back to the desk chair and the direct lamplight.

The chess-board is the world, the pieces are the phenomena of the universe, the rules of the game are what we call the laws of Nature. The player on the other side is hidden from us. We know that his play is always fair, just, and patient . . .

Ellery arrghed and clapped the book shut. That's what you get when you go bird-dogging for analogies! They strike close enough to make a noise, but then they go ricocheting off into the irrelevant. (What caliber bullet does it take to kill the irrelevant? he thought inexcusably; and: The irrelevant never forgets. He was warned by this that his brain was running too fast for its own good, and he put *Familiar Quotations* and Huxley aside and sat down quietly to think.)

He sat thinking for some time, unmoving except when he crossed his legs the other way. Once he muttered, "But it's my move." After a while his eyes drooped shut. But he had never been further from sleep.

And the move came to him.

Instantly he rejected it. Don't be a fool, he advised himself, you'll lose your knight . . . If only he could recall which head went on which piece! Especially . . . The move came creeping back to him; he stepped on it. He thought of other moves. *The* move, uncrushed, laid its warm head on his ankle and purred and purred. He tried to kick it off. But now it had its claws in him. He sighed in surrender and took it up into his lap. And stroked its unusual carcass, and said, Let's have a look at you . . .

He knew, when he rose, that he had made up his mind long before. He knew the dangers. He knew, also, the infernal nuisance of persuasion and argument he was going to have to go through. None of which mattered.

Ellery shuffled doggedly through the apartment, shot open the door of the Inspector's bedroom so that the knob cannoned into the socket it had dug for itself in the bedroom plaster (a concession which always brought his father up standing, though he might not truly waken for ten minutes or more) and stood patiently waiting while the old man beat the end of blanket away from his ears and snarled, *Wurra, wurra, wurra,*" and similar incantations, ending with, "What in time time is it?"

Then Ellery said, "Dad, we'll have to let Walt go."

Hell broke loose.

PART THREE

End Play

25 · Waiting Moves

Mr. J. H. Walt went back to York Square, and a miracle was passed by the fourth estate.

On booking Walt for Myra York's death, Inspector Richard Queen had asked the newsmen to sit on it. He took his oath on a long-term better break if they would go along with him now. Therefore three papers had mentioned Walt's arrest not at all; three had mentioned it, but harmlessly ("held for questioning") in the back pages. The seventh paper, honoring its promise, reported nothing in its news columns; but, alas, from its editorial page crawled That Certain Columnist, who had chewed and spewed as follows:

> . . . *Anyone for a handyman's job? There's one open at a downtown private park surrounded by crackerjack castles. Seems the incumbent can't explain away evidence connecting him with the latest obit in a dead-millionaire epidemic they've been enjoying like on the square. Up to now the police score was 0 for 3, but maybe they're getting the old batting eye back and the Commissioner will be able to point with pride to the Kitty-Korner Killings down at Kosy-Kastle Square.*
>
> *Maybe. Because grim suspicion: Trickling down the left side of this (coff-coff) "liberal" administration could be the sludgy notion that scot-free murder is quicker and neater than taxing the rich to death.*

Now it may be that some of the newspapers went along with Inspector Queen because they respected and trusted him. Or it may be—it may indeed well be— that other columnists had sharply pointed things to say and had them ready to jab, but slipped them back into the scabbard when Brother Rat ratted. And this in turn may have been from contempt for That Certain Columnist's politics (pro-mom, anti-sin, and for anything and everything that promised to incite hatred in the breasts of the masses); or from dislike of his person, which looked, felt and smelled like aging yeast; or from envy of his income, which was counted by computers. Whatever the motivations, the betrayed all worked together to leave T. C. C. high and dry on an uncharted reef, belatedly aware that a scoop is not a scoop unless floated by a tide of like-thinking late-comers. And there he clung until the morning editions swept down on his stranded scoop, with an elemental howl, a typhoon that smashed its hull to the bilge.

For now—said *all* the papers, including the derelict's own—it appeared that Myra was a suicide, consequently John Henry Walt was released from custody; Emily was an accident; and such progress had secretly been made on Robert's case that an arrest could be expected at any hour.

None of this came (officially) from Centre Street.

The Curious Incident of the Embarrassing Moment came about in this way:

Because no man can remain in an immovable state of fear, perplexity or anger and keep his sanity, Ellery swung out into a brief light-heartedness. It was evoked, perhaps, by the sun on Ann Drew's hair. She was walking her little beast in York Square, and Tom Archer was with her; and Ellery was to reflect later that if any one of these entities had been absent he would not have made so erroneous an error.

"Queen!" called Archer. "Do you know what she's going to do?"

"Good morning," said Ellery to Ann Drew; and to the dog, "Good morning, Bud," and to young Archer, "First tell me which of these ladies you're talking about."

"It isn't Bud, it's Bub," said Archer. "She's going to work with me. How do you like those apples! Finishing the collection."

"Bud is? Oh, licking stamps."

"Not Bub! Ann. She's agreed to stay on in the Square and work for me, and the trustees at the bank have okayed a salary for her."

"You actually crave a career of stamp-licking?" Ellery asked the girl, while saying to himself, Would God I were a tender 1869 Gambia 6d. pale blue no-watermark imperf.

"You don't lick these stamps—" Archer began indulgently.

But Ann Drew smiled, an act somehow equivalent to daybreak, which immediately darkened because she also touched Tom Archer's arm. So Ellery sighed and said to the dog, "You and I are in the wrong business, Bud."

"Bub," Archer corrected him again. "It's short for Beelzebub. But don't ask Ann why," he added, fondly teasing. "It shocks her."

"Oh, yes," Ellery recalled. "The thing Miss Drew said she would *never* tell me." And then, perhaps because her hair and her smile had made his head spin, or this sustained whimsy had passed its proper peak, he tossed off words which at once he would gladly have given lifetime first North American serial rights to recall. All he meant was, "Why did you call the dog that?" but what actually emerged from his mouth was "And just what would shock the likes of you, milady?"

In that split second it came to Ellery in a flood: what she had done as a girl, and how terrified she was lest Tom Archer ever hear of it. Ellery's immediate predicament all but overwhelmed him, for her stricken face was scalding: and "Hey!" cried

Tom Archer in swift concern, and stroked her. "Hey, there, it's not as bad as all *that*."

That was when Ellery said, "Look, I have to run, I'm late for the mumble mumble," and fled.

And there in the sunlight they watched him go; and to Archer's astonishment and delight Ann said to him, "Hold me, Tom, hold me tight . . ." so that he forgot to question what any of it meant.

Living ghosts invaded York Square. Among the strollers and rubbernecks on wheels—among the wiring inspectors, meter readers, inventory men from the estate's bank, postmen, laundrymen and newsmen—a high percentage came from Inspector Queen's and the D.A.'s offices. These ghosts were both seen and invisible. Above and behind, around and under, in manholes with listening bugs and in neighboring buildings with field glasses and cameras, the cordon was thrown around Percival York. He was of necessity informed of what was going on, but he liked it not and he took it dimly. Some of his protection he could see; but a great deal of it was kept secret from him, and therefore Percival never felt that he was getting enough.

Yet it was impossible to rely on him. Not four hours after unreservedly promising the Queens to stay in sight at all times, or to notify the nearest guard when he felt he had to leave York Square, Percival slipped his tails (and was neatly tailed again without his knowledge, thanks to a man on Emily's tower with a handie-talkie and another on a neighboring rooftop with a tight-beam flashlight), and took a taxi to the estate's bank. Here he demanded to know if the terms of his residence in the Square under old Nathaniel's will could be stretched far enough to allow his taking a cruise until the danger was past. The bank official who told him solemnly that, were he to do such a thing, he might forfeit the entire fortune was frankly lying, because Ellery had been there against just such a contingency. Not since that magnificent miser, Jack Benny, was asked by a holdup man, "Your money or your life," had a man seemed in such anguished indecision as Percival York. Living bait, he acted as if he feared the worst by the moment, by the breath, the bite and the swallow (Ellery remarked to his father that York must fear a dozen deaths; no man could be that afraid of only one). The alternative, to flee and lose his pending millions, must have been to him—judging by his behavior—quite as dreadful a prospect as death itself.

Of all things Percival feared, he feared Walt the most.

The handyman had slipped back into his routine without a sign of trauma. He was no trouble to watch; he was thoroughly preoccupied. He had regained his tongue with his freedom; but he had never exercised it lavishly, and he obeyed Inspector Queen's injunction to the letter: to answer no questions about his arrest from anyone, and to refer the persistent questioners to the Inspector.

"Not that he'd spill anything," the old man growled. "You can make Walt answer questions by the yard without learning a blasted thing."

And Ellery nodded, himself preoccupied.

Walt did what he was told. He was told to do little, for he had a sharpshooter's eye for a fleck of plaster, a bald spot on a lawn, a dripping faucet; for the rest, he spent most of his time in his room, since the passing of three of the four Yorks left him largely maintenance duties.

The toy printing set, on which no prints had been found but Walt's, had been returned precisely to its hiding place; so had the letters from Y—after being photostated and microphotographed by the lab. The letters, too, had yielded no fingerprints but

Walt's; hence the microphotographs. If they should reveal any sign of latent prints, the originals could always be repossessed for further examination.

"This case, though," said the Inspector sourly, "will hang by no easy threads like that. This is a fall-on-your-face kind of case."

"This case," retorted his son, "is a drop-dead kind of case."

There was little chance that Walt might destroy the letters, both Queens felt. They meant so much to him that, to preserve their wonderful testimony to his worth, he had risked the displeasure of his guardian angel—the only thing in which apparently he had disobeyed Y.

Walt's course and Percival's seldom crossed; but when they did, the result was ludicrous. Small and stocky Walt, with that queer glide-on-tracks gait, the oddly non-reflecting eyeballs, the withdrawn glance—Walt would proceed from here to there like a natural event, a distant flight of birds, or an oncoming winter, unchangeable by anything outside itself. Ambling, shambling, bag-eyed Percival, who ordinarily managed a jaunty step, would—at his first glimpse of Walt—wobble on his feet like a suddenly pierced balloon . . . not so much from weakness as from sheer indecision about which way to go.

At the same time Percival's pressures were not all directed toward escape; he seemed to have a stubborn desire to fluff the whole thing off like a man. If Walt's course seemed to be taking him by at a safe distance, Percival might tremble and flutter, but he would hold his ground; or, if there was a wall or a tree behind him, he backed toward it slowly, never taking his eyes off his enemy, until he stood with his bent-bow spine hard-pressed against solidity . . . breathing noisily, nostrils aflutter, beady eyes peering out over their discolored shelves. So he would stand until Walt was unequivocally past; after which he would slump, and sigh, and straighten up and go about his business. If, of course, the encounter was direct, Percival unhesitatingly ran. It was as if he knew that Walt not only had, but was, some sort of fragmentation bomb.

As for Walt, at a distance or in close, he sidled by at never-changing speed, on a never-changing course, oblivious.

So matters held for almost a week, while the Queens, *pater* and *filius*, waited for the next move.

He was not displeased.

True, there had been delays. But then, the universe itself was created force against force, each modifying the other. The forces seldom balanced; so often there was a flow one way or the other. The hand of God met resistance in the clay it molded, or the molding would have been impossible.

He contemplated the night city through the dirty window of the hotel room. The city's lights danced nervously. He smiled.

He turned, and crossed the dreary little room, and patted the patiently waiting typewriter, and went to the door.

He put out the light.

He locked the door.

He left.

Ann Drew and Tom Archer saw a play in Greenwich Village, took the subway for the short journey home, and a little past midnight found themselves in the dark warmth of York Square. They paused to kiss briefly before the plaque bearing

Nathaniel York, Junior's name, because there they had almost quarreled once; and it was from there that they heard the distant sound of weeping.

For a shocked moment they looked toward each other in the gloom. Then Ann hurried off in the direction of the ugly sound, and Archer hurried after her.

The sound drew them halfway around the Square, to Percival York's house; and here they found its source, on the top step, weeping and rocking.

Ann ran up the walk, Tom running after with a warning word. But before she could reach the step, or the word could be spoken, a tall blackness separated itself from a deeper blackness and said sharply, "Hold it, there!" and then said softly, "Oh, Miss Drew, Mr. Archer. Evening."

"*Gosh*," breathed Ann. "I didn't see you at all."

"Inspector Queen's know-how, Miss Drew," said Detective Zilgitt amiably. "Inspector knows the value of assigning a black detective to a dark night."

Ann smiled a faint smile. Her pupils had adjusted to the darkness by now, and she could just make out the glow of the city detective's answering smile. "Is that . . . Mr. York?"

"Nobody else."

"But he's crying."

"Been crying for close to an hour."

"Can't you do anything for him?"

"I'm just my brother's keeper," said Zillie dryly. "Holding his hand isn't my department."

Ann licked her lip, braced, began the swift movement to kneel by the weeping, rocking Percival. Instantly the detective checked her, with the same gesture taking her purse. Archer, squinting, saw how deftly the man passed it from one hand to the other, weighing it, taking inventory. "Let Mr. Archer hold this for you," said Zilgitt kindly. He handed it over.

"But this *is* your department," said Archer.

"That's right," said the detective, and he drifted in close as Ann sank down before the sobbing man.

"Percival." Ann shook his shoulder gently. "It's me, Ann."

"Didn't want you to—see me—this way," sobbed Percival.

"Ah, now, listen," said Tom Archer. He hauled Ann to her feet from behind. "Let the guy be. Didn't you ever see a crying jag before?"

She shrugged his hands away. "He has *not* been drinking, Tom! Don't you see he's in trouble?" She knelt again. Archer, feeling foolish, stepped back. "Percival?"

"Didn't want you to—see me—like this," wept Percival stubbornly.

"What is it? What's wrong?"

He put down his hands. She reached past to snare his display handkerchief, shook it out and gave it to him. Reflexively he wiped his face. "Annie—I mean, Miss Snff."

"Ann," she said.

Not noisily, Tom Archer spat.

"Don't bother about me. Please."

"Isn't there something we can do for you?"

"Nobody can do anything. I wish I never heard of this place. Or the money."

"You don't have to stay here."

"But I do. You think I've got the moxie to walk away from eleven million bucks? But—"

"Go on," Ann Drew crooned.

Percival slapped his own face angrily with the handkerchief. "But I can't stand it here, either. I've got nobody, nothing."

Tom Archer said, "You'll have eleven million bucks."

"And what's that, all by yourself?" Percival sniffed and blew his nose. "Look at you two, what you've got. Each other. Work you like, that pays your way. And people who like *you*. Know anybody that likes me? In forty-six years I've never had anybody."

"You could still have it," Ann said emotionally.

He shook his head. "I never learned how. You know, Ann," he said, very quietly, "I really did *not* want you to see me like this. This thing's done something to me. You won't believe it, but I've quit drinking—I haven't been near a single horse parlor—I got rid of . . . Well." He made a difficult little laugh. "And here I am, having to *tell* it to people! Where do you start if you want to be like everyone else and you don't know how?"

Tom Archer squatted on a heel beside Ann and looked into Percival's face from a distance of six inches. "You actually mean what you're saying?"

"Tom, he does!" cried Ann. "Percival—Mr. York—look I know at least three people who'll help. Tom and me—"

"And who else?" It was part leaping hope, part wry disbelief.

"You."

Young Archer rose. "Perce, you be at Robert's house nine o'clock tomorrow morning. I've got a deadline on those stamps, and Ann and I are swamped. I can use your help. Will you come?"

The last known survivor of the Yorks leaned eagerly toward the two young faces, peering in astonishment. Then—"All right!" Percival York said. "All *right!*"

The hardest thing Ellery had had to do was con his father into taking the tails off John Henry Walt after releasing him from custody. The hardest thing Inspector Queen had had to do was con his superiors into looking the other way. By some magic, possibly the alchemy of desperation, both succeeded.

"They're examining my reports," mumbled the Inspector, "when they ought to be examining my head. I've got everybody so dazzled by this thing that no one's opened his eyes wide enough to see that I'm letting an indictable killer run around loose with a completely bare bottom."

"It makes sense," Ellery insisted. "Now that we have positive evidence that Walt's a mere tool, with Mr. Y—why couldn't he have called himself X!—with Y directing his every move, it stands to reason that Y watches Walt closely. When we let Walt go, Y had every right to smell a trap—to expect us to keep Walt under around-the-clock surveillance. We can't afford to scare Y off; we have to force his hand; so no tails on Walt; and maybe Y will think it's on the level—that the Walt make was from hunger, and we saw it couldn't be he. After all, Y doesn't know we're on to those letters of his to Walt. By the way, has the clipboard been checked recently?"

"Yesterday afternoon, by Johnson. He skinned up there while Walt was mixing a little cement to set a loose flagstone behind Emily's house. Nothing's changed."

"You're afraid Y's seen through us?"

"Well, I just said it. Nothing's changed."

"I think we're pulling a successful deception play. Anyway, Dad, it's a chance we've got to take."

The Inspector grunted and poured the breakfast coffee.

"All right, I know how worried you are," said Ellery. ("Who, me?" said the Inspector with a hollow laugh.) "But look, there'd be even less sense to this mishmash if Percival weren't marked for slaughter, too. Well, we have Percival sewed up tight, haven't we? So there's really not much to worry about."

"Maybe we've got Percival sewed up *too* tight." The old man snatched the marmaladed toast out of his mouth and shot a look ceilingward. "Lord forgive me."

"Amen!" muttered Ellery. "More toast, please."

"Maybe that's why this Y hasn't hit."

"Up to now, probably. Percival's led such an unpredictable life—he's ordinarily here, there, yonder and out all night to boot. Y studies his victims' routines and plans accordingly; our Perce hasn't had any routines. But now . . . now, suddenly, he's on time, he's in position."

"And how about that," said the Inspector. "My boys still haven't got over it."

"Maybe there's been another Percival hiding out in that rotten hulk all the time, waiting for a chance to take over."

"Maybe."

"Anyway, the new Perce is bound to tempt Y into a move."

They sat with their thoughts, munching toast and sipping coffee: Ellery thinking painfully of a girl so good she needed no salvation (and why *had* the pooch been named Beelzebub?), and of an evil man, about to be Croesus-rich, who had within him an ordinary and quite decent fellow aching to be born; and the old gentleman recalling the shy, laughing one peeping out from Miss Sullivan's weathered hulk.

"Maybe," repeated the Inspector. "But my innocent-eyed watchdogs are saying—"

"Don't tell me, I know," sighed Ellery. "They're saying it can't last."

The Inspector shrugged.

"It's very possible. Percival's the kind who turns over a new leaf in the way he's always done everything, to excess."

"According to the reports, he's been so damn punctual on that stamp job this week he makes the late Robert look like a slob. Now when Perce says he's going to be somewhere, that's where he is. Except twice."

"Except twice?" Ellery put down his cup. "Except twice what?"

"Except twice this week," said the Inspector with the fretful guilt of the executive who accepts full responsibility for his subordinates' booboos, "when our reborn friend slipped away."

"What!"

"Once," nodded the old man, "he asked Archer for time off to go get his polio shot—his duty, he said, his *civic* duty, for Pete's sake! Archer was up to his ears and forgot to alert the man on duty; the man on duty didn't 'expect' Percival to cut out and was sneaking a coffee break—and where *he* is now," the Inspector interpolated grimly, "he doesn't have much expectation of *anything*. And the other night our boy slipped his leash—don't worry, we've plugged that one—and got back to York Square just as we were pushing the panic button. Apologized, said he went for a walk, didn't mean to cause trouble! It won't," said Inspector Queen through his dentures, "happen again."

"It—had—better—not," said Ellery. The moisture he wiped from his upper lip with his napkin was true fear-sweat. And he picked up a toast crust, looked at it, put it down and began to nibble on his thumb instead.

"Well," said the Inspector, shoving his chair back.

"Dad, before you go." Ellery shut his eyes and flapped his head like a dog drying himself. Then he opened his eyes and said, "Nothing new on the letters, I suppose?"

"You mean from the lab? No, and they blew up those micro-slides as big as a barn door. Just Walt's prints, period. Why? Did you expect this Y to be careless about a thing like prints?"

"No, but . . ."

"But *what?*"

"I was looking over those print photos yesterday—I mean the original set the lab took. There's something about them that's been bugging me."

His father stared. "Go on."

Ellery shut his eyes again. "I was sitting there, staring at them, trying to visualize Walt reading them, gloating over them—I mean the letters. Judging by the prints the lab brought out, he handled those letters a lot."

"Yes? So?"

"Well, if you really *look* at those prints of his—the way they're distributed"—Ellery opened his eyes suddenly—"you have to see Walt holding the letters by the top corners. As if . . . well, as if he repeatedly held them up to the light, or something."

"If you mean hidden messages," the Inspector said dryly, "forget it. They've been checked for that."

"I *know*. But why would he hold each page by the upper corners? With his thumbs? Because those upper-corner prints are all thumbprints. Why, Dad?"

"If I thought I'd get an answer," said the old man in a voice one part irascibility and one part perplexity, "I'd ask him."

And this time he did get up from the table, because the phone rang.

Inspector Queen came back tautly. "We'd better hop to it. That was the post office."

"Post office?"

"They have a letter down there addressed to Mr. Percival York."

"The same kind as—?" Ellery was twisted about in his chair. "A card-letter?"

"A card-letter."

26 · Attack Culminated

He inserted the fresh sheet in the typewriter and, without hesitation in the special silence of the dingy hotel room, began to write with great speed:

My Dear Walt:
  Here is your final task, the glorious culmination of all you have done for me and, through me, for yourself.
  You will take the enclosed card and, with the usual care to get a clean impression with the rubber stamp and to center it on the card (and remembering that to be correct in this instance the diagonal edge of the card must be at the lower left) imprint the card with the proper stamp so that it looks like this:

  Place it in the envelope, address it to Mr. Percival York at York Square, and mail it at any time before midnight of the day you receive this.
  In the following day go about your duties in the ordinary way. Do not worry about Percival York's keeping to his new work schedule. He will almost certainly stick to it.
  When you are finished with your work on that day, go to your room. At exactly five minutes past eight o'clock you will step out of your room, ready to discharge your last great work for me.
  Just outside your door you keep a foil-lined peach basket which you use for waste paper. Lift the basket. Beneath it you will find a flat package wrapped in white paper. Unwrap it quietly. Drop the paper and string into the basket. Take what is in the package with you.
  By this time it will be dark. You will have left the light on in your room and the blind drawn. This is important.
  You will then go down the stairs and slip out the side door of the garage. Do not concern yourself about the police; they are

not watching you. But be careful not to be seen or heard by anyone.

When you are satisfied that no one is in sight or hearing, go into the rear garden. Stay in the shadows while you step onto the terrace. Move without a sound to the French doors leading from Mr. Robert's study. You will then see Mr. Percival seated at Mr. Robert's desk with his back to you, still at work.

Use what is in the package. You will know exactly how when you see it.

And that, my Dear Walt, will be the end of it. All you need do subsequently is let come what may. Things will happen quickly, but do not be afraid. You will remain unharmed, as befits the lord of all you survey. I, I say this to you.

Dispose of this letter as you have disposed of the others.

I do not say good-bye, as you will soon understand. I remain, My Dear Walt, as ever, and always,

Y

He prepared the white card and folded the letter, and inserted them in an unaddressed envelope and departed from his past procedures in other ways as well.

Among these unprecedented actions:

He strolled over to the street directly west of York Square and, using the apartment-house alley behind Robert York's corner, swiftly climbed the fence between the rear of the apartment building and the York garage.

He slid along the garage wall to the side door, entered the garage, shut the door silently, stood still for a moment listening, then in the darkness crept to the rear of the garage and up the narrow stairway to the landing before Walt's room.

He squatted here, and felt about to the left of Walt's door, and located Walt's peach-basket waste container.

He raised the basket with infinite patience and slipped a flat small package wrapped in white paper under it.

He lowered the basket until it stood squarely on the package, concealing it.

He pushed the unaddressed envelope containing the new card and Walt's latest instructions through the crack between Walt's door and the floor.

He then rose and made a groping, noiseless retreat—down the stairs and out of the garage and along the garage wall and over the fence and through the apartment-house alley, to the street west of York Square.

He slept soundly indeed that night.

27 · Open File

Ellery had himself let out of the cruiser a block from York Square and—by consuming gobbets of will power—he walked, did not run, to Robert York's house; rang, did not batter; and, when the door was answered, spoke, did not shout. (The Inspector, meanwhile, like a stage manager on the afternoon of Opening Night, slipped anxiously behind the scenes to immerse himself in detail.)

"Good morning Ann, is Percival York here? Is he all right?" Ellery asked; and only when she frowned did he realize he had said it as if it were a single compound word in German. She rose to the occasion, however, for behind that exquisitely rippled brow was a quick mind; she nodded. "On time and working hard." Quietly she added, "Isn't it wonderful?"

Ellery entered and she took his hat. He could see, down the hallway, the patient bulk of the plainclothesman who waited by the stairs, and through the study doorway Tom Archer leaning over Percival York, who was seated at the desk.

Ellery nodded toward the double doors of the dining room, and Ann caught his meaning instantly. "There's no one there but Bub," she said, and both opened the door and closed it behind them. The shepherd bitch lurched to her feet and padded over to them. She was developing into a splendid animal. Ellery let the puppy sniff his hand and then sought the sleek head, working his fingers around to scratch behind her left ear. Bub issued him a membership card.

"What is it?" Ann asked him; and her trusting face sharply reminded him of another time he had requested an interview with her, and how it had hurt.

"Percival's card is in the mail, Ann. The fourth card."

She went quite pale. "How could you possibly know that?"

"The post office, gentlemanly to the core, refused to let us intercept and examine his mail, but they did agree to watch for just this envelope addressed just this way, and to notify us before delivery. What time does the mailman get here?"

"About ten. Oh, dear. This means someone is still trying . . . What are you going to do?"

"Give him his mail."

She put her hands together. "How awful."

"How awful what?" Ellery demanded. "Letting him get the card when we might spare him the shock? Or do you mean the shock itself is awful? Or this whole devilish business?"

"I was thinking of Percival," Ann said earnestly. "He's come so far. It's been fascinating to watch—how he pushed himself into this, into a work discipline, a hard schedule, regular meals and sleep. And suddenly you could see him light up as if two wires had touched to complete a circuit. Stamps stopped being what he used to call 'nothing.' Now he holds a stamp with his tongs and it isn't colored paper to him any more. It's a messenger of ideas and feelings between people as well as history and geography and politics and so many other things. You know, for a while Perce was *angry?* In a how-long-has-this-been-going-on way? Ellery, I don't want him hurt. It's too soon. He's too—too *new.*"

"He won't get hurt," Ellery assured her, "although he's got to get shocked, and scared. There's somebody in the offing who's expecting exactly that, and that somebody mustn't be disappointed."

"What are you intending to do?"

He smiled at her, but not with his eyes. "Restricted information, Ann," and quickly, "Here he comes—and goes. That fellow takes the 'swift completion of his appointed rounds' business seriously, doesn't he?"

Through the dining-room window, diagonally across the little park, they saw the mailman. He was a young one, who leaped up Percival York's front steps, barely paused and was off again. Something in Ellery was whimsically nettled by the speed and casualness. There should have been—at the least—a sting of menacing music. And here, oblivious in his cousin's house, Percival York, instead of releasing a booming laugh (as he did), chased by Archer's comradely cackle (as now happened), should have begun to shrivel under the shadow of a great and featureless foreboding. Mighty poor mood-writing, Ellery told it in his heart.

Ann asked tremulously, "Are you going to let Perce just . . . find it there when he gets home?" He knew she was thinking of how alone he would be at the moment of truth, with no one to turn to.

"Certainly not," Ellery said. "You watch."

And so Ann Drew watched—watched the closed door of the castle oblique to their vantage post, its blind lamps, the grin of its slit-lipped mail slot . . . watched as the door swung inward and the sturdy little figure of Mrs. Schriver appeared, bearing something in two dimensions, a white rectangle.

"She's under orders," said Ellery to the stricken girl. "Complete the delivery," and he left the dining room so abruptly that Beelzebub started and woofed.

Ellery strode to the study, knuckled the door frame to announce himself to Percival York and Tom Archer, and stepped inside.

Because it was uncluttered and otherwise unused, Inspector Queen had set up his field headquarters, as it were, in the little bedroom-workroom of the late Emily York's house directly north of the battle site.

The Inspector and three of his lieutenants were studying a detailed plan of York Square, its four castles and environs, when Sergeant Velie thundered in.

"Jonesy just called, Inspector. He's nosed out a flop joint where some character's been coming in late at night and rattling away on a typewriter in the room he rented."

Quiet settled. The tip of the Inspector's nose had changed color. He stared at the good sergeant as if he had never seen that grizzled enormity before.

"Velie. Tell him to seal that room—"

"Jonesy did that first thing."

"—keep the manager under wraps till I get there—"

"He's got the manager practically hog-tied."

"—get his hooks on the typewriter—"

"That," Sergeant Velie rumbled uneasily, "Jonesy can't do, Inspector. It's gone. The guy checked out."

The old man cursed and jumped up. "What name was he registered under?"

"W-y-e, Jonesy said. Wye."

"Tell Jones to sit on this till I get there!" Velie, for all his bulk, took off like a sparrow. "Piggott, buzz the Robert York house and tell my son to wait outside—now. Then go relieve Hesse—you'll find him in the bushes beside the terrace. Zillie, I'm leaving you in charge of Percival York's skin, and right now it's a hell of a lot more valuable than yours, I don't care what the NAACP says!" Detective Zilgitt grinned. "Now hop."

Sergeant Velie had the cruiser waiting, and he burned rubber down the Square to Robert York's. Ellery made it in one bound, and they headed west.

"What's going on?"

"Somebody leaked," said Inspector Queen through his teeth. "Jones found some fleabag hotel where a man's been staying who used a typewriter at night and calls himself Mr. W-y-e."

Ellery blinked. "Anyone we know?"

"We'll soon find out."

Ellery shifted on his lean rump. "Leaked? How do you mean?"

"He's gone," spat the Inspector. "*And* his typewriter."

"Not necessarily a leak, Dad."

"He's lit out, hasn't he? How else would you figure?"

"Period," said Ellery. "Project accomplished. He's through, that's all."

The Inspector chewed on a thumbnail. "Sure. Of course. This case is getting me . . . Velie!" he howled. "Don't *park* here. Get going!"

"Now he's going to take it out on me," Sergeant Velie said in an aggrieved tone. "What am I supposed to do, Inspector, fly this thing?" They were caught in an intersection jam-up.

"What's bothering me," murmured Ellery, "is—Walt should have received the usual letter of instruction from Y. It ought to be on the clipboard in Walt's ceiling right now. When was it last checked, Dad?"

"About an hour ago, and it wasn't there. Maybe this time the robot destroyed it. What bothers *me*," muttered the Inspector, massaging his rigid neck, "is the post office promised to tip us to any letter addressed to Walt, too, and they didn't. *Why?*"

"Maybe because it didn't go through the mail."

"Then it would have to have been delivered by hand! And the men all swear it wasn't."

"Not this morning. But how about last night?"

"Last *night?*" the old man said blankly.

"Yes. The security force moves as Percival moves. Last night Perce went back to his house, as usual, and the men went back with him. Leaving," Ellery said savagely, "leaving Robert's premises unguarded. Meaning that Y himself, in person, could have slipped up to Walt's, dropped his letter of instructions in *re* Operation Percival, and slipped away. Mr. W-y-e plays a mighty cool game. I'm beginning to feel like an idiot." Then he shouted, "Velie! Can't you get us out of this mess?"

"You, too?" mourned the sergeant; and he once more activated his siren. The traffic tangle slowly unsnarled.

The Inspector began a bitter mumble, "That's what comes—"

"I know," yelled Ellery. "That's what comes of my insistence on taking the tails off Walt! All right, it's my fault! Does that satisfy you?"

His father, startled, subsided. Ellery, ashamed immediately, also subsided. They sat, each man an island side by side, in silence. Just as Sergeant Velie got in the clear Ellery said, "I'm sorry, Dad," and the Inspector said, "For what, for what?" and they both felt better. But not much.

With surface irrelevance, as the sergeant rocketed them toward their objective, Ellery found himself thinking of Percival York, and how he had taken the arrival of his white card with the second H on it. First Percival had shut his eyes. Then he had opened them. Then he had begun to perspire. Then he had turned yellowish and had seemed about to faint. But when Ellery had reached quickly for the carafe and a glass, Percival had shaken his head and said, "It's all right, Mr. Queen. In a way I'm glad. The waiting, the not knowing, is a lot worse. I'll be fine. Let the devil come. I'm ready." Percival York had rejoined the human race.

Which I'd better do, too, Ellery thought grimly; and he leaned forward, approximately himself again, as the sergeant shot the cruiser up to the curb before the Hotel Altitude.

The word "Hotel" in its title may have had technical justification, but otherwise it was as relative to the conjuration of whispering elevators, cut flowers in spanking rooms all foam and chrome, and noiseless waiters as the one-hoss shay to Cape Canaveral.

The Altitude was an old-law, five-story rattletrap of once-red brick, with flaking fire escapes on its shade-lidded, embarrassed façade, and the mean smell of poverty. Everything about it, outside and in, spoke of dirt and secrets.

The lobby was tiny and so, except for his ears, was the ancient desk clerk. He was bald and unshaven and all but toothless; and he was frightened almost to death by the towering young plainclothesman, Jones.

"This is the manager, Inspector," said Jones smartly. "Doubles as desk clerk."

"You've done a good day's work, Jones," growled Inspector Queen; and, "You," he rapped to the little bald man, "what's your name?"

The flaccid chin wobbled. Finally, "Gill."

"All right, Gill, let's see your book."

"Book."

"Registry!"

"Oh. Use cards, I do."

"I don't care if you use toilet paper! Let me see the record for this Mr. Wye." The ancient's hand shook its way through a five-and-dime store tin-box file, located a card.

"No, hold it by the edges! That's right. Now drop it on this." The Inspector had spread his handkerchief on the cigarette-stippled desk.

He stooped over it tautly, Ellery taut by his side. Name: Wye comma dash. Address: New York City. Mr. Wye-comma-dash had checked in seven weeks before, checked out the preceding night. The handwriting on the registration card was as uncertain as a kindergarten exercise.

"Funny handwriting," muttered Ellery; but: "Oh, I wrote this card up," quavered Mr. Gill.

They looked at each other.

"How come?" snapped the Inspector.

"Had to. He made the reservation by phone, said he'd be checking in late, wanted everything ready for him, asked how much the room'd be by the month. Told him, and he said he'd mail it to me. When the money come in, I put the key in Room Three-twelve and left the door unlocked, like he told me to do."

"Did he spell his name for you?" asked Ellery. "This W-y-e?"

"Well, sure. No . . . wait . . . Guess he didn't at that."

"This is your spelling, then?"

"Well, yes."

"Why isn't there a first name on the card?"

"Didn't give me none. I asked him over the phone, and he mumbled something I didn't get. So I put in a dash."

Inspector Queen retrieved his handkerchief in disgust, picked up the card. "When Wye paid the second month's rent in advance—was that by cash, too?"

"Yep." Mr. Gill was losing his fear; his answers came readily now, as if he had suddenly mastered a difficult situation.

"All right," said the Inspector, and leaned toward the ancient across the desk. "Now listen to me very carefully, Mr. Gill. And answer the same way! What did this man look like?"

Mr. Gill retreated into apprehension. "I dunno."

"You don't *know?*"

"He never come by the desk. Left the second month's money on the night table in his room, sticking out of the Gideon."

"Well, you must have seen him—"

"Thought I did once," Mr. Gill said hurriedly. "About three A.M., must have been. Course, it could have been somebody else. I was kind of dozing like."

Again the Queens looked at each other. Plainclothesman Jones looked on in sympathy.

"All *right,*" said the Inspector with iron patience. "You thought you saw him once. What did he look like?"

"I dunno, I tell you. Just saw him—I guess it was him—going out the door. Don't keep much light going, three o'clock and all."

"Well was he tall, short, big, skinny, blond, brunet, limping? *Anything?*"

Mr. Gill looked helpless. "Dunno. Just a feller going out."

"His voice," said Ellery. "You said—"

"Dunno."

"Wait a second! You *said* you talked to him on the phone when he made the reservation. What kind of voice did he have?"

Mr. Gill seemed about to burst into senile tears. "I tell ye I dun*no!* Voice. Man's voice. Just a man's voice."

"Deep? Medium? High?"

"I dunno," Mr. Gill said, vocally wringing his hands. "I don't hear so good over the phone no more."

Ellery stepped back. "I give up," he said.

"Well, not me!" snarled his father. "Look, Gill! Did this Mr. Wye have any luggage? Do you know *that?*"

"Oh, yes, sir. Little black case, typewriter like. Kept it under the bed. Wasn't here much, just nights every now and then. Some sort of a salesman is my guess," the manager added in an eager-to-please tone. But then he spoiled it. "Though Tillie says he never used the bed."

"Tillie's the maid, I take it?" the Inspector grunted. At the ancient's nod he yapped, "Well, tell her to stay out of Three-twelve until further notice!"

Officer Jones inserted a delicate cough. "The maid's been and gone, sir. Sorry about that, Inspector. It was before I got here."

"Tillie cleans real good," said Mr. Gill anxiously.

"Bro-ther," said Inspector Queen. "Okay, Gill—"

"Hold it," said Ellery, returning suddenly from retirement. "If you've had no contact with him, Mr. Gill, how do you know he's checked out? He's paid up through next week, isn't he? Or did he turn in his key?"

"I can answer that, Mr. Queen," said the young plainclothesman. "Seems he dropped it on the desk here last night while the old man was snoozing. That's how Gill knew he checked out—he'd always retained possession of the key before that, or stashed it somewhere outside the room. That, and the fact that the typewriter's gone. He's always kept it here before this. I talked to the maid on the phone."

"Where's the key now?" demanded the Inspector.

"I've snagged it, Inspector, for the print boys."

"Okay, let's go on up."

Sergeant Velie was waiting for them outside a door with 312 nailed to it in rusting tin digits.

"You find anything in here," announced the sergeant, "and I'll eat it."

"Alert the print men, Velie."

"They're already on their way, Inspector. I called in."

The sergeant opened the door and they trooped into Y's room. A chipped enamel bedstead with a hilly mattress; a carpet thin and scabrous as a Biblical leper; a sagging bureau; a chair; a night table and a drunkenly leaning lampstand; a sour-smelling cubby of a bathroom; and that was all.

Nothing.

They waited for the technical men, and watched while the men worked.

Nothing.

"Tillie cleans real good, all right," said the Inspector bitterly; and they left.

In the cruiser, on the way back to York Square, Inspector Queen actually said, "Nothing."

"Something," murmured Ellery. "He's cleared out. He *is* thorough, except for the minor detail."

"What minor detail?"

"Giving it to Percival. And that's the job of his good, strong, stupid right arm, Walt."

"And that's another thing," muttered the old man. *"When?"*

"Soon, I'd say. Probably tonight."

"I wish I had your crystal ball!"

"Dad," Ellery said, nibbling his thumb, "if there's anything at all we can be sure of, it's that Y knows his victims inside and out. He's got to every one of them by knowing them in the most personal sense—where they'd be, what they'd do, when they'd do it. So Y must be pretty familiar with Percival. I don't think he'd have much confidence in Percival's suddenly getting religion. Y has to figure that Perce is a cracked chalice, likely to lapse into the old unpredictable sinner at any moment. Therefore Y can't afford to wait. He's got to grasp this opportunity, when he knows just where Percival will be and exactly what he'll be doing. Tonight's the night, all right."

"Yeah, you listen to the Maestro, Inspector," said Sergeant Velie. "Did he ever steer you wrong?"

"Plenty of times," mumbled the old man; and he sunk into the lightless deeps of his misery.

28 · Capture

Ann Drew invited them both to dinner. Inspector Queen smiled feebly and excused himself, pleading catch-up work at his office. But Ellery accepted; and, the young couple having persuaded Percival York, not to return to his house for a lonely meal, the four made a pleasant occasion of it, with Mrs. Schriver serving and the gargantuan Velie helping out between the kitchen and the dining room, having his own troubles with the housekeeper's sharp tongue and the German shepherd puppy, which growled big-doggishly every time the sergeant came near. The very size of Velie and the proximity of Ellery, not to mention Archer, seemed to stimulate Percival; he exuded friendship and good will, as he had exuded fear at his first sight of the small white card in the shape of his castle plot.

He was pathetically anxious to learn all about stamps, his new-born interest; and Ellery and Archer found themselves taking turns in feeding his philatelic hunger: how to tell the difference between flatbed and rotary-printed postal paper; how it was that a stamp could be immersed in benzine for watermark examination and dry again in minutes with no damage to the ink, the paper or the adhesive—the simplest things. Percival kept asking greedy questions, unappeasable; until it occurred to Ellery that this was his way of keeping his mind off the dreadful situation developing about him.

It grew dark outside.

After dinner they went into the study. Here they chatted for a few minutes, while Percival York seated himself at his late cousin Robert's desk, his back to the terrace doors, and Tom Archer retreated to the library table piled high with albums. Mrs. Schriver finished the dishes and departed; Sergeant Velie disappeared; and, finally, Ann Drew said good night and went upstairs.

Ellery stepped into the hall, retrieved his hat, returned to the study and stood for another moment by the desk. For a long time afterward he was to remember his good-night conversation with Percival York.

"This is so nice," the last of the Yorks said. "I could take a lot of it, Mr. Queen. Sometimes . . ."

"Yes?" Ellery encouraged him, curious.

Percival laughed with embarrassment. "Sometimes I think I have the Sadim touch."

"What's *that?*"

"Midas spelled backwards. It means every bit of gold I touch turns to dlog."

"Gold spelled backwards?" Ellery afterward recalled saying with a smile.

"That's it, and you know what *that* means. I'd explain it, but I don't want to corrupt young Archer there."

But young Archer looked up and defined it precisely; whereupon Ellery shook hands all around, laughing, and left.

On the dot, Walt paused in the black shadow of the garage to peer behind, to the side, and then straight ahead to the illuminated terrace. The only light came streaming through the French doors of the study.

Above him, prone and motionless on the garage roof, Detective Zilgitt touched the *Press to Talk* button on the tiny Citizen's Band transceiver he carried and tapped gently and rapidly on the speaker grille with his thumbnail.

Inside Robert York's house, in the dark hallway, the rasping crackle sounded in the soft rubber earphone in Sergeant Velie's ear. He pulled the pen-sized flashlight out of his breast pocket and flashed it; Ellery Queen, standing in the study, saw it. The same faint crackle sounded in the ears of two detectives concealed at one side of the terrace, a third at the other, in some bushes. None of the three moved.

Clinging to the shadows, Walt oozed from the corner of the garage to a point directly across the rear lawn from the terrace. The black oval of Percival York's sports jacket, its frazzled pale topping of head and hair, were perfectly visible to him.

Walt felt for the flat object in his pocket.

Overhead a pink thumbnail tapped again. Cars rolled noiselessly across the mouths of the alleys and stopped. A darker shadow, man-shaped, appeared at the garage corner where Walt had first paused. It made no sound at all.

Suddenly Walt melted and hardened, like a flow of lava.

Ellery Queen, hat in hand, had approached the desk in the study and he was talking to Percival York.

Walt waited. Far off, a car rushed by, blatting. Nearer, a boyish voice yelled an obscenity. There was a tinkle somewhere, as if a rock had gone through a window, and the thudding retreat of derisive feet. None of this moved Walt in the slightest. He waited.

Ellery laughed, waved, was gone.

Immediately Walt slid to his left and to the blackly looming bushes. His hand went again to the flat object in his pocket.

And just as he reached the protection of the bushes, the lights went off. Everything blacked out—the study, the terrace, the dim sheen on the lawn.

From the study Walt could hear Percival's hoarse shout: "The lights are out! The lights are out!" and Tom Archer's "Just a fuse, Perce. Hang on a minute. Don't go banging around in the dark—sit still."

Sit still.

Walt leaped across the lawn, its imprint perfectly clear in his brain. He vaulted surely the low margin of the terrace, sprang to the left-hand jamb of the French doors. He waited.

He was crouched there, the little flat cold gun in his hand, when the lights blazed back on like a nova.

Walt fired five shots. Three grouped themselves in the middle of Percival York's sports jacket. The fourth splintered the top right-hand desk drawer. The fifth plowed a long clean furrow along the top of the desk and knocked a stamp album off the table beyond. He managed to squeeze off the fourth shot and the fifth even though his legs were snatched from under him, even though he was struck from above and both sides and grabbed and held and buried under the mass of men diving in over the terrace edges and from the study itself.

Ellery, lunging for breath, stood over the squirming mound.

The detectives slowly disentangled themselves, panting; but even as they separated, at least one hand of each man was tightly pinned to some part of John Henry Walt—flat on his back on the brick-red tiles, smiling like a seraph.

Looking down at that unafraid, relaxed, coldly smiling countenance, Ellery felt his skin crawl.

"For the love of heaven," he said in an unsteady voice, "take it—him—away."

Ellery sat on his shoulder blades and through bloodied eyes stared at the Eleventh Edition. He thought: Suppose they'd climbed Everest and, pulling themselves up on the last crag, had found themselves standing at the bottom? Suppose a man ran what he knew was a three-minute mile and then found they'd forgotten to wind the watches?

He thought: Come on, now, don't wallow in all the things that don't suit you. When feeling low, take an inventory of the good. What have we got that's good?

Our murderer, of course, John Henry Walt in the clink, cheerfully signing a full statement of four premeditated capital crimes. John Henry Walt doesn't defend himself; he denies nothing; he admits everything.

Everything, that is, but the important things.

The why of it all he will not answer.

He still does not know that we have Y's letters. Ask him: "Did you have help?" "Is there anyone else involved?"—and he smiles.

Ellery thought: Oh, that queer little dead-faced man, he has the prettiest smile. Want to see that smile at its prettiest? Ask him what the final H on Perce York's card means. Walt smiles and smiles.

And Ellery thought: The man is crazy, of course. Crazy in the worst way, with a craziness consistent as the law of gravity. With a craziness so consistent as to make him a more reliable tool for Y's mysterious purposes than a sane triggerman would have made.

Ellery brought his fist down on the arm of his chair, jarringly. It was wrong. It was *wrong*. It was like arresting the gun for murder.

The player on the other side . . .

He was brought back by the grate of a key and the thump of a door.

"Dad?"

"Hi," said the old man. He came into Ellery's workroom and dropped his hat on the floor and sank wearily onto the sofa.

"Still working on Walt?"

The Inspector nodded. "I've got what I thought we wanted. And all it's going to get me is that nothing's going to get *him*. He'll be committed. He'll spend the rest of his life on free grub and rent, with movies on Saturdays and no income tax. You know what? I'll bet that's what he keeps smiling about."

"You got nothing out of him."

"Nothing but more smiles." And the Inspector gave such a gruesome imitation of Walt that Ellery winced and said, *"Please."*

They were silent for a while.

"Anything on the gun?" asked Ellery finally.

"No."

"Did you tell him about the other letters?"

"No, I'm still operating from the one we found on him."

"Prints—?"

"Just Walt's."

They were silent for another while.

Then Ellery muttered, "Did you ask the lab if this latest letter from Y had Walt's thumbprints all over the top corners?"

"No," said the old man, "I looked for myself. They're there, all right."

"Many?" Ellery asked eagerly. "I mean—more than on the other letters, or fewer, or the same?"

"I'd say about the same."

Ellery made a puzzled sound far back in his throat. He reached over and picked up a piece of *Ellery Queen's Mystery Magazine* stationery and held it, dangling, with his thumbs in the upper corners, before his eyes. "Why in the name of Sam Lloyd would Walt—even Walt!—read a letter in this position? I wonder . . . Dad, has he been doing any reading in his cell?"

"Not that way," sighed his father. "Stop badgering me, son. I've had a rough day."

"Wait, Dad. Has anyone said anything to him about Percival?"

"No. He never even asked. By the way, how is our hero today? I haven't had time to call."

"According to Archer, still in mild shock." Ellery found, rather to his chagrin, that he was feeling annoyed with Percival York. Everything had been carefully outlined to him in advance; how the entire evening was a vast trap; how the rear lawn and environs were to be flooded with infra-red light, invisible to Walt, in which a police sharpshooter with a snooperscope on the garage roof beside Detective Zilgitt would have Walt on the crosshairs every second; how the script Ellery and the Inspector had worked out called for a bit of acting on the part of everyone, with the blackout as its climax to provide darkness in which to yank Percival from behind the desk and made a swift substitution in the chair of a bolster wrapped in Percival's jacket, surmounted by a department-store dummy's head. "I guess Perce isn't the new man he thinks he is. Shock! He couldn't have been safer if he'd been locked up for the night in Fort Knox."

"Where's your Christian charity?" jeered the Inspector. "I thought you were pro-Percival now. Look, El, I'm dog-tired and I want a shower—"

"Dad."

"What now?" The Inspector sank back.

"I think we ought to reconsider Percival," said Ellery slowly.

"*Again?*"

"Well, he is the only one who gains from these murders."

"And he planned this last attack—on himself? Hmm?"

"If Percival is Y, why not? If you had planned to get rid of three co-heirs, wouldn't a fourth attack—on yourself—make a good smoke screen?"

"This thought," said the old man, "has crossed my feeble mind, too." He snorted. "Kind of chancy, though, wouldn't it be? If Percival is Y, Walt doesn't know it. And that's one customer, once you give him an order, who can't tell let's-pretend from the real thing."

"It wasn't chancy at all. Percival could count on our not risking his life."

"All the same, those were real bullets, not spitballs."

"And the stakes were real high, if you'll pardon the syntax."

The Inspector rubbed his gray brush of mustache fretfully. "I don't know, son . . . If Perce is behind all this, he ought to apply for an Equity card. Because he sure put on a performance every time Walt got near him. And he knew he was safe then, too.''

But Ellery shook his head. "The more you look at it the more attractive it gets. You can't blink the fact that the deaths of Robert, Emily, and Myra York leave Perce York all eleven of the millions. There just isn't anyone else who benefits by the three murders. Percival certainly knew the habits, characters and routines of his three cousins. He's had an insider's opportunity to watch and evaluate Walt. And to hire that hotel room. And type and mail those letters.''

"All of a sudden," remarked his father, "it sounds as if you've got something against Percival."

"No but . . . Well, I think I've rather resented the concept of Walt as the player on the other side. I'm actually relieved to know now that he can't be. A pigeon!"

"Of courrrrse," said the Inspector wickedly. "Whereas my famous son rates nothing less than an eagle."

"Oh, cut it out, Dad. Anyway, this isn't an eagle-type case. Not if it's Perce York we're hunting. As the criminal—if this were a detective story—he'd be about as satisfying as the butler.''

"It's been my experience," sighed the father, "that in the real McCoy you take 'em as and where you find 'em.''

"Exactly! So don't give me that eagle stuff." Ellery began to inspect a pipe, sniffing its bole, blowing through the mouthpiece; it had been so long since Ellery had smoked a pipe that the Inspector stared. "The notion's been picking away at me ever since dinner the other night at Robert's. Think of Perce as Mr. Y, Dad. Is he smart enough? Is he weird enough?"

"You've got a point there," said the Inspector, and closed his eyes.

"Look at the offbeat touch—the cards bearing letters of the alphabet. JHW, the patsy's initials. The signed crime. That's always the mark of a certain kind of nut, the kind who likes to pull the strings from out of sight, the god of the machine. But what good are his power and his cleverness if he personally can't take a public bow for them? So—the signature. Sometimes it's a message in lipstick. Sometimes it's a zig-zag symbol, like the Mark of Zorro. Sometimes, by God, it's on a global scale and he strews swastikas around. Our boy goes for initials.''

"My son the psychiatrist," murmured his father, keeping his eyes closed.

"My point is," Ellery continued doggedly, "that, having tacked Walt's initials onto the evidence—and all the time resenting having to give the credit to the wrong man—our mastermind can't resist adding *his* exalted hallmark to the murders he's manipulated Walt into committing for him.''

The old man's eyes flew open at that. "His *hallmark?*"

"Certainly. And it's a very clever hallmark, because it could have two meanings . . . The other day I mourned the fact that the writer of the letters didn't sign his letters 'X.' I forgot that 'Y' is a symbol of unknown quantity, too. So . . . Y, the unknown quantity; and that's to tell us we don't know who he is. But there's a Y in this case who's also a *known* quantity; and when he types that Y at the end of his letters, that's to tell us that we *do* know who he is.''

"York," said the Inspector, sitting up straight. "The *initial* Y!"

"And Q and E and D," said Ellery; but he said it glumly, as if he were still not satisfied.

"I'll be damned," said the Inspector. But then he frowned. "Wait a minute, Ellery, you left something out. There were four letters, the first three giving us J,

H and W. But the fourth gave us another H—on Perce's letter. Where does that come in?''

"There," confessed Ellery, "you've got me. That extra H is the pain that's been attacking my neck ever since the Percival letter came. I can't seem to fit it in anywhere. J, H, W—and then another H.'' He shook his head. "Anyway, how does my argument sound to you?—Percival York, as Mr. Y?''

"The way I feel right now," said Inspector Richard Queen of police headquarters, "I'd even take *that* mess of non-evidence to the D.A. if I got one more little push.''

It would make nice dramatic unity here to report that the telephone rang, bringing Inspector Queen the information that would afford him the one more little push he craved.

Actually, nothing of the sort happened. And when it did happen, there was no fanciness in it about symbols and initials and such.

For the following morning the Inspector received a note, marked *Urgent,* giving him a telephone number to call; and, on calling it, the old workhorse of Centre Street was told by a certain blonde that she was now prepared to sign a statement implicating Percival York in the York Square murders. He went to see her clippety-clop; and very shortly afterward he galloped to York Square and formally arrested Percival York.

It was mid-morning, and Percival was working away at Robert York's—now Percival York's—stamps in concert with Archer and Ann Drew.

When the Inspector intoned the arresting formula, Percival blinked slowly and said to Ann and Archer, "I told Mr. Queen I had the Sadim touch. I *told* him,'' and, with tears in his eyes, he patted Beelzebub good-bye and went docilely.

29 · Discovered Check

When Ellery dropped in at the Robert York house two days later he found Tom Archer sullen, Ann Drew anxious, and both resentful.

"Because if Perce did what they say he did," Archer argued hotly, "he *used* us. As cold-bloodedly and cunningly as he used Walt. It's more than just being shoved around by a greedy megalomaniac. It's that he played on Ann's soft heart. My—my goodfellowism. Our sympathy, forgiveness, generosity. Damn it, Ellery, that's worse than highway robbery!"

Ellery said wryly, "If it pains you to discover that a Nice Man can be a crumbum, Tom, it's life you've got to object to, not Percy in particular."

Ann's anxiety and resentment had a different base. "Ellery," she demanded, "what really happened to make your father decide to arrest him?"

"It's been pretty well covered in the newspapers."

"No, it hasn't," said Ann angrily. "Walt was caught in the act of shooting what he thought was Percival York. Walt's some kind of psycho, and he's confessed to all the crimes. Perce in turn was arrested for having incited Walt to the commission of the murders. Pages and pages of this. But it's all they really say. Why do they leave out so much?"

"In tackling a criminal case," murmured Ellery, his heart not really in it, "you look for motive and opportunity. For the murders themselves Walt had opportunity; his motive was the motive of whoever directed him. Percival's motive is as old as private property; and he had the opportunity to do all the things the writer of the letters had to do. What more do you want?"

"A lot more," retorted Ann. "For one thing, Perce hasn't confessed."

"The law doesn't require a confession for an indictment," said Ellery evasively. "The case against him—"

"If the case against him is good enough," the girl said with equivalent irrelevance, "it doesn't matter how good the *man* is—is that it?"

"The question is," growled Tom Archer, "how good *is* he?"

"Oh, you be quiet!" said Ann Drew, stamping her tiny foot.

"Ann," said Ellery. "In this state a person charged with first-degree murder is given an automatic not-guilty plea. Perce will have his day in court."

"Big deal!" She shook her head, shook it again, Ellery watching the untouchable interplay of highlights in her hair with yearning admiration. "I suppose what really bothers me," Ann said, "is that Perce seemed to be getting so much *better*—"

"For whose benefit?" snapped Tom. "And at whose expense? Look, honey, exercise your female prerogative of deciding guilt or innocence by intuition, but until the courts operate likewise *I* string along with the juridical system."

"You would," said Ann, as if she had suddenly discovered a grave flaw in his character; at which Tom Archer uttered inchoate protest and registered an ocular appeal toward the ceiling. "Ellery, when is Perce to be indicted?"

"The Grand Jury gets the case day after tomorrow. Until then, at least, he's safe enough."

Ann examined him with great thoroughness. "Well, anyway, *you* seem to be sure."

"In my profession and in this life I," said Ellery humbly, "am sure of nothing, ma'am."

Then followed an awkward silence, during which the three looked at one another, and away. Ann said brightly, "Well," and found herself out of words. Tom Archer turned to Robert York's bookshelves, as if inspiration would come to him emblazoned on the spine of some fortuitous volume. Ellery understood perfectly. The unspoken decision was to drop the subject of Percival York and talk about something else. The trouble was—they made the discovery in simultaneous independence—there was nothing else for them to talk about; they knew nothing of one another aside from York Square and its recent events.

It was Bub, the German shepherd puppy, who saved the day.

She said, "Woof!"

Ellery could have kissed her muzzled. "Got to do something about those ears," he said, frowning critically. The top third of her ears drooped.

"I've been feeding her lots of stiffener," said Archer, in gratitude.

"Bub-baby!" Ann cried, throwing her arms about the puppy's neck. "They're so nasty. You're *perfect*."

"She is not," said Ellery. "Ears have to stand at attention."

"We could send her to the laundry," said Tom. "Medium starch, and so on."

"Monster," said Ann. "Don't think he wouldn't, Ellery. According to him, dogs aren't human."

"They're better than human," said Tom. "Ever know a human puppy to turn a somersault at Bub's age? Or even a shepherd child? One of my talents is to achieve the impossible. Want to see?"

"A man who'd steal the credit from a puppy is a—is a dirty dog."

"Shush, woman, I'm performing. Okay, Bub." Young Archer got down on one knee and held out his hands. The dog came, wagging her hind end furiously. He grasped her overgrown front paws, elevated them, set himself . . . *"Hup!"* he yelped; and rising quickly, he flipped the paws up and back.

The somersault was creditable, although Bub staggered when she landed. She promptly bounded back, to leap on Archer and swab his face with her built-in squeegee.

"Very good," said Tom Archer. "Now I'll do it with both her paws on my forearm. You see, a puppy-dog of this weight . . . What the devil?"

Archer broke off, staring.

"Ellery!" Ann Drew cried. "What's wrong?"

For Ellery stood stiff and still, eyes screwed shut. When she called his name he silenced her with a chopping gesture. The two exchanged apprehensive glances. It was either a stroke or a voice from beyond; and since Inspector Queen's pride and sometimes joy refused to topple, it was evidently the latter.

Suddenly the Queenian eyes opened wide and out of the mouth came a strange, frightful sound—the wordless screek of a man who, having cut himself, sees the gleaming of his own bone.

And then he ran.

Archer and Ann, clutching each other, watched him through the front window. Hatless, the great man dashed out into York Square, glanced frantically north, south, east and west, leaped at sight of a police car, beckoned with furious urgency, spoke imperiously to the driver, then snatched the door open and flung himself into the rear seat.

And the cruiser scorched off, smoking.

30 · Interpose

The radio room called Inspector Queen and told him that his son was hellbent for the jail, and would the Inspector meet said son there immediately. The Inspector, who was up to his ears, said no and hung up. The radio room called back. Mr. Queen had asked that this message be relayed verbatim: *I need you.* The Inspector left on the double.

"I've got to see York. *Right now,*" was Ellery's greeting. He had been waiting on the curb when the Inspector's car pulled up; and he had opened the door, lunged halfway in to say these words, then taken his father by the wrist and yanked. Whatever seethed and crackled within the Inspector remained unvented at sight of his son's oyster-toned face.

As he hustled the old man across the pavement and up the steps, Ellery banged his head with the heel of his free hand and babbled hoarsely, "Why don't I see what I'm looking at when I'm looking at it?"

"What?" panted his father; but by then they were inside, and he had to forgo questions in favor of the prescribed amenities.

They hurried down echoing stone steps and along a stark corridor to a short desk and a tall gate. The guard unlocked the gate with a crash, and locked it with a crash. Ellery began to run, the old man stiff-legging it after him.

"What the devil am I running about? Couldn't this wait for tomorrow? Or tonight?"

"No, Dad—"

"You," gasped the Inspector grimly, "had damn well better be right!"

He was right, but too late.

Another gate, another guard, this one accompanying them.

A cell bank.

Percival's cell.

And Percival hanging by his neck from the high window bars.

31 · Isolated Pawn

Mr. Ellery Queen, that great man, stood aside to let his father and the guard rush in and cut Percival York down. The great man stood aside, not because he was great, but because he was not. He was simply unable to help, or even to think very much. And after a moment he was unable even to stay there.

He smiled over to the guard at the cross-corridor. "Where's Walt's cell?"

"Walt who?" said the guard.

"Walt nobody." That's very good, Ellery thought: Walt Nobody. "J. H. Walt. John Henry Walt."

"Oh, the kook." The guard gave directions. Ellery listened. He said thank you. He slogged away.

Mr. Ellery Queen passed a cell immuring a man snoring; a cell containing a man pacing it off; an empty cell; an empty cell; a turn in the corridor and first-cell-to-the-right. This was indeed occupied by J. H. Walt, Human Murder Weapon.

Mr. Ellery Queen came up close, bilge sloshing, on waterlogged legs, with a salty swell trying to share his eye sockets. He clung to the bars—and which is the monkey? he thought—and he looked at J. H. Walt.

J. H. Walt sat like a good little citizen, neatly, cleanly, knees and feet together, reading his Bible. At the corners of his mouth dwelt the shadows of a smile, a serene smile, a smile of peace. ". . . and all's right with the world," the smile said. He did not look up. He was absorbed in his Book.

The bars insisted on trying to slide upward through Ellery's hands. He gripped them, which had the extraordinary effect of squeezing two tears out of his eyes. They scalded; he was glad that they hurt, glad that they turned the prim Bible reader into a blur; glad masochistically, childishly. Pain in any amount would at this moment, he felt, be just. He wished he could be sure that a fit punishment would seal off his bottomless self-scorn; oh, if it would, he would seek out the stern wielder of the nine-tailed cat, whoever he might be, confess his criminal stupidity and be thankfully flogged for it. Fantasy, of course: there would be no escape, ever, from the fury and contempt in which Ellery Queen held the great man.

A hand grasped his shoulder. No matter what policeman this might be, Ellery thought, he can never make a case against me; and this, really, was the core of his despair.

The hand squeezed his shoulder, and the Inspector's voice said, "It's all right, son. We got here in time after all. He did a sloppy job. He's going to be all right."

Ellery felt his hands slip from the bars and his body turn toward the source of the voice. He did not wipe his face or feel embarrassment; in a warm, all-but-forgotten sense, this was his father.

"Hey . . . hey . . ." A soft, drawn-out breath; Ellery recalled its use over barked knees and broken treasures. "Hey, now, son."

Ellery went with his father down the corridor. He could draw a clean breath now, remember his handkerchief, stand six feet tall once more. And it was rue and wry he felt, blowing his nose and trying to grin.

"Want to tell me what happened to you, son?" Inspector Queen asked gently.

"You bet," said Ellery. "I've solved it."

"Solved what?"

"The mystery of Y."

"The what?" cried the old man. "How do you mean, Ellery?"

"I know who it is."

32 · Combination

In the car Ellery subsided into a corner. "Call in," Inspector Queen instructed the driver. "Tell 'em I can be reached at home. And if they reach me at home it had better be important."

After a moment they swung uptown, and Ellery opened his eyes. "Dad, you don't have to make a production of this. You're busy—"

"You've scraped something off the bottom of this case, right?" growled the old man. Ellery nodded. "Well, whose case is it? The quicker you get started, the sooner I'll know what you've got."

"You ought to hang out a shingle," Ellery said. The Inspector kept a knowledgeable silence. After a while Ellery said, "The best way to do this sort of thing is to test every brick as you build. Why don't I ever learn that lesson?" Still silence. Defensively Ellery said to the dome light above him, symbolically unlit, "Yes, sir, I think I go pretty much to the point."

"And *I* think," said his father, "that it would be lovely if you started talking English. Is it all right for me to ask a few questions?"

"Ask away."

"How in the name of Houdini did you know Percival York was going to commit suicide?"

"I didn't. I just saw it as a possibility when I realized that he's innocent. That he isn't Y."

"Whoa!" exploded the Inspector. "What are you giving me, Ellery? He *isn't?* I've never known you to blow so hot and cold about anything—"

"I'm sure," Ellery said; and from the way he said it his father knew that now, at last and forever, the pieces would fit.

"If York's not Y, who is?" demanded the old man.

"I'll be coming to that—"

"Okay, I'll play," said the Inspector with a sigh, and he sank back. "How about this: What made you rush to the jail like that?"

"I wanted to tell Perce York I was sure he was innocent, and not to hang, so to speak, but to hang on." Ellery touched his own neck absently, squinting into some distance. "Dad, I saw this fellow—before his arrest—straightening the kinks out of himself. Working hard. Keeping regular hours. I saw it, I recorded it, but I didn't compute it. Electronic clog, you might call it.

"Here was a man," Ellery frowned at the driver's neck, "taking a good look at himself for the first time in his life. So much so that he could even see past and around a bequest of eleven million dollars, which is a mighty hard trick. He'd faced the ugly fact of what he'd been, and he was doing something about it.

"Now I don't think anybody has liked Perce York since the day he sneered his first word. And at the head of that numerous company you can put Perce York

239

himself. All he really wants is to be like other people, because up to now he's lived with the absolute belief that he's less than other people. The only thing in his whole life he's ever done reasonably well is to mount Robert's stamps in those albums; it was his first, his *first* positive achievement. Know what he said to me, Dad?'' Ellery swallowed. "He said, 'I've got the Sadim touch. That's Midas turned backwards.' What he meant was that anything good he touched was bound to turn bad. In a different time he might have said, 'I'm accursed.' ''

"Come to think of it," said the Inspector thoughtfully, "when we cut him down and he opened his eyes and found he was still in the land of the living, he looked me square in the kisser and croaked, 'I botched this one, too, Inspector, didn't I?' ''

Ellery nodded. "That's it. Now. I think all along he felt he'd never live to get the money, or if he did he wouldn't get to use it. His arrest must have been the end of the world to him and, at the same time, just the sort of thing he expected would happen. In that state he was what a head-candler I know calls 'a psychological emergency,' the result of which is often the victim's destroying himself—either by literal suicide or schizoid withdrawal. The one thing Perce York needed at that crisis was to be told that somebody believed in him, that somebody knew he was innocent. That somebody gave a damn about what happened to him—''

"Ellery Queen, say.''

"All right. Now you see why I was in such a rush, Dad. I held the only thing that could help him, and I was the only one who did.''

"Well, how about sharing the wealth?" his father goaded him gently. "It's about time, wouldn't you say?''

"Don't jostle me, I'm getting there," scowled Ellery. "Very well. Mr. Y wasn't Percival. Then who?''

"Archer," said the old man suddenly. "Tom Archer. He's smart enough to have seen how to use Walt as his murder weapon. And God knows Archer's been smack in the middle of the premises from the beginning—''

Ellery shook his head. "Not Tom Archer.''

"You leading me by the nose really far out?" asked the Inspector sarcastically. "Okay! Let's dress up little Ann in men's clothing and keep trying to believe she was Mr. Wye of the Hotel Altitude.''

Ellery smiled faintly. "Let's do no such thing.''

"How about Mrs. Schriver?" demanded the Inspector. "She far enough out for you?''

Ellery managed a chuckle at this. "It's not Mrs. Schriver.''

"You can bet your sweet asafetida it's not! That would be almost as ridiculous as saying it's Miss Sullivan. Far out . . . Mallory. How about Mallory? He's pretty far out. Boston.''

"Not far enough, Dad.''

"Look, son, can we stop playing games? There's nobody left!''

"But there is," said Ellery; and he said it in such a peculiar way that the old man's nostrils began to itch. He was rubbing them vigorously when Ellery said, "Here we are.''

The Inspector stopped rubbing and saw the familiar 87th Street brownstone façade. He dismissed the driver, and Ellery got out his key, and they trudged up the interior stairs like two very tired men coping with the heavy burden of their unspoken thoughts. When they were in the Queen apartment, Ellery automatically made for the living-room bar, his hands became independently active and he began again.

"What's torn me up so much," he said, "is realizing how plop under my nose it's been, practically from the start. It isn't as if I didn't *notice*. My alleged brain recorded it, all right—it just didn't compute."

The Inspector had long ago learned the lesson of inhuman patience at times like these. There was no point, he now saw, in any further prodding. In the climactic stages Ellery had to be given his head; in his own mysterious time he'd head for home.

"Don't be so hard on yourself, son."

"I couldn't be," said Ellery with profound disgust. He stood a while, then gradually focused on the two glasses he held. He came around the bar, handed his father the highball and retired to the couch with his cocktail.

"The evidence was evident all along the path," Ellery went on. "It was to be seen even in the first murder, Robert's, that this was the work of some species of madman. A madman with a systematized madness."

"But we didn't know then that he was intending to work his way all around the Square, son," Inspector Queen said intently.

"But we did know he'd sort of warned Robert with that kooky J card. Do sane killers—to make a fine distinction—warn their victims of their homicidal intentions?"

The Inspector waved his hand, keeping the wave genial by main force. "All right, that told us—you—that he was crazy."

"Don't give me any premature credit, Dad. I couldn't stand it." Ellery took a swallow. "We—I should have left that itty-bitty door wide open. But no, I had to keep whittling my sights down to ordinary motivations. Instead of bearing in mind that anything—*anything*—could figure into this man's plans, I—oh, well, it's too late to pick *those* nits."

He emptied his glass and banged it down on the coffee table. "With an open mind I might have guessed the truth by the time we laid eyes on that second card. Because by then we had two letters of the message, J and H. But again . . . I suppose it's because I'm not conditioned to madness. A madman has his logic, but it's not a sane man's logic—and, although I know you sometimes have your doubts, I think I'm more on the sane side than the other way."

"I'll give you that much," said the Inspector. "Skoal."

"Skoal," said Ellery absently. "Where I really fumbled the ball, of course, was in Myra's murder. Even before it *was* a murder. Remember I spoke to Walt not ten minutes after he'd dropped the rat poison into Myra's water jug? He had just left Myra's house, and I stopped him and questioned him."

"So?"

"I'll get to it later," and the old man could have screamed. "Anyway, that was the afternoon I decided to take off and find Mallory."

"Take off is right. We had one dilly of a time finding you."

"I didn't know it would take that long. And my Mallory notion seemed so far-fetched, I thought you'd laugh me off the case. Wait till you see how far-fetched it really was."

"My son," sighed the Inspector, "I reckon I'm just about the best li'l ol' waiter ever."

Ellery ignored this. "I still have the nagging feeling that if I'd picked up my cues and clues, if I hadn't gone to Boston just then, maybe Myra . . . All right, I'll quit being iffy."

"That third case, Myra's. The one with the W. Adding W to J and H and giving us J.H.W.; obviously—what could be more obvious?—the initials of John Henry Walt. Bingo! this so-called mind closes down to any other possibility." Ellery scowled at his empty glass. "Charles Fort, who made a career out of jeering at conventional scientific thinking, wrote somewhere that it takes a special species of idiot—or was it fool?—always to concede that any answer is the *only* answer. All I could see was that JHW were initials, and that the initials stood for Walt's full name. Perfect example of recording and not computing. If I'd remembered that principle I might—I just might—have added insanity to the murder of these particular people, plus J and H and W, and summed up accurately. I had the opportunity to do the simple arithmetic again, when we found the typewritten letters signed with a Y—those do-my-bidding, I-own-the-universe letters. I could have applied Fort's dictum *then*. And I'd have known. I'd even have been able to prophesy that the next card would have another H on it."

"Do tell," murmured the Inspector, his pulse at last beginning to accelerate. This must be it! "How does that figure?"

Ellery frowned at his father. "The letters JHWH have no meaning for you?"

"Not a glimmer."

"Coupled with someone who calls himself Y?"

"Y? 'York' satisfies me there. Or," added the Inspector wryly, "did."

"You insist on joining Fort's special-species-of-fool club along with me, don't you? No, it isn't York."

"Here we go again," muttered the old man. "Okay. Yoicks. Yehudi. Yuk-yuk. Will you stop diddling, son, and get to it?"

"JHWH," said Ellery, "makes up the Tetragrammaton."

"JHWH," said Inspector Queen, "makes up the Tetragrammaton. What in God's name is *that* supposed to mean?"

"You," and Ellery, to his father's consternation, burst into frenetic laughter, "you have said it!"

"What have I said?"

"God's name—that's what Yod Ho Waw Ho—JHWH—represents. The Name of Names. In Old Testament times it was forbidden to speak the true name of the Lord. JHWH—in its ancient Hebrew, Greek and other equivalents—was the Hebrew way of writing down what could not be uttered. They used the consonants, and substituted the vowels from the words Adonai or Elohim—both scriptural terms for 'God' or 'the Lord'—so that JHWH became *Jehovah*. Or *Yahweh*, the other of the two best-known versions. Yahweh, with a Y."

"JHWH, Jehovah, on the cards—Yahweh, the Y, on the letters . . . Jehovah, Yahweh . . ." Inspector Queen glanced suspiciously at his son. "What are you trying to hand me? That Walt actually thought he was getting mail from *God?*"

"Before sheer merriment overcomes you," said Ellery, "I advise you to reread Y's letters with that thought in mind. 'You know who I am.' 'Have faith in me and I shall guard you and keep you.' 'There is no thing I cannot do.' 'I am with you wherever you go.' 'For I possess all powers, and I am everywhere.' 'You may not speak my name.' And so on. That constant, soothing, reassuring, intimate, *omnipotent* refrain."

Over the old man's face came a look that was very like terror. He actually, in the flesh, shivered.

"Think of poor little lonely, boxed-in, blank-past Walt," said Ellery with the same wincing frown. "No one notices him. No one is concerned about him. No one cares enough about him to like him or even to dislike him as far as he can tell. Erased as he is, he still contains within himself the faint impression of the human matrix.

"And suddenly," said Ellery, "suddenly he's noticed, he's liked, he's admired—he's even asked for *favors!*—by none other than the Lord God Himself. Do you wonder that Walt did as the letters told him to do? Do you wonder that he's never been frightened, has never felt worried, by what might happen to him? That he's refused with the greatest of ease, happily, consistently, to be trapped or cajoled or browbeaten into saying that Name? How could mere mortals touch him? Walt's had it made. In the very biggest way."

"Four Bibles in his room," murmured the Inspector. *"Four."*

"Yes, and they mean something rather different now, Dad, don't they? Now that we know what fits in. That time I bumped into him outside Myra's, for instance. I questioned him about Tom Archer's saying Walt had crept up on him and Ann. I asked Walt what Archer had said, and Walt said simply, 'He saw me and he said, "God." ' It wasn't exclamatory the way Walt said it; it was quite matter-of-fact. God *is* a fact to Walt; they're on the most personal terms . . . And then those initials of his. Coincidence? Miracle? Whatever it was in reality, in Walt's book—or maybe I ought to capitalize it—it was just another manifestation of Him Who was the Author of the letters . . . Meaningless in themselves, these things. But in context, a giveaway. And there I was, day after day, in the thick of it, recording and not computing."

"God!" said the Inspector; and it was impossible to judge how he used the word. "What put you onto this finally, son?"

"Ann's dog, Beelzebub. Familiarly—Bub."

"Ann's *dog?*" His father gasped.

"Yes. After Perce was arrested. When I went over to see Archer. We were kidding around about the dog, and Archer was showing Ann and me how he was teaching it to do a somersault."

"Hold it, hold it," said the Inspector faintly. "A few seconds ago we were talking about the Old Testament."

"Exactly. That's it. Don't you see? I watched Archer show the dog off—lift up its front paws and flip it over backwards. *Backwards.* Something in my brain went—*snick!* clean as can be—and dropped into place. Talk about divine intervention. Something's been bugging me for days to look—just look—and I'd see it. But I didn't, I didn't. Till Archer flipped the dog."

"Simmer down, Ellery," muttered the old man. "Try to make sense, for my sake. What's with this backwards-dog business?"

"Dog," said Ellery. "Backwards."

"Dog, backwards," repeated the Inspector. "Dog, backwards. D-o-g . . . g-o-d. G-o-d." And, suddenly, his lips clamped shut.

"God," said Ellery, nodding. He rose and took his father's empty glass and his own over to the bar. "That was it. It made me think, 'God.' And the next thing I knew, I was in the Old Testament, thinking 'Jehovah,' 'Yahweh.' Thinking JHWH. Thinking Y."

The Inspector was silent.

Fumbling with the ice, Ellery said, "Now Jehovah, Yahweh, was a member of no Trinity, was represented by no lambs, suffered no little children. He was an almighty vindictive deity. He meddled in individual lives. And He was always right because He *was*. In Genesis. Exodus. Remember Job. Think of what He did to Onan, to Lot's wife, to everybody in Noah's time.

"And now," said Ellery grimly, "imagine His intrusion into the here and now, into York Square. And let's say that you're Walt. Couldn't He have done these things as far as you, Walt, are concerned? Isn't it perfectly reasonable that He chose to choose you, Walt, as his instrument simply because He felt like it?"

Ellery handed his father the freshened highball, but the old man shook his head and set the glass down. "I'm still foggy on this, Ellery. I mean, what kind of mentality would conceive of pretending to be God Almighty, just to get that poor little slob Walt to do his dirty work?"

"Dad, you haven't been following." Ellery's eyes were quite bright. "No one *pretended* to be Yahweh. The writer of those letters *is* Yahweh."

"Oh, come on, now!" shouted the Inspector.

"In his own mind, to the best of his own devoutest belief and conviction, Y is exactly what he says he is. Walt has no monopoly on unshakable faith."

The old man thrashed about. "That's as wild a theory—"

"It is not," said Ellery with slow and chilling emphasis, "a theory, Dad. I can prove it. I'll go further. I'll take you to Him."

"Gosh," said the Inspector, but the sneer had an undernote of brute anger. "Meet Yahweh in person. I better change into my best suit."

"He's satisfied that he's Yahweh," said Ellery, unmoved. "Whether *you* think so or not is, I assure you, a matter of complete unconcern to him."

"I've had enough of this," snarled his father, jumping up. "I don't know what's got into you, Ellery, but I'm not going to sit here all day listening to a lot of mystical—mystical *boloney* mishmash! Just tell me one thing: Who is he?"

"I've told you," said Ellery, positively luminous. "He's Yahweh."

"All *right!*" howled the old man. "There's some crazy thing you want to do—want *me* to do—I can tell by your eyes. We're going to have a fight about it. We'll wind up doing it. And you'll scare the devil into me!"

Ellery did not deny it. He folded his arms and waited.

Inspector Queen inhaled hugely. Then, in a patient—a more than patient—voice, he asked, "Ellery—son—what is it you want me to do?"

"Turn Walt loose again."

At which hell really broke loose.

There were four of them, crouched on the grimy fire escape outside Room 312 of the Hotel Altitude. Two of them were named Queen. Each of the others represented a round of the wild battle they had fought all afternoon and evening and up to this midnight moment, and which they were still fighting. The third man's presence was the result of the Inspector's last-ditch refusal to go on with any such harebrained and dangerous and disastrous scheme, because the Police Commissioner would never agree.

"Then invite him along," Ellery had said.

The fourth man was here as a result of the Commissioner's total objection that the D.A. wouldn't allow it. "Then let's invite him, too," the Queens had said, in one voice. To enlist co-workers of such substance had proved sound strategy; it handled every human obstacle of lesser weight, like jail wardens. Weightier obstacles were simply not informed; they could be presented with the *fait accompli* "that you've proved your point," the District Attorney had put it grimly, "or that somebody else can figure out three murders and a flubbed suicide on a fire escape." And besides, Ellery had pointed out, there was just not room enough on the fire escape for the Mayor, too. His Honor ran to bulk.

Ellery was inspired, exalted. He planned like a Metternich, he drove like a Legree.

Walt had been released. Someone had said something to him about "insufficient evidence," but he had hardly listened; release was no more than his expectation and due. He was taken to the prison hospital, given his clothes (in which $200 had been planted) and abruptly marched into a private room containing a bed containing Percival York.

Reports on this encounter could describe nothing of interest but a moment of suspended-animation stillness, Walt's specialty. Then they had led him out and turned him loose.

"That's why it has to work," Ellery had expounded in setting up the encounter. "Since we jumped him on the terrace he's been cooped up in a cell with only a Bible to read. Nobody's ever told him he failed to kill Percival York. Seeing Percival alive, his antlike mentality will perceive the unalterable necessity to finish the unfinished job. Still, he's Walt; and he won't know how to go about it. Unless and until he gets another letter. He has to have another letter. He'll get it."

Gill, the gnomelike manager of the Hotel Altitude, had been scooped up. His false teeth chittered and his big ears jerked. He didn't want trouble. Room 312 hadn't been cleaned, it was the maid's night off. Or no, there was a paying guest in 312. Or was there? And anyway, who's going to pay for the room? Faithfully promised the personal vendetta of Inspector Richard Queen and the vacuum-cleaner scrutiny of the Department of Fire Inspection, the Board of Health, the Commissioner of Licenses and the Morals Squad, Manager Gill was suddenly anxious to co-operate.

Walt was not followed. There was no need. He was watched. He was watched in ways that would have been the envy of the city, state, federal and international security forces which had once been assigned the nerve-twitching task of providing protection to Nikita Khrushchev and Fidel Castro during their simultaneous stay in New York.

From the jail steps Walt had only two directions to choose between; both routes were congested with pedestrians, loungers holding up buildings, watchers from windows and watchers from cars, both parked and on the move.

Walt chose to go north. The men who had been deployed to the south were instantly redeployed, to intercept all possible random developments. Around the little handyman, as he oozed along, there was observably nothing out of the ordinary. But by his movements he unknowingly commanded the shifting and shuttling of a small army of men.

The equipment for Operation Walt was a policeman's delight. Ellery had urged the Commissioner to use a logistical maximum, cunningly justifying the whole, mad, awesome operation as not only the pursuit and capture of a vengeful deity but the equivalent of a high-level, top-secret emergency drill of the first importance. The Commissioner was charmed, and the police and citizens' radio bands soon set up an elbowing clamor of calls. Minute transistor sets relayed messages from one pedestrian to another, from the second pedestrian to a parked or moving car, from car to radio dispatch to Morse flasher and then back to pedestrian again.

Everything was collated and filtered and passed to the Commissioner's earplugs; checked and monitored and refiltered and cross-checked. Sets were pulled off emergency racks and found to contain dead batteries, or no batteries at all. Channel control crystals turned out to be mislabeled; and so on. There was not too much of this, however; and when all was in readiness everyone concerned granted that these equipment delinquencies might not have been discovered for years if not for Ellery Queen's Operation Walt. (Officially, of course, it was known as the Commissioner's Operation Walt.)

The Commissioner's dearest joy was the transistorized squealer, broadcasting on 27.215 megacycles (Band 21), fixed automatically by direction-finders on a whole echelon of mobile stations, and mounted—batteries and all, and all unbeknownst— in the heel of Walt's left shoe.

No, it could be said with confidence that they weren't about to lose John Henry Walt.

33 · Checkmate

At first it seemed like much ado about very little, for Walt made no attempt to get lost; in the manner of the ant, he forged ahead as if activated by instinctive forces, without a backward or sidelong glance.

But at one point Walt turned a corner; and when the nearest watchers re-established visual contact they sensed a wariness in him, as if something had suddenly happened to alert his mechanic faculties. Now he occasionally glanced over his shoulder; he readjusted his carriage and his stride lengthened, as if to disguise himself. Had the robot become suspicious? It certainly seemed so; and the word, in various inflections, flashed hither and about, new orders were rapped, the lines tightened, reserve forces slipped in to take over from men whose recurrent faces might have caused Walt's sudden caution. The measures apparently had their effect; Walt became preoccupied, he began to hurry, his movements turned purposeful.

He went first to a chain drug store, where he purchased a cheap tablet of lined paper and some plain white envelopes.

He went next to a pawnshop (hair-raisingly, within four minutes of its closing) and came out with a second-hand portable typewriter.

He then stepped into a second drug store and put a coin into the slot of a a stamp-dispensing machine.

And at twenty minutes past the eleventh night hour he came to rest on the dissolute sidewalk in front of the Hotel Altitude.

And, of all things, lit a cigarette.

He had bought a pack in the second drug store; they had wondered about that. Walt did not smoke—at least, the Queens had never seen him smoke; the detectives on the case had never noted his smoking in their reports; no one in York Square had ever mentioned his smoking; and there was no evidence in his room above the garage that he was addicted to the habit.

Still, here he was on the sidewalk before the entrance to the Hotel Altitude, smoking with large, unhurried puffs; smoking, and watching through the plate-glass door the tiny desk with the tiny desk clerk behind it visible at the tiny end of his line of sight, like Alice looking down the rabbit-hole.

A signal was passed.

Gill, the manager, came round the end of the desk to stand in full view of the entrance; he stretched; he yawned; then he shuffled over to a door marked MEN and opened it and disappeared, the door closing behind him.

Walt immediately stopped smoking. He did not toss the cigarette into the gutter; he did not drop it and step on it. He did a rather curious thing: he crushed out its burning end between thumb and forefinger, not quickly, with no evidence of pain, but deliberately and thoroughly; and then, when he was satisfied that the cigarette was out, he tossed the butt over his shoulder with the oddest gesture of contempt and stepped forward and entered the Altitude.

This was the anxious time. Ellery had not been at all sure what Walt would do. Mr. Wye at his last departure had left the passkey to 312 at the desk; Walt had no key.

Eyes watched, ears listened, from everywhere.

He did not go to the desk and behind it, where in the cubicle plainly labeled 312 the tagged key lay in plain sight for his convenience. He did not even glance beyond, or even at, the desk. He strode smoothly and quietly and directly to the stairs.

Between the second and third floors he met a man coming down. At once Walt set the typewriter on the stair and stooped over his left shoe. When the man was gone Walt rose, picked up the machine and resumed his ascent.

At the third floor he made unhesitatingly for Room 312.

Here Ellery's reserve plan proved its efficacy. Before the door tin-figured 312, Walt set the typewriter down again and put his right hand in his pocket. When his hand emerged empty, he frowned. But then the frown cleared and he turned the knob and pushed, and the door swung inward into darkness, and he picked up the typewriter and walked into the darkness as if he had expected nothing less; and he shut the door and touched the light switch, evoking a low thin illumination from a little gooseneck lamp corded to the socket in the ceiling—it left the upper part of him in tantalizing gloom. The duplicate key they had inserted in the keyhole on the room side of the door Walt immediately turned, locking himself in. The miraculous appearance of the key he accepted with utter calmness.

On the fire escape outside 312's window Ellery gave a nervous cluck, and nodded. "Yes," he muttered. "Of course."

Room 312 was at the rear of the Hotel Altitude, so that its fire escape faced nothing but the grimy backs of loft and other business buildings, all untenanted and dark at this hour. They had nothing to fear from curious eyes.

Ellery crouched against the dirty brick wall, eye glued to the eyepiece of a magnifying periscope. His father, the District Attorney, the Commissioner were listening to reports in their earplugs; but now all sounds ceased, and as one man they turned to Ellery.

He nodded. "It's Walt."

"You sure this Y is meeting him here?" whispered the D.A.

"I'm sure."

"That's all right, then," said the Commissioner with satisfaction. The room was bugged; the tapes of recorders in adjacent and opposite rooms were winding.

"Get away!" said the Inspector swiftly. He had a periscopic device, too. Walt had laid down his typewriter and was approaching the window. The four men glued themselves to the wall, two to each side of the window.

Walt tried the window; it was stuck fast. After a moment he turned back. And this was a small triumph for Inspector Queen; it had been his notion to grease the window carefully with a silicone compound and install a quick-release lock, invisible from the room, on the fire-escape side.

"Watch this," said Ellery softly. He had his periscope back in place. The Inspector followed suit.

They had arranged the small night table at the foot of the bed; the gooseneck lamp was standing on one corner of it. The position of the night lamp and the chair at which Y had sat had been predetermined by examination of impressions on the carpeting.

Walt set the typewriter on the little table and removed its cover. He placed the cover, the envelopes and the cheap tablet on the bed. Then he sat down at the table, his left profile to the window, and reached over to adjust the angle of the lamp. The light sprang strongly to his face.

Inspector Queen made a throaty noise. He straightened up, knuckled his eyes, then peered into the eyepiece once more. Finally he sat back on his heels and looked up at the others in the dim glow from the window.

And he whispered, *"That's not Walt."*

The Commissioner stooped, and looked, and his tough cop's face rippled with shock.

"My God, Burt," he said to the District Attorney. "Look!"

The D.A.'s lips parted audibly; his jaw dropped; and when he shifted from the eyepiece he glanced at Ellery as if he had never seen Inspector Queen's son before. But Ellery merely bit down on his own teeth and kept watching the man in the room.

The man was reaching over now to the bed. He flipped the cover of the tablet open and removed the top sheet of paper. The Queens hastily adjusted the knurled brass rings of their eyepieces, got the field onto the blur that represented the sheet of paper and focused until they could see it sharply.

"The pale blue lines," muttered the Inspector. "The identical paper!"

The man in the chair slipped the sheet into the carriage of the portable and began adjusting it, apparently for exact alignment with the blue lines.

Choked the Inspector: "I'll be damned . . ."

"What, Dick, what?" asked the Commissioner excitedly.

But the old man's response was to his son. "So that's how you knew. A somersaulting dog, and thumbprints at the top corners of the Y letters!"

"It had to be that," nodded Ellery, without looking away. "From adjusting the paper on the machine so that it typed precisely on the blue lines. From doing it on line after line, because the spacing between the paper's blue line-spacing obviously didn't conform to the machine's line-spacing. The conclusion had to be: Whoever left all those thumbprints at the top corners of the letters typed the letters. Simple." And Ellery added in so bitterly low a tone that only his father heard him, *"Very simple. It took me a mere three murders and an almost-fourth to figure it out."*

And now the man who had been Walt was launched on his letter. He was typing with two fingers; steadily, evenly, rapidly unrolling a stream of words. At each succeeding line he stopped to realign the paper, as Ellery had predicted.

"What's he typing?" moaned the Inspector. "I can't make it out—"

"I can." And Ellery read off the words as they appeared on the blue-lined sheet:

> *"My Dear Walt:*
> *"You have been all I asked you to be. You have done all I asked you to do. But, because of developments beyond your understanding, our last task remains uncompleted.*
> *"I assure you out of the depths of my admiration and approval of you, My Dear Walt, that this temporary failure is not of your making, and I absolve you of blame.*
> *"There must come now a time of waiting.*
> *"All things in their season.*

"Be observant, My Dear Walt.
"Be patient, and be yourself.

"He's stopped typing," Ellery mumbled.

"I think," said the Commissioner, "that's enough. Don't you, Burt?"

The District Attorney's lips were set in a long thin line. "Plenty enough."

"Okay," said the Inspector, "let's take him."

The Commissioner spoke a word into the grille of his little transceiver.

Ellery put a thumb on the window-lock and the other fingers at the bottom edge of the sash, and he gathered his legs under him.

Out in the hall a man drifted, like smoke in a draft, from the room directly opposite to the door of 312, placed his fingers on the jamb and yanked. The entire doctored jamb swung outward, bringing the strike plate and lockbolt with it.

The door swung open at the exact second that the window slammed up and Ellery dived into the room.

Electrically quick, the typist's face flashed toward Ellery; the man half rose.

"Hold it," said the detective in the doorway. The face in the light turned toward the detective slowly, slowly and phlegmatically glanced at the revolver in his hand and seemed amused. The man got to his feet and deliberately faced Ellery.

"If I raise my hand, of course," he said in a voice so deeply and surely unlike Walt's that Ellery's scalp crept, "you will cease to exist."

There was a long silence. At the window behind Ellery the faces of Inspector Queen, the Police Commissioner and the D.A. were plaster masks. The detective in the doorway, now joined by two others, began a movement; Ellery checked it with the slightest gesture.

And in the silence they all took in the strange man's imperial stance; his bright, sharp eyes; his almost lipless mouth.

"Please be good enough to tell me," Ellery said with the softest courtesy, "why the Yorks had to die?"

"For the sins of the father," intoned the man at the table.

"Not the fath*ers?*" Ellery stressed the sibilant.

"I have said it."

Ellery bowed his head. "Thank you," he said. At the slight sound of the Inspector preparing to put his leg over the window sill, Ellery casually put a hand behind his back and with it made a peremptory gesture. "We will meet again," he said with deference.

"If I . . . will . . . iiiii . . ."

The *it* dribbled off into silence. And the bright, sharp eyes dulled and blunted and opened wide and opened wider until they were quite round. And the almost lipless mouth began to materialize, to inflate, to become fleshy and wet. And the imperial set of the shoulders wilted, rounding them. And the corded demarcations of jawbone and cheek muscles and neck tendons all softened and sagged and ran together.

And there was Walt.

"Hello, Walt," said Ellery.

"Mr. Queen." And there was Walt's flat, unencumbered voice. The round eyes blinked past Ellery to the window, took in the Commissioner, the District Attorney, Inspector Queen, returned to Ellery.

"Walt, we'd like you to come back with us," said Ellery.

A smile spread the slack lips. A gentle, happy, I-have-secrets-I-am-loved smile.

"Yes," said Walt.

"Dr. Morton Prince," said Ellery a century later. "He pioneered in this thing. But it didn't become general knowledge until those two psychiatrists, Doctors Thigpen and Cleckley, published their remarkable report in The Three Faces of Eve, and Evelyn Lancaster herself followed it up, with the help of James Poling, in *The Final Face of EVE*. So I suppose there's hardly anyone who hasn't heard of multiple personality."

Inspector Queen was still incapable of coherent speech.

"I imagine," Ellery chuckled, "that the Commissioner and the D.A. would still be debating whether to put me under psychiatric observation at Bellevue if they hadn't seen with their own eyes how Walt slipped from his second personality back into his first. I don't know why two disassociated personality manifestations in the same body should be so tough to credit. Evelyn Lancaster had three before developing her final one. Dr. Prince documents as many as five in one body, none of them knowing the existence of the others."

The Inspector cleared his throat and found his voice at last. "Poor devil. How do you handle a thing like this? I mean legally?"

"The psychiatrists and the lawyers will have to battle this one out, Dad. I don't think there's any doubt that in the end Walt will be 'protected,' as his *alter ego* Y promised. He'll be studied and treated and taken care of for the rest of his life. And who knows? Maybe he'll develop a third personality, as socially responsible as Walt and Mr. Y can never be."

The Inspector shook his head. "I guess I'll never really *believe* it. It's too much like black magic. That little schmo Walt and that egomaniac Y in the same body!"

"Well, Dr. Prince and others have pointed out that alternate personalities are most often extremely opposite expressions of the bottled-up ego. In one kind of dual personality the ultra-prim, teetotaling spinster will abruptly produce a gin-loving party girl. Robert Louis Stevenson instinctively made Dr. Jekyll the embodiment of goodness, and Mr. Hyde just about as evil as a man could be.

"So here's Walt. It wouldn't be easy to locate another human being who scores nearer zero in looks, intelligence, wit, social and economic standing and what-have-you. It's no surprise, really, that he produces an alternate personality who's very close to infinity."

His father shuddered and was silent again. But then he looked up and asked, "And you really think Walt didn't know he was writing those letters to himself?"

"The head boys will probably have an answer for that. It's happened before, Dad. As I understand it, down deep at the heart of such cases is a demanding hunger, a kind of dictatorial want. Walt *wanted* God to like him and send him messages, therefore he *didn't want* to know who wrote them. Or rather, he'd want not to know."

"And why the Yorks, son? Why did Walt—I mean Y!—pick on the Yorks?"

Ellery twisted his nose thoughtfully. "I really had no idea until the other night—until 'Y,' before he reverted to Walt, gave me that curious answer when I asked him the same question."

"He said something about the sins of the fathers."

"No," Ellery said, "what he said was 'of the father.' Singular. When you stop to think of it, that's a singularly revealing statement. The only father in this game was Nathaniel York, Senior—whose son became so fed up with old Nat's dictatorial ways that he threw up everything, lit out and never came back.

"Dad, I think Walt-Y made an identification in a weird sort of way with young York, Nathaniel Junior, whose jungle death Nathaniel Senior could never get himself to believe. Remember that the old man's will left everything to Junior if he should turn up alive. Walt—Y, I think, took upon himself not only young Nat's grievances but also his right to the inheritance. In a sense, Walt-Y took upon himself young Nat."

"Could be," the Inspector grumbled. "Far as I'm concerned, son, in this case anything could be."

"Including the possibility that Walt actually knew young Nathaniel."

The old man stared.

"It might pay, in fact, to do some backtracking along the trail that ended with Junior's death. You might find that his path crossed Walt's somewhere, that the two might even have been friends. This would have to have been, of course, before Walt broke into two personality pieces. It would clear up a lot, Dad. Why Walt gravitated to this vicinity. Why he drifted—if he did—into the Walt-young Nat syndrome. Who Walt really is, for that matter—or, rather, who he originally was— and where he came from and so on. But I'm pretty sure that somehow, somewhere, Walt knew Nathaniel York, Junior."

Ellery shrugged. "For no reason at all, by the way, I once looked up that birth date chiseled into Junior's plaque in York Park. April 20, 1924. Know when that fell, Dad? On Easter.

"So meek Walt gradually talked himself into inheriting the earth—began to feel it was his due—then began to be outraged that the York cousins were getting it instead.

"What may well have tipped him overside was the discovery, one time when he was poring over his Bibles, that JHW—his own initials—constituted part of the Tetragrammaton. For Walt it was quite logical for 'part' of the Tetragrammaton to become 'most' of it, and finally 'all' of it. That may well have been the exact point in time when Mr. Y made his bow. JHWH. Jehovah. Yakweh. Y.

"And then," said Ellery, squinting through his cigarette smoke at his silent father, "and then Yahweh went to work with a vengeance, as you might say."

Ellery got up to refill his coffee cup, and the Inspector's. Neither had drunk anything stronger than strong coffee since the phantasmagoria in Room 312 of the Altitude.

"So now we have God-and-Nat-identified-Walt brooding over the Yorks of York Square," Ellery resumed. "They had, or would have, so much; and what they would have was rightfully his. Or maybe Yahweh's sense of justice was outraged. A lot of quite sane monopersonality people wouldn't hesitate to charge that not one of the Yorks deserved the treasure. Myra and Percival in particular. Even Robert and Emily, on the at least arguable ground that neither had the slightest notion of the right way to spend that kind of loot. That used to be Percival's point about Robert and Emily, remember? By the way, Dad, is he suing the city?"

"Nah," said the Inspector. "Percival is saintly now. An honest mistake, he calls it; he's ready to forgive and forget."

"Forgive," murmured Ellery, "and ye shall receive?"

"I'll admit," said his father dryly, "that the thought has occurred to me. Retaliatory forgiveness. Perce may have turned over a whole set of new leaves, but there's a lot still in print on the flip side."

"What do you mean?"

"He's forgiven his blonde, too."

"No!"

"Yes. And a sickening sight it was, too. After she read in the papers about his attempted suicide, she camped at the jail until they let her in just to get rid of her. She cried salty tears all over the prison infirmary, and Perce patted her shoulder in a sad and fatherly way and told her it was okay, he understood." The old man grimaced. "Ellery, I wanted to set her down on her fat rump for coming to me the way she did with that out-and-out lie about Percy 'confiding' in her how he'd talked Walt into doing his dirty work. But there's nothing I can do—her statement wasn't made in court or under oath."

"How did she know anybody persuaded Walt to do anything? We sat on that pretty hard."

"A shrewd guess. There's some sort of brain under that mop of hair dye. She lay awake nights thinking it up, to get even with Perce for giving her the boot."

"So now they'll live happily ever after?"

"Guess again," chuckled the Inspector.

"Don't tell me," said Ellery, his cup in midair, "Perce has another doll already!"

"Yump. I was the one brought 'em together. Suggested they could help each other."

"Miss Sullivan?"

"That's my boy," nodded the old man, grinning. "I'll bet you didn't know there's going to be—actually going to be—a rehabilitation center near the city that'll be the biggest thing since Father Damien invented leprosy."

"And I'll bet," Ellery grinned back, "that Miss Sullivan gets York Square, too."

"No takers—she does. With Mrs. Schriver thrown in, who's so smitten by the new Percival York she's ready to follow him to hell and back."

To hell and back . . .

Even aside from esoteric terrors like multiple personality, the human mind was an awesome thing. There were apparently key words in key situations, a chance encounter of all the right ingredients.

Ellery sat in silence and thought how, throughout this mad case, while the answer eluded him and he chased it like a cat after a moth, a hidden power had been trying to call it to his attention.

How early had it been that Ann Drew refused to tell him why the puppy-dog was named Beelzebub? How close had he been then, and how much closer that later time when he had turned whimsy into a whip? At any stage in the game Tom Archer could have—would have—told him, had Ellery had the wit to ask.

To hell and back . . .

Beelzebub: the Devil. Archer had wickedly named the dog for the Devil because the Devil is God's opposite . . . and "dog" is "God" spelled backwards.

Well, Ellery thought (and he smiled), perhaps it was too much to expect, even from himself.

"What, Dad?" he said. "I wasn't listening."

"I said, so that ends your game. The one you weren't going to play."

"Yes."

It seemed so long ago. And all of it seemed to have happened to a driveling stranger with a pure bone head. A stranger who had felt he must go on to something else because technology had deprived him of opponents. Such nonsense. Madness, or aberrance—or, for that matter, "that rare disorder" from which John Henry

Walt suffered—were outside the jurisdiction of the mechanical equalizers. Someone had to be standing by for such times as the Devil possessed the Player on the Other Side.

"Dad," he said out of his reverie. "Do you remember the Huxley quotation? 'The chess-board is the world, the pieces are the phenomena of the universe, the rules of the game are what we call the laws of Nature. The player on the other side—' "

"What?" said the Inspector, roused from a reverie of his own.

" 'The player on the other side is hidden from us. We know that his play is always fair, just, and patient.' When I first read that," Ellery frowned, "I couldn't buy the 'fair, just, and patient' part. Now . . . Well, I mean, who's to judge fairness, justice? Fairness and justice really aren't absolute, are they? They're conditioned by time and place. They emerge as a function of the rules; what *he* thinks they mean has to affect what *I* think they mean. So . . . I've been standing myself in a corner and memorizing the rest of what Huxley said."

"What was that?" asked his father.

" 'But also we know, to our cost, that he never overlooks a mistake, or makes the smallest allowance for ignorance.' "

"To our cost," said the Inspector thoughtfully.

"It reminds me," Ellery went on, "of something Rimbaud, the French poet, once wrote to a friend: *'Je est un autre.'* Not *ju suis,* you'll note. *'Je* est *un autre'*— 'I *is* someone else.' Sounds like something out of Joel Chandler Harris. Until you start mouthing it. Then, all of a sudden, it becomes: 'I . . . is-some-one-else.' "

But it was too much for the old man, and he stopped listening.

"It's a tough one," Ellery reflected aloud. "It calls on the head. I is someone else . . . Then I ran across Archibald MacLeish's interpretation of Rimbaud's line. MacLeish interprets it as meaning: 'One is played *upon,* not player.' One is played upon, not player," he repeated, savoring it. "Tasty, isn't it?"

But—*to our cost,* thought the Inspector; and he let his eyelids droop, the better to see the board, and the taken pieces lying, discards, in the margins: the bronze plaque to the living memory of Nathaniel York, Junior, kept loving-bright by the machines of Walt's hands; the demolished head that had belonged to Robert York; the country dreams of Emily York, thrown into the mandibles of the great steel underground worm; the little pre-sleep nip of juniper juice in Myra York's little pink mouth, and the instant quiet flash of agony; and, off by itself, in a strange terrain, a place of distortions seen through another dimension . . . off by itself the checkmated king, writhing with hideous life. And, in some hideous way, happy. All for the lack of a bit of regard here, a warming hand there, a spoonful of loving concern in a critical hour.

"To our cost," Inspector Queen sighed.

Inspector Queen's Own Case

1 · At First the Infant

The dove-colored Chevrolet was parked fifty feet from the hospital entrance. The car was not new and not old, just a Sunday-hosed-looking family job with a respectable dent here and there in the fenders.

The fat man squeezed behind the wheel went with it like a used tire. He wore a home-pressed dark blue suit with a few food spots on the lapels, a white shirt already damp from the early morning June sun, and a blue tie with a wrinkled knot. A last summer's Macy's felt hat with a sweat-stained band lay on the seat beside him.

The object in point was to look like millions of other New Yorkers. In his business, the fat man liked to say, visibility was the worst policy. The main thing was not to be noticed by some nosy noonan who could lay the finger on you in court afterwards. Luckily, he did not have to worry about impressing his customers. The people he did business with, the fat man often chuckled, would avail themselves of his services if he came to work in a Bikini.

The fat man's name was Finner, A. Burt Finner. He was known to numerous laboring ladies of the nightclubs as Fin, from his hobby of stuffing sharp five-dollar bills into their nylons. He had a drab little office in an old office building on East 49th Street.

Finner cleaned his teeth with the edge of a match packet cover, sucked his cheeks in several times, and settled back to digest his breakfast.

He was early, but in these cases the late bird found himself looking down an empty worm hole. Five times out of ten, Finner sometimes complained, they wanted to change their confused little minds at the last second.

He watched the hospital entrance without excitement. As he watched, his lips began to form a fat O, his winkless eyes sank deeper into his flesh, the pear-shaped face took on a look of concentration; and before he knew it he was whistling. Finner heard his own music happily. He was that rarity, a happy fat man.

The tune he whistled was *Ah! Sweet Mystery of Life*.

My theme song, he called it.

When the girl came out of the hospital the fat man was on the steps to greet her, smiling.

"Good morning!" the fat man said. "All checked out okay?"

"Yes." She had a deep, slightly hoarse voice.

"No complications or anything?"

"No."

"And our little arrival is well and happy, I hope?" Finner started to raise the flap of the blue blanket from the face of the infant the girl was carrying, but she put her shoulder in the way.

"Don't touch him," she said.

"Now, now," the fat man said. "I'll bet he's a regular lover-boy. How could he miss with such a doll for a ma?" He was still trying to get a look at her baby. But she kept fending him off.

"Well, let's go," Finner said curtly.

He took the rubberized bag of diapers and bottles of formula from her and waddled to his car. She dragged after him, clutching the blanketed bundle to her breast.

The fat man had the front door open for her. She shook his hand off and got in. He shrugged.

"Where do you want I should drop you?"

"I don't care. I guess my apartment."

He drove off cautiously. The girl held the blue bundle tight.

She wore a green suède suit and a mannish felt pulled down over one eye. She was striking in a theatrical way, gold hair greenish at the scalp, big hazel eyes, a wide mouth that kept moving around. She had put on no makeup this morning. Her lips were pale and ragged.

She lifted the blanket and looked down at the puckered little face with tremendous intentness.

"Any deformities or birthmarks?" the fat man asked suddenly.

"What?"

He repeated the question.

"No." She began to rock.

"Did you do what I told you about his clothes?"

"Yes."

"You're sure there are no identifying marks on the clothes?" he persisted.

"I told you!" She turned on him in fury. "Can't you shut up? He's sleeping."

"They sleep like drunks. Had an easy time, did you?"

"Easy?" The girl began to laugh. But then she stopped laughing and looked down again.

"Just asking," Finner said, craning to see the baby's face. "Sometimes the instruments—"

"He's perfect merchandise," the girl said.

She began to croon in a sweet and throbbing contralto, rocking the bundle again. The baby blatted, and the girl looked frantic.

"Darlin', darlin', what's the matter? Don't cry . . . Mama's got you . . ."

"Gas," the fat man said. "Just bubble him."

She flung him a look of pure hate. She raised the baby to her shoulder and patted his back nervously. He burped and fell asleep again.

A. Burt Finner drove in delicate silence.

All at once the girl burst out, "I can't, I won't!"

"Sure you can't," Finner said instantly. "Believe me, I'm no hard-hearted Hannah. I got three of my own. But what about *him*?"

She sat there clutching her baby and looking trapped.

"The important thing in a case like this is to forget yourself. Look," the fat man said earnestly, "every time you catch yourself thinking of just you, stop and think what this means to this fine little fella. Do it right now. What would it mean to him if you goofed off now?"

"Well, what?" she said in a hard voice.

"Being raised in a trunk, is what. With cigar smoke and stinking booze fumes to fill his little lungs instead of God's wonderful fresh air," the fat man said, "that's what. You want to raise a kid that way?"

"I wouldn't do that," the girl said. "I'd never do it like that! I'd get him a good nurse—"

"I can see you been thinking about it," A. Burt Finner nodded approvingly, "even though we got an ironbound agreement. Okay, you get him a good nurse. So who'd be his mother, you or this nurse? You'd be slaving all day and night to pay her salary, and buy certified milk and all, and it's her he'd love, not you. So what's the percentage?"

The girl closed her eyes.

"So that's out. So there he is, back in the trunk. So who'd baptize him, some hotel clerk in Kansas City? Who'd he play with, some rubberlips trumpet player on the junk? What would he teethe on, beer openers and old cigar butts? And," the fat man said softly, "would he toddle around from table to table calling every visiting Elk from Dayton daddy?"

"You bastard," the girl said.

"Exactly my point," the fat man said.

"I could get married!"

They were on a side street on the West Side, just passing an empty space at one of the curbs. Finner stopped, shifted, and backed the Chevrolet halfway in.

"Congratulations," he said. "Do I know this Mr. Schlemihl who's going to take another guy's wild oat and call him sonny-boy?"

"Let me out, you fat creep!"

The fat man smiled. "There's the door."

She backed out, her eyes blazing.

He waited.

Not until her shoulders sagged did he know that he had won. She reached back in and laid the bundle carefully on the seat beside him and just as carefully shut the door.

"Good-by," she whispered to the bundle.

Finner wiped the sweat off his face. He took a bulky unmarked envelope from his inside pocket and reached over the baby.

"Here's the balance of your dough," he said kindly.

She looked up in a blind way. Then she snatched the envelope and hurled it at him. It struck his bald head and burst, showering bills all over the seat and floor.

She turned and ran.

"Nice to have met you," the fat man said. He gathered up the scattered bills and stuffed them in his wallet.

He looked up and down the street. It was empty. He leaned over the baby, undid the blanket, examined it. He found a department-store label on the beribboned lawn nightgown, ripped it off, put the label in his pocket. He found another label on the tiny undershirt and removed that, too. Then he looked the sleeping infant over. Finally, he rewrapped it in the blanket and replaced it beside him.

Then he examined the contents of the rubberized bag. When he was satisfied, he rezipped it.

"Well, bubba, it's off to a long life and a damn dull one," he said to the bundle on the seat. "You'd have had a hell of a lot more fun with her."

He glanced at his wristwatch and drove on toward the West Side Highway.

On the highway, driving at a law-abiding thirty, with an occasional friendly glance at the bundle, A. Burt Finner began to whistle.

Soon his whistle changed to song.

He sang, *"Ahhhhh, sweet mys-tery of life and love I found youuuuuuuuuu . . ."*

The seven-passenger Cadillac was parked in a deserted lane just off the Hutchinson River Parkway, between Pelham and New Rochelle. It was old-fashioned, immaculate, and wore Connecticut plates. A chauffeur with a red face and white hair was at the wheel. A buxom woman with a pretty nose sat beside him. She was in her late forties. Under her cloth coat she wore a nurse's nylon uniform.

In the tonneau sat the Humffreys.

Sarah Stiles Humffrey said, "Alton, isn't he *late?*"

Her husband smiled "He'll be here, Sarah."

"I'm nervous as a cat!"

He patted her hand. She had a large hand, beautifuly groomed. Mrs. Humffrey was a large woman, with large features over which she regularly toiled and despaired.

Her husband was an angular man in a black suit so dreary it could only have been planned. A Humffrey had made the Mayflower crossing; and from the days of Cole's Hill and Plimoth Plantation Humffreys had deposited their distinguished dust among the stones of New England. His wife's family was very nearly as distinguished.

Alton K. Humffrey withdrew his hand quickly. Tolerant as he could be toward his wife's imperfections, he could not forgive his own. He had been born without the tip of the little finger on his right hand. Usually he concealed the offending member by curling it against his palm. This caused the ring finger to curl, too. When he raised his hand to hail someone the gesture looked Roman, almost papal. It rather pleased him.

"Alton, suppose she changed her mind!" his wife was saying.

"Nonsense, Sarah."

"I wish we could have done it in the usual way," she said restlessly.

His lips compressed. In crucial matters Sarah was a child. "You know why, my dear."

"I really *don't.*"

"Have you forgotten that we're not exactly the ideal age?"

"Oh, Alton, you could have managed it." One of Sarah Humffrey's charms was her clinging conviction that her husband could manage anything.

"This way is safest, Sarah."

"Yes." Sarah Humffrey shivered. Alton was so right. He always was. If only people of our class could live like ordinary people, she thought.

"Here he comes," the white-haired chauffeur said.

The Humffreys turned quickly. The dove-colored Chevrolet was pulling up behind them.

The buxom nurse with the pretty nose got out of the Cadillac.

"No, I'll get him, Miss Sherwood!" Alton K. Humffrey said. He sprang from the limousine and hurried over to the Chevrolet. The nurse got into the tonneau.

"Oh, dear," Mrs. Humffrey said.

"Here he is," Finner beamed.

Humffrey stared in at the blue blanket. Then without a word he opened the Chevrolet door.

"Time," Finner said.

"What?"

"There's the little matter of the scratch," the fat man smiled. "Remember, Mr. Humffrey? Balance C.O.D.?"

The millionaire shook his head impatiently. He handed over a bulky unmarked envelope, like the one Finner had offered the girl in the suède suit. Finner opened the envelope and took out the money and counted it.

"He's all yours," Finner said, nodding.

Humffrey lifted the bundle out of the car gingerly. Finner handed out the rubberized bag, and the millionaire took that, too.

"You'll find the formula typed on a plain slip of paper in the bag," the fat man said, "along with enough bottles and diapers to get you started."

Humffrey waited.

"Something wrong, Mr. Humffrey? Did I forget something?"

"The birth certificate and the papers," the millionaire said grimly.

"My people aren't magicians," the fat man said, smiling. "I'll mail them to you soon as they're ready. They'll be regular works of art, Mr. Humffrey."

"Register the envelope to me, please."

"Don't worry," the fat man said soothingly.

The tall thin man did not stir until the Chevrolet was gone. Then he walked back to the limousine slowly. The chauffeur was holding the tonneau door open, and Mrs. Humffrey's arms were reaching through.

"Give him to me, Alton!"

Her husband handed her the baby. With trembling hands she lifted the flap of the blanket.

"Miss Sherwood," she gasped, "look!"

"He's a little beauty, Mrs. Humffrey." The nurse had a soft impersonal voice. "May I?"

She took the baby, laid it down on one of the jumpseats, and opened the blanket.

"Nurse, he'll fall off!"

"Not at this age." The nurse smiled. "Mr. Humffrey, may I have that bag, please?"

"Oh, why is he crying?"

"If you were messed, hungry, and only one week old, Mrs. Humffrey," Nurse Sherwood said, "you'd let the world know about it, too. There, baby. We'll have you clean and sweet in no time. Henry, plug the warmer into the dashboard and heat this bottle. Mr. Humffrey, you'd better shut that door while I rediaper Master Humffrey."

"Master Humffrey!" Sarah Humffrey laughed and cried alternately while her husband stared in. He could not seem to take his eyes from the squirming little body.

"Alton, we have a son, a *son*."

"You're actually excited, Sarah." Alton Humffrey was pleased.

"Nurse, let's not use the things from that bag, shall we? All the nice new things we've brought for you, baby!" Mrs. Humffrey zipped open a morocco case. It was full of powders, oils, sterilized cotton, picks. The nurse took a bottle of baby oil and a tin of powder from it silently. "The first thing we'll do is have him examined by that pediatrician in Greenwich . . . *Alton*."

"Yes, dear?"

"Suppose the doctor finds he's not as . . . not as represented?"

"Now, Sarah. You read the case histories yourself."

"But not knowing who his people are—"

"Must we go back to that, my dear?" her husband said patiently. "I don't want to know who his people are. In a case like this, knowledge is dangerous. This way there's no red tape, no publicity, and no possibility of repercussions. We know the child comes of good Anglo-Saxon stock, and that the stock is certified as having no hereditary disease on either side, no feeble-mindedness, no criminal tendencies. Does the rest matter?"

"I suppose not, Alton." His wife fumbled with her gloves. "Nurse, why doesn't he stop *crying?*"

"You watch," Miss Sherwood said over the baby's furious blats. "Henry, the bottle should be ready." The chauffeur hastily handed it to her. She removed the aluminum cap and shook some of the milk onto the back of her hand. Nodding, she popped the nipple gently into the little mouth. The baby stopped in mid-blat. He seized the nipple with his tiny jaws and began to suck vigorously.

Mrs. Humffrey stared, fascinated.

Alton K. Humffrey said almost gaily, "Henry, drive us back to the Island."

The old man turned over in bed and his naked arms flew up against the light from somewhere. It was the wrong light or the wrong direction. Or wasn't it morning? Something was wrong.

Then he heard the surf and knew where he was and squeezed his eyelids as hard as he could to shut out the room. It was a pleasant room of old random furniture and a salt smell, with rusty shrimp dangling from bleached seaweed on the wallpaper. But the pale blue wavery water lines ran around and around like thoughts, getting nowhere, and they bothered him.

The night air still defended the room coolly, but he could feel the sun ricocheting off the sea and hitting the walls like waves. In two hours it would be a hotbox.

Richard Queen opened his eyes and for a moment looked his arms over. They're like an anatomical sketch of a cadaver, he thought, wornout cables of muscle and bone with corrugated covers where skin used to be. But he could feel the life in them, they could still hold their own, they were useful. He brought his hands down into focus, examined the knurls of joints, the rivuleted skin, each pore like a speck of dirt, the wiry debris of gray hairs; but suddenly he closed his eyes again.

It was early, almost as early as when he used to wake in the old days. The alarm would go off to find him already prone on the braided rug doing his fifty pushups— summer or winter, in green spring light or the gray of the autumn dawn. The hot shave and cold shower, with the bathroom door shut so that his son might sleep on undisturbed. The call-in from the lieutenant, while breakfast was on the hod, to report any special developments of the night. The Sergeant waiting outside, the drive downtown. Headed for another working day. Listening to the general police calls on the way down, just in case. Maybe a direct word for him on the radiophone from the top floor of the big gold-domed building on Centre Street. His office . . . "What's new this morning?" . . . orders . . . the important mail . . . the daily teletype report . . . the 9 A.M. lineup, the parade of misfits from the Bullpen . . .

It was all part of a life. Even the corny kidding, and the headaches and heartaches. Good joes sharing the raps and the kudos while administrations came and went, not touching them. Not really touching them, even in shake-ups. Because when the dust settled, the oldtimers were still there. Until, that is, they were shoved out to pasture.

It's hard to break the habits of a lifetime, he thought. It's impossible. What do those old horses think about, munching the grass of their retirement? The races they'd won? The races they could still win, given the chance?

The young ones coming up, always coming up. How many of them could do fifty pushups? At half his age? But there they were, getting set, getting citations and commendations if they were good enough, a Department funeral if they stopped a bullet or a switchblade . . .

There they were. And here am I . . .

Becky was stirring carefully in the next room. Richard Queen knew it was Becky, not Abe, because Abe was like a Newfoundland dog, incapable of quiet; and the old man had been visiting in the beach house with its papery walls long enough to have learned some intimate details of the Pearls' lives.

He lay in the bed idly.

Yes, that was Becky creeping down the stairs so as not to wake her husband or their guest. Soon the smell of her coffee, brown and brisk, would come seeping up from the kitchen. Beck Pearl was a small friendly woman with a big chest and fine hands and feet that were always on the move when her husband was around.

On the beach the gulls were squabbling over something.

Inspector Queen tried to think of his own wife. But Ellery's mother had died over thirty years ago. It was like trying to recall the face of a stranger glimpsed for an instant from the other end of a dark corridor.

Here comes the coffee . . .

For a while the old man let the drum and swish of the surf wash over him, as if he were lying on the beach below the house.

As if he were the beach, being rhythmically cleaned and emptied by the sea.

What should he do today?

A few miles from where Richard Queen was lying in the bed swam an island. The island was connected to the Connecticut mainland by a private causeway of handsome concrete. A fieldstone gatehouse with wood trim treated to look like bleached driftwood barred the island end of the causeway. This gatehouse was dressed in creeper ivy and climber roses, and it had a brief skirt of garden hemmed in oyster shells. A driftwood shingle above the door said:

Nair Island
PRIVATE PROPERTY
Restricted
For the Use of
Residents & Guests
ONLY

Two private policemen in semi-nautical uniforms alternated at the gatehouse in twelve-hour shifts.

Nair Island had six owners, who shared its two hundred-odd acres in roughly equal holdings. In Taugus, the town on the mainland of which the island was an administrative district, their summer retreat was known—in a sort of forelock-tugging derision—as "Million-Nair" Island.

The six millionaires were not clubby. Each estate was partitioned from its neighbors by a high, thick fieldstone wall topped with shells and iron spikes. Each owner had his private yacht basin and fenced-off bathing beach. Each treated the road serving the six estates as if it were his alone. Their annual meetings to transact the trifling business of the community, as required by the bylaws of the Nair Island Association, were brusque affairs, almost hostile. The solder that welded the six owners together was not Christian fellowship but exclusion.

The island was their fortress, and they were mighty people. One was a powerful United States Senator who had gone into politics from high society to protect the American way of life. Another was the octogenarian widow of a railroad magnate. Another was an international banker. A fourth was an aging philanthropist who loved the common people in the mass but could not stand them one by one. His neighbor, commanding the seaward spit of the Island, was a retired Admiral who had married the only daughter of the owner of a vast shipping fleet.

The sixth was Alton K. Humffrey.

Inspector Queen came downstairs shaved and dressed for the day in beige slacks, nylon sports shirt, and tan-and-white shoes. He carried his jacket over his arm.

"You're so early, Richard." Beck Pearl was pouring her husband's coffee. She was in a crisp housedress, white and pink. Abe was in his uniform. "And my, all spiffed up. Did you meet a woman on the beach yesterday?"

The old man laughed. "The day a woman messes with me."

"Don't give me that. And don't think Abe isn't worried, leaving me alone in the house every day with an attractive man."

"And don't think I'm not," Abe Pearl growled. "Squattez-vous, Dick. Sleep all right?"

"All right." He sat down opposite his friend and accepted a cup of coffee from Becky. "Aren't you up kind of early yourself this morning, Abe?"

"My summer troubles are starting. There was a brawl during the night—some tanked-up teenagers at a beach party. Want to sit in, Dick, just for ducks?"

The Inspector shook his head.

"Go on, Richard," Beck Pearl urged. "You're bored. Vacations are always that way."

He smiled. "Working people take vacations. Not old discards like me."

"That's fine talk! How do you want your eggs this morning?"

"Just this coffee, Becky. Thanks a lot."

The Pearls glanced at each other as the old man raised the cup. Abe Pearl shook his big head slightly.

"What do you hear from your son, Dick?" he said. "I noticed you got a letter from Rome yesterday."

"Ellery's fine. Thinking of visiting Israel next."

"Why didn't you go with him?" Mrs. Pearl demanded. "Or weren't you invited?" Her two sons were married, and she had definite ideas about what was wrong with the younger generation.

"He begged me to go. But I didn't feel it would be right. He's roaming around Europe looking for story ideas, and I'd only be in his way."

"He wasn't fooled by that poppycock, I hope," Beck Pearl snorted.

"He wanted to cancel his trip," Richard Queen said quietly. "He only went because you and Abe were kind enough to ask me up here for the summer."

"Well! I should think so."

Abe Pearl rose. "You're sure you won't sit in, Dick?"

"I thought I'd do a little exploring today, Abe. Maybe take your boat out, if you don't mind."

"Mind!" Abe Pearl glared down at him. "What kind of dribble is that?" He kissed his wife fiercely and pounded out, making the dishes on the sideboard jingle.

Through the window Inspector Queen watched his host back the black-and-white coupé with the roof searchlight out of the garage. For a moment the sun sparkled on the big man's cap with the gold shield above the visor. Then, with a wave, Abe Pearl was gone.

With his ability and popularity, the old man thought, he can hold down this Chief's job in Taugus for life. Abe used his head. He got out of the big time when he was still young enough to set up a new career for himself. He isn't much younger than I am, and look at him.

"Feeling sorry for yourself again, Richard?" Beck Pearl's womanly voice said. He turned, reddening.

"We all have to adjust to something," she went on in her soft way. "After all, it isn't as if you were like Abe's older brother Joe. Joe never had an education, never got married. All he knew was work. He worked all his life on a machine, and when he got too old and sick to work any more he had nothing—no family, no savings, nothing but the few dollars he gets from the government, and the check Abe sends him every month. There's millions like Joe, Richard. You're in good health, you have a successful son, you've led an interesting life, you've got a pension, no worries about the future—who's better off, you or Joe Pearl?"

He grinned. "Let's give Abe something to be jealous about." And he got up and kissed his friend's wife tenderly.

"Richard! You devil." Becky was blushing.

"Old, am I? Bring on those eggs—sunnyside, and don't burn the bacon!"

But the lift was feeble. When he left the house and headed for Abe Pearl's second-hand sixteen-foot cruiser, the old man's heart was bitter again. Every man tasted his own brand of misery. You needed more than a successful past and a secure future. Becky had left one thing out, the most important thing.

A man needed the present. Something to do.

The engine coughed its way into the basin and expired just as the sixteen-footer slid alongside the dock. Richard Queen tied up to a bollard, frowning, and looked around. The dock was deserted, and there was no one on the beach but a buxom woman in a nurse's nylon uniform reading a magazine on the sand beside a net-covered perambulator.

The old man waved. "Ahoy, there!"

The nurse looked up, startled.

"Could I possibly buy some gas here?" he bellowed.

The woman shook her head vigorously and pointed to the pram. He walked down to the beach end of the dock and made his way across the sand toward her. It was beautiful sand, clean as a laundered tablecloth, and he had the uneasy feeling that he should not be making tracks in it.

"I'm sorry," he said, taking off his hat. "Did I wake the baby?"

The nurse was stooping over the carriage intently. She straightened up, smiling.

"No harm done. He sleeps like a little top."

Richard Queen thought he had never seen a nicer smile. She was big and wholesome-looking; her pretty nose was peeling from sunburn. Close to fifty, he judged, but only because he had had long experience in such matters. To the amateur eye she would pass for forty.

She drew him off from the pram a little way. "Did you say you were out of gas?"

"Forgot to check the tank before I shoved off. It's not my boat," he said apologetically, "and I'm afraid I'm not much of a sailor. I just about made it to your dock when I saw your pump."

"You're a trespasser," she said with her crinkly smile. "This is private property."

"Nair Island," he nodded. "But I'm desperate. Would you allow me to buy some juice for that contraption?"

"You'd have to ask Mr. Humffrey, the owner, but I'm sure it wouldn't do you any good. He'd like as not call the Taugus police."

"Is he home?" The old man grinned at the picture of Abe Pearl running over to Nair Island to arrest him.

"No." She laughed. "They've taken the cabin cruiser down to Larchmont to watch some yacht racing. Mrs. Humffrey hasn't stuck her nose out of the house since the baby came."

"Then if I helped myself nobody would know?"

"I'd know," she retorted.

"Let me take a few gallons. I'll send Mr. Humffrey a check."

"You'll get me in trouble . . ."

"I won't even mention your name," he said solemnly. "By the way, what is it?"

"Sherwood. Jessie Sherwood."

"My name is Richard Queen, Mrs. Sherwood."

"*Miss* Sherwood, Mr. Queen."

"Oh," he said. "Glad to meet you."

"Likewise," Nurse Sherwood murmured.

For some absurd reason they both smiled. The sun on the old man felt good. The blue sky, the sparks flying off the water, the salt breeze, everything felt good.

"I really don't have any place to go, Miss Sherwood," he said. "Why don't we sit down and visit?"

The crinkles went out of her smile. "If it got back to Mr. and Mrs. Humffrey that I'd entertained a strange man on the beach while I was minding the baby they'd discharge me, and they'd be perfectly right. And I've got awfully attached to little Michael. I'm afraid I can't, Mr. Queen."

Nice, he thought. Nice woman.

"Of course," he said. "It's my fault. But I thought . . . You see, I'm an old friend of Chief of Police Pearl's of Taugus. In fact, I'm spending the summer with him and Mrs. Pearl in their shack on the beach."

"Well!" she said. "I'm sure Mr. Humffrey wouldn't mind *that*. It's just that they're so nervous about the baby."

"Their first?"

"Well, yes."

"They're smart. Parents can't be too careful about their children, especially if they're rich."

"The Humffreys are multimillionaires."

"Chief Pearl tells me they're all loaded on Nair Island. I remember a snatch case I investigated a few years ago—"

"Case? Are you a police officer, too, Mr. Queen?"

"Was," he said. "In New York. But they retired me."

"Retired you! At your age?"

He looked at her. "How old do you think I am?"

"About fifty-five"

"You're just saying that."

"I never just say things. Why, are you older?"

"I quote Section 434-a dash two one point O of the Administrative Code of the City of New York," he said grimly, "which states as follows: 'No member of the police force in the department except surgeons of police,' etcetera, 'who is or hereafter attains the age of 63 years shall continue to serve as a member of such force but shall be retired and placed on the pension rolls of the department.' " He added after a moment, "You see, I know it by heart."

"Sixty-three." She looked skeptical.

"My last birthday."

"I wouldn't have believed it," she murmured.

From the depths of the pram came a squawk. Nurse Sherwood hurried to its source, and he followed. He could not help taking in the curve of her hips, the youthful shoulders, the pretty legs and ankles.

It was just a cry in the baby's sleep. "He'll be waking up for his feeding soon," she said softly, fussing with the netting. "Is your wife visiting with Chief and Mrs. Pearl, too?"

Strong hands.

"I've been a widower almost as long as you're old, Miss Sherwood."

"That's impossible!" She laughed. "How old do you think I am?"

"Thirty-nine, forty," he lied.

"Aren't you sweet! I'll be fifty in January. Why, I've been an R.N. for almost twenty-five years."

"Oh, you're a trained nurse. Is this a sick baby?"

"Heavens, no. He's a sturdy little monkey."

He was, too. He had chubby arms and legs, a formidable little chest, and fat cheeks. He was sleeping with his arms defending his head in a curious attitude of defiance and helplessness; his silky brows were bunched in a troubled way. Richard Queen thought, They look so . . . so . . . He could not think of the word. Some feelings there were no words for. He was surprised to find that he still had them.

"It's just that Mrs. Humffrey is so nervous," Jessie Sherwood was saying. "She won't trust an ordinary nursemaid. And I've been a pediatric and maternity nurse practically my entire career. Ordinarily I wouldn't take a case like this—a perfectly healthy baby—I could be taking care of someone who really needs me. But I've rather overdone it the past few years, and Mr. Humffrey's offer was so generous—"

She stopped abruptly. Why was she telling all this to a perfect stranger? She was appalled.

"Never married?" the old man asked casually.

"Beg pardon? Oh, you mean me." Her face changed. "I was engaged once. During the war."

It was her eyes that were crinkled now, but not with laughter.

"He was a doctor," she explained. "He was killed in Normandy."

The old man nodded. They stood over the carriage side by side, looking through the netting at the tiny sleeping face.

What am I thinking of? he thought. A vigorous, attractive woman . . . and what am I but a withering old fool?

He fumbled with the button of his jacket. "I can't tell you how nice it's been talking to you, Miss Sherwood."

She looked up quickly. "You're going?"

"Well, I'd better lift some of Mr. Humffrey's gas and start back. Becky—Mrs. Pearl—will be having fits if I don't show up for lunch. She's been trying to put some meat on my bones."

"I don't see why," Jessie Sherwood said warmly. "I think you're built beautifully for—"

"For a man my age?" He smiled. "I hope we meet again some time."

"Yes," she said in a low voice. "I don't know a soul here. On Thursdays I go crazy. That's my day off—"

But he merely said, "I know what you mean. Well." His smile was fixed. "Good-by, Miss Sherwood. And thanks. I'll mail Mr. Humffrey a check tonight."

"Good-by," Jessie Sherwood said.

He did not even wave to her as he pulled away from the dock.

Independence Day was a Monday, and it developed into the noisiest Fourth Nurse Sherwood could remember. In spite of the ban on their sale, fireworks crackled, hissed, swooshed, and screeched into the skies over Nair Island all day.

The continuous barrage had made little Michael fret and wail, and his displeasure infected the household. Mrs. Humffrey wrung her hands and hovered all day; Mrs. Charbedeau, the cook, overdid the roast and exchanged bickering sarcasms with Mrs. Lenihan, the housekeeper; Mrs. Lenihan snapped the head off Rose Healy, the upstairs maid, and reduced Marie Tompkins, the downstairs maid, to the sullen verge of Notice. Even old Stallings, the gardener, ordinarily the most unaffected of men, threatened wrathfully to bust Henry Cullum in the snoot if the chauffeur ever again backed a car five feet onto his lawn in the poorly planned apron behind the Humffrey garage.

Alton Humffrey was annoyed. The Island's one road was as crowded all day as Front Street in Taugus; the surrounding waters splashed and spluttered well into the evening with hundreds of holiday craft from the mainland; and Cullum had to be delegated to stand guard on the Humffrey beach to chase trespassing picnickers away.

Worst of all, Ronald Frost made a scene. Frost was Humffrey's nephew, the only child of the millionaire's dead sister. He lived on a small income from his mother's estate, spending most of his time as a house guest of his numerous socialite friends, making a partner for an odd girl or teaching someone's cousin to play tennis.

The young man had come up to spend the weekend, along with some relatives of Sarah Humffrey's from Andover, Malden and Cambridge; and whereas the Stiles clan, all elderly people, had sensibly left on Sunday night to get the jump on the northbound traffic, Ronald Frost lingered well into Independence Day. What the attraction was Jessie Sherwood failed at first to see, unless it was his uncle's liquor cabinet; certainly he made no secret of his boredom, and his visits to the cabinet were frequent.

Ron was a younger edition of his mother's brother—tall, thin, shoulderless, with lifeless brown hair and slightly popping eyes. But he had an unpleasant smile, half unction, half contempt; and he treated servants vilely.

Jessie Sherwood heard the row from the nursery that afternoon while she was changing the baby; Alton Humffrey's upstairs study was across the hall. Apparently Ron Frost was mired in a financial slough and expected his uncle to pull him out.

"I'm afraid, Ronald, you'll have to look for relief elsewhere this time," Jessie heard the older man say in his chill, nasal voice.

"What?" Young Frost was astounded.

"This avenue is closed to you."

"You don't mean it!"

"Never more serious in my life."

"But Uncle Alton, I'm in a rotten jam."

"If you must get into jams, it's time you learned to get out of them by your own efforts."

"I don't believe it." Frost was dazed. "Why, you've never turned me down before. And I'm in the damnedest spot just now . . . What's the idea, Uncle? Don't tell me *you're* in a pecuniary pickle."

"I don't get into pecuniary pickles, Ronald." Jessie Sherwood could almost see Alton Humffrey's glacial smile. "I take it this request was the real purpose of your visit, so—"

"Wait a minute." Ron Frost's tone was ugly now. "I want clarification. Is this a peeve of the moment because your precious castle has been fouled up all day by the common people, or is it a permanent freeze-out?"

"Translated into English," his uncle said, "you're apparently inquiring whether this is a whim or a policy. It's a policy, Ronald. I find now that I have a better use for my money than to pay your gambling debts and enlarge the bank accounts of your heartbroken ladyfriends."

"The brat," mumbled Frost.

"I beg your pardon?"

"This mongrel you picked up somewhere—"

"You're drunk," Alton Humffrey said.

"Not so drunk I can't put two and two together! All your wormy talk about the Humffrey blood—the family name—the promises you made my mother—!"

"You have an obligation, too," his uncle snapped. "Principally, to stop following the life cycle of a sponge. By the way, you'll apologize for the disgusting manner in which you've just referred to my son."

"Your son!" shouted Frost. "What is he if he isn't a mongrel?"

"Get out."

"Can't stand the truth, hey? You gave me every reason to expect I'd be your heir, not some puking little—"

"So help me God, Ronald," Alton Humfrey's voice said clearly, "if you don't leave at once I'll throw you down the stairs."

There was a silence.

Then Jessie Sherwood heard young Frost say with a nervous laugh, "I'm sorry, Uncle. I guess I am tight. I apologize, of course."

There was another silence.

"Very well," Humffrey said. "And now I take it you're about to leave?"

"Right, right," Ron Frost said.

She heard him stagger up the hall. A few minutes later his footsteps returned and stopped in the study doorway.

"Please say good-by and thanks to Aunt Sarah for me, Uncle. Under the circumstances—"

"I understand." The Humffrey voice sounded remote.

"Well . . . so long, Uncle Alton."

"Good-by, Ronald."

"I'll be seeing you and Aunt Sarah soon, I hope."

There was no reply.

Young Frost stumbled down the stairs. Shortly after, Jessie heard his Jaguar roar away.

So the day was intolerable, and she sank into bed thankfully that night, punched her pillow, murmured her nightly prayer, and sought sleep.

At two in the morning she was still seeking.

Nair Island had long ago settled down to silence and to darkness. The rustle of surf that soothed her every night was the only sound she could hear, except for an occasional late guest's car leaving the Island; but tonight its rhythm seemed to clash with her pulse rate. Everyone in the house was asleep; the two rooms above the garage, where Stallings and Cullum had their quarters, had been dark for hours. Her bedroom was not even hot; a cool breeze had swept in from sea at eleven, and she had had to get up for a quilt.

Then why couldn't she sleep?

It was a nuisance, because usually she fell asleep at will. She had always had the gift of instant relaxation. It was one of her assets as a nurse.

It certainly wasn't the baby. Jessie had been a little concerned about his behavior during the day, but with bedtime he had become his healthy little self again, and he had finished his bottle, bubbled mightily, and fallen asleep like an angel. When she had checked him before turning in, his tiny face was serene and he was breathing with such untroubled lightness that she had actually stooped over his crib. Nor was it an imminent feeding that was keeping her wakeful; little Michael had broken himself of his 2 A.M. bottle ten days before, and he had slept peacefully through every night since.

It was the whole disagreeable day, Jessie decided—the fireworks, the general confusion, Mrs. Humffrey's flapping about, the tension in the household climaxed by the row between uncle and nephew. And perhaps—she felt her cheeks tingle—perhaps it had something to do with that man Richard Queen.

Jessie had to admit that she had been acting like a moony teenager ever since their meeting on the Humffrey beach. Thinking about a man of sixty-three! Hinting to him about Thursday being her day off . . . The burn in her cheeks smarted. She had even gone over to the public beach in Taugus on her next day off and sat on the sand under a rented beach umbrella all afternoon, hoping against hope and feeling silly at the same time. What if he had shown up? Her figure in a bathing suit wasn't bad for her age, but she could hardly compete with those skinny brown three-quarters-naked young hussies flitting about the beach. So she had left that day relieved, angry at herself, and yet disappointed. He'd seemed so nice, so youthful-looking, and so troubled about his age and his retirement . . . Of course, he had stayed away. He must know plenty about women, having been a police officer all his life. Probably put her down right off as a coy old maid on the prowl for a victim.

Still, it was a pity. They could have found lots to talk about. Some of her more interesting cases, people of note she had nursed. And he must have had hundreds of exciting experiences. And actually she hadn't looked half bad in her bathing suit. She had studied herself in the bathroom mirror very critically before making up her mind to go that day. At least she had some flesh on her bones. And her skin was really remarkably unlined for a woman of forty-nine. How old was Marlene Dietrich . . . ?

Jessie Sherwood heaved over and buried her face in the pillow.

And in the silence that followed the groan of the bed she heard a sound that drove all other thoughts from her head.

It was the sound of a window being opened in the nursery.

She lay stiffly, listening.

The nursery was at the rear of the house, a corner room with two windows. One overlooked the driveway and gardens at the side, the other faced the sea. At the baby's bedtime she had opened both windows wide, but when the breeze came up and she had had to get a quilt for herself, she had gone into the nursery to tuck an extra satin throw around the baby and shut the seaward window. The temperature had dropped so low that she had even removed the screen and pulled the driveway window most of the way down, leaving it open no more than three or four inches.

It seemed to her the sound had come from the driveway window.

There it was again.

Again!

They were short, soft, scrapy sounds, as if the window were being opened an inch or two at a time, little secretive upward nudges, with listening pauses between.

"Parents can't be too careful about their children, especially if they're rich . . ."

He had said that.

"A snatch case I investigated a few years ago . . ."

A kidnaper!

With a leap Jessie Sherwood was out of bed. She grabbed her robe, flung it over her cotton nightgown, and dashed through the communicating doorway into little Michael's room.

In the faint glow of the baseboard nightlight she saw a man. He had one leg over the sill of the driveway window. The other was apparently braced against the top rung of a ladder. His head was cut off at the neck by the half-raised venetian blind. He was all flat and colorless. It was like seeing a lifesized cutout made of black paper.

Nurse Sherwood yelled and sprang to the crib. The figure in the window disappeared.

There was a great deal of confusion after that. Mr. Humffrey ran in buttoning his pajama coat over his gaunt, furry torso; Mrs. Humffrey flew by him, shrieking, to tear the baby from his nurse's arms; Mrs. Lenihan, Mrs. Charbedeau, the two maids thronged the stairway from the third floor, pulling on assorted negligees and gasping questions; and the men's quarters over the garage lit up. The baby wailed louder, Mrs. Humffrey shrieked harder, Mr. Humffrey roared demands for an explanation, and through the bedlam Jessie Sherwood tried to make herself heard. When she was finally able to communicate, and Alton Humffrey thrust his head out the window, the driveway was empty except for old Stallings and Henry Cullum, in pajamas and barefoot, looking up and asking wildly what was the matter.

A long ladder was leaning against the window.

"Search the grounds," Alton Humffrey shouted to the two white-haired men below. "I'll phone the gatehouse."

When he came back he was fuming. "I don't know what we pay those guards for. Either that imbecile Peterson was asleep or he's drunk. Sarah, *stop* that, please. Give Michael to Miss Sherwood. You're frightening him half to death."

"Oh, Alton, suppose it was a *kidnaper*," Sarah Humffrey said hysterically.

"Nonsense. It was some housebreaker, and Miss Sherwood scared him off. Here, let me have him."

"I'll take him, Mr. Humffrey," Jessie Sherwood said. "Mrs. Lenihan, would you get me a bottle of formula from the refrigerator? I think, darlin', we'll make an exception tonight. But first let's change this diaper . . ." She took the baby into the nursery bathroom and firmly shut the door.

When she came out with him, Alton Humffrey was alone in the nursery watching the bottle in the electric warmer.

"Is Michael all right?" he asked abruptly.

"He's fine, Mr. Humffrey.'

"You're sure it was a man?"

"Yes, sir."

"Nothing familiar about him?" His tone was odd.

"I really can't say," Jessie said quietly. "I didn't see his face at all, and the rest of him was just a black silhouette against the moonlight. Mr. Humffrey, I don't think it was a housebreaker."

"You don't?" He glanced at her sharply.

"Why should a housebreaker try to enter through an upper window? The windows aren't locked downstairs."

Alton Humffrey did not reply. Jessie took the bottle from the warmer, sat down in the rocker, and began to feed the baby.

"Mr. Humffrey?" It was Cullum, from below.

Humffrey strode to the window. "Yes?"

"No sign of a soul," the chauffeur said. Stallings, beside him, nodded.

"You two had better get some clothes on and stay out there for a while." He put the nursery screen with the animal cutouts on it before the window. Jessie noticed how careful he was not to touch the window.

When he turned back his brow was all knots.

"Don't you think you'd better call the police, Mr. Humffrey?" Jessie murmured.

"Yes," he said.

The telephone rang on the other side of the flimsy wall and the old man was instantly awake. He heard Abe Pearl's sleepy growl say, "Yes?" and then, not sleepily at all, "I'll go right over. Have Tinny and Borcher meet me there."

When Chief Pearl let himself out of his bedroom, there was the old man in the hall in his robe, waiting.

"Dick. What are you doing up?"

"I heard the phone, Abe. Trouble?"

"Something funny over on Nair Island," the big man grunted. "Maybe you'd like to sit in on it."

"Nair Island," Richard Queen said. "What kind of trouble?"

"Somebody tried to break into one of those millionaires' homes. Kid's nursery. Might be a snatch try."

"It wouldn't be at the Humffreys', would it?"

"That's right." Abe Pearl stared.

"Anybody hurt?"

"No, he was scared off. But how do you know, Dick?"

"I'll be with you in three minutes."

The Humffrey house was lit up. They found one of Abe Pearl's men examining the ladder in the driveway and another in the nursery talking to Humffrey and the nurse. The screen was around the crib now, and Sarah Humffrey was in the rocker, gnawing her lips but quieted down.

The old man and Jessie Sherwood glanced at each other once, then looked away. He remained in the background, listening, looking around. Her color was high, and she drew her robe more closely about her. It would have to be the *cotton* nightgown tonight! she thought. Why didn't I wash out the orlon?

When they had repeated their stories, Chief Pearl went to the window.

"Is that your ladder, Mr. Humffrey?"

"Yes."

"Where is it usually kept?"

"In the tool shed where Stallings, my gardener, keeps his equipment."

"Take a look, Borcher."

The detective went out.

Abe Pearl turned to Jessie. "This man," he said. "Would you know him if you saw him again, Miss Sherwood?"

"I doubt it."

"He didn't say anything? Make any sound?"

"I didn't hear anything but the window being slid up little by little. When I ran in he disappeared."

"Did you hear a car?"

"No. I mean, I don't recall."

"Did you or didn't you?"

Jessie felt herself growing hot. "I tell you I don't know!"

"That's all right," Chief Pearl said. "People get excited." He turned his back on her, and Richard Queen blinked. He knew what his friend was thinking: Tag the nurse as a possible question mark. Of course, Abe didn't know her. He was surprised to find himself thinking of her as if he had known her for a long time. "Did you hear a car drive away, Mr. Humffrey?"

"I can't say. There was a great deal of noise here, naturally, after Miss Sherwood screamed."

Abe Pearl nodded. "The chances are, if he came in a car, he parked on the road off your grounds. You didn't find a note of any kind, did you?"

"No."

Sarah Humffrey whispered, *"Note?"*

Her husband said sharply, "Sarah, don't you think you'd better go to bed?"

"No, Alton, no, please. I couldn't sleep now, anyway. I'm all right, dear."

"Sure she is, Mr. Humffrey. Think you can answer a few questions, Mrs. Humffrey?" The chief's tone was deferential.

"Yes. But I can't tell you anything—"

"About your servants, I mean."

"The *servants?*" Sarah Humffrey repeated.

"Just a matter of form, Mrs. Humffrey. You never know in cases like this. How many you got, and how long they been with you?"

"Our housekeeper, Mrs. Lenihan, has been with us since our marriage," Sarah Humffrey said. "Mrs. Charbedeau, the cook, has worked for us almost ten years. Rose Healy and Marie Tompkins, the maids, are Boston girls who have been with us for a number of years."

"How about those two old fellows out there?"

"Stallings, the gardener," Alton Humffrey said, "is a local man, but we've employed him since we purchased this property. He stays on as caretaker during the winters. Henry Cullum, the chauffeur, drove for my father as a young man. I'll vouch for both of them. For that matter, for the women, too. We're very careful about our servants, Mr. Pearl.''

"How about Miss Sherwood?" Chief Pearl asked casually.

Jessie said, "I resent that!"

"Miss Sherwood has been with us only since a week or so before the baby came. However, she was highly recommended both by Dr. Holliday of Greenwich, our pediatrician, and Dr. Wicks of Taugus, who is our famly physician during the summers."

"Check her references, Mr. Humffrey?"

"Very thoroughly indeed."

"I've been a registered nurse for twenty-three years," Jessie Sherwood snapped, "and I've taken an awful lot in my time, but this is the limit. If I'd been in cahoots with some psychopath to kidnap this darling baby, do you think I'd have let out a yell and chased him away?"

Chief Pearl said mildly, "Just getting the picture," and went out.

Inspector Queen said to nobody in particular, "Don't blame the chief. It's his job."

Nurse Sherwood tossed her head.

When Abe Pearl came back he said to Humffrey, "There's dust on the ladder. We might get some prints. Miss Sherwood, I suppose you can't say whether the man you saw was wearing anything on his hands?"

"I can't say," Jessie replied shortly.

"Well, there's nothing else we can do tonight, Mr. Humffrey. Personally, I don't think you've got anything to worry about. But if you want me to leave a man, I'll leave one."

"I wish you would," Alton Humffrey said slowly. "And, Mr. Pearl."

"Yes, sir?"

"I don't want any publicity about this."

"I'll see that the boys over at Headquarters keep quiet about it. Dick?" The chief glanced at his friend.

"One thing." Richard Queen stepped forward. "If you don't mind my asking, Mr. Humffrey—is this your own child?"

Sarah Humffrey started. Alton Humffrey looked at the old man almost for the first time.

"No offense," Inspector Queen went on, "but you told Chief Pearl you have no other children. It struck me you people are a little on in years to be having a first baby."

"Is this one of your men, Chief?" the millionaire demanded.

"Inspector Queen of the New York police department, retired," Abe Pearl said quickly. "He was my lieutenant when I pounded a Manhattan beat, Mr. Humffrey. He's visiting me for the summer."

"The man who sent me a check for a dollar and fifty cents," Alton Humffrey said. "Are you in the habit of helping yourself to other people's gasoline, sir?"

"I explained that in my note."

"Yes. Well, Inspector, I don't see the relevance of your question."

"You haven't answered it," Richard Queen smiled.

"Michael is an adopted child. Why?"

"There might be something in his background to explain this, Mr. Humffrey, that's all."

"I assure you that's quite impossible." The millionaire's tone was frigid. "If there's nothing else, gentlemen, will you excuse Mrs. Humffrey and me?"

Jessie Sherwood wondered if Chief Pearl's friend was going to say anything to her before he left.

But he merely glanced politely in her direction and followed the chief out.

Tuesday evening after dinner, Jessie Sherwood went upstairs, peeped in at the baby, changed into a cool blue summer cotton, tidied her hair, powdered her nose, and slipped out of the house.

Jessie wondered as she sauntered down the driveway what the Humffreys talked about when they were alone. They were on the terrace now, sipping cherry brandy and staring silently to sea. In company they were articulate enough—Mrs. Humffrey was a positive chatterbox, of the corded-neck variety, while her husband had a caustic volubility—but Jessie had come upon them dozens of times alone together, and not once had she interrupted a conversation. They were strange people, she thought.

And jumped. A man had stepped suddenly from behind a tall clump of mountain laurel at the driveway entrance and flashed a light on her face.

"Oh. Sorry, Miss Sherwood."

"It's all right," Jessie said untruthfully, and strolled into the road. He was the second of the three guards hired by Alton Humffrey early that morning from a private detective agency in Bridgeport. They were rockfaced men who turned up and disappeared like alley cats.

When she rounded the curve in the road she began to walk fast. The air was salty sweet from the sea breeze and flowering gardens; and the road lights, great wrought-iron affairs shaped like sailing-ship lanterns, were besieged by platoons of moths and beetles cheerfully banging away. It was all very peaceful and lovely, but Jessie hurried on.

The gate was across the road at the Island end of the causeway.

"Mr. Peterson?"

The big private guard loomed in the gatehouse doorway. "You walking across?" His voice was sulky.

"No, I'm just out for some air. What's the matter, Mr. Peterson? You sound sour on the world."

"You'd think I'd had a picnic this weekend," the guard grumbled, unbending. "You know how many cars came through here last night? And then they want me to remember who went in and out!"

"That's a shame," Jessie said sympathetically. "With all that outbound traffic, I wouldn't have blamed you if you'd simply left the gate open all night."

"That's what I did, Miss Sherwood."

"Even at two in the morning, I suppose."

"Sure. Why not? How was I to know?"

"Well, of course. And by that time you must have been darn tired. Were you sitting in the gatehouse, resting?"

"I'll say!"

"So of course you didn't see the car that drove in some time after midnight and left around 2 A.M."

Peterson scowled. "I saw the back of it."

Jessie drew a long breath in the perfumed moonlight. "I'll bet it was a car you knew, and that's why you didn't stop him."

"Something like that. I didn't see his face, but him and the car looked familiar."

"What kind of car was it, Mr. Peterson?"

"Foreign job. A Jaguar."

"I see." Jessie's heart was beating faster.

"Like the one run by Mr. Humffrey's nephew—what's-his-name—Mr. Frost. Matter of fact," the guard said, "I thought it was Frost. He'd been off and on the Island all weekend."

"Oh, then you're not sure."

The guard said uncomfortably, "I can't swear to it."

"Well." Jessie smiled at him. "Don't you worry about it, Mr. Peterson. I'm sure you do your job as well as anyone could expect."

"You can say that again!"

"Good night."

"Good night, Miss Sherwood," Peterson said warmly.

He went back into the gatehouse, and Jessie began to retrace her steps, frowning.

"Nice going," a man's voice said.

Jessie's heart flopped. But then she saw who it was.

"Mr. Queen," she cried. "What are you doing here?"

He was in the roadway before her, spare and neat in a Palm Beach suit, looking amused.

"Same thing you are, only I beat you to it. Playing detective, Miss Sherwood?" He chuckled and took her arm. "Suppose I walk you back."

Jessie nodded a little stiffly, and they began to stroll along beside high fieldstone walls clothed in ivy and rambler roses, with the moon like a cheddar cheese overhead and the salty sweet air in their nostrils. How long is it, she wondered, since I last took a moonlight stroll with a man holding my arm? The last one had been Clem, on leave before shipping out . . .

The old man said suddenly, "Did you suspect Ron Frost all along?"

"Why are you so interested?" Jessie murmured.

"Let's say I don't like cases involving nursery windows." He sounded gruff. "And I can lend a hand to Abe Pearl . . ."

Some tireless patriot out at sea sent up a Roman candle. They stopped to watch the burst and drip of fireballs. For a few seconds the Island brightened. Then the darkness closed in again.

She felt his restless movement. It was like a dash of cold sea.

"I'd better be getting back," Jessie said matter-of-factly, and they walked on. "About your question, Mr. Queen. I suppose I shouldn't be saying this while I'm taking the Humffreys' money, but I like threats to babies even less than you do. Ronald Frost quarreled with Mr. Humffrey over Michael yesterday." And she told him what she had overheard from the nursery.

"So Frost expected to be his uncle's heir, and now he figures the baby's queered his act," Richard Queen said thoughtfully. "And Frost was tanked up when he left, you say?"

"Well, he'd had quite a bit to drink."

"He was nursing a beaut of a hangover this morning, and there was an empty bourbon bottle on his bureau. So he must have worked himself up to a real charge by late last night. Could be . . ."

"You saw him?" Jessie exclaimed.

"I dropped over to his place in Old Greenwich. Sort of as a favor to Abe Pearl."

"What did Frost say? Tell me!"

"He said he came straight home last night and went to bed. He lives alone, so no one saw him. In other words, no alibi."

"But did he actually deny having driven back here?"

"Would you expect him to admit it?" She knew he was smiling in the darkness. "Anyway, he's had a good scare—I'll guarantee that. If Frost was the man who tried to climb in through that window, I don't think he'll try it again."

"But what could he have been thinking of?" Jessie shivered.

"Drunks don't make much sense."

"You think . . . ransom? He told Mr. Humffrey he was badly in debt."

"I don't think anything," the Inspector said. "Whoever it was wore gloves—there wasn't an unaccounted-for print anywhere in the nursery or shed, and smudges were evident on the ladder. We have nothing on Frost but a questionable identification by Peterson. Even if we had, I doubt if Mr. Humffrey would press a charge, from the way he talked to Abe Pearl on the phone today. The best thing for you to do is forget last night ever happened, young lady."

"Thank you." Jessie felt herself dimpling, and it made her add tartly, "Young lady!"

He seemed surprised. "But you are young. Some people never age. My mother was one of them. You're very much like her—" He stopped. Then he said, "This is it, isn't it? It's so blasted dark—"

"Yes." Jessie hoped fiercely that the guard from the Bridgeport detective agency would have the decency to remain behind his bush and keep his finger off the flashlight button. "You were saying, Mr. Queen?"

"It wasn't anything."

There was a silence.

"Well," Jessie said. "I must say you've relieved my mind, Inspector. And thanks for walking me back."

"It was my pleasure." But from the way he said it, it sounded more like a sadness. "Well, good night, Miss Sherwood."

"Good night," Jessie said emptily.

She was standing there in the dark, listening to his footfalls retreat and wondering if she would ever see him again, when the light suddenly blinded her.

"Who was that with you, Miss Sherwood?" the private detective said.

"Oh, go away, you—you beagle!" Nurse Sherwood said, and she ran up the driveway as if someone were after her.

So that seemed the end of a promising friendship. The weeks went by, and although during little Michael's nap times on the Humffrey beach Jessie kept glancing up at passing small craft, or on her Thursdays off found herself scanning the crowds on Front Street or the Taugus public beach, she did not catch even a glimpse of that wiry figure again.

What children men are! she thought angrily.

If not for the baby, she would have given notice and quit Nair Island. She was desperately lonely. But little Michael needed her, she kept telling herself, trying not to feel the old jealous twinge when Mrs. Humffrey took him from her arms and exercised her proprietary rights.

Sometimes Jessie thought she ought to leave for the baby's sake, before he became too attached to her. But she kept putting it off. In the gloom that had suddenly set in, he was the only sunny thing. Besides, she told herself, there was always that disturbing incident of the night of July 4th. Suppose the attempt should be repeated and she weren't there to protect him?

So the weeks passed, and July drew to a close, and nothing happened. On the 31st, almost four weeks to the day from the date of the nursery incident, Alton Humffrey dismissed the three private detectives.

The following Thursday morning Jessie bathed and dressed the baby, fed him his gruel and bottle, and turned him over to Sarah Humffrey.

"You're sure you're up to it?" Jessie asked her anxiously. Mrs. Humffrey was sniffling with a slight summer cold. "I'll gladly forgo my day off. I can make it up some other time."

"Oh, no." Mrs. Humffrey peered at Michael through her white mask. Jessie privately wished she wouldn't insist on wearing a mask at the least provocation; the baby didn't like it. Besides, Jessie held the unprofessional view that the more an infant was shielded from common germ and virus infections in his early months, when he still had certain immunities, the more susceptible he became later. But Mrs. Humffrey went by the book, or rather by the books; she had a shelf full of them over her bed. "It's not the least bit necessary, Miss Sherwood. It's just a little head cold. We'll be fine without Nursie, love, won't we?"

"Maybe I'd better plan on coming back tonight, though," Jessie said, setting herself for squalls. Michael was staring up at the white mask with apprehension, and his little mouth was beginning to droop at the corners.

"I won't hear of it." Mrs. Humffrey took this moment to tickle his abdomen. "Kitchy-kitchy! Come on, darling, *laugh.*"

"I really wouldn't mind," Jessie said, choking back a sharp command to stop. Michael solved the problem by throwing up and howling. Mrs. Humffrey guiltily backed off. "It's nothing," Jessie said, taking him. "It's just not a very good idea to tickle an infant, especially on a full stomach." She burped him, cleaned him up, and handed him back.

"Oh, dear," Sarah Humffrey said "There's so much I have to learn."

"Not so much," Jessie couldn't help saying. "It's really only a matter of common sense, Mrs. Humffrey. I do think I'll come back tonight."

"I absolutely forbid you. I know how you've looked forward to a night in town . . ."

In the end Jessie was persuaded. Driving her sturdy little 1949 Dodge coupé, she told herself all the way to the railroad station that she really must stop being so possessive. It would do Mrs. Humffrey good to have to care for her baby around the clock. Women had no business turning their children over to someone else. But if they were that kind—and it seemed to Jessie that she rarely encountered any other kind—the more responsibility that was forced on them the better off they and the children were.

Still, Jessie was uneasy all day. It rather spoiled the good time she had planned. She met an old friend, Belle Berman, a supervisor of nurses at a New York hospital; and although they shopped at Saks's, had luuch in a winy-smelling restaurant on 45th Street with French travel posters on the walls, and took in a matinée, Jessie found her thoughts going back to Nair Island and the unhappy little face on the bathinette.

They had dinner in Belle Berman's apartment on West 11th Street. All during the meal Jessie kept glancing at her watch.

"What *is* the matter with you?" her friend demanded as she began to collect the dishes. "Anyone would think you'd left a dying patient."

"I'm sorry, Belle, but I'm worried about the baby. Mrs. Humffrey does have a cold, and if she starts moaning and pampering herself . . . Besides, she's so helpless about the simplest things."

"Heavens, Jessie," Belle Berman exclaimed. "Is there anything more indestructible than an infant? Anyway, it will do the woman good. These rich mothers! Now you stop this foolishness—no, *I'll* wash the dishes, and you're going to sit on your fanny and talk to me. By the way, how do you keep your figure? You eat like a horse!"

Belle Berman had a few friends in after dinner, and Jessie tried hard to catch up on hospital gossip and join in the good-natured character assassination of certain doctors and nurses they all knew. But as the evening wore on she grew more and more restless. Finally, she jumped up.

"Belle, I know you're going to think I'm menopausal or something, but would you mind very much if I change our plans and I don't stay overnight after all?"

"Jessie Sherwood."

"Well, I can't bear the thought of my precious lamb being mishandled by that woman," Jessie said fiercely. "Or suppose she got really sick today? Those maids don't know one end of a baby from the other. If I leave now and take a cab, I can catch the 11:05 . . ."

She just made the train. The trip was stifling and miserable. Jessie lolled all the way in a sickish stupor, dozing.

It was a few minutes past midnight when she got off at the Taugus station and unlocked her car. Even here the night was a humid swelter, and the inside of the Dodge was like an oven. She rolled down the windows, but she did not wait for the car to cool off. She drove off at once, head throbbing.

She thought Charlie Peterson would never come out of the gatehouse. He finally appeared, yawning.

"What a night," he said, slapping at the mosquitoes.

"Yes."

"Hot in town, too, Miss Sherwood?"

"Beastly."

"At least you could go to an air-cooled movie. What makes this job so tough is having to look at this damn water while you're boiling to death—"

"I have such a headache," Jessie murmured. "Would you please let me through, Mr. Peterson?"

"Sorry!" He raised the barrier, offended.

Jessie drove up the Nair Island road, sighing. Now that she was here, it all seemed rather silly. The Humffrey house up ahead was dark. If the baby were sick or wakeful the house would be blazing with lights. Mrs. Humffrey took it for granted that her employees were delighted to share her troubles and got them all out of bed the moment anything went wrong. Well, this was one night when none of them was going to be disturbed. She'd leave the car just inside the grounds and let herself in the front door quietly and tiptoe upstairs and go to bed. The sound of the car going around the driveway to the garage might wake someone up.

Jessie turned off her ignition, locked the car, and groped toward the front of the house. She located the key in her bag by touch, let herself in, shut the door carefully, felt around until she found the newel post, and climbed the stairs, grateful for the heavy carpeting.

Then, at the door of her room, after all her caution, she dropped her purse. In the silence of the dark house it sounded like a bomb going off.

Jessie was feeling around on all fours, trying to locate the purse and keep her head from falling, too, when a whiplash voice a few feet away said, "Don't move."

"Oh, dear," Jessie said with an exasperated laugh. "It's only me, Mr. Humffrey. I'm sorry."

A light flashed on her.

"Miss Sherwood." As her eyes accommodated to the glare she saw his robed figure utterly still, a flashlight in one hand and a gun in the other. "I thought you were spending the night in New York."

Jessie plucked her purse from the floor, feeling like a fool. "I changed my mind, Mr. Humffrey. I developed a headache, and the city was so hot . . ."

Why did he keep the gun pointing at her that way?

"Alton! What is it?"

"Oh, dear," Jessie said again. She wished he would lower the gun.

Light flooded the master bedroom doorway. Mrs. Humffrey peered out, clutching one of her exquisite negligees at the bosom. Her face looked pinched and old with fear.

"It's Miss Sherwood, Sarah." Only then did Alton Humffrey drop the gun into the pocket of his robe. "That was foolish of you, Miss Sherwood, stealing in this way, without warning. You might have been shot. Why didn't you phone?"

"I didn't have time. I made my mind up at the last minute." Jessie began to feel angry. Questioning her as if she were a criminal! "I'm terribly sorry my clumsiness woke you up. Is the baby all right, Mrs. Humffrey?"

"He was the last time I looked in." Sarah Humffrey came out into the hall and switched on the lights. Her husband went back to their room without another word. "Have you been in to Michael yet?"

"No. How is your cold?"

"Oh, it's all right. Baby was cross all day, I can't imagine why. I didn't leave him for a moment. And I've been in to him twice since I put him beddy-bye. Do you suppose he could have caught my cold?"

"I'll have a look," Jessie said wearily. "But I'm sure he's all right, Mrs. Humffrey, or this noise would have made him restless. Why don't you go back to bed?"

"I'll look with you."

Jessie shrugged. She opened her door, turned on her bedlamp, and tossed her hat and gloves on the bureau.

"I hope I did all the right things," Mrs. Humffrey said. "He was so fretful at 10:30 the last time I looked at him before I went to bed, that I put a big pillow between his head and the headboard. I was afraid he'd hurt himself. Their tender little skulls . . ."

Jessie wished her tender little skull would stop aching. She tried to keep the irritation out of her voice. "I've told you, Mrs. Humffrey, that's not a wise thing to do when they're so tiny. The bumpers give him all the protection necessary." She hurried toward the nursery.

"But he's such an active child." Sarah Humffrey stopped in the doorway, a handkerchief pressed hygienically over her mouth and nose.

The nursery was hot and close, although Jessie noticed in the faint glow of the nightlight that the Venetian blind on the window overlooking the driveway was drawn all the way up and the window was wide open. Also, someone had removed the window screen, and the room was full of bugs.

She could have slapped the ineffectual woman in the doorway.

She tiptoed over to the crib.

A vise closed over her heart, and squeezed. The baby had kicked his covers off. He was lying on his back, his fat little legs helter-skelter, and the pillow was over his face and torso.

It seemed to Jessie Sherwood that a million years passed between the constriction of her heart and its violent leap. In that infinite instant all she could do was stare down at the motionless little body, paralyzed.

Then she snatched the pillow away, kicked the side of the crib down, and bent over.

"Put the overhead light on," she said hoarsely.

"What? What's the matter?" quavered Mrs. Humffrey.

"Do as I say. The light!"

Mrs. Humffrey fumbled for the switch on the wall, the other hand still over her mouth and nose.

Jessie Sherwood, R.N., went through the motions as prescribed, her fingers working swiftly, by training and habit as cool as a surgeon's—as if they were, in fact, the fingers of a surgeon, or of anyone not herself. Inside a sick something was forming, a nausea of disbelief.

Two months old. Two months.

And as she worked over the cold little limbs, trying not to see him as he was but only as he had been—in her arms, in his bath, in his pram on the beach—she knew he would never be any older.

"He's dead," Jessie said without stopping, without looking up. "He's suffocated, I'm giving him artificial respiration but it's useless, he's been dead for some time, Mrs. Humffrey. Call your husband, call a doctor—not Dr. Holliday, Greenwich is too far away—call Dr. Wicks, and don't faint till you do, Mrs. Humffrey. Please don't faint till you call them."

Mrs. Humffrey screamed piercingly and fainted.

With some surprise Jessie found herself a long time later wrapping another blanket around Sarah Humffrey in the master bedroom. The spirits of ammonia were on the bed shelf near the books on infant care, with the stopper out, so she knew she had done the right things automatically, or perhaps it was at Dr. Wicks's direction— she could hear his voice from the hall. Mrs. Humffrey was lying across the bed, her head hanging over the side; she was conscious, moaning, and Jessie thought it a pity that her professional training had made her bring the woman out of the blessed land of shock. In fact, Jessie thought, Sarah Humffrey would be better off dead.

Then she remembered, and the memory brought her to her senses.

Dear God, she thought.

She hauled the moaning woman to a comfortable position on the bed and walked out on her.

Now she remembered everything. Where had she been? How long was it? It would have taken some time for Dr. Wicks to dress and drive over. How long had he been here?

The doctor was in the hall talking to Alton Humffrey. The gaunt millionaire was leaning against the wall, shading his eyes as if the light hurt them.

"It's always a question, Mr. Humffrey," Dr. Wicks was saying. "I'm afraid we don't know very much about this sort of thing. In some cases we find a widespread, diffuse infection, probably viral, that simply doesn't show up except on autopsy, and not always then. It could have been that. If you'd consent to an autopsy—''

"No," Alton Humffrey said. "No."

She remembered his running into the nursery at Sarah Humffrey's scream, the look on his face as he caught sight of the body in the crib, the terrible frozen look, like the *risus sardonicus* of tetanus. For fully a minute that look had held possession of him as he watched her trying to restore the function of the dead lungs, trying to coax the flaccid little rib cage into an elasticity it would never have again, trying to revive a tiny heart that had stopped beating long ago.

Then he said, "He's really dead."

And she had said, "Phone Dr. Wicks, *please.*"

And he had picked up his wife and carried her out, and a moment later Jessie had heard him phoning Dr. Wicks in a voice as frozen as his look had been.

After a while Jessie had stopped working the cold baby arms, covered the body, and gone to Mrs. Humffrey. Her husband was trying to revive her.

"I'll do it," Jessie had said, and he had gone out with long strides, in a release of stopped-up energy, as if his need for expending himself were overwhelming. As she worked over the unconscious woman she had heard him talking to the servants in a strangely considerate tone, and there were weepy female sounds and a sudden unbelievable shout from him—the patrician who never raised his voice!— a shout of pure rage, and immediately shocked silence. After that he had merely prowled downstairs and up, in the room and out, until Dr. Wicks arrived.

Jessie went up to them and leaned against the wall, too.

"Oh, Miss Sherwood." Dr. Wicks looked relieved. He was a fashionable little man with a sun-blotched scalp. "How is Mrs. Humffrey?"

"She's conscious, Doctor."

"I'd better have a look at her. You're going to have to handle your wife very carefully for a while, Mr. Humffrey."

"Yes," Alton Humffrey said, rousing himself. "Yes."

Dr. Wicks picked up his bag and walked quickly into the master bedroom. The gaunt man unfolded himself and followed. Jessie shuffled after, her feet dragging. A wave of weakness surged over her, and for a moment the hall rocked. But she steadied herself and went into the bedroom.

Sarah Humffrey was weeping now, her bony shoulders jerking like something at the end of a fisherman's line. Dr. Wicks was saying as if to a child, "That's all right, Mrs. Humffrey, don't mind us at all. It's nature's way of relieving tension. A good cry will make you feel better."

"My baby," she sobbed.

"It's terribly unfortunate, a great tragedy. But these things do happen. I've seen babies go like that in the best-regulated nurseries."

"The pillow," she wept. "I put the pillow there to protect him, Doctor. Oh, God, how was I to know?"

"There's no point in dwelling on it, Mrs. Humffrey, is there? What you need now is sleep."

"I shouldn't have let Miss Sherwood go off. She offered to stay. But no, I had to pretend I knew all about taking care of him . . ."

"Mrs. Humffrey, if you're going to carry on like this—"

"I loved him," the woman sobbed.

Dr. Wicks glanced at Jessie as if for professional support. But Jessie was standing there like a stone, stuck fast, wondering how to say it, wondering if it could be true, knowing it was true and loathing the knowledge.

I'm going to be sick any minute, she thought. Sick . . .

"I think," Dr. Wicks said with a show of firmness, "we'll have to give you something."

Jessie heard him with surprise. Did it show that much? But then she saw that he was still talking to Mrs. Humffrey.

"No!" the woman screamed. "No, no, *no!*"

"All right, Mrs. Humffrey," the doctor said hastily. "Just quiet down. Lie back . . ."

"Dr. Wicks," her husband said.

"Yes, Mr. Humffrey."

"I assume you're intending to report this to the County Coroner's office?" The millionaire had sheathed himself like a sword.

"Yes. A formality, of course—"

"I needn't tell you how abhorrent all this is to me. I have some influence in Hartford, Doctor. If you'll be good enough to cooperate—"

"Well, now, I don't know, Mr. Humffrey," Dr. Wicks said cautiously. "I have a sworn duty, you know."

"I understand." Jessie and the feeling that he was holding himself in the scabbard by sheer will. "Still, there are sometimes considerations above a sworn duty, Dr. Wicks. In exceptional cases, let us say. Haven't you found it so in your practice?"

"I can't say I have," the physician replied in a stiffening tone. "Whatever it is you have in mind, Mr. Humffrey, I'm afraid the answer must be no."

The millionaire's mouth tightened. "All I'm asking is that Mrs. Humffrey and I be spared the ordeal of a coroner's inquiry. It will mean newspaper reporters, an inquest, public testimony. It's intolerable to have to face that, Doctor. Certainly my wife can't in her condition. As her physician, surely you know that."

"I'm as unhappy about this misfortune as you are, Mr. Humffrey. But what can I do?"

"It was an accident! Are people to be crucified in public because of an accident?"

Jessie Sherwood thought if they did not stop she would scream.

"I know it was an accident, Mr. Humffrey. But you're placing me—"

She heard herself saying in a very loud voice, "No, it wasn't."

Dr. Wicks turned sharply. "What did you say, Nurse?"

Mrs. Humffrey's body swiveled on the bed as she tried to focus her swollen eyes on Jessie.

"I said, Dr. Wicks, it was not an accident."

For a faraway moment Jessie thought Alton Humffrey was going to spring at her throat. But he merely said, "What do you mean, Miss Sherwood?"

"I mean that somebody else entered the nursery after Mrs. Humffrey went to bed."

The tall man looked at her with burning eyes.

Jessie steeled herself and returned his look.

"That baby was murdered, Mr. Humffrey, and if you don't call the police—this minute—I'm going to."

2 · Creeping like Snail

Faces kept floating about the steamy room. All the weight had bobbed out of Jessie's head. It felt taut and airy, like a balloon. In the nightmare she knew with curious certainty that her alarm would go off any minute. She would wake up in a solid world, jump out of bed, listen for the baby's gurgling, shuffle into the nursery with a bright good morning . . .

"Sit down, Jessie."

"What?"

It was miraculously Richard Queen. He was urging her back into the rocker, putting a glass to her dehydrated lips. He had called her Jessie, so it was still the nightmare. Or perhaps the nightmare was turning into a harmless dream.

"Drink it."

The flow of cold water down her throat awakened her. She saw the room now as it was. The nursery was full of men peering, measuring, talking, weighing, as impersonal as salesmen—state troopers and Taugus policemen and an unshaven man without a tie whom she distantly recalled as having arrived carrying a briefcase.

"Are you feeling better now, Miss Sherwood?" That was Chief Pearl's rumble.

"It's just that I haven't had any sleep," Jessie explained. What had they been talking about when the room began to swim? She couldn't remember. All she could remember was Chief Pearl's bass voice, the enormous mass of him, his drilling eyes.

"All right. You went into the nursery with Mrs. Humffrey, you bent over the crib, you saw the pillow lying on the baby's face, you grabbed it away, you saw that he had suffocated, and you automatically began to give him first aid, artificial respiration, even though you had every reason to believe he was dead.

"Now think back, Miss Sherwood. How long would you say it took you— starting from your first sight of the pillow over the baby's face—to get past the shock and snatch that pillow off him?"

"I don't know," Jessie said. "It seemed like an eternity. But I suppose it wasn't more than a second or two."

"One or two seconds. Then you grabbed the pillow and did what with it?"

Jessie knuckled her eyes. What was the matter with him?

"I tossed it aside."

"Tossed it where?" the Taugus police chief persisted.

"Toward the foot of the crib."

The tieless, unshaven man said, "Would you remember exactly where at the foot of the crib the pillow landed, Miss Sherwood?"

They were all touched by the heat, that was it, Jessie decided. As if where it landed made any difference!

"Of course not," she said acidly. "I don't think I gave it a glance after I threw it aside. My only thought at that time was to try and revive the baby. I didn't really think back to what I'd seen on the pillow until a long time afterward. Then it came back to me with a rush, and I realized what it meant."

"Suppose you tell us once more just what you think you saw on that pillow, Miss Sherwood," the tieless man said again. Had she imagined someone's saying he was from the State's Attorney's office in Bridgeport?

"What I think I saw?" Jessie flared. "Are you doubting my word?"

She glanced at Richard Queen in her anger, to see if he was on their side after all. But he merely stood over her rubbing his gray stub of mustache.

"Answer the question, please."

"I *know* I saw a handprint on the pillow."

"An actual, recognizable human handprint?"

"Yes! Someone with a dirty hand had placed it on that pillow."

"What kind of dirt, Miss Sherwood?"

"Kind? How should I know?"

"What color was it? Black? Brown? Gray?"

"I really couldn't say. Maybe grayish. Like dust."

"Well, was it grayish, like dust, or wasn't it?"

"I think it was."

"You *think* it was?"

"I'm not sure about the color," Jessie said tiredly. "How can I be? My impression is that it looked like a dust print. I could be wrong about that, but I don't think I am. That it was dirt of some kind I'm positive."

"You say it was as if someone had placed a dirty hand on the pillow," the tieless man said. "Placed it how, Miss Sherwood? Flat? Doubled up? Partially?"

"Perfectly flat."

"Where on the pillow?"

"Just about in the middle."

"Was it a clear impression? That is, could you tell unmistakably that it was a human handprint?"

"Well, it wasn't really sharp, as I recall it. Sort of blurry—a little smudged. But it couldn't be mistaken for anything but what it was. The print of a hand." Jessie shut her eyes. She could see it with awful clarity. "The print was indented. I mean . . . there had been pressure exerted. Considerable downward pressure." She opened her eyes, and something happened to her voice. "I mean someone with a filthy hand had pressed that pillow hard over the baby's face, and kept pressing till he stopped breathing. That's why I told Mr. and Mrs. Humffrey that Michael had been murdered. At first, as I say, it didn't register. I saw it, and my brain must have tucked it away, but I wasn't conscious of it till later. Then I told them to call the police. Why are you asking me these questions? Why don't you just examine the pillow and see for yourselves?"

"Stand up, Miss Sherwood," Chief Pearl growled. "Can you stand?"

"Oh, I'm all right." Jessie got to her feet impatiently.

"Go over to the crib. Don't touch it. Just take a look at the pillow."

Jessie was convinced now that it was the treacherous kind of dream where you thought you'd waked up but even that thought was part of the dream. Look at the pillow! Couldn't they look at it themselves?

Suddenly she felt a reluctance to go to the crib. That was queer, because she had seen death regularly for many years, in a thousand forms. Jessie had feared death only three times in her life, when her parents died and when she received the telegram from the War Department about Clem. So it was love, perhaps, that made the difference . . . because it was she who had tended his unhealed navel . . . because it was on her face that he had kept his bright new eyes fixed with such absolute trust while she fed him.

Let him not be there, she prayed.

"It's all right, Jessie," Richard Queen's voice murmured close to her. "The little boy's been taken away."

He knew, God bless him.

She walked over to the crib blindly. But then she shook her head clear and looked.

The expensive pillow was at the foot of the crib, one corner doubled over where it lay against the footboard.

The lace-edged pillowcase was spotless.

Jessie frowned. "It must have flipped over when I tossed it aside."

"Borcher, turn it over for Miss Sherwood," Chief Pearl said.

The Taugus detective took the lace between thumb and forefinger at one corner and turned the pillow carefully over.

The other side was spotless, too.

"But I don't understand," Jessie said. "I saw it with my own eyes. I couldn't possibly have been mistaken."

"Miss Sherwood." The voice of the man from the State's Attorney's office was unpleasantly polite. "You would have us believe that you had your attention fixed on this pillow for no more than a second or two, in a room illuminated only by a dim baseboard nightlight, and not only saw a handprint on the pillow, but saw it clearly enough to be able to say that it seemed made by a human hand filthy with dust?"

"I can't help what you believe," Jessie said. "That's what I saw."

"It would be a feat of observation even if we found the handprint to back it up," the tieless man said. "But as you see, Miss Sherwood, there's not a mark on either side of the pillow. Isn't it possible, in your shock and excitement—and the feeble light in the room—that it was an optical illusion? Something you imagined you saw that never was there?"

"I've never had an optical illusion in my life. I saw it just as I've described it."

"You stick to that? You don't want to reconsider your recollection?"

"I most certainly do not."

The tieless man seemed displeased. He and Chief Pearl conferred. The old man caught Jessie's eye and smiled.

Then they went to the window overlooking the driveway, where a man was doing something with some bottles and a brush, and the tieless man looked out and down whlle the chief said something about an aluminum extension ladder.

"Ladder?" Jessie blinked over at Richard Queen.

He came quickly to her. "Just like that night last month, Jessie. The same ladder, in fact. Didn't you notice it standing against the wall when you drove into the driveway?"

"I didn't drive into the driveway. I left my car on the road."

"Oh, that was your car." His face said nothing at all.

"Then that's how that—that monster's hand got all dirty! The dust on the ladder while he was climbing up." Jessie was staring at the pillow. "Why didn't I notice that before?"

"Notice what, Jessie?" He was instantly alert.

"This isn't the same pillow slip!"

"Isn't the same as what?"

"As the one I saw that had the handprint on it. *Inspector Queen, this is a different slip.*"

The old man looked at her. Then he called his friend and the State's Attorney's man over.

"Miss Sherwood says she now notices that this isn't the same pillowcase that had the handprint on it."

"It isn't?" Chief Pearl glanced at the tieless man. "That's an interesting addition to the story, Merrick."

The tieless man said to Jessie, "How can you tell?"

"The edging—Mr. Merrick, is it? The other slip was edged with a different kind of lace. Both slipcases are made of very fine batiste, but the edging of the other one was Honiton lace, while this, I think, is an Irish crochet. Anyway, it's not the same."

"You're sure of this, Miss Sherwood?" Merrick demanded.

"Positive."

"Changed," Richard Queen remarked. "If you accept Miss Sherwood's story, somebody removed the soiled case from the pillow afterward and substituted this clean one. It's a break, Abe."

The big policeman grunted, looking around the nursery. He pointed to what looked like a drawer in the wall near the door. "Is that a laundry chute, Miss Sherwood?"

"Yes."

He went over to the wall and opened the chute door, trying to peer down. "Where does this lead to?"

"To the laundry in the basement."

"Who does the laundry here?"

"Mrs. Smith, Mrs. Sadie Smith."

"Sadie Smith." Abe Pearl's heavy brows bunched. "Who's she? There's nobody of that name in the house."

"She's an outside laundress from Norwalk. She comes in twice a week to do the hand laundry and ironing for the better things. The . . . baby's diapers I've been doing myself." Jessie closed her eyes. Friday was one of Mrs. Smith's days. Tomorrow—today—she would show up, and she would wash and iron those exquisite little garments of Michael's . . .

"Tinny, Borcher." Chief Pearl's two detectives came over. "Take a couple of men and split up. Look for a pillowcase with a lace edging, a case with a dirty handprint on it. Cover the laundry basement, hampers, linen closets, fireplaces, garbage—the likely ones first. If you don't find it, tear the place apart."

People with watery outlines and sounds that mixed and jangled endlessly kept floating in and out of Jessie's awareness. She knew she had to sit there and hold on to herself in this strange world outside time, or horrible things would happen. Through it all she strained to hear little Michael's voice, more than ever convinced by the unsubstantial quality of things that it had all happened in a dream, or a film. Sooner or later there would be a snap, the film would break, and the world would be restored to sanity and rightness.

Occasionally she felt Richard Queen's touch on her shoulder. Once he put his palm to her forehead. His hand felt dry and cool, and Jessie looked up at him. "Please keep it there. It feels good." But he took it away after a moment, embarrassed.

One of the fragments involved Sarah Humffrey and their attempts to question her. Jessie heard the commotion going on in the master bedroom without much interest. The frantic woman kept screaming that it was all her fault, that she had killed her baby, her blessed baby, she deserved to die, she was a monster, a criminal, let her die, oh her poor innocent baby. The men's voices came up and through and around her self-accusing aria in discordant counterpoint, her husband's by turns soothing, mortified, pleading, like a violin twanging the gamut; Dr. Wicks's snappish and brittle—he's the oboe, Jessie thought, pleased with her fancy; the insinuating trombone of Merrick, the Bridgeport man, sliding in and out of the conversation; Chief Pearl's bass horn underscoring the whole crazy fugue. Finally the men came out, the chief and the State's Attorney's man bleak with anger at Dr. Wicks, Alton Humffrey almost female in his distress and irritation.

"She's not a well woman," the millionaire kept exclaiming in a high excited voice, oddly unlike the voice Jessie knew. "You've got to understand that, gentlemen . . . my wife has never been strong emotionally . . . hypersensitive . . . this shocking experience . . ."

Dr. Wicks snapped, "Mrs. Humffrey is in a dangerous state of emotional agitation. As a matter of fact, her distress is so severe that I doubt whether her judgment can be relied on. I'm speaking as her physician, gentlemen. If you insist on keeping this up, you'll have to assume the responsibility."

"I can't allow it, Mr. Pearl," Alton Humffrey said, waving his long arms. "I can't and I won't, do you hear?"

Abe Pearl glanced at Merrick, and Merrick shrugged.

"I know when I'm licked, I guess," the chief growled. "All right, Doctor, put her under"; and Dr. Wicks disappeared.

Jessie heard his voice going in the other room, on and on like a go-to-sleep record for insomnia, and the clash of bedsprings as Sarah Humffrey threw herself about. Finally the sobs and shrieks stopped.

Later Jessie became aware of a shift in focus. They were back at her again. The house had been ransacked from basement to attic, it seemed, and the searchers had failed to turn up a pillowslip such as she had described, a lace-edged case with a dirty handprint on it.

Yes, the nightlight in the nursery had been quite dim. But no, she had not been mistaken. There was enough light to see the handprint by.

No, she didn't wear glasses. Yes, she had 20/20 vision.

No, it couldn't have been a trick of lighting, a conformation of shadows that just looked like a handprint. It *was* a handprint. Of a right hand.

"How do you know it was a *right* hand?"

"Because the thumb part of the print was on the left side."

Someone laughed, a masculine sound halfway between a chuckle and a snort. Jessie found herself not caring at all.

"Either she was seeing things, or it's been burned or cut to pieces and flushed down a toilet."

"What do they have on the Island, septic tanks?"

"No, regular city sewage installations. Emptying into the Sound, like in Taugus."

"Then we'll never know."

"Looks like it."

They were just voices. But the next one had that precious quality of nearness. Strange how every time he made a sound, even an ordinary sound, she felt safer.

"It's the big point, Abe," Richard Queen was saying mildly. "If you don't mind my horning in—"

"Don't be a jackass, Dick."

"It's the difference between murder and accident. I wouldn't give up on that pillowcase if I were you."

"We aren't even sure it exists!"

"Miss Sherwood is."

"Hell, Dick, she could be—"

"I don't think so, Abe."

The voices drifted off and became a mumble. Jessie was tickled. He's defending me, she thought gleefully. How kind of him. No one's ever done that before. Or not for a long, long time. Then she thought: How silly can you get. He knows I'm telling the truth and he's merely sticking to his point.

The joy went out of Jessie's thoughts and she sat blankly, dozing.

The voices swept up suddenly, startling her. Chief Pearl sounded harassed.

"Well, what about the ladder, Dick!"

"It confirms the murder theory."

"It does not. Mr. Humffrey put it there himself. Mr. Humffrey, would you mind telling Inspector Queen how the ladder came to be there?"

The millionaire's exhausted voice said, "I heard a banging sound from the nursery about ten o'clock. A wind had come up from sea and pulled one of the shutters loose outside the driveway window. I was afraid the noise would wake the baby. I removed the screen, tried to secure the shutter from the nursery, and found I couldn't reach it. Stallings and Cullum were out—they have Thursday evenings off—so I had no choice but to get the ladder out of the shed, climb up, and fix it myself. Then the baby did wake up, my wife became very nervous, and by the time we got him back to sleep I'd completely forgotten about the ladder. I can't see that any of this has any relevance."

"Mr. Humffrey's right, Dick. The ladder doesn't mean a thing."

"It certainly doesn't disprove murder, Abe. If this was murder, the killer simply came along and used the ladder he found standing here. And Miss Sherwood is so positive about that pillowslip—"

"Dick, for God's sake, what do you want me to do?"

"Keep looking for the slip till you find it."

"Mr. Humffrey, did you see a pillowslip with a handprint on it?"

"No."

"Did you, Dr. Wicks?"

The doctor's voice said shortly, "I'd have reported it if I had."

"And about the only thing Mrs. Humffrey said that made sense was that she didn't see it, either. And she was in the same room, Dick."

"She was in the doorway," the familiar voice said. "The footboard of the crib might have limited her range of vision. How about the servants, Abe?"

The big man made a disgusted sound. "The gardener and the chauffeur didn't pull in till almost 1 A.M. The women know from nothing."

"Jessie Sherwood against everybody."

And that was her own voice. What a funny thing to have said. Jessie heard herself laugh, a shrill hoppy sort of laugh that wasn't like her laugh at all.

Immediately the noises swooped away, leaving silence.

The next thing she knew was she was lying on something softly embracing, and Dr. Wicks was forcing her to swallow the bitter contents of a spoon.

After that everything stopped.

Inspector Queen was wandering along the water's edge when Chief Pearl came tramping down to the Humffrey beach. The sky over the sea was all pearl shell and salmon belly as the dawn turned to day.

"I've looked all over for you," the Taugus policeman bellowed. "What the hell are you doing?"

The old man looked up. "Nothing much, Abe. Just checking to see if a boat mightn't have beached here last night."

Abe Pearl stared. "Why a boat?"

"Because he'd have been a fool to try his luck twice at getting past that gatehouse in a car."

"You mean Frost?" the chief said in an odd tone.

"Who else? But there's nothing. Tide's almost all the way in. I should have thought of it when we got here." He glanced at his friend. "All through at the house?"

"Yeah."

They went up through the belt of trees side by side in silence, the big man and the small one, an invisible something between them. As they crossed the perfect lawns Chief Pearl spoke to several of his men, who were still searching the grounds.

"Keep looking till I call you off," he ordered. "Tell the boys in the house ditto."

They got into the black-and white police car, and the big man turned on his ignition.

"Talk to that gatemen, Peterson?" the old man asked.

"The state troopers talked to him. He didn't see anything." Abe Pearl grunted. "Dumb as they come, sure. But on the other hand, Dick, a man can't see what isn't there."

The old man did not reply.

At the gatehouse Chief Pearl crooked his finger at Peterson. Inspector Queen listened quietly.

"All right, Peterson, let's have it all over again," Abe Pearl said.

The guard pushed his fleshy lips forward. "I'll give it to you just once, Chief, then I'm getting the hell off this Island and so help me I'll never come back! The last car that went through this gate last night before the Humffrey kid was found dead, like I told the troopers, was that Dodge coop belongs to the nurse up there, that Miss Sherwood, who came in around 12:30 A.M. Before Miss Sherwood, there was an incoming car about an hour earlier, some of old Mrs. Dandridge's servants coming back from the Taugus movies. Before that, around 11 P.M., the Senator's chauffeur—"

"Did a car drive through at any time since you came on duty, going in or out," the chief interrupted, "that you didn't recognize? Had to check?"

"No."

Richard Queen's voice startled Peterson. "Did anyone walk through?"

"Huh?"

"Somebody on foot? Going either way?"

"Nope."

"But somebody could have come through on foot without your seeing him. Isn't that so?"

"Listen, friend," Peterson snarled, "this gatehouse is a joke. I got to sit down sometimes. I got to step into the bushes once in a whlle. I got to feed my face. There's a hundred ways a guy can get onto this Island without being seen. Go look for your patsy some place else. I'm taking no fall but for nobody."

"You know, Abe, Peterson's right," the old man murmured as they crossed the causeway. "Nair Island is accessible to anyone who wants to go to a little trouble. A rowboat to one of the private beaches at night . . . a sneak past the gate . . . a young fellow like Ron Frost could even have swum over from one of the Taugus beaches and got back the same way."

His friend glanced at him. "You're dead set that this is murder, Dick, aren't you? And that the Frost kid pulled it?"

"I'm not dead set on anything. It's just that I believe Jessie Sherwood saw something on that pillowslip. *If* it was a handprint she saw, murder is indicated. And *if* it was murder, young Frost is your hottest suspect."

"Not any more he isn't. The report came in while you were nosing around the beach for rowboat tracks. Frost can't possibly have been on Nair Island last night."

"Why not?"

"The baby died on the Island between 10:30 P.M. and around half-past midnight. In that two-hour period Ronald Frost was in Stamford, unconscious."

"Unconscious?"

"He was rushed to Stamford Hospital in an ambulance from a friend's house on Long Ridge Road about 9 P.M. He was operated on for an emergency appendectomy at 10:07 P.M., and he didn't come out of the anesthetic till three o'clock this morning." Abe Pearl grinned as he swung his car into the street of little beach houses. "What do you think of your Nurse Sherwood's pillowslip yarn now?"

Richard Queen blinked.

His friend pulled up, turned off the motor, and clapped him on the back. "Cheer up, Dick! Do you have to see a murder to make time with the Sherwood number? Take her out like a man!" He sniffed mightily. "I can smell Becky's bacon from here. Come on, Dick—hot breakfast—few hours' shuteye—"

"I'm not hungry, Abe," the old man said. "You go on in. I'll sit here for a while."

He sat there for a long time.

Jessie Sherwood braked up to the barrier and honked impatiently for Monty Burns, the day guard, to come out of the gatehouse and pass her through. It was a week after the tragedy, seven days that had dragged like years. The weekend had brought with it the first hurricane of the season; some Nair Island cellars were flooded, and fifteen-foot breakers had weakened the causeway—it was still under repair.

But it would have taken more than a hurricane to keep Nurse Sherwood on the Island that Thursday. The week had been hellish. A dozen times she had regretted giving in to Alton Humffrey's stiffish request that she stay on to nurse his wife. The big house was too full of the dead baby, and Sarah Humffrey's antics had Jessie's nerves at the shrieking point. But what else could I have done? she thought. That Mrs. Humffrey was on the verge of a nervous breakdown Jessie's professional eye told her quite without the necessity of Dr. Wicks's warnings. *Mea culpa* . . .

ELLERY QUEEN

The inquest and funeral by themselves would have unnerved a healthy woman, let
alone a guilt-ridden hysteric.

Her chief recollection of the inquest was of sweaty bodies, goggling eyes, and
her own humiliation and anger. They had treated her as if she were some malicious
trouble-maker, or a psychopath. By contrast Sarah Humffrey had got off lightly.
Alton Humffrey, Jessie thought grimly, had seen to that.

The verdict had been death by inadvertence, an accident. Accident!

And the funeral . . .

The coffin had been white and woefully tiny. They had tried to keep the time
and place secret, but of course there had been a leak, and the pushing, craning
crowds . . . the shouting reporters . . . that hideous scene in the Taugus cemetery
when Sarah Humffrey screamed like an animal and tried to jump into the grave
after the little flower-covered coffin . . .

Jessie shuddered and leaned on the horn. Monty Burns came out of the gatehouse,
hastily buttoning his tunic.

She got over the workman-cluttered causeway at last, and she was about to kick
the gas pedal when a familiar gray-mustached figure stepped out from under a
maple tree into the road, holding up his hand and smiling.

"Morning!"

"What are you doing here?" Jessie asked confusedly.

"Remembered it was your day off, and decided to walk off Beck Pearl's breakfast
in your direction. I've been waiting for you. Going anywhere in particular?"

"No."

"How about going there together?"

"I'd love it."

He's got something on his mind, Jessie thought as he got in. She drove slowly
north, conscious of the intentness under his smile.

Signs of hurricane damage were everywhere. Between Norwalk and Westport
the shore road was still under water in places. Jessie had to detour.

"A sailboat would have been more practical!" Jessie said. "What have you been
doing with yourself, Inspector Queen?"

"This and that. You know," he said suddenly, "when you let your face relax,
Jessie, you get pretty as a picture."

"Do I, now," Jessie laughed. She was laughing! She scaled her black straw
behind her and threw her head back. "Isn't this breeze scrumptious?"

"Lovely," he agreed, looking at her.

"It's making a mess of my hair, but I don't care."

"You have beautiful hair, Jessie. I'm glad you keep it long."

"You like it that way?" Jessie said, pleased.

"My mother's hair reached to her knees. Of course, in those days no women
bobbed their hair but suffragettes and prostitutes. I guess I'm old-fashioned. I still
prefer long hair in a woman."

"I'm glad," Jessie murmured. She was beginning to feel glad about everything
today.

"How about lunch? I'm getting hungry."

"So am I!" Jessie cried. "Where shall we go?"

They found an artfully bleached seafood place overlooking an inlet of the Sound.
They sat behind glass and watched the spray from the still-agitated water trying to
get up at them, hurtling from the pilings and dashing against the big storm window

almost in their faces. They dipped steamed clams into hot butter, mounds of them, and did noble archeological work on broiled lobster, and Jessie was happy.

But with the mugs of black coffee he said abruptly, "You know, Jessie, I spent a whole day this week in Stamford. Part of it at the Stamford Hospital."

"Oh," Jessie sighed. "You saw Ronald Frost?"

"Also his hospital admission card, and the doctor who operated on him. Even talked to the people he was visiting when he got the appendix attack. I wanted to check Frost's alibi for myself."

"It stands up, of course."

"Yes. It was a legitimate emergency appendectomy, and from the times involved, Frost couldn't physically have been on Nair Island when the baby died."

"Lucky emergency." Jessie frowned out the window. "For him, I mean."

"Very," Richard Queen said dryly. "Because he *was* the one who made that first attempt on the night of July 4th."

"He admitted it?" Jessie cried.

"Not in so many words—why should he?—but I'm convinced from what he said and how he said it that he was the man that night, all right. God knows what he thought he was trying to do—I don't think he knew, or knows, himself. He was drunk as a lord. Anyway, Jessie, that's that. As far as the murder is concerned, Frost is out."

Jessie picked up her coffee mug, set it down again. "Are you trying to tell me you don't think it was murder after all, Inspector Queen?"

He stirred his coffee carefully. "How about dropping the Inspector Queen stuff, Jessie? If you and I are going to see a lot of each other—"

"I didn't know we were," Jessie murmured. I'll really have to go into the ladies' room and fix my hair, she thought. I must look like the Wild Woman of Borneo. "But of course, if you'd like . . . Richard . . ."

"Make it Dick." He beamed. "That's what my friends call me."

"Oh, but I like Richard ever so much better."

His beam died. "I guess Dick sounds pretty young at that."

"I didn't mean *that*. It has nothing to do with age. Goodness!" Jessie prodded her hair. "And don't change the subject. Was it or wasn't it murder? And don't tell me the coroner's jury called it an accident!"

"Well, look at it from their viewpoint," he said mildly. "Your testimony about that dim nightlight, for instance. Those couple of seconds you'd mentioned as being the maximum period you had the handprint in view, for another. And on top of that, Jessie, your detailed description of the print. You'll have to admit, with the pillowslip not produced, it takes a bit of believing."

Jessie felt tired suddenly.

"I could only testify to what I saw. What *happened* to that pillowslip?"

"Probably destroyed. Or disposed of in some way."

"But by whom?"

"By somebody in the house."

"But that's ridiculous!" Jessie was appalled.

"If you start from the existence of the handprint, it's the logical conclusion."

"But who in the Humffrey house would do a thing like that, Richard?"

He shrugged. "Your guess is as good as mine."

Jessie said, "You do believe me, don't you? Somebody has to . . ."

"Of course I believe you, Jessie," he said gently. "And that's where I'm jumping off from."

"What do you mean?"

"I had a talk with Abe Pearl last night. Abe's the salt of the earth, and he was a good big-city cop, but maybe he isn't as good a judge of character as I am." He grinned. "Your character, anyway."

But Jessie did not smile back. "In other words, Chief Pearl has made up his mind not to believe my story, either."

"Abe's not prepared to kick up a fuss about a murder when there's nothing concrete to back it up. And then, of course, the inquest jury did bring in a verdict of accidental death. Put that together with Frost's alibi for last Thursday night, and you see the spot Abe's in."

"What you're trying to tell me," Jessie said bitterly, "is that he's dropping the case."

"Yes." Richard Queen rubbed his jaw. "That's why I informed the Pearls last night that they'd soon be losing their star boarder."

"You're going to leave?" And suddenly the spray on the window made an empty sound, and the lobster began to weigh heavily. "Where are you going?"

"Back to New York."

"Oh." Jessie was silent. "But I thought you said—"

He nodded wryly. "I've been doing a lot of thinking about the case and I've decided New York is the place to start an investigation. Abe can't, the Humffreys won't—who else is there but me? I have nothing to do with myself, anyway."

Tears sprang into Jessie's eyes. "I'm so glad. So glad, Richard."

"In fact . . ." He was looking at her across the table with the oddest expression. "I was hoping you'd go with me."

"*Me?*"

"You could help in lots of ways," he said awkwardly. He fumbled with his cup.

Jessie's heart beat faster. Now don't be foolish, she kept saying to herself. He's just being kind. Or . . . after all, what do I really know about him? Maybe . . .

"I think I'd have to know in what ways, Richard," she said slowly. "For one thing, I've promised to stay on at Nair Island for a while to keep an eye on Mrs. Humffrey—"

"Let Humffrey get another nurse."

"No, I gave my word."

"But how long—?"

"Let's talk about it in the car," Jessie said abruptly. "If I'm getting into something, I want to know just what it is. Do you mind?"

He leaned forward suddenly and took her hand. "You're quite a woman, Jessie. Did anyone ever tell you that?"

"And none of your blarney!" Jessie laughed as she withdrew her hand and rose. "I'll meet you in the car."

Richard Queen watched her make her way among the empty tables toward the rest rooms. She walks like a young girl, he thought. A young girl . . .

He signaled the waitress and caught himself staring at his hand.

He pulled it quickly down and out of sight.

In the end, it was Alton Humffrey's wife who made up Jessie's mind. The following Tuesday—it was the 16th of August—Sarah Humffrey slipped out of her bedroom while Jessie was in the kitchen fixing a tray, ran down to the Humffrey beach in her nightgown, waded out into the Sound, and tried to drown herself. She might have succeeded if Henry Cullum had not been on the dock tinkering with the engine of the Humffrey cruiser. The white-haired chauffeur jumped in and pulled the hysterical woman out. She was screaming that she wanted to die.

Dr. Wicks put her under deep sedation and spoke to her husband grimly.

"I'm afraid you're going to have to face it, Mr. Humffrey. Your wife is a damned sick woman, and I'm not the doctor for her. She needs specialized help. This obsession of hers that she killed the baby, these hysterical feelings of guilt about the pillow, now an attempt at suicide—I'm over my depth."

Alton Humffrey seemed all loosened, as if the binder that held him together was crumbling away. Jessie had never seen him so pale and depressed.

"Your wife is on the edge of a mental collapse," Dr. Wicks went on, blotting the freckles on his bald spot. "In her unstable condition, in view of what happened here, this house is the last place in the world she ought to be. If you'll take my advice—"

"What you're trying to tell me, I believe, is that I ought to put Mrs. Humffrey in a sanitarium?"

"Er, yes. I know a very good one up in Massachusetts. In Great Barrington. The psychiatrist in charge has an excellent reputation—"

"And can he keep his mouth shut?" the millionaire said. "This running down into the water business . . . if the newspapers should get wind of it—"

Dr. Wicks's lips flattened. "I wouldn't recommend him otherwise, Mr. Humffrey. I know how you feel about publicity."

"A psychiatrist, you say?"

"One of the soundest."

"I'll have to think about it." And Humffrey rose with an imperious gesture of dismissal.

The physician was red-faced when he came into the adjoining bedroom for a final look at his patient. He snapped some instructions to Jessie and left.

It was Dr. Wicks's last visit to Sarah Humffrey.

On Wednesday afternoon Jessie heard the door open and looked up from her patient's bedside to see Alton Humffrey crooking a bony forefinger at her.

"Can you leave her for a few minutes, Miss Sherwood?"

"I've just had to give her another hypo."

"Come into my study, please."

She followed him across the hall to the study. He indicated an armchair, and Jessie sat down. He went to the picture window and stood there, his back to her.

"Miss Sherwood, I'm closing this house."

"Oh?" Jessie said.

"I've been considering the move for some time. Stallings will stay on as caretaker. Henry and Mrs. Lenihan will go along with me to the New York apartment. I'm sending Mrs. Charbedeau and the maids back to the Concord house. The best part of the summer is gone, anyway."

"You're intending to spend most of your time in New York?"

"All winter, I should think."

"The change ought to be good for Mrs. Humffrey."

"Mrs. Humffrey is not coming with me." His voice was nasally casual. "I'm sending her to a sanitarium."

"I'm glad," Jessie said. "She needs sanitarium care badly. I heard Dr. Wicks telling you yesterday about a place in Great Barrington—"

"Wicks." The narrow shoulders twitched. "In matters as important as this, Miss Sherwood, one doesn't rely on the Wickses of this world. No, she's not going to Great Barrington."

It's the psychiatry that's scared you off, Jessie thought. "May I ask which sanitarium you've picked out, Mr. Humffrey?" She tried to keep her voice as casual as his.

She thought his long body gathered itself in. But then she decided she had been mistaken. When he turned he was smiling faintly.

"It's a convalescent home, really—that's all nonsense about her need for psychiatric treatment. Mrs. Humffrey is in a highly nervous state, that's all. What she requires is complete rest and privacy in secluded surroundings, and I'm told there's no better place in the East for that than the Duane Sanitarium in New Haven."

Jessie nodded. She knew several nurses who had worked there—one, Elizabeth Currie, had been on Dr. Samuel Duane's nursing staff for eight years. The sanitarium was an elaborate closet for distinguished skeletons, restricted to a rigidly classified clientele at exclusive rates. It was surrounded by a tall brick wall topped with four-foot pickets ending in lance points, and it was patrolled by a private police force.

Exactly the sort of place Alton Humffrey would choose! Jessie thought. Once Sarah Humffrey was safely inside Dr. Duane's luxurious prison, her husband could relax. Dr. Duane's guards could smell a reporter miles away.

"When is Mrs. Humffrey leaving?" Jessie asked.

"This evening. Dr. Duane is calling for her personally in a sanitarium limousine, with a nurse in attendance."

"Has Mrs. Humffrey been told?" At the millionaire's frown, Jessie added hastily, "The reason I ask, Mr. Humffrey, is that I've got to know just how to handle preparing her to go away—"

"I haven't told her, no. Dr. Duane prefers that I break the news when he's present."

"You'll be going out with her?"

"I don't know. That will depend entirely on Duane." His wedge of face lengthened. "You'll keep all this confidential, of course, Miss Sherwood."

"Of course."

He went over to his desk, sat down, and began to write a check. She watched his long white fingers at their deliberate work, the little finger curled in hiding, as secretive as the rest of him.

"I suppose this means," Jessie said, "that you want me to leave as soon as possible."

"Oh, nothing like that. You're entirely welcome to stay on for a few days. The staff isn't leaving until next week some time."

"I'm a restless sort, Mr. Humffrey. It's kind of you, but I think I'll go tomorrow morning."

"As you wish."

He blotted the check carefully and reached over to lay it on the desk near her.

"Oh, but Mr. Humffrey," Jessie protested. "This is far too much. You're paid up through last week—"

"I see no reason why you should be penalized by my sudden decision about Mrs. Humffrey," he said, smiling. "So I've paid you for a full week, and I've added a little something in appreciation of all you've done for Mrs. Humffrey and Michael."

"A little something." Jessie shook her head. The bonus was five hundred dollars. "You're awfully kind, Mr. Humffrey, but I really can't accept this."

"Heavens, Miss Sherwood. Why not?" He seemed genuinely surprised.

"Well . . ." Her hands felt clammy. But she looked straight at him. "Frankly, Mr. Humffrey, I'd rather not be under obligation to you."

"I don't understand." Now his tone was icy.

"If I felt differently about little Michael, I could take this. As it is, I'd rather not."

He made it easy for her. "You mean if you felt differently about the cause of his death?"

"Yes, Mr. Humffrey."

The four whole fingers drummed on the desk, their maimed companion curled tightly. Then he leaned back in his leather chair.

"You still don't agree it was an accident, Miss Sherwood."

"It was murder," Jessie said. "That baby was deliberately and wickedly smothered to death with the pillow in the pillowcase that's disappeared."

"But no pillowcase has disappeared."

"Oh, yes, it has. They just haven't found it."

"My dear Miss Sherwood." His tone was patient. "The coroner's jury are satisfied it was an accident. So are the police. So am I. How can you set yourself up as the sole dissenting judge?"

"I saw the pillow with the handprint, Mr. Humffrey," Jessie said quietly. "No one else did."

"Obviously you were mistaken."

"I was not mistaken."

"There's not a scintilla of evidence—I believe that's the approved phrase—to back your opinion up."

"It's not an opinion, Mr. Humffrey. It's a fact. I know what I saw."

"Show me one competent person who agrees with you—"

"Richard Queen."

Humffrey arched his sparse brows. "Who?"

"Chief Pearl's friend. He used to be an inspector in the New York police department. He believes me."

The millionaire shrugged. "These old fellows have nothing to do but poke their noses into other people's affairs. He was probably retired for senility."

"He's only sixty-three, and he's in complete possession of his faculties, I assure you!" Jessie bit her lip; Humffrey was regarding her with amusement. "Anyway, Inspector Queen agrees with me it was murder, and we're going to—"

Jessie stopped.

"Yes?" Alton Humffrey no longer looked amused. "You and this man are going to what, Miss Sherwood?"

"Nothing." Jessie jumped up nervously. "I'll have to be getting back to Mrs. Humffrey—"

"Miss Sherwood." He had his hands flat on the desk. For a moment Jessie had the queerest feeling that he was going to spring at her. She remembered having had the same feeling about him once before. "Do you suppose for an instant that if I thought the child was murdered I'd let the case drop?"

"I'm sure I can't answer that, Mr. Humffrey." She was actually backing away. When she realized it, she stopped herself. "Please, I must go to Mrs. Humffrey.

But I do wish you'd tear up this check and make out another simply for the amount you owe me.''

But his eyes kept bulging and burning. "Don't you know what that baby meant to me, Miss Sherwood?''

"I'm sure he meant everything to you," Jessie said desperately. "But . . . you force me to say this . . . now that little Michael's dead you want the whole thing buried, along with his remains. You'd rather see the case written off as an accidental death than involve your family name in a murder case. I don't understand people like you, Mr. Humffrey. There are some things in this world a lot worse than getting your name bandied about by the common people. Letting a baby killer get off scot free is one of them.''

"Are you finished?" Alton Humffrey said.

"Yes," Jessie whispered.

"No, wait, Miss Sherwood. Before you go.''

Jessie turned at the door, praying for escape.

"You know my wife's condition." The nasal tones dripped venom. "I don't know what it is you and this man Queen are up to, but if through any act of yours my wife gets worse or my name is exposed to further public humiliation, you will account to me. To *me*. Do you understand?''

"Perfectly." Jessie's throat was dry. "May I go now, Mr. Humffrey?''

"By all means.''

She fled those unwinking pop-eyes, fixed on her like something in a museum.

Ten minutes later Jessie was on the phone, crying. "Richard, please ask Mrs. Pearl if I can come over tonight. I don't care where I stay. I'll sleep in my car or bed down on the floor. Anywhere! But I won't stay in this house another night.''

Inspector Queen was waiting for her on the other side of the causeway in Beck Pearl's Plymouth. He got out, waving wildly, as Jessie pulled up.

"Jessie! You all right?''

"Oh, Richard, I'm so glad to see you.''

"But what happened?''

"Nothing, really. Mr. Humffrey's sent his wife to a sanitarium and discharged me, and I'm afraid I let on that you and I weren't going to let the case drop, and he sort of threatened me—''

"He did, did he?" the old man said grimly.

"I don't know what you're thinking of me. I've never acted this way before in my life. Mrs. Pearl must be having visions of some hysterical female throwing fits all over her rug—''

"You don't know Beck Pearl.''

"I'd go back home—I have a little house in Rowayton—but I rented it to some summer people till after Labor Day. I'm so ashamed, Richard. I'll go to a motel or some place for the night—''

"Becky says if I don't bring you right over I don't have to come back myself. You follow me, Jessie!'' . . .

In the plain sanity of the Pearls' little beach cottage Jessie felt safe for the first time in weeks. Mrs. Pearl looked into her eyes and smiled approvingly at Richard Queen, and Chief Pearl blundered about making her feel as if she were an honored guest.

"You're not really an ogre after all, Mr. Pearl," Jessie told him. "Do you know I was afraid of you?''

The big man glanced guiltily at his wife.

"Did he bully you?" Beck Pearl looked at her husband.

"I'll get your bag out of your car, Miss Sherwood." Abe Pearl went out hurriedly.

"Put it up in Richard's room, Abe!"

"Mrs. Pearl, I won't hear of it—"

"You'll have Richard's room, Abe and Richard will sleep in our room, and I'll take the daybed down here. It's the most comfortable bed in the house."

"Oh, no—"

"That's the way it's going to be," Mrs. Pearl said firmly. "Now I'm going to fix you and Richard some supper. Then Abe and I are going to the movies . . ."

When the Pearls were gone, Jessie said softly, "You're lucky to have such friends, Richard."

"You like them."

"They're absolute darlings."

"I'm glad," he said simply. "Now you tackle this casserole, or Becky will feel terrible. Abe says she can do more things with clams than a Siwash Indian."

Afterward, Jessie washed the dishes in Beck Pearl's tiny kitchen and Richard Queen dried them and put them away, while he told her about his summer with the Pearls and never once referred to what had brought her flying to him. Jessie listened mistily. I mustn't feel so happy about this, she kept thinking. I'll just build myself up to another letdown, the way I did with Clem . . . It was hard to keep from comparing them, hard and unfair. It had been so many years ago. Clem had been so much younger—tall and self-sufficient, with quick surgeon's fingers and his eyes always tired-looking. Thinking about him even now, when he had been dead such a long time, Jessie felt her pulse quicken . . . This, this was so different. Working over a kitchen sink and drainboard side by side. She couldn't visualize herself doing that with Clem. Clem had meant excitement, a life of high spots and crises, and long stretches of loneliness. This quiet man, with his fine-boned face and gray brush of mustache, his reserve of strength and knowledge about ordinary people—it was hard to think of anything they couldn't do together, the everyday little things that made up a life. And she could be very proud of him, she knew that instinctively. Proud and complete . . . I *mustn't* let myself run on this way! Jessie thought despairingly.

"You're tired," Richard Queen said, looking at her. "I think, Jessie, I'm going to send you to bed."

"Oh, no," Jessie cried. "I'm enjoying this so much. I want to tell you everything that's happened in the past few days, Richard. Please."

"All right. But just for a few minutes. Then up you go."

He put the dish towel over the towel bar to dry, and they went into the little living room. He sat her down in the most comfortable chair, lit her cigaret for her, and listened noncommittally while she told him about Sarah Humffrey's suicide attempt and the substance of her conversation with Alton Humffrey. He made no comment beyond, "He's a queer duck, all right," and then he said, "Time's up, Miss Sherwood."

"But aren't we going to talk about your plans?"

"Not tonight."

"Then how about mine?"

He laughed. "I've made six-foot police sergeants shake in my time, but I guess I'll never learn how to handle a woman. All right, Jessie, shoot."

"I'm coming with you."

"I know that."

"You don't!" Jessie said, piqued.

"I'm not flattered," he said dryly. "I didn't do it. It's Alton Humffrey who's made up your mind."

"Well, it's true I don't like to be threatened," Jessie said, pinching her skirt down, "but that's not the only reason."

"The baby."

"*And* other reasons."

The old man looked at her searchingly. "It might not be a picnic, Jessie." He got up suddenly and began to walk about. "In fact, I'm wondering if I haven't let you in for something risky out of plain selfishness. This is a very peculiar case. *Why* was the baby murdered? While Frost was a suspect, with his inheritance motive, it made some sort of crazy sense. With Frost eliminated, the Humffrey fortune doesn't seem to be involved. So the motive must lie in a different direction. Do you see a lead, Jessie?"

"I've thought about it, too," Jessie said quietly. "The only thing I can think of is that it must be connected with Michael's adoption."

"Ah," the Inspector said, and he sat down again, eagerly. "You saw that. Where does it take you, Jessie?"

"It may have something to do with the real parents. You know, Richard, neither side knows who the other side is. The whole adoption was handled by a lawyer acting for *both* sides."

He nodded. "A lawyer named A. Burt Finner. That was his name, wasn't it?"

"Yes. Do you know him?"

"I know of him. He's a clever shyster who specializes in black-marketing babies for people who either can't swing a legitimate adoption or for some reason would rather handle it under the counter. If Humffrey's had dealings with him, it's probably because Finner guarantees no trouble and no publicity. The important thing, Jessie, is that Finner knows the real parentage of that baby. So that's where we start."

"With Finner?"

"With Finner."

"But if the real parents don't know who got Michael—"

"One step at a time," Richard Queen said. "We'll go into the city in the morning. Meanwhile, you're going to bed."

He got up and took her hand.

Jessie giggled. "You make me feel like a little girl. Don't I have any say about things like where I'm going to stay?"

"Not a word," he said firmly. "You're staying at my apartment in town."

"*Inspector* Queen," Jessie murmured. "I'm going to do no such thing."

Even his neck reddened. "I mean I'll go to the Y or some place. Ellery isn't due back from abroad for a long time yet—"

"Silly. I'm hardly at the age when I'm worried about my reputation." Jessie giggled again, enjoying his embarrassment. "But I wouldn't dream of putting you out of your own home."

"I'd come up every morning and have breakfast with you—"

"No, Richard," Jessie said softly. "I have loads of friends in New York, nurses who live alone in little apartments and don't particularly like it. But . . . thank you. So much."

He looked so forlorn that Jessie impulsively squeezed his hand. Then she ran upstairs.

For some reason he felt very good suddenly. He walked about the cottage with long strides, smiling at his thoughts and occasionally glancing at the ceiling, until the Pearls came home.

Jessie spent nearly an hour Thursday morning on the telephone, running up New York City toll calls.

"I'm in luck," she told Richard Queen. "Belle Berman, she's a supervisor I know, wants me to move right in with her. And Gloria Sardella, a nurse I took my training with, is leaving tomorrow on her vacation. She's going on a six-week cruise, and she's offered me her apartment."

"Where are the two places?"

"Belle's down in the Village—West 11th Street. Gloria's place is on 71st Street off Broadway, in a remodeled walkup."

"The Sardella apartment," he said promptly.

"That's my thought, because I'll get Gloria to sublet it to me for whatever her rent is, whereas Belle wouldn't hear of my sharing expenses." Jessie looked at him. "What's your reason, Richard?"

"Geography," he said sheepishly. "I'm on West 87th. We'd be less than a mile apart."

"You want to watch this man, Jessie," Beck Pearl said. "He's a regular wolf."

"Don't I know it!"

He mumbled something about having to pack, and beat a retreat.

Jessie phoned her friend again to arrange for her stay in the West 71st Street apartment, paid for the calls over Mrs. Pearl's protests, and at last they were off in Jessie's car, Beck Pearl waving from her doorway like a happy relative.

"She's such a lamb," Jessie said, turning into the Taugus road that led to the Merritt Parkway. "And so is Abe Pearl. Do you know what he said to me this morning before he left?"

"What?"

"He said you were a changed man since—well, since the Fourth of July. He seemed tickled to death, Richard. The Pearls have been very worried about you."

He seemed flustered aud pleased. "A man needs an interest in life."

"Yes. This case—"

"Who's talking about the case?"

"You know, I do believe you are a wolf!"

They chattered happily all the way into New York.

Jessie had decided to take her coupé into the city because Richard Queen had no car, and his son's car was in summer storage. "What good is an assistant without a car?" she had said. "It isn't as if you still had a police driver at your disposal, Richard. My jalopy may come in handy."

"All right, if you'll let me pay the garage bills."

"Richard Queen. Nobody pays my bills but me!"

They stopped at the old brownstone on West 87th Street to drop his bags. Jessie got one whiff of the Queen apartment aud threw the windows wide. She aired the beds, inspected the kitchen with horror, and began opening closets.

"What are you looking for?" he asked feebly.

"Fresh linen, a vacuum cleaner. You have to sleep here tonight! Who takes care of your apartment, anyway?"

"A Mrs. Fabrikant. She's supposed to have come in once a week—"

"She hasn't stuck her nose in this place for two months. You go on—make your phone calls, or whatever you have to do. I'll make your bed and straighten up a bit. First chance I get I'll do a thorough housecleaning. Imagine your son coming home to this!"

He retreated to Ellery's study with a warm feeling. He did not even think about the blank space on his bedroom wall, where his direct line to Headquarters used to be.

When he went back to the bedroom he found Jessie moaning. "It's hopeless. Take *hours* to do just this room properly."

"Why, it looks as clean as a hospital room," he exclaimed. "How'd you do it so fast?"

"Well, you'll be able to sleep here without getting cholera, but that's about all," Jessie grumbled. "Fast? A nurse does everything fast. Did you get that man Finner?"

"Finally, after about a dozen calls. He'll be in all afternoon, he said. I didn't fix a time, Jessie, because I don't know how long you'll take getting settled."

"Forget about me. I can't get into Gloria's place until 4:30 or a quarter of five, anyway. She's on an eight-to-four case."

"But she's going away tomorrow!" he said, astonished.

"Nurses don't live like people. Let me wash some of this grime off, and I'll be right with you to tackle Mr. Finner."

"You're going to tackle some lunch at the Biltmore first. *With* cocktails."

"Oh, wonderful. I'm hungry as a wolf."

"I thought I was the wolf," he said gaily.

"There are she-wolves, aren't there?"

He found himself whistling like a boy to the homey sound of splashing from the bathroom.

The building was on East 49th Street, an old-timer six stories high with a clanky self-service elevator. His name was on the directory in the narrow lobby: *Finner, A. Burt 622*.

"Jessie, let me do most of the talking."

"As if I'd know what to say!" Then Jessie thought of something. "I wonder, Richard . . ."

"What about?" he asked quickly.

"When we drove out to that rendezvous near Pelham the morning we picked up the baby, Finner drove right up behind where we were parked. I'd gone along to take charge of the baby. Finner may recognize me."

"Not likely, but I'm glad you remembered to tell me." He looked thoughtful. "All right, we'll use it just on the chance. And, Jessie."

"Yes?" Her heart was beginning to thump.

"It's going to cut some corners for us if Finner thinks I'm still with the Department. Don't act surprised if I make like a police officer."

"Yes, sir," Jessie said meekly.

Six-twenty-two was on the top floor at the other end of the corridor from the elevator. The corridor had dirty tan walls, and there was a smell of old floor polish and must.

The old man smiled at her, then suddenly opened the door.

A. Burt Finner half rose behind the desk in the small office, scowling.

"Come in, Miss Sherwood," Richard Queen snapped. "It's all right, he won't bite you. He's an old dog at this game, aren't you, Finner?"

Jessie stepped into the office gingerly. She did not have to act scared. She was.

The fat man crashed back in his swivel chair. As far as Jessie could recall, he was wearing the same wrinkled blue suit and sweaty white shirt he had driven up in that morning near Pelham. The dingy office was stale with his odor. There was nothing in the room but a burn-scarred metal desk, a sad-looking imitation leather chair, a costumer leaning to one side with a dirty felt hat hanging from it, an old four-unit filing cabinet with a lock, and the swivel chair creaking under Finner's weight. No rug, nothing on the walls but a large calendar put out by a baby foods company showing a healthy-looking infant in a diaper. The blind on the single window was limp and streaked. The walls were the same grubby tan shade as the corridor, only dirtier.

Richard Queen shut the door, took Jessie by the arm, and steered her over to the unoccupied chair.

"Have a seat, miss," he said. He looked coldly at the fat man. "Now."

"Wait a minute." A. Burt Finner's little pale-blue eyes went from Jessie to the old man and back to Jessie. He seemed puzzled. My face looks familiar to him, Jessie thought, but he can't place it. She wondered why she was so nervous. He was just a fat man, not at all dangerous-looking. Maybe it's his professional relations with women, she thought. He doesn't leer; he's seen it all. "What is this? Who are you people?"

"I phoned you two-three hours ago," the old man said. "Remember the $64,000 word I dropped, Finner?"

"What word?"

"Humffrey."

The moon face widened. "Oh, yes. And I told you I didn't know what you were talking about."

"But to drop in, anyway, you'd be here all afternoon." Richard Queen stared at him with contempt. "Well, here we are, Finner. You're up to your fat face in real jam this time, aren't you?"

"Who are you?" Finner asked slowly.

"The name is Queen." He brought out a small flat leather case and flipped it open. A gold shield glittered for a moment in the sunshine struggling through the dusty window.

Finner blinked.

The old man put the case back in his pocket.

"Inspector's shield," Finner said. "Well, well, this is a real pleasure, Inspector. And this lady is—?"

The pale eyes turned on Jessie again. Jessie tried not to fumble with her skirt.

"Don't you recognize her, Finner?"

"No." The fat man was worried. He immediately broke into a smile. "Should I, Inspector?"

"I'd say so," Inspector Queen remarked dryly, "seeing that she's the baby nurse who was in the Humffrey car that day."

"What car, what day, what baby?" Finner asked amiably. "And that about somebody named Humffrey. I don't know anybody named Humffrey."

"Counselor, you and I will get along a lot chummier if you cut out the mullarkey and start recollecting your sins. Miss Sherwood, is this the man you saw pull up behind the Humffrey limousine on a deserted back road near Pelham on Friday morning, June 3rd, behind the wheel of a Chevvy and hand over to Mr. Alton K.

Humffrey of Nair Island, Connecticut, a blue blanket wrapped around a week-old baby?''

"That's the man, Inspector Queen!" Jessie said shakily. She wondered if she ought to point at the fat lawyer, the way they did in movie courtooms, but she decided against it.

"The lady is mistaken." Finner beamed, aud cleared his throat. "She never saw me in any such place at any such time doing any such thing."

"How can you lie like that?" Jessie cried indignantly. "I saw you with my own two eyes and you're not exactly an ordinary-looking man!"

"I've built a whole career, miss," the fat man remarked, "on being just that. However, my memory could be failing. Got anything else to give it a jab, Inspector? Like, say, a corroborating witness?"

"Three, Finner," Inspector Queen said, as if he were enjoying himself. "Mr. and Mrs. Humffrey are two, and their chauffeur—white-haired party with rosy cheeks—he's the third."

"The chauffeur driving the Humffrey car that morning, you mean?" Finner said reflectively.

"That's right."

"But how do you know he'd corroborate this lady's identification, Inspector? I don't see him here."

"Well, we can soon find out. Mind if I use your phone?"

Finner said, "Skip it." He sucked his rubbery lower lip, frowning, then swiveled to clasp his hands behind his overlapping folds of neck and stare out the window. "Supposing I was weak-skulled enough to admit having been there that day," he asked the window, "then what, Inspector?"

Jessie glanced at Richard Queen. But he shook his head.

"You mean, Finner, what do I have?"

"Put it any way you want."

"Well, it's like this. You work deals with an angle. You specialize in unmarried mothers. You shop around for a buyer, you arrange for the girl to give birth in a hospital under a false name, with a phony background, you pay the girl—with the buyer's money—and you take possession of the baby when the mother is discharged from the hospital. Then you turn the baby over to your buyer, collect the balance of your fee, probably furnish a forged birth certificate, and you're ready for the next client. It's a sweet racket, Finner, and the sweetest part of it is that everybody involved has a vested interest in protecting you. You see, I've been looking you up."

"I haven't heard a thing," Finner said, still to the window, "and I'm listening with both pink ears."

"I'm not passing judgment on the dirty way you earn those fins you scatter around the night spots, Finner," Richard Queen said. "Some day the boys are going to prove it on you. But if it's the black-market baby rap you're worrying about, right now I'm not interested in you at all. I'm after other game."

"What do you mean?" Finner spun about so suddenly the spring under his chair squealed.

"You're going to tell me who the Humffrey baby's real parents are."

Finner stared at him. "Are you kidding?"

"Tell me, Finner," the old man said.

Jessie held her breath.

The fat man laughed. "Even supposing this junkie jive you been popping around the premises were the McCoy, Inspector—and I'm not admittimg a goddam thing—why should I tell? An operator in a racket like that—I'm told—works on a confidential basis. Run off at the tonsils and you're out of business. You know that."

"I know you're in this up to your top chin, Finner," Richard Queen smiled. "Of course you know the baby's dead."

"Dead, uh?" Finner squinted along the top of his desk and hunched down to blow some dust off. With fascination, Jessie watched his fat lips working. "Seem to recall reading about some baby named Humffrey up in Connecticut being found suffocated in his crib. Was that the same baby you're trying to hook me up to, Inspector?"

"That's the one."

"Tough. I got a soft spot for kids. Got three of my own. But so what? It was an accident, wasn't it?"

"It was a murder, Finner."

Finner's bulk came up like a whale surfacing. "The hell you say. I read the papers, too. Coroner's jury brought in a verdict of accidental death. The case is closed. What you trying to pull on me, Inspector?"

"It was a murder, Finner."

Finner swallowed. He picked up a steel letter-knife from his desk, made as if to clean his fingernails, put the knife down again.

"New evidence?"

Richard Queen said nothing. He merely kept looking at the fat man's fat hands. Finner's hands vanished below the level of the desk.

"Look, Inspector," he said rapidly. "You got me on something of a spot here. Without incriminating myself in any degree, you understand, maybe I can get some information for you. About the kid's real parents, I mean. One of my contacts might . . ."

"I don't care what you call yourself, Counselor. I want those names."

"Tell you what. What's today?—Thursday. Maybe I can do even better for you, Inspector. I'm not promising, see, but maybe."

"Maybe what?"

"Maybe my contact can get them right here in my office for you."

The old man's lips drew back. "That would be just dandy, Finner. When?"

"Say this Saturday. That's the 20th. Four P.M. okay with you?"

"When the building's empty, eh? Nothing like a deserted office building for a little get-together, I always say."

"With me murder is strictly sucker." Finner was breathing noisily. "If I pull this off for you, Inspector, no cross-up? I got your word?"

"No deals, Finner. But co-operation never hurt anybody." Richard Queen looked down at Jessie Sherwood. "That's it, Miss Sherwood. Thanks for the make."

"The make?" Jessie said, bewildered.

"The identification." He poked her to her feet. "You come through for me Saturday afternoon, Finner."

Finner nodded sadly.

Jessie phoned Richard Queen Friday morning from Gloria Sardella's apartment to say that she would be busy all day getting her friend off on the cruise and herself settled. When he pressed her to meet him for dinner Jessie hesitated, then asked him to phone her later in the day. He called promptly at five o'clock and she said she was so fagged she would be poor company. She was going to make a sandwich and go to bed. Did he mind very much?

"Seems to me I haven't seen you for years," he complained.

Jessie laughed uncertainly.

"It's been a long day, and it's going to be a longer evening," he said. "At least let me take you to breakfast tomorrow morning."

"Make it lunch," Jessie said, "and it's a date . . . I admit I'm a little nervous about tomorrow, Richard. Maybe having to shake the hand that pressed the pillow over Michael's little face . . ."

"Not much chance of that."

"What do you mean? Finner said—"

"I know what Finner said," he retorted. "That guff about getting them down to his office Saturday was a stall. Finner wants time to put the screws on them, see what information he can squeeze out of them."

"But if he doesn't produce them tomorrow—"

"He'll either produce them or he'll produce their names. In the end, A. Burt Finner will protect A. Burt Finner. What time tomorrow, Jessie?"

"Make it one-ish."

"That late?" He sounded dismayed.

"Why, your appointment isn't until four o'clock. How many hours do you usually take for lunch?"

He hung up, feeling deserted. He had spent most of the day down at Centre Street, wandering into the Squad Room, leafing through recent copies of *General Orders* to see who had been cited, commended, promoted—gabbing with old cronies in the Central Office bureaus and squads in the Annex at the corner of Broome Street. They had been glad to see him, but he had come away miserable. Friday was the working officer's busiest day of the week, and he had had the sickening feeling that he was in the way.

The Queen apartment was no sanctuary. It seemed to him dull and empty.

What did men on the shelf *do* with their days and nights? the old man wondered. How many newspapers could you read? How many movies could you see? How many hours could you spend on a Central Park bench watching cooing humans and pigeons? How long could you hang around men you'd worked with who were still active, before you got into their hair and they began to show it?

Richard Queen went to bed Friday night at a quarter past nine, wishing fiercely it was four o'clock Saturday afternoon.

He muttered: "Now I don't know what I'm going to run into. You remember what I told you."

"But *why* can't I go in with you, Richard?" Jessie whispered.

"We're tangling with a lot of unknowns. The chances are Finner's in there all alone, but a detective's life is full of surprises."

"I'm some assistant," she said disconsolately.

"You listen to me, Jessie. I'll go in and you'll wait here at the end of the hall. Keep the cage slide open so the elevator can't get away from you, just in case. If I think it's all right, I'll signal you from the doorway. Otherwise stay out of sight. If you hear anything that sounds like trouble, get out quick."

"You just watch me!"

"You hear me, Jessie?"

"You'd better go."

"You won't forget?" He looked up the corridor. "If you got hurt, Jessie, I'd never forgive myself."

"Funny," Jessie said with a shaky laugh. "I was just thinking the same thing."

He stared at her. Then he grinned, pressed her hand, and walked quickly up the hall.

She saw him stop before 622, put his ear to the door. After a moment he straightened and knocked. He immediately tried the door. It gave, and he went in.

The door did not close at once.

But then, suddenly, it did.

The office building made a pocket of silence in the noisy world.

The door stayed closed.

Now don't be a goop, Jessie told herself. This is the kind of thing he's done all his life. He couldn't have become a veteran police officer without learning how to handle violence. Anyway, there's nothing to be afraid of. The fat man is certainly harmless; he'd run like a rabbit rather than risk his skin. The other . . . the others, whoever they are . . . they're probably more scared right now than I am.

But her heart kept galloping.

He'd been so awkwardly high-spirited when he called for her at Gloria's, and over lunch. Like a boy on a heavy date. And looking so spruce. He'd pressed his suit and his tan-and-white shoes gleamed. And he'd shown up with a corsage of mignonette for her.

"The florist thought I was crazy," he had said, embarrassed. "Seems nobody buys mignonette for corsages any more. But I remember how my wife used to love it . . ."

She had not had the heart to tell him that the greenish mignonette was just the wrong thing for the green linen suit she was wearing. Or that a woman wasn't necessarily thrilled by being given flowers loved by a dead wife, even one dead thirty years. She had exclaimed over the corsage while pinning it on, and then she had gone into Gloria's bedroom and changed her hat, with which the mignonette clashed, too.

The trouble is, Jessie thought, it isn't really me. It's just that he's rediscovered the world of women.

In the solitude of Gloria Sardella's two disordered rooms yesterday, the dismal thought had come to her like a headache. Any woman could have done it. Any woman could still do it. Any other woman . . .

What was going on in there?

Jessie strained, but she could hear nothing except the tumult of the 49th Street traffic.

She had spent a miserable day and night examining herself. How could she have maneuvered herself into a sublet apartment in New York . . . New York, which she loathed! . . . into an adventure with a man she hardly knew? And that call from Belle Berman—"What's this I hear about you and some *man*, Jessie?" Gloria, of course, who had met him Thursday after the visit to Finner's office. And Gloria's probing afterward . . . Endlessly Jessie had debated phoning him to say it was all a mistake, they were both too old for this sort of thing, let's part good friends and I'll go back to my bedpans and catheters and you to sunning yourself on a beach . . .

Oh, I oughtn't to be here! Jessie told herself. I ought to be coming onto a maternity case, checking the chart, being oh so cheery to Mrs. Jones, wondering if my feet will hold out till the midnight relief whlle she yakkety-yaks about her nine hours of labor and how she'll make that husband of hers pay through the nose for what she's been through . . .

He was in the hall.

Jessie started. She hadn't even heard the door of 622 open. He was standing in the hall and he was beckoning to her. Jessie hurried to him.

He was all tightened up, careful. His eyes had a tight careful look, too. He had the door open no more than an inch, his hand on the knob holding it that way.

"Yes, Richard?" Jessie whispered breathlessly. "It's all right for me to go in?"

"That depends on *you*, Jessie." Even his voice was on the alert. "On how much you can take."

"What? Isn't Finner in there?"

"He's in there, all right. He's dead."

3 · And Then the Lover

The fat man looked different dead. He looked like a jumbo balloon with the air leaking out. He was wedged in the swivel chair, head flopped over, flippers dangling. The chair was half turned from the desk, as if he had been struggling to get up. His whole left side was soaked with blood.

The metal handle of a knife stuck out of his chest. Jessie recognized it as the handle of the steel letter-knife she had seen on his desk Thursday.

"Stay where you are, Jessie," Inspector Queen said. He had shut the door. "And hold your purse with both hands. That'll keep them out of trouble. You don't have to look at him."

"I've seen a homicide case or two in my time," Jessie said. She was holding on to her purse for dear life.

"Good girl."

He went around the desk, looked under it, rose, looked out the window.

"It's a cinch nobody saw anything." The vista from the window was a tall blank wall, the rear of a photoelectric plant on the next street.

"Key-ring on the floor behind the desk. Torn from loop on his pants. Key still in the lock of the filing cabinet. Somebody was in a hurry, Jessie. But careful, careful."

"Maybe we ought to—"

"Don't move from that spot."

Forty-eight hours ago that fat man had been sitting in that same chair, wearing the same suit and a shirt just as gray with damp, and now it was half-dyed with his heart's blood and he looked like nothing so much as a Macy's Thanksgiving Day balloon with the paint running and a knife stuck in it. So there would be no more under-the-counter arrangements for babies, and the unmarried mothers would have to seek elsewhere. And how many satisfied customers would read about the fat man and look at their wives or husbands and clutch their purchases tight? And would Mrs. A. Burt Finner erect a headstone saying HUSBAND AND FATHER and weep for the vanished provider? And how many nightclub girls would shed a blackened tear over the baby-made five-dollar bills that would invade their nylons no more?

Jessie stifled an impulse to laugh.

The Inspector wrapped a handkerchief around his right hand and went to the swivel chair again and leaned over Finner. When he drew up straight there was a wallet in his swathed hand. He flicked it open.

"Crammed with bills, Jessie."

He put the wallet back as carefully as he had taken it out.

"Not robbery," Jessie's voice was as tight as his had been.

309

"No."

He looked over the top of the desk. There was an afternoon newspaper folded back to the sports section, a well-pen, a telephone with a memorandum pad clipped to it, a pack of filter cigarets almost empty, a pocket lighter, and a cheap glass ash tray with chipped corners. The ash tray was filled with half-smoked butts and ashes. The old man squatted to desk level and squinted along the surface of the memo pad. Then he turned some of the butts in the tray over with one fingernail.

"Nothing written on a torn-off sheet of pad. No lipstick on any of the butts. And the basket under the desk is empty except for an empty cigaret pack, same brand as this one. All Finner's. This was a cool operator, Jessie. Clue-conscious."

"How about the desk drawers?" Jessie wet her lips.

He grinned. "I'll leave those to Homicide. Finner wouldn't have kept anything in this desk. No locks on the drawers." He glanced at her. "Just at a guess, Jessie—seeing that you're in the respectable branch of this business—how long would you say he's been dead?"

"That's very hard to say."

"Say it anyway."

"It's a hot day. The window is shut . . . At the least, I'd have to touch him."

"Without touching him."

"I've handled dead bodies, Richard. I'll do it."

"Without touching him."

"Not long." Jessie considered. "From the appearance of the blood maybe an hour. I don't know. I could be way off."

He placed the back of his left hand lightly against the dead man's cheek, nodded. Then he went over to the filing cabinet and tugged at the handle of the top drawer. The drawer slid out with a rasp that made Jessie's teeth ache.

The drawer contained file envelopes with identifying plastic tab holders containing white slips of cardboard on which names had been hand-printed in red ink. The first envelope in the drawer was marked ABRAMSON, the last DUFFY. He shut the top drawer and opened the drawer below it. The file envelopes were separated slightly about two-thirds of the way in. The tab on the exposed envelope said HYAMS. The tab on the envelope immediately preceding it said HUGHES.

There was no envelope in between.

"No Humffrey," Richard Queen said softly.

"Maybe the names on the tabs are of the mother," Jessie mumbled. "Not the adopter."

He looked at her. "You're a smart woman, Jessie." He checked a file at random, using his swathed hand. "However, you're wrong. The names are of the adopters."

He replaced the file and ran his eye over all the tabs on the envelopes. He shut the drawer and checked the tabs of the third drawer, then of the bottom one.

He shut the bottom drawer and rose.

"No doubt about it, Jessie. Finner's kill is tied in with the Connecticut case. Finner used our Thursday visit to try to screw some inside information about Michael's death out of one or both of the real parents. So they've shut his mouth about the parentage and walked off with the whole file on the case. Finner probably was the only outsider who knew at least who the mother was, the hospital Michael was born in, and every other fact that might have led to an identification."

"The same one who murdered the baby," Jessie said slowly. "That means we're on the right track."

"We're stranded on a siding in Podunk," Richard Queen said grimly. "With the contents of that envelope destroyed we're at another dead end. The question is, where do we go from here?"

He gave A. Burt Finner a glum look. But Finner wasn't talking.

"I think, Jessie—"

The telephone rang.

Jessie's heart landed in her mouth with a bump.

He moved nearer the desk, eying the telephone thoughtfully.

"You're not going to answer it?" Jessie said in terror. "Richard, for heaven's sake!"

"Shh."

His right hand was still bound round with the handkerchief. He used it to lift the phone from its cradle.

He said hoarsely, "Yes?" in a fair approximation of Finner's voice.

Jessie shut her eyes. She heard a phone operator's unmistakable cadence. The old man said, "Yes?" again in the same hoarse voice and the operator said something back and then there was silence.

"New Haven calling," he told her.

"New Haven?" Jessie opened her eyes wide.

"Always play a hunch. This may foul me up with my old friends, but I'm here and they aren't.—Yes?"

The man's voice was clipped, successful-sounding. "This is Dr. Samuel Duane calling. Is Mr. Alton K. Humffrey there?"

"Humffrey?" Richard Queen said in the Finner voice. "What do you want him for?"

"It's confidential." The doctor's tone had an urgent, almost a harried, vibrato. "I must speak to Mr. Humffrey."

"You'll have to tell me what it's about, Dr. Duane." He glanced over at Jessie, winking.

"I'm Mrs. Humffrey's physician. She's . . . worse, and I must find her husband. Do you know—?"

"How bad is she?"

"See here, is Mr. Humffrey there, or isn't he?"

"Well, no, Doctor, but maybe I can find him for you. Did you call his summer place in Connecticut?"

"Good lord, man, do you think I'm an idiot? His housekeeper tells me he left Nair Island yesterday driving the small car and saying he wouldn't be back till tonight or tomorrow. Is—?"

"Didn't he say where he was going?"

"No! She gave me the phone numbers of all the places he might be—clubs, Park Avenue apartment, his home in Concord, even Mrs. Humffrey's relatives in Massachusetts. But I haven't been able to trace him. Have you any idea where he might have gone? I understand you've done some confidential legal work for him."

"Who told you that?"

"The chauffeur, I think, suggested your name. What difference does it make?" Dr. Duane sounded at the point of explosion. "Will you give me something definite or won't you? I tell you this is urgent!"

"I guess I can't help you at that, Doctor. But if I should hear from him . . ."

Dr. Duane slammed his receiver.

Richard Queen looked at Jessie as he hung up. "Queer . . ."

"What did he *say*, Richard?"

He told her.

"But I don't see anything queer about it. Except the coincidence of calling here just when . . ."

He was shaking his head, frowning, staring at Finner.

Finally he said, "Jessie, I want you to go home."

"Without you?"

"I've got to notify the police. A homicide has to be reported as soon as it's discovered."

"Then why didn't you pick up the phone and call the minute you walked in here?" Jessie retorted.

"You're a hard woman, Jessie," he murmured. "All right, maybe I've come to feel that this is my case. Mine and yours . . . You and I know the two homicides are connected, but with the Humffrey envelope gone, there's no reason for them to link Finner's murder up with a Connecticut baby-smothering case that's been written off as an accidental death. Not right away, anyway. Meanwhile, we'll have some room to stretch in."

"Wouldn't it be better to ask for reinstatement, Richard?" Jessie asked quietly. "If they knew you'd been in on this from the start, maybe they'd give you a special assignment to take charge of the case."

He smiled faintly. "It doesn't work that way. The New York police department has two thousand detectives working out of precincts and Headquarters, not to mention some twenty or so thousand men and women in other police jobs. They don't need old man Queen. Come on, Jessie, I'll see you out of the building. I don't want some night man to spot you."

Jessie looked back just before he shut the door.

The fat man was still sitting there like an abandoned balloon.

It was after eleven that night when the phone rang.

"Jessie?"

"Richard, why haven't you called before? Where are you?" Jessie exclaimed. "Is everything all right?"

"Fine," he said. "I'm down at Headquarters chewing the fat with the boys. Going to bed?"

She understood that he couldn't talk freely and wouldn't be able to come over.

"You can't see me tonight, is that it?"

"Right. I'll ring you in the morning."

"Good night, Richard."

Jessie hung up and surveyed the table she had set. She had bought minute steaks, frozen French fries, and some salad vegetables in a delicatessen on 72nd Street, thinking to treat him to a home meal when he came. So that's what policemen's wives' lives were like . . .

What am I thinking of! Jessie thought guiltily, and she went to bed.

She was still in curlers and an old wrapper Sunday morning when the doorbell rang. She opened the door to the width of the latch chain, wondering who it could be.

"*Richard!*"

"Thought I'd surprise you," he grinned. "I've got the Sunday papers, frozen juice, fresh rolls, eggs—got any ham? I forgot the ham. Jessie? Where are you?"

"You mustn't *do* things like this," Jessie moaned, flat against the door. "Don't you know how a woman looks first thing in the morning? I'll undo the chain, but don't you dare walk in till you finish counting ten!"

"All right," he said, stricken.

When she came out of the tiny bedroom, he was sitting on the edge of a chair with the paper sack in his lap.

"Richard Queen, I could strangle you. Is anything more hideous than a woman in curlers? Don't just sit there. Let me have that bag."

"I'm sorry." He looked so deflated that Jessie laughed. "Anyway, I thought you looked fine. It's a long time since I saw a woman in curlers."

"I suppose it is at that," Jessie said. She took the bag to the kitchen alcove and got busy.

"Did I say something wrong, Jessie?" he asked anxiously.

"Heavens, no. Make yourself useful. I don't have any ham, but you'll find a couple of minute steaks in the fridge and a box of French fries in the freezer drawer. How does that sound?"

"Oh, boy!" It was not until she was pouring his second cup of coffee that Jessie asked, "Well, what happened yesterday?"

"Nothing much," he said in a careless tone. "The first men there were a patrolman and sergeant, radio patrol car, 17th precinct—I know both of them pretty well. Then a couple of detectives from the 17th I know very well, and after that a lot of old buddies of mine—Deputy Chief Inspector Tom Mackey in charge of Manhattan East, Chief of Detectives Brynie Phelan, the Homicide boys—it was like Old Home Week."

"And when they asked their old buddy how he happened to stumble over a corpse," Jessie said, "what did their old buddy say?"

He set his cup down, shrugging. "All right, I lied. The going was rough for a while, but I think I pulled it off." He sounded ashamed. "I suppose an honorable lifetime in and out of uniform counts for something, especially when the men you're lying to are friends of yours."

"What was your story, Richard?" Jessie asked quietly. "I have to know, in case they get to me."

He glanced at her with admiration. Then he stared at the floor. "I said I'd been going crazy doing nothing, began thinking about some rats I'd known in harness whom we'd never been able to collar, and remembered Finner and his vicious racket. I said I thought it would be nice to get something on him—he doesn't even have a yellow sheet down at the B.C.I., no record at all. So I dropped in on Finner Thursday, I said, and let him think I was still on active duty and that we'd come up with something on him at last . . . on the theory that if you rattle a rat, he'll panic. I said Finner hinted at a payoff to keep the boys off his back, and I said I pretended to play along and made a date to visit his office again Saturday afternoon, and I said when I got there I found him dead. That's what I said, Jessie, and may the Lord have mercy on my soul."

"But that wasn't really a lie," Jessie said quickly. "It's not so far from the truth."

"Only about a million miles," he snarled. "It's the worst kind of lie there is. It doesn't tell them a single thing I know that could help them. Jessie, I think I'll have another cup of coffee."

She emptied the pot into his cup in silence.

"So they're off to the races," he said, swishing the coffee around. "They figure the killer's somebody who wanted to get at Finner's files for blackmail purposes but was maybe scared off. They don't discount the possibility that the answer may lie in one of the night spots Finner patronized. So they're checking all the babes he's fooled around with, some of them linked with some pretty tough characters. They've got every angle covered except the right one." He nudged the Sunday papers, which were lying on the floor, with his toe. "Read all about it."

"Don't feel so bad, Richard." Jessie leaned across the table to put her hand on his.

He gripped it and held on.

After a moment, pink-cheeked, she withdrew it and began to collect the dishes. "What do we do now?"

He got up and began to help her. "Well, the problem is still to find out who the baby's parents are."

"I don't see how we possibly can, now."

"There's a way."

"There is?" Jessie stared. "How?"

"Isn't every child born in a hospital handprinted for identification purposes?"

"Or footprinted." Jessie nodded. "Most hospitals take footprints these days."

"Knowing Finner's methods, it's likely he had the mother give birth in a hospital. What we've got to do is get hold of Michael's prints. It means an exhumation, of course—"

Jessie said, without turning from the sink, "What would you say, Inspector, if I told you I have his footprints?"

"What!"

"Mrs. Humffrey'd bought one of those baby books put out by the Chicago Lying-In hospital—you know, where you keep a record of feeding, teeth growth, and so on. There's a place in them for recording the footprints. I pressed his feet on that page myself."

"And you have it?" he asked incredulously.

"Yes. After the funeral I asked Mrs. Humffrey where she wanted me to put the book. She got hysterical and told me to take it away, she never wanted to see it again. So I appropriated it," Jessie said defiantly. "He was a lot more my baby than hers . . . Wait, I'll get it for you. It's in one of my bags."

She hurried into the bedroom and came out with an oversized book with a baby-blue cover.

"Of course, we couldn't fill in the birth data except for the date of birth—" Jessie gasped. "The date of birth!"

"This is going to be a cinch," he chortled. "With these footprints and the birth date, it's only a question of locating the hospital. Finner brought the baby to that Pelham meeting in the morning, so the odds are he picked him up in a New York hospital. I'll have these prints photostated first thing tomorrow, and . . . Jessie, what's the matter?"

She was staring blearily down at the tiny black feet impressions. "Nothing, Richard." She fumbled for a handkerchief, turning away.

He started to touch her, withdrew his hand awkwardly. "It's a brutal business, Jessie . . ."

"He was so little," Jessie sobbed. "That perfect body . . . his feet . . . I used to kiss his toes one at a time reciting Piggy, and he'd gleep . . ." She blew her nose angrily. "I'm sorry. I don't know what's happened to me lately."

"You're a woman," he muttered. "Maybe you haven't had time to find that out before, Jessie."

She kept her face averted. "What do I do, Richard?"

"The first thing you do is recognize the spot you're in."

"The spot *I'm* in?" She swung about at that.

"If I'd known about your having this baby book, I'd never have let you get into this. It's a dangerous thing for you to have. Finner was murdered because he was a link in the chain leading to little Mike's mother. This book, with his footprints, is another such link. Who knows you've got it?"

Jessie sank into a chair, staring at him. "Only Sarah Humffrey, I suppose. For all I know, maybe even she doesn't know. She may have assumed I destroyed it."

He scowled. "Maybe the killer's assumed the same thing. Or doesn't know it exists. All the same, Jessie, you're going to have to watch your step. In fact, the more I think of it the less I cotton to the idea of your living in this apartment alone. I wish—"

"Yes?" Jessie said.

"Well, I can be your bodyguard in the daytime, anyway." He smiled down at her. "What would you like to do today?"

Before they set out Monday afternoon with the photostats, Richard Queen said, "It's going to be a long pull, Jessie. There must be seventy-five or eighty hospitals in Manhattan and the Bronx alone, not to mention Brooklyn, Queens, Staten Island, Westchester, Long Island, and nearby Jersey."

"Why not start off with the maternity hospitals?" Jessie suggested. "Those would be the logical places."

"Which is why Finner would have avoided them. And he'd certainly not use places like the New York Foundling Hospital or the Shelter for Unmarried Mothers. No, I think he'd figure a big general hospital would give his brood mares a better choice of getting lost in the shuffle. Let's start with those."

"All right, suppose we make a list and split it up. That would halve the time."

"I'm not letting you out of my sight," he said firmly. "Besides, I doubt if you could get access to hospital files, even in the places where they know you. I've got a natural in with this shield."

On Wednesday afternoon, the third day of their hunt, they were leaving a hospital in the East 80s when Jessie said, "What's wrong, Richard? You've acted strange all day. You said yourself it's going to be a long search."

He steered her across the street to her coupé. "I didn't think it showed," he said dryly.

"You can't fool me. When you're worried about something you get all tight and quiet. What is it?"

"Watch. In the rear-view mirror."

He started the Dodge and moved out into traffic, heading north. Jessie slid over close to him and kept her eyes on the mirror. As they passed a corner, a black Chrysler sedan badly in need of a washing moved out from the side street and turned in after them. For a moment it was just behind them and Jessie caught a glimpse of the driver's face. It was all jaw and cheekbone in sharp angles, hard and gray. The man was alone.

Then the Chrysler fell back, other cars intervened, and Jessie lost sight of it. But when the Inspector turned west a few blocks north of the hospital, Jessie saw the gray-faced man turn west, too.

"We're being followed." Her mouth felt sticky.

"He's been on our tail all day."

"A city detective?"

"City detectives generally work in pairs."

"Then who is he?"

"A small-time private detective named George Weirhauser. Fleabag office near Times Square. Mostly divorce evidence jobs. He rates pretty low downtown—he's pulled plenty of shady stuff—but he's always managed to steer clear of open violations. Enough to hold on to his license, anyway."

"But what's he doing watching us?"

"I don't know." Richard Queen looked grim. "Well, there's no point trying to shake him with what he's seen today already. A tail can work two ways—he keeps an eye on us, we keep an eye on him. Maybe we'll find a use for him."

"He looks awfully hard."

"That's Weirhauser's stock-in-trade," he said contemptuously. "It's all front, Jessie. Don't worry about him."

Weirhauser tailed them until after ten o'clock, when they put Jessie's car away for the night in the garage on 70th Street where she had arranged for a month's parking. When they walked over to 71st and stopped before Gloria Sardella's walkup, the Chrysler drove past, picked up speed, aud did not come back.

"Thank goodness," Jessie said. "He makes me nervous. Won't you come up, Richard? I'll make some coffee."

"No, you're going to bed, Jessie."

"I am a little weary," Jessie confessed. "And you're a dear to have seen it.— *Richard.*" She clutched his arm.

"Yes?"

"There's another one!"

"Another what, Jessie?" He seemed calm.

"Another man following us! I noticed him lounging around near the garage when we drove in. And now he's across the street in a doorway!"

"You certainly missed your calling," he said.

"Richard, what are you doing—?"

He was guiding her by the elbow across the street toward the offending doorway. The man who had been watching them retreated into the dimness of the vestibule. To Jessie's consternation, Richard Queen marched her right in after him.

"Shame on you, Wes," he said, chuckling. "Jessie, this is Wes Polonsky, ex-detective first grade, Automobile, Forgery, and Pickpocket Squad, retired."

"Good heavens," Jessie said. "How do you do, Mr. Polonsky."

"Glad to meet you, Miss Sherwood," the man said sheepishly. "Or maybe not so glad. I'm sure rusty." He was a massive old man with a mashed nose and white hair and innocent blue eyes. He looked as if he had once been powerful, but his chest was sunken and Jessie noticed his puffy hands trembling as he lit a cigaret. "You going to take me off, Inspector? This is the first kicks I've had in eight years."

"Don't be silly. This woman has eyes in the back of her head." Richard Queen sounded proud. "Wes, we were tailed today."

"I noticed a black Chrysler sedan ambling after you just now," Polonsky said, "but I couldn't get a good look at the driver."

"He wasn't around here last night, was he?"

"No. At least not in that car."

"It's George Weirhauser."

"That crum." Polonsky made a disgusted sound. "Want me to run him off if he shows again?"

"Let him be. Just don't let him get near Miss Sherwood."

"Okay, Inspector."

"But what is all this?" Jessie demanded. "I don't understand, Richard!"

"Now don't get mad, Jessie," he said placatively. "I ran into Wes Sunday night while I was walking home from your place—he lives in this neighborhood—and, well, Wes was saying how sick he was of being idle—"

"I'd get me a job," Polonsky said apologetically, "but it's impossible for a man my age to find anything."

"So," Richard Queen said, "one thing led to another, and before I knew it Wes was begging me to declare him in."

"And that's how Mr. Polonsky came to be my guardian angel, is it?"

"Since Sunday night," the ex-detective said, beaming.

"It's only for the night trick, Jessie. The times when I'm not with you."

"It's very sweet of you, Mr. Polonsky," Jessie said in a low voice.

The second old man said, "It's my pleasure, miss."

Jessie slept soundly that night.

They struck the trail in the seventh day of their search.

It was at one of the big general hospitals on the West Side, in midtown. The old man was going through a file of baby footprints when Jessie felt him stiffen. He turned a pocket magnifying glass from the hospital record he was examining to the photostat and back again several times.

"We've found it, Jessie," he muttered.

"I don't believe it! Are you sure?"

"Positive."

The name identifying the set of footprints was "Baby Exeter."

"Let's see what they have on the mother."

He came back with some scribbled notes, and they sat down on a sofa in the waiting room.

"Mother's name Mrs. Willis P. Exeter, maiden name Lois Ann Edwards. Phonies, of course. Address . . . this house number on East 55th is misleading, Jessie. It's actually a small residential hotel. My guess is Finner maintained a room there under the name of Willis P. Exeter—probably had a number of such rooms around town under different aliases—and simply assigned one of them with a 'Mrs.' attached to every girl he did business with, for purposes of hospital registration."

According to his notes "Mrs. Willis P. Exeter" was twenty-four years old, white, with blond hair and hazel eyes. She had been admitted to the hospital on May 26th at 9:18 A.M., the baby had been born on May 27th at 3:56 P.M., and mother and baby had been discharged on June 3rd as of 10:15 A.M. The woman had occupied a semi-private room in the Maternity wing.

"I wonder if the doctor was in on it," Jessie said balefully. "What's his name?"

The old man shook his head. "Finner worked through legitimate doctors who never knew he existed. He simply sent the girl during her pregnancy to this doctor under the name of Mrs. Willis P. Exeter, armed with a phony background, and the doctor took care of her in good faith. All Finner had to do was use a different doctor for each girl, and he was all right. No, this tells us nothing." He squinted at Jessie. "Ever work this hospital?"

"Yes."

"Then you'd probably know the floor nurses in Maternity."

"Some of them."

"Why don't you go up and scout around? Maybe you'll run into one who remembers this girl. It's only three months back."

"What excuse do I give?"

"You're helping to trace Mrs. Exeter for a lawyer. She's come into an inheritance and the lawyer can't locate her." He grinned. "That one never fails."

When Jessie came back her eyes were sparkling. "Genevieve Fuller. She'll meet us in the Coffee Shop in ten minutes."

"I certainly do remember Mrs. Exeter, Mr. Queen," Nurse Fuller said. Jessie's friend was a small lively woman with gray hair and inquisitive eyes. "She was so sad all the time. Hardly said a word. The other patient in her room thought she was a drip, but I knew there was something special about her. Pretty girl in a kind of hard way. She had the sweetest baby. A little boy."

Jessie took a gulp of coffee.

"Did she ever tell you anything about herself, Miss Fuller?" Richard Queen asked.

"No, and I didn't press her. I knew she'd had some tragedy in her life. Do you know her husband never showed up once?"

"Really?"

"Some men! I'd drop in on her when she was in heavy labor, and she'd grab my hand and cry, she was so glad to see a sympathetic face. *No* one showed up. No parents, no sister, no brother, no friends—what kind of family she comes from I can't imagine. They must be animals."

"Didn't she ever say anything that might give us a clue to her present whereabouts, Miss Fuller?"

"No." The nurse looked around the Coffee Shop, lowering her voice. "But I am practically a hundred per cent sure Exeter wasn't her real name!"

"Is that so?" Inspector Queen said. "Well, now, that may account for it. Why did you think that?"

"Because from the second I laid eyes on her I knew I'd seen her somewhere before. Only I couldn't place her. Then one morning she gave herself away."

"How?" Jessie exclaimed.

"Oh, I didn't let on that it meant anything to me. Just made an offhand remark about what a nice voice she had. *You* know."

"But I don't, Gen! What's her voice got to do with it?"

"One morning," Genevieve Fuller looked around again "—it was the day before she was discharged—I was passing her room when I heard somebody singing in a low, sweet, sexy voice. It really gave me a turn. I looked in, and darned if it wasn't this Exeter girl. The screen was around her bed and they'd brought her the baby for a feeding—that's another thing I liked about her, a girl in her line insisting on nursing her own baby, not like some of the parasite sluts we get around here who sit around Schrafft's all day in their minks while strangers prepare their children's formulas. They seem to think God gave them breasts for just ornaments—"

"In her line, Miss Fuller?" Richard Queen prompted.

"I started to tell you. She was nursing her baby and *singing* to him. Well, you can't fool me about voices. You know, Jessie, what a bug I am on pop singers. Well, I'd have recognized that voice anywhere. You can have your Rosemary

Clooneys and Dinah Shores and Jo Staffords and Patty Pages and Doris Days—oh, they're very good, of course, and they're a thousand times better known than this girl, she's only made a few recordings, but she'll hit the top one of these days, you mark my words, she'll be the biggest seller of them all instead of just somebody a few people rave about."

"And her real name is—?"

"I'm not sure it's her *real* name, Mr. Queen. Her professional name is Connie Coy." And Nurse Fuller leaned back, narrowing her eyes to get the full effect of her revelation. She seemed disappointed. "Anyway, I figured she was incognito, and I wouldn't have let on for the world. Besides, as I say, I knew she was in some kind of trouble. But I'll swear on a stack of Bibles that was Connie Coy, the nightclub singer. And you say she's come into money! I think that's wonderful. God bless her. Too many people with real talent wither away on the desert air unseen. When you find her, Mr. Queen, will you tell her I'm her absolute number one fan? And what a darling baby she has! . . ."

When Genevieve Fuller had left, the old man said, "Connie Coy. Ever hear of her, Jessie?"

Jessie said, "I haven't been inside a nightclub since December 18, 1943. No, Richard."

But he ignored her sally. "If it wasn't Sunday, I could get her address in any one of a dozen ways. As it is, we'll have to hold it over till tomorrow."

"I know a thirteenth way," Jessie murmured.

"What's that?"

"Look in the phone book."

He stared at her. "Sometimes, Jessie," he said solemnly, "I wonder what I ever did without you. Excuse me!"

When he came back he was waving a slip of paper.

"It's up on 88th near West End Avenue," he said exultantly. "After you, Commissioner!"

"Still no sign of Mr. Weirhauser," Jessie remarked as Inspector Queen started the car. They had not caught a glimpse of the black Chrysler all day.

"Funny," he muttered.

"Maybe he doesn't work Sundays. Or he's been called off the job."

The old man said nothing. But he kept stealing glances in his rear-view mirror all the way uptown.

The apartment house was turn-of-the-century, a fancy production of stone scrollwork and false balconies, cracked and weatherstained, with bleached awnings that had once been striped, scabby iron-grilled doors, and a sidewalk chalked over with hopscotch squares. The whole building cowered as if it were ashamed.

They entered a lobby powerful with food odors. At a wall switchboard, doubled up on a three-legged stool under a 25-watt light, sat a skinny pimpled youth in a uniform too large for him, reading a comic book.

"Who you want?" The boy did not look up.

"Miss Connie Coy."

"She ain't in."

"When do you expect her?"

"I dunno."

Jessie suggested, "There's a door there says Superintendent."

The old man grunted. They went over to the door and he rang the bell.

A heavy-set man in a collarless shirt, with a green paper napkin stuck in the neckband, opened the door.

"Yeah?"

"I'm looking for some information about one of your tenants, Miss Connie Coy."

"I can't give out information about my tenants." The man began to shut the door, but it refused to shut. He glanced down coldly. "Guys can get their feet knocked off that way. You want I should call a cop?"

The gold shield flashed in Inspector Queen's palm.

"That's a hot one," the man grinned. "Come on in."

"We can talk here. By the way, what's your name?"

"McKeown. Joseph N."·

"Do you know where Miss Coy is, McKeown?"

"Out of town. She left three weeks ago Friday. She was supposed to be gone only a week, but she didn't come back so I guess they held her over."

"Oh, a professional engagement?"

"Yeah, she's a club singer. You know, a shantoose." McKeown glanced sidewise at Jessie.

"Then she might be back any day?"

"I'd say so."

"She live here long?"

"Seven-eight months."

"Where's she singing?"

"Chicago." McKeown peered over at the switchboard boy and lowered his voice. "Wha'd she do, Cap?"

"Nothing. She may have to be a witness in a case."

"Glad to hear it," the superintendent said. "Nice quiet gal. Too bad about her husband."

"Oh," the old man said. "She's got a husband?"

"A GI. He's in Korea. And he never even got to see his kid. He's still over there." McKeown looked sad. "Hard lines getting your wife pregnant and having to ship out, then she has the kid all alone and loses it in childbirth in the bargain. Came back from the hospital all broke up."

"I see," Richard Queen said. "What hospital was she at, do you know?"

"Some Army hospital over in Jersey, she said. She was just beginning to show when she moved in here. Tough."

"It certainly is," Jessie murmured. "Does she use her married name here in the building?"

"Yeah. Mrs. Arthur Dimmesdale."

"How do you spell that, McKeown?" He took out a ballpoint pen and a wrinkled envelope with an Italian postmark. McKeown spelled the name, and the Inspector wrote it down on the back of the envelope.

Arthur Dimmesdale . . . Jessie thought, Where have I heard that name?

"Then I take it, McKeown, since Miss Coy—Mrs. Dimmesdale—didn't move in here till after her husband shipped out to Korea, that you've never seen him?"

"Never laid eyes on him."

"Any idea of his branch of service? Rank?"

"I think she said he's a second looey in the Army."

The old man made a note. "Couple more questions, McKeown, and I'll let you get back to your Sunday dinner. What's Miss Coy's apartment number?"

"5-C. That's on the top floor."

"Apartment C, fifth floor. She live alone?"

"All by her lonely, Cap."

"She ever have anybody sleep over?"

McKeown grinned. "This ain't the Barbizon, my friend. We don't keep a check. She don't run no brawls, and that's good enough for me."

"Don't mention this to Miss Coy when she gets back, McKeown."

"I get you, Cap."

As they walked toward Broadway, Jessie said, "But where are we going, Richard? Why didn't we get into the car?"

"You've got to have your dinner, Jessie. There's a nice restaurant on Broadway and 87th—"

"That's not the reason. What is it?"

"I can't keep anything from you, can I? We were wrong about Weirhauser. I just spotted him in a parked car as we came out of the apartment house. He was trying to hide behind a newspaper, but I got a look at him."

"I don't understand it," Jessie exclaimed. "I've kept on the lookout for his Chrysler all day."

"So have I. That's why we didn't see him. Don't turn around, Jessie. He's about to go into the apartment house." Richard Queen steered her around the corner into Broadway. "He pulled a fast one today. Ditched the old Chrysler and tailed us in a new Ford."

"How clever of him," Jessie tried to keep her tone amused. "Then he's finding out right now that we've been asking for Connie Coy. If McKeown doesn't tell him, that pimply boy will."

"More important, he knows we've found her. And by tonight, whoever's paying him to tail us will know it, too." He was preoccupied as they entered the restaurant.

"What are we going to do, Richard?"

He squeezed her arm. "Have dinner."

He took a table commanding a view of the door. But the private detective did not appear.

Over the chicken noodle soup Jessie said, "Do you think she's really married?" He shrugged.

"Maybe that's why she had her baby under the name of Exeter, Richard. And told the super she'd given birth in a New Jersey hospital when she actually had the baby in New York. If she's married and her husband wasn't the baby's father . . ."

"She'd use a phony name at the hospital if she wasn't married, too. I'll check Washington first thing in the morning on a Lieutenant Arthur Dimmesdale." He stopped talking until the waiter removed the soup plates. "Either way we slice this, Jessie, it comes out the same. If Connie's married, Dimmesdale isn't the father. If she's an unmarried mother, and invented Dimmesdale to make life simpler for herself at the apartment house, we've still got to look for the man who got her pregnant."

"And for the other man," Jessie said grimly.

"Which other man?"

"The man who's hired that private detective to shadow us."

He buttered a roll and remarked, "They might be the same man."

Jessie looked surprised. "That's so, isn't it? Or . . . Richard! Do you suppose Weirhauser's client could be Arthur Dimmesdale?"

"From Korea?"

"Don't smile. Suppose the husband does exist. Suppose Dimmesdale knew he hadn't left his wife pregnant. Then some snoopy 'friend' writes to Korea that Connie's having, or had, a baby. He's furious. He goes AWOL, or wangles a leave or something—anyway, gets back to the States. First he traces the baby to the Humffreys and murders him—"

"That would make him a psycho, Jessie. And what about Finner's murder?"

"When Michael was murdered, Finner might have figured the husband did it, pussyfooted around, and decided he was right. If Finner then tried to blackmail Dimmesdale—"

But the Inspector was shaking his head. "I'm pretty sure, from the way Finner reacted, that he'd had no idea the baby was murdered. Hold it. —Fine, waiter. Yes, just the way I like it. Jessie, dig into this roast beef."

There was no sign of George Weirhauser when they left the restaurant. They walked back up to 88th Street, where they had parked Jessie's coupé, and Richard Queen rubbed his jaw.

"He's gone."

There was no sign of Weirhauser's new Ford, either.

"Well!" Jessie said "That's a relief."

"Is it?" he said oddly. "It probably means that instead of his client knowing tonight that we've located Connie Coy, he's learning it right now."

When he came downstairs from Jessie's apartment that night he strolled up the street a way and then suddenly pulled open the door of a blue Studebaker parked at the curb and climbed in.

"Evening, Inspector," Polonsky said.

"See anything of a gray-and-salmon Ford this evening, Wes?"

The retired officer looked concerned. "I thought Weirhauser was driving a black Chrysler."

"He switched on us today."

Polonsky swore. "Somebody's been teaching that punk his trade. I couldn't say I didn't, Inspector. I wasn't watching out for Fords."

"Neither was I." The Inspector began gnawing on his mustache. "Wes, what ever happened to Pete Whatzis? You know, the Pete you used to team up with."

"Pete Angelo? Pete's wife died two years after he retired. His married daughter's husband got transferred to Cincinnati, the younger daughter is away at college, and his son's a Navy career man. Pete worked for a protection agency a few years and then quit." Polonsky sighed. "At least he tells everybody he quit. He was fired on account of his age. Age! Pete Angelo could still wade into a gang of street corner hoodlums and stack 'em like cordwood."

"Ever see Angelo?"

"All the time. He lives here on the West Side. We meet in the cafeteria, have four cups of coffee apiece, and tell each other how good we used to be."

"Then Angelo's not doing anything?"

"Just going nuts, like the rest of us."

"Do you suppose I could get Pete to handle a plant for me?"

"Inspector, he'd throw his arms around your neck and kiss every hair on your mustache."

"Can you think of any other retired cop who'd be willing to team with Angelo? I'd need them both right away."

The ex-detective pondered. Then he smacked the wheel. "Murph! I ran into him this past week. You remember Sergeant Al Murphy, Inspector—he used to be on radio car patrol in the 16th. Murph was retired this past June, and he told me he's still undecided what to do with himself. Never saw a guy so itchy.''

"Anybody else you can think of, Wes? I'd like two teams, one for the night trick, one for daytimes.''

"I'll bet Pete or Murph'll come up with a couple. When do you want them for?''

"If possible, starting tonight.''

Polonsky climbed out of his Studebaker. "You take this stakeout for a while, Inspector. I'll be right back.''

When he slipped behind the wheel again Polonsky was grinning. "Pete Angelo and Al Murphy'll meet you in the cafeteria on 72nd in fifteen minutes. Pete says not to worry, he can get you ten teams. Your problem, he says, is going to be to fight off the ones you can't use.''

Richard Queen sat there in silence. Then he pressed Polonsky's arm and got out. The old man in the car watched the old man on the sidewalk stride toward Broadway like a very young man indeed.

On Monday morning Richard Queen phoned to tell Jessie he had started the ball rolling on Lieutenant Dimmesdale with a connection of his at the Pentagon, and that he would have to stick close to his phone all day.

"What are your plans, Jessie?'' he asked anxiously. "I haven't got you covered daytimes.''

"Oh, I'll be all right. I have some laundry and a few other things to do, and then I thought I'd hop a cab and give that bachelor's sty of yours the thorough house-cleaning I promised. If you wouldn't mind my coming, I mean.''

"Mind,'' he said in a fervent tone. "And here I was all gloomed up. But be careful on the way, Jessie!''

Jessie arrived a little past noon. At her ring he bellowed that the door was off the latch, and she went in to find him on the phone in Ellery's study, waving at her through the study doorway.

"Richard Queen, why didn't you tell me your Mrs. Fabrikant had been here? Or is this your work?''

He grinned and went on talking.

"Not that it still doesn't need doing,'' Jessie sniffed. She hung her taffeta coat and her hat in the foyer, prepared to take her handbag into the bathroom, change into a housedress, and sail in. But when she got further into the living room, there was the gateleg table set for two with winking silver and fancy paper napkins. He had decorated a big platter artistically with assorted cold cuts, deviled eggs, potato salad, parsley, and tomato slices, and the aroma from the kichen told her the coffee was perking.

Jessie turned the gas down under the coffeepot with the strangest thrill of proprietorship.

So they lunched tête-à-tête, and he told her that he had just finished arranging for an around-the-clock watch on Connie Coy's apartment.

"But who's watching?'' Jessie asked, astonished.

"Four retired members of the Force,'' he grinned. "Al Murphy and Pete Angelo signed up last night. Pete got Hughie Giffin for me this morning, and that was ex-Lieutenant of Homicide Johnny Kripps just now trying to climb through the phone. Murphy and Angelo for daytime duty, Giffin and Kripps for dark-to-dawn. And four better officers you couldn't find between here and the west forty.''

"Connie Coy is back, then?''

"No. That's one of the reasons I want the building covered. This way I'll know the minute she gets home."

When Jessie came out of the bathroom after lunch, in a housedress and with her hair bound in a scarf, she found him washing the lunch dishes.

"Here, Richard, I'll do those."

"You go on about your business. I'm a pearl diver from way back."

But afterward he trailed her around the apartment in a pleased way, making a nuisance of himself.

"Haven't you anything to do?" She was washing the living-room windows, and she suspected she had a dirt smudge on her nose. "Goodness!"

"I'll go call Abe Pearl," he said hastily. "Been meaning to do it all day."

"Are you going to tell him about Finner's death and how it ties in with the baby?"

"I called Abe on that early last week."

"You never told me. What did he say?"

"I couldn't repeat it."

"Then Chief Pearl's not so sure about my optical illusions," Jessie couldn't help saying.

"I'm afraid Abe's not sure about anything any more."

He went into the study and called Taugus police headquarters.

"Abe? Dick Queen."

"Dick!" Abe Pearl roared. "Wait a minute." Richard Queen heard him say, "Borcher, shut that door, will you?" and the slam of a door. "Okay, Dick—"

"I thought you were going to call me back last week."

"Call you back? I've called that damn number of yours two dozen times. Don't you ever stay home? What's going on, Dick? Honeymoon—or something—with the Sherwood number?"

"Don't be funny," the old man said huffily.

"All right, all right. But you've tied my hands, I don't dare buzz Centre Street for information—I'm sitting out here like a bump on a log. Come on, Dick, give!"

He told Abe Pearl about their success in tracking down the mother of the dead baby.

"I'm waiting now for the girl to get back to town, Abe. Meanwhile, I'm trying to get a line on this alleged husband of hers, Dimmesdale. What did you find out about the Humffreys? How is Mrs. Humffrey?"

"I can't get to first base on that. This Duane is closer-mouthed than the FBI. I even got a friend of mine, a New Haven doctor who's sent patients to the Duane sanitarium and knows Duane well, to make some wild heaves from left field, but all Jerry could learn was that they'd called in some big specialist for her."

"How about Alton Humffrey, Abe? When did he get back from that mysterious fadeout weekend before last?"

"A week ago Sunday night, late. The help must have told him about Dr. Duane's trying frantically to get hold of him, because my information is Humffrey turned right around and drove up to New Haven. He was back Monday morning."

"That was Monday a week ago? The 22nd?"

"Yeah. The next day—last Tuesday—he closed up the Nair Island house and went into New York for good. The only one left is the gardener, Stallings."

Richard Queen was silent. Then he said, "Abe, were you able to find out where Humffrey was during his two-day disappearance?"

"Nope. What the devil is this all about, Dick? It's a lot of fog to me."

"Move over," the old man chuckled.

But he looked worried as he hung up.

At 4:12 P.M. the phone rang. It was the operator with a call from Washington.

"This is it, Jessie," Richard Queen shouted. "Hello?"

Two minutes later he hung up.

"The Pentagon says that no such person as Arthur Dimmesdale—either as officer, enlisted man, draftee, or even civilian employee—is carred on the rolls of the United States Army, in Korea or anywhere else."

"So she did make him up," Jessie said slowly. "Poor girl."

"I wish your poor girl would show," he snapped. "I wish something would show!"

Something did. At 4:25 he answered the doorbell to find himself staring into the hard blue eyes of his old friend, Deputy Chief Inspector Thomas F. Mackey in charge of Manhattan East.

If Inspector Mackey's eyes were not affable, the rest of him was. He remarked how long it had been since his last visit to 87th Street, asked after Ellery, complimented his old friend on his taste in cleaning women (Jessie, hurriedly taking her mops into the study at a glance from her confederate, felt a shiver wiggle up her spine), and did not get down to business until he was offered a drink.

"Thanks, Dick, but I'm on duty," Inspector Mackey said awkwardly.

The old man grinned. "I'll go quietly, Tom."

"Don't be a jerk. Look, Dick, you and I can talk frankly. We're up a tree on the Finner homicide. Just a big nothing. We've run down hundreds of leads, mostly from those files of his. His night-spot romances have pretty much washed out. There's something wrong. Not a whisper of anything has come in from the stools. Wherever we turn—in a case that should have been cracked in forty-eight hours—we run up against a blank wall. Dick, are you sure you told us the whole story a week ago Saturday?"

The Queen face got red. "That's a funny question to ask me, Tom."

His friend's face got red, too. "I know. I've been debating with myself all week should I come up here. The damn thing is, I got the queerest feeling that day that you were holding something back." He was miserable, but his glance did not waver. "Were you, Dick?"

"I'm not going to answer that, Tom!"

They stared at each other. For a moment the old man thought his equivocation had been unsuccessful. But Chief Deputy Inspector Mackey misread the emotion in his friend's voice.

"I don't blame you. It was a rotten question to ask a man who's given the best part of his life to the City of New York. Forget I ever asked it, Dick. And now, before I shove off, I think I'll take that hooker!"

When Inspector Mackey had left, Jessie came out of the study. She went over to Richard Queen, slumped in his big armchair, and put her hand on his shoulder.

"You couldn't do anything else, Richard."

"Jessie, I feel like a skunk." His hand crept up and tightened over hers. "And yet I can't turn this over to the Department. The minute I do I'm through with the case. It's our case, Jessie, yours and mine. Nobody else wanted it . . ."

"Yes, Richard," Jessie murmured.

They had had dinner and were in the living room watching television when the phone rang again. Jessie snapped off the set and glanced at her watch as the old man hurried into the study. It was almost 8:30.

"Inspector? Johnny Kripps."

"Johnny. Did Giffin turn up to help you take over from Angelo and Murphy?"

"Hughie's watching the front right now. I'm phoning from a drugstore on Broadway. She's back, Inspector."

"Ah," the old man said. "You're sure she's our gal, Johnny?"

"She pulled up in a cab full of luggage about ten minutes ago, alone. Her bags have the name Connie Coy on them. And Giffin overheard the night man in the lobby call her Mrs. Dimmesdale. What do we do?"

Richard Queen said quietly, "Keep your eyes open and stay under cover. I'm on my way."

They walked over; it was only a few blocks. The night was hot and humid, but Inspector Queen set a quick pace. There was no sign of George Weirhauser.

"I wonder why," Jessie panted. Her girdle was killing her, but she would have died rather than ask him to slow down.

"Either his job is done or our staying in all day's fooled him." He shrugged. "It doesn't matter."

The curbs on both sides of 88th Street were packed with cars. How he knew Jessie could not imagine, but he stopped suddenly near one of the parked cars to light a cigaret, and a man's voice from inside the car said, "Okay, Inspector."

"Where's Giffin staked out, Johnny?"

"Up there on the floor somewhere. If you don't want the lobby man to see you, there's a side service entrance. This side of the building. Delivery elevator is self-service."

"You're clairvoyant, Johnny."

Kripps laughed. Jessie wondered what he looked like.

The Inspector strolled her slowly toward a shadowed area near the service entrance. The entrance had a weak caged bulb over it. He stopped her in the shadow. A car was cruising by, and a portly man in a Hawaiian shirt was trudging toward them from West End Avenue followed by a woman who was walking as if her feet hurt. The woman was jabbering a steady stream; the man kept wading on, deaf. He turned into the apartment house entrance and the woman went in after him.

"Now, Jessie."

Jessie found herself stumbling down three steps into a sort of tunnel. Ahead was darkness. He took her hand and led the way, trailing his other hand along the inner wall.

"Here's the door."

They entered a cluttered, sour-smelling basement, dimly lit. There was a trash can in the elevator.

The elevator went up creaking and groaning. It seemed to Jessie it was making enough noise to be heard over on Broadway. But the old man merely watched the floors move by.

"Why are we sneaking in this way, Richard?"

"We're not exactly in a position to operate openly. What the lobby man can't see won't hurt us." He sounded grim.

The elevator stopped, swaying. He opened the door and they stepped into a dingy rear hall. He shut the elevator door noiselessly.

There were four apartment doors, lettered A, B, C and D. He went over to the fire stairway to look down into the well. Then he moved over to the stairs leading up, and peered. They were on the top floor. This flight undoubtedly led to the roof exit, but the whole upper part of the staircase was in darkness.

"Giffin?"

"Yeah, Inspector." The ex-detective's voice sounded a little surprised. "I thought with Kripps covering the street, I'd cover the back stairs."

"Okay."

He went to the door lettered C and put his forefinger on the bell button. C was one of the two rear apartments.

Jessie held her breath. Little Michael's mother at last . . .

A latch chain rattled. The door opened a couple of inches.

"Who is it?"

She had a deep, slightly hoarse voice. Jessie caught a glint of gold hair, a slash of lipstick.

"Miss Connie Coy?"

"Yes?"

Richard Queen held his shield-case up for her inspection. "May we come in?"

"Police?"

Just the merest tremble of fear, Jessie thought, in that sugared voice. One large hazel eye, heavily mascaraed, shot a glance in Jessie's direction.

"What do you want with me?" She made no move to open the door.

"Let us in, please, Miss Coy," he said quietly. "I don't think you want the neighbors in on this."

She undid the latch chain then, stepping back with the door fast.

Connie Coy was clutching a green terry cloth housecoat about her, glancing from Richard Queen to Jessie and back again. Jessie saw now that her gold hair had greenish roots and that the makeup did not entirely conceal tired, biting lines. She was wearing dark green sandals. Her toenails were painted gold.

The old man shut the door and hooked the chain back.

"Sorry to barge in on you this way, Miss Coy, but it couldn't be helped. I'm Inspector Queen, this is Miss Sherwood. Where can we talk?"

"But what's this all about?" She was openly frightened now.

"Is that your living room in there?"

He went swiftly through the neat little kitchen into a big studio room.

"Don't be afraid, Miss Coy," Jessie said in her soft voice.

The girl gave her a puzzled look. Then she laughed and poked at her hair. "I've never had a visit from the police before," she said. "Are you a policewoman?"

"I'm a trained nurse."

She seemed rooted to the floor. But then she said, "Won't you come in?" and stepped aside.

They went into the studio room. Richard Queen was in the bedroom, looking into the bathroom. Open suitcases were strewn about the bed and the floor. Evening gowns lay everywhere.

"What are you looking for, Inspector?" the girl asked nervously.

"Just making sure we're alone." He came back, frowning.

It was a gay room in a theatrical way. The furniture was nondescript modern, but the upholstery was brightly colored and there was a striking batik throw over the back of the sofa. An ivory-and-gilt Steinway stood to one side of a big studio window. She had thrown the window wide open to the humid night, and through it Jessie could see the starlit roofline of an apartment building on the other side of a narrow inner court, no more than twenty feet away. The window hangings were of dramatic red velvet. The walls were covered with inscribed theatrical photographs, mostly of jazz musicians, but there were several Degas reproductions of ballet dancers, an airy Dufy, and two small Japanese prints of subtle coloring that looked old. From an Egyptian copper vase on the mantelpiece over the false fireplace drooped some dead red roses. Half of one wall held floor-to-ceiling shelves crammed with books and recordings. There was a hi-fi player, a television set, a tiny bar.

"I'd offer you folks a drink," Connie Coy said with a strained smile, "but I'm out of everything and I only just got back tonight from out of town. Please sit down."

Jessie seated herself on the sofa near an iron-and-glass end table. A book lay open on the table. She wondered what it was.

The girl sat down in a wing chair, stiffly.

"Well?" she said. "I'm ready."

Inspector Queen went over to the fireplace, fingered a dry rose petal that lay on the brass knob of the andiron, suddenly whirled.

"Miss Coy, when did you see your baby last?"

The brutality of his question struck Jessie like a blow. She gave him an angry glance, but he was looking at the blonde girl. Jessie looked at her, too.

She was pale, but under control. She's been expecting it, Jessie thought. She took it better than I did.

"Baby? I don't know what you're talking about."

"Miss Coy." His voice was perfectly flat. "Seven or eight months ago you leased this apartment under the name of Mrs. Arthur Dimmesdale. There is no Arthur Dimmesdale. Some time between then and May of this year you were approached by a lawyer named Finner. You were pregnant, and he offered to see you through in safety to yourself providing you turned the baby over to him. He was in the adoption business, he told you, and he would see to it that your child was placed in a very good home with foster-parents who couldn't have children of their own and wanted to adopt one. All expenses would be paid; you would receive a large sum of money; Finner would take care of all the 'legal' details. You were desperate, and you agreed. Finner sent you to a reputable gynecologist who knew you only as 'Mrs. Willis P. Exeter,' a name Finner provided, and when your time came you entered the hospital Finner designated under that name. The date was May 26th. On May 27th you gave birth to a male child. He weighed six pounds thirteen ounces, was nineteen centimeters long, had blue eyes and blond hair. On June 3rd you and your baby were discharged from the hospital and you turned him over to Finner. He paid you the promised fee and took the baby away. Are you ready to answer my questions now?"

"I threw the money in his fat face!"

The girl was trembling violently. She buried her face in her hands and began to cry.

Jessie made an instinctive move toward her. But the Inspector shook his head emphatically, and she sank back.

"I'm sorry." The Coy girl stopped crying as suddenly as she had begun. "Yes, I was desperate, all right. That slug Finner hung around a club I was singing at. I don't know how he knew I was pregnant. I suppose one of the girls suspected and sold him the information. What do you want to know?"

"Was that morning—June 3rd—the last time you saw your baby?"

"Yes."

She was twisting her hands in her lap, biting her lip.

"Now tell me this. Where were you on the afternoon of August 20th? That would be Saturday a week ago."

"I was in Chicago," she said dully. "That's where I just got back from. I did a three-week singing engagement at the Club Intime."

"Do you remember what you were doing that Saturday afternoon?"

"Sure. I was working a TV show. The club press agent arranged it."

"You were in a TV studio in Chicago all afternoon?"

"All day. We went on the air at 4:30."

For the first time his face softened. "That's an alibi nobody can improve on. I'm glad for your sake."

The girl was staring at him. "What do you mean, Inspector? Alibi for what?"

"On Saturday mid-afternoon, August 20th, A. Burt Finner was murdered in his office on East 49th Street in New York."

"Finner . . . murdered?"

"Didn't you know that, Miss Coy?"

"No! Finner murdered . . . Who did it?"

"That," the old man said gently, "is why we're here."

"I see," she said. "You thought I murdered him . . . I hope you never get the one who did! She ought to get a medal. Maybe you didn't know Finner the way I got to. He was the lowest thing that crawled. He was a creep, a fat creep. This baby racket wasn't just business with him. He got kicks out of it. The filthy bastard."

He let the bitter voice run on. His silence finally stopped her.

"You're keeping something from me," she said slowly. "Does Finner's murder have something to do with my baby?"

"Miss Coy." He stopped. Then he said, "Miss Coy, don't you know about the baby, either?"

"Know? About my baby?" The girl clutched the arms of her chair. "Know what, Inspector?"

"Don't you know who bought your baby from Finner?"

"No. That was part of the deal. I had to sign all kinds of papers Finner pushed in front of me. Promise never to try to find out who the adopters were. Promise never to look for him." She jumped up. "You know who they are! Who are they? Tell me! Please?"

"A millionaire Massachusetts couple with a summer home in Connecticut and an apartment in New York. Mr. and Mrs. Alton K. Humffrey."

Her mascara had run, and she kept blinking at him, blinking as if she could not stop. Suddenly she went over to the end table and snatched a cigaret from an open box. Her gesture pushed the book lying there into Jessie's lap. The girl turned away, thumbing a table lighter savagely.

"Tell me more," she said. "These Humffreys. They bought my baby from Finner, and what happened? Because something happened, I know it. What was it, Inspector?"

He glanced at Jessie.

"Well, Miss Coy, I'll tell you—"

"I'll tell her, Richard." Jessie got up, holding the book, and went close to the girl. "Take a good drag, Miss Coy. This is going to be very hard. I was your baby's nurse in the Humffrey household. He's dead."

She touched the girl's shoulder.

Connie Coy turned around. Her lips were apart and the smoldering cigaret was dangling from her lower lip. Jessie took it from her mouth and put it in an ashtray.

"You may as well hear the rest of it," Richard Queen muttered. "Your baby was murdered."

"Murdered . . . ?"

Jessie lunged, and he bounced forward. But the girl pushed their arms blindly aside, went over to the wing chair, sat down on the edge with her hands clasped between her knees, staring.

Jessie hurried into the kitchen. She came back with a glass of water.

"Drink this."

Connie Coy sipped mechanically, still staring.

"No, that's enough. Murdered. When did it happen?"

"August 4th, a Thursday night," the old man said. "Over three weeks ago. Didn't you read about the death of a child named Michael Stiles Humffrey up on Nair Island in Connecticut? It was in all the papers."

"So that's the name they gave him. Michael. I always called him just Baby. In my thoughts, I mean. Michael . . ." She shook her head, as if the name meant nothing to her. "Papers? No, I guess I didn't. Thursday night, August 4th . . . I left for Chicago on the 5th. I was busy packing, I didn't get a paper that Friday. I didn't see a New York paper all the time I was away." She shook her head again, violently this time. "It's so confusing. You know? Getting hit this way . . . Murdered . . . All this time I've kept kidding myself it was for his good, the advantages he'd have, and never knowing he was illegitimate. How he'd grow up tall and happy and well adjusted, and . . . And he's murdered. At two months old." She laughed. "It's crazy, man, crazy."

She threw her head back and laughed and laughed. Jessie let her laugh it through. After a while the girl stopped laughing and said, "Can I have a cigaret?"

"I wish I had a good stiff drink to give you," Jessie said. She lit a cigaret and put it between the girl's lips. "How about some coffee?"

"No, thanks. I'm all right." She seemed completely composed, as if the laughter, the enormous hazel stare, had never happened. "Let's get this straight. A rich couple named Humffrey bought my baby from Finner. The baby was murdered. A couple of weeks later Finner was murdered. I don't see the connection."

"We don't know yet why the little tyke was murdered, Connie." The Inspector dragged a chair over to her and sat down eagerly. "But the way we see it, Finner got it because he was the only outsider who knew the baby's real parentage. A while ago you said you didn't know how Finner found out you were pregnant— you supposed one of the girls at the club you were singing in suspected and sold him the information. Did you have any real reason for believing that?"

"No," she said slowly. "I never let on to anybody, and it certainly didn't show at that time. But it's the only way I can imagine Finner got to know it."

"It isn't likely. But there's one way Finner could have found out that is likely. Connie, tell me: Did the man who got you pregnant know it?"

Her eyes flickered.

"Yes," she said. "I told him. He wanted me to go to some dirty abortionist. But I was afraid. So then he bowed out." She shrugged. "I didn't blame him. It was my own fault. I thought I loved him and found out I didn't when it was too late. I knew all the time he was married." Then she said, "Pardon me for going into my memoirs. You were saying?"

"Three people knew it," Richard Queen said. "You, the man, Finner. You didn't tell Finner. Then how did Finner find out? *The man must have told him.*"

"That's real touching," Connie Coy murmured. She got up and ground the cigaret out in the ash tray on the end table. She ground it hard. "Keep going, Inspector."

"So Finner knew the identity of both parents. If he was killed because he knew—" the old man rose, too—"then you're in danger, Connie."

"Me?" She swung about to face him, expressionless. "How do you figure that?"

"The only ones with reason to shut Finner's mouth for good about the child's parentage are the parents themselves. You're one of them, but you have a solid alibi for the day of Finner's murder. That leaves the other parent. It's my belief, Connie, that Finner was murdered by the baby's real father, and if that's so he may well come after you, too. With Finner dead, you're the only one left who can expose him. That's why I want you to tell us who the father is."

The blonde girl walked over to her grand piano. She ran her left hand soundlessly over the keys.

"Certainly you can't have any sentiment left about him." The Inspector spoke softly from the center of the room, above Jessie's head. "You say he's married. Am I right in supposing he's also somebody prominent—someone who might be ruined if a story like this came out? A certain type of man will run amok under a fear like that. Your protection is to share your information, Connie. The more people know who he is, the safer you are. He can't kill us all. Who is he? Tell us."

There was another cigaret box on the piano, and the girl took a cigaret from it and put it to her mouth. She looked around. He picked up the lighter from the end table and walked over to her.

"Tell us," he said again. He held the lighter up, but he did not finger the flint lever. She took the lighter from him and worked the lever herself.

"Arthur Dimmesdale," Jessie said from the sofa.

The flame remained an inch from the cigaret.

"What, Jessie?" Richard Queen said, puzzled.

The open book from the end table was still in Jessie's hand. She tapped it. "I thought it sounded familiar, Richard. Arthur Dimmesdale is the name of Hester Prynne's lover in Hawthorne's *Scarlet Letter*."

"Oh, that." Connie Coy laughed. "I picked the book up one day in a secondhand shop. I'd always meant to read it. And I'd just found out I was pregnant. *A* for *Adultery* . . . Hester's lover's name seemed like just the thing when I had to invent a husband. My mother always warned me my romantic streak would get me into trouble."

"Only a person who's married can commit adultery, Connie," Jessie said. "You're not the adulterer. He is. And now it seems he's a murderer, too. That's the thing to remember, isn't it?"

"So," Inspector Queen repeated, "who is he?"

"All right," the blonde girl said suddenly. "I'll tell you."

She brought the flame of the lighter to the tip of the cigaret.

The flame seemed to explode with a sharp crack, and a black hole appeared in the middle of her forehead.

Then the hole gushed red, and the lighter fell, and the cigaret fell, and the girl fell.

She fell sideways, glancing off the piano keys. She crashed to the floor before the brilliant clang of the keys stopped.

"Get down, Jessie!"

Jessie found herself in a crouch on the floor, with the sofa between her and the studio window. The old man was skittering like a crab toward the wall switch. Jessie heard two more explosions. Something shattered behind her.

The room plummeted into darkness.

He was pounding through the kitchen now. Undoing the latch chain.

The service door opened and closed. The sounds were definite but not loud Before the door closed she heard the voice of the ex-detective, Giffin. And soft running steps.

Then silence.

Jessie Sherwood sat up in the dark, rested her head against the sofa seat. Her ears were ringing and it bothered her.

She shut her eyes.

But even with her eyes shut she could see him.

He had shot a gun off from the roof of the house twenty feet on the other side of the court, through the open window. The flame of the lighter had made Connie Coy's blonde head a perfect target. A blurry-black figure against the glow of the city sky. As the girl fell. With a glinting something held in front of him. A figure vaguely male. Then she had tumbled off the sofa.

Amazing how quiet everything was.

Not really quiet. Just normal-quiet. As if there had been no man on the roof, no sharp crack, no hole in a human head. It wasn't quiet. TV sets were going all over the place. The court was full of them. Auto sounds from the streets. Buses going by on Broadway. Not the kind of sounds they would make if they knew a girl had been shot. Not the rasp of windows, cries, questions, doors, running.

Girl shot.

Jessie came alive.

The girl . . .

She crawled toward the window, reached up, got hold of the short end of the drape pull, and yanked. Before she climbed to her feet she felt for the drapes to make sure they were drawn.

She located the lamp on the piano, felt for the button, found it. The lamp remained dark. Why didn't it turn on? The wall switch. It controlled all the lights in the room.

She groped toward where Richard Queen had scuttled at the first shot. After a while she located the switch.

Connie Coy was lying between the Steinway and the pulled-out piano bench, on her back. Her robe had twisted open in her fall. She was wearing nothing underneath.

The blonde girl was staring intently at the ceiling, as if something were written there that she could not understand.

4 · Even in the Cannon's Mouth

"Don't touch anything, Jessie."

Jessie had not heard him come in. He was just inside the doorway from the kitchen, breathing in heaves, getting his breath. Perspiration was streaming down his cheeks.

"She's dead, Richard."

"I know."

He had a handkerchief on his right hand again. He went into Connie Coy's bedroom, wiped the knob of the bathroom door. He came back and went to the piano and picked up the fallen lighter and wiped it clean and put it back on the end table. He wiped the chair he had used. He glanced at the glass of water Jessie had brought the girl from the kitchen, then at Jessie's hands.

"You're still wearing your gloves. That's good." He went over to the sofa, picked up Jessie's purse, looked around the living room. "You've pulled the drapes." He did not sound angry. He said it like a man taking inventory. He came over to her and led her to the kitchen doorway. "Stay right here." He went to the wall switch and rubbed it with the handkerchief.

Then he flipped the switch.

The room got dark again.

She heard him making his way to the window. The drapes hissed open again.

"Let's go, Jessie." He was back by her side.

"No," Jessie said.

"What?" He sounded surprised, grabbed her arm.

"Just one more minute." She began to pull away.

He held on, pulling gently the other way. "You can't do anything for her, Jessie. Don't you understand that we've got to get out of here? Come on, now."

"I won't leave her exposed like that," Jessie said stubbornly. "It isn't fair. All I want to do is close her robe, Richard. Let me go."

But he did not. "We mustn't touch anything."

"All those men looking at her! A woman's nakedness is her own. It isn't fair."

"She's dead, Jessie."

The street was just the same. No, not quite. Kripps's car was gone. Where Richard Queen had paused to light a cigaret and talk to the retired policeman in the car there was space, signifying flight or chase.

Jessie walked stiff-legged, letting him lead her.

They walked over to Broadway, waited for the light, crossed to the east side, headed downtown.

Jessie kept moving one stiff leg after the other. Once in a while it would come to her that she was somebody named Jessie Sherwood, a registered nurse, and that behind her a blonde girl with her robe open to the navel lay under a grand piano and that none of it should be that way.

The old man did not speak to her. He was busy strolling along, her right arm tucked beneath his left, stopping for signals at corners, nudging her ahead, glancing into shop windows, pausing to light a cigaret, wipe his face, let the cigaret go out, pause to light it again. He lit a great many cigarets.

At 72nd Street he suddenly stepped up their tempo. He hurried her across the intersection, steered her briskly into a cafeteria. The cafeteria was crowded. He picked up a tray, two spoons, two paper napkins. He made her stand on line with him behind the railing. He put two cups of coffee on the tray. He had their tickets punched, paused to look around as if for a table. Then he took her over to where a pair of elderly men were sitting over cups of coffee, too. One had a scar on his face, the other wore heavy glasses. The other two chairs at the table were unoccupied; they were tilted against the third and fourth sides as if they were reserved.

Richard Queen set the tray down, pulled out one of the tilted chairs for her, seated himself in the other.

Only then did he say, "Giffin. Kripps. What happened?"

"We lost him, Inspector."

"You first, Giffin."

The elderly man with the scar stirred some sugar into his coffee, talking to the coffee as if it had ears. "I ducked out onto the roof and shot a flash across the court to the other side. Nobody. I beat it down the stairs into the basement and got over to the other street through the back court. Lots of people walking, kids horsing, plenty of traffic moving in both directions. Nobody running, nobody pulling away from the curb, nobody acting like anything had happened. And as far as I could see, not an empty parking space. I talked to the kids, but they hadn't noticed anybody come out of the house. I knew it was a waste of time, but I checked the stairs, elevators, basement, and roof over there. The roof is absolutely clean. The way I figure it, he cut across the roofs of several buildings and came out near the corner of West End—maybe had a getaway parked there. Anyway, it was a bust."

"You, Johnny?" Inspector Queen said.

The other elderly man looked like a teacher or a librarian, Jessie thought, with his black-rimmed glasses and distinguished white hair. "I drove around to 89th when you ran outside with the news, Inspector. By the time I got there it was either too early or too late, I didn't know which. I hung around for a few minutes with nothing to latch onto. Then a car pulled away from the curb fast, and I tailed it. It turned out to be some college kid late for a date."

"It's the legs," Giffin said gloomily to his coffee. "Let's face it, we're not as spry as we used to be."

"We needed more men is all." Johnny Kripps breathed on his glasses. "Hell, I'm not even packing a gun."

"Who was it?" Jessie thought. To her surprise, the thought was audible.

The men glanced at her curiously.

"Take it easy, Jessie," the old man said. "As a matter of fact, boys, I'm not getting you in any deeper." He sipped some coffee and looked at them. "I want you to go home and forget it."

They laughed. Giffin said, "We haven't met the lady, Inspector."

"I beg your pardon. Miss Sherwood, John Kripps, Hugh Giffin."

"How do you do," Jessie said. "He shot her between the eyes as if she were something in a shooting gallery. Then he fired two more shots. It couldn't have been at her, she was flat on the floor. He shot at us, Richard."

"I know, Jessie," he said gently. His hand came to her under the table. "I want you boys to go home, and one of you phone Pete Angelo and Al Murphy and tell them to forget it, too."

"How about a little something to go with that coffee, Miss Sherwood?" Hugh Giffin asked.

"Maybe a nice cheese Danish?" Johnny Kripps said. "They're tops in here."

"About this deal," the Inspector said insistently. "I appreciate your attitude, boys. But this is murder. I can't let you endanger your pensions, maybe wind up in jail. Jessie and I," his hand tightened, "we're in so far now we couldn't get out if we wanted to. But you—"

"You're wasting your breath," Kripps said. "I'm talking for Pete and Murph, too. Who takes care of the call-in?"

"I will!" the old man said.

"The hell you will," Giffin said hotly. "Your voice is too well known, Inspector. Johnny or I'll do it."

"Call-in?" Jessie said.

"Notifying the police, Miss Sherwood," the ex-homicide man explained. He *did* look like a scholar. "We can't let her lie on that floor till the super's nose brings him up there."

"An anonymous call?" Jessie said.

The three men flushed and picked up their cups.

Jessie picked up her cup, too. She remembered now that she hadn't touched it.

He took the key from her cold fingers. He unlocked the apartment door and shoved it open and reached for the switch and ducked all in one movement. Then he stood there looking. After a moment he went into Jessie's bedroom.

He came back.

"All right."

He shut the apartment door and latched it.

"Why am I so cold?" Jessie shivered. "Did the temperature drop?"

He felt her forehead, her hand.

"It's the nervous reaction," Richard Queen said. "I used to break out in a sweat afterward, even in the dead of winter. You're going to bed, young woman."

"I'm not a young woman," Jessie said, standing there trying to keep her teeth from clacking. "I'm an old woman and I'm scared."

"I could kick myself for letting you in for this." He took her purse and gloves, clumsily removed her hat. "I'd send you back to Connecticut tomorrow—"

"I won't go."

"—only I want you where I can keep an eye on you. For all he knows, she told us his name."

"He shot at us," Jessie said. "A bullet hit something behind me and broke it. He doesn't take chances, does he?"

"He's taking all kinds of chances," the old man said gently. "But we'll talk about it tomorrow. You go in there and get undressed. Do you have any phenobarb?"

"What are you going to do, Richard?" Now her teeth *were* clacking.

"Stay over."

She knew she should protest, send him home, or at least make up the daybed for him in the living room. But the connection between her larynx and her will seemed broken. On the edge of things lay the body of Connie Coy with the spattery hole in her forehead and the greenish roots of her gold hair slowly dyeing red. But the core of herself felt a great warmth. As long as he was here nothing like that hole and that bloody dye could happen to *her*. All she had to do was drift . . . let go . . . Goodness, Jessie thought dreamily, I'm getting to be a female woman.

"Can you make it by yourself all right?" he asked anxiously.

"Why do you ask?" Jessie giggled at the consternation that flooded his face. He was so easy to tease . . .

Later, when she was in bed, he knocked and she said, "Come in," and he came in with a cup of warm milk and a sleeping tablet.

"Take this."

"Yes, sir," Jessie said obediently.

It was hard lifting her head from the pillow. He hesitated, then slipped his arm around her shoulders and sat her up. The coverlet dropped away and Jessie thought, Now, Jessie! But she really didn't have the strength to pull it back up . . . And me in my most décolleté nightgown. How shameless can you get? He'll think I purposely . . .

Jessie drank the milk very slowly.

"It's hot."

"I'm sorry. Take your time." His voice sounded funny.

When she sank back he removed his arm as if it hurt.

"Thank you, Richard." Is this really *me?* Jessie thought.

"Feeling better?" He was addressing the badly reproduced Van Gogh still-life over Gloria Sardella's bed.

"Worlds."

But it's so nice . . . Jessie slipped under the covers, giggling again.

He went over to the window and looked out. The fire escape seemed to disturb him. He pulled the window down and locked it, lowered the Venetian blind, closed the vanes. Then he went into the bathroom.

One second her forehead was smooth and white, the next it had a hole in it, a real hole, black and then red . . .

"I've opened the bathroom window, Jessie. I'll leave the door to the living room open for circulation. Unless light bothers you?"

"Just don't go away." She began to shiver again.

"I won't. Remember, I'll be in the next room. At anything—for any reason—sing out."

"Yes . . . The linen's in that closet next to the kitchenette. Richard, she's dead."

"Go to sleep now, Jessie."

"I don't know what's the matter with me. I don't seem to have any strength at all."

"It's been a rough night. If you're not better in the morning I'll call a doctor."

"Oh, no . . ."

"Oh, yes."

The light snapped off, but she could not hear him move.

"Good night," Jessie said drowsily.

"Sleep well, Jessie."

He went out then, in a sort of stumble.

He *didn't* look at me as if I were just any woman. He looked at me as if . . .

The last thing Jessie heard as she fell asleep was the scream of police sirens heading uptown.

The voice of Abe Pearl at the other end of the wire was so loud the old man glanced over at the bedroom doorway.

"Stop bellowing, Abe," he grumbled. "I'm not deaf yet."

"Where in the name of God have you been?" Chief Pearl demanded angrily. "I've been trying to reach you all night. Where you calling from?"

"Jessie Sherwood's place in New York."

"Look, Dick, if you want to shack up, shack up, but the least you can do is leave me her phone number so I can contact you. I didn't start this, you did!"

"You cut that out, Abe," Richard Queen growled. "I'm not shacked up with anybody—"

"Okay, so she's playing hard to get—Becky, will you shut up! . . . Can you give me five minutes?"

"Go ahead," he said shortly.

"I got a call tonight from New Haven, from this Dr. Duane. He's been phoning all over creation trying to reach Humffrey again. He finally contacted me out of desperation, wanted me to run over to Nair Island and see if maybe Humffrey hadn't gone back there—he'd tried to reach Stallings, but there was no answer. I've found out that Stallings had gone to a movie; anyway, he hadn't seen or heard from Humffrey. The point is, Mrs. Humffrey is bad again, and it sounded to me like Duane's got hold of a hot knish and would like to let go. You don't know where Humffrey is, Dick, do you? I thought I'd check with you before calling Duane back."

"I haven't seen Humffrey, no," Richard Queen said slowly. "Abe."

"Yes?"

"What time did Humffrey leave his Park Avenue apartment today? Did Duane talk to Mrs. Lenihan?"

"She told him he'd left early this morning and didn't say where he was going. At the time Duane called me, which was about nine tonight, Humffrey still hadn't got back."

"Did Cullum chauffeur him? Or did Humffrey leave alone?"

"I don't know." Abe Pearl paused. "Dick, what's happened? Something happened tonight."

"Connie Coy's been knocked off."

"The *mother?*"

When Abe Pearl heard the story, he said, "One minute, Dick. Just hang on." The silence was prolonged. "I'm trying to piece this together—"

"It's complicated," Richard Queen said dryly.

"Dick. Why did you ask me what time Humffrey left his New York apartment today?" He said, "Dick? You there?"

"I'm here." The old man said rapidly, "Abe, doesn't it strike you as queer that the day Finner is murdered Humffrey's movements can't be accounted for, and the night Connie Coy gets it—ditto?"

Abe Pearl said, *"What?"*

"You heard me."

His friend was silent.

Then he said, "You're crazy! There might be a dozen explanations—"

"Sure."

"It's just a coincidence—"

"I can't prove it isn't."

"The whole idea is ridiculous. Why . . ." Abe Pearl paused. "You're not serious."

The old man said, "Oh, yes, I am."

Silence again.

"How long has this bee been buzzing around in your bonnet?" the Taugus chief finally demanded.

Inspectcr Queen did not answer.

"Don't you see you've got nothing to back it up? So Humffrey couldn't be located around the time of either murder. So what? Maybe now that his wife is tucked away in New Haven, he's picked himself up some tasty blonde—"

"Now?" The old man sounded grim. "That could have happened a year ago."

"Dick, you're off your trolley. Alton Humffrey? You have to be human to start chick-chasing. Even if Humffrey had the yen, he wouldn't put himself in such a position. He thinks too damn much of himself and his precious name."

"Be consistent, Abe. One minute you're saying Humffrey might be having an affair with some woman to account for his absences, but when I suggest the woman was Connie Coy and he had the affair with her last year you start telling me he isn't the type. Sure he's the type. Under given circumstances, any man's the type. And especially the Humffreys of this world."

"Humffrey . . ." He could almost see Abe Pearl shaking his head.

"I admit it's mostly hunch. But there isn't much else to go by, Abe. Up to now it's been one stymie after another. First the nephew, Frost, comes up with an airtight alibi for the baby's murder. Then the killer lifts the Hummfrey folder from Finner's files and chokes off the obvious lead to the child's mother. When we finally get to the Coy woman by a roundabout route and she's about to come through with the baby's father's name, she stops a bullet between the eyes. I can't wait for the next stymie, Abe. I've got to take the initiative."

"You're heading for big trouble," Chief Pearl said in a mutter. "You can't go after a man like Humffrey with a popgun."

"I don't intend to. I won't move in till I have some man-sized ammunition. And I think I know where I can get some."

"Where?"

"I'll let you know when I get it. Give my love to Becky, will you?"

After he hung up, the old man sank into a chair, scowling.

A long time later he reached for the Manhattan classified directory and began hunting for an address under *Detective Service*.

The gray-skinned man got off the elevator and walked erratically up the hall reading page three of the *Daily News*. He seemed fascinated and slightly sick. He was a big man of about forty in a slim-drape lounge suit and a hat with a Tyrolean feather. The gray skin was drawn angularly over his face bones in flat planes and straight lines. He looked like a cartoon.

He stopped before a pebbled glass door and fumbled in his pants pocket for a keycase without taking his eyes from the newspaper. The door said:

G. W. DETECTIVE AGENCY
Civil—Criminal—Personal
DOMESTIC TROUBLES OUR SPECIALTY
Complete Photographic Service
WALK IN

He unlocked the door and stepped into the ante-room, still reading. The typewriter on the receptionist's desk was in a shroud. There was no window in the room.

His left hand groped near the door, located the light switch, snapped it on. Absorbed in his morning paper, he walked on through, into the inner office, over to the window. He pulled up the blind, sank into the chair behind the desk. As he continued to read he tilted back, nibbling his lip.

"Interesting story?"

The gray-faced man looked up quickly.

Richard Queen was seated in a chair behind the partition wall of the anteroom.

"I said that's an interesting story about that girl's murder last night," he said. "From the way you're reading it, Weirhauser, you agree with me."

The private detective put the newspaper down on his desk carefully.

"Am I supposed to know you, pop?" He had a rough, nasty voice. "Or is this a stickup?"

"Come, come, George, cut the clowning," the old man said mildly. "I thought we could talk before your girl got here, and I didn't feel like waiting in the hall." He rose, put his hat on the chair, and walked over to the desk. "I want some information from you. Who hired you to tail me?"

The investigator looked blank. "Am I supposed to be tailing you?"

"You were pulled off the job Sunday, whether temporarily or permanently I don't know." The Inspector's tone was patient. "I asked you a question."

"See that word *Private?*" Weirhauser said. "Get going."

"You haven't changed a bit, Weirhauser. Still doing a take off on George Raft." The Inspector laughed.

Weirhauser got up. "You going to get out, or do I have to heave you out?"

The old man stared at him. "Don't you realize what you've stepped into? Or are you even stupider than you act?"

The gray was taking on a brick color. Weirhauser set his knuckles on the desk. "Who the hell do you think you're talking to?"

Inspector Queen glanced at his watch. "I don't have any time to waste, Weirhauser. Let's have it."

"You talk like you're somebody." The man's tone was jeering, but there was an uncertain note in it.

"You know who I am."

"I know who you were. The trouble with you has-beens is you don't know enough to lay down and roll over. You're not Inspector Queen any more, remember?"

"Hand me that phone."

Weirhauser's color changed back to its normal gray. "What are you going to do?"

"Call Headquarters and show you whether I'm a has-been or not."

"Wait."

"Well?"

The investigator said, "You know I can't give out that kind of information, Inspector." He was trying to sound rueful and put-upon. "Agency work is confidential—"

"You should have stuck to chasing dirty divorce evidence." The old man looked amused. "How do you like being mixed up in a murder? You didn't bargain for that, did you?"

Weirhauser said quickly, "Who's mixed up in a murder? I took a tailing job. I was told to tail you and the woman and to report your movements to my client and I did and that's all."

"You tailed me from hospital to hospital, you tailed me to an apartment house on 88th near West End, you found out I was asking for a girl named Connie Coy and that she was expected back from out of town shortly, and you reported that to your client Sunday evening. This morning, Tuesday, you open your paper and find that a girl named Connie Coy got back from Chicago last night and within the hour was shot to death through her window from a nearby roof. And you say you're not mixed up in it, Weirhauser? You walked in here this morning trying to remember your prayers."

"Look, Inspector," Weirhauser began.

"Suppose we go downtown and tell one of the brass that you, George Weirhauser, holding a license to conduct private investigations, fingered Connie Coy for a client you refuse to name? How long do you think you'd hold your license? In fact, how long do you think it would be before you began yelping for a bail bondsman?"

"Look," Weirhauser said again, licking his lips. "You're way off base on this thing, Inspector. My client couldn't have had anything to do with this—"

"How do you know he couldn't?"

"Well, he's . . ."

"He's what? All right, maybe he didn't have anything to do with it. Do you know where he was all day yesterday, Weirhauser? Can you alibi him for the time of the girl's murder?"

The private detective shouted, "I didn't go near the guy yesterday! Didn't even talk to him on the phone. He told me Sunday night when I spoke to him that he'd changed his mind, the information I had for him wasn't what he was after at all, he was calling the whole thing off. That's all I know."

The Inspector shook his head. "Try again, Weirhauser."

"What d'ye mean? I tell you that's all I know!"

"You've left one thing out."

"What's that?"

"The name of your client."

Weirhauser got up and went to the window, fingering his lip. When he came back and sat down again his sharp eyes were sly.

"What side of the street you working in this deal . . . Inspector?"

"That," the old man snapped, "is none of your business."

"It just occurred to me." The investigator grinned. "You might be in this up to your eyeballs yourself—you and this dame."

"I am."

"You are?" The man looked surprised.

"Sure," the old man said. "I'm after your client, and I'm going to get him. And the less you know about it, Weirhauser, the longer you'll sleep in your own bed. I've thrown away enough time on you. Who is he?"

"Okay, okay, but give me a break, will you? Honest to God, if I'd known this was going to wind up in a homicide, I'd have spit on his retainer and run like hell."

"Who is he?" the old man repeated. His eyes were glittering.

"It's understood you'll keep me out of this?"

"Personally, I don't give a damn about you. As far as I'm concerned you're out of it right now. Who is he, Weirhauser?"

Weirhauser got up again and shut the door to the anteroom.

"Well, he's a rich muckamuck, lives on Park Avenue—" Even now the gray-faced man sounded grudging, as if he were being forced to sell a gilt-edged security far below its market value.

"His name!"
Weirhauser cursed. "Alton K. Humffrey."

"Are you all right, Jessie?"
Jessie said, "I'm fine."
They were in the tall-ceilinged foyer outside the Humffrey apartment on Park
Avenue. The wall opposite the elevator was an austere greenish ivory, with plaster
panel-work of cupids and wreaths. The elevator had just left them, noiselessly.
"Don't be afraid," Richard Queen said. "This is the one place where he won't
try anything. I wouldn't have asked you along if I thought there was any danger."
"I'm not afraid." Jessie smiled faintly. "I'm numb."
"Would you rather sit this out?"
"I'm fine," Jessie said again.
"We've got to move in on him, Jessie. See just how tough a nut he's going to
be. So far he's had it all his own way. You see that, don't you?"
"I suppose the trouble is I don't really believe it." Jessie set her lips to keep
them from quivering. "I want to look at his face—really look at it. Murder must
leave a mark of some kind."
The Inspector blotted the perspiration from his neck and pressed the apartment
bell. He had given their names to the flunkey in the lobby with a confidence Jessie
could only admire. There had been no unpleasantness. Mr. Humffrey had said on
the house phone yes, he would see them. In a few minutes. He would call down
when they might be sent up.
It was Friday evening, the second of September, a sizzling forerunner of the
Labor Day weekend. The city had been emptying all day, leaving a sort of tautness
in the vacuum.
Like me, Jessie thought.
It had been a curious three days since Richard Queen came back from George
Weirhauser's office. He had summoned his aging assistants that evening to a council
of war. It was surely the strangest conference, Jessie thought, in the unlikeliest
place . . . a gathering of old men on a bench in a secluded spot in Central Park.
The handsome ex-Lieutenant of Homicide, Johnny Kripps, had been there; the scar-
faced Hugh Giffin; ex-Sergeant Al Murphy of the 16th, chunky, brick-skinned,
with all his red hair, the youngest of the group; big Wes Polonsky, of the shaking
hands; and Polonsky's old partner, Pete Angelo, a slim tough dark man whose face
was a crisscross of wrinkles, like a detail map of his seventy years.
They had listened in happy silence as Richard Queen spoke, lonely men being
handed straws and grasping them thankfully. And when they had walked off into
the night, one by one, each with his assignment, Jessie had remarked, "I feel sorry
for him in a way."
"For whom, Jessie?"
"Alton Humffrey."
"Don't waste your sympathy," the old man had muttered. "We've got a long
way to go."
"Good evening," the millionaire said.
He had opened the door himself. He stood there sharp and shoulderless in a satin-
faced smoking jacket, at disciplined ease, the chill Brahmin with nothing on his
wedge of face but remoteness—like a high Army officer in mufti or a Back Bay
man of distinction—framed in a rectangle of rich wines and hunt-club greens and
leather browns; and Jessie thought, No, it isn't possible.
"You're looking well, Miss Sherwood."

"Thank you."

"I'm not sure I can say the same about you, Mr. Queen. Won't you come in? Sorry the servants aren't here to greet you. Unfortunately, I gave them the evening off."

"Within the last fifteen minutes?" Richard Queen said.

Alton Humffrey shook his head, smiling. "You're an extremely suspicious man."

"Yes," the old man said grimly, "I suppose you could say that."

The apartment was like a strange land, all mysterious woods and coruscating chandeliers, antiques, crystal, oil paintings, old tapestries, glowing rugs—rooms twice as large as any Jessie had ever set foot in, with no cushion crushed, no rug scuffed, no receptacle with a crumb of ashes. The study was like the drawing room, indigestibly rich, with monumental furnishings and impossibly tall walls of books that looked as if they were going to topple over.

"Please sit down, Miss Sherwood," Humffrey said. "May I give you some sherry?"

"No, thanks." The thought was nauseating. "How is Mrs. Humffrey?"

"Not too well, I'm sorry to say. Mr. Queen, whisky?"

"Nothing, thanks."

"Won't you have a seat?"

"No."

"Forbidding," the millionaire said with a slight smile. "Sounds like an inspector of police."

Richard Queen did not change expression. "May I begin?"

"By all means." Humffrey seated himself in the baronial oak chair behind his desk, a massive handcarved piece. "Oh, one thing." His bulbous eyes turned on Jessie, and she saw now that they were cushioned by welts she had not noticed on Nair Island. "I take it, Miss Sherwood, from your being here tonight with Mr. Queen, that you're still pursuing your delusion about poor Michael's death?"

"I still believe he was murdered, yes." Jessie's voice sounded too loud to her ears.

"Well, at least let me thank you for pursuing it so discreetly."

"Are you through?" the old man asked.

"Forgive me, Mr. Queen." The millionaire leaned back attentively. "You were about to say?"

"On the 20th of this month," the inspector began, "a shyster lawyer named Finner was murdered in his office on East 49th Street."

"Oh, yes."

"Finner, of course, was the man who turned the baby over to you back in June."

"He was?"

"Come, Mr. Humffrey, you're hardly in a position to deny it. Jessie Sherwood went along with you and Mrs. Humffrey to take charge of the child. She saw Finner at that time. So did your chauffeur, Cullum."

"I did not deny it, Mr. Queen," Humffrey smiled. "I was merely making some appropriate sounds."

"On Thursday the 18th, possibly the next day, Finner got in touch with you, told you I was putting pressure on him, and asked you to be present at a meeting in his office with me and Miss Sherwood on Saturday the 20th, at 4 P.M. You agreed to come."

"Now you've moved from the terra firma of fact," Humffrey said, "into the cuckooland of speculation. Of course I can't permit unfounded allegations to pass unchallenged. Pardon me for interrupting, Mr. Queen."

"You deny those allegations?"

"I will not dignify them by a denial. In view of your failure to mention the slightest corroboration, none is necessary. Go on."

"You agreed to be there," Richard Queen continued, unmoved. "But you had a little surprise up your sleeve for Finner, Mr. Humffrey. And, I might add, for us. You went to Finner's office that Saturday afternoon, all right, but not at four o'clock. You got there about an hour and a half early—from the contents of Finner's stomach, according to accounts of the autopsy findings, it must have been right after Finner came up from his lunch. You picked up Finner's letter-knife from his desk and buried it in his heart. Then you rifled his files for the folder marked 'Humffrey' that contained the papers and proofs of the baby's parentage, and out you walked with it. By this time, of course, you've destroyed it."

Jessie was watching Alton Humffrey's face, fascinated. There was no twitch or flicker to indicate that the millionaire was indignant, alarmed, or even more than mildly interested.

"I can only ascribe this extraordinary fantasy to a senile imagination," Humffrey said. "Are you accusing me—in all seriousness—of murdering this man Finner?"

"Yes."

"You realize, of course, that without proof of any sort—an eyewitness, let us say, a fingerprint, something drearily unfantastic like that—you're exposing yourself to a suit for criminal slander, defamation of character, and probably half a dozen other charges my attorneys will think of?"

"I'm relying on your well-known dislike for publicity to restrain them, Mr. Humffrey," the old man said dryly. "May I proceed?"

"My dear man! Is there more?"

"Lots more."

Humffrey waved his long white hand with its curling fingers as if he were bestowing a benediction.

"On the following Monday morning," Richard Queen went on, "you walked into a Times Square detective agency run by a fellow named Weirhauser and hired him to shadow Miss Sherwood and me. Weirhauser reported to you that we were visiting the maternity sections of one metropolitan hospital after another, trying to match up a set of infant footprints with the hospital birth records. This went on for about a week."

"I see," Humffrey said.

"Last Sunday evening, Weirhauser reported to you that we had presumably found what we'd been looking for. Our hospital find had taken us to an apartment house on West 88th Street, where we asked a lot of questions about a tenant named Connie Coy. Connie Coy, Mr. Humffrey."

"You pause significantly. Is the name supposed to mean something to me?" the millionaire asked.

"Weirhauser told you that Connie Coy was out of town filling a singing engagement in a Chicago nightclub, but that she was expected back soon. You then gave Weirhauser a clumsy story about being on the wrong tack and called him off the job."

Suddenly the room turned stifling. Jessie sat very still.

"And for this allegation, Mr. Queen, you're also drawing on your imagination?"

"No," the old man said, smiling for the first time. "For this one, Mr. Humffrey, I have an affidavit sworn to and signed by George Weirhauser. Would you care to see it? I have it right here in my pocket."

"I'm tempted to say no," Humffrey mumured. "But as a man who has played poker with Harvard undergraduates in his day—yes, I think I would care to see it."

Inspector Queen took a folded paper from his pocket and laid it defenselessly on the desk. Jessie almost cried out. But the millionaire merely reached for it, unfolded it, read it through, and politely handed it back.

"Of course, I don't know this man Weirhauser's signature from yours, Mr. Queen," he said, clasping his bony hands behind his head, "But even if this is a legitimate affidavit, I fancy Weirhauser hasn't too sweet a reputation, and if it became a matter of his word against mine—"

"Then you're denying this, too?"

"As among the three of us here," and Humffrey smiled coldly, "I see no harm in admitting that yes, I engaged a detective to follow you and Miss Sherwood last week, simply to see what mischief you were up to. I'd gathered from what Miss Sherwood let drop that you and she were bent on following up her hysterical belief that the baby was murdered; and I felt—in my wife's protection, if not in mine— that I was justified in keeping myself informed. When my man's report indicated that you were chasing some will-o'-the-wisp involving a woman I'd never heard of, I of course lost interest. My only regret is that in hiring Weirhauser I seem to have made a mistake. I detest mistakes, Mr. Queen, particularly my own."

"Then your position is that you never knew Connie Coy, the nightclub singer?"

"Yes, Mr. Queen," the millionaire said gently, "that is my position."

"Then I can't understand your activities the day after you fired Weirhauser. Last Sunday night Weirhauser told you we were asking questions about the Coy girl and that she was expected back soon from Chicago. The next day—this past Monday, Mr. Humffrey—*you spent the entire day and a good deal of the evening at Grand Central Terminal watching the arrival of trains from Chicago.* Why would you have done that if you didn't know Connie Coy and had no interest in her?"

Humffrey was silent. For the first time a slight frown drew his brows toward each other. Then he said, "I think I'm beginning to be bored with this conversation, Mr. Queen. Of course I was not in Grand Central Terminal that day, to watch the Chicago trains or for any other absurd purpose."

"That's funny," the old man retorted. "A red-cap and a clerk at one of the newsstands have identified a Stamford, Connecticut news photo of you as that of a man they saw hanging around the Chicago incoming train gates at Grand Central all day."

The millionaire stared at him.

Richard Queen stared back.

"Now you annoy me, Mr. Queen," Humffrey said icily. "Your so-called identifications don't impress me at all. You must know, from your days as a competent police officer, how unsatisfactory such identifications are. I must really ask you to excuse me."

He rose.

"Just when I was getting to the most interesting part, Mr. Humffrey?"

The old man's grin apparently changed Humffrey's mind. He sat down again.

"Very well," he said. "What else have you dreamed up?"

"The Coy girl got in at Grand Central that evening. She took a taxi uptown, and you followed her to 88th Street."

"And you have a witness to that?"

"No."

"My dear Queen."

"At least not yet, Mr. Humffrey."

Humffrey settled back. "I suppose I should hear this fairy tale out."

"You followed Connie Coy home, you took up a position on a roof overlooking her top-floor apartment, and when you saw me pumping her you aimed at a point midway between her eyes with a gun you were carrying, and you shot her dead.

"Don't interrupt me now," the old man said softly. "Finner was killed because he had the file on the case and knew who the baby's parents were. Connie Coy was killed because, as the mother of the baby, she certainly knew the identity of its father. The only one who benefits by destroying those papers and shutting Finner's and the real mother's mouth, Mr. Humffrey, is the baby's real father.

"You've committed two cold-blooded murders to keep your wife, her relatives, your blue-nosed friends, me, Jessie Sherwood, from finding out that you'd adopted not a stranger's child, but *a child you yourself fathered in a cheap affair with a nightclub entertainer.*"

Humffrey opened a side drawer of his desk.

Jessie's heart gave a wicked jump.

As for the old man, his hand flashed up to hover over the middle button of his jacket.

But when the millionaire leaned back, Jessie saw that he had merely reached for a box of cigars.

"Do you mind, Miss Sherwood? I rarely smoke—only, in fact, when I'm in danger of losing my temper." He lit a cigar with a platinum desk lighter and looked at Richard Queen with a mineral brightness. "This has gone beyond simple senility, Mr. Queen. You're a dangerous lunatic. You claim that I not only committed two atrocious murders, but that I did so in order to conceal from the world that I was the blood-father of the unfortunate little boy I adopted. I can't imagine your laying any other heinous crimes at my door, but from the beginning you and Miss Sherwood have insisted Michael was murdered. How does your diseased mind reconcile his alleged murder with my subsequent crimes? Did I murder my own child, too?"

"I think you got the idea when your nephew made that drunken, senseless attempt to break into the baby's nursery the night of July 4th," the Inspector said quietly. "What you couldn't have known, of course, was that Frost would suffer an appendix attack and have to have an emergency operation—an ironbound alibi—for the very night *you* picked. I think you murdered Michael, Mr. Humffrey, yes. I think you selected a night when you knew Miss Sherwood would be off. I think that after your wife fell asleep you deliberately suffocated the baby, and that in the confusion after Miss Sherwood's arrival to find the baby dead you noticed the pillowslip in the crib with its telltale handprint that indicated murder, and disposed of it. And from that moment on, of course, you kept insisting that Jessie Sherwood had been seeing things and that the baby's death was an unfortunate nursery accident. Yes, Mr. Humffrey, that's exactly what I think."

"Making me out a monster with few precedents." Humffrey's nasal tones crackled. "Because only a monster murders his own flesh and blood—eh, Mr. Queen?"

"If he does it believing it *is* his own flesh and blood."

"I beg your pardon?" The millionaire sounded amazed.

"When you found out that Connie Coy was pregnant and arranged through Finner to adopt the baby without her knowledge when it was born, Mr. Humffrey, you did it because you wanted possession of your own child. But suppose after you

arranged for the secret purchase of your baby, with a forged birth certificate, with
Finner paid off, with Connie Coy not knowing you had the baby and your wife not
knowing the baby was yours—suppose after all this, Mr. Humffrey, you suddenly
began to suspect you'd been made a fool of? That you'd gone to all that trouble
and skulduggery to pass your name on to a baby that wasn't yours at all!''

Humffrey was quite still.

''A woman who'd had an affair with one man might have had affairs with a
dozen, you told yourself. Suppose you even checked back and found that the Coy
girl had been sleeping around with other men at the same time you were her lover?
You being what you are—a proud, arrogant man with an exaggerated sense of
family and social position—your love for the child you'd thought was yours might
well have turned to hate. And so one night you murdered him.''

The cigar had gone out. Humffrey was very pale.

''Get out,'' he said thickly. ''No, wait. Perhaps you'll be good enough to spell
out for me just what further incredible flights of your fancy, Mr. Queen, I must
protect myself against. According to you, I fathered that child in a sordid affair, I
murdered the child, I murdered Finner, I murdered the child's mother. Against
these insanities you have abducted just two alleged pieces of evidence—that I hired
a private detective to follow you two for a week, which I have explained, and that
I was seen in Grand Central Terminal last Monday watching for Chicago trains,
which I deny. What else have you?''

''You were in the Nair Island house on the night of the baby's murder.''

''I was in the Nair Island house on the night of the baby's accidental death,''
the millionaire said coolly. ''A coroner's jury supports my version of the slight
difference in our phraseology. What else?''

''You had the strongest motive of anyone in the world to remove the folder
marked 'Humffrey' from Finner's filing cabinet and destroy it.''

''I cannot grant even the existence of such a folder,'' Humffrey smiled. ''Can
you prove it? What else?''

''You have no alibi for the afternoon of Finner's murder.''

''You state an assumption as a fact. But even if your assumption were a fact—
neither have ten thousand other men. What else, Mr. Queen?''

''You have no alibi for the evening of Connie Coy's murder.''

''I can only repeat my previous comment. Anything else?''

''Well, we're working on you,'' the old man drawled. ''A whole group of us.''

''A whole group?'' Humffrey pushed his chair back.

''Oh, yes. I've recruited a force of men like myself, Mr. Humffrey, retired police
officers who've become very interested in this case. So, you see, it wouldn't do
you the least good to kill Miss Sherwood and me, as you tried to do Monday night.
Those men know the whole story . . . *and you don't know who they are.* Come,
Jessie.''

All Jessie could think of was that her back was to him; she could almost hear
the blast of doom exploding behind her as she went to the door. But nothing
happened. Alton Humffrey simply sat in the baronial chair at his desk, thinking.

''One moment.'' The millionaire came slowly around the desk toward them.

Richard Queen moved over to block the doorway. Humffrey stopped a few feet
away, so close Jessie could smell the after-shave lotion on his gaunt cheeks.

''After reflection, Mr. Queen,'' he said good-humoredly, ''I must conclude that
you and your aging cronies have exactly nothing.''

''Then you've got exactly nothing to worry about, Mr. Humffrey.''

''We're in a sort of stalemate, aren't we? I won't go to the police to make you stop annoying me, because I prefer being annoyed in private rather than in public. You won't go to the police with your fantastic story, because your activities could land you in jail. It looks as if you and I are going to have to grin and bear each other. By the way, that is a gun you're carrying under your left armpit, isn't it?''

"Yes," the old man said, showing his denture for a moment. "And I imagine you have a permit for the gun you decided not to take out of that drawer a few minutes ago."

"Now your imagination is back within bounds, Mr. Queen," the millionaire smiled.

"He pointed a gun at me once, Richard," Jessie said in a piping voice. "The night I came back from New York to find the baby dead. Even after I identified myself he kept pointing it at me. For a minute I thought he was going to shoot me."

"Perhaps I should have." With those eyes turned on her, Jessie felt absurdly like running. Something womanish insinuated itself into Humffrey's voice, taunting and cruel. "I've given you considerable thought, Miss Sherwood. But now I've solved you. You're that most dismal of people, her brother's keeper. Good night."

Late that night Richard Queen snapped to the five silent old men, "It's going to be rough. He's an ice-cold customer, and smart. He's not going to be stampeded into anything stupid. As I said the other night, our best bet is to go backwards. We've got to tie him in with the Coy girl. They must have had a love nest somewhere before he dropped her and she moved to 88th Street. Maybe there's a record of his having paid her rent or hospital bills. We've got to find witnesses who saw them together—in restaurants, nightclubs, hideaways, rooming houses, motels . . ."

He talked until two in the morning to the attentive men. Jessie fell asleep on his shoulder. He did not disturb her.

New York came back from its holiday weekend. Autumn set in suddenly. Children prepared to return to school. Department stores were jammed. Another hurricane threat petered out. A sensational bank robbery in Queens seized the headlines, elbowing out the dwindling followup stories on the Finner and Coy cases.

Alton Humffrey was followed wherever he went. But his comings and goings were exemplary. The homes of friends, the ballet, his attorney's offices, Wall Street, the Harvard Club. He did no entertaining.

They discussed a wire tap. Johnny Kripps was for it.

"We're in so far, Inspector, we may as well go the whole way."

But Inspector Queen vetoed it.

"He's too smart to say anything incriminating over a phone, Johnny. Besides, whom would he say it to? He's cleaned his slate. There's no business pending on his agenda except keeping an eye on us . . . I wonder why he hasn't gone up to New Haven."

"He's probably keeping in touch with Dr. Duane by phone," Jessie said.

The old man looked troubled.

The reports from Angelo, Murphy, and Giffin were discouraging. If Humffrey had set up a love nest for Connie Coy, they could find no trace of it. Before moving to the West Side apartment the Coy girl had lived in a theatrical hotel in the 40s. The ex-detectives, armed with photographs of Humffrey snapped by Kripps with a concealed candid camera, could turn up no one at the hotel who recognized the millionaire. The trace-back of the girl's New York club dates around August and September of the previous year, when conception must have taken place, was without result.

"She played a lot of dates out of town around that time," Pete Angelo reported. "One of them was a week's engagement in Boston. The Humffreys closed up the Nair Island place right after Labor Day last year and went back to Massachusetts. I better run up to Boston, Inspector."

"All right, Pete. But watch your step. He's a lot better known there than he is here."

"In the hot spots?" Angelo's wrinkles writhed. "If you ask me, this is a case of a guy slipping on his one and only banana peel. They won't know who he is unless they've seen him in their joint. Don't worry, Inspector."

Angelo came back three days later.

"Nothing definite," he reported. "The maitre-dee *thought* he looked familiar, but couldn't place him. He remembered Coy singing there, but he says she kept pretty much to herself. I had to shy off, because he began to get nosy. Said 'another New York detective' had been around asking questions about Coy."

"Routine," the Inspector muttered. "Out of desperation, sounds like. Did the New York cop show this fellow a man's photo, Pete?"

"Nothing but Coy's, and no mention of any particular man. They're still chasing their tails. While I was there," Angelo added, "I checked on the hotel she'd stayed at, and some likely hideaway eateries and motels. But no dice. I get the feeling Boston or around Boston was where they met, but it was a year ago, and it looks pretty hopeless to me."

"He must have seen her in New York early last winter, when she got back to town," ex-Sergeant Murphy said. "But he sure was cagey."

"Cagey," Richard Queen said glumly, "is his middle name."

Kripps and Polonsky shared the shadowing assignment. They kept reporting nothing but tired feet.

On the 14th of the month Jessie announced that she had to go up to Rowayton. Her summer tenants' lease was expiring the next day and she was a little anxious about the condition of her house.

"It isn't much," Jessie said, "but I do have a few nice things and I don't cherish the thought of finding them smashed or made love to."

"I think I'll go with you," the Inspector said suddenly.

"That isn't necessary, Richard. Nothing can happen to me while he's being followed day and night."

"It isn't that, Jessie. I can't understand Humffrey's staying away from the sanitarium so long. You'd think with his wife so ill he'd go up to see her at least once a week. I'm going to tackle Dr. Duane."

"I'll drive you to New Haven."

"I'd rather not risk your being seen there. Not just yet, anyway. Are your tenants vacating tomorrow?"

"In the morning. I've called them."

"Well, we'll drive up to Connecticut around noon, and if you don't mind my borrowing the Dodge, I'll drop you off at your place and go on to New Haven. I shouldn't be gone more than a few hours."

He gave Johnny Kripps, who had the day trick, special instructions. The next morning Kripps called to say that Humffrey had a luncheon appointment in town with an investment banker, and another with some friends for late afternoon at one of his clubs.

Richard Queen found the Duane Sanitarium without difficulty. It was a colossal white Colonial building, with sky-reaching pillars, on a rise of hill overlooking acres of barbered gardens and lawns. But it was entirely surrounded by a high iron-spiked brick wall, and there was a guardhouse at the iron entrance.

The guard was grim-faced. "Sorry, sir, no one gets in without an appointment or pass. You'll have to write or phone."

He flashed his gold shield. "You tell your Dr. Duane that a police inspector from New York wants to see him—and not next week, but right now."

Ten minutes later an attendant was ushering him through a vast flower-spotted reception room and up a flight of marble stairs to the director's private office.

Dr. Duane was waiting for him beside his secretary's desk. He was a tall impressive man with a carnation in his lapel.

"Come in, come in," he said testily, indicating the open door of his office. "Miss Roberts, I'm not to be disturbed." He followed the old man in and shut the door. "And you are Inspector—?"

"Queen." He looked around. The office was like an M-G-M set, with massive blond furniture, potted plants, and tropical fish tanks inset in the walls. "I know you're a busy man, so I'll get right to the point. I want to see Mrs. Sarah Humffrey."

Dr. Duane frowned. He seated himself at his immaculate desk and straightened a pile of medical charts.

"Impossible, I'm afraid."

The old man's brows went up. "How come, Doctor?"

"She's in no condition to see anyone. Besides, Mr. Humffrey's instructions were specific."

"Not to allow his wife to speak to a police officer?" Inspector Queen asked dryly.

"I didn't say that, Inspector. The circumstances under which Mrs. Humffrey came to us, as I take it you know, make Mr. Humffrey's wishes quite understandable. She has seen no once since being admitted here except our staff and her husband."

"How is she?"

"Better. The prognosis now is considerably more optimistic. However, any emotional upset . . ."

The man was nervous. He kept fidgeting with his bow tie, the papers, the telephone cord.

"Incidentally, just what's wrong with her?"

"Now, Inspector Queen, you can't expect me to tell you that. If Mr. Humffrey wishes to discuss his wife's illness, that's his affair. As her physician, I can't."

Queen took out a small black notebook and leafed through it. Duane watched him alertly.

"Now, Doctor, there's that business of your phone call on the afternoon of Saturday, August 20th, to the New York office of a lawyer named Finner—"

Dr. Duane stiffened as if his chair were wired. "*My* call?" he cried. "Why do you say that?"

"Because you made it."

"You people are hounding me! I told those detectives long ago I knew nothing about a phone call to such a person."

"Oh, some of the boys were up here on that?" the Inspector murmured. "When was this, Dr. Duane?"

"The last week in August. It seems that in investigating the murder of this man—Finner, was it?—the New York police claimed to have found a telephone company record of a toll call from this New Haven number to the man's office . . . Didn't you know they'd been here?'' he asked, breaking off suspiciously.

"Of course. I also know, Doctor, that you did make that call."

"Prove it," Dr. Duane snapped. "You people prove it! I told your men at the time that it was a mistake. We have never had a patient named Finner here, or a patient directly connected with a person of that name. I showed them our records to prove that. It's always possible some member of my staff put in such a call, but they have all denied it, and the only explanation I can offer is the one I gave— that someone here did call a New York number but got this fellow Finner's number by mistake . . ."

"In a way it's a break," Richard Queen said thoughtfully to Jessie when he got back to her cottage in Rowayton. "His lie about the phone call to Finner's office the afternoon of the murder stopped New York cold. Their one lead to Humffrey in this case was choked off at the source."

"You haven't said one word about whether you like my house," Jessie said. She was surrounded by mops and pails, and she was furious.

"It's pretty as a picture, Jessie. But about Duane's lying. Privacy means money to Duane. His whole high-toned establishment is based on it. He can't afford to have his name kicked around in a murder case. He's not protecting Humffrey, he's protecting himself." He scowled into his coffee cup.

"Those *people!*"

"What people?"

"My tenants! The condition they left my beautiful little matchbox in! Pigs, that's what they must be. Look at this filth, Richard!"

"I think I'll run over and see Abe Pearl while I'm in the neighborhood," he said philosophically.

"Would you? That will give me a chance to clean at least *some* of this mess."

He grinned. "Never knew a woman who could look at a dirty house and think of anything else. All right, Jessie, I'll get out of here."

Abe Pearl almost tore his arm out of the socket.

"What's happening, for God's sake?" When the old man brought him up to date, he shook his head. "That Humffrey dame might just as well be rotting in solitary somewhere. Do you suppose she's gone clean off her rocker, Dick, and that's why they won't let anyone see her?"

"No," Richard Queen said slowly. "No, Abe, I don't think so. What happened up there today only confirms a suspicion I've had."

"What's that?"

"I think Humffrey's main reason for putting his wife out of circulation in a place where he can be sure she can't be got at—and himself staying away, now that he's being tailed day and night—is to keep us from her."

"I don't get it," Chief Pearl said.

"He's put her where nobody can talk to her. He'd like us to forget she ever existed. Abe, *Humffrey is scared to death of something his wife might tell us.*"

"About him?" The big man was puzzled.

"About him and the baby's death. It's got to be about little Mike's murder— she probably hasn't even been told about the other two. And if it's something Alton Humffrey doesn't want us to know, then it's something we've got to find out. The problem is, how to get to Sarah Humffrey . . ."

Jessie wanted to stay over, claiming that it would take a week to clean her house properly. But he hurried her back to the city.

They found Hugh Giffin picking disconsolately at his scar, and Al Murphy staring at the backs of his red-furred hands.

"Hospital," Giffin said. "Nothing, Inspector. The trail goes back to Finner, and Finner only. Even Finner didn't pay the bills directly. Connie Coy paid them with the cash Finner provided. Humffrey kept a million miles away from it."

"Murph," the Inspector said. "Any luck with the cabs?"

"Nope," the ex-sergeant said gloomily. "I must have tackled every hackie stationed around Grand Central. Just didn't hit it, that's all. Either this Humffrey hopped a cruising cab when he followed the girl home that night, or else he used a private car."

The old man shook his head. "He'd have felt safer taking a public carrier, Murph. Actually, all he had to do when he saw her climb into a cab with her luggage at Grand Central was take another cab, maybe on Madison or Lexington, and be driven to the general neighborhood of the apartment, then walk over. After the shooting he probably just walked away—another pedestrian out for some air."

Murphy looked unhappy.

"It's all right," Inspector Queen shrugged. "We'll just have to keep digging." He clapped the two men on the shoulder and sent them home.

The following night, when Johnny Kripps came up with his day's report on Humffrey, the old man said, "I'm calling you off the tail, Johnny. Pete Angelo can take over."

"You firing me, Inspector?" the bespectacled ex-Homicide man asked, not altogether humorously.

"At the salary you're getting?" He grinned, not humorously either. "Johnny, have you been spotted by any of the working details?"

"I don't think so."

"We'll have to start cutting corners. We're getting nowhere. Here's what I want you to do—I'd do it myself, but you're the logical man for the job. Drop in at Homicide and see some of the boys. A friendly visit to your old pals, you understand."

"Steer the talk around to the Coy and Finner cases?"

"Especially the Coy case. Find out what they've got. Don't overdo it, Johnny— I don't want to have to bail you out of 125 White Street!"

Kripps reported the next afternoon. "They've drawn a skunk egg, Inspector. All they had on the Finner case was that New Haven toll call, and Duane's pooped them on that. The fact that he's an M.D. running a private sanitarium gave them the bright idea at first that he was mixed up with Finner in the baby racket, but the more they've investigated Duane the cleaner he washes. Finner's case files they've exhausted without a lead."

"And Coy?" Richard Queen asked grimly.

"Bellve it or not, they haven't been able to come up with a single witness who saw a damn thing the night she got it. By the way, they think too that the killer hopped three or four roofs before he hit for ground level. Just walked down, and out, and away, probably on West End Avenue."

The inspector tormented his mustache.

"All they've got in the Coy case is the bullet they've taken from her head and the ones from the plaster." Kripps shrugged. "Three slugs from the same gun. .38 Special ammo."

"Pete dug out the gun permit information on Humffrey today," the old man muttered. "One of the revolvers he owns is—or was—a Colt Cobra, which would fit with the ammo. But the gun is gone, Johnny. That we can be sure of. He probably dropped it in the Hudson the same night he shot Connie."

"Quite a guy," Kripps said unadmiringly.

"How do you know?" Jessie said.

"That he's quite a guy, Miss Sherwood?"

"That he's disposed of the gun?"

They looked at her.

"But Jessie," Richard Queen protested, "possession of the weapon that fired the bullet that killed Connie Coy would be enough by itself to warrant a murder indictment. Humffrey wouldn't be so foolish as to hold on to it. A ballistics comparison test, if we or the police got our hands on it, would mean curtains for him."

"Clever people are often so clever they're stupid," Jessie said. "He might be holding on to the gun out of plain cussedness, just because he figures you think he wouldn't. He strikes me as that type of man."

Ex-Inspector Queen and ex-Lieutenant Kripps examined each other.

"What do you think, Johnny?"

"What have we got to lose?"

"Plenty if we get caught at it."

"Let's not be."

"It might throw a scare in him, too," the old man chuckled. "Maybe even turn up something. I should have thought of it myself! Let's talk to Murph and Giffin and the others and see how they feel about it."

"Feel about what?" Jessie asked. "What are you talking about, Richard?"

He grinned at her. "There's only one way to take the bull, Jessie, and that's by the horns. We're going to raid Humffrey's apartment."

The opportunity came two nights later. Cullum drove Alton Humffrey out to Oyster Bay to visit friends. The women on the staff had been given the night off.

The raiding party gained entrance to the Park Avenue building by way of an adjoining roof and a boarded-up penthouse. They got into the Humffrey apartment through the service door.

"No ripping, tearing or smashing," Richard Queen ordered. "But give it a real going-over."

They found nothing—no gun, no love letters, no receipted bills that tied in with Connie Coy, no correspondence with Finner . . . not a scrap of evidence to link Alton Humffrey with the murdered girl, or the murdered lawyer, or for that matter with the murdered baby.

The phone rang at three in the morning.

"Mr. Queen?" said a familiar nasal voice.

"Yes." He was wide-awake instantly.

"I'm disappointed in you."

"Are you, now."

"Did you really think you'd find anything in my apartment that could possibly nourish your fantasies?"

"For the record, Mr. Humffrey," Richard Queen said, "I don't know what you're talking about."

"Yes. Well." Humffrey sounded nasty but amused. "When you get over your attack of amnesia, you might take stock. Having me followed, ransacking my apartment, investigating my past—none of it will get you anywhere. You're in a pitiful condition, Mr. Queen. Have you considered consulting a palmist?"

His phone clicked gently in the old man's ear.

There was nothing in the next day's newspapers about a robbery attempt on Park Avenue.

The Inspector called another conference.

"Humffrey's right," he said grimly. "I'm calling you all off."

"What?" Jessie cried.

"The tail, too?" Wes Polonsky said.

"The tail, too, Wes." The five old men stared at the sixth incredulously. "We'll get nowhere attacking Humffrey's strength," he went on without excitement. "All we've done is waste time, money, and shoe leather. He's covered his tracks from way back where Finner and Coy were concerned, and he has nothing to do now but sit tight. What we've got to do is attack his weakness."

"Does he have one?" Jessie asked bitterly.

"Yes. It's mixed up with what happened on the night of August 4th on Nair Island. It doesn't matter which murder we pin on Humffrey, remember. He can only take the long sleep once."

"Sarah Humffrey? You keep coming back to her, Richard."

He nodded. "I should have stuck to her from the beginning. I'm convinced Mrs. Humffrey knows something about the baby's murder that Humffrey is dead scared she'll spill." He looked down at Jessie. "We've got to worm that information out of her. And that means an inside job."

"In other words," Jessie said, "me."

He took her hand clumsily. "I wouldn't ask you to do it if I could see a better way, Jessie. Do you think you could get into the Duane Sanitarium as a nurse?"

5 · And Then . . . Justice

"Where is this woman?" Richard Queen snarled. "She's half an hour late now."

"She'll be here," Jessie said soothingly. "My, you don't sound like an engaged man at all. More like a husband."

He colored. "How about another cocktail?"

"I'd *love* another cocktail."

He signaled the waitress hastily.

Jessie felt warm inside. It was not entirely the Pink Lady. Pretending to be engaged for Elizabeth Currie's benefit had been his idea. He had insisted on coming along, and they had to have a reason for his presence.

"Dr. Duane saw you that night on Nair Island, when he came to take Mrs. Humffrey to the sanitarium," he had said stubbornly. "I'd rather sit in on this."

"But he hardly glanced at me," Jessie had said. "Doctors never look at a nurse's face unless she's young and pretty."

"Then he took a good look!"

Not that Dr. Duane was going to be present. It was an exploratory lunch in a Stamford restaurant with Jessie's friend Elizabeth Currie, who had been on the nursing staff of the Duane Sanitarium for years. Approaching the problem of getting inside the sanitarium—and eventually inside Sarah Humffrey's room—through Elizabeth Currie had been Jessie's idea. Still, Richard had insisted. ("I want to feel this out, Jessie. I may still change my mind. After all, once you got in there you'd be cut off from me . . .")

Elizabeth Currie turned out to be a tall Scotswoman with iron hair, steel jaws, and bone eyes.

"So this is *the* man, Jessie. Let me look at you . . . Well! He's a little older looking than I expected, but then . . . I think it's marvelous, two people of your age finding each other after all hope had fled, haha! However did you do it, Jessie?"

"It was love at first sight," Jessie said lightly. "Wasn't it . . . darling?"

"Smack between the eyes," Richard Queen mumbled. "Cocktail, Miss Currie?"

"I'll say! Double Manhattan."

"Double Manhattan," he said to the waitress. "Maybe we'd better order the food now . . ."

An hour later he nudged Jessie under cover of the tablecloth, desperately.

"Well, no, Elizabeth," Jessie said, nudging him back. "As a matter of fact, our plans are a little vague. Richard's firm is sending him abroad for a few months, and we probably won't be . . . married till he gets back."

"What a hor'ble idea," the nurse said. "Why don't you get married now, you fool, and go with him?"

354

"We uh—we can't afford it," the Inspector said. "So Jessie's looking around for something to do to while away the time—"

"I can't face going back to private cases, Elizabeth. I wish I could find a staff job somewhere."

"You're crazy," Elizabeth Currie said.

"Elizabeth, I just thought! Do you suppose there's an opening at the Duane Sanitarium?"

"There's always an opening at the Duane Sanitarium. Staff turnover is something terrific. But I still think you're crazy, Jessie."

"Could you find out? First thing tomorrow? I'd be ever so grateful."

"I'll talk to Dr. Duane myself." Jessie's friend giggled. "I'm tight, do you know? Don't worry, I'll fix it for you, but you're absolutely balmy."

"Maybe Elizabeth has something on this," Richard Queen said. "What sort of place is it, Miss Currie? I wouldn't want Jessie getting into something—"

"That's just what she'd be doing," the nurse said confidentially. "Oh, it's a lovely place and all that—like a lovely prison, that is. Those patients. Phoo."

"Pretty sick people?"

"Pretty sick my eye. Bunch of hypochondriacs, most of 'em. Drive a nurse to drink. Which reminds me. Could I have another Manhattan, you nice man?"

"Better not, Elizabeth," Jessie said. "Talking about patients. You get some pretty important people up there, don't you?"

"Filthy rich people. Could I—?"

"Isn't the Duane Sanitarium where they took that wealthy society woman—what was her name? You know, Elizabeth—that woman from around here somewhere, tragic case of the baby that suffocated in its crib. Last month."

"Huh," the nurse said. "Mrs. Humffrey."

"Mrs. Humffrey!" Jessie said. "She's the one." She thought, If Elizabeth remembers the newspaper stories, I'm sunk. She glanced at her confederate doubtfully, but he nodded for her to go ahead. "She had a nervous breakdown or something, didn't she?"

"Absolutely no control over herself," Elizabeth Currie nodded contemptuously. "'Bereavement shock,' they called it. All right, it was a ter'ble experience, but my God. She had everybody running around in circles."

"Had?" Richard Queen said. "'Had,' Miss Currie?"

"Huh?" the nurse said owlishly.

"Doesn't she still have everybody running around in circles?"

"No, indeedy, you nice man."

"Why not?" Jessie didn't dare glance at him this time. "Elizabeth, you talk as if she isn't at the Duane Sanitarium any more."

"She isn't. Big private limousine with two husky nurses in it took her away last Friday morning. And was Dr. Duane glad to see the last of her."

"I wonder where they took her."

"Nobody knows. Big hush-hush. Who cares? Richard—I may call you Richard, mayn't I?—just one more teeny Manhattan? He's real nice, Jessie . . ."

It was late afternoon before they got rid of Elizabeth Currie, blearily bewildered at Jessie's sudden decision not to apply for a nursing job at the Duane Sanitarium after all.

He drove in a fury. "Last Friday morning! And I was up there Thursday asking about her. Duane must have phoned Humffrey, or Humffrey called and Duane mentioned my visit, and bango! the next morning Humffrey hauls her out of there."

"But Richard, he was being followed."

"He didn't go himself. Didn't you hear, Jessie?" He honked savagely at a slowpoke driver. "Arranged the switch to a new hideout by phone, and drew us off while the transfer was made by the new people, who could be anybody, anywhere— maybe Arizona, for all we know. He's smart, Jessie. Smart and quick on his pins."

Jessie shivered. "What do we do now?"

"Who knows? It might take us months to locate her. If ever."

He stared ahead.

A few miles later Jessie touched his arm. "Richard."

"Yes?"

"Why don't we give up?"

"No!" he said.

"But it seems so hopeless."

To Jessie's surprise, he smiled. "Maybe not, Jessie."

"What do you mean?"

"It's his round, all right. But we've just learned something about Mr. Alton K. Humffrey."

"We have?" Jessie sounded dubious.

"This business of snatching his wife out from under our noses confirms my belief that the murder of that baby is his weak spot. It's not theory any more. We've learned something else, too. The way to get at Humffrey is to force his hand. If we can surprise him, get him off balance . . ."

"You've thought of something!"

He nodded. "If it works, it could finish this off at one stroke."

"What is it, Richard?"

"Let me think it through."

For some reason, Jessie felt no elation. The title of an old Robert Benchley book, *After 1903, What?*, crossed her mind, *After Alton Humffrey, What?* She slumped down and closed her eyes . . .

She opened them to see the airy span of the George Washington Bridge moving by on her right.

"I fell asleep," Jessie murmured.

"And looked like a young chicken," he said in a peculiar way.

Jessie grimaced and sat up. "I'd make pretty tough chewing, I'm afraid."

"Jessie."

"Yes, Richard."

"Wasn't it a funny feeling? Back there in Stamford, I mean?" He said it with a laugh.

"You mean whan Elizabeth said Sarah Humffrey had been spirited away? I thought I'd die."

"No, I mean you and me." He was very red. "Pretending to be engaged."

Jessie stared straight ahead at the traffic. "I didn't see anything funny about it," she said coldly. "I thought it was nice."

"Well . . ."

Yes? Jessie thought. Yes?

But when he spoke again, it was to explain the plan he had worked out.

"It's that one over there, Jessie," Richard Queen said.

It was Wednesday evening, the 28th of September.

Jessie turned the coupé into the Pearl driveway and switched off her ignition. It was a spready old white clapboard house covered with wisteria and honeysuckle vines on a peaceful side street in Taugus. Great maples shaded the lawns, and on the old-fashioned open porch there were two rockers and a slide-swing.

He got out of the car, handling a large square flat package as if it contained eggs.

But Jessie was looking at the house. "What a lovely place for two people to live out their lives together."

"It's too big for two people, Abe says."

"I'll bet that's not what Mrs. Pearl says."

"You'd win," he chuckled. "Becky's children were born in this house, and to her that makes it holy. When Abe bought the beach shack, he had to fight to get her to go out there during the summer months. She isn't really happy till they close it up in September and come back here."

"She's lucky."

"So is Abe." He added. "In more ways than one."

Jessie sighed and got out. They went up on the porch, Richard Queen carrying the package carefully.

The door opened before he could ring the bell. "Richard, Jessie." Beck Pearl embraced them enthusiastically. "Let me look at you two! Abe, they're positively blooming. Did you ever see such a change in two people?"

"Well, get out of the way and let them come in," Abe Pearl grumbled. "I don't know why you wouldn't let me go to the door till they came up on the porch—"

His wife's glance withered him. "Let me have your things, Jessie. I can't imagine why Abe didn't insist on your coming for dinner. He's so stupid about some things!"

She carted Jessie off, and Abe Pearl took his friend into the living room.

"I thought you'd never get here. What held you up, Dick?"

"Daylight." The Inspector laid his package gently on the mahogany refectory table. "Mind if I pull the blinds?"

"You're acting damn mysterious. What's up?" The Taugus chief kept eying the package.

"Let's wait for the women." He drew all the shades down to the sills. Then he went back to the table and stood there.

The women came in chattering. But when Beck Pearl saw the old man's face she stopped talking and sat down in a corner. Jessie took a chair near her and folded her hands in her lap.

"Abe," Inspector Queen said, "what would you say if I told you we've finally got the goods on Alton Humffrey?"

The Taugus policeman looked from him to the package.

"In that thing?"

"Yes."

"So it's back in my lap." The big man came slowly to the table. "Let's have a look."

The Inspector undid the twine and removed the heavy wrappings, with loving care. Then he stepped back.

Abe Pearl said, "My God, Dick."

The package contained two sheets of thick plate glass. Between them, spread flat but showing wrinkle marks, as if it had been found crumpled but had been smoothed out, lay a lace-edged pillowslip. The slip was of some dainty fabric; the lace was exquisite. By contrast the dirty imprint of a man's hand, a trifle blurry but unmistakable, was an offense. The print lay just off-center, the impression of a right hand from which the tip of the little finger was missing to the first joint.

"Where did you find this?" Abe Pearl demanded.

"You like it, Abe?"

"Like it!" The chief bent over the glass, scrutinizing the pillowslip eagerly. "That missing fingertip alone—! Wait till Merrick sees this."

"You owe Jessie an apology, Abe, don't you?" Richard Queen said smiling.

"I guess I do; Miss Sherwood! I can't wait to see that iceberg's face when he gets a squint at this," Abe Pearl chortled. "But Dick, you haven't told me where you got it."

The old man said quietly, "We made it."

The big man's jaw dropped.

"It's a forgery, Abe. And judging by your reaction, a successful one. That's what I wanted to find out. If it's fooled you, it'll fool Humffrey."

"A forgery . . ."

"We've been working on this for a week. Jessie went around from store to store in New York till she found a pillowcase exactly like the one that disappeared. What's this lace called again, Jessie?"

"Honiton. The case itself is batiste." Jessie glanced at the big policeman. "So of course, Mr. Pearl, I'll let you take your apology back."

He made an impatient gesture and turned away. But he turned back at once. "Tell me more, Dick."

"One of the boys, Pete Angelo, went up to Boston. We figured because of Humffrey's missing fingertip he'd likely have his gloves made to order, and we were right. Pete located his glovemaker, and got hold of a pair of gloves the old fellow'd made for Humffrey that Humffrey didn't like. Then we enlisted Willy Kuntzman, who used to be one of the best men in the Bureau of Tech Services—" the old man grinned—"retired, of course—and Willy went to work on the right glove. He came up with a cast of Humffrey's right hand in that plastic, or whatever it is, that looks and feels like flesh. Then, with Jessie describing the handprint she'd seen on the original pillowcase, Willy doctored the duplicate, and this is the result."

"Isn't this taking a hell of a chance?"

Richard Queen returned his friend's look calmly. "I'm willing to take it, Abe. I was hoping you'd be, too."

"You want me to pull this on Humffrey."

"The preliminary work, yes."

The big man was silent.

"Of course, Abe, it's not absolutely necessary. I can do the whole thing. But it would have more of an effect if you set it up. The crime was committed in your jurisdiction. You're the logical man to have found this."

"Where?"

"You don't tell him where. It won't even occur to him to ask. The sight of this ought to throw him for a loop. If he should ask, toss it to me. I'll be in on the kill."

"Listen, Dick, you've got a rock in this," the police chief said slowly. "All right, Humffrey left his right handprint on a pillowcase just like this, and disposed of it that night before we got there. How? It must have been burned up, we said.

Or it was cut to pieces and flushed down a toilet. Humffrey knows how he disposed of it, doesn't he? If he burned it, how could we produce it? If he cut it up, how come it's whole again?'' Abe Pearl shook his head. "It won't work. He'll know in a flash we're trying to pull one.''

"I don't think so, Abe." The Inspector seemed unperturbed. "I didn't agree with you and Merrick when you discussed it that night, although I didn't want to put my two cents in with Merrick there. It's highly unlikely that Humffrey'd have burned the pillowslip. It was a hot night in August. He'd hardly have risked making a fire that might have been seen or smelled by somebody in the house—Jessie here, a servant, Dr. Wicks, even his wife—and remembered later just because it was a hot night in August.

"As for cutting it to pieces, he didn't have to, Abe. The material is so fine you can take this thing and crumple it into a small ball. He could have flushed it down a drain in one piece. A man who's just taken the life of an infant and expects the police any minute—no matter what substitute for blood is flowing through his veins—isn't going to go in for anything fancy. That only happens in my son's books. Humffrey had only one thought in mind, to get rid of the pillowcase in the quickest and easiest way.

"Sure, Abe, I don't deny the risk. But the way I see it, the odds are way over on our side." He shrugged. "Of course, if you'd rather not have anything to do with it—''

"Don't be a horse's patoot, Dick. It's not that." Abe Pearl began to pull on his fleshy lower lip.

The old man waited.

"It is that, Abe." It was Beck Pearl's soft voice. "You're thinking of me."

"Now Becky," her husband shouted, "don't start in on me!"

"Or maybe I'm flattering myself. Maybe it's yourself you're thinking of. Your job."

"Becky—" he thundered.

"The trouble is, dear, you're going soft in Taugus. It's a nice fat easy job, and you've gotten nice and fat and easy along with it.''

"Becky, will you stay out of this? Damn it all—!''

"How would you feel if that little boy had been Donny? Or darling little Lawrence?''

"You would throw my grandchildren up to me!" The big man hurled himself into the armchair with a crash that made the room shake. "All *right,* Dick! What's your plan?''

The next morning two police cars shot across the Nair Island causeway, drove into the Humffrey grounds, and eight Taugus detectives and uniformed men, headed by Chief Pearl, jumped out.

Stallings, the caretaker-gardener, was on his knees in one of the flower beds, planting bulbs.

"Something wrong again, Chief?''

"Nothing that concerns you, Stallings," Chief Pearl said gruffly. "Get on with your work. Borcher, you and Tinny take the house. You other men, fan out on the grounds—you know what we're after. One of you go down to the beach and keep an eye on that dredger, in case they make the strike.''

"One minute," Stallings said uneasily, as the officers began to scatter. "I'm responsible, Chief. What are you up to?''

"This is a search party," the chief barked. "Out of my way.''

"But Mr. Pearl, I got my instructions from Mr. Humffrey. He specially said I was to keep cops and reporters out."

"He did, did he? Ever hear of a search warrant, my friend?"

"A warrant?" Stallings blinked.

Chief Pearl waved an official-looking document before the old fellow's nose and immediately put it back in his pocket and turned away. "All right, men."

He went into the Humffrey house on the heels of his two detectives.

Stallings waited.

When all the officers had disappeared, he stole up the driveway to the service entrance, slipped inside, shut the door quietly, and went to the telephone extension in the butler's pantry. He gave the Taugus operator the Humffrey apartment number in New York City.

"The Humffrey residence," Mrs. Lenihan's Irish voice answered.

"Lenihan," Stallings muttered. "Is his nibs there?"

"Who is this?"

"Stallings. Got to talk to Mr. Humffrey. Shake a leg."

"You old fool, what are you up to now?" the housekeeper sniffed. "Drunk again, like as not. Mr. Humffrey isn't here."

"Where is he?"

"I don't know. All he said was for Henry to have the limousine ready. They drove off early this morning." Mrs. Lenihan lowered her voice. "Something doing?"

"Plenty. Cops all over the place. Chief Pearl with a search warrant. Don't you have *no* idea where they went?"

"Mercy," Mrs. Lenihan said faintly. "I don't, Stallings. What are they looking for?"

"How should I know?" Stallings sounded disgusted. "Well, I done my duty." He hung up and returned to his bulbs.

In Alton Humffrey's upstairs study, Abe Pearl replaced the study extension on its base softly.

At a few minutes past two that afternoon Stallings phoned Mrs. Lenihan again. This time he sounded agitated.

"Isn't Mr. Humffrey back yet, Lenihan?"

"Not yet," the housekeeper said. "What's the latest?"

"They just left."

"That's good."

"Maybe not so good," Stallings said slowly. "Maybe not so good, my fine Mrs. Lenihan."

"Now what? You and the voice of doom! What did they do? What did they say?"

"Nothing. Wouldn't tell me nothing. But Chief Pearl cracked me on the back, and do you know what he says to me?"

"What?"

" 'Stallings,' he says, 'I got the funniest feeling you're going to be looking for a new job,' he says."

"He didn't!" the housekeeper gasped.

"That's what he says to me, Lenihan, word for word."

"What do you suppose it *means*?"

"I don't know," the caretaker muttered. "But I don't like it . . . You better make good and damn sure Mr. Humffrey calls me the minute he gets in!"

Abe Pearl began phoning the Humffrey apartment from his office in Taugus police headquarters at a little past 3 P.M. He called again at 3:30, and again at 4:00.

When he phoned at 4:15 Mrs. Lenihan answered in a voice shrill with tension. "No, he *isn't* here yet, Chief Pearl. I told you I'd tell Mr. Humffrey the minute he comes in. Mercy!"

"Make sure you do, Mrs. Lenihan," Chief Pearl growled. He hung up and said, "Well, that's it. Let's hope it works."

"It'll work, Abe," Richard Queen said confidently.

It was almost 6 P.M. when Abe Pearl put his hand over the mouthpiece and said, "Here he is!"

Richard Queen hurried into the anteroom. The police operator handed him the earphones and he slipped them on and waved a go-ahead through the open doorway.

Abe Pearl removed his hand and said grimly, "Okay, Phil. Put Humffrey on."

Alton Humffrey's voice rasped in the earpiece. "Chief Pearl!"

The chief said coldly, "So you finally got my messages, Mr. Humffrey."

"I've only just got in. May I ask what in the name of common sense has been going on today? My housekeeper is in tears, Stallings keeps babbling some nonsense about a police raid on my Nair Island property—"

"Oh, you've talked to Stallings."

"Certainly I've talked to Stallings! He's been calling all day, too. Is he out of his mind, Chief, or are you?"

"I'd rather not discuss it over the phone."

"Really? By what right do you invade my privacy, ransack my house, trample my flowers, put dredgers to work off my beach? By what right, Chief Pearl?" The millionaire's twang vibrated with anger.

"By the right of any police officer who's got the jurisdiction to search for evidence in a murder case."

"*Murder* case? You mean the baby? Good heavens, are you people singing that tune again? Don't you remember, Mr. Pearl? That case is closed. You closed it yourself."

"An unsolved murder case is never closed."

"It wasn't an unsolved murder case! It was an accident."

"It was a murder case, Mr. Humffrey," Abe Pearl said. "And now we've got the evidence to prove it."

There was a pause.

Then the millionaire said in an altogether different way, "Evidence, you say? What evidence?"

"I'd appreciate it if you came out to police headquarters in Taugus right away, Mr. Humffrey. Tonight."

"Tonight? I'm not going anywhere, any time, until I have more information! What evidence?"

The chief glanced over into the anteroom. Richard Queen nodded.

"Well, you might say," Abe Pearl said into the phone, "you might say it's something we should never have stopped looking for in the first place."

There was another pause.

"I see," Humffrey said. "You wouldn't be referring, by any chance, to that pillowslip the Sherwood woman—that nurse—kept babbling about?"

The police chief glanced over at Richard Queen again. The old man hesitated this time. But then, grimly, he repeated the nod.

"That's right," Abe Pearl said.

"You've found it?" The bitterness in Humffrey's voice was startling.

"I can't say any more over the phone. Will you come out here so we can have a talk about this, Mr. Humffrey? Voluntarily? Or—?" He deliberately left Humffrey dangling.

The wire was quiet.

"Very well," the millionaire said slowly. "I'll be out in an hour."

The instant the connection was broken, Richard Queen snatched the earphones from his head and ran into Abe Pearl's office.

"Convinced now?" he cried. "You heard the way he asked if you'd found it! He'd never have said it that way if he knew the pillowslip was gone beyond recall. He *accepted* the possibility that the slip could be produced! Look, let's get that tape recorder hooked up. Better be sure you plant the bug where he won't spot it . . . I tell you, Abe, we've got him!"

"Chief Pearl," Alton Humffrey said.

"Who wants him?" The desk man kept writing.

"Alton K. Humffrey."

The officer looked up.

"Humffrey?" he said in a hard voice. He rose. "Have a seat."

"I'll stand," Humffrey said.

"That's up to you." The uniformed man disappeared in a hall beyond the water cooler.

The millionaire looked around the room. He was very pale. Several patrolmen and two detectives were lounging in silence, staring at him. Humffrey's pallor deepened. He looked away, fingering his collar.

The burly figure of Chief Pearl appeared from the hall.

"I made good time, you see, Chief," Alton Humffrey said. He sounded nervously friendly.

The chief said, "Reynolds, better fill in at the desk. Harris has to take stenographic notes. No calls of any kind. I don't care if there's a riot."

"Yes, sir." One of the patrolmen went behind the desk and sat down.

"This way, Mr. Humffrey." Abe Pearl stepped back. Alton Humffrey moved toward him slowly. The millionaire seemed puzzled as well as nervous now.

The two detectives got up and sauntered across the room after him. Humffrey glanced over his shoulder at them, looked ahead quickly.

"That door at the end of the hall," Chief Pearl said.

Humffrey walked up the hall, the chief close on his heels. The two detectives followed.

At the door Humffrey hesitated.

"Go in and have a seat, Mr. Humffrey. I'll be there in a minute."

Abe Pearl turned his back and began to whisper to his two detectives.

Humffrey stepped into the chief's office uncertainly. The man who had been on desk duty in the outer room was at one of the windows operating a pencil sharpener. On a chair beside the chief's big swivel chair lay a stenographic notebook. The officer glanced at Humffrey, went to the smaller chair, picked up the notebook, flipped it open, and sat down, waiting.

There was only one other chair in the office. It was straightbacked and uncomfortable-looking. The millionaire hesitated again. Then he sank into it.

Chief Pearl came in alone. He went around his desk and seated himself. Humffrey stole a glance at the door. The shadows of the two detectives were silhouetted on the frosted glass.

"This is all very formidable, Mr. Pearl," Humffrey said with a smile. "Anyone would think you were preparing to arrest me."

The swivel chair squealed as the Taugus chief leaned back, scowling.

"Perhaps I should have brought my attorney," Humffrey went on in a jocular way.

"There's nothing your attorney can do for you tonight," Chief Pearl said. "Tonight you're going to be shown something, and I expect you to make a statement. After that you can call ten attorneys for all I care."

"Shown something?" the millionaire said. "That would be the pillowslip, Mr. Pearl?"

The big man got up and went over to the door of the anteroom. He opened it and said, "All right, Dick."

Humffrey half-rose.

Richard Queen came in with the glass-protected pillowslip. It was wrapped in brown paper.

"Queen," Humffrey said. He was staring from the old man to the paper-covered object.

"You, too, Miss Sherwood," Abe Pearl grunted.

Jessie walked in.

The millionaire got to his feet.

"I might have known," Humffrey said slowly. "I might have known."

"It's your show, Dick. Take over." The chief glanced at the uniformed man with the notebook. "Start taking notes, Harris."

The sharpened pencil poised.

"If you don't mind, Abe, I'll set this down on your desk." The Inspector laid the package on the desk. He loosened the wrappings, but did not remove them. Humffrey's eyes were on the brown paper. The old man straightened up and faced the millionaire. "This is quite an exhibit, Mr. Humffrey. No wonder you didn't want us to find it."

Humffrey was all gathered in now, almost crouching. He could not seem to tear his glance from the brown paper.

"It's a whole case by itself," Richard Queen went on. "It not only knocks that inquest jury's verdict of accidental death into the next county, it proves that Michael Stiles Humffrey was deliberately murdered, as Miss Sherwood insisted from the beginning. But it does even more than that, Mr. Humffrey. It not only proves the baby was murdered, it shows who murdered him."

He whirled and whipped the paper off the glass.

"Miss Sherwood," he said swiftly, "for the record I want you to identify this pillowslip. Is this the pillowslip you saw lying over Michael Stiles Humffrey's face and torso on the night of August 4th, when you found the baby dead of suffocation?"

Jessie stepped up to the desk.

"It is," she said in a stiff voice, and stepped back.

Humffrey quivered. His pallor was yellowish now. He moved toward Abe Pearl's desk in a jerky way, slowly, and stared down at the pillowslip under the glass.

"You never thought we'd find it, did you?" Inspector Queen said softly. "There's the dirty handprint—the dirty print of a right hand, just as Miss Sherwood said. But it's not just the dirty print of a right hand, Mr. Humffrey, as you can see. It's the dirty print of a right hand that has the tip of the little finger missing to the first joint!''

Abe Pearl reached over suddenly and seized the millionaire's right hand in his big paw. He uncurled the little finger as if it were a child's, exposing its deformity.

"You murdering louse," Abe Pearl said. "A man who'd kill a two-month old baby, a kid he'd given his own name to, for God's sake! . . . You won't bull or buy your way out of this one, Humffrey. You're through. With this pillowslip as evidence, you haven't got a chance. The best thing you can do is sit down in that chair and start talking. I want a full confession, and I want it now.''

He flung the hand from him contemptuously and pointed to the straightbacked chair. Then he turned away.

"Congratulations, Chief, on a superb performance.''

Abe Pearl swung about. Alton Humffrey was smiling. There was nothing uncertain in his smile. It was a smile without humor, angry and cruel.

"What did you say?'' Abe Pearl said.

"I should have warned you about Queen, Mr. Pearl. Apparently his lunacy is contagious." He began to stroll about the police chief's office, glancing here and there with fastidious distaste, as if he were slumming. He ignored Richard Queen and Jessie Sherwood utterly. "Beautifully staged, I'll grant you that. The meaningless raid on my property. The repetitious phone calls. The menacing summons. The policemen sitting about, waiting to pounce on the big bad wolf and cart him off to the pound. And finally—" the millionaire's glance shriveled Richard Queen and Jessie Sherwood, shattered the glass-protected pillowslip—"finally, these two mountebanks, and the production of this work of art. Who manufactured it, Chief, you or Queen? I suppose it was you, Queen, and your West 87th Street Irregulars. It has the metropolitan touch. Unfortunately, you slipped. The moment I glanced at this I knew it was a fake. But you couldn't have known that, could you? And so it's all gone to waste. All this loving labor, the stage designing, the suspense, the superb acting, the extras in the wings . . .''

Alton K. Humffrey suddenly strode over to the hall door and yanked it open.

The two detectives looked around, startled.

Humffrey laughed.

"Do we haul him in now, Chief?'' one of the detectives asked.

"Oh, get out of my way, you fool,'' Alton Humffrey snapped; and he walked out.

"I don't understand it," Inspector Queen said. "I don't, I don't.''

Abe Pearl said nothing. Patrolman Harris was gone; the three were alone in the office.

"I never should have involved you in this, Abe. Or you, Jessie.''

"Please, Richard.''

"Up to a certain point he was our fish," the old man muttered to the pillowslip on the desk. "He was hooked. Right through the gills. Then he takes one look at the slip and he knows it's a frameup. What did we do wrong? Could it be the pillowslip itself, Jessie? The wrong material, wrong lace, wrong size or something?''

"It can't have been that, Richard. This is an exact duplicate of the one that disappeared. I'd seen the slip many times, told Mrs. Humffrey how lovely I thought it was.''

"Then it's what we did with it. The position of the print?''

"To the best of my recollection, it was just about where I told Mr. Kuntzman to put it."

"Maybe it's what we *didn't* do with it," he said suddenly. "After all, Jessie, you did see it in a dim light for only a couple of seconds. Suppose there was some other mark on it, a mark you missed? Maybe a dirt streak, a smudge, a tear. Something you just didn't notice."

"I suppose that's it," Jessie said lifelessly. "You see how misguided you were to put any confidence in me. Look what I've got you into."

"Let's not talk about who got whom into what." Richard Queen grimaced. "Here's Abe, ready to strangle me—"

"You didn't hold any gun to my head, Dick," Abe Pearl said heavily. "I'm just trying to figure out what gives now. Think he's going to make an issue of this?"

"Not a chance."

"He could make it pretty hot for us."

"He can't afford to, Abe. The last thing Humffrey wants is to stir up a full-scale investigation." The Inspector looked up. "You know, this isn't a total loss. It's confirmed two important points. One, that he substituted the clean pillowslip that night for the dirty one, otherwise he wouldn't have spotted the discrepancy. Two, that he didn't destroy the dirty slip—he was all ready to believe we'd found it. We're not licked yet!"

Jessie stared at him. "Richard, you sound as if you're going on with this."

"Going on with it?" He seemed puzzled. "Of course I'm going on with it, Jessie. How can I stop now? We've got him on the run."

Jessie began to laugh. Something in her laugh alarmed him, and he stepped quickly to her side. But she stopped laughing as suddenly as she had started. "I'm sorry, Richard. It just struck me funny."

"I don't see anything funny about it," he growled.

"I am sorry." She touched his arm.

"Aren't you going on with it, Jessie?" he asked grimly.

Her hand dropped to her side.

"Richard, I'm so tired . . . I don't know."

Their return to the city was a strain on both of them. He seemed depressed, resentful, frustrated—a combination of things that Jessie with her throbbing head did not attempt to analyze. When he dropped her off at 71st Street, promising to park her car in the garage, he drove off without another word.

Jessie floundered all night. For once aspirin did not help, and tension made her skin itch and prickle unmercifully. Toward morning she took a seconal and fell into a heavy sleep. She was awakened by various bumps and crashes to find the clock hands standing at five minutes to noon and Gloria Sardella dumping various bags and packages on the living room floor.

Holy Mother! Jessie thought. It's the 30th!

She decided then and there.

"I'm going home, Richard," Jessie said over the phone.

"So you've made up your mind." And he was silent.

Jessie thought, Is it possible this is the way it's going to end?

"I've sort of had my mind made up for me," she said, trying to sound chatty. "I'd forgotten all about Gloria's saying when she left that she'd be back on the

30th. I guess I've lost track of time, along with everything else. Are you there, Richard?"

"I'm here," he said.

"I felt like such a ninny when she walked into the apartment this morning. The least I might have done was meet the boat! Of course, Gloria was awfully sweet— said I was welcome to stay as long as I wanted—"

"Why don't you?" He was having some trouble clearing his throat.

"It wouldn't be fair to Gloria. You know how small her apartment is. Besides, what's the point? The whole thing's been a mistake, Richard." Jessie stopped, but he didn't say anything. "Last night in Taugus was the straw that broke the lady camel's back, I guess. I'd better go home and back to being a nurse again."

"Jessie."

"Yes, Richard."

"Do we have to talk over the phone? I mean—unless you'd rather not see me any more—"

"Richard, what a silly thing to say."

"Then can I drive you up to Rowayton?" he asked eagerly.

"If you'd like to," Jessie murmured.

He drove so slowly that irate cars honked and swooshed around them all the way up to Connecticut.

For a while he talked about the case.

"I went over some of the boys' reports, from when they were tailing Humffrey. Couldn't sleep last night, anyway. I noticed something that hadn't meant anything at the time.

"That Friday morning when Humffrey'd had his wife removed from the Duane Sanitarium, the report said that his chauffeur left town early, alone, driving the big limousine. Remember Elizabeth Currie saying that Mrs. Humffrey was taken away in a big private limousine? My hunch is that Humffrey sent Cullum up to New Haven while he stayed in town to draw us off. Cullum must have picked up the two nurses on the way, and then gone up to the sanitarium. At least, it's a possibility. I'm going to work on that right away—today."

"Richard, you should have told me. I'd never have let you waste all this time driving me home."

"It can wait till I get back to the city," he said quickly.

"What are you going to do, pump Henry Cullum?"

"Yes. If I can find out through him where Sarah Humffrey is . . ."

But for the most part they were silent.

In Rowayton he carried her bags into the cottage, fixed the leaky kitchen faucet, admired her zinnias, accepted her offer of coffee; but it was all done on a note of withdrawal, and Jessie's head began to ache again.

I won't help him, she told herself fiercely. I won't!

He refused to let her drive him to the Darien station. He phoned for a cab instead.

Then, at the last moment, with the taxi waiting outside, he said suddenly, "Jessie, I can't go without—without—"

"Yes?"

"Without, well, saying thank you . . ."

"Thank *me?*" You're overdoing it, old girl, she thought in despair. How do women manage these things? "What on earth for, Richard?"

He toed her living-room rug. "For just about the two most wonderful months of my life."

"Well," Jessie said. "I thank *you*, Mr. Queen. It hasn't been exactly dull for me, either." *And there's a brilliant remark.*

"I don't mean this Humffrey thing." He cleared his throat twice, the second time irritably. "You've come to mean—well, a lot to me, Jessie."

"I have, Richard?" *Oh, dear . . .*

"An awful lot." He scowled at the rug. "I know I have no right . . ."

"Oh, Richard."

"I mean, a man of my age—"

"Are we back to *that* again?" Jessie cried.

"And you so youthful, so pretty . . ."

My goodness, Jessie thought. Now if my stomach doesn't start making blurpy bilge-pump sounds, the way it always does when I'm fussed . . . *And there it goes!*

"Yes, Richard?" Jessie said loudly.

The taxi man took that moment to start blasting away on his horn. Richard Queen flushed a profound scarlet, grabbed her hand, shook it as if it were a fighting fish, mumbled, "I'll call you some time, Jessie," and ran.

Jessie sat down on her floor and wept.

He'll never call, Jessie assured herself. Why should he? I got him into it, and now I've run out on him. He won't come back.

She swallowed the two aspirins dry, as a punishment, and resumed putting her clothes away.

Murdered babies.

My righteous indignation.

The truth is, Jessie Sherwood, she told herself pitilessly as she banged hangers about in the closet, you're a hopeless old maid. You're a hopeless old maid filled with hopeless guilt feelings, and don't blame it on menopause, either. You've got plenty to feel guilty about, old girl. Not just running out on him. Not just acting like an irresponsible neurotic, throwing yourself at him, leading the poor man on till he began to feel young again, and then making it as hard for him as you could.

It's that pillowslip.

When Jessie thought about the pillowslip, something inside cringed and curled up. She tried not to think of it, but the more she tried the faster it bounced back. She had been so positive the doctored slip was just like the one she had seen. But it hadn't been. One look, and Humffrey had known it was a forgery. How could he have known? What hadn't she noticed, or forgotten? Maybe if she could remember it now . . . That would be helping. That would be making it up to Richard!

So Jessie shut her eyes tight and thought and thought, right there in the closet, seeing the nursery again, seeing herself stooping over the crib in the nightlight, the pillow almost completely covering the motionless little body . . . the pillowcase . . . the pillowcase . . .

But she could not add anything to the pillowcase. It remained in her mind's eye as she thought she had seen it that night.

She dropped the dress to the floor and went over to the chintz-backed maple chair near the window, where she could look out at her postage-stamp back garden. The morning-glories were still in bloom, and the petunias; the berries on the dogwood tree were big and shiny and red, and disappearing fast down the gullets of the birds; and Jessie thought, I will do it for him. I *will*.

So she sat there and thought, desperately.

How *had* that monster disposed of the pillowslip? He hadn't burned it, he hadn't cut it to pieces . . . He had been under pressure, the pressure of his own guilt, the pressure of his wife's hysterics, the pressure of Dr. Wicks's presence, the pressure of the police-on-the-way . . . Pressure. Pressure makes people do things quickly, without much thought. Richard had remarked himself Wednesday night that Humffrey had had only one thought in mind, "to get rid of the pillowcase in the quickest and easiest way."

Suppose I'd been the one, Jessie thought with a shudder.

Suppose I've smothered the baby and the baby's body has been found by that nosy nurse and the house is in confusion and Dr. Wicks is there and the police are coming and suddenly, like a dash of seawater, I notice the pillow with my dirty handprint on the slip. It mustn't be found . . . they'll know it was murder . . . get rid of the slip quick, quick . . . is that someone coming? whose voice is that? I mustn't be found in here . . . I'm in the nursery—I've got to get rid of it—got to hide it—where? where?

The laundry chute!

Now wait, Jessie said to her racing pulse, wait, wait, that came too easy. . . .

Easy? But that's just it. The easiest way! One step to the door of the chute, one flip of the wrist, one shove, another flip of the wrist . . . and the pillowslip is gone. Gone down into the basement, into the laundry-sized canvas hamper under the chute opening . . . gone to mingle with the rest of the household's soiled laundry. The easiest, the quickest way to get rid of it.

At least temporarily.

Later—later I'll get hold of it, destroy it. As soon as I can. As soon as I can get down into the basement plausibly, safely . . .

And suppose just then the police arrived. And you couldn't, you simply couldn't call attention to yourself by disappearing. Not with a hysterical wife needing attention, policemen's questions to be answered, the dead little body in the crib . . . not with the awful guilt clamoring to be guarded . . . and the servants downstairs whispering over their coffee, in the path of anyone wanting to get to the basement unseen. And always and constantly the need to hear every whisper, to observe every change of expression, every coming, every going, to make sure you were still unsuspected . . .

Jessie frowned. It sounded fine—except for one thing. The police had searched the house thoroughly. "The laundry basement, the hampers . . ." Chief Pearl had ordered. And they hadn't found the pillowslip. So maybe . . .

So maybe they overlooked it.

That's what must have happened! Jessie thought exultantly. They didn't find the slip somehow and Alton Humffrey must have died a thousand deaths while they were looking and was reborn a thousand times when they failed to find it, and kept waiting, waiting for them to leave so he could sneak down into the basement and rummage through the canvas hamper and retrieve the fateful piece of batiste. But dawn came, and daylight, and still Abe Pearl's men were on the premises searching, and still he was afraid to risk being seen going to the basement.

And then, of course, Sadie Smith came, Sadie Smith from Norwalk, driving up in her 1938 Olds that made such a clatter early Tuesday and Friday mornings . . .

Sadie Smith to do the wash.

Jessie burrowed deeper in the maple chair, surprised to find herself shaking.

For of course after that Alton Humffrey thought he was safe. That day passed, a week, a month and the pillowslip vanished into the limbo of forgotten things.

Sadie Smith had washed the pillowslip along with the other hand laundry, not noticing, or ignoring, the dirty handprint; and that was the end of that.

The end of it.

Jessie sighed.

So much for "helping" Richard.

But wait!

Surely Sadie could not have been deaf and blind to what was going on in the house that Friday. Surely Mrs. Lenihan, or Mrs. Charbedeau, or one of the maids, must have told Sadie about the pillowslip the policemen were turning the house and grounds upside down for. Even if the police had missed it in the hamper, *wouldn't Sadie have been on the lookout for it?*

Yes!

Then why hadn't she found it?

It was still light when Jessie parked before the neat two-story brick housing development in Norwalk. She found Sadie Smith changing into a clean housedress. Mrs. Smith was a stout, very dark woman with brawny forearms and good-humored, shrewd black eyes.

"Miss Sherwood," she exclaimed. "Well, of all people! Come in! I just got home from work—"

"Oh, dear, maybe I ought to come back some other time, Mrs. Smith. It was thoughtless of me to pop in just before dinner, and without even phoning beforehand."

"We never eat till eight, nine o'clock. My husband don't get home till then. You go on into the parlor and set, Miss Sherwood. I'll fix us some tea."

"Thank you. But why don't we have it here in your kitchen? It's such a charming kitchen, and I get so little chance to be in my own . . ."

Mrs. Smith said quietly, as she put the kettle on the range, "It's about the Humffreys, Miss Sherwood, ain't it?"

"Yes," Jessie admitted.

"I knew it." The dark woman seated herself at the other end of the table. "You don't have to tell me you're still all bothered about how that little child died. It's a terrible thing, Miss Sherwood, but he's dead, and nothing can bring him back. Why don't you just forget the Humffreys? They ain't your kind of people."

"I'd very much like to, but there are reasons why I can't. Do you mind if I call you Sadie?"

"Not you I don't," Mrs. Smith said grimly.

"Do you remember that Friday you came to do the wash, Sadie? The morning after little Michael was found dead?"

"I surely do."

"Did you run across one of those batiste pillowslips with the delicate lace that day—a slip that was very dirty? In fact, that had the print of a man's dirty hand on it?"

Sadie Smith cocked an eye at her. "That's what the detectives kept asking me that day."

"Oh, they did? Did anyone else ask you about it? I mean . . . people of the household?"

"Mrs. Lenihan mentioned it to me first thing I set foot in the house. Told me about the child, and said the policemen were turning the house inside out looking for a dirty pillowslip like that. I told her I'd keep an eye out for it, and I did."

"Anyone mention the pillowslip to you besides Mrs. Lenihan and the detectives?"

"No."

"I take it you never found it."

"That's right. Picked that wash over a dozen times, but it just wasn't there. There's the kittle!" The stout woman jumped up and began bustling about.

"Were there *any* pillowslips in the wash that day?" Jessie persisted.

"Nary one."

"Not one?" Jessie frowned. "That's queer."

"I thought so, too. You take sugar and cream, Miss Sherwood?"

"Neither, thanks," Jessie said absently. "No pillowslips at all . . ."

"Well, you're going to taste some of these sweet buns I just got from the bakery, or I'll take it real unfriendly of you. But about those pillow slips. First thing I thought was that snippety upstairs maid of theirs had stuffed too big a bundle into one of the laundry chutes. She'd done it a couple times, and the laundry'd got stuck, and we had to go fishing for it in the chute with a plumber's snake they have in the basement."

A stopped-up chute!

"Do you suppose that's what could have happened to the pillowslip they were looking for, Sadie?" Jessie asked excitedly. "A chute already stopped up, and the slip just didn't go all the way down?"

Mrs. Smith shook her head. "Wasn't no stopped-up chute. I took some clothespins and dropped one down each chute that morning to see if they was clear, and they was. Then I remembered. Friday mornings was the upstairs maid's day to strip the beds and change linen, and the way things was in the house that morning she just didn't get to do it. You eat one of those buns, Miss Sherwood."

"Delicious," Jessie said, munching. "You checked *all* the chutes, Sadie? The one in the nursery, too?"

"Well, not the nursery one, no. First place, they wouldn't let me in there. Second place, never was any stopping-up trouble in the nursery chute, 'cause *you* always slid the wash down from that room."

Could that be it? Jessie thought hungrily.

But she had been the only one who used the nursery chute. She always stripped and remade the baby's crib herself. And she had always been automatically careful to throw one piece down the chute at a time, even though the sheets were only crib size.

Jessie sipped her tea hopelessly.

"—though there was that trouble with the nursery chute when they was installing it," the laundress was saying. "I'd forgot about that. Maybe 'cause nothing ever happened."

"What?" Jessie looked up. "What did you say, Sadie?"

"When they was installing it. Before you came to work there, Miss Sherwood. Wasn't no nursery or room off it—the one you slept in—till just before Mr. and Mrs. Humffrey adopted the baby. That all used to be an upstairs sitting room. They had it made over into two rooms for the baby and a nurse, and that was when they installed the chute in the nursery. Hadn't been one there before."

"But you said something about some trouble with the nursery chute during installation—"

"And it only just come to mind," Mrs. Smith nodded. "Mr. Humffrey was fit to be hogtied. Seems after the chute was put in and all, and the man was testing it, throwing things down it, he found out there was a defect in it—it had a little piece of metal or something sticking out some place down the chute—and every once in a while something would catch on it. The man poked some kind of tool down in and felt around till he found the snag, and sort of sawed away at it. I guess he smoothed it down, 'cause you never had nothing stick in that chute, Miss Sherwood, did you?''

No, Jessie thought, I never did.

But suppose that was just luck!

Suppose the night Alton Humffrey dropped the damning pillowslip down that chute . . . *suppose that time it caught on what was left of the snag?*

So Sadie Smith hadn't found the slip, and Alton Humffrey thought Sadie Smith *had* found it and washed it out, and all the time it was stuck in the nursery chute *and it was still there.*

Jessie hung up, collected her coins, and sat in the telephone booth nibbling her nails. Richard's phone in New York didn't answer, so he must be out after Henry Cullum. Taugus police headquarters said that Chief Pearl had left for the night, and there had been no answer at the Pearls' house—they must have gone visiting, or out to dinner and a movie.

Jessie sat there, frustrated.

I've *got* to know, she thought. And not tomorrow, but tonight.

Suddenly she thought, I can do it myself.

She accepted the thought instantly, and without attempting to think through the difficulties. If I think about it, she told herself, I won't do it. So I won't think about it.

She left the drugstore, got into her coupé, and set out for Taugus.

The electrified ship's lantern over the gatehouse looked lost against the black bulk of Nair Island.

Jessie drove across the causeway slowly. Did they maintain guards after the season? If they did, she was sunk. The closer she got to the gatehouse the more foolhardy the project became.

A burly figure in a uniform stepped out of the gatehouse and held up his hand. And the gate was *down.*

So much for private enterprise, Jessie thought.

"Hey," a familiar voice said. "It's Miss Sherwood."

Charlie Peterson!

"Why, Mr. Peterson," Jessie said warmly. "What are you doing here? I thought you'd quit. At least you said you were going to."

"Well, you know how it is," the big guard said. "It ain't such a bad job, especially after the summer."

"And when policemen aren't driving you crazy," Jessie smiled. What can I say to him? she thought.

"That's a fact." The guard planted his elbow on the edge of her window. "How you been, Miss Sherwood?"

"Just fine. And you?" *I'll have to think of a plausible excuse. But what?*

"No complaints. Say, I never expected to see you again." Peterson looked at her in the oddest way, and Jessie thought, Here it comes. "What brings you to the Island?"

Jessie wet her lips. "Well . . ."

He pushed his big face close to hers, exhaling an aroma of bourbon. "It wouldn't be me, now, would it?"

Jessie almost laughed aloud. Problem solved!

"Why, Mr. Peterson," she said archly. "And you a family man and all."

He guffawed. "Can't blame a redblooded guy for a little wishful thinking! You going up to the Humffrey house? Nobody's there."

How lucky can you get! Jessie thought exultantly.

"Oh, dear," she said. "Nobody, Mr. Peterson? Where's the caretaker?"

"Stallings had to drive up to Concord, Mass. tonight. Mr. Humffrey phoned him to take some bulbs or something there for transplanting. That's their winter place."

"I don't know what to do," Jessie wailed. "Is Stallings going to be back tonight?"

"Tomorrow night, I guess."

"I suppose I could come back tomorrow, but as long as I'm here . . ." She turned her eyes on him appealingly, hoping the bourbon hadn't worn off. "Do you think anybody'd mind if I went up there for a few minutes? Like a fool I forgot some of my things when I packed, and I've just got to have them."

"Well." Peterson scratched his bulging jaw. You big oaf, Jessie thought, I'll— I'll vamp you if I have to. "Seeing it's you, Miss Sherwood . . ." But then he said, with his hand on the barrier, "Wait a minute."

Now what?

"How you going to get in?"

"Oh, I'll manage," Jessie said quickly. How, she had no idea.

"Hold it." Peterson went into the gatehouse. In a moment he was back, flourishing a key. "Stallings always leaves the key with me in case Mr. Humffrey should show up while he's off the Island. Need any help, Miss Sherwood?" he shouted after her gallantly.

"No, thanks," Jessie shouted back, clutching the key.

She felt rather bourbonish herself as she drove up the Nair Island road.

Stallings had left the nightlight burning over the service entrance. Jessie parked in the driveway near it, turned off her ignition and lights, and jumped out.

Her feet crunched loudly on the gravel, and Jessie hesitated, her skin itching. What am I so nervous about? she thought. Nobody can hear me.

Still, she found herself putting her feet down as if she were in a bog.

She unlocked the service door and slipped thankfully into the Humffrey house. But with her back against the door, thankfulness melted away.

She had never seen such dark darkness.

This is what comes of being an honest woman, she thought. Nobody here, nobody on the Island but Peterson, whose blessing I have, and yet . . . It seemed to her the house was full of furtive noises. As if the wood and plaster were breathing.

Remember Michael, she told herself rigidly. Remember that little dead body. She filled her lungs with air, deliberately, then let the air out.

Immediately the house became a house, the darkness friendly.

Jessie pushed away from the door and stepped confidently forward. Her hand touched the basement door. She opened it, felt for the switch, found it, and snapped it on.

The basement sprang at her.

She ran down the stairs. The steps were cushioned and carpeted and her descent was soundless.

At the bottom she paused to look around.

She knew where the outlet of the nursery chute was. She could see it from where she stood, with the big canvas laundry basket still in place under the vent. She had always done the baby's diapers and undershirts herself, refusing to allow Mrs. Humffrey to employ a diaper service.

"I like to know what my babies' diapers are washed in," she said to Mrs. Humffrey. "I've seen too many raw little bottoms."

Funny the things you thought about when . . . Jessie forced herself to think about the problem at hand.

Sadie Smith had mentioned a "plumber's snake." Jessie had only the vaguest notion of what a plumber's snake might be. She supposed it was some device for getting into clogged pipes and things that might choke up and be hard to clean. Where would such a thing be kept? Then she recalled that one of the basement walls was covered with shelving for the storage of tools, light bulbs, and odds and ends of housewares and hardware. The snake would probably be there. Wasn't it at the far end of the basement, behind the oil burner?

Jessie walked past the set tubs where Mrs. Smith had done the hand washing, past the washing machine and dryer, around the burner . . .

There it was.

She found the snake on the bottom shelf among some wrenches, pipe elbows, and other plumbing accessories. It was unmistakable, a large coil of metal cable with a loopy sort of head on it.

She took the snake over to the vent of the nursery chute, set the canvas basket to one side, inserted the head of the cable in the opening, and pushed. As she unwound the snake, she kept pushing upward. The cable made a raspy, rattly sound going up. She kept wiggling it, shaking it, making it go from side to side.

It went up, up, up. Finally it banged against something far overhead, refused to go further. It had obviously struck the door of the chute in the nursery.

And nothing had come down.

Jessie sat down on the basement floor and laughed.

Exit Jessie Sherwood, Female Sleuth.

The only thing to do was return the snake to the shelf, turn off the light, get into her car, and go back where she belonged.

Still seated on the floor under the vent, Jessie began to coil the cable. It came down, scraping, as she rewound it. The head appeared.

And something crumpled and white appeared with it and dropped into her lap.

The material was batiste. It had a lace edging. Honiton lace.

With trembling fingers Jessie took the pillowslip by two corners and held it up. The imprint of a dirty right hand showed plainly just off the center of the square.

"Why, I've done it," Jessie said aloud in an amazed voice. "I've found it."

A horribly familiar voice behind her replied, "So you have, Miss Sherwood."

Jessie's head screwed around like a doll's.

Her eyeballs froze.

Alton K. Humffrey was standing at the foot of the basement stairs.

In his right hand there was a gun, and the gun was aimed at her heart.

The eye of the gun came steadily nearer, growing bigger and bigger.

Richard, Jessie thought. *Richard*.

"First, Miss Sherwood," the horrible voice said, "I'll relieve you of this."

She felt the pillowslip jerked out of her hand. From the corner of her paralyzed eye she saw his left hand crumple it, stuff it into his pocket.

The gun receded.

Not far.

"You're frightened, Miss Sherwood. I sympathize. But you have only yourself to blame. Not a particularly consoling last thought, I suppose. Believe me, I dislike this almost as much as you do. But what recourse have you left me?"

Jessie almost said, *None*. But she knew that if she opened her mouth, nothing would come out but a chatter of teeth.

Richard, Richard. You don't even know where I am. Not you, not Chief Pearl, not anybody but Charlie Peterson, and what good is he? Alton Humffrey has seen to that, or he wouldn't be here pointing a gun. You're going to die alone, Jessie, like an idiot, sitting on a basement floor in an empty house on an empty island. Die.

The voice was saying, without bite or pinch, "You must see that I have no choice. You've found the slip, you've examined it. You're probably incorruptible. In any case, you're too close to that busybody Queen. So I must kill you, Miss Sherwood. I must."

This isn't happening, Jessie thought. It's just—not—happening.

"Not that the prospect pleases. I'm not a compulsive murderer. It's easier to commit murder then one would think, I've found, but it isn't pleasant. Your death is even dangerous to me. Peterson knows you're here. I could shoot you as an intruder, saying that I fired before I realized who you were, but Peterson's told me you were here. By the same token, he also knows I'm here. So I'm forced to take a great risk."

I'm going to wake up any second . . .

"When you disappear, suspicion will naturally fall on me. After I row your body out and sink it in deep water, I shall have to concoct a story. They won't believe the story, of course, no matter how plausible it is. But without a body, with no evidence of a crime, what can they do, after all? I think I'll come out of it all right. This is a soundproof room, Miss Sherwood, and—forgive me—I shall be very careful about removing all traces afterward."

It's silly. He's just trying to scare me. Nobody could talk as calmly as this and mean to take a human life. Nobody.

Richard, Richard.

"I still don't understand what brought you here tonight." The millionaire's voice this time was slightly flavored with petulance. "I certainly had no idea I was going to run into anyone. I came for the very purpose you accomplished, to check the nursery chute. That farce in Chief Pearl's office—before Queen produced the forgery—set me to wondering how they could possibly have found the pillowslip. And that reminded me of the obstruction in the chute when it was installed. How did you learn about that, Miss Sherwood?" Jessie stirred, and he said sharply, "Don't move, please."

"I have to," Jessie heard herself say. "My legs have fallen asleep. My neck."

"I'm sorry," he said, as if he really were. "You may stand up."

Jessie got to her feet. Her knees gave, and she leaned against the wall of the chute.

"In a way it was unfortunate for you that I employ a caretaker," the millionaire droned on. "If not for Stallings's being on the premises, I would have examined the chute last night. As it was, I had to go back to New York and find an excuse to send Stallings away. What did make you come here tonight to look the chute over?"

"Does it matter?" How lightheaded she felt.

Jessie shut her eyes.

"I suppose not."

She heard a click.

Her eyes flew open and she stared wildly. He was stepping back, his arm was coming up, it was extending, the gun was glowing softly blue at the end of it, she could see the stump of his little finger at the base of the grip, the index finger was beginning to whiten . . .

"Don't kill me, Mr. Humffrey, I don't want to die, please don't kill me."

"I must," Alton Humffrey muttered.

"*Don't!*" Jessie screamed, and she shut her eyes tight.

The basement rocked with the explosion.

Why, there's no pain, Jessie thought. Isn't that odd? There's no pain at all. Just the roar of the gun and the smash of glass—

Glass?

She opened her eyes. Alton Humffrey's right hand was a bloody pulp. His gun was on the floor and he was gripping his right wrist with his left hand convulsively. His mouth and nose were curled back in agony. A man's hand, holding a smoking revolver, was just withdrawing from a broken window high in the basement wall and two other men were vaulting down the basement stairs to fling themselves on the wounded millionaire and bring him crashing to the floor.

Then an incredibly dear figure appeared at the head of the stairs and Jessie saw that it was he who had fired the shot through the basement window and he was running down the stairs like a boy with the smoking gun still in his hand and she was in his arms.

"Richard," Jessie said.

Then she fainted.

Jessie found herself staring at a white ceiling. There was something familiar about the light fixture and the molding, and she turned her head and looked around. Of course. Her room. The nursery next door. The baby would be gleeping in a moment and the alarm would go off and she would jump out of bed . . .

Then she remembered.

Jessie sat up.

Mrs. Pearl was sitting in the rocker beside the bed, smiling at her.

"How do you feel, Jessie?"

"All right, I guess." Jessie looked down. Someone—she hoped it had been Beck Pearl—had removed her dress and girdle. "Did you . . . ?"

The little woman nodded. She got up to switch off the nightlight and turn on the overhead lights.

"What time is it?" Her wristwatch was gone, too.

"About 3 A.M. You've had quite a sleep. Dr. Wicks gave you a needle. Don't you remember?"

"I'm trying to, Becky. But how is it you're here?"

"They located Abe and me at a friend's home in Westport. When I heard about your terrible experience, I made Abe bring me along. Richard wanted to take you to a hospital, but Dr. Wicks said it wasn't necessary. You're sure you feel well enough to get out of bed?"

"Yes." Jessie swung her legs to the floor stiffly.

"Where's Richard?"

"He's still here. They all are. They don't want to move Humffrey yet. He lost a lot of blood and they've got him in bed, under guard." Beck Pearl's soft mouth set hard. "It's funny what good care they take of murderers. I'd have let him bleed to death."

"Becky, you mustn't say a thing like that."

"You're a nurse, Jessie," the little woman said quietly. "I'm just a woman who's had babies. And I have grandchildren. He murdered a baby."

Jessie shivered.

"I'd better get dressed," she said.

"Let me help you, dear."

"No, please. You might tell Richard I'm up."

Beck Pearl smiled again and went out.

It's all over, Jessie kept telling herself as she wriggled into the girdle. It's really all over.

He was waiting for her in the hall.

"Richard."

He took her by the arms. "You're sure you ought to be up?"

"You saved my life."

"You're so pale."

"You saved my life, Richard," Jessie said again.

He flushed. "You'd better sit down."

He drew her over to the big settee opposite Alton Humffrey's upstairs study. How tired he looked. Tired and . . . something else. Disturbed?

"What were you doing here, Jessie? When I looked through that basement window and saw you standing down there facing Humffrey's gun, I couldn't believe my eyes."

"I tried to phone you before I came, but I couldn't get an answer. I couldn't even locate Chief or Mrs. Pearl." Jessie told him what she had found out from Sadie Smith, and how on impulse she had decided to investigate the chute when she was unable to reach him or the Taugus chief of police. "What I don't understand, Richard, is what *you* were doing here. I thought you were in town chasing Henry Cullum."

"I started to, but I ran into Johnny Kripps and Wes Polonsky." He grinned. "They were watching Humffrey's Park Avenue apartment on their own. That was luck, because Wes had his car. We sat around waiting for Cullum to show, so we could pump him about Mrs. Humffrey's whereabouts, when we saw Humffrey trying to take a sneak. He was alone, and he was acting so queer we decided to tail him. He dodged around to his garage, got his car out, and headed for the West Side Highway. We tailed him all the way to Nair Island, and that was that."

Jessie laid her head on his shoulder. "It's all over, Richard."

"No, it isn't."

His shoulder was rigid. Jessie sat up quickly.

"It isn't?" she said. "It isn't what, Richard?"

"Isn't over." He pressed his fingers to his eyes. "I don't know how much more you can take tonight, Jessie. Can you stand a big shock?"

"Shock." Dear God, what is it now? Jessie thought.

"What's happened!"

"We sure picked a lulu when we stuck our noses into this one. I don't know that I've ever run across a case like it."

"Like *what?*"

He got up and took her by the hand.

"I'll show you, Jessie."

Chief Pearl's two detectives, Borcher and Tinny, were in the study. Borcher was reading a copy of Plato's *Republic* with a deep frown. Tinny was napping in a leather armchair.

Both jumped up when Richard Queen opened the door. When he waved, Borcher returned to his puzzled reading and Tinny sank down and closed his eyes again.

"Over here, Jessie."

The dirty pillowslip was spread out on Humffrey's desk. Everything else had been removed.

"I was the one who found it," Jessie said. "I fished it out of the nursery chute. Then he—he came in and took it away from me."

"Then you've seen it."

"Just a glance."

"Examine it, Jessie."

Jessie bent over the pillowslip. Now that she saw it in strong light, at leisure, it was remarkable how well she had remembered the position of the handprint in supervising the forgery.

She shook her head. "I can't see anything special about this, Richard. Is there something on the back? I never did see the back."

"As a matter of fact, there is." He took hold of the tip of the lace edging at the upper right corner of the slip and turned it back a little. Just below the reverse of the lace Jessie saw a small stain, rusty brown in color. "That's a bloodstain, probably from a scratched finger. However, remember that Humffrey didn't get a look at the back of our forgery. We had it face up on Abe's desk under glass." He flipped the corner back. "You still don't see where we went wrong?"

Jessie stared and stared. "No."

"Take another look at that handprint, Jessie. A real look this time."

And then she saw it, and her mind leaped back to that August night in the nursery aud her brief glimpse of the pillow over the baby's face. And for the first time since that moment Jessie Sherwood saw the pillow as she had seen it then.

What she had forgotten until now was that the little finger of the handprint was a whole finger.

There was no missing fingertip.

"That's how Humffrey knew the slip we showed him was a fake," Inspector Queen shrugged. "We showed him a handprint with the tip of the pinkie gone. He knew that the original pillowcase had a handprint showing five full fingers."

"But I don't understand," Jessie cried. "Alton Humffrey's pinkie does have the tip missing. How could his right hand possibly have made this print?"

"It couldn't."

"But—"

"It couldn't. Therefore it didn't."

Jessie gaped at him. The silence became so intense that Borcher looked up from his Plato uneasily and Tinny opened one eye.

"But Richard . . ."

"Humffrey didn't murder the baby, Jessie. I guess they knew what they were doing when they retired me." The old man sighed. "I was so sure Humffrey knocked off Finner and the Coy girl that I had to wrap it up in one neat package.

One killer. But it wasn't one killer, Jessie. Humffrey murdered Finner and Connie Coy, all right, but someone else murdered the baby.''

Jessie squeezed her forehead with both hands, trying to force some order into her thoughts.

"Humffrey never doubted for a minute that the baby was his—I was wrong about that, too. He knew it was his. That was the whole point. And when he spotted the pillowcase that night he knew his baby had been murdered, and he knew who'd murdered it. That's when he got rid of the pillowcase. He was determined to make the death look like an accident. That's what made him say *he* had put the ladder there, when he hadn't touched the ladder. It was the baby's killer who'd put the ladder there, thinking to make the murder look like the nephew's work.

"And when Finner got in touch with Humffrey and told him to meet us in Finner's office, Humffrey realized that unless he shut Finner's mouth the story of Michael's real parentage might come out and lead right back to Michael's death. So he killed Finner and removed all the evidence from the file. And when we got to Connie Coy in spite of everything and she was about to name Humffrey as the real father of Michael, he killed Connie Coy.

"It was all coverup, Jessie. Coverup to keep us from learning the true reason for the baby's murder. To keep the whole nasty story out of the papers. To protect the sacred name of Humffrey.''

"Someone else," Jessie said, clinging to the thought. "What someone else, Richard? Who?''

"Jessie," Richard Queen said. "Who had the best reason to hate Alton Humffrey's illegitimate child? Who's the only one in the world Humffrey would have a guilt feeling about, a compulsion to cover up? Whose exposure as an infant-killer would smear as much muck on the Humffrey name as if he himself were tagged for it? Who's the one who kept hysterically insisting—until Humffrey got her out of the way and kept her out of the way—that she'd been 'responsible' for little Mike's death? . . . only we all misunderstood her?''

He shook his head. "There's only one possible candidate for the baby's murder, Jessie. It's Sarah Humffrey's handprint on this pillowcase.''

Chief Pearl stuck his big head into the room. "Hi, Jessie. You okay now? Dick, he's fully conscious and ready to make a statement. You'd better come.''

Jessie went as far as the doorway of the master bedroom. The room was full of men. Taugus police. The State's Attorney's man, Merrick, tieless again. Dr. Wicks. A lot of state troopers. Wes Polonsky and Johnny Kripps.

And Alton Humffrey.

Humffrey was lying on the great bed, propped on pillows, his right arm swathed in bandages. His skin was not sallow now. It was colorless. The narrow wedge of face was without expression or movement, a face in a coffin. Only the eyes were alive, two prisoners struggling to escape.

Jessie said faintly, "I'll wait with Beck Pearl, Richard," and she stumbled away.

"That," Richard Queen remarked, leaning back in happy surfeit, "was the best darned Sunday dinner I've ever surrounded.''

"Delicious, Jessie!" Beck Pearl said, not without a slight mental reservation about the wine in the sauce. "She's really a wonderful cook, Dick. Imagine being a trained nurse and having a talent like this, too!''

"It's just a veal roast," Jessie said deprecatingly, as if she were in the habit of standing over a hot oven every Sunday for hours and hours basting with an experimental sauce of garlic salad dressing, lemon juice, sauterne, bouillon and Parmesan cheese, and praying that the result would be edible.

"But as I was saying," Abe Pearl said, and he belched.

"Abe!" his wife said.

"Beg pardon," Abe Pearl said.

It was Sunday, October 9th, a brisk and winy day, a day for being alive. Jessie had planned and slaved for this day, when Richard Queen's two friends should sit in her little dining alcove in Rowayton and tell her—and him—what a marvelous cook she was. Only Abe Pearl insisted on talking about what Jessie had hoped and hoped would not be talked about.

"Wonderful," Richard Queen beamed. "Just wonderful, Jessie."

"Thank you," Jessie murmured.

"—she's as cold turkey as any killer I ever heard of," Abe Pearl went on. "Match that big mitt of hers to the handprint on the pillowcase—a perfect fit. Analyze her perspiration—it gives the same lab result as the sweat traces in the slip. Analyze her blood—it's just like the blood in the stain on the back of the slip, which got on there when she scratched her hand on the ladder. Dust on ladder same as dust on slip. And, by God, when they work over the slip and bring out some fingerprints left by the mixed dust and perspiration, they're her prints!" Chief Pearl pressed his paws to his abdomen to discourage another belch. "And yet," he thundered solemnly, "I tell you Sarah Humffrey will never go to the Chair. If she wasn't as nutty as a fruit cake—I mean after they got the baby, when she overheard Humffrey talking to Finner over the phone and realized her saintly husband had palmed off his own bastard on her—if she wasn't as nutty as a fruit cake then, she sure is now. She'll get sent to a bughouse on an insanity verdict, and I don't see how the State can stop it."

"Abe," Beck Pearl said.

"What?"

"Wouldn't you like to walk off your dinner?"

So finally they were alone in Jessie's little garden. Abe Pearl was wandering in Coventry somewhere along the waterfront, and his wife was in Jessie's kitchen banging dishes around to show that she wasn't listening through the kitchen window.

And now that they were alone together, there seemed to be nothing to say. That same peculiar silence dropped between them.

So Jessie picked some dwarf zinnias, and Richard Queen sat in the white basket chair under the dogwood tree watching the sun on her hair.

If he doesn't say something soon I'll shriek, Jessie thought. I can't go on picking zinnias forever.

But he kept saying absolutely nothing.

So then the flowers were tumbling to the ground, and Jessie heard herself crying, "Richard, what in heaven's name is the matter with you?"

"Matter?" he said with a start. "With me, Jessie?"

"Do *I* have to propose to *you?*"

"Prop . . ." The sound came out of his mouth like a bite of hot potato. "*Propose?*"

"Yes!" Jessie wept. "I've waited and waited, and all you ever do is pull a grim face and feel sorry for yourself. I'm a woman, Richard, don't you know that? And you're a man—though you don't seem to know that either—and we're both lonely, and I think we l-love each other . . ."

He was on his feet, clutching his collar and looking dazed. "You mean . . .
you'd *marry* me, Jessie? Marry *me?*"

"What do you think I'm proposing, Richard Queen, a game of Scrabble?"
He took a step toward her.
And stopped, swallowing hard. "But Jessie, I'm an old man—"
"Oh, fish! You're an old fool!"
So he came to her.

A long time later—the sun was going down, and the Pearls had long since
vanished—Richard Queen's arm shifted from Jessie Sherwood's shoulders to her
waist, and he muttered blissfully, "I wonder what Ellery's going to say."

Cat of Many Tails

1

The strangling of Archibald Dudley Abernethy was the first scene in a nine-act tragedy whose locale was the City of New York.

Which misbehaved.

Seven and one-half persons inhabiting an area of over three hundred square miles lost their multiple heads all at once. The storm center of the phenomenon was Manhattan, that "Gotham" which, as the *New York Times* pointed out during the worst of it, had been inspired by a legendary English village whose inhabitants were noted for their foolishness. It was a not entirely happy allusion, for there was nothing jocular in the reality. The panic seizure caused far more fatalities than the Cat; there were numerous injured; and what traumata were suffered by the children of the City, infected by the bogey fears of their elders, will not be comprehended until the psychiatrists can pry into the neuroses of the next generation.

In the small area of agreement in which the scientists met afterward, several specific indictments were drawn. One charged the newspapers. Certainly the New York press cannot disclaim some responsibility for what happened. The defense that "we give John Public the news as it happens, how it happens, and for as long as it happens," as the editor of the *New York Extra* put it, is plausible but fails to explain why John Public had to be given the news of the Cat's activities in such necrotic detail, embellished by such a riches of cartoonical crape and obituary embroidery. The object of this elaborate treatment was, of course, to sell more newspapers—an object which succeeded so admirably that, as one circulation manager privately admitted, "We really panicked 'em."

Radio was named codefendant. Those same networks which uttered approving sounds in the direction of every obsessionist who inveighed against radio mystery and crime programs as being the First Cause of hysteria, delinquency, seclusive behavior, *idée fixe,* sexual precocity, nailbiting, nightmare, enuresis, profanity, and other antisocial ills of juvenile America saw nothing wrong in thoroughly airing the depredations of the Cat, with sound effects . . . as if the sensational were rendered harmless by the mere fact of its being not fiction. It was later charged, not without justice, that a single five-minute newscast devoted to the latest horror of the strangler did more to shatter the nerves of the listening population than all the mystery programs of all the networks percussively put together. But by that time the mischief was done.

Others fished deeper. There were certain elements in the Cat's crimes, they said, which plucked universal chords of horror. One was the means employed. Breath being life and its denial death, their argument ran, the pattern of strangulation was bound to arouse the most basic fears. Another was the haphazard choice of victims—

"selection by caprice," they termed it. Man, they stated, faces death most equably when he thinks he is to die for some purpose. But the Cat, they said, picked his victims at random. It reduced the living to the level of the sub-human and gave the individual's extinction no more importance or dignity than the chance crushing of an ant. This made defenses, especially moral defenses, impossible; there was nowhere to hide; therefore panic. And still a third factor, they went on, was the total lack of recognition. No one lived who saw the terrorizer at his chill and motiveless work; he left no clues to his age, sex, height, weight, coloration, habits, speech, origin, even to his species. For all the data available, he might well have been a cat—or an incubus. Where nothing was to be perceived, the agitated imagination went berserk. The result was a Thing come true.

And the philosophers took the world view, opening casements to the great panorama of current events. *Weltanschauung!* they cried. The old oblate spheroid was wobbling on its axis, trying to resist stresses, cracking along faults of strain. A generation which had lived through two global conflicts; which had buried millions of the mangled, the starved, the tortured, the murdered; which rose to the bait of world peace through the bloody waters of the age and found itself hooked by the cynical barb of nationalism; which cowered under the inexplicable fungus of the atomic bomb, not understanding, not wishing to understand; which helplessly watched the strategists of diplomacy plot the tactics of an Armageddon that never came; which was hauled this way and that, solicited, exhorted, suspected, flattered, accused, driven, unseated, inflamed, abandoned, never at peace, never at rest, the object of pressures and contrary forces by the night and the day and the hour—the real victims of the universal War of Nerves . . . it was no wonder, the philosophers said, that such a generation should bolt screaming at the first squeak of the unknown. In a world that was desensitized, irresponsible, threatened and threatening, hysteria was not to be marveled at. It had attacked New York City; had it struck anywhere in the world, the people of that place would have given way. What had to be understood, they said, was that the people had welcomed panic, not surrendered to it. In a planet shaking to pieces underfoot it was too agonizing to remain sane. Fantasy was a refuge and a relief.

But it remained for an ordinary New Yorker, a 20-year-old law student, to state the case in language most people could understand. "I've just been reading up on Danny Webster," he said. "In one case he was mixed up in, trial of a fellow named Joseph White, Webster tossed this one over the plate: *Every unpunished murder takes away something from the security of every man's life.* I figure when you live in our cockeyed kind of world, when some boogyman they call the Cat starts sloughing folks right and left and nobody can get to first base on it, and as far as Joe Schmo can see this Cat's going to keep right on strangling the population till there's not enough customers left to fill the left field bleachers at Ebbets Field— or am I boring you and by the way whatever happened to Durocher?" The law student's name was Gerald Ellis Kollodny and he made the statement to a Hearst reporter on sidewalk-interview assignment; the statement was reprinted in the *New Yorker,* the *Saturday Review of Literature,* and *Reader's Digest; M-G-M News* invited Mr. Kollodny to repeat himself before its cameras; and New Yorkers nodded and said that was just about how it had stacked up.

2

August 25 brought one of those simmering subtropical nights in which summer New York specializes. Ellery was in his study stripped to his shorts, trying to write. But his fingers kept sliding off the keys and finally he turned off his desk light and padded to a window.

The City was blackly quiet, flattened by the pressures of the night. Eastward thousands would be drifting into Central Park to throw themselves to the steamy grass. To the northeast, in Harlem and the Bronx, Little Italy, Yorkville; to the southeast, on the Lower East Side and across the river in Queens and Brooklyn; to the south, in Chelsea, Greenwich Village, Chinatown—wherever there were tenements—fire escapes would be crowded nests in the smother, houses emptied, streets full of lackadaisical people. The parkways would be bug trails. Cars would swarm over the bridges—Brooklyn, Manhattan, Williamsburg, Queensborough, George Washington, Triborough—hunting a breeze. At Coney Island, Brighton, Manhattan Beach, the Rockaways, Jones Beach, the sands would be seeded by millions of the sleepless turned restlessly to the sea. The excursion boats would be scuttling up and down the Hudson and the ferries staggering like overloaded old women to Weehawken and Staten Island.

Heat lightning ripped the sky, disclosing the tower of the Empire State Building. A huge photographic process; for the shutterflash of a citysized camera taking a picture of the night.

A little to the south hung a bright spume. But it was a mirage. Times Square would be sweltering under it; the people would be in Radio City Music Hall, the Roxy, the Capitol, the Strand, the Paramount, the State—wherever there was a promise of lower temperatures.

Some would seek the subways. The coupled cars kept their connecting doors open and when the trains rushed along between stations there was a violent displacement of the tunnel air, hellish but a wind. The choice position was in the front doorway of the head car beside the motorman's cubicle. Here the masses would be thickest, swaying in a grateful catalepsy.

In Washington Square, along Fifth Avenue, 57th Street, upper Broadway, Riverside Drive, Central Park West, 110th Street, Lexington Avenue, Madison, the busses would accept the few and spurn the many and they would rush up and down, north and south, east and west, chasing their tails like . . .

Ellery blundered back to his desk, lit a cigaret.

No matter where I start, he thought, I wind up in the same damned place.

That Cat's getting to be a problem.

He tilted, embracing his neck. His fingers slithered in the universal ooze and he tightened them, thinking that he could stand an over-all tightening. Nonskid thoughts. A new lining job on the will.

The Cat.

Ellery smoked, crookedly.

A great temptation.

In the Wrightsville Van Horn case Ellery had run into stunning treachery. He had found himself betrayed by his own logic. The old blade had turned suddenly in his hand; he had aimed at the guilty with it and it had run through the innocent. So he had put it away and taken up his typewriter. As Inspector Queen said, ivory tower stuff.

Unhappily, he had to share his turret with an old knight who jousted daily with the wicked. Inspector Richard Queen of the New York Police Department being also the unhorsed champion's sire, it was a perilous proximity.

"I don't want to hear about a case," Ellery would say. "Just let me be."

"What's the matter?" his father would jeer. "Afraid you might be tempted?"

"I've given all that up. I'm not interested any longer."

But that was before the Cat strangled Archibald Dudley Abernethy.

He had tried to ignore the murder of Abernethy. And for some time he had succeeded in doing so. But the creature's round little face with its round little eyes had an annoying way of staring out at him from his morning newspaper.

In the end he had brought himself up to date.

It was interesting, an interesting case.

He had never seen a less meaningful face. It was not vicious, or kind, or sly, or stupid; it was not even enigmatic. It was nothing, a rotundity, a 44-year-old fetus-face; one of nature's undeveloped experiments.

Yes, an interesting homicide.

And then the second strangling.

And the third.

And . . .

The apartment door *blupped!*

"Dad?"

Ellery jumped, banging his shin. He limped hurriedly to the living room.

"Hi there." Inspector Queen already had his jacket and necktie off; he was removing his shoes. "You look cool, son."

The Inspector looked gray.

"Tough day?" It was not the heat. The old man was as weatherproof as a desert rat.

"Anything on the ice, Ellery?"

"Lemonade. Quarts of it."

The Inspector shuffled into the kitchen. Ellery heard the icebox open and close. "By the way, congratulate me."

"Congratulate you on what?"

"On being handed today," said his father, reappearing with a frosty glass, "the biggest pig in the poke of my alleged—I say alleged—career." He threw his head back and drank. Throat showing, he looked even grayer.

"Fired?"

"Worse."

"Promoted."

"Well," said the Inspector, seating himself, "I'm now top dog in the Cat chase."

"The Cat."

"You know, the Cat?"

Ellery leaned against the study jamb.

"The Commissioner called me in," said the Inspector, folding his hands about the glass, "and he told me he'd had the move under consideration for some time. He's creating a special Cat squad. I'm in full charge. As I said, top dog."

"Caninized." Ellery laughed.

"Maybe you find this situation full of yuks," said his father, "but as for me, give me liberty and lots of it." He drained what was left in the glass. "Ellery, I damn near told the Commissioner to his face today that Dick Queen's too old a bird to be handed a deal like this. I've given the P.D. a pretty full lifetime of faithful service. I deserve better."

"But you took it."

"Yes, I took it," said the Inspector, "and God help me, I even said, 'Thanks, Commissioner.' And then I got the feeling," he went on in a worried way, "that he had some angle he wasn't putting on the line and son, I wanted to duck out even more. I can still do it."

"You talking about quitting?"

"Well, I'm just talking. Anyway, you can't say you don't come by it honestly."

"Ourrrrch." Ellery went to one of the living room windows. "But it's not my brawl," he complained to New York. "I played around a little, that's all. For a long time I was lucky. But when I found out I was using loaded dice—"

"I see your point. Yes. And this crap game's for keeps."

Ellery turned around. "Aren't you exaggerating?"

"Ellery, this is an emergency."

"Oh, come."

"I said," said the old man, "an emergency."

"A few murders. Granted they're puzzling. That's hardly a new twist. What's the percentage of unsolved homicides? I don't understand you, Dad. I had a reason for quitting; I'd taken on something and I flubbed it, causing a death or two by the way. But you're a pro. This is an assignment. The responsibility for failure, if you fail, is the Commissioner's. And suppose these stranglings aren't solved—"

"My dear philosopher," said the Inspector, rolling the empty glass between his palms, "if these stranglings aren't solved, and damned quickly, something's going to pop in this man's town."

"Pop? In New York? How do you mean?"

"It hasn't really got going yet. Just signs. The number of phone calls to Headquarters asking for information, instructions, reassurance, anything. The increase in false alarm police calls, especially at night. The jitters of the men on duty. A little more all-around tension than there ought to be. A . . ." the Inspector groped with his glass . . . "a sort of concentration of interest on the part of the public. They're too interested. It isn't natural."

"Just because an overheated cartoonist—"

"Just because! Who cares a hoot in Hell Gate what's caused it? It's on its way, Ellery. Why is the only smash hit on Broadway this summer that ridiculous murder farce, *The Cat?* Every critic in town panned it as the smelliest piece of rat cheese to hit New York in five years, and it's the only show doing business. Winchell's latest is 'Cat-Astrophes.' Berle turned down a cat joke, said he didn't think the subject was funny. The pet shops report they haven't sold a kitten in a month. They're beginning to see the Cat in Riverdale, Canarsie, Greenpoint, the East Bronx, Park Row, Park Avenue, Park Plaza. We're starting to find alley cats strangled with cords all over the city. Forsythe Street. Pitkin Avenue. Lenox. Second. Tenth. Bruckner Boulevard—''

"Kids."

"Sure, we've even caught some of them at it. But it's a symptom, Ellery. A symptom of something that scares the stiffener out of me, and I'm man enough to admit it.''

"Have you eaten anything today?''

"Five murders and the biggest city in the world gets the shakes! Why? How do you explain it?''

Ellery was silent.

"Come on,'' said the Inspector sarcastically. "You won't endanger your amateur standing."

But Ellery was only thinking. "Maybe,'' he said, "maybe it's the strange feel of it. New York will take fifty polio cases a day in its stride, but let two cases of Asiatic cholera break out and under the right conditions you might have mass hysteria. There's something alien about these stranglings. They make indifference impossible. When a man like Abernethy can get it, anyone can get it.'' He stopped. The Inspector was staring at him.

"You seem to know a lot about it."

"Just what I've happened to catch in the papers.''

"Like to know more? Worm's eye view?''

"Well . . .''

"Sit down, son.''

"Dad—''

"Sit down!''

Ellery sat down. After all, the man was his father.

"Five murders so far,'' said the Inspector. "All in Manhattan. All stranglings. Same kind of cord used in each.''

"That tussah silk number? Indian silk?''

"Oh, you know that.''

"The papers say you've got nowhere trying to trace them.''

"The papers are correct. It's a strong, coarse-fibered silk of—so help me—Indian jungle origin, and it's the only clue we have.''

"What?''

"I repeat: not a single cursed other clue. Nothing! Nothing, Ellery. No prints. No witnesses. No suspects. No motives. There isn't a thing to work on. The killer comes and goes like a breeze, leaving only two things behind, a corpse and a cord. The first victim was—''

"Abernethy, Archibald Dudley. Aged 44. Three-room apartment on East 19th Street near Gramercy Park. A bachelor left alone by the death of his invalid mother a few years ago. His father, a clergyman, died in 1922. Abernethy never worked a lick in his life. Took care of mama and afterward of himself. 4-F in the war. Did his own cooking, housekeeping. No apparent interests. No entangling alliances. No anything. A colorless, juiceless nonentity. Has the time of Abernethy's death been fixed more accurately?''

"Doc Prouty is pretty well satisfied he was strangled around midnight of June 3. We have reason to believe Abernethy knew the killer; the whole setup smacked of an appointment. We've eliminated relatives; they're scattered to hell and gone and none of them could have done it. Friends? Abernethy didn't have any, not one. He was the original lone wolf.''

''Or sheep.''

''As far as I can see, we didn't miss a trick,'' said the Inspector morosely. ''We checked the super of the building. We checked a drunk janitor. Every tenant in the house. Even the renting agent.''

''I understand Abernethy lived off the income from a trust—''

''Handled by a bank for umpty years. He had no lawyer. He had no business—how he occupied his time since his mother's death God only knows; we don't. Just vegetated, I guess.''

''Tradesmen?''

''All checked off.''

''Barber, too?''

''You mean from the killer's getting behind his sweet petit point chair?'' The Inspector did not smile. ''He shaved himself. Once a month he got a haircut in a shop off Union Square. He'd gone there for over twenty years and they didn't even know his name. Just the same we checked the three barbers. And no dice.''

''You're convinced there was no woman in Abernethy's life?''

''Positive.''

''And no man?''

''No evidence that he was even a homo. He was a small fat skunk egg. No hits, no runs, no errors.''

''One error. At least one.'' Inspector Queen started, but then his lips tightened. Ellery sloshed a little in his chair. ''No man can be the total blank the facts make out Abernethy to have been. It's just not possible. And the proof that it's not is that he was murdered. He had a feeble life of *some* sort. He did *something*. All five of them did. What about Violette Smith?''

''Violette Smith,'' said the Inspector, closing his eyes. ''Number 2 on the Cat's hit parade. Strangled just nineteen days after Abernethy—date, June 22, sometime between 6 P.M. and midnight. Unmarried. 42. Lived alone in a two-room apartment on the top floor of a bug trap on West 44th, over a *pizzeria*. Side entrance, walkup. Three other tenants in the building besides the restaurant downstairs. Had lived at that address six years. Before that on 73rd and West End Avenue. Before that on Cherry Street in the Village, where she'd been born.

''Violette Smith,'' said the Inspector without opening his eyes, ''was the opposite of Archie Abernethy in just about every conceivable way. He was a hermit, she knew everybody around Times Square. He was a babe in the woods, she was a she-wolf. He'd been protected by mama all his life, the only protection she knew was the kind she had to pay. Abernethy had no vices, Violette had no virtues. She was a dipso, a reefer addict, and she'd just graduated to the hard stuff when she got hers. He never earned a penny in his life, she made her living the hard way.''

''Sixth Avenue mostly, I gather,'' said Ellery.

''Not true. Violette never worked the pavements. Her hustling was on call; she had a mighty busy phone.

''Whereas in Abernethy's case,'' the Inspector droned on, ''we had nothing to work on, in Violette's we hit the jackpot. Normally, when a woman like her gets knocked off, you check the agent, the girl friends, the clients, the dope peddler, the mobster who's always in the background somewhere—and somewhere along the line you hit the answer. Well, this setup was normal enough; Vi had a record of nine arrests, she'd done some time, she was tied up with Frank Pompo, all the rest of it. Only nothing got anywhere.''

"Are you sure—"

"—it was a Cat job? As a matter of fact, at first we weren't. If not for the use of the cord—"

"Same Indian silk."

"The color was different. Pinkish, a salmony kind of color. But the silk was that tussah stuff, all right, same as in Abernethy's case, only his was blue. Of course, when the third one came along, and the fourth and fifth, the pattern was clear and we're sure now the Smith woman was one of the series. The more we dig in the surer we get. The picture, atmosphere, are the same. A killer who came and went and didn't even leave a shadow on a windowshade."

"Still—"

But the old man was shaking his head. "We've worked the vine overtime. If Violette was slated to go we'd get some hint of it. But the stools don't know a thing. It's not that they've clammed up; they just don't know.

"She wasn't in any trouble. This definitely wasn't a crackdown for holding out, or anything like that. Vi was in the racket for a living and she was smart enough to play ball without a squawk. She took shakedowns as part of the hazards of the business. She was well-liked, one of the old reliables."

"Over 40," said Ellery. "In a wearing profession. I don't suppose—"

"Suicide? Impossible."

Ellery scratched his nose. "Tell me more."

"She wasn't found for over thirty-six hours. On the morning of June 24 a girl friend of hers who'd been trying to reach her by phone a whole day and night climbed the stairs, found Violette's door shut but not locked, went in—"

"Abernethy's body was found seated in an easychair," said Ellery. "Exactly how was the Smith woman found?"

"Her flat was a bedroom and sitting room—kitchenette was one of those wall-unit jobs. She was found on the floor in the doorway between the two rooms."

"Facing which way?" asked Ellery quickly.

"I know, I know, but there was no way of telling. She was all bunched up. Might have fallen from any position."

"Attacked from which direction?"

"From behind, same as Abernethy. And the cord knotted."

"Oh, yes, there's that."

"What?"

"The cord was knotted in Abernethy's case, too. It's bothered me."

"Why?" The Inspector sat up.

"Well . . . there's a sort of finality about it."

"A what?"

"Decorative, but was it necessary? You'd hardly let go till your victim was dead, would you? Then why the knot? In fact, it would be pretty hard to tie a knot while the victim was strangling. It suggests that the knots were tied after they were dead."

His father was staring.

"It's like putting a bow on a package that's quite adequately wrapped. The extra—I almost said the artistic—touch. Neat, satisfying. Satisfying a . . . what would you say? a passion for completeness? finality? Yes, so damned final."

"What in the world are you talking about?"

"I'm not sure," said Ellery mournfully. "Tell me—was there a sign of forcible entry?"

"No. The general opinion is that she expected her killer. Like Abernethy."

"Posing as a client?"

"Could be. If he was, it was only to get in. The bedroom wasn't disturbed and while she was found wearing a wrapper, she had a slip and panties on underneath. The testimony is she nearly always wore a negligee when she was home. But it could have been anybody, Ellery. Someone she knew well or someone she didn't know so well or even someone she didn't know at all. It wasn't hard," said the Inspector, "to make Miss Smith's acquaintance."

"The other tenants—"

"Nobody heard a thing. The restaurant people didn't even know she existed. You know how it is in New York."

"Ask no questions and mind your own business."

"While the lady upstairs is getting herself dead."

The Inspector got up and fussed to a window. But immediately he returned to his chair, scowling. "In other words," he said, "we drew a blank in the Smith case, too. Then—"

"Question. Did you find any connection between Abernethy and Violette Smith? Any at all?"

"No."

"Go on."

"Cometh Number 3," said the Inspector in a sort of liturgical mutter. "Rian O'Reilly, 40-year-old shoe salesman, living with his wife and four kids in a Chelsea tenement. Date, July 18; twenty-six days after the Smith murder.

"O'Reilly's kill," the Inspector said, "was so damn . . . so damn discouraging. He was a hardworking fellow, good husband, crazy father, struggling to keep his head above water and having a tough time of it. To keep his family going O'Reilly held down two jobs, a full-timer in a lower Broadway shoe store, a night relief job in a shop on Fulton and Flatbush across the river in Brooklyn. He'd have managed to scrape along if he hadn't run into such hard luck. One of his children got polio two years ago. Another got pneumonia. Then his wife splashed herself with hot paraffin putting up grape jelly and he paid a skin specialist for a year trying to heal her burn. On top of that another kid was run over by a hit-and-run driver who was never identified and spent three months in a hospital. O'Reilly's borrowed the limit against his $1000 insurance policy. His wife had hocked her measly engagement ring. They'd had a '39 Chevvy—O'Reilly sold it to pay doctors' bills.

"O'Reilly liked his nip now and then, but he gave up drinking. Even beer. He held himself down to ten cigarettes a day, and he'd been a heavy smoker. His wife put up box lunches and he didn't eat supper till he got home, usually after midnight. In the past year he'd suffered a lot from toothache, but he wouldn't go to a dentist, said he didn't have time for such foolishness. But he'd toss around some at night, his wife said."

The heat flowed through their windows. Inspector Queen wiped his face with a ball of handkerchief.

"O'Reilly was no Saturday night Irishman. He was a little guy, thin and ugly, with heavy eyebrows that made him look worried even when he was dead. He used to tell his wife he was a physical coward, but she thought he'd had plenty of guts. I guess he did, at that. He was born in Hell's Kitchen and his life was one long battle. With his drunk of a father and with the street hoodlums when he was a boy, and after that with poverty and sickness. Remembering his old man, who used to beat up his mother, O'Reilly tried to make up for it to his own wife and children. His whole life was his family.

"He was wild about classical music. He couldn't read a note and he'd never had a lesson, but he could hum snatches of a lot of operas and symphonies and during the summer he tried to take in as many of the free Sunday concerts in Central Park as he could. He was always after his kids to tune in WQXR, used to say he thought Beethoven would do them a lot more good than *The Shadow*. One of his boys has a talent for the violin; O'Reilly finally had to stop his lessons. The night that happened, Mrs. O'Reilly said, he cried like a baby all night.

"This was the man," said Inspector Queen, watching his curling toes, "whose strangled body was found early in the morning of July 19 by the janitor of the building. The janitor was mopping the entrance hall down when he noticed a heap of clothes in the dark space behind the stairway. It was O'Reilly, dead.

"Prouty fixed the time of death as between midnight and 1 A.M. of the 18th-19th. Obviously, O'Reilly was just coming home from his night job in Brooklyn. We checked with the store and the time he left jibed, sure enough, with his movements if he'd gone directly home and been attacked as he entered the house on the way upstairs. There was a lump on the side of his head—"

"The result of a blow, or from a fall," asked Ellery.

"We're not sure. A blow seems more likely, because he was dragged—there are rubberheel scrapes on the marble—from just inside the front door to the spot under the stairs where the janitor found him. No struggle, and nobody heard anything." The Inspector pinched his nose so hard the tip remained whitish for a few seconds. "Mrs. O'Reilly had been up all night waiting for her husband, afraid to leave the kids alone in the apartment. She was just going to phone the police—they held on to their phone, she said, because O'Reilly always said suppose one of the kids got sick in the middle of the night?—when the cop the janitor'd called came up to give her the bad news.

"She told me she'd been scared and nervous ever since the Abernethy murder. 'Rian had to come home from Brooklyn so late,' she said. 'I kept at him to quit the night job, and then when that woman on West 44th Street was choked to death too I nearly went out of my mind. But Rian only laughed. He said nobody'd bother to kill *him*, he wasn't worth killing.' "

Ellery planted his elbows on his naked knees and his face secretively between his hands.

The Inspector said, "Seems like it's getting hotter," and Ellery mumbled something. "It's against nature," complained the Inspector. He took off his shirt and undershirt and he plastered them with a smack against the back of his chair. "Leaving a widow and four children, with what was left of his insurance going to pay for his burial. I understand his priest is trying to do something, but it's a poor parish and O'Reilly's heirs are now enjoying City relief."

"And now his kids will be listening to *The Shadow* if they can hang on to their radio." Ellery rubbed his neck. "No clues."

"No clues."

"The cord."

"Same silk, blue."

"Knotted at the back?"

"Plenty of rhyme," muttered Ellery. "But where's the reason?"

"You tell O'Reilly's widow."

And Ellery was quiet. But after a while he said, "It was about that time that the cartoonist was inspired. I remember the unveiling of the Cat. He jumped out at you from the editorial page of the *Extra* . . . such as it was and is. One of the great monsters of cartoonical time. The man should get the Pulitzer prize for Satanism. A diabolical economy of line; the imagination fills in what the artist leaves out. Guaranteed to share your bed. *How Many Tails Has the Cat?* asks the caption. And we count three distinct appendages, curling at the ends back upon themselves. Not thick true tails, you understand. More like cords. Ending in nooselike openings just right for necks . . . which aren't there. And one cord bears the number *1*, and the second cord bears the number *2* and the third cord the number *3*. No *Abernethy, Smith,* or *O'Reilly.* He was so right. The Cat is quantitative. It's numbers that equalize all men, the Founding Fathers and Abe Lincoln to the contrary notwithstanding. The Cat is the great leveler of humanity. It's no accident that his claws are shaped like sickles."

"Sweet talk, but the point is the day after August 9 there was the Cat again," said the Inspector, "and he'd grown a fourth tail."

"And I remember that, too," nodded Ellery.

"Monica McKell. August 9. Twenty-two days after O'Reilly."

"The perennial debutante. A mere 37 and going strong."

"Park and 53rd. Café society. A table jumper they got to call Leaping Lena."

"Or in a more refined phrase of Lucius Beebe—Madcap Monica."

"That's the one," said the Inspector. "Also known as McKell's Folly, McKell being her old man, the oil millionaire, who told me Monica was the only wildcat he'd never brought in. But you could see he was proud of her. She was wild, all right—cut her teeth on a gin bottle, came out during Prohibition, and her favorite trick when she was tight was to get behind the bar and outmix the bartender. They say she mixed the best Martini in New York, drunk or sober. She was born in a penthouse and died in the subway. Downhill all the way.

"Monica never married. She once said that the only unrelated male she'd ever known that she could stand having around for any length of time was a horse named Leibowitz, and the only reason she didn't marry him, she said, was that she doubted she could housebreak him. She was engaged a dozen times, but at the last minute she'd take a walk. Her father would yell, and her ma, who's a handkerchief-twister, would get hysterics, but it was no deal. They had high hopes about Monica's last engagement—it looked as if she was really going to marry this Hungarian count—but the Cat put a crimp in that."

"In the subway," said Ellery.

"Sure, how did she get there. Well, it was this way. Monica McKell was the biggest booster the New York subway system ever had. She'd ride it every chance she got. She told Elsa Maxwell it was the only place a girl could get the feel of the people. She took a particular delight in dragging her escorts there, especially when they were in tails.

"Funny," said the Inspector, "that it should have been the subway that did her in. Monica was out clubbing that night with Snooky—her count—and a bunch of their friends. They wound up in some Village dive, and around a quarter of four in the morning Monica got tired tending bar and they decided to call it a night. They began piling into cabs—all except Monica, who stood her ground and argued that if they really believed in the American way they'd all go home in the subway. The others were game, but the count got his Hungarian up—he was also tanked on vodka-and-Cokes—and said something like if he wanted to smell peasants he'd have stayed in Hungary and he'd be damned if he'd lower himself, into the ground or any other way, and she could bloody well go home in the subway herself if she wanted to so bad. And she did.

"And she did," said the Inspector, licking his lips, "and she was found a little after 6 A.M. lying on a bench near the tailpiece of the platform of the Sheridan Square station. A trackwalker found her. He called a cop and the cop took one look and went green. There was the salmon-colored silk cord around her neck."

The Inspector got up and went into the kitchen and came back with the pitcher of lemonade. They drank in silence and then the Inspector put the pitcher back in the icebox.

When he returned, Ellery said with a frown, "Was there time for—?"

"No," said the Inspector. "She'd been dead about two hours. That would place the murder attack at around 4 A.M. or a little later, just about time for her to have walked over to Sheridan Square from the night club and maybe wait around a few minutes—you know how the trains run at that hour of the morning. But Count Szebo was with the others until at least 5:30. They all stopped in at an allnight hamburger place on Madison and 48th on their way uptown. Every minute of his time is accounted for well past the murder period. Anyway, what would the point have been? Old man McKell had contracted to settle a hot million on Szebo when the knot was tied—excuse me, that was a bad figure of speech. I mean the count would have strangled himself before he'd lay a finger to that valuable throat. He doesn't have a Hungarian pretzel.

"In Monica McKell's case," said the Inspector, shaking his head, "we were able to trace her movements right up the entrance of the Sheridan Square station. A nighthawk cab spotted her about halfway to the station from the club, pulled up alongside. She was on foot, alone. But she laughed and said to the hack, 'You've got me wrong, my friend. I'm a poor working girl and I've just got a dime to get home on,' and she opened her gold mesh bag and showed him; there was nothing in it but a lipstick, a compact, and a dime, he said. And she marched off down the street, the hack said, the diamond bracelet on her arm sparkling under the street lights. Squinting along like a movie star, was the way he put it. Actually, she was wearing a gold lamé creation designed like a Hindu sari, with a jacket of white mink thrown over it.

"And another cab driver parked near the station saw her cross the Square and disappear down the steps. She was still on foot, still alone.

"There was no one on duty at the change booth at that hour. Presumably she put her dime in the turnstile and walked down the platform to the end bench. A few minutes later she was dead.

"Her jewelry, her bag, her jacket weren't touched.

"We've found no evidence that anybody else was on the platform with her. The second cab driver picked up a fare right after he saw Monica go down the subway steps, and apparently he was the only one around. The Cat may have been waiting on the platform; the Cat may have followed Monica down from the street after ducking into doorways to avoid being seen by the two cab drivers; or the Cat may have got off at Sheridan Square from an uptown train and found her there—there's nothing to tell. If she put up a battle, there's no sign of it. If she screamed, no one heard it. And that was the end of Monica McKell—born in New York, died in New York. From penthouse to subway. Downhill all the way."

After a long time Ellery said, "A girl like that must have been mixed up in a thousand pulp story plots. I've heard a lot of scandal . . ."

"I am now," sighed his father, "the world's foremost authority on the Mysteries of Monica. I can tell you, for instance, that she had a burn scar just under the left breast that she didn't get from falling on a hot stove. I know just where she was, and with whom, in February of 1946 when she disappeared and her father had us and the FBI chasing our tails looking for her, and despite what the papers said at the time her kid brother Jimmy had nothing to do with it—he'd just got out of the Service and he was having his own troubles readjusting to civilian life. I know how Monica came to get the autographed photo of Legs Diamond that's still hanging on her bedroom wall, and it's not for the reason you'd think. I know why she was asked to leave Nassau the year Sir Harry Oakes was murdered, and who asked her. I even know something J. Parnell Thomas never found out—that she was a card-carrying member of the Communist Party between 1938 and 1941, when she quit to become a Christian Fronter for four months, and then jumped that to take a course in Yoga Breathing Exercises under a Hollywood swami named Lal Dhyana Jackson.

"Yes, sir, I know everything there is to know about Leaping Lena, or Madcap Monica," said the Inspector, "except how she came to be strangled by the Cat . . . I can tell you this, Ellery. If when the Cat walked up to her on that subway platform he said, 'Excuse me, Miss McKell, I'm the Cat and I'm going to strangle you,' she probably moved over on the bench and said, 'How perfectly thrilling. Sit down and tell me more.' "

Ellery jumped up. He took a turn around the living room, busily, like a runner limbering up. Inspector Queen watched the sweat roll down his back.

"And that," said the Inspector, "is where we're hung up."

"Nothing—?"

"Not a bastardly thing. I suppose," the old man said angrily, "I can't blame McKell Senior for offering $100,000 reward, but all it's done is give the papers another angle to play up and flood us with a barrage of happy gas from ten thousand crackpots. And it hasn't been any help having McKell's high-priced prima donna dicks underfoot, either!"

"What about the current mouse?"

"Number 5?" The Inspector cracked his knuckles, clicking off integers in a bitter arithmetic. "Simone Phillips, 35, lived with a younger sister in a coldwater flat on East 102nd Street." He grimaced. "This mouse couldn't even rustle her own cheese. Simone'd had something wrong with her spine since childhood and she was paralyzed from the waist down. Spent most of her life in bed. What you might call a pushover."

"Yes." Ellery was sucking a piece of lemon and making a face. "Doesn't seem cricket, somehow. Even from the Cat."

"It happened last Friday night. August 19. Ten days after the McKell woman. Celeste—the younger sister—fixed Simone up, turned on the radio for her, and left for a neighborhood movie. Around 9 o'clock."

"Pretty late?"

"She went for just the main feature. Celeste said Simone hated being left alone, but she simply had to get out once a week—"

"Oh, this was routine?"

"Yes. The sister went every Friday night—her only recreation, by the way. Simone was helpless and Celeste was the only one she had. Anyway, Celeste got back a little after 11. She found the paralytic strangled. Salmon-colored silk cord tied around her neck."

"The crippled woman could hardly have let anyone in. Weren't there any signs—?"

"Celeste never locked the apartment door when she had to leave Simone. Simone was deathly afraid of gas leaks and fires, afraid she'd be caught helpless in bed sometime when her sister wasn't there. Leaving the door unlocked eased her mind. For the same reason they had a phone, which they certainly couldn't afford."

"Last Friday night. Almost as hot as tonight," mused Ellery. "In that district the people would all be congregated on the stoop, hanging out the windows. Do you mean to tell me no one saw anything?"

"There's so much testimony to the effect that no stranger entered the building through the front entrance between 9 and 11 that I'm convinced the Cat got in through the rear. There's a back door leading out to a court, and the court is accessible, from one of a half-dozen different directions, the backs of the other houses and the two side streets; it runs right through. The Phillips flat is on the ground floor, rear. The hall is dark, has only a 25-watt light. That's the way he got in, all right, and out again. But we've been over the square block a dozen times, inside the buildings and out, and we haven't turned up a thing."

"No screams."

"If she did yell, nobody paid any attention to it. You know what a tenement district's like on a hot night—kids out on the street till all hours and screams a dime a dozen. But my hunch is she didn't make a sound. I've never seen such fright on a human face. Paralysis on top of paralysis. She didn't put up the scrawniest kind of scrap. Wouldn't surprise me if she just sat there with her mouth open, pop-eyed, while the Cat took his cord out and tied it around her neck and pulled it tight. Yes, sir, this was his easiest strike."

The Inspector pulled himself to his feet. "Simone was very fat, from the waist up. The kind of fat that gives you the feeling that if you poked it you'd go clear through to the other side. As if she had no bones, no muscle."

"*Musculus,*" said Ellery, sucking the lemon. "Little mouse. The shrunken little mice to the mouse. Little atrophies."

"Well, she'd been parked in that bed over twenty-five years." The old man trudged to one of the windows. "Sure is a scorcher."

"Simone, Celeste."

"What?" said the Inspector.

"Their names. So Gallic. Maternal poetry? And if not, how come 'Phillips'?"

"Their father was French. The family name was originally Phillippe, but he Anglicized it when he came to America."

"Mother French, too?"

"I think so, but they were married in New York. Phillips was in the import-export business and he made a fortune during the First World War. He dropped it all in the '29 crash and blew his brains out, leaving Mrs. Phillips penniless."

"With a paralyzed child. Tough."

"Mrs. Phillips managed by taking in sewing. They made out fine, Celeste says— in fact, she was enrolled as a freshman in N.Y.U. downtown when Mrs. Phillips died of pleurisy-pneumonia. That was five years ago."

"Must have been even tougher. For Celeste."

"It couldn't have been a peach parfait. Simone needed constant attention. Celeste had to quit school."

"How'd she manage?"

"Celeste has a modeling job in a dress shop her mother did business with. Afternoons and all day Saturday. She has a beautiful figure, dark coloring—pretty goodlooking number. She could make a lot more somewhere else, she told me, but the store isn't far from their home and she couldn't leave Simone alone too long. I got the impression Celeste was pretty much dominated by Simone and this was confirmed by the neighbors. They told me Simone nagged at Celeste all the time, whining and complaining and making the younger sister, who they all think is a saint, run her legs off. Probably accounts for her beatup look; she really was dragging her chin when I saw her."

"Tell me," said Ellery. "On Friday night last did this saintly young character go to the movies alone?"

"Yes."

"Does she usually?"

The Inspector looked surprised. "I don't know."

"Might pay to find out." Ellery leaned far forward to smooth out a wrinkle in the rug. "Doesn't she have a boy friend?"

"I don't think so. I gather she hasn't had much opportunity to meet men."

"How old is this Celeste?"

"23."

"Ripe young age. —The cord *was* tussah silk?"

"Yes."

The rug was now smooth.

"And that's all you have to tell me?"

"Oh, there's lots more, especially about Abernethy, Violette Smith, and Monica McKell."

"What?"

"I'll be happy to open the files to you."

Ellery was silent.

"Want to go over them?" asked his father.

"You found no connection among any of the five victims."

"Not a particle."

"None of them knew any of the others."

"As far as we can tell."

"They had no common friends, acquaintances, relatives?"

"So far we haven't hit any."

"Religious affiliation?" asked Ellery suddenly.

"Abernethy was a communicant of the Episcopal Church—in fact, at one time, before his father died, he was studying for the ministry. But he gave that up to take care of his mother on a regular basis. Certainly there's no record that he ever went after his mother died.

"Violette Smith's family are Lutherans. As far as we know, she herself went to no church. Her family threw her out years ago.

"Monica McKell—all the McKells—Presbyterian. Mr. and Mrs. McKell are very active in church affairs and Monica—it sort of surprised me—was quite religious.

"Rian O'Reilly was a devout Roman Catholic.

"Simone Phillips came of French Protestants on both sides, but she herself was interested in Christian Science."

"Likes, dislikes, habits, hobbies . . ."

The Inspector turned from the window. "What?"

"I'm fishing for a common denominator. The victims form a highly conglomerate group. Yet there must be some quality, some experience, some function they shared . . ."

"There's not a single indication that the poor mutts were tied up any way at all."

"As far as you know."

The Inspector laughed. "Ellery, I've been on this merry-go-round since the first ride and I tell you there's as much sense in these killings as there was in a Nazi crematorium.

"The murders haven't followed any time pattern or recognizable sequence. The intervals between the various crimes have been nineteen days, twenty-six, twenty-two, ten. It's true that they all occurred at night, but that's when cats walk, isn't it?

"The victims came from all over the City. East 19th near Gramercy Park. West 44th between Broadway and Sixth. West 20th near Ninth. Park and 53rd, in this case the victim actually getting it under Sheridan Square in Greenwich Village. And East 102nd.

"Economically? Upper crust, middle class, the poor. Socially? You find a pattern that includes an Abernethy, a Violette Smith, a Rian O'Reilly, a Monica McKell, and a Simone Phillips.

"Motive? Not gain. Not jealousy. Not anything *personal*.

"There's nothing to indicate that these have been sex crimes, or that a sex drive is even behind it.

"Ellery, this is killing for the sake of killing. The Cat's enemies are the human race. Anybody on two legs, will do. If you ask me, that's what's really cooking in New York. And unless we clamp the lid on this—this *homicide*, it's going to boil over."

"And yet," said Ellery, "for an undiscriminating, unselective, blood-lusting and mankind-hating brute, I must say the Cat shows a nice appreciation of certain values."

"Values?"

"Well, take time. The Cat uses time the way Thoreau did, as a stream, to go fishing in. To catch Abernethy in his bachelor apartment he'd have to run the risk of being seen or heard entering or leaving, because Abernethy was an early-to-bed man. What's more, Abernethy rarely had a visitor, so that going to his door at a normal hour might have aroused a neighbor's curiosity. So what does the Cat do? He contrives to get Abernethy to agree to an appointment at an hour when the building's settled down for the night. To accomplish this called for the considerable feat of making an ossified bachelor change a habit of years' standing. In other words, the Cat weighed the difficulties against the time and he chose in favor of the time.

"In Violette Smith's case, whether it was done by appointment or as a result of careful study of her business practices, you can't deny that the Cat did pick a *time* when a very busy lady was in her flat alone.

"O'Reilly? Most vulnerable when he came home from his Brooklyn night job. And there was the Cat lying in wait in the downstairs hall. Nicely timed, wouldn't you say?"

The Inspector listened without comment.

"Monica McKell? A woman obviously running away from herself. And that kind of woman—from that kind of background—loses herself in crowds. She was always surrounded by people. It's no accident that she adored the subway. Monica must have presented a problem. Still—the Cat caught her alone, in a place and at a time which were most favorable for his project. How many nights did he trail her, I wonder, watching for just the right *moment?*

"And Simone, the paralytic. Easy pickings once he got to her. But how to get to her without being seen? Crowded tenement, the summer—daytime was out of the question, even when Celeste was away at work. But at night her sister is always with her. Always? Well, not exactly. On Friday nights the annoying Celeste goes to the movies. And Simone is strangled when? On a Friday night."

"You finished?"

"Yes."

Inspector Queen was remote. "Very plausible," he said. "Very convincing. But you're arguing from the premise that the Cat picks people in advance. Suppose I argue from the premise that he does nothing of the sort?—a premise, incidentally, that's borne out by the total lack of connection among the victims.

"Then the Cat happened to be prowling on West 44th Street one night, picked a likely-looking building at random, chose the top floor apartment because it was closer to a roof getaway, pretended to be a salesman for nylons or French perfume— anything to get in—and that was the end of somebody whose name happened to be Violette Smith, call girl.

"On the night of July 18 he was feeling the urge again and chance took him to the Chelsea district. It was around midnight, his favorite hunting hour. He follows a tired-looking little guy into a hall and that's the end of a hard-working Irishman named O'Reilly. It might just as well have turned out to be William Miller, a shipping clerk who came home from a date with a Bronx girl around 2 A.M. and walked up the stairs under which O'Reilly's body was lying, still warm.

"In the early morning hours of August 9 the Cat was on the loose in the Village. He spotted an unescorted woman, walking. He followed her to the Sheridan Square subway and that was the end of Well-Known New York Socialite, who should have stuck to her twelve-cylinder job.

"And on the night of August 19 he was up around 102nd Street hankering after another neck, and he got into a nice dark court and pussyfooted around until he saw through a ground floor window a fat young woman lying in a bed, alone. And that was the end of Simone Phillips.

"Now tell me something—anything—that says it didn't happen that way."

"Abernethy?"

"You left Abernethy out," said Ellery. "Abernethy the Vague. Admittedly not a hard thing to do. But he is dead, he *was* strangled with one of those silk cords, and didn't you yourself say it was by appointment?"

"I said the whole setup smacked of an appointment. But we don't *know* it. Something could have made him sit up past his usual bedtime that night, maybe a radio program, or he fell asleep in the easychair. The Cat could have been in the building on the loose and seen the light under Abernethy's door and knocked—"

"At which Abernethy let him in?"

"All he'd have to have done was unlock the door."

"An Abernethy? At midnight?"

"Or maybe he'd forgotten to check his spring latch and the Cat just walked in, releasing it on his way out."

"Then why didn't Archibald use his lungs? Or run? How is it he permitted the Cat to get behind him while he sat in his chair?"

"He might have been—like Simone Phillips—scared stiff."

"Yes," said Ellery, "I suppose that's possible."

"I know," muttered the Inspector. "The Abernethy thing doesn't conform. Nothing conforms." He shrugged. "I'm not saying you're not right, Ellery. But you see what we're up against. And the whole blasted thing's in my lap now. It would be bad enough if that's all I had to worry about. But he's not through; you know that. There's going to be another one, and another one after that, until we catch him or he drops dead from overexercise. How can we prevent it? There aren't enough cops in the U.S. to make every nook and cranny of a city like New York murderproof. We can't even be sure he'll keep restricting his activities to Manhattan. And the other boroughs know it. They're getting identical reactions from the public in the Bronx, Brooklyn, Queens, Richmond. Hell, it's being felt on Long Island, in Westchester, Connecticut, New Jersey, all the commuter places. Sometimes I think it's a bad dream. Ellery—"

Ellery's lips parted.

"Don't answer till I'm finished. You feel that you failed in the Van Horn case and that because you failed two people went to their deaths. Lord knows I've tried to help you get it out of your system. But I guess nobody can talk away another man's conscience . . . I've had to sit by and watch you crawl into a hole while you kept swearing by the beards of all the Prophets that you'd never mix into another case.

"But son," said the old man, "this is a special kind of deal. This one is tough. It's tough not only on its own merits—which are tough enough—but because of the atmosphere it's creating. This isn't just a matter of clearing up a few murders, Ellery. It's a race against—against citywide collapse. And don't make with the eyebrow: I tell you it's coming. It's only a question of time. Just one murder in the wrong place . . . Nobody downtown's out to rob me of the glory: not in this one. They're all feeling sorry for the old duck. Let me tell you something." The Inspector stared down at 87th Street, bracing himself against the window frame. "I mentioned earlier that I thought the Commissioner had an angle in putting me at the head of this special Cat squad. The boss thinks you're a screwball, but he's often asked me when you're going to snap out of the sulks and get back to using the crazy talents God gave you. Well, my opinion, Ellery, is that he's put me on the spot deliberately."

"For what reason?"

"To force you into the case."

"You're not serious!"

His father looked at him.

"But he wouldn't do a thing like that." Ellery's face was dark. "Not to you. That's the dirtiest kind of slap in the face."

"To stop these stranglings, son, I'd do a lot worse. Anyway, what's the odds? You're no superman. Nobody expects miracles. It's even a sort of insult to you. In an emergency people will try anything, even tough old eggs like the Commissioner."

"Thanks," mumbled Ellery. "That sets me up. It really does."

"Kidding aside. It would hit me pretty hard to think that when I needed you most you let me down. Ellery, how about getting into this?"

"You," said the son, "are an extremely clever old man."

The Inspector grinned.

"Naturally if I thought I could help out in a thing as serious as this I'd . . . But, damn it, Dad, I feel virginal. I want to and I don't want to. Let me sleep on it. I'd be no use to you or anybody in my present state."

"Fair enough," said his father briskly. "Good grief, I've been making speeches. How do these politicians do it? How about some more lemonade, son, with a shot of gin in it to take the bite off?"

"In my case, it'll take more than a shot."

"Motion seconded."

But neither meant it.

The Inspector sat down at the kitchen table with a groan, thinking that with Ellery the usual psychology was a waste of breath. The Cat and Ellery seemed two twinges of the same pain.

He leaned back against the tiled wall tipping his chair.

The blasted heat . . .

He opened his eyes to find the Police Commissioner of the City of New York leaning over him.

"Dick, Dick," the Commissioner was saying. "Wake up."

Ellery was in the kitchen doorway, still in his shorts.

The Commissioner was hatless and the gabardine around his armpits was soaked. Inspector Queen blinked up at him.

"I told them I'd notify you in person."

"Notify me about what, Commissioner?"

"The Cat's got another tail."

"When?" The old man licked his lips.

"Tonight. Between 10:30 and midnight."

"Where?" He brushed past them, darted into the living room, grabbed at his shoes.

"Central Park, not far from the 110th Street entrance. In some bushes behind a rock."

"Who?"

"Beatrice Willikins, 32, single, sole support of an aged father. She'd taken him to the Park for some air and left him on a bench to go looking for water. She never came back and finally he called a Park patrolman. The patrolman found her a couple of hundred feet away, strangled. Salmon-colored silk cord. Purse not touched. Hit over the head from behind and signs of dragging into the bushes. The strangulation took place there, probably while she was unconscious. No superficial indication of rape."

"No, Dad," said Ellery. "Those are wet. Here's a fresh shirt and undershirt."

"Bushes, Park," said the Inspector rapidly. "That's a break. Or is it? Prints on the ground?"

"So far, nothing. But Dick," said the Commissioner, "something new's been added."

The Inspector looked at him. He was trying to button his shirt. Ellery did it for him.

"Beatrice Willikins lived at West 128th Street."

"West," said the Inspector mechanically, sticking an arm into the jacket Ellery was holding up. Ellery was staring at the Commissioner.

"Near Lenox."

"Harlem?"

The Commissioner swabbed his neck. "This one might do it, Dick. If someone lost his head."

Inspector Queen ran to the door. He was very pale. "This means all night, Ellery. You go to bed."

But Ellery was saying, "This one might do what if someone lost his head, Commissioner?"

"Push the button that blows New York higher than Hiroshima."

"Come on, Commissioner," said the Inspector impatiently from the foyer.

"Wait." Ellery was looking politely at the Commissioner, and the Commissioner was looking just as politely at him. "If you'll give me three minutes, I'll go with you."

3

The sixth tail of the Cat, which went on display on the morning of August 26, offered a delicate departure from the mode. Where its five fellows were hairlines enclosing white space, this tail was solidly inked in. Thus New York City was informed that the Cat had crossed the color line. By the glowing encirclement of one black throat, to the seven million pale necks already within the orbit of the noose were joined five hundred thousand others.

It was notable that, while Inspector Queen occupied himself in Harlem with Beatrice Willikins's demise, the Mayor called a dawn press conference at City Hall which was attended by the Police Commissioner and other officials.

"We are convinced, gentlemen," said the Mayor, "that there is no race angle to Beatrice Willikins's murder. The one thing we've got to avoid is a repetition of the kind of tension that brought on the so-called Black Ides of March in 1935. A trivial incident and false rumor resulted in three deaths, thirty-odd people hospitalized for bullet wounds, and over two hundred others treated for injuries, cuts, and abrasions. Not to mention property damage amounting to more than $2,000,000."

"I was under the impression, Mr. Mayor," remarked a reporter for one of the Harlem newspapers, "that—to quote from the report of the bi-racial commission appointed by Mayor La Guardia to investigate the riot—it was caused by 'resentments against radical discrimination and poverty in the midst of plenty.' "

"Of course," replied the Mayor quickly. "There are always underlying social and economic causes. Frankly, that's what we're a little apprehensive about. New York is a melting pot of every race, national origin, and creed under the sun. One out of every fifteen of our fellow New Yorkers is Negro. Three out of every ten are Jewish. There are more Italians in New York City than in Genoa. More Germans than in Bremen. More Irish than in Dublin. We've got Poles, Greeks, Russians, Spaniards, Turks, Portuguese, Chinese, Scandinavians, Filipinos, Persians—everything. That's what makes us the greatest city on earth. But it also keeps us on the lid of a volcano. Postwar tensions haven't helped. These stranglings have made the whole City nervous and we don't want anything foolish to touch off public disorders. Naturally, that last remark is off the record.

"Gentlemen, our most sensible course is to treat these murders, uh, as routine. Non-sensationally. They're a bit off the beaten path and they present some rather tough problems, but we have the finest crime-investigating agency in the world, we're working on the murders night and day, and the break may be expected at any time."

"Beatrice Willikins," said the Commissioner, "was strangled by the Cat. She was Negro. The five other victims have all been white. That's the thing for you boys to emphasize."

"Our angle might be, Commissioner," said the reporter for the Harlem paper, "that the Cat is a firm democratic believer in civil rights."

In the shout that followed, an atmosphere was created which enabled the Mayor to close the conference without disclosing that the latest murder was giving the head of the new Cat squad a very bad time.

They were sitting around in the squad room of the main Harlem precinct weighing reports on Beatrice Willikins. The investigation on the scene, in the Park, had yielded nothing. The ground behind the boulder was rocky and if the Cat had left the print of his pads on it the first confusion following the discovery of the young woman's body had scuffed it out. An inch-by-inch examination of the grass, soil, and paths in the vicinity of the boulder produced only two hairpins, both identified as coming from the victim's head. Laboratory analysis of certain particles scraped from under the victim's fingernails, at first thought to be coagulated blood or bloody tissue, proved that they consisted principally of lip rouge, of a shade popular with Negro women and which matched exactly the rouge still on the dead girl's lips. There was no trace of the weapon with which the Cat had struck her head and the bruise gave no clue to its nature: it could only be described by that most inconclusive of terms, "blunt instrument."

As for the catch of the police dragnet, thrown around the area within minutes of the body's discovery, it consisted of a great many citizens of both colors and sexes and all ages, uniformly overheated, excited, frightened, and guilty-looking; none, however, gave off precisely the whiff for which Ellery's nostrils were sniffing. It took the entire night to screen them. At the end with echoes of bedlam still in their ears, the police had only two likely fish, a white and a black, the white an unemployed jazz trumpet player 27 years old found lying on the grass smoking a marijuana cigaret, the black a skinny, undersized runner for a Lenox Avenue drop. The Negro, a middleaged man, was caught in the act of peddling the numbers. Each was stripped to the skin and thoroughly examined without result. The policy employee was released when Negro detectives rounded up witnesses who accounted for his whereabouts for an hour preceding the general crime period, and for some time after that; at which everyone, remembering the Black Ides, looked happy. The white musician was taken to Headquarters for further questioning. But, as Inspector Queen remarked, it didn't look promising: if he was the Cat, he had been in New York on June 3, June 22, July 18, August 9, and August 19; whereas the trumpet player claimed to have left New York in May and returned only five days before. He said he had been employed during that period on a round-the-world luxury boat. He had described the boat, the captain, the purser, and other members of the ship's orchestra; and, in some detail, several feminine passengers.

So they tackled it from the other end and hoisted the victim to the scales. Which tipped depressingly on the side of rectitude and good works.

Beatrice Willikins had been a responsible member of the Negro community, belonging to the Abyssinian Baptist Church and active in many of its groups. Born and raised in Harlem, and educated at Howard University, she had been employed by a child welfare agency and her work had been exclusively with the underprivileged and delinquent children of Harlem.

She had contributed sociological articles to *Journal of Negro Education* and poetry to *Phylon*. Occasional freelance pieces under her byline had appeared in the *Amsterdam-Star News, Pittsburgh Courier,* and the Atlanta *Daily World.*

Beatrice Willikins's associations had been impeccable. Her friends were Negro educators, social workers, writers, and professional people. Her work had taken her from Black Bohemia to San Juan Hill; she had come in frequent contact with dope peddlers, pimps, the streetwalkers of "The Market Place"; Puerto Ricans, Negro Moslems, French Africans, Black Jews, darkskinned Mexicans and Cubans, Negroid Chinese and Japanese. But she had gone among them as a friend and healer, unresented and unmolested. The police of Harlem had known her as a quietly determined defender of juvenile delinquents.

"She was a fighter," the precinct captain told Inspector Queen, "but she wasn't any fanatic. I don't know of anybody in Harlem, white or black, who didn't respect her."

In 1942 she had been engaged to a young Negro physician named Lawrence Caton. Dr. Caton had gone into the Army and he had been killed in Italy. Her fiancé's death had apparently sealed off the girl's emotional life; there was no record that she had ever gone out with another man.

The Inspector took a Negro lieutenant aside, and the detective nodded and went over to the bench on which the girl's father was seated, beside Ellery.

"Pap, who do you figure did the girl in?"

The aged man mumbled something.

"What?"

"He says," said Ellery, "that his name is Frederick Willikins and his father was a slave in Georgia."

"That's fine, that's okay, Pap, but what man was she messing around with? White man?"

The old man stiffened. They could see him struggle with something. Finally he drew back his brown skull, like a snake, and struck.

The Negro detective stooped and wiped the old man's spittle from his shoe.

"I guess old Pappy here figures I insulted him. On two counts."

"It's important." The Inspector moved toward the bench.

"Better let me, Inspector," said the detective. "He's got a spitting eye." He stooped over the old man again. "Okay, Pap, your daughter was a gal in a million. Now you want to bring down the wrath on the one who give it to her, don't you?"

He mumbled again.

"I think he said, Lieutenant," said Ellery, "something about the Lord providing."

"Not in Harlem," said the detective. "Pap, you keep your mind on this. All we want to know is, did your girl Bea know some white?"

The old man did not answer.

"It's all this pale hide around here," said the Negro lieutenant apologetically. "Pap, who is he? What did he look like? Bea ever tell a white skin off?"

The brown skull drew back again.

"Better save that juice," growled the lieutenant. "Come on, Pappy, all I want is one answer to one question. Bea had a phone. Did a white man keep calling her up?"

The withered lips drew back in a tormented grin. "She has truck with a white, I kill her with my own two hands." Then he shrank into the corner of the bench.

"Say."

But the Inspector was shaking his head. "He's 80 if he's a day, Lieutenant. And look at his hands. All crippled up with arthritis. He couldn't strangle a sick kitten."

Ellery got up. "There's nothing here. I need a few hours' sleep, Dad. And so do you."

"You go along home, Ellery. If I get a chance I'll stretch out on a cot upstairs. Where will you be tonight?"

"At Headquarters," said Ellery. "With those files."

On the morning of August 27 the Cat was at his old stand on the editorial page of the *New York Extra* doing a brisk business in fear. But business can be brisker, and during the day the circulation manager of the *Extra* earned a bonus, the reason for which became evident on the morning of the 28th. In that issue the Cat moved over to Page 1, cartoonically speaking, on a longterm lease; a new tenancy so successful that by midmorning not a copy was to be found on any newsstand in the City.

And, as if to celebrate his leasehold, he waved a new tail.

It was ingenious. At first glance—there was no caption—the picture advertised a new horror: There were the six numbered tails and the giant-sized seventh, a scratchline arrogance. The reader seized the paper and hunted in vain among the headlines. Puzzled, he returned to the drawing; whereupon he saw it as it was, the noose shaped by the great tail numbered 7 being no noose at all but a question mark.

In the places of authority there was sharp disagreement as to precisely which question the question mark marked. The *Extra's* editor, in an interesting telephone conversation with the Mayor on the afternoon of the 28th, protested in a wide-eyed tone of voice that the question was, obviously, *Is the Cat going to claim a seventh victim?*— a logical, ethical, public-service, newsworthy query, the editor said, arising smack from the facts of record. The Mayor replied carbolically that it seemed to him, and to a great many other New Yorkers who had seen the cartoon and who were even now harrying the City Hall and Police Headquarters telephone operators, that the question it posed was, crudely and brutally, *Who's going to be the Cat's seventh victim?*—executed, moreover, in a drooling-whiskered, chop-licking style which was distinctly not in the public service, quite the contrary, and which he, the Mayor, might have expected from an opposition newspaper which was incapable of subordinating dirty politics to the public interest. The editor retorted that he, the Mayor, ought to know, as he was lugging around a rather large bundle of soiled laundry himself, and the Mayor shouted, "What do you mean by that slanderous remark?", at which the editor replied that he yielded to no man in his admiration for the rank and file of New York's Finest but everybody who knew the score knew that the Mayor's appointee, the present Commissioner, was an old party fire-horse who couldn't catch a pop fly let alone a desperate animal, and if the Mayor was so deletedly concerned about the public interest why didn't he appoint somebody sharp to the top police post?—then maybe the people of the City of New York could go back to sleeping nights. What was more, this was a suggestion the *Extra* intended to toss off in its lead editorial tomorrow—"in the public interest, Mr. Mayor, you understand." With which the editor of the *Extra* hung up to receive a circulation report that left him glowing.

He glowed too soon.

As the Mayor angrily sniffed the green carnation in his lapel, the Commissioner said, "Jack, if you want my resignation—"

"Don't pay any attention to that rag, Barney."

"It has a lot of readers. Why not cross it up before that editorial hits the streets tomorrow?"

"By firing you? I'll be damned if I will." And the Mayor added thoughtfully, "And I'll be damned if I won't, too."

"Exactly," said the Commissioner, lighting a cigar. "I've given the whole situation a lot of thought. Jack, what New York needs in this crisis is a hero, a Moses, somebody who'll capture their imaginations and—"

"Distract their attention?"

"Well . . ."

"Come on, Barney, what's on your mind?"

"Well, you appoint this fellow something like . . . well, like Special Cat Catcher for the Mayor."

"Pied Piper of Gotham, hm?" muttered His Honor. "No, that was rats. We've got plenty of those, too."

"No connection with the P.D. A roving assignment. Sort of advisory. And you could break the story just too late for the *Extra* to yank that editorial."

"Don't you mean, Barney," murmured the Mayor, "that you want me to appoint a fall guy who'll absorb the heat and take all the raps, while you and the Department get off the spot and back to everyday operations?"

"Well, it's a fact," said the Commissioner, looking critically at his cigar, "that the men, from the brass down, have been thinking more of headlines than results—"

"Suppose this fellow," asked the Mayor, "beats you to the Cat?"

The Commissioner laughed.

Rather abruptly, the Mayor said, "Barney, whom did you have in mind?"

"A real glamor boy, Jack. Native New Yorker, no political ax to grind, nationally known as a crime investigator, yet he's a civilian. He can't refuse, because I softened him up first by dropping the whole hot potato in his old man's lap."

The Mayor slowly brought his swivel chair back to the vertical.

The Commissioner nodded.

The Mayor reached for his private line. "Barney," he said, "this time I think you've outfoxed yourself. Oh, Birdy. Get me Ellery Queen."

"I'm overcome, Mr. Mayor," said Ellery. "But certainly my qualifications—"

"I can't think of a better man to become Special Investigator for the Mayor. Should have thought of it long ago. I'll be frank with you, Mr. Queen—"

"Yes," said Ellery.

"Sometimes a case comes along," said the Mayor, one eye on his Police Commissioner, "that's so off the trail, so eccentric, it licks even the finest cop. I think this Cat business needs the kind of special talents you've demonstrated so brilliantly in the past. A fresh and unorthodox approach."

"Those are kind words, Mr. Mayor, but wouldn't a thing like this create hard feeling on Centre Street?"

"I think I can promise you, Mr. Queen," said His Honor dryly, "the full cooperation of the Department."

"I see," said Ellery. "I suppose my father—"

"The only one I've discussed this with is the Commissioner. Will you accept?"

"May I take a few minutes to think it over?"

"I'll be waiting here at my office for your call."

Ellery hung up.

"Special Investigator to the Mayor," said the Inspector, who had been listening on the extension. "They're really getting fussed."

"Not about the Cat," Ellery laughed. "The case is getting too torrid to touch and somebody's looking for a potential burnt sacrifice to stand up and take the heat."

"The Commissioner . . ."

"He's really played that angle, hasn't he?"

The Inspector scowled. "Not the Mayor, Ellery. The Mayor's a politician, but he's also an honest man. If he fell for this, it's for the reason he gave you. Why not do it?"

Ellery was silent.

"All this would do would make it official . . ."

"And tougher."

"What you're afraid of," said his father deliberately, "is being committed."

"Well, I'd have to see it through."

"I hate to get personal, but doesn't that make two of us? Ellery, the move might be important in another way."

"How?"

"Just the act of your taking this job might scare the Cat off. Thought of that?"

"No."

"The publicity alone—"

"I meant no, it won't."

"You underestimate your rep."

"You underestimate our kitty. I have the feeling," said Ellery, "that nothing can scare him off."

His voice conveyed such a burdensome knowledge that the Inspector started. "For a second there you had me thinking . . ." But then he said slowly, *"Ellery, you've spotted something."*

Between them lay the archaeology of murder. Detail photographs of the victims, full and side views. General views of the scenes of the crimes, interiors, exteriors, closeups, from various angles. Cross-sketchings, neatly compass-directed and drawn to specified scale. The file of appurtenant fingerprints. A whole library of reports, records, assignments, details of work complete with notations of time, place, names, addresses, findings, questions and answers and statements and technical information. And, on a separate table, *res gestae* evidence, the originals.

Nowhere in this classified heterogeneity had a recognizable clue been discovered.

In a sharper tone the Inspector said, "Have you?"

Ellery said, *"Maybe."*

The Inspector opened his mouth.

"Don't ask me any more. Dad. It's something, but where it may lead . . ." Ellery looked unhappy. "I've spent forty-eight hours on this. But I want to go over it again."

Inspector Queen said into his phone, "Get the Mayor. Tell him Ellery Queen."

He sounded at peace for the first time in twelve weeks.

The news burst upon the City with a roar that soothed even the Police Commissioner. The noise was largely jubilant. The Mayor's mail increased fivefold and the City

Hall switchboard was unable to handle the volume of telephone calls. Commentators and columnists approved. It was noted that within twenty-four hours the gross number of false alarm police calls had been reduced by half and the strangulation of alley cats all but stopped. A small section of the press scoffed, but its collective voice was too feeble to register against the applause. As for the *New York Extra,* Ellery's appointment caught it with the issue containing its editorial blast all but run off; and although in a followup edition the paper excoriated the Mayor for "undermining the morale of the finest police force in the world," the Mayor's announcement took the sting out of the charge.

"Mr. Queen's appointment," the Mayor's handout had said in part, "in no way conflicts with, weakens, or is an expression of lack of confidence in, the regular police authority. The homicide record of the New York Police Department speaks for itself. But in view of the rather peculiar nature of this particular series of homicides, I have felt it advisable to enlist the aid of an expert who has specialized in unusual crimes. The suggestion that Ellery Queen be appointed Special Investigator came from the Police Commissioner himself, with whom Mr. Queen will work in the closest co-operation."

The Mayor repeated his statement over the air the same night.

At City Hall, after the swearing-in ceremony, punctuated by flashlight shots of the Mayor and Ellery Queen, of Ellery Queen and the Police Commissioner, of the Police Commissioner and the Mayor, and of the Mayor, the Police Commissioner, and Ellery Queen, Ellery read a prepared statement.

"The Cat has been at large in Manhattan for almost three months. In that period he has murdered six people. The file on six homicides weighs just about as much as the responsibilities I have accepted in taking this post. But while I have a great deal of catching up to do, I am sufficiently familiar with the facts to feel justified in stating even at this time that the case can and will be solved and the killer caught. Whether he will be caught before he commits another murder remains, of course, to be seen. But if the Cat should claim another victim tonight, I ask everyone to bear in mind that more New Yorkers are killed by automobiles in one day on our streets than the Cat has killed in three months."

Immediately he finished reading the statement, Ellery was asked by the reporter for the *Extra* if he was not already "withholding information": "Did you mean by saying 'I am sufficiently familiar with the facts to feel justified in stating that the case will be solved' that you've got a hot lead?"

Ellery smiled faintly and said: "I'll stand on my statement as read."

In the next few days his course was puzzling. He did not act like a man who has found something. He did not act at all. He retired to the Queen apartment and remained invisible to the public eye. As for the public ear, he took his telephone off the cradle, leaving Inspector Queen's direct line to Headquarters as his sole contact with the City. The Queen front door he kept locked.

It was not quite what the Commissioner had planned, and Inspector Queen heard rumblings of his discontent. But the old man merely continued to lay reports before Ellery as they came in, without comment or question. One of these concerned the marijuana-smoking trumpet player detained in the Beatrice Willikins investigation: the musician's story had been substantiated and he had been released. Ellery scarcely glanced at the report. He balanced on his coccyx chainsmoking as he studied the lunar topography of his study ceiling, that epic issue between the Queens and their wily landlord. But the Inspector knew that Ellery was not thinking of the unattainable calcimine.

During the evening of August 31, however, Ellery was back at the reports. Inspector Oueen was about to leave his office after another day which had contrived to be both full and empty when his private line came to life and he picked up the phone to hear his son's voice.

"I've been going over the reports on the cords again—"

"Yes, Ellery."

"I was thinking of a possible way to determine the Cat's manual preference."

"What do you have in mind?"

"The technique worked out years ago on the Continent by the Belgian, Goddefroy, and others."

"With rope?"

"Yes. The surface fibers will lie in the direction opposite to that of the pulling or other motions involving friction."

"Well, sure. We've settled a few hanging cases that way where the question was suicide or murder. What of it?"

"The Cat loops the silk cord around his victim's neck from behind. Before he can start pulling and tightening the noose, he's got to cross the ends over each other. Theoretically, therefore, there ought to be a point of friction where the noose crosses itself at the nape of the neck.

"In two of these cases, O'Reilly and Violette Smith, the neck photos show that during the stranglings—before knots were tied—the two ends of the cord did make contact in crossing."

"Yes."

"All right. He's pulling with both hands, one to each end of the cord, in opposite directions. But unless he's ambidextrous, he's not pulling with equal force. One hand will tend to hold, while the other—his favored hand—will tend to pull. In other words, if he's righthanded the end of the cord held by his left hand ought to show a point of friction, and the end of the cord held by his right hand ought to show a line of friction. Vice versa if he's lefthanded. Tussah silk is coarse-fibered. There may be observable effects."

"It's a thought," muttered the Inspector.

"Call me back when you find out, Dad."

"I don't know how long it'll take. The lab's been overworked and it's late. You'd better not wait up. I'll stick around here till I find out."

The Inspector made several telephone calls, leaving word that he was to be notified the moment a finding was made. Then, because he had a couch hauled into his office several weeks before, he stretched out on it thinking he would close his eyes for just a few minutes.

When he opened them, the September 1 sun was pouring in speckled splendor through his dusty windows.

One of his phones was ringing.

He tottered over to his desk.

"What happened to you?" asked Ellery.

"I lay down for a cat nap last night and the next thing I knew the phone was ringing."

"I was about to call a policeman. What about those cord findings?"

"I haven't . . . Wait, the report's on my desk. Damn it, why didn't they wake me?" After a moment, the Inspector said: "Inconclusive."

"Oh."

"Their opinion is that O'Reilly and the Smith woman thrashed about from side to side during the attacks just enough to make the Cat alternate his pull from one hand to the other and back. In a sort of seesaw movement. Maybe O'Reilly was only stunned and fought back. Anyway, there's no point of friction determinable. What slight friction areas are detectable in the silk are about equally divided between right and left."

"And there you are." But then Ellery said in an altogether different tone, "Dad, come right home."

"Home? I'm just starting my day, Ellery."

"Come home."

The Inspector dropped the phone and ran.

"What's up?" Inspector Queen was breathing hard from his sprint up the stairs.

"Read these. They came in this morning's mail."

The Inspector sat down slowly in the leather armchair. One envelope bore the brash imprint of the *New York Extra,* the address typewritten; the other was small, pinkish, and secretive-looking and it had been addressed by hand.

From the *Extra* envelope he took a slip of yellow scratch-pad paper.

> DEAR E.Q.—What did you do, rip out your phone? Or are you looking for the Cat in Bechuanaland? I've been up to your place six times in the past couple of days and no answer.
>
> I've got to see you.
>
> JAMES GUYMER MCKELL
>
> P.S. Known to the trade as "Jimmy Leggitt." Leg-It, get it? Call me at the *Extra.*
>
> J.G.M.

"Monica McKell's kid brother!"

"Read the other one."

The notepaper of the second letter matched the envelope. This was elegance unaccustomed, a yearning after effect. The hand was hurried and a bit wretched.

> DEAR MR. QUEEN,
>
> I have been trying to reach you by telephone ever since the radio announced your appointment as Special Investigator of the Cat murders.
>
> Can you possibly see me? This is *not* an attempt to get your autograph.
>
> *Please.*
>
> Sincerely,
> CELESTE PHILLIPS

"Simone Phillip's sister." The Inspector laid the two letters down on an endtable, carefully. "Going to see them?"

"Yes. I phoned the Phillips girl at her home and I reached McKell at his paper. They both sound pretty young. I've seen some of McKell's stuff on the Cat cases under the name of Leggitt, but nothing that connected him personally with any of them. Did you know Leggitt and McKell were the same man?"

'No.'' The Inspector seemed disturbed by his ignorance. "I've seen him, of course, but in the McKell home on Park Avenue. I suppose being a legman is the thing to do just now in his set. Did they say what they wanted?''

"Celeste Phillips said she'd rather tell me in person. I told McKell if it was an interview he was after for that ragbag he works for I'd heave him out on his ear, but he assured me it was personal.''

"Both in the same morning,'' muttered the Inspector. "Did either mention the other?''

"No.''

"When are they due?''

"I violated a cardinal rule of the Manual. I'm seeing them at the same time. 11 o'clock.''

"Five of! I've got to shower, shave, and get into clean clothes.'' The old man, hurrying to his bedroom, added over his shoulder, "Hold them here. By force, if you have to.''

When the refurbished man emerged, his son was gallantly applying the flame of a lighter to a cigaret held by two slim gloved fingers to two female lips of distinction. She was sleekly modish from her hairdo to her shoetips, but young—the New York woman as she would like to be, but not quite grown up to it. The Inspector had seen girls like her on Fifth Avenue in the late afternoons, alone and unapproachable, the healthy raw material of youth covered by a patina of chic. But she was never upper crust; there was no boredom in her. *Vogue* just graduated from *Seventeen*, and very beautiful.

The Inspector was confused. It was Celeste Phillips. But what had happened to her?

"Hello, Miss Phillips.'' They shook hands; her grip was quick, withdrawing. She wasn't expecting me, he thought; Ellery didn't say I was home. "I almost didn't recognize you.'' It was incredible; less than two weeks. "Please sit down.''

Over her shoulder as she turned he glimpsed Ellery being quizzical. The Inspector recalled his description of Simone Phillips's sister and he shrugged in reply. It was impossible to see this spick-and-span girl against the smeary background of the flat on 102nd Street. Yet she still lived there; Ellery had reached her there. Inspector Queen decided that it was the clothes. Probably borrowed for the occasion from that dress shop she models in, he thought. The rest was makeup. When she got home and returned the finery and washed her face she would be again the Cinderella he remembered. Or would she? He was really not so sure. The sunny shallows under her bright black eyes, which had replaced the purple deeps he remembered, would not blot off with a towel. And certain planes then in her face had . . . been buried with her sister?

By the pricking of my thumbs . . .

"Don't let me interrupt anything,'' said the Inspector with a smile.

"Oh, I was just telling Mr. Queen how impossible the apartment situation still is.'' Her fingers were unclasping and reclasping the catch on her bag with a life of their own.

"You're intending to move?" At the Inspector's glance the fingers flew to a stop.

"As soon as I can find another place."

"Yes, you'll be starting a new life," the Inspector nodded. "Most people do. In cases like this." Then he said, "Did you get rid of the bed?"

"Oh, no. I sleep in it." She said very quickly, "I've been sleeping on a cot for years. Simone's bed is so comfortable. She'd want me to. And then . . . I'm not afraid of my sister, you see."

"Well," said Ellery. "That's a good healthy attitude. Dad, I'd just about got round to the point of asking Miss Phillips why she wanted to see me."

"I want to help, Mr. Queen." She had a *Vogue* voice this morning, too. So careful.

"Help? In what way?"

"I don't know. I don't even know . . ." She covered her distress with a *Vogue* smile. "I don't understand it myself. Sometimes you feel you just have to do something. You don't know why."

"Why did you come, Miss Phillips?"

She twisted in the chair. But then she snapped forward and she was no longer a figure in a magazine but a very young woman stripped all but bare. "I pitied my sister terribly. She was a cripple in more ways than one. Anybody would be, chained to a bed so long. Absolutely helpless. I hated myself for not being a cripple, too. I always felt so *guilty*.

"How can I explain it?" she cried. "Simone wanted to live. She was, oh, greedy about it. She was interested in everything. I had to tell her how people in the streets looked, what the sky was like on a cloudy day, the garbage men, the lines of wash across the court. She kept the radio going from morning to night. She had to know all about the movie stars and the society people, who was getting married, who was getting divorced, who was having a baby. When I went out with some man, which wasn't too often, I had to tell her what he said, how he said it—what his line was, the passes he made, how I felt about the icky phase of going out.

"And she hated me. She was jealous. When I came home from work I used to wipe the makeup off before I stepped into the house. I never . . . dressed or undressed in front of her if I could help it. Only—she'd make me. She seemed to like being jealous; she'd get a kick out of it.

"And then there were other times when she'd cry and I knew she loved me very much.

"She was right," Celeste Phillips said in a hard voice. "There was no justice in her being a cripple. It was a punishment she didn't deserve and she was determined not to give up. She wanted to live much more than I do. Much more.

"Killing her wasn't—wasn't *fair*.

"I want to help find the one who killed her. I don't understand it and I can't believe yet that it really happened to us—to her . . . I've got to be part of his punishment. I can't just stand around doing nothing. I'm not afraid or kittenish or silly. Let me help, Mr. Queen. I'll carry your briefcase, run errands, type letters, answer your phone—anything. Whatever you say. Whatever you think I can do."

She looked down at her white doeskins, blinking angrily.

The Queens kept looking at her.

"I'm really awfully, terribly sorry," said a voice, "but I rang and rang—"

Celeste jumped up and ran to the window. A long wrinkle ran like a crack from one shoulder to the opposite hip and the young man in the doorway seemed spellbound by it. As if he half-expected a shell to fall off.

He said again, "I can't tell you how sorry," not taking his eyes from her back, "but I lost a sister by that route myself. I'll come back later."

Celeste said, "Oh!" and she turned around quickly.

They stared at each other across the room.

Ellery said, "Miss Phillips and—I gather—Mr. McKell."

"Ever see New York the way it's going to look the day after God Almighty strikes us all dead because He's sick and tired of us?—I mean, Wall Street on Sunday morning?" Jimmy McKell was saying to Celeste Phillips ten minutes later. As far as he was concerned, the Almighty had already begun, with the Queens. "Or Big Liz coming up the bay? Or the mid-Hudson from the Yonkers ferry in June? Or Central Park from a Central Park South penthouse looking north any old time? Ever taste a *bagel? Halvah?* Chopped liver with chicken fat and a slice of black radish? *Shish kebab?* Anchovy *pizza?*"

"No," said Celeste primly.

"This is ridiculous." He waved his absurd arms. He looks like young Abe Lincoln, thought Ellery. All length and enthusiasm, awkward and lovely. An ugly, humorous mouth and eyes not so frank as his voice. His brown suit was positively disreputable. 25 or 26. "And you call yourself a New Yorker, Celeste?"

Celeste stiffened. "Maybe, *Mister* McKell, being poor all my life has something to do with it." She has the French heritage of middleclass propriety, Ellery thought.

"You sound like my saintly father in reverse," said James Guymer McKell. "He never ate a *bagel,* either. Are you anti-Semitic?"

"I'm not anti-anything," gasped Celeste.

"Some of my father's best friends are anti-Semitic," said young McKell. "Listen, Celeste, if we're going to be friends you've got to understand that my father and I—"

"I've got my own tender heart to thank for this," said Celeste coldly. "That and the fact that my sister—"

"And mine."

She said, flushing, "I'm sorry."

Jimmy McKell flung a grasshopper leg up and over. "I live on a legman's stipend, my girl, and not because I like it, either. It's that or go into oil with my father. I wouldn't go into oil if I was— if I was a Portuguese sardine."

Celeste looked suspicious but interested.

"I thought, McKell," remarked the Inspector, "that you lived with your people in that Park Avenue museum."

"Yes," smiled Celeste. "How much board do you pay?"

"Eighteen bucks a week," said Jimmy, "just about enough to buy the butler's cigars. And I don't know that I'm getting my money's worth. For my silken flop, with running hot toddies, I have to take long sermons on class distinction, a Communist in every garage, how we must rebuild Germany, what this country needs is a Big Businessman in the White House, my-boy-marry-into-Steel, and that grand old favorite, The Unions Be Damned. The only reason I stay to take it is that I'm kind of sentimental about my mother. And now that Monica . . ."

"Yes?" said Ellery.

Jimmy McKell looked around. "What? Say, I've kind of forgotten what I came for, haven't I? It's that old debbil sex again. Pin-up GI McKell, they used to call me."

"Tell me about your sister," said Celeste suddenly, pinching her skirt forward.

"Monica?" He pulled a cigaret with the texture of a prune from his pocket, and a large match. Celeste covertly watched him light up and lean forward in a jackknife, one eye cocked against the smoke, his elbows on his shanks and an overgrown hand tossing the match stump up and down. Jimmy Stewart and Gregory Peck, Celeste thought. And—yes—the teeniest dash of Raymond Massey around the mouth. Young-wise and boy-old. Homely and sweet. Probably had every woman in New York running after him. "A good joe. Everything they said about Monica was true, yet they never got to know her. Least of all father or mother. It was her own fault; she was misery-misery-misery inside, and she put up a front to cover it that was tougher to get through than a tank trap. Monica could be mean, and cruel, and toward the end she was getting worse."

He tossed the match into an ashtray. "Father had always spoiled her rotten. He taught her what power was and he gave her his own contempt for people. His attitude toward me's always been different; he made me toe the line from the start. We used to have some pretty rough times. Monica was a grown woman when I was still in knee pants, and it was Monica who slugged it out with father in my defense. He never could stand up to Monica.

"Mother was always afraid of her."

Jimmy hooked a garter-revealing leg over the arm of the chair. "My sister grew up—as long as you're asking—without a slum kid's chance to find out what she really wanted out of life. Whatever it was, it wasn't what she had, and that's what made my father into an even meaner old man than he'd ordinarily have been, because in his view she had everything. I found out by spending three years in the Army as a doughfoot, two of them crawling around the Pacific mosquito parks on my belly. Monica never did find out. The only outlet she had was kicking the rules in the pants. And all the time, underneath, she was scared and mixed up . . . It's a funny deal, Celeste," said Jimmy suddenly, staring at her.

"Yes . . . Jimmy?"

"I know a lot about you." She was startled at that. "I've been covering the Cat cases since the Abernethy murder—I get special privileges at the Bastille because they find me useful for dirt-digging purposes in the upper crust. I actually talked to you after your sister was murdered."

"You did? I didn't . . ."

"Naturally, I was just one of the vultures, and you were pretty numb. But I remember thinking at the time that you and I had a lot in common. We were both way out of our class and we both had sisters who were cripples and whom we loved and understood and who got the same nasty, sickening deal."

"Yes."

"I've been meaning to look you up when you'd had a chance to unpack the bags under your eyes and get your defenses up a little. I was thinking about you when I walked up those stairs."

Celeste looked at him.

"Cross my heart and hope to die in the oil business." Jimmy grinned, but only for an instant. He turned abruptly to Ellery. "I run off at the mouth, Queen, but only when I'm with fellow-workers. I'm a great lover of humanity and it comes out here. But I also know how and when to button up. I was interested—as a reporter—when Abernethy, Violette, and O'Reilly were knocked off; when my own sister got it, it got personal. I've got to be on the inside in this cat race. I'm no boy genius, but I've learned to toddle around this town and I think you can use me. If my newspaper connection rules me out, I'll quit today. Myself, I think it's an advantage; gives me entree I wouldn't have otherwise. But that's strictly up to you. Maybe before you say no I ought to go on record before witnesses that I wouldn't write anything for that lousy bedsheet I work for that you nixed. Do I get the job?''

Ellery went to the mantelpiece for a pipe. He took a long time filling it.

"That makes two questions, Mr. Queen," said Celeste in a tense voice, "you haven't answered."

Inspector Queen said, "Excuse us a minute. Ellery, I'd like to talk to you."

Ellery followed his father into the study and the Inspector shut the door. "You're not considering it."

"Yes."

"Ellery, for God's sake. Send them home!"

Ellery lit his pipe.

"Are you out of your mind? A couple of hopped-up kids. And they're both connected with the case!"

Ellery puffed.

"Look here, son. If it's help you want, you've got the entire Department on call. We've got a flock of ex-GIs who'd give you everything this youngster could and a lot more—they're trained men. If you want a pretty girl, there's at least three I can think of right now in the Policewomen's Bureau who'd give the Phillips number a run for her money. And they're trained, too."

"But they're not," said Ellery thoughtfully, "connected with the case."

The Inspector blinked. Ellery grinned and went back to the living room.

"Very unorthodox," he said. "I'm inclined to go for it."

"Oh, Mr. Queen."

"What did I tell you, Celeste?"

The Inspector snarled from the doorway, "Ellery, I've got to phone my office," and he slammed the door.

"But it might be dangerous."

"I know some judo," said Jimmy helpfully.

"It's not funny, McKell. Maybe very dangerous."

"Listen, son." Jimmy was growling. "The little folks we kids played tag with in New Guinea didn't wrap a cord around your neck. They cut it. But you'll notice mine is still in one piece. Of course, Celeste here—that's different. Inside work, I'd say. Something exciting, useful, and safe."

"How about Celeste's speaking for herself, Jimmy?"

"Go on, Miss Alden."

"I'm scared," said Celeste.

"Sure you are! That's what I—"

"I was scared when I walked in and I'll be scared when I walk out. But being scared won't stop me from doing anything I can to help catch Simone's murderer."

"Well, now," began Jimmy.

"No," she said. Distinctly.

Jimmy reddened. He mumbled, "My mistake," and dug another refugee cigaret from his pocket.

"And we've got to have something else understood," said Ellery, as if nothing had happened. "This is no fraternity of rollicking companions, like the Three Musketeers. I'm Big Chief Plotto and I take nobody into my confidence. I give unexplained orders. I expect them to be carried out without protest, without questions, in confidence . . . and without consultation even between yourselves."

They looked up at that.

"Perhaps I should have made that part of it clear first. You're not co-workers in this little QBI. Nothing as cosy as that. You're accountable always and solely to me, what I give you to do is your personal assignment not to be communicated to each other or anyone else; and for the support of this declaration I expect you to pledge your lives, your fortunes, and your sacred honor if any. If you feel you can't join me under these conditions, say so now and we'll write this session off as a pleasantly wasted hour."

They were silent.

"Celeste?"

She clutched her bag. "I said I'd do anything. I accept."

But Ellery persisted. "You won't question your instructions?"

"No."

"No matter what they happen to be?"

"No."

"No matter how unpleasant or incomprehensible?"

"No," said Celeste.

"And you agree not to disclose your instructions to anyone?"

"I agree, Mr. Queen."

"Even to Jimmy?"

"To anybody."

"Jimmy?"

"You're a tougher boss than the human oak knot who holds down the city desk at the *Extra*."

"Amusing," smiled Ellery, "but it doesn't answer my question."

"I'm in."

"On those precise terms?"

"Yes, sir."

Ellery looked at them for a moment.

"Wait here."

He went quickly into his study, shutting the door.

As Ellery began to write on a tablet, his father came in from his bedroom. The old man stood at the desk watching, his lips pushed out.

"Anything new downtown, Dad?" murmured Ellery, writing.

"Just a call from the Commissioner asking—"

"Asking what?"

"Just asking."

Ellery tore the sheet off the pad, put it into a plain envelope, sealed the envelope, and wrote on its face, "J."

He began to write on another sheet.

"Nothing at all, hm?"

"Oh, it's not all Cat," said the Inspector, watching. "Murder on West 75th and Amsterdam. Double header. Betrayed wife trails hubby to apartment and lets both sinners have it. With a pearl-handled job, .22."

"Anybody I know?" Ellery cheerfully tore the second sheet off the pad.

"Dead woman was a nightclub dancer, Oriental numbers a specialty. Dead man was a wealthy lobbyist. Wife's a society woman prominent in church affairs."

"Sex, politics, society, and religion," said Ellery as he sealed the second envelope. "What more could anyone ask?" He wrote on the envelope, "C."

"It'll take the heat off for a few days, anyway." As Ellery got up his father demanded, "What's that you just wrote?"

"Instructions to my 87th Street Irregulars."

"You're really going through with this Hollywood dam-foolery?"

Ellery went back to the living room.

The Inspector paused in the doorway again, bitterly.

To Celeste Ellery handed the sealed envelope marked "C," to Jimmy the sealed envelope marked "J."

"No, don't open them now. Read, destroy, and report back to me here when you're ready."

Celeste was a little pale as she tucked her envelope into her bag. Jimmy crammed his into his outside pocket, but he kept his hand there.

"Going my way, Celeste?"

"No," said Ellery. "Leave separately. You first, Jimmy."

Jimmy jammed his hat on and loped out.

To Celeste the room seemed empty.

"When do I go, Mr. Queen?"

"I'll tell you."

Ellery went to one of the windows. Celeste settled back again, opened her bag, took out a compact. The envelope she did not touch. After a while she replaced the compact and shut her bag. She sat looking at the dark fireplace. Inspector Queen, in the study doorway, said nothing at all.

"All right, Celeste."

About five minutes had passed. Celeste left without a word.

"Now," exploded the Inspector, "will you tell me what you wrote in those damned notes?"

"Sure." Ellery was watching the street. "As soon as she comes out of the house."

They waited.

"She stopped to read the note," said the Inspector.

"And there she goes." Ellery strolled over to the armchair. "Why, Dad," he said, "in Celeste's note I instructed her to find out all she can about Jimmy McKell. In Jimmy's note I instructed him to find out all he can about Celeste Phillips."

Ellery relit his pipe, puffing placidly.

"You conniver," breathed his father. "The one thing I didn't think of, and the only thing that makes sense."

"If Heaven drops a date, the wise man opens his mouth. Chinese proverb."

The Inspector launched himself from the jamb, steaming around the room like Scuffy the Tugboat.

"Beautiful," he chortled. "They'll have to head for each other like two—" He stopped.

"Cats?" Ellery took the pipe from his mouth. "That's just it, Dad. I don't know. This could be brutal. But we can't take chances. We simply mustn't."

"Oh, it's ridiculous," snapped the old man. "A couple of romantic kids."

"I thought I detected the inspectorial nose twitch once or twice during Celeste's true confession."

"Well, in this business you suspect everybody at least once. But when you stop to think about it, you—"

"You what? We don't know a thing about the Cat. The Cat may be male, female, 16, 60, white, black, brown, or purple."

"I thought you told me a few days ago that you'd spotted something. What was it, a mirage?"

"Irony really isn't your long suit, Dad. I didn't mean something about the Cat himself."

The Inspector shrugged. He started for the door.

"I meant something about the Cat's operations."

The old man pulled up, turned around.

"What did you say?"

"The six murders have certain elements in common."

"Elements in *common?*"

Ellery nodded.

"How many?" The Inspector sounded choked.

"At least three. I can think of a fourth, too."

His father ran back. "What, son? What are they?"

But Ellery did not answer.

After a moment the Inspector hitched his trousers up and, very pale, marched out of the room.

"Dad?"

"What?" His angry voice shot in from the foyer.

"I need more time."

"For what? So he can wring a few more necks?"

"That was below the belt. You ought to know these things can't be rushed sometimes."

Ellery sprang to his feet. And he was pale, too. "Dad, they mean something. They must! But what?"

4

Ellery was nervy that weekend. For hours he occupied himself with compass, ruler, pencil, graph paper. Plotting the curves of statistical mysteries. Finally he hurled his co-ordinates into the fireplace and sent them up in smoke. Inspector Queen, coming upon him that broiling Sunday apparently warming himself at a fire, made the feeble remark that if he had to live in purgatory he was going to do something about lowering the temperature.

Ellery laughed disagreeably. "There are no fans in hell."

And he went into his study and made a point of closing the door.

But his father followed.

"Son."

Ellery was standing at his desk. Glaring down at the case. He had not shaved for three days; under the rank stubble his skin was green and mortal.

Looks more like a vegetable gone to seed than a man, thought his father. And he said again, "Son."

"Dad, I'd better give up."

The Inspector chuckled. "You know you won't. Feel like talking?"

"If you can suggest a cheerful topic of conversation."

The Inspector turned on the fan. "Well, there's always the weather. By the way, heard from your—what did you call those two—Irregulars?"

Ellery shook his head.

"How about a walk in the Park? Or a bus turned cherry-colored in ride?"

"Nothing new?" muttered Ellery.

"Don't bother shaving. You won't meet anybody you know; the City's half-empty. What do you say, son?"

"That's another thing." Ellery looked out. There was a crimson hem on the sky. It brushed the buildings. "This damned weekend."

"Now look," said his father. "The Cat's operated strictly on working days. No Saturday, no Sunday, and he bypassed the only holiday since he got going, Fourth of July. So we don't have to get the jitters about the Labor Day weekend."

"You know what New York's like on Labor Day night." The buildings bloodied. Twenty-four hours from now, he thought. "Bottlenecks at every road, bridge, tunnel, terminal. Everybody cramming back into town at the same time."

"Come on, Ellery! Let's take in a movie. Or, I'll tell you what. We'll rustle up a revue. I wouldn't mind seeing a leg show tonight."

Ellery failed to smile. "I'd only take the Cat with me. You go on and enjoy yourself, Dad. I'd be no fun at all."

The Inspector, a sensible man, went.

But he did not go to a leg show.

With the assistance of a busman, he went downtown to Police Headquarters instead.

The dark the heat as the French blades swished toward his neck. He held himself ready. He was calm, even happy. The tumbril below was jammed with cats knitting solemnly with silk cords of blue and salmon-pink and nodding their approval. A small cat, no larger than an ant, sat just under his nose looking up at him. This cat had black eyes. As he all but felt the flick of the knife and the clean and total pain across his neck it seemed to him the night lifted and a great light flew over everything.

Ellery opened his eyes.

His cheek throbbed where something on the desk had corrupted it and he was wondering that the screeching agony of the dream persisted past its borders when it occurred to him that the telephone in his father's bedroom was ringing in a nasty monotone.

He got up and went into the bedroom and turned on the light.

1:45.

"Hello." His neck ached.

"Ellery." The Inspector's voice stung him awake. "I've been ringing for ten minutes."

"I fell asleep at my desk. What's up, Dad? Where are you?"

"Where would I be on this line? I've been hanging around all evening. Still dressed?"

"Yes."

"Meet me right away at the Park-Lester apartment house. It's on East 84th between Fifth and Madison."

1:45 A.M. It is therefore Labor Day. The 25th of August to the 5th of September. Eleven days. Eleven is one more than ten. Between Phillips, Simone, and Willikins, Beatrice, it was ten days. One more than ten makes . . .

"Ellery, you there?"

"Who is it?" His head ached abominably.

"Ever hear of Dr. Edward Cazalis?"

"Cazalis?"

"Never mind—"

"The psychiatrist?"

"Yes."

"Impossible!"

You crept along the catwalk of a rationale while the night split into a billion tinsel fragments.

"What did you say, Ellery?"

He felt hung up in far space. Lost.

"It couldn't be Dr. Cazalis." He mustered his forces.

The Inspector's voice said craftily, "Now what would make you say a thing like that, son?"

"Because of his age. Cazalis can't be the seventh victim. It's out of the question. There's a mistake somewhere."

"Age?" The old man floundered. "What the devil has Cazalis's age got to do with anything?"

"He must be in his mid-60s. It can't be Cazalis. It's not in the scheme."

"What scheme?" His father was shouting.

"It's not Dr. Cazalis, is it? If it's Dr. Cazalis . . ."

"It just happens it isn't!"

Ellery sighed.

"It's Cazalis's wife's niece," said the Inspector peevishly. "She's Lenore Richardson. The Park-Lester is where the Richardsons live. The girl, her father and mother."

"Do you know how old she was?"

"Late or middle 20s, I think."

"Not married?"

"I don't think so. I have very little information. I've got to hang up now, Ellery. Get a move on."

"I'll be right there."

"Wait. How do you know Cazalis wasn't—?"

Just across the Park, Ellery was thinking, staring at the phone on the cradle. He had already forgotten having put it there.

The phone book.

He ran back to the study, grabbed the Manhattan directory.

Richardson.

Richardson Lenore 12¹/₂ E. 84.

There was also a *Richardson Zachary 12¹/₂ E. 84* listed at the same number.

Ellery went about shaving and changing his clothes in a blissful nirvana.

Later, it was possible to synthesize his nightlong impressions into one complex. The night itself was a jumble. Faces flowed and crossed and hung apart; fragments of things said, voices broken, tears shed, looks passed, men coming, telephones ringing, pencils writing; doors, a chaise, a photograph, photographers, measurements, sketches, a small bluish fist, the dangle of a silk cord, a gold Louis XVI clock on an Italian marble fireplace, an oils nude, a torn book jacket . . .

But Ellery's mind was a machine. The unselective evidence of his senses stoked it, and after a while out came a product.

Tonight's production, by a squirrel instinct, Ellery stored away, sensing a future need.

The girl herself told him nothing. He could see what she might have been, but only from a photograph; the flesh, hardened at the supreme moment of the struggle not to die, was the usual meaningless petrifaction. She had been small and cuddlesome, with soft brown curly hair. Her nose was saucy and her mouth—from the photograph—had been pettish. She was manicured and pedicured and her hair had been recently set. The lingerie under her pongee negligee was expensive. The book she had been reading at the pounce of the Cat was a tattered reprint of *Forever Amber*. The remains of an orange and a few cherry pits lay on the inlaid occasional table beside the chaise. On the table also were a bowl of fruit, a silver cigaret box, an ashtray with fourteen lipstick-tipped butts in it, and a silver table lighter in the shape of an armored knight.

In the withering lividity of death the girl looked 50; in the photograph, a recent one, untouched 18. She had been 25 and an only child.

Ellery dismissed Lenore Richardson as a regrettable intrusion.

The living told no more.

They were four: the father and mother of the murdered girl; the girl's aunt—Mrs. Richardson's sister—Mrs. Cazalis; and the eminent Dr. Cazalis.

There was no family fellowship in their grief. This Ellery found stimulating, and he studied them carefully one by one.

The mother passed what was left of the night in uncurbed hysterics. Mrs. Richardson was a superb woman of middle age, rather too fashionably gowned, and overjeweled. Ellery thought he discovered in her a chronic anxiety, unrelated to her sorrow; like the frown of a colicky infant. She was apparently the kind of woman who hoards life like a miser. The gold of her youth having tarnished, what little remained she kept gilding and packaging in extravagant self-delusion. Now she writhed and shrieked as if, in losing her daughter, she had found something long mislaid.

The father, a gray little rigid man of 60, looked like a jeweler, or a librarian. Actually, he was the head of Richardson, Leeper & Company, one of the oldest wholesale drygoods houses in New York. Ellery had passed the Richardson, Leeper & Company building often in his prowls about the City. It stood nine stories high on half a square block on Broadway and 17th Street. The firm was known for its old-fashioned merchant virtues: sternly nonunionized, run on the benevolent-patron system, with employees who tottered comfortably along in the traces until they dropped. Richardson would be unswervingly honest, unalterably stubborn, and as narrow as a straight line. This was all quite beyond him. He could only sit by himself in a corner glancing bewilderedly from the tormented woman in the evening gown to the tumbled little mountain range under the blanket.

Richardson's sister-in-law was much younger than his wife; Ellery judged Mrs. Cazalis to be early-fortyish. She was pallid, slender, tall, and self-contained. Unlike her older sister, she had found her orbit; her eyes went often to her husband. She had a submissive quality Ellery had found frequently in the wives of brilliant men. This was a woman whose marriage was the sum of existence to her, in a pitifully arithmetic way. In a society composed largely of Mrs. Richardsons, Mrs. Cazalis would tend to have few friends and few social interests. She comforted her middleaged sister as a mother might soothe a child in a tantrum; it was only during Mrs. Richardson's wilder vocalisms that the younger woman's ministrations took on an edge of rebuke and resentment. It was as if she felt herself cheapened and cheated. There was a virginal, unthawed sensitivity in her, a chill delicacy of feeling, which recoiled from her sister's exhibitionism.

It was during one of these moments that an amused male voice said in Ellery's ear, "I see you've noticed it."

Ellery turned quickly. It was Dr. Cazalis, big and stoop-shouldered and powerful, with cold milky eyes and masses of icegray hair; a glacier of a man. His voice was deliberate and carried a musical undertone of cynicism. Ellery had heard somewhere that Dr. Cazalis had an unusual history for a psychiatrist; meeting the man for the first time, he was disposed to acceptance of the report. He must be 65, Ellery thought, possibly older; in semi-retirement, taking only a few cases, chiefly women, and those on a selective basis—it all added up to failing health, the declining phase of a medical career, the coronary age; and yet Dr. Cazalis seemed, aside from a certain restlessness of his large thick surgeon's hands, a vigorous and functioning personality; certainly not a man to spare himself. It was a puzzle, not the less interesting for its irrelevance. His rather encyclopedic eyes were unavoidable. He sees everything, thought Ellery, and he tells exactly nothing; or what he tells is automatically conditioned by what he thinks his hearer ought to know.

"Noticed what, Dr. Cazalis?"

"The difference between my wife and her sister. Where Lenore was concerned, my sister-in-law was criminally inadequate. She was afraid of the child, jealous and overindulgent. Alternated between pampering and screaming at her. And in the sulks ignored Lenore entirely. Now Della's in a panic overwhelmed by feelings of guilt. Clinically speaking, mothers like Della wish for the death of their young and when it happens they set up a terrified howl for forgiveness. Her grief is for herself."

"It seems to me Mrs. Cazalis is as aware of that as you are, Doctor."

The psychiatrist shrugged. "My wife's done what she could. We lost two babies in the delivery room within four years of our marriage and Mrs. Cazalis was never able to have another. She transferred her affections to Della's child and it compensated each of them—I mean my wife and Lenore—for her own lack. It couldn't be complete, of course; for one thing, the biological but otherwise inadequate mama is always a problem. Essentially," said the doctor dryly, glancing over at the sisters, "essentially unsatisfactory even in mourning. The mother beats her breast and the aunt suffers in silence. I was rather fond of the little chicken," said Dr. Cazalis suddenly, "myself." He walked away.

By 5 A.M. they had the facts orderly. Such as there were.

The girl had been home alone. She was to have accompanied her father and mother to a party in Westchester at the home of one of Mrs. Richardson's friends, but Lenore had begged off. ("She was due for her mensis," Mrs. Cazalis told Inspector Queen. "Lenore always had a hard time. She told me in the morning over the phone that she wouldn't be able to go. And Della was cross with her.") Mr. and Mrs. Richardson had left for Westchester shortly after 6 o'clock; it was a dinner party. One of the two domestics, the cook, was away for the holiday, having left Saturday afternoon to visit her family in Pennsylvania. The other, a maid, had been given the night off by Lenore herself; since she did not sleep in, she was not expected until morning.

The Cazalises, who lived eight blocks away, at Park Avenue and 78th Street, had been worried about Lenore all evening. At 8:30 Mrs. Cazalis had telephoned. Lenore had said she was "in the usual crampy dumps" but otherwise all right and that her aunt and uncle were not to "throw fits" about her. But when Mrs. Cazalis learned that Lenore had characteristically failed to eat anything, she had gone over to the Richardson apartment, prepared a warm meal, forced Lenore to eat it, made the girl comfortable on the chaise in the living room, and had spent perhaps an hour with her niece afterward, talking.

Lenore had been depressed. Her mother, she had told her aunt, had been hounding her to "get married and stop running from one man to another like a stupid high school girl." Lenore had been deeply in love with a boy who was killed at St.-Lô, a poor boy of Jewish origin of whom Mrs. Richardson had violently disapproved; "Mother doesn't understand and she won't let him alone even when he's dead." Mrs. Cazalis had let the girl pour out her troubles and then had tried to get her to bed. But Lenore said "with all this pain" she would stay up reading; the heat was bothering her, too. Mrs. Cazalis had urged her not to stay up too late, had kissed her good night, and left. It was about 10 P.M. She had last seen her niece reclining on the chaise, reaching for a book, and smiling.

At home, Mrs. Cazalis had wept, her husband had soothed her, and he had sent her to bed. Dr. Cazalis was staying up over an involved case history and he had promised his wife he would call Lenore before turning in, "as the chances are Della and Zach won't be rolling in till 3 or 4 in the morning." At a few minutes past midnight the doctor phoned the Richardson apartment. There was no answer. Five minutes later he tried again. There was an extension in Lenore's bedroom so that even if she had gone to sleep the repeated rings of the phone should have aroused her. Disturbed, Dr. Cazalis had decided to investigate. Without awakening his wife, he had walked over to the Park-Lester and found Lenore Richardson on the chaise with the salmon-colored silk cord imbedded in her flesh, dead of strangulation.

His in-laws had still not returned. Except for the dead girl, the apartment was empty. Dr. Cazalis had notified the police and, finding the telephone number of Mrs. Richardson's Westchester friends on the foyer table—"I left it for Lenore in case she felt sick and wanted me to come home," sobbed Mrs. Richardson—he had notified them that something had "happened" to Lenore. He had then phoned his wife to come at once, as she was, in a taxi. Mrs. Cazalis had hurried over with a long coat thrown over her nightgown to find the police already there. She collapsed, but by the time the Richardsons arrived she had recovered sufficiently to take charge of her sister—"for which," muttered Inspector Queen, "she ought to get the Nobel peace award."

The usual variation on the theme, thought Ellery. Chips of incident and accident, the death-colored core remaining. The non-crackable nut.

("I took one look at the silk cord around her neck," said Dr. Cazalis, "and I recall only one coherent thought. 'The Cat.' ")

Pending daylight examination of the terrace and roof—the living room French doors had stood open all evening—they were inclined to the belief that the Cat had gained entrance boldly through the front door by way of the self-service penthouse elevator. Mrs. Cazalis recalled having tried the front door from the foyer on her way out at 10 o'clock and, at that time, the door was locked; but on her husband's arrival about 12:30 A.M. the door was wide open, held ajar by a doorstop. Since the doorstop revealed the dead girl's fingerprints, it was evident that Lenore had propped the apartment door open after her aunt's departure, probably to encourage some slight circulation of air; it was a stifling night. The night doorman remembered Mrs. Cazalis's arrival and departure and Dr. Cazalis's arrival after midnight; but he admitted that he had slipped out several times in the course of the evening to get a cold bottle of beer at the delicatessen at 86th Street and Madison Avenue and that, even while he was on duty in the lobby, a prowler could have got past him unnoticed: "It's been a hot night, half the tenants are out of town, and I snoozed on the lobby settee on and off the whole evening." He had seen and heard nothing out of the ordinary.

Neighbors had heard no screams.

The fingerprint men turned up nothing of interest.

Dr. Prouty of the Medical Examiner's office was unable to fix the time of death more accurately than the limits defined by Mrs. Cazalis's departure and her husband's arrival.

The strangling cord was of tussah silk.

"Henry James would have called it," said Dr. Cazalis, "the fatal futility of facts."

They were sitting around at dawn in the wreckage of the night over cold ginger ale and beer. Mrs. Cazalis had prepared a platter of cold chicken sandwiches to which no one applied but Inspector Queen, and he only under Ellery's bullying. The body had been removed on the official order; the sinister blanket was gone; a breeze blew from the penthouse terrace. Mrs. Richardson was asleep in her bedroom under sedation.

"With all respect to the Great Casuist," replied Ellery, "it's not the futility of facts that's fatal, Doctor, but their scarcity."

"In seven murders?" cried the doctor's wife.

"Seven multiplied by zero, Mrs. Cazalis. Well, perhaps not quite, but it's very difficult."

Inspector Queen's jaws were going mechanically. He seemed not to be listening.

"What can I do!"

They were startled. Lenore's father had been still so long.

"I've got to do something. I can't just sit here. I have a great deal of money . . ."

"I'm afraid money won't do it, Mr. Richardson," said Ellery. "Monica McKell's father had the same idea. His offer of $100,000 reward on August 10 hasn't even been threatened. It's simply increased the work of the police."

"How about turning in, Zach?" suggested Dr. Cazalis.

"She didn't have an enemy in the world. Ed, you know that. Everyone was mad about her. Why did this . . . why did he pick Lenore? She was all I had. Why my daughter?"

"Why anybody's daughter, Mr. Richardson?"

"I don't care about the others. What do we pay our police for!"

Richardson was on his feet, his cheeks cerise.

"Zach."

He sagged, and after a moment he mumbled something and went out very quietly.

"No, dear, let him go," said the psychiatrist quickly to his wife. "Zach has that sturdy Scotch sense of the fitness of things and life is very precious to him. But I've got to worry about you. Your eyes are drooping out of your head. Come on, darling, I'll take you home."

"No, Edward."

"Della's asleep—"

"I won't go without you. And you're needed here." Mrs. Cazalis took her husband's paw. "Edward, you are. You can't stay out of this now. Tell me you'll do something."

"Certainly. I'll take you home."

"I'm not a child!"

The big man sprang to his feet. "But what can I do? These people are trained to this sort of thing. I wouldn't expect them to walk into my office and tell me how to treat a patient!"

"Don't make me seem stupid, Edward." Her voice had sharpened. "You can tell these gentlemen what you've told me so many times. Your theories—"

"Unfortunately, that's all they are. Now let's be sensible. You're going home this—"

"Della needs me." The taut voice was stretching.

"Darling." He seemed startled.

"You know what Lenore meant to me." Mrs. Cazalis broke. "You know, you know!"

"Of course." His glance warned Ellery and Inspector Queen off. "Lenore meant a great deal to me, too. Now stop, you'll make yourself very ill."

"Edward, you know what you said to me!"

"I'll do what I can. You've got to cut this out, dearest. Stop it." Gradually, in his arms, her sobs subsided.

"But you haven't promised."

"You needn't go home. I think you're right. Della will need you. Use the guest room, dear. I'll give you something to make you sleep."

"Edward, promise!"

"I promise. Now I'm putting you to bed."

When Dr. Cazalis returned, he looked apologetic. "I should have seen those hysterics coming on."

"I'd welcome a good old-fashioned emotional binge myself right now," murmured Ellery. "By the way, Doctor, which theories was Mrs. Cazalis referring to?"

"Theories?" Inspector Queen looked around. "Who's got theories?"

"Why, I suppose I have," said Dr. Cazalis, seating himself and reaching for a sandwich. "Say, what are those fellows doing out there, anyway?"

"Examining the terrace and roof. Tell me about these theories of yours, Doctor." The Inspector took one of Ellery's cigarets; he never smoked cigarets.

"I suppose everybody in New York has one or two," smiled the psychiatrist. "The Cat murders would naturally not pass a psychiatrist by. And even though I don't have the inside information at your disposal—"

"It wouldn't add much to what you've read."

Cazalis grunted. "I was about to say, Inspector, that I'm sure it wouldn't make any material difference. Where it seems to me you people have gone off is in applying to these murders the normal investigatory technique. You've concentrated on the victims—admittedly the sensible methodology in ordinary cases, but in this one exactly wrong. In this case you stand a better chance concentrating on the murderer."

"How do you mean?"

"Isn't it true that the victims have had nothing in common?"

"Yes?"

"Their lives crossed nowhere?"

"As far as we can tell."

"Take my word for it, you'll never find a significant point of contact. The seven seem unrelated because they are unrelated. At no time did they stand a greater chance of interrelationship than if the murderer had shut his eyes and opened the telephone directory, let's say, to seven different pages at random, determined to kill the forty-ninth person listed in the second column of each page."

Ellery stirred.

"We have, then," continued Dr. Cazalis, swallowing the last of his sandwich, "seven persons dying by the same hand who have no interidentity or contiguity. What does this mean in practical terms? A series of apparently *indiscriminate* acts of violence. To the trained mind, this spells psychosis. I say 'apparently' indiscriminate, by the way, because the conduct of the psychotic appears unmotivated only when judged in the perspective of reality—that is, by more or less healthy minds viewing the world as it is. The psychotic has his motivations, but they proceed from distorted views of reality and falsification of facts.

"My opinion, based on an analysis of the data available to me, is that the Cat—damn that cartoonist! an infamous libel on a very well-balanced beast!—suffers from what we call a systematized delusional state, a paranoid psychosis."

"Well, naturally," said the Inspector, who seemed disappointed, "one of our first theories was that the killer's insane."

"Insanity is the popular and legal term," said Dr. Cazalis with a shrug. "There are any number of individuals who, though not insane in a legal sense, are nevertheless subjects of a psychosis. I suggest we stick to the medical terminology."

"Psychotic, then. We've checked the mental hospitals time and again without result."

"Not all psychotics are institutionalized, Inspector Queen," said the psychiatrist dryly. "That's exactly my point. If, for example, the Cat is a paranoid psychotic of the schizophrenic type, he may well be as normal in appearance and behavior—to the untrained eye—as any of us. He might remain unsuspected for a long time, during which he could do plenty of damage."

"I never yet talked to one of you birds," said the Inspector wearily, "that I didn't come away with my chin dragging."

"I gather, Dad," said Ellery, "that Dr. Cazalis has more to disseminate than gloom. Go on, Doctor."

"I was merely going to suggest the alternative, which is that he may be undergoing treatment, or may have been recently under treatment, by a private doctor. It would seem to me whoever's committing these crimes is a local product, all seven murders having taken place in Manhattan, so a good place to start checking would be right in the borough here. It would mean, obviously, getting the co-operation of every man in the field. Each one, being briefed on what to look for, could comb his own records for patients, either current or discharged, who might be possibilities; and those possibilities would have to be questioned by trained people for clinical clues as well as investigated by you people in the routine way. It might be a total frost, of course, and there'd be a dickens of a lot of work—"

"It's not the work," muttered Inspector Queen. "It's the trained personnel that's bothering me."

"Well, I'd be glad to do what I could to help. You heard my wife! I don't have many patients these days—" the psychiatrist made a face—"I'm tapering off to retirement—so it wouldn't work any special hardship on me."

"Handsome offer, Dr. Cazalis." The Inspector rubbed his mustache. "I'll admit this has opened up a field we haven't scratched. Ellery, what do you think?"

"By all means," said Ellery promptly. "It's a constructive suggestion and might well lead straight to our man."

"Do I detect the faintest note of doubt?" smiled Dr. Cazalis. His powerful fingers were drumming on the table.

"Perhaps."

"You don't agree with my analysis."

"Not entirely, Doctor."

The psychiatrist stopped drumming.

"I'm not convinced that the crimes are indiscriminate."

"Then you have information I haven't."

"No. I base my opinion on the same data, I'm sure. But, you see, there's a pattern in these crimes."

"Pattern?" Cazalis stared.

"The murders have a number of elements in common."

"Including this one?" rasped the Inspector.

"Yes, Dad."

Dr. Cazalis began to drum again. "I take it you don't mean consistency of methods—the cords, strangling—"

"No. I mean elements common to the seven victims. I'm convinced they signify a plan of some sort, but what it arises from, what its nature is, where it's going . . ." Ellery's eyes clouded.

"Sounds interesting." Dr. Cazalis was studying Ellery surgically. "If you're right, Mr. Queen, I'm wrong."

"We may both be right. I have the feeling we are. 'Though this be madness, yet there is method in 't.' " They laughed together. "Dad, I'd emphatically recommend that Dr. Cazalis's suggestion be followed up, and right away."

"We're breaking every rule in the book," groaned his father. "Doctor, would you consider taking full charge?"

"I? Of the psychiatric end?"

"That's right."

Dr. Cazalis's fingers stopped exercising. But they remained, as it were, available.

"This is going to be as big a selling as a medical job. It won't work unless every doctor in the field co-operates. With you heading that phase of the investigation—with your reputation and professional connections, Doctor—it's a guarantee of thorough coverage I don't think we'd get another way. As a matter of fact," said the Inspector thoughtfully, "it wouldn't be a bad arrangement for other reasons. The Mayor's already appointed my son special investigator. We're covering the official end. With you in charge of a medical inquiry, it would give us a three-pronged offensive. Maybe," said the Inspector, exhibiting his denture, "maybe we'd even turn up a little something."

He said abruptly, "I'd have to get confirmation of this downtown, Dr. Cazalis, but something tells me the Mayor and the Commissioner will be very happy about the whole thing. Pending an okay, can I tell them you're available?"

The psychiatrist threw up his hands. "What was that line from a movie I once saw? 'Bilked by my own chicanery!' All right, Inspector, I'm hooked. What's the procedure?"

"Where are you going to be later today?"

"Depends on how Della and Zach behave themselves. Either here or at home, Inspector. This morning I'm going to try to get a few hours' sleep."

"Try?" Ellery stretched, rising. "In my case it won't be the least problem."

"Sleeping is always a problem with me. I'm a chronic insomniac—a symptom which is generally part of the clinical picture," said the psychiatrist with a smile, "of dementia, general paresis, and so on, but don't tell my patients. I keep well supplied with sleeping pills."

"I'll phone you this afternoon, Dr. Cazalis."

Cazalis nodded to the Inspector and strolled out.

The Queens were silent. The men working on the terrace were beginning to drift away. Sergeant Velie was crossing the terrace in the sun.

"What do you think?" asked the Inspector suddenly.

"Think? About what, Dad?"

"Cazalis."

"Oh.—Very solid citizen."

"Yes, isn't he."

"Nothing doing," said Sergeant Velie. "No sign of a damn thing, Inspector. He got in by that penthouse elevator, all right."

"The only thing is," mumbled the Inspector, "I wish he'd stop those figure exercises of his. Makes me nervous.—Oh, Velie. Knock off and get some shuteye."

"What about those newspaper guys?"

"They've probably ganged up on Dr. Cazalis. Run interference for him and tell them I'll be right there. With my own pet line of double talk."

The sergeant nodded and clumped off, yawning.

"How about you, Dad?"

"I'll have to go downtown first. You going home now?"

"If I can get away in one piece."

"Wait in the hall closet. I'll decoy 'em into the living room here and then you can make the break."

They parted rather awkwardly.

When Ellery woke up he found his father perched on the edge of the bed, looking at him.

"Dad. What time is it?"

"Past 5."

Ellery stretched. "Just pull in?"

"Uh-huh."

"Anything new in crime?"

"P.m. shows nothing so far. The cord's a washout. It's the other six continued."

"How's the atmosphere? Safe?"

"I wouldn't say so." Inspector Queen hugged himself as if he were cold. "They're really laying into this one. Every line into Headquarters and City Hall jammed. The papers have taken the gloves off and they're yelping for blood. Whatever good the announcement of your appointment did has gone up the flue with the murder of the Richardson girl. When I walked into the Mayor's office with the Commissioner this morning to confer on the Cazalis thing His Honor practically kissed me. Phoned Cazalis then and there. First thing he said over the phone was, 'Dr. Cazalis, when can you hold a press conference?' "

"Cazalis going to do it?"

"He's doing it right this minute. And going on the air tonight."

"I must be a great disappointment to His Honor." Ellery laughed. "Now hit the sack or you'll be a candidate for a medical conference yourself."

The Inspector failed to move.

"There's something else?"

"Ellery." The old man pulled up his left leg and began slowly to untie his shoelace. "There's been some nasty talk downtown. I wouldn't ask you this except that if I'm to keep taking it on the chin I've got to know what round it is."

"Ask me what?"

"I want you to tell me what you've spotted." He began on the other shoe. "For my own information, you understand," he explained to the shoe. "Or let me put it another way. If I'm to keep singeing my pants I want to know what the hell I'm sitting on."

It was a kind of declaration of independence, conceived in grievance and delivered for just cause.

Ellery looked unhappy.

He reached for a cigaret and an ashtray and lay back with the tray balanced on his chest.

"All right," he said. "From your standpoint I'm a disloyal dispenser of nothing and from your standpoint I suppose I am. Now let's see whether what I've been holding out on you could prove of the slightest utility to you, me, the Mayor, the Commissioner, or the shade of Poe.

"One: Archibald Dudley Abernethy was 44 years old. Violette Smith was 42 years old. Rian O'Reilly was 40 years old. Monica McKell was 37 years old. Simone Phillips was 35 years old. Beatrice Willikins was 32 years old. Lenore Richardson was 25 years old. 44, 42, 40, 37, 35, 32, 25."

The Inspector was staring.

"Each victim's been younger than the victim preceding. That's why I was so positive Dr. Cazalis couldn't have been Number 7; he's older than any of them. To have been seventh on the list he'd have to have been under 32, the sixth victim's age . . . that is, if there was a descending-age pattern. And it turned out that Number 7, the Richardson girl, was 25, and I was right. There *is* a descending-age pattern. Mathematically irregular differences, but they're always younger, younger."

The old man gripped his right shoe. "We didn't see that. Nobody saw it."

"Well, it's one of those exasperating little fragments of sense in a jumble. Like the hidden-face puzzles. You look and look, and suddenly there it is. But what does it mean? It's sense, all right, but what sense? It springs from a cause, but what cause? It can't conceivably be the result of coincidence; not seven! And yet the longer you examine it, the less it seems to signify. Can you think of a single satisfactory reason why anyone should go to the trouble of killing successively younger people—who haven't the faintest connection with one another? I can't."

"It's a poser, all right," his father muttered.

"It's true I might announce tonight that no New Yorker 25 years old or older had anything to worry about because the Cat's going down the actuarial tables and he's passed Age 25 . . ."

"Very funny," said the Inspector feebly. "It sounds like—like something out of Gilbert and Sullivan. They'd all think you were crazy and if they thought you were sane it would only pack all the anxiety down into the—the lower brackets."

"Something like that," nodded Ellery. "So I kept it to myself.

"Two." He crushed the cigaret out and cradled his head, staring at the ceiling. "Of the seven victims, two have been male, five female. Until this last one, the victims have been 32 years old or older. Well past the minimum age of consent, wouldn't you say?"

"The what?"

"I mean, we live in a connubial society. All the roads of our culture lead to the American Home, which is not conceived as the citadel of celibacy; if the point requires any proof, we have only to consider, gentlemen, the delicious sense of naughtiness we get out of the mere phrase 'bachelor apartment.' Our women spend their maidenhood catching a husband and the rest of their lives trying to hold on to him; our men spend their entire boyhood envying their father and consequently can't wait when they grow up to marry the next best thing to their mother. Why do you suppose the American male is obsessed with the mammae? What I'm trying to say—"

"Well, for heaven's sake, say it!"

"—is that if you picked seven American adults at random, all of them over 25 years of age, six of them over 32, what are the odds that all but one of them will be unmarried?"

"O'Reilly," said the Inspector in an awed voice. "By God, O'Reilly was the only one."

"Or you could put it another way. Of the two men, Abernethy was a bachelor and O'Reilly was married. That seemed to cancel out the men. But of the five women, all have been single! When you stop to think of it, that's really remarkable. Five women between the ages of 42 and 25 and not one of them succeeded in the great American rat race. As in the case of the descending ages, coincidence is unthinkable. Then the Cat deliberately chooses—among his female victims, at least—only unmarried ones. Why? Inform me."

Inspector Queen gnawed his nails. "The only thing I can think of is that he dangles the marriage bait in order to get in close. But—"

"But that just isn't the explanation, right. No such Lothario's turned up, or the slightest trace of one.

"Of course, I could have cried the glad tidings to Mrs. New York that the only females who need fear the embrace of the Cat are virgins, misogamists, and Lesbians, but—"

"Go on," snarled his father.

"Three: Abernethy was strangled with a blue silk cord, Violette Smith with a salmon-colored one, O'Reilly blue, Monica McKell salmon, Simone Phillips salmon, Beatrice Willikins salmon, Lenore Richardson salmon. There's even a report on that."

Mumbled the Inspector: "I'd forgotten that."

"One color for the males, another for the females. Consistently. Why?"

After a time the Inspector said, rather timidly: "The other day, son, you mentioned a fourth point . . ."

"Oh. Yes. They *all* had phones."

His father rubbed an eye.

"In a way, the very prosiness of the point makes it the most provocative. To me, anyway. Seven victims, seven phones. Even Simone, the poor cripple. They all had phones or, where the subscriber was someone else—as in the cases of Lenore Richardson, Simone Phillips, and Monica McKell—they had separate listings in the directory; I checked.

"I don't know the figures, but I should imagine there's a ratio of some twenty-five phones in the United States per hundred population. One out of four. In the big urban centers, like New York, the percentage may be greater. Let's say in New York one out of three. Yet of the seven victims tagged by the Cat, not one, not two, not four, but all seven had phones.

"The first explanation to suggest itself is that the Cat picks his dainties out of the phone book. Pure lottery. But in a lottery the odds against picking seven victims successively each of whom turns out to be younger than the last would be literally incalculable. Then the Cat makes his selections on some other basis.

"Still, all his victims are listed in the Manhattan directory. Those phones are a point, a point."

Ellery set the ashtray on his night table and swung his legs off the bed to squat, mourner-fashion. "It's damnable," he moaned. "If there were one break in the sequence—one victim older than the last, one woman strangled who was married

or who'd ever been married, one man found necktied in salmon—or heliotrope!—
one who didn't have a phone . . . Those points in common exist for *reasons*. Or
maybe,'' said Ellery, sitting up suddenly, ''or maybe the points in common exist
for the *same* reason. A sort of great common denominator. The Rosetta stone. One
key to all the doors. Do you know, that would be nice.''

But Inspector Queen was mumbling as he stripped. ''That getting-younger business.
When you think of it . . . Two years' difference in age between Abernethy and
Violette. Two years between Vi and O'Reilly. Three years between O'Reilly and
McKell's sister. Two years between her and Celeste's sister. Three years between
her and Beatrice Willikins. Two and three. Never more than three. In six cases.
And then—''

''Yes,'' said Ellery, ''and then Lenore Richardson and we find a jump in the
age differential from a previous maximal three to seven . . . That haunted me all
last night.''

And now the Inspector was denuded, his little sexagenarian hide impaled on the
point of a needle.

''What's haunting me,'' he mumbled, ''is who's next?''

Ellery turned away.

''And that's all you had, son?''

''That's all I *have*.''

''I'm going to bed.'' The little naked man shuffled out.

5

Inspector Queen overslept. He came galloping out at 9:45 Tuesday morning like a late starter under the whip, but when he saw who was having coffee with Ellery he slowed to a walk which neatly ended at the breakfast table.

"Well, look who's among us," beamed the Inspector. "Good morning, McKell."

"Morning, Inspector." said Jimmy McKell. "On your way to the abattoir?"

"Mmmmmmmmmch," inhaled the Inspector. "I think I'll have a slup or two of the life-giving mocha myself." He pulled out a chair and sat down. "Morning son."

"Morning, morning," said Ellery absently, reaching for the coffeepot. "Jimmy came up with the papers."

"Do people still read?"

"Cazalis's interview."

"Oh."

"Goodnaturedly but firmly neutral. The calm voice of organized knowledge. We promise nothing. But one has the feeling that an Osirian hand directed by a radiant eye has taken over. The Mayor must be in the eleventh heaven."

"I thought it was seven," said Jimmy McKell.

"Not in the Egyptian cosmography, Jimmy. And there is something Pharaonic about Cazalis. 'Soldiers, from these pyramids forty centuries look down upon you.'"

"Napoleon."

"In Egypt. Cazalis is soothing syrup to the general. Simply wonderful for morale."

"Don't mind him," grinned the Inspector, reading the paper. "You'll never win . . . Say, this is pretty good medicine at that. You given up journalism, McKell? I didn't spot you among the rest of the scavengers yesterday."

"The Richardson deal?" Jimmy looked secretive. "Yesterday was Labor Day. My day. I'm a working stiff."

"Took off, eh?"

"Who labors best and so on," said Ellery. "Or was it in line of duty, Jimmy?"

"Something like that."

"You had a date with Celeste Phillips."

Jimmy laughed. "And not just yesterday. It's been one sweet journey through time. You give the most interesting assignments, dearie. You should have been a city editor."

"I take it you two have been getting along."

"We manage," replied Jimmy, "to tolerate each other."

"Nice girl," nodded the Inspector. "Son, that tasted like a refill."

"Ready to talk about it, Jimmy?"

"Say, it's getting to be my favorite subject."

"Let's have another all around." Ellery poured, amiably.

"I don't know what you two witch doctors are up to," said Jimmy, "but I'm happy to report that this is a wench of exceptional merit, and in my circles I'm known as Iconoclast McKell, Female Images a Specialty." He fingered his cup. "All kidding aside, I feel like a heel."

"Heeling is a hard profession," said Ellery. "Would you mind itemizing the assignment's virtues, as you found them?"

"Well, the gal has looks, brains, personality, guts, ambition—"

"Ambition?"

"Celeste wants to go back to college. You know she had to quit in her freshman year to take care of Simone. When Simone's mother died back in—"

"Simone's mother?" Ellery frowned. "You make it sound as if Simone's mother wasn't Celeste's mother."

"Didn't you know that?"

"Know what?"

"That Celeste wasn't the daughter of Mrs. Phillips?"

"You mean those two weren't sisters?" The Inspector's cup rattled.

Jimmy McKell looked from Queen to Queen. He pushed his chair back. "I don't know that I'm fond of this," he said. "In fact, I know damn well I'm not."

"Why, what's the matter, Jimmy?"

"You tell me!"

"But there's nothing to tell," said Ellery. "I asked you to find out what you could about Celeste. If we now have something new on her—"

"*On* her?"

"I mean about her, something we didn't know, why, you've only justified my confidence in you."

"May we dispense with the horse droppings, sleuth?"

"Jimmy, sit down."

"I want to know what cooks!"

"Why all the heat?" growled Inspector Queen. "You'll have me thinking in a minute . . ."

"Right." Jimmy sat down suddenly. "There's nothing to think. Simone was Celeste's third cousin or something. Celeste's parents were killed in a gas stove explosion when she was a baby. Mrs. Phillips was her only relative in New York and took her in. That's all there is to it. When Mrs. Phillips died, Celeste naturally took care of Simone; they always considered each other sisters. I know a hell of a lot of real sisters who wouldn't have done what Celeste did!"

"Even speaking not Delphically," said Ellery, "so do I."

"What?"

"Go on, Jimmy."

"She's crazy to get a college education—it half-killed her when she had to give it up at Mrs. Phillips's death. The books that kid's read! Deep stuff—philosophy, psychology—why, Celeste knows more right now than I do, and I've got a Princeton sheepskin acquired by sweat, toil, and grand larceny. Now that Simone's gone, the kid's free to live her own life again, go back to school and make something of herself. She's going to enroll this week in Washington Square College for the fall semester. She wants a B.A., majoring in English and philosophy, and then she'll go on to graduate work. Maybe teach.''

"She must want it a great deal to cut out a program like that for herself on a night school basis."

"Night school? Who said anything about night school?"

"We still live in a competitive economy, Jimmy. Or," said Ellery cheerfully, "were you thinking of taking that problem off her hands?"

"Maybe," said the Inspector with a wink, "maybe that question is irrelevant, immaterial, and none of our business."

Jimmy gripped the table. "Are you crumbums suggesting—?"

"No, no, Jimmy. With benefit of clergy, of course."

"Oh. Well . . . let's leave me out of it." His homely face was angry and watchful.

"She can't work as a model daytimes and go to day college too, Jimmy," said Ellery.

"She's giving up that job."

"Really?" said the Inspector.

"Oh," said Ellery, "she's got herself a night job."

"No job at all!"

"I'm afraid," said Ellery mournfully, "I lost you somewhere back in the third canto. No job at all? How is she going to support herself?"

"With Simone's nestegg!" Jimmy was shouting now.

"Nestegg?"

"What er . . . what nestegg would that be, Jimmy?" asked the Inspector.

"Look." Jimmy inflated his chest. "You asked me to do a dirty chore and I've done it. I don't understand this, any of it. But assuming you're a big wheel in the gray cell department, Queen, and I'm just a little screw rattling around, will you tell me what the devil difference any of this makes?"

"No more difference than the truth ever makes."

"Sounds profound, but I suspect a gimmick."

"McKell." Inspector Queen was grim. "I've had a lot of men working on this case and I've been in it myself up to my Adam's apple. This is the first I've heard about Simone Phillips's leaving anybody anything but a lower back ache. Why didn't Celeste tell us?"

"Because she only found it last week! Because it's got nothing to do with the murder!"

"Found it?" murmured Ellery. "Where?"

"She was cleaning out Simone's junk. There was an old wooden table clock, a French deal that was a family heirloom or something—it hadn't run for ten years and Simone would never let Celeste have it fixed, kept it on a shelf over her bed. Well, when Celeste took it down last week it slipped out of her hands and cracked open like an egg on the floor. There was a big roll of bills inside, bound with a rubber band."

"Money? I thought Simone—"

"So did Celeste. The money had been left by Simone's father. There was a note in his handwriting bound in with the bills. According to the note, written just before he committed suicide, from the date on it, he managed to save $10,000 out of the wreckage when he dropped his fortune in the '29 market crash. He had left the ten grand to his wife."

"And Celeste knew nothing about it?"

"Mrs. Phillips and Simone never mentioned it to her. Most of the dough is there, about $8600. Celeste thinks the missing $1400 went toward Simone's doctors' bills in the early days, when Mrs. Phillips still had hopes she could be cured. Certainly Simone knew all about it, because she had fits if Celeste went anywhere near the clock. Well, now the money is Celeste's and it's going to make life tolerable for her for a while. And that's the great big mysterious story," said Jimmy with outthrust jaw, "the moral of which—if you ask me—is that, invalid or no invalid, Simone was a firstclass drip. Imagine letting that poor kid nurse her in the Black Hole of Calcutta and shag her legs off trying to support both of them when all the time Simone had almost nine grand stashed away! What was she keeping it for, the junior prom? . . . What's the matter? Why the steely looks?"

"What do you think, Dad?"

"Any way you slice it, Ellery, it's a motive."

"*Motive?*" said Jimmy.

"The first one we've found." The Inspector went to a window, looking unhappy.

Jimmy McKell began to laugh. But then he stopped laughing.

"I wondered last week if there might be a motive," said Ellery, thoughtfully. "When she came here."

"*Celeste?*"

Ellery did not reply.

"I know," said Jimmy. "This is something out of H. G. Wells. An unknown gas drifts into the earth's atmosphere out of interstellar space and everybody in the world goes fay. Including the great Ellery Queen. Why, Queen," he snarled, "she came here to help you *find* the killer of Simone!"

"Who, it develops, wasn't her sister and had deliberately held her in peonage for years."

"Give me air. Sweet, sane air."

"I'm not saying it's so, Jimmy. But by the same token can you say it isn't?"

"Damned right I can! That kid is as pure as I was till I stumbled into this Siberian Casbah this morning and got polluted! Besides, I thought you were looking for the Cat—seven-times strangler!"

"Ellery." Inspector Queen came back to the table. He had apparently fought an engagement with himself and won it. Or lost it. "It's out of the question. Not that girl."

"Now there's a man," shouted Jimmy, "who's still got one toenail on the ground!"

Ellery stared into his cooling coffee. "Jimmy, have you ever heard of the ABC theory of multiple murder?"

"The *what?*"

"X wants to kill D. X's motive isn't apparent, but if he killed D in the ordinary way the police investigation would disclose eventually that the only person, or most likely person, with motive to kill D was X. X's problem is, How can he kill D and gain his object without having his motive stand out? X sees that one way to accomplish this is by surrounding D's murder with a smokescreen of other murders, deliberately committed with the same technique in order to tie them up as a series of interrelated crimes. Consequently, X first murders A, B, and C . . . wholly innocent people, you understand, with whom he's not in the least involved. Only then does he murder D.

"The effect of this is to make the murder of D appear merely a single link in a chain of crimes. The police will not be looking for someone with motive against D, they will look for someone with motive against A, B, C, *and* D. But since X had no motive whatever for murdering A, B, and C, his motive against D is either overlooked or ignored. At least, that's the theory."

"How to become a detective in one easy lesson," said Jimmy McKell. "In a series of murders, last one with motive is It and leave my fee in the hypodermic needle, please."

"Not quite," said Ellery, without rancor. "X is smarter than that. To stop at the one murder which incriminates him, he realizes, is to bring it into exactly the prominence he has been trying to avoid by making it one of a series. Therefore X follows the relevant murder of D with the irrelevant murders of E, F, and G—and H and I and J, if necessary. He kills as many nonsignificant persons as he feels will successfully obfuscate his motive against the significant one."

"Pushing my way through the thicket of scholarly language," grinned Jimmy, "I now get it. This 23-year-old she-gorilla with the detachable chassis, this fiend in human form, strangles Abernethy, the Smith babe, O'Reilly, Monica, Beatrice Willikins, and little Lenore Richardson just so she can sandwich in the bumpoff of her crippled cousin Simone. Queen, have you seen a good doctor lately?"

"Celeste gave up five years of her life to Simone," said Ellery patiently. "She faced the prospect of giving up—how many more? Ten? Twenty? Simone might have lived on and on. Evidently Celeste had given her excellent care; the medical report indicates no bedsores, for example, the prevention of which in such cases requires constant attention.

"But Celeste wants desperately to make something of herself. Celeste would like to get away from the cheerless and limiting environment to which Simone's existence condemns her. Celeste is also young, pretty, and hot-blooded, and her life with Simone is frustrating emotionally. On top of all this, Celeste finds one night—not last week, but last May, let's say—a young fortune, which Simone has kept a secret from her all these years and possession of which would enable Celeste to satisfy her needs and wants for a considerable period. Only one thing stands in the way of possessing it—and putting it to use—and that's her cousin Simone. She can't bring herself to leave a helpless invalid—"

"So she kills her," chuckled Jimmy. "Along with six other folks."

"We've obviously hypothesized a person of confused motivations and personality—"

"I take it back. You don't need a checkup, Queen. You need a checkdown. From the scalp."

"Jimmy, I haven't said Celeste killed Simone and the others. I haven't even indicated an opinion as to its likelihood. I'm putting the known facts together in one possible way. In a shambles that's already seen seven people slaughtered and for all we know may eventually include a great many more, would you have me ignore Celeste simply because she's young and attractive?"

"Attractive. If what you're 'hypothesizing' about Celeste is true, she's a maniac."

"Read yesterday's interview with Dr. Edward Cazalis, Noted Psychiatrist. A maniac—of a very deceptive type—is exactly what Noted Psychiatrist is looking for, and I must say he makes out a convincing case."

"*I* am the type maniac," said Jimmy through his large teeth, "who can take just so much sanity. Watch out below!" And he went over the breakfast table as if it were the edge of a pool.

But Ellery was on his feet and to one side rather more quickly, and Jimmy McKell landed on his nose in a splash of tepid coffee.

"I must say that was silly, Jimmy. Are you all right?"

"Leggo, you character assassin!" yelled Jimmy, swinging.

"Here, sonny-boy." The Inspector caught Jimmy's arm. "You've been reading too many of Ellery's books."

Jimmy shook off the Inspector's hand. He was livid. "Queen, you get somebody else to do your stooling. I'm through. And what's more, I'm going to tell Celeste what she's up against. Yes, and how you suckered me into collecting your garbage for you! And if she upchucks at the mere proximity of McKell, it'll be no more than the yokel deserves!"

"Please don't do that, Jimmy."

"Why not?"

"Our agreement."

"Produce it in writing. What did you buy, Mephisto—my soul?"

"No one forced you into this, Jimmy. You came to me, offered your services, I accepted them on explicit conditions. Remember that, Jimmy?"

Jimmy glowered.

"Granted it's a quadrillion-to-one shot. Just on that remote possibility, will you keep your mouth shut?"

"Do you know what you're asking me to do?"

"Keep your promise."

"I'm in love with her."

"Oh," said Ellery. "That's really too bad."

The Inspector exclaimed: "So soon?"

Jimmy laughed. "Did they clock it in your day, Inspector?"

"Jimmy. You haven't answered my question."

Then the doorbell rang.

The Queens looked at each other quickly.

"Who is it?" called the Inspector.

"Celeste Phillips."

But it was James Guymer McKell who reached the door first, swooping down like a stork.

"Jimmy. You didn't tell me you were—"

His long arms dropped around her.

"Jimmy." She struggled, laughing.

"I want you to be the last to know," snarled Jimmy McKell. "I love you."

"Jimmy, what . . . !"

He kissed her angrily on the lips and took off, sailing down the stairs.

"Come in, Celeste," said Ellery.

Celeste went crimson. She came in fumbling for her compact. Her lipstick was smeared and she kept looking at it in her mirror.

"I don't know what to say. Is Jimmy plastered? This early in the morning?" She laughed, but she was embarrassed and, Ellery thought, a little scared.

"Looked to me," said the Inspector, "as if he knew just what he was doing. Hey, Ellery?"

"Looked to *me* like the basis for a nuisance charge."

"*All* right," laughed Celeste, eying the repairs. "But I really don't know what to say." She was dressed less modishly this morning, but it was a new dress. Her own, thought Ellery. Bought with Simone's money.

"It's a situation not covered by Miss Post. I imagine James will go into it in detail at the first opportunity."

"Sit down, Miss Phillips, sit down," said the Inspector.

"Thank you. But what's the matter with him? He seemed upset. Is anything wrong?"

"First time I told a girl I loved her, I found myself making pleats in her father's best derby. Ellery, were you expecting Miss Phillips this morning?"

"No."

"You told me to come when I had something to report, Mr. Queen." Her black eyes were troubled. "Why did you ask me to find out everything I could about Jimmy McKell?"

"Remember our compact, Celeste?"

She looked down at her manicured nails.

"Now, Ellery, don't be a fuddy-duddy before your time," said the Inspector genially. "A kiss cancels all contracts. Why, Miss Phillips, there's no mystery about it. Jimmy McKell is a newspaperman. This might have been a dodge for him to get in on the inside of the Cat case, beat other reporters to news breaks. We had to be sure Jimmy's interest was personal, as he claimed. Do you find him a straightshooter?"

"He's simply drearily honest. If that's what you're worried about . . ."

"Well, that's that, isn't it?" beamed the Inspector.

"But as long as you're here, Celeste," said Ellery, "you may as well tell us the rest."

"I really can't add anything to what Jimmy told you about himself last week. He's never got along with his father and, since he got out of the Service, they hardly speak to each other because Jimmy insists on living his own life. He really does pay his father $18 a week for board." Celeste giggled. "Jimmy says he's going to make it $75 as soon as the lawyers unwind all the red tape."

"Lawyers?"

"Oh, that business of his grandfather's estate."

"His grandfather," said the Inspector. "Now, let's see. That would be . . ."

"Mrs. McKell's father, Inspector. He was a very rich man who died when Jimmy was 13. Jimmy and his sister were their mother's father's grandchildren and he left a big estate for them in trust. The income from the estate was to start being paid when each grandchild reached the age of 30. Monica'd been collecting her share for seven years, but Jimmy wasn't due to start for five years more, or whenever it is. The only thing is, now Jimmy will get the whole thing, because under his grandfather's will if one of the two grandchildren died the entire estate—principal and income—was to go to the survivor at once. There's millions in the estate and Jimmy's sick about the whole thing, I mean the way it's coming to him. Through Monica's death and all . . . what's the matter?"

Ellery was looking at his father. "How was that missed?"

"I don't know. None of the McKells said a word about an existing trust from an outside source. Of course, we'd have found out eventually."

"Found out *what?*" asked Celeste fretfully.

Neither man answered.

After a moment she got up. "Do you mean . . ."

"The fact is," said Ellery, "the death of Monica McKell means a fortune to her brother, who lives on a reporter's salary. It's what's known in our depressing profession, Celeste, as a motive."

"*Motive.*"

Rage reshaped her. It was an alteration that began deep inside, like the first tiny release of energy in the heart of an explosive. Then it burst, and Celeste sprang.

Even as he felt the rip of her fingernails, Ellery thought absurdly: Like a cat.

"To use me to trap him!"

She kept screaming as Ellery seized the clawing hand and his father came up fast from behind.

"To think Jimmy'd do a thing like that! To *think* it! I'm going to tell him!"

Sobbing, she wrenched away and ran.

They saw Jimmy McKell step out of the basement areaway as the front door burst open and Celeste Phillips flew out. He must have said something, because the girl whirled, looking down. Then she ran down the brownstone steps and hurled herself at him. She was crying and talking wildly. When she stopped, he said something to her very quietly and she put her hand to her mouth.

Then a cab veered inquiringly toward the curb and Jimmy held the door open and Celeste crept in. He got in after her and the cab raced off.

"End of an experiment," sighed Ellery. "Or the beginning of one."

Inspector Queen grunted. "Do you believe that baloney you sliced for McKell about ABC, D, X, and what have you?"

"It's possible."

"That somebody connected with only one of the seven murders is behind all of them as a coverup?"

"It's possible."

"I know it's possible! I asked you if you believe it."

"Can you be certain someone connected with only one of the seven murders isn't behind all of them?"

The Inspector shrugged.

Ellery tossed the stained handkerchief on the sofa. "As far as Celeste and Jimmy are concerned, the way they came to me logically admitted of suspicion. The fact that each one has just disclosed information damaging to the other, viewed without sentiment and on its own merits, only enlarges the suspicion area. Still, I'm willing to go on belief—I don't believe either is the Cat, no. There's a factor that goes beyond logic. Or maybe," said Ellery, "maybe I'm rusty. Do you suppose that could be it?"

"You're not convinced."

"Are you?"

"You'll be questioning me next!"

"Or myself."

The Inspector reached for his hat, scowling. "I'm going downtown."

6

The Cazalis phase of the investigation ran into shoal water immediately.

As originally charted by Dr. Cazalis, the psychiatric inquiry was to be a fishing expedition of all the specializing physicians in the local field, a sort of grand fleet sailing under a unified command. But it became evident that the expedition would have to be remapped. Each specialist, it appeared, was his own captain, guarding his nets and lines and the secrets of his fishing grounds with Japanese zeal. He regarded his catch as his exceptional property and no other fisher should have them.

To the credit of most, their scruples were largely ethical. The sanctity of the physician-patient confessional could not, *in propria persona*, be invaded even by other physicians. Dr. Cazalis surmounted the first obstacle by proposing the adoption of a published-case history technique. Each psychiatrist was to go through his files, select his possibilities on the broadest base, and make transcripts in which all identifying allusions were to be altered, leaving only the initials of the patient for reference. This suggestion was approved. When the case histories came in a five-doctor central board, headed by Dr. Cazalis, was to go to work. The board was to consider each history, rejecting those which in the consultative view were unlikely. By this method many persons would be screened out while being spared the violation of their privacy.

Here, however, agreement went aground.

How were the remaining cases to be treated? Anonymity could be preserved only so far. Then names must be disclosed.

The inquiry almost foundered on this reef.

For therapeutic reasons the type and class of suspect Dr. Cazalis's plan involved could not be handled as the police handled the daily haul of the dragnet, even assuming that the problem of protecting the confidences of the consulting room could be solved. Inspector Queen was directing and co-ordinating the activities of over three hundred detectives under orders to stop at nothing. Since early June each morning's lineup had been crowded not merely with dope addicts, alcoholics, old sex offenders, and criminal psychopaths with penal or institutional records but also with vagrants, prowlers, "suspicious characters" of all descriptions—a category which in three months had swollen alarmingly from the internal pressures of the case. In the high prevailing temperature, civil rights had tended to shrink as official frustration expanded. There had been typhoons of protest from all quarters. The courts had been showered with writs. Citizens had howled, politicians had roared, judges had thundered. But the investigation was plunging ahead in the teeth of all this. Dr. Cazalis's colleagues would have been reluctant to submit their patients to normal police procedures; how, they demanded, could they be expected to turn their patients over to the authorities in this stormy, overheated atmosphere? To many of their charges even an ordinary questioning session would raise dangers. These people were under treatment for mental and emotional disorders. The work of months or years might be undone in an hour by detectives callously intent only on finding a connection between the suspect and the Cat.

There were other difficulties. The patients originated for the most part in the prominences of the cultural geography. Many were socially well-known or came from well-known families. The arts and sciences were heavily represented, the theatrical world, business, finance, even politics. Democracy or no democracy, said the psychiatrists, such people could not be thrown into the lineup as if they were poolroom loiterers or park prowlers. How were they to be questioned? How far might the questions go? Which questions should be avoided and who was to decide? And who was to do the questioning, and when, and where?

The whole thing, they said, was impossible.

It took the better part of the week to work out a plan satisfactory to the majority. The solution took shape when it was recognized that no single *modus operandi* was practicable. There would have to be a separate plan, as it were, for each patient.

Accordingly a list of key questions, carefully composed so as to conceal their origin and objective, was drawn up by Dr. Cazalis and his board in collaboration with Inspector Queen. Each doctor co-operating received a confidential copy of this list. The individual physician was to do his own questioning, in his own office, of those patients on his suspect roll whom he considered it therapeutically risky to turn over to others. He agreed to file reports of these sessions with the board. Patients who in the judgment of their doctors could be safely interviewed by others were to be handled directly by the board at any one of their several offices. The police were not to come into contact with any patient except in the final stage of the medical inquiry, and then only where the findings compelled it. Even at this point the procedure was to emphasize the protection of the patient rather than the overriding hunt for damaging facts. Wherever possible in these cases the investigation was to proceed around the suspect instead of through him.

To the police it was a clumsy and irritating plan; but as Dr. Cazalis, who had begun to look haggard, pointed out to the Police Commissioner and Inspector Queen, the alternative was no investigation at all. The Inspector threw up is hands and his superior said politely that he had been looking forward to a rather more alluring prospect.

So, it appeared, had the Mayor. At an unhappy meeting in City Hall, Dr. Cazalis was inflexible: there were to be no further interviews with the press on his part or on the part of anyone associated with him in the psychiatric phase of the investigation. "I gave my professional word on that, Mr. Mayor. Let one patient's name leak to the newspapers and the whole thing will blow up in my face."

The Mayor replied with a plaintive, "Yes, yes, Dr. Cazalis, I hadn't thought it through, I'm sure. Good luck, and keep right on it, won't you?"

But when the psychiatrist had left, the Mayor remarked bitterly to his private secretary, "It's that damned Ellery Queen business all over again. By the way, Birdy, whatever happened to that fellow?"

What had happened was that the Mayor's Special Investigator had taken to the streets. Ellery might have been seen these days—and he was seen, by various Headquarters men—at eccentric hours lounging on the sidewalk across from the building on East 19th Street where Archibald Dudley Abernethy had come to an end, or standing in the hall outside the ex-Abernethy apartment, which was now occupied by a Guatemalan member of the United Nations secretariat and his wife, or wandering about Gramercy Park and Union Square; silently consuming pizza in the Italian restaurant on West 44th Street over which Violette Smith had flirted successfully with death, or leaning against the banister of the top floor hall listening to a piano stammer along behind the apartment door to which was thumbtacked a large sign:

This Is IT—Yes!!!!
All Squares, Visiting
Firemen, Ear Benders,
Pearl Divers, and
Peeping Toms
KEEP OUT!!

SONG WRITER AT WORK!!

poking about beneath the staircase in the lobby of a Chelsea tenement at the spot where the body of Rian O'Reilly had been found; sitting on a bench at the end of the Sheridan Square subway-station platform, uptown side, with the shade of Madcap Monica McKell; prowling beneath the washlines in a certain rear court on East 102nd Street and never once catching a glimpse of the emancipated cousin of fat little Simone Phillips; standing before the brassrailed stoop of a house on West 128th Street in a swarm of dark children, or strolling down Lenox Avenue among brown and saffron people to the 110th Street entrance to Central Park, or sitting on a park bench not far from the entrance or on the nearby boulder which had been the rock, if not the salvation, of Beatrice Willikins; or trudging along East 84th Street from Fifth Avenue to Madison past the canopied entrance of the Park-Lester and up Madison and back again to circumambulate the block, or taking the private elevator in the Park-Lester's neighbor to a boarded-up penthouse whose occupants were away for the summer to stare frankly across the parapet at the terrace beyond which Lenore Richardson had gripped *Forever Amber* in the convulsion of strangulation.

Ellery rarely spoke to anyone on these excursions.

They took place by day as well as by night, as if he wished to view the sites in both perspectives.

He returned to the seven localities again and again. Once he was picked up by a detective who did not know him and spent several hours as a suspicious character in the nearest precinct house before Inspector Queen hurried in to identify him.

Had he been asked what he was about, the Mayor's Special Investigator would have been at a loss for a communicable reply. It was difficult to put into words. How materialize a terror, much more see him whole? This was one whose feet had whispered over pavements, displacing nothing larger than molecules. You followed his trackless path, sniffing upwind, hopefully.

All that week the eighth tail of the Cat, the now familiar question mark, hooked and held the eye of New York.

Ellery was walking up Park Avenue. It was the Saturday night after Lenore Richardson's murder and he was drifting in a vacuum.

He had left the night life of the City behind. In the 70s only piles of articulated stone kept him company, and an occasional goldbraided doorman.

At 78th Street Ellery paused before the royal blue-awninged house where the Cazalises lived. The ground-floor Cazalis apartment, with its private office entrance directly off the street, showed lights, but the vanes of the Venetian blinds were closed and Ellery wondered if Dr. Cazalis and his fellow-psychiatrists were at work behind them. Brewing the potion, stirring the caldron; wrapping truth in darkness. They would never find the Cat in their co-wizard's notes. He did not know how he knew this, but he knew it.

He walked on and some time later found himself turning into 84th Street.

But he passed the Park-Lester without breaking the rhythm of his torpor.

At the corner of 84th and Fifth, Ellery stopped. It was still early, the evening was warm, but the Avenue was a nervous emptiness. Where were the Saturday night arm-in-arm strollers? Even the automobile traffic seemed lighter. And the busses whined by carrying remarkably few passengers.

Facing him across Fifth Avenue was the Metropolitan Museum of Art, a broad-beamed old lady sitting patiently in darkness.

He crossed over on the green light and began to walk uptown along the old lady's flank. Beyond her lay the black and silent Park.

They're beginning to stick to the well-lighted areas, he thought. *O comfort-killing night, image of Hell.* No friendly darkness now. Especially here. In this part of the jungle the beast had pounced twice.

He almost cried out at the touch on his arm.

"Sergeant."

"I tailed you for two blocks before I recognized you," said Sergeant Velie, falling into step.

"On duty tonight?"

"Naw."

"Then what are you doing around here?"

"Oh . . . just walking around." The big fellow said carelessly, "I'm baching it these days."

"Why, where's your family, Velie?"

"Sent the wife and kid to my mother-in-law's for a month."

"To Cincinnati? Is Barbara-Ann—?"

"No, Barbsy's okay. And as far as school is concerned," said Sergeant Velie argumentatively, "she can catch up any time. She's got her ma's brains."

"Oh," said Ellery; and they ambled on in silence.

After a long time the Sergeant said, "I'm not intruding on anything, I trust?"

"No."

"I mean, I thought you might be on the prowl." The Sergeant laughed.

"Just going over the Cat's route. For the umpteenth time. Backwards, Sergeant. Richardson, Lenore, to Willikins, Beatrice. Number 7 to Number 6. East 84th to Harlem. The Lord's anointed to His unshorn lamb. One mile or so between and the Cat jumps it by way of the moon. Do you have a light?"

They stopped under a street lamp and the Sergeant struck a match.

"Talking about the Cat's route," he said. "You know, Maestro, I've been giving this case a lot of thought."

"Thanks, Velie."

They crossed 96th Street.

"I long ago gave up," the Sergeant was saying—"I'm speaking only for Thomas Velie, you understand—gave up trying to get anywhere on this carrousel. My personal opinion is when the Cat's knocked off it will be by dumb-bunny luck. Some rookie cop'll walk up to a drunk bent over like he's regretting the whole thing and bingo, it'll be the Cat tying a bow in the latest neck. But just the same," said the Sergeant, "you can't help figuring the angles."

"No," said Ellery, "you certainly can't."

"Now I don't know what your impression is, and of course this is all off the record, but I got busy the other night with a map of Manhattan and environs that I traced off my kid's geography book and I started spotting in the locations of the seven homicides. Just for the hell of it." The Sergeant's voice lowered. "Well, sir, I think I got something."

"What?" asked Ellery. A couple were passing, the man arguing and pointing to the Park and the woman shaking her head, walking very fast. The Sergeant stopped abruptly; but Ellery said, "It's all right, Velie. That's only a Saturday night date with ideas."

"Yeah," said the Sergeant sagely, "sex suckers all men."

But they did not move until they saw the man and woman climb into a southbound bus.

"You'd got something, Velie."

"Oh! Yeah. I put a heavy dot on each location on the map, see. The first one—Abernethy's, East 19th—I marked that one *1*. The second one—Violette Smith's on West 44th off Times Square—I mark *2*. And so forth."

"You," said Ellery, "and that *Extra* cartoonist."

"Then when I've got all seven spotted and numbered, I begin drawing lines. A line from *1* to *2*. A line from *2* to *3*. Et cetera. And what do you think?"

"What?"

"It's got a kind of design."

"Really? No, wait, Sergeant. The Park gives me nothing tonight. Let's strike crosstown." They crossed 99th and began to make their way east through the dark and quiet street. "Design?"

"Look." Sergeant Velie pulled a wad of tracing paper from his pocket and unfolded it on the corner of 99th and Madison. "It's a kind of double-circular movement, Maestro. Straight up from *1* to *2*, sharp down again but westerly from *2* to *3*, keeps going southwest to *4*, then what? Sharp up again. A long one this time, crossing the 1-2 line. Up, down, over and up again. Now look! Now it starts all over again! Oh, not at exactly the same angles, of course, but close enough to be interesting, hmmm? Again it's up and over from *5* to *6*—northwesterly—then sharp down to *7* . . ." The Sergeant paused. "Let me show you something. If you assume there's a sort of scheme behind this, if you continue that same circular movement, what do you find?" The Sergeant pointed to his dotted line. "You can predict just about where Number *8*'s going to come! Maestro, I'd almost bet the next one's in the Bronx." He folded his piece of paper, restored it carefully to his pocket, and they resumed their eastward way. "Maybe up around the beginning of the Grand Concourse. Around Yankee Stadium or some place like that." And after a few moments, the Sergeant asked, "What do you think?"

Ellery frowned at the passing sidewalk. "There's a little thing that comes out of *The Hunting of the Snark,* Sergeant," he said, "that's always stuck in my mind.

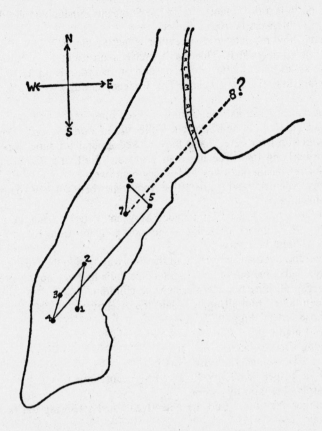

"He had bought a large map representing the sea,
  Without the least vestige of land:
And the crew were much pleased when they found it to be
  A map they could all understand."

"I don't get it," said Sargeant Velie, staring at him.

"I'm afraid we all have our favorite maps. I had one recently I was extremely attached to, Sergeant. It was a Graph of Intervals. The intervals between the various murders expressed in number of days. The result was something that looked like a large question mark lying flat on its face. It was a lesson in humility. I burned it, and I advise you to do the same with yours."

After that, the Sergeant just strode along, muttering occasionally.

"Why, look where we are," said Ellery.

The Sergeant, who had been acting dignified, started as he glanced up at the street sign.

"So you see, Sergeant, it's the detective who returns to the scene of the crime. Drawn by a sort of horizontal gravity."

"Drawn by my garter belt. You knew just where you were going."

"Unconsciously, maybe. Shall we press our luck?"

"Last one in is a dirty name," said the Sergeant, unbending; and they plunged into the noisy breakers of 102nd Street.

"I wonder how my female ex-Irregular is getting along."

"Say, I heard about that. That was a pretty smart trick."

"Not so smart. The shortest collaboration on record.—Hold it, Velie."

Ellery stopped to fish for a cigaret. The Sergeant dutifully struck a match, saying, "Where?"

"In that doorway behind me. Almost missed him."

The flame snuffed out and Sergeant Velie said in a loud voice, "Darn it all, old man, let's get on over here," and they moved around a frantic hopscotch game toward the building line. The big man grinned. "Hell, it's Piggott." He struck another match near the doorway and Ellery bent over.

"Evening, evening," said the detective from somewhere. "I saw you two amateurs coming a block away."

"Is there a law against it?" demanded Sergeant Velie. "What are you working tonight, Piggo? Yeah, I'll have one." He took a cigaret from Ellery.

"Watch it! Here he comes."

Ellery and the Sergeant jumped into the doorway beside the Headquarters man. A tall fellow had come out of an unlighted vestibule halfway up the street, on their side. He began pushing his way through the children.

"I've been tailing him all night," said the detective.

"On whose orders, Piggott?"

"Your old man's."

"How long has this been going on?"

"All week. Hesse and I are divvying him."

"Didn't the Inspector tell you?" asked Sergeant Velie.

"I've hardly seen him this week."

"It's nothing exciting," said the detective. "Just satisfying the taxpayers, the Inspector said."

"How's he been spending his time?"

"Walking and standing still."

"Up here much?"

"Till last night."

"What's he been up to in that vestibule tonight?"

"Watching the entrance of the girl's house across the street."

Ellery nodded. Then he said, "Is she home?"

"We all pulled in here about a half hour ago. She spent the evening in the 42nd Street Library. Reference Room. So that's where we were, too. Then he tailed her here, and I tailed him, and here we are."

"Has he gone in there?"

"No, sir."

"He hasn't approached her, spoken to her?"

"Hell, she didn't know he was following her. It's been kind of like a Humphrey Bogart movie, at that. Johnson's been tailing *her*. He's been in the back court across the street since we pulled in here."

"Sounds like a Canarsie clambake." Then the Sergeant said swiftly, "Piggo, get *lost*."

The tall man was coming directly toward their doorway.

"Well, well," said Ellery, stepping out. "Hi."

"I thought I'd save you some wear and tear." Jimmy McKell stood innerbraced, looking from Ellery to Sergeant Velie and back again. Behind them, the doorway was empty. "What's the significant idea?"

"Idea?" said Ellery, considering it.

"I saw you two rubberheels sneak into this doorway. What are you doing, watching Celeste Phillips?"

"Not me," said Ellery. "Were you, Sergeant?"

"I wouldn't do a thing like that," said the Sergeant.

"Very funny." Jimmy McKell kept looking at them. "Why don't you ask me what I'm doing here?"

"All right, Jimmy. What are you doing here?"

"The same thing you are." Jimmy excavated a cigaret, brushed off the linty detritus, and stuck it like a flag between his lips. His tone was amiable, however. "Only my angle is maybe different. I'm told there's somebody doing the town collecting necks. Now that woman has one of the prettiest head supports in Christendom." He lit the cigaret.

"Protecting her, huh?" said the Sergeant. "You play long shots, reporter."

"Two-Million-to-One McKell, they call me." Jimmy tossed the match; it glanced off Velie's ear. "Well, I'll be seeing you. If that's my kismet." He began to walk away.

"Jimmy, wait."

"For what?"

"What do you say we drop in on her?"

Jimmy sauntered back. "For what?"

"I've been meaning to have a talk with you two."

"For what?"

"You're both entitled to an explanation, Jimmy."

"You don't have to explain anything to me. My nose knows."

"No kidding."

"I'm not. It really does."

"I don't blame you for being griped—"

"Hell, who's griped? What's a little thing like being suspected of seven murders? I mean between pals?" He stepped close all at once and Sergeant Velie stirred. Jimmy's lips were out. "Queen, that was the most two-faced, poisonous deal since the days of the Medicis. To sick me onto Celeste and Celeste onto me. I ought to boff you for that."

The Sergeant said, "Here."

"Take that ham hock off me."

"It's all right, Sergeant." Ellery was preoccupied and morose. "But Jimmy, I had to make some test."

"Some test is right."

"Yes, it was on the silly side. But you both came to me at such a convenient moment. I couldn't close my eyes to the possibility that one of you—"

"Is the Cat." Jimmy laughed.

"We're not dealing with normality."

"Do I look abnormal? Does Celeste?"

"Not to my eyes, no. But then I don't have psychiatric vision." Ellery grinned. "And dementia, for example, is a youthful disease."

"Praecox McKell. Well, they called me a lot worse in the late Hot War."

"Jimmy, I never really believed it. I don't believe it now."

"But there's always the mathematical chance."

"Come on, let's drop in on Celeste."

"I take it if I refuse," said Jimmy, not budging, "Charley the Anthropoid here will pinch me?"

"I'll pinch you," said Sergeant Velie. "Where it hurts."

"See what I mean?" said Jimmy bitterly. "We're just not compatible." And he strode away, breaking up the hopscotch game and pursued by the curses of little children.

"Let him go, Velie."

After a few moments Detective Piggott's voice said, "There goes my bread and butter. Night, Brother Elks." When they looked around, Piggott was gone.

"So he's been watching Celeste to save her from the Cat," said Ellery as they began to cross the street.

"In a swine's eyeball."

"Oh, Jimmy means it, Sergeant. At least he thinks he does."

"What is he, feebleminded?"

"Hardly." Ellery laughed. "But he's suffering from a severe attack of what our friend Cazalis might call—though I doubt it—confusional inanity. Otherwise known as the love psychosis."

The Sergeant grunted. They stopped before the tenement and he looked around casually. "You know what I think, Maestro?"

"After that double wingback map of Manhattan of yours I wouldn't even attempt a guess."

"Go ahead and horse," said the Sergeant. "But I think you put a bee in his buzzer."

"Explain."

"I think maybe McKell thinks maybe Celeste *is* the Cat."

Ellery glanced up at the behemoth as if he had never really seen him before.

"You know what I think, Velie?"

"What?"

"I think you're right." And, looking slightly ill, he said, "Let's go in."

The hall was cheaply dim and pungent. A boy and a girl jumped apart as Ellery and Velie walked in; they had been clutching each other in the shadows beside the staircase. "Oh, *thank* you, I had such a lovely time," said the girl, running up the stairs. The boy smirked. "I ain't complaining, Carole." He slouched out, winking at the two men.

A door at the rear stood open, a line of wash clipping its upper corner to the dark sky.

"Piggott said Johnson was out there, Maestro."

"Not any more Johnson isn't," said a voice from under the stairs. "I got an old camp chair in here, Sarge."

" 'Lo, Johnson," said the Sergeant, not turning. "How's the trick?"

"With those two juvenile delinquents that were just here it was colossal. You calling on C.P.?"

"Is she still up?" Ellery asked the darkness.

"There's the light under her door, Mr. Queen."

"That door there," said the Sergeant.

"Alone, Johnson?"

"Uh-huh." There was a yawn.

Ellery went over and knocked on the door. Sergeant Velie moved to one side, out of range.

After a moment, Ellery knocked again.

"Who is it?" She sounded frightened.

"Ellery Queen. Please open, Celeste."

They heard her undo the latch chain very slowly.

"What do you want?"

In the box of light she stood bristling. One hand clutched a large book to her breast. It looked like an old book, one fingered with respect.

Survey of English Literature—First Year.

Saturday night on East 102nd Street. A voom with the Venerable Bede. Bebop with *Beowulf.* Holding hands with Hakluyt's *Divers Voyages.* Jive print in double columns, kneedeep in footnotes.

She blocked his view of the room. He had never seen this room, only photographs.

She was dressed in a full black pleated skirt and a tailored white blouse and her hair was disordered, as if she had had her fists in it as she read. There was blue ink on one finger. What he could make out of her face was a little shocking. The violet stains had spread and her skin was blotchy, cupped to bitter heads.

"May I come in?" asked Ellery with a smile.

"No. What do you want?"

"In this neighborhood, Maestro," said Sergeant Velie, "you couldn't run for your life."

Celeste took a quick look out. She immediately withdrew her head. "I remember *him.*"

Sergeant Velie stiffened.

"Haven't you done enough damage?"

"Celeste—"

"Or did you come to arrest me? Not that I'd put it past you. I suppose Jimmy McKell and I were accomplices. We strangled all those people together. Each of us pulling on one end of the silk cords."

"Celeste, if you'll let me—"

"You've spoiled everything. *Everything.*"

The door slammed in his face. They heard the furious turn of the key, the lash of the latch chain.

"Each on one end," mused Sergeant Velie. "Think that's such a crosseyed idea? Did anybody take that into consideration? Two of them?"

Ellery muttered, "They've had a blowup."

"Sure, last night. It was just terrible," said Johnson's voice cheerfully. "He says she suspected him of being the Cat and she says nonono it's him who suspected *her* of being the Cat. Then they both deny it like mad. Going at it hot and heavy— I was out in the court there and I was afraid they'd collect a crowd and I'd have to fade. Well, sir, she starts bawling like she means it and what does he do but say a naughty word and damn near bust the hinges off the door blasting his way out."

"Love's sweet young stuff," said the Sergeant. "Do you suppose it could have been an act? Maybe they're wise to you, Johnson. Hey, Maestro. Where you going?"

Ellery sounded miserable. "Home."

All during the week following Ellery had a sense of marking time. Nothing occurred of the least interest. He saw the reports on Jimmy McKell and Celeste Phillips; they had made up, they had quarreled again, they had made up again. Other reports had all but stopped coming in. One morning Ellery dropped in to view the lineup performance. As entertainment it was depressing, and it told nothing, but he experienced the satisfaction of a man who has performed a duty. He did not go again. He cleverly refrained from venturing below Centre Street and the good Magistrate at City Hall seemed to have forgotten his existence, for which Ellery was abysmally grateful. He saw little of his father and he purposely avoided asking questions about the progress of Dr. Cazalis's investigation . . . And the Cat's eighth tail remained a question mark on the front page of the *Extra*.

Even the newspapers were marking time.

It was curious. The *status quo ante* in American journalism is not a standing still; it is a going backward. A Page 1 story remains there only so long as it grows. Let it stop growing and it finds itself on Page 6, and it will continue this oblivious process until it backs right out of the paper. But the Cat story blandly bucked the rule. If it got nowhere, neither did it lose headway. It rode anchor on the front page. It was news even when it was not.

In a way, it was more news when it was not than when it was, when the Cat lay napping in his den than when he padded out to hunt another neck. His inactivity exerted a special attraction, horrid and hypnotic: the magnetism of suspense. It was like a smolder between bursts of flame. If, as Jefferson said, newspapers "serve to carry off noxious vapors and smoke," the New York press could only obey the physics of the times.

It was during these intervals that the public nervousness was most remarkable. The waiting was worse than the event. When the Cat killed, people were actually relieved for a few days, in a semi-hysterical way; they and theirs were safe once more. But their dread was not destroyed; it was merely becalmed. Relief soon wore off, suspense surfaced again, the night anxieties, the counting of the days, the pitching wonder as to who would be next.

It was no use pitting the mathematical improbabilities against the individual's fears. The psychological laws of lottery ruled, the only difference being that in this policy game the prize was not money but extinction. Tickets were free to all New Yorkers, and each holder knew in his heart he would win at the next drawing.

So the week wore on.

Ellery was thankful to see the week end; by Saturday it had become insupportable. His absurd Graph of Intervals persisted in haunting him. Between Victims 1 and 2, nineteen days; between Victims 2 and 3, twenty-six days; between Victims 3 and 4, twenty-two days; between Victims 4 and 5—Monica McKell to Simone Phillips—the teasing, inexplicable drop to six days; and then the reascending curve of eleven days between Victims 6 and 7. Was this the beginning of a new upward spiral? Were the intervals leveling off? It was now the twelfth day after the strangling of Mrs. Cazalis's niece.

In the uncertainty, each moment excreted fear.

Ellery spent that Saturday chasing police calls. It was the first time he had used any of the vague powers conferred on him by the Mayor's appointment. He was not even sure it would work. But when he commandeered a car with a police radio, a black seven-passenger limousine with no identifying insignia occupied by a plainclothes chauffeur and his plainclothes companion showed up promptly. Most of the time Ellery slumped low in the tonneau listening to interminable accounts of "real baffling cases." Each detective was the size of Sergeant Velie and each was equipped with inexhaustible lungs.

Ellery kept wondering on and off through the long tiresome day what had happened to his father. No one seemed to know where Inspector Queen was; he had left the apartment before Ellery rose, he had not been to Headquarters, he had not called in.

They roared with open siren from the Battery to the Harlem River, from Riverside Drive to First Avenue. They were in on the breakup of a teenage street fight in San Juan Hill and the arrest of a cocaine addict caught trying to slip a forged prescription by an alert Yorkville pharmacist. They visited the scenes of holdups, traffic accidents, minor assaults; on the agenda in order were a queue-pulling match off Chatham Square, an attempted rape in a Hell's Kitchen hallway, the case of a getaway car in a Third Avenue pawnshop robbery. They witnessed the bloodless capture of a meek gangster in Little Italy wanted for questioning in an old homicide, the escape of a Lithuanian cook from a Little Hungary restaurant where he had suddenly gone berserk. There were four suicides—above the average for such a short period, the detectives explained, but it had been a bad summer, one in the Bowling Green subway station, an elderly Brooklynite who had thrown himself in the path of an incoming IRT express; another a Herald Square window-jumping case, a girl registered in a hotel from Chicopee Falls, Mass., identified as an eloper; another a gas range job in a Rivington Street tenement, a woman and a baby; the fourth an alcoholic case in the West 130s who had slashed his wrists. There were two homicide calls: the first, shortly before noon, a knifing in a Harlem poolroom; the second, at 6:30, a woman beaten to death with a Stillson wrench in the East 50s by her husband, an advertising agency executive. This last aroused some interest in the detectives since it involved another man, a Broadway character, and they were disposed to linger; but Ellery waved them on.

There were no strangulations, with or without cords.

"Just another day,"said the detective at the wheel as he slid the squad car into 87th Street. He sounded apologetic.

"Why not keep going tonight?" suggested the other detective as Ellery got out. "Saturday night's always lively, Mr. Queen, and maybe it's the Cat's night out."

"By the twitching of my left ventricle," said Ellery, "I can tell it isn't. Doesn't matter, anyway—I can always read about it in the papers. Will you boys join me in a friendly glass?"

"Well, now," said the driver.

But the other detective said, "Give your old woman a break for once, Frank. And I've got a long haul, Mr. Queen. Out to Rockville Centre. Thanks just the same."

Upstairs, Ellery found a note from his father.

It was a scribble marked *7 P.M.*

> *EL—Been phoning since 5. Dashed home to leave this note. Meet me at Cazalis's the minute you get in. Big powwow set for 7:30.*

7:35.
Ellery ran.

When the uniformed maid ushered him into the Cazalis living room, the first person he saw was the Mayor of the City of New York. That harrowed servant of the people was lying back in an easychair, hands clasped about a tall glass, glaring at a bust of Sigmund Freud above Ellery's head.

The Police Commissioner, seated beside the Mayor, was studying the fume of his cigar.

Dr. Cazalis sat on a Turkish divan, bolstered by silk pillows. His wife held on to his hand.

At a window stood Inspector Queen, cocooned in silence.

The air was chill.

"Don't tell me, please," said Ellery. "It's a washout."

No one replied. Mrs. Cazalis rose and prepared a Scotch-and-soda, which Ellery accepted with genuine gratitude.

"Ellery, where have you been today?" But the Inspector failed to sound as if he cared.

"Out chasing radio calls. Don't be misled, Mr. Mayor," said Ellery. "It's the first time since I took over. Hereafter I'll do my special investigating from an armchair—that is, if there *is* a hereafter?"

The Mayor's glance touched him briefly, almost with loathing. "Sit down, Queen, sit down."

"Nobody's answered my question."

"It wasn't a question, it was a statement," said Dr. Cazalis from the pillows. "And as a statement it exactly states the case."

"Sit down, Queen," snapped the Mayor again.

"Thank you, Mr. Mayor. I'll keep my father company." Ellery was startled by Dr. Cazalis's appearance. His pale eyes were inflamed and his skin was plowed so raw that Ellery thought of floodwater soil eroded into gullies; the glacier had given way. And he recalled Cazalis's remark about his insomnia. "Doctor, you look depreciated."

"There's been considerable wear and tear."

"He's worn out," said Mrs. Cazalis shrilly. "He drives himself so. No more sense than an infant. He's been at this day and night since . . ."

Her husband squeezed her hand. "The whole psychiatric attack, Mr. Queen, is a fizzle. We've got exactly nowhere."

Inspector Queen said curtly: "This week I've been working close to Dr. Cazalis, Ellery. We wound up today. There were a number of possibilities. We ran every one of them down."

"Quietly, you understand," said the Mayor bitterly. "No toes stepped on. Not a word in the papers."

"Well," said Dr. Cazalis, "it was a long chance at best. My fault entirely. It seemed a notion at the time."

"At the time, Edward? Isn't it still?" Mrs. Cazalis was regarding her husband in a puzzled way.

"Humpty Dumpty, dear."

"I don't understand."

"I take it, Queen," said the Mayor, "you haven't got to first base?"

"I never took the bat off my shoulder, Mr. Mayor."

"I see." Here goes a Special Investigator, thought Ellery. "Inspector Queen, what's your feeling?"

"We have a very touchy case, Mr. Mayor. In the usual murder investigation, the range of suspicion is limited. The husband, the 'friend,' the handyman, the rival, the enemy, and so on. Motive begins to stick out. The field narrows. Opportunity narrows it even further. We've got human material to work on. Sooner or later in even the most complicated case we make a rap stick. But in this one . . . How are you going to narrow the field? Where do you start? No connection among the victims anywhere. No suspects. No clues. Every murder a dead end. The Cat could be anybody in New York."

"You can still say that, Inspector?" cried the Mayor. "After all these weeks?"

The Inspector's lips thinned. "I'm ready to hand in my shield right now."

"No, no, Inspector, I was just thinking aloud."

The Mayor glanced at his Police Commissioner. "Well, Barney, where do we go from here?"

The Commissioner tapped a long ash very carefully into a tray. "When you get right down to it, there's no place we can go. We've done, and we're doing, everything humanly possible. I could suggest a new Police Commissioner, Jack, but I doubt if that would satisfy anybody except the *Extra* and the other crowd, and I'm Irish enough to believe it wouldn't necessarily bag your Cat, either."

The Mayor waved impatiently. "The question is, *are* we doing everything possible? It seems to me where we may have gone off is in assuming that the Cat is a New Yorker. Suppose he comes from Bayonne? Stamford? Yonkers? He may be a commuter—"

"Or a Californian," said Ellery.

"What? What was that?" exclaimed the Mayor.

"A Californian, or an Illinoisan or a Hawaiian."

The Mayor said irritably, "Queen, I can't see that that sort of talk gets us anywhere. The point is, Barney, have we done anything outside the City?"

"Everything we can."

"We've had every community within a radius of fifty miles of the City alerted for at least six weeks," said the Inspector. "From the start they've been requested to keep their eyes peeled for psychos. But so far—"

"Jack, until we get a concrete reason for believing otherwise, nobody can crucify us for concentrating on Manhattan."

"My personal opinion," added the Inspector, "has been all along that he's a Manhattanite. To me this Cat smells local."

"Besides, Jack," said the Commissioner with a certain dryness, "our jurisdiction ends at the City limits. After that we've got a tin cup in our hands and take what the saints provide."

The Mayor set his glass down with a little bang and went over to the fireplace. Ellery was nuzzling his Scotch with a faraway look, the Commissioner was back at his cigar examination, Dr. Cazalis and Inspector Queen were blinking at each other across the room to keep awake, and Mrs. Cazalis sat like a grenadier.

The Mayor turned suddenly. "Dr. Cazalis, what are the chances of extending your psychiatric investigation to include the entire metropolitan area?"

"Manhattan is the concentration point."

"But there are other psychiatrists outside?"

"Oh, yes."

"What about them?"

"Well . . . it would take months, and then you wouldn't get anything like satisfactory coverage. Even here, in the heart of things, where I exert a pretty direct professional influence, I haven't been able to get better than 65 to 70 per cent of the men in the field to co-operate. If the survey were extended to Westchester, Long Island, Connecticut, New Jersey . . ." Dr. Cazalis shook his head. "As far as I personally am concerned, Mr. Mayor, it would be pretty much out of the question. I haven't either the strength or the time to tackle such a project.''

Mrs. Cazalis's lips parted.

''Won't you at least continue covering Manhattan, then, Dr. Cazalis? The answer may well lie in the files of one of the 30 or 35 per cent you say refused to play along. Won't you keep after those people?''

Dr. Cazalis's fingers pumped rapidly. ''Well, I've been hoping . . .''

''Edward, you're not giving up. You're not!''

''*Et tu,* darling? I thought I had no more sense than an infant.''

''I mean for going at it the way you have. Ed, how can you stop altogether? Now?''

''Why, dear, simply by doing so. I was paranoid to attempt it.''

She said something in such a low tone that Dr. Cazalis said, ''What, dear?''

''I said what about Lenore!''

She was on her feet.

''Darling.'' Dr. Cazalis scrambled off the divan. ''All this tonight's upset you—''

''Tonight? Did you think I wasn't upset yesterday? And the day before?'' She sobbed into her hands. ''If Lenore had been your sister's child . . . had meant as much to you as she did to me . . .''

''I think, gentlemen,'' said the Mayor quickly, ''we've imposed on Mrs. Cazalis's hospitality long enough.''

''I'm sorry!'' She was really trying to stop. ''I'm so sorry. Edward, let me go. Please. I want to . . . get something.''

''Tell you what, darling. Give me twenty-four hours' sleep, a two-inch T-bone when I wake up, and I'll tackle it where I left off. Good enough?''

She kissed him suddenly. Then, murmuring something, she hurried out.

''I submit, gentlemen,'' said the Mayor, ''that we owe Mrs. Cazalis a few dozen roses.''

''My only weakness,'' laughed the psychiatrist. ''I never could resist the diffusion of the female lachrymal glands.''

''Then, Doctor,'' said Ellery, ''you may be in for a bad time.''

''How's that, Mr. Queen?''

''If you'll run over the ages of the seven victims, you'll find that each victim had been younger than the one preceding.''

The Commissioner's cigar almost fell out of his mouth.

The Mayor went brick-red.

''The seventh victim, Doctor—your wife's niece—was 25 years old. If any prediction is possible in this case, it's that Victim Number 8 will be under 25. Unless you're successful, or we are, we may soon be investigating the strangulation of children.'' Ellery set his glass down. ''Would you say good night to Mrs. Cazalis for me?''

7

The so-called "Cat Riots" of September 22-23 marked the dread appearance in New York City of *mobile vulgus* for the first time since the Harlem disorders of almost fifteen years before. But in this case the mob was predominantly white; as a wry vindication of the Mayor's dawn press conference of the previous month, there was no "race angle." The only racial fears involved were the primitive ones of all mankind.

Students of mob psychology found the Cat Riots interesting. If in one sense the woman whose hysterical outburst set off the panic in Metropol Hall exerted the function of the inevitable *meneur*—the leader each mob tends to throw up, who starts the cheering or the running away—if the hysterical woman represented the fuse which sparked the explosion, she in her turn had been ignited by the inflammatory Citizens' Action Teams which had sprung up all over the Greater City during the immediately preceding Four Days and whose activities were responsible for her presence in the Hall. And no one could say with certainty who originally inspired those groups; at least no individual responsibility was ever determined.

The shortlived movement which came to be known as the Four Days (although from inception to culminating riot it spanned six days) was first publicly taken note of early on Monday, September 19, in the late morning editions of the newspapers.

An "association of neighbors" had been formed over the past weekend on the Lower East Side under the name of "The Division Street Vigilantes." At an organizing meeting held Saturday night a series of resolutions had been drawn up in the form of a "Declaration" which was ratified "in full convention assembled" on the following afternoon. Its "Preamble" asserted "the rights of lawabiding American citizens, in the failure of regular law enforcement," to band together "for common security." Anyone in the prescribed neighborhood was eligible to join. World War II veterans were especially solicited. Various patrols were to be set up: a Streets Patrol, a Roofs Patrol, an Alleys Patrol. There was a separate Unit Patrol for each dwelling or other building in the area. The function of the patrols was "to stand guard against the marauder who has been terrorizing the City of New York." (There was some intra-organizational protest against the use of "fancy language," but the language stood when the Resolutions Committee pointed out that "on Division Street and around here we're supposed to be a bunch of pigs.") Discipline was to be military. Patrolmen were to be equipped with flashlights, armbands, "and available weapons of defense." A 9 P.M. curfew for children was to be enforced. Street level lighting was to be maintained until daybreak; special arrangements were being made with landlords of dwellings and stores.

In the same news story was noted the simultaneous formation of three similar organizations, apparently unconnected with one another or with the Division Street

Vigilantes. One was in the Murray Hill section and called itself "The Murray Hill Committee of Safety." Another took in the area between West 72nd Street and West 79th Street and was named "The West End Minutemen." The third centered in Washington Square, "The Village Home Guard."

Considering the differences among the three groups culturally, socially, and economically, their avowed purposes and operating methods were astonishingly similar to those of the Division Street Vigilantes.

Editorials that morning commented on "the coincidence of four widely separated communities getting the same idea over the same weekend" and wondered "if it is so much of a coincidence as it appears." The anti-Administration papers blamed the Mayor and the Police Commissioner and used phrases like "the traditional American way" and "the right to defend the American home." The more responsible journals deplored the movement and one of them was "confident that the traditional good humor of New York will laugh these well-meaning but overexcited people back to their senses." Max Stone, editorial writer of the leading liberal paper, wrote: "This is fascism on the sidewalks of New York."

By 6 P.M. Monday the newscasters were reporting to their audiences that "at least three dozen action committees have spung up in scattered neighborhoods of the five boroughs since the announcement this morning of the organization of the Division Street, Murray Hill, West End Avenue, and Greenwich Village groups."

The late evening editions of the newspapers were able to say that "the idea is spreading like an oldfashioned prairie fire. By press time the number of action committees was over a hundred."

By Tuesday morning the count was reported as "hundreds."

The term "Citizens' Action Teams" seems to have first appeared in a Tuesday *Extra* story on the amazing citywide phenomenon. The story was bylined "Jimmy Leggitt." The phrase took hold when Winchell, Lyons, Wilson, and Sullivan noted in their columns that its initials spelled "cat." And CATs they remained.

At an emergency meeting in the Mayor's office Monday night, the Police Commissioner expressed himself as being in favor of "taking tough police measures to stop this thing dead in its tracks. We can't have every Joe, Moe, and Schmo in town a selfappointed cop. It's anarchy, Jack!" But the Mayor shook his head. "You're not going to put out a fire by passing a law against it, Barney. We can't stop this movement by force; it's out of the question. What we've got to do is try to control it."

At his press conference Tuesday morning the Mayor said with a smile, "I repeat that this Cat thing has been exaggerated far out of proportion and there is absolutely no basis for public alarm with the Police Department working on it twenty-four hours a day. These groups will function much more in the public interest with the advice and assistance of the authorities. The Police Commissioner and his various heads of department will be on hand all day today to receive delegations of these groups with the end in view of systematizing and co-ordinating their activities, in much the way that the splendid ARP groups operated during the War."

Disturbingly, the groups did not appear to be received.

On Tuesday night the Mayor went on the air. He did not in the slightest impugn the integrity and good intentions of the people forming home defense groups, but he felt sure all reasonable people would agree that the police power of the greatest city in the world could not be permitted to be usurped by individual citizens, no matter how honest or well-intentioned, in defiance of legal authority. "Let it not be said that the City of New York in the fifth decade of the twentieth century resorted to frontier town vigilante law." The dangers implicit in this sort of thing were recognized by all, he was certain, as far exceeding any possible threat of one homicidally inclined psychotic. "In the old days, before the establishment of official police systems, night patrols of citizens were undoubtedly necessary to protect communities from the robberies and murders of the criminal element; but in the face of the record of New York's Finest what justification is there for such patrols today?" He would regret, the Mayor stated, having to resort to countermeasures in the allover public interest. He knew such a step would prove unnecessary. "I urge all already functioning groups of this nature, and groups in the process of organizing, to get in touch immediately with their police precincts for instructions."

By Wednesday morning the failure of the Mayor's radio appeal was apparent. The most irresponsible rumors circulated in the City: that the National Guard had been called out, that the Mayor had made an emergency-flight personal appeal to President Truman in the White House, that the Police Commissioner had resigned, that in a clash between a Washington Heights CAT patrol and police two persons had been killed and nine injured. The Mayor canceled all appointments for the day and remained in continuous conference. Top officials of the Police Department were unanimous in favor of presenting ultimatums to the CAT groups: Disband at once or face arrest. The Mayor refused to sanction such action. No disorders had been reported, he pointed out; apparently the groups were maintaining internal discipline and restricting themselves to their avowed activities. Besides, the movement by now embraced too many people for such measures. "They might lead to open clashes and we'd have riots all over the City. That might mean calling for troops. I'll exhaust every peaceful means before I lay New York open to that."

By midafternoon Wednesday word came that "the central committee" of "the combined Citizens' Action Teams of New York City" had engaged the vast and windy Metropol Hall on Eighth Avenue for "a monster mass meeting" Thursday night. Immediately after, the Mayor's secretary announced a delegation of this committee.

They filed in, a little nervous but with stubborn looks on their faces. The Mayor and his conferees regarded the deputation with curiosity. They seemed a cross-section of the City's people. There were no sharp or shady faces among them. The spokesman, a tall man in his 30s with the look of a mechanic, identified himself as "Jerome K. Frankburner, veteran."

"We've come here, Mr. Mayor, to invite you to talk at our mass meeting tomorrow night. Metropol Hall seats twenty thousand people, we'll have a radio and television setup, and everybody in the City will be sitting in. It's democracy, it's American. What we'd like you to tell us, Mr. Mayor, is what you've done to stop the Cat and what plans you and your subordinates have for the future. And if it's straight talk that makes sense we guarantee that by Friday morning there won't be a C.A.T. in business. Will you come?"

The Mayor said, "Would you gentlemen wait here?" and he took his people into a private office next door.

"Jack, don't do it!"

"Why not, Barney?"

"What can we tell them that we haven't told them a hundred times already? Let's ban the meeting. If there's trouble, crack down on their leaders."

"I don't know, Barney," said one of the Mayor's advisers, a power in the Party. "They're no hoodlums. These people represent a lot of good votes. We'd better go easy."

There were other expressions of opinion, some siding with the Police Commissioner, some with the Party man.

"You haven't said anything, Inspector Queen," said the Mayor suddenly. "What's your opinion?"

"The way I see it," replied Inspector Queen, "it's going to be mighty tough for the Cat to stay away from the meeting."

"Or to put it another way," said the Mayor—"although that's a very valuable thought, Inspector—I was elected on a people's platform and I'm going to stay on it."

He opened the door and said, "I'll be there, gentlemen."

The events of the night of September 22 began in an atmosphere of seriousness and responsibility. Metropol Hall was filled by 7 P.M. and an overflow crowd gathered which soon numbered thousands. But there was exemplary order and the heavy concentration of police had little to do. The inevitable enterprising notions distributor had sent hawkers out to peddle ticklers with a cat's head on the end and oversized C.A.T. lapel buttons of cardboard, and others were peddling orange-and-black cats' heads with grisly expressions which were recognizably advance stocks of Hallowe'en gimcrackery, but there were few buyers in the crowd and the police hustled the vendors along. There were noticeably few children and an almost total absence of horseplay. Inside the Hall people were either quiet or spoke in whispers. In the streets around the Hall the crowds were patient and well-behaved; too patient and too well-behaved, according to old hands of the Traffic Division, who would have welcomed, it appeared, a few dozen drunks, a rousing fistfight or two, or a picket line of Communist demonstrators. But no drunks were visible, the people were strangely passive, and if Communists were among them it was as individuals.

The Traffic brass, testing the wind, put in a call for more mounted police and radio-patrol cars.

A noose dropped quietly around the entire area at 8 P.M. Between 51st and 57th Streets south to north, and between Seventh and Ninth Avenues east to west, solid lines of police appeared to screen off each intersection. Automobile traffic was detoured. Pedestrians were permitted to penetrate the police lines entering the area, but none were allowed to leave before identifying themselves and answering certain questions.

Throughout the district hundreds of plainclothesmen circulated.

Inside the Hall there were hundreds of others.

Among them was one Ellery Queen.

On the platform sat the central committee of the combined Citizens' Action Teams of New York. They were a polyglot group in which no single face stood out; they might have been a jury in a courtroom, and they all wore the intent but self-conscious expressions of jurymen. The Mayor and his official party occupied the seats of honor—"which means," as the Mayor remarked behind his hand to Dr. Edward Cazalis, "where they can keep an eye on us." The speaker's rostrum was flanked with massed American flags. Radio and public address microphones clustered before it. The television people were set up and waiting.

The meeting was opened at 9 P.M. by Jerome K. Frankburner, acting chairman of the evening. Frankburner wore a GI uniform. On the breast of his tunic glittered several decorations, and his sleeve carried an impressive weight of overseas stripes. Above the military figure hung a grim face. He spoke without notes, quietly.

"This is the voice of a New Yorker," Frankburner began. "It doesn't matter what my name is or where I live. I'm speaking for hundreds of New York neighborhood groups who have organized to protect our families and our neighbors' families from a citywide menace. Lots of us fought in the last war and we're all lawabiding Americans. We represent no self-seeking group. We have no axes to grind. You won't find any chiselers, racketeers, or Commies among us. We're Democrats, Republicans, Independents, Liberals, Socialists. We're Protestants, Catholics, Jews. We're whites and we're Negroes. We're business people, white collar people, laboring people, professional people. We're second-generation Americans and we're fourth-generation Americans. We're New York.

"I'm not going to make a speech. We're not here to listen to me. All I want to do is ask a few questions.

"Mr. Mayor, people are being murdered right and left by some lunatic. It's almost four months since the Cat got going and he's still on the prowl. All right, you can't catch him or you haven't been able to yet. Meanwhile what protection do we have? I'm not saying anything against our police. They're a hardworking bunch like the rest of us. But the people of New York ask you: What have our police done about it?"

A sound went through the Hall and met another from outdoors. It was very little, a distant flutter of thunder, but in the Hall and throughout the surrounding streets police nervously fingered their clubs and tightened ranks and on the platform beside the speaker the Mayor and his Police Commissioner were seen to go a little pale.

"To the last man and woman," said Frankburner, a ring coming into his voice, "we're against vigilante law. But we're asking you, Mr. Mayor, what other recourse we have. My wife or my mother might be feeling that silk cord around her throat tonight, and the police wouldn't be in on it till it was all over but the funeral arrangements.

"Mr. Mayor, we've invited you here tonight to tell is what plans you and the law-enforcement authority have for giving us the protection we feel we haven't got.

"Ladies and gentlemen. His Honor, the Mayor of New York."

The Mayor spoke for a long time. He spoke in a sober, neighborly way, exercising his considerable charm and knowledge of the City's people. He traced the history of the New York Police Department, its growth, its gigantic organization, its complexity. He cited the record of its eighteen thousand men and women in guarding law and maintaining order. He gave some reassuring statistics on homicide arrests and convictions. He went into the legal and social aspects of vigilantism and its threats to democratic institutions, its tendency to degenerate from original high purposes to mob rule and the satisfaction of the worst passions of the lowest elements. He pointed to the dangers—violence begetting violence, leading to military intervention, to martial law, and to the suppression of civil liberties, "the first step on the road to fascism and totalitarianism."

"And all this," the Mayor said goodhumoredly, "because temporarily we have failed to locate a single homicidal maniac in the haystack of a city of over seven and one-half millions of people."

But the Mayor's speech, for all its ease and sanity and persuasiveness, was not eliciting those little signs and responses by which veteran public speakers gauge the success or failure of their exertions. This audience gave no signs and responses whatever. It simply sat, or stood, listening. A multibreathing, unstirred entity waiting for something . . . a loosening word.

The Mayor knew it; his voice took on an edge.

His party knew it; they whispered to one another on the platform with exaggerated ease, conscious of the eyes, the television cameras.

Rather abruptly, the Mayor asked the Police Commissioner to give an accounting of the specific measures already taken and "being planned" for the apprehension of the Cat.

As the Commissioner approached the rostrum, Ellery rose in the audience and began to walk down the central aisle toward the press section, scanning the ranks of human heads.

He spotted Jimmy McKell shortly after the Commissioner began to speak.

McKell was twisted about in his seat, glaring at a girl three rows behind him. The girl, pink, was looking at the Commissioner.

Celeste Phillips.

Ellery could not have said what thought, feeling, intuition kept him in the vicinity. Perhaps it was merely the sight of familiar faces.

He dropped to his heels in the aisle at the end of Celeste's row.

He was uneasy. There was something in the air of Metropol Hall that affected him unpleasantly. He saw that others were in the grip of the same disquiet. A sort of mass auto-intoxication. The crowd breathing its own poisons.

And then he knew what it was.

Fear.

The crowd breathing its own fear. It came out of people in invisible droplets, loaded down the air.

What had seemed patience, passivity, expectancy . . . nothing but fear.

They were not listening to the voice of the man on the platform.

They were listening to the inner voice of fear.

"THE CAT!"

It came as the Commissioner turned a page of his notes in the silence.

He looked up very quickly.

The Mayor, Dr. Cazalis, half-rose.

Twenty thousand heads turned.

It had been a woman's scream, pitched to a rare level and held there. It raised the flesh.

A group of men were pushing their way with flailing arms through the standees at the rear of the Hall.

The Commissioner began to say: "Get that woman qui—"

"THE CAT!"

A little eddy of noise began to spin; another; another. A man rose from his seat, a woman, a couple, a group. Craning.

"Ladies and gentlemen, please be seated. Just a hyster—"

"THE CAT!"

"Please!" The Mayor, on the rostrum beside the Commissioner. "Please! Please!"

People were running along the side aisles.

At the rear, a fight was going on.

"THE CAT!"

Somewhere upstairs a man's voice bellowed. It was choked off, as if he were being throttled.

"Take your seats! Officers!"

Bluecoats materialized all over the auditorium.

The disturbance at the rear was now a yeasty corruption, eating into the main aisle, nibbling at the seats.

"THE CAT!"

A dozen women began to scream.

"HE'S HERE!"

Like a stone, it smashed against the great mirror of the audience and the audience shivered and broke. Little cracks widened magically. Where masses had sat or stood, gaps appeared, grew rapidly, splintered in crazy directions. Men began climbing seats, using their fists. People went down. The police vanished. Trickles of shrieks ran together. Metropol Hall became a great cataract obliterating human sound.

On the platform the Mayor, Frankburner, the Commissioner, were shouting into the public address microphones, jostling one another. Their voices mingled; a faint blend, lost in the uproar.

The aisles were logjammed, people punching, twisting, falling toward the exits.

Overhead a balcony rail snapped; a man fell into the orchestra. People were carried down the balcony staircases. Some slipped, disappeared. At the upstairs fire exits hordes struggled over a living, shrieking carpet.

Suddenly the whole contained mass found vents and shot out into the streets, into the frozen thousands, in a moment boiling them to frenzy, turning the area about Metropol Hall into a giant frying pan. Its ingredients sizzled over the police lines, melting men, horses, machines, overflowing the intersections and pouring uptown and down, toward Broadway and toward Ninth Avenue—a smoking liquid that burned everything in its path.

Ellery remembered shouting Jimmy McKell's name as the stampede began, remembered pointing to a petrified Celeste Phillips, trying himself to buck the wall of flesh which pushed him back. He managed to struggle on to a seat, keep his footing there. He saw Jimmy fight his way slowly over three rows, reach the terrified girl, seize her waist. Then they were sucked into the mass and Ellery lost them.

He devoted himself thereafter to keeping off the floor.

A long time afterward he found his father helping the Mayor and the Commissioner direct rescue operations. They had no time for more than a few words. Both were hatless, bleeding, in tatters; all that was left of the Inspector's jacket was the right sleeve. No, he had not seen McKell or the Phillips girl. Or Dr. Cazalis. His eye kept stealing toward the neat and lengthening line of the dead. Then the Inspector was called away and Ellery plodded back into Metropol Hall to help with the casualties. He was one of an impromptu army: police, firemen, ambulance doctors, Red Cross workers, volunteers from the streets. Sirens kept up their outcry, silencing the moans of the injured.

Other horrors took shape as reports kept pouring in. The mob in fleeing had accidentally broken some shop windows in the side streets between Eighth Avenue and Broadway. Looting had begun, led by hoodlums, loiterers, kid gangs. Bystanders who had tried to interfere had been beaten; shopkeepers had been assaulted and in some instances knifed. For a long time the looting had threatened to get out of hand; there was a furious hour as theaters emptying into Broadway had fed the chaos. Hotels had locked their doors. But the police drove patrol cars into the mobs, mounted patrolmen charged concentrations of rioters, and gradually they were dispersed. Hundreds of stores had sustained broken windows and rifled stocks as far south as 42nd Street. Polyclinic Hospital was bedding the injured in corridors; Red Cross emergency first-aid stations had been set up throughout the Times Square

area. Ambulances were speeding into the district from as far north as Fordham
Hospital. Lindy's, Toots Shor's, Jack Dempsey's, other restaurants in the vicinity
were sending coffee and sandwiches to the relief workers.

At 4:45 A.M. one Evarts Jones, an attorney, handed the following statement to
the press:

> *I am authorized by Jerome K. Frankburner, chairman of tonight's
> disastrous meeting, and by the central committee of the so-called
> CATs of Greater New York City, to announce that all units will
> be immediately disbanded and organized patrol activities will
> cease.*
>
> *Mr. Frankburner and the committee speak for all citizens who
> joined in this well-meant but ill-advised popular movement when
> they express their great sorrow and profound regret over what
> occurred in Metropol Hall last night.*

Pressed by reporters for a personal statement, Frankburner shook his head. "I'm
too punchy to say anything. What can anybody say? We were dead wrong. The
Mayor was dead right."

At dawn the Cat Riots were quelled and the Four Days were a bloody paragraph
in the unwritten almanacs.

Later, the Mayor in silence distributed the statistics of the night's disorders to
the press.

The Dead

Women	19
Men	14
Children	6
TOTAL	39

Seriously Injured

Women	68
Men	34
Children	13
TOTAL	115

Minor Injuries, Fractures, Abrasions, etc.

Women	189
Men	152
Children	10
TOTAL	351

Arrested on Charges of Looting, Unlawful Assemblage,
  Inciting to Violence, etc.
        127 persons (including minors)

Property Damage (estimated)
    $4,500,000

The woman whose screams touched off the panic and the rioting that followed, said the Mayor, was trampled to death. Her name was Mrs. Maybelle Legontz, 48, a widow, childless. Her body was identified at 2:38 A.M. by a brother, Stephen Chorumkowski, steamfitter, of 421 West 65th Street. Persons in the audience in the immediate vicinity of Mrs. Legontz had testified that to the best of their recollection she had not been attacked or molested by anyone; but the standees had been packed together and an accidental nudge by some bystander may have exploded her nervous fears.

Mrs. Legontz had a medical history of neurasthenia, a condition which first appeared following the death of her husband, a sand-hog, of the "bends."

There was no possibility that she had been the Cat.

It had been, the Mayor agreed with the reporters, one of the worst outbreaks in New York's history, perhaps the worst since the draft riots of 1863.

Ellery found himself in the milky darkness seated on one of the benches of Rockefeller Plaza. There was no one else in the Plaza but Prometheus. Ellery's head was dancy and the chill of the New York morning against the torn places on his hands and face was deliciously personal, keeping him in a rare consciousness.

Prometheus spoke from his watery niche in the sunken court and Ellery took a certain comfort in his company.

"You're wondering how it all came about," began the golden giant, "that this beast in human form you call the Cat has been able, through the mere bawling of his name, to drive thousands of men out of their heads and send them like frightened animals to an animal death.

"I'm so old I don't recall where I originally came from, except that it's supposed to have been without women—which I find very unconvincing—but I seem to remember that I found it necessary to bring to men the gift of fire. If I really did that, I'm the founder of civilization, so I feel qualified to make certain extended remarks on the late unpleasantness.

"The truth is, what happened last night had nothing to do with the Cat at all.

"The world today reminds me of the very old days, when religions were being born. I mean, modern society resembles primitive society to an amusing degree. There's the same concentration on democratic government, for example, while certain of your number who claim to be in touch with higher powers push to the top to rule. You make the same virtue out of common names and common bloods, investing both with mystic mumbo jumbo. In sexual affairs, your women are equally overrespected and kept inside a convenient cage of sanctity, while important affairs are arrogated to themselves by your males. You've even reverted to food taboos in your worship of diets and vitamins.

"But I find the most interesting similarity," continued Prometheus, apparently impervious to the cold dawn which was making Ellery rattle like an old gourd, "in the way you react to your environment. The crowd, not the individual, is the thinking unit. And the thinking power of a crowd, as last night's unfortunate events demonstrated, is of an extremely low order. You're bursting with ignorance, and ignorance breeds panicky fears. You're afraid of nearly everything, but most of all you're afraid of personal contact with the problems of your time. So you're only too happy to huddle together inside the high magic wall of tradition and let your leaders manipulate the mysteries. They stand between you and the terrors of the unknown.

"But once in a while your priests of power fail you and suddenly you're left to face the unknown in person. Those on whom you relied to bring you salvation and luck, to shield you from the mysteries of life and of death, no longer stand between you and the dreadful darkness. All over your world the magic wall has crumbled, leaving your people paralyzed on the edge of the Pit.

"In such a state of affairs," said Prometheus, "is it to be wondered at that a single hysterical voice, screaming a single silly taboo, can frighten thousands into running away?"

Ellery awoke on the bench to pain and an early sun burnishing his tutor. There were people in the Plaza and automobiles were rushing by. It seemed to him that someone was making an awful lot of noise and he got up angrily.

The cries were coming from the west, hoarse and exultant.

Boys' voices, booming in the canyons.

Ellery limped up the steps, crossed the street, and made his way stiffly toward Sixth Avenue.

There's no hurry, he thought. They're peddling the obituary of the C.A.T. So many dead, so many injured, so many dollars' worth of wreckage. Read all about it.

No, thank you. Hot coffee will do nicely instead.

Ellery limped along trying not to think at all.

But bubbles kept bobbing up.

Obituary of C.A.T. Obituary of *Cat* . . . now that would be something. Obituary of Cat. Come seven.

Our wishes lengthen as our sun declines.

Ellery laughed.

Or as another immortal put it, I should of stood in bed.

Brother Q, you're through. Only you had to rise from the dead. To chase a Cat. What next?

What do you do?

Where do you look?

How do you look?

In the fresh shadow of the Music Hall marquee the boy's mouth was going through an acrobatic exercise under his popping eyes.

Never an ill wind, thought Ellery as he watched the pile of papers dwindle.

And he began to pass, to cross Sixth Avenue for his coffee, when a shouted syllable made sense and something on top of the heap flew up and lodged in his brain.

Ellery fumbled for a coin. The coin felt cold.

"*Extra.*"

He stood there being elbowed right and left.

There was the familiar Cat, but he had an eighth tail and it was not a question mark.

8

Her name was Stella Petrucchi. She lived with her family on Thompson Street, less than a half a mile below Washington Square. She was 22 years of age; of Italian parentage; of the Roman Catholic faith.

For almost five years Stella Petrucchi had been employed as a stenographer in the same law office on Madison Avenue and 40th Street.

Her father had been in the United States for forty-five years. He was a wholesale fish merchant in Fulton Market. He came from Livorno. Stella's mother was also from the province of Toscana.

Stella was the sixth of seven children. Of her three brothers, one was a priest and the two others were in business with George Petrucchi. Of her three sisters, the eldest was a nun of the Carmelite order, one was married to an Italian cheese and olive oil importer, the third was a student at Hunter College. All the Petrucchi children but the priest, who was the eldest, had been born in New York City.

They had thought at first that Stella was part of the immortal debris littering the vicinity of Metropol Hall, overlooked in the streetcleaning. But the silk cord around the girl's neck gave her the special distinction conferred by the Cat and they found that when they pulled her head back by the tumbled black hair and exposed her throat.

A pair of patrolmen had run across her body a block and a half from Metropol Hall at just about the time the Mayor was giving reporters the statistics of the carnage. It was lying on the cement of an alley between two stores, ten feet from the Eighth Avenue sidewalk.

She had been strangled, said the Medical Examiner's man, some time before midnight.

The identification was made by Father Petrucchi and the married sister, Mrs. Teresa Bascalone. Mr. and Mrs. George Petrucchi collapsed on being informed of the tragedy.

A man, Howard Whithacker, 32, who gave a West 4th Street rooming house address, was closely questioned.

Whithacker was a very tall, lean, blackhaired man with closely set diamond black eyes, a horny skin, and Gothic cheekbones. He looked considerably older than the age he gave.

His occupation, he stated, was "unsuccessful poet." On being pressed, he grudgingly admitted that he "kept body and soul together" by working as a counterman in a Greenwich Avenue cafeteria.

Whithacker said that he had known Stella Petrucchi for sixteen months. They had met in the cafeteria late one night the previous spring. She had been out on a date and had stopped in with her escort at two in the morning. The escort, "a deep Bronx troglodyte with handpainted mermaids on his tie," had jeered at Whithacker's midwestern speech. Whithacker had picked up a baked apple from the counter between them, leaned over, and crammed the apple into the offending mouth. "After that, Stella used to drop in almost every night and we became kind of friendly."

He denied angrily having had an affair with the girl. When this line of questioning persisted, he became quite violent and had to be subdued. "She was a pure, sweet soul," he yelled. "Sex with her was out of the question!"

Whithacker talked reluctantly about his background. He hailed from Beatrice, Nebraska. His people were farmers; the original stock had been Scotch—a great-grandfather had come up out of Kentucky in 1829 in a group of Campbellites. There was Pawnee blood in the family and a splatter of Bohemian and Danish. "I'm one of the percentage Americans," said Howard Whithacker. "All decimal points. You know?" At home, he said, he attended the Disciples of Christ church.

He was a graduate of the University of Nebraska.

At the beginning of the war he had enlisted in the Navy, "winding up in the Pacific. I was blown into the water by a kamikaze who darn near made it. My ears still ring sometimes. It had a remarkable effect on my poetry."

After the war, finding Beatrice confining, he went to New York—"financed by my brother Duggin, who thinks I'm poetry's gift to Gage County, Nebraska."

His sole published work since his arrival two years before consisted of a verse entitled "Corn in the Coral." It had appeared in Greenwich Village's newspaper, the *Villager,* in the spring of 1947; Whithacker produced a greasy clipping to prove it. "My brother Duggin is now convinced I'm not another John Neihardt. However," he said, "I have received considerable encouragement from fellow-poets in the Village, and of course Stella adored me. We have regular 3 A.M. poetry-reading sessions in the cafeteria. I live Spartanly but adequately. The death of Stella Petrucchi leaves an empty pigeonhole in my heart; she was a dear child without a brain cell in her head."

He denied indignantly having taken money from her.

As to the events of the night of September 22, Whithacker stated that Thursday night being his night off, he had met Stella outside her office building to take her to the Metropol Hall mass meeting. "A cat poem had been taking shape in my mind for some time," he explained. "It was important that I attend. Stella, of course, always looked forward to our Thursday nights together."

They had walked crosstown, stopping in at an Eighth Avenue spaghetti house "owned by a cousin of Stella's father. I discussed the Citizens' Action Teams movement with Mr. Ferriquancchi and we were both surprised to find that the subject made Stella extremely nervous. Ignazio said we oughtn't to go if Stella felt that way and I offered to go alone, but Stella said no, she wanted to go, at last somebody was doing something about the murders. She said she asked the Virgin Mother every night to keep everyone she knew safe."

They had managed to get into Metropol Hall and had found downstairs seats well to the front of the auditorium.

"When the stampede started, Stella and I tried to hold on to each other, but the damn cattle tore us apart. The last I saw of her she was being carried off in a crowd of lunatics, screaming something at me. But I couldn't hear. I never saw her alive again."

Whithacker had been lucky, suffering no more than a torn pocket and some pummeling.

"I crowded with a few other people in a doorway across from the Hall to keep out of harm's way. When the worst was over I started searching for Stella. I couldn't find her among the dead or injured at the Hall so I began looking along Eighth Avenue, the side streets, Broadway. I wandered around all night.''

Whithacker was asked why he had not telephoned to the Petrucchis; the family had been up all night frantic over Stella's failure to come home. They had not known about her appointment with him.

"That's the reason. They didn't know about me. Stella said it was better that way. She said they were strict Catholics and it would only cause a ruckus if they found out she was going around with a non-Catholic. She didn't mind her father's cousin Ignazio knowing about us, she said, because Mr. Ferriquancchi is anti-Papist and nobody in the Petrucchi family has anything to do with him anyway.''

At 7:30 A.M. Whithacker had returned to Metropol Hall for another checkup, intending to telephone the Petrucchis ''despite their religious scruples'' if this last effort to locate Stella failed.

At his first question he was seized by the police.

"I must have passed the entrance to that alley a dozen times during the night," Howard Withacker said. "But it was dark, and how was I to know Stella was laid out in there?''

Whithacker was held ''for further questioning.''

"No," Inspector Richard Queen told reporters, "we have absolutely nothing on him. But we want to check his story, and so on.'' The "and so on" was taken by the press—correctly—to refer both to related matters in the recent past and to a certain interesting wildness of eye, manner, and speech in Stella Petrucchi's friend.

There was no medical evidence of rape or attempted rape.

The girl's purse was missing; but it was found later, its contents intact, in the debris of the Hall. A gold religious medal on a fine chain about her neck had not been touched.

The strangling cord was of the familiar tussah silk, dyed salmon-pink. It had been knotted at the nape exactly as in the previous cases. Laboratory examination of the cord turned up nothing of significance.

It seemed clear that Stella Petrucchi had taken refuge in the alley after being hurled into the street with the rest of the Metropol audience. But whether the Cat had been waiting for her in the alley, or had entered with her, or had followed her in, there was no way of telling.

The probability was that she had suspected nothing until the clutch of the silk. She might well have entered the alley at the Cat's invitation, assuming he caught up with her and offered to ''protect'' her from harm at the hands of the mob.

As usual, he had left no trail.

It was past noon when Ellery pulled himself up the stairs to find the door of the Queen apartment unlocked. Wondering, he went in; and the first thing he saw on entering his bedroom was a torn nylon stocking dangling from the seat of his ladderback chair. Over one of the chair posts was hooked a white brassiere.

He bent over his bed and shook her.

Her eyes popped open.

"You're all right."

Celeste shuddered. "Don't *ever* do that again! For a split century I thought it was the Cat.''

"Is Jimmy . . . ?"

"Jimmy's all right, too."

Ellery found himself sitting on the edge of his bed; the back of his neck throbbed again. "I've often dreamed about this situation," he said, rubbing it.

"What situation?" She stretched her long legs stiff under the sheet, moaning, "Oh, I ache."

"I know," said Ellery. "This all happened in a Peter Arno drawing."

"What?" said Celeste sleepily. "Is it still today?"

Her black hair coursed over his pillow in sweet poetic streams. "But exhaustion," Ellery explained, "is the enemy of poetry."

"*What?* You look kind of dilapidated. Are *you* all right?"

"I will be once I get the hang of sleeping again."

"I am sorry!" Celeste clutched the sheet to her and sat up quickly. "I wasn't really awake. Er, I'm not . . . I mean, I didn't want to poke around in your bureau . . ."

"You cad," said a stern voice. "Would you boot out an unclothed maiden?"

"Jimmy!" said Celeste happily.

Jimmy McKell was in the bedroom doorway, one arm about a large, mysterious-looking paper sack.

"Well," said Ellery. "The McKell. Indestructible, I see."

"I see you made it, too, Ellery."

They grinned at each other. Jimmy was wearing one of Ellery's most cherished sports jackets, which was too small for him, and Ellery's newest tie.

"Mine were torn clean off me," explained Jimmy. "How you feeling, woman?"

"Like September Morn at an American Legion convention. *Would* you two step into the next room?"

In the living room Jimmy scowled. "You look beat, old-timer. What's with the Petrucchi girl?"

"Oh, you know about that."

"Heard it on your radio this morning." Jimmy set the sack down.

"What's in that bag?"

"Some hardtack and pemmican. Your larder'd run dry. Have you eaten anything, bud?"

"No."

"Neither have we. Hey, Celeste!" Jimmy shouted. "Never mind making with the clothes. Rustle us some breakfast!"

Celeste laughed from Ellery's bathroom.

"You two seem awfully gay," remarked Ellery, feeling for the armchair.

"Funny how it hits you." Jimmy laughed, too. "You get mixed up in something like last night's fandango and all of a sudden everything drops into the slot. Even stupidity. I thought I'd seen everything in the Pacific, but I hadn't. The war was murder, all right, but organized. You wear a uniform and you carry a gun and you take great big orders and somebody cooks your chow and you kill or get killed, all according to the book. But last night . . . tooth and claw. Man stripped to the bloody bones. Disintegration of the tribe. Every fellow-cannibal your enemy. It's good to be alive, that's all."

"Hello, Celeste," said Ellery.

Her clothes were macerated and although she had evidently brushed them and applied pins to secret parts, they looked like hardening lava. Her legs were rowdy: she carried her stockings.

"I don't suppose you'd have an old pair of nylons around, Mr. Queen?"

"No," said Ellery gravely. "My father, you know."

"Oh, dear. Well! I'll fix you men something in a jiffy," and Celeste went into the kitchen with the sack.

"Superior, hey?" Jimmy stared at the swinging door. "You'll note, Brother Queen, that the lady made no apology for her appearance. Definitely superior."

"How'd you two manage to keep together last night?" asked Ellery, closing his eyes.

"Now don't cork off on us, Ellery." Jimmy began setting the dropleaf table. "Why, the fact is we didn't."

"Oh?" said Ellery, opening one eye.

"We lost each other right after I got to her. She doesn't remember how she got out, and neither do I. We kept hunting for each other all night. I found her around 5 A.M. sitting on the steps of Polyclinic Hospital, bawling."

Ellery closed the eye.

"How do you like your bacon, Mr. Queen?" called Celeste.

Jimmy said, "Are you there?" and Ellery mumbled something. "Curly and wet, he says!—What, Ellery?"

"The last word," said Ellery, "was 'bawling.' "

"Her eyes out. I tell you, I was touched. Anyway, we had some coffee at an allnight joint and then we went looking for you. But you'd disappeared. We thought you'd probably got out all right and gone home, so we came up here. Nobody home, so I said to Celeste, 'He won't mind,' and I climbed up the fire escape. For an eye, Ellery, you're very careless about your windows."

"Go on," said Ellery, when Jimmy stopped.

"I don't know if I can explain it. Why we came, I mean. I don't think Celeste and I said two dozen words to each other after we clutched this morning. I think we both realized your position for the first time and we wanted to tell you we've been a couple of firstclass *schlemihls* and didn't quite know how to do it." Jimmy straightened a spoon. "This thing is awfully gross," he said to the spoon. "The war all over again. In another form. The individual doesn't mean a damn. Human dignity gets flushed down the drain. You have to get up to your elbow in muck to hold on to it. I didn't see that till last night, Ellery."

"Neither did I." Celeste was in the kitchen doorway with a piece of toast in one hand and a buttery knife in the other. Ellery thought, Piggott and Johnson lost them last night; they must have. "You were right, Mr. Queen. After what we saw last night you were right."

"About what, Celeste?"

"About suspecting Jimmy and me. Jimmy and me or anybody."

"I guess what we wanted to hear you say was 'Come back, all is forgiven,' " grinned Jimmy. But then he began on the cutlery again.

"So you waited here for me."

"When we heard the news we knew what was keeping you. I made Celeste get into your bed—she was dead on her feet—and I parked on the sofa in here. Anything to connect the Petrucchi girl with the others?"

"No."

"What about this cornhusker-poet character? What's his name?"

"Whithacker?" Ellery shrugged. "Dr. Cazalis seems interested in him and they're going to examine him carefully."

"I'm one hell of a newspaperman." Jimmy banged a spoon down. "All right, I'll say it. Do you want us back?"

"I don't have anything for you to do, Jimmy."

"For me!" cried Celeste.

"Or for you."

"You don't want us back."

"I do. But I have no work for you." Ellery got up, groping for a cigaret. But his hands dropped. "I don't know where to turn. That's the truth. I'm absolutely hung up."

Jimmy and Celeste looked swiftly at each other. Then Jimmy said, "You're also absolutely pooped. What you need is to slice a herring with Morpheus. Hey, Celeste! *The coffee!*"

Ellery awoke to the sound of a loud voice.

He switched on the night light.

8:12

The voice was driving. Ellery crawled out of bed, pulled on his robe and slippers, and hurried to the living room.

The voice was the radio's. His father was lying back in the armchair. Jimmy and Celeste crouched on the sofa in a nest of newspapers.

"You two still here?"

Jimmy grunted. His long chin was nuzzling his chest and Celeste kept rubbing her drawnup bare leg in a reassuring way.

The Inspector was all bones and gray wilt.

"Dad—"

"Listen."

"—reported tonight," said the voice. "A third-rail short circuit on the BMT subway at Canal Street caused a panic and forty-six persons were treated for injuries. Trains out of Grand Central Terminal and Pennsylvania Station are running from ninety minutes to two hours behind schedule. The parkways out of the City are a solid double line of cars as far north as Greenwich and White Plains. Traffic is clogged for a large area around the Manhattan approaches to the Holland and Lincoln Tunnels and the George Washington Bridge. Nassau County authorities report that traffic conditions on the major Long Island parkways are out of control. New Jersey, Connecticut, and upstate New York police report—"

Ellery snapped the radio off.

"What is it?" he asked wildly. "War?" His glance flew to the windows, as if he expected to see a flaming sky.

"New York's turned Malay," said Jimmy with a laugh.

"The *amok.* They'll have to rewrite the psychology books." He began to get up, but Celeste pulled him back.

"Fighting? Panic?"

"That Metropol Hall business last night was just the beginning, Ellery." The Inspector was fighting something, nausea or rage. "It snapped a vital part. Started a sort of chain reaction. Or maybe it was the Petrucchi murder on top of the panic and riot—that was bad timing. Anyway, it's all over the City. Been spreading all day."

"They're running," said Celeste. "Everybody's running."

"Running where?"

"Nobody seems to know. Just running."

"It's the Black Death all over again," said Jimmy McKell. "Didn't you know? We're back in the Middle Ages. New York is now the pesthole of the Western Hemisphere, Ellery. In two weeks you'll be able to shoot hyenas in Macy's basement."

"Shut up, McKell." The old man's head rolled on the back of his chair. "There's a lot of disorder, son, a lot. Looting, holdups . . . It's been particularly bad on Fifth Avenue, 86th around Lexington, 125th, upper Broadway, and around Maiden

Lane dowtown. And traffic accidents, hundreds of traffic accidents. I've never seen anything like it. Not in New York.''

Ellery went to one of the windows. The street was empty. A fire engine screamed somewhere. The sky glowed to the southwest.

"And they say," began Celeste.

"Who says?" Jimmy laughed again. "Well, that's the point, my friends, whereupon today I'm proud to be one of the capillaries in the circulation system of organized opinion. We've really swung it this time, comrades." He kicked a drooping newspaper. "Responsible journalism! And the blessed radio—"

"Jimmy," said Celeste.

"Well, old Rip's got to hear the news, hasn't he? He's slept through history, Miss Phillips. Did you know, sir, that there's a citywide quarantine? It's a fact. Or is it? That all schools will be shut down indefinitely—O happy day? That Father Knickerbocker's chickens are to be evacuated to camps outside the metropolitan area? That all flights from La Guardia, Newark, and Idlewild have been nixed? That the Cat's made of extremely green cheese?''

Ellery was silent.

"Also," said Jimmy McKell, "Beldame Rumor hath it that the Mayor's been attacked by the Cat, that the FBI's taken over Police Headquarters, that the Stock Exchange positively will not open its doors tomorrow—and that's a fact, seeing that tomorrow's Saturday." Jimmy unfolded himself. "Ellery, I went downtown this afternoon. The shop is a madhouse. Everybody's busy as little beavers denying rumors and believing every new one that comes in. I stopped on my way back to see if Mother and Father are maintaining their equilibrium and do you know what? I saw a Park Avenue doorman get hysterics. Brother, that's the end of the world." He swiped his nose backhandedly, glaring. "It's enough to make you cancel your membership in the human race. Come on, let's all get drunk.''

"And the Cat?" Ellery asked his father.

"No news."

"Whithacker?"

"Cazalis and the psychiatrists have been working on him all day. Still are, far as I know. But they're not doing any backbends. And we didn't find a thing in his West 4th Street flop.''

"Do I have to do it all by myself?" demanded Jimmy, pouring Scotch. "None for you, Celeste.''

"Inspector, what's going to happen now?"

"I don't know," said the Inspector, "and what's more, Miss Phillips, I don't think I give an Irish damn." He got up. "Ellery, if Headquarters calls, I've gone to bed.''

The old man shuffled out.

"Here's to the Cat," said Jimmy, lofting his glass. "May his giblets wither.''

"If you're going to start toping, Jimmy," said Celeste, "I'm going home. I'm going home anyway.''

"Right. To mine.''

"Yours?''

"You can't stay up in that foul nest of underprivilege alone. And you may as well meet Father now and get it over with. Mother, of course, will be nightingale soup.''

"It's sweet of you, Jimmy," Celeste was all olive-pink. "But just impossible.''

"You can sleep in Queen's bed but you can't sleep in mine! What is this?''

She laughed, but she was angry. "It's been the ghastliest and most wonderful twenty-four hours of my life, darling. Don't spoil it."

"Spoil it! Why, you proletarian snob!"

"I can't let your parents think I'm some dead-end kid to be taken in off the streets."

"You are a snob."

"Jimmy." Ellery turned from the fireplace. "Is it the Cat you're worrying about?"

"Always. But this time the rabbits, too. It's a breed that bites."

"You can stop worrying about the Cat, at any rate. Celeste is safe."

Celeste looked bewildered.

Jimmy said, "The hell you say."

"For that matter, so are you." Ellery explained the diminishing-age pattern of the murders. When he had finished he packed a pipe and lit it, watching them, and all the time they stood peering at him as if he were performing a minor miracle.

"And nobody saw that," muttered Jimmy. "Nobody."

"But what does it mean?" Celeste cried.

"I don't know. But Stella Petrucchi was 22; and you and Jimmy being older than that, the Cat's passed your age groups by." Just relief, he thought, wondering why he was disappointed.

"May I print that, Ellery?" Jimmy's face fell. "I forgot. *Noblesse oblige.*"

"Well, I think," said Celeste defiantly, "that people ought to be told, Mr. Queen. Especially now, when they're so frightened."

Ellery stared at her. "Wait a minute."

He went into his study.

When he returned he said, "The Mayor agrees with you, Celeste. Things are very bad . . . I'm holding a press conference at 10 o'clock tonight and I'm going on the air with the Mayor at 10:30. From City Hall. Jimmy, don't double-cross me."

"Thanks, pal. This descending-age business?"

"Yes. As Celeste says, it ought to quiet some fears."

"You don't sound hopeful."

"It's a question which can be more alarming," said Ellery, "danger to yourself or danger to your children."

"I see what you mean. I'll be right back, Ellery. Celeste, come on." He grabbed her arm.

"Just put me in a cab, Jimmy."

"Are you going to be pork-headed?"

"I'll be as safe on 102nd Street as on Park Avenue."

"How about compromising in a—I mean on a hotel?"

"Jimmy, you're wasting Mr. Queen's time."

"Wait for me, Ellery. I'll go downtown with you."

They went out, Jimmy still arguing.

Ellery shut the door after them carefully. Then he went back to the radio, turned it on, and sat down on the edge of the chair, like an audience.

But at the first blat of the newscaster he leaped, throttled the voice, and hurried to his bedroom.

It was afterward said that the press conference and radio talk of the Mayor's Special Investigator on that topsyturvy night of Friday, September 23, acted as a brake on the flight of New Yorkers from the City and in a matter of hours brought the panic phase of the case to a complete stop. Certainly the crisis was successfully passed that night and never again reached a peak. But what few realized who were following the complex psychology of the period was that something comparably undesirable replaced it.

As people straggled back to the City in the next day or so, it was remarked that they no longer seemed *interested* in the Cat case. The cataract of telephone calls and in-person inquiries which had kept City Hall, Police Headquarters, and precincts all over the City swamped for almost four months ebbed to a trickle. Elected officials, who had been under continuous bombardment from their constituents, discovered that the siege had unaccountably lifted. For once, to their relief, ward politicians found their clubhouses deserted. *Vox populi,* which had kept the correspondence columns of the newspapers in an uproar, sank to a petty whisper.

An even more significant phenomenon was observed.

On Sunday, September 25, churches of all denominations throughout the City suffered a marked drop in attendance. While this fall from grace was deplored by the clergy, it was almost unanimously regarded by lay observers as an agreeable evil, considering "the recent past." (Already the panic had dwindled to the size of a footnote in the City's history, so dramatic was the change.) The unusually heavy church attendance during the summer, these observers said, had been inspired largely by Cat-generated fears and a panic flight to spiritual reassurance; the sudden wholesale defection could only mean that the panic was over, the pendulum had swung to the other extreme. Shortly, they predicted, church attendance would find itself back in the normal rhythm.

On all sides responsible people were congratulating one another and the City on "the return to sanity." It was recognized that the threat to the City's young people had to be guarded against, and special measures were planned, but everyone seemed to feel—in official quarters—that the worst was over.

It was almost as if the Cat had been caught.

But there were contrary signs to be seen by those who were not blinded by sheer relief.

During the week beginning Saturday, September 24, *Variety* and Broadway columnists began to report an extraordinary increase in night club and theater attendance. The upswing could not be ascribed to seasonal change; it was too abrupt. Theaters which had not seen a full house all summer found themselves under the pleasant compulsion to rehire laidoff ushers and haul out ropes and S.R.O. signs. Clubs which had been staggering along were regarding their jammed dance floors with amazement; the famous ones were haughtily turning people away again. Broadway bars and eating places sprang to jubilant life. Florist shops, candy shops, cigar stores were crowded. Liquor stores tripled their sales. Scalpers, barkers, and steerers began to smile again. Bookmakers rubbed their eyes at the flow of bets. Sports arenas and stadiums reported record receipts and new attendance marks. Pool room and bowling alleys put on extra employees. The shooting galleries on Broadway, 42nd Street, Sixth Avenue were mobbed.

Overnight, it seemed, show business and its feedline subsidiaries began to enjoy boomtime prosperity. Times Square from sundown to 3 A.M. was roaring and impassable. Taxi drivers were saying, "It's just like the war all over again."

The phenomenon was not restricted to midtown Manhattan. It was simultaneously experienced by the entertainment districts of downtown Brooklyn, Fordham Road in the Bronx, and other localities throughout the five boroughs.

That week, too, advertising agency executives were bewildered by advance reports from their radio-polling services. At a time when most major radio shows had returned to the air to begin the fall and winter broadcasting cycles and an appreciable rise in listener-response should have become apparent, the advance ratings unaccountably dropped in the metropolitan area. All networks were affected. The independent stations with local coverage had Pulse and BMB make hasty special surveys and discovered that the bottom had fallen out of their program-response and listener-circulation tables. The most significant of all—in all surveys—were those showing the percentage of sets-in-use. They were unprecedentedly small.

A parallel drop was noted in television surveys.

New Yorkers were not listening to the radio and watching the telecasts.

Account executives and broadcasting company vice-presidents were busy preparing explanations to their clients, chiefly masochistic. The truth seemed to have occurred to none of them, which was that radio and television sets could not be turned on in the home by people who were not there or who, if they were, were absent spiritually.

Police were puzzled by the abrupt rise in drunkenness and disorderly conduct cases. Routine raids on gambling houses bagged huge takes and a type of burgher clientele not ordinarily found throwing its money away. Marijuana and narcotics cases took a disturbing jump. The Vice Squad was compelled to put on a co-ordinated drive in an attempt to curb the sudden spread and acceleration of prostitution activities. Muggings, car thefts, holdups, common assaults, sex offenses increased sharply. The rise in juvenile delinquency was especially alarming.

And of peculiar interest was the reappearance all over the City of strangled alley cats.

It was evident to the thoughtful few that what had seemed a healthy loss of interest in the Cat case on the part of New Yorkers was not that at all. Fear had not died; the City was still in the mob mood and mob psychology was still at the panic stage; it had merely taken a new form and direction. People were now in flight from reality on a psychic rather than a physical level. But they were still fleeing.

On Sunday, October 2, an unsurprisingly large number of clergymen took as their texts Genesis XIX, 24-25. It was natural to cite Sodom and Gomorrah that day, and brimstone and fire were generously predicted. The ingredients of moral disintegration were all present in the melting pot, bubbling to the boil. The only trouble was that those whom the lesson would have profited were atoning for their wickedness in a less godly fashion, elsewhere.

By a sly irony the ninth life of the Cat proved the crucial one.

For the break in the case came with the ninth murder.

The body was found a few minutes after 1 A.M. on the night of September 29-30, exactly one week after the Cat Riots and less than two miles from the site of Stella Petrucchi's murder. It lay sprawled in deep shadows on the steps of the American Museum of Natural History, at 77th Street and Central Park West. A sharpeyed patrolman spotted it on his rounds.

Death was by strangulation. A cord had been employed, of tussah silk, dyed blue as in the cases of Archibald Dudley Abernethy and Rian O'Reilly.

According to a driver's license found in his untouched wallet, his name was Donald Katz, he was 21 years old, and he lived on West 81st Street. The address proved to be an apartment house between Central Park West and Columbus Avenue. His father was a dentist, with offices at Amsterdam Avenue and West 71st Street near Sherman Square. The family was of the Jewish faith. The victim had an elder sister, Mrs. Jeanne Immerson, who lived in the Bronx. Donald was enrolled in extension courses in radio and television engineering. He had been, it seemed, a bright quixotic boy given to quick enthusiasms and dislikes; he had had many acquaintances and few friends.

The father, Dr. Morvin Katz, officially identified the body.

It was from Dr. Katz that police learned about the girl his son had been out with that evening. She was Nadine Cuttler, 19, of Borough Park, Brooklyn, a student at the New York Art Students' League. Brooklyn detectives picked her up during the night and she was brought to Manhattan for questioning.

She fainted on viewing the body and it was some time before she could give a coherent story.

Nadine Cuttler said that she had known Donald Katz for almost two years. "We met at a Palestine rally." They had had "an understanding" for the past year, during which period they had seen each other three or four times a week. "We had practically nothing in common. Donald was interested in science and technology, and I in art. He was politically undeveloped; not even the war taught him anything. We didn't even agree about Palestine. I don't know why we fell in love."

The previous evening, Miss Cuttler stated, Donald Katz had met her at the Art Students' League after her classes and they had walked down Seventh Avenue from 57th Street, stopping in at Lum Fong's for a chow mein dinner. "We fought over the check. Donald had juvenile ideas about this being a man's world, and that women ought to stay home and have babies and smooth their husbands' brows when the men came home after an important day, and all that sort of thing. He got very angry with me because I pointed out to him it was my turn to pay. Finally, I let him pay the check just to avoid a scene in public."

Afterward, they had gone dancing in a little Russian night club on 52nd Street, The Yar, across from 21 and Leon and Eddie's.

"It was a place we liked very much and often went to. They knew us there and we called Maria and Lonya and Tina and the others by their first names. But last night it was crowded and after a while we left. Donald had had four vodkas and didn't touch any of the *zakuska,* so when we hit the air he got lightheaded. He wanted to go clubbing, but I said I wasn't in the mood and instead we strolled back uptown on Fifth Avenue. When we got to Fifth and 59th, Donald wanted to go into the Park. He was feeling very . . . gay; the drinks hadn't worn off. But it was so dark in there, and the Cat . . ."

At this point Nadine Cuttler broke down.

When she was able to continue, the girl said: "I found myself awfully nervous. I don't know why. We'd often talked about the Cat murders and neither of us ever felt a personal threat, I'm sure of it. We just couldn't seem to take it seriously, I mean really seriously. Donald used to say the Cat was anti-Semitic because in a City with the biggest Jewish population in the world he hadn't strangled a single Jew. Then he'd laugh and contradict himself and say the odds were the Cat was Jewish because of that very fact. It was a sort of joke between us which I never thought very funny, but you couldn't take offense at anything Donald said, not really, he . . ."

She had to be recalled to her story.

"We didn't go into the Park. We walked crosstown on Central Park South, sticking to the side of the street where the buildings are. On the way Donald seemed to sober up a bit; we talked about the murder of the Petrucchi girl last week and the Cat Riots and the stampede out of the City, and we agreed it was a funny thing but it was usually the older people who lost their heads in a crisis while the young

ones, who had most to lose, kept theirs . . . Then, when we got to Columbus
Circle, we had another quarrel.''

Donald had wanted to take her home, ''even though we'd had an absolute compact
for months that on weeknight dates I'd go back to Brooklyn by myself. I was really
exasperated with him. His mother didn't like him to get in late; it was the only
basis on which I allowed myself to see him so often. Why didn't I let him, why
didn't I let him?''

Nadine Cuttler cried again and Dr. Katz quieted her, saying that she had nothing
to condemn herself for, that if it was Donald's fate to become a victim of the Cat
nothing would have changed the result. The girl clung to his hand.

There was little more to her story. She had refused to let the boy accompany her
to Brooklyn and she had urged him to hop a cab and go right home, because ''he
was looking sick and besides I didn't like the idea of his being alone on the streets
in that condition. That made him even madder. He didn't even . . . kiss me. The
last I saw of him was when I was going down the subway steps. He was standing
at the top talking to somebody, I think a taxi driver. That was about 10:30.''

The taxi driver was found. Yes, he remembered the young couple's tiff. ''When
the girl sails off down the steps I open my door and say to this kid, 'Better luck
next time, Casanova. Come on, I'll take you home.' But he was sore as a boil.
'You can take your cab and shove it,' he says to me. 'I'm walking home.' And he
crossed the Circle and turns into Central Park West. Headed uptown. He was pretty
rocky on his pins.''

It seemed clear that Donald Katz had tried to carry out his intention, walking
uptown along the west side of Central Park West from Columbus Circle for almost
a mile to 77th Street, just four blocks short of his home. There seemed no question
but that the Cat had followed him all the way, perhaps had followed the couple all
evening, although nothing developed from inquiries made at Lum Fong's and The
Yar, and the taxi driver could not recall having seen anyone acting suspiciously as
Donald Katz left him. The Cat had undoubtedly bided his time, waiting for an
opportunity to pounce. The opportunity had come at 77th Street. On the steps of
the Museum, at the spot where Donald was found, there was a mess of regurgitated
matter; some of it was on Donald's coat. Apparently as he was passing the Museum
his intoxication reached the stage of nausea and Donald had sat down on the steps
in a dark place and he had been ill.

And the Cat had approached him from the side and got behind him as he sat
retching.

He had struggled violently.

Death occurred, said the Medical Examiner, between 11 P.M. and midnight.

No one heard screams or choked cries.

The most thorough examination of the body, the clothing, the strangling cord,
and the scene turned up nothing of importance.

''As usual,'' said Inspector Queen at the dawn's early light, ''the Cat's left not
a clue.''

But he had.

The fateful fact emerged obliquely during the morning of the 30th in the Katz
apartment on West 81st Street.

Detectives were questioning the family, going through the familiar motions of
trying to establish a connection between Donald Katz and the persons involved in
the previous eight murders.

Present were the boy's mother and father; their daughter; the daughter's husband, Philbert Immerson. Mrs. Katz was a lean brown-eyed woman of bitter charm; her face was undressed by weeping. Mrs. Immerson, a chubby young woman without her mother's mettle, sobbed throughout the interview; Ellery gathered from something Mrs. Immerson said that she had not got along with her young brother. Dr. Katz sat by himself in a corner, as Zachary Richardson had sat on the other side of Central Park three and a half weeks before; he had lost his son, there would be no others. Donald's brother-in-law, a balding young man with a red mustache, wearing a sharp gray business suit, stood away from the others as if to avoid being noticed. He had freshly shaved; his stout cheeks were perspiring under the talcum.

Ellery was paying little attention to the automatic questions and the surcharged replies; he was dragging himself about these days and it had been a particularly depleting night. Nothing would come of this, he felt sure, as nothing had come of any of the others. A few slight alterations in the pattern—Jewish instead of Christian, seven days since the last one instead of seventeen, or eleven, or six—but the bulk features were the same: the strangling cord of tussah silk, blue for men, salmon-pink for women; the victim unmarried (Rian O'Reilly was still the baffling single exception); the victim listed in the telephone directory—Ellery had checked that immediately, and the ninth victim younger than the eighth who had been younger than the seventh who had been . . .

"—no, I'm positive he didn't know anybody of that name," Mrs. Katz was saying. Inspector Queen was being perversely insistent about Howard Withacker, who had disappointed the psychiatrists. "Unless, of course, this Whithacker was somebody Donald met in training camp."

"You mean during the war?" asked the Inspector.

"Yes."

"Your son in the war, Mrs. Katz? Wasn't he too young?"

"No. He enlisted on his eighteenth birthday. The war was still on."

The Inspector looked surprised. "Germany surrendered in May, I think it was, of 1945—Japan in August or September. Wasn't Donald still 17 in 1945?"

"I ought to know my own son's age!"

"Pearl." Dr. Katz stirred in his corner. "It must be that driving license."

The Queens both made the slightest forward movement.

"Your son's license, Dr. Katz," said Inspector Queen, "gives his birth date as March 10, 1928."

"That's a mistake, Inspector Queen. My son made a mistake putting down the year on his application and never bothered to have it corrected."

"You mean," asked Ellery, and he found himself clearing his throat, "you mean Donald was *not* 21 years old, Dr. Katz?"

"Donald was 22. He was born on March 10, 1927."

"22," said Ellery.

"*22?*" The Inspector sounded froggy, too. "Ellery. Stella Petrucchi."

Abernethy, 44. Violette Smith, 42. Rian O'Reilly, 40. Monica McKell, 37. Simone Phillips, 35. Beatrice Willikins, 32. Lenore Richardson, 25. Stella Petrucchi, 22. Donald Katz . . . 22.

For the first time the diminishing-age sequence had been broken.

Or had it?

"It's true," Ellery said feverishly in the hall, "it's true that up to now the age drop's been in years. But if we found . . ."

"You mean this Katz boy might still be younger than Stella Petrucchi," mumbled his father.

"In terms of months. Suppose the Petrucchi girl had been born in January of 1927. That would make Donald Katz two months younger."

"Suppose Stella Petrucchi was born in *May* of 1927. That would make Donald Katz two months *older*."

"I don't want to think about that. That would . . . What month *was* she born in?"

"I don't know!"

"I don't remember seeing her exact birth date on any report."

"Wait a minute!"

The Inspector went away.

Ellery found himself pulling a cigaret to pieces. It was monstrous. Fat with meaning. He knew it.

The secret lay here.

But what secret?

He tried to contain himself as he waited. From somewhere he heard the Inspector's voice, in tones of manhood. God bless the shade of Alexander Graham Bell. What secret?

Suppose it turned out that Donald Katz had been older than Stella Petrucchi. By so little as one day. Suppose. What could it mean? What *could* it mean?

"Ellery."

"Well!"

"March 10, 1927."

"What?"

"Father Petrucchi says his sister Stella was born on March 10, 1927."

"*The same day?*"

They glared at each other.

Later they agreed that what they did was reflexive; on its merits it promised nothing. Their inquiry was a sort of conditioned response, the detective organism reacting to the stimulus of another uncomprehended fact by calling into play the nerves of pure habit. The futility of any conscious consideration of the identical-natal day phenomenon was too painfully apparent. In lieu of explanation—even of reasonable hypothesis—the Queens went back to fundamentals. Never mind what the fact might mean; first, was it a fact?

Ellery said to his father, "Let's check that right now," and the Inspector nodded and they went down into West 81st Street and climbed into the Inspector's car and Sergeant Velie drove them to the Manhattan Bureau of Vital Records and Statistics of the Department of Health.

Neither man uttered a sound on the ride downtown.

Ellery's head hurt. A thousand gears were trying to mesh and failing to do so. It was maddening, because he could not rid himself of the feeling that it was all so very simple. He was sure there was a rhythmic affinity in the facts but they were not functioning through a silly, aggravating failure of his perceptive machinery.

Finally, he shut the power off and was borne blank-minded to their destination.

"The original birth certificates," said Inspector Queen to the Registrar of Records. "No, we don't have the certificate numbers. But the names are Stella Petrucchi, female, and Donald Katz, male, and the date of birth in each case is, according to our information, March 10, 1927. Here, I've written the names down."

"You're sure they were both born in Manhattan, Inspector?"

"Yes."

The Registrar came back looking interested. "I see they were not only born on the same day, but—"

"March 10, 1927? In both cases?"

"Yes."

"Wait, Dad. Not only born on the same day, but what?"

"But the same doctor delivered them."

Ellery blinked.

"The same . . . doctor delivered them," said his father.

"May I see those certificates, please?" Ellery's voice was cracked again.

They stared at the signatures. Same handwriting. Both certificates signed:

Edward Cazalis M.D.

"Now, son, let's take it easy," Inspector Queen was saying, his hand muffling the phone. "Let's not jump. We don't know a thing. We're just bumbling around. We've got to go slow."

"I'll go as I damn please. Where's that list?"

"I'm getting it. They're getting it for me—"

"Cazalis, Cazalis. Here it is! Edward Cazalis. I told you it was the same one!"

"He delivered babies? I thought—"

"Started his medical career in the practice of obstetrics and gynecology. I knew there was something queer about his professional history."

"1927. He was still doing O.B. work as late as 1927?"

"Later! Here. It says—"

"Yes, Charley!"

Ellery dropped the medical directory. His father began writing as he listened. He wrote and wrote. It seemed as if he would never stop writing.

Finally, he did.

"Got 'em all?"

"Ellery. It just isn't reasonable that *all* of them—"

"Would you please get the original birth certificates," Ellery said, handing the Inspector's paper to the Registrar, "of the people listed here?"

"Dates of birth . . ." The Registrar ran his eye down the list. "All Manhattan born?"

"Most of them. Maybe all of them. Yes," said Ellery. "I think all of them. I'm sure of it."

"How can you be 'sure' of it?" snarled his father. "What do you mean, 'sure'? We know about some of them, but—"

"I'm sure of it. All born in Manhattan. Every last one. See if I'm wrong."

The Registrar went away.

They kept walking around each other like two dogs.

The clock on the wall crept along.

Once the Inspector said in a mutter: "This could mean . . . You know this could mean . . ."

Ellery turned around, baring his teeth. "I don't want to know what this 'could' mean. I'm sick of thinking of 'possibilities.' First things first, that's my motto. I just invented it. One thing per time. Step by step. B follows A, C follows B. One and one make two, and that's the limit of my arithmetic until I have to add two more."

"Okay, son, okay," said the Inspector; after that he muttered to himself.

And then the Registrar came back.

He was looking baffled, inquisitive, and uneasy.

Ellery set his back against the office door. "Give it to me slowly, please. One at a time. Start with Abernethy. Abernethy, Archibald Dudley—"

"Born May 24, 1905," said the Registrar. Then he said. "Edward Cazalis, M.D."

"Interesting. Interesting!" said Ellery. "Smith. Violette Smith."

"Born February 13, 1907," said the Registrar. "Edward Cazalis, M.D."

"Rian O'Reilly. Is good old Rian O'Reilly there, too?"

"They're all here, Mr. Queen. I really . . . Born December 23, 1908. Edward Cazalis, M.D."

"And Monica McKell?"

"July 2, 1912. Edward Cazalis, M.D. Mr. Queen . . ."

"Simone Phillips."

"October 11, 1913. Cazalis."

"Just 'Cazalis'?"

"Well, of course not," snapped the Registrar. "Edward Cazalis, M.D. See here, I really don't see the point of going through this name by name, Inspector Queen. I said they're all here—"

"Give the boy his head," said the Inspector. "He's been reined in a long time."

"Beatrice Willikins," said Ellery. "I'm especially interested in Beatrice Willikins. I should have seen it, though. Birth is the universal experience along with death; the two always played footsie under God's table. Why didn't I see that at once? Beatrice Willikins."

"April 7, 1917. The same doctor."

"The same doctor," nodded Ellery. He was smiling, a forbidding smile. "And that was a Negro baby, and it was the same doctor. A Hippocratic physician, Cazalis. The god of the maternity clinic, no doubt, on alternate Wednesdays. Come all ye pregnant, without regard for color or creed, fees adjusted according to the ability to pay. And Lenore Richardson?"

"January 29, 1924. Edward Cazalis, M. D."

"And that was the carriage trade. Thank you, sir, I believe that completes the roll. I take it these certificates are the untouchable trust of the Department of Health of the City of New York?"

"Yes."

"If anything happens to them," said Ellery, "I shall personally come down here with a derringer, sir, and shoot you dead. Meanwhile, no word of this is to get out. No whisper of a syllable. Do I make myself clear?"

"I don't mind telling you," said the Registrar stiffly, "that I don't like either your tone or your attitude, and—"

"Sir, you address the Mayor's Special Investigator. I beg your pardon," said Ellery, "I'm higher than the much-abused kite. May we use your office and your telephone for a few minutes—alone?"

The Registrar of Records went out with a bang.

But immediately the door opened and the Registrar stepped back into his office, shut the door with care, and said in a confidential tone, "A doctor who would go back to murder the people he himself brought into the world—why, gentlemen, he's nothing but a lunatic. How in hell did you let him weasel his way into your investigation?"

And the Registrar stamped out.

"This isn't," said the Inspector, "going to be easy."

"No."

"There's no evidence."

Ellery nibbled a thumbnail on the Registrar's desk.

"He'll have to be watched day and night.. Twenty-four out of twenty-four. We've got to know what he's doing every minute of every hour of the day."

Ellery continued to nibble.

"There mustn't be a tenth," said the Inspector, as if he were explaining something abstruse, top-secret, and of global importance. Then he laughed. "That cartoonist on the *Extra* doesn't know it but he's run out of tails. Let me get to that phone, Ellery."

"Dad."

"What, son?"

"We've got to have the run of that apartment for a few hours." Ellery took out a cigaret.

"Without a warrant?"

"And tip him off?"

The Inspector frowned.

"Getting rid of the maid ought to present no problem. Pick her day off. No, this is Friday and the chances are she won't be off till the middle of next week. I can't wait that long. Does she sleep in?"

"I don't know."

"I want to get in there over the weekend, if possible. Do they go to church?"

"How should I know? That cigaret won't draw, Ellery, because you haven't lit it. Hand me the phone."

Ellery handed it to him. "Whom are you going to put on him?"

"Hesse. Mac. Goldberg."

"All right."

"Police Headquarters."

"But I'd like to keep this thing," said Ellery, putting the cigaret back into his pocket, "exclusive and as far away from Centre Street as you can manage it."

His father stared.

"We really don't know a thing . . . Dad."

"What?"

Ellery uncoiled from the desk. "Come right home, will you?"

"You going *home?*"

But Ellery was already closing the door.

Inspector Queen called from his foyer, "Son?"

"Yes."

"Well, it's all set—" he stopped.

Celeste and Jimmy were on the sofa.

"Hello," said the Inspector.

"We were waiting for you, Dad."

His father looked at him.

"No. I haven't told them yet."

"Told us what?" demanded Jimmy.

"We know about the Katz boy," began Celeste. "But—"

"Or has the Cat walked again?"

"No." Ellery scrutinized them. "I'm ready," he said. "How about you?"

"Ready for what?"

"To go to work, Celeste."

Jimmy got up.

"Sit down, Jimmy." Jimmy sat down. "This time it's the McCoy."

Celeste grew quite pale.

"We're on the trail of something," said Ellery. "Exactly what, we're still not sure. But I think I can say that for the first time since the Cat got going there's something encouraging to work on."

"What do I do?" asked Jimmy.

"Ellery," said the Inspector.

"No, Dad, it's safer this way. I've thought it over very carefully."

"What do I do?" asked Jimmy again.

"I want you to get me a complete dossier on Edward Cazalis."

"Cazalis?"

"Dr. Cazalis?" Celeste was bewildered. "You mean—"

Ellery looked at her.

"Sorry!"

"Dossier on Cazalis," said Jimmy. "And?"

"Don't jump to conclusions, please. As I said, we don't know where we are . . . Jimmy, what I want is an intimate sketch of his life. Trivial details solicited. This isn't just a *Who's Who* assignment. I could do that myself. As a working newspaperman you're in a perfect position to dig up what I want, and without arousing suspicion."

"Yes," said Jimmy.

"No hint to anyone about what you're working on. That goes in spades for your people at the *Extra*. When can you start?"

"Right away."

"How long will it take you?"

"I don't know. Not long."

"Do you suppose you could have a good swatch of it for me by . . . say . . . tomorrow night?"

"I can try." Jimmy rose.

"By the way. Don't go near Cazalis."

"No."

"Or anyone connected with him closely enough so that word might get back to him that somebody's asking questions about him."

"I understand." Jimmy lingered.

"Yes?" said Ellery.

"What about Celeste?"

Ellery smiled.

"Got you, got you," said Jimmy, flushing. "Well, folks . . ."

"Celeste has nothing to do yet, Jimmy. But I do want you to go home, Celeste, pack a bag or two, and come back here to live."

"What?" said the Inspector and Jimmy together.

"That is, Dad, if you have no objection."

"Er, no. None at all. Glad to have you, Miss Phillips. The only thing is," said the Inspector, "if I'm to get any rest I'd better stake out *my* bed right now. Ellery, if there's a call—anything at all—be sure and wake me." And he retreated to his bedroom rather hurriedly.

"Live *here* you said," said Jimmy.

"Yes."

"Sounds tasty, but is it kosher?"

"Mr. Queen." Celeste hesitated.

"On second thought," said Jimmy, "this is a very delicate situation. It raises all sorts of possible conflicts."

"I'm going to need you, Celeste—when I do—on a moment's notice." Ellery frowned. "I can't predict when it will be. If it's late at night and you weren't at my fingertips—"

"No, sir," said Jimmy, "I can't say I'm wild about this development."

"Will you be quiet and let me think?" cried Celeste.

"I should tell you, too, that it may be quite dangerous."

"So taking it all in all," said Jimmy, "I don't think it's such a hot idea, darling. Do you?"

Celeste ignored him.

"I'll say it's dangerous! It's also downright immoral! What will people say?"

"Oh, muffle it, Jimmy," said Ellery. "Celeste, if my plans work out you're going to be right up there on the razor's edge. Now's the time for you to jump off. If you're going to do any jumping at all."

Celeste rose. "When do I move in?"

Ellery grinned. "Sunday night will do."

"I'll be here."

"You'll have my room. I'll bed down in the study."

"I hope," said Jimmy bitterly, "you'll both be very happy."

He watched Jimmy boost Celeste rudely into a taxi and then shamble angrily up the street.

Ellery began wandering about the living room.

He felt exhilarated. Jumpy.

Finally, he sat down in the armchair.

The hand that cut the cord.

Tightened it.

The end flows from the beginning.

The circular madness of paranoia.

God in the fingertips.

Was it possible?

Ellery had the feeling that he sat on the brink of a vast peace.

But he had to wait.

From some stronghold he had to summon the reserve to wait.

9

Inspector Queen phoned home a little after noon on Saturday to announce that everything was arranged for the following day.

"How long will we have?"

"Long enough."

"The maid?"

"She won't be there."

"How did you work it?"

"The Mayor," said Inspector Queen. "I got His Honor to invite the Cazalises for Sunday dinner."

Ellery shouted. "How much did you have to tell the Mayor?"

"Not very much. We communicated mostly by telepathy. But I think he's impressed with the necessity of not letting our friend go too soon after the brandy tomorrow. Dinner's called for 2:30 and there are going to be bigshot guests in afterward. Once Cazalis gets there, the Mayor says, he'll stay there."

"Brief me."

"We're to get a buzz the minute Cazalis sets foot in the Mayor's foyer." On that signal we shoot over to the apartment and get in through the service door by way of the basement and a back alley. Velie will have a duplicate key ready for us by tomorrow morning. The maid won't be back till late; she gets every other Sunday off and it happens tomorrow is her off-Sunday. The building help are being taken care of. We'll get in and out without being seen. Have you heard from Jimmy McKell?"

"He'll be up around ninish."

Jimmy showed up that night needing a shave, a clean shirt, and a drink, "but I can dispense with the first two items," he said, "providing Number 3 is produced forthwith," whereupon Ellery planted the decanter, a bottle of seltzer, and a glass at Jimmy's elbow and waited at least ten seconds before he made an encouraging sound in his throat.

"I'll bet the seismograph at Fordham is going crazy," said Jimmy. "Where do you sphinxes want it from?"

"Anywhere?"

"Well," said Jimmy, admiring his glass in the light, "the story of Edward Cazalis is kind of lopsided. I couldn't find out much about his family background and boyhood, just a few details. Seems he got away from home early—"

"Born in Ohio, wasn't he?" said the Inspector. He was measuring three fingers of Irish whiskey with care.

"Ironton, Ohio, 1882," nodded Jimmy McKell. "His father was a laborer of some sort—"

"Ironworker," said the Inspector.

"Whose report is this, anyway?" demanded Jimmy. "Or am I being checked up on?"

"I just happen to have a few facts, that's all," said the Inspector, holding his glass up to the light, too. "Go on, McKell."

"Anyway, Papa Cazalis was descended from a French soldier who settled in Ohio after the French and Indian War. About Mama I couldn't find out." Jimmy looked at the old gentleman belligerently, but when that worthy downed his wiskey without saying anything Jimmy continued. "Your hero was one of the youngest of fourteen ill-fed, ill-clothed, and ill-housed brats. A lot of them died off in childhood. The survivors and their descendants are strewn around the Middle West landscape. As far as I can tell, your Eddie's the only one who made anything of himself."

"Any criminals in the family?" asked Ellery.

"Sir, don't asperse the rank and file of our glorious heritage," said Jimmy, pouring another drink for himself. "Or are you taking a refresher course in sociology? I couldn't find anything special in that line." He said suddenly, "What are you digging for?"

"Keep going, Jimmy."

"Well, Edward seems to have been a very hep cookie. Not a prodigy, you understand. But precocious. And very ambitious. Poor but honest, he burned the midnight oil, worked his industrious little fingers to the bone, and got a southern Ohio hardware king all hopped up about him; in fact, he became this tycoon's protégé. A real Horatio Alger character. Up to a point, that is."

"What do you mean by that?"

"Well, in my book young Eduardo was something of a heelo. If there's anything worse than a rich snob, it's a poor one. The hardware hidalgo, whose name was William Waldemar Gaeckel, lifted the bloke clean out of his lousy environment, scrubbed him up, got him some decent clothes, and sent him away to a fancy prep school in Michigan . . . and there's no record that Cazalis ever went back to Ironton even on a visit. He ditched pa and ma, he ditched Tessie, Steve, and the other fifty thousand brothers and sisters, and after old Gaeckel sent him proudly to New York to study medicine he ditched Gaeckel, too—or maybe Mr. G. got wise to him; anyway, they had no further relations. Cazalis got his M.D. from Columbia in 1903."

"1903," murmured Ellery. "Aged 21. One of fourteen children, and he became interested in obstetrics."

"Very funny," grinned Jimmy.

"Not very." Ellery's voice was chill. "Any information on the obstetrical specialty?"

Jimmy McKell nodded, looking curious.

"Let's have it."

Jimmy referred to the back of a smudged envelope. "Seems that back in those days medical schools weren't standardized. In some the courses were two years, in others four, and there weren't any obstetrical or gynecological internships or residencies . . . it says here. Very few men did obstetrics or gynecology exclusively, and those who did became specialists mostly by apprenticeship. When Cazalis graduated from Columbia—with honors, by the way—he hooked onto a New York medico named Larkland—"

"John F.," said the Inspector.

"John F.," nodded Jimmy. "East 20s somewhere. Dr. Larkland's practice was entirely O.B. and gyne but it was apparently enough to keep Cazalis with him about a year and a half. Then in 1905 Cazalis started his own specializing practice—"

"Just when in 1905?"

"February. Larkland died that month of cancer, and Cazalis took over his practice."

Then Archibald Dudley Abernethy's mother had been old Dr. Larkland's patient and young Cazalis had inherited her, thought Ellery. It soothed him. Clergymen's wives in 1905 were not attended by 23-year-old physicians except in extraordinary circumstances.

"Within a few years," continued Jimmy, "Cazalis was one of the leading specialists in the East. As I get the picture, he'd moved in on the ground floor and by 1911 or '12, when the speciality had become defined, he had one of the biggest practices in New York. He wasn't a money-grubber, I understand, although he made pots. He was always more interested in the creative side of his profession, pioneered a couple of new techniques, did a lot of clinic work, and so on. I've got lots of dope here on his scientific achievements—"

"Skip it. What else?"

"Well, there's his war record."

"World War I."

"Yes."

"When did he go in?"

"Summer of 1917."

"Interesting, Dad. Beatrice Willikins was born on April 7 that year, the day after Congress declared war on Germany. Must have been one of Cazalis's last deliveries before getting into uniform." The Inspector said nothing. "What about his war record?"

"Tops. He went into the Medical Corps as a captain and came out a full colonel. Surgery up front—"

"Ever wounded?"

"No, but he did spend a few months in a French rest area in '18, and in early '19 after the war ended. Under treatment for—I quote—'exhaustion and shell shock.' "

Ellery glanced at his father, but the Inspector was pouring his fourth, fifth, and sixth finger of whiskey.

"Apparently it wasn't anything serious." Jimmy glanced at his envelope. "He was sent home from France as good as new and when he was mustered out—"

"In 1919."

"—he went back to his specialty. By the end of 1920 he'd worked up his practice again and was going great guns."

"Still doing obstetrics and gynecology exclusively?"

"That's right. He was then in his late 30s, approaching his prime, and in the next five years or so he really hit the top." Jimmy hauled out another envelope. "Let's see . . . yes, 1926. In 1926 he met Mrs. Cazalis through her sister, Mrs. Richardson—and married her. She was one of the Merigrews of Bangor. Old New England family—blood transparent, blue, and souring, but I'm told she was a genetic sport, very pretty, if you went for Dresden china. Cazalis was 44 and his bride was only 19, but apparently he had Dresden china ideas; it seems to have been an epic romance. They had a fancy wedding in Maine and a long honeymoon. Paris, Vienna, and Rome.

"I find," said Jimmy McKell, "I find nothing to indicate that the Cazalises have been anything but happily married—in case you're interested. No whisper about him, in spite of all the ladies in his medical life, and for Mrs. Cazalis there's never been any man but her husband.

"They ran into hard luck, though. In 1927 Mrs. Cazalis had her first baby and early in 1930 her second—"

"And lost both in the delivery room," nodded Ellery. "Cazalis mentioned that the night I met him."

"He felt terrible about it, I'm told. He'd taken fanatical care of his wife during both pregnancies and he'd done the deliveries himself—what's the matter?"

"Cazalis was his wife's obstetrician?"

"Yes." Jimmy looked at them both. Inspector Queen was now at the window, pulling at his fingers behind his back.

"Isn't that unethical?" asked the Inspector casually. "A doctor delivering his own wife?"

"Hell, no. Most doctors don't do it because they're emotionally involved with the woman in labor. They doubt their ability to maintain—where's that note?—to maintain 'the necessary objective, detached professional attitude.' But many doctors do, and Dr. Edward Cazalis of the Tearing Twenties was one of them."

"After all," said the Inspector to Ellery, as if Ellery were arguing the point, "he was a big man in his field."

"The type man," said Jimmy, "so supremely egocentric he'd maybe become a psychiatrist. Hm?"

"I don't think that's quite fair to psychiatrists," laughed Ellery. "Any data on the two babies he lost?"

"All I know about it is that both babies were toughies and that after the second Mrs. Cazalis couldn't have any more children. I gathered that they were both breeches."

"Go on."

The Inspector came back and sat down with his bottle.

"In the year 1930, a few months after they lost their second child, we find Cazalis having a breakdown."

"Breakdown," said Ellery.

"Breakdown?" said the Inspector.

"Yes. He'd been driving himself, he was 48—his collapse was attributed to overwork. By this time he'd been practicing obstetrical and gynecological medicine for over twenty-five years, he was a wealthy man, so he gave up his practice and Mrs. Cazalis took him traveling. They went on a world cruise—you know the kind, through the Canal up to Seattle, then across the Pacific—and by the time they reached Europe Cazalis was practically well again. Only, he wasn't. While they were in Vienna—this was early in '31—he had a setback."

"Setback?" said Ellery sharply. "You mean another breakdown?"

" 'Setback' was the word. It was nerves again, or mental depression or something. Anyway, being in Vienna, he went to see Béla Seligmann and—"

"Who's Béla Seligmann?" demanded Inspector Queen.

"Who's Béla Seligmann, he says. Why, Béla Seligmann is—"

"There was Freud," said Ellery, "and there's Jung, and there's Seligmann. Like Jung, the old boy hangs on."

"Yes, he's still around. Seligmann got out of Austria just in time to observe *Anschluss* from an honored bleacher seat in London, but he went back to Vienna after the little cremation ceremony in the Berlin Chancellery and I believe he's still there. He's over 80 now, but in 1931 he was at the height of his powers. Well, it seems Seligmann took a great interest in Cazalis, because he snapped him out of whatever was wrong with him and aroused in the guy an ambition to become a psychiatrist."

"He studied with Seligmann?"

"For four years—one under par, I'm told. Cazalis spent some time in Zürich, too, and then in 1935 the Cazalises returned to the States. He put in over a year getting hospital experience and early in 1937—let's see, that would have made him 55—he set himself up in the practice of psychiatry in New York. The rest is history." Jimmy laced his flagging glass.

"That's all you got, Jimmy?"

"Yes. No." Jimmy referred hastily to his last envelope. "There's one other item of interest. About a year ago—last October—Cazalis broke down again."

"Broke down?"

"Now don't go asking me for clinical details. I don't have access to medical records. Maybe it was plain pooping out from overwork—he has a racehorse's energy and he's never spared himself. And, of course, he was 66. It wasn't much of a breakdown but it must have scared him, because he started to whittle down his practice. I understand he hasn't taken a new case in a year. He's polishing off the patients under treatment and transferring long-termers to other men when he can. I'm told that within a short time he'll be retiring." Jimmy tossed his collection of disreputable envelopes on the table. "End of report."

The envelopes lay there.

"Thanks, Jimmy," said Ellery in a curiously final voice.

"Is it what you wanted?"

"What I wanted?"

"Well, expected."

Ellery said carefully, "It's a very interesting report."

Jimmy set his glass down. "I take it you shamans want to be alone."

Neither man replied.

"Never let it be said," said Jimmy, picking up his hat, "that a McKell couldn't recognize a brush."

"Fine job, McKell, just fine," said the Inspector. "Night."

"Keep in touch with me, Jimmy."

"Mind if I drift in with Celeste tomorrow night?"

"Not in the least."

"Thanks! Oh." Jimmy paused in the foyer. "There's one little thing."

"What's that?"

"Let me know when you clap him in irons, will you?"

When the door closed Ellery sprang to his feet.

His father poured another drink. "Here, have one."

But Ellery mumbled, "That touch of so-called shell shock in the first war. Those recurring breakdowns. And in the middle age the obvious attempt to compensate for something in that sudden, apparently unprepared-for interest in psychiatry. It fits, it fits."

"Drink it," said his father.

"Then there's the whole egocentric pattern. It's unusual for a man of 50 to begin studying psychiatry, to set up in practice at 55, and to make a success of it to boot. His drive must be gigantic.

"Look at his early history. A man who set out to prove something to—whom? himself? society? And who wouldn't let anything stand in his way. Who used every tool that came to hand and tossed it aside when it outlived its immediate usefulness. Professionally ethical always, but in the narrowest sense: I'm sure of it. And then marriage to a girl less than half his age—and not just any girl; it had to be a Merigrew of Maine.

"And those two tragic confinements, and . . . guilt. Guilt, decidedly: immediately that first breakdown. Overwork, yes; but not his body. His conscience."

"Aren't you doing an awful lot of guessing?" asked Inspector Queen.

"We're not dealing with clues you can put on a slide. I wish I knew more!"

"You're spilling it, son."

"The conflicts set in, and from then on it's a question of time. A gradual spreading of the warp. A sickening, a corruption of the whole psychic process—whatever the damned mechanism is. Somewhere along the line a personality that was merely paranoid in potential crossed over and became paranoid in fact. I wonder . . ."

"You wonder what?" asked his father when Ellery paused.

"I wonder if in either of those deliveries the infant died of strangulation."

"Of *what?*"

"Umbilical. The umbilical cord wound around its neck."

The old man stared.

Suddenly he bounced to his feet.

"Let's go to bed."

They found the white index card marked *Abernethy, Sarah-Ann* within twenty seconds of opening the file drawer labeled 1905-10. It was the eleventh card in the file. A blue card was clipped to it marked *Abernethy, Archibald Dudley, m., b. May 24, 1905, 10:26 A.M.*

There were two old-fasioned filing cabinets of walnut, each containing three drawers. Neither had locks or catches, but the storage closet in which they found the cabinets had to be unlocked, a feat Sergeant Velie performed without difficulty. It was a large cabinet filled with the memorabilia and bric-a-brackery of the Cazalis household; but on the side where the cabinets stood were also a glass case of obstetrical and surgical instruments and a worn medical bag.

The records of his psychiatric practice were housed in modern steel cabinets in his inner office. These cabinets were locked.

The Queens, however, spent all their time in the crowded musty-smelling closet.

Mrs. Abernethy's card recorded an ordinary case history of pregnancy. Archibald Dudley's recorded the data of birth and infant development. It was evident that Dr. Cazalis had provided the customary pediatric care of the period.

Ninety-eight cards later he ran across one marked *Smith, Eulalie* to which was clipped a pink card marked *Smith, Violette, f., b. Feb. 13, 1907, 6:55 P.M.*

One hundred and sixty-four cards beyond the Smith cards they found the entries for *O'Reilly, Maura B.* and *O'Reilly, Rian, m., b. Dec. 23, 1908, 4:36 A.M.* Rian O'Reilly's card was blue.

In less than an hour they located the cards of all nine of the Cat's victims. There was no difficulty. They were arranged in chronological order in the drawers, each drawer was labeled with its year-sequence, and it was simply a matter of going through the drawers card by card.

Ellery sent Sergeant Velie for the Manhattan telephone directory. He spent some time with it.

"It's so damnably logical," complained Ellery, "once you have the key. We couldn't understand why the Cat's victims should be successively younger when there was no apparent connection among them. Obviously, Cazalis simply followed the chronology of his records. He went back to the beginning of his medical practice and systematically worked his way forward.''

"In forty-four years a lot had changed," said the Inspector thoughtfully. "Patients had died off. Children he'd brought into the world had grown up and moved to other localities. And it's nineteen years at a minimum since he had any medical contact with any of them. So most of these cards must be as obsolete as the dodo.''

"Exactly. Unless he was willing or prepared to undertake a complicated search, he couldn't hope to make a clean sweep. So he'd tend to concentrate on the cards bearing names most easily traced. Since he'd had a Manhattan practice, the obvious reference was to the Manhattan phone book. Undoubtedly he began with the first card in his files. It's Sylvan Sacopy, a boy born to a Margaret Sacopy in March of 1905. Well, neither name is to be found in the current Manhattan directory. So he went on to the second card. Again no luck. I've checked every name on the first ten listings and not one is to be found in the Manhattan book. Abernethy's the first card with a current listing. And Abernethy was the first victim. And while I haven't checked all the names on the ninety-seven cards between Abernethy and Violette Smith, I've taken enough of a sampling to indicate that Violette Smith became the Cat's second victim for exactly the same reason: despite the fact that her card is Number 109, she had the misfortune to be Number 2 in the phone book checkback. There's no doubt in my mind that the same thing is true of all the others.''

"We'll check.''

"Then there was the baffling business of the nonmarital status of all but one of the victims. Now that we know how Cazalis picked them, the answer is childishly clear. Of the nine victims, six were women and three were men. Of the three men, one was married and two were not—but Donald Katz was a youngster: it was a reasonable average. But of the six women not one was married. Why were the female victims consistently single? Because when a woman marries *her name changes!* The only women Cazalis could trace through the phone book were those whose names had remained the same as the names appearing on his case cards.

"And the curious color notes that ran through the crimes,'' continued Ellery. "That was the most obvious clue of all, damn it. Blue cords for males, salmon-pink for females. Maybe it was the salmony cast of the pink that threw me off. But salmon *is* a shade of pink, and pink and blue are the traditional colors for infants.''

"It's a sentimental touch,'' muttered his father, "I could do without.''

"Sentimental nothing—it's as significant as the color of hell. It indicates that deep in the chasm of his mind Cazalis regards his victims as infants still. When he strangled Abernethy with a blue cord he was really strangling a boy baby . . . using a cord to return him to limbo? The umbilical symbolism was there from the start. The murderous colors of childbirth.''

From somewhere in the apartment came the peaceful sounds of drawers opening.

"Velie,'' said the Inspector. "God, if only some of these cords are here.''

But Ellery said, "And that tantalizing gap between Victims 6 and 7—Beatrice Willikins to Lenore Richardson. Up to that point the age differential between successive victims was never more than three years. Suddenly, seven.''

"The war—''

"But he was back in practice by 1919 or '20, and Lenore Richardson was born in '24.''

"Maybe he couldn't locate one born during those years.''

"Not true. Here's one, for instance, born in September 1921, Harold Marzupian. It's in the directory. Here's another, January 1922, Benjamin Treudlich. And he's in the directory. I found at least five others born before 1924, and there are undoubtedly more. Still, he bypassed them to strike at Lenore Richardson, 25. Why? Well, what happened between the murders of Beatrice Willikins and Lenore Richardson?"

"What?"

"It's going to sound stuffy, but the fact is that between those two homicides the Mayor appointed a Special Investigator to look into the Cat murders."

The Inspector raised his brows.

"No, think about it. There was an enormous splash of publicity. My name and mission were talked and written about sensationally. My appointment couldn't fail to have made an impression on the Cat. He must have asked himself what the sudden turn of events meant to his chances of continuing his murder spree with safety. The newspapers, you'll recall, spread out the whole hog. They rehashed old cases of mine, spectacular solutions—Superman stuff. Whether the Cat knew much about me before that, you may be sure he read everything that was printed and listened to everything that was broadcast afterwards."

"You mean he was scared of you?" grinned Inspector Queen.

"It's much more likely," Ellery retorted, "that he welcomed the prospect of a duel. Remember that we're dealing with a special kind of madman—a man trained in the science of the human mind and personality and at the same time a paranoiac in full flight, with systematized delusions of his own greatness. A man like that would likely consider my appearance in the investigation a challenge; and it's borne out by the seven-year jump from Willikins to Richardson."

"How so?"

"What's the outstanding fact about the Richardson girl in relation to Cazalis?"

"She was his wife's niece."

"So Cazalis deliberately skipped over any number of available victims to murder his own niece, knowing that this would draw him into the case naturally. Knowing he'd be bound to meet me on the scene. Knowing that under the circumstances it would be a simple matter to get himself drawn into the investigation as one of the investigators. Why did Mrs. Cazalis insist on her husband's offering his services? Because he'd often 'discussed' his 'theories' about the Cat with her! Cazalis had prepared the way carefully by playing on his wife's attachment to Lenore even before Lenore's murder. If Mrs. Cazalis hadn't brought the subject up, he would have volunteered. But she did, as he knew she would."

"And there he was," grunted the Inspector, "on the inside, in a position to know just what we were doing—"

"In a position to revel in his own power." Ellery shrugged. "I told you I was rusty. I was aware all along of the possibility of such a move on the Cat's part. Didn't I suspect Celeste and Jimmy of exactly that motive? Couldn't get it out of my mind. And all the while there was Cazalis—"

"No cords."

They jumped.

But it was only Sergeant Velie in the closet doorway.

"They ought to be here, Velie," snapped the Inspector. "How about those steel files in his office?"

"We'd have to get Bill Devander down to open them. I can't. Not without leaving traces."

"How much time do we have?" The Inspector pulled on his watch chain.

But Ellery was pinching his lip. "To do the job properly would take more time than we have today, Dad. I doubt that he keeps the cords here, anyway. Too much danger that his wife or the maid might find them."

"That's what I said," said Sergeant Velie heatedly. "I said to the Inspector—remember?—I said, Inspector, he's got 'em stashed in a public locker some place . . ."

"I know what you said, Velie, but they might also be right here in the apartment. We've got to have those cords, Ellery. The D.A. told me the other day that if we could connect a find of the same type of blue and pink cords with some individual, he'd be willing to go into court pretty nearly on that alone."

"We can give the D.A.," said Ellery suddenly, "a much better case."

"How?"

Ellery put his hand on one of the walnut filing cabinets.

"All we have to do is put ourselves in Cazalis's place. He's certainly not finished—the cards on Petrucchi and Katz took him only as far as March 10, 1927, and his obstetrical records extend over three years beyond that."

"I don't quite get it," complained the Sergeant.

But the Inspector was already at work on the drawer labeled *1927—30*.

The birth card following Donald Katz's was pink and it recorded the name "Rhutas, Roselle."

There was no Rhutas listed in the directory.

The next card was blue. "Finkleston, Zalmon."

There was no such name in the directory.

Pink. "Heggerwitt, Adelaide."

"Keep going, Dad."

The Inspector took out another card. "Collins, Barclay M."

"Plenty of Collinses . . . But no Barclay M."

"The mother's card gives her Christian name as—"

"It doesn't matter. All his victims have had personal listings in the phone book. I checked a few parents' names before, where the victim wasn't listed, and I found two in the book; there must be lots of others. But he passed those up, I imagine because it would have increased the amount of investigating he'd have to do and by that much increased the risk. So far at least he's taken only directly traceable cases. What's the next card?"

"Frawlins, Constance."

"No."

Fifty-nine cards later the Inspector read, "Soames, Marilyn."

"How do you spell that?"

"S-o-a-m-e-s."

"S-o-a . . . Soames. Here it is! Soames, Marilyn!"

"Let me see that!"

It was the only Soames listed. The address was 486 East 29th Street.

"Off First Avenue," muttered the Inspector. "Within spitting distance of Bellevue Hospital."

"What are the mother's and father's names? On the white card?"

"Edna L. and Frank P. Father's occupation given as 'postal employee.' "

"Could we get a quick check on Marilyn Soames and her family? While we're waiting here?"

"It's getting late . . . I'll ring the Mayor first, make sure he hangs on to Cazalis. Velie, where's the phone?"

"There's a couple in his office."

"No household phone?"

"In a phone closet off the foyer."

The Inspector went away.

When he returned, Ellery said, "They're not calling back here, are they?"

"What do you think I am, Ellery?" The Inspector was peevish. "We'd be in a fine mess if we answered a personal call! I'm calling them back in half an hour. Velie, if the phone rings out there don't answer it."

"What do you think *I* am!"

They waited.

Sergeant Velie kept tramping about the foyer.

The Inspector kept pulling out his watch.

Ellery picked up the pink card.

Soames, Marilyn, f., b. Jan. 2, 1928, 7:13 A.M.

Add to population of Manhattan one female. Vital statistics of birth. Recorded by the hand of death.

Onset of labor	*Natural*
Position at delivery	*L.O.T.*
Duration of labor	*10 hrs.*
Normal	*Normal*
Anaesthesia	*Morphine-scopalamine*
Operative	*Forceps*
Crede—prophylaxis	*Crede*
Period gestation	*40 wks.*
Respiration	*Spontaneous*
Method of resuscitation	*None*
Injuries at birth	*None*
Congenital anomalies	*None*
Medication p-n.	*None*
Weight	*6 lbs. 9 oz.*
Length	*49cm.*

And so on, unto the tenth day. *Behavior of Baby . . . Type of supplemental or complemental feeding . . . Disturbances noted: Digestive, Respiratory, Circulatory, Genito-urinary, Nervous system, Skin, Umbilicus . . .*

A conscientious physician. Death was always conscientious. Digestive. Circulatory. Umbilicus. Especially umbilicus. *The place where the extraembryonic structures are continuous with those of the body proper of the embryo,* anatomical and zoological definition. *To which is attached the umbilical cord connecting the fetus of the mammal with the placenta . . . Jelly of Wharton . . . Epiblastic epithelium . . .* No mention of tussah silk.

But that was to come twenty-one years later.

Meanwhile, pink cards for females, blue cards for males.

Systematized. The scientific mumbo jumbo of parturition.

It was all down here on a card in faded pen-marks. God's introductory remarks on another self-contained unit of moist, red, squirming life.

And even as the Lord giveth, He taketh away.

When the Inspector set the telephone down he was a little pale. "Mother's name Edna, nee Lafferty. Father's name Frank Pellman Soames, occupation post office clerk. Daughter Marilyn is public stenographer. Aged 21."

Tonight, tomorrow, next week, next month, Marilyn Soames, aged 21, occupation public stenographer, of 486 East 29th Street, Manhattan, would be plucked from the files of Dr. Edward Cazalis by the hand that had pulled her into the world and he would begin measuring her for a salmon-pink cord of tussah silk.

And he would set out on his quest, cord in hand, and later the cartoonist of the *New York Extra* would sharpen his pens and refashion his Cat to wave a tenth tail and an eleventh in the form of a question mark.

"Only this time we'll be waiting for him," Ellery said that night in the Queen living room. "We're going to catch him with a cord in his hands as close to the actual instant of attack as we can safely manage. It's the only way we can be sure of slapping the Cat label on him so that it sticks."

Celeste and Jimmy were both looking frightened.

From his armchair Inspector Queen kept watching the girl.

"Nothing's been left to chance," said Ellery. "Cazalis has been under twenty-four-hour observation since Friday, Marilyn Soames since late this afternoon. We're getting hourly reports on Cazalis's movements in a special office at Police Headquarters, where Sergeant Velie and another man are on continuous duty. These two officers are instructed to call us on our private line the moment a suspicious movement on Cazalis's part is phoned in.

"Marilyn Soames knows nothing of what's going on; no one in her family does. To let them in on it would only make them nervous and their actions might get Cazalis suspicious. Then we'd have the whole thing to do over again or it might scare him off permanently—or for a very long time. We can't afford to wait. We can't afford to miss.

"We're getting hourly reports on the girl, too. We're almost completely set."

"Almost?" said Jimmy.

The word hung among them in a peculiarly unpleasant way.

"Celeste, I've been holding you in reserve," said Ellery. "For the most important and certainly the riskiest job of all. As an alternate to Jimmy. If Cazalis's next available victim had turned out to be male, I had Jimmy. Female—you."

"What job would that be?" asked Jimmy cautiously.

"My original idea was to substitute one of you for the next victim indicated by Cazalis's files."

And there was McKell, out of the cubist tangle of his arms and legs and glaring down at Ellery. "The answer is no. You're not going to turn this woman into a slaughterhouse beef. I won't have it—me, McKell!"

"I told you we should have locked this character up as a public nuisance, Ellery."

The Inspector snapped, "Sit down, McKell."

"I'll stand up and you'll like it!"

Ellery sighed.

"You're so cute, Jimmy," said Celeste. "But I'm not going to run out no matter what Mr. Queen has in mind. Now won't you sit down and mind your own business like a lambie-pie?"

"No!" roared Jimmy. "Do you enjoy the prospect of getting your silly neck wrung? Even this vast intellect here can have his off-days. Besides, when was he ever human? I know all about *him*. Sits in this control tower of his and fiddles with little dials. Talk about delusions of grandeur! If he runs your neck into Cazalis's noose, what's the difference between him and Cazalis? They're both paranoiacs! Anyway, the whole idea is plain damn imbecility. How could you fool Cazalis into thinking you were somebody else? Who are you, Mata Hari?"

"You didn't let me finish, Jimmy," said Ellery patiently. "I said that was my original notion. But on second thought I've decided it's too dangerous."

"Oh," said Jimmy.

"Not for Celeste—she'd have been as well protected as Marilyn Soames is going to be—but for the sake of the trap. The Soames girl is going to be his objective; he's going to scout her, as he's scouted the others; it's safest to string along with her."

"I might have known even your reason for *not* making Cat bait out of her would be non-human!"

"Then what's my job, Mr. Queen?—Jimmy, shut up."

"As I said, we have every reason to believe Cazalis makes some sort of preliminary investigation of his victims. Well, we've got Marilyn covered every time she steps out of the Soames flat. But obviously with detectives we can only work from outside. That takes care of physical protection, but it doesn't give us a line on— for example—telephone calls.

"We could tap Cazalis's phones, on the chance that he'll try to contact Marilyn or her family from his home. But Cazalis is informed as well as shrewd, and the public's been made conscious of official wiretapping in the past year or two—the technique, what to listen for, have been well publicized; we can't chance Cazalis's getting suspicious. Besides, it's unthinkable that he'd be foolish enough to use his own phones for such a purpose; that he's cautious as well as daring is proved by his operations. So if he tries a phone approach it will undoubtedly be from a public booth somewhere, and that we can't prepare for.

"We could tap the Soames phone, but here again we can't run the risk of arousing the family's suspicions; too much depends on the Soameses behaving normally in the next few weeks.

"Or Cazalis may not phone at all. He may try a correspondence contact."

"It's true we've found no evidence of approaches by letter in previous cases," put in the Inspector, "but that doesn't mean there haven't been any; and even if he's never done it before, that's no guarantee he won't do it now."

"So a letter under an assumed name is possible," said Ellery. "And while we could intercept the United States mail . . ." Ellery shook his head. "Let's say it just wouldn't be practicable.

"In either event, our safest course is to plant somebody we can trust in the Soames household. Somebody who'll live with the family on a round-the-clock basis for the next two or three weeks."

"And that's me," said Celeste.

"Will somebody please tell me," came a choked voice from the sofa, "if this is or is not a nightmare concocted by Dali, Lombroso, and Sax Rohmer?"

But no one paid any attention to him. Celeste was frowning. "Wouldn't he recognize me, though, Mr. Queen? From the time when he—?"

"Scouted Simone?"

"And from those pictures of me in the papers afterward."

"I rather think he concentrated on Simone and didn't pay too much attention to you, Celeste. And I've checked the file on your newspaper photos and they're uniformly execrable. Still, it's possible he'd recognize you—yes. If he saw you, Celeste. But we'd make very sure," smiled Ellery, "that he didn't. This would be strictly an inside job and you'd never come out on the streets except under rigidly controlled conditions."

Ellery glanced at his father, and the Inspector got up.

"I don't mind telling you, Miss Phillips," began Inspector Queen, "that I've been dead set against this. This job calls for a trained operative."

"But," said Jimmy McKell bitterly.

"But two facts exist which made me let Ellery change my mind. One is that for years you nursed a paralyzed invalid. The other is that one of the younger children in the Soames family—there are four, with Marilyn—a boy of 7, broke his hip a month ago and he was brought home from the hospital only last week in a cast.

"We've had a medical report on this boy. He's got to stay in bed and he's going to need a lot of care for the next few weeks. A trained nurse isn't necessary, but a practical nurse is. We've already had an intermediary in touch with the family doctor, a Dr. Myron Ulberson, and it turns out that Dr. Ulberson had been trying to find a practical nurse for the child but so far hasn't had any luck." The Inspector shrugged. "The boy's accident could be a great break for us, Miss Phillips, if you felt qualified to act the part of a practical nurse in a broken hip case."

"Oh, yes!"

"Besides being fed, washed, and amused," said Ellery, "the boy will need massages, I understand, and care of that sort. Do you think you could handle it, Celeste?"

"I did exactly that kind of nursing for Simone, and Simone's doctor often told me I was better than a lot of trained nurses he knew."

The Queens looked at each other, and the Inspector waved.

"Tomorrow morning, Celeste," said Ellery crisply, "you'll be taken to see Dr. Ulberson. He knows you're not a working practical nurse and that your presence in the Soames household is required for a highly secret purpose not connected with the ostensible one. Dr. Ulberson's been very tough—we had to get a high official of the City to give him personal reassurances that this is all in the interests of the Soames family. Just the same, he's going to test you unmercifully."

"I know how to move patients in bed, give hypos—I'll satisfy him, I know I will."

"Just turn on some of that charm," growled Jimmy. "The kind you befogged me with."

"I'll do it on merit, McKell!"

"I have a hunch you will," said Ellery. "By the way, you'd better not use your real name, even with Dr. Ulberson."

"How about McKell?" sneered McKell. "In fact, how about changing your name to McKell and to hell with this lady-dick opium dream?"

"One more crack out of you, McKell," snapped the Inspector, "and I'll personally escort you to the door on the end of my foot!"

"Okay, if you're going to be that selfish," muttered Jimmy; and he curled up on the sofa like an indignant sloth.

Celeste took his hand. "My real family name is Martin, pronounced the French way, but I could use it as just plain English-sounding Martin—"

"Perfect."

"—and then Mother Phillips used to call me Suzanne. It's my middle name. Even Simone called me Sue sometimes."

"Sue Martin. All right, use that. If you satisfy Dr. Ulberson, he'll recommend you to Mr. and Mrs. Soames as a live-in nurse and you can go right to work. You will charge, of course, the prevailing practical nurse fee, whatever it happens to be. We'll find that out for you."

"Yes, Mr. Queen."

"Stand up a minute, Miss Phillips," said Inspector Queen.

Celeste was surprised. "Yes?"

The Inspector looked her up and down.

Then he walked around her.

"At this point," said Jimmy, "they usually whistle."

"That's the trouble," rasped the Inspector. "Miss Phillips I suggest you deglamorize yourself. Meaning no disrespect to the highly important profession of practical nursing, if you look like a practical nurse I look like Olivia de Havilland."

"Yes, Inspector," said Celeste, blushing.

"No makeup except a little lipstick. And not too vivid."

"Yes, sir."

"Simplify your hairdo. Take off your nail polish and clip your nails. And wear your plainest clothes. You've got to make yourself look older and more—more tired-looking."

"Yes, sir," said Celeste.

"Do you have a white uniform?"

"No—"

"We'll get you a couple. And some white stockings. How about low-heeled white shoes?"

"I have a pair that will do, Inspector."

"You'll also need a practical nurse's bag, equipped, which we'll provide."

"Yes, sir."

"How about a pearlhandled heater?" suggested Jimmy. "No eye-ette genuine without one."

But when they ignored him he got up and went to the Scotch decanter.

"Now as to this detective business," said Ellery. "Aside from nursing the Soames boy, you're to keep your eyes and ears open at all times. Marilyn Soames operates her stenographic business from home—she does manuscript typing and that sort of thing; that's why she has a phone in her name. Marilyn's working at home is another break; it will give you an opportunity to get friendly with her. She's only two years your junior and, from the little we've been able to learn so far, a nice, serious-minded girl."

"Gads," said Jimmy from the cellaret. "You have just described Operative 29-B." But he was beginning to sound proud.

"She seldom goes out socially, she's interested in books—very much your type, Celeste, even physically. Best of all, she's mad about her kid brother, the sick boy, so you'll have something in common right off."

"You're to pay particular attention to phone calls," said the Inspector.

"Yes, find out the substance of every conversation, especially if the caller is a stranger to the Soameses."

"And that goes whether the call is for Marilyn or anyone else."

"I understand, Inspector."

"You'll have to manage to read every letter Marilyn gets, too," Ellery said. "The whole family's mail, if possible. In general, you're to observe everything that happens in the household and to report it to us in detail. I want daily reports as a matter of routine."

"Do I report by phone? That might be hard."

"You're not to use the phone there except in an emergency. We'll arrange meeting places in the neighborhood of East 29th and First and Second Avenues. A different spot each night."

"Me, too," said Jimmy.

"At a certain time each night after Stanley's gone to sleep—you'll have to set the time for us after you get in and find out more about the setup—you'll go out for a walk. Establish the habit the very first night, so that the family comes to take your nightly absences as matter of course. If something should come up to prevent your leaving the house at the agreed time, we'll wait at the meeting place till you can get away, even if it means waiting all night."

"Me, too," said Jimmy.

"Any questions?"

Celeste pondered. "I can't think of any."

Ellery looked at her rather nakedly, Jimmy thought. "I can't stress too much how important you may be in this thing, Celeste. Of course, the break may come from outside and you won't be involved at all, which is what we're all hoping. But if it doesn't, you're our Trojan filly. Everything may then depend on you."

"I'll do my best," said Celeste in a smallish voice.

"By the way, how do you feel about this?"

"Just . . . fine."

"We'll go over all this again in greater detail after you've seen Dr. Ulberson tomorrow." Ellery put an arm around her. "You'll stay here tonight as we arranged."

And Jimmy McKell snarled, *"Me, too!"*

10

Celeste would have felt better about having to play female Janus in the Soames household if she had found Marilyn's father a burly lecher, Mrs. Soames a shrew, Marilyn a slut, and the youngsters a pack of street rats. But the Soameses turned out insidiously nice.

Frank Pellman Soames was a skinny, squeezed-dry-looking man with the softest, burriest voice. He was a senior clerk at the main post office on Eighth Avenue at 33rd Street and he took his postal responsibilities as solemnly as if he had been called to office by the President himself. Otherwise he was inclined to make little jokes. He invariably brought something home with him after work—a candy bar, a bag of salted peanuts, a few sticks of bubble gum—to be divided among the three younger children with Rhadamanthine exactitude. Occasionally he brought Marilyn a single rosebud done up in green tissue paper. One night he showed up with a giant charlotte russe, enshrined in a cardboard box, for his wife. Mrs. Soames was appalled at his extravagance and said she just wouldn't eat it, it would be too selfish, but her husband said something to her in a sly *sotto voce* and she blushed. Celeste saw her put the little carton carefully away in the ice chest. Marilyn said that in charlotte russe season her parents always got "whispery." Next morning, when Celeste went to the chest for milk for Stanley's breakfast, she noticed that the box was gone.

Marilyn's mother was one of those naturally powerful women whose strength drains off in middle age, leaving raw debility behind. She had led a back-breaking, penny-balancing life and she had not had time to spare herself; besides, she was going through a trying menopause. "I've got change of life, falling of the room rent, varicose veins, and bad feet," Mrs. Soames said to Celeste with grim humor, "but I'd like to see the Sutton Place lady who can bake a better berry pie," adding, "when there's money for berries." Often she had to lie down from weakness, but it was impossible to keep her in bed during the day for longer than a few minutes. "You know what Dr. Ulberson said, Edna" her husband would say anxiously. "Oh, you and your Dr. Ulberson," she would snort. "I've got the week's wash to do." Mrs. Soames was obsessive on the subject of her laundry. She would never let Marilyn touch it. "You girls these days expect soap to do your scrubbing for you," she would say scornfully. But to Celeste Mrs. Soames once said, "She'll have wash enough to do in her life." Mrs. Soames's single self-indulgence was the radio. There was only one machine in the house, a small table model which usually occupied the center of the catchall shelf above the kitchen range; this Mrs. Soames had placed with a sigh at little Stanley's bedside. When Celeste ruled that Stanley might listen to the radio for no more than two hours a day, at selected times—and selected those times which did not conflict with his mother's favorite programs—Mrs. Soames looked guiltily grateful. She never missed Arthur Godfrey, she told Celeste, or *Stella Dallas, Big Sister,* and *Double or Nothing.* And she confided that "when our ship comes in, Frank's going to get me a television set," adding dryly, "At least, that's what Frank says. He's that sure one of those Irish Sweepstakes tickets he's always buying will come through."

Stanley was the youngest child, a thin little boy with blazing eyes and an imagination which ran to mayhem and gore. In the very beginning he was suspicious of Celeste and she could get hardly a word out of him. But late that first day, when she was giving his bony body a massage, he suddenly said: "You a real nurse?" "Well, sort of," smiled Celeste, although her heart skipped a beat. "Nurses stick knives into you," Stanley said glumly. "Whoever told you a story like that?" "Yitzie Frances Ellis, that's my teacher." "Stanley, she didn't. And where did you get that awful nickname of 'Yitzie' for a perfectly nice lady teacher?" "The principal calls her that," said Stanley indignantly. *"Yitzie?"* "The principal calls Miss Ellis Yitzie-Bitzie when nobody's around." "Stanley Soames, I don't believe a single—" But Stanley had screwed his little head about, his eyes bugging with horror, "Lie still! What's the matter?" "You know something, Miss Martin?" whispered Stanley. Celeste heard herself whispering back, "What, Stanley, what?" *"I got green blood."* After that, Celeste digested Master Stanley's remarks, revelations, and confidences with great quantities of salt. She often had to exercise judgment to distinguish fact from fancy.

Stanley was thoroughly familiar with the Cat. He told Celeste solemnly that he *was* the Cat.

Between her patient and Marilyn there were two other children: Eleanor, 9, and Billie, 13. Eleanor was a large calm child with an unhurried attitude toward life; her rather plain features were illuminated by a pair of remarkably direct eyes, and Celeste hastened to make friends with her. Billie was in junior high, a fact which he accepted philosophically. He was clever with his hands and the apartment was always turning up things he had built for his mother out of "nothing," as Mrs. Soames said. But his father seemed disappointed. "We'll never make a student out of Billie. His heart isn't in it. All he does is hang around garages after school learning about motors. He can't wait till he's old enough to get his working papers and learn some mechanical trade. The scholars in my family are the girls." Billie was in the weedy age, "a regular Ichabod Crane," as Mr. Soames put it. Frank Soames was something of a reader; he generally had his nose buried in some library book and he owned a prize shelf of decrepit volumes which he hoarded from young manhood—Scott, Irving, Cooper, Eliot, Thackeray—authors whom Billie characterized as "squares"; Billie's reading was restricted almost entirely to comic books, which he acquired in wholesale quantities by some complex barter-system incomprehensible to his father. Celeste liked Billie—his overgrown hands, his rather furtive voice.

And Marilyn was a darling; Celeste fell in love with her immediately. She was a tall girl, not pretty: her nose was a little broad and her cheekbones were pitched too steep; but her dark eyes and hair were lovely and she carried herself with a defiant swing. Celeste understood her secret sorrow: the necessity of earning a living to help her father carry the weight of the family's needs had kept her from going on from high school to the higher education she craved. But Marilyn was no complainer; outwardly she was even serene. Celeste gathered that she had another, independent life, a vicarious one: through her work she kept in touch with a sort of malformed, teasing shadow of the creative and intellectual world. "I'm not the best manuscript typist in the business," she told Celeste. "I get too blamed interested in what I'm typing." Nevertheless, she had built up a good clientele. Through a former high school teacher she had got in with a young playwrights' group whose art was, if nothing else, prolific; one of her accounts was a Columbia full professor who was engaged with writing a monumental work of scholarship, "a psychological outline of world history"; and her best client was a famous journalist author who, Mr. Soames said proudly, swore by her— "and sometimes at me," added Marilyn. Her earnings were capricious and the importance of maintaining them kept Marilyn a little on the grim side. For the sake of her father's self-esteem she preserved the fiction that her coproducing role in the family was a temporary one, "to tide us over the high prices." But Celeste knew that Marilyn knew there would be no escape for many years, if ever. The boys would grow up, marry, and move off; there was Eleanor's education to provide for—Marilyn was firm that Eleanor should go to college, "she's really a genius. You ought to read the poetry she writes right now, at 9"; Mrs. Soames was headed for invalidism; Frank Soames was not a well man. Marilyn knew her fate and was prepared for it. Because of this she discouraged the romantic advances of several men who were pursuing her, "at least one of them," Marilyn said with a laugh, "with honorable intentions." Her most persistent pursuer was the journalist author—"he's *not* the one. Every time I have to call for a new chapter—he writes in longhand—or deliver one I've typed, he chases me around his apartment with an African war club he picked up in his travels. It's supposed to be a gag, but it's gagging on the level. One of these days I'm going to stop running and poke him one. I'd have done it long ago if I hadn't needed his work." But Celeste suspected that one of these days Marilyn would stop running and not poke him one. She persuaded herself that the experience would do Marilyn good; Marilyn was a passionate girl who had kept herself, Celeste was sure of it, rigidly chaste. (It also occurred to the sophisticate that this was true of a certain Celeste Phillips as well; but at this point Miss Phillips dropped the whole subject out of her thoughts.)

The Soameses lived in a two-bedroom, five-room apartment in an ancient walkup; because they needed three sleeping rooms, the "front room" had been converted into a third bedroom, and this room served both as the girls' bedroom and Marilyn's workshop. "Marilyn ought to have her own room," sighed Mrs. Soames, "but what can we do?" Billie had rigged up a partition—a drape on a long curtain pole— to cut off part of the room for Marilyn's "office"; here she had her work table, her typewriter, her stationery, her telephone; there was a modest illusion of separate quarters. The arrangement was also necessary because Marilyn often had to work at night and Eleanor went to bed early.

The location of the telephone prompted Celeste to make an ulterior suggestion. When she arrived to take up her duties she found Stanley occupying his own bed in the boys' room. On the plea that she could not very well share a bedroom with a boy as big as Billie—and obviously she had to be within call of her patient during the night—Celeste moved Stanley into the front bedroom, to Eleanor's bed, and Eleanor moved to the boys' room. "You're sure this won't interfere with you?" Celeste asked Marilyn anxiously; she was feeling wretched about the whole thing. But Marilyn said she had trained herself to work under impossible conditions: "With a boy like Stanley in the house you either learned how to turn your ears off or you cut your throat." Marilyn's easy reference to "throat" made Celeste sick; on her third day she became aware that she had been unconsciously avoiding that part of Marilyn's generous anatomy. It was a strong throat, and in the days that followed it became for Celeste a sort of symbol, a link between the lives of all of them and the death that waited outside. She trained herself to look at it.

The transfer of Eleanor to Stanley's bed created a problem and sharpened Celeste's feeling of guilt. Mrs. Soames said it was "not good" for brother and sister to share a bedroom at Eleanor's and Billie's ages. So Billie was sent to his parents' room and Mrs. Soames moved over to the boys' room to sleep with Eleanor. "I feel as if I've created a revolution," Celeste wailed, "upsetting your lives this way." And when Mrs. Soames said, "Why, Miss Martin, don't give a thought to us. We're so grateful you could come nurse our baby," Celeste felt like the most callous doubledealing spy. There was a small portion of consolation for her in the thought that the bed she had to sleep on in the front room, an antique cot borrowed from a neighbor, was as hard as the floor of a flagellant's cave. On this she did penance for her chicanery. She almost angrily rejected the family's offer of any one of their own beds in exchange.

"It's so mean," Celeste moaned to the Queens and Jimmy during their second-night rendezvous in a First Avenue areaway. "They're so sweet about everything I feel like a criminal."

"I told you she's too peasant-like for this job," jeered Jimmy; but in the dark he was nibbling her fingertips.

"Jimmy, they're the nicest people. And they're all so grateful to me. If they only knew!"

"They'd smother you with onions," said Jimmy. "Which reminds me . . ."

But Ellery said, "What's the mail situation, Celeste?"

"Marilyn goes downstairs for it first thing in the morning. Mr. Soames leaves the house before the first delivery—"

"We know that."

"She keeps her current correspondence in a wire basket on her desk. I won't have any trouble reading it," said Celeste in a trembly voice. "Last night I managed to do it in the middle of the night, when Marilyn and Stanley were asleep. There are opportunities during the day, too. Sometimes Marilyn has to go out in connection with her work."

"We know that, too," said the Inspector grimly. Marilyn Soames's unpredictable excursions, sometimes in the evening, were keeping them all on the edge of ulcers.

"Even if she doesn't, she always eats lunch in the kitchen. I can even read her mail while Stanley's awake, because of the heavy curtain."

"Wonderful."

"I'm glad you think s-so!" And Celeste found herself irrigating Jimmy's dusty-blue tie.

But when she returned to the Soames flat she had color in her cheeks and she told Marilyn that the walk had done her oceans of good, really it had.

Their meeting time was set by Celeste at between 10 and 10:15. Stanley was not tucked in for the night much before 9, she said, and he rarely fell asleep until 9:30 or so. "Being in bed all the time he doesn't need so much sleep. I can't leave till I'm sure he's dropped off, and then too I've been helping with the supper dishes."

"You mustn't overdo that, Miss Phillips," said the Inspector. "They'll get suspicious. Practical nurses don't—"

"Practical nurses are human beings, aren't they?" sniffed Celeste. "Mrs. Soames is a sick woman who slaves all day and if I can save her some work by doing the supper things I'm going to do it. Would it put me out of the spy union if I told you I also pitch in to the housework? Don't worry, Inspector Queen, I shan't give anything away. I'm quite aware of what's at stake."

The Inspector said feebly that he just thought he'd mention it, that was all, and Jimmy reeled off some verse that he said he had made up but which sounded remarkably like one of the Elizabethan things.

So they met at 10 o'clock or a little later, each night in a different place by prearrangement the night before. For Celeste, at least, it took on the greenish cast of fantasy. For twenty-three and a half hours a day she worked, ate, spied, and slept among the Soameses; the half hour away was a flight to the moon. Only Jimmy's presence made it bearable; she had come to dread the taut, questioning faces of the Queens. She had to brace herself as she walked along the dark street to the appointed spot, waiting for the signal of Jimmy's soft wolf-whistle. Then she would join them in the doorway, or under the store awning, or just inside the alley—wherever the agreed rendezvous was—and she would report the increasingly pleasant monotonies of the past twenty-four hours and answer questions about the Soames mail and the telephone calls, all the while clinging to Jimmy's hand in the darkness; and then, feeling the pull of Jimmy's eyes, she would run back to what had come to signify for her the endearing sanity of the little Soames world.

She did not attempt to tell them how much the aroma of Mrs. Soames's rising bread reminded her of Mother Phillips or of how, by some witchery, Marilyn had become the best of remembered Simone.

And of how frightened, how icily frightened, she was during every moment of every waking hour, and beyond.

To tell any of them.

Especially Jimmy.

They speculated interminably. Beyond meeting Celeste each night, there was nothing else to do.

Over and over they came back to the reports on Cazalis. They were exasperating. He was acting exactly as if he were Dr. Edward Cazalis, Noted Psychiatrist, and not a cunning paranoiac bent on satiating his appetite for death. He was still working with his board on occasional private case histories sent in by psychiatric stragglers. He even attended a meeting called by the Mayor at which the Queens were present. At this meeting Cazalis was studied closely by men trained in the art of dissimulation; but it was a question who was the best actor present. The psychiatrist was affably discouraging; he said again that he and his board were wasting their time; they had cracked a few of their reluctant colleagues but the remainder were adamant and nothing was to be expected of them. (And Inspector Queen reported to the Mayor with a garmented face that in the trickle of suspects turned over by Dr. Cazalis and his coworkers there was exactly none who could be the Cat.) "Haven't you fellows made any progress at all on your end?" Cazalis asked the Inspector. When the Inspector shook his head, the big man smiled. "It's probably someone from outside the metropolitan area."

Ellery thought it unworthy of him.

But he was looking poorly these days, and that was provocative; thinned out, fallen in, the ice of his hair crumbling. His heavy face was sludgy and cracked; he had developed twitches under both eyes; his large hands, when they were not drumming on the nearest object, kept drifting about his person as if seeking an anchorage. Mrs. Cazalis, who was in miserable attendance, said that the work her husband had done for the City had taken too much out of him, it was her fault for having pounded at him to continue investigating. The doctor patted his wife's hand. He was taking it easy, he said; what bothered him was that he had failed. A young man "rises above failure," he said, an old man "sinks under it." "Edward, I want you to go away." But he smiled. He was considering a long rest, he said. As soon as he tied off certain "loose ends" . . .

Was he mocking them?

The metaphor remained with them.

Or had he become suspicious and was uncertainty or the fear of detection strong enough to check the continuing impulse to kill?

He might have caught sight of one of his pursuers. The detectives were sure he had not.

Still, it was possible.

Or had they left a trace of their visit to his apartment? They had worked systematically, touching and moving nothing until they had fixed in their memories the exact position and condition of each object to be touched and moved. And afterward they had restored each object to its original place.

Still, again, he may have noticed something wrong. Suppose he had set a trap? He might have had a little signal for himself, a trivial thing, unnoticeable, in the storage closet or in one of the drawers. A psychotic of a certain type might have taken such a precaution. Elaborately. They were dealing with a man whose brilliance overlapped his psychosis. In certain flights he might be prescient.

It was possible.

Dr. Cazalis's movements were as innocent as those of a man walking across a field under the sunny sky. A patient or two a day in his office, chiefly women. An occasional consultation with other psychiatrists. Long nights when he did not step out of his apartment. Once a visit with Mrs. Cazalis to the Richardsons'. Once a concert at Carnegie, when he listened to the Franck symphony with open eyes and clenched hands; and then, curl-lipped and calm, listening with enjoyment to Bach and Mozart. Once a social evening with some professional friends and their wives.

At no time did he venture near East 29th Street and First Avenue.

It was possible.

That was the canker.

Anything was *possible*.

By the tenth day after the strangulation of Donald Katz, and in the sixth day of "Sue Martin's" practical-nursing career, they were sweating. They spent most of their time now in the report room at Police Headquarters. In silence. Or, when the silence became intolerable, snapping at one another with a querulousness that made silence a relief.

What was digging new hollows in Inspector Queen's face was the thought that Cazalis might be outwaiting them. Madmen had been known to exercise extraordinary patience. Sooner or later—Cazalis might be thinking—they would conclude that he had reached the end of his string . . . if only he did nothing long enough. Then they would call off their watchdogs. Sooner or later.

Was that what Cazalis was waiting for?

If, of course, he knew he was being watched.

Or, if he foresaw that this was one case in which the watchers would never be withdrawn, he might deliberately be waiting until he tired them into carelessness. And then . . . an opening. And he would slip into the clear.

With a tussah silk cord in his pocket.

Inspector Queen kept harrying his operatives until they hated him.

Ellery's brain performed more desperate acrobatics. Suppose Cazalis *had* set a trap in his storage closet. Suppose he *did* know someone had been looking through his old files. Then he knew they had exposed the heart of his secret. Then he knew they knew how he chose his victims.

In such case it would not be overcrediting Cazalis's acumen to say that he would also guess their plan. He had merely to do what Ellery was now doing: to put himself in the adversary's place.

Then Cazalis would know that they had gone beyond Donald Katz to Marilyn Soames, and that with Marilyn Soames they had baited a trap for him.

If I were Cazalis, said Ellery, what would I do then? I would give up all thought of snaring Marilyn Soames's card to the card of the next regularly indicated victim. Or, to play it even safer, I would skip the next regularly indicated victim to the one following on the chance that the enemy had taken out insurance as well. Which we haven't done . . .

Ellery writhed. He could not forgive himself. There was no excuse, he kept saying. To have failed to take the precaution of searching Cazalis's cards past Marilyn Soames to the next-indicated victim, and the next, and the next, and protecting them all—even if it meant going to the end of the file and having to guard a hundred young people all over the City . . .

If these premises were sound, Cazalis might even now be waiting for the detectives trailing him to relax their vigilance. And when they did, the Cat would slink out to strangle a tenth, unknown victim at his leisure, laughing all the while at the detectives he knew were guarding Marilyn Soames.

Ellery became quite masochistic about it.

"The best we can hope for," he groaned, "is that Cazalis makes a move toward Marilyn. The worst, that he's already moved against someone else. If that happens, we won't know about it till it's over. Unless we can keep Cazalis at the other end of the tail, Dad. We've got to hang on to him! How about assigning a few extra men . . . ?"

But the Inspector shook his head. The more men, the greater the chance of giving the game away. After all, there was no *reason* to believe that Cazalis suspected anything. The trouble was that they were getting too nervous.

"Who's nervous?"

"You are! And so am I!—though I wasn't till you started your old fancy mental gynmastics!"

"Tell me it couldn't happen that way, Dad."

"Then why not go after those records again?"

Well, muttered Ellery, they were better off stringing along with what they had. Let well enough alone. Watchful waiting. Time will tell.

"The master of the original phrase," snarled Jimmy McKell. "If you ask me, your morale is showing. Doesn't anybody give a slup in bloody borscht what happens to my girl?"

That reminded them that it was time to go uptown for the nightly meeting with Celeste.

They jostled one another getting through the door.

The night of Wednesday, October 19, was uncharitable. The three men huddled in the alley entrance between two buildings on the south side of East 29th Street, near Second Avenue. There was a cutting wet wind and they kept up a little dance as they waited.

10:15.

It was the first time Celeste had been late.

They kept yapping at one another. Swearing at the wind. Jimmy would poke his head out of the alley and say under his breath, "Come onnnnnn, Celeste!" as if she were a horse.

The lights of Bellevue over on First Avenue were no comfort.

The reports on Cazalis that day had been discouraging. He had not left his apartment. Two patients had called during the afternoon, both young women. Della and Zachary Richardson had shown up at 6:30 on foot; apparently for dinner, as by 9 P.M., the time of the last report the Queens had received before leaving Headquarters, they had still not come out.

"It's nothing, Jimmy," Ellery kept saying. "Cazalis is safe for the night. Can't mean a thing. She just couldn't get away—"

"Isn't that Celeste now?"

She was trying not to run and not succeeding. She would walk faster and faster, then break into a trot, then slow down suddenly, then run. Her black cloth coat kept flopping around her like birds.

It was 10:35.

"Something's up."

"What could be?"

"She's late. Naturally she'd hurry." Jimmy whistled the signal; it came back all dry and blowy. "Celeste—"

"Jimmy." She was gulping.

"What is it?" Ellery had her by both arms.

"He phoned."

The wind had dropped and her words shrilled through the alley. Jimmy shouldered Ellery aside, put his arms around her. She was trembling.

"There's nothing to be scared of. Stop shaking."

She began to cry.

They waited. Jimmy kept tumbling her hair.

Finally, she stopped.

Inspector Queen said instantly: "When?"

"A few minutes past 10. I was just leaving—out in the hall with my hand on the doorknob—when I heard the phone ring. Marilyn was in the dining room with Billie and Eleanor and their father and mother and I was nearest to the front room. I ran and got the phone first. It was . . . I know it was. I heard his voice over the radio the day he gave his press conference and talk. It's low and musical and at the same time sort of sharp."

"Cazalis," said the Inspector. "You mean this was Dr. Edward Cazalis's voice, Miss Phillips?" He said it as if he did not believe it at all and as if it were of the greatest importance to corroborate his disbelief.

"I tell you it was!"

"Well, now," said the Inspector. "Just from hearing it on the radio." But he moved closer to Celeste.

"What did he say?" This was Ellery. "Word for word!"

"I said hello, and he said hello, and then he gave me the Soames phone number and asked if that was the number and I said yes. He said, 'Is this the public stenographer, Marilyn Soames, speaking?' It was his voice. I said no and he said, 'Is Miss Soames in—it is *Miss* Soames, isn't it, not Mrs.? I believe she's—the daughter of Edna and Frank Soames.' I said yes. Then he said, 'I want to talk to her, please.' By that time Marilyn was in the room so I handed her the phone and hung around pretending I had to fix my slip."

"Checking up," muttered the Inspector. "Making sure."

"Go on, Celeste!"

"Give her a chance, will you!" growled Jimmy.

"I heard Marilyn say yes once or twice and then she said, 'Well, I am kind of piled up, but if it's that kind of deal I'll try to get it out for you by Monday, Mr.— What was your name again, sir?' When he told her, Marilyn said, 'I'm sorry, would you mind spelling that?' and she spelled it after him.''

"The name.''

"Paul Nostrum. N-o-s-t-r-u-m.''

"Nostrum.'' Ellery laughed.

"Then Marilyn said yes, she could call for the manuscript tomorrow, and she asked him where she was to pick it up. He said something and Marilyn said, 'I'm tall and dark and I have a mashed nose and I'll be wearing a cloth coat, big white and black checks, you can't miss it, and a beanie. How about you?' and after he answered she said, 'Well, then, maybe you'd better do all the looking, Mr. Nostrum. I'll be there. Good night,' and she hung up.''

Ellery shook her. "Didn't you get the address, the time?''

Jimmy shook Ellery. "Give her a chance, I said!''

"Wait, wait.'' Inspector Queen pushed them both aside. "Did you get any other information, Miss Phillips?''

"Yes, Inspector. When Marilyn hung up I said as offhandedly as I could, 'New client, Marilyn?' and she said yes, she wondered how he knew about her, some writer she did work for must have recommended her. 'Nostrum' had said he was a writer in from Chicago with his new novel to see his publisher, that he'd have to revise his last few chapters and he needed them retyped in a hurry. He hadn't been able to get a hotel accommodation and he was staying with 'friends,' so he'd meet her tomorrow at 5:30 in the lobby of the Astor to give her his manuscript.''

"Lobby of the Astor!'' Ellery was incredulous. "He couldn't have picked a busier spot at a busier hour in the whole City of New York.''

"You're sure it's the Astor, Miss Phillips.''

"That's what Marilyn said.''

They were silent.

Finally, Ellery shrugged. "No use beating our brains out—''

"No, indeed, for time will tell,'' said Jimmy. "Meanwhile what happens to our heroine? Does Celeste stay in that rat cage? Or does she show up at the Astor tomorrow in a checked coat, garnished with parsley?''

"Idiot,'' Celeste rested her head on his arm.

"Celeste stays where she is. This is just his opening move. We'll play along.''

The Inspector nodded. "What time did you say he made that call?'' he asked Celeste.

"It was just about five minutes past 10, Inspector Queen.''

"You go back to the Soameses'.''

Ellery squeezed her hand. "Stick to that phone, Celeste. If there's a call tomorrow from 'Paul Nostrum'—or anyone else—changing the time and place of Marilyn's appointment, that's one of the emergencies I mentioned. Phone Police Headquarters immediately.''

"All right.''

"Ask for Extension 2-X,'' said the Inspector. "That's a code signal that will put you right through to us.'' The old man patted her arm awkwardly. "You're a good girl.''

"Good, schmood,'' muttered Jimmy. "Give me a kiss.''

They watched her walk down the windy street, not moving until she disappeared in the entrance of 486.

Then they ran toward Third Avenue, where the squad car was parked.

According to Sergeant Velie, Detective Goldberg's 10 P.M. report had stated that at 9:26 Mr. and Mrs. Richardson, accompanied by Dr. and Mrs. Cazalis, had left the Cazalis apartment house. The two couples had strolled up Park Avenue. According to Detective Young, Goldberg's partner, Cazalis had been in high spirits; he had laughed a great deal. The four had turned west on 84th Street, crossed Madison Avenue, and they stopped before the Park-Lester. Here the couples separated, the Cazalises walking back to Madison, turning north, and stopping in at a drugstore on the corner of 86th Street. They sat at the counter and were served hot chocolates. This was at two minutes of 10, and at 10 o'clock Goldberg had telephoned his hourly report from a coffee shop across the street.

Ellery glanced at the wall clock. "Ten after 11. What about the 11 o'clock report, Sergeant?"

"Wait," said Sergeant Velie. "Goldie called in again at 10:20. A special."

The Sergeant seemed to be expecting exclamations and excitement, for he paused dramatically.

But Ellery and Jimmy McKell were doodling on pads at opposite sides of the desk and all that the Inspector said was, "Yes?"

"Goldberg said he'd no sooner got off the phone in the coffee shop at 10 when Young signaled him from across the street and Goldie walked over and saw Mrs. Cazalis sitting at the soda counter—all by her lonesome. Goldie thought he was seeing things because he doesn't spot Cazalis any place and he says to Young, Where's our man, where's our man? Young points to the back of the drugstore and Goldie sees Cazalis in a booth back there, phoning. Young told Goldberg that right after Goldie left Cazalis looked at his watch like he'd all of a sudden remembered something. Young said it was a great big take and it looked phony to him, Cazalis putting on an act to fool his wife. He said a few words—like he was excusing himself—gets off the stool, and goes to the back. He looks up a number in one of the phone books on the rack, then he goes into the booth and makes a call. Time of entry into booth: 10:04."

"10:04," said Ellery. "10:04."

"That's what I said," said the Sergeant. "Cazalis is on the phone around ten minutes. Then he comes back to Mrs. Cazalis, drinks the rest of his hot chocolate, and they leave."

"They took a cab, Cazalis giving the hack his home address. Young tailed them in another cab and Goldie went into the drugstore. He'd noticed that the directory Young said Cazalis had looked a name up in was open on the stand, and he wanted a gander at it because nobody had used it after Cazalis. It turned out to be the Manhattan book, and it was open at the pages with . . ." Velie paused impressively, . . . "with the S-O names."

"The S-O names," said Inspector Queen. "Did you hear that, Ellery? The S-O names." His denture was showing.

"Would you think," said Jimmy, drawing a set of fangs, "that a kindly old gent like that could look so much like a Brontosaurus?"

But the Inspector said genially, "Go on, Velie, go on."

"There's nothing more," said the Sergeant Velie with dignity. "Goldberg said he thought that rated a hurry-up special report, so he phoned right in before leaving to go back to Park Avenue after Young."

"Goldberg was so right," said the Inspector. "And the 11 o'clock report?"

"The Cazalises went right home. At ten minutes to 11 their lights went out. Unless the doc is figuring on a sneak tonight, after his old woman is in dreamland—"

"Not tonight, Sergeant, not tonight," said Ellery, smiling; "5:30 tomorrow, at the Astor."

They saw him enter the Astor lobby through the 44th Street doorway. The time was 5:05 and they had already been there an hour. Detective Hesse was close on his tail.

Cazalis was dressed in a dark gray suit, a rather seedy dark topcoat, and a stained gray hat. He came in with several other people, as if he were one of their group, but well in the transverse corridor at the rear of the lobby he took himself off, bought a copy of the *New York Post* at the cigar counter, stood for a few moments glancing at the front page, and then began a strolling tour of the lobby. Moving a few feet at a time, with long pauses between.

"Making sure she hasn't come yet," said the Inspector.

They were on the balcony of the mezzanine, well hidden.

Cazalis kept circulating. The lobby was crowded and it was hard to keep him in sight. But Hesse had taken a central position; he had to move very little, and they knew he would not lose his man.

There were six other Headquarters men planted in the lobby.

When Cazalis had completed his tour, he edged alongside five people, men and women, who were standing near the Broadway entrance talking and laughing. He held an unlighted cigaret.

On the steps outside they caught an occasional glimpse of the broad back and accented waistline of Detective Zilgitt. He was a Negro and one of the most valuable men at Headquarters; Inspector Queen had especially detailed him to work with Hesse for the day. Zilgitt, who was a modest dresser, had rigged himself out in sharp clothes for his assignment; he looked like a Broadway character waiting for a heavy date.

At 5:25 Marilyn Soames arrived.

She came hurrying into the lobby, out of breath. She paused by the florist's shop to look around. She wore a big-checked cloth coat and a little felt cap. She carried an old simulated-leather briefcase.

Detective Johnson walked in, passed her, and mingled with the crowd. But he kept within fifteen feet of her. Detective Piggott entered the florist's shop from Broadway; he took some time buying a carnation. He had a perfect view of both Marilyn and Cazalis through the glass walls of the shop. A little later he sauntered out into the lobby and stopped almost at the girl's elbow, looking around as if for a familiar face. She glanced at him doubtfully and seemed about to speak to him; but when his glance passed over her she bit her lip and looked elsewhere.

Cazalis had spotted her instantly.

He began to read his newspapers. Leaning against the wall, the cigaret between his fingers still unlighted.

From where the Queens stood watching they could see his glance fixed on her face above his paper.

Marilyn had begun scanning the area within her orbit from the side of the lobby opposite to which Cazalis stood. Her glance searched slowly. When it had all but completed its half-circle, just as it was about to reach him, Cazalis lowered his newspaper, murmured something to one of the men in the group by his side, and the man produced a packet of matches, struck a match, and held the flame to the tip of Cazalis's cigaret. For that moment Cazalis looked like one of the group.

Marilyn's glance passed him as if he were invisible.

He inched back. Now he stood with the group between them, studying her frankly.

The Soames girl remained where she was until 5:40. Then she moved off, walking around the lobby and searching among the men who were seated. A few smiled and one said something to her. But she frowned and walked on.

As she walked, Cazalis followed.

He made no attempt to get close to her.

At times he even stood still, his eyes taking up the hunt.

He seemed to be committing her to memory—her gait, the swing of her body, the plain strong profile.

He was flushed now, breathing heavily. As if he were tremendously excited.

By ten minutes to 6 she had gone completely around the lobby and returned to her original position near the florist's shop. Cazalis passed her. It was the closest he had come to her—he could have touched her, and Johnson and Piggott could have touched him. She actually studied his face. But this time his glance was elsewhere and he passed her briskly, as if he were going somewhere. Apparently he had given her a false description of himself, or no description at all.

He paused in the nearest doorway.

It was just inside the entrance where Detective Zilgitt waited. Zilgitt glanced at him casually and moved off the steps.

The girl's foot began tapping. She did not look behind her and Cazalis was able to study her without subterfuge.

At 6 o'clock Marilyn straightened up and with determination began to push toward the bell captain's desk.

Cazalis remained where he was.

A few moments later a bellboy began to call: "Mr. Nostrum. Mr. Paul Nostrum."

Immediately Cazalis went down the steps, crossed the sidewalk, and got into a taxicab. As the cab moved away from the curb into the Broadway traffic, Detective Hesse jumped into the next cab at the stand.

At 6:10 Marilyn Soames, looking very angry, left the Astor and walked with long strides down Broadway toward 42nd Street.

Johnson and Piggott were just behind her.

"Marilyn was fit to be tied," Celeste reported that night. "I almost kissed her when she got home, I was so relieved. But she was so mad at being stood up she didn't notice. Mr. Soames said writers were temperamental and she'd probably get a bouquet of flowers from him as an apology, but Marilyn snapped that she wasn't going to be blarneyed out of it, he was probably drunk in some bar and if he phoned again she'd meet him just so she could tell him where to get off." The Inspector was annoying his mustache. "Where on earth did he go from the Astor?"

"Home." Ellery seemed disturbed, too. "Where is Marilyn, Celeste? She hasn't gone out again, has she?"

"She was so mad she had supper and went right to bed."

"I'd better take a walk around and tell the boys to keep an extra eye out tonight," muttered the Inspector.

They watched him hurry down the street.

Finally Celeste pushed away from Jimmy. "Do you think he'll phone again, Mr. Queen?"

"I don't know."

"What was the idea today?"

"He's had to play this one differently. Marilyn doesn't go out to work, hasn't a predictable routine. He's probably too cagey to hang around here day after day hoping to catch a glimpse of her, so he had to use a trick to get a good look.''

"That's . . . right, isn't it. He didn't know what Marilyn looked like.''

"Not since he spanked her rosy bottom," said Jimmy. "Now can I have five minutes alone in this palatial hallway with my future wife? Before the bell tolls, Fairy Godfather, and I turn into a pumpkin.''

But Celeste said, "When do you think he'll . . .''

"It won't be long.'' Ellery sounded remote. "Any night now, Celeste.''

And they were quiet.

"Well,'' said Celeste at last.

Jimmy stirred.

"I'd better be getting back.''

"Keep checking the phone calls. And pay particular attention to Marilyn's mail.''

"Right.''

"You've got to give me my five lousy minutes!'' wailed Jimmy. Ellery stepped out into the street.

Inspector Queen came back before Jimmy and Celeste were finished in their hallway.

"Everything all right, Dad?''

"They're scratching fleas.''

Afterwards, the three men went back to Headquarters. The latest word, delivered in Detective Goldberg's 11 P.M. report, was that the Cazalises were entertaining a large number of people who had arrived in chauffeur-driven limousines. The party, Goldberg had said, was gay. Once, prowling in the court, he heard the boom of Cazalis's laugh, accompanied by a chatter of crystal. "The doc,'' Goldberg had said, "sounded just like Santa Claus.''

Friday. Saturday. Sunday.

And nothing.

The Queens were scarcely on speaking terms. Jimmy McKell found himself functioning as part peacemaker, part interpreter. He suffered the usual fate of middlemen; sometimes they both turned on him. He was beginning to wear a haunted look himself.

Even Sergeant Velie was antisocial. When he spoke at all it was in an animal growl.

Once an hour the telephone rang. Then they all leaped.

The messages varied, but their gist was the same.

Nothing.

They began to share a common loathing for the report room, which was only surpassed by their loathing for one another.

Then, on Monday, October 24, the Cat moved.

The announcement came from Detective MacGayn, who was Hesse's partner on the regular day trick. MacGayn called only a few minutes after his hourly report, in considerable excitement, to say that their man was taking a powder. Several suitcases had just been carried out of the Cazalis apartment by the doorman. Hesse had overheard him instruct a taxi driver to wait as he had "some people going to Penn Station to catch a train.'' Hesse was set to follow in another cab; MacGayn had run to phone in the news.

Inspector Queen instructed MacGayn to go immediately to Pennsylvania Station, locate Hesse and their man, and then wait at the 31st Street entrance nearest Seventh Avenue.

The squad car screamed uptown.

Once Ellery said angrily, "It isn't possible. I don't believe it. It's a trick." Otherwise, there was no conversation.

On order, the driver cut his siren out at 23rd Street.

MacGayn was waiting for them. He had just found Hesse. Dr. and Mrs. Cazalis were standing in a crowd at the gate of a Florida train. They had been joined by Mr. and Mrs. Richardson. The gate was not yet open. Hesse was standing by.

They made their way cautiously into the station.

From the windows of the south waiting room MacGayn pointed out the Cazalis-Richardson group and, nearby, Hesse.

"Take Hesse's place," said Inspector Queen. "And send him here."

Hesse walked in briskly a few moments later.

Ellery kept his eyes on Cazalis.

"What's going on?" demanded the Inspector.

Hesse was worried. "I don't know, Inspector. There's something offbeat, but they're a little in the clear out there and I can't get close enough to listen in. His wife keeps arguing with him and he keeps smiling and shaking his head. The luggage has gone down. The Richardsons', too."

"Oh, so they're also going," said Ellery.

"Looks like it."

He was not wearing Thursday's disreputable topcoat. His coat looked new and fashionable, he wore a smart Homburg, a small 'mum in his lapel.

"If he ever wiggles out of this one," remarked Jimmy McKell, "he can always make himself a tidy zloty by posing as a Man of Distinction."

But Ellery muttered, "Florida."

The gate opened and the crowd began squeezing through.

Inspector Queen seized Hesse's arm. "Get down there after him and stick. Take MacGayn and if anything happens send him back up. We'll be waiting at the gate."

Hesse hurried away.

The gate had opened late; train-departure time, according to the figures posted above the gate, was only ten minutes off.

"It's all right, Ellery," said the Inspector. "They won't pull out on time." His tone was paternal.

Ellery looked wild.

They strolled out into the shed and mingled with the people gathering before a gate marked *Philadelphia Express: Newark-Trenton-Philadelphia.* The stairway to the Florida train was two gates away. They kept glancing from the gateway to the big clocks.

"I told you," said the Inspector.

"But why Florida? Suddenly!"

"He's called Operation Necktie off," said Jimmy.

"No."

"Don't you want him to?"

"Who says he's called it off?" Ellery scowled. "He's given up on the Soames girl, granted. Spotted something Thursday, maybe. Or figured she was too tough. Or this might be a trick to put us off guard, if he suspects something. After all, we don't know how much he knows. We don't know anything! . . . If he doesn't suspect, this mean he's gone on to somebody else—"

"Somebody who he found out is vacationing in Florida," nodded Inspector Queen.

Jimmy said, "New York papers please copy. Dateline Miami, Palm Beach, or Sarasota. *Cat Hits Florida.*"

"It could be," said Ellery. "But somehow I can't get myself to believe it. It's something else. Some other trick."

"What do you need, diagrams? I'll bet he's got those silk cords in his bags. What are you waiting for?"

"We can't chance it." Inspector Queen looked dour. "We just can't. If we have to we'll work through the Florida locals. We'll have him watched down there and set him up on his return to New York. It means doing the whole thing over again."

"The hell it does! Not with Celeste, Old Sleuth. I can't wait that long, see?"

And just then MacGayn came running out of the gateway making frantic signals. The trainman was looking at his watch.

"MacGayn—"

"Get back, he's coming back up!"

"What?"

"*He's not going!*"

They scuttled into the thick of the crowd.

Cazalis appeared.

Alone.

He was smiling.

He cut diagonally across the shed toward the corner marked *Taxicabs* with the happy stride of a man who has accomplished something.

Hesse shuffled after him studying a timetable.

As he walked he rubbed his left ear; and MacGayn wriggled through the crowd and began to saunter along behind.

When they got back to the report at Headquarters they found a message from MacGayn.

Their man had cabbed directly home.

Now they could look back on the four weeks just past and see what had undoubtedly happened. Cazalis had out-smarted himself. Ellery pointed out that in murdering his wife's niece and insinuating himself into the Cat case as a psychiatric consultant Cazalis had seriously hobbled himself. He had not foreseen the demands on his time; he had failed to take into account the white light in which he would have to operate. Before his murder of Lenore Richardson he had had only to deceive a submissive, trusting wife; in semi-retirement, he had moved very nearly at will and in satisfactory shadows. But now he was crippled. He had made himself accountable to officialdom. He was linked with a board of fellow-psychiatrists. Colleagues were communicating with him about their patients. His failing health was causing Mrs. Cazalis to take sharper notice of his activities. And there was the little family matter involving the Richardsons which he could scarcely ignore.

"He strangled Stella Petrucchi and Donald Katz under difficulties," said Ellery. "Conditions were not as favorable to him in those two murders as in the previous ones. Undoubtedly he had to run bigger risks, invent more lies to account for his absences at least in the Katz case; how he managed it in the Petrucchi case, especially on the night of the murder itself, after the Cat Riot, I'd love to know. It's reasonable to suppose that his wife, the Richardsons, began to ask embarrassing questions.

"Significantly, it's those three who've gone to Florida.

"Hesse saw Mrs. Cazalis 'arguing' with Cazalis at the gate to the train. It's an argument that must have started days ago, when Cazalis first suggested the Florida trip. Because it's a certainty Cazalis was the one who suggested it, or who saw to it that the suggestion was made.

"I'm inclined to think he worked it through his sister-in-law. Mrs. Richardson was his logical tool. In her Cazalis had an excellent argument for his wife, who must have been hard to persuade: Della could stand a rest and a change of scene after what had 'happened,' she leaned heavily on her sister, and so on.

"However Cazalis managed it, he got the Richardsons to leave town and his wife to accompany them. Unquestionably he explained his inability to go with them on the double ground of his remaining patients and his promise to the Mayor to clean up his end of the investigation.

"Anything to get his wife and in-laws out of the way.

"Anything to give himself freedom of movement."

Jimmy said. "There's still the maid."

"He's given her the week off," said the Inspector.

"And now they're all out of the way," nodded Ellery, "he has unlimited opportunity and mobility, and the Cat can really go to work on the delightful problem of Marilyn Soames."

And he did. Cazalis went to work on Marilyn Soames as if getting his noose around her throat was of the utmost importance to his peace of mind and he could no longer hold himself in.

He was so eager he was careless. He went back to his shabby topcoat and old felt hat; he added a motheaten gray wool muffler and scuffed shoes; but otherwise he neglected to alter his appearance and it was child's play to keep track of him.

And he went hunting in daylight.

It was evident that he felt completely sure.

He left his apartment early on Tuesday morning, just after Detectives Hesse and MacGayn took over from Goldberg and Young. He left by way of the service entrance, slipping out into the side street and walking rapidly toward Madison Avenue as if his destination lay westward. But at Madison he veered south and walked all the way down to 59th Street. On the southeast corner he looked casually around. Then he jumped into a parked taxicab.

The taxi headed east. Hesse and MacGayn followed in separate cabs to minimize the danger of losing him.

When Cazalis's cab turned south on Lexington Avenue the detectives tensed. It kept going south but as it did it worked its way farther eastward until it reached First Avenue.

It went straight down First Avenue to 28th Street.

Here Cazalis's taxi made a four corner turn and drew up before Bellevue Hospital.

Cazalis got out, paid his driver. Then, briskly, he began to stride toward the hospital entrance.

The cab drove off.

Immediately Cazalis stopped, looking after the cab. It turned a corner, heading west.

He retraced his steps and walked rapidly toward 29th Street. His muffler was high around his neck and he had pulled the snapbrim of his hat over his eyes as low as it would go without looking grotesque.

His hands were in the pockets of his topcoat.

At 29th he crossed over.

He walked past 486 slowly, looking the entrance over but without stopping or changing his pace.

Once he looked up. It was a four-story building of dirty tan brick.

Once he glanced back.

A postman was trudging into 490.

Cazalis continued to amble up the street. Without pausing he strolled around the corner to Second Avenue.

But then he reappeared, coming back at a fast clip, as if he had forgotten something. Hesse barely had time to step into a doorway. MacGayn was watching from a hallway across the street, out of sight. They knew that at least one of the detectives assigned to guard Marilyn Soames was in 486, probably at the rear of the downstairs hall, in the gloom behind the staircase. Another was on MacGayn's side of the street somewhere.

There was no danger.

No danger at all.

Still, their palms were sweating.

Cazalis strode past the house, glancing in as he passed. The postman was now in the vestibule of 486, slipping mail into the letter boxes.

Cazalis stopped before 490, looking at the number inquiringly. He fumbled in an inner pocket and produced an envelope which he consulted elaborately, glancing from time to time at the house number above the entrance, like a collector of some sort.

The postman emerged from 486, shuffled up the street, turned into 482.

Cazalis walked directly into 486.

Detective Quigley in the hall saw him look over the letter boxes.

He studied Soames's box briefly. The paper name plate bore the name *Soames* and the apartment number *3B*. There was mail in the box. He made no attempt to touch the box.

Quigley was having a bad time. The mail was delivered at the same time every morning and it was Marilyn Soames's habit to come downstairs for it within ten minutes of the regular delivery.

Quigley fingered his holster.

Suddenly Cazalis opened the inner door and walked into the hall.

The detective crouched in the blackest corner behind the stairs.

He heard the big man's step, saw the thick legs pass and disappear. He did not dare to make the slightest movement.

Cazalis walked up the hall, opened the back door. The door closed quietly.

Quigley shifted his position.

Hesse ran in and joined him under the stairs.

"In the court."

"Casing it." Then Hesse whispered, "Somebody coming down the stairs, Quig."

"The girl!"

She went into the vestibule, unlocked the Soames box.

Marilyn wore an old bathrobe; her hair was in curlers.

She took out the mail, stood there shuffling letters.

They heard the snick of the rear door.

Cazalis, and he saw her.

The men said afterward they expected the Cat case to be written off then and there. The setup was ideal: the victim in the vestibule in a bathrobe, bound to come back into the gloomy hall in a matter of seconds; no one about; the street outside almost deserted; the court for an emergency getaway.

They were disappointed. Hesse said, "Hell, he'd probably have tried to drag her behind the stairs, the way he did O'Reilly over in Chelsea. Where Quigley and I were parked. The crazy bastard must have had a premonition."

But Ellery shook his head. "Habit," he said. "And caution. He's a night worker. Probably didn't even have a cord along."

"I wish we had as standard equipment X-ray eyes," mumbled Inspector Queen.

Cazalis stood there at the end of the hall, pale eyes burning.

In the vestibule Marilyn was reading a letter. Her flattish nose, her cheekbones, chin, were tacked against the glass of the street door.

She stood there three minutes.

Cazalis did not move.

Finally she opened the inner door and ran upstairs.

The old boards rattled.

Hesse and Quigley heard him let his breath go.

Then Cazalis walked down the hall.

Dejected. Furious. They could tell by the slope of his thick shoulders, the mauls of his fists.

He went out into the street.

He was back after dark, watching the entrance of 486 from a hallway across the street.

Until a quarter of 10.

Then he went home.

"Why didn't you jump him?" cried Jimmy McKell. "And end this Grand Guignol? You'd have found a cord in his pocket!"

"Maybe we would and maybe we wouldn't," said the Inspector. "He's trying to fix her habits. This may go on for a couple of weeks. She's a toughie for him."

"He'd certainly have one of those cords on him!"

"We can't be sure. We'll just have to wait. Anyway, an actual attack will put him away. A cord might slip. We can't risk anything." Jimmy heard Ellery's teeth grinding.

Cazalis prowled about the neighborhood all day Wednesday; with the night, he settled down in the doorway across the street again.

But at ten minutes to 10 he left.

"He must be wondering if she ever leaves the house," said the Inspector that night, when Celeste reported.

"I'm beginning to wonder myself," rapped Ellery. "Celeste, what the devil is Marilyn doing?"

"Working." Celeste sounded muffled. "On a rush job for one of her playwright customers. She says she won't be finished with it till Saturday or Sunday."

"He'll go nuts," said the McKell voice.

No one laughed, least of all the quipster.

Their nightly meetings in the dark had taken on the weightless flow of dreams. Nothing was real but the unreality they watched. They were conscious only occasionally that the City ground and grumbled somewhere below. Life was buried under their feet; they marked time above it, a treadmill experience.

On Thursday he repeated himself. Only this time he gave up at two minutes past 10.

"Later each night."

Jimmy was fretful. "At this rate, Ellery, he'll be seeing Celeste leave the house. I won't have that."

"He's not after me, Jimmy." Celeste was sounding shrill.

"It's not that," said Ellery. "It's the regularity. If he spots Celeste coming out every night at the same time, he may get curious."

"We'd better change the time, son."

"Let's do it this way: Celeste, those third-floor windows are in the Soameses' front room, aren't they? The room where Stanley is?"

"Yes."

"From now on don't leave until 10:15, and then only under certain conditions. Is your wristwatch accurate?"

"It keeps very good time."

"Let's synchronize." Ellery struck a match. "I have 10:26 exactly."

"I'm about a minute and a half off."

He struck another match. "Fix it." When she did, he said, "From now on be at one of those front windows every night between 10:10 and 10:15. We'll meet you, starting tomorrow night, somewhere along First Avenue in the immediate neighborhood—tomorrow night let's make it in front of that empty store near the corner of 30th."

"We met there Sunday night."

"Yes. If between 10:10 and 10:15 you see a light flash three times from one of the doorways or alleys across from 486—we'll use a pocket pencil flash—that will mean Cazalis has left for the night and you can come down and make your report. If you see no signal, stay upstairs. It will mean he's still around. If he should leave between 10:10 and 10:25 you'll get the signal between 10:25 and 10:30. If there's no signal in those five minutes, he'll still be around; stay put. We'll operate on the same system till he leaves. Watch for a signal every fifteen minutes. All night if necessary."

By MacGayn's 5 P.M. report Friday Cazalis had still not left his apartment. It puzzled them. He did not leave until dusk. Friday night it was necessary to keep Celeste waiting until 11:15. Ellery flashed the signal himself and trailed her to the rendezvous.

"I thought that flash would never come." Celeste was white. "He's gone?"

"Gave up a few minutes ago."

"I tried to get a call in all afternoon and evening but Stanley was demanding and fidgety today—he's much better—and Marilyn stuck to her typewriter . . . He phoned a little after 1 P.M."

They pressed around her in the dark.

"Paul Nostrum, again. Apologized for having stood her up at the Astor, said he was taken sick suddenly and that he's been laid up till today. He wanted her to meet him . . . tonight." Celeste was trying to sound steady. "I've been leaping."

"What did Marilyn say to him?"

"She refused. Said she was all tied up on a special piece of work and he'd have to get somebody else. Then he tried to date her."

"Go on!" Inspector Queen's voice was shaky.

"She just laughed and hung up."

Jimmy drew her away.

"He's getting impatient, Dad."

"That maid of his comes back Monday."

They milled a little.

"Celeste."

Celeste came back, Jimmy protesting.

"How much did she actually tell him about the work she's doing?"

"She said she couldn't possibly be finished before tomorrow night, probably Sunday, and then she'd have to deliver it—" Celeste caught her breath. Then she said in the queerest way, "Deliver it. She did say . . ."

"This weekend," said Ellery.

The Saturday sky was overcast; a glum rain fell intermittently on the City all day. It stopped at dusk and a fog settled over the streets.

The Inspector cursed and passed the word around: he did not consider an act of God sufficient for failure to keep their man covered. "If necessary, take chances. But stick with him." He added, gratuitously: "Or else."

It was a bad day.

The whole day was bad. During the morning Detective Hesse was seized with cramps. MacGayn put in a hurry call. "Hesse has to knock off. He's writhing. Step on it, he's all alone over there." By the time Hagstrom reached Park Avenue MacGayn was gone. "I don't know where," gasped Hesse. "Cazalis came out at 11:05 and walked off toward Madison, MacGayn covering him. Put me in a cab before I foul myself up." It took Hagstrom over an hour to locate MacGayn and his quarry. Cazalis had merely gone to a restaurant. He returned to his apartment immediately afterward.

But a little past 2 found Cazalis leaving in his working clothes, by way of the court. He headed for East 29th Street.

Then, shortly before 4 o'clock, Marilyn Soames walked out of 486. Celeste Phillips was with her.

The two girls hurried west on 29th Street.

The fog had not yet come down; it was still drizzling. But the sky was threatening to black out.

Visibility was poor.

Cazalis moved. He moved in a glide, very rapidly. His hands were in his pockets. He kept to the opposite side of the street. MacGayn, Hagstrom, Quigley, the Queens, Jimmy McKell followed. Singly, in pairs.

Jimmy kept mumbling. "Is Celeste out of her mind? The fool, the fool."

The Inspector was mumbling, too. A rather stronger characterization.

They could see Cazalis's rage. It told in his pace. He would lunge ahead, then walk, then trot, then come to a dead stop. As he followed the girls his head thrust itself forward.

"Like a cat," said Ellery. "There's the Cat."

"She's out of her mind," whispered Jimmy.

"She's out of her mind!" Inspector Queen was close to tears. "We set him up— we set him up all this time. His tongue is hanging out. He'd have tried it in this bad light sure. And she . . ."

The girls turned into Third Avenue and entered a stationery store. The man in the store began wrapping reams of paper, other articles.

It was growing quite dark.

Cazalis was beyond caution. He stood eagerly in the rain on one of the corners of Third Avenue and 29th Street before a drugstore window. The lights came on as he stood there, but he did not move.

The head was still thrust forward.

Ellery had to hang on to Jimmy's arm.

"He won't try anything while Celeste is with her. Too many people on the streets, Jimmy. Too much traffic. Take it easy."

The girls came out of the store. Marilyn carried a large package.

She was smiling.

They walked back the way they had come.

For a moment, fifty feet from the tenement, it looked as if Cazalis were going to take the plunge. The drizzle had thickened and the girls were running for the vestibule, laughing. Cazalis gathered himself, actually jumped into the gutter.

But a car drove up to the curb before 490 and three men got out. They stood on the opposite pavement, shouting to one another in the rain, arguing hotly about something.

Cazalis stepped back.

The girls disappeared into 486.

He walked heavily down the street, stepped into a hallway opposite the Soames building.

Goldberg and Young arrived to take over from MacGayn and Hagstrom.

They worked in close, for the fog had descended.

Cazalis lingered all evening, not moving except to change hallways when someone headed for the one he occupied.

Once he chose Young's, and the detective was within fifteen feet of him for over a half hour.

A few minutes after 11 o'clock he gave up. His bulky figure plunged along in the fog, chin on his breast. They saw him pass from their own observation post near Second Avenue and, a few seconds later, Goldberg and Young.

The three vanished going west.

With some grimness, Inspector Queen insisted on flashing the all-clear signal to Celeste himself.

The meeting place for the night was a dim-walled bar-and-grill on First Avenue between 30th and 31st Streets. They had used it once before; it was crowded, smoky, and mindful of the rights of man.

Celeste came in and sat down. Without waiting for anything she said, "I couldn't help it. When she ran out of onionskin second sheets and said she was walking over to Third Avenue for some, I almost died. I knew he wouldn't dare try anything if somebody was with her. Now give me ten demerits."

Jimmy glared. "Are you out of your everloving mind?"

"Did he follow us?" She was bloodless tonight, very nervous. Ellery idly noticed her hands. They were cracked and red; her nails were chewed-looking. There was something else about her, too, but it insisted on being elusive.

What was it?

"He followed you," said the Inspector. Then he said "Miss Phillips, nothing would have happened to her." He said, "Miss Phillips, this case has cost the City of New York I don't know how many tens of thousands of dollars and months of work. Today by acting like an irresponsible moron you undid every last bit of it.

We may never get as good a chance again. It could mean not getting him at all. Today he was desperate. If she'd been alone, he'd have jumped. I can't tell you how put out I am with you. In fact, Miss Phillips, I'm not irreverent when I say I wish to God Almighty I'd never seen or heard of you.''

Jimmy started to get up.

Celeste pulled him down, rested her cheeks on his shoulder. "Inspector, I just couldn't find the strength to let her walk out into that street alone. What do I do now?''

The old man raised his glass of beer with shaking hands and drained it.

"Celeste." What was it?

"Yes, Mr. Queen.'' Jimmy's clutch tightened and she smiled up at him.

"You're not to do that again.''

"I can't promise that, Mr. Queen.''

"You did promise it.''

"I'm so sorry.''

"We can't pull you out now. We can't disturb the status quo. He may try another trick tomorrow.''

"I wouldn't leave. I couldn't.''

"Won't you promise not to interfere?''

Jimmy touched her face.

"This may all be over by tomorrow night. He hasn't the remotest chance of hurting her. She's covered, so is he. Let him get that cord out, make one move toward her, and he'll be jumped by four armed men. Did Marilyn finish the play she's typing?''

"No, she was too exhausted tonight. She has a few more hours' work on it tomorrow. She says she's going to sleep late, so that means she won't have it done till late afternoon.''

"She's to deliver it immediately?''

"The writer is waiting for it. It's overdue now.''

"Where does he live?''

"The Village.''

"Weather forecast for tomorrow is more rain. It will be dark or almost dark when she leaves the house. He'll make his pitch either on East 29th Street or in the Village. One day more, Celeste, and we can bury this with the rest of our bad dreams. Won't you let her go alone?''

"I'll try.''

What *was* it?

Inspector Queen snarled, "Another beer!''

"You're making this awfully tough, Celeste. Did you leave Marilyn all right?''

"She's gone to bed. They all have. Mr. and Mrs. Soames and Billie and Eleanor are going to church early tomorrow.''

"Good night.'' Ellery's chin angular. "I'd hate to think you let us down.''

Jimmy said, "Cheese it. The aborigine.''

The waiter slapped a beer down before the Inspector. He lisped, "What's for the lady?''

"Nothing,'' said Jimmy. "Remove yourself.''

"Listen, pally, this is a going concern. She drinks, or you do your smooching someplace else.''

Jimmy slowly uncoiled. "Listen yourself, no-brow—''

The Inspector barked, "On your way.''

The waiter looked surprised and backed off.

"Go on back, baby," crooned Jimmy. "I would have a word or two with our associates here."

"Jimmy, kiss me?"

"Here?"

"I don't care."

He kissed her. The waiter glowered from afar.

Celeste ran.

The fog swallowed her.

Jimmy got up to lean over the Queens with a bitter expression. He opened his mouth.

But Ellery said, "Isn't that Young?" He was squinting through the murk.

They jerked about like rabbits.

The detective was in the open doorway. His glance darted along the bar, from booth to booth. There were deep yellowish lines around his mouth.

Ellery laid a bill on their table.

They got up.

Young spotted them. He was breathing through his mouth.

"Now listen, Inspector, listen." There was sweat on his upper lip. "It's this goddam fog, you can't see your hand in front of your face in this goddam fog. Goldberg and I were right on his tail when all of a sudden he doubled back on us. Back east. Back here. Like he got the urge again and decided to make a night of it. He looked crazy-mad. I don't know if he saw us or not. I don't think so." Young inhaled. "We lost him in the fog. Goldie's out there roaming around, looking for him. I've been looking for you."

"He headed back here and you lost him."

Inspector Queen's cheeks were damp and hardening plaster.

Now I remember.

"That checked coat," said Ellery mechanically.

"What?" said his father.

"She was so upset tonight she put it on instead of her own. *He's loose and Celeste is out there in Marilyn's coat.*"

They tumbled after Jimmy McKell into the fog.

11

They heard Celeste's shriek as they sprinted along First Avenue between 30th and 29th Streets.

A man was running toward them from the 29th Street corner waving them back wildly.

"Goldberg . . ."

Not on 29th Street, then. It was here, along First Avenue.

The scream gurgled. It gurgled again, like a song.

"That alley!" yelled Ellery.

It was a narrow opening between the 29th Street corner building and a block of stores. The alley was nearer to Goldberg but Jimmy McKell's praying mantis legs got him there first.

He vanished.

A radio-patrol car tore up, its headlights splashing against the fog. Inspector Queen shouted something and the car backed and lurched to train its brights and side light on the alley entrance.

As they dashed in, Johnson and Piggott skidded around the corner with drawn guns.

Sirens began sawing away on 29th, 30th, Second Avenue.

An ambulance shot diagonally across First Avenue from Bellevue.

In the boiling fog the girl and the two men were struggling casually. Staggered: Celeste, Cazalis, Jimmy; caught in the molecular path of a slow motion projection. Celeste faced them, arched; a bow in the arms of a bowman. The fingers of both hands were at her throat defending it; they had deliberately trapped themselves between her neck and the pinkish cord encircling it. Blood sparkled on her knuckles. Behind Celeste, gripping the ends of the noose, swayed Cazalis, bare head wrenched back by Jimmy McKell's stranglehold; the big man's tongue was between his teeth, eyes open to the sky in a calm expressionless glare. Jimmy's free hand was trying to claw Cazalis's clutch loose from the cord. Jimmy's lips were drawn back; he looked as if he were laughing.

Ellery reached them a half-step before the others.

He smashed Cazalis directly behind the left ear with his fist, inserted his arm between Jimmy and Cazalis and smacked Jimmy's chin with the heel of his hand.

"Let go, Jimmy, let go."

Cazalis slid to the wet concrete, his eyes still open in that curious glare. Goldberg, Young, Johnson, Piggott, one of the patrolmen, fell on him. Young kneed him; he doubled under them, screeching like a woman.

"That wasn't necessary," said Ellery. He kept nursing his right hand.

"I've got a trick knee," said Young apologetically. "In a case like this it goes pop! like that."

Inspector Queen said, "Open his fist. As if he were your mother. I want that cord smoking hot."

An intern in an overcoat was kneeling by Celeste. Her hair glittered in a puddle. Jimmy cried out, lunging. Ellery caught him by the collar with his other hand.

"But she's dead!"

"Fainted, Jimmy."

Inspector Queen was scrutinizing the pink cord with love. It was made of thick, tough silk. Tussah.

He said, "How's the girl, Doctor, hm?" as he eyed the noose dangling from his upheld hand.

"Neck's lacerated some, mostly at the sides and back," replied the ambulance doctor. "Her hands got the worst pressure. Smart little gal."

"She looks dead, I tell you."

"Shock. Pulse and respiration good. She'll live to tell this to her grandchildren till it's coming out of their ears." Celeste moaned. "She's on her way out of it now."

Jimmy sat down in the wet of the alley.

The Inspector was snaking the silk cord carefully into an envelope. Ellery heard him humming "My Wild Irish Rose."

They had Cazalis's hands manacled behind his back. He was lying on his soaked right side with his knees drawn up, staring through Young's big legs at an overturned trash can a few feet away. His face was dirty and gray, his eyes seemed all whites.

The Cat.

He lay in a cage whose bars were the legs of men, breathing ponderously.

The Cat.

They were taking it easy, waiting for the intern to get finished with Celeste Phillips; joking and laughing. Johnson, who disliked Goldberg, offered Goldberg a cigaret; Goldberg had lost his pack somewhere. Goldberg accepted it companionably and struck a match for Johnson, too, who said, "Thanks, Goldie." Piggott was telling about the time—it was during a train wreck—when he had been cuffed to a homicidal maniac for fourteen solid hours: "I was so jittery I smacked him on the jaw every ten minutes to keep him quiet." They guffawed.

Young was complaining to the patrolman, "Hell, I was on the Harlem run for six years. Up there you use your knee first and ask questions afterward. Shiv artists. The whole bastardly lot of 'em."

"I don't know," said the patrolman doubtfully. "I've known some that were white men. You take Zilgitt."

"What difference does it make?" Young glanced down at their prisoner. "He's squirrel bait, anyway. Where there's no sense there's no feeling."

The man lying at their feet had his mouth going a little, as if he was chewing on something.

"Hey," said Goldberg. "What's he doing that for?"

"Doing what?" Inspector Queen shouldered in, alarmed.

"Look at his mouth, Inspector!"

The Inspector dropped to the concrete and grasped Cazalis's jaw.

"Watch it, Inspector," someone laughed. "They bite."

The mouth opened docilely. Young flashed a light into it over Inspector Queen's shoulder.

"Nothing," said the Inspector. "He was chewing on his tongue."

Young said, "Maybe the Cat's got it," and most of them laughed again.

"Hurry it up, Doctor, will you?" said the Inspector.

"In a minute." The intern was wrapping Celeste in a blanket; her head kept lolling.

Jimmy was trying to fend off the other ambulance man. "Scatter, scatter," he said. "Can't you see McKell is in conference?"

"McKell, you've got blood all over your mouth and chin."

"I have?" Jimmy felt his chin, looked at his fingers with surprise.

"Mister, you bit halfway through your lower lip."

"Come onnnnn, Celeste," crooned Jimmy. Then he yelped. The ambulance man kept working on his mouth.

It had turned colder suddenly, but no one seemed to notice. The fog was thinning rapidly. There was a star or two.

Ellery was sitting on the trash can. "My Wild Irish Rose" was going patiently in his head, like a hurdy-gurdy. Several times he tried to turn it off but it kept going.

There was another star.

The back windows of the surrounding buildings were all bright and open; it was very cheerful. Crammed with heads and shoulders. Box seats. Arena, that was it. The pit. *It*. They couldn't possibly see *It*, but they could hope, couldn't they? In New York, hope dwells in every eye. A dwindling old building. A sidewalk excavation. An open manhole. A traffic accident. *What was it? What's happened? Who got hit? Is it gangsters? What are they doing down there?*

It didn't matter.

The Cat's in his Hell, all's right with the world.

New York papers please copy.

"Jimmy, come here."

"Not now."

"*Extra*," called Ellery, with significance. "Don't you want a bonus?"

Jimmy laughed. "Didn't I tell you? They fired me last week."

"Get to a phone. They'll make you editor."

"The hell with them."

"It's worth a million to them."

"I've got a million."

Ellery rocked on the trash can. The screwball was really a card. Swell kid, Jimmy. Ellery laughed again, wondering why his hand felt so queer.

The third floor windows at the rear of 486 East 29th were all filled, too.

They don't know. The name of Soames goes down in history and they're sitting up there wondering whose name they'll read in the papers.

"Here she is," announced the intern. "Greetings, Miss, and may I be the first to congratulate you?"

Her bandaged hands went to her throat.

Jimmy mumbled to the other one, "Will you get the devil off my lip? Baby, it's me. It's all over. *Fini*. Jimmy, baby. Remember me?"

"Jimmy."

"She recognizes me! All over, baby."

"That horrible . . ."

"It's all over."

My Wiiiiild Irish Rooooose . . .

"I was hurrying along First Avenue."

"Practically a grandmother. This iodine dispenser said so."

"He pulled me in as I passed. I saw his face and then it was dark. My neck."

"Save it, save your strength for a little later, Miss Phillips," said the Inspector genially.

"All over, baby."

"The Cat. Where is he? Jimmy, where is he?"

"Now stop shaking. Lying right over there. Just an alley cat. See? Look. Don't be afraid."

Celeste began to cry.

"It's all over, baby." Jimmy had his arms around her and they rocked together in a little puddle.

Wonder where they think Celeste is. Down here "helping out," probably. Clara Barton stuff . . . And is it not a battlefield? The Battle of First Avenue. After sending McKell's Marauders out on cavalry reconnaissance, General Queen feinted with Phillips's Corps and engaged the enemy with his Centre Str . . . Ellery thought he spied the dark head of Marilyn Soames among the other heads, but then he untwisted his neck and rubbed the back of it. *What was in that beer?*

"Okay, Doc, okay," the Inspector was saying. "Over here now."

The intern stooped over Cazalis, looked up. "Who did you say this is?" he asked sharply.

"He got a hard one in the groin. I don't want to move him till you say it's all right."

"This man is Dr. Edward Cazalis, the psychiatrist!"

Everybody laughed.

"Thanks, Doc," said Detective Young, winking at the others. "We're beholden to you."

They laughed again.

The intern flushed. After a while he got to his feet. "Hold him up and he'll make it. Nothing serious."

"Upsadaisy!"

"Say, I'll bet he was pulling a fakeroo all the time."

"Young, you better practice up that knee action."

"Watch him, watch him."

He was making a strong effort to move his legs, mincing along half on his toes like a student ballet dancer, his knees not quite supporting him.

"Don't look," Jimmy said. "It's not the least bit important."

"It is. I want to. I promised my—" But then Celeste shuddered and looked away.

"Keep that street out there cleared." The Inspector looked around. "Hold it." The procession stopped and Cazalis seemed grateful. "Where's Ellery?"

"Over there, Inspector."

"Hey."

"What's the matter with him?"

My Wiiiiild Ir . . .

The trash can clattered and rolled a few feet.

"He's hurt."

"Doctor!"

The intern said, "He passed out. His hand is fractured. Easy . . ."

Easy. Easy does it, a mere five months' worth of sniff and dig and hunt and plot—twenty-one weeks of it; to be exact, twenty-one weeks and one day, one hundred and forty-eight days from a soft rap on the door of an East 19th Street apartment to a hard smash to a man's head in a First Avenue alley; from Abernethy, Archibald Dudley to Phillips, Celeste, alias Sue Martin, Girl Spy; from Friday, June 3, to Saturday, October 29; point four-o-four per cent of a single year in the life of the City of New York, during which period one of the City's numerous hatchetmen cut down the population of the Borough of Manhattan by nine lives although, to be sure, there was that little matter of the Metropol Hall panic and the rioting that followed; in the sum, however, statistical chicken feed lost in Bunyan's barnyard, and what was all the excitement about?

Easy does it.

Easy does it, for the Cat sat in a hard chair under photographic light and he was not the tails-lashing chimera of the broken metropolitan dream but a tumbledown old man with shaking hands and an anxious look, as if he wanted to please but not quite sure what was required of him. They had found a second salmon-pink cord of tussah silk on his person and at the rear of one of the locked filing cabinets in his Park Avenue office a cache of two dozen others of which more than half were dyed the remembered blue; he had instructed them where to look and he had picked out the right key for them from the assortment in his key case. He said he had had the cords for many years; since late in 1930, when he was on a tour around the world after returning from his obstetrical practice. In India a native had sold him the cords, representing them to be old strangling cords of thuggee origin. Later, before putting them away, he had dyed them blue and pink. Why had he saved them all these years? He looked bewildered. No, his wife had never known about them; he had been alone when he purchased them in the bazaar and he had kept them hidden afterward . . . His head slanted readily to their questions and he answered in a courteous way, although there were stretches when he became uncommunicative or slightly erratic. But the rambling episodes were few; for the most part he caught the pertinent past in brilliant focus, sounding quite like the Dr. Cazalis they had known.

His eyes, however, remained unchanged, staring, lenslike.

Ellery, who had come there directly from Bellevue Hospital with Celeste Phillips and Jimmy McKell, sat to one side, his right hand in a splint, listening and saying nothing. He had not yet run down; he still had a feeling of unreality. The Police Commissioner and the District Attorney were also present; and at a little past 4:30 A.M. the Mayor hurried in, paler than the prisoner.

But the grimy old man in the chair seemed not to see any of them. It was a deliberate avoidance, they all felt, dictated by a kind of tact. They knew how plausible such madmen could be.

In the main, his account of the nine murders was remarkable for its detail. Barring his few lapses from clarity, which might well have resulted from pain, confusion, emotional and physical exhaustion—had they not known what he really was—his confession was excellent.

His least satisfactory reply came in response to Ellery's only contribution to the night's inquisition.

When the prisoner had nearly concluded, Ellery leaned forward and asked: "Dr. Cazalis, you've admitted that you hadn't seen any of these people since their infancy.

As individuals, therefore, they couldn't possibly have meant anything to you. Yet obviously you had something against them. What was it? Why did you feel you had to kill them?''

Because the conduct of the psychotic appears unmotivated only when judged in the perspective of reality—that is, by more or less healthy minds viewing the world as it is . . .

Said Dr. Cazalis.

The prisoner twisted in his chair and looked directly at the source of Ellery's voice, although because of the lights beating on his bruised face it was plain that he could not see beyond them.

"Is that Mr. Queen?" he asked.

"Yes."

"Mr. Queen," said the prisoner in a friendly, almost indulgent tone, "I doubt that you're scientifically equipped to understand."

Sunday's morning was full-grown when they got away from the reporters. Jimmy McKell sprawled in a corner of the taxi with Celeste in his arms and in the other corner Ellery pampered his immobilized hand, looking out the window on his side not for reasons of delicacy but because he wanted to see through it.

The City looked different this morning.

Felt, smelled, sounded different.

New.

The air had a tune in it. Maybe it was the churchbells. Churches were bellowing their wares downtown and up, East Side to west. *Adeste fideles!* Come and get it!

In the residential sections delicatessens, bakeries, newsstands, drugstores were busy opening.

An El train went bucketing by somewhere.

A newsboy, bluepawed.

Occasionally an early riser appeared, rubbing his hands together, walking smartly.

At taxi stands cabs stood parked. Bootleg radios going. Drivers intent.

People began collecting around them.

New York was stretching.

Waking up.

12

New York awoke and for a week or two the ugly vision tarried. Had radio's celebrated planetary invasion of Earth been real, people would have stood in long lines afterward to view the Martian remains and wonder at their gullibility. Now that the monster was localized in a cage, where it could be seen, heard, pinched, reported, read about, even pitied, New York queued up. The clarity of hindsight engaged the facts of postmortem and out of it came citywide conversation pieces in shame, a safe and even enjoyable exercise for all. The Cat was merely a demented old man; and what was one lunatic against a city? File and forget; Thanksgiving was coming.

New York laughed.

Still, like his British cousin from Cheshire, the Cat lingered in his grin after the rest of him had vanished. It was not the grin of the old man in the cell; that old man did not grin. It was the grin of the dream monster. And there were the children, with shorter memories but fresher senses. Parents had still to contend with nightmares. Not excluding their own.

Then, on the morning after Armistice Day, the body of a young girl later identified as Reva Xavinzky, of Flushing, was found in various places about Jamaica Bay. She had been ravished, mutilated, dismembered, and decapitated. The familiar horrors of this case, its recognizably atrocious details, instantly diverted public attention; and by the time the murderer, an ex-Army deserter with a typical history of the sexual psychopath, was caught, the diversion—at least insofar as adults were concerned—was complete. Thereafter the word "cat" raised no grislier image in the mind's eye of the average New Yorker than that of a small domestic animal characterized by cleanliness, independence, and a useful appetite for mice. (That the case of Reva Xavinzky, performed a like service for younger New York may be questioned; but most parents seemed to feel that with Thanksgiving and Christmas hovering, the Cat would be supplanted in their children's dreams by turkey and Santa Claus. And perhaps they were right.)

There was a minority with special interests, however, who hung on. For some— certain City officials, reporters, psychiatrists, the families of the Cat's victims— this was a matter of duty, or specific assignment, or professional or personal implication. For others—the sociologists, the psychologists, the philosophers—the capture of the nine-times murderer signaled the opportunity to launch a socio-scientific investigation of the City's behavior since early June. The second groups were wholly unconcerned with Edward Cazalis; the first were concerned with no one else.

The prisoner had retreated to a sullen phase. He refused to talk, he refused to exercise, for a time he refused to eat; he appeared to exist only for the visits of his wife, for whom he called constantly. Mrs. Cazalis, accompanied by her sister and brother-in-law, had flown back from Florida on October 30. She had refused to believe the reports of her husband's arrest as the Cat, protesting to reporters in Miami and New York that "there's some mistake. It can't be. My husband is innocent." But that was before her first meeting with him. She emerged from it deathly pale, shaking her head to the press, going directly to the home of her sister. She was there for four hours; then she returned to her own apartment.

It was noted in those first excited days after the monster's capture that it was his mate who took the full impact of the City's animus. She was pointed out, jeered at, followed. Her sister and brother-in-law vanished; no one could or would say where they had gone. Her maid deserted her and she was unable to engage another. She was asked to vacate her apartment by a management that made it frantically clear they would use every means within their power to evict her if she resisted. She did not resist; she placed her household furnishings in storage and moved to a small downtown hotel; and when the hotel management discovered who she was the next morning, she was asked to leave. This time she found quarters in a lugubrious rooming house on Horatio Street in the Village; and it was here that her eldest brother, Roger Braham Merigrew of Bangor, Maine, located her.

Merigrew's visit to his sister did not outlast the night. He had come accompanied by a shadlike man carrying a briefcase; when the two emerged from the Horatio Street building at 3:45 in the morning and found the reporters waiting, it was Merigrew's companion who covered his factor's escape and gave the statement which appeared in the newspapers later that day. "As Mr. Merigrew's attorney I am authorized to state the following: Mr. Merigrew has attempted for several days to persuade his sister, Mrs. Cazalis, to rejoin her kin in Maine. Mrs. Cazalis refused. So Mr. Merigrew flew down to renew his appeal in person. Mrs. Cazalis still refuses. There is nothing further Mr. Merigrew can do, therefore he is returning home. That's all there is to this." Asked by reporters why Mr. Merigrew did not remain by his sister's side in New York, the Maine attorney snapped, "You'll have to ask Mr. Merigrew that." Later, a Bangor paper managed to get a few words from Merigrew. He said, "My sister's husband is insane. There's no cause to stand by a murdering lunatic. It's not fair to us, the publicity and so on. Any further statement will have to come from my sister." The Merigrews owned large conservative business interests throughout New England.

So Mrs. Cazalis faced her ordeal alone, living in a squalid Village room, dogged by reporters, visiting her husband, and growing daily wilder-eyed and more silent.

She engaged the famous attorney, Darrell Irons, to defend her husband. Irons was uncommunicative, but it was rumored that he was having his hands full. Cazalis, it was said, "refused" to be defended and would not co-operate with the psychiatrists Irons sent endlessly to his cell. Stories began to circulate of maniacal rages, attempted physical violence, incoherent ravings on the part of the prisoner; those who knew Darrell Irons stated that he had inspired them and that most likely, therefore, they were not true. It was clear what Irons's defense would be, for the District Attorney seemed determined to prosecute Cazalis as a man who knew the nature and quality of his acts, who had demonstrated in his daily life even during the period of his crimes his capacity to act rationally and who therefore, under legal definition, must be considered "sane," no matter what he may have been under the medical definition. The District Attorney set considerable store, it was said, by the prisoner's conversations with the Mayor's Special Investigator and Inspector Richard Queen of Police Headquarters on the night of the Lenore Richardson investigation, when he had outlined his "theory" of the Cat case as pointing to a psychotic pure and simple. This had been the calculated act of a calculating murderer, the D.A. was said to hold, purposely turning the investigation into a channel of "gibbering idiocy" the more effectually to divert attention from the responsible mentality behind the stranglings.

A dramatic trial was forecast.

Ellery's interest in the case flagged early. He had lived with it far too long at too steep a pitch to experience anything but exhaustion after the events of the night of October 29-30. He found himself trying not merely to forget the past but to dodge the present. The present, at least, would not be evaded; it insisted on applying pomp to circumstance. There were Athenian honors, press and radio-television interviews, a hundred invitations to address civic groups and write articles and investigate unsolved crimes. He managed to back away from most of these with approximate grace. The few he could not avoid left him irritable and profane. "What's the matter with you?" demanded his father. "Let's say," snapped Ellery, "that success has gone to my head." The Inspector puckered; he was no stranger to migraine, either. "Well," he said cheerfully, "at least this time it's not caused by failure."

Ellery continued to fling himself from chair to chair.

One day he decided he had located the infection. It was the boil of pressure. But not of the past or the present; of the future. He was not finished. On the morning of January 2, in one of the larger courtrooms under the gray dome of the Supreme Court building in Foley Square, a Mr. Justice-Somebody would make his blackrobed entrance from chambers and one Edward Cazalis, alias the Cat, would go on trial charged with murder. And in this trial one Ellery Queen, Special Investigator to the Mayor, would be a major witness for the people. There would be no release for him until that ordeal was passed. Then he could go about his business purged of the whole corrupting mess.

Why the trial should cause him such twinges Ellery did not attempt to diagnose. Having discovered—as he thought—the source of his malady, he adjusted his psychic screws to the inevitable and turned to other matters. By this time Reva Xavinzky had been collated and the spotlight probed elsewhere. He was able almost to relax. Even to think about getting back to writing. The novel he had neglected since August 25 lay in its lonely grave. He exhumed it and was surprised to find it as alien as any tax roll papyrus dug out of the Nile delta after three thousand years. Once, long ago, he had labored greatly on this, and now it had the historic smell of shards. *Look on my Works, ye Mighty, and despair!* Despairing, Ellery dropped the primitive effort of his pre-Cat days into the fire.

And sat him down to compose a newer wonder.

But before he could settle his feet on the bottom drawer, there was an agreeable interruption.

Jimmy McKell and Celeste Phillips were being wed and it seemed that Mr. Queen, in his single person, was to constitute the wedding party.

"Exclusive," grinned Jimmy, "by McKell."

"Jimmy means," sighed Celeste, "that his father hit the roof and won't come."

"He's biting the Chippendale," said Jimmy, "because his hitherto invincible weapon—disownery? disownment?—has turned to womanish water in his hand, now that I'm buckled into Grandfather's millions. And Mother'd no sooner got over sopping up the tears than she started planning a twenty-thousand guest wedding. So I said the hell with it—"

"And we got our license, we've taken our Wassermanns—"

"Successfully," added Jimmy, "so would you hand my bride over to me in City Hall at 10:30 tomorrow morning, Mr. Q?"

They were married between the Arthur Jackson Beals of Harlem and the Gary G. Cohens-to-be of Brownsville, Brooklyn; the City Clerk did them distinguished honor by going no more than half so rapidly as usual; Mr. Queen bussed the bride with a fervent "At last!"; and afterward there were only eighteen reporters and cameramen waiting for them in the hall. Mrs. James Guymer McKell exclaimed that she couldn't imagine how in the world they had all known, because she and Jimmy hadn't breathed a word to anyone but Ellery . . . and her groom growled an invitation to his ex-fellow-journalists to hoist a few on him, whereupon the augmented party set out for La Guardia Airport and the wedding luncheon was imbibed in a cocktail lounge, with Parlay Phil Gonachy of the *Extra* crying the square dance which somehow followed. At the climax of the thunderous quadrille the Airport police appeared; causing certain strict constitutionalists among the working guests to defend with camera, bottle, and bar stool the sacred freedom of the press and enabling the happy couple to slip away with their sponsor.

"Whither do you fly with your unravished bride?" inquired Mr. Queen in a slightly wobbly tone. "Or is said question none of my olfactory business?"

"It is entirely *comme il faut*," replied Mr. McKell with the grandeur of one who has also given generous lip service to the sacraments of Reims and Epernay, "since we fly no-whither," and he steered his bride gallantly exitward.

"Then why La Guardia?"

"A ruse to mislead those roistering anteaters. Equerry!"

"We're spending our honeymoon at the Half-Moon Hotel," confided the bride with a blush as a cab rushed up. "You're positively the only one who knows *that*."

"Mrs. McKell, I shall guard your secret with my honor."

"Mrs. McKell," murmured Mrs. McKell.

"All my life," said her husband in a whisper that shot heads around twenty feet away, "I have yearned for a winter's honeymoon among the frolicking Polar Bears of Coney Island." And Mr. McKell yelled to the apprehensive hack, "Okay, White Fang. Mush!"

Ellery observed their exhaust fondly as they rode off into the smog.

After that he found it joy to settle down to work. Ideas for a new mystery novel flowed like the wedding party's champagne; the only problem was to keep a sober judgment.

One morning Ellery looked around to find Father Christmas breathing down his neck. And he saw with some astonishment that New York's Yule was to be white; overnight, 87th Street sparkled. A Samoyed rolling in the snow across the street made him think of the arctic huskies; and thus he was reminded of the James McKells and their Coney Island honeymoon among the curious tribe of New Yorkers who called themselves the Polar Bears. Ellery grinned, wondering why he had not heard from Jimmy and Celeste. Then it occurred to him that he had, and he began looking through his deserted mail, an accumulation of several weeks.

He found Jimmy's note in the middle of the heap.

> *We like it Ellery. We like it.*
> *If you have a mind to crack a friendly jeroboam for auld lang*
> *syne, the McKells are receiving in the back room of Kelly's Bar*
> *on East 39th at 2 P.M. tomorrow for all of the tribe of Jurgen.*

We still haven't found an apartment and are bedding down with
various disreputable characters. I won't take my wife to a hotel.

James

P.S. If you don't show, we'll see you at the Assizes.
P.P.S. Mrs. McK. sends love.   *J.*

The postmark was ten days old

The McKells and, Christmas . . . This called for heroism.

A half hour later Ellery was up to his armpits in lists, and a half hour after that he was sallying forth in galoshes.

Fifth Avenue was already a speckled swamp. The plows were still working in the side streets but along the Avenue they had toiled all night like beetles rolling dung and the brown-spattered snowplows challenged the agility of jaywalkers and squeezed motor traffic into an impossible bottleneck.

A white Christmas, everybody was saying, shuffling through the slush, sneezing and coughing.

At Rockefeller Center Noel was being caroled and in the Plaza, dwarfed by a hundred-foot tree raped from some Long Island estate, the skaters were whizzing along to a determined version of "Jingle Bells."

Santas in wrinkled red suits clanged at almost every corner, shivering. Shop windows were faery glimpses into the magic wood of advertising. And everywhere people slipped and sloshed, and Ellery slipped and sloshed with them, wearing the glazed frown by which you may know all New Yorkers in the last week before Christmas.

He dodged in and out of great stores, trampling on little children, pushing and being pushed, clawing at merchandise, shouting his name and address, writing out checks—until, in midafternoon, his master list was reduced to a single uncrossed-off name.

But beside that name stood a large, repulsive question mark.

The McKells were the nice problem. Ellery had not sent them a wedding gift in view of the uncertainty surrounding their future habitat. At the time he had thought that by Christmas they would surely be settled, whereupon he could combine the nuptial gift with the seasonal; and here was the annual Miracle and neither the problem of the McKells' residence nor the nature of his gifts to them had been solved. He had kept an eye alerted for inspiration all day. Silver? Glass? Silk?—no, not silk, definitely not silk. Ceramic? He saw a glossy Bubastis and shuddered. Native wood carving, something primitive? An antique? Nothing came, nothing at all.

Until, in late afternoon, Ellery found himself on 42nd Street between Fifth and Sixth Avenues. Before Stern's a Salvation Army lass, a strapping soldier of charity, sang hymns accompanied by a bluing comrade at a portable organ set down in the slush.

The organ made tinkly sounds in the treble and for a moment sounded like a musicbox.

Musicbox.

Musicbox!

They were originally a fad of French exquisites, dispensing snuff to little metallic tunes, but centuries of delight had made them currency in the realm of childhood and their pure elfishness purchased smiles from lovers.

Ellery dropped a dollar in the tambourine and considered his idea excitedly. Something special . . . featuring the Wedding March . . . yes, that was a must . . . inlays of precious woods, mother-of-pearl, cunning stonework . . . a big one, artfully made. An import, of course. The most delicate pieces came from central Europe . . . Swiss. A Swiss musicbox of the most elaborate craftsmanship would be expensive, but hang the expense. It would become a household treasure, a little chest of golden sentiment unawed by the McKell millions, to be kept at their bedside until they were eigh—

Swiss.

Swiss?

Switzerland!

ZÜRICH!

In a twinkling musicboxes, Wedding Marches, Christmas itself were forgotten. Ellery waded wildly across 42nd Street and dashed through the side entrance into the New York Public Library.

For a point in his plot-in-progress had been bothering him for days. It concerned phobias. Ellery was postulating a significant relationship (of such is the kingdom of mystery writers) among morbid fear of crowds, of darkness, and of failure. Just how he had come to juxtapose these three phobias plotwise he did not know; it was his impression that he had read about their interrelationship, or heard about it, somewhere. But research had failed to turn up the source. It was holding him up.

And now Zürich. Zürich on the Limmat, Athens of Switzerland.

Zürich rang that bell!

For now Ellery remembered having either read or been told that in Zürich, at some recent international meeting of psychoanalysis, precisely such a phobic relationship had been the subject of a paper.

Search in the foreign periodical section of the Library rewarded him in less than an hour.

The source was a *Züricher* scientific journal, one of a pile Ellery was leafing through as he exercised his stiffened German. The entire issue was given over to the proceedings of the convention, which had lasted ten days, and all scientific papers read before it were reprinted in full. The paper he was interested in bore the alarming title of *Ochlophobia, Nyctophobia, and Ponophobia;* but when he glanced through it he found it to contain exactly what he was looking for.

He was about to go back to the beginning to start rereading carefully when an italic note at the end of the article caught his eye.

A familiar name.

—Paper read by Dr. Edward Cazalis of the United States . . .

Of course! It was Cazalis who had been responsible for the birth of the idea. Ellery recalled it all now. It had come up during that September night in the Richardson apartment, in the first hours of the on-scene investigation of Lenore's murder. There had been a lull and Ellery found himself in conversation with the psychiatrist. They had talked about Ellery's fiction and Dr. Cazalis had remarked with a smile that the field of phobias offered Ellery's craft rich stores of material. On being pressed, Cazalis had mentioned work he himself had done on "ochlophobia and nyctophobia" in relation to the development of "ponophobia"; in fact, Ellery remembered his saying, he had read a paper on the subject at a convention in

Zürich. And Cazalis had talked for a little about his findings, until they were interrupted by the Inspector and recalled to the sorry business of the night.

Ellery made a face. The brief conversation had sunk into his unconscious under the weight of events, to emerge two months later under pressure, its source forgotten. *Sic semper* the "original" idea.

It was an irony of coincidence that Cazalis should prove responsible for it. Smiling, Ellery glanced at the footnote again.

> *—Paper read by Dr. Edward Cazalis of the United States at the night session of 3rd June. This paper was originally scheduled for presentation at 10 P.M. However, the preceding speaker, Dr. Naardvoessler of Denmark, exceeded his allotted time and did not conclude the reading of his paper until 11:52 P.M. A motion to adjourn was withdrawn when President Dr. Jurasse of France, Chairman of the Convention, asserted that Dr. Cazalis had attended all the sessions patiently awaiting the Convention's pleasure and that, notwithstanding the lateness of the hour, in view of the fact that this was the concluding session of the Convention, the distinguished Members present should extend the adjournment hour to enable Dr. Cazalis to present his paper. This was done* viva voce, *Dr. Cazalis presented his paper, concluding at 2:03 A.M., and the Convention was adjourned for the year by President Dr. Jurasse as of 2:24 A.M. 4th June.*

Still smiling, Ellery flipped the journal to the front cover and glanced at the year of issue.

Now he did not smile. Now he sat staring at the last digit of the date as it grew rapidly larger, or as he himself rapidly shrunk.

"*Drink Me.*"

He felt—if it could be called feeling—like Alice.

The *Züricher* rabbit-hole.

And the Looking-Glass.

How did you get out?

At last Ellery got up from the table and made his way to the information desk outside the main reading rooms.

He crouched over copies of *Who's Who* and the latest annual roster of the American Psychiatric Association.

Who's Who . . . Cazalis, Edward.

The national roster of the American Psychiatric Association . . . Cazalis, Edward.

In each case a single Cazalis, Edward.

In each case the same Cazalis, Edward.

It was really not to be borne.

Ellery returned to his Zürich journal.

He turned the pages slowly.

Calmly.

Anyone watching me is saying: There's a man who's sure of himself. He turns pages calmly. Knows just what's what."

There it was.

> *Dr. Fulvio Castorizo, Italy*
> *Dr. John Sloughby Cavell, Great Britain*
> *Dr. Edward Cazalis, United States*

Of course he'd be listed.
And that old man? Had he been present?
Ellery turned the page.

> *Dr. Walther Schoenzweig, Germany*
> *Dr. Andrés Selborán, Spain*
> *Dr. Béla Seligmann, Austria*

Someone tapped Ellery on the shoulder.
"Closing time, sir."
The room was empty.
Why hadn't they caught it?
He trudged into the hall. A guard directed him to the staircase when he made the wrong turn.
The District Attorney knows his business. His office is topnotch. They're old hands.

He supposed they had backtracked from Katz, Donald, to Petrucchi, Stella, past Richardson, Lenore, to Willikins, Beatrice, the way growing fainter as they retreated in time until, at the five-months-ago mark, it had disappeared to become impassable. But that wouldn't have stopped them. They probably had one or two or even three others they hadn't been able to fix. It would actually not seem necessary to fix each one. Not in so many murders. Not over such a long period in such a peculiar case where the identity of the victim was a detail hardly meriting notice. Six, say, would do the District Attorney nicely. Plus the caught-in-the-act attempt on Celeste-Phillips-thinking-she-was-Marilyn-Soames and the minute-to-minute evidence of his Soames stalk in the days preceding the attempt.

Ellery walked uncertainly up Fifth Avenue. The weather had turned very cold and the slush had frozen in serrated little icehills of dirty gray, rutted and pocked, a relief map of nowhere on which he teetered along.
This will have to be done from home . . . I've got to have a place where I can sit and feel safe.
When the ax falls.
Executions brought to your door.
At no extra charge.
He stopped at a shop window through which a faceless angel with a needlethin torch was trying to fly, and he looked at his watch.
In Vienna it's the middle of the night.
Then I can't go home.
Not yet.
Not till it's time.
He drew back from the thought of facing his father like a turtle rapped on the nose.

Ellery let himself in at a quarter of 4 in the morning.

On the tips of his toes.

The apartment was dark except for a night light in the majolica lamp on the living room table.

He felt refrigerated. The mercury had dropped to five above in the streets and the apartment was only a little less icy.

His father was snoring. Ellery went to the bedroom door and shut it, thievishly.

Then he stole into his study and turned the key. He did not remove his overcoat. Switching on the desk light, he sat down and drew the telephone to him.

He dialed the operator and asked for the Overseas Operator.

There were difficulties.

It was almost 6 o'clock. The steam had just begun to rattle the radiators and he kept his eye apprehensively on the door.

The Inspector was a 6 o'clock riser.

Finally, he got through.

Ellery prayed that his father oversleep as he waited for the Vienna operator to settle matters at her end.

"Here is your party, sir."

"Professor Seligmann?"

"*Ja?*"

It was an old, old voice. Its bass cracked and a little peevish.

"My name is Ellery Queen," said Ellery in German. "You do not know me, Herr Professor—"

"Incorrect," said the aged voice in English, Oxonian English with a Viennese accent. "You are an author of *romans policiers,* and out of guilt feelings for the many crimes you commit on paper you also pursue malefactors in life. You may speak English, Mr. Queen. What do you want?"

"I hope I haven't caught you at an inopportune moment—"

"At my age, Mr. Queen, all moments are inopportune except those devoted to speculations about the nature of God. Yes?"

"Professor Seligmann, I believe you are acquainted with the American psychiatrist, Edward Cazalis."

"Cazalis? He was my pupil. Yes?" There was nothing in the voice, nothing at all.

Is it possible he doesn't know?

"Have you seen Dr. Cazalis in recent years?"

"I saw him in Zürich earlier this year. Why do you ask?"

"On which occasion, Herr Professor?"

"At an international convention of psychoanalysis. But you do not tell me why, *mein Herr.*"

"You don't know the trouble Dr. Cazalis is in?"

"Trouble? No. What is this trouble?"

"I can't explain now, Professor Seligmann. But it's of the greatest importance that you give me exact information."

The line wheezed and keened and for a moment Ellery thought: *Let us pray.*

But it was only the mysterious defects of the transoceanic process coming up through Professor Seligmann's silence.

He heard the old voice again.

Growling this time.

"Are you Cazalis's friend?"

Am I?

"Yes, I'm Cazalis's friend," said Ellery.

"You hesitate. I do not like this."

"I hesitated, Professor Seligmann," said Ellery carefully, "because friendship is a word I weigh."

He thought he had lost, but there was a faint chuckle in his ear and the old man said: "I attended the last few days of the Zürich meeting. Cazalis was present, I heard him read his paper on the night of the last session and I kept him up until long past dawn afterward in my hotel room telling him how absurd I thought it was. Are you answered, Mr. Queen?"

"You have an excellent memory, Herr Professor."

"You question it."

"Forgive me."

"I am reversing the usual process of senescence. My memory is apparently the last to go." The old voice sharpened. "You may rely on the accuracy of the information."

"Professor Seligmann—"

There was a word, but it was swallowed up by such a howl of atmospheric expletive that Ellery snatched the receiver from his ear.

"Herr Professor Seligmann?"

"Yes. Yes. Are you—?" But then he faded, bolting into space.

Ellery cursed. Suddenly the line was clear.

"Herr Queen! Yes?"

"I must see you, Professor Seligmann."

"About Cazalis?"

"About Cazalis. If I fly to Vienna at once, will you see me?"

"You would be coming to Europe for this alone?"

"Yes."

"Come."

"Danke schön. Auf Wiedersehen."

But the old man had already broken the connection.

Ellery hung up.

He's so damned old. I hope he lasts.

His European flight was a bother from beginning to end. There was trouble about his visa, long talks with the State Department, much questioning and headshaking and form-filling. And passage seemed an impossibility; everyone was flying to Europe, and everyone who flew was a person of terrestial importance. Ellery began to realize what a very small tuber he was in the vast potato patch of world affairs.

He spent Christmas in New York after all.

The Inspector was magnificent. Not once in those days of pacing did he question the purpose of Ellery's trip. They merely discussed ways and means and the impediments.

But the Inspector's mustache grew noticeably ragged.

On Christmas Day Ellery cabled Professor Seligmann that he was being delayed by transportation and other nuisances but that he expected clearance at any hour.

The hour arrived late on December 28, in time to save the crumbs of Ellery's sanity.

Exactly how his father managed it Ellery never learned, but at dawn on December 29 he found himself on a conspicuously special plane in the company of persons of obvious distinction, all of whom were unmistakably bound on missions of global gravity. He had no idea where the plane was going or when it was scheduled to arrive. He heard murmurs of "London," "Paris," and such, but he could detect no Strauss waltzes, and to judge from the pursed blankness that met his worried inquiries the *Wiener Wald* was something in Moscow.

Neither his nails nor his stomach survived the Atlantic crossing.

When they did touch soil, it was fog-choked and British. Here a mysterious delay occurred. Three and a half hours later they took off again and Ellery sank into a doze. When he awoke it was to no thunder of motors. He sat in a great hush. As far as he could make out through his window, they had landed on an Arctic ice field; his very corpuscles were frozen. He nudged his companion, a U.S. Army officer. "Tell me, Colonel. Is our destination Fridtjof Nansen Land?"

"This is France. Where you going?"

"Vienna."

The colonel pushed out his lips and shook his head.

Ellery doggedly began to work his glaciated toes. Just as the first motor exploded, the co-pilot tapped his shoulder.

"Sorry, sir. Your space is required."

"What!"

"Orders, sir. Three diplomats."

"They must be very thin," said Ellery bitterly, getting up. "What happens to the bum?"

"You'll be put up at the field, sir, till they can find space for you on another ship."

"Can't I stand? I promise not to sit on anybody's lap and I'll gladly drop off over the Ringstrasse by parachute."

"Your bag's already off, sir. If you don't mind . . ."

Ellery spent thirty-one hours in a whistling billet, surrounded by the invisible Republic of France.

When he did reach Vienna, it was by way of Rome. It seemed impossible, but here he was on a frozen railway station with his bag and a little Italian priest who had unaccountably clung to him all the way from Rome and a sign somewhere that said *Westbahnhof,* which was certainly in Vienna so he was in Vienna.

On New Year's Day.

Where was Professor Seligmann?

Ellery began to worry about the Viennese fuel situation. He had a frostbitten recollection of engine trouble, a forced landing after tumbling over and over among the stars like a passenger on a space ship out of control, and a miserable railway train; but his chief memory was of the cold. As far as Ellery could make out, Europe was in the Second Ice Age; and he fully expected to locate Professor Seligmann imbedded in the heart of a glacier, like a Siberian mastodon, in a perfect state of preservation. He had telephoned Seligmann from Rome, giving the old man such information as he had had about his Italian plane's scheduled arrival. But he had not foreseen the journey through outer space and the groaning aftermath of the miserable train. Seligmann was probably getting pneumonia at . . . which airfield had that been?

The hell with it.

Two figures approached, crunching the icy platform. But one was a saber-toothed porter and the other a *Schwester* of some Austrian Roman Catholic order and neither satisfied Ellery's conception of a world-famous psychoanalyst.

The *Schwester* hurried the little Italian priest away and the saber-toothed porter came dashing up, full of colloquialisms and bad breath. Ellery found himself engaged in a battle of unconquerable tongues. Finally he left his bag in the fellow's charge, although not with confidence; the porter looked exactly like Heinrich Himmler. And he went sleuthing for a telephone. An excited female voice answered. "Herr Kavine? But is not Herr Professor with you? *Ach,* he will die in the cold! He must meet you. You are to wait, Herr Kavine, to wait where you are. *Westbahnhof?* Herr Professor will find you. He said it!"

"Bitte schön," muttered Herr Kavine, feeling like Landru; and he returned to the platform and the glacial epoch. And waited again, stamping, blowing on his fingers, and catching only every fifth word of the porter's. Probably the coldest winter Austria's had in seventy-nine years, he thought. It always is. Where was the *Föhn,* that lecherous Lurleian breeze from the Austrian Alps which reputedly caressed the jeweled hair of Danube's Queen? Gone, gone with all the winds of myth and fantasy. Gone with *Wiener Blut, leichtes Blut,* now a sullen mass of crimson icicles; gone with the *Frühlingsstimmen,* the spring voices, stilled by the throttling winter and the shrilling of boys crying the postwar *Morgenblätter,* such as they were; gone with the *Geschichten aus dem Wiener Wald,* now tales imprisoned in an antique musicbox which was forever broken . . . Ellery shivered, stamped, and blew as the disguised Himmler whined to him about *die guten, alten Zeiten.*

In the gas chambers, Ellery thought unreasonably. Tell it to Hitler, he thought. *An der schönen, blauen Donau . . .*

Ellery kept his refrigerated feet pumping and blew *pfuis* on the whole postwar European world.

Professor Seligmann came along at a little after 10 o'clock. The mere sight of that huge body, made huger by the black sheeplined greatcoat collared with Persian lamb and topped with a Russian-style *bashlyk,* was thawing; and when he took one of Ellery's disembodied members in his great, dry, warm hands Ellery melted to the inner man. It was like wandering lost over the earth and coming unexpectedly upon the grandfather of your tribe. The place did not matter; where the patriarch was, there was home. Ellery was struck by Seligmann's eyes particularly. In the lava of that massive face they were eternal fumaroles.

He barely noticed the changes in the Karlsplatz and on the Mariahilferstrasse as they rode in the psychoanalyst's ancient Fiat, driven by a scholarly looking chauffeur, into the Inner City through toppling streets toward the Universität district where the old man lived. He was too agreeably occupied in warming himself at his host.

"You find Vienna not as you expected?" asked Professor Seligmann suddenly.

Ellery started; he had been trying to ignore the shattered city. "It's been so many years since I was here last, Herr Professor. Since long before the War—"

"And the Peace," said the old man with a smile. "We must not overlook the Peace, Mr. Queen. Those difficult Russians, *nyet?* Not to mention those difficult English, those difficult French, and—*bitte schön*—those difficult Americans. Still, with our traditional *Schlamperei,* we manage to drag along. After the first War there was a song popular in Vienna which went, *'Es war einmal ein Walzer; es war einmal ein Wien.'* And we survived. Now we are singing it again, when we do not sing *'Stille Nacht, heilige Nacht.'* Everywhere in Vienna people are speaking of *die guten, alten Zeiten.* How do you say this? 'The good old days.' We Viennese swim in nostalgia, which has a high saline content; that is how we remain afloat.

Tell me about New York, Herr Queen. I have not visited your great city since 1927.''

Ellery, who had flown an ocean and crisscrossed half a continent to talk about something else, found himself giving a Times Square sightseeing busman's description of postwar Manhattan. And as he talked his sense of time, numbed by his hyperborean flight, began to revive and tick away; and he experienced the shock of recognition, as if this—now—were something very old insisting in a flash on being re-experienced. Tomorrow the trial of Edward Cazalis began and here he was, gossiping with a very old man over four thousand miles away by any route. A pulse began to clamor, and Ellery fell silent as the car drew up before a shellpocked apartment building on some broad *Strasse* whose name he had not even bothered to watch for.

Frau Bauer, Professor Seligmann's housekeeper, greeted her aged employer with aspirin, tea, a hot-water bag, and imprecation—and Ellery with a reminiscent frigidity; but the old man brushed her aside with a smiling *"Ruhe!"* and led Ellery by the hand, like a child, into the land of *Gemütlichkeit*.

Here, in Seligmann's study, were the best of the grace and charming intelligence of *Alt Wien*. The décor was twinkly with wit; it had animation, a leisurely joyousness, and it was a little sly in a friendly way. Here the self-conscious new did not intrude; there was nothing of Prussian precision; things had a patina, they were fine and they glowed.

Like the fire. Oh, the fire. Ellery sat in the lap of a motherly chair and he felt life. And when Frau Bauer served a starving man's breakfast, complete to melting, wonderful *Kaffee-kuchen* and pots of rich and aromatic coffee, he knew he was dreaming.

"The best coffee in the world," Ellery said to his host, raising his second cup. "One of the few national advertising claims with the merit of exact truth."

"The coffee, like almost everything else Elsa has served you, comes to me from friends in the United States." At Ellery's blush Seligmann chuckled. "Forgive me, Herr Queen, I am an old *Schuft,* as we say, a scoundrel. You have not crossed an ocean to indulge in my bad manners." He said evenly, "What is this now about my Edward Cazalis?"

So here it was.

Ellery left the motherly chair to stand before the fire like a man.

He said: "You saw Cazalis in Zürich in June, Professor Seligmann. Have you heard from him since?"

"No."

"Then you don't know what's been going on in New York this summer and fall?"

"Life. And death."

"I beg pardon?"

The old man smiled. "I assume it, Mr. Queen. Has it not always? I do not read newspapers since the war begins. That is for people who like to suffer. I, I do not like to suffer. I have surrendered myself to eternity. For me there is today this room, tomorrow cremation, unless the authorities cannot agree to allow it, in which case they may stuff me and place me in the clock tower of the *Rathaus* and I shall keep reminding them of the time. Why do you ask?"

"Herr Professor, I've just made a discovery."

"And what is that?"

Ellery laughed. "You know all about it."

The old man shook silently. He didn't when I phoned him from New York, thought Ellery, but he's done some catching up since.

"You do, don't you?"

"I have made some inquiries since, yes. Was it so evident? Sit down, Mr. Queen, sit down, we are not enemies. Your city has been terrorized by a paranoid murderer who strangled nine people, and now Edward Cazalis has been arrested for the crimes."

"You don't know the details."

"No."

Ellery sat down and related the story, beginning with the discovery of Archibald Dudley Abernethy's body and ending with the capture of Cazalis in the First Avenue alley. Then he briefly indicated the subsequent conduct of the prisoner.

"Tomorrow, Professor Seligmann, Cazalis's trial begins in New York, and I'm in Vienna—"

"To what purpose?" The old man regarded Ellery through the reek of his meerschaum. "I treated Cazalis as a patient when he came first to Vienna with his wife eighteen years ago, he studied under me subsequently, he left—I believe in 1935—to return to America, and since that time I have seen him once. This summer. What is it you want of me, Herr Queen?"

"Help."

"Mine? But the case is concluded. What more can there be? I do not understand. And if there is more, in which way could I be of assistance?"

"Yes." Ellery fingered his cup. "It must be confusing. Especially since the evidence against Cazalis is so damning. He was captured in the act of attempting a tenth murder. He directed the police to the hiding place of a stock of strangling cords and they were found where he said they would be, in the locked medical files in his office. And he confessed to the previous nine murders in considerable detail." Ellery set his cup down with care. "Professor Seligmann, I know nothing of your science beyond, let's say, some intelligent layman's understanding of the differences among neurotic behavior, neurosis, and psychosis. But in spite of—or perhaps because of—my lack of knowledge in your field I've been experiencing my own brand of tension, arising from a rather curious fact."

"And that is?"

"Cazalis never explained his . . . forgive me for hesitating . . . his motive. If he's psychotic, his motives proceed from false views of reality which can have only clinical interest. But if he's not . . . Herr Professor, before I'm satisfied, I've got to know what drove Cazalis to those murders."

"And you believe I can tell you, Herr Queen?"

"Yes."

"How so?" The old man puffed.

"You treated him. Moreover, he studied under you. To become a psychiatrist he had himself to be analyzed, a mandatory procedure—"

But Seligmann was shaking his great head. "In the case of a man so old as Cazalis was when he began to study with me, Mr. Queen, analysis is not a mandatory procedure. It is a most questionable procedure, Mr. Queen. Very few have been successfully analyzed at the age of 49, which is how old he was in 1931. Indeed, the entire project was questionable because of his age. I attempted it in Cazalis's case only because he interested me, he had a medical background, and I wished to experiment. As it happened, we were successful. Forgive me for interrupting—"

"At any rate, you analyzed him."

"I analyzed him, yes."

Ellery hitched forward. "What was wrong with him?"

Seligmann murmured: "What is wrong with any of us?"

"That's no answer."

"It is one answer, Mr. Queen. We all exhibit neurotic behavior. All, without exception."

"Now you're indulging your *Schufterei,* if that's the word." The old man laughed delightedly. "I ask you again, Herr Professor: What was the underlying cause of Cazalis's emotional upset?"

Seligmann kept puffing.

"It's the question that's brought me here. Because I know none of the essential facts, only the inconclusive superficial ones. Cazalis came from a poverty-laden background. He was one of fourteen children. He abandoned his parents and his brothers and sisters when a wealthy man befriended and educated him. And then he abandoned his benefactor. Everything about his career seems to me to point to an abnormal ambition, a compulsive overdrive to success—including his marriage. While his professional ethics remained high, his personal history is characterized by calculation and tremendous energy. And then, suddenly, at the apex of his career, in his prime—a breakdown. Suggestive."

The old man said nothing.

"He'd been treated for a mild case of what they called 'shell shock' in the first war. Was there a connection? I don't know. Was there, Herr Professor?"

But Seligmann remained silent.

"And what follows this breakdown? He abandons his practice, one of the most lucrative in New York. He allows his wife to take him on a world cruise, apparently recovers . . . but in Vienna, world's capital of psychoanalysis, another breakdown. The first collapse had been ascribed to overwork. But to what was the second collapse, after a leisurely cruise, ascribable? Suggestive! Professor Seligmann, you treated him. What caused Cazalis's breakdowns?"

Seligmann took the pipe from his mouth. "You ask me to disclose information, Mr. Queen, of which I came into possession in my professional capacity."

"A nice point, Herr Professor. But what are the ethics of silence when silence itself is immoral?"

The old man did not seem offended. He set the pipe down. "Herr Queen. It is evident to me that you have come not for information so much as for confirmation of conclusions wich you have already reached on the basis of insufficient data. Tell me your conclusions. Perhaps we shall find a way of resolving my dilemma."

"All right!" Ellery jumped up. But then he sat down again, forcing himself to speak calmly. "At the age of 44 Cazalis married a girl of 19 after a busy life devoid of personal relationships with women although in his work all his relationships were with women. During the first four years of their married life Mrs. Cazalis gave birth to two children. Dr. Cazalis not only cared for his wife personally during her pregnancies but performed both deliveries. Neither infant survived the delivery room. A few months after the second fatality in childbirth, Cazalis broke down— and retired from obstetrics and gynecology, never to go back to them.

"It seems to me, Professor Seligmann," said Ellery, "that whatever was wrong with Cazalis reached its climax in that delivery room."

"Why," murmured the old man, "do you say this?"

"Because . . . Professor Seligmann, I can't speak in terms of libido and mortido, Ego and Id. But I have some knowledge of human beings, and the sum of whatever observations I've been able to make of human behavior, and of my own and others' experience of life, impels me to the conclusion.

"I observe the fact: Cazalis turns his back with cold purpose on his childhood. Why? I speculate. His childhood was predominated by a mother who was always either carrying a child or having a child, by a laborer-father who was always begetting them, and by a horde of other children who were always getting in the way of his wishes. I speculate. Did Cazalis hate his mother? Did he hate his brothers and sisters? Did he feel guilt because he hated them?

"And I observe the career he sets for himself, and I say: Is there a significant connection between his hate for maternity and his specialization—as it were—in maternity? Is there a nexus between his hate for the numerous progeny of his parents and his determination to make himself an expert in the science of bringing more children into the world?

"Hate and guilt—and the defenses against them. I've put two and two together. Is this permitted, Herr Professor? Is this valid?"

Seligmann said, "One tends to oversimplify in your sort of mathematics, *mein Herr*. But go on."

"Then I say to myself: Cazalis's tensions lie deep. His guilts are profound. His defenses against the unconscious becoming conscious—if that's a fundamental identification of neurotic behavior—are elaborate.

"Now I observe his marriage. Immediately, it seems to me, new tensions—or extensions of old ones—set in. Even a so-called normal man of 44 would find a first marriage, after a life of overwork and little socializing—would find such a marriage, to a 19-year-old girl, unsettling and conflicting. In this case the young bride was from a thinblooded New England strain. She was emotionally of delicate balance, rather rarefied, on the frigid side, and almost certainly inexperienced. And Cazalis was as he was. I speculate.

"I say: It seems to me Cazalis must at once have found himself involved in serious sexual dissatisfactions, frustrations, and disagreeable conflicts. I say: There must have been recurrent episodes of impotence. Or his wife was unresponsive, unawakened, or actually repelled. He began to feel an erosive inadequacy, perhaps? Yes, and a resentment. It wouldn't be unnatural. He, the highly successful entrepreneur of the biological process, can't master the technique of his own marriage. Also, he loves his wife. She is an intelligent woman, she has a fragile charm, reserve, breeding; even today, at 42, she's handsome; at 19 she must have been extremely attractive. Cazalis loves her as only a man can love who is old enough to be the father of the highly desirable object of his affections. And he's inadequate.

"So I say: A fear is born. Undoubtedly his fear arises from altogether different causes, but it expresses itself in a disguised form: he becomes afraid he will lose his young wife to another man."

Ellery drank some coffee and Seligmann waited. The ormolu clock on the mantelpiece kept a sort of truce between them.

"The fear is nourished," continued Ellery, "by the great difference in their ages, temperaments, backgrounds, interests. By the demands of his practice, his long hours at the hospital assisting other men's wives to bring other men's children into the world, by his enforced professional absences from Mrs. Cazalis—frequently at night.

"The fear spreads like cancer. It gets out of control. Cazalis becomes violently suspicious of his wife's relationships with other men, no matter how slight. no matter how innocent—especially of her relationships with younger men.

"And soon this fear grows into an obsession.

"Professor Seligmann." Ellery eyed the old Viennese. "Was Edward Cazalis obsessively jealous of his wife during the first four years of their marriage?"

Seligmann picked up his pipe and rather deliberately set about knocking it out. "Your method, Mr. Queen, is one unknown to science," he said with a smile. "But this is of great interest to me. Continue." He stuck the empty pipe in his mouth.

"Then Mrs. Cazalis becomes pregnant." Ellery frowned. "One could imagine at this point Cazalis's fears would recede. But no, he's passed the point of reasonableness. Her very pregnancy feeds his jealousy and becomes suspect. Isn't this a confirmation of his suspicions? he asks himself. And he insists—he insists—on taking care of his wife himself. He is undoubtedly excessively devoted, solicitous, and watchful. Gestation unfortunately takes nine months. Nine months in which to watch a fetus grow. Nine months in which to torture himself with a question which at last bursts forth in the full deformity of obsession: Is this child mine? Is it?

"Oh, he fights it. He fights an endless battle. But the enemy is discouraging. Kill it in one place and it springs up, viciously lively as ever, in another. Does he ever tell his wife of his suspicions? Accuse her outright of infidelity? Are there scenes, tears, hysterical denials? If so, they only serve to strengthen his suspicions. If not, if he keeps his raging fears bottled up, then it's even worse.

"Mrs. Cazalis comes to term, goes through labor.

"And there she lies.

"In the delivery room.

"Under his hands.

"And the baby dies.

"Professor Seligmann, do you see how far I've traveled?"

The old man merely waggled the pipe in his jaws.

"Mrs. Cazalis becomes pregnant a second time. The process of suspicion, jealousy, self-torment, and uncertainty-certainty repeats itself. Again Cazalis insists on seeing his wife through her pregnancy. Again he insists on performing the delivery.

"And again his baby dies in the delivery room.

"His second child, dead like the first.

"*Under his hands*.

"Under those powerful, delicately nerved, practiced surgeon's hands.

"Professor Seligmann." Ellery loomed over the old man. "You're the only being on the face of the earth in a position to tell me the truth. Isn't it fact that when Edward Cazalis came to you eighteen years ago for psychiatric treatment he had broken down under a dreadful load of guilt—*the guilt of having murdered his own two children in the act of delivery?*"

After a moment old Seligmann took the empty pipe from his lip. He said carefully, "For a physician to murder his own unborn children under the delusion that they were another's—this would be psychosis, Herr Queen, no? You could not expect him to follow his subsequent brilliant, stable career, most particularly in the field of psychiatry. And my position, what would that have been? Still, you believe this, Herr Queen?"

Ellery laughed angrily. "Would it make my meaning clear if I amended my question to conclude: 'the guilt of *fearing* he had murdered his own two children'?"

The old man looked pleased.

"Because it was the logical development of his neurosis, wasn't it? He had excessive feelings of guilt about his hates and a great need for punishment. He, the eminent obstetrician, had brought thousands of other men's children into the world alive, but under his hands his own children had died. *Did I kill them?* he agonized. *Did my obsessive jealousy and suspicions make my hands fail? Did I want them to be born dead and my hands saw to it that they were? I did want them to be born dead. And they were born dead. Therefore I killed them.* The terrible illogic of neurosis.

"His common sense told him they had been breech births; his neurosis told him he had performed countless other breeches successfully. His common sense told him that his wife, let's say, was not ideally constructed for motherhood; his neurosis told him her babies were fathered by other men. His common sense told him he had done his efficient best; his neurosis told him that he had not, that he might have done this or that, or not done that or this, or that had he not insisted on performing the deliveries himself but placed his wife in the hands of another obstetrician, his children would have survived. And so on.

"Because he had an overwhelming compulsion to believe it, within a short time Cazalis had convinced himself that he'd murdered both babies. A little of this mental *Schrecklichkeit* and he broke. When his wife took him traveling and he came to Vienna—odd coincidence, wouldn't you say, Professor?—lo, he collapsed again. And went to you. And you, Professor Seligmann, you probed and analyzed and treated and . . . you cured him?"

When the old psychoanalyst spoke, his rumbling voice held a growl. "It is too many years and I know nothing of his emotional problems since. Even at the time there was a menopausal complication. If in the past few years he has been pushing himself too hard—at the present stage of his life . . . Often in the middle age people are unable to defend themselves by means of neurotic symptoms and they break down completely into a psychosis. We find, for example, that paranoid schizophrenia is frequently a disease of late middle age. Still, I am surprised and troubled. I do not know. I should have to see him."

"He still has guilt feelings. He must have. It's the only explanation for what he's done, Professor."

"What he has done? You mean, Mr. Queen, murdering nine persons?"

"No."

"He has done something else?"

"Yes."

"In addition to the nine murders?"

"To the exclusion," said Ellery, "of the nine murders."

Seligmann rapped the bowl of his meerschaum on the arm of the chair.

"Come, *mein Herr.* You speak in riddles. Precisely what is it that you do mean?"

"I mean," said Ellery, "that Cazalis is innocent of the charge for which he is going to trial in New York tomorrow morning."

"*Innocent?*"

"I mean, Professor Seligmann, that Cazalis did not kill those nine people. Cazalis is not—and never was—the Cat."

13

Seligmann said "Let us expose Fate, whose other name is Bauer." He bellowed, "Elsa!"

Frau Bauer appeared, pure jinni.

"Elsa—" began the old man.

But Frau Bauer interrupted, stumbling from a secure "Herr Professor" into uncertain English so that Ellery knew her remarks were intended for his ears also. "You have breakfast eaten when it is already lunch. Lunch you have not eaten. Now comes your time to rest." Fists on bony hips, Frau Bauer glared challenge to the non-Viennese world.

"I'm so very sorry, Professor—"

"For what, Mr. Queen? Elsa." The old man spoke gently, in German. "You've listened at the door. You've insulted my guest. Now you wish to rob me of my few remaining hours of consciousness. Must I hypnotize you?"

Frau Bauer whitened. She fled.

"It is my only weapon against her," chuckled the old man. "I threaten to put her under hypnosis and send her into the Soviet zone to serve as the plaything of Moscow. It is not a matter of morals with Elsa; it is sheer horror. She would as soon get in bed with the Antichrist. You were telling me, Mr. Queen, that Cazalis is innocent after all?"

"Yes."

The old man sat back, smiling. "Do you arrive at this conclusion by way of your unique scientifically unknown method of analysis, or is it based upon fact? Such fact as would, for example, satisfy your courts of law."

"It's based on a fact which would satisfy anyone above the mental age of five, Professor Seligmann," Ellery retorted. "Its very simplicity, I think, has obscured it. Its simplicity and the fact that the murders have been so numerous and have dragged on for so long. Too, it's been the kind of case in which the individuality of the victims has tended to blur and blend as the murders multiplied, until at the end one looked back on a homogeneous pile of carcasses, so many head of cattle passed through the slaughter pen. The same sort of reaction one got looking at the official pictures of the corpses of Belsen, Buchenwald, Oswiecim and Maidanek. No particularity. Just death."

"But the fact, Mr. Queen." With a flick of impatience, and something else. And suddenly Ellery recalled that Béla Seligmann's only daughter, married to a Polish Jewish doctor, had died at Treblinka. Love particularizes death, Ellery thought. And little else.

"Oh, the fact," he said. "Why, it's a mere matter of beginners' physics, Professor. You attended the Zürich convention earlier this year, you told me. Exactly when this year?"

The white brows met. "The end of May, was it not?"

"The meeting lasted ten days and the concluding session was held on the night of June 3. On the night of June 3 Dr. Edward Cazalis of the United States read a paper entitled *Ochlophobia, Nyctophobia, and Ponophobia* in the convention hall before a large audience. As reported in a *Züricher* scientific journal, the speaker scheduled to precede Cazalis, a Dane, ran far over his allotted time, to virtually the adjournment hour. Out of courtesy to Dr. Cazalis, however, who had attended all the sessions—according to a footnote in the journal—the American was permitted to deliver his paper. Cazalis began reading around midnight and finished at a few minutes past 2 o'clock in the morning. The convention was then adjourned for the year. The official adjournment time was 2:24 A.M. 4th June."

Ellery shrugged. "The time difference between Zürich and New York being six hours, midnight of June 3 in Zürich, which is when Cazalis began reading is paper to the convention, was 6 P.M. June 3 in New York; 2 A.M. June 4 in Zürich, which is about when Cazalis finished reading his paper there, was 8 P.M. June 3 in New York. Assuming the absurd—that Cazalis whisked himself from the convention hall immediately on adjournment or even as he stepped off the platform at the conclusion of his talk, that he had already checked out of his hotel and had his luggage waiting, that the slight matter of his visa had been taken care of, that there was a plane ready to take off for the United States at the Zürich airport the instant he reached there (for which specific plane Cazalis had a ticket, notwithstanding Dr. Naardvoessler's windiness, the unusual hour, or the impossibility of having foreseen the delay), that this plane flew to New York nonstop, that at Newark airport or La Guardia Cazalis found a police motorcycle escort waiting to conduct his taxi through traffic at the highest possible speed—assuming all this nonsense, Herr Professor, at which hour could Edward Cazalis have reached midtown Manhattan, would you say? The earliest conceivable hour?"

"I have a poor acquaintance with the progress—if that is the word—of aeronautics."

"Could the entire leap through space—from a platform in Zürich to a street in Manhattan—have been accomplished in three and a half to four hours, Professor Seligmann?"

"Obviously not."

"So I telephoned to you. Whereupon it came out that Edward Cazalis did not go from the convention hall to an airfield that night. Came out not as speculation but as fact. For you told me you had kept Cazalis up talking in your hotel room in Zürich all through that night until 'long past dawn.' Surely that would mean, at the very earliest, 6 A.M.? Let's say 6 A.M., Professor, to please me; it must have been, of course, even later. 6 A.M. in Zürich on the 4th of June would be midnight in New York on June 3. Do you recall my giving you the date of the first Cat murder? The murder of the man named Abernethy?"

"Dates are a nuisance. And there were so many."

"Exactly. There were so many, and it was so long ago. Well, according to our Medical Examiner's report, Abernethy was strangled '*around midnight*' *of June 3*. As I said, a matter of simple physics. Cazalis has demonstrated many talents, but the ability to be in two places thousands of miles apart at the same moment is not one of them."

The old man exclaimed, "But, as you say, this is so basic! And your police, your prosecutors, have not perceived this physical impossibility?"

"There were nine murders and an attempted tenth. The time-stretch was almost exactly five months. Cazalis's old obstetrical files, the strangling cords hidden in his psychiatric case history files, the circumstances of his capture, his detailed and voluntary confession—all these have created an over-whelming presumption of his guilt. The authorities may have slipped through overconfidence, or carelessness, or because they found that in the majority of the murders Cazalis could physically have committed the crimes. Remember, there is no direct evidence linking Cazalis with any of the murders; the people's entire case must rest on that tenth attempt. Here the evidence is direct enough. Cazalis was captured while he was in the act of tightening the noose about the throat of the girl who was wearing Marilyn Soames's borrowed coat. The noose of tussah silk. The Cat's noose. *Ergo,* he's the Cat. Why think of alibis?

"On the other hand, one would expect the defense attorneys to check everything. If they haven't turned up Cazalis's alibi, it's because of the defendant himself; when I left New York, he was being extremely difficult. After attempting to get along without legal help altogether. And then there's no reason why a lawyer, merely because he is a lawyer for the defense, should be immune to the general atmosphere of conviction about his client's guilt.

"I suspect, however, a more insidious reason for the alibi's remaining undiscovered, one that goes to the roots of the psychology which has operated in this case virtually from its outset. There has been a neurotic anxiety of epidemic proportions to catch the Cat, drive a stake through his heart, and forget the whole dreadful mass incubus. It's infected the authorities, too. The Cat was a *Doppelgänger,* his nature so tenuously drawn that when the authorities actually laid their hands on a creature of flesh and blood who fitted the specifications . . ."

"If you instruct me whom to address, Mr. Queen," rumbled old Seligmann, "I shall cable New York of my having detained Cazalis all night until past dawn of the 4th June in Zürich."

"We'll arrange for you to make a formal deposition. That, plus the evidence of Dr. Cazalis's attendance throughout the Zürich convention and of his return passage to the United States, which can't have begun earlier than June 4, will clear him."

"They will be satisfied that, having been unable physically to murder the first one, Cazalis did not murder the others?"

"To argue the contrary would be infantile, Professor Seligmann. The crimes were characterized and accepted as the work of the same individual almost from the beginning. And with abundant reason. The source of the supply of victims' names alone confirms it. The method used in selecting the specific victims from the source of supply confirms it. The identical technique of the strangulations confirms it. And so on. The strongest point of all is the use in all nine murders of the strangling cords of tussah silk—cords of East Indian origin, exotic, unusual, not readily procurable, and obviously from the same source."

"And, of course, in a sequence of acts of violence of a psychotic nature showing common characteristics—"

"Yes. Multiple homicides of this kind are invariably what we call 'lone wolf' operations, acts of a single disturbed person. There won't be any trouble on that score . . . Are you sure you wouldn't like to rest now, Professor Seligmann? Frau Bauer said—"

The old man dismissed Frau Bauer with a scowl as he reached for a tobacco jar. "I begin to glimpse your destination, *mein Herr.* Nevertheless, take me by the hand. You have resolved one difficulty only to be confronted by another.

"Cazalis is not the Cat.

"Then who is?"

"The next question," nodded Ellery.

He was silent for a moment.

"I answered it between heaven and earth, Professor," he said at last with a smile, "in a state of all but suspended animation, so you'll forgive me if I go slowly.

"To arrive at the answer we must examine Cazalis's known acts in the light of what we've built up about his neurosis.

"Just what was it Cazalis *did?* His known activities in the Cat cases begin with the tenth victim. His very choice of 21-year-old Marilyn Soames as the tenth victim must have arisen from his application of the same selective technique employed by the Cat in hunting through Cazalis's old obstetrical case cards—I used the technique myself and arrived at the same victim. Anyone of reasonable intelligence could have done it, then, who had access to both the facts of the preceding nine crimes and the files.

"Having employed the Cat's method in selecting the next victim in the series, what did Cazalis then proceed to do?

"As it happened, Marilyn Soames works at home, she was extremely busy, and she didn't regularly come out into the streets. The Cat's first problem in each case must have been to become familiar with the face and figure of the victim he had marked for destruction. Had the real Cat, then, been working on Marilyn Soames he would have attempted to lure her from her home in order to be able to study her appearance. This was precisely what Cazalis did. By a subterfuge, he lured Marilyn Soames to a crowded public place where he could 'study' her in 'safety.'

"For days and nights Cazalis scouted the girl's neighborhood and reconnoitered the building where she lives. Just as the Cat would have done. Just as the Cat must have done in the previous cases.

"While he was apparently on the prowl, Cazalis exhibited eagerness, cunning, disappointment of an extravagant nature at temporary frustrations. The kind of behavior one would have expected the unbalanced Cat to evince.

"Finally, on that climactic, October night, Cazalis waylaid a girl who resembled Marilyn Soames in height and figure and who was accidentally wearing Marilyn Soames's coat, dragged this girl into an alley, and *began* to strangle her with one of the tussah silk cords associated with the Cat's previous homicidal activities.

"And when we captured him Cazalis 'confessed' to being the Cat and reconstructed his 'activities' in the nine previous murders . . . including an account of the murder of Abernethy, committed when Cazalis was in Switzerland!

"Why?

"Why did Cazalis imitate the Cat?

"Why did he confess to the Cat's crimes?"

The old man was listening intently.

"This was patently not the case of a deluded man's identifying himself with the violent acts of another by merely claiming, as many psychotics did in those five months—every sensational crime brings people forward—to have committed the Cat's crimes of record. No. Cazalis *proved* he was the Cat by thought, plan, and action; by creating a new and typical Cat crime based upon exact knowledge and a clearly painstaking study of the Cat's habits, methods, and technique. This was not even imitation; it was a brilliant interpretation, consisting of omissions as well as of commissions. For example, on the morning when Cazalis actually entered the Soames apartment house, while he was out in the court, Marilyn Soames came downstairs to the vestibule and stood there for several minutes looking over her mail. At this moment Cazalis re-entered the hall. No one was apparently about except Cazalis and his victim; it was early morning, the street beyond was deserted. Nevertheless, at that time Cazalis made no move to attack the girl. Why? Because to have done so would have broken the consistent pattern of the Cat's murders; those had been committed, to the last one, after dark—and this broad daylight. Such scrupulous attention to detail could not conceivably have come out of an ordinary psychotic identification. Not to mention the self-restraint exhibited.

"No, Cazalis was rational and his deliberate assumption of the Cat's role in all its creative vigor was therefore rationally motivated."

"It is your conclusion, then," asked Seligmann, "that Cazalis had no intention of strangling the girl to death in the alley? That he merely made the pretense?"

"Yes."

"But this would presuppose that he knew he was being followed by the police and that he would be captured in the act."

"Of course he knew, Professor. The very fact that he, a rational man, set out to prove he was the Cat when he was not raises the logical question: Prove it to whom? His proof did not consist merely of a confession, as I've pointed out. It consisted of elaborate activities stretching over a period of many days; of facial expressions as well as of visits to the Soames neighborhood. A deception presupposes that there is someone watching to be deceived. Yes, Cazalis knew he was being followed by the police; he knew that each move he made, each twist of his lips, was being noted and recorded by trained operatives.

"And when he slipped the silk cord around Celeste Phillips's neck—the girl he mistook for his victim—Cazalis was playing the final scene for his audience. It's significant that the tenth case was the only case in which the intended victim was able to cry out loudly enough to be heard. And while Cazalis tightened the cord sufficiently to leave realistic marks on the girl's neck, it's also significant that he permitted her to get her hands between the noose and her throat, that he did not knock her unconscious as the Cat had done in at least two of his assaults, and that Celeste Phillips was able within a short time of the attack to speak and act normally; what slight and temporary damage she sustained was chiefly the result of her own struggles and her terror. What Cazalis would have done had we not run into the alley to 'stop' him is conjectural; probably he would have permitted the girl to scream long enough without fatal injury to insure interference from some outside source. He could be certain detectives weren't far away in the fog, and it was a congested section of the City.

"He wanted to be caught in the act of a Cat murder-attempt, he planned to be caught in the act of a Cat murder-attempt, and he was successful in being caught in the act of a Cat murder-attempt."

"Whereupon it becomes evident," murmured the old man, "that we approach our destination."

"Yes. For a rational man to assume another's guilt and to be willing to suffer another's punishment, the rational mind can find only one justification: the one is shielding the other.

"Cazalis was concealing the Cat's identity.

"Cazalis was protecting the Cat from detection, exposure, and punishment.

"And in doing so Cazalis was punishing himself out of deeply buried feelings of his own guilts as they centered about the Cat and his emotional involvement with the Cat.

"Do you agree, Professor Seligmann?'

But the old man said in a curious way: "I am only an observer along this road you travel, Mr. Queen. I neither agree nor disagree; I listen."

Ellery laughed. "What did I now know about the Cat?

"That the Cat was someone with whom Cazalis was emotionally involved. With whom he was therefore in a close relationship.

"That the Cat was someone whom Cazalis had an overpowering wish to protect and whose criminal guilt is tied in Cazalis's mind to his own neurotic guilts.

"That the Cat was a psychotic with a determinable psychotic reason for seeking out and murdering people who a generation and more before had been brought into the world by Cazalis the obstetrician.

"That, finally, the Cat was someone who has had equal access with Cazalis to his old obstetrical records, which have been stored in a locked closet in his home."

Seligmann paused in the act of putting the meerschaum back into his mouth.

"Is there such a person, I asked myself? To my certain knowledge?"

"There is. To my certain knowledge," said Ellery. "Just one.

"Mrs. Cazalis."

"For Mrs. Cazalis," said Ellery, "is the only living person who fits the specifications I have just drawn.

"Mrs. Cazalis is the only living person with whom Cazalis is emotionally involved in a close relationship; in his closest relationship.

"Mrs. Cazalis is the only living person whom Cazalis would have a compulsion to protect and for whose guilt Cazalis would feel intensely responsible . . . whose criminal guilt would be tied in his mind to his own neurotic guilt feelings.

"Mrs. Cazalis has a determinable—the only determinable—psychotic reason for seeking out and murdering people her husband had brought into the world.

"And that Mrs. Cazalis has had equal access with her husband to his obstetrical records is self-evident."

Seligmann did not change expression. He seemed neither surprised nor impressed. "I am chiefly interested in pursuing your third point. What you have called Mrs. Cazalis's 'determinable psychotic reason' for murdering. How do you demonstrate this?"

"By another extension of that method of mine you've characterized as unknown to science, Herr Professor. I knew that Mrs. Cazalis had lost two children in giving birth. I knew, from something Cazalis told me, that after the second delivery she was no longer able to bear children. I knew that she had thereafter become extremely attached to her sister's only child, Lenore Richardson, to the point where her niece was more her daughter than her sister's. I knew, or I had convinced myself, that Cazalis had proved inadequate to his sexual function as a husband. Certainly during the long period of his breakdowns and subsequent treatment he must have been a source of continual frustration to his wife. And she was only 19 when they married.

"From the age of 19, then," said Ellery, "I saw Mrs. Cazalis as leading an unnatural, tense existence, complicated by strong maternal desires which were thwarted by the deaths of her two infants, her inability to have another child, and what could only have been a highly unsatisfactory and unsettling transference of her thwarted feelings to her niece. She knew that Lenore could never really be hers; Lenore's mother is neurotic, jealous, possessive, infantile, and interfering—a source of unending trouble. Mrs. Cazalis is not an outgoing individual and apparently she never was. Her frustrations, then, grew inward; she contained them . . . for a long time.

"Until, in fact, she was past 40.

"Then she cracked.

"I say, Professor Seligmann, that one day Mrs. Cazalis told herself something that thenceforward became her only reason for living.

"Once she believed that, she was lost. Lost in the distorted world of psychosis.

"Because, Professor, I believe the oddest thing occurred. Mrs. Cazalis did not have to know that her husband thought he had murdered their children at birth; in fact, she undoubtedly did not know it—in her rational life—or their marriage would hardly have survived the knowledge for so many years. *But I think she arrived at approximately the same point in her psychosis.*

"I think she finally told herself: *My husband gave thousands of living babies to other women, but when I was to have my own babies he gave me dead ones. So my husband killed them. He won't let me have my children, so I won't let them have their children. He killed mine; I'll kill theirs.*" And Ellery said, "Would it be possible for me to have more of that wonderful non-Viennese coffee, Professor Seligmann?"

"*Ach.*" Seligmann reached over and tugged at a bellpull. Frau Bauer appeared. "Elsa, are we barbarians? More coffee."

"It's all ready," snapped Frau Bauer in German. And as she returned with two fat, steaming pots and fresh cups and saucers, she said, "I know you, you old *Schuft.* You are in one of your suicidal moods." And she flounced out, banging the door.

"This is my life," said the old man. He was regarding Ellery with bright eyes. "Do you know, Herr Queen, this is extraordinary. I can only sit and admire."

"Yes?" said Ellery, not quite following but grateful for the gift of the jinni.

"For you have arrived, by an uncharted route, at the true destination.

"The trained eye looks upon your Mrs. Cazalis and one says: Here is a quiet, submissive type of woman. She is withdrawn, seclusive, asocial, frigid, slightly suspicious and hypercritical—I speak, of course, of the time when I knew her. Her husband is handsome, successful, and in his work—his obstetrical work—he is constantly in contact with other women, but in their married life her husband and she have disturbing conflicts and tensions. She has managed nevertheless to make an adjustment to life; in—as it were—a limping fashion.

"She has done nothing to warrant special notice. In fact, she has always been overshadowed by her husband and dominated by him.

"Then, in her 40s, something occurs. For years, secretly, she has been jealous of her husband's rapport with younger women, his psychiatric patients—for it is interesting to note that in recent years, as Cazalis told me in Zürich, he has had an almost totally female clientele. She has not required 'proof,' for she has always been of a schizoid tendency; besides, there was probably nothing to 'prove.' No matter. Mrs. Cazalis's schizoid tendency bursts forth in a delusional state.

"A frank paranoid psychosis.

"She develops the delusion that her own babies were killed by her husband. In order to deprive her of them. She may even think that he is the father of some of the children whose successful deliveries he performed. With or without the idea that her husband is their father, she sets out to kill them in retaliation.

"Her psychosis is controlled in her inner life. It is not expressed to the world except in her crimes.

"This is how the psychiatrist might describe the murderer you have delineated.

"As you see, Mr. Queen, the destination is the same."

"Except that mine," said Ellery, his smile slightly bitter, "seems to have been approached poetically. I recall the artist who kept depicting the stranger as a cat and I warm to his remarkable intuition. Doesn't a tigress—that grandmother of cats—go 'mad' with rage when she is robbed of her cubs? Then, Professor, there's the old saying, *A woman hath nine lives like a cat*. Mrs. Cazalis has nine lives to her debit, too. She killed and she killed until . . ."

"Yes?"

"Until one day Cazalis entertained a ghastly visitor."

"The truth."

Ellery nodded. "It could have come about in one of a number of ways. He might have stumbled on the hiding place of her stock of silk cords and recalled their visit to India years before and her purchase—not his—of the cords. Or perhaps it was one or two of the victims' names striking a chord of memory; then it would require merely a few minutes with his old files to open his eyes. Or he may have noticed his wife acting oddly, followed her, and was too late to avert a tragedy but in quite sufficient time to grasp its sickening significance. He would go back in his mind to the recent past and discover that on the night of each murder he could not vouch for her whereabouts. Also, Cazalis suffers from chronic insomnia and he takes sleeping pills regularly; this, he would realize, had given her unlimited opportunities. And for purposes of slipping in and out of the building at night unobserved by the apartment house employees, there was always Cazalis's office door, giving access directly to the street. As for the daytimes, a woman's daytime excursions are rarely examined by her husband; in our American culture, in all strata, 'shopping' is the magic word, explaining everything . . . Cazalis may even have seen how, in the cunning of her paranoia, his wife had skipped over numerous eligibles on the list in order to strike at her niece—the most terrible of her murders, the murder of the unsatisfying substitute for her dead children—in order that she might maneuver Cazalis into the investigation and through him keep informed as to everything the police and I knew and planned.

"In any event, as a psychiatrist Cazalis would immediately grasp the umbilical symbolism in her choice of cords to strangle—as it were—babies; certainly the infantile significance of her consistent use of blue cords for male victims and pink cords for females could not have escaped him. He could trace her psychosis, then, to the traumatic source upon which her delusion had seized. It could only be the delivery room in which she had lost her own two children. Under ordinary circumstances this would have been a merely clinical, if personally agonizing, observation, and Cazalis would either have taken the medical and legal steps usual in such cases or, if the prospect of revealing the truth to the world involved too much pain, mortification, and obloquy, he would at the least have put her where she could do no more harm.

"But the circumstances were not ordinary. There were his own old feelings of guilt which had expressed themselves through and revolved about that same delivery room. Perhaps it was the shock of realizing what lay behind his wife's mental illness that revived the guilt feelings he had thought were dissolved. However it came about, Cazalis must have found himself in the clutch of his old neurosis, its tenacity increased a thousandfold by the shock of the discovery that had brought it alive again. Soon he was persuaded by his neurosis that it was all his fault; that had he not 'murdered' their two babies she would not have erupted into psychosis. The sin, then, was his; he alone was 'responsible,' therefore he alone must suffer the punishment.

"So he sent his wife south in the care of her sister and brother-in-law, he took the remaining silk cords from his wife's hiding place and stored them in a place indentifiable with him alone, and he set about proving to the authorities that he, Edward Cazalis, was the monster the City of New York had been hunting frantically for five months. His subsequent 'confession' in detail was the easiest part of it by far; he was fully informed through his affiliation with the case of all the facts known to the police, and upon a foundation of these facts he was able to build a plausible, convincing structure. How much of his behavior at this point and since has been playacting and how much actual disturbance I can't, of course, venture to say.

"And that, Professor Seligmann, is my story," said Ellery in a tightened voice, "and if you have any information that controverts in, this is the time to speak out."

He found that he was shivering and he blamed it on the fire, which was low. It was hissing a little, as if to call attention to its plight.

Old Seligmann raised himself and devoted a few minutes to the Promethean chore of bringing warmth back to the room.

Ellery waited.

Suddenly, without turning, the old man grumbled: "Perhaps it would be wisdom, Herr Queen, to send that cable now."

Ellery sighed.

"May I telephone instead? You can't say much in a cable, and if I can talk to my father a great deal of time will have been saved."

"I shall place the call for you." The old man shuffled to his desk. As he took the telephone, he added with a twitch of humor, "My German—at least on the European side, Mr. Queen—will undoubtedly prove less expensive than yours."

They might have been calling one of the more distant planets. They sat in silence sipping their coffee, attuned to a ring which did not come.

The day was running out and the study began to blur and lose its character.

Once Frau Bauer stormed in. Her bristling entrance startled them. But their unnatural silence and the twilight they sat in startled her. She tiptoed about, switching on lamps. Then, like a mouse, she skittered out.

Once Ellery laughed, and the old man raised his head.

"I've just thought of something absurd, Professor Seligmann. In the four months since I first laid eyes on her, I've never called her or thought of her or referred to her as anything but 'Mrs. Cazalis.' "

"And what should you call her," said the old man grumpily, "Ophelia?"

"I never did learn her Christian name. I don't know it at this moment. Just Mrs. Cazalis . . . the great man's shadow. Yet from the night she murdered her niece she was always there. On the edges. A face in the background. Putting in an occasional—but very important—word. Making idiots of us all, including her husband. It makes one wonder, Herr Professor, what the advantages are of so-called sanity."

He laughed again to indicate that this was pleasantry, a sociable introduction to conversation; he was feeling uneasy.

But the old man merely grunted.

After that, they resumed their silences.

Until the telephone rang.

The line was miraculously clear.

"Ellery!" Inspector Queen's shout spurned the terrestrial sea. "You all right? What are you still doing in Vienna? Why haven't I heard from you? Not even a cable."

"Dad, I've got news for you."

"News?"

"The Cat is Mrs. Cazalis."

Ellery grinned. He felt sadistically petty.

It was very satisfactory, his father's reaction. "Mrs. Cazalis. *Mrs*. Cazalis?"

Still, there was something peculiar about the way the Inspector said it.

"I know it's a blow, and I can't explain now, but—"

"Son, I have news for *you*."

"News for me?"

"Mrs. Cazalis is dead. She took poison this morning."

Ellery heard himself saying to Professor Seligmann: "Mrs. Cazalis is dead. She took poison. This morning."

"Ellery, who are you talking to?"

"Béla Seligmann. I'm at his home." Ellery took hold of himself. For some reason it was a shock. "Maybe it's just as well. It certainly solves a painful problem for Cazalis—"

"Yes," said his father in a very peculiar tone indeed.

"—because, Dad, Cazalis is innocent. But I'll give you the details when I get home. Meanwhile, you'd better start the ball rolling with the District Attorney. I know we can't keep the trial from getting under way tomorrow morning, but—"

"Ellery."

"What?"

"Cazalis is dead, too. He also took poison this morning."

Cazalis is dead, too. He also took poison this morning. Ellery thought he was thinking it, but when he saw the look on Seligmann's face he realized with astonishment that he had repeated these words of his father's aloud, too.

"We have reason to believe it was Cazalis who planned it, told her just where to get the stuff, what to do. She's been in something of a fog for some time. They weren't alone in his cell more than a minute or so when it happened. She brought him the poison and they both swallowed a lethal dose at the same time. It was a quick-acting poison; before the cell door could be unlocked they were writhing, and they died within six minutes. It happened so blasted fast Cazalis's lawyer, who was standing . . ."

His father's voice dribbled off into the blue. Or seemed to. Ellery felt himself straining to catch remote accents. Not really straining to catch anything. Except a misty, hard-cored something—something he had never realized was part of him—and now that he was conscious of it it was dwindling away with the speed of light and he was powerless to hold on to it.

"Herr Queen. Mr. Queen!"

Good old Seligmann. He understands. That's why he sounds so excited.

"Ellery, you still there? Can't you hear me? I can't get a thing out of this goddam—"

A voice said, "I'll be home soon, goodbye," and somebody dropped the phone. Ellery found everything calmly confusing. There was a great deal of noise, and Frau Bauer was in it somewhere and then she wasn't, and a man was sniveling like a fool close by while his face was hit by a blockbuster and burning lava tore down his gullet; and then Ellery opened his eyes to find himself lying on a black leather couch and Professor Seligmann hovering over him like the spirit of all grandfathers with a bottle of cognac in one hand and a handkerchief in the other with which he was gently wiping Ellery's face.

"It is nothing, nothing," the old man was saying in a wonderfully soothing voice. "The long and physically depleting journey, the lack of sleep, the nervous excitements of our talk—the shock of your father's news. Relax, Mr. Queen. Lean back. Do not think. Close your eyes."

Ellery leaned back, and he did not think, and he closed his eyes, but then he opened them and said, "No."

"There is more? Perhaps you would like to tell me."

He had such a fantastically strong, safe voice, this old man.

"I'm too late again," Ellery heard himself saying in the most ridiculously emotional voice. "I've killed Cazalis the way I killed Howard Van Horn. If I'd checked Cazalis against all nine murders immediately instead of resting on my shiny little laurels Cazalis would be alive today. Alive instead of dead, Professor Seligmann. Do you see? I'm too late again."

The grandfatherly voice said, "Who is being neurotic now, *mein Herr?*" and now it was not gentle, it was juridical. But it was still safe.

"I swore after the Van Horn business I'd never gamble with human lives again. And then I broke the vow. I must have been really bitched up when I did that, Professor. My bitchery must be organic. I broke the vow and here I sit, over the grave of my second victim. What's the man saying? How do I know how many other poor innocents have gone to a decenter reward because of my exquisite bitchery? I had a long and honorable career indulging my paranoia. Talk about delusions of grandeur! I've given pronunciamentos on law to lawyers, on chemistry to chemists, on ballistics to ballistic experts, on fingerprints to men who've made the study of fingerprints their lifework. I've issued my imperial decrees on criminal investigation methods to police officers with thirty years' training, delivered definitive psychiatric analyses for the benefit of qualified psychiatrists. I've made Napoleon look like a men's room attendant. And all the while I've been running amok among the innocent like Gabriel on a bender."

"This in itself," came the voice, "this that you say now is a delusion."

"Proves my point, doesn't it?" And Ellery heard himself laughing in a really revolting way. "My philosophy has been as flexible and as rational as the Queen's in *Alice*. You know *Alice*, Herr Professor? Surely you or somebody's psychoanalyzed it. A great work of humblification, encompassing all the wisdom of man since he learned to laugh at himself. In it you'll find everything, even me. The Queen had only one way of settling all difficulties, great or small, you'll remember. 'Off with his head!' "

And the fellow was standing. He had actually jumped off the couch as if Seligmann had given him the hotfoot and there he was, waving his arms at the famous old man threateningly.

"All right! All right. I'm really through this time. I'll turn my bitchery into less lethal channels. I'm finished, Herr Professor Seligmann. A glorious career of *Sclamperei* masquerading as exact and omnipotent science has just been packed away forever without benefit of mothballs. Do I convey meaning? Have I made myself utterly clear?"

He felt himself seized, and held, by the eyes.

"Sit down, *mein Herr*. It is a strain on my back to be forced to look up at you in this way."

Ellery heard the fellow mutter an apology and the next thing he knew he was in the chair, staring at the corpses of innumerable cups of coffee.

"I do not know this Van Horn that you mention, Mr. Queen, but it is apparent that his death has upset you, so deeply that you find yourself unable to make the simple adjustment to the death of Cazalis which is all that the facts of the case require.

"You are not thinking with the clarity of which you are capable, *mein Herr*.

"There is no rational justification," the deliberate voice went on, "for your overemotional reaction to the news of Cazalis's suicide. Nothing that you could have done would have prevented it. This I say out of a greater knowledge of such matters than you possess."

Ellery began to assemble a face somewhere before him. It was reassuring and he sat still, dutifully.

"Had you discovered the truth within ten minutes of the moment when you first engaged to investigate the murders, the result for Cazalis would have been, I am afraid, identical. Let us say that you were enabled to demonstrate at once that Mrs. Cazalis was the psychotic murderer of so many innocent persons. She would have been arrested, tried, convicted, and disposed of according to whether your laws admitted of her psychosis or held that she was mentally responsible within the legal definition, which is often absurd. You would have done your work successfully and you would have had no reason to reproach yourself; the truth is the truth and a dangerous person would have been removed from the society which she had so greatly injured.

"I ask you now to consider: Would Cazalis have felt less responsible, would his feelings of guilt have been less pronounced, if his wife had been apprehended and disposed of?

"No. Cazalis's guilt feelings would have been equally active, and in the end he would have taken his own life as he has done. Suicide is one of the extremes of aggressive expression and it is sought out at one of the extremes of self-hate. Do not burden yourself, young man, with a responsibility which has not been yours at any time and which you personally, under any circumstances, could not have controlled. So far as your power to have altered events is concerned, the principal difference between what has happened and what might have happened is that Cazalis died in a prison cell rather than on the excellently carpeted floor of his Park Avenue office."

Professor Seligmann was a whole man now, very clear and close.

"No matter what you say, Professor, or how you say it, the fact remains that I was taken in by Cazalis's deception until it was too late to do more than hold a verbal post-mortem with you here in Vienna. I did fail, Professor Seligmann."

"In that sense—yes, Mr. Queen, you failed." The old man leaned forward suddenly and he took one of Ellery's hands in his own. And at his touch Ellery knew that he had come to the end of a road which he would never again have to traverse. "You have failed before, you will fail again. This is the nature and the role of man.

"The work you have chosen to do is a sublimation, of great social value.

"You must continue.

"I will tell you something else: This is as vital to you as it is to society.

"But while you are doing this important and rewarding work, Mr. Queen, I ask you to keep in mind always a great and true lesson. A truer lesson than the one you believe this experience has taught you."

"And which lesson is that, Professor Seligmann?" Ellery was very attentive.

"The lesson, *mein Herr*," said the old man, patting Ellery's hand, "that is written in the Book of Mark. *There is one God; and there is none other but he.*"

A NOTE ON NAMES

If one of the functions of fiction is to hold a mirror up to life, its characters and places must be identified as in life; that is, through names. The names in this story have had to be numerous. For verisimilitude they are common as well as uncommon. In either category, they are inventions; that is to say, they are names deriving from no real person or place known to the Author. Consequently if any real person finds a name in this story identical with or similar to his or her own, or if any place in this story has a nominal counterpart in life, it is wholly through coincidence.

The story has also required the introduction of certain official- and employee-characters of New York City. Where names have been given to characters in this category, if such inventions should prove identical with or similar to the names of real officials and employees of New York City, again the resemblance is coincidental and the Author states in the most positive terms that no real official or employee of New York City has been drawn on in any way. Where names have not been used, only official titles, the same assurance is given. A special point should be made in the case of the characters of the Mayor ("Jack") and the Police Commissioner ("Barney"). Neither the present Mayor and Police Commissioner of the City of New York, nor any past Mayor or Police Commissioner, living or dead, has been drawn on in any way whatsoever.

The list of person- and name-places invented follows. If any occur in the text which do not appear on the list, it is through failure of a weary proofreading eye and the reader should assume its inclusion.

Abernethy, Archibald Dudley
Abernethy, Mrs. Sarah-Ann
Abernethy, Rev.

Bascalone, Mrs. Teresa
Bauer, Frau Elsa, *Austria*
Beal, Arthur Jackson

Castorizo, Dr. Fulvio, *Italy*
Caton, Dr. Lawrence
Cavell, Dr. John Sloughby, *Great Britain*
Cazalis, Dr. Edward
Cazalis, Mrs. Edward
Chorumkowski, Stephen
Cohen, Cary G.

Collins, Barclay M.
Cuttler, Nadine

Devander, Bill

Ellis, Frances

Ferriquancchi, Ignazio
Finkleston, Zalmon
Frankburner, Jerome K.
Frawlins, Constance

Gaeckel, William Waldemar
Goldberg (Detective)
Gonachy, Phil

Hagstrom (Detective)
Heggerwitt, Adelaide
Hesse (Detective)

Immerson, Mrs. Jeanne
Immerson, Philbert
Irons, Darrell

Jackson, Lal Dhyana
Johnson (Detective)
Jones, Evarts
Jurasse, Dr., *France*

Katz, Donald
Katz, Dr. Morvin
Katz, Mrs. Pearl
Kelly's Bar
Kollodny, Gerald Ellis

Larkland, Dr. John F.
"Leggitt, Jimmy"
Legontz, Mrs. Maybelle

MacGayn (Detective)
"Martin, Sue"
Marzupian, Harold
Mayor of New York City ("Jack")
McKell, James Guymer
McKell, Monica
Merigrew, Roger Braham
Metropol Hall
Miller, William

Naardvoessler, Dr., *Denmark*
"Nostrum, Paul"

O'Reilly, Mrs. Maura B.
O'Reilly, Rian
O'Reilly, Mrs. Rian

Park-Lester Apartments
Petrucchi, Father
Petrucchi, Mr. and Mrs. George
Petrucchi, Stella
Phillips, Celeste
Phillips, Simone
Piggott (Detective)

Police Commissioner of New York City
   ("Barney")
Pompo, Frank

Quigley (Detective)

Registrar of Records, Manhattan Bureau
   of Vital Records and Statistics of the
   Department of Health
Rhutas, Roselle
Richardson, Mrs. Della
Richardson, Leeper & Company
Richardson, Lenore
Richardson, Zachary

Sacopy, Mrs. Margaret
Sacopy, Sylvan
Schoenzweig, Dr. Walther, *Germany*
Selborán, Dr. Andrés, *Spain*
Seligmann, Dr. Béla, *Austria*
Smith, Mrs. Eulalie
Smith, Violette
Soames, Billie
Soames, Mrs. Edna Lafferty
Soames, Eleanor
Soames, Frank Pellman
Soames, Marilyn
Soames, Stanley
Stone, Max
Szebo, Count "Snooky"

Treudlich, Benjamin

Ulberson, Dr. Myron

Velie, Barbara-Ann

Whithacker, Duggin
Whithacker, Howard
Willikins, Beatrice
Willikins, Frederick

Xavinzky, Reva

Young (Detective)

Zilgitt (Detective)

Double, Double

Tuesday, April 4

Ellery had thought he was through with Wrightsville. He had even developed a nostalgia about it like the man who looks back on his boyhood home through the filtering lens of a sentimental eye. He liked to say that, although he was born in New York City, Wrightsville was his spiritual birthplace—a town of complacent elms, wandering cobbles, and crooked sidestreets nestled in the lap of a farmers' valley and leaning against the motherly abdomen of one of New England's most matriarchal mountain ranges. Here it was always forest green or immaculate with snow. Orderly fields to look at, spiced air to breathe, the unfolding satisfaction of the hills. The whole place glittered in his memory like a diamond, or an emerald.

Never a ruby, because the blood color was uncomfortably close to the mark.

The envelope cast a ruby glow.

Ellery examined it again, not touching its contents.

It was a long envelope of flawed slick bluish paper, the correspondence offering of every five-and-ten cent store in America. This one, he felt sure, came from the stationery counter of the High Village Five-and-Dime. A few doors away dozed J. C. Pettigrew, Real Estate, and at the Five-and-Dime's Upper Whistling side glared Miss Sally's Tea Roome, where the ladies of Wrightsville's *haut monde* forgathered daily to sample Miss Sally's celebrated calorie specialty, Pineapple Marshmallow Nut Mousse. O Wrightsville! If you sighted due west along Lower Main from the entrance of the Five-and-Dime you could just make out the limy bronze back of Founder Jezreel Wright lording it over the rustcaked horse trough in the center of the Square (which was round) and beyond on the Square's western arc, the new marquee of the old Hollis Hotel, in certain of whose rooms could still be found the forthright china receptacles which the managment in an earlier generation had provided for the nighttime convenience of its guests. And if you looked across the street, next door to Louie Cahan's Bijou you saw the cheap white glare of the Kut-Rate Drug Co. Thunder mugs and fluorescence—in focus, this was Wrightsville; and rather peevishly Ellery flipped over the envelope which had photographed his illusion.

There was no return address.

Of course there wouldn't be. People who addressed an envelope in penciled capitals, deliberately crude, announced their passionate shyness in the act. An anonymous letter. Ellery was tempted to scale it into his April fire.

He slit the envelope with care.

It contained some newspaper clippings held together at their upper lefthand corners by an ordinary steel pin.

There was nothing else in the envelope.

The topmost clipping advertised the masthead of the *Wrightsville Record,* Wrightsville's only daily newspaper, and the date: *Wednesday, February 1.*

Two months old, then. Ellery read the story through.

It reported the death from heart failure of Luke MacCaby, 74, of 551 State Street, High Village.

Ellery did not recall the name, but there was a one-column cut of the dead man's house and he thought he recognized it.

It was a very large porched, peaked, gabled, and turreted building painted the inescapable Victorian dirty tan; it was fancy with wooden embroidery and stained-glass fanlights and it drooped against the dreary earth on which it had stood for six or seven decades. State Street, which is the northeast spoke leading from the Square's hub, is the broadest thoroughfare in town, and for several blocks it is stately and beautiful. But farther up it goes seedy. This was the fashionable residential district of Wrightsville around the turn of the century, before the old families moved up to the Hill. Now the down-at-the-heel mansions are populated by the lower middle class; some of them are rooming houses. Porches sag everywhere. Latticework is broken-toothed. Walks are cracked and hairy. The entire district cries out for carpentry and paint.

If the MacCaby house was the one Ellery recalled, it stood on the corner of State and Upper Foaming and it was the largest house and it cried out in the loudest tones of any house in the neighborhood.

MacCaby, said the *Record,* had been The Town Hermit. He had rarely ventured from the dilapidated premises in which he crept mysteriously about; he had not been seen around the Square or Lower Main, testified High Village trademen, for many years. In the old days MacCaby had been thought a miser, gloating over hypothetical piles of gold and diamonds in the gaslit interior of his ancestral hovel; but this rumor, whether made of myth or matter, apparently lacked vitality, for it had faded and died off; and for a long time now The Town Hermit had been considered a pauper subsisting on crusts. This was obviously not true, since he employed a caretaker, or companion, or servant—the story was vague as to the man's status; but that Luke MacCaby had been in poor circumstances was attested by his physician, the well-known High Village general practitioner Dr. Sebastian Dodd (of whom Ellery had never heard, either). Dr. Dodd, interviewed by the *Record,* reluctantly confessed that for years he had kept sending the old man bills, until "I realized the poor old codger simply didn't have enough to live on decently, so I stopped dunning him." Nevertheless, Dr. Dodd had continued to take medical care of MacCaby to the day of MacCaby's death. The old man had been suffering from a chronic heart ailment. To relieve his attacks Dr. Dodd had given him certain tablets.

As far as was known, Luke MacCaby was the last of his line; his wife had died in 1909 and they had had no "issue," according to the *Record.* He left behind only the questionable memories of his caretaker-companion-servant, Harry Toyfell. Toyfell had cared for MacCaby for fifteen years. He was an old man himself—another of the town characters, it seemed, for he was known as The Town Philosopher. Even better, Toyfell was often seen at Gus Olesen's Roadside Tavern on Route 16 in the company of Tom Anderson and Nicole Jacquard. At the encounter with Tom Anderson, Ellery warmed; here at last was an old acquaintance, he who was known to Wrightsville not unaffectionately as The Town Drunk and/or The Town Beggar. Nicole Jacquard eluded him for a moment. Unless . . . By gar! Back in '40 or '41 Ellery had been told of a Low Village French Canadian (in Wrightsvillese, "Canuck") family named Jacquard, the heads of which had specialized in production of children; hadn't there been something about "another" set of triplets . . . ? If Nicole Jacquard was that Jacquard, as seemed likely, he was not exactly a model of Low Village deportment. That Jacquard—and Ellery hoped he was motivated by nothing more reprehensible than the necessity of keeping the innumerable little Jacquard mouths filled—had been frankly known as The Town Thief. Ellery felt a positive glow; it was like coming home again.

There was little more to the newspaper story. Toyfell and his queer employer had been known "to fight like a cat and a dog." Asked why he had remained in the sour ruin for so many years tending a crotchety hermit who (presumably) paid him little or nothing, Toyfell had replied in four profound words: "He liked flowers, too." Toyfell had green fingers; he had worked miracles in the MacCaby garden, the only vital spot on the premises, with cuttings allegedly raped from North Hill estates as his material. The MacCaby Giant Gladiolus was a seasonal feature of Andy Birobatyan's Wrightsville Florist Shop on Washington Street.

Now that his employer was dead, Toyfell was asked his "plans." He replied: "For five years Mr. John Hart's been pesterin' me to take over his gardenin'. Guess I'll do it now." John Hart—John Spencer Hart—was the millionaire owner of "the old cotton mill" in Low Village, the *Record* reminded its readers. Knowing Wrightsville, Ellery was not astonished to learn that this was a locutionary tie with the past; no cotton had been milled in the old cotton mill for twenty years. Mr. John Spencer Hart's millions came from dyes, and over the ugly plant at Washington and Lower Whistling ran the stainless steel legend, WRIGHTSVILLE DYE WORKS.

"So ends another romantic chapter in Wrightsville history. Services for the deceased will be conducted by Dr. Ernest Highmount, assistant pastor of the First Congregational Church on West Livesey Street. Interment will be at East Twin Hill Cemetery, in the MacCaby family plot."

Requiescat in pace. And Harry Toyfell, may your new gardening job with Millionaire John Spencer Hart add material peace to your philosophy. But why in hell should anyone think I'd be interested?

Ellery glanced at the byline at the head of the clipping.

By Malvina Prentiss.

He shook his head and flipped the clipping back.

A second excerpt from the *Wrightsville Record*. A later one: *Monday, February 13*. And this second story was scareheaded. The *Record* had a sensation by the tail and it was shouting. (Somehow, it did not seem like the *Record* of Frank Lloyd's day, or even of Diedrich Van Horn's. It was blary. Under new publishership, apparently.)

The second clipping followed up the obituary story of February 1. Luke MacCaby, the eccentric old pauper, had been no pauper at all. He had died one of the wealthiest men in Wrightsville!

So there is matter in myth after all.

Secretly, MacCaby had been a full partner in the Wrightsville Dye Works.

Why MacCaby had chosen to remain a silent partner in a multimillion-dollar plant which had mushroomed during the war and had been spreading ever since "will never be known. According to Mr. Hart, Mr. MacCaby insisted that their business relationship be kept a secret without ever revealing his reason. Mr. Hart believes that Mr. MacCaby's eccentricity," etc.

It appeared that MacCaby had kept his stock, his dividends, virtually all his assets, in a large safe deposit box in the vaults of the Wrightsville National Bank;

even the officers of the bank (said Mr. Wolfert Van Horn, president) had been
ignorant of MacCaby's partnership in the Wrightsville Dye Works. Hart had established
a special account in a Connhaven bank; all partnership checks went into this account
and MacCaby's funds came to him—at his request, said Hart—in cash.

Sensation.

The story came out, said the *Record,* when Otis Holderfield, a local attorney,
filed a will for probate with the County Surrogate which, said Holderfield, Mr.
MacCaby had had him draw only a few weeks before the old man's death.

But this was nothing compared with the revelation to come. Luke MacCaby had
willed his entire estate to a well-known Wrightsvillian, a worthy man known for
his good works; in fact—hold your breath, now—to none other than . . . Dr.
Sebastian Dodd!

Sensation!

Dr. Sebastian Dodd's fees were still two dollars "at the office," three on house
call. Dr. Sebastian Dodd's patients were poor farmers, poor Low Villagers, poor
High Villagers; he specialized in poverty. He was known to own only two suits
and he ran an antediluvian "tin lizzie." He could not have survived without the
occasional Hill patient who, since Dr. Milo Willoughby's death, came to him instead
of to one of "the young men." Dr. Sebastian Dodd's waiting room was always
full and his checking account always empty. He was so busy being a failure that
he had even taken a young associate, Dr. Kenneth Winship, to help him stay poor.

This was the man who had come into an estate worth over four million dollars,
The *Record* waxed ecstatic. Who said Virtue went Unrewarded?

Dr. Sebastian Dodd was flabbergasted. "Why, what can I say? I don't know
what to say. I never had the least idea . . . he never let on . . ." At first the elderly
physician had insisted feebly that it must be a hoax. Four *million* dollars! But when
Attorney Otis Holderfield cited him clause and codicil, and Mr. John Spencer Hart
confirmed it, Dr. Dodd turned sparkly-eyed. He began to speak of the deplorable
condition of the Wrightsville General Hospital. Until 1946, Dr. Dodd pointed out,
Wrightsville's only hospital had not even possessed a private pavilion. Its equipment
was out-of-date and inadequate and its bed capacity far too small to cope with the
medical needs of a community numbering ten thousand souls. " 'When I took over
as chief of staff from the late Milo Willougby in '48,' said Dr. Dodd," said the
Record, " 'I promised myself by golly I wouldn't rest till the Wrightsville General
got at least the modern children's wing we need so awfully bad. Now, through Mr.
MacCaby's generosity, I can endow one.' "

To Harry Toyfell, The Town Hermit had left exactly nothing.

The Town Philosopher came nobly to the support of his reputation when the
Record reporter asked him how he felt about having been overlooked in the will
of the old man he had served for so long. " 'Thy money perish with thee,' " he
said, the *Record* identifying the source of this wisdom as Acts VIII, 20. "The grave
manured by gold grows weeds," Toyfell had added, quoting himself this time (or
the *Record* was unable to locate the quotation). "Money wouldn't make me a better
man, now would it? In the eyes of the Lord all men are equal. Read your Jesus.
Read your Paine." The *Record* commented on Toyfell's Christian character and
said there was a deep lesson for all its readers in this humble old man's stern
spirituality. The *Record* did a little quoting of its own, mentioning the needles's
eye.

No, Harry Toyfell had not suspected MacCaby's affluence.

The story was bylined: *By Malvina Prentiss.*

Ellery, frowning, turned to the next-underlying clipping.

This one—it was the last—was dated *Monday, February 20*. One week later the story had shot up like the Beanstalk. John Spencer Hart had committed suicide.

This time Ellery read with naked devotion.

On learning that he was Luke MacCaby's sole heir to some four millions of dollars, Dr. Sebastian Dodd had retained Otis Holderfield, the lawyer who had drawn MacCaby's astonishing will, to watch over his legal interests. Accordingly, Holderfield had presented a letter for his new client's signature which was addressed to Mr. John Spencer Hart, president of the Wrightsville Dye Works, requesting a preliminary accounting of the plant's financial status. Dr. Dodd had signed the letter, Attorney Holderfield had mailed it to Mr. Hart by Registered Mail, Return Receipt Requested, the receipt had come back duly signed by addressee; and that night the milllonaire had pleaded a grippey feeling, he had handed his wife into the Harts' town-and-country job, watched her drive off to a housewarming at the Hallam Lucks'—who had just moved from Hill Drive to a magnificent new house on Skytop Road—stepped back into his house, and he had dismissed the four inside servants for the evening. Hart had then gone into his library, locked the door, written a note to his wife, and blown his brains out.

This spectacular effect had obviously rocketed from a cause, which could only have been the slightly dangerous legal letter the late millionaire had just received. (To the *Record,* faithfully reflecting Wrightsville mores, all "lawyer letters" had a sinister undertone.) But what was the fireworks ingredient? Investigation soon isolated it. Unknown even to his wife, Hart had been gambling and speculating like a madman for years, his acumen apparently having been restricted to the dye business. His personal fortune had been consumed; his interest in the Wrightsville Dye Works was eaten away; he had even gnawed a chunk out of his silent partner's interest. Hart had teetered on the brink of ruin and prison at the very moment when his new partner's formal request for an accounting arrived. A well-placed bullet seemed the reasonable solution.

A report from Finegold & Izzard, Certified Public Accountants (108 Upham Block, on the Square), revealed that the Wrightsville Dye Works was still in sound shape despite Hart's reckless inroads. " 'No cut in personnel is contemplated, no,' says Dr. Dodd, now sole owner of the dye works," said the *Record,* " 'at least at present. As for management, I have had several long talks with George Churchward, who ran the plant under Mr. Hart since early in the war, and I'm convinced Mr. Churchward knows his business. As soon as the legal mess is cleaned up, Churchward becomes vice-president in full charge of plant operations. Meanwhile, he will continue in his present capacity.' " The *Record* pointed out that George Churchward had long been one of the most up-and-coming young plant managers in the industrial county and that he was 41, married to Angel Asperley Stone, popular daughter of Willis Stone (the well-known High Village mortician), and father of three of Wrightsville's brightest "sun-suit set," Charline Willis, 5, Love Asperley, 3, and George, Jr., 16 months. "Congratulations, George Churchward!"

John Spencer Hart was survived by his widow, Ursula Hart (nee Brooks), and their son Carver B., sophomore at Yale. " 'I understand John Hart left very little insurance,' stated Dr. Sebastian Dodd today to the *Record* in an exclusive interview, 'having borrowed the limit against his policies and let others lapse, so that Mrs. Hart and her son are being left practically destitute. I'm writing to her today. As soon as the dye works tangle and the MacCaby will are straightened out, Mrs. Hart will begin receiving a monthly income from the Works and this will continue for the rest of her life. And if young Carver wants a job, there's one waiting for him.' "

Plans for the MacCaby-Dodd Children's Wing of the Wrightsville General Hospital were being held up, explained Dr. Dodd in this interview, pending clarification of "the state of the Works," viewed in the light of the late J. S. Hart's "unfortunate personal investments."

A human interest footnote to this latest chapter in what Ellery had already entitled The Adventures of Sebastian Dodd was appended by the *Record* reporter. Harry Toyfell, who had scarcely had time to take up his duties as head gardener of the Hart estate on North Hill Drive, "now finds himself out of a job for the second time in less than three weeks through the scythe of the Grim Ripper. However, Harry is taking 'the slings and arrows of fortune' like the grand old philosopher he is. He has already accepted a new job as gardener for one of Wrightsville's leading citizens. We refer to none other than Dr. Sebastian Dodd."

The story was signed: *By Malvina Prentiss*.

Ellery got up and tossed a fresh briquet into the fire.

But light was called for as well as heat.

Who had sent him the *Record* clippings? And why?

His first thought had been Emmeline DuPré. Emmeline DuPré was a hatpin of a woman, all length and steel and sting, who dwelt among the gentry at 468 Hill Drive, two doors from the great Wright place, and represented Art and Culture in Wrightsville by giving Dancing and Dramatic Lessons to the gentry's youth. Miss DuPré had richly earned the sobriquet—in the Wrightsville nomenclature—of The Town Crier; the clapper of her tongue usually struck the tocsin of bad news. But on reflection Ellery decided this was subtler work. Emmeline Dupré dealt in black and white, not sinister gray.

That there was something sinister behind all this Ellery felt in his marrow. But what? Wrightsville knew him in his criminological capacity. But where was the crime? John Spencer Hart had committed a crime, but the criminal himself had solved his mystery. Was there a hidden crime? Did the anonymous clippings-sender suspect, or know, that foul play had occurred? But the editorializing news accounts from the typewriter of Malvina Prentiss gave no hint of any such possibility. Luke MacCaby had apparently died of a heart attack; he had had a long cardiac history and, even if he had not had a long cardiac history, life at 74 is routinely unreliable. As for Hart's suicide, its motivation was thorough and convincing and the *Record* story had even observed, *passim,* that his suicide note to Mrs. Hart had been in his verified handwriting: the widow and son had both identified it at the inquest held by Coroner Grupp, whose scalpel eye no corruption would have escaped.

It was an annoyance.

Finally, Ellery put the envelope and its contents away in his odds-and-ends drawer.

It was probably a belated April Fools' Day joke.

Still the little mystery kept yapping at his heels.

Friday, April 7

When the second envelope arrived by special delivery three nights later, Ellery tore it open with shameless eagerness. That the sender was the same required two glances. The size and paper of the envelope, the crudely penciled address, the Wrightsville postmark, the blank reverse were identical.

One clipping from the *Record*, dated *Monday, April 3*, floated to his desk.

The Town Drunk had disappeared.

Tom Anderson was no more.

Ellery glared.

Investigation by Chief of Police Dakin had established, "almost to a dead certainty," that Anderson was dead. His coat and hat had been found early Sunday morning, April 2, at the edge of Little Prudy's Cliff in The Marshes. (The Marshes, Ellery recalled, was a tangle of sulphurous swamp just outside the eastern boundary of Low Village; it was the bogeyland of Low Village's young and the breeding place of a superior strain of mosquito.) There was "unmistakable evidence," said Chief Dakin, "of a tussle at the edge of the cliff," in the course of which Anderson must have toppled into the quicksand below. The *Record* pointed out that the quagmire at the foot of Little Prudy's Cliff was "bottomless" and that any object was immediately sucked beneath the surface. Attempts to drag the bog had been abandoned as hopeless. "Who struggled with Tom Anderson at the edge of Little Prudy's Cliff?" demanded the *Record* hotly. "Who hurled him over to his horrible end? This is the question Wrightsville wants answered right away!"

The deceased, concluded the *Record*, was survived by a daughter, Rima Anderson, 22 years of age.

Byline: *By Malvina Prentiss*.

Ellery laid the clipping down.

Here was puzzle compounded. What was the connection between The Town Drunk's murder—if it was murder—and the saga of Sebastian Dodd?

For there was a connection. There must be. In the earliest clipping there was no correlation between Anderson and Luke MacCaby, the central figure of that story. And in the second and third stories Anderson was not even mentioned as background. Suddenly—in story number 4—Anderson again, this time as protagonist. But isolated. No cross-reference to MacCaby, or Hart, or Dr. Dodd, or even to his crony Harry Toyfell.

Yet they were all related, perhaps even Nicole (The Town Thief) Jacquard. They were related by the fact that someone in Wrightsville had related them. Anonymous suspected, or had, inside information. Anonymous had reason to believe that Town Drunk Anderson was pushed to his death. Anonymous knew that Town Drunk Anderson's murder arose from the events reported in the first three *Record* stories.

Was that it? Did Anonymous mean to convey that MacCaby and Hart were also murdered? Or one of them?

Then there was Tom Anderson himself. Anderson had clearly been a man of culture and respectability before his fall from sobriety. Even drunk as Chaucer's ape, lolling on the rotten imitation-stone pedestal of the Low Village World War I Memorial—against a background of smutty red brick factories, stoop-shouldered two-story crackerbox houses, cramped shops with embarrassing pinchbeck fronts like Sidney Gotch's General Store . . . in the humped and dingy shadow of the old cotton mill—now the Wrightsville Dye Works!—even then The Town Drunk had aroused regret, not laughter or revulsion. Ellery could have sworn there was no evil in the derelict. If he was dead of violence, the evil lay elsewhere.

And the surprising news that Anderson had had a daughter. *Survived by a daughter, Rima Anderson, 22 years of age, period.* Bad reporting, Malvina. Was she a drudge in some High Village tourist home? Hired girl on one of the meaner valley farms? Or a regular in a four-bit bawdy house on Barking Street? But the name Rima . . . It irritated him, because it sounded and looked familiar and it kept just out of reach. And because, unoriented, it still refused to fit into his visual memory of the Wrightsville slums and sinks. It evoked an image of grace, solitude, greenery . . . But he was certain he had never met anyone in Wrightsville with such a name.

Well, he thought, this isn't getting me anywhere. At all.

Ellery threw the second envelope into his catchall drawer.

I'll sleep on it, he said to himself.

Saturday, April 8

As Ellery was setting down his second cup of coffee the next morning his doorbell rang. He opened the door to find a child in the hall. The foyer and hallway were murky and he had to peer. It was evident that the little girl had put on a costume of her mother's—who must be a character!—and she was pluckily fighting off nervousness.

"Yes?" said Ellery with an encouraging smile.

"Ellery Queen?"

He squinted past her, searching the shadows. The voice had been a woman's.

"Did you say that?" he asked sharply.

"My name is Rima Anderson. Could you talk to me?"

The next few minutes Ellery devoted to re-stabilization. The world of fiction is made up of heroines, he caught himself philosophizing, industriously contrived by their authors to be all that no woman ever is. Yet here was a girl, in flesh, with blood, who might have stepped out of a book. In fact, as Ellery soon discovered, Rima Anderson *had* stepped out of a book.

She had a special, unbelievable quality of . . . *consistency*. Women are made of skin, hair, muscle, sweat glands, ten thousand things; this girl had the harmony of a figurine. She was of one piece. He kept thinking of Tanagra and terra cotta, and of how breakable she seemed. Yet when she came in her step was soundless. He thought of elves and birds.

When he saw her in the full light there was nothing fragile about her. She was like a miniature fruit at its ripest. A child giving off a womanly disturbance. The child-woman paradox was most emphatic in her eyes. They were as serenely un-cluttered, as without guile or guilty knowledge, as the eyes of any little girl; still, under scrutiny, they veiled themselves as no child's eyes had ever done. The effect was enchanting and fresh, but it carried no conviction. You had to talk yourself into it.

Even her voice. It had a lilt, the music of something formless but significant in nature. The voice of a brook, or a dryad. That's it, thought Ellery. She's a nymph who lives in the heart of a tree. And then he remembered who "Rima" was. Rima was the child-woman, the bird-girl of the Venezuelan jungle, in a book he had not read for twenty years.

And here she sat.

But where was old Nuflo, her grandfather? And his dogs Susio and Goloso? One had a right to expect them, and the mora tree, and the hummingbird, and the little silkhaired monkey.

"Is Rima the name you were given when you were born?"

"Rima is the name I was given when I was born."

By her father. By The Town Drunk. He had named her Rima by benefit of W.
H. Hudson and he had made her Rima in fact. To shape a child in the mold of a
name is brutal, but poetry. Ellery saw Tom Anderson in a suddenly altered light.
Chief Dakin and the *Record* might still be wrong. Such a man could have poised
himself on the edge of Little Prudy's Cliff and, like Icarus, taken off.

No one in Wrightsville had known this girl well; perhaps she had been a sort of
myth to the town, a creature of folklore in the making. The Town Drunk must have
hidden her away, protecting the delicate product of his creative energy from the
corrosive influence of the community. And Ellery knew without asking that Rima
Anderson's playmates had been birds and small animals, and that her playground
had been the natural world in which Wrightsville squats—plain and hill and stream
and wood, the wilder woods where hardly anyone ventured. And if her skin had a
sheen, and if her hair was waved, and if her lips were as redly soft as young
raspberries, it was because Rima had been taught to patronize the cosmeticians of
nature, the sun and the wind and the rain. In the world of beauty parlors and cutrate
toiletries she walked alone.

The girl wore a house dress of the cheapest cotton, black coarse stockings,
flatheeled and papery-looking white "store" shoes, a shrieking bonnet. Everything
about her added up to "country store" in some remote rural district; Ellery could
recall no shop even in Low Village which carried such outlandish merchandise.
She must have walked over to Fidelity, the very poor community west of Wrightsville,
or down to Shinn Corners, deep in the southwestern farm country, to get them.
Things would be cheaper there, and there would be fewer eyes. Like a bird, she
was shy. There was a pallor under her brown skin which told him what contact
with New York had done to her. Probably this was her first visit to a big city.
Absurdly, he wished he had a finch, or a field mouse, to offer her . . . and wondered
how he could manage to get her back to Wrightsville in some less outrageous
costume. It was a problem; and he decided to let inspiration or opportunity solve
it.

"How did you happen to come all the way to New York to see me, Miss
Anderson?"

She laughed—the unprepared outburst of a bird. "Call me Rima!"

"All right. But why did you laugh, Rima?"

"Nobody's ever called me Miss Anderson before." When he repeated his first
question, she said, "My father, Thomas Hardy Anderson, used to talk about you."
Thomas Hardy Anderson . . .

"Tom Anderson?" Ellery asked involuntarily.

"The Town Drunk." She said it naturally. It was a fact, like the bad reputation
of gophers; one stated it and passed on. She has the quick acceptance of all wild
things, he thought; a fawn doesn't question the morals of its father.

"What did he say about me, Rima?"

"Oh, that you were the kind of man who had a compulsion to look for the truth.
He told me that if I was ever in trouble and he was gone, I was to come to you.
And I'm in trouble."

"So you've come to me."

"Yes."

Ellery got up and fiddled with the Venetian blind. When he turned around he
said, "I know about his disappearance."

"I think my father is dead." It was hard to adjust to her directness. She did not
question the source of his information; his knowledge did not surprise her.

"Apparently the Wrightsville police think so, too."

"Chief Dakin told me that. And a woman from the newspaper. I don't like her, but I like Chief Dakin."

"And that's why you think your father is dead, Rima? Because they've told you so?"

"I knew it before they told me." She was up and over at the window.

"What do you mean, you 'knew it before'? Do you know something the others don't?"

"I just know it. If he were alive he'd come back to me, or write. He's dead." She kept looking down at 87th Street, with interest, as if the death of her father was of no importance. But again Ellery had to readjust. The rules didn't apply to her. What seemed curiosity about a New York street was probably caution. The sparrow soars from the pavement crumb to a safe telephone wire, and from there he watches. His watching is mysteriously tied up with his wants.

"People have been known to go away, Rima. Without explanation or warning. Because—let's say—they're in trouble."

"He may have been in trouble, but he would have told me if he had to go away. He's dead."

"The struggle on Little Prudy's Cliff—"

"He was pushed over. He was murdered."

"Why?"

She fluttered about at that. "I don't know, Mr. Queen. That's why I've come to you." Just as suddenly she returned to the sofa, tucked her legs under her, smiled at him. They had turned a corner. Or the sparrow had decided that the man on the pavement was harmless. "May I take off my shoes? They hurt."

"Please do."

She took them off, wiggling her toes. "I hate shoes, don't you?"

"Can't stand them."

"Then why don't you take yours off?"

"Well, I . . . think I will!" said Ellery, and he removed his shoes.

"I'm going to take off these stockings, too, if you don't mind. They itch so. Mmmm . . ." Her legs were honey-colored, beautiful running legs covered with brisk scratches. But the soles of her feet were not at all beautiful; they were covered with a horny integument, like a coating of plastic. She noticed his glance and frowned. "They're ugly, aren't they? But I can't abide shoes." Ellery could see her flying through the woods. He wondered what she wore in her natural habitat. "At first I thought of talking with his two friends," Rima went on. "But—"

She makes no transitions, he thought. You follow her flight or you lose her.

"Nick Jacquard? Harry Toyfell?"

"But I don't like them. Jacquard is no good. And Toyfell makes me . . ." She grew still.

"Makes you what, Rima?"

"I don't know . . . They weren't good for Daddy. Until a short time ago, they had a bad influence on him."

"You think Jacquard or Toyfell, or both, had something to do with what happened to your father?"

"Oh, no. They were really his friends. But I don't want to talk to them. I don't like them."

And it seemed perfectly logical to Ellery at the moment not to question your father's only close associates about his disappearance on the ground that you disliked them.

He got up and began that hungry patrol of his preserves which in Ellery follows uneasiness. Rima watched him trustfully.

"Tell me all about your father, Rima. Was he originally from Wrightsville? What did he use to do for a living?"

"He was born in Wisconsin somewhere. He never talked about his family. I think he'd had very strict, ignorant parents and they quarreled and he left home in his teens. He wanted to write poetry. He worked his way East and got into Harvard, tutoring to support himself. Some famous Harvard professor told him he'd never be anything but a third-rate poet but that he had the makings of a first-rate teacher. He took graduate courses in education and afterwards got a job teaching English literature at Merrimac University in Connhaven . . . Hardy wasn't his real middle name. His real middle name was Hogg. He took Hardy when he enrolled in Harvard."

Ellery nodded.

"He'd been teaching at Merrimac for eighteen years when he met my mother. She was a graduate student there. By this time he was a full professor and one of the most popular teachers in the university. He was 44, Mother was my age. Neither had ever loved anyone before. They fell in love."

A bachelor over 40, with a background of family antagonisms and creative frustration, who was forced to sublimate his passion for verbal sound and shape in the teaching of literature, Anderson had poured everything into the first love of his life. Rima's mother had been a beauty and a poet of promise. "Daddy used to say Mother got more poetry into a grocery list than he'd ever pounded into an ode." Rima's mother had come from the Middle West, one of the numerous daughters of a *nouveau riche* family. Her parents had social plans for her and violently opposed her alliance with a small-salaried college professor "stuck up in the New England woods." Rima's mother broke with her family and married her professor.

"They lived on the Merrimac campus and the next year I was born. Daddy named me Rima after the heroine in *Green Mansions*. When I was 2 he built a little house up in the hills near Connhaven and we moved there, away from everybody. Daddy went in to college every day, mother tended house and me and wrote poems on the backs of envelopes and on grocery sacks, like Emily Dickinson, and I played in the woods. On weekends we'd all three do it. We wore practically no clothes and at night we'd sleep on spruce boughs under blankets and we'd have wonderful times. I think we were the happiest family in the world. When I turned 5, Daddy drove me down to school every day and picked me up again in the afternoons. What I learned I learned from him and Mother and the woods, though . . . Then, when I was almost 10, Mother took sick and died. Overnight. I don't know what it was—some rare disease. One day she was with us, the next day she wasn't."

Rima sat still.

"I'll never forget what Daddy said at Mother's grave, when everybody'd gone away. He hadn't said a word since her death, just held my hand. 'This is black wickedness, Rima. There's no beauty or justice in it,' he said; and that night, after he put me to bed, he went down to Connhaven and came back very late, drunk."

Rima's recollections of those days were of staggering steps, shouts, whisky fumes, wild weeping in the night, and wilder tenderness. Anderson had periods of abstinence, when he would go about pale and silent, his hands trembling; at these times he often reread his wife's poems to Rima. But the temperate episodes became less and less frequent, and finally they stopped altogether. For the most part Rima was looked after by friends, the wives of faculty members; later, there were threats of legal action if Anderson did not stop drinking or turn the child over to welfare authorities. But Rima herself thwarted all attempts to separate them. "I must have run away from various places a dozen times," she told Ellery. "Daddy was always kind to me, even when he was very drunk. Nobody could keep me, and after a while nobody tried." Then the last of a series of painful incidents in class and Professor Anderson was dismissed from the Merrimac faculty.

"That's when we came to Wrightsville," Rima said. "Somehow Daddy got an appointment to teach English at Wrightsville High. We lived in Mrs. Wheatley's rooming house on Upper Purling Street. Mrs. Wheatley looked after me during the day. She's dead now."

Tom Anderson's position on the high school faculty lasted eight months. When Principal Martha E. Coolye caught him with a glass of whisky on his desk during class, he was summarily discharged.

"Five weeks later Mrs. Wheatley put us out for nonpayment of rent. Daddy said, 'Don't blame her, Rima. She's a poor woman and we're taking up space she could get money for. We'll find another place to live as soon as I straighten myself out and get a job.' "

Rima's next recollection was of the shack on the edge of The Marshes. It had been built by some engineers during a survey of The Marshes in one of the periods when public agitation for its drainage threatened to upset Wright County political applecarts. Its roof leaked and its tarpaper covering was all but peeled away. They managed to make it weatherproof and in the intervening years Rima had built an additional room onto it and a new floor from salvaged lumber, and she had grown ivy all over the outer walls. "It's pretty now," laughed Rima. "More like a flowerbox than a house." And the mosquitoes of the Marshes? asked Ellery. "Mosquitoes don't bite me," said Rima.

And there they had lived ever since. The land belonged to no one, so far as Rima knew; at least, they had never been molested. In those earlier years repeated attempts were made by the Ladies' Aid and the town welfare authorities to separate the child from her father, but Rima always broke loose and came back to him. "He needed me. I knew that the day my mother died. He needed somebody who loved him and didn't condemn him for being drunk all the time. He needed somebody to take his clothes off when he came home, or hold his head when he was more than usually drunk, or read to him, or put him to bed. Where did we get beds, furniture, a stove? I don't know. Daddy managed to get eveything we needed. We didn't need much." Finally the attempts to give the girl "a proper home" were abandoned and the Andersons were let alone. "They've forgotten all about me!" They had no money beyond the few dollars Tom Anderson earned occasionally doing an odd job and a small sum which arrived monthly, in cash, addressed to "Thomas Hogg Anderson" in care of General Delivery, Wrightsville, bearing the postmark "Racine, Wis." but no return address. I think it's from a brother, or sister, of Daddy's out there," said Rima indifferently. "Daddy never talked about it but once that I recall. He said, laughing, 'I'm the Pariah of the Anderson tribe, darling. Their blood boils from contact with the Untouchable, but they soothe their glossy souls by the payment of a pittance in conscience-money. It's all for you, baby. I won't touch a scummy cent of it.' " But he always did. They had made a ritual out of it. Each month her father walked to the post office at Lower Main and the Square, brought back the envelope, Rima opened it with ceremony, she hid the money in a cracker tin on a shelf above the stove while he turned his back; and later Tom Anderson—and the money—would disappear for a day or so. "It went on that way for years. He always insisted that I hide it, and I always did, just to please him. Sometimes he even made me hide it in a different place." Occasionally, when the need was acute, Rima took a dollar or two from the box before the remittance vanished. But in general she got along very well without money. She raised her own vegetables in a little garden behind the shack, and her father had developed a skill that amounted to art in supplying their household with flour, fowl, fruit, bacon. "You know," said Rima matter-of-factly, "they called him The Town Beggar just about as often as The Town Drunk. He always resented that. 'I give them value for consideration,' he used to say. 'I amuse them. In the Middle Ages I would have been a jester. I've never begged in my life.' " But he had, and she knew it. "It was for me," she told Ellery. "If it was just for himself, he'd have starved first." Silently, Ellery doubted this. The hard moral fiber of Tom Anderson had been buried with his wife. The flabby residue sagged to every whim, and most weakly to his craving for forgetfulness.

At times he killed rabbits and other small game in the woods north of The Marshes. Rima never touched them. "They're my friends," she laughed. "I couldn't eat my friends."

Rima spent her days in the hills and backwoods surrounding Wrightsville. There were sweet wild berries to be plucked, streams to bathe in, injured birds and animals to nurse, hot long-grassed meadows to lie on while her father sat crosslegged by her side lecturing and questioning, book in hand. For the School Board had discovered the uselessness of trying to keep Rima Anderson in a classroom, and there had been talk of a truancy proceeding which would have placed her behind the bars of the County Corrective Home for Girls at Limpscot, upstate. Tom Anderson had roused himself. He stopped drinking for forty-eight hours, Rima mended and brushed his clothes, and then he had marched into town to demand a special Board hearing. At the hearing he pleaded brilliantly his pedagogic qualifications and pledged that he would teach his daughter privately, following the curriculum prescribed by the State Regents. After a confused session the Board voted its assent to this unusual arrangement, on the condition that Rima present herself each semester for examinations in the prescribed high school courses of study, the penalty for failure being punitive Board action.

"We made them eat crow," gurgled Rima, doubled over. "Daddy never let me get away with anything and I always passed their old exams with high marks." Rima's highest marks had come in English literature. "They called him names and sneered at him and said he wasn't fit to be a father, and a lot of what they said was true, but Daddy never neglected my education and because I loved him and he was a wonderful teacher I learned more than most of the Wrightsville kids. In literature I think I could teach their teachers a thing or two! We had nothing— according to Wrightsville—and if we did have anything they said Daddy pawned it or sold it to get money for liquor. But he never touched our books, no matter how desperate he was, and if you come to Wrightsville, Mr. Queen, I'll show you a library that will open your eyes."

And now Tom Anderson was gone. Dead, Rima insisted.

"I want to know what happened to him. How it happened." Her eyelids came down. "Who did it." He saw that her hands were in perfect repose. She's learned an animal discipline, he thought.

"Rima." Ellery sat down opposite her again. "A few minutes ago, in talking about your father's two friends—Nick Jacquard and Harry Toyfell—you said they'd exerted a bad influence on him 'until a short time ago.' Exactly what did you mean by that? Had he stopped seeing Jacquard and Toyfell? Given them up?"

"He stopped drinking. He gave liquor up."

Ellery looked at her.

"You think he didn't. That he couldn't have. I know he did. In all the years since Mother died he never once tried to give up drinking. Even when he stayed sober for two whole days that time when he had to see the School Board about me, it was for just those two days; he didn't pretend he was reforming. About a month ago, without any warning, he told me he was through being The Town Drunk. I was surprised and I asked him what had happened. He wouldn't tell me. 'Let's wait and see,' he said.

"He'd never said anything like that to me before. I suppose that's why I believed him. At first I thought he just *wanted* to. But then, as the days and nights passed and he'd come home walking as straight as anybody else and with no whisky on his breath, I knew he was actually doing it. His hands would shake and he'd toss around half the night. There were times when he'd get almost wild and run around the shack as if he were crazy. Once when he thought I was asleep he crawled out of bed and lit a stub of candle and got a bottle of whisky out of a hole in the floor. He put it on the table next to the candle and pulled out the cork and he sat down with his hand on the bottle and looked at it. I could see a big artery jumping under his skin and the sweat was pouring down his face. He sat there that way for fully an hour. Then he put the cork back into the bottle, put the bottle back in the hole in the floor, replaced the floor board, and went to bed again."

Ellery wondered why she was making such a story up. It couldn't possibly be true. Not an alcoholic with such a long history of addiction as Tom Anderson. But then he saw the strange clarity of her eyes and he found himself doubting his own doubt.

"Maybe it wouldn't have lasted," said Rima calmly. "But it did last for a month. Until the night he died."

"He continued to see Toyfell and Jacquard?"

"Yes. But he told me it was to test himself. He said that he still went to the Roadside Tavern with them and that while they drank he sat with an empty glass before him. Jacquard laughed at him, he said—he was angry about it. Maybe being angry helped him."

"So when he quarreled with somebody on Little Prudy's Cliff a week ago tonight, you think he was sober?"

"I'm positive he was." She couldn't possibly be, but she was. And, unreasonably, Ellery was, too.

"And he didn't get around to telling you why he'd suddenly decided to give up drinking?"

"No. I knew he'd tell me in time. I didn't want to press him. Daddy couldn't take much pressure."

And Ellery, nodding, began to drift about again. After a while he came to a decision. It was an uneasy decision, because Rima was an enigma he had not entirely solved. The case was difficult and called for improvisation. He said to her, "Rima, have you ever sent me a letter?"

It was a ridiculous question. But then Anonymous was always a shy bird, too. It seemed the right shot at the moment. It might flush a look, a tremor, a breath.

But Rima merely shook her head.

Ellery kept looking at her. "Did you know an old man in High Village named MacCaby?"

"Luke MacCaby? I've heard about him through Daddy. Harry Toyfell worked for him. But Luke MacCaby is dead. He died leaving a lot of money to a doctor in High Village named Dodd, Sebastian Dodd."

"Did your father ever talk to you about MacCaby's death?"

"He told me what he'd heard, especially from Toyfell. But everybody in town was talking about it, he said. Everybody was very excited."

"Did he know MacCaby?" persisted Ellery.

"I don't know. Why do you keep asking about MacCaby?"

"Do I ask you why you keep performing tonsillectomies on ailing meadowlarks, Rima? I manage to keep in touch with Wrightsville," said Ellery manfully, "one way and another. Tell me: What do you know about John Spencer Hart?"

No flash or flicker. She was really trying to remember. "Hart . . . Wasn't he connected with Luke MacCaby in some way? I think a man of that name died recently in town, too. I don't know much about Wrightsville," confessed Rima. "I hardly ever go into town. The only people I see are kids who wander off into the woods to pick berries and get lost and have to be taken back home. I know more Wrightsville dogs than people. There's always a gang of them around the shack, scratching themselves and wagging their tails."

"Did your father know John Spencer Hart?"

"Oh, I'm sure he didn't! Because now I remember. Wasn't Mr. Hart a very rich man who lived on a huge estate on North Hill Drive?"

"Did your father ever mention John Spencer Hart?"

"I don't recall his saying . . ."

"Did your father know Dr. Dodd, Rima?"

"Dr. Dodd? I don't know." She was distressed now; her exquisite little hands fluttered. "You must think I'm stupid. But it's just that I've had no interest in Wrightsville affairs and I never questioned Daddy about whom he knew or what he did or where he went. Not because I didn't want to know but because he didn't like being pushed. If he wanted to tell me something, I listened. If he needed my help, I gave it. Otherwise I let him alone. People were lecturing him all the time. I was the only one who took him as he was and respected his rights as a human being, even if according to Wrightsville he was a very poor human being . . . I just don't know, Mr. Queen."

"I understand Dr. Dodd does a great deal of work in Low Village, and I thought—"

"But we're never sick. I mean, we never were."

"Not even your father?"

"He was a funny man in some respects. He thought going to a doctor was a sign of weakness. He'd fight off things that would put other people into bed."

"Rima, you're the world's most unsatisfactory client. There's nothing to go on."

"I'm so sorry—"

"I suppose you'll tell me your father hadn't an enemy in the world."

"He hadn't."

"He must have had at least one!"

"No . . . Daddy charmed people. Even Mrs. Coolye, the principal who kicked him out of Wrightsville High—the day she dismissed him she cried. Chris Dorfman, the radio car policeman who was brought up last year on charges of breaking the nose of Big Tootsie's girls in a drunken brawl, used to bring Daddy home instead of running him in; he'd tell me, 'It's a shame about your old man. He's a great old guy.' Nobody'd want to hurt Daddy because of anything Daddy *was*."

"What do you mean by that?" Ellery stared at her.

"Some people will kill a ladybug. Not because the ladybug is harmful but because it happens to get in their way. Nothing personal. Just a matter of convenience."

Ellery kept staring.

"If there's nothing to go on . . ." Rima got off the sofa, slowly this time. "You won't take the case."

"Rima, how much money do you have?"

The blood flooded her cheeks. "I'm stupid. Of course, your fee. Mr. Queen, I'm sorry. I—"

"I didn't say anything about my fee. I asked you how much money you have."

She looked at him. Then, as suddenly as she did everything, she opened her imitation leather purse and held it out to him.

The purse contained a handkerchief, a railroad ticket, a box of wild cherry drops, and some coins. Perhaps fifty cents.

"It's what I had left after I bought my ticket to New York and return, and paid my bus fare here from Grand Central Terminal. Daddy hadn't touched the money from Racine last time. Otherwise I couldn't have come."

"Bad." Ellery scowled.

"Bad?"

"It interferes with my plans."

"Plans? I don't—"

"I wanted you to look big-cityish when we went back to Wrightsville."

"You're coming back with me!" That bird peal again.

"What? Oh, certainly," said Ellery. "I mean to say, it's important that you look . . . smart, Rima. Up-to-the-minute. New York chic, as it were—"

"You want me to buy different clothes." He blushed slightly as she glanced down at herself, up at him. "I know these are awful," she said helplessly. "But I couldn't afford any better. I have no wardrobe."

"It's a bother," said Ellery with a fierce frown. Then his forehead cleared. "See here, I don't see why we should endanger my plan of action merely because of the lack of a little money. Suppose I advance you a couple of hundred, Rima."

"Dollars?"

"Why, yes."

"But I couldn't ever pay that much back." She trilled at his childishness.

"Of course you could. You're not going to keep living in that mosquito-infested flowerpot, are you?"

She was amazed. "Where else would I live?"

"I'm sure I don't know. But you've got to get yourself a job of some sort—"

"Why?"

"Why? Because . . . because you'll owe me two hundred dollars!" He grasped her arm and was surprised to find it as pliantly tough as a gull's wing. "Now we've had enough talk. We're going out to get you a suit, blouses, hat, underthings, stockings, shoes, a hairdo, manicure, pedicure . . ."

It was the best he could muster on the moment.

Weekend, April 8–9

They passed over another bridge or two before the weekend was out. The first crossing from formality proved to be their shopping excursion. Ellery smuggled Rima into Lachine's on Fifth Avenue, where you may buy everything from a bobby pin to an ermine wrap and whose salespeople are never surprised by anything. He spent most of the afternoon worrying his thumbs and wondering what magics were being performed in the dressing room. At 4:30 he saw and was awed. Then there was an interminable session with François on the fifth floor. Rima emerged at last, accompanied by an agitated Gallic male who kept wailing that one does not gild a lily and what should one do to improve such a complexion, Monsieur?—but the hair, Monsieur, and the feet, Monsieur! Ellery replied hotly that the hair, Monsieur, and the feet, Monsieur, were as God had made them, François retorted that if such was the case, Monsieur, why in the sacred name of a paper bag had Monsieur brought Mad'moiselle to his salon, and Rima sat down in her new clothes and put her manicured fingers to her made-up eyes and wept all over them, reducing both François and Ellery to agonized silence. At this point a motherly saleswoman sent them both away, and when Ellery next saw Rima she was cool, and perfect, and she smiled a New York smile and said, "Am I according to plan, Pygmalion?" whereupon his shame melted in a warm gush of something and he found himself suddenly adoring her.

Then he took her off to dinner at the snootiest place he could think of.

He no longer thought of her as a child. Quite the contrary. In fact, he found himself glaring at the Van Johnson type at the next table. Afterwards, back on 87th Street, he saw the admiration in Inspector Queen's eyes; and when the Inspector, who was an absolute Englishman about the inviolability of his room, actually offered Rima the use of his bed for the night, Ellery knew the worst. Hastily, he took her to a women's hotel in the 60s, where it would be necessary to say goodnight under the frigid eye of an elderly female desk clerk.

He returned to 87th Street slightly damp under the collar.

He found his father waiting up for him.

"Back so soon?" asked Inspector Queen.

"The question answers itself," said Ellery coldly. "What did you think I'd be doing?"

"Odd type, that girl," said the Inspector in an absent way. "From Wrightsville, you said?"

"Yes."

"And you're going back with her tomorrow?"

"Yes!"

"I see," said the Inspector, and he went to bed.

She was a nuisance all night.

On the train the next day, rather hollow-eyed, Ellery tried to analyze it. It wasn't the clothes. All the clothes did was to point up what she was. But what was she? he thought as he felt her fingers withdrawn from his. After a moment he attacked the question negatively. She *wasn't* a . . . She wasn't a great many things, but when you added the all up you still had a positive something left that remained as irritating a mystery. In the end he decided that the secret of her lay in the child-woman dichotomy somewhere. She was neither, and she was both. Like a child, she took your hand; like a woman, she suddenly let go. At bottom it was probably—he winced—unbelievable innocence. You simply didn't find innocence like hers. She had no tactile experience of the world. Of the world of books, yes; of nature, decidedly; but of man, none at all. It came of being brought up in the woods like a wild animal. Something Thomas Hardy Anderson hadn't figured on. A girl like this could do devastating damage, to others as well as to herself. You couldn't depend on either her actions or her reactions; she moved in other spheres. Where values were indecipherable. Normal contact with parents, friends, relatives, strangers, teachers, bigots, bullies, lovers—with terrestrial life—the contact of bruises and caresses which prepares the growing individual for maturity had been kept from her during the formative years. There were blank spaces in her, to an extent and of a nature no one could fathom, least of all Rima herself. You had to keep remembering how she had been brought up, how green she was, how alone.

And of a sudden Ellery saw the danger that she might attach herself to him like a motherless doe. There were signs. She had stopped calling him Mr. Queen and was addressing him as "Ellery" and "darling." She had put her hand in his a dozen times. She was asking no questions; she seemed to have no concern about what he proposed doing with her when they got to Wrightsville; she had put herself utterly in his keeping. After lunch in the dining car she had kicked off her smart shoes, lain down on the long seat of their compartment with her head in his lap, burrowed for a moment like a puppy, and then fallen asleep with a happy sigh. As if she were Mowgli and he were the branch of a tree. The trouble was—and it was a trouble—he wasn't the branch of a tree. He doubted if any normal man, similarly situated, could feel like the branch of a tree. Ellery found himself determining to marry her off to a deserving young poet—he would have to be a poet—just as quickly as one could be found. She simply couldn't be allowed to run around loose.

When Rima woke up she yawned and stretched and wriggled, but she made no move to sit up.

"Hello, darling." Her voice was sleepy, and her smile. He felt her hand in his again.

"Had a good nap?" Ellery tried to keep his tone on a fatherly level.

"Aery light, from pure digestion bred," laughed Rima.

"What?"

"Didn't you ever read *Paradise Lost?* You're funny, Ellery."

"Comical, or queer?"

She laughed again, throwing her head back. "My error! Oh, I like you so much."

"I like you, Rima." The skirt of her new suit had ridden up well over her knees and in spite of himself Ellery reached over to pull it down.

She watched him curiously. "Why did you do that?"

"Why did I do it?"

"Because my legs are ugly?"

"Because they're not."

"Then why cover them?"

"See here, Rima," Ellery began angrily.

"I've never quite understood that. I've seen girls at Slocum Lake and the lake at Pine Grove parading around in bathing suits that made them practically naked. But when they got dressed they'd keep pulling their skirts down. Over the same legs."

"Yes. Good point. Exactly. There's a time and a place for everything, you see, Rima."

"But we're alone, Ellery. Don't you want to see my legs?"

"No. I mean yes, very much. That's why the rules say you mustn't let me."

"Rules?"

"Haven't you ever gone to church?"

"No."

"You should. You should, Rima."

"But I don't mind your seeing my legs, Ellery."

"Perhaps I do!"

That was when she withdrew her hand. "You want to see my legs but you *mind* seeing them? What's the matter with you?"

"Would you let any man see your legs who wanted to?"

"No . . ."

"Well, there you are."

"I mean, it would depend on the man and why he wanted to see them. Which rules?"

"What? Oh! The rules of society, morality, good manners, er . . . any number of things." Ellery said desperately, "Didn't your father ever teach you anything but English literature?"

"He taught me everything."

"Well, he appears to have left one or two things out—"

"You mean about sex?"

"Look there, Rima! In another two weeks the countryside will be simply beautiful—"

The problem of Rima Anderson, it seemed, was going to present even greater difficulties than the problem of her father.

It was twilight when they reached Wrightsville. And there was old Gabby Warrum in the doorway of the stationmaster's cubby waggling his one tooth and waving to the trainman. And the two boys in jeans swinging their bare feet from the handtruck might have been the very same boys who had sat there on a certain summer day in 1940 when Ellery had stepped off the same train onto the Wrightsville station platform for the first time.

Nothing had changed. Well, almost nothing. The chrome on Phil's Diner had a less pristine glitter and the blue of its awnings was considerably faded; the garage which had been a smithy cowered under a new neon sign; there was a three-story "hotel" (nameless) among the shanties across the tracks which had not been there before; and the gravel about the station had disappeared along with the horse droppings, replaced by paving. But there was the same crackerbarrel skyline above Low Village, the same fat-behinded bus marked *Wrightsville Omnibus Company* backing up to the station platform, the same broad fields to the south, the same crooked thread of Lower Whistling Street wandering west and north to become Upper Whistling when it reached High Village and respectability. And there were

Lower Dade and Washington, from the west side of town, and Lower Apple and Piney Road and Shingle Street from the east side of town—they all squeezed close to one another as they ran down to the station in the extreme southeast corner of the municipality.

And they all looked good and the air, Low Village notwithstanding, smelled as if it had been washed, washed and hung out in the sun to dry.

"You like Wrightsville," said Rima as Ellery handed her into Ed Hotchkins's taxi. She sounded amazed.

"Very much, Rima."

Rima looked at him and then at Wrightsville, through the window, a little frown between her eyes.

"Where to?" said Ed.

"You don't remember me, do you?" asked Ellery with a smile.

Ed Hotchkiss scratched his nose. He was heavier; he had another chin. "I hacked you years ago. Say!"

"You do remember."

"Green. No . . . Queen! By Christmas, Mr. Queen!"

"Hi, Ed."

"Say!" They pumped each other's arms. "Paying the old dump another visit, hey? Who's the bad news for this time?" Ed started his motor. "Or is it a honeymoon?"

"Does he mean me?" murmured Rima.

Ed looked around at Rima, glanced at Ellery, and winked.

"Upham House," said Ellery. It was impossible to stop at the same hotel. Simply impossible. Not in Wrightsville. As Ed Hotchkiss swung the cab into Washington Street Ellery took Rima's hand and said, *sotto voce,* "That wink did it. It's Wrightsvillese for naughty-naughty."

"He thinks we're married!" Rima doubled up, laughing silently.

"I doubt it. I'm going to register at the Hollis—"

"But you told him Upham House."

"That's where you're registering."

"Me? In a Wrightsville hotel?"

"Now don't start that business about Mosquito Manor again. They'll be nice to you—you'll be alone, and you have a respectable-looking suitcase."

"Is this part of your plan?"

"I want you to take this money."

She stared at the bills he had pressed into her hand. "But I owe you so much already."

"My plan," said Ellery firmly. He had no idea what his plan was, except as it got her decently clothed, housed, fed, and protected. "We'll worry about the business details later. Er, Rima. Have you ever been in a hotel before?"

"No."

Another problem.

"But I know what to do," Rima went on, a bit dryly. "If that's what's worrying you. You seem to think I'm some sort of savage."

"It does sound that way, doesn't it?" Ellery said feebly. "Books, I suppose. They're full of hotels."

"It can't be very hard. You sign your name on a card and you tip the bellboy a quarter."

"And lock your door!"

"Yes, Ellery." And this time she didn't sound like a child at all.

He dropped her at Upham House, reviling himself for the nasty caution which told him not to be seen taking her in, and he had Ed drive him around the Square to the Hollis.

Ed seemed puzzled.

They had dinner at the Hollis Gold Gardens, a rather unsuccessful affair, since Rima was unaccountably cool and unimpressed with the Gold Gardens décor, whose lamé-like balloonings and gilded tablecloths were Wrightsville's pride. She did not even respond to the "dinner music" of Floyd Lycoming and His Hollis Hummadours, but this was probably because Ellery forgot himself and asked her to dance. "The fact that I know a fork from a knife has fooled you," Rima said sweetly. "I'm a barbarian, remember?" And afterwards she said she was tired and would he take her back to Ma Upham's. So Ellery took her back to Mrs. Upham's chaste Revolutionary hostelry and they said goodnight on the steps between the Colonial pillars, with their fingertips. He half-suspected that as soon as he was gone she would slip off her New York shoes and sprint downtown through Low Village to the shack in The Marshes.

Ellery was definitely depressed as he wandered back to the Square. Of course, Wrightsville was not at its best on Sunday nights. Most of the shops were closed. The streets were empty, except for Lower Main between the Square and Upper Whistling, and there was little activity even here because everyone was in the Bijou. The Gold Gardens had had its sprinkling of diners, and probably the Upham House Colonial Terrace was half-full of old ladies, but most of the upper crust, he knew, were visiting one another's homes on the hill, North Hill Drive, Twin Hill-in-the-Beeches, and Skytop Road; it was the Sunday night tradition. If there was any liveliness, it could be found only on Route 16, along the three-mile stretch between Low Village and Wrightsville Junction, where the roadhouses were.

But it was not Wrightsville that depressed him.

It was himself.

He couldn't seem to get hold of anything,

The facts of the MacCaby-Hart-Dodd hodgepodge were meaningless, or he was dull. He had no idea where to begin . . .

And perhaps Rima had something to do with it.

Ellery found himself on State Street, outside the County Court House. It was about 10 o'clock and everything was properly dark, the old elms nodding overhead and the occasional flash of headlights darting across State and Upper Whistling barely jerking the neighborhood from its drowse. Across State the Northern State Telephone Company, the Wrightsville Light & Power Company, the tomblike Chamber of Commerce, the Carnegie Library buildings were almost nonexistent. The entrance to Memorial Park, fronted by the long concavity of the Our Boys Memorial, whose gilded roster was already flaky and half-illegible, gaped vacantly. Beyond, the marble apron on the lap of Town Hall glimmered clean under the "eternal light" surmounting the flagstaff. Ellery was tempted to invade the dark park and sit down on one of the benches near the American Legion Bandstand to commune with the bracing ghost of Sousa. He actually started for the entrance. But then he noticed the green lights in the driveway between the park and the Court House, and he stopped.

Wrightsville police headquarters.

Chief Dakin.

He went in. A little, black-tonsured officer sat behind the desk, his chin on his breast.

At the opening of his door, Dakin grasped the arms of his swivel chair.

"Positively not an apparition," said Ellery. "Excuse me for not knocking. But I didn't want to wake Lieutenant Gobbin up."

"Mr. Queen!"

"I said to myself," said Ellery cheerfully, "that the state of crime in Wrightsville might be sufficient to make you pass up your Sunday night church choir, and it seems I was absolutely solid. How are you, Dakin?"

"Oh, you baby doll." Dakin pumped for all he was worth. "What are you doing in Wrightsville?"

"I hardly know." Dakin was an old man. That lean Yankee look was swelling and showed little red veins.

"I'm tickled to see you anyway. Sit down, sit down! Just get in?"

"Few hours ago."

"How long you figurin' on staying?"

"That," said Ellery, "depends on what you can tell me about Little Prudy's Cliff."

Dakin's colorless eyes crimped at the corners. "The Anderson girl?"

"She came to me in New York. I came back with her."

"So you're fixing to find out what happened to Tom Anderson."

"Can you save me the trouble?"

Dakin laughed. "Do I look that contented?"

"Tough?"

"Tougher than a preacher on Sunday." Chief Dakin swiveled to stare at a photograph of J. Edgar Hoover above his water cooler. "I've sat here night after night thinkin' on it. It's got so it's almost a personal issue between me and Anderson. What's another case? An old rummy . . . he'd have got his sooner or later, one way or another—a knife in the ribs some night at Vic Carlatti's, or drowned in Willow River when he was too full to navigate, like Matt Mason in '26. Just the same . . ."

"How do you know Anderson was murdered?"

"His coat was torn fresh in half a dozen places. Two buttons yanked off. His hat trampled. There was some blood." Dakin turned around. "The way I figure it, Anderson had an appointment with somebody. He was jumped, he fought back, and he lost. I couldn't trace his movements past 11 o'clock Saturday night—the night before the morning his coat and hat were found on the Cliff. He was last seen around that hour walking along Congress Avenue in Low Village, alone."

"Sober?"

"Walking straight as a Baptist deacon. And headed east, to the outskirts of Low Village, where The Marshes begin. But Anderson didn't get home that night, his daughter says. I figure at 11 that Saturday night he was headed for his appointment at Little Prudy's Cliff. It was Garrison Jackson saw him on Congress Avenue— Abe L. Jackson's kid brother. Garry says Anderson was walking like he was bound somewhere. My guess is he was dead by midnight.

"The aggravating thing about this case, Mr. Queen," said the chief of police slowly, "is that it don't add up to nothin'. Nobody stood to gain by Anderson's death. No enemies. Hadn't had any trouble. Harmless and friendly. Everybody liked him. He couldn't have been killed by mistake; full moon that night, brightest night in a month. Maniac? Hophead? We've checked and checked. But we wasted our time. It wasn't an accident, it wasn't a freak, it wasn't a mistake. Tom Anderson was lured to his death by somebody who knew just what he was doing. But who, and why?'' *Nothing personal. Just a matter of convenience.* "What's that you said, Mr. Queen?''

"I was thinking about ladybugs,'' said Ellery. "I take it you didn't neglect Anderson's soul-mates?''

"Who?''

"Harry Toyfell. Nick Jacquard.''

"First ones I questioned. If either of 'em did it, he did a mighty fine job of covering up afterwards.''

"Neither had any idea whom Anderson might have been meeting?''

"They say no.'' Dakin swiveled to stare out at State Street. "Anyway, they're small potatoes. This is big. I feel it in my bones.''

"Anderson had given Jacquard and Toyfell no hint about anything unusual in his life?'' persisted Ellery.

"No. Though talking about something unusual in his life, you know Anderson had taken the pledge.''

"So Rima told me.''

"I have a sneaky notion,'' muttered the chief to State Street, "that had something to do with it.''

"If that's true, it points a hard moral.''

Dakin turned back, smiling faintly. He was a teetotaler.

"What did you mean this thing is 'big,' Dakin? Big how? Importance? Ramifications? Involving well-known people?''

"Maybe.''

"Give me an example.''

"I can't.'' Dakin pulled himself to his feet, angrily. "You see, I'm a useless old man. Worn down to the nub and bellywappin' on the raw material. Have a cigar?''

Ellery had a cigar and for a half hour they talked about pleasanter things. Governor Cart Bradford was making the pork-barrel fraternity in the State Capital rear back and howl. "You mark my words, that boy'll wind up in the White House yet.'' Prosecutor Chalanski, the idol of Low Village, had cracked a scandalous embezzlement case wide open and there was talk of running him for Congress next year. Everybody was complaining about the four-mill jump in the tax rate. Judge Eli Martin had had a mild stroke the previous winter, after the death of his wife Clarice, but he was fine now, although retired from his law practice and raising prize asters which he gave away to all comers; Andy Birobatyan of the Wrightsville Florist Shop was looking pained. Wolfert Van Horn had been caught *in flagrante delicto* last fall at his Lake Pharisee summer lodge in the upper Mahoganies with one of the young Watkins girls, the giggly one, and Jess Watkins had beaten him up good with an old buggy whip and afterwards refused to prosecute—"Leave it to Jess to turn a profit on a deal.'' Julie Asturio had got religion and had left town in the wake of a foaming evangelist. The Busy Bee Stores were building a supermarket on the California plan on Slocum Street, between Washington and Upper Whistling, next door to the Bluefield Block; Bloody Logan across the street was chewing his nails to the quick. One of Jorking's sows over on the pig farm on Route 478 had dropped a five-legged piglet. Doc Sebastian Dodd had come into something like four million dollars by the will of old Luke MacCaby, and Doc was planning a new wing for the hospital.

"Oh, yes,'' said Ellery. "I've heard about your Dr. Dodd. Fellow who seems determined to earn the title of Town Saint.''

"He's earned it," said Dakin. "Lord knows Doc deserved a break."

"Unsuccessful?"

"Heck, no. Most successful doctor in town, if you count patients. Only thing is," chuckled Dakin, "his patients don't have the scratch. Doc still lives in the house he was born in—big three-story turkey on the corner of Wright and Algonquin. Dates back to the Civil War. It's so darn big the spare bedrooms on the third floor ain't even used. Doc's a bachelor—never been married."

"Then why does he need such a big house?"

"Who'd buy it? And he's got to live somewhere. At that, he's got a houseful. There's Doc's housekeeper and cook, Regina Fowler—Mrs. Fowler's a distant cousin of old John F. Wright's, his middle name was Fowler; know he'd died?— and then there's the maid, Essie Pingarn, and Tom Winship's boy Kenneth, and now old Harry Toyfell."

"Tom Winship. Is that the Thomas Winship who testified in the Haight trial for the State in '41? Head cashier of the Wrightsville National?"

"That's the one. Well, Tom died about six years ago. Didn't leave much, because his wife was an invalld and nearly every cent went to hospitals and sanitariums and fancy big-city specialists. Not that it did Mrs. Winship any good—when their only child, Kenneth, came back from his hitch overseas he found his ma dead, too. Well, it sort of broke Kenny up and he went to pieces for a while. And who d'ye think—?"

"Dr. Sebastian Dodd."

"Right. Doc Dodd took Kenny in hand, straightened him out, sent him back to college to finish up his medical course that was interrupted by the war, and now Kenneth is Doc's assistant and protégé. Doing a fine job, too, Doc tells me. He's mighty proud of that boy, says he's going to be a big doctor some day. Cast your bread upon the waters, that's Doc's motto."

"I must meet this paragon," murmured Ellery. "I really must. In fact, I think I'll walk over and look in on him tomorrow if I can find a spare half hour. And Harry Toyfell's working for him now. And living there. It certainly is a blessing to have a man like Dodd around. By the way, Dakin, I understand old Luke MacCaby's having all that wealth came as something of a surprise to Wrightsville."

"Set the town right on its hams."

"And that partner of MacCaby's—what was his name?—Hart, John Spencer Hart, Wrightsville Dye Works. Must have come as quite a shock when Hart blew the top of his head off."

"How long'd you say you've been in Wrightsville, Mr. Queen?" said Chief Dakin dryly.

Ellery laughed. "I suppose you're satisfied that Hart did die by his own hand? And MacCaby by God's?"

"What?"

"I know about the Hart inquest, but did anybody go into the question of MacCaby's death?"

Dakin was sitting still. "I didn't know it was a question. No. Why?"

"Just curious."

"Luke MacCaby was 74 years old," said the chief of police slowly, "He'd had heart trouble near twenty years. Doc Willoughby once told me MacCaby would have died years ago if not for Doc Dodd's care. And old Luke knew it; that's why he left his bundle to Doc. So it all adds up just dandy. Except that you're curious, Mr. Queen. I thought we were talkin' about the Anderson case. Or were you?"

Ellery was silent. A flick of eagerness scudded over Dakin's face. "You know something I don't!"

"I don't *know* anything, Dakin." Ellery got to his feet. "But there are two sides to every coin. Take the Anderson case. You're convinced Anderson is dead. But you can't produce his body, Dakin. I always turn the coin over. Have that type of mind." Dakin was gripping the rim of his desk. "As for MacCaby and Hart, maybe they died as advertised, and maybe they didn't. And maybe their deaths had nothing to do with Tom Anderson's disappearance, and maybe their deaths had everything to do with it."

"And maybe I'm crazy!"

"Keep that reversible mind, Dakin. Keep that coin on edge, where you can take a quick look at either side." Ellery laughed and shook Dakin's slack hand.

Dakin was still staring at him as he shut the door.

Of course, thought Ellery charitably as he crossed the Square to the Hollis, poor Dakin doesn't have an obliging friend named Anonymous.

Monday, April 10

In the morning Rima was pitifully interrogative. It was apparent that during the night life had crept up on her. Or the Monday morning austerity of Upham House, smelling of slop suds and floor polish, had settled over her like an uneasy dew. She no longer took the future on faith. Tomorrow was a question mark; even today. How long did he expect her to remain at Mrs. Upham's? Didn't he realize she was running up a debt to him it would take her years to pay back? When could she go back to the Marshes? Why did she have to stay at Upham House at all? What had the redheaded bellboy meant last night when he had said that if she was expecting anybody he'd be glad to leave the side door unlocked? Where had Eliery gone after leaving her last night? (So Rima was the one who had phoned the Hollis, leaving no message.) Did he find out anything? Did he see anybody? Her feet were swollen from these shoes; when could she take her clothes off? What were his plans? Were they getting anywhere? Where were they going this morning?

"To answer *omega* first," sighed Ellery, "to breakfast. I can't talk before I've had my coffee."

On the walk over to Miss Sally's Tea Roome, he thought furiously. He had had a bad night not entirely ascribable to Manager Brooks's Himalayan mattress. And when he had fallen asleep, it had been not Anderson but the daughter of Anderson who darkened last in his consciousness. He could not improvise with twenty-dollar bills indefinitely. Sooner or later he would have to settle the question of Rima's immediate future.

Miss Sally's was providentially deserted. When they were seated, Ellery said: "Rima, if you had the problem of earning your livelihood, how would you go about solving it?"

"I don't know," said Rima coldly.

"Well, what can you do? I mean, besides doctoring birds?"

"Nothing."

"I don't suppose you can operate a typewriter or anything like that?"

"That's right."

"If worst came to worst, you might get a job as a salesgirl . . . ?"

"And be cooped up in a stuffy store all day? I'd die."

"How about a tutoring job? There must be children of well-to-do parents in town who'd—"

"Cooped up."

"But you've got to do something!"

"Oh, your money. It's worrying me, too. But I'll find a way of paying you back."

Ellery ordered breakfast.

With the coffee, the questions began again. Ellery listened glumly. Finally he said, "See here, Rima. I have only one plan and you may as well get it clear now.

"Everything else is irrelevant.

"I have reason to believe that what happened to your father is connected with a series of events that began here in Wrightsville two months or so ago. The death of Luke MacCaby. His secret partnership with John Spencer Hart. MacCaby's bequest to Dr. Sebastian Dodd." Rima clutched a piece of cooling toast, a little pale. "How your father fits into that picture is, I think, the major question. If it can be answered, we may be able to figure out that business of Little Prudy's Cliff.

"I saw Chief of Police Dakin last night," continued Ellery, "and he hasn't any idea that your father's fate is tied up with these other matters. So Dakin's no help. We're on our own.

"I can see only one way to make a start. The man who treated Luke MacCaby for years, who signed MacCaby's death certificate, is Dr. Sebastian Dodd. The man to whom MacCaby left his unsuspected fortune is Dr. Sebastian Dodd. The man who through MacCaby's will became in effect the business partner of John Spencer Hart is Dr. Sebastian Dodd. The man whose sudden association with the Hart-MacCaby dye works resulted in Hart's suicide is Dr. Sebastian Dodd. Dodd seems to be the great common denominator of all the events preceding your father's disappearance. So the first thing we've got to do is try to find out if Dodd was in any way involved with your father, too."

Rima nodded wordlessly.

"I phoned the Dodd house this morning and made an appointment for 11 A.M. at the doctor's office. He's expected back from the hospital then and it will be before his office hours, so we'll have some time to reconnoiter.

"I don't know what we'll run into. Maybe nothing. Maybe a great deal. I'll have to develop a strategy as we go along.

"That's where we stand, Rima. Now finish your eggs."

But Rima said, "I see. I see," and Ellery was startled to see tears in her eyes. He said gruffly, "What's the matter?"

"I don't really come into it at all."

That made him think again of how alone she was, which was exactly the thought he had been dodging. He found himself melting like the butter on her toast, which made him think that she wasn't eating, and he snapped, "You eat your breakfast!" Dutifully she crunched off a piece of toast and he reached over and took her hand, so that she looked at him, surprised. "Rima, I've always believed in being forearmed. You do come into it. How, I haven't any idea. But I've got you ready. You're Tom Anderson's daughter. What involved him may involve you. By your existence you assert the emotional, if not the moral, right to enter the problem. No one's going to question your intercession but the author of your father's fate, whatever it was; but that's exactly what we're aiming at. And that's the technical reason for our visit Saturday to Lachine's, the reason why you've got to keep limping around in those shoes if they kill you.

"Something may come up. We may be able to wing an opportunity. Of course, it may be dangerous. I've got to emphasize that. In fact, it will almost certainly be dangerous. Do you know what you really want, Rima?"

She looked down at her plate, saying in a low voice, "Daddy and I were very close. Much closer, I think, than normal people. Yes, I know what I want." She looked up, almost with anger. "Do understand. This has all been horribly new to me. You've been so patient . . . kind . . . I won't give you any more trouble. I promise, Ellery. From now on I'll do just what you say.''

The house on the corner of Wright Street and Algonquin Avenue was suffering from all the diseases of neglected old age. Its porch, which ran around the side as well as the front, had a feeble-looking, crippled floor. Its squat wooden pillars were cracked and chipped. Its blistered brownish paint erupted in pustules, as if it had an advanced case of acne. The shingled roof sagged in places, curling up with a sort of arthritis in others; and the dormer windows of the sloping top story looked for all the world like the bulging eyes of a row of old blind men. Some shutters were broken, others missing. On its Algonquin Avenue side it elbowed a four-story remodeled apartment building in zippy blue stucco, on its Wright Street side it threatened to topple over on a one-story crate of a shop with a window full of dummy whisky bottles and placards of long-legged toothy women—the crudely painted script on the window said JACK'S PALACE BAR & GRILL.

But the old house was set well back from the street and its rejuvenating lawn was beginning to sprout new grass. There was a flagged walk, bordered by files of freshly manured earth, which meandered around to the side of the house and beyond to what was apparently a rear garden. A great elm in the center of the lawn loomed higher than the house; in summer it would shade the lawn and porch almost agreeably.

A small black-painted sign on a wrought iron standard beside the front gate announced in uncertain gilt lettering:

SEBASTIAN DODD, M.D.
KENNETH WINSHIP, M.D.

"It doesn't look so bad," said Rima doubtfully as they went up the three precarious wooden steps.

"I imagine it could have its gruesome side," said Ellery. "At night, under an orange moon." He pressed his thumb on an iron button marked: RING FOR DOCTOR.

The pebbled glass door was opened by a rawboned, empty-eyed female with a broom. "Which one do you want?" she said.

"Dr. Dodd, please."

"Ain't here yet. Office hours start noontime."

A piercing female voice screamed, "Now Essie, who is that?"

A glint of rebellion sparked in Essie's glassy eyes. "Body would think a body couldn't answer a darn door," she muttered. But then she screamed back, "They're for Dr. Dodd, Mis' Fowler!"

"You let 'em in, Essie," Mis' Fowler screamed in retort. A stout elderly woman in a white house dress appeared at the rear of the hall. She wore an earpiece and the cord was speckled with flour. "You the man called this mornin'?" she shouted.

"That's right," said Ellery.

"Essie, show these folks into the waitin' room. Dr. Winship's in there. Don't rile him. He's in an awful stew about Miss Pinkle."

"But they want to see Dr. Dodd!" bawled Essie.

"It's Dr. Winship I spoke to this morning," put in Ellery.

"Course it is," yelled the stout woman cheerfully. "Don't pay Essie no mind. She's got a surgical sponge where her brains ought to be. Essie, you get a move on!" The housekeeper disappeared.

There was a strong, baffling odor in the hall, warm, yeasty, and antiseptic. Then Ellery identified it: baking bread and Lysol.

The hall was dark, flanked with wide panels of aged walnut interspersed with panels of a wallpaper whose original design had faded beyond recognition. There was a stained-glass chandelier, and a walnut stairway which curved gracefully to the upper floors. On the midway landing there was more stained glass.

A double French door to the left, heavily curtained in ecru lace, was shut. Essie preceded them to the right and marched through a wide archway from which the doors had been removed into a waiting room. Standing about like prehistoric monsters was a congregation of hideous overstuffed furniture; on the floor was a handhooked rug so old and worn that its colors were gone. There was a door marked *Dr. Dodd* and there was a door marked *Dr. Winship*. The walls were painted a dingy green and on them hung some ancient color-prints of Western scenes by Frederic Remington. Several verses or mottoes printed artistically on imitation woodgrain cardboard dangled by tasseled cords. One of them said:

> *As a rule a man's a fool,*
> *When it's hot he wants it cool,*
> *When it's cool he wants it hot,*
> *Always wanting what is not.*

Another began:

> *Laugh and the world laughs with you,*
> *Weep, and you weep alone.*
> *For the . . .*

Ellery was fascinatedly trying to make out the rest when Essie, with a leer, poked him in the ribs.

"That's him," she said.

A very large young man in a white office jacket looked up from the secretarial desk at which he was rather peevishly going through a disorderly heap of filing cards.

"They want to see Dr. *Dodd*," said Essie, and she tramped off in triumph, holding her broom like a lance.

"Yes?" snapped the young man.

"I'm Ellery Queen, Dr. Winship."

"Oh!" Dr. Winship scrambled to his feet, knocking his chair over backwards. His big, serious face reddened as he stooped and yanked the chair upright. "Not functioning this morning. Ever try to make sense out of the filing system of a secretary who's always mooning about last night's date? Damn all the Pinkles of this world! Dr. Dodd's not back from the hospital yet, Mr. Queen." He looked as if he would have been more at home in the dressing room of a college stadium. He came around the desk and seized Ellery's hand. "It's a pleasure to make your acquaintance. I'm an admirer of yours from way back. Remember when you first came to town. '40, wasn't it?" His grin was as broad as his shoulders. "Won't you and the young lady sit down?'' Then his rather battered brown eyes took in "the young lady," and they lost their fatigue.

"Miss Anderson, Dr. Winship," said Ellery.

"How do you do," said Miss Anderson.

"How do *you* do," said Dr. Winship.

They stared at each other.

And at that moment Ellery's idea was born. It was tiny and vague and, like most inspirations, it preceded its rationale. But even afterward Ellery found very little of a concrete nature to go on: a large, sober young man immersed in his work, showing the physical effects of long hours, insufficient sleep, a monkish life; and a pixy of a girl with a temporarily Fifth Avenue look and a naked yearning to be back among her butterflies and mosquitoes. Not much. But perhaps enough. It was necessary to revise his previous notion about deserving young poets, for—and Ellery could not have said why he was so sure of this—there was work to be done here.

"There's a button missing from your coat," said Rima. She pointed.

Dr. Winship looked down. "There always is." Then he looked at her again as if she had said a wonderful thing. "You're not from Wrightsville," he said.

Rima laughed. Her shrill sweet bird laughter.

"You *are?*"

Ellery said casually, "Miss Anderson, Dr. Winship, is Tom Anderson's daughter."

It was too easy.

"The Town . . ." The young doctor bit his lip, glancing quickly at Ellery. Ellery smiled and nodded. Eagerly Winship dragged a chair forward. And Rima lowered her eyes and slipped into the seat. He remained over her, with joy. He'd hardly have believed it. Where had she been keeping herself? But he supposed the thing that had happened to her father . . . Did she ever get down to the hospital? She must be awfully alone these days. Loneliness wasn't wise at her age. He ought to know! But then she was probably kept pretty busy—and by the way, what did she do with herself? Say, on weekends? Did she ever get over to Connhaven for the summer series of concerts? He found music wonderfully relaxing . . . did she know Fauré's "Pavane"? Vaughan Williams's "Fantasia on a Theme of Tallis"? The slow movement of the Schubert Quintet? He had a pitiful collection of records— couldn't afford what he'd like—but if she'd care to spend a musical evening with him sometime . . .

He's been badly bruised, thought Ellery. Hurts all over. He'd shy away from most girls. But she's as soothing as a brook. There's no danger in her. He wants those wounds laved.

Rima was acting remarkably coy. Answering in dovelike murmurs. Not like herself at all. She was afraid her musical education had been neglected. Unless you consider poetry to be music. Which of course it is. Did he know Lovelace? Marvell? Henry Vaughan?

I saw eternity the other night
Like a great ring of pure and endless
light.

Ellery listened, smiling.

But then Dr. Sebastian Dodd came in and Ellery had something else to think about.

Dr. Dodd's appearance shocked him.

Ellery had visualized the beneficiary of Luke MacCaby's will as a rather sad-eyed little man with a workworn body and a halo of silvery hair—a slender, almost fragile, saint at peace with himself and the universe. The man who came swiftly, almost furtively, into the waiting room and stopped in his tracks in the archway was a harried brute. His great body was powerful and grossly fleshed; had he been smaller, he would have been fat. He was all but bald and his glossy skull was stippled with liverish-looking pigment, like the spots on his big, unsteady hands. His face was startling. It was a great jowled face, its jowls shaking. The eyes were buried in pits of deeply sagging flesh, like pouches, and the pouches quivered, too. They twitched and jerked. The eyes themselves, small and overbrilliant, were never still. They kept darting from side to side like minnows. And his skin was lifeless and of a yellow color, as if some poison was sapping its vitality.

Had his voice been in tune with his appearance, Dr. Dodd would have been monstrous, a vast obscenity. But when he spoke the sounds that came out of his throat were grave and sweet and slowly given. His voice was the only part of him with beauty. It suggested what he might have been, or what perhaps he once was.

"No, no, Mr. Queen. Dr. Winship phoned me at the hospital; I was expecting you. Pretty nearly bowled me over. Been as flustered as a girl. Kenneth, you know who Mr. Queen is, don't you?"

"What?" said Dr. Winship.

"You'll have to forgive Dr. Winship, Mr. Queen. He's one of these born healers of humanity—always worrying about the incidence of next year's diseases." Dr. Dodd chuckled, his jowls flying. "At that, he's got a dietary theory that I think is going to make medical history. Get him to tell you sometime about the 'metabolic personality.' And who'd you say this very pretty little girl is?"

"Rima Anderson, Dr. Dodd."

"Ri . . . Tom Anderson's daughter?"

Rima said, "Thomas Hardy Anderson." Distinctly.

The minnows darted about in a sort of pain. Then Dr. Dodd took Rima's little hands in his and he said in a rumble, "I'm sorry about your father, Rima. I knew him well. He was a fine man, and now that I've seen you I know he didn't waste his life. Won't you both come into my office?"

Dr. Winship automatically followed, as if Rima led him on an invisible leash.

Dr. Dodd's consulting room was big and old-fashioned, with an antiquated-looking oak-framed fluoroscope in one corner and an apothecary's cubby in another. One wall was solid with dusty medical magazines and books. Through an open door Ellery saw an examining room: a stirruped examining table, a case of surgical instruments, a scale, a sterilizer.

But he noted these things by habit. His mind was busy with Dr. Dodd, and his remarkably fluid appearance, and his words, *I knew him well.* Poor Yorick Anderson. I think we've come to the right place . . .

"What, Doctor? Oh, yes! I'm looking into Tom Anderson's death for Rima," said Ellery. "Frustrating case. So little to go on. We don't actually know that Anderson died of violence. We don't even *know* that he's dead." And all the time Ellery was speaking he was fascinated by those two unquiet eyes in that unquiet face, and by the big hands that kept playing with things on the desk. What's worrying him? Ellery kept thinking. Most worried man I ever saw. Whatever it is, it's put him under enormous tension. Getting him down. No man could go on under such pressure for very long. Is it the money? "So I decided to talk to everyone who might have known him, Doctor. And since I was told you're so well acquainted with the people of Low Village particularly . . .''

Dr. Dodd nodded. "Matter of fact, Mr. Queen, your coming here today to see me is something of a coincidence. I said to Kenneth only yesterday that I really ought to drop in on Chief Dakin, or call him up. I don't know that it has a thing to do with what happened to Tom, but it might well have, and if I hadn't been so blamed busy, what with my patients and this diphtheria scare we're having, and—'' he grinned suddenly, rubbing his chin in a sheepish way—''and certain developments recently in my personal life, why, I'd have gone to Dakin right off. Remember my saying that to you yesterday, Kenneth?''

"Hm? Oh. Oh, yes, you did," said Dr. Winship. "And I said you darned well ought to, and you said you'd do it first thing this morning, only I suppose you've forgotten as usual."

"Well, Shumley Purvis's wife is pretty bad," said Dr. Dodd apologetically. "You might have to do a tracheotomy on her. If that swelling gets any worse—''

"You don't know that *what* has anything to do with what happened to Tom Anderson, Dr. Dodd?" asked Ellery.

"Beg pardon? Why, that money I gave him."

"You gave Daddy money?" exclaimed Rima. She glanced quickly at Ellery. He gave no sign, but she said no more, looking down at her hands.

"Which money was that, Doctor?" said Ellery.

"Oh, it's something of a yarn," replied Dr. Dodd with a sigh. "I have a confounded meddlesome streak in me, Mr. Queen. Always interfering in people's lives. I remember when Tom Anderson first showed up in Wrightsville—taught at the high school. It wasn't so many years ago, Rima, was it? He was a fine-looking man, with a lot of trouble in his face. A gentleman and a scholar, I always thought. I was sorry to see him lose his grip on himself that way. An awful waste.

"Well, I'd meet him on the street every so often and ask him to stop in and see me. Finally he did. I saw right away that what was wrong with him couldn't be diagnosed on *my* examining table, anyway. It was a case for a psychiatrist and we don't have any psychiatrists in these parts. But we talked things over. Well, he got to crying and feeling penitent and I knew I wasn't doing him any good. I knew he'd go right out and hunt up another drink."

Unexpectedly, Rima started to cry. In silence, putting her hands to her face and shaking all over. Dr. Winship looked as if someone with a large foot had kicked him in the groin. But Dr. Dodd caught Winship's eye and shook his head, and Ellery signaled to the big man to go on. And in a moment Rima had stopped crying and her hands were back in her lap and she was staring at them. "Then, a short time ago," Dr. Dodd went on, "I came into all this money through the will of Luke MacCaby—''

"—blessed be his name," muttered Dr. Winship with an eye on Rima, and he brightened when she laughed. "But the trouble is, Dr. Dodd won't use it for himself. All he does—''

"Now Kenneth," said Dr. Dodd. "The will isn't through probate and what I've been able to squeeze out of Otis Holderfield is by mercy of the Surrogate, whom I used to whale the daylights out of when we were boys playing hooky from Miss Schoonmaker's schoolhouse over on Piney Road . . . when it was a road, not a damned death trap of a garbage dump. Well, anyway, not long after the MacCaby business came out I bumped into Tom Anderson. Almost literally. I'm sorry, my dear," said Dr. Dodd gently to Rima, "but he was sitting in the middle of Polly Street reciting poetry and I almost ran over him."

"It's all right, Dr. Dodd," said Rima. Then she added, oddly: "Daddy wasn't half as unhappy as people thought he was."

"Well, Rima, he wasn't leaping for joy that day," retorted Dr. Dodd. "I got him into my jalopy and pulled over to the curb and we had a long gabfest. He started to cry again—your dad always seemed to cry when I talked to him,"

"What was he crying about, Doctor?" asked Rima very quietly.

"You."

"Me!" She looked incredulous.

"That's right. Said he'd been worrying a lot about you lately. That he realized he hadn't brought you up right." Rima was getting pale around the nostrils. "Now, my dear, I'm just telling you what he said—"

"My father brought me up very well!"

"Course he did," said Dr. Dodd. "And look at the results. Just remarkable. But Tom seemed to feel he hadn't prepared you for life, Rima. That if anything happened to him you'd be left all alone without a friend or a way of getting along."

"Rima," said Ellery.

"Yes." Rima was angry.

"A squatter's shack in a swamp, he said. No place for a fine girl—"

"He was playing on your sympathies, Dr. Dodd. He didn't mean it. I knew my father." Rima's eyes flashed. "I don't think anyone can understand how well we knew each other. He knew he couldn't have kept me for five minutes if I hadn't wanted to stay with him and The Marshes. I won't have even Daddy spoiling what he and I had together!"

"Now maybe," said Dr. Dodd mildly, "maybe you didn't know your father as well as you think you did, Rima."

"I remember my father," said the young doctor in a low voice. "I thought I knew him, too. But the letters he sent me while I was overseas . . ." Then he grinned. "You listen to old Doc Dodd, Miss Anderson. He dispenses pretty sound medicine."

"And I want to hear the end of this yarn," said Ellery with a smile. "Won't you go on, Dr. Dodd?"

"Well, I said it was a pretty late date for him to be talking that way, and Tom said he knew that, and he cried some more, and it went on that way for some time. But then he said something that gave me a notion."

"What was that, Doctor?"

"He said he wished he could quit drinking. And he stopped crying when he said it. Really seemed to mean it. I asked him why he didn't, and he said, 'A man has to have something to work for. Or to. I'd like to rehabilitate myself. Open a little bookshop, maybe. Make a decent home for my daughter. But I'm weak, Doctor. I can't seem to get started on it.' Well," said Dr. Dodd, screwing and unscrewing the cap of his ancient fountain pen, "I'd heard alcoholics talk that way before. But, as I say, he'd stopped crying. And just then Mrs. Gonzoli's daughter's child, 'Tita, came running up Polly Street holding something up high and screaming, 'Look what I found! A four-leaf clover!' "

"Four-leaf clover," said Ellery.

Dr. Dodd said slowly, "Four-leaf clover. It's not very scientific, Mr. Queen, I know. But then I'm just an old country practitioner . . . Got one of my blamed sudden impulses. I said to Tom, 'Tom, I'm not sure I believe you. But by golly

I'm going to give you your chance.' And I made a deal with him. I'd make the down payment on a new life for him. Provide the finances if he'd provide the will power and stick-to-it. Kind of a partnership. He had to give up the bottle. Not gradually. But all at once. And not touch the stuff again. I said to him, 'Tom, you come to me one week from today. If you're cold sober and haven't had a drop in the meantime, I'll give you five thousand dollars in cash. And if six months from now you're still on the wagon, I'll settle an annuity on your girl.' You know, a week is a long time in the life of an alcoholic. I figured it would be a good test.''

Dr. Dodd put his left thumb into his mouth. He began to worry the nail with his teeth, producing swift uneven little clicking sounds.

"And what did he say to that, Doctor?'' asked Ellery. The big man's nails were bitten away painfully.

"Why, he didn't say a word for a long time. Just put his hands on my arm and looked at me. He was pretty bleary-eyed and he couldn't focus very well, but he kept trying. Then all of a sudden he said, 'I wouldn't want the money. Not till I'd proved something to myself.' I said, 'No, Tom, I want you to have it. A man has to feel solid ground under his feet.' He kept quiet again. But he was thinking, I could see that, thinking hard. Finally he said, 'Maybe you're right, Doc. All right, but I won't spend a penny of it till I've earned the right.' He got out of my car on all fours and when I tried to help him he shook my hand off. So I let him do it by himself; I could see it was important to him. And then he staggered up the street.''

And Rima's eyes were big and full of tears.

"The next time I saw him was a week later. He was among the people in my waiting room out there. Sober and looking as if he'd been having a pretty bad time. He said, 'Doctor, if you want the proof—' I said, 'No, Tom, I don't ask for proof. Just looking at you is proof enough,' and I called up Otis Holderfield—I'd given him his instructions just in case—and told Holderfield I was sending Mr. Anderson over to his office. A man who's had a bad time,'' said Dr. Dodd apologetically, "needs little rewards like that—being called Mister, I mean. It certainly did something for Tom. I could see him sort of straighten up as he walked out . . . Well, about an hour later, there was Tom back in my waiting room. When I was able to see him again, he pulled an envelope out of his pocket. Didn't say a word. I said 'Well, Tom, is it all there?' and he said, 'Yes, Doctor, it's all there. I don't think I believed it before. Now I do.' And then he said something that kind of embarrassed both of us, and this time we shook hands and he walked out with his shoulders way back, like a man.

"Last time I ever saw him,'' muttered Dr. Dodd. "But I kept hearing about him. He was holding to his word. Kind of made me feel there was hope for the human race. That's why it was such a stunner when I heard about his death. And more than once it's passed through my mind that maybe my giving him that money had something to do with what happened to him.''

And the big man in the shiny blue serge suit was silent, the floppy places on his face jerking as if they had life of their own, his thick fingers prowling around his desk.

And then he cried out. It was almost a cry of fear. Because Rima had flashed from her chair to his desk and she had snatched one of his restless paws and put it to her lips. And then, with the swiftness which always surprised Ellery, she was at the window facing the blue stucco wall of the apartment building next door, her back to them.

Dr. Dodd was on his feet. His yellow skin had turned burnt orange. He stood leaning his heavy body on his fists, apparently at a loss for what to say. Dr. Winship sat rigid. And Ellery merely sat.

Finally Dr. Dodd rumbled, "Well, Rima, that money ought to take the pressure off you, give you a start. Don't let any sharpers take it away from you . . . Kenneth, I think I hear the mob gatherin' out there. Mr. Queen, if there's nothing else—"

Ellery said, "But Rima doesn't have the money, Dr. Dodd."

"Eh?"

"She knew nothing about it. She never saw it and he never mentioned it to her." The two doctors stared.

"May I use your phone?" And when Ellery set the telephone down, he said, "I didn't think he had, but it's always best to check. Dakin says he found no money in the coat on Little Prudy's Cliff. No money at all."

"Robbery!" exclaimed Dr. Winship.

Rima was facing them.

"Oh, no," said Dr. Dodd. "Oh, I hope not." He sank into his chair, the nerves and muscles doing a dervish dance. His skin was yellow again.

"Two sides to every coin," said Ellery. "Maybe it was robbery. And on the other hand maybe it wasn't." He added smoothly, but with just the right touch of urgency, "Well, Rima, these good men are going to be busy in a moment and we've still got the problem of your immediate future to settle, so—"

Dr. Dodd had sunk into himself again, twitching and shaking, but young Dr. Winship rose nobly to the fly. "What do you mean by that, Mr. Queen?"

"Rima can't go back to that shack in The Marshes, Dr. Winship," said Ellery. "And to live anywhere else—I mean, to lead any sort of normal life—she'll have to find employment somewhere. Kind of you to be interested. Come on, Rima— oh, by the way, Doctor," said Ellery, turning back, "you wouldn't know someone who needs an intelligent girl with a superior educational background, would you?"

"Wait a minute. There's still some time—" Dr. Winship glanced quickly at his wristwatch. "Plenty of time! Wait just one minute, Mr. Queen. Doc!"

Dr. Dodd came back with a start. "Yes? Yes?"

"Y'know, I've meant to talk to you about Pinkle—"

"Miss Pinkle. Oh. Yes."

"She's got the case cards in such a mess it's taken me most of the weekend and all of this morning and I'm still not through straightening them out. Pinkle's going steady with Rafe Landsman and half the time she's still back in Memorial Park last night, smooching on the grass. She broke my sterilizer through downright carelessness Saturday and when I bawled her out she said she wouldn't have to take my 'abuse' much longer because she and Rafe were going to elope any day now and he didn't want his wife working, or some such slop. Why, she hasn't even showed up this morning."

"Hasn't showed up this morning. Oh," said Dr. Dodd. "Lord, what are we going to do?"

"Well, I think we might give her a couple of weeks' pay and our good wishes and give her to Rafe. Just a second now, Mr. Queen—"

"But Kenneth," said Dr. Dodd helplessly, "we'd have to go all through that awful business of finding a new girl—"

"Oh, I don't know," said Dr. Winship. "How about . . . well, how about Miss Anderson here?"

Dr. Dodd turned slowly.

"Oh," said Rima. "Oh, I don't know if I—" Ellery pinched her ankle as he stooped to pick up the cigaret he had dropped. Rima stopped.

"There's certainly nothing in the job that ought to tax an intelligent girl like Miss Anderson," said Dr. Winship carelessly. "If that Pinkle troglodyte could mangle the job . . . Don't you agree, Mr. Queen?"

"Well, it's certainly providential. But I don't know," said Ellery craftily. "Rima doesn't know how to type—"

"Is that all?" cried young Winship. "You ought to see samples of Pinkle's alleged typing. If Rima can't do better in one lesson I'll—I'll kiss Pinkle's foot! I'll bet Miss Anderson can at least spell. And what ever help Dr. Dodd and I need with patients—I mean, preparing them for examination, working the sterilizer, and so on—why, she could learn that in no time. You know we lost our regular office nurse during this damn diphtheria outbreak in Low Village and every trained nurse in town is needed for case work, and at the hospital. So we've been more or less limping along here, anyway. Doc, what do you say? It would tide us over and sort of help Miss Anderson out at the same time."

Dr. Dodd was swabbing his forehead with a soggy handkerchief. "Yes, I . . . think you'd like that, Rima?" He sounded feeble.

"I don't know, Dr. Dodd. I've never been cooped up in a—"

"Sooner or later you'll have to start being cooped up, Rima," said Ellery crossly. He felt like spanking her. "You can't live like a butterfly indefinitely. And this is really wonderful luck, Dr. Winship's suggestion."

"Maybe you're worried about the salary?" said Dr. Winship anxiously. "Pinkle's been getting thirty a week but, Doc, I think we might stretch a point and make it thirty-five for Rima—Miss Anderson—"

"Yes, yes, Kenneth. The only thing that's bothering me," said Dr. Dodd painfully, "is that I promised Henry Pinkle I'd give Gloria every chance. You know she hasn't been able to hold a job and the Pinkles need the money—"

"I tell you the nitwit is planning to elope!"

"Well . . . let's talk to Gloria again, Kenneth—see if this marriage business is definite." Dr. Dodd looked relieved, as if he had solved a difficult problem. "If it is, Rima, it would be just fine having you work with us."

Dr. Winship looked dissatisfied.

"Fair enough," said Ellery cheerfully. "You can let Rima know how it works out through me, Dr. Winship. I guess we can manage to hold out another day or so, eh, Rima?"

"Yes," said Rima.

Dr. Dodd's hands were shaking so badly that he dropped his handkerchief. "It's all right, Kenneth. Got 'em worse than usual today! Meanwhile, child, if you need any money—"

"Thank you, Dr. Dodd." Rima's voice was soft. "You've done . . . enough already."

"And Mr. Queen, if there's anything further I can do—"

"I'll certainly not hesitate to call on you, Doctor. Dr. Winship, it's been a pleasure—Oh! Just one thing." This is insanity, Ellery thought. But nothing's gone right, anyway. "Has either of you gentlemen sent me a letter recently?"

Rima looked at him sharply. And then at the two doctors. But they were merely looking bewildered; and I can't say I blame them, Ellery said to himself. He shook Dr. Dodd's hand—it was unpleasantly moist—and Dr. Winship walked them out.

The waiting room was crowded. A fullblown young woman in spike-heeled shoes and a transparent peekaboo blouse was making her lips up at the desk, fretfully.

"See what I mean?" hissed Dr. Winship, and he glared all the way to the front door.

Outside, Ellery said: "And what happened to your promise in Miss Sally's Tea Roome this morning, Rima? Wasn't it fundamentally obvious that I wangled that offer for you? And you went ahead and spoiled it!"

"Dr. Dodd didn't want me."

"Oh. Sensitive, too."

"He didn't, Ellery."

"You're wrong. Dodd's a chronic do-gooder. Whatever's messed him up expresses itself through acts of charity and loving kindness. More power to him. He's genuinely worried, I think, about his promise to the Wrightsville peony's father. But Rima, you're on his conscience, too. We're working in the dark, groping for a little light on a man's death. We've got to take advantage of every glimmer. We can't afford to have scruples. With a little intelligent assistance from you—" He was fuming.

"I'm sorry." Rima was staring at the lawn, where beside the walk an old man on his knees was transplanting seedlings from a flat. "It seemed like taking advantage. Dr. Dodd was so kind to Daddy. And Dr. Winship—"

"Ah, Dr. Winship. The tone changes. I didn't think you knew how, but apparently the art is bred in the bone. What about Dr. Winship?"

"You don't like him."

"I love him! But he's still only a piece in a puzzle as far as I'm concerned. What about Dr. Winship?"

"Well, he was so nice. And I don't know anything about office work."

She looked so small and isolated. "Well, well," Ellery said, "we'll talk about it some more . . . That old man. Is that—?"

"That's Harry Toyfell." Toyfell's knobby hands were working swiftly in the soil. He wore a grim suit of what had once been black cloth, patched in odd places and earthstained at the knees and cuffs. A violent blue shirt. And an incredible high stiff collar with a string tie. He was long and narrow, with sucked-in cheeks and a gritty skin. His skull was a squeezed bone thinly striated with hair. Put a stovepipe hat with a ribbon around its crown on that skull, thought Ellery, and you'd have Old Bluenose in person. Strange philosopher.

"Let's talk to him, Rima."

"No!"

"Are you afraid of him?" he asked her gently.

"Yes!"

"Stay behind me."

Rima followed reluctantly.

"Toyfell."

The gardener looked around and up with a jerk. Trying to give the impression he hadn't noticed us, thought Ellery.

"Yes, Mister?"

Ellery said sharply, "I'm a detective. Ellery Queen. Investigating the death of Tom Anderson. You were a crony of his, Toyfell. What do you know about it?"

"What do I know 'bout it?" Toyfell got to his feet in sections. "Why, Mister, I know that man is mortal and I know that death is sad. That's what I know 'bout it. Do you know any more?'' His voice was a rusty abomination. His little blue eyes shifted. "Ain't that Rima Anderson?''

Ellery squeezed her hand.

"Hello, Mr. Toyfell,'' she said quickly.

"Didn't know ye at first in those togs. Make ye look like a real grownup young woman.'' The mineral eyes stared.

Rima's grip tightened.

"When is the last time you saw Anderson?'' Ellery snapped.

"Night he disappeared. We were settin' in Gus Olesen's. Tom, Nick Jacquard, and me,'' Toyfell kept glancing at Rima, his Adam's apple bobbing. "On Route 16,'' he said.

"All leave together, did you?''

"No, Mister. Tom left first.''

"Time?''

" 'Bout 10:30. After a spell Nick, he got up and left, too. Then me.''

"Anderson was sober?''

"Hadn't drunk a lick. 'A ginger ale,' he says to Gus.'' The old man spat on the grass.

"Didn't you or Jacquard ask Anderson where he was going?''

Toyfell looked at Ellery. "Want to make your own liberty secure, guard your enemy from oppression. That's Paine. And I say to that, Amen, brother.''

"I thought Tom Anderson was your friend.''

"He was. Therefore I say, How can a man do less unto his friend?'' Toyfell spat again.

Valuable philosophy, thought Ellery. Especially in a homicide investigation. "And you didn't see him again?''

"Not in this life.'' Toyfell grinned, but then Ellery saw that the old gardener was drawing his lips back over his empty gums in a grimace of genuine sadness. And he thought that many of Toyfell's disagreeable aspects might be similarly the result of physical distortion; but he thought this for only a moment. There were those flinty eyes, and Rima holding herself in by his side.

And Ellery found himself repeating the foolish litany: "Did you send me a letter or two recently?''

The old man stared. "Now that's a question I just don't get, Mister.''

"To Ellery Queen. West 87th Street, New York City. Two letters.''

"Haven't writ a letter in twenty-five years.''

"See the *Record* regularly, do you?''

"I see it, but I don't read it. There's no truth in newspapers, only facts. Do you want to argue the case?''

"Some other day,'' smiled Ellery. "But Toyfell, I must say I admire you. You seem to be standing up under blows that would have knocked the starch out of a lesser man. In a short time death's taken two employers and a friend, and here you are—still philosophizing.''

"Know theyself,'' said Harry Toyfell, getting down on his knees again. "The soul of man is immortal and imperishable.''

"You're a religious man?''

"A pagan said that, Mister. Read your Plato. But people don't read Plato any more. Just newspapers. As for my religion, I worship God in every seed. When did you find anything in a church but cut flowers? Not that it's any of your business, Mister.''

They left The Town Philosopher crawling about among his young plants, dealing with them tenderly. He did not look up as they left him. Not even to look at Rima Anderson.

Rima said no, she didn't care for any lunch, thank you, she wasn't hungry, and unless he had some special reason for wanting her she'd like to go back to the hotel and take off her shoes, she really would. Also, she was used to taking a nap in the afternoon, and so on. No, he needn't bother to take her back, really he needn't; she didn't want to interfere in any way with his plans.

"I'll pick you up in a couple of hours, Rima. Some things I want to do." Ellery took her hand.

"At Upham House?" She withdrew it.

"Yes."

"All right."

He watched her swing away. Hurrying strides. He would not have been surprised if she had broken into a run.

Ellery walked up Algonquin to State and west on State to the County Court House.

Chief Dakin grabbed him. "What's this about did I find money?" he cried.

Ellery told him.

Dakin got red. "Now that wasn't right," he spluttered. "Doc Dodd should have told me about that right off. Five thousand dollars! Where is it?"

Ellery tapped his teeth with a thoughtful fingernail.

"There wasn't a brass cent in that coat. And no sign of anything on the cliff or around it."

"He might have hidden it, Dakin. Probably did. Did you search the shack?"

"Tore it apart. Looking for anything we could find. But all we turned up was three bottles of whisky in different hiding places under the floor."

"No money. In any amount."

"Not a Confederate dime. But that's it, Mr. Queen. There's the motive and there's the crime." The chief of police rubbed his hands. "He had that five thousand on him and he was lured to that spot, attacked, robbed, and flung over the cliff."

Ellery pushed his lips out.

Finally he said. "Maybe," and rose.

"Where you goin'?"

"There's still a byroad or two. By the way. Dakin, none of your local riffraff's been displaying unusual riches lately, I suppose."

"Haven't heard of any, but I'm goin' to get busy on that first thing."

"Might pay to keep this under your visor for a while, Dakin."

"I wasn't figuring on getting up in Town Meetin' about it. Who else knows besides Doc Dodd and Kenny Winship and you and me?"

"Rima, of course. And Otis Holderfield."

"Well, you can take care of Rima, and Otis's father on his mother's side was a clam—"

"By the way, what about this fellow Holderfield? What's his reputation in Wrightsville?"

"Otis," said Chief Dakin with a grin, "is black and blue from pinchin' himself. How Luke MacCaby came to pick him when he needed a lawyer nobody's been able to figure out. For years he's scrabbled along on accident and rent-collection cases, doing an insurance business to pay for the butter. Mysterious little guy always full of secrets and you always know most of it's hot air. The Rotary bunch groan when they see him comin'. That is, up to the last month or so. Otis sure has blossomed. From rags to riches. Got into a big new office in the Granjon Block, smokes quarter cigars, has his shoes shined every day, calls Donald Mackenzie and J. C. Pettigrew by their first names, and Clint Fosdick told me the other day he'd seen Otis over at Marty Zilliber's agency looking over a Buick convertible. Mostly on prospect of course—the money hasn't started to come in yet, but they'll be through probate any day now and when they are—why, Doc Dodd's retained Otis to represent his legal interests and I guess Otis will be rolling in clover. But he's a smart one, Otis is, considering his limitations. At least he doesn't make the mistake of shootin' off his face. We might slip this five thousand dollar deal by the *Record,* at that. If they haven't got hold of it by this time . . ."

"The *Record,*" said Ellery; and he looked thoughtful as he left.

He walked slowly up State Street, past the Our Boys Memorial, past the Town Hall, into the Square.

Here he paused, facing south. One spoke away was Lower Main, and on the south corner of Lower Main the *Record* building stood. Ellery became aware for the first time that the *Record* building was not what it had been. It had been a blackish green affair of decayed woodwork with a gingerbread cornice and a stubborn look. The mordant woodwork was no more; the face of the building was now bright coral stucco and chrome, off which the sun ricocheted angrily. The old dingy sign, which had stretched across the building under the cornice, was gone, replaced by an intricate mechanism on the roof of neon tubing. The whole structure had a coltishly rejuvenated air, and it tickled his interest. He actually started across State Street.

But then he about-faced and made his way along the rim of the Square to the Wrightsville National Bank.

Scowling, he went in.

Fifteen minutes later he came out, crossed Upper Dade, passed the old Bluefield store, J. P. Simpson's Loan Office, Dunc MacLean—Fine Liquors, the Hollis entrance, Sol Gowdy's Men's Shop, the Atomic War Surplus Outlet Store. At the corner of the Square and Lincoln Street, where Hallam Luck (the First) in 1927 had erected his Greek temple of finance, the Public Trust Company, Ellery stopped again.

After a moment he went into Wrightsville's other bank.

Ellery was back on the sidewalk in twelve minutes.

He hesitated, staring vacantly across Lincoln Street at the Bon Ton, and the High Village Pharmacy and the New York Department Store beyond. The Square was lively with Monday morning commerce and he was elbowed a little.

Finally he walked back along the western arc of the Square to the Hollis Hotel.

There was one cab at the taxi stand and a man he had never seen before sat behind the wheel reading a copy of *Record.*

"Cab, sir?"

"Well. I wasn't intending to walk all the way to Slocum," said Ellery grumpily; and he got in.

At three o'clock in the afternoon Ellery was back in Wrightsville, on the ground floor south wing of Upham House, knocking on the door of Room 17.

He knocked again.

"You Mr. Queen?"

A redhaired bellboy was at his elbow, leering.

"Yes."

"Miss Anderson said to tell you she got clau—clau—"

"Claustrophobia?"

"Yes, sir. I had it written down but I guess I lost it. Anyway, she said to tell you she's over in Memorial Park somewhere, holding down a tree."

Ellery hurried back to State Street.

He found Rima deep in the park, at its hilly northern side lying under a willow tree on the bank of Mullins Creek. Her skin was halfway to her waist and her bare toes were wiggling in the water like little pink fish: he saw her shoes and stockings ten feet away, as if they had been flung. As he approached, a dozen birds rose from the grass about her and raced up into the willow, from which they scolded him.

"Bird talk for 'Unclean! Unclean!' " said Ellery. "Your name should have been Avis, or at least Rara. How do you do it?"

"I just lie very still and talk softly to them. Did you have any trouble finding me?" She was all dreamy friendliness again, as she had been on the train.

"Natty Bumppo Queen?" He looked down at her. "Feeling better?"

"Oh, ever so much." She sat up abruptly, pulling her skirt quickly over her knees. When he grinned, she laughed and jumped to her feet. "Where have you been, Ellery?"

"Here and there. Hungry?"

"No."

"Do you eat like a bird, too? Suppose you pull those instruments of torture back on, Rima—"

"We going somewhere?"

"Calling."

"Again? Where?" Her whole face flashed.

"The Granjon Block."

"Oh."

They strolled back through the park. After a while Rima's hand slipped into his. Ellery squeezed and she smiled faintly and did not let go until they reached the American Legion Bandstand opposite the Town Hall steps and flushed two teenagers from under the latticework.

The Granjon Block was the building on the southwest corner of Washington and Slocum Streets, across Slocum from the Professional Building. Unlike the Professional Building, whose copestone said that it had been built in 1879, the Granjon Block was "new"; it was less than thirty years old and it advertised elevator service for its four stories. According to the directory in the lobby, it was tenanted chiefly by lawyers and other professional men. The legend, HOLDERFIELD, OTIS, ATTORNEY-AT-LAW . . . 401, glistened.

A bulky old man in a black alpaca jacket took them up in the elevator. "Aren't you Mr. Queen?" he asked Ellery.

"That's right. And you're Buzz Congress. You used to be the 'special' at the Wrightsville National in John P. Wright's day."

"Recongnized you right off, Mr. Queen."

"Can't beat a trained eye. Know if Otis Holderfield's in his office?"

"Took him up from lunch an hour ago."

"I hear Holderfield's in the chips."

"Changed man. Why, seems only yesterday he was goin' around with a handkerchief tucked into his collar and holes in his shoes." The old man's tone was without irony; it was even respectful. "Nobody'd hardly talk to Otis. He'd have to hang onto their lapels. Now the same folks who'd been uppity to him come up here to shake his hand and give him their law business." Buzz Congress wheezed—not at Otis Holderfield, it was clear, but at the folks who had been uppity. "It's that office there, sir. With the gold letters."

The outer office was shiny and new, the furniture was shiny and new, the law books were shiny and new, and even the secretary looked as if she had just been unpacked. Her blouse plunged steeply at the neckline, her eye was cold and wise, her figure insolent; she was what Wrightsville still terms "a hot number." Ellery's pre-estimate of Otis Holderfield underwent a modification. He began to feel sorry he had brought Rima.

Wrightsville's newest legal comet zipped out of his private office. He was the newest-looking little man Ellery had ever seen—a haberdasher's dream and a barber's delight; he stood in an almost visible field of eau de cologne. His suit, his striped silk shirt, his handpainted silk necktie, his suède shoes, the diamond on his stubby finger—their wearer was obscured by the blaze. And a good thing, too, thought Ellery; for Holderfield was no beauty. He was bullt on the lines of a small keg, with womanish hips and shoulders whose meagerness was only accentuated by the sharp pads which broadened them. The top of his head was perfectly flat, a pinkish plateau covered with a sparse scrub of oily black hair; he had small cunning features, crooked teeth, and a nervous little bounce.

"Ellery *Queen? The* Ellery Queen from New York? Say!" Ellery's hand was wrung by two moistly eager members. "Couldn't believe my ears when my secretary announced you." His secretary was looking Ellery over frankly. "Come in, come in, Mr. Queen! Can't get the little old ham-burg out of your blood, hey? Haha! Say, I used to read about you in the *Record* and I remember saying to myself, 'Now there's a smart cookie I'd like to meet up with some day,' and, by damn, here you are! Walking into Otis Holderfield's private office like you owned the place. Well, sir, you do, you do. Here, take this one—that's real leather. Should have given me a buzz, Mr. Queen. I'd have set up a lunch with some of the boys— you know, Donald and J.P. . . . Say! I almost didn't see this little lady. New York stock, hey?" The little man's left eyelid drooped and the left side of his face screwed up for a moment. "Hiya, little gal. Here, you take this chair where we galoots can both get an eyeful, haha! What did you say this cute trick's name is, Mr. Queen?"

"Rima Anderson," said Ellery.

Holderfield's animation died. His little eyes narrowed and he shot a quick glance at Ellery.

"The Old Soak's girl, hey?" he said pleasantly. "I'll be a monkey's uncle. Just goes to show—never judge a book by its bookie, haha! Well, well, I suppose this visit has something to do with your father, honey, hm? Though, Mr. Queen, I don't see . . .

"I saw Dr. Dodd this morning, Holderfield."

"You did?" He was behind his desk now, tilting his swivel chair, fingertips meeting in a juridical way. Very attentive.

"Dr. Dodd told me all about the five thousand dollars."

"Five thousand dollars?"

"That he instructed you to get for Tom Anderson."

"Dr. Dodd told you that, did he?"

"I'm looking for additional information."

Otis Holderfield was silent. Then he said, smiling, "You understand, Mr. Queen, Dr. Dodd's an important client, and the client-attorney relationship . . ."

"You mean you'd rather not talk about it?"

"I didn't say that," said the attorney with a slight sharpness.

"Dr. Dodd didn't seem reticent."

"He didn't. Well that's fine. By the way, did Dr. Dodd tell you to come to see me, Queen?"

"No."

The little man looked regretful. "In that case . . ."

"May I use your phone?"

"What?" Holderfield was alarmed. "Who you going to call?"

"Your client. You seem worried about the propriety of discussing this with me, Holderfield. I think Dr. Dodd will relieve your mind—"

"Say, don't think about it." Holderfield was all smiles again. "Not the least bit necessary, Mr. Queen. It's just that Dr. Dodd's one of my big clients and naturally an attorney . . . I mean, my father used to say to me, 'Otis, two things a man has to keep buttoned if he's going to stay out of trouble. The other one is his mouth.' Haha! Never forgot that bit of wisdom. Though we all ignore even the best advice at times, now, don't we, haha! Don't mind telling you about the Anderson business, Mr. Queen—don't mind at all. Though, as I told Dr. Dodd, I thought it was ill-advised in the first instance, and then the old barfly disappearing that way—"

"He's dead," said Rima.

"Now, now, little girl, we don't *know* that, do we? Not as a fact. No, sir, if I were you I'd put that thought clean out of my head, little girl. That hat and coat on the cliff don't constitute a corpus delicti and that's my legal opinion. Won't cost you a penny, either, haha."

"He's dead," repeated Rima.

Holderfield scowled. "Well, this is a free country. But I can't see that that kind of talk does anybody any good. I'm a great believer in facts—"

"So am I," said Ellery. "But I believe we're still ambling around in the realm of opinion. Why was Dodd's gift to Tom Anderson ill-advised?"

"Well, you give an old rummy—I mean, The Old Soak hadn't had five silver dollars to rub against one another for years—now had he, Miss Anderson? A fact's a fact. And then . . . Of course, it was Dr. Dodd's money and I'm a great believer in following through on my clients' wishes—within reason, of course, haha!—even though in this case it meant putting myself and my client under obligation to the Surrogate. At that, I had the devil of a time . . ."

"In other words, Holderfield, you were against Dodd's giving Anderson that money."

"Yes, sir, I was." The little man looked stern. "Sebastian Dodd's got a heart as big as Wright County. Too darn big for his own good. Got absolutely no conception of the value of—Excuse me. What is it, Floss?"

The secretary was in the doorway, leaning. "Dave Waldo."

"Dave? Say! Mr. Queen, this won't take a minute. Matter of fact—Send him in, Floss. Mr. Queen, seeing you're from New York, I'd like your reaction to this. Come in, David!"

As the lawyer bounced from his chair Ellery glanced at Rima, shaking his head slightly. Rima relaxed.

The man who hurried into the office was tiny and anxious looking. He was so small that he had to look up to Holderfield. His little narrow shoulders were curved inward, his eyes stared myopically, his skin was a clayish gray, and there were innumerable pricks in his fingers. It was no surprise to learn that he was a tailor—"Dave Waldo, runs the tailoring shop downstairs, he and his brother Jonathan. David and Jonathan—pretty good, uh? They're twins, haha! But they certainly know how to make a suit. Wouldn't have my clothes made anywheres else, hey, Dave?" David Waldo smiled nervously as he laid a bolt of cloth on Holderfield's desk. "Just came from New York, Mr. Holderfield. You said you wanted to see it in the bolt, so I ran right up with it. Finest lightweight camel's hair. Imported." "How's it look to you, Ellery?—y'know, Dave, this is Ellery Queen, you've heard of *him:* From New York. Going to have Dave make me up a spring topcoat. Hollywood style. You know, big shoulders, loose cut, lots of material, tie belt. Think it'll be worth a hundred and fifty with this material?" Ellery murmured something sage about relative values, wondering where he had seen David Waldo before, and Otis Holderfield examined the cocoa-colored material critically, finally saying it would do all right—"I'll be down for a fitting on that garbadine suit, Dave, first chance I get. Charge the oxford gray to my account, Davey-boy"—and the little tailor looked grateful and scurried out. Holderfield seemed sorry to see him go.

Ellery said abruptly, "I have one or two other things to do today, Holderfield. I'm trying to locate that five thousand."

"Locate it?"

"It's disappeared."

Holderfield looked unhappy.

"It wasn't in the coat Dakin found on Little Prudy's Cliff. It wasn't hidden in the Anderson house. I've spent part of today checking back to see if Anderson mightn't have deposited it in a bank or hired a safe deposit box somewhere. The two Wrightsville banks have no record of either an account or a box. I've been to Slocum with no luck, either. There's no bank at the Junction, or in Fidelity or Bannock, and I hardly think Anderson would have gone so far afield as Connhaven. Holderfield, have you any idea what he may have done with that five thousand dollars?"

"Think it has something to do with his disappearance, do you, Mr. Queen?"

"I don't know whether it has or not. That's what I'm trying to find out."

"Well, it hasn't or I'd have advised my client long ago to tell the whole story to the police . . ." Holderfield was perspiring, swabbing down the flat of his head with a handrolled, Irish linen handkerchief.

"Where is that money, Holderfield?"

The little man bounced to his feet. "Dang it, it's a nuisance!" he cried. "Don't know why I'm placed in this position. Try to keep your client happy . . . Few days after Dr. Dodd phoned me and Anderson came over and I handed him the envelope with the money in it, why, Anderson came back. Came back with the envelope."

"Here? To your office?" asked Ellery sharply.

"That's right!"

"The same envelope?"

"Same envelope. My imprint. But sealed—double-sealed. With Scotch tape. It wasn't sealed when I'd given it to him."

"Then you didn't actually see the money when he visited you for the second time?"

"No. But it was in there, all right—it had been in twenties, fifties, and hundreds and it made a whopper of an envelopeful. Besides, Anderson said so. Said he was too nervous to hide the money and too nervous to keep carrying it around, and would I hold onto it for him till he proved something to himself, or words to that effect." Holderfield's expression was distinctly disagreeable. "I should have had my head examined! Tried to argue with him—asked him why he didn't put it in a bank—and he said no, if anything happened to him the money'd get all tangled up in legal red tape and he'd rather it was in a place where it could be got to without a fuss. Asked me to keep it in my office safe. Well, I was jammed up that day, had an office full of people, so I didn't stop to think and I said I'd do it. He handed me the envelope and I noticed he'd written on it, 'If anything happens to Thomas Hardy Anderson, this envelope is to be turned over to Nicole Jacquard.' "

"Nick *Jacquard?*"

"That's right."

"That's the second time you say he referred to something possibly happening to him. Did you get the impression, or did he specify—?"

"Not a bit of it. It was more like a man's making out a will. He indicates a disposition of his property just in case—"

"But why Jacquard?"

"Of all people," said Rima. Her eyes were sad.

Holderfield shrugged. "I didn't ask him and he didn't say. He just said there was a letter of instructions to Jacquard included in the envelope, telling Jacquard just what to do with the contents. I thought myself it was sort of queer, his picking Jacquard, I mean, but as I say I was busy, so I put the envelope in my safe and Anderson left." Holderfield used his handkerchief again. "Well, when his hat and coat turned up on Little Prudy's Cliff, that certainly came under the heading of something 'happening' to Anderson, so I sent word to Nick Jacquard and he dropped into my office here and I gave him the envelope. I've got a receipt for it signed by Jacquard," Holderfield added quickly, "so everything's hunky-dory, as the old rubes around here say, haha!"

"May I have that receipt, please?"

"Well, now, Mr. Queen, I don't want to seem uncooperative, but the fact is that receipt's my only proof I gave Jacquard Anderson's envelope—"

"Then may I see it?"

"Well, it's in my safe and I've got a client coming up any second now, Mr. Queen—"

"Let it go," said Ellery. "But everything's not quite as hunky-dory as you'd have me believe, Holderfield. In the first place, the moment you heard about Anderson's death—"

"Disappearance," said Holderfield rather breathlessly.

"—you should have hotfooted it over to Dakin's office and told Dakin the whole story—"

"Not at all, not at all," said the lawyer. "That money involved my client. I mean, it brought him into what might have been a mess. My duty is to my client first and foremost—"

"Your duty, Holderfield, is to the law first and foremost."

"It was my client's place to go to the police if he saw fit, and, if he didn't, it was my place as his attorney to back him up—"

"It was your place as his attorney to advise him to go to the police and you know it. But, aside from that, you certainly had no right to give that envelope up to Jacquard or anyone else. It was material to a suspected homicide. Anderson was dead, following a felonious assault. That's murder—''

"You prove it!" said Holderfield triumphantly. "You prove Anderson was murdered. You prove he's even dead! All anybody knows for a fact is that he's disappeared. Not a particle of evidence to any other effect. I held that envelope of his as a confidential trust. I had my instructions: If anything 'happened' to him, I was to turn the envelope over to Nicole Jacquard. Mine not to reason why, as the poet says, hey, Mr. Queen? You can't get around that, no, siree-bob.''

"What you wanted to do, and what you did," said Ellery rising "was to get rid of that envelope just as fast as you could. Holderfield, you're in a mess, and you know it, and I know it, and none of your pettifogging legalisms can change the fact." Otis Holderfield was pale, but whether with fear or with anger Ellery could not decide. The man sat worrying his lower lip and turning the diamond ring on his fat finger. It seemed an excellent moment for his standard question, so Ellery went on, "And talking about envelopes, Holderfield, did you address a couple of same to me recently?''

"Me? Send you letters?''

"Yes.''

"If you got any letters on my stationery," said Holderfield excitedly, "they were forged. I never sent you a letter in my life. And you can't prove I did!''

"A simple negative would have served the purpose," sighed Ellery, nodding to Rima. "Oh, by the way, Holderfield." Ellery detained Rima in the doorway. "I'm curious about one other matter. How did Luke MacCaby come to call you in when he wanted to make a will?''

The little man bounced to his feet, purple. "And what's the matter with me?" he shouted.

"I didn't say anything was the matter. I just asked you a question.''

"I've drawn a will or two in my time!''

"I'm sure you have. But how did MacCaby happen to pick you when he wanted his drawn?''

"Mr. Queen, you've got no right asking me questions like that! I don't have to take that sort of thing!''

"I seem to have stumbled on your sore toe, Holderfield—''

"And anyway, what's MacCaby got to do with this Anderson business? I don't get it, Mr. Queen, I don't get it!''

"I don't either, Holderfield, which is why I'm trying. Sorry if I've offended you—''

"Just because I was scraping along in this town—! All right, I was lucky. If you must know, MacCaby got my name out of the classified directory. But I had a break coming, fella! And all these wiseacres who used to look down their noses at me—why, I've got 'em eating out of my hand. I'm big potatoes in this hamlet now and, Brother Queen, I mean to stay that way!'' Holderfield's high color slowly faded, but some of it lingered on his cheekbones. He began to fuss with some papers on his desk, a little blindly.

"Did your father ever say anything to you about Nick Jacquard's being his executor, so to speak, in case anything happened to him?" Ellery asked Rima when they were on Washington Street again.

"No.''

"Did Jacquard ever get in touch with you after your father disappeared?''

"No." Rima shivered.

"Dodd to Holderfield to Jacquard," muttered Ellery, taking Rima's arm. "Town Saint to Town Rabbit's-Foot to Town Thief. Fascinating gambit. Let's go smoke out Nick Jacquard."

They found him immediately, for Ellery said the logical place to start looking was Gus Olesen's on Route 16 and when they took a cab to the Roadside Tavern and walked into its malty interior there was Jacquard, alone, spreading his shoulders over the bar, his battered hands closed about a glass of beer. Jacquard was a hulk, with all the hulk's derelict nature; he may have been a trim vessel once, but brawls and hunger and liquor had left him dismantled and unfit, a huge and dirty piece of uselessness lapped by the brown waters of a drunken daydream. He was unshaved, unshorn, and unwashed and his costume was improvised from crooked bits of a once-honest workman's wardrobe.

He spied them in the bar mirror and it seemed to Ellery Jacquard's seaglass eyes sparkled briefly at sight of Rima, but the man did not turn on his stool, he kept guard over his beer and stared into the mirror and beyond.

Gus Olesen was not about and the bartender was a new man, for which Ellery gave thanks. He ordered a root beer for Rima and a Martini for himself, and then he set Rima down to one side of Jacquard and he took the flanking stool, so that Jacquard sat humped between them. The man stirred.

"Don't go away, Nick," said Rima. "My friend wants to talk to you."

" 'Allo," said Nick Jacquard. His diction was half-slurred and difficult. "They find your old man?"

"My friend, Nick," said Rima. "On the other side of you."

"You got a friend?" Jacquard's eyes shined. "Pretty quick."

"On this side," said Ellery.

Jacquard turned.

"My name is Queen. Ellery Queen."

The bloodshot eyes blinked. "Pleased to meet you. I got to go—"

"Sit down, Jacquard."

After a moment Jacquard settled back on his stool. "What you want?"

"To talk about your old pal Tom Anderson."

"You're a bull," said Jacquard heavily. "I know about you. I tell Dakin everything I know. I got nothing to tell you."

"Nick, you're lying," said Rima.

Jacquard muttered something in patois and tossed his beer down with a jerk.

Ellery tried to focus the three cronies at this very bar. Tom Anderson, Nick Jacquard, Harry Toyfell. The gentle, the dull, the sharp. Town Drunk, Town Thief, Town Philosopher. An ex-professor of English literature, an illiterate bum, an iconoclastic gardener. Tom, Nick, and Harry. Ellery wondered what bitter cement had held them together.

"Maybe you lie," said Jacquard, cocking his shaggy head at Rima. "Maybe you pull a trick on me, *hein?*" He laughed, but he was alarmed, his glances caroming off the mirror toward Ellery and back to Rima, his murderous hands gripping the edge of the bar.

"No, Jacquard. We know the whole story of the envelope that lawyer, Holderfield, gave you after Tom Anderson disappeared."

Jacquard sat still.

"Holderfield did give you an envelope, didn't he? With your name on it in Anderson's handwriting. A thick one, sealed with Scotch tape."

Jacquard said nothing.

"And you gave Holderfield a receipt for it, Jacquard."

"Then okay!" the man burst out. His little eyes were prowling now.

"What was in it?" Jacquard's tongue came out. "Jacquard, what was in the envelope?"

"Papers."

"Papers? What kind of papers?"

"Papers . . . letters. Old letters. That Tom writes one time."

"Letters he wrote to you?" smiled Ellery.

"No. To—Yes! To me."

"Can you read, Jacquard?"

"You're lying, Nick," said Rima.

"I can read better as you!" Jacquard licked his lips again. He's furious and dull-witted, thought Ellery.

"How much money did the envelope have in it, Jacquard?"

"Money?"

"Money."

"You crazy! There is no money in that! No money, you hear?" He waved his thick arms, getting off the stool.

"Jacquard, there were five thousand dollars in that envelope."

"No money!" He backed away.

"And a letter of instructions from Anderson to you. What were Anderson's instructions, Jacquard?"

"No money." Jacquard lurched through the swinging doors, at the last with a lunge. His hoarse voice came back. "No money!" he cried, as if with each repetition his cry became more believable, to himself as well as to them.

They heard him scuffing rapidly away through the gravel.

Rima laughed. "Poor Daddy." But her lips were trembling.

"Nature of the beast." said Ellery reflectively. "He's dazed with the immense, the immense good luck of it all. Five thousand dollars. To Jacquard five million wouldn't be more. Could you hold a starving tiger from the helpless kill? He means to keep it, Rima. He's dazed and he's scared, and he's sick to his stomach, but he means to keep it. Maybe not even to spend; how could a Jacquard spend five thousand dollars? What amazes me, Rima, is not Jacquard's childish lying and his dishonesty. It's your father's sublime folly."

"Jacquard was his friend. Daddy had only two friends in the world. Besides me." The last was said to her root beer, which she had not touched.

"Two friends. Of whom one was a thief and the other a philosopher. And he entrusts his money to the thief."

"My father," said Rima, "was a wonderful man."

"The exact word," nodded Ellery, throwing a bill down on the bar. "Possibly, Rima, he had even less faith in the honesty of the philosopher than in the crookedness of the thief. Friendship isn't necessarily based on trust. A man who's lonely will cling to his worst enemy . . . Or he might have been borrowing a leaf from the golden book of Sebastian Dodd—giving the crooked man his chance to straighten out." Ellery said gently, "Come, Rima."

But Rima kept staring into her glass. "Why didn't Daddy give it to me? Didn't he trust me?" She laughed again. "Or did he trust Nick Jacquard more?"

It was a question Ellery had been asking himself for some time. "You should know the answer to that."

"I should, but I don't."

"He had to prove something to himself. For all their cronyism, Jacquard and Toyfell were outsiders to him. They didn't touch him. They weren't part of him. I think your father felt the necessity of doing this on his own. And then maybe he kept thinking of you as a child . . . Damn it, I didn't ask Jacquard my favorite question." When she said nothing, he said, "About those anonymous letters."

She looked up this time. "Which anonymous letters?"

"Not that it would have told me anything. And that reminds me. How tired are you?" It was successful. She was interested once more.

"I'm not."

"Then we'll have our friend outside drive us back to town. Do you know a newspaper gal named Malvina Prentiss?"

"She's the one who kept asking me things when Daddy . . ."

"She's the one we're going to see."

The old scarified front door of the *Record* building was gone. In its place hung a squarish production of coral-colored plastic bossed with fat chrome studs. A circular window in the door, resembling a porthole, added a puzzling marine touch.

The homely interior was no more. You had always gone from the street directly into the *Record's* business office; now you found yourself in a foyer whose walls were of coral plastic aud stainless steel. In a circular well in the center of the foyer rotated a large globe of the Earth illuminated from below. Stainless steel chairs stood about and a young woman in a *Vogue* blouse asked your business icily from behind a stainless steel grille.

"I'd like to see one of your reporters. Malvina Prentiss."

The ice broke. The young woman giggled. "Better not let Malvina hear you say that!"

"Say what?"

"That's she's a reporter. She owns this paper. Owner, publisher, Editor-in-Chief, and Lady High Muckamuck—Lady Muck, we call her for short, but don't tell her I said so. Who's calling, please?"

Ellery told her, feebly. The plastic, coral, chrome, steel . . . a lady publisher it would have to be. Inherited wealth, two trips to Paris with stopovers in London, and a secret yen to look like Rosalind Russell. Smoked cigarets in a footlong holder, gowned by Jacques Fath via an exclusive Boston shop, and loathed men. Native habitat doubtful, but almost certainly not Wrightsville. There might have been a newspaper publisher in her bloodline. Crisp would be the word for her. She must have swooped into town when she heard of the suicide of Diedrich Van Horn, former owner-publisher of the *Record,* and bought it out from Wolfert Van Horn to work her will on it.

A bucktoothed page in a green corduroy jacket took them in tow, leading them to a gem of a little elevator. The business office was unrecognizable, a tone poem in silver and forest green, with grim stainless-steel-edged green counters and half a dozen metal desks with silvery telephones at which sat selfconscious-looking young women in identical tailored green skirts and white blouses.

"Any second now," Ellery mumbled to Rima, "a hidden orchestra will strike up and the members of the ensemble will leap as one into a ballet number." To place a mere five-line ad at one of these counters would take courage.

He wondered what the incredible Miss Prentiss had done with Phinny Baker's old press room.

The big catchall editorial room on the upper floor had always been a cheerful chaos—comfortably dirty, with mutilated rolltop desks, men sitting around in paper cuffs, spittoons on the naked floor, and behind everything a manly bedlam. Now it was a kind of industrial cloister—hushed, disapproving, cold—divided into gleaming little shells of offices in which unhappy-looking people sat toiling. Ellery could spy no one he knew. Gladys Hemmingworth, Frank Lloyd's bustling Society Editor, had given way to a mannish female in velveteen slacks who was honking into one of the prevailing silvery telephones. There was no sign of stout Clara Peacher, who under the name of "Aunt Peachie" had written the domestic column; or of Obie Gilboon, who had covered spots for twenty-six years and whose tie was always smoldering from the droppings of his palsied bulldog pipe. And the plate on eyeshaded Woodie Wentworth's old city desk now said freezingly, DEAN ST. A. ST. JOHN, which was certainly not a Wrightsville-sounding name.

With a bleeding heart, Ellery followed Rima and the page through the coral door on which stern steel letters spelled out M. O. PRENTISS.

The lady publisher's office was what he had expected, and so was the lady publisher, except more so. Here not only were the walls covered with the lecherous green plastic material, but the ceiling was cushioned, too. The steel desk was as big as a baby tank; the desk set was of sterling silver; the Venetian blinds were of aluminum. The lady herself, as anticipated, was a Rosalind Russell type, but in a superproduction by Ernst Lubitsch. She was tall, svelte, and dressed as "smart woman executive" in a business suit which would have looked merely expensive if it had not also been of a disturbing silver-sheened material. Silver seemed her passion: her fingernails were painted silver, her footlong cigaret holder (as predicted) was of silver, she wore silvery harlequin glasses which emphasized the frozen quirk of her eyebrows, and her hair was platinum-dyed. There were so many points of wonder about her that it was some time before Ellery realized that in a normal setting and costume—off the set, as it were—Malvina Prentiss was probably an attractive woman. As she was, and in Wrightsville, she was an absurdity.

She said, "Ellery Queen?" in an insolent contralto, looking him over as if he were a horse. Then she stared at Rima, and Rima blushed. "And who's this?"

"Rima Anderson."

Malvina Prentiss threw back her head, exhibiting a set of powerful, immaculate teeth. "What have you done to our little wood nymph, Queen? Ever see such a transformation, Spec?"

Then Ellery realized that seated beside her desk was a redhaired man in his mid-thirties who was trying not to look miserable and being thoroughly unsuccessful. Exactly the type of male claque-leader Malvina Prentiss would keep in her private employ—intelligent eyes behind hornrimmed glasses, hair parted in the middle, unpadded shoulders, a studious pallor to offset a nonexistent waistline, and a meek, almost suffering, manner. All togged out in a conservative business suit and a correct pindot tie.

The man said, "Yes, Miss Prentiss, I mean no! Miss Prentiss," his freckled skin turning old rose; and he clutched the back of his chair, from which he had jumped, as if to hold himself up.

"Mr. Queen, Francis O'Bannon. My executive assistant. Pure Back Bay. Harvard, of course. Sound politics, fair brain, but very nearly distracted about everything, especially me. We like to have him around, though, Spec, don't we?" The old rose deepened. She was enjoying her cruelty in a contemptuous way. "Knows a surprising lot about running a newspaper—"

"Not as much as you do, of course, Miss Prentiss."

She glanced at O'Bannon sharply. "And that's the truth," she said; but then she laughed. "Well, well, Mr. Queen, and what's a twelve-cylinder smartiepants like you doing in little Wrightsville?" She glanced surgically at Rima. "Or is it love?— or something?"

Rima said, "I don't like you."

Malvina Prentiss stopped smiling. "That was clever of you, darling. Who's been teaching you the finer shades of meaning?"

"I know enough to interpret a nasty remark like that, Miss Prentiss."

They stared at each other. Then the lady publisher shrugged. "Well, the best people don't like me, dear, but I didn't think it had filtered down into the lower classes quite so soon." And she jabbed a cigaret into her holder. O'Bannon leaped for the silver lighter on her desk. "All right, Mr. Big. Come to the point."

"To take the points one at a time," said Ellery. "this girl has just lost her father under tragic circumstances, she's pretty much alone in the world, and kindness would make an awfully good starting one, don't you think, Miss Prentiss?"

"Does she have to kick me in the face?" She laughed again. O'Bannon, who had been transfixed on the point of her desk, immediately laughed too. "What's on your mind. Mr. Queen?"

Ellery placed two envelopes before her. "Look at the contents of these, Miss Prentiss."

After a moment the platinum-haired woman looked up. "What about them?"

"They were mailed to me in those two envelopes. Did you send them?"

"Certainly not. Spec, did you?"

O'Bannon quivered under the lash. "No—no, Miss Prentiss," he stammered.

"We seem to have a press agent in our midst." She frowned. "Sit down, Mr. Queen. You, too, Rima. There's more to this than meets the eye."

"There certainly is," said Ellery. "For instance, note the curious juxtaposition of subject matter. The death of Luke MacCaby. His bequest to Sebastian Dodd. The suicide of John Spencer Hart. And the disappearance, with strong suspicion of murder, of Thomas Hardy Anderson."

"The MacCaby-Dodd-Hart business is all part of the same story. The Anderson thing stands on its own. Why should anyone string them together?"

"That's the question, Miss Prentiss, that I came up here to ask you."

Malvina Prentiss stared at him, then at Rima, and finally at Francis O'Bannon. "Any ideas, Spec?" she asked crisply.

O'Bannon said, "Not a glimmer," with regret, but it seemed to Ellery the redhaired man's interest had quickened. Ellery was sure of it when O'Bannon removed his eyeglasses and began to polish the lenses with a pinked rectangle of yellow cloth.

"Miss Prentiss, I'm convinced Anderson's death is linked in some way with the events that preceded it. If you have any information that would confirm this, let me in on it."

"You're not serious?"

"You're not withholding information?"

"Why would I withhold information in a murder case?"

"I'm sure I don't know, Miss Prentiss. Why would you?"

She smiled sweetly. "You're fumbling, Mr. Q. The *Record* doesn't withhold information, conceal evidence, or suppress news. Not this *Record,* Mr. Q. On the contrary. The publisher of this *Record* will print anything that sells more papers and attracts more advertisers."

"Anything covers a large area, Miss Prentiss."

"Now you've got it." She might have been talking about her religion, or her lover. "When I bought this sheet from the Van Horn estate it was a typical do-gooder rag, country style. The eternal verities. Elbert Hubbard and those-men-in-the-State House. And before that Frank Lloyd, coming through the rye, the farmer's friend. Lofty sentiments, or personals, never built a moneymaker. Of course, we have to keep it more or less at the ruben level. Folksy writing. Lots of local news and issues. But for expanding circulation give me a nice dirty adultery, a divorce suit with a motel in it, suicide of a big shot, murder of anybody. They call me Lady Muck around here! I don't mind, I love it. Do you know what the circulation of this miserable rural rag had dropped to at the time I took it over? Twenty-eight hundred-odd! Do you know what it is today? Paid circulation?"

Without looking at him, she snapped her fingers at O'Bannon.

"Thirty-two thousand, two hundred and ninety-one," said Francis O'Bannon.

"In a town of ten thousand. Are we magicians? In a way. We muscled into the other guys' territory. Bannock. Slocum. Limpscot. Fyfield. Even Connhaven. We're blanketing the southern part of the county. You ought to see our mail subscription list. And we've only started. Merchants who used to take a thirty-line ad in Lloyd's and Van Horn's day now fight for full pages. Before I'm through the *Wrightsville Record's* going to be the leading newspaper in Wright County, maybe in the State. Next month I start a puzzle contest—ten thousand dollars in prizes. Not bad for a hick sheet. Of course, I have a slight edge over my yokel rivals—I have money and they don't—O'Bannon, why don't you stop me?"

O'Bannon mumbled something.

"Letting me show off this way. Was I awfully girlish?" Malvina Prentiss leaned far back in her chair, eying Ellery. "So you're taking little Rima in hand," she said. "Spec, why didn't we play up this little beauty?"

"We did, Miss Prentiss."

"That back-to-Nature stuff," said the woman impatiently. "Who's interested in a bird-girl? Unless she's got two heads." She looked Rima over. "Darling, where did you get those clothes? I mean, who paid for them?"

"We're wandering," said Ellery. "If you don't know any more about the Anderson case than you've printed, Miss Prentiss—"

"What's your hurry? Do you really think there's real muck in the Anderson disappearance?—I mean, that ties in to MacCaby, Hart, and Dr. Dodd?" Malvina was regarding Ellery speculatively, tapping her teeth with a long silver pencil.

"What I think," said Ellery, "isn't for publication. Rima—"

"Why not?"

"Why not what, Miss Prentiss?"

"Why not for publication? I'd like you to go to work for the *Record*."

"Oh?"

"Run of the case. Give me an exclusive on your investigation. A daily column, say. We'll feature it. The Anderson thing needs a shot in the arm and your name would be a big asset to me right now. It's a cinch to attract the syndicates, too. We'd need a catchy column title . . . Spec!" O'Bannon gave a little leap. "Get into gear. A name for Queen's column."

"*It's Murder*," said O'Bannon mechanically, knitting his salmony brows. "*Queen's Evidence. Queen Quiz. Queen—*"

"Quits," said Ellery.

"Oh, come," snapped Malvina. "You're not that good. I'm not haggling with you, Queen. You can waltz in here pretty much to your own music. You'd have the full facilities of my organization—legmen, stenos, blond or brunette, take your choice, unlimited expense account and no kicks about the bourbon. Your own office, mine if you want it. Set your own figure. I can use you and I'll pay for you. Malvina O. Prentiss is the name—O for Opulent."

"Ellery N. Queen is mine—N for No," said Ellery, taking Rima by the elbow. "Thanks awfully, though," and he guided Rima to the door. Glancing back, he caught Francis O'Bannon in an unguarded pose, gazing after him with admiration and envy.

"If you should change your celebrated mind—" the lady publisher shouted, but the rest was lost in the refined mutter of the editorial rooms.

On Lower Main again Rima made a chest and looked around with relief.

"I know," grinned Ellery. "I need a bath, too."

"But does she really mean all that, Ellery? I've never dreamed there were people like her."

"There aren't, Rima. She's an illusion. The silver motif is symbolism. She comes directly off the screen from her original habitat, which was a book. I confess it with shame—I once invented a character like Malvina myself."

"But I've never read," began Rima with a frown.

"A gap in your cultural education we're going to bridge right now." Ellery led her up the street to Ben Danzig's High Village Rental Library and Sundries. "Your literary background, Miss Anderson, is incomplete without a study of the fictitonal prototype of specimen Malvina Prentiss . . . Hm. Yes. Chandler. Or Cain, or Gardner. Wait here a minute." He went into Ben Danzig's and came out a few minutes later flourishing a crimson-jacketed book. Rima took it wonderingly. "You read this in bed tonight. It's not the purest example of its type—Ben's stock seems to run more to fantasy fiction these days—but it's virile enough to introduce you to the subject."

"But isn't *this* fantasy?"

"My dear child!" said Ellery in an injured tone. "Read the blurb. 'Brute realism'— here, see it?"

"All right," said Rima doubtfully. She tucked the book under her arm.

They stood before Ben Danzig's window, out of the way of the late afternoon crowds. A band of high school girls and boys were chattering outside Al Brown's Ice Cream Parlor next door, making dates for Saturday night at Danceland, in Pine Grove. A few early moviegoers were lined up at the box office of the Bijou. Across the street people were dashing into the post office, Mr. Graycee was standing glumly at the door of his travel agency, J. C. Pettigrew was winding up the awning of his real estate office, girls hurried into the Lower Main Beauty Shop, and the doors of the Five-and-Dime were in continuous motion. Outside the *Record* building a tired-looking mob heaved as a bus placarded SLOCUM TOWNSHIP rounded the corner from the Square for its return trip.

"I can see what you like in it, Ellery," said Rima suddenly. "I wish that . . ." He knew she was thinking of her father.

"You're dragging," he said cheerfully, "and I don't wonder. The Prentiss woman on top of a futile day."

"This morning it looked . . ."

"And then all our shiny images faded out. Hungry, Rima?"

"Yes."

"It's about time. Let's get something to eat and call it a day. Gold Gardens?"

"Oh, no. Some place not so . . . Not Miss Sally's Tea Roome, either." She was trying not to cry.

"How about the Square Grill? That little counter joint around the corner on the Square. Caters to the elk-tooth boys, coffee without saucers, and I once had a surprising steak there."

"Oh, yes!"

As they passed the *Record* building again, Ellery said casually, "It's always this way. You look and look and you find yourself with a lot of nothing for your pains. Till one day you turn a corner and there it is." Her hand tightened on his arm. "I think tomorrow, Rima," he said briskly, "we'll take stock. Since the best position for seeing where you stand is on your back, we'll have to go off somewhere—"

"Ellery!"

"—get away from town."

"Can we?"

"Let's see. We'll need a few trees, a bush or two, and a couple of mossy boulders. Pine needles to lie on, if possible. Oh, and maybe a bit of bubbling water."

"I know just the place," cried Rima.

"Wonderful. Where?"

"I found it once when I was poking around in the hills. Nobody in Wrightsville knows about it."

"How far away is it?"

"Not far at all. But you won't find it on the map. It's mine by right of discovery. I've even given it a name."

"What?"

"Guess!" Rima laughed.

"Nova Rima?"

"Way off."

"Mount Anderson?"

"Try again."

"Of course. Ytaioa."

"That's it!" Rima fairly flew into Mike Polaris's Square Grill.

Tuesday, April 11

The next morning, when Ellery called at Upham House, the desk clerk handed him a note.

> DEAR ELLERY—I couldn't wait. I've paid my bill with your money and gone home. Follow my map.
>
> RIMA
>
> P.S.—Bring a pair of swimming trunks if you feel especially stuffy this morning.

She had sketched a route through Low Village. The shack was indicated by a black X.

Ellery walked down Washington Street, passed Crosstown Avenue—the dividing line between High Village and Low Village—and turned into Plum. Here he sought and found Homer Findlay's garage, whose placard in the Hollis lobby advertised a Drive Urself service. He drove out in a 1939 Plymouth coupé (or "coop," in Homer's version) with 92,000-odd miles on its mileage meter.

Back uptown he found an empty space by a parking meter on Wright Street. He strolled up Washington toward Slocum, searching the shop windows. In the middle of the block he spied PURDY'S—DRY GOODS & FURNISH'GS, and he went in. He purchased two large bath towels.

"Anythin' else today?" asked Mr. Purdy.

Ellery hesitated. He was feeling not the least bit stuffy this morning. On the other hand . . . "Yes," he said firmly. "A pair of swimming trunks."

Mr. Purdy said he didn't have his summer stock in yet, but he might fish out an odd pair . . . He returned with a dusty box which revealed three one-piece swimming suits seasoned with moth crystals. Mr. Purdy held one up.

"Left over from one or two seasons back," he said.

Eying the long limp shanks, Ellery decided that Mr. Purdy's mathematics were at fault and he said no, he didn't think so. Mr. Purdy nodded gloomily.

"Might try the Waldo brothers next door. In the Granjon Block. They're tailors, but ever since Otis Holderfield found himself a gold mine and began toggin' himself out like a movie star, the Waldos been getting ideas—puttin' in bathrobes, sport jackets, what-all . . . talkin' about carryin' a full line of gents' furnishings! Wouldn't surprise me if they got just what you want. Direct from Paris, likely."

There was no reason why the name Waldo in Mr. Purdy's rather bitter accent should have startled Ellery. On the sidewalk, his package of towels under his arm, Ellery stared at the shop next door. It showed evidences of a new prosperity—freshly painted, one window draped elegantly with bolts of men's suiting, the other displaying men's furnishings of apparently good quality. There was a brand-new sign over the front: WALDO BROS. EXCLUSIVE TAILORS. Still, his scalp itched and the backs of his hands were fizzy. As if he were on the verge of a discovery.

Ellery entered the shop. Here prosperity had not yet penetrated: the fixtures were aged and few, the triple mirror was tarnished in streaks, and from what he could see of the workroom in the rear, past the calico curtain, it was dingy and miserably lit.

A very small man in his shirt sleeves, vest covered with snips of thread, a tape measure about his neck, appeared at the curtained doorway. "Yes?" Then he brightened. "Oh, you're the gentleman was in Mr. Holderfield's office yesterday afternoon. Something in a suit?"

Ellery could hear nothing from the workroom. Apparently David Waldo was alone in the shop.

"Would you have a pair of bathing trunks? Mr. Purdy next door said—"

The itch and fizz were really pretty bad. And they seemed to get worse the longer he was in the shop. Or perhaps it was the soft touch of the little tailor's hands as he measured Ellery's waist. What was it?

"We've only just put in this line—"

"Fine. Just what I want. By the way, did you know Tom Anderson?"

"Who? Oh! No, not to talk to. Too bad, the way he went. Got some fine-quality gabardine here—"

"I'm not surprised. I mean, I imagine your clientele is a little more exclusive. Didn't John Spencer Hart get his clothes made here?"

"Wish he had. But Mr. Hart had his tailoring done in Boston, I heard. That camel's hair we're making up for Mr. Holderfield—"

"Maybe you're lucky. Didn't Hart die owing a lot of money? It's a bad habit that partner of his didn't get into, I understand—what was his name again? . . ."

"MacCaby."

"That's it. Wasn't MacCaby the original miser?"

"I wouldn't know. If you're thinking of going swimmin' this early in the year, maybe a beach robe—?"

"Oh, you didn't know MacCaby."

"No. Will that be all?"

"I was saying to Dr. Dodd just the other day—"

Waldo said quickly, "You know Doc Dodd?"

"My, yes. Is he a customer of yours?"

"Say." David Waldo smiled. "If we had to depend on Doc Dodd for a living, we wouldn't stay in business long. Fine man, though. Six ninety-five."

Ellery walked out with the trunks, still tingling.

What was it?

He crossed the street and went into Jeff Hernaberry's Sporting Goods store, where he bought a picnic hamper and a Thermos jug. Then he visited The Delicatessen Caravansary, which lay between Logan's Market and Miss Addie's Anticipation Shop. Here he found food for digestion as well as reflection and when he came out he was weighted. It was all he could do to get back to Homer Findlay's coupé.

After studying Rima's map, Ellery drove down Washington Street into Low Village and turned left into Congress. The map instructed him to follow Congress across town as far as it went.

Congress Street rapidly turned more dilapidated, noisome, and depressing. It paralleled Polly, with the nasty trickle of Willow River between. Here the refuse of Low Village factories floated past the back doors of workmen's barrows. There was an occasional blotch of green, chiefly weeds; there were no trees at all. Yet

Ellery drove slowly. Tom Anderson had taken this route countless times, yawing along its broken walks; how many times had he run aground on the reefs of the jagged asphalt? And along about here was where Abe L. Jackson's younger brother Garrison must have met him that Saturday night when Anderson was presumably sober and headed for his baffling rendezvous on Little Prudy's Cliff. Whom had Rima's father been meeting that night? The answer might lie on this crippled back street behind one of these shaky walls, in the undigested memory of some sodden millhand or his sagging wife or one of his wild children.

Or it might lie in the infinite land of chance. *Nothing personal* . . .

The narrow street came to an abrupt end in a mound of dirt, broken brick, tin cans, and assorted debris. The street fell away in a declivity to a deep gulley which was choked with the accumulated refuse of years. From this gulley rose a stench which turned Ellery pale. The thought of having to wade through its sour fumes on the rickety footbridge which spanned the chasm daunted him. Beyond the bridge stretched a skimpy belt of scrub, rubbish, and wasteland. Behind that glowered The Marshes.

Ellery locked the coupé and put a handkerchief to his nose. He was about to step onto the footbridge when he saw Rima Anderson running from a stand of crazily twisted trees a hundred yards down gulley on the opposite side. She was barefoot and wore a sarong-like garment apparently sewn together from the remains of a man's old suit. She sped across the bridge, hair streaming.

"I've been watching for you."

It seemed to Ellery that she was tense and unhappy. "Anything wrong, Rima?"

"Wrong? Of course not." But there was.

"These Congress Street kiddies look predatory. Is it all right to leave the car while we go over to your place?"

"We're not going to my place."

"What!" Rima walked to the coupé and Ellery followed her, protesting. "But why not, Rima? I want to see it."

"Some other time."

"But only last night you said—"

"Why did you bring a car?"

"So we could go picnicking. Wasn't that the idea?"

"We could have walked. I always do."

"You mean you don't swing through the trees, like Tarzan?"

"Who's Tarzan?"

Ellery told her as he unlocked the car and they got in.

"Oh, a grownup Mowgli." Rima's voice was listless. "I've always loved Baloo and Bagheera. And hated Shere Khan. Turn right into Shingle Street, Ellery. That's Route 478A. You follow it up to just before Twin Hill-in-the-Beeches, then you turn off." She curled up beside him, staring ahead.

This was not humor, or even mood. Something painful had happened this morning. It had arisen on her return to the shack, not before; her Upham House note had told him to come. Was it that after a journey into the world she had come back to see her home for the pitiful hovel it was? Or . . .

He could not overlook the possibility that there might be something darkly different behind it.

He drove along in silence.

After a while Rima squirmed. "I read that book last night."

"Oh? What did you think of it?"

"I laughed. Is that what's known as a detective story?"

"One kind of detective story."

"Detectives aren't that way in life, are they? Kissing or slapping every girl they meet, beating up people, shooting off guns all the time?"

"Most detectives I've known have forty-eight waistlines, chronically sore feet, don't handle a gun from one year to another, and can't wait for the weekend to water their lawns."

"And then that girl Ginger, the one Dave Dirk called 'Gin' and 'Gingivitis'—"

"His secretary."

"She made me tired. Getting into one silly mess after another. And why did she keep calling Dirk 'Chief'? He wasn't a policeman."

"He was her chief."

"Slang," said Rima thoughtfully. "I wondered about that. Do all detectives' secretaries call them Chief?"

"All who have secretaries, I suppose."

"Do you have one?"

"Not at the moment. But then, Rima, I'm not in a book."

"You ought to be!" They both laughed, and the day brightened.

They were in the northeastern part of town now, climbing into the hills above High Village. The name "Shingle Street" on the signs had disappeared. Young cottages roosted above them. And when they rounded a curve, there were Twin Hills' big breasts straight ahead, below which twined the expensive girdle of Twin Hill-in-the-Beeches. Beyond Twin Hill lay exclusive Skytop Road, Wrightsville's newest residential district; and far in the distance nodded the old head of Bald Mountain.

At Rima's instructions Ellery turned the coupé into a narrow dirt road, little more than a firebreak, hacked, pitted, and ungraded. Three miles of this and the road ended at a boulder. As far as Ellery could see, they were walled in by thick forest. There was nothing in sight that resembled a trail except the road behind them.

"What now? Aviation?"

"Just plain walking."

Ellery's recollections of the hour that followed were a flicker of wicked bushes, nettles, emery-barked trees, ground that rolled underfoot; he was stabbed, flogged, and tripped. Rima flitted ahead, slipping by the malignant spirits of the woods as if she carried an aerial immunity. Occasionally she paused to hack a path with a machete-like knife which she carried at the waist of her sarong. At such times he embraced a tree, gasping. At the end of eternity, just as he was about to mutiny, he found himself staggering into the anteroom of paradise.

They were in a small glade which was carpeted with moss and pine needles and guarded on three sides by immense pines, hundred-foot beeches, red spruce, balsam, hemlock, birch, cedar. On the fourth side lay a clear pool. It was fed by a tiny waterfall which came frisking down a sluice of gleaming granite, replenished the pool, and disappeared somewhere in burbly darkness. The sun sparkled on the pool, but in the glade the air was washed and cool and full of wood and earth scents. Birds flashed and chirruped everywhere.

"Ytaioa."

"Like it?"

Ellery lay back on the aromatic carpet and shut his eyes.

He opened them to catch the glint of a brown body splitting the surface of the pool. The knife, the tweedy sarong, lay on an outcropping of rock above the water.

Her head appeared and a wet brown arm came up and grasped the ledge.

"Aren't you coming in?"

"If you'll . . ."

"Oh, piffle."

"Well, damn it all!" began Ellery, but she was gone again, laughing. He got into his swimming trunks behind a modest beech, feeling like a fool.

They splashed and dived and romped in the pool; they dried off on the ledge, Rima disdaining his towel for any purpose whatever so that, in all conscience, he had to close his eyes; and when he awoke Rima was squatting crosslegged—in the sarong—beside one of the towels, on which she had spread the contents of the hamper.

"Come on, Ellery, I'm hungry."

They had a feast in the glade, after which Rima plaited a wreath of vine leaves for his hair while, like a lactic Bacchus, Ellery swigged the last of the milk in the Thermos jug.

"And now if you'll be very still," said Rima, "I'll have some of my friends in for tea. There's the loveliest doe—"

"I'll meet Bambi's ma some other time," said Ellery, lying back. "Make yourself into an audience, Rima. I feel a monologue coming on."

It seemed to him the gladness went out of her; but she stretched out on the moss obediently, her head on his chest.

Ellery blew a smoke ring at the dappled ceiling.

"Rima," he began, "a thing isn't always what it seems. In fact, there have been whole schools of thought whose scholars have insisted that a thing isn't ever what it seems. I choose the middle road: Truth and the appearance of truth. Some things are true, and some things merely seem true when they're not.

"The smart investigator of a crime is always aware of this ambivalence, and it's his job to separate the conflicting elements of a case and put his fingertip on what is true in them and what is false. Some cases are more two-faced than others, and I'm beginning to believe this one bears the stamp of Janus."

"You and Daddy," murmured Rima; and then she was silent, not explaining what she meant. But Ellery thought he knew, and for a moment he squinted at a squirrel racing for his hole, giving Rima time to come back.

"Three deaths," he went on. "Or two and a probable. Luke MacCaby's by heart disease—presumably; John Spencer Hart's by a bullet in his brain—called suicide; your father's in the quicksand below Little Prudy's Cliff—again presumably, and presumably as the result of violence. A great many presumptions. Appearances of truth which may be truth and, on the other hand, may be quite otherwise.

"Now let's follow up the premise laid down by my mysterious correspondent, Anonymous: that the three deaths, or rather the three events, are connected. If they are . . . if they are, is there evidence of the connection? Does some common factor exist in each event? Yes, Dr. Sebastian Dodd. Dr. Dodd proved to be MacCaby's heir. Dr. Dodd became Hart's business associate and, as a result, Hart died in a shooting. And Dr. Dodd presented your father with five thousand dollars a short time before your father's disappearance.

"Truth and the appearance of truth. Either the three events are what they seem, or they're not. Either Dodd, who figures importantly in all of them, is what *he* seems . . . or *he* is not."

Ellery sighted along his nose. Rima's eyes were turned on him, startled. "Dr. *Dodd?*"

"I didn't say Dr. Winship. Why not Dr. Dodd? If all three events are what they seem, they were natural developments of natural means. If the three events are not what they seem, they were unnatural developments of contrived means—in other words, they were criminally brought about. And if we accept Dr. Dodd's story in each instance as being the whole truth, then Dr. Dodd is what he seems, a good and kind and innocent man; and if we do not accept Dr. Dodd's story in each instance as being the whole truth, or part of the truth, or any of the truth, then Dr. Dodd may be the reverse of what he seems: that is, an evil, scheming, guilty man. A criminal, Rima."

"A criminal?"

"There were three deaths," said Ellery. "Or two and a probable."

"A *murderer?*"

Ellery relit his cigaret, which had gone out.

"Be careful of that match!" And Rima took it from him and buried it. Then she said, "But why should Dr. Dodd have murdered Mr. MacCaby? Or Mr. Hart? Or Daddy?"

"Well, let's see," said Ellery. "First MacCaby. Is Dodd what he seems in the MacCaby case—a good, kind, innocent man? Then it's true, as Dodd states, that MacCaby died naturally—that is, of heart disease. Then it's true, as Dodd states, that he, Dodd, was unaware before MacCaby's death of MacCaby's wealth. Then it's true, as Dodd says, that he had no idea that with MacCaby's death he, Dodd, would become a very rich man.

"But suppose Dodd is not what he seems? Suppose he's an evil schemer, cleverly garbing his wickedness in the daily garment of straitened living and good works? Then shortly before his death MacCaby told Dodd he was a wealthy man and that Dodd would inherit MacCaby's wealth. Then Dodd hastened MacCaby's death. How? Dodd was MacCaby's doctor; he was giving the old man certain tablets for his heart ailment. Then Dodd gave MacCaby a rather different box of similar-appearing tablets and, when the next attack occurred and MacCaby took a tablet, MacCaby died. And Dodd, who was called, took back his little box. Truth and the appearance of truth. The two faces of the coin. Look at the obverse and Dr. Dodd is innocence incarnate. Look at the reverse and he may be the devil himself."

"I don't believe it," said Rima. "Not Dr. Dodd."

"Belief has nothing to do with it," said Ellery. "It seems to me I've said that before, but in my line of work you can't afford to forget it. Cover yourself with the other towel if you're cold, Rima. Now let's take up the case of the late John Spencer Hart. Possibility the first: that Dodd is innocent. In this case, as he says, he sent Hart a routine request through Attorney Otis Holderfield for a preliminary accounting of the dye works' financial condition, not suspecting that Hart had embezzled part of the assets of the business. Being unaware that Hart had stolen from the company, Dr. Dodd of course could not have anticipated that his request for an accounting would drive Hart to suicide.

"But—possibility the second: that Dodd is guilty. Suppose MacCaby had told Dodd not only about his riches and Dodd's heir-apparency, but also about one other matter. Because if MacCaby was shrewd enough to invest in a business that proved as successful as the Wrightsville Dye Works, and if MacCaby was as canny in money matters as his pennypinching indicated, then he may well have kept an eye cocked on his partner and found his own way of checking on Hart's management of the Works. Then suppose MacCaby told Dr. Dodd that he knew of Hart's wild gambling sprees, his reckless speculation, his embezzlement. In this case, once he had murdered MacCaby, Dodd would have known that his request for an accounting before Hart could cover his tracks might well come to Hart as a deathblow. This is a close-knit community and the character and personality of a man as prominent as Hart must have been common knowledge. So Dodd must have known that John Spencer Hart could not take exposure, disgrace, social ostracism; that to a man like Hart the prospect of trial, conviction, imprisonment was intolerable. So, if Dodd is guilty and has been lying about his actual relationship with Hart, his request for an accounting became as murderous a weapon as the gun which ended Hart's life."

"He drove Mr. Hart to suicide?"

"Only on the face of the coin we're considering. And then—your father's disappearance." Ellery scowled. "Obverse: that Dodd is innocent. In that case, as he says, he gave your father five thousand dollars to help rehabilitate a man who needed and wanted rehabilitation. A kind, a generous, a magnificently unselfish act.

"But on the reverse, with Dodd lying . . . Suppose your father, Rima, had stumbled on some evidence that connected Dodd criminally with Luke MacCaby's death. For example, the pillbox which should have contained heart tablets. We've surmised, if Dodd gave MacCaby a lethal box of tablets, that Dodd took the box away after MacCaby died. But suppose your father got to that box first? He was a friend of Harry Toyfell's; he might well have been *persona grata* in the MacCaby house; a fortuitous visit, and something about MacCaby's death may have excited his suspicious. Since he was an intelligent man, suspicion would lead him to the tablets. And there we have Tom Anderson in possession of the evidence which could send Sebastian Dodd to the electric chair. In this case Dodd's investment in your father's rehabilitation may not have been entirely altruistic. In fact, it may have been—impure and simple—hush money."

"Blackmail?" What he saw in Rima's eyes made him study an arrangement of branches overhead. "You mean my father blackmailed Dr. Dodd? Is that what you mean?"

"We're only theorizing, Rima. A lot of ifs stand between the theory and the fact."

"I *don't* believe it!"

"In the end, your faith will probably triumph. I certainly hope it does. But at this stage of the game, Rima, we've got to stick to reason. And reason points to blackmail as one face of this particular coin.

"Let's look at it for another moment.

"Tom Anderson has demanded five thousand dollars for not turning the box of tablets over to Chief Dakin, and Dr. Sebastian Dodd has paid it. Some weeks pass. And there's Tom Anderson again, with a demand for more—no, Rima, listen. Blackmail is a disease which manifests itself in recurrent attacks. It's an insatiable hunger. A second demand is inevitable if you postulate a first and a reason for the first.

"Now the victim of a blackmailer has three courses open to him: He can continue to pay, he can refuse to pay, or he can so arrange matters that he has to do neither. If Tom Anderson made a second demand so soon after his first, Dr. Dodd would be far less intelligent than he actually is if he did not get a grim preview of the future . . . demands at increasing frequency, perhaps increasing demands, and continued over as many years as were left to him or as he submitted meekly to the squeeze. This is a prospect that attracts no guilty man, most particularly one who has other plans for his money. But suppose Dodd refused to pay the second time. Anderson might take his evidence to the police; the threat of exposure is the blackmailer's weapon. In this case exposure meant death. Defiance was therefore out of the question. That left the third way."

"Murder."

"According to this set of premises, the conclusion seems to follow that Sebastian Dodd arranged to meet your father at Little Prudy's Cliff that night, presumably to hand over another payment for silence, actually to push him over the edge."

Rima sat up, shivering. She looked so forlorn sitting there, so cold and bloodless and abandoned, that Ellery sat up too and put his arms around her.

"Remember, none of this may be true."

"And all of it may be true."

"Well," said Ellery, "yes."

Rima said passionately, "And maybe I don't want to hear any more 'truth'!"

"Maybe the decision, Rima, is no longer in your hands." She twisted out of his embrace, resting far back on her heels, staring at him. "Once you take this kind of beast by the tail, you can't let go. *I* can't let go. Are you going to walk out on me?"

She dropped her glance to the moss. "I'd like to."

"Run away?"

"Yes. But I won't. You know I couldn't."

"I was hoping you couldn't. All right, then." Ellery got to his feet, tossing the wreath of vine leaves away. "Our job is to eliminate one of the two sets of possibilities. We've got to establish as a fact what Dodd is."

"How would you go about doing a thing like that?"

"The proper study of Dodd is Dodd. He's got to be watched, investigated, interpreted. If evidence exists—one way or the other—it has to be found. One of us, Rima, has to get into that Victorian antique on the corner of Wright and Algonquin and stay there. You're indicated."

"That's why you said yesterday—!'

"My assistant. In the most romantic Dave Dirk tradition. I'll even call you Gingivitis. And, in time, I'll probably get used to your calling me Chief."

But Rima failed to smile in return. "I never should have come to you. What you want is a spy and a lady liar. I'm sure I haven't the talent to be either. And it all seems so silly. Just on the mathematical chance . . . Ellery, I don't think I could do it."

"Then don't. I'll find another way."

"You're angry with me."

"Not at all."

"You are. You think it's because of . . . Dr. Winship, or something."

"Isn't it?"

"No!"

"It's really too bad," said Ellery, "because Winship's the chink in Dodd's armor. I mean, the way he went for you—"

"Went for me? Where?'

"I forgot, yours is a classical education. Succumbed to your charms."

"You're reading so much into—"

"And that beautiful Pinkle situation. Made to order. Well, forget it. Help me pack up, Rima, will you? Or do you want another plunge before we go? It's getting kind of chilly."

"I didn't say I wouldn't do it."

"Plunge?"

"Be your spy. It's just that . . ."

"It's so hard—I know, darling. Murder is a hard business. And smelling it out is even harder. The Thermos jug?"

Rima drifted somehow to her feet. Like a snowflake in reverse. She looked miserably about to dwindle and vanish. "Ellery, what do you want me to do?"

Ellery failed to feel triumphant. He said carelessly, "Be my eyes, ears, and legs. It's ten to one when I get back to the hotel I'll find a message from Winship saying he's arranged everything on the Gloria Pinkle business to Dr. Dodd's satisfaction and that the job of office assistant is yours. If I'm wrong, I'll do some more spadework on it. But I'll work you in, Rima. Leave that to me."

"And when I get in?"

"Watch for a chance to look over Dodd's records on Luke MacCaby, his personal papers. Listen to what he says and to whom he says it. Find out from Winship—without giving yourself away—everything about Dodd that you can which may tie in with what we're hunting for. And report to me whatever you run across. No matter how little it seems to mean." Ellery said gently, "Don't worry about Winship. He's intense, and lonely, and I'm being very generous to him."

Rima smiled. "And to me?"

Ellery flushed. "There's a larger ethic. I'll discuss it with you sometime. You've got to stop wearing your heart on your sleeve, Rima. Are you in love with him?"

"Love?"

"Your poets' glibbest word—"

"I don't know what love is. I've only seen him once."

"Yes," said Ellery. "Bear that in mind." And for a moment he looked like a man who has lost something. But only for a moment. "At this point, baby, Dave Dirk usually grabs his doll, gets a half nelson on her, plants a few cynical smacks on her perfect mouth, and sends her off with a slap on the rump to the villain's lair, so that ten pages later he can stroll in and cuff her from the jaws of somebody else's lust. Ready?"

"Ellery, don't be silly."

"You don't seem to get the point, babe. You *never* use my first name." Ellery hissed, "Got that straight, Gingivitis?"

This time she laughed. "Got you, Chief."

"With more humility."

"Chief."

"Yes. And don't forget who is."

"Who is what?"

"Head man."

"Oh, you are, Chief."

"I doubt it." And Ellery looked so woebegone that Rima laughed and laughed, in a hysterical way.

Ellery picked Rima up at 7:30 that night at the Congress Street end of the footbridge. She was again dressed in her New York finery and she was leaning against the peeling guardrail beyond the cairn of refuse surrounded by admiring children.

Rima shooed them off and got into Homer Findlay's car quickly.

"Well?"

"I thought we'd run down Slocum way for dinner, Rima," said Ellery. "Barred Rock Inn. What's the shortest way from here?"

"South on Shingle for five blocks and then east on the Old Low Road and across the railroad tracks to Route 478. But I didn't mean that. I meant . . ."

"The Dodd thing?" Ellery backed and shifted, dispersing the wild seed of the underprivileged. "Why, I won my bet."

"He'd called." She sat back, letting her breath out.

"He?"

"All right. Dr. Winship."

"Only three times. I was a little disappointed in him."

"What did he say?"

"Miss Gloria Pinkle is no longer associated with Doctors Dodd and Winship. It seems she's been secretly married to Rafe Landsman for about ten days and hasn't had the nerve to tell anybody, much to Mr. Landsman's dismay. They've been honeymooning in parks. Dr. Dodd sent her off with four weeks' salary, his goodman's blessing, and an order on Myers & Manadnock, Jewelers, Hill Village's 'Gemporium,' for a hundred-and-fifty-dollar set of silver. You're hired in Gloria's place. Salary, thirty-five dollars per week, board and room. That last," said Ellery, guiding the Plymouth warily over the uncertain boards of the Willow River bridge, "I'm rather proud of."

"I'm to live there? I couldn't!"

"And let's have no more of the caged bird routine. You'll live there and you'll like it."

"Yes, Chief." Her laughter was candid joy.

"It's very nearly the whole point. Actually, it was no feat; Dr. Winship did it almost unassisted. He agreed instantly that a girl who's alone in the world, an innocent and inexperienced girl who has nowhere to live but a shanty, and who owes a New York sharper some hundreds of dollars, needs both a respectable home and the opportunity to save as much of her earnings as possible so that she can get out of the fellow's clutches. It's all painfully proper; Dr. Winship repeated that, as if I were a suspicious relative."

"Aren't you?" Rima was giggling.

"Mrs. Fowler and Essie are there to chaperon you. I'm triply assured that there will be a lock on your chamber door, aud your evenings are strictly your own." Ellery honked at the intersection, not looking at her. Giggling! He turned left into a narrow macadamized road which badly needed repaving. "Is this the Old Low Road?"

"Yes . . . I didn't think I'd have to live there."

"Adjust, adjust. You start tomorrow morning at eight. Dr. Winship is calling for you in his car."

"No. All right."

"Be where I just picked you up. At 7:45 . . . Oh, don't be flattered. Dr. Winship told me he picked Gloria Pinkle up on her first morning, too. A sort of standard office courtesy—"

"All *right*."

"Chief."

"Chief!"

Ellery scrutinized her uneasily during dinner. Rima was brilliant. She flashed, trilled, chattered.

Wednesday–Thursday,
April 12–20

Early on Wednesday afternoon, after a morning of coffee-nursing in the Hollis
Coffee Shoppe, *Record*-reading, chair-warming in the lobby, haircutting in Joe
Lupin's chair in Luigi Marino's Hollis Hotel Tonsorial Parlor, pavement-clumping
through High Village—even book-hunting in the Carnegie Library on State Street;
Dolores Aikin failed to recognize him from her sentrybox, and he was obscurely
grateful—Ellery finally permitted himself a telephone call.

It was Rima who answered, and she sounded professional and secretive. Oh,
yes, she was getting along just beautifully. Dr. Winship had been very helpful. He
had spent an hour with her at the very beginning (over breakfast and later) explaining
about the sterilizers and the routine with patients and so on, and then he had had
to go to the hospital, but he'd found time to dash back well before office hours to
take her over to the Square for a more appropriate office outfit than the Fifth Avenue
suit; because of the diphtheria epidemic the Bon Ton was featuring nurses' nylon
uniforms and she'd felt almost like the real thing. They dried in three hours, you
know, and didn't have to be ironed . . . and, yes, flat-heeled white shoes and white
stockings and . . . Ellery said something snide, about not recalling Gloria Pinkle,
Miss Anderson's predecessor, in such trained attire, or did the nylon uniform come
with a plunging neckline, and did Winship pay for it?—but Rima laughed in his
ear and said not to be silly, *you* paid for it, or rather I did with your money, which
I'm going to start paying back next week, Dr. Winship had wanted to but I wouldn't
let him. How cosy, said Ellery, at which Rima stopped laughing and said coldly
he needn't be cynical, given half a chance people were human beings in the best
sense, anxious to be friendly and even to extend themselves—even old Harry Toyfell
had said an encouraging word this morning and Mrs. Fowler had given her the
freedom of the icebox and shown her into the loveliest old-fashioned bedroom,
ever so much nicer than the patriotic stereotypes at Upham House . . . in fact, she
had learned a great deal today about life. Yes, said Ellery, no doubt you have, but
have you learned—? But Rima, either because she was not alone or for some
perverse female reason, refused to talk business and instead she said she wouldn't
have the least bit of trouble, except possibly with the typing, and Dr. Dodd was
so nice, though she'd only seen him once before office hours, in the morning as
he was leaving for the hospital, and . . . Dinner? Well, she'd try. Dr. Winship had
mentioned . . . Anyway, her first day . . . And then the Pinkle girl had left things
in such a mess, and she simply had to spend some extra time familiarizing herself
with the filing system—"Yes, Dr. Winship! Goodbye, Ellery," and Ellery was
left holding the receiver.

He tried her again at 6:30. But when Essie Pingarn said Miss Anderson was eatin' with Dr. Winship, Ellery said never mind, to tell her Uncle Ellery had called, and he hung up.

He waited in his room at the Hollis until almost 10 o'clock.

The next day was equally unsatisfactory. He could get nothing out of her over the phone beyond a certain tarnishing of tone, as if the glitter of newness had worn off and she did not quite know how to rub it shiny again. At 5:30 he was in Dr. Dodd's house.

Rima was alone in the waiting room. She was tapping painfully away at the typewriter keys with a puffy forefinger. She looked ill.

"The mountain comes to Fatima. Anything wrong?"

She said quickly, "I couldn't very well talk to you over the phone . . ."

"How's it going, Rima?"

"The work? All right."

"I don't mean the work." He did not bother to lower his voice; from where he was standing, he could see Harry Toyfell watering the front lawn, and Essie and Mrs. Fowler were arguing in the rear somewhere. The doctors' offices were empty. "Found anything?"

"No."

"Have you looked?"

"No!"

"I thought something of the sort was going on," said Ellery. "Well, Rima, what do you suggest?"

"Ellery, I can't."

"Can't what?"

"Sneak. Open drawers like a thief."

Ellery said softly, "Anybody would think I was Fagin. Certainly I don't have to go over the whole bloody works again. Have you overheard anything?"

"No . . ."

"Get anything out of Winship?"

She did not reply.

Ellery pursed his lips. "Rima, I'll tell you what I'm going to do."

"I'm sorry, Ellery."

"I'm going back to New York."

She was silent.

"This is the only course I can plot, and if you can't follow it I'm helpless." He took her hand. "I don't blame you, Rima. It's very hard. And I've been something of a brute. If you change your mind, write me. Better still, phone. Give me a piece of paper . . . Here's my phone number."

She began to cry.

Ellery stood over her for a few moments, feeling angry and incompetent.

Then he tousled her hair as if she were a child and he went back to the Hollis and checked out.

He was back in Wrightsville at her summons a week later. As soon as he had dropped his suitcase in Room 835 at the Hollis he picked up the phone.

"Ellery." She sounded cool and perfect, as if wrapped in a secret. Not at all the way she had sounded long distance.

"Shall I pick you up?"

"Don't bother. I'll meet you in the Square Grill at 7 o'clock."

"All right."

He was sampling Mike Polaris's coffee when Rima walked in. He was surprised, although he told himself he shouldn't have been. Of course she couldn't live in that one suit. She was wearing a skirt made of burlap and a bolero of the same astounding material; the blouse was Lachine's.

"It's the latest thing." She laughed, slipping onto the next stool. "Didn't you know?"

"Burlap?"

"Al Hummel says it's being featured by *Vogue*. Al's Dress Shop, on Slocum, next door to Jeff Hernaberry's Sporting Goods store. Five dollars down and the rest in weekly payments. I had to get a number of things. And by the way." She laid a small envelope on the counter.

"What's this?" Her hair was done differently, too. Lower Main Beauty Shop, no doubt.

"First installment on my debt."

"Rima—"

"No."

"All right." He pocketed it and ordered two steaks. Then he said, "Well?"

"It isn't much. I don't know if it's anything." She was rummaging in her bag, but not as if she were looking for something. "I've been through the files."

"MacCaby?"

"I couldn't find anything wrong. Unless a gun—"

"Where?"

"In D's office desk. I didn't touch it."

"Most doctors up here have them. How about personal stuff? Did you get a peek?"

"Yes, but there's nothing there, I'm sure. He has a study at the rear of the house downstairs—I've managed to look there. None of his drawers is locked."

"Is there a safe in the study?"

"I don't think so. Not one you can see anyway."

"Get anything out of K.W.?"

"Only that he's worried about Dr. Dodd."

"Why?"

"Because Dr. Dodd is so worried. Ken—" it came out easily—"Ken can't put his finger on the cause. The physical symptoms, he says, are all those of a man on the verge of a nervous collapse. But Dr. Dodd won't talk about it, gets very angry, says it's just nerves and overwork. He won't take a vacation or see a neurologist."

But that's of long standing, thought Ellery. Those twitches didn't develop overnight. "It's more than that, Rima."

She knew what he meant. She was staring at the counter, twisting her fork. "Yes. I think it has something to do with that room on the top floor, though I didn't tell Kenneth so."

"Room on the top floor?"

"On the attic floor. Dr. Dodd won't allow anyone in there. Not even Mrs. Fowler or Essie to clean up. He keeps it locked and there's only one key. At the end of his watch chain."

Ellery smiled. "Bluebeard?"

"I told you it was probably nothing." Mike slammed the steaks down and Rima began to eat, slowly.

"Does he visit the room often?"

"Once a day."

"Really? Every day?"

"Yes, in the mornings. It's the first thing he does after he dresses. He unlocks the door, goes in, and locks it after him."

"How long does he stay usually?"

"Sometimes only a few minutes, sometimes longer. It's never very long, though. Then he comes out, locks the door, and goes downstairs to breakfast. Essie told me about it. So I watched."

"Mrs. Fowler doesn't know what's in the room?"

"No."

"Winship? Have you discussed it with him?"

"I couldn't very well without explaining how I knew. And he's never mentioned it. I don't think he knows about it."

They ate in silence.

Finally Ellery said, "And how are you coming along, Rima? Are you happy there?"

"Well, I miss the outdoors, but . . ." She put her hand on his arm. "I'm sorry I brought you out here for nothing. I didn't know, Ellery. But you said—"

"It wasn't for nothing."

"You think it's important?"

"Yes."

"But what can it mean?"

"I don't know. Rima, that room has to be inspected."

She went quite pale. After a moment she said, "All right, I'll try. But I don't know how . . . and the key . . ."

"No," said Ellery. "That's my department."

Friday, April 21

Ellery's department began functioning the next morning. He walked over to Algonquin Avenue shortly after 11. Harry Toyfell was manuring the lawn. The man did not look up.

"Morning. Doc Dodd in?"

"Don't ye see his car over there?" Toyfell straightened, resting the heavy bag on his hip. "Long as you're here . . ." he said slowly. "Find out anything about Tom Anderson?"

"Nothing conclusive, Toyfell. I don't suppose you've run across anthing?"

But the man was back at his manure scattering.

Ellery found Rima and Dr. Winship with their heads together over a stack of case cards. Through the doorway of Dr. Dodd's office he could see Dodd getting into his white office coat. Ellery thought Rima and young Winship jumped rather too quickly; there was a slight flush on Winship's face.

"Rima said you were back," he said, shaking hands. "She's missed you."

"I've missed her, Dr. Winship. But then I probably haven't been as busy as you people. Hello, Dr. Dodd."

The burly man had come in with his surprising stride. He was looking wretched. The twitches were continuous and his jowls had a steady underswell. But he sounded genial.

"Busy. We can barely keep supplied with diphtheria toxoid. Giving Schick inoculations all over the place and not getting too much sleep, I'm afraid. This little girl has been just fine, Mr. Queen. Wonderful help to Kenneth and me."

Rima went scarlet and disappeared in Dr. Winship's office with some cards.

"I was kind of surprised when Rima said you'd gone back to New York, Mr. Queen. Thought you'd given up."

"No," said Ellery, and he primed his big gun. "It's hotels, Dr. Dodd."

"Hotels?"

"Can't stand 'em longer than a night or two. Anything beyond that is insomniac torture. I'm not as lucky this time as I've been. On most of my visits to Wrightsville I've been able to avoid staying in a hotel—generally managed to bed down with some private family. But I haven't seen Hermy Wright or the Foxes for years, and of course the Van Horns . . ."

He saw at once that he had misfired. Dr. Dodd's tormented eyes blinked rapidly and he said, "Oh. That's too bad," in a vague way and immediately went on to ask, "Then you haven't got very far in your investigation of Tom Anderson's disappearance?"

"Haven't got anywhere. Well, Doctor, I won't take any more of your time—"

"No, no, Mr. Queen. Does me good to see a foreigner once in a while—"

"Seeing that he's so crazy about your company, Mr. Queen," grinned Dr. Winship, "maybe you can talk him into knocking off for a couple of days. Doc, why don't you run up to Lake Pharisee?"

"This early in the year? Rot, Kenneth."

"What's at Lake Pharisee?" asked Ellery, as if he didn't know.

"It's north of Quetonokis Lake, Mr. Queen—high up in the Mahoganies," said Dr. Dodd. "Summerin' place. Lots of us have summer cabins up there. If it was the fishing season . . ."

"You could open the cabin, Doc," argued Dr. Winship. "Get her ready."

"No, Kenneth—"

"Must be beautiful up there this time of year," said Ellery. "Especially having the whole place to yourself . . . Couldn't you get away, Dr. Dodd? I'd like to invite myself to a day's work with an axe."

"Would be sort of a change," muttered the doctor. "But I don't see how the hospital, clinic, my patients . . ."

"For a couple of days?" cried his young associate. "Who do you think you are, God? If necessary, I'll get Walter Flacker to pitch in—he's mildewing up in that rarefied Hill office of his, anyway. I'm not worried about your patients Doc. Suppose you dropped dead from overwork? What good would you be to them then?"

It seemed to Ellery that Dr. Dodd's vital machinery sputtered and stopped. For just a moment.

It was curious how yellow he got and how quickly he took hold of himself.

But perspiration stippled his bald skull and Ellery knew he would have at least one day in which to make a proper study of Dr. Sebastian Dodd.

Saturday, April 22

Rima lay on the overstuffed waiting-room couch in the three-quarter darkness. A golden clear youth's voice was singing something tender and longing in a queer language to the accompaniment of a native stringed instrument and beside her, through the song, she could hear Kenneth Winship breathing in masculine rhythm to the music and feel the still heat of his hand on her ankle, like a minor sun, strengthening but full of fiery danger. She did not know what time it was; she supposed it was close to midnight, and it was Saturday night, but what was time? A way of spacing things that happened, and she was in no statistical mood tonight. The day had been too full of pain and flushed faces, whistling breaths, high temperatures, submissive people at the clinic, the hiss of the sterilizer, the croak of sick children. She was so exhausted that she felt lightheaded. Or perhaps it was that odd antique music.

Or the burning place on her ankle.

The voice stopped and the heat lifted as she felt and heard him get up from the couch. The record was scratching away in the living room across the hall and she saw his big figure cross under the dim night light in the hallway chandelier and get lost in the darkness beyond. A moment later the scratching stopped and then it began again. The same golden young voice accompanied by the same childish instrument was lifted in a grave and fervid plea of some sort; and Dr. Winship came back across the hall and took his place again.

"What was that, Ken?" Rima murmured.

"An Italian ballade of the fourteenth century. Remember the *Decameron?* Boccaccio's young rakes who fled the plague of the city and found so much time on their hands in the country? That was one of the songs they sang to the accompaniment of the viol."

"And this?"

" 'Gloria in Cielo.' Same period. It's rather different, isn't it?"

"Yes."

Yes, thought Rima. This is all proper things and the other had been, had been . . . She felt her hand taken and she made a convulsive movement, half sitting up.

And suddenly he was saying the most absurd things. She heard his voice and she knew what the words meant but none of them seemed real; it was like the language of the ballade singer, incomprehensible but clear as the sun on leaping water, full of turbulent things in a dream.

"I loved you the second I saw you, Rima. I knew I couldn't ever really be satisfied again unless you were in the same room. I'm a clumsy ox and you're so little and wonderful, but I'll try I'll try awfully hard, Rima, so awfully hard, Rima . . ."

And she was saying as the record went round and his voice went round, "I love you, Ken, I love you. I don't know what love is but whatever it is I'm full to the brim and it's all for you, darling, it's been that way since . . ."

And then only the record went round and round, although things in Rima's head seemed to be doing it too in the same sweet unbearable rhythm.

It was hours or years later when the light sprang up in the living room across the hall and Rima heard Dr. Dodd's voice saying, "Funny, this record on. Where's everybody?" But now time was spacing things again and she found herself on her feet, the backs of her legs bracing her against the couch, and Ken's big hand steadying her and his voice saying, "It's all right, dearest. Just Doc and Queen back from Pharisee." And then the light came on in the waiting room and there were Dr. Dodd and Ellery in the doorway, startled and aware in the same moment; and everything was over.

Later, they sat around in the darkened living room, the three men and Rima, talking about the miracle and making plans for its consecration, and it was a very happy time. Or so it seemed to Rima. She leaned against Ken's shoulder content to drift and listen, not thinking of her father or the dark colors of her recent trouble, only wishing that Ellery would talk less and Ken more, so that she could keep hearing his voice. But Ellery was all over the place. Now he was telling about the day's outing and what a cunning old woodsman Dr. Dodd was, and all the time he chattered he avoided looking at Rima, so that gradually she became conscious of his avoidance and some of the joy went out of things.

When suddenly he broke off, Rima thought he was being very erratic and she began to laugh; but when Ken put his hand over her mouth she felt a little thrill of alarm.

"Did you hear that, Ken?" asked Ellery in an undertone.

"A window. At the back of the house somewhere."

"Funny," said Dr. Dodd.

They listened again.

This time Rima heard it. A creaky window was being slowly opened. There was a squeak, then silence, then another squeak, then another silence.

"Burglars?" asked Rima facetiously.

But no one smiled. Dr. Dodd got up.

"Doc, where you going?"

"I'll be right back." He passed quickly under the night light in the hall and disappeared in the darkness of the waiting room.

"What the devil," muttered Kenneth Winship.

Dr. Dodd recrossed the hall. Something was glinting in his right hand.

"Oh, no, you don't. Doc, give me that!"

"Kenneth—"

"For heaven's sake. You'd probably shoot yourself with it." The younger man took the revolver. "Now, Doc, there's nothing to be afraid of." Dr. Dodd's teeth were actually rattling. Ken put his hand on the burly man's arm. "Now, Doc," he said. The little sounds stopped and Ellery heard Dodd mumble something. "You all stay here—"

"No!" whispered Rima.

"Don't . . . leave me," said Dr. Dodd with some difficulty.

Ken was already in the hall. Rima flew after him.

Dr. Dodd began to shake again.

"It's all right, Doctor," said Ellery. He took the man's arm; it was rigid as wood. "We'll trail along. There's no danger. Ken's had army training." Of course, Winship was right. The day in the woods had told Ellery only one thing: Sebastian Dodd lived in a monster-infested jungle, the prey of—what? Ellery did not know.

Ken was at a door at the rear of the hall, listening, Rima against the wall. Ken looked back; Ellery nodded toward the hall chandelier and, still gripping Dr. Dodd's arm, moved over and touched the switch button.

In the darkness, Dr. Dodd's breath whistled a tune.

The door at the other end of the hall crashed open and there was a streak of light from the room beyond, wheeling in a surprised arc, then a blaze as Ken's left hand sprang into view against an invisible wall, fixed on a light switch.

And they heard Ken say, "Hold it, you," quietly.

Ellery ran up the hall, brushed by Rima, stopped.

The room was a study, with an old mission desk and chair and a black leather couch and mission bookcases and two windows beyond, one of which was open to the night. Several of the desk drawers were open and in one of them a large dirty hand was caught while the other gripped a flashlight. Behind loomed the bulk of Nicole Jacquard.

"Jacquard, what do you think you're doing?" asked Ken.

The man's tongue came out of hiding, darted in again.

"What," asked Ellery, "were you looking for?"

But Jacquard only glared.

"Nick." Dodd's voice. Shaking. "Did I ever send you a bill for Emilie's operation? For saving little André's leg? For delivering your wife of your last three children? Is this the way you pay me back, Nick?"

Jacquard said nothing. The glassy eyes were hunting.

"You won't get anything out of him," said Rima. "He knows only two things, drinking and stealing. Not even my father could do anything with him." All of the past was in her voice.

Jacquard moistened his lips again.

"Queen, take this gun and cover him," said Ken Winship. "While I get some rope to tie those hams of his—"

That'll teach you never to take your eyes off a cornered man, Ellery thought as he flung his arms up and backward, bowling Rima over and doubling up Dr. Dodd. And then he was sprawled on both of them, covering them with his body. At the slight turn of Winship's head Jacquard had sprung with animal agility, his paws flashing for the gun. The two men went down with a crash, Ken hanging on to the weapon. There was no time for Ellery to help; he jumped backward against Rima and the older doctor as Jacquard leaped; they all struck the floor at the same instant. And immediately after there was a shot, and all motion stopped.

For a moment the two men lay entangled.

Then Rima screeched, clawing her way from under Ellery just as he lunged toward the antagonists.

He felt the warm blood on his hand as he pulled.

"Ken!" Rima screamed. Then she cried joyfully, "It wasn't Ken! It wasn't Ken!"

Everything on Ken's face was straining to open wider. Ellery pulled him to his feet. He tried to pull away, staring down at Nick Jacquard. But Ellery said, "No, Ken, no. Let Dr. Dodd do it."

Dr. Dodd looked up after a while, his face alive with some mysterious yeast. "He's dead."

"Dead?" said Ken in an outraged voice.

"In the heart, Kenneth. He's dead."

"I killed him."

"Darling, he was fighting you for the gun," said Rima rapidly, holding on to him. "We all saw it. It's not your fault, Ken. We all saw it."

"I killed a Jerry once. In Italy. Big bruiser. Big as Jacquard. He spun around like a ballet dancer and then his knees buckled and he fell on his face and lay there on his knees with his behind in the air like a praying Arab. Dead?"

"Get him out of here," muttered Ellery to Dr. Dodd and Rima. "Doctor, give him something. Keep telling him it wasn't his fault. Go on, now! I've got to phone Dakin."

Chief of Police Dakin, who had been decently in bed, was there by 1:45 A.M. and Prosecutor Chalanski, who had been at a party on Skytop Road, did not arrive until 2:15—which was a valuable lesson, said Chalanski, for the good shall inherit the headaches—"though talking about headaches . . . what was *in* those Manhattans? . . . this doesn't promise much of one at all, eh, Queen?"—and the prosecutor of Wright County shook hands limply, adding that crime seemed to follow Ellery around like a bill collector and prompting Ellery to mumble that he rather thought— at least he hoped—it was the other way around.

No one, with the interesting exception of Harry Toyfell seemed to take the death of The Town Thief very seriously, at least in a social sense. Ken was immersed in his own psychological troubles; Rima was immersed in Ken; Essie Pingarn, who flew downstairs in tight rag curlers and a surprisingly elegant quilted bathrobe covered with big red roses, fainted and, on being revived by Dr. Dodd, immersed herself in the roaring waters of her faith; Mrs. Fowler, pale but showing the iron of her Puritan genes, bustled about with pots of coffee, fumbling with the control box of her earpiece and saying that the Lord had His own way of punishing shiftlessness and sin; Dr. Dodd turned very nearly cheerful, joking with Chief Dakin about his gun license, telling stories of other gunshot deaths in his experience, and generally being—not altogether to Ellery's surprise, for he had seen men falsely bucked up by death before—a tower of strength; and Dakin and Chalanski handled Jacquard as if he were a card in a file. As for Harry Toyfell, he appeared like some medieval monk in a long earthcolored bathrobe and tattered carpet slippers and took his place over the hulk of his old crony, now a total wreck, with a hardbitten stoicism. Toyfell slept in a room above the garage, which was to the rear of the house and had once been a coach house; he had shuffled through the rear garden and the earth crumbs on his carpet slippers were very near his friend's dead face.

"No, I sleep hard," he replied to Prosecutor Chalanski, "Didn't hear a thing till your siren woke me up."

"Better for Jacquard if you had, maybe," remarked Dakin.

But Toyfell shook his head. "He'd got in a bad mess one way or 'nother," he said. "Nick was an angry man," he said. "All his life he was lost and couldn't find his way out."

"Well, he's found it now," said Chalanski with a laugh, turning away.

Toyfell remained out of everyone's way, near the body.

Malvina Prentiss descended out of space with a flash. Ellery got to the window just in time to witness her landing in a rocket-shaped convertible, its iridescent silver paint reflecting the amazed street lights. Dakin's men had roped off the area before the Dodd house; beyond pressed a crowd; and they were all gaping, police included, at the silver monster. Apparently, like Chalanski, the publisher had been to a party: she was half-dressed in a silver lamé evening gown of Polynesian *décolletage* and a billowing evening cape of some other silvery material; and as she sailed up the walk pulling Francis O'Bannon along in her airstream, she looked about as indigenous to Wrightsville as a Venusian warlord. O'Bannon, at least had been to no Saturday night social. He needed a shave, his neat Boston suit was rumpled, the laces of one shoe dragged. If he looked surly and rebellious, it was only in transit. By the time they were in the house he had a pad and pencil out and was trotting after his employer with not a shirttail of independence showing.

Miss Prentiss was there, it seemed, to see justice done.

When the facts were presented to her—Chalanski was gracious and tumblehaired, as befitted a man nuzzling a Congressional candidacy and counting on his boy-of-the-people personality to get over to the electorate by way of the press—Miss Prentiss's highborn nostrils quivered as if she detected the odor of corruption and she demanded an interview "with the murderer of this poverty-stricken father of twelve orphaned children." Mayhem, in the small person of one Rima Anderson, was averted by the gentleman from New York. That authority pointed out with a smile that the shooting was accidental and wholly the result of the dead man's own folly, and that any attempt on the part of the *Record* to needle public sentiment against Dr. Winship in advance of the inquest would be cynical, unjust, prejudicial, and a damned dirty piece of xanthous journalism, and how are you again, Miss Prentiss? Miss Prentiss laughed and so the disagreeable incident was squashed, threatening to arise again only once, when Harry Toyfell said thoughtfully: "Man who expects truth from a newspaper would look for mercy from a Japanese beetle."

When Miss Prentiss finally took off in a puff of silver, trailed by her exhaust, Mr. O'Bannon, with his padful of curlicues and pothooks, everyone drew an extra breath.

They were all accountably sober as two men from Duncan's Funeral Parlors packed Nicole Jacquard off for temporary safekeeping and the pleasure of Coroner Grupp and a jury of Dr. Winship's peers, Dr. Dodd mumbling something about having to see what could be done for Jacquard's widow and children. Harry Toyfell shuffled after the undertaker's men as far as the elm on the front lawn. His long face was set in a deep and monkish wisdom.

Dakin conferred with Chalanski and the prosecutor said that it would not be necessary to put Dr. Winship to the nastiness of cell detention until the inquest; he could be booked for the record and released on his own recognizance until the hearing. So they all went out to the cars.

Ellery's ascent into Dr. Dodd's decrepit vehicle was accomplished not without a groan or two, for he was feeling a dragging weariness. Nothing seemed right, nothing came to a point; the fate of Anderson, the significance of the deaths of MacCaby and Hart, were as far from comprehension as ever; perhaps further. The events of the night had only piled nonsense on confusion. And yet he could not escape the puzzle. It pressed on him so heavily that his head ached. I'm bushed, he thought as Dr. Dodd started the car. I've got to—

Then he was bushed no longer.

A sort of double exposure, he was thinking at the jump of his blood, because they were really one face duplicated. Two tiny men in undershirts, their pants sagging, with lumberjackets identically hung over their pigeon shoulders, stood side by side on the porch of a small frame house directly across Algonquin Avenue from the Dodd house.

Watching.

The little elderly tailors of the Granjon Block on Washington Street.

The identical Waldo twins.

Which was David and which Jonathan? He had never seen Jonathan. Not that it mattered. Seeing Jonathan was seeing David. There were probably differences if you used X-rays and micrometers, even differences in skills; but this was nature in an antic mood—and even so, why should anyone care? As Dr. Dodd's car spluttered away, Ellery kept asking himself why his nervous system should jangle an alarm at learning the surely extraneous fact that the Waldo brothers, who made Otis Holderfield's clothes, were across-the-street neighbors of Attorney Holderfield's patron saint, the fortunate Dr. Sebastian Dodd?

Sunday, April 23

"What?" said Ellery. He was still hearing the carillon spiel of the First Methodist barker and Dakin's axhead face was still blurry around the edges. He rubbed his eyes; Rima was there, too, seated on the edge of Manager Brooks's bed, and without Ken Winship. "I thought Jacquard was dead. Or did I dream it all, Dakin?"

"I didn't say Jacquard. I said Jacquard's house. Y'know, Mr. Queen," said the chief of police, "he lived in a house. More like a chicken coop than a house, with all those youngsters underfoot, but a house you'd have to call it even though it's on Polly Street and the rats eat out of your hand."

"*Or* your hand," said Rima.

"The point is, I found Rima's father's five thousand dollars over there this morning."

Now the last lingering bong was gone and Dakin was his proper hatchet self again, and Ellery said, "So," like little Hercule Poirot, and he went over and shut one of the windows, shivering. It would happen on a cold Sunday in April. "So what, Dakin?"

"So I thought you'd be surprised," said Dakin in a surprised voice.

"So did I," said Rima.

"Really you should have brought some coffee up with you," said Ellery. "Where do you think Jacquard would hide money that didn't belong to him?"

"Then why didn't you look there?" Dakin was being awfully disagreeable so early in the morning, thought Ellery; a Sunday, too. "Now ask me why *I* didn't look there. Well, sir, I didn't look there because nobody bothered to tell me about Anderson's coming back to Holderfield with Dodd's five thousand in an envelope and turning it over to Holderfield with instructions to turn it over to Nick Jacquard if somethin' happened to him, and Holderfield's doing so. That's why *I* didn't look there, Mr. Queen. And I've got a little business with Mr. Holderfield this morning, too, that's goin' to make Mr. Holderfield remember me."

"You're so right, Dakin," groaned Ellery. "It's this damned zippermouth training I got in my youth. By the way, who did tell you?"

"I did," said Rima. "I woke up early this morning after bad dreams and I went right to Chief Dakin. Didn't tell Ken or Dr. Dodd or anybody—Ken had gone to the hospital and Dr. Dodd was still asleep."

"Got me out of bed with it, bless her heart," said Dakin, "and don't give her that wait-till-I-get-you-alone look, Mr. Queen, 'cause she's a better friend of mine than you are. Or were you waiting for Jacquard to cash in so you could find that five thousand yourself?"

"This is unworthy of our long friendship," said Ellery with dignity. "I really must have some coffee . . . Well, anyway, you've got it, and that's the main thing,

642

and now that you have, what are you going to do with it? Oh, did you find the envelope and the letter Tom Anderson told Holderfield he had enclosed with the money?''

"To the second question, no, Jacquard must have destroyed it. To the first,'' said the police chief, "why, Dr. Dodd gave that money to Tom Anderson, and Tom Anderson no longer being with us . . .''

"That's why I'm here,'' said Rima, looking Ellery in the eye. "I don't want that money. Dr. Dodd gave it to Daddy for a purpose and Daddy didn't live long enough to accomplish the purpose, so the money ought to go back where it came from. And that's just where it's going.''

Dakin looked at Ellery hopefully. "Well,'' he said after a moment. Then he went to the door and Rima followed him.

"Wait,'' said Ellery. They both stopped. "Rima, I'll meet you in the lobby. I won't be five minutes dressing.''

Dakin looked reproachful as they went out.

Ellery took Rima into the coffee shop and they sat down five tables away from the nearest traveling man. Rima said she would have just coffee, thank you, so Ellery ordered two pots of coffee and said, "What else did you tell Dakin?''

"Nothing else.''

"Why did you tell him anything at all?''

"I thought he ought to know.''

"You thought he ought to know. Do you know, in war you'd be shot for this?''

"I didn't know Mr. Dakin was the enemy.''

"You argue like a Levantine,'' growled Ellery. "Of course, he's not. But you're sworn. Head man—chief. That was supposed to be me, remember?''

"Ellery.''

"What?''

"I'm resigning.''

Ellery nodded and for a few moments they devoted themselves to their coffee. Finally Ellery lit a cigaret and blew a question mark.

"Yes. After what happened last night—Ken and me . . . Ellery, I couldn't. Not and stay in love with Ken. It's something neither you nor I knew would happen when we made our bargain. Of course you understand.''

"Of course.'' Of course. But it had not occurred to him before. This is what comes, he thought ruefully, of thinking of people not as people but as chess pieces. "You're perfectiy right, Rima. There can't be any other basis for your relationship. Only . . . respect my position, will you?''

"You mean I'm not to tell Ken anything?''

"Because of Ken's loyalty to Dodd. He'd probably boil over and in his anger tip off Dodd. And that might spoil everything.''

"You're going ahead with this?'' Rima was astonished.

Ellery looked astonished at her astonishment. "Why, certainly.'' And then he said, irrelevantly, "You know, Rima, Dodd is a very sick man.''

"You mean his nervousness?''

"His phobia.''

"Phobia?''

"It isn't just worry or anxiety, Rima. It's fear. And not an ordinary intermittent fear—a pathological fear. Obsessive. I suppose that's what's really keeping me in Wrightsville. What in the world is Dodd so unreasonably terrified of? And whatever it is, how is it connected with the deaths of MacCaby and Hart? And with what happened to your father? And to Jacquard?''

"To *Jacquard?*''

"Yes.''

"But Jacquard's death . . .'' She was bewildered.

"Exactly. First MacCaby's death, then Hart's death, then presumably your father's death, and now Jacquard's death. All connected. Or are they? Two possibilities, Rima. Remember? The double play.''

"But—it was his own fault!''

"Good heavens, I'm not turning a beady eye on your beloved. Poor Ken in any event would be an instrument of fate. I didn't mean that. I meant—in theory—the two faces of the coin. One possibility: Jacquard, a petty thief, broke into the house of the town's newest rich man. Past midnight when it was in almost total darkness, you'll recall. Why? For the obvious purpose of stealing something. What? Anything he could lay his hands on. Place, time, circumstances, intended victim, known character of the culprit—they all fit the simple interpretation. As, incidentally, did the previous events.

"But the reverse? Dodd the wicked man? In the grip of a deathly fear? . . . Follow him through to Jacquard.''

"I don't see . . .''

"Suppose, again, Dodd murdered MacCaby for the fortune, drove Hart to suicide to gain sole control of the dye works, killed your father to avoid paying more blackmail. If that's the truth, your father had some evidence that proved Dodd's guilt—the box of pills Dodd gave MacCaby, or something else. It doesn't matter what.

"Now Tom Anderson. Tom Anderson is an intelligent man. He knows Dodd is a murderer and that a man who has murdered twice will murder a third time. And he, Anderson, is putting pressure on that Dodd. He sees the dreary possibility. So he hides his evidence.

"He hides his evidence, and what does he do? He leaves a sealed letter with Holderfield with instructions that, if anything should happen to him—Anderson— Holderfield is to turn the envelope over to Nick Jacquard. And in this envelope he has not only placed the five thousand dollars he got from Dodd but also a letter of instructions to Jacquard telling Jacquard all about Dodd's guilt, about the evidence, its nature and where Anderson has hidden it. So that if Dodd thought to resolve his difficulties by killing Anderson, Jacquard could disillusion him by carrying the blackmail on. They were friends, weren't they? And Tom Anderson had come a long way from his poetry and his mortarboard.''

Rima said nothing, but her scorn was explicit.

Nevertheless, Ellery went on. "And where had Tom Anderson hidden the evidence of Dodd's guilt? Well, what did Jacquard, Anderson's heir, so to speak, do last night? He broke into Dodd's study. Then suppose Anderson's letter to Jacquard had said: *I hid the evidence in the last place Dodd would think of looking for it— his own study.* At Dodd's own word, Anderson had been in Dodd's house at least twice. Suppose it had been, however, not in Dodd's waiting room as he said, but in Dodd's study, that their conversations about the five thousand dollars took place. And suppose Dodd had been called out for a few minutes, leaving Anderson in the study alone? You see where the other fork of the road takes us, Rima? To Jacquard breaking into Dodd's house to get possession of the evidence by which Anderson had blackmailed Dodd and for the suppression of which Dodd had killed Anderson.

Dodd, Dodd, and Dodd. Dodd the frightened man. Always Dodd. That's why I want so badly to get into that house, Rima. It's only one of two possible theories, but finding that evidence—which Jacquard didn't get—would block off one road and take us down the other to a destination. Now, wouldn't it?''

Rima smiled. "Sorry, Mr. Queen. I don't believe it. Except as perverted poetry, perhaps. But it's pure imagination. You should have lived in Coleridge's day. Or smoked opium with De Quincey. I'm going back to Ken and Dr. Dodd, who's a sweet, troubled man . . . maybe sick from overwork, from nervous exhaustion, but not a murderer, not the nemesis of a rich man and a foolish man, a pauper and a thief . . . Ellery, what's the matter?''

For Ellery was crouched there watching his cigaret scorch the flesh of his forefinger as if he were a Yogi.

"Ellery!" She slapped his hand and the butt fell into his coffee with a frustrated hiss. "What's ailing you?''

He came back to the Hollis Coffee Shoppe with a start. And almost upset the table, he jumped up so wildly.

"Ellery! Where are you going?''

"Dodd! . . . Pay the check. I mean . . . Oh, hell, I can't wait for change. Still asleep, you said? Rima, come on!''

"What *are* you raving about?''

But he was already waving to the taxi parked outside.

Ellery said: "Dr. Dodd, I'm going to tell you a fairy tale.''

They had found Dodd in his study, in pajamas and a frayed black silk dressing gown, behind the desk where Nick Jacquard had made his last stand the night before. He was sipping black coffee with both hands about the dancing cup, staring through the window at his garden. Nothing was visible but Harry Toyfell turning up the earth around a row of narcissus shoots. Ken was giving the doctor a report on some patient he had just seen at the hospital, but the older man seemed not to have been listening.

Dodd was not so much shaking this morning as being shaken by a personal earthquake.

He tried to smile; the smile burst into fragments, leaving a stubbled chaos, everything in trembling motion. He seemed fascinated by Toyfell's movements, the rise and fall of the bits of earth.

Ken Winship was frazzled himself this morning; Rima gently stroked his lids. "Ellery, I don't think this morning is a good time.''

The best time, thought Ellery.

"A fairy tale,'' he repeated. "But it has to be believed. And because it has to be believed, Dr. Dodd, I ask you to open your mind as wide as it can go.''

Now he had Dodd's attention; an unpleasant victory, for this man was shaking to pieces before his eyes.

"I said—'' began Ken.

"Darling, listen,'' said Rima.

"I'll have to start at the beginning. I came to Wrightsville with a theory. My theory was that Tom Anderson's death was only a link in a chain. My theory was that it was the third link, the first link having been the death of Luke MacCaby and the second link the death of John Hart. Last night Nick Jacquard died. My theory last night was that Jacquard's death was the fourth link.''

"What the devil are you talking about, Ellery?''

"Ken. Listen."

"Dr. Dodd, this morning the theory became a fact. The deaths of MacCaby, Hart, Anderson, Jacquard are positively connected. In that exact order, by the way. As to what counects them . . ."

"What?" croaked Dr. Dodd.

"I want you to work it out with me, Doctor," said Ellery. "MacCaby was the first to die. How would you describe MacCaby?"

Dodd was squeezing the edge of his desk. "How do you mean?"

"Not physically. As a personality."

"An eccentric."

"No. In social terms. The thing Wrightsville talked about most when they discussed him after his death." Ellery paused. "Everyone thought he was—?"

"A poor man?" Dodd was squinting across the desk.

"When he was actually—?"

"A wealthy man."

"The second casualty, Hart. In exactly the same sense, Doctor, how would you describe Hart?"

"He turned out to be an embezzler."

"Yes, but what's the fact that brought Hart down to the level of the lowliest Low Villager?"

"Everyone thought he was a millionaire when he was really penniless?"

"Yes, the have turns out to be the have-not. In our society, where the accumulation of wealth is the preoccupation of most individuals, the loss of it is the most tragic— that is, the most dramatic—of possible turns of the plot. So—in the scale of our social plot values—just as the most significant thing about Luke MacCaby was that, thought to be a poor man, he was actually rich, so the most significant thing about John Spencer Hart was that, thought to be a rich man, he was actually poor.

"And now," said Ellery, "describe Tom Anderson."

"It's all right, Doctor," began Rima.

"No," said Ellery, "let's stick to socio-economics. It's obvious that we've been dealing with classifications of property, isn't it? Riches, poverty. In that frame, Dr. Dodd, what was Tom Anderson?"

"Poverty."

"More than poverty. Or, rather, less. Poverty is a relative term, Doctor, like vacuum. But Tom Anderson was an absolute. The economic untouchable. Rima, you told me in New York what Wrightsville called your father when they weren't pinning the drunkenness label on him."

"The Town Beggar."

"He was also called The Town Beggar. And Jacquard, who followed The Town Beggar in this mystifying sequence? What was Jacquard noted for?"

"Petty thievery. The Town Thief."

"MacCaby the rich man, Hart the poor man, Anderson the beggar, Jacquard the thief. In that order." Ellery paused. Then he said lightly, "Rich man, poor man, beggar, thief." And paused again. And when they said nothing, when they glanced blankly back at him, Ellery whipped his jacket open, flung his necktie over one shoulder, and jabbed at the top button of his shirt with a furious forefinger. *"Rich man—"* the button below—*"poor man—"* the button below that—*"beggar-man—"* the fourth button—*"thief!"*

Now they saw, and he pulled his tie back straight and rebuttoned his jacket and shook himself a little. "All right, I'm off my chump. Four men die, each under perfectly . . . adult circumstances, and here the fellow comes along and works out a child's jingle, a counting game of the young, a fortune-telling abracadabra. 'What are you going to be when you grow up, Junior? Tell your beads—I mean your buttons.' And Junior puts his chubby littie finger on his shiny little buttons, and he pipes, 'Rich man, poor man, beggar-man, thief . . .' Well, say it! Or do you see, Dr. Dodd, that mad or not, that's the incantation arising out of the ghosts of MacCaby, Hart, Anderson, and Jacquard? You're a man who believes in four-leaf clovers! Will you believe that four deaths can follow a jingle?''

The sweat was rolling down Dodd's speckled skull. "I don't know what to say," he stammered.

"You've got to believe! Try it youself. Test it any way you want to. Sleep on it. Be scientific. What else can it mean? What else can it be? Four men die, following the patter of a child's counting game. Ridiculous! Insane! But true.''

"Coincidence." Ken Winship was angry.

"Four? One certainly, two possibly, three conceivably, but four, Ken? No, not coincidence. Plan.''

"Whose?''

Rima said nothing, but she had grown very pale.

Dr. Dodd wiped his skull.

"Oh, for heaven's sake, Doc. Look, Ellery.'' Ken was being reasonable now. "This would be great stuff for one of your books, but chase those romantic cobwebs away for a minute. MacCaby's heart quit. Hart put a bullet through his brain. Anderson—we don't even know he's dead. Jacquard . . . And you say there's a directing *mind* behind this?''

"And yet . . . *rich man, poor man, beggar-man, thief*. Plan, Ken. A directing mind. Not necessarily hand, but a mind. I believe it. I have to. What's more,'' Ellery leaned on the desk, and he was not speaking to Dr. Winship now, *"you* have to, Doctor.''

"Me?'' Dr. Dodd's eyes kept roving. "Why?''

"It's not finished.''

"What's not finished?'' demanded Ken irritably.

Rima was terribly still.

"Wait, Kenneth.'' The shaking man remarkably stopped shaking. And he said slowly, *"Rich man, poor man, beggar-man, thief; doctor . . .''*

"No, Rima.'' Winship laughed, on his feet. "So that's the way it works out.''

"Doctor,'' nodded Ellery. "Dr. Dodd, Ken. Indicated. Next on the list.''

Dodd began shaking again. It was hard to look at him.

"The fifth character in the jingle is 'doctor,' so that means Dr. Sebastian Dodd. In a town with thirteen doctors of medicine, four doctors of dentistry, and I don't know how many doctors of other sorts, 'doctor' in a jingle means Doc Dodd. Queen, who's pulling whose leg? And why?'' And now Ken sounded almost ugly.

"I don't blame you, Ken,'' said Ellery without rancor. "On the surface it's lunacy or worse. But dig in. Dr. Dodd is the only doctor in Wrightsville who's had an important connection with MacCaby's death, Hart's death, Anderson's death, and Jacquard's death—with all four. MacCaby was Dodd's patient and Dodd inherited his fortune. Dodd became Hart's business partner and then sole owner of the Hart-MacCaby business through Hart's suicide. Dodd gave Anderson five thousand dollars a short time before Anderson's disappearance. And it was in Dr. Dodd's home, with Dr. Dodd's gun, that Nick Jacquard met his death. That's why 'doctor' in the rhyme means Dr. Dodd to me, Ken. Call it hunch, paranoia, superstition, but that's why I'm convinced that Dr. Dodd is down in somebody's book as victim number five. You people have to see it. You have to take precautions. I'll help, if you'll accept help—''

"Ken!"

At Rima's shriek Dr. Winship whirled. But Ellery was already pushing him aside.

Sebastian Dodd was on his feet behind the desk. His mouth was flapped back. His eyes glassed terror in, like cages.

He pitched forward just as Ellery got to him.

Shock, said Ken, his tone official. They were outside Dodd's bedroom. Rima was keeping watch over the doctor. Each man was stiffly on edge.

"There's nothing wrong with his heart. If there were, Queen, you'd have killed him."

"He's sicker than I thought. But I had no choice. He's tagged. I had to warn him. He's got to watch himself."

"I'll watch him. He'll be up by tomorrow morning."

"I'd like to help, Ken."

Winship did not reply.

"There's no point in our acting like two strange dogs. You've got Rima and a long life ahead of you and I've got my conscience to live with. We both owe Dodd something. The job is to take care of him and find out what this is all about." Ellery said patientiy, "I'm going to do it anyway."

"But I don't believe any of this," Ken Winship snarled.

"Dodd does. You heard what he said when you revived him. Do we join forces, Ken, or square off?"

Ken relaxed suddenly. "Oh, hell, pull out of the Hollis and move into one of these rooms. If you're right, Ellery, I'll . . . buy you a whole set of nursery rhymes!"

Monday, April 24

He could have taken the key from the chain while Dodd was asleep under sedation, Ellery reflected, but there had been Ken, big brass and bridling, and Rima, little and loyal as the sergeant of his own conscience in her enlistment on the other side. Afterward, he hàd had to go to the Hollis for his suitcase, and when he got back to the Dodd house Ken, an ally who kept his weapons primed, made it impossible to be alone.

Sunday night, on the pretext of "looking the house over," Ellery had maueuvered the young doctor to the attic floor, and they had opened doors and poked into cubbies stored with historic furniture and the opulent whatnots of the last century—these had been servants' quarters in the mansion's heyday—until finally they had come to a narrow door with a modern lock, and this door did not open. "What's in here?" Ellery had asked casually. "Darned if I know. The plusher Dodd family heirlooms, maybe. I don't think Doc ever said," and Ken had passed on. So that had been that; and later, when they looked in on Dr. Dodd, they had found him sitting up in bed like an aged frog in the stillness of some hopeless disease, a spready blotch against the lily pad of the wornout patchwork counterpane.

Their discussion with him, a tragic sonata in which the Winship and Rima variations were unsuccessfully lively, produced an unexpected coda. The doctor was grateful for Ellery's interest and Ellery was more than welcome to stay, it seemed, but he had had time to think things out and he knew now that ordinary precautions were a waste of time. "I don't need watching, Mr. Queen. I'm to die and it won't be a hand that does it. Some things you can't do a biopsy on. With all our sulfas and atomic bombs and electronic microscopes and two hundred inch telescope lenses we don't begin to know the powers that fill the universe. Any more than the ameba in that glass of water knows what's going on in this room. All we can do is wait and try not to be too afraid." He had even managed a smile that was more depressing than the dreary burnside set of his jowls. And all the time he spoke his clothes lay on a chair beside his bed with that bit of watch chain peeping out, unattainable as the Little Dipper.

And when, at two in the morning, Ellery had crept down the hall in his naked feet, he had found Dr. Dodd's door locked. In his peevishness it had struck him as an infantile defense against a Juggernaut, although effective enough against softer material. Ellery had crept back to bed cursing.

Which is how the indifferent dawn came to find him barefooted, pajamaed, and shivering, spreadeagled on the perilous pitch of the rearward Dodd roof and inching his way over to the armored eye of one of the dormers, the window of the little attic room that was locked. He had made up his mind about this after a predawn inspection—from the garden behind the house—of the mysterious dormer three floors above. The beam of his flashlight, a powerful one that occupied a permanent niche in his suitcase, had revealed a battered blind; and on this slender thread he had climbed to the top floor, entered the cubby next to the locked room, opened the cubby's dormer window, and crawled out to the roof. Fortunately, there was a sound if ancient copper gutter along the edge of the eaves, and he was able to brace himself against this in getting over to the next dormer. Arrived at his goal, he found that the only rent in the blind of any promising size required him to hang on to the bulging eyelid of the dormer like a crooked lash, with half of him unsupported by anything more substantial than the heavy dawn air.

It was light enough by now, and the tear in the blind was sufficiently flapped away, to enable him to see most of the attic room. If he had expected dead bodies (or live ones), he was disappointed; what he could see of the room was unoccupied. It was small and meagerly furnished. There was a desklike table on the uncovered floor, a grayish mission "library table" of a previous generation, and an angular slatted armchair of the same style and period; on the interior shelf of the one end of the table which he could see stood some books; along the braceboard below the tabletop ranged an assortment of objects he could not identify; on the tabletop itself lay what appeared to be two decks of playing cards, stacked face down; and there was nothing else in the room that he could see except dust and spiderwebs.

Ellery drew back and sat down with his knees up and his bare heels in the copper gutter. He lit a cigaret from the pack he had cannily slipped into his pajama pocket and he smoked under the rising sun of Wrightsville on a crumbling roof watched by the northerly hills. He was filthy, and thoughtful. An elderly country doctor rose every morning and locked himself into a secret room in his attic and did . . . what?

Played solitaire? Read books? Prayed?

The sun was only a finger higher and his legs were only a little stiff. The doctor would be an early riser and this morning he would have reason to rise even earlier . . . The roof was shedding with age and through its thin skin Ellery heard the little door begin to beat.

He took his time getting his eye back to the peephole. Finally the dormer was embraced. About the sun at his back and his shadow on the blind he could do nothing; that was in the hands of God.

But Dr. Dodd was blind to changes in light. He was dressed in his working suit of blue serge. The key dangled from its chain, touching his thigh. He stood at the table staring down; and, yes, perhaps his lips were moving. Behind him the little door barred everyone.

Suddenly the doctor sat down, his big hand closing shakily about one of the decks of cards.

He sat there, arm resting on the edge of the library table, hand about the deck.

It came away in a spasm, severing the deck like an executioner. For a moment he was motionless, part of the deck on the table, part of the deck in his hand. Then he exposed the card he had cut to.

The ace of spades.

Dr. Dodd slammed the cards back and heaved to his feet. He ran to the door clawing for the key at his thigh. His thick blue back looked armored, as if he expected a blow from behind. He could not get the key into the lock; Ellery saw him seize his right hand with his left to steady it.

But then his hands dropped and he stood still again. Offering his back as a target? But Ellery was wrong. This was not surrender. Dr. Dodd turned—slowly, but he turned—and went heavily back to his altar.

And conducted a second service.

This was done very slowly indeed. The man who goes twice to question his god knows there can be no third appeal.

Dr. Dodd put his hand on the second deck of cards. It came away with part of the deck concealed in it. After an infinity of meditation he looked.

And this was the strangest thing of all, that he no longer quaked or leaned upon the table but simply stood in the hardening seizure of a kind of death, strong and sure of itself and not to be struggled against.

Stood looking at another ace of spades.

After a long time Dr. Dodd dropped the cards on the other deck and with remarkable steadiness marched to the door, unlocked it, and went out, leaving the little room only a shade altered.

Ellery found himself some time later squatting on the curled shingles contemplating the garden below his navel, a meager and perplexed Buddha. There was an earthstained spade beside a tulip bed by the wall of the garage, but it was not nearly so mordant as the memory of those other spades, of ink and pasteboard, in the hand of Dr. Dodd. The nine of diamonds had served the butcher duke of Cumberland in another age to put the curse of death on the Jacobites of Scotland. That card, fresh from Culloden Moor, had had writing on it; was there a sentence on Dr. Dodd's two aces of spades?

And who was the butcher duke of Wrightsville?

Dr. Dodd would have said the noble Fiend, that teller of black fortunes. Telling death twice, as if he would not be misunderstood.

Ellery sat on Dr. Dodd's roof thoroughly confused.

At last he crept over to the other dormer and prepared to re-enter the house. He had just scrambled through and was shutting the window when he spied a slotlike face at another window, a window below him and the garden's width away, in the upper story of the garage.

Harry Toyfell.

Ellery let himself into the attic hall. The house was churchly; nor was there sign or sound of Dr. Dodd. As he tried the door of Dodd's dusty chapel and found it locked again, Ellery fretted over more than the doctor's secretiveness.

How long had the slabjawed gardener been peering from behind the curtain of his room above the garage? Had Toyfell witnessed the acrobatics on the roof? Would he drop a philosophical word to his new employer?

It was a nuisance; and Ellery went down to his bedroom, showered, washed out his grimy pajamas, and dressed, all in an unsettled haste.

In the hall again, he took stock. Rima's door was shut, Ken Winship's door was shut; Dr. Dodd's door was open, as were the doors of Mrs. Fowler and Essie.

Ellery went downstairs.

Dr. Dodd was not in his office, not in his study.

Coffee warmed the kitchen. "No, just coffee, Mrs. Fowler. Thought I heard Dr. Dodd stirring. Is he up?"

"Doctor's always up with the birds," Mrs. Fowler shouted cheerfully. "Never saw such a man for early risin'. Though he'd have prescribed staying in bed for a body looked as peaked as he did this mornin'. No breakfast, thank you, and he takes his hat and marches out. I declare all men are infants and doctors are the worst of all! ''

"Where did he go Mrs. Fowler? Oh, thanks. Hospital?"

"He didn't say, though I expect that's where he is. Just said to say he'd meet you, Miss Anderson, and Dr. Winship at the inquest this afternoon. Oh, that awful Jacquard!''

Ellery put down his cup and went back to his bedroom, walking softly as he passed the closed doors. Of course I might ask Dodd, he thought. But a man who keeps locking a door with a key doesn't usually open it with a word. In any language. And afterward he'd be hysterically on his guard.

Ellery opened his suitcase, which had an uncandid side to it. From the false bottom, where he regretfully carried certain tools of his trade, he took this and that; and he went out and past the sleeping doors to the attic stairs.

A little later he balanced himself on the edge of Chief Dakin's desk and he said, "Dakin, I'm going to ask you to help me commit an illegal act.''

"Sure," said Dakin, rising with alacrity. "But we'll have to work fast if we're to make that inquest this afternoon. What crime do I commit?''

"You arrange the technical details. Is there a locksmith in town?''

"Millard Peague. Got a little shop down on Crosstown and Foaming.''

"How good is he?''

"He's done a job or two for the county in his time, and once in a while he gets a call from as far away as Connhaven. What do you want Millard to do?''

"Make a key from a wax impression I just happen to have on me.'' And Ellery placed a little carefully wrapped bundle on Dakin's desk.

Dakin sat down again. "Whose?''

"That," said Ellery, "is surely irrelevant and immaterial?''

"I could hold you up, Mr. Queen.''

"And I," smiled Ellery, "could let you down.''

"Suppose we make a dicker—''

"On my terms, Dakin. You get this little job done for me without questions or publicity and I'll tell you what door the key fits when I think you ought to know.''

"Tell me this," said the chief of police. "You going to take anything?''

"No.''

"You going to *put* anything?''

"Cold, Dakin, cold.''

"Then what do you want to get in for?''

"Let's say murder, shall we, and let it go at that?''

"You're a hard man," said Chief Dakin, rising and reaching for his cap, "and I'm just wax in your hands. If you'll give me that thing I'll go see what Millard Peague can do.''

The inquest into Nicole Jacquard's death went off like an operation under the surgical hands of Coroner Grupp, presiding in Judge Eli Martin's old courtroom in the County Court House. Grupp cut deftly through issues and skillfully tied off arterial impediments like the flowing Widow Jacquard and her distressed priest, Father Crétien of Low Village; and he handled the jury as if they were his masters, which they were not. It was all over in a wonderfully short time. Dr. Ken Winship, to his and Rima's piteous relief, was exonerated by his peers, and the widow—though not in her hearing—was congratulated by the jury, for she had not only been cut free from the deadweight of her humorless husband but it was rumored that Dr. Sebastian Dodd was settling a far more substantial weekly sum on her and Nicole's progeny than the corpse had provided in the most successful days of his pilferage. The verdict of the coroner's jury was "It's a good thing all around," although expressed in more formal terms; and the atmosphere in the courtroom when the inquest broke up was such as to make Prosecutor Chalanski wish, humorously aloud to Mr. Queen, that he could hurry the date of the Congressional primaries.

Ellery's interest in the proceedings was narrow. He had eyes chiefly for Sebastian Dodd. They had found Dr. Dodd seated heavily in the courtroom; he seemed to have signed a temporary truce with events. He said nothing of where he had been all morning. And afterward, Dodd had gone straight to the house on Algonquin and Wright and locked himself in his bedroom. He thought he would take it easy for the rest of the day, he said; his office hours had been canceled by Rima in the morning and Kenneth could take his evening house calls. He was happy, he said, very happy that the inquest had turned out so well, and would Mrs. Fowler leave a tray outside his door? This had been a sop to Mrs. Fowler, whose remedy for any sort of distress was invariably hot food in quantity. Ellery, passing Dodd's door later that evening, found the tray cold, as Mrs. Fowler had not left it; he resisted an impulse with difficulty to kick it and blow up the charged silence of the house.

They were all affected by Dr. Dodd's peculiar suppressions, even Essie, who just before dinner suddenly burst into tears and fled to her room; even Harry Toyfell, whose elongated jaws ground away in the kitchen to the exclusion of all possibility of communication. Mrs. Fowler served, and it was a question which was worse, her loquacity or the silence at the supper table. Ken did not even pretend to be hungry; he kept glancing upward. Rima watched him anxiously, a little island of helplessness. And Ellery nibbled, feeling the cold burn on his thigh of the key Chief Dakin had slipped into his hand as they were leaving the courtroom.

Finally Ken tossed his napkin down. "I've got to get out on those calls."

"Ken. Don't you think you ought to do something about Dr. Dodd?" At last it was out.

"What, darling? Take his blood pressure?" Dr. Winship sounded savage. He kissed Rima, excused himself, and they heard him drive away in a rush.

"Rima," began Ellery.

But Rima said steadily, "No, I won't listen to *anything*. I don't understand and I have Ken's and Dr. Dodd's bills to make out and if you don't mind, Ellery, I'd like to get to it."

Nobody seemed to want to talk but Mrs. Fowler; and it was Mrs. Fowler's conversation that eventually drove Ellery upstairs.

From his room he could hear the sputter of Rima's typewriter, the offended bang of Mrs. Fowler's dishes; punctuations to the silence. Ellery hurled himself about the bedroom under the spur of the duplicate key in his pocket. His was a corner bedroom, in a small ell, and from his window he could see the windows of Dr. Dodd's room. Dodd's light was on; it had been on all evening. Occasionally Ellery could see his bulk drift past like a paramecium on a slide.

It was impossible to investigate the locked attic room while Dodd was awake. It was almost directly above Dodd's bedroom and the floors, dryboned with age, squealed and tattled with every step.

At 9:30 Ellery heard Mrs. Fowler's heavy step come up the hall. He heard her knock on Essie Pingarn's door and Essie's sniveling reply. A moment later Mrs.

Fowler's light came on and a moment after that there was a muffled swoosh of water. Ellery groaned, Mrs. Fowler's bedtime tub the night before had taken exactly one hour and ten minutes.

He left his room and went down the hall. There was the taunting moat of light under Dodd's door. The tray was gone; Mrs. Fowler must have taken it away.

He knocked.

He knocked again.

"Yes? Who's that?"

"Queen."

"Oh." He sounded hoarse, as if he had been addressing audiences. "Yes?"

"I saw your light on, Doctor. May I come in and visit?"

"Well, the fact is I was just going to sleep—" The moat blacked out. Ellery heard the clash of springs.

"Feeling all right, Doctor?"

"Fine. Had a wonderful rest this evening. You comfortable, Mr. Queen? Have your dinner? Everything you want?"

"Yes, thanks. Good night. Sleep well."

"Thanks . . ."

Ellery continued loudly down the hall. At the head of the stairs he stopped.

He waited one hour by his watch. Then he went back; it took him ten minutes to retrace the fifteen feet to Dr. Dodd's door. He braced himself with both hands and put his ear to the panel.

The breathing was deep and slow, with a slight snore in it occasionally. And once a whimper.

Ellery straightened. Rima's typewriter was still going downstairs; Ken had still not returned. Toward the other end of the hall the transom above Mrs. Fowler's door was dark.

Carefully Ellery went back to the stairs and started for the attic.

He used a pencil-sized flash this time.

The key had a film of oil on it and he eased it into the lock of Dr. Dodd's sanctuary with no sound.

Then he put the flashlight between his jaws, like a cigar, grasped the knob firmly with his left hand, and with his right he twisted.

The key would not turn.

Ellery could have sat down on the attic floor and cried.

Then he was angry. It was the most ridiculous case he had ever stuck his nose into. It was made of froth and dancing flecks and the look in a man's eyes, with not enough substance to keep a dwarf going.

He made his way back to the second floor, and he rummaged in his suitcase again, and then he returned to the attic and with gritted teeth made another wax impression of the lock.

As he finished, he heard a car in the driveway, and by the time he got downstairs with his hat Rima was sitting on Ken's lap in the waiting room, her arms about his neck.

"Don't get up," said Ellery, smiling. "I'm just passing through. You look beat, Ken."

"He's going right to bed. Which is where I thought you were, Ellery," said Rima.

"Itchy. By the way, Dr. Dodd's asleep."

"I was just going up to see him," said Ken guiltily. "But if he's sleeping— Where you going?"

"I thought I might walk this flea mood off. Talking of sleep, Ken, this female you've captivated has been working on your damned bills all evening."

"I know it, and I've been giving her hell. Darling, I told you . . ."

Ellery let himself out. There was a raw edge to the night and he shivered as he hurried around the corner to Wright Street. The alcoholic heat of Jack's Palace Bar and Grill was almost pleasant. Ellery went to the bar and ordered a beer. He sipped it long enough to outwait the interest his entrance had stirred up, and then he slipped into the telephone booth.

"Dakin? Don't you ever go home?"

"Well, since my wife died there's not much to go home for. But I was on my way. What's up?"

"The key Peague made doesn't work. I've got another impression."

"Where are you?"

"It doesn't matter. I'll be right over."

Dakin was waiting for him on the steps between the green lights. "No point to popping Gobbin's popeyes," Dakin said mildly. "He's got a direct pipeline to Malvina Prentiss's office. Where is it?"

Ellery gave it to him and Chief Dakin put it carefully into a Boston bag he was carrying. They began to walk east on State Street, past the Court House.

"Too late to do anything on this tonight, Mr. Queen."

"When will you get it to Peague?"

"First thing in the morning. You'll have it by noon tomorrow. Any news for me?"

"No. Any news for me?"

"No."

They parted at State and Upper Whistling in silence.

Tuesday, April 25

Nick Jacquard was down on all fours on the rocky ledge staring into the pool which seemed made of brown sugar and sparkled like a million fireflies under the moon, and Ellery peered over Jacquard's thick back to see a face imbedded in the sugar below which was suddenly not sugar but writhing lava, smoke drifting over the face just in time to prevent identification although there had been a plea in it for recognition of some sort. At this the moonrays turned scarlet, pouring into the lava pit, and Nick Jacquard threw back his shaggy head, Ellery seeing that he was a dog howling in unfeeling agony at the incomprehensible nature of the night. There was such a piercing note in his canine grief that Ellery cried out and covered his ears. Now the howls muffled, and Ellery awoke to find himself pressing the ends of his damp pillow to his ears.

The dog still howled.

Ellery sat up in bed, blinking at his wrist. After three. His skin was still slick and he irritably got out of bed and lurched to the window, trying to rouse himself.

The dog was howling in or beyond the garden in the monotonous terror of the dream. There was no moon. The only light came from a window toward the other end of the house.

Dodd's bedroom window.

And Dodd was at the window, his arms raised as he hung on to his drapes, a gross, supplicating silhouette.

The howling persisted.

The howling persisted and Ellery's head cleared suddenly, his hairs prickling.

He kept staring across at the man in the window.

A dog howling in the night. And recently there had been an ace of spades, twice dealt.

The noise persisted. Ellery wondered how anyone could sleep. Dodd, at his window, never moved.

It stopped just before dawn and only then did Dr. Dodd come alive. The black arms dropped, the window was blank. A moment later the light went out.

Ellery crept back to bed, inviting sleep. But sleep was a sensitive plant tonight, shrinking from the breath of the dog. And there was always that infernal jingle. *Rich man, poor man, beggar-man, thief; doctor . . .* Something Sisyphean about it; a stone he kept pushing endlessly toward a conclusion and which rolled endlessly back on him.

And in the morning there was another vexation.

Ellery was dragging his tail down the stairs when he froze on the landing above the front hall. Something between a scream and a bellow had suddenly split the early morning silence. Immediately there were sounds of feet which one moment ran, the next scuffled violently; then a crash and a thud, aud the bullish voice rose again in maddened anger.

He found himself at the rear of the downstairs hall looking about wildly.

"Mrs. Fowler! Essie! Where's that coming from?"

"The doctor's study," shrieked Mrs. Fowler. "They're murderin' him, Mr. Queen!"

From the noise, they certainly were. Ellery hurled himself at the study door and almost broke his neck. It gave at a touch.

Dr. Dodd was running about his study brandishing a rolled-up copy of the *Wrightsville Record,* flailing away at walls, desk, bookcases, floor in a grotesque balletry of rage. The dancing doctor accompanied himself with a song half prayer and half imprecation, fitting music to his choreography. In one of the windows, open to the rear garden, old Toyfell's gloomy face was framed.

Then Ellery solved the mystery. Dodd was not executing a ritual dance; he was trying to kill a bird. It was a small dreary-colored bird, a sparrow or bunting, which had evidently blundered into the study through the open window, and Dodd and the bird had surprised each other when he came downstairs. Why the sight of the trapped and frightened little creature, which swooped and soared desperately among the invisible parabolas of the doctor's blows, should have upset Dodd so eluded Ellery for the moment.

"Dr. Dodd. Doctor—"

"Get that damned thing out of here!" panted the doctor. "Get it out!"

"Ellery—" Rima was in an old wrapper of Mrs. Fowler's, pale.

"See what you can do with Mr. Sparrow—he's probably an old friend of yours. Doctor. Dr. Dodd! Stop that, now."

He managed to get the big man in an armchair while Rima stood still in the center of the study and made chirruping sounds. The bird, perched on the highest bookcase, gave a querulous reply. And in a little while, apparently reassured by Rima's conversation, it flew down and perched on her shoulder. But only for a moment. Then it streaked for the opening in the window and whistled past Harry Toyfell's head like a bullet and was gone.

"A bird." Rima sounded shocked. "And you tried to kill him, Doctor."

Dr. Dodd cowered in the armchair.

"Drink this," Ellery held a glass to the doctor's liverish lips. "Rima, where's Ken?"

"He had to be at the hospital early this morning for a consultation. Dr. Dodd, what was the matter?"

Dodd did not reply. He pushed the glass from his lips.

"We'd better get Ken or somebody right away," said Rima in a low voice. At the window Harry Toyfell's saturnine face still hung. Mrs. Fowler and Essie clung to the doorway.

"No doctor." His mouth seemed stiff. "I'm all right. Just let me lie down on the couch. I'll be fine."

They left him stretched out on the black leather couch, face turned to the wall.

"Always was the nervous kind," Mrs. Fowler whispered loudly in the hall, "but I declare, lately he's a wreck. I don't see how he can go on much longer this way."

"Scared of a little old bird," sniffed Essie Pingarn. "If you ask me, Miss Fowler, it's his ma all over again."

"Essie!" hissed the housekeeper; and Essie flounced off.

"What did Essie mean—'his ma all over again'?"

Mrs. Fowler took refuge in her earpiece. "What?"

Ellery repeated the question.

"Don't seem to hear you, Mr. Queen. I've got to get your breakfast started—"

"Bother my breakfast, and you heard Essie perfectly. If she knows about it, it can't be much of a secret. What about Dr. Dodd's mother, Mrs. Fowler?"

"You ask Dr. Winship. You do that. Got my laundry to sort, and—"

"He's not here and you are. Tell me."

The housekeeper glanced fearfully at the closed study door. Then she whispered, "His ma died in Slocum State Hospital," and fled.

It accounted for a great deal.

But not enough.

Ellery looked into the waiting room. Rima was on the phone trying to locate Dr. Winship.

Ellery waved and went across the hall to the dining room.

As he cracked his first egg a partial answer came to him.

A bird coming into a house was one of the oldest of evil omens. A bird coming into a house. Like a dog howling in the night. Or an ace of spades.

They all announced the imminent visit of death.

Ellery returned from Dakin's office at a little past noon with the second duplicate key in his pocket to find the waiting room crowded and Rima and Dr. Winship running about like harassed store clerks in a going-out-of-business sale. He managed to see Winship for a moment.

"It's the Jacquard shooting," said Ken despairingly. "Half the people out there have nothing wronger with 'em than an acute case of rubberneck. Local politics and other people's troubles are Wrightsville's two main interests."

"Where's Dodd, Ken? He's not in his study."

"He ducked out just before office hours, said he wanted some air. I told him to go. He'd be no good here in the condition he's in."

"Ken, what's the matter with Dodd?"

"I wish I knew. He's in a highly nervous state, bordering on hysteria."

"Bordering hell. Didn't Rima tell you what happened this morning?"

"Of course. If this keeps on I'm going to call in a psychiatrist. He can't go on this way, something's bound to give. I wish I had more time for him. But now that I have to take care of two practices—"

Rima came in hurriedly and said, "I've got Mrs. Broadbeck on the table, Ken. She *knows* it's a tumor."

"Tumor my left ovary. I told her last month she was pregnant. Rima, did I say it today?"

"No, darling."

"I love you. Who's after Broadbeck?"

Ellery went out. He had passed Harry Toyfell on the front lawn spading some rose bushes. Essie Pingarn's vacuum cleaner was whining in the dining room. He poked his head into the kitchen; Mrs. Fowler was on the extension, reading a grocery list to Logan's Market.

So he went upstairs, rubbing his thumb over the key in his pocket.

Now that he was in the attic room, with the door locked behind him, Ellery was let down. He did not quite know what he had expected to find in the part of the room which had been beyond the line of his vision when he hung over the roof, but it was certainly nothing so unexciting as the rusty iron sink and small electric burner that he now saw.

The rest were as he had last seen them. The two decks of cards on the table, the row of objects on the braceboard shelf below. The mission chair.

The room was close and musty. Browning wallpaper curled everywhere.

He picked up one of the decks of cards and glanced through it; then the other. Perfectly ordinary cards. He replaced them on the table as he had found them.

Now he squatted on his heels for a closer look at the shelf which ran the length of the table underneath. It supported a conglomeration of things, as random and unrelated as the contents of a boy's pocket. A heap of pebbles. A carton of salt. A little box of assorted finger rings, some antique-looking, others of modern design; none was valuable. A pair of red dice. A rusty sadiron that looked as old as the house. Absurdly, a bundle of arrows—old Indian arrows, he thought; at Creecher's Barn, over toward Connhaven, you could pick up anything from the petticoat of a Salem witch to Increase Mather's shoe buckle. For that matter, all you had to do was dig almost anywhere. Boys were always turning up arrowheads, maize pestles, and whatnot; this had been congested Indian country. Seven arrows, and other things equally childish.

But as he squatted there, taking inventory of Sebastian Dodd's haphazard treasures, pebbles, salt, rings, dice, sadiron, arrows and the rest ranged themselves along the shelf like instruments in an orchestra of different materials, shapes, and sizes but all bound by a common function to a common destiny.

And now Ellery heard and apprehended the music of A. Dodd's queer orchestra; but comprehension was still beyond him, for Ellery was a man of simple sanity and certain things of which he knew remained just outside the grasp of his understanding.

The Dodd who had collected these objects was not to be salvaged by an ordinary man. That was a reclamation job for experts.

As Ellery relocked the little door from the outside, he tasted a guilty brash. On Sunday he had quoted Dodd a jingle, prophesying doom. No wonder Kenneth Winship had been furious. It had been like putting out the light in the room of a child who was screaming because he was afraid of the dark.

When Ellery got downstairs, Rima jumped up from her desk and took him into the hall.

"Dr. Dodd's back and, Ellery, what do you think?"

"What?" asked Ellery quickiy.

"He's back in his office examining patients!"

"Funny," muttered Ellery.

"You and Ken. Ken said the same thing. 'It isn't natural,' he said—"

"It isn't."

Rima stamped back into the waiting room.

Ellery saw Dodd after the last patient left. The doctor was looking tired but calm. "That silliness this morning, Mr. Queen—"

"I'm delighted to see you back in harness."

"Must have overdone it. It creeps up on you at my age." He even laughed. "I can't guess what you've been thinking. Mrs. Fowler treating you all right?" He actually put his hand on Ellery's shoulder in a friendly way.

But Ellery felt it tremble.

Thursday, April 27

The household brightened quickly snatching a half portion as the whole. At the same time there was a common watchfulness which centered on Dr. Dodd, responsive to the slightest twitch of his jowls. But the doctor seemed really better. He was nimbly in and out on calls at all hours of the day and night; he went back to his clinic duties; he visited the hospital frequently. He even made little jokes about "Mrs. Kenneth Winship" and young Dr. Kildares in love. Rima worked and trilled and made them laugh, recounting Ken's exasperated attempts to teach her to drive his car in the odd hours they were able to snatch together. Mrs. Fowler broke out in a rash of cookies and pies. Essie Pingarn unpacked her bag. Even Harry Toyfell looked less glum as he worked over his flats and transplanted seedlings; on Wednesday Ellery heard him rustily whistle a tune.

If Ken remained skeptical, he was at considerable pains to conceal it.

Still, there was something artificial in the doctor's gaiety and their grateful responses. They were like people on a stage going through carefully rehearsed emotions.

Ellery lounged about the house. There was nothing to be done except to go over the same shifty ground retesting his footing. But he could find solidity nowhere. There was the past, and there was the jingle, and between them the mysterious quicksand. Dakin knew nothing. Nothing had happened, nothing had changed. A rich man was dead, a poor man was dead, a beggar-man was gone if not dead, a thief was indubitably dead; and there was the doctor, playing the scherzo of his tragic symphony. Who was composing what in purgatory?

As he dropped off to sleep Wednesday night, Ellery was thinking that he might as well give up and go home.

But that was Wednesday night.

On Thursday Dr. Dodd's composition came to its end with a crash, double forte.

Ellery was at breakfast with Winship when Rima came hurrying down, yawning guiltily. "I am sorry, Kenny. *Good* morning, Ellery! Oversleeping, I mean—"

Ken kissed her. "You and Doc. I'd have waited for breakfast, but I'm due at the hospital. Dr. Flacker has a tracheotomy scheduled and he's a little touchy about it—"

"Did you say," said Ellery, " 'you and Doc'?"

"What?"

"Dr. Dodd? Oversleeping?"

"Yes. He hasn't been down yet."

"He has been. I looked into his room on my way down and he'd been up and gone."

"But Mrs. Fowler said—" And Ken stopped.

There was a little interlude.

"Don't be silly," said Rima gaily. "It was probably a night call, an emergency or something. He has an extension by his bed and now I remember I thought I heard a phone ringing during the night. Will you two," cried Rima crossly, "stop looking that way?"

"Are you sure, Rima, you heard his phone ring during the night?"

"Of course I'm not sure. I may have dreamed it. Or he got up early and went out for a walk before breakfast. He's done that twice since I've been living here. I don't know why everyone has to be so . . . There he is now! Ringing the front door bell. Forgot his key. Essie? Is that Dr. Dodd?"

"It's a policeman," came Essie's nasal voice. "Wouldn't you be Mis' Gotch's boy Dodie? That was in the navy? Sakes, how you've shot up."

They were in the hall not conscious of having run. Mrs. Fowler's head was caught in the swinging door to the kitchen. Harry Toyfell, with egg on his chin, pushed it wider.

"Mr. Queen? Dr. Winship?" He was a young officer, tall and serious; the new crop. Ellery did not know him. "Chief Dakin's sent me to get you."

Ken said, "Something's happened to Doc."

"Yes, sir," said Mrs. Gotch's boy Dodie respectfully. "We found his jalopy over on Route 478 in a culvert. Just past the railroad tracks. He'd crashed through the concrete wall on the curve of the overpass there. Car's a junk heap."

"But Dr. Dodd," said Ken. "Dr. Dodd!"

The young officer said with an awkward tact, "I guess, Doc, he's pretty dead."

Dr. Dodd was very dead. At the impact with the concrete wall he had been hurled headfirst through his windshield into the culvert and the car had followed, landing on top of him. They had been an hour extricating the body. One of the policemen, as new on the force as Mrs. Gotch's Dodie, had had to be sent home.

Coroner Grupp was there, and Prosecutor Chalanski, and Malvina Prentiss and Francis O'Bannon and a photographer from the *Record*. And for a short time the chubby startled face of Attorney Otis Holderfield appeared, but after talking to Dakin and Chalanski he disappeared. There were two ambulances, one from Wrightsville General and the other from the County Hospital beyond Slocum. Cars were lined up on both sides of the overpass; the edge of the culvert was jammed with people. In a nearby field a farmer was screaming at some boys who were racing through his radish and lettuce plants. The sun was warm and everything was clear and beautiful.

"No, Doc," Dakin was saying to Ken at the bottom of the culvert, "I'm not goin' to let you see him. Now, I'm not."

"I'm a doctor!" shouted Ken. "Get out of my way!"

"No, sir, I don't think it would be a good idea," said Dakin. Rima took Ken by the arm and led him off to a rock where they sat down, Rima holding his hand.

Dakin nodded to Ellery.

So Ellery saw Dr. Dodd; or rather he saw enough of Dr. Dodd to tell that it was Dr. Dodd, but such a Dr. Dodd as even he was barely able to stomach. But he steeled himself and asked them to turn the body over. He looked down at what had been the back of Dr. Dodd's head and turned away to stumble over to where the coroner and the prosecutor were talking to Malvina Prentiss. Francis O'Bannon stood at her elbow holding his notebook at the ready.

"The back of his head, Dr. Grupp—" began Ellery, swallowing.

"I know all about the back of his head," said Grupp in a querulous voice. "How would the back of your head look if you were tossed through a windshield, bounced twenty-five feet off sharp rocks, and then had a car fall on top of you?"

"Mr. Queen, are you on Miss Prentiss's payroll?" asked Prosecutor Chalanski with a slight smile. "She's interested in the back of his head, too."

"Why aren't you, Chalanski?" demanded Malvina Prentiss. The sun on her silver harlequin glasses as she tossed her head made Chalanski shift to the other foot. "Seems to me you people are in an awful hurry to write this off as a common highway accident."

"Now what do you mean by that?" asked the prosecutor without the smile.

"Coroner, didn't you say it looks to you as if he's been dead since about five?"

"A snap opinion. Completely unofficial."

"What was Dodd doing on the road at 5 A.M.?"

"He was a doctor," said a dry voice, "and he never refused a sick call in his life." It was Chief Dakin. "And he had his medical bag with him, Miss Prentiss."

"Well, who called him? Have you located this hypothetical patient? That oughtn't to be too hard, even for a Wrightsville policeman."

Dakin's colorless eyes flickered. But he said mildly,

"You might give us a chance, Miss Prentiss. This only just happened."

"And even if you do locate somebody, suppose Dodd was followed? Suppose he was cut off near the overpass and stopped? Suppose he was cracked on the head? Suppose his car was sent tearing at that wall up there with an unconscious man at the wheel?"

"Then I'd say somebody committed the pefect murder," replied Chalanski, smiling again. "Miss Prentiss, you have to have *some* fact to start supposing things with. If somebody stopped his car, there's no sign of it on the road up there. If somebody cracked Dodd on the head—which is possible and wouldn't be detectable now, Coroner Grupp has admitted—we haven't found the weapon it was done with, or it's part of that pile of bloody junk there and won't ever be identified. If Dodd's car was sent crashing at high speed against the retaining wall *we* can't tell it, because the tire marks visible up there are just such marks as the car would have made if Dodd ran off the road in an ordinary accident. In other words, Miss Prentiss, the facts we have to this point indicate an accident, like thousands of similar accidents messing up our roads every year. When we turn up something that points in the opposite direction you've got my word, Miss Prentiss, you'll be the first to be notified."

"Oh, come on, Chalanski," said Coroner Grupp; and the prosecutor followed him abruptly. Chief Dakin followed both.

The lack of a fact, thought Ellery. Again. How true. Bringing up, again, two possibilities. Either-or. Accident or murder. Natural or contrived. Obverse or reverse.

Rich man dead, poor man dead, beggar-man dead, thief dead, and now doctor dead.

"What?" said Ellery. "I beg your pardon, Miss Prentiss, I'm afraid I wasn't listening."

"I said," said the publisher, eying him frigidly, "What are you waiting for, Mr. Queen, a sign from heaven? *They're* waiting for Charlie Duncan's dead-wagon to cart off the pieces, but you're not an undertaker. Or are you?"

"I'm afraid—"

Francis O'Bannon said placatively, "It's all these deaths, Mr. Queen. MacCaby, Hart, Anderson, Jacquard, now Dodd. We're bothered, too—"

"Though in a different way, Spec, a different way," said his employer briskly. "The point is the great sleuth has been in our fair township for how long is it now?—and the longer you stay, Mr. Queen, the more people die. When do you make more history with some big deductions? When do you start sleuthing?"

Suppose I said to her right now, thought Ellery, with the wreckage of Dodd and his car not cold: Would you like to know, Miss Prentiss, who's going to be next? Because I can tell you, Miss Prentiss. And you'd laugh, and I'd have to laugh with you. Because we'd know and we wouldn't know. We'd see and we'd be blind. We'd act and we'd be running around in a circle.

"Tell me," she was saying—"since you don't seem to want to answer those fundamental questions—tell me, Mr. Queen. Do *you* think it was an accident?"

"I don't know," said Ellery.

The woman smiled. It was a radioactive smile, and Ellery thought: O you would-be Rosalind Russells of this world. He watched her as she turned to O'Bannon, everything about her flashing, "Use the murder tag with question marks, Spec. Connect Dodd with the others by association. MacCaby, Hart, Anderson, Jacquard, Dodd. What's behind it? Who's out to depopulate Wrightsville? Why? *And who's next?* That's our lead, Spec: *Who's Next?* Pratt!" she shouted at her photographer. "Did you shoot Queen? Well, why not?—come down here! 'Famous Sleuth at Scene of Crime Question Mark?' " Malvina Prentiss smiled atomically at Ellery. "We'll drag you into this yet, Ellery."

Francis O'Bannon, his redhead's face earnest and preoccupied, wrote and wrote.

Monday, May 1

"It was fear of the ultimate," said Ellery.

"Fear of what?" said Kenneth Winship.

"Fear of death."

They were sitting about in the Dodd living room waiting for Otis Holderfield. Until now they had avoided talking about the past four days—the police, the autopsy report, the inquest, the funeral, Mrs. Fowler's lamentations, Essie's hysterics, the dry and tasteless titbits of Harry Toyfell's philosophy, the prying telephone, the visits of the curious, the demands of the *Record* . . . the house fuller of Sebastian Dodd now that he was gone than when he had clumped through its halls. But Attorney Holderfield, looking put upon, raised a petulant voice Sunday afternoon after the funeral, announcing that he would be over the next morning with the deceased's will, which, Holderfield snapped, Dr. Dodd had drawn up only a few days before the accident; and this had brought a certain resurgence of interest in all quarters. Prosecutor Chalanski had indicated that he would be present; Chief Dakin had remarked that he'd likely be along, too. And Malvina Prentiss promised grimly that the press would not evade its responsibillty to report the proceedings. In fact, her Monday edition—an advance copy of which lay on the living room floor, hurled there by Dr. Winship—cried the probability that with the reading of Sebastian Dodd's will "the motive of his murderer" would be revealed. (Friday's *Record* had merely raised the question of murder; by Monday—to the *Record,* at least—the question had been answered and was beyond dispute. Which was exasperating to Coroner Grupp and prosecutor Chalanski, since nothing had come out in the interim to add a crumb's weight to the evidence; in fact, Wesley Hardin, 54, truck farmer, whose farm was located on Route 478 roughly halfway between Wrightsville and Slocum, came forward with the statement that it was he who had telephoned Dr. Dodd a little after 4 A.M. Thursday to come right away as Calvin, 9, was delirious and he was afraid the boy'd caught the diphtheria; when Dr. Dodd failed to arrive, Mr. Hardin had phoned the hospital and they sent an ambulance and Calvin was placed in the isolation ward—diphtheria sure enough. So that had been that and the coroner's jury had brought in a prompt verdict of "accidental death," to which the *Record* paid no attention whatever.)

"Fear of death," repeated Ellery as they sat waiting for Holderfield, Dakin, Chalanski, and the *Record.* "It had become a phobia. Unless you understand that . . . Didn't you know, Ken, that Dr. Dodd was obsessive on the specific subject of death?"

"No! A doctor—who sees it all the time—"

"Fears it all the more if there's something wrong with him to begin with. Dodd was so terrified of death that he took steps regularly to thwart it."

"To do what?" asked Rima bewilderedly.

"Well, the practice of divination is largely devoted to foretelling the future; and no diviner tries to foretell the future who doesn't have the frantic hope that somehow he can forestall it."

"Divination?"

"Only the practice of divination," nodded Ellery, "explains the variety of things Dodd kept in that locked room I showed you this morning. A pile of pebbles, books, finger rings, flatiron and burner, salt, dice, playing cards, and so on. Divination is practiced in many forms and each form is respectable with tradition, to the point of having scientific names like 'pessomancy,' for example, divination through the use of pebbles. Books, finger rings, redhot iron, salt, dice—and playing cards, of course—each has its prescribed divining uses and ritual, and each is represented in Dodd's locked room. I haven't seen anything like it in a long time."

"But Dr. *Dodd?*" said Rima faintly.

"You doubt it. Well, take the arrows, seven of them. Our Christian world has no monopoly on the practice of divination; the Mohammedans, for instance, are old hands at it and one of their favorite forms employs arrows to the number seven. There are seven 'divining arrows' in the great mosque at Mecca. Some authorities claim the Arabs actually employed only three. It doesn't matter. What does matter is that with that bundle of arrows upstairs, on top of all the other objects—every one of which is used in some form of divination—you simply have to conclude that Dr. Dodd for a long time had been trying to find out what the future held for him, using numerous prescribed methods, including the Mohammedan. And since the most important question about anyone's future is when and how he is going to die, it's obvious that the subject of his phobia was death. I myself saw him knocked galley-west by a couple of aces of spades. A dog howled and he was up all night. A bird got into his study and he had hysterics. All death omens . . . if you believe that sort of thing. He believed. And when he was convinced death was coming, he stopped fighting. You saw how he acted the last couple of days."

There seemed nothing to say, and no one said anything further until Essie Pingarn whined from the doorway, *"They're* here."

Otis Holderfield marched in followed by Chalanski, Dakin, O'Bannon of the *Record,* and a man who looked like an aged and prosperous Sherlock Holmes and was introduced as Dr. Farnham Farnham, internist and member of the Board of Directors of Wrightsville General Hospital. A moment later Mrs. Fowler and Toyfell appeared, remaining in the doorway beside Essie.

Attorney Holderfield made no attempt to dissemble his feelings. He slammed his antelope gloves and fawn Homburg on the fireplace mantel and opened his alligator briefcase with a yank of zipper disapproval that included not only his late client but all said client's earthly connections.

"It's nothing to me, you understand," Holderfield began, resuming a conversation he had apparently been having with himself. "Less than nothing. I'm just the instrument of my client's will, haha! Man has a right to dispose of his worldly goods as he sees fit, doesn't he? Ours not to reason why, hmm? Unless someone wants to raise the question of *non compos mentis,* which I doubt, seeing that my late client died unwed and without issue and leaving no blood relations that he knew of. Not that it would make any difference. My client certainly knew what he wanted to do with his estate, once he got going. He'd never had a will before last week—kept putting it off."

"People who are afraid to die," said Ellery, "generally do."

"Read it, Holderfield, read it," said the prosecutor indulgently. "Wills usually speak for themselves."

"Yes," said O'Bannon with a surprising incisiveness. "The *Record's* very interested in this will." Then he glanced at Ellery in a startled way. "Did you say Dodd was afraid to die?"

"Who isn't?" said Chief Dakin. "Come on, Holderfield."

Otis Holderfield had taken an elegantly bound legal paper out of his briefcase and was gazing down at it with a scrubbed and shaven bitterness. Now, with almost a smile, he flipped back the blue cover.

"I, Sebastian Dodd, now residing in Wrightsville, do hereby make, publish, and declare this to be my will . . ."

The little laywer attacked Dodd's will as if it were an enemy to be dispatched as quickly and venomously as possible. Testator directed that the Wrightsville Dye Works, which constituted the bulk of his estate, was to be liquidated. Out of the general estate legal fees, taxes, and all claims against the estate were to be paid. The mortgage on his house at Algonquin Avenue and Wright Street, which was large, was to be paid off. The house with its office equipment, furniture, furnishings, personal property and effects, et cetera, was to be placed at the disposal of "my associate, Dr. Kenneth Winship, for his residence and use should he so elect, rent free, for a period up to five years from the date of my decease, provided however that said Dr. Winship maintains the property in reasonable condition, pays taxes, et cetera, during his occupancy; thereafter, or at any time within said five years when said Dr. Winship may at his election vacate the premises, the house, its furnishings, et cetera, shall be sold and the proceeds added to my general estate."

The sum of one thousand dollars in cash was bequeathed to "my housekeeper, Mrs. Regina Fowler." (Mrs. Regina Fowler started then fumbled for her apron.)

The sum of five hundred dollars in cash was bequeathed to "Essie Pingarn, housemaid." (Essie Pingarn looked incredulous, then joyful, then she burst into tears.)

The principal remainder of the estate was to be placed into a Fund. Said Fund was to be known as "The MacCaby-Dodd Wrightsville Municipal Health Center and Receiving Hospital Fund" and was to be administered by the Board of Directors of the Wrightsville General Hospital as Trustee, who were also to act as Executor of the estate, to rebuild said hospital "from the ground up and in its entirety, if necessary, in order to give Wrightsville the modern hospital facilities its size and needs warrant. The rebuilt hospital is to include a modern Children's Wing along the lines indicated in my memorandum to the Board of February 19 of this year." (Dr. Farnham Farnham permitted himself a gratified smile.)

There was a little more legal language, and then Attorney Holderfield slammed the cover over the document and said malevolently, "That's that."

"Any comment, Dakin?" asked Prosecutor Chalanski after a silence.

"No comment." Chief Dakin rose. It was impossible to tell whether he was disappointed or relieved. Ellery, eying him closely, had to decide on a psychic basis that Dakin was relieved.

"And you, Mr. O'Bannon?" asked the prosecutor, turning a rather amused eye on Malvina Prentiss's shadow.

"What I think personally, Mr. Chalanski," replied O'Bannon, "hardly matters. And what the *Record* thinks it will undoubtedly print." And with a dyspeptic

Harvard smile O'Bannon went away, tucking his notebook soberly into his pocket as he did so.

"I'll go over everything with your Board. Dr. Farnham," said Otis Holderfield coldly, "at your convenience. I'll be at my office for the rest of the day if your attorneys are interested. I don't believe, gentlemen, there's anything else—"

"—except his bill for services rendered," said Chalanski dryly when Holderfield had gone, "which I'd examine under the microscope, Dr. Farnham. Well, good people, I think I may say the county authorities are satisfied. Glad it worked out this way. Hey, Mr. Queen? Nice, clean disposition. Miss Anderson, Dr. Winship . . . Coming, Dakin, Dr. Farnham?"

"You know, Winship," said Dr. Farnham, speaking for the first time as he shook hands, "with Dodd's death there's a vacancy on the Board. In the light of this magnificent gift of Sebastian Dodd's, I think it's no more than right that you should take his place on the Board, and I'll certainly recommend it to—"

But Ken, smiling, was shaking his head. "Thanks, Doctor, but I'm afraid I'd have to decline. I'm goin' to be pretty busy making a living. See me five years from now."

Everybody laughed, but when the others were gone a silence settled rather heavily. It was stirred up after a while by Ellery.

"You can understand Holderfield's pique. To have the whole suety pudding kicked out of his hungry little fingers like this must be maddening. All of those wonderful plums he expected—for negotiating the sale of the dye works, the nourishing fees he'd have commanded as Trustee and Executor of the estate—snatched. Poor old Otis. I wonder when the Waldo brothers will start dunning him to pay those tailoring bills he's been running up."

"And O'Bannon," grinned Ken, "did you see his face? The *Record* can hardly accuse the Wrightsville General of having murdered Doc. Or Mrs. Fowler for the thousand dollars he left her or Essie for her five hundred."

"Or Harry Toyfell," murmured Ellery, "for his nothing."

"Or me for mine! Well, baby, what do we do about our handsome legacy? Do we accept Doc's offer?"

"It's entirely up to you, darling," said Rima seriously. "With Dr. Dodd gone I imagine many of his patients will go elsewhere, so it might come in handy to have no rent to pay. Ken . . ."

"What?"

"I'm glad he didn't leave you anything."

"Huh?" Ken and Ellery exchanged glances. "Why?"

"Oh, nothing. I'm just . . . glad."

Ken laughed and enfolded her in his big arms. "You're about as subtle as a *Record* editorial. Darling, you're engaged to a guy who'll never have a dime. All I've ever wanted out of life is a little security, you, and enough surplus to buy some good recordings every once in a while. The rest is love and medicine—money doesn't come into it. And talking about love, you won't mind living here?"

"With you? I'd live in a tree. Oh, I wish we could!"

There was some kissing. Then Ken said, "Then let's get married."

"When?"

"Now. Tomorrow."

"But Ken—!"

"Hold it," said Ellery. "I have to see a street about some ozone."

"Ellery, no!" Rima was laughing. "Ken proposed long ago; this is just arrangements. You've *got* to be here to protect my interests."

"You can bloody well protect your own interests. I'm sick of being your Uncle Patsy."

"Oh, be quiet and listen. Ken, it's so soon."

"All right, move out of here," growled her swain. "Tongues are going to clack if you don't, Mrs. Fowler and Essie notwithstanding. Not that I give a curse, you understand, but Wrightsville can make it awfully tepid for anyone they drop into their kettle. Rima, Doc's forced our hand. We've *got* to get married."

"Ken's right," said Ellery. "You two couldn't go on living here together with Dodd gone, and to go off and live alone in a rooming house or that marsh-surrounded shanty—which I haven't seen yet, by the way!—would be inane. If you've actually made up your mind to marry young Dr. Kildare, Rima, you may as well shut your eyes and jump now as later."

So it was decided that they would get a license from Town Clerk Caiaphas Truslow at Town Hall in the morning and then run over to Justice of the Peace Burleigh Pendleton's place near the Junction on Route 16. "Of course," said Ken, " 'Aphas will spread the good word, but we'll be spliced before he can do much damage and a phone call to the *Record* right afterward ought to calm everybody." Ken glowered. "I wish we could take a couple of weeks off for a honeymoon."

"Dearest, I don't care—"

"I've got not only my patients on my hands, but Doc's. With the diphtheria epidemic still jamming everybody up there's no one I could turn them over to."

"Ken, I *adore* your being the reincarnation of Hippocrates. Really I do."

"Maybe you'd better forget the whole thing. Doc always said a doctor had no business getting married. And what can I offer you, after all? Certainly not what I'd hoped to be able to."

"Darling, I don't *want* a honeymoon."

"Well, I do! A man getting married is entitled to a honeymoon!"

It went on that way for some time, somewhere in between Ellery finding himself invited to be Ken's best man and the Winships' house guest afterward.

"Are you mad?" Ellery howled. "Camp with a couple of newlyweds? What do you think I'm made of, salt water taffy? Winship, I'll have you understand I've cracked a ventricle or two over this wench, too."

"Then you're giving up," said Rima before Ken could say anything.

"Giving up? What?"

"What brought you here. Not that I blame you, poor dear—"

"No such thing," said Ellery testily. "It's simply—"

"Then you'll have to stay," retorted Rima with supreme logic. "And since you're staying, you can't move to a hotel now or the *Record* will dream up all sorts of nasty things to print."

"Ellery, the house is huge. Rima and I'll have acres of privacy. That's settled." Ken got up, looking for his pipe. "The only thing is, where do we go from here?"

"There's that." Rima found it for him. "Ellery, what is the next step?"

"Well . . . now that Dodd's gone," said Ellery gloomily, "I'm pretty much locked on my course."

"What do you mean?"

"You know the two sets of possibilities I've had to keep juggling, Rima. They're reduced to one. It simplifies matters wonderfully." But he failed to look starry-eyed.

"Two sets of possibilities?" demanded Ken. "How? About what?"

"Oh, dear, it's kind of intricate, darling." Rima was looking anxiously at Ellery. When he nodded, she brightened. "Ellery said there were two viewpoints you had to look at the case from. Looked at one way, Dr. Dodd was what everybody thought he was. Looked at the other way, he was . . ." She stopped, seeing something in her lover's eye.

"He was what?"

"Criminally involved," finished Ellery.

"You suspected Doc of . . . of *what,* for pete's sake! "

"Of murdering MacCaby. Of driving Hart to suicide. Of being blackmailed by Tom Anderson and pushing him over Little Prudy's Cliff to loosen Anderson's hold."

"Of all the dribbling . . . pus!"

"Now, yes. But before Dodd died—no."

"How the devil does his death change anything?"

"Alive, Dodd was possibly a murderer. Dead, he's possibly a victim, certainly an innocent man. Innocent, he told the truth. Then, as Dr. Dodd said, Luke MacCaby died of coronary whatever-it-was; Dodd did not deliberately drive John Spencer Hart to suicide; and when he gave Anderson the five thousand dollars, it wasn't because Anderson was blackmailing him but simply out of the goodness of his heart. With Anderson not a blackmailer, the letter he left with Holderfield in the envelope containing the five thousand dollars probably instructed Jacquard to hold the money for Rima—nothing else. And when Jacquard, after appropriating the money, Rima, broke in here it wasn't to find 'blackmail evidence' but merely to burglarize the house.

"With Dodd innocent, we're on a straight track, with no alternate route. We're back where we started from: in a series of deaths following the precise pattern of a child's game. Rich man MacCaby, poor man Hart, beggar-man Anderson, thief Jacquard, Doctor Dodd."

"But *why?*"

"That," mourned Ellery, "remains the question."

Ken shook his head, his pipe waggling. "It's no question at all, Ellery. I think you're shadowboxing. An old man with chronic heart trouble dies of it, a businessman caught embezzling blows his brains out, a penniless man who suddenly came into possession of five thousand dollars is killed in what was probably an attempted robbery by somebody who didn't know he'd deposited the money for safekeeping with a lawyer, a petty thief breaks into a house and when he's caught tries to grab a gun and gets shot in the scuffle, an overworked and highly neurotic doctor on a night call runs off the road. Every damned one has a natural explanation. Why try to string them together because they happen to fit a hunk of nursery nonsense?"

"That's why," said Ellery. "Because they do. Oh, it's silly. But how do you explain it?" When they did not answer, he said, "I have an inbred mind. Eats itself up alive. This is the sort of problem that drives me crazy. I couldn't let go of it if I wanted to. Especially," he said suddenly, "since it isn't over."

"What isn't over?"

"The deaths."

"Oh, for God's sake."

"Wait a minute, Ken," said Rima.

"Dodd blinded me. There was someone else wound up with MacCaby, Hart, Anderson, and Jacquard. And with Dodd, for that matter."

"Who's that?" demanded Ken.

"Otis Holderfield. It's Holderfield who drew the MacCaby will. When Dodd retained Holderfield to look after his interests, it was Holderfield who suggested and composed the letter to Hart for Dodd's signature which was the direct cause of Hart's killing himself. It was Holderfield who turned Dodd's five thousand dollars over to Tom Anderson. It was Holderfield who at Anderson's request regained possession of the money, allegedly in trust. It was Holderfield who turned Anderson's sealed envelope over to Nick Jacquard. And it was Holderfield who, as Dodd's attorney, drew up the Dodd will."

"You mean that shiny little squirt," said Ken, "is behind everything that's happened?"

"No, because—don't hit me, Ken—there's reason to believe Holderfield is going to be the next victim."

"Here we go again!"

But Ellery kept chanting through his teeth, *"Rich man, poor man, beggar-man, thief; doctor, lawyer . . ."* He spread his hands. "A lawyer is next in the series, and Holderfield is the only lawyer up to his neck in everything that's happened so far."

They were silent until a voice said from the doorway, " 'Scuse me."

It was Harry Toyfell.

"I'd like to talk to ye, Dr. Winship."

"What about, Harry?"

"It's Doc Dodd give me this job, Dr. Winship. Maybe this ain't the time. But I'd like to know where I stand."

"Oh." Ken looked embarrassed. "Matter of fact, I've been meaning to talk to you. I'm going to have to take over the running of the house, the expense is considerable . . . Maybe, Harry, it would be better if you looked around for another job. Right away."

Harry Toyfell did not seem surprised. It was as if he never expected anything but the worst and could be surprised only by something short of it.

He shuffled out of sight beyond the doorway.

"Mr. Toyfell, wait!" Rima said in a low voice, "Darling, I know it's practical to start by cutting expenses, and I've never cared for him . . . much myself, but couldn't we keep him on a little while? He *has* had such a hard time . . ."

"Hell, it isn't the expense," said Ken, redfaced. "He's a damned Jonah!"

"So you've noticed it, too," murmured Ellery.

"I'm not blind! Toyfell worked for MacCaby and MacCaby died. He went to work for Hart and Hart committed suicide. He had two friends, Tom Anderson and Nick Jacquard—and where are they? And he no sooner goes to work for Doc Dodd than Doc dies. Damn it all, baby, we're starting a new life. Call me superstitious—"

"No, darling. I hadn't thought of it that way . . . Ken, do you mind if I do something for him?"

"Cripes, *I'll* do something for him. I just don't want him around here. Toyfell!"

The gardener shuffled back into view.

"Harry, this is kind of sudden, I know. Suppose I pay your salary till you find another job."

"And you can stay at my shack in The Marshes, Mr. Toyfell," added Rima, "till you do. There's some canned food there, and I planted some vegetables that . . ."

But Toyfell was shaking his long head, his crocodile jaws parted in the imitation of a smile. "Tom brought ye up right, Rima. Mighty Christian. But it's better to give than to take. The giver gains and the taker loseth. That's wisdom ye won't find in the medical books. I'll be out of here tonight."

He went away without once having glanced at Ken, the only sign that his philosopher's skin had been scratched.

It was a remarkably different Otis Holderfield who received Ellery in his office that afternoon. Holderfield was in high spirits. One of the Waldo brothers—Ellery could not determine which—was hurrying away with a handful of swatches; the nubile secretary was still very much in evidence; and the little lawyer himself had his British-last shoes higher than his head in an attitude of nabob comfort.

"Sit down, Mr. Queen! Tickled to see you. Hope you didn't think I made a darn jackass of myself this morning. Attorney ought never to let his emotions get the better of him; it's absolute death, haha! When I got back and thought it over, things didn't look so bad. No, sir. Of course, it's a blow losing an estate like Dodd's; but we'll make out, we'll make out. What's on your mind?"

"You."

"Me?" Holderfield was startled. "How do you mean?"

"Holderfield, do you carry any life insurance?"

The lawyer took the cigar from his teeth. "What's the joke?"

"Suppose I tell you I have reason to believe you're going to die."

Holderfield stared. Then his swivel chair squealed as he sat up. "So are you."

"But not before my time, I hope."

"You mean I will before mine?" smiled the little man.

"Any day now."

"What is this," he asked genially, "the introductory remarks to a shakedown? Who—I mean whom—do I pay, and for what?"

"I don't blame you," said Ellery morosely. "And yet I couldn't have slept tonight if I hadn't warned you. There are times, Mr. Holderfield," he said, looking out the window at Washington Street, "times of peculiar crisis, when almost everything goes wrong, nothing makes sense, all that's left is a common language. And I don't suppose you have the faintest notion what I'm babbling about."

"That's right," grinned the lawyer. But his eyes were watchful.

"So I'll have to tell you my favorite fairy tale these days. Once upon a time there was a miserly old man named MacCaby," began Ellery; and he proceeded to relate the story of the five men whose deaths followed the specifications of a jingle. *"Doctor, lawyer . . ."*

Ellery turned from the window. Otis Holderfield's head was thrown back, his hands held his jiggling sides, and he was laughing so hard his eyes ran over.

"You find it funny, Holderfield?"

"Funniest thing I ever heard!"

It's not this funny, thought Ellery. And suddenly it came to him that Holderfield knew something, something he had never revealed, and that it was this knowledge which made him laugh now. Not because he was amused, but because he was not. He's covering up, thought Ellery. I've hit him somewhere. If I only knew where!

"Course, you're only pulling my leg," gasped the lawyer as he wiped his eyes.

"No."

"You're serious?"

"Yes."

"For heaven's sake. See here, Mr. Queen, I'm a man with no imagination at all." Holderfield waved his cigar. "Don't misunderstand me. I take it kindly of you to warn me. But—haha!—I can see myself asking Chief Dakin for protection because—"

"I doubt that he could give it to you," said Ellery, picking up his hat.

"Wait just a minute, Mr. Queen!" His telephone was ringing. "Who, Floss! . . . Huh? All right, put him on. Hello? . . . Yes . . . Oh . . . Well, maybe I could at that. Matter of fact, I could . . . No, no, entirely selfish on my part. Wait till you see the condition it's in, haha! What? . . . Now wait a minute. I'm not one of your Wrightsville millionaires. Let's say eighty-five a month and maintenance. Best I can do . . . You know where it is? . . . Okay, see you tonight." Holderfield hung up. "And you hanging crape, Mr. Queen. Why, this is my lucky day. Here, I'll see you out."

"Lucky day?" said Ellery.

"I've got a little place over on Upper Curling. Pretty much gone to seed. I've been thinking about a gardener and handyman, and by crickmajiggy, as old Ivor Crosby used to say, I've just hired me the best damn one in the county. Much obliged, Mr. Queen, I'll remember you in my will, haha!"

Harry Toyfell had found a new employer.

Waiting for Buzz Congress and the elevator, Ellery felt icy mice scamper along his spine. It was ridiculous, but there they were.

Tuesday, May 2

Rima and Ken were married after Ken's office hours Tuesday afternoon in Burleigh Pendleton's parlor, with Ellery and a beaming Mis' Pendleton to witness.

"It's an omen," chortled Ken as they walked back to his car. The homegoing Junction traffic was zipping joyously by. "Burleigh never has Mis' Pendleton to witness except when she's sober. Did you hear that extra zing in his delivery? We've got a mighty good start, Mrs. Winship."

"Bless them. Bless everybody." Rima was hanging on to her husband's arm as if she were afraid he might vanish.

"Get in, Ellery."

"Not this time," said Mr. Queen hollowly. "There's a limit to every man's endurance, and this marks mine. You two go on about your business and let me get quietly potted. I'll notify the *Record,* so don't bother to stop in town."

"Oh, Ellery . . ."

"Oh Ellery nothing. I don't even want to know where you're going."

"Up to Durkee's Falls."

"Just for overnight, but we thought you'd at least have our wedding supper with us."

"There is a dreadful noise of waters in mine ears, as the poet says, and they hear not. God speed and bless your union and may neither of you ever scab. Now get the hell out of here before I break down and blub."

"We'll be back first thing in the morning!" shouted Ken as they drove off.

Ellery stood at the justice of the peace's gate until the exhaust of Hymen's chariot mingled with the haze of the hills.

He began to trudge up Route 16 with his hands in his pockets, wondering what it must feel like to be happy. Rima was happy, so happy she was numb. Ken was happy, with a masuline exuberance he had tried decently to control. Mis' Pendleton had been happy, perhaps in anticipation of the bottle she was reputed to keep stashed in her chicken coop. About dour Burleigh Pendleton Ellery was not sure; he was a Yankee of Scotch blood; but at least he dispensed happiness. Life went on in and about Wrightsville, working, drinking, quarreling, copulating; people died and people married, everybody exercised some function.

And here he was, about as useful as an extra appendix.

Ellery found himself before Gus Olesen's Roadside Tavern. It was only a hundred yards or so up the road from Burleigh Pendleton's, a juxtaposition both merchants had found profitable.

He went in.

Gus's was crowded with people decently having a beer or a shot or two before going home from the mill or the office. Everybody seemed to be enjoying himself except one man alone in a booth, who was plainly suffering. Ellery walked over and said, "I'm a desperate man and there's nowhere else to park. May I share this, or do I fight you for it?"

The man said belligerently, "Sit and be damned to you," and when he looked up Ellery saw under the fedora—which looked as if an elephant had trampled on it—the once-precise red hair and countenance of Francis O'Bannon. "Haven't we met? Don't answer. I'm really not interested."

"Why, O'Bannon." Ellery sat down, pleased. O'Bannon crocked seemed another man. His pink plastic glasses hung from one ear and a splash of what was probably whisky debauched his chaste tie; but it was more than that. The glare in his eye reflected a fire from which the damper had been lifted. He gave out a fierce exhalation of manhood. "What's happened? You and Malvina have a bit of a thing, old boy?"

"Look, sucker—"

"The name is Queen."

"Queen, look. Have a drink."

Ellery filled one of the numerous vessels strewn about the table from the incumbent bottle. "Cheers."

"Just drink it. What did you say the name was?"

"Queen. How about you and Malvina—"

"Queen, when you bandy the name of that bitch about a bistro you insult an honorable profession. That silver-plated houri. That svelte-rumped Hitler. The brass of a gold brick, the conscience of a bookie, the soul of a press agent, and the ambition of a body louse. And no more heart than a frozen fryer. She flicks her tail in your face and dares you to think of anything lower than last week's paid advertising. There is a broad, Mr. Queen, who defies analysis. She buys a ninety-five-thousand-dollar house on Skytop Road, fills it with fifty grand worth of decorators' daydreams, and she sleeps in a whitewashed cubbyhole with nothing in it but a hospital bed and a straightbacked chair. She has a ten-thousand-dollar collection of classical recordings and a twenty-five-hundred-dollar machine and all she plays on it are Bozo, Babar, Christopher Robin, and Frank Luther singing Mother Goose. And she hates kids. Contradictory, see?"

"Maybe she once lost a child. Has she ever been married?"

"Thrice. Number one was a millionaire pork packer, around seventy, number two was a ballet dancer, number three was a society fungus who wore corsets and paraded around the ancestral keep in a Japanese kimono and a riding crop. Maybe you've got something there. But me, I'm a primitive soul. One of these days I'm going to beat her brains in with an eight-column head of pi."

"Tell her off. It's not so messy."

"Mr. Green," said O'Bannon morosely, "every man goes nuts in his own way."

"Why not quit if it's so unbearable?"

"What's it to you?"

"I try to render service where it's in obvious demand. O'Bannon, if you ever saw Harvard Square it was only to get a story on the mating habits of the Crimson undergraduate for the *America Weekly*. Why this flowering-of-New-England getup?"

"Yikes, the fellow undoes me. Would you really like to know?"

"We have the evening before us."

"You wouldn't believe it."

"I'm a specialist in fantasy. Try me."

"Then get a load of this—Breen, is it? I just spot this Prentiss calamity at one of the last presidential conventions. She irks me—you know what I mean? Right off the bat. Ever see a dame who the first time you saw her you wanted to make like you're milking a cow with her neck? Gorgeous, knows all the shots, just the slightest curl around the edges, and don't-touch-me-peasant-I'm-for-your-betters. Hell, for all I know she was there trying to get herself nominated; I wouldn't put it past her. Anyway, I kind of follow her around like a dog. You can't deny it, Feeney, she's got racy lines. But a sort of instinct tells me, 'O'Bannon, don't let this hunk of frozen Chanel get her hooks in you.' So, I hang back, see? Well, I get back to New York where I'm wiping up after a city editor at the time and, Sweeney, the first thing I see is a Guild piece about this lady publisher in a jerk New England town who's bought up an alleged newspaper and is making large motions in the direction of the national screwball prize. And what should her name be but Malvina Prentiss, my convention dream-girl! I make a few reckless inquiries among some unemployed beagles I know and I find out Malvina is hunting for an editorial assistant on this bumpkin bedsheet with bigtime, brass-knuckle newspaper experience. But there's a catch. I discover a lot of guys are tripping over who would like to bury themselves in the hay for a couple of semesters for personal reasons, and otherwise qualify. And that is that the successful candidate must also be refined, of Pilgrim stock, and—I quote—'with a sound Harvard background.' What she wants, apparently, is a sort of journalistic thug type who was baptized in the Charles River and cut his first incisors on the silver service of the Copley-Plaza. Well, my name isn't O'Bannon by accident. Every Irishman in America has at least one cousin in Boston and mine is also named Francis O'Bannon. Cousin Francis has pale hands, Back Bay manners, a crampy look, and he got an M.A. from Harvard and is now running a suds parlor at Revere Beach. So after spending a couple of weeks with him getting the feel of my Back Bayground again and brushing up on my memories of the Common, the Yard, Copey, and Radcliffe, another week in Cambridge studying the lingo of the natives, their peculiar habits and customs and so forth, buying me these plate glass cheaters for twenty bucks, and finally visiting a Harvard Square funeral parlor at four in the morning to borrow the clothes from an old alumnus who had no further use for them, I entrained sedately for Wrightsville with Cousin Francis's sheepskin under my arm and a letter of introduction from President Conant, which I forged, and I was in. Quickest thing you ever saw.

"The question is," said O'Baanon, refilling his glass bitterly, "who took whom and who gets it in the end? Mr. Greeley, sex is the third leg of humanity. It ought to be abolished along with falsies, mint-flavored potato chips, and inherited wealth. Here's blood in your eye."

"And in Malvina's," said Ellery, "in case you're interested."

O'Bannon straightened up as if he had been shot in the back. "Where is she?" he asked cautiously.

"Standing in the doorway having herself a panoramic look."

"The hell with her."

"She's advancing."

"I'll tell her off. That's what I'll do."

"Uh-uh," said Ellery. "She's spotted me."

O'Bannon turned toward the wall, shoulders high. "Decoy her, for God's sake. Get off your fanny." His fingers fumbled with his tie.

"Too late."

O'Bannon sprang to his feet. "So! You thought you could get me intoxicated, did you?" he cried scornfully, leveling an indignant forefinger at Ellery. "You scoundrel, I'll have you know most of this liquor you've been urging upon me has been secretly poured on the floor! Oh, hello there, Miss Prentiss. Miss Prentiss—"

"Spec." The word dropped as softly as snow on a cake of ice. "Do you know how long I've been looking for you? You're drunk."

"Miss Prentiss, the cur phoned me. He had me meet him in this low saloon on a vary plausible excuse that escapes me at the moment. He's been plying me with bourbon and asking insidious questions, Miss Prentiss, a great many insidious questions. Oh, he'll deny it—what's your name, again?—"

"Queen," said Ellery. "Won't you join us, Miss Prentiss?"

"Thank you." She sat down beside Francis O'Bannon, eying him curiously. "Sit down, Spec, you look ridiculous. And fix your hat. I didn't know you were human." O'Bannon sat down, muttering. "But why Spec, Queen? Not very sporting of you. Where I come from we throw those back."

Ellery's heart bled for O'Bannon. "I think you underestimate O'Bannon, Miss Prentiss. He didn't give a thing away."

"What would there be to give? You must be desperate if you're looking for clues in the *Record's* direction."

"Exactly what I told the fellow, Miss Prentiss!"

"Shut up, Spec." Malvina laughed. "I've been looking you up, Ellery. This is your fourth crack at Wrightsville and your score is perfect. A string of . . . what do they call them in the sports department, Spec?"

"Skunk eggs," said O'Bannon.

"Skunk eggs, Ellery. And from the look of things, you're preparing to set on still another striped pussy."

"I don't think," said Ellery with a secretive smile, "that that's quite what I'm hatching this time, Miss Prentiss." Her laughter had recalled Otis Holderfield's, and it had occurred to him that Holderfield was Wrightsville, which endows the printed word with a magic that transforms hearsay into fact. To read it in the *Record* might stop Holderfield's hilarity.

Malvina Prentiss frowned; O'Bannon blinked and looked interested.

"You've found out something."

"The name of the next candidate."

"Oh, come!"

"You talk like his campaign manager," said O'Bannon in an angry tone.

"You flatter me," said Ellery. "However, I've begun to detect some of the strings. Number one, MacCaby, was a rich man, for instance. Number two, Hart, turned out to be a poor man. Rich man, poor man. Tom Anderson was known as The Town Beggar. Beggar-man. Nick Jacquard, number four to leave us, was The Town Thief—"

"Rich man, poor man, beggar-man . . . thief?" mumbled O'Bannon. He started. *"Rich man, poor man, beggar-man, thief; doctor . . . Dr. Dodd!"*

"Lawyer," said Malvina Prentiss swiftly. "Spec—"

"Oh, no," groaned O'Bannon. "No, Miss Prentiss."

"You chanted it yourself. What else could it mean?"

"You can't print a thing like that!"

"Why not?"

"They'd be howling from the lobster beds of Maine to the perfumed strand of Baja California!"

"Queen isn't howling."

"He made it up."

"Not I," said Ellery. "You needn't squirm so, O'Bannon. Think of it in terms of lunacy and it at once becomes reasonable."

"You're a fiction writer!"

"I didn't write this fiction."

Malvina Prentiss was tapping the table with her silver fingernails. "Are you through, Spec? This is the tieup we've been looking for. Whether it makes sense or not. For all I know, it does. Anyway, it doesn't matter. I'll handle it from the editorial end. You run over to Boston first thing in the morning—no, make it tonight; take my Caddy—and track down the source of that rhyme, or game, or whatever it is. Bring back every book you can find that gives anything on it. Are you in condition to drive tonight?"

"Please, Miss Prentiss," said O'Bannon, offended.

The woman in silver rose. "That was sharp, Queen. Your spotting that. My offer of a column is still open. At your own figure."

Ellery shook his head. "I'm allergic to millstones, Miss Prentiss. By the way, Rima Anderson and Kenneth Winship were married this afternoon by Justice of the Peace Burleigh Pendleton. They're on a one-night honeymoon and don't ask me where."

Malvina seemed surprised. But all she said was, "Our bird-girl does all right, doesn't she? Spec, get a move on," and she strode off.

O'Bannon muttered, "Thanks for not crabbing my act, chum," pushing himself to his feet. His hand collided with the bottle and he looked around furtively. But then he called, "Coming, coming, Miss Prentiss!" and hurried after her.

Ellery stared at O'Bannon's bottle.

Dark brown secrets guaranteed.

Besides, what else was there to do?

Ellery reached for the bottle.

Saturday, May 13

O'Bannon disappeared, Rima and Ken came back, Malvina Prentiss went to town on the front page of the *Record,* O'Bannon returned; and Ellery simmered in the May sunshine like an emptying kettle or sulked in the gloomier parts of the Dodd house trying not to hear the music of the newlyweds. Rima reminded him of a newly mated bird busy with her nest. She shopped, tore down curtains, changed drapes, made diplomatic changes in Mrs. Fowler's and Essie Pingarn's routine, received patients, typed case cards, answered the telephone, hauled her books over from the shack, took her driver's test in Ken's aging but faithful Packard, announced that she was going to repaper the house herself and spent snatched hours at Whitby's Paint Store poring over wallpaper books, overhauled her husband's wardrobe—which she declared a disgrace—and at night dropped into bed tired and ecstatic. And Ken could be heard whistling at all hours, even when the record player Ellery had given them as a wedding present was silent. At other times the house was full of Mozart, Hayden, and Bach—good round geometric beauty which succeeded only in mocking the insoluble mathematics in Ellery's head. Sometimes the music drove him into the garden with a hoe or the insecticide spray, but this invariably invoked the departed image of Harry Toyfell and from this it was but a frame to the picture of little Otis Holderfield; so gardening was no escape, either.

The *Record* recited its deadly rhyme and O'Bannon was avenged. Everybody howled. From the refuse heaps of Low Village to the cathedral aisle of the Hill *Rich man, poor man* raised its treble voice in glee. It became a proud Wrightsville property and strong businessmen took it into their councils whenever the moment called for hilarity. Floyd Lycoming set it to music and His Hollis Hummadours gave its premiere at the annual May dance of Wrightsville High. The next day the whole town was singing it, and it was the feature of Lycoming's broadcast over KWRI the following week.

The *Record's* editorial retorted—against O'Bannon's advice—that fiddling was an old custom but Rome burned just the same. The ineffable Malvina, it seemed, had a tarnish spot on her polished armor: she could let pique make her tilt at windmills. The laughter only infuriated her and *Who Is the Lawyer?* remained her stubborn head. Even the halls of the County Court House and the County Lawyers' Block rang, and Judge Lysander Newbold, presiding over the spring term, was heard for the first time within the memory of court attendants to utter a witticism: When an attorney for the defense failed to answer at the opening of court one morning, Judge Newbold smiled and said archly, *"Cherchez l'avocat."*

Prosecutor Chalanski and Chief of Police Dakin were monotonously reported in the *Record* as declining comment. But one day Essie Pingarn called Ellery to the phone and he picked it up to hear Dakin's bitter voice remark, "I suppose this is your doings, Mr. Queen. Who is this lawyer that's tagged to be next?"

"Otis Holderfield, I think," said Ellery humbly. "Maybe Holderfield will listen to you, Dakin. Or if he won't promise to be careful, put him under guard."

"I haven't the time, manpower, or budget to play games, Mr. Queen," rasped Dakin. "Got a town of ten thousand to police. Besides, Holderfield came to *me* and told me what you'd told him. He's blaming you for this whole thing. Otis ain't laughing, and I'm not either!"

"Well, I'm glad to hear he doesn't find it funny any more."

"Mr. Queen I made up my mind about something and I may as well tell you right now."

"What's that?"

"This *Rich man, poor man* tripe did it. There's not been a crime in the carload. I can't go along with you any more on this." And Chief Dakin hung up abruptly.

Ellery crept away.

Ellery was alone in the living room one Saturday afternoon, leafing listlessly through a copy of *Mother Goose* which he had borrowed from the Carnegie Library the night before. Ken was out making house calls; Rima had gone over to Logan's Market to place her weekly order, an act of housewifely initiative to which Mrs. Fowler had not yet become inured—Ellery could hear her rattling pots around in the kitchen; Essie was pushing a carpet sweeper somewhere upstairs. Then the front door banged, and Ellery looked up to see Rima, panting.

"Otis Holderfield . . ."

As he raced for his coat and hat, Rima gasped out what she knew. She had been in Logan's waiting her turn at the meat counter when she heard screams from the street. People were converging from every direction on the Granjon Block diagonally across the street. She had caught one glimpse of something sprawled on the pavement before the Waldo Brothers' tailoring shop and then the crowd had closed in.

"A taxi driver said it was Lawyer Holderfield . . . fell out of a window . . ."

Ellery found the southeast corner of Washington and Slocum Streets roped off. Saturday afternoon was High Village's busiest time of the week and several hundred people pressed against the police lines. In the doorways of the shops within the lines pale faces were packed; among them Ellery glimpsed the duplicate Waldos. A bluecoat was leaning far out of a fourth-floor window of the Granjon Block on which was lettered OTIS HOLDERFIELD, ATTORNEY-AT-LAW. On the sidewalk directly below him Chief Dakin, Malvina Prentiss, Francis O'Bannon, and several uniformed men stood about a newspaper-covered heap.

Ellery shouted; Dakin spied him and said something and an officer let him through.

Ellery lifted a corner of the papers. Holderfield was lying in an impossible position, like a double-jointed acrobat. He was coatless. His custom-made trousers were no longer immaculate and his silk shirt was a camouflage in oily grime, dust, and blood.

An emergency truck from the Volunteer Fire Department on Minikin Road and Lincoln Street, two squares away, was backed up to the curb a few feet from the heap.

The crowd watched in silence.

When Ellery rose, Chief Dakin said, "A lawyer it was, Mr. Queen," in hostile accents.

"Not just a lawyer, Dakin. Lawyer Holderfield."

"Yeah."

"Well, it's done, Dakin. Can't be undone."

"Yeah."

Ellery looked at him, the hostility penetrating. "You sound as if you blame me for this, Dakin," he said pleasantly.

"Not talkin' about blame. But sometimes . . . you put an idea in a man's head and he makes it come true."

"Oh, I see," said Ellery.

Dakin said abruptly, "They'll take care of him. Come on upstairs. Chalanski's there checking my boys."

There were some law books open on Holderfield's desk and on a pad of ruled yellow paper Holderfield's handwriting told that he had been working on a brief in a case in which Prosecutor Chalanski said the lawyer had been scheduled to appear the following week. Holderfield's beautiful suit jacket poised over the back of his chair and on the clothestree floated his twenty-dollar hat.

"Holderfield let his secretary, Flossie Bushmill, go at around 2:30," said the prosecutor. "She's usually off at one on Saturdays, but she says she had a lot of correspondence to get out. He went down with her and they walked over to the Kelton grill and had a bite of lunch together. He left her outside the Kelton and she saw him walk back toward the Granjon Block. Buzz Congress took him up in the elevator, alone."

"Buzz says he was moody," said Chief Dakin, "not his usual wise-cracking self. So does Flossie Bushmill." He added "They say he'd been that way ever since Dr. Dodd died, and specially bad this week."

"Buzz saw him unlock the office door and go in. And that's the last anyone saw him alive."

"Except his killer," said Malvina Prentiss.

"No evidence of that at all, Miss Prentiss," said Chalanski mildly. "At some point in his work Holderfield got up from his desk and went to the window, which was open, by the way. It's been hot for May and he probably wanted a breath of air. And he fell out—"

"Or threw himself out," put in Dakin. He was staring at Ellery.

But the prosecutor shook his head. "Doubt it, Dakin. Some of the letters Holderfield dictated this morning referred to appointments for Monday, and so on. And his brief is lucid and concise, not like the work of a man whose mind was playing around with thoughts of suicide. No," said Chalanski, "this was an accident. It wouldn't be the first time a man went to a window on a warm day, feeling dizzy, and fell out."

"Or was pushed out," smiled Miss Prentiss.

The prosecutor glanced heavenward and went to the window.

Ellery stirred. "Have you talked to the other tenants in the building?"

"Nobody to question," Dakin said. "The last tenant but Holderfield to leave the building was Lawyer Wendell Wheeler, third floor, who was late for a golf date at the Country Club and left at 4:15; Buzz Congress took him down. Buzz went home at five, his regular Saturday quittin' time; there's no night man and after hours late tenants walk down. We questioned the storekeepers on the street floor—"

"Including the Waldo brothers?" Ellery found himself murmuring.

"Sure including the Waldos," snapped Dakin. "They're no privileged characters. But nobody saw anyone enter or leave the building after five."

"And if somebody had," remarked Francis O'Bannon, "would the storekeepers have noticed? Or were they all sunning themselves on the sidewalk between five and six on their busiest afternoon of the week?"

"Good point, Spec," said his employer. "The thing is, gentlemen, this could have been murder and you know it. Either Holderfield's killer got in by the Washington Street door or the back entrance via Granjon Alley, either from Slocum Street or Wright. And out the same way."

Chalanski turned around. "I'd like something a little more concrete in the way of evidence, Miss Prentiss."

"Read the *Record*," she retorted. "*Rich man, poor man, beggar-man, thief; doctor, lawyer—*"

"*Indian chief*," finished the prosecutor with a broad smile. "Dakin, do we have any redskins in Wrightsville? Because, according to Miss Prentiss—and Mr. Queen? —somebody named Hiawatha is going to be the next victim of Phantom Killer."

"Do you have any Indians in Wrightsville?" asked Ellery.

"No!" shouted Dakin.

"I don't mean necessarily a character in breechclout and turkey feathers," said Ellery. "A remoter connection will do. For instance, someone with Indian blood who's descended from—forgive me—a chief."

"Far as I know, Mr. Queen," replied Chalanski with gravity, before Dakin could explode again, "no one in town qualifies. However, you might ask Dolores Aikin over at the Library. She has the genealogy of Wrightsville at her fingertips."

"Make a note of that, Spec," said the newspaper publisher.

"I asked the Aikin woman that last week," replied O'Bannon. "No Indian chief."

"What," demanded the chief of police in a howl, "has all this fiddlededee got to do with Otis Holderfield? Now, you tell me! Mr. Chalanski, I'm through here! And if you are, too—"

"Just another moment or two," said Ellery. "As far as Holderfield's death is concerned, gentlemen, you can shout your Yankee horse sense hoarse but you can't get by the fact that a lawyer was called for next in the rhyme and a lawyer was the next to die. And not merely a lawyer, but a lawyer up to his chubby dimple in the MacCaby-Hart-Anderson-Jacquard-Dodd case. You can't ignore it. You can't laugh it off . . . Yes, Holderfield might have fallen out of that window—accident. Yes, he might have thrown himself out on impulse—suicide. But he also might have been pushed out by someone who got into the building at a time when there was no risk of being seen. And of the three theories it's the murder theory that is supported by our miserable rhyme. Don't ask me to explain it; that's why I've been hanging around Wrightsville. I can't explain it. Nor do I expect your coroner's jury, Mr. Chalanski, to bring in anything but a verdict of accidental death. The legal mills properly reject fantastic grist like this. But I ask you—and you, Dakin— to open your minds unofficially to it. And to keep them open to the last possibility."

"What last possibility?" snarled Dakin.

"With no Indians in Wrightsville, there's only one other place the rhyme can go."

"Is there more to it?" exclaimed Chalanski.

"Not in that version, no. But it happens that the rhyme, or verse, or game, exists in two forms" That everlasting dualism, thought Ellery. "In one version it's *Rich man, poor man, begger-man, thief; doctor, lawyer, Indian chief.* In the other version it's *Rich man, poor man, beggar-man, thief; doctor, lawyer—*"

"*Merchant chief,*" said O'Bannon.

"Exactly."

Dakin made a despairing sound and Chalanski threw up his hands.

"Frankly," said Ellery, "if I owned a successful retail business in this town—especially if I were the leading merchant in my line—I shouldn't sleep too well tonight. This last one adds a nice touch. There's no 'merchant chief' who's been involved in any of the deaths so far. Not only can't we prevent the last death, we can't even hazard a guess as to who's going to be honored. Perhaps, Miss Prentiss," said Ellery, turning to the silver woman in the very silent office, "that's a fact which in the interest of Wrightsville's peace of mind you won't care to print in your newspaper."

That night Ellery walked over to Upper Curling Street under black young leaves to find a group of High Villagers standing on the broken walk before the house he was seeking. They were women as well as men and some of the men had been drinking. He did not like the suspended faces or their lack of conversation. Ellery made his way through them very carefully.

It was a shabby little building in need of paint, with the shrunken look of so many of Wrightsville's very old houses, and its interior was harmoniously minature and seedy. He'd have got rid of this if things had gone differently for him, Ellery thought in the flickering entrance hall; as it is, it's getting rid of him.

He found Dakin in the yellowlit parlor going through a sagging breakfront, watched by Harry Toyfell. Toyfell wore a torn gray sweater buttoned on his rootlike neck, as if he were cold. His eyes were just visible.

"Going through Holderfield's personal stuff," grunted the chief of police. "Begins to look like Otis's death is going to make lots of folks in town mighty sad. Didn't leave much beside debts."

"Oh?" said Ellery. As Toyfell turned, he said, "Don't go yet, Toyfell. I came over to see you."

Toyfell stopped.

"Carried a second mortgage on the house, they'll repossess his car, and if there's two hundred dollars' worth of cash value in his household effects I'll eat 'em with molasses. A hundred and sixty-four dollars in his checking account, no savings, no stocks or bonds, and no insurance. Some accounts receivable outstanding, and course there's what the Dodd estate owes him, but that's going to take months and balancin' it off against his bills, when it's all settled there won't be enough left over to buy him a grave marker. He owes the Waldos alone over a thousand dollars for tailoring."

"*Vanitas, vanitas,* eh, Toyfell?" said Ellery.

"Live a fool and die a pauper," said Harry Toyfell. "Live a pauper and die a fool. It comes to the same thing in the end. Riches are all around us, and every man is free to partake."

"That's what Nick Jacquard thought, too," said Dakin dryly. "And in his own way Otis Holderfield. Then you can't think of anything Holderfield said or did, Harry, that might explain the way he died?"

Toyfell bared his gums, and Ellery wondered if he was laughing. "No more than the others."

"What others?" Dakin was looking through papers.

"Doc Dodd, Nick Jacquard, Tom Anderson, Mr. Hart, Mr. MacCaby."

"Oh, you think they're all connected, too."

"Maybe."

"How?"

"Don't know," said Toyfell. "Maybe by me."

"By you!" Dakin rose. "How d'ye mean?"

Toyfell shrugged. "Every one of 'em I worked for or had anythin' to do with up and died. They're sayin' I'm a Jonah. If this was tar-and-feather country, I'd likely be rid out on a rail." He stopped, but his jaws kept working. "Maybe I won't find me another job so easy."

Dakin considered this for a long time. Finally he closed the breakfront decisively. "I'll see you're not pestered, Harry. Course, you'll have to clear out of here. Somebody from the Sheriff's office'll be here tonight or tomorrow."

"Have anywhere to go, Toyfell?" asked Ellery.

"I'll find some place."

"That's why I walked over tonight. There's still the Anderson shack. Rima asked me to tell you again you're welcome to use it."

"Thank Rima kindly. Now maybe I will."

He accompanied them to the front door.

"Better lock it, Harry," said Dakin.

"No, sir."

"That's an ugly bunch out there."

"I'm as good as they are, Mr. Dakin. No better, no worse. I ain't goin' to run and I ain't goin' to hide behind a lock."

He was shuffling down the dim hall before the door closed.

Dakin said something to one of his men and after a few minutes the people before the house dispersed. The two men stood in the lilac shadows of the porch until the street was empty. The house behind them grew dark.

"Mighty hard man to figure," grunted Dakin finally.

"So was Tom Paine," said Ellery. "No thanks, Dakin, I'll walk. Good night."

"Good night," said Dakin stiffly.

Wednesday, May 24

The fire occurred eleven days later.

Ellery was awakened in the middle of the night by the sirens. He scrambled wildly for his robe and slippers, certain he could feel the heat of flames underfoot. The hiss of water under high pressure and the cry of the engines were very close by.

Rima and Ken were struggling into robes in the hall. Essie blubbered somewhere. From dowwstairs Mrs. Fowler was shrieking, "Fire! It's a fire!"

From the glare and heat the whole street might have been going up. But when they joined Mrs. Fowler and Essie at the front gate they saw that the heart of the blaze was a small frame house directly across Algonquin Avenue.

"The Waldos," cried Ken. He dashed into the street and Ellery ran after him, Rima screaming at them to come back.

Four engines were pumping away. The street swarmed with firemen and volunteers. But it was clear that they could only try to keep the fire from touching off the adjoining buildings. The Waldo house was unapproachable; the entire structure glowed with flame.

A smoke-blackened figure lay in the middle of the street.

"Here's Dr. Winship!"

"This one's smoked up bad, Doctor. Ambulance hasn't come yet."

Ken shouted at Rima and a few moments later she came racing from the house with blankets and his medical bag.

The little man was writhing and moaning.

"Which one are you?"

"David. Is my . . . ?" He fainted.

Ellery ran over to Fire Chief Everitt Apworth, an elongated countryman who might have been Dakin's brother. Chief Apworth was chewing tobacco mechanically and spitting in the direction of the fire.

"Where's Jonathan Waldo, Chief?"

"Still in there. Couldn't get to him. Lucky we got David. They were sleepin' 'sthough they were drugged."

A voice said, "They were," and Ellery looked down at Rima.

"Drugged?"

"They were Dr. Dodd's patients. I've seen their case cards in the file. They suffered from chronic insomnia and Dr. Dodd used to prescribe nembutal so they could sleep. They took it regularly."

"So that's it." Chief Apworth ran off, swearing at one of his firemen.

When the ambulance took David Waldo away, Ken said, "He's not bad at all. They didn't get the other one out?"

At dawn they did. The little body was a cinder.

"Merchant chief?" said Dakin patiently. "Not Jonathan, Mr. Queen. Not hardly. A two-by-four tailor. Besides, Jonahan wasn't even Dave's partner, at least legally. I've had a talk with Mr. Gonzales at the Wrightsville National and he tells me the business was owned by Dave. Even the house is in Dave's name. So where's your merchant chief?"

"I don't know," groaned Ellery.

"This time you're surely barking up the wrong tree."

But Ellery gritted his teeth. "The Waldos were Otis Holderfield's tailors and Sebastian Dodd's patients. They shared in the prosperity that began with the death of Luke MacCaby. And now they've shared in the deaths, Dakin."

"Pretty thin, Mr. Queen." Then Dakin's face softened. "Why don't you give up? Darned if it wasn't gettin' me, too, till I got hold of myself."

"Where did the fire start?"

"In the cellar. A neighbor saw the flames shoot out of the cellar windows. Then the whole house went up."

"Doesn't that sound like arson to you?" Ellery said desperately.

"No. The Waldos stored a lot of cleaning fluid in their cellar; used it in the shop. The house was one of the oldest on Algonquin Avenue. Just a tinderbox. No, Mr. Queen."

"The fire started by itself, I suppose."

"It's called," said Dakin gently, "spontaneous combustion. Or did you ever hear of defective electric wiring?"

"Any evidence of either?"

"You saw the ashes this morning. A smolderin' lot."

"Have you questioned David Waldo?"

"He can't be talked to yet."

Ellery left Dakin's office and wandered over to the Square in the twilight. He had begun the day in a gyroscopic activity and his progress had been gyroscopic, too. Nothing was resolved. The fire might have been an accident and it might have been set. At the hospital David Waldo, while pronounced out of danger, was unapproachable. Jonathan Waldo was not a merchant chief, but he was dead. Either-or.

Dakin was right. The sensible thing was to pack up and take the first train back to New York.

The neon sign on the *Record* building was already glowing. Ellery turned into the Square.

He had never been so confused. Failure was an old story, but this was chaos. He could not even be sure the death of Jonathan Waldo and the narrow escape of his twin were part of the pattern. Their connection with the others was remote. He could not blame Dakin. Dakin was being reasonable.

Maybe that's the trouble, Ellery thought. He's being reasonable. And this isn't a reasonable case.

He found himself before the coral front door of the *Record*.

On impulse, he went in and asked to see O'Bannon.

Malvina Prentiss's editorial assistant was framed in a boudoir of an office jabbing with two lackadaisical fingers at a rose-colored typewriter.

"If it's a shakedown," he said without looking up, "you can tell her and to hell with you. I'm about fed up, anyway."

"By which I take it Malvina isn't on the premises. O'Bannon, did you find the books in Boston?"

"Books in Boston," said O'Bannon. "Hey?"

"Source books for the rhyme."

"Oh! They're around on the shelves somewhere." O'Bannon began to peck again. "I'm roughing out a followup for Lady Muck on the Waldo conflagration. What do you know, Joe?"

"About what you do, I imagine." Ellery located the books. "All these shelves need is some pink ruching and they'd look like lace panties. Are these all of them?"

Ellery sat down with the books in a chartreuse plastic chair. They were only an armful: Burton Stevenson's *Home Book of Modern Verse*, William H. Newell's *Games and Songs of American Children*, a volume called *The Music Hour* by Osbourne McConathy, a few others. He began turning pages.

"You won't find anything in them," said O'Bannon. "Original author of the lines unknown. Thrilling. Were you able to talk to David Waldo?"

"No."

"Neither was I. What did Dakin tell you?"

"What did he tell you?"

"Check. I've interviewed the representative of the fire underwriters and he's very unhappy. Are you happy, Queen?"

"No."

"Nobody's happy. Not even Malvina. Do you know this town is on the thin edge of group diarrhea?" Ellery had stopped turning pages and he was staring at some words. "Queen, tell me. Were the Waldos part of this mishmash?"

"Yes."

The typewriter stopped. "Did you say yes?"

"Yes."

"Say . . ."

"Yes!" Ellery got up. The books tumbled to the floor.

"Wait a minute!"

But Ellery was gone. O'Bannon picked up the books, puzzled.

"Two possibilities," Ellery said after dinner that night.

"Two again. But that's not the important thing. The important thing is a comma." Rima glanced at her husband. Ken was scrutinizing Ellery with a frown.

"Comma, comma." He was striding about the living room smoking furiously. "O'Bannon saw it with his own eyes and didn't see it at all. Nobody's seen it. What's the alternate version of that rhyme? *Rich man, poor man, begger-man, thief—*"

"*Doctor, lawyer, Indian chief,*" said Rima.

"No, that was out long ago on sufficient grounds. The other one."

"*Doctor, lawyer, merchant chief.*"

"Gives us seven victims of lunacy. Seven corpses. But oh, that comma." He chuckled and rubbed his hands.

"What," said Ken, "are you gassing about!"

"Why, Dr. Winship, it seems that of the second version there are two sub-versions. Two again, see? In the first sub-version the rhyme winds up with *Doctor, lawyer, merchant chief.* But go to the source books and you find the second sub-version: *Doctor,* comma, *lawyer,* comma, *merchant,* COMMA, *chief.*"

"Merchant comma chief," Rima repeated. "Merchant *and* chief? Two separate—?"

"Beautiful, isn't it? Yes, two separate words, Rima. Merchant. Chief. Makes eight items where there were seven. Does it fit? Oh, yes. The Waldos weren't 'merchant chiefs'—but they were merchant tailors . . . merchants. So somebody's following the second sub-version, the one with eight characters. Number seven was Jonathan Waldo."

"Then there's an eighth to come," said Rima damply.

"*Chief?*" muttered Ken.

"Chief what, Ellery? What kind of chief?"

Ellery's glee faded. "Now there you've got me. The only chiefs in Wrightsville I know of are the chief of police and the fire chief." Ellery hurled his butt into the fireplace. "Damn it, don't look at me that way! Of course Dakin and Apworth will have me committed! But what else can I think? What else can I do? I'm going to bed!"

Thursday, June 8

Decoration day it poured, but the annual exercises in Memorial Park were dampened by more than the heavens. Mrs. Holmes of Wrightsville High, who taught Comparative Lit., was heard to murmur something Hardyesque about the Greek unities. Other comments were less highfalutin. Some said the exercises had never been the same since 1939, which was the year Murdock Wheeler, Wrightsville's last surviving veteran of the Grand Army of the Republic, passed away; others ascribed the flickering of the patriotic fire to more recent passings.

Everyone seemed glad to go home.

The weather turned nice the next day, but Wrightsville's mood remained glum. No one knew why, but you could feel it all over town.

At least this was the litmus reaction of one outsider. Ellery admitted to himself that it might be his chemistry, not Wrightsville's, which turned everything blue. He had taken to wandering about town at all hours, leaving the doves on Algonquin Avenue to their hearty cooing.

Nothing came up. Nothing.

One day Ellery hunted up the Anderson shack in The Marshes. He located it after blundering about in a state of growing excitement, as if at last he faced a clarifying issue. But all he found was a pretty hut, blackweathered and overgrown with roses, lilac, and lily-of-the-valley, complete with backhouse, mossy well, and vegetable garden. And inside Harry Toyfell with some of the books Rima had not removed.

The Town Philosopher was serene. "What more does a man need? Tell me I'm not the equal of the richest man on the Hill. What's he got I haven't? Worries. And what have I got he'll never have? Liberty. Yes, sir, I couldn't ask for better 'n this . . . The Waldos? Too bad. Well, at least they can't set the blame for that on me!"

On the way back Ellery detoured to Little Prudy's Cliff. He spent a few minutes trying to read the soft mass at its foot. It remained illegible.

Another day, with a sudden yearning for the company of the late Otis Holderfield's secretary, he walked over to the Granjon Block.

"Where does she live?" Ellery asked the old elevator man.

Buzz Congress chuckled. "With Flossie Bushmill ye have to work fast, Mr. Queen. She's lit out."

"Gone? From town?"

"Yep. With some drummer for a Boston, now, ladies' underwear company. I seen it comin', Mr. Queen! And then she'll ditch him and latch onto somebody else. Itchy feet, that Floss. Always had, 'specially since her dad died. Jake Bushmill, the blacksmith. Real pioneer type, Flossie." The old man cackled.

And still another day, learning from Ken Winship that David Waldo was on the mend, Ellery visited the Wrightsville General Hospital. But the intern on duty in the men's ward shook his head.

"He gets hysterical when anyone tries to question him. Chief Apworth, a man from the *Record,* and the fire insurance people didn't get a thing out of him. Better come back next week, Mr. Queen."

When Ellery went back to the hospital the following Thursday, Waldo was gone. He had left the hospital three days before.

Rather annoyed, Ellery set about finding him. His annoyance soon vanished.

On Waldo's release from the hospital on the morning of June 3 he had gone to Slocum Township. In Slocum he had sought out a tailor named Elbert Scolly who, it seemed, had been trying for a year to buy out the Waldos. Waldo had signified to Scolly that he was now willing to sell, but only for spot cash and provided the sale could be effected in twenty-four hours. Scolly, a down-Easter, had driven a smart bargain. Waldo had agreed to accept a sum far below the actual value of his stock, fixtures, lease, and good will and the two men had driven over to Wrightsville in Scolly's delivery truck for a session with Sam Izzard of Finegold & Izzard, Upham Block, who were the Waldos' accountants. The papers were then drawn up at the Wrightsville National Bank, Scolly had returned to Slocum to arrange matters with his bank there, and David Waldo—after a short visit to his shop in the Granjon Block—had disappeared; Ellery could not discover where he had spent the night. However, he had turned up again on Tuesday morning, closed out his accounts at The Public Trust Company and the Wrightsville National, paid all his bills, met Scolly and the bank officials and consummated the sale, and at 2:30 P.M. he was driven by Ed Hotchkiss to the railroad station with a new suitcase and a considerable amount of cash in a wallet he had purchased from saleswoman Eppie Simpson at the leather goods counter of the Bon Ton, along with the suitcase. The settlement of his fire insurance claim he had left in the hands of Lyman Hinchley, the insurance broker in The Public Trust Company building.

Gabby Warrum, the stationmaster, could not recall David Waldo's having appeared at the ticket window. "Saw him climb onto the southbound, though," said Gabby. "Figure he bought his ticket on the train. The 3:12."

The 3:12 was a Connhaven local, stopping at every station.

Waldo had left no forwarding address. He had told Lyman Hinchley, "I'll get in touch with you in a few weeks." Scolly, Izzard, Mr. Lorrie Preston of the Wrightsville National, Hinchley, Eppie Simpson, and everyone else who had been in contact with Waldo during those twenty-four hours agreed that he was "the most jittery man" they had ever seen. They ascribed it to the horror of his experience in the fire and the shock of his brother Jonathan's death. "You know how it is with identical twins," said Lyman Hinchley, whose aunt, Sara Hinchley of the Junction Hinchleys, had been a trained nurse. "Very delicate and sympathetic nervous systems."

There was no evidence, however, that David Waldo had visited his brother's grave in Twin Hill Cemetery before disappearing.

"Dakin, you've got to find Waldo for me," Ellery said in the police chief's office Thursday night. Ellery looked tired and sounded urgent.

"But *why?*"

"I can't tell you why. I don't know why."

"You've got to have a reason!"

"Maybe it's because I think Waldo knows something. Maybe he doesn't even know he knows it—"

Dakin held his head. "Doesn't even know he knows what?"

"That's what we've got to find out, Dakin, don't you see?" said Ellery patiently. "Dave Waldo may be the key to the whole thing."

The chief of police glared at Ellery like a paralytic confronted by a hornet. "You're the man recites kiddie rhymes ending in 'chief,' " he said bitterly. "But I'm still breathin' and Ev Apworth says he never felt better in his life. Why don't you let me be?"

"If you won't do it, Dakin, I'll have to do it myself. But it's going to take me a lot longer than it would take you, with your facilities, and by the time I got to him . . ."

In the end Dakin flung up his hands and agreed to look for David Waldo.

Saturday–Sunday, June 10–11

Rima and Ken were at the Bijou seeing a movie, Ellery having begged off, and Ellery was alone in the living room listening to the Huddersfield Choral Society's recording of Holst's "Hymn of Jesus"—which seemed to him for the first time very distant music—when the telephone rang in the waiting room.

"It's for you, Mr. Queen," said Essie. "Long distance."

He almost knocked her down getting by.

"Dakin?"

"Hello." Dakin sounded weary.

"You've found him!"

"In a farmhouse in Huxton—that's northwest of Connhaven. We talked him into coming with us and we've got him holed up in a room at the Hotel Dorcas in Connhaven."

"Where is that?"

"It's just as you pull into Connhaven on 478. Room 412."

"Dakin, hang on to him. I'll be there in two hours."

"And then what?" said Dakin sourly; but Ellery hung up.

He turned off the record player, thrust Holst back between Haydn and Humperdinck, scribbled an explanatory note to Rima and Ken, and raced upstairs for his coat and hat. On his way out he halted; then he went back and opened his suitcase. Absolute rot, he kept saying to himself as he rummaged in the false bottom. He wondered if it was still there. It had been given to him years before by his father—a birthday gift which was a joke of long standing. It was there; and when he came out of the bedroom its weight made him feel silly.

Homer Findlay's newest used car, a Buick Roadmaster, was waiting for him at the curb. It had been waiting there with a full tank since Friday morning.

In three minutes he was on Route 478, whistling in the wind and stretching his legs for the seventy-five mile run through Slocum, Bannock, Agunquin, Scottstown, and Fyfield to Connhaven.

Dakin rose from the lobby settee. "I was beginning to worry about you. It's almost midnight."

"I didn't figure on that ten-mile detour south of Fyfield. Does he know I'm coming?"

"I told him. He didn't do a jig about it."

"Done any talking"

"No."

One of Dakin's younger men, in plainclothes, nodded from an alcove near the elevator. They crossed the hall and Dakin opened the door of 412 without knocking.

David Waldo was lying on the bed with the candlewick spread drawn up to his little chin. Beyond the fact that his eyebrows and hair looked singed, Ellery could see nothing wrong with him. Another young officer sat in the single armchair under a lamp with a newspaper over it. He got up as they came in.

"Tried to get Mr. Waldo to take his clothes off and make himself comfortable," he said, "but he wouldn't even douse his shoes."

"All right, Jeep."

The officer went out.

Ellery took the newspaper off the lamp and went over to the bed. "How are you, Mr. Waldo?"

The little tailor kept his eyes shut.

"Mr. Waldo." Waldo blinked. "Does the light bother you?"

"No." The eyes opened. They were bloodshot and fixed on some inner object.

Ellery sat down on the edge of the bed. "I've spent the past two months of my life up here because I'm convinced there's a killer loose in Wrightsville, a killer who covers his tracks so well he leaves no evidence of murder. I think the fire that killed your brother and so nearly killed you, Mr. Waldo, is part of a murder pattern that began with Luke MacCaby's death. Now I can't prove that—or anything else— so it's of tremendous importance that you give me what help you can. Of importance to you personally if you're to stay alive. That's why I asked Chief Dakin to find you and why I drove here from Wrightsville tonight to talk to you."

David Waldo quivered. "I'm going to die."

"No. Not if we compare notes and see this thing through together."

"But I don't know anything."

"Why did you run away?"

"I'm afraid."

"Of what? Of whom?"

"I don't know, I don't know. The fire was set. Somebody was out to kill us. I was just lucky or I'd be dead, too."

"Why do you think the fire was set? Did you see or hear anything? Get a warning of any kind?"

"No. But the *Record* . . . the rhyme . . . merchant . . . I'm no merchant now! I sold out! You're not going to take me back to Wrightsville! I won't go!" The little man grew hysterical. Ellery and Dakin had to muffle his cries. Finally he began to weep quietly into the pillow.

Ellery sat doubled on the edge of the armchair, frowning at the elderly little figure on the bed.

"Never was one to kick a man when he was down," came Dakin's dry voice, "but between you and the Prentiss woman, Mr. Queen, you've given poor Dave a bad case of frozen toes, and that's about the story."

"No," said Ellery absently.

"You're just a mule. Well, I can't hang around here. What are you going to do?"

"Stay with it." Ellery got up. "Dakin, would you leave your men here with me?"

"Now look, Mr. Queen—"

"Suppose you're wrong, Dakin. Suppose tomorrow morning the Connhaven police called you and said—"

"Cripes!" Dakin yanked the door open and a moment later the officers came in. "I'm going back to town. You're under Mr. Queen's orders till you hear from me." He clumped off down the hall toward the stairs, tugging angrily at his hat.

"You're Jeep. I remember you from the Van Horn case, but I never did know your last name."

"Jorking, sir. My dad's the pig farmer just off the Old Low Road, on 478."

"And I don't know you at all," Ellery said to the other officer.

"Plaskow, sir. Phil Plaskow."

"Oh, yes. Well, boys, I'm going to try to get some information out of this man. You're here to protect him. Can we get some sandwiches and coffee?"

"There's an all-night diner about three squares into town," said Jorking.

"Swell. Get enough for the four of us, Jeep, with a couple of quarts of black coffee." Ellery gave him a ten-dollar bill. "Phil, you hole up in that alcove across the hall and keep your eyes open. This looks like a long session."

At 1 A.M. David Waldo was sitting up in the armchair with a blanket around him—although it was a warm night and he had swallowed two cups of scalding coffee he kept complaining of the chill. But there was color in his face and he seemed touched by their solicitude.

"Now you understand, Mr. Waldo," Ellery said, setting his cup down on the bureau, "I haven't any idea where this is going. Let's begin where the case did. Did you know Luke MacCaby?"

"Not to talk to, Mr. Queen."

"Does that mean you did see him occasionally?"

"Once or twice, years ago, on the street. He was pointed out to me."

"By whom?"

"A storekeeper, I think. Maybe it was Jeff Hernaberry—the sporting goods store." He was stumbling, and Ellery kept smiling at him. "Yes, it was Hernaberry."

"MacCaby never had a suit made by you or your brother? Or any mending, cleaning, pressing—?"

"No."

"Do you recall anybody ever discussing MacCaby with you?"

"Jeff Hernaberry—"

"Aside from Jeff Hernaberry."

"No, I don't."

"Not even Otis Holderfield?"

"Well . . . no . . . I don't think so. No, sir. Maybe Mr. Holderfield might have mentioned something to Jonathan—"

The tailor's voice trembled, and Ellery quickly left Otis Holderfield. He asked a few more questions, more to restore Waldo's confidence than out of any hope, and then he switched to John Spencer Hart.

"No, Mr. Hart had his clothes made in Boston, I think. I think I once told you that."

"Yes, the day I bought those bathing trunks from you. How about his pressing?"

"No, sir, Mr. Hart had his own vallay did that. Everybody knew that. We never did any work for him."

"Were any of the employees of the Wrightsville Dye Works customers of yours?"

"Dye works. Well, there was George Churchward, the plant manager, he had two or three suits made at one time. But we didn't do his pressing and cleaning."

"Did Churchward ever mention Mr. Hart?"

"Not that I remember."

"Did he ever mention MacCaby?"

"I don't think so . . .''

Ellery abandoned John Spencer Hart after a while and brought up Thomas Hardy Anderson. Waldo reiterated his ignorance. He had not known Anderson except as one of the town characters; Anderson had never done any odd jobs for the brothers; neither David nor, to his knowledge, Jonathan had ever given Anderson any money; they had had no contact with Anderson's cronies, Toyfell and Jacquard; and so on.

He fared no better on the subject of Nicole Jacquard.

When he came to Sebastian Dodd, however, Waldo's replies were meatier. Yes, David and Jonathan had been patients of Dr. Dodd's for years. Nothing of any importance—their yearly bout of flu, Jonathan's touch of rose fever every June— nothing important, that is, except their insomnia, which was very important; the doctor prescribed nembutal and they had taken it rather more regularly than he had advised, but a tailor was like a fiddle player, his hands were his livelihood, and if he didn't sleep they shook so he couldn't ply a needle for beans. Oh, yes, they'd thought a lot of Doc Dodd; salt of the earth, right smart and obliging. And then, it was convenient having him just across the street—

"When did you see Dodd last?" interrupted Ellery.

"Let's see. When did he die, again?"

"Very early in the morning of April 27th. A Thursday, before dawn."

"Thursday. Yes, I saw him two days before he died."

"On Tuesday the 25th? Where, Mr. Waldo?"

"In Mr. Holderfield's office."

So that was where Dodd had been late that morning. It was the morning of the trapped bird, and later Ellery had gone over to Dakin's office to pick up the second duplicate key made by Millard Peague and when he had returned to the house Dodd was gone.

"You saw Dodd in Holderfield's office two days before Dodd's death. What was he doing there, M. Waldo?"

"Making his will."

"Oh.—What were you doing there?"

"Witnessing it, Mr. Queen. My brother and me. Mr. Holderfield phoned down to our store and said he needed two more witnesses to a will, would Jonathan and me come up. We came up and Dr. Dodd was sitting there, looking peaked. Mr. Holderfield called in his secretary, that Flossie Bushmill, Dr. Dodd said the paper in front of him was his will, he signed it, and Floss Bushmill and my brother and I signed as witnesses. Then we went back downstairs, I mean Jonathan and me. Whole thing didn't take five minutes. Course, the will was all made out beforehand."

Ellery switched to Otis Holderfield. He asked a great many questions : about the Waldos' relationship with the dead lawyer, when they had got to know him and under what circumstances; he asked Waldo to recall each occasion on which he had been in contact with Holderfield, each consultation about new clothes, each fitting, each delivery, and the substance of Holderfield's remarks in every case, to the best of Waldo's recollection. He brought Waldo up to the Saturday of Holderfield's death and went over the day like a doctor searching for broken bones, feeling for some splinter of fact, some detail, some incident not known to him. He was sure one lurked in David Waldo's memory; at least one. It was infantile to feel sure on the basis of nothing whatever, but he felt sure.

And he found nothing.

Waldo began to nod. His lids, yellowswollen with exhaustion, would crawl down over his eyes like grubs over two rotting berries, then they would draw back with a start.

"Are you too tired to go on? Would you like to sleep a bit now?"

"I couldn't. Run out of nembutal. It's the light now. Please turn the light down."

Ellery put the newspaper back over the lamp and went to the door. Phil Plaskow was in the alcove by the elevator and Jorking was down the hall near a door through which loud, mixed laughter was coming. Jorking came back quickly.

"Broadminded hotel. That's quite a party going on in there. How's it coming, Mr. Queen?"

"By way of Okinawa. Jeep, do you suppose you could rustle more coffee?"

"There's some left in the container. Phil, is it still hot?"

"Warm."

Ellery shut the door and held the container to Waldo's lips. The tailor gulped, choked.

"No more!"

"Then let's start all over again."

Waldo moaned.

MacCaby.

Hart.

Anderson.

Jacquard.

Dodd.

Holderfield.

Jonathan Waldo.

The room was beginning to feel unstable; the floor developed a tilt.

MacCaby.

Hart.

Put two men in a hotel room for a few hours, thought Ellery, and it begins to smell like a tomb.

Anderson.

Jacquard . . .

At one point Waldo was sick and Ellery had to take him to the bathroom. He was sweating himself and the floor was really unreliable.

MacCaby.

Hart.

Anderson . . .

They had worked their way back to Dodd again and Ellery was saying through his teeth, "The time you witnessed Dodd's will, Mr. Waldo. Do you recall Dodd's saying anything to Holderfield, or Holderfield's saying anything to Dodd, about . . ."

"No," whimpered David Waldo. "Let me alone."

". . . about some third person, say? Or about being afraid? Or about anything that might have struck you at the time as being queer in any way?"

"You're just trying to kill me. I answered you a thousand times. You're killing me."

"I'm trying to keep you alive. Think, man! Anything like that? Answer me!" Ellery shook him.

"What was the question?"

Ellery had to think a little himself. Then he repeated it.

"I can't remember." Waldo's eyes were brimming over with self-pity. "How can a man remember things like that? In the middle of the night?"

"You've got to!"

"We just came upstairs . . ."

"You came upstairs, you and Jonathan. And—?"

"We came upstairs when Mr. Holderfield phoned down. It was three days before Doc Dodd died. There was my brother Jonathan, there was me, there was that floozy—"

"Yes," sighed Ellery. It was no use. The man simply had nothing to offer. Another dead end. Might just as well—

"It was three days before Doc Dodd died," Waldo said miserably. "My brother, me . . ."

"What did you say, Mr. Waldo?"

"You've got no right holdin' me here. I haven't done anything. I'm a citizen—"

"Yes, sure you are and we don't and you haven't, but what did you just say, Mr. Waldo? How many days before Dodd died?"

"Three."

"Three?"

"Three!"

"I wish you'd be consistent," said Ellery fretfully. "Aren't you making a mistake, Waldo? That would have made it Monday. You said before it was two days before Dodd's death that you witnessed his will. On Tuesday. Make up your mind, will you?"

Waldo kept blinking. "My head's goin' around, Mr. Queen. That's what's the matter."

"Which was it, Waldo—two days before Dodd's death, or three?"

"Two . . . or three?" muttered the tailor. "Let me see, now . . ."

"The day Holderfield phoned you to come up to his office to witness Dodd's will. Was that on Monday or on Tuesday of the week the doctor died?"

To Ellery's consternation, Waldo began to cry. "You keep pesterin' me!" he wept angrily, "I'm in no condition, you can see that! I can't think. I can't!"

Ellery braced himself. "Of course you can't, Mr. Waldo. But try. *Don't fall asleep!*" He pounded the little man's back and Waldo's eyes blinked open. "It's a small point, but those are the ones that bother me. Waldo, was it Tuesday or Monday?"

"What difference does it make? One day or another . . ."

"Waldo. You witnessed Dodd's will. Was it two days before the accident you did that, or three? Tuesday or Monday?"

"Chnnh . . . ?"

"Waldo, I'll snap that skinny windpipe of yours with my bare hands if you fall asleep now! *Tuesday or Monday?*"

"It was . . ." Waldo's voice cracked with hate. "It was . . . both days," he said triumphantly. "Yes, sir, that's it! Both days. Now I've answered your question and that's that. I stand on my rights. I'm goin'—"

"Both days? Now, Waldo, that's not very likely, is it? You're just making that up to satisfy me. Nobody witnesses a will two days in succession. You're *not* getting out of here! Answer me!"

Waldo's teeth rattled. "Both days, I tell you. We witnessed it twice. I remember it clear as anything now, Mr. Queen. Can't we stop now? I'm going to be sick again. I just feel it—"

"Dr. Dodd's will witnessed twice? Was Dodd there both times? On Monday, then again on the following day?"

"That's right, and Mr. Holderfield called us up both times. Jonathan and me. That no-good secretary witnessed both times, too. You don't have to believe me. Go ahead, ask *her*. She'll tell . . . you . . ."

"You're certain of this."

Waldo did not reply.

"Waldo! You're positive it was two successive days?"

Waldo's head rolled. "Wha . . ."

"Positive! Certain! Sure!" Ellery stooped over him, a drop of perspiration falling from the end of his nose into Waldo's thin gray hair. "Waldo? . . . *Waldo*."

The little tailor's chin was buried in the blanket. His skin was waxy with exhaustion.

Ellery pulled on his coat. The noise from the party down the hall had stopped. Waldo's snuffly breathing was very loud.

Ellery opened the door. Jorking had found a chair somewhere and he was nodding against the corridor wall. He got up, yawning. "What time is it, sir?"

"3:40. Waldo's fallen asleep in the chair, Jeep; don't disturb him." Phil Plaskow joined them from across the hall. "I suggest you boys start working in shifts, one resting while the other stands guard. Both of you had better go into the room with him. I want at least one pair of eyes working at all times. Order meals in the room and park here till you hear from Dakin or me. I may be back and I may not. In any event, stick with Waldo till you're called off. I don't think he'll give you any trouble."

Ellery remained outside the door until he heard the lock turn over.

Then he rang for the elevator.

The night wind had a streamlike coolness that was delicious after the heated air of the hotel room. Ellery opened the Buick's window to its widest.

He drove slowly along the deserted highway.

The persistency of twoness in this case was certainly remarkable. Either-or. Obverse or reverse. Even the rhyme had two versions. The last line of the second version had two punctuations. And now there had been two witnessings of Dodd's will, on two successive days.

In any case each suspect may be two-faced, each piece of testimony may be double talk, each act may conceal a double-cross, each motive may be double-dyed, each clue double-edged . . . right enough; that was what you always kept in mind. But here alternativeness had reached into death itself. Each death offered two faces, the story of each victim was twice told depending on the twin choice of viewpoints.

The eyes of a car glared in his rear-vision mirror, getting rapidly larger. Ellery slowed down further and the car pushed by into the darkness ahead.

. . . It was as if the case as a whole, the complete fabric of confusion, concealed a double meaning. A deadly sampler with its secret woven in.

Some time later a car tore past again, this time headed the other way.
Ellery paid no attention.
But it was the same car.

And a few minutes later the fast car was northbound again, pulling up rapidly behind the Buick until a hundred yards separated them.
Now it followed meekly, keeping its distance.

Some time passed before the car behind began to close up. Its lights annoyed Ellery into alertness. But suddenly the lights swung away and he forgot them.
The second car had turned off into a side road, a dirt lane. Its lights went out, then its motor, a few yards from the turnoff under the lee of an embankment.

Ellery kicked his brake and the Buick squealed with indignation. He had almost overrun a roadblock.

He was on the ten-mile stretch of detour between Connhaven and Fyfield, on a poor-relation county road whose two ragged lanes had been further chewed by the teeth of the steam shovel tractors and big gravel and dirt-carting trucks which were working on the state highway paralleling it a few hundred yards away. Shoring, sections of pipe, wooden trestles, the jointed carcass of a small bridge were stockpiled along the soft shoulders. Flarepots were everywhere.

The two trestles which barred the road stood side by side. Each said DANGER.
Ellery stopped the car.

He had come south on this road just before midnight and it had been open all the way. The same clutter along the shoulders, flarepots flickering, work stopped for the night and workmen gone.

Had they come back to resume work in the middle of the night?
Ellery turned off his lights, let his eyes adjust to the dark.

But aside from the smoky little flames at road level there was no sign of activity ahead, and the road was straight—to judge from the line of pots—for as far as he could see.

Boys, probably; some country kids' notion of a Saturday night prank.

The road here was hemmed in by crowding woods. He could hear crickets and bullfrogs. But no human sound, and there was no light anywhere except from the pots.

Still, he felt uneasy.

Ellery turned on his lights again. He felt a definite diffidence about getting out of the Buick. There was something hostile in the dark and sibilant countryside with its hundreds of flaming little eyes. But then he became angry with himself and he opened the door and stepped onto the road.

He went forward in the path of the headlights rather quickly.

As he heaved on the righthand trestle, he thought he heard a flat secretive sound behind him, like a footfall.

Ellery turned.

But there were only the Buick, breathing patiently, and the dark road behind.

He pushed the other trestle to the left side of the road and hurried back to the car. He jumped in, pulled the door to, and released the handbrake.

As he began to straighten up he heard the sound again.

This time it was close by. By the car. By the driver's seat.

He hurled himself over sidewise, knowing as he did so that he was too late and that the stabbing glint the corner of his left eye had caught in the light of his dashboard was the reflection of a revolver barrel as it flashed over the rim of the open window at his elbow.

He heard two explosions at the same time that a searing agony tore through his left side.

And in the splinter of time between the two shots and the blow of the upholstered seat Ellery underwent a profound experience. It was as if the lightning of death had ripped away the whole concealing roof of the structure, exposing the truth inside for a timeless moment before the darkness closed down.

Ellery returned to life in a slow mangle of images and pain. When he opened his eyes there were lights before them and it was some time before he realized that he was lying on his right side on the car seat and that the lights came from the dashboard. He tried to sit up and after a while he managed it by pushing with his right arm; his left was a dangling uselessness and his whole left side was in flames. When he had succeeded in getting upright he inspected himself. From his shoulder down the left side of his jacket was stained a lively color.

Everything went dark again.

The second time he came to he was still in a sitting position and through the pain he was able to take note of his surroundings. Nothing seemed to have changed since the episode began. The world was still in that talkative darkness, the flarepots still twinkled, the trestles were where he had left them. He tried to lift his left arm to see what time it was but the arm refused to move. Then he became conscious of pain in it and soon the arm was on fire, too. But he was unable to make it function. The stain on his sleeve and side had spread considerably. He knew a warm adhesive satisfaction.

The motor was running. The emergency was off. He wondered if he could do it and then he knew he must and he got his feet in position and his right hand on the wheel and he began to drive.

Later he was turning with caution into Wrightsville's State Street. The night was backing away before a pale and nervous dawn; the elms lining the street looked pleased, and Ellery looked pleased as he parked the Buick before the County Court House. He turned off the ignition and the lights, edged over to the righthand door, and got out. He walked carefully into the alley toward the green twin lights of the police station and on the steps he tripped and fell on his left side. He felt the rip of coagulation and a warm flow. From where he lay he saw with faraway interest a new stain begin.

He tried to rise, thought better of it, and crawled to the front door. The problem was to get the door open, but to do that he had to support himself with his left arm and that was out of the question. He frowned over the problem for some time. He could raise himself with his right arm but then he had no way of completing the action. Finally he rolled over on his back before the door and struck it with his right fist.

After a long time the door opened and a baldpated man with a rim of black hair was looking down at him, startled.

"Dakin. Get Dakin," said Ellery clearly. He tried to look reassuringly back at Lieutenant Gobbin; but then it was night again.

When he came to this time he was on a couch looking at a photograph of J. Edgar Hoover, half of whose face was spread alarmingly behind the edge of a water cooler, and a man in a collarless shirt held together at the neck with a large gold collar button was winding bandage around his left arm.

"Here he is, Dakin," said the man with a grin.

A man who had been standing at a window came to Ellery and Ellery saw that it was Chief Dakin, in a suit of old rose ski pajamas and a black rubber policeman's cape.

"You're Coroner Grupp," said Ellery in a happy voice, as if he had made a delightful discovery.

"How do you feel?"

Ellery saw that he was naked from the waist up. The skin over the ribs on his left side was a brilliant yellow-green-purple-cerise and his left arm was bandaged to the shoulder.

"Not good," he said.

"Drink this."

Ellery swallowed something foul. He sank back, tired.

"He's all right," he heard Coroner Grupp say a long distance away. "Mostly shock and loss of blood. I'd get him to the hospital."

"No, no hospital," said Ellery. "I won't have it."

"He won't have it," said Dakin.

"I've got something to do, Dakin."

"He's got something to do," said Dakin.

"Well, then keep him warm and don't let him get up for a few hours, Dakin."

The next thing Ellery knew Dakin was dressed and there was sun in the room. He was lying under a blanket. His arm beat like a drum and his torso felt flayed.

"Feel any better?" asked Dakin.

Ellery tested himself cautiously and found to his joy that he could sit up on the couch. "Oh, wonderful."

"I'll bet. I've talked to Jorking and Plaskow on the phone and they didn't know a thing about this."

"How is Waldo?"

"All right. How come you wearing this?" Dakin held up an odd-looking garment.

Ellery took it. "Hunch." A splat of shapeless metal was imbedded in it. "No wonder I felt as if I were kicked by a horse. Right over the heart. Why, Dakin, I carry a few odds and ends in my bag and last night I felt near enough to the payoff to warrant putting on a bulletproof vest before I drove to Connhaven. Too bad it's sleeveless. How big a hole was blasted in my arm?"

"Big enough. The gun couldn't have been more than a few inches from you when it went off. Did you see who fired the shots?"

"No."

"I thought Fire Chief Apworth or me was tagged for the last killing," said Dakin dryly. "How did it go? *Doctor, lawyer, merchant, chief?* Or's the game changed to *Ring Around the Rosie?*"

"It's the same game, Dakin," said Ellery with a faint smile. "You see, I'd
forgotten I was a chief, too. To one person in this town, anyway." And he was
silent.

Dakin grunted and went to the window. "When you're ready to talk American
let me know."

Ellery lay back, tidying his thoughts.

Finally, he said, "Dakin, I know the whole story." Dakin turned. "It's an
incredible story, and yet it's a very ordinary story, too. Simple as a kiddie game.
The only thing is, you have to see it. Do you suppose Chalanski's up yet?"

"What?" Dakin sounded helpless.

"Because I think we'd better have Chalanski in on this. There's a great deal
both of you have to understand before we can do what's called for. Would you
phone him to come right over—and bring along one of his shirts? I'm afraid this
one's a bit messy."

They closed in on the Dodd house in three cars. One shot around to the rear to
cover the kitchen door, garden, and alley of the blue stucco apartment building.
Another discharged three officers at the curb; one took his stand at the front gate,
one ran up to the front porch, and the third strolled across the street to the blackened
rubble where the Waldo house had stood. From the third car came Ellery, his left
arm in a sling, Chief Dakin, Prosecutor Chalanski, and two plainclothesmen. By
the time they reached the porch the patrolman from the second car, Officer Dodie
Gotch, had the front door open and was standing just inside the hall with one hand
clamped on Essie Pingarn's petrified elbow. Mrs. Fowler was at the rear of the
hall, frantically fumbling with the control box of her hearing aid.

Rima and Ken were at their Sunday breakfast. Both got up slowly, staring at
Ellery's arm, Dakin, Chalanski, the two big plainclothesmen with drawn guns, one
of whom blocked the doorway to the hall, the other moving over to the kitchen
door and setting his back against it.

"Ellery."

"We found your note last night—"

"What's happened to your arm?"

"What is this?"

Ellery lowered himself carefully into a chair, smiling across the table. "I don't
get shot at every day, Rima. I know you'll understand."

"Shot."

"*What's this all about?*"

"Why, Ken," said Ellery, "it's about something I wish it weren't. I'm afraid
you won't like it either and if I thought it would do any good I'd ask you to leave."

Ken blinked. He glanced at Rima. But there was no enlightenment there. There
was nothing there except pallor.

"It's about a child's game," said Ellery. "A harmless game, or it was until a
diseased mind used it as a pattern for a series of murders. *Rich man, poor man,
beggar-man, thief; doctor, lawyer, merchant, chief.* Until last night the first seven
deaths occurred on schedule. In the early hours of this morning, the eighth was
attempted on a detour between Connhaven and Fyfield. Somebody put up a roadblock,
got behind me, waited until I stopped, then stuck a gun over the rim of my window
and pulled the trigger twice six inches from my heart. Number eight didn't come

off because for no good reason I wore a bulletproof vest last night. So 'chief' didn't die.

"But the attempt on my life wasn't a total loss. It identified me as a 'chief.' But I'm not a chief. Or am I? Then I remembered that for one short period, in this one town, to exactly one person, I was. It was a gag, of course, but any specialist in mental illness will tell you that the disturbed mind has no sense of humor. The one person who knew me as 'chief,' therefore, is the one person who could have plugged me. But why resort to these circumlocutions? Let's name names—shall we, Rima?"

There was no color in her cheeks at all.

"Shall we what?" roared Ken.

Ellery got up. "Ken, Rima is the only one in Wrightsville or anywhere else who's ever called me, or thought of me as, chief."

Ken blinked and blinked. "That makes Rima . . . what?"

"There have been seven deaths in Wrightsville," Ellery said to him gently, "and all seven followed the child's counting game. First a man who was revealed as rich died. Then a man who was revealed as poor died. Then a man who was known as a beggar as well as a drunkard—what price heredity? Then a man who was known as a thief. Then a doctor, a lawyer, a merchant. In that exact order. And finally the attempt on my life . . . 'chief.' Since it was Rima who tried to kill 'chief,' it was Rima who also killed merchant, lawyer, doctor, thief, beggar, poor man and rich man. That's what it makes Rima, Ken."

"Wait a minute," Ken said. "Wait a minute." He seemed to be trying to concentrate. "Last night. She was home. With me."

"I'm afraid," began Prosecutor Chalanski in a delicate way, "your testimony as her husband, Dr. Winship . . ."

"Just between us, Ken," said Chief Dakin dryly, "can you swear she didn't leave you snorin' last night, take your car, follow Mr. Queen to Connhaven, ambush him on his return trip, and slip back into bed before you woke up this morning?"

Ken sat down suddenly.

"The way we see it, Dr. Winship," said Chalanski with a slight cough, "your wife is . . . I mean, that child's game business . . . after all. Er, mental trouble is the only explanation that makes sense to me—at least at this stage of the game. I assure you she'll get every consideration from my office consistent with—"

"But you can't be serious," muttered Ken. He looked up, and then he sprang to his feet, shouting. "You're all crazy! Making out a case against my wife on the strength of some kid nonsense dreamed up by a deluded paranoid! I'll sue for false arrest, defamation of character—!"

He stopped. A plainclothesman had appeared in the hall and was making surreptitious signals to Chief Dakin.

"It's all right, Charlie. What is it?"

"See you a minute?"

Dakin went into the hall. The plainclothesman talked to him in an undertone. In the dining room the only thing that happened was that Kenneth Winship moved around the table to stand beside Rima. As he moved the detective at the kitchen door moved, too. Rima was holding on to the back of her chair, eyes shut. Chalanski's lips were pursed, but there was no tune. And Ellery shifted to the other foot.

Dakin said, "All right, Charlie, have it towed in," and at his words Chalanski stopped pursing, Ellery straightened, and Rima opened her eyes.

Ken was looking wildly at the chief of police.

Dakin was back in the doorway, squared off. Chalanski hurried to him and after a moment Ellery joined them. Dakin whispered something, smiling a little. Ellery said, in an exhausted way, "Then that's it," and stepped by the two men into the hall as if there were no longer any reason for remaining.

"What in the name of hell," asked the doctor thickly, "is going on here?"

Chalanski's sharp face was settled. "You may as well know now, Dr. Winship. Comparison between fresh tire marks found near the scene of the attempt on Mr. Queen's life and the tires of your Packard show they're identical. Since you have only one car, that places your wife where Mr. Queen stopped two bullets. No, it's not airtight, but I imagine a few days' steady grilling at the jail will get the whole story out of her. I don't have to tell you, Doctor, that she'll be protected to the best of our ability. The town's been very nervous about these killings lately and there's a lot of ugly talk. However, I'm pretty sure we can handle any trouble that may arise. So don't worry about that." The prosecutor growled suddenly, "Oh, come on, Dakin, get this over with."

Dakin pulled a paper out of his pocket. "I have here a warrant for the arrest of Mrs. Rima Winship, nee Rima Anderson, on a charge—I guess, Mr. Chalanski, I better read this the way it's written?"

Chalanski agreed.

Dakin began to read in a colorless voice. He droned on and on, Kenneth Winship's mouth was slightly open, his breathing noisy. Rima's eyes were closed again.

Then Dakin was saying, "Take her in, Crabbe."

The big detective near the Winships sprang, his shoulder catching Ken's and sending Ken spinning to one side; he almost fell. Before he could recover his balance there was a click, and Rima was staring down at her wrists.

"Come on." The detective clamped his hand about her upper arm and began to hustle her across the room. He looked as if he were holding her aloft with one hand.

Rima cried out at the pain, once.

And then, somehow, Dr. Kenneth Winship was in the doorway before them, arms spread to their widest.

"Dakin."

"Don't make this tougher on yourself, Kenny," said Chief Dakin.

"Dakin . . ."

"There's a man behind you with a gun. Don't be a fool. One side."

"Take the handcuffs off her. She didn't do it."

"I know, Kenny. Come on, out of the way."

"She didn't do it, I tell you! I ought to know! She knows—that's why she's kept quiet! She didn't use that car last night, Dakin—and she's guessed who did!"

"She didn't, huh?" said Dakin patiently. "Then who did, Kenny? The man in the moon?"

"I did. I shot Queen. I was behind the whole thing. I killed five of them. Anderson, Jacquard, Doc Dodd, Holderfield, Waldo. I planned it, I tell you! The whole bloody thing."

"I had to do it this way, Rima," Ellery said. "There was no proof. I had only one available weapon, Ken's love for you. So we rigged it, Rima—the impressive attack in force, your carefully staged arrest, the timed entrance of Charlie Brady with the fictitious information that the tire marks matched . . . there weren't any tire marks . . . It was crude, and it was cruel, but Rima, there just wasn't any other way to establish Ken's guilt.''

The house was quiet, as if another death had taken place and the people gathered in Algonquin Avenue watching in silence were waiting for a casket to be carried out. As perhaps they were. Rima lay on her bed immovably.

"Ken thought he was going after the only thing in the world he wanted," continued Ellery. "He failed to get it. But, in failing, he found you. That was a great moment in his life, Rima, and if murder were erasable, like pencil marks, then in finding you Ken might have found himself. But murder can't be wiped away. Ken found out something else. Past a certain point the murderer loses control of events and events begin to control him. It was too late, Rima.

"And it was too late for you, Rima. Sooner or later you'd have seen that something was terribly wrong. Sooner or later you'd have suspected what it was. And eventually you'd have known." He had prepared himself to say a great deal more, about how young she was, about the curative properties of time, and so on, but her withdrawn silence, an unapproachable quality in her suffering, like the sinking of a bird, made him stop. He rose undecidedly. Finally he said, "Rima, is there anything I can do?''

The two—edged irony of his question struck him as he stood over her unresponsive little figure. But then, he thought, sighing as he left her, his Wrightsville "triumphs" had never left anything but the taste of mockery in his mouth.

At least there was consistency in that!

Tuesday, June 13

"But we can't get a thing out of Chalanski or Dakin," said Malvina Prentiss. "If they know anything of importance, which I doubt."

"The only one besides you," said Francis O'Bannon in his most precise Harvard accent, "who can give us the whole story is Winship, and it seems he won't talk even to his lawyer."

"Why did he do it, Ellery, and how did you crack it? That's what the *Record* wants to know—before AP and UP and INS get onto you—and if you think you're sneaking off on that train . . ."

It was the hour of doldrums at the Roadside Tavern, midafternoon of a greengold day, when the saloon seemed becalmed on an empty sea, Gus reading a racing form on the bridge and over everything the cool smell of suds. There was simply no wriggling out. Ellery had played back to Chalanski, in adequate periods, the epitasis of the Winship tragedy; the legal business was all attended to; he would not be needed again until the trial; nothing had remained, it seemed, but to take the first train south. Still, a feeling of incompletion had made him linger. Rima, of course. For one thing, Rima's predicament appalled him. What would she do? Where would she go? How would she live? She had nothing. When this was over she would have no home, no husband, no income, no money—no friends. Ellery had applied himself to the problem with ferocity. Finally he remembered the Natural History Museum in Slocum, and Dr. Josiah Bull. And afterwards, when he had come back from Slocum, he could not even communicate with her. She had locked herself in at the Dodd house, refusing to see anyone, refusing to come to the phone. So he had sent a note over to Algonquin Avenue by Hosy Dowling, the elderly messenger boy of the telegraph office in the Bluefield Block, and that was that, and Ellery had negotiated his departure. Only . . . he still lingered. How could he leave Wrightsville without a goodbye? He had even indulged in a brief fantasy in which he revisited Ytaioa with her. The delay had been fatal. Rosalind Russell and her man Friday had caught him at the station, and now he was in their hot clutch having to ransom himself like Scheherazade to get back to his checked suitcase and the next through train, which was the 6:02.

"The thing that threw me most of all throughout," Ellery began with a sigh, "Was the dull question of motive. The more I beat my everloving brains out over what was happening, the more convinced I became that the crimes were not the work of a homicidal maniac. The homicidal maniac makes no attempt to conceal his crime—usually he flaunts them—but in these deaths there was never any certainty that it was murder at all; every death, until I was shot at, might have been natural or accidental. And when it became positive that the deaths were following a preconceived sequence, I was sure a rational mind was directing events. Because the homicidal maniac doesn't kill in a precise, undeviating pattern, either.''

Ellery swallowed some of his beer without zest. O'Bannon was writing furiously in his notebook.

"I went over every conceivable motivation. Hate. Revenge. Jealousy. Fear of dangerous knowledge. Elimination of obstacles to what-have-you. Self-protection. Protection of another, or others. To every motive I thought of there were strong objections. Except one—gain.''

"Gain?" frowned Malvina Prentiss. "But—''

"I know. But you couldn't avoid that allover sheen of property, Miss Prentiss. There was money in everything, at least up to a certain point; either money, or the couspicuous absence of it. Gain seemed the reasonable theory.

"But when I broke it down gain didn't make sense, either. MacCaby left a large fortune when he died and it went to Dodd. Carry Dodd. John Spencer Hart's death left Dodd a clear field for the operation of the Wrightsville Dye Works. Carry Dodd again. As for Hart, he died not merely penniless, but bankrupt. Tom Anderson died possessed of five thousand dollars, given to him by Dodd, and this five thousand was appropriated by Nick Jacquard—through Anderson's folly, incidentally—but Jacquard himself subsequently died and Anderson's money was found by Dakin, refused by Rima, and made its way back to its original donor. Carry Dodd a third time. All right, there's Dodd, who so far benefited from everything. But what happened to Dodd? He willed the bulk of his inherited estate to the Wrightsville General Hospital! Dead end. Holderfield? Died broke. Jonathan Waldo? His death benefited no one; his brother David owned the tailoring business and the house was in David's name all the time. I had to reach the puzzling conclusion that while gain was the only plausible motive, still nobody gained from any of the seven deaths.

"There were other perplexities," continued Ellery, slumping to his tail and addressing Gus Olesen's measled tin ceiling. "Were the deaths all natural-or-accidental or were they all criminal? Were some of the deaths natural-or-accidental and others criminal? If so, which deaths were natural-or-accidental and which were criminal? There was no means of telling. There were no clues. If these were crimes, they were flawless.

"Then I got my first break in two months.''

"What was that?" asked Malvina Prentiss. O'Bannon's pencil waited.

"Saturday night in a Connhaven hotel room David Waldo revealed to me a fact I hadn't known before. The Waldo twins, who had been witnesses to Sebastian Dodd's will, had acted in that capacity *not once but twice, on two successive days*—on the third day, and again on the second day, preceding Dodd's death.

"To be called upon to witness the same man's will twice within twenty-four hours could mean only one thing: in that twenty-four hours testator had changed his mind about the provisions of his first will and had his lawyer draw up a new one.

"What did the new, or second, will provide? That we've known: except for a few times, Dodd left everything for the financing of a new hospital. What did the first, the superseded, will provide?''

"What?" asked O'Bannon sharply.

"Well, O'Bannon," said Ellery with a faint smile, "I had no more information than you. But I felt that that first, discarded will concealed a fact of great importance. It was no use hammering away at Waldo; he'd merely witnessed Dodd's signature. Only three people knew what was in that first will—Otis Holderfield, who prepared it; Flossie Bushmill, Holderfield's 'secretary,' who undoubtedly typed it; and Dr. Dodd. Holderfield and Dodd were dead, and Flossie'd run off heaven knows where with some salesman. So I had to puzzle over it.''

Ellery studied his suds. ''Whatever the provisions of that first will were, I could be sure that they were *different* from the provisions of the later one. But that reopened the whole question of motive.

''In a rather odd way,'' Ellery added, looking up. ''*Cui bono*, future tense. Not who benefits, but who *expects* to benefit.''

He was silent, and after a momont Malvina Prentiss said intently, ''I don't entirely follow.''

''Dodd changed his will. We know what he changed it *to*—his chief beneficiary is a hospital. But what had he changed it *from*? Whose loss was the hospital's gain? Who could have been Dodd's chief beneficiary before his overnight change of mind?

''Only one person. Dodd left no family. The only one close to him was a young fellow whose career he had financed and sponsored, whom he had sent through medical school, whom he had taken into his home afterward as his companion, protégé, and professional associate. And then I remembered a remark of Ken Winship's the day Otis Holderfield came to the house to read the will-in-force. After Holderfield left, Ken unwisely said to Rima that he couldn't offer her as much as he'd 'hoped' to be able to. It meant nothing at the time; in retrospect now, the remark took on a significant shade of red.

''There was no doubt in my mind, then, that it was Kenneth Winship whom Dodd had named in his first will. And it was equally obvious that, considering his sole and unique relationship with Dodd, Ken had every right to *expect* to be named in Dodd's will. And that,'' said Ellery, ''was just about that.

''Why Dodd cut Winship off at the last moment? I really couldn't say. There are possibilities. Toward the end Dodd wasn't exactly stable. Or the hospital's needs had grown to such proportions in his mind as to overshadow personal considerations. Or, in a flash, Dodd saw or suspected the truth.

''Anyway, I finally had a clear motive—the expectation of gain—and someone to pin it on.''

Ellery made rings with his beer glass. ''Dr. Kenneth Winship wanted those millions of dollars, and he didn't want to wait for them. Besides, Dodd was so free-handed. Planned a children's wing for the hospital the moment he found out he was MacCaby's heir. Gave Hart's widow an income for life. Handed Tom Anderson five thousand dollars. Settled an income on Nick Jacquard's widow and children. At that rate, even millions wouldn't last long. It was apparent to Ken that if he was to get that fortune in anything like its original size, he had to hurry things a bit.

''But there was a rub here, too. Dodd had not made out a will. At all. You heard Holderfield that morning—he'd been after Dodd for some time to do that very thing. As it was, Dodd didn't have it done until the week of his death.

''In law, if Dodd died intestate, Ken had no claim whatever; he and Dodd had no legal relationship. So while he was hurrying things along, Ken had to be sure Dodd left a will. The problem, in principle, must have seemed simple to Ken. If Dodd made his will, Ken would be the heir. Whom else did the childless country doctor have to leave his money to? Ken was as interested in medicine as he was; he looked on Ken as a son, and he was as proud of Ken as if he were Ken's father.''

Malvina Prentiss looked disturbed, and O'Bannon looked sick.

Ellery growled, "But in practice the problem wasn't simple at all. Ken knew all about Dodd's death phobia, of course, long before I smoked it out. Naturally. He was a doctor and he lived in the same house. Ken knew all there *was* to know about Dodd.

"Now a man who morbidly dreads death rarely makes a will of his own volition; to such a man, the very act seems like tempting fate. That's why Dodd kept putting it off. How could Ken force Dodd, in the face of that phobia, to go to a lawyer and have a will drawn? Ken found the answer; he was very resourceful. The man morbidly afraid to die resists the act of will-making because he is desperately hanging on to life and the hope of its indefinite continuance. But suppose he could be made to come to believe that the hope is nonexistent? *That his death is not merely inevitable but imminent?*

"As Ken saw it, he had to smash Dodd's hold on hope. He had to convince Dodd beyond the quiver of a doubt that death was a matter of days and that nothing he or anyone else did could stop it."

"My God," breathed O'Bannon.

"And then Winship got one of the most diabolical inspirations in the history of murder. There had been two deaths in Wrightsville recently which involved and affected Sebastian Dodd: the death of old Luke MacCaby from heart disease and the suicide of John Spencer Hart. Winship noticed that MacCaby, always considered a pauper, died a rich man, and that Hart, always considered one of the town's nabobs, died a poor man. The contrast struck him. Rich man-poor man. Rich-man-poor-man.

"Into Ken's brain, sharpened by acquisitiveness, sickened by his war experiences— Dakin told me Winship went to pieces when he got back from overseas—into Ken's mind leaped the old children's jingle.

"Immediately," said Ellery, "Immediately Ken saw his implementation whole. *Rich man, poor man, beggar-man, thief*—and then *doctor*. If the death of MacCaby, who had willed his fortune to Dodd, and the death of Hart, which left Dodd in sole possession of the great Wrightsville Dye Works, should be followed by the deaths of a 'beggar' and a 'thief,' two people with whom Dodd also had a connection, and if that sinister progression were to be brought forcefully to Dodd's notice, then Dodd would be convinced of two things: first, that a doctor would certainly be the next to die, and second, that he, Dodd, would certainly be that doctor. And if Dodd were so convinced, he would make a will."

"And if he didn't?" said O'Bannon.

"But he did, O'Bannon," said Ellery dryly. "Anyway, that's the chance a murderer takes. There's at least one in every crime. Ken took his, and won."

"Go *on!*" said Malvina Prentiss.

"Winship got going immediately. His first step was to find somebody in town who fitted the third character in the rhyme. He hadn't far to look. Tom Anderson was known as The Town Beggar as well as The Town Drunk, and Dodd had given him a large sum of money. Winship arranged a meeting with Anderson at Little Prudy's Cliff late one night and tossed Anderson into the quicksand below. And once Anderson's disappearance was accepted as death, Ken mailed newspaper clippings concerning the three deaths—MacCaby's and Hart's, with which he had utterly nothing to do and which were exactly what they purported to be, and Anderson's—to me, anonymously."

"Why did he do that?"

"Oh, that was very nearly the most important part of his plans, Miss Prentiss,'' smiled Ellery. "The key objective of his campaign was to convince Dodd absolutely that death was just around the corner. Ken knew my weakness for the bizarre and he reasoned that if I could be brought into it to expound the death rhyme to Dodd, the job was done. If I didn't bite, or if I failed to see the death scheme, Ken could always 'discover' it himself, or disclose the rhyme pattern through an unsigned letter to the *Record*. But I was the ideal instrument. Wrightsville knew me. I had reputation and authority. A disclosure by me to Dodd would insure Dodd's acceptance of the inevitability of his early death . . . Of course, Ken couldn't have known Rima would ask me to investigate her father's disappearance. But I probably would have come to Wrightsville, anyway, on the strength of those three clippings he sent me. Once I showed up in Wrightsville he knew he was on the right track. And he prepared his next move.''

"Jacquard.''

"Yes. The problem there was to get Jacquard to break into the Dodd house. Exactly how he managed it I don't know—it doesn't matter. What matters is that Ken duped Jacquard into attempting a burglary. When Ken turned his head, ostensibly to hand me the gun so he could get some rope, it was not an act of carelessness. He was inviting Jacquard to jump him. Had Jacquard failed to do so, Ken would have tried something else—conned him into trying to make a break for it, perhaps. In any event, it's perfectly clear what Ken's plan was: to shoot Jacquard in cold blood, but under such circumstances that the shooting would seem an unavoidable and justifiable act. This was the most daring murder of them all, committed before three competent witnesses all of whom swore with perfect honesty that it was an act of self-defense. Ken must have got quite a kick out of that.''

Ellery lit a cigaret. "Now his stage was set. Four Wrightsvillians had died—a rich man, a poor man, a beggar, and a thief. All he had to do was wait for me to see it. And I saw it, as he'd schemed and hoped, and I rushed to Dodd to recite the doggerel and warn Dodd he was next on the list. Dodd accepted the idea of his doom at once. And how Winship must have preened himself on that.''

"This is,'' said Malvina Prentiss, moistening her lips, "this is fabulous.''

"Yes,'' said Ellery. "Only more so. Winship was a master of detail. I'd obligingly shattered the living hope in Dodd, but there might be fragments that still squirmed. Ken went methodically to work to destroy them. He turned Dodd's own weapons against him . . . Which weapons? Oh, you don't know about Dodd's secret belief in divination, do you?''

"In *what?*''

"In divination.'' Into their incredulous ears he poured the story of Sebastian Dodd's attic room and its contents.

"You may be sure Ken knew all about that room and what went on there; in fact, his knowledge of Dodd's superstitious practices may have been the spark that inspired Ken's whole plan. He undoubtedly had a duplicate key to the room, unknown to Dodd. How many times he secretly watched Dodd probe the future in that room only he knows, but by the time he was ready to move he was perfectly sure of his ground.

"First, Ken engineered the illusion of the death card, the ace of spades, that grand old standby of bad omens—the double death card, because I myself watched Dodd cut two decks of cards and both times uncover the spade ace. How Ken managed this? Suppose it was your problem. The solution is obvious. You'd buy a hundred and four decks of cards of the same design as the decks Dodd was using, you'd remove the ace of spades from each deck, and with your hundred and four spade aces you'd make up two decks of fifty-two spade aces each. Can't miss. Unfortunately, by the time I was able to get a workable duplicate key to the attic door, Ken had slipped into the room, removed the planted decks, and restored Dodd's originals. Those perfectly normal decks of cards gave me rather a bad time."

"Risky," mumbled O'Bannon.

"No," said Ellery. "Dodd never looked at the other cards when he cut for fortune, apparently. A habit is as predictable as a thing. Ken's knowledge of Dodd was thorough.

"Having dealt Dodd the twin blow of the black pip, Ken followed it with the dog that howled in the night, another common omen of death. He wasn't aware that he had already won the game, that Dodd had visited Otis Holderfield the morning after my revelation of the jingle and had made his will—the first will. Unaware of this, Ken kept hammering away. He planted a bird in Dodd's study, still another omen of death.

"It may be," said Ellery, dropping his cigaret butt moodily into his beer, "that Ken's own perfectionism defeated him. He kept adding little artistic touches—the car, the dog, the bird—when, as events proved, they weren't needed. Under the added pressures, completely demoralized, Dodd not merely made a will—he made two. With one hand he gave, with the other he took away. For twenty-four hours, as it were, Kenneth Winship had his day and didn't know it. Then it was the morning after. But he still didn't know it. He must have learned of Dodd's visits to Holderfield's office after the bird incident, naturally assumed them to mean a single will, assumed that his objective had been won, and prepared himself for the last move, the mop-up. He waited until an emergency night call took Dodd into an outlying district and then he simply followed and forced Dodd off the road at a spot where death was sure. Or perhaps he listened on the extension, learned Dodd's destination, went off in advance, waylaid Dodd, hit him on the head, and sent Dodd's car spinning into the gulley. So it was done.

"It was done," said Ellery, "and Ken Winship went through all the easy motions of dazed grief, and Dr. Dodd was buried, and the day came when the doctor's will was read. And Winship, brilliant schemer, artist of crime, three-times murderer, learned that for his great exertions he was going to get his rent free for a few years—and that was all."

And Ellery was silent again.

Malvina Prentiss stirred. "But the murders didn't stop. Why, when he had nothing to gain—?"

"That's true. He had nothing to gain, and he knew it better than anyone in the world. So at first Ken Winship did the only thing he could do: he accepted his defeat. He made the best of it. Wrote the past off. He had something powerful to help him over the hump. He'd fallen in love and he was loved in return. By some crippled ethic he may have consoled himself that his failure to win a fortune through murder was what made it morally possible for him to marry Rima. At any rate, he married her and settled down to the unexciting life of a country doctor. As far as Ken was concerned, considering his failure, he was in a pretty fair position. The fact that he gained practically nothing from Dodd's death left him above suspicion. There was still the hanging loose end of the child's rhyme, but he was quite content to let me break my head over it.

"And then a queer thing happened," said Ellery, "and, O'Bannon, you might put this down in double pothooks, because it's the really beautiful part of the story.

"Up to this time, Ken had manipulated events.

"Now events began to manipulate Ken.

"You know," said Ellery, "every once in a while I'm caught up short. There's no explaining some things in feet, minutes, or pounds. There are times when nature, fiddled with, cracks down with a sort of cynical intelligence. Determinism seems proved and fate seems to work in a dark humor. What Hardy called satires of circumstance. Certainly Kenneth Winship must have found himself in the grip of a force he didn't grasp. He had brought a certain pattern of events into being. When he tried to stop, by a tremendous irony he found he couldn't."

"What do you mean?" asked Malvina Prentiss.

But Ellery went on talking as if he were alone. "Where does coincidence end and the force of circumstances begin? It's a fine point. In the last analysis there may be no such thing as coincidence. At least it wasn't coincidence that kept Ken's pattern going. It couldn't have been. It was too implacably right.

"What do I mean?" Ellery looked up. "I mean that the pattern, entirely aside from Ken, insisted on completing itself.

"Holderfield drew both of the Dodd wills. Therefore Holderfield knew that in the first—the revoked—will Kenneth Winship had been Dodd's heir. Under his lard Otis Holderfield was a sharp, shrewd citizen. He solved the mystery. He saw that Winship, and Winship alone, had a motive for murder.

"At one point in this game," said Ellery, "I played with the theory that Tom Anderson might have been blackmailing Sebastian Dodd. There was a blackmailer in the case, all right, only it wasn't Anderson. After Dodd's death Holderfield must have talked to Winship, told Winship what he knew, and promised silence on the damning fact of the first will—for a consideration.

"Ken had no money that would satisfy a blackmailer, but he had inherited Dodd's practice, or most of it. It's likely, therefore, that Holderfield proposed a steady bleeding, a share of Ken's earnings on a businesslike basis. That's why Holderfield, who on the morning he read Dodd's will to us was angry and embittered, shortly afterward was all smiling heartiness again. He'd figured out his blackmail scheme . . . And there was Ken, with nothing to show for his crimes, and now he was in even a worse position : now he had to pay for them.

"Ken saw what he had to do. He was not the kind of a man who submits meekly to blackmail, as Holderfield should have known. One murder more would hardly stop him. He stole into the Granjon Block late one Saturday afternoon, when the building was deserted, and tossed Holderfield out of his own window. If Holderfield had a copy of that first will in his office, as he undoubtedly did, Ken looked for it, found it, and destroyed it.

"Another murder, committed without hope of gain, entirely against his wishes, I'm sure, and only because of expediency. The murder of a blackmailer named Holderfield. The only thing was . . . in murdering a blackmailer named Holderfield, *Ken murdered a lawyer,* and a lawyer was what the pattern called for to follow the doctor. Coincidence? I can't think so."

"Kind of odd, at that," muttered O'Bannon, scribbling away.

"If this had been the end of it, merely 'odd' might have described it. But it wasn't. Having eliminated Holderfield, Winship found he still couldn't stop. The Waldo twins had witnessed that will, the will which established Winship's sole motive. For all he knew, the Waldos knew its contents. But even if they did not, they knew there were two wills a day apart, and that knowledge was dangerous, too . . . The Waldos took nembutal to make them sleep, they lived directly across from the Dodd house, and their house was an old tinderbox. Ken set a fire in their cellar and went back to bed.

"He may have planned the murder, too, of Floss Bushmill, Holderfield's secretary, who had been the third witness to the will—after all, if he got nothing out of all his work, the least he could do was remove all trace of his involvement. But then everything went to pot and by the time he was bogged down in stickier problems Floss had skipped Wrightsville for greener fields.

"*Doctor, lawyer, merchant* . . . He had planned to murder two brothers who possessed some dangerous knowledge. In setting that fire Ken may have overlooked the fact that tailors are merchants, but it's obvious that some higher authority had not."

"Incredible," said Malvina Prentiss.

"The authority I'm referring to, Miss Prentiss," said Ellery with a smile, "specialized in incredibilities. Only this doesn't happen to be one of them. A law almost as natural as Newton's controlled Winship's 'happening' to murder a merchant after a lawyer when the jingle called for precisely that sequence. For how did the 'merchant' Waldos get on Winship's list? They were called in by Lawyer Holderfield to witness Sebastian Dodd's will. Now note that Lawyer Holderfield's office was in an office building, and that the office building, like virtually all office buildings, contains retail stores on its ground floor, and that the building is in the heart of the business district of Wrightsville, which is largely composed of retail storekeepers. Nine out of any ten people Holderfield called in to witness Dodd's will would therefore have been merchants of one sort or another. The two who were called happened to be merchant tailors. They might just as well have been Mr. Purdy of the drygoods store or Jeff Hernaberry of the sporting goods store. No, not incredible, Miss Prentiss; not coincidence.

"But to get on to the end of this. Fate was coming to enjoy the game. One of the Waldo brothers failed to die in the fire.

"At this point everything began to move rapidly. Ken realized that in David Waldo's survival lay the very danger he had tried to stave off by setting fire to the Waldo house. He could hardly murder Waldo in the hospital—far too great a risk of detection. Then Waldo, frightened witness, got out, secretly cleaned up his Wrightsville affairs, and disappeared.

"Ken knew I was determined to find Waldo. If I did, I might pry out of him the story of that first will. When Waldo was found, therefore, and I left a note at the Dodd house telling Rima and Ken where I was going, Ken waited until there was a night call for his professional services, or more likely invented one for Rima's benefit, got his car out, and followed me to Connhaven. All along, by the way, his profession gave him beautiful mobility. No one dreams of questioning a doctor's going out in the middle of the night.

"He followed me, he set a trap, the trap worked, and he fired two shots at my heart from a distance of six inches.

"And fate had a good belly laugh at his expense. First, I was wearing, of all things, a bulletproof vest. And second, I was—and utilized in my countertrap—a 'chief.' Winship must have thought he was having a nightmare—he certainly wasn't trying to fill out the last line of that rhyme when he shot me!

"It's true that 'chief' didn't die. But it's also true that I was 'chief only in the most absurd and narrow of senses. The pattern is going to fulfill itself quite realistically. There's still a death to come.''

O'Bannon's pencil point snapped and Malvina Prentiss sat up very straight.

"Ken's, for his crimes," said Ellery. "And there, without a note of sophistry, you'll have the supreme satire of circumstance. Because the truth is Ken was the chief of everything. The chief criminal, the chief planner, the chief of operations, the chief victim. The perfect ending to his rhyme, although I doubt that he'll fully appreciate it until it's too late. Are you people as dry as I am? I'd like another beer.''

The place was half full now, workmen from the mills, businessmen on their way home. It took some time to get Gus's attention. Meanwhile, Francis O'Bannon was staring at his notebook in a thoughtful way. Malvina Prentiss tapped her silver fingernails on the table absently. Ellery lit another cigaret.

"What'll it be?'' asked Gus.

"One beer," said the publisher of the *Record*. "For Mr. Queen." She laid a bill on the table and rose.

"Make mine a bottle of bourbon," said Francis O'Bannon.

She stared coldly down at his red thatch. "I thought we'd gone all through that, Spec. Get off your bottom and back to the shop. We've got quite a haul ahead of us.''

"Bourbon," said O'Bannon.

"Yes, sir," said Gus doubtfully.

"Spec," said Malvina Prentiss. "I spoke to you.''

"You spoke to me. What do you know about that." Harvard's crimson was slowly rising in O'Bannon's neck. "What am I supposed to do?''

"What you're paid to do. Jump through a hoop!''

"Malvina," said O'Bannon softly, "you can damn well go back to the shop yourself. Gus, bourbon.''

"Back Bay," said Malvina contemptuously. "You sound more like a New York garbage collector.''

"Well, that's what I am, you silverplated refugee from Madame Tussaud's!'' O'Bannon sprang to his feet. He snatched off his glasses and broke them excitedly before her eyes.

"Spec." She was horrified.

"Spec your left one! Gus, you get me that bottle of bourbon or I break up the joint. Why, Malvina honey, I'm a phony, didn't you know that? I let you wipe up the *Record* floor with me because I liked it. Well, I don't like it any more!'' he yelled. "You can take your powder room job and stuff it!''

"Spec—'' she stammered.

"Francis Vincent Xavier O'Bannon is the name, and now I'm going to call you a few, my proud hunk of beauty!'' And Francis Vincent Xavier O'Bannon did so, with a blasphemous fluency that brought respectful silence from Gus's customers. And all the time she was being so graphically described, Malvina Prentiss stood in the booth with her mouth open, a vision of stupefaction. And when O'Bannon had concluded, and he had downed a quarter of a fifth of bourbon via the mouth of the bottle Gus had fetched, and he had saluted Ellery and stalked from the tavern to the accompaniment of whistles and applause from the multitude, Malvina Prentiss shut her mouth, looked around fearfully, blushed to the roots of her platinum hair, and fled.

And now two will be one, thought Ellery. Life goes on, unifying dualities.

He looked up from his watch to see Rima in the doorway.

They met in the middle of the barroom, beside a table at which an overalled man with a grease streak on his nose was lining up four glasses of whiskey, carefully.

"Are you a detective, too?" asked Ellery, not smiling.

"You weren't hard to find. You're very famous."

"I'm glad you came, Rima."

"That was sweet of you—getting me a job."

"You've spoken to Dr. Bull?"

"I phoned him."

"What did he say?"

"He asked me a great many questions. He's putting me in the Wild Life wing—assistant to the curator. It was very sweet of you, Ellery."

"I'm sure you'll be happy there, Rima. There's a great deal of field work involved, I understand. When do you start?"

"Dr. Bull said any time at my convenience. I picked tomorrow morning."

"Well," said Ellery with a smile. Then he said, "I'm glad you picked tomorrow. It's an excellent day for it."

Rima looked as if she did not quite agree.

"Besides," she said, "I couldn't let you leave without saying goodbye."

"I'll be back, Rima."

"Oh, yes. For the trial."

"Not entirely for the trial."

A big fellow in a checkered shirt yelled, "Gus!"

"Not . . . entirely, Ellery?" It pained him to look at the purple-brown underscoring of her eyes.

"Have you forgotten my lecture in Ytaioa? Rima, I've got to go. Cab down to the station with me."

"Lecture?" Rima said.

"There are always," said Ellery, "two possibilities."

The color of something alive entered her face, and as Ellery took Rima outside to where Ed Hotchkiss was waiting in his hack he kept thinking, not very originally, that it was like seeing the sun come up on a darkened world.